PRAGATI

MATHEMATICS

MCQs

(MULTIPLE CHOICE QUESTIONS)
FOR
JEE (MAINS & ADVANCED) & OTHER COMPETITIVE EXAMS

Tijo Jacob

LEARNING SIMPLIFIED

★ **Author of Great Repute**
★ **Latest Inputs as per CBSE Syllabus**
★ **Complete Chapterwise MCQs**
★ **More than 4500 MCQs**
★ **Questions from Competitive Exams included**
★ **Latest Papers with Answers included**

PRAGATI BOOKS

PP034

Pragati - Mathematics (MCQs)	ISBN 978-93-86353-32-0

First Edition : **January 2017**

© : **Author**

Published By :   Polyplate

NIRALI PRAKASHAN

Abhyudaya Pragati, 1312, Shivaji Nagar,
Off J.M. Road, PUNE – 411005
Tel - (020) 25512336/37/39, Fax - (020) 25511379
Email : niralipune@pragationline.com

☞ **DISTRIBUTION CENTRES**

PUNE

Nirali Prakashan : 119, Budhwar Peth, Jogeshwari Mandir Lane, Pune 411002, Maharashtra
Tel : (020) 2445 2044, 66022708, Fax : (020) 2445 1538
Email : bookorder@pragationline.com, niralilocal@pragationline.com

Nirali Prakashan : S. No. 28/27, Dhyari, Near Pari Company, Pune 411041
Tel : (020) 24690204 Fax : (020) 24690316
Email : dhyari@pragationline.com, bookorder@pragationline.com

MUMBAI

Nirali Prakashan : 385, S.V.P. Road, Rasdhara Co-op. Hsg. Society Ltd.,
Girgaum, Mumbai 400004, Maharashtra
Tel : (022) 2385 6339 / 2386 9976, Fax : (022) 2386 9976
Email : niralimumbai@pragationline.com

☞ **DISTRIBUTION BRANCHES**

JALGAON

Nirali Prakashan : 34, V. V. Golani Market, Navi Peth, Jalgaon 425001,
Maharashtra, Tel : (0257) 222 0395, Mob : 94234 91860

KOLHAPUR

Nirali Prakashan : New Mahadvar Road, Kedar Plaza, 1st Floor Opp. IDBI Bank
Kolhapur 416 012, Maharashtra. Mob : 9850046155

NAGPUR

Pratibha Book Distributors : Above Maratha Mandir, Shop No. 3, First Floor,
Rani Jhanshi Square, Sitabuldi, Nagpur 440012, Maharashtra
Tel : (0712) 254 7129

DELHI

Nirali Prakashan : 4593/21, Basement, Aggarwal Lane 15, Ansari Road, Daryaganj
Near Times of India Building, New Delhi 110002, Mob : 08505972553

BENGALURU

Pragati Book House : House No. 1, Sanjeevappa Lane, Avenue Road Cross,
Opp. Rice Church, Bengaluru – 560002.
Tel : (080) 64513344, 64513355,Mob : 9880582331, 9845021552
Email:bharatsavla@yahoo.com

CHENNAI

Pragati Books : 9/1, Montieth Road, Behind Taas Mahal, Egmore,
Chennai 600008 Tamil Nadu, Tel : (044) 6518 3535,
Mob : 94440 01782 / 98450 21552 / 98805 82331,
Email : bharatsavla@yahoo.com

niralipune@pragationline.com | www.pragationline.com
Also find us on f www.facebook.com/niralibooks

PREFACE

The entrance examination scenario has witnessed many changes in the pattern of question papers varying from subjective to multiple choice questions, since the time prestigious institutions such as IITs and AIIMS have come into existence.

This book is an attempt to provide an updated and in-depth coverage of the latest syllabus and pattern of question papers for all the Entrance Examinations i.e. IIT-JEE, JEE (MAINS), MHT-CET and other Competitive Exams. The book has been shaped entirely according to the student perspective and a sincere effort has been made to present the material in a very functional and practical manner so that students enjoy the learning process as they proceed through the lesson rather than experiencing it as an ordeal. Each unit has been designed with the objective of testing an aspirant's grasp and understanding of concepts. This book will equip the students with the necessary speed, accuracy and confidence for the entrance examinations.

The author shall be grateful to the readers for any constructive suggestions or inputs for the improvement of the text. The author wishes to record his thanks to the publisher whose efforts went a long way in bringing out this work.

Suggestions for the improvement and further enhancement of the scope of the book will be welcome.

Author

CONTENTS

1.	Set Theory	1.1 – 1.7
2.	Quadratic Equations and Inequations	2.1 – 2.14
3.	Trigonometric Ratios and Identities	3.1 – 3.10
4.	Trigonometric Equations	4.1 – 4.9
5.	Inverse Trigonometric Functions	5.1 – 5.10
6.	Properties and Solution of Triangle	6.1 – 6.10
7.	Heights and Distances	7.1 – 7.5
8.	Complex Numbers	8.1 – 8.10
9.	Sequences and Series	9.1 – 9.13
10.	Permutations and Combinations	10.1 – 10.16
11.	Binomial Theorem	11.1 – 11.14
12.	Exponential and Logarithmic Series	12.1 – 12.5
13.	Co-ordinate Geometry and Straight Lines	13.1 – 13.8
14.	Circle	14.1 – 14.12
15.	Parabola	15.1 – 15.8
16.	Ellipse	16.1 – 16.7
17.	Hyperbola	17.1 – 17.9
18.	Functions	18.1 – 18.13
19.	Limits	19.1 – 19.10
20.	Continuity and Differentiability	20.1 – 20.13
21.	Differentiation	21.1 – 21.11
22.	Applications of Derivatives	22.1 – 22.20
23.	Indefinite Integration	23.1 – 23.16
24.	Definite Integral and Area	24.1 – 24.26
25.	Differential Equations	25.1 – 25.11
26.	Matrices	26.1 – 26.11
27.	Determinants	27.1 – 27.18
28.	Statistics	28.1 – 28.9
29.	Probability	29.1 – 29.21
30.	Vectors	30.1 – 30.29
31.	Three Dimensional Geometry	31.1 – 31.13
32.	Mathematical Logic	32.1 – 32.3
	Question Papers of Previous Exams (JEE MAINS 2013 to 2016)	P.1 – P.12

•••

Chapter 1

SET THEORY

MULTIPLE CHOICE QUESTIONS

1. If A and B are two sets such that A has 12 elements, B has 17 elements and $A \cup B$ has 21 elements, then $A \cap B$ has how many elements ?
   (a) 6   (b) 8
   (c) 4   (d) None of these.

2. If $n(U) = 700$, $n(A) = 200$, $n(B) = 300$, $n(A \cap B) = 100$, then $n(A' \cap B') =$
   (a) 400   (b) 300
   (c) 240   (d) None of these.

3. In a committee, 50 people speak French, 20 speak Spanish and 10 speak both. The number of people speaking atleast one of these two languages is :
   (a) 60   (b) 38
   (c) 40   (d) None of these.

4. Out of 20 members in a family, 12 like tea and 15 like coffee. Assuming that each one likes atleast one of the two drinks, the number of people liking :
   (a) only tea and not coffee is 5
   (b) only coffee and not tea is 8
   (c) both tea and coffee is 7
   (d) All the above

5. In a group of 65 people playing basket ball or lawn ball, 40 like basket ball, 10 like both basket ball and lawn ball. The number of people liking lawn ball only and not basket ball is :
   (a) 15   (b) 21
   (c) 25   (d) None of these.

6. $U = \{1, 2, 3, 4, 5, 6, 7, 8, 9, 10\}$, $A = \{1, 2, 3, 4\}$, $B = \{2, 4, 6, 8, 10\}$ then :
   (a) $(A \cup B)' = \{5, 7, 9\}$
   (b) $(A \cap B)' = \{1, 3, 5, 6, 7\}$
   (c) $(A \cap B)' = \{1, 3, 7, 8, 9, 10\}$
   (d) None of these.

7. If $A = \{1, 2, 3, 4\}$, $B = \{2, 3, 5, 6\}$ $C = \{3, 4, 6, 7\}$ then :
   (a) $A - (B \cap C) = \{1, 3, 4\}$
   (b) $A - (B \cap C) = \{1, 4\}$
   (c) $A - (B \cup C) = \{2, 3\}$
   (d) $A - (B \cup C) = \{1\}$

8. For two sets X and Y, $X \cap (X \cup Y)' =$
   (a) X   (b) Y
   (c) ϕ (d) None of these.

9. If $A = \{2, 3, 4\}$, $X = \{0, 1, 2, 3, 4\}$, then :
   (a) $\{0\} \in A'$ w.r.t. X
   (b) $\phi \in A'$ w.r.t. X
   (c) $\{0\} \subset A'$ w.r.t. X
   (d) $0 \subset A'$ w.r.t. X

10. If $n(U) = 60$, $n(A) = 35$, $n(B) = 24$, $n(A \cup B)' = 10$, then $n(A \cap B) =$
    (a) 9   (b) 6
    (c) 8   (d) None of these.

11. The members of a group of 400 people speak either English or Hindi or both. If 270 people speak Hindi only and 50 people both English and Hindi, the number people speaking English only is :
    (a) 45   (b) 60
    (c) 80   (d) None of these.

12. In a group of 26 people, 8 like pepsi but not coke and 16 like pepsi. Number of people who like coke but not pepsi is :
    (a) 10   (b) 8
    (c) 6   (d) None of these

13. In a city , 42% of people read TOI, 51% read HT and 68% read ET. 30% read TOI and HT, 28% read HT and ET, 36% read TOI and ET, and 8% do not read any of the 3 newspapers. The percentage of people who read all the three newspapers is :
    (a) 25%   (b) 20%
    (c) 18%   (d) None of these

14. Every student in a class of 42 students, studies at least one of the subjects, Maths, Physics or Chemistry. 14 study Maths, 20 Chemistry and 24 Physics. 3 study Maths and Chemistry, 2 Physics and Chemistry and no student studies all the three subjects. The number of students who study Maths but not Chemistry is :

(a) 11   (b) 5

(c) 6   (d) None of these

15. Of the members of an athletic teams in a school, 21 play basket ball, 26 hockey and 29 football. 14 play hockey and basket ball, 15 play hockey and football, 12 play football and basket ball and 8 play all the three games. The total number of members are :

(a) 18   (b) 43

(c) 32   (d) None of these

16. Suppose $A_1, A_2, ..., A_{30}$ are 30 sets, each with 5 elements and $B_1, B_2, ..., B_n$ are n sets, each with 3 elements. Let $\bigcup_{i=1}^{30} A_i = \bigcup_{j=1}^{n} B_j = S$. If each element of S belongs to exactly 10 of A_i's and exactly 9 of the B_j's, then n =

(a) 45   (b) 35

(c) 40   (d) None of these.

17. A relation R on the set of complex numbers defined by $z_1 R z_2 \Leftrightarrow \dfrac{z_1 - z_2}{z_1 + z_2}$ is real, is :

(a) reflexive   (b) symmetric

(c) transitive   (d) All of these

18. Let R be a relation such that R = {(1, 4), (3, 7), (4, 5), (4, 6), (7, 6)} then :

(a) $R^{-1} o R^{-1}$ = {(5, 1), (6, 1), (6, 3)}

(b) $R^{-1} o R^{-1}$ = {(4, 1), (6, 1), (6, 3)}

(c) $(R^{-1} o R)^{-1}$ = {(3, 3), (4, 4), (7, 7), (4, 7)}

(d) None of these

19. If $Y \cup \{1, 2\}$= {1, 2, 3, 5, 9} then :

(a) minimum n (Y) = 2

(b) minimum n (Y) = 4

(c) maximum n (Y) = 4

(d) maximum n (Y) = 5

20. If A = {x:|x| < 2}, B = {x : |x – 5| ≤ 2},

C = {x : |x| > x} and D = {x : | x | < x} then :

(a) A ∪ B = (– 2, 2) ∪ [3, 7]

(b) A ∩ C = (– 2, 0)

(c) A ∩ D = φ

(d) All of these.

21. The solution of $3x^2 – 12x = 0$ when :

(a) x ∈ N is {4}

(b) x ∈ I is {0, 4}

(c) x ∈ S = {a + bi : b ≠ 0, a,b ∈ R} is φ

(d) All of these.

22. If A = {1, 2, 3}, B = {3, 4} and C = {4, 5, 6}, then $(A \times B) \cap (B \times C)$ is :

(a) {(3, 4)}   (b) {(1, 4), (3, 4)}

(c) {(1, 4), (2, 3)}   (d) None of these

23. If n (A) = 3 and n (B) = 6, then minimum number of elements in A ∪ B is :

(a) 6   (b) 3

(c) φ   (d) None of these

24. If X = {$4^n – 3n – 1$: n ∈ N} and Y = {9 (n – 1) : n ∈ N}, then :

(a) $X \subset Y$ (b) $Y \subset X$

(c) X = Y   (d) None of these.

25. If a N = {ax : x ∈ N}, then 3N ∩ 7N =

(a) 3N   (b) 7N

(c) N   (d) 21 N

26. Let R be a relation defined as α R β, if α ⊥ β, α, β are straight lines in a plane, then the relation R is :

(a) reflexive   (b) symmetric

(c) transitive   (d) None of these.

27. Let R be a relation defined by R = {(4, 5), (1, 4), (4, 6), (7, 6), (3, 7) }then :

(a) RoR = {(1, 5), (1, 6), (3, 6)}

(b) RoR = {(1, 5), (1, 6), (1, 7), (3, 6)}

(c) $R^{-1} o R$ = {(4, 4), (1, 1), (4, 7), (7, 4), (7, 7)}

(d) None of these.

28. Let S be the set of all points in a plane and R be a relation on S such that for any two points a and b, aRb iff b is within 1 cm of a, then R is :
    (a) reflexive only
    (b) reflexive and symmetric
    (c) symmetric and transitive
    (d) equivalence relation.

29. Let R be a relation defined as aRb iff $1 + ab > 0$. The relation R is :
    (a) equivalence
    (b) reflexive only
    (c) symmetric and transitive
    (d) reflexive and symmetric

30. A relation R on $N \times N$ is defined as $(a, b) R(c, d) \Leftrightarrow a + d = b + c$, where N is set of natural numbers, then R is :
    (a) reflexive only
    (b) symmetric only
    (c) transitive only
    (d) equivalence relation

31. $n R m \Leftrightarrow n$ is a factor of m, then R is :
    (a) reflexive and symmetric
    (b) reflexive and transitive
    (c) equivalence relation
    (d) None of these

32. Let $A = \{x : x \in R, |x| < 1\}$, $B = \{x : x \in R, |x - 1| \geq 1\}$ and $A \cup B = R - D$, then set D is :
    (a) $\{x : 1 < x \leq 2\}$
    (b) $\{x : 1 \leq x < 2\}$
    (c) $\{x : 1 \leq x \leq 2\}$
    (d) None of these

33. Consider the set 'A' of all determinants of order 3×3 containing only 0 and 1 as its elements. Let B be subset of A, consisting of all determinants with value 1 and C be subset of A, containing determinants with value – 1. Then :
    (a) C is empty
    (b) $A = B \cup C$
    (c) $n (B) = n (C)$
    (d) $n (B) = 2 \cdot n (C)$

34. If R_1 and R_2 are symmetric relations (not disjoint), on a set A, then the relation $R_1 \cap R_2$ is :
    (a) reflexive
    (b) symmetric
    (c) transitive
    (d) equivalence

35. If $n(U) = 700$, $n(A) = 200$, $n(B) = 300$, $n(A \cap B) = 100$, then $n(A' \cap B') =$
    (a) 300
    (b) 350
    (c) 400
    (d) None of these.

36. The set of intelligent students in a class is :
    (a) a null set
    (b) a singleton set
    (c) a finite set
    (d) not defined

37. The number of non-empty subsets of set $\{1, 2, 3, 4\}$ is:
    (a) 15
    (b) 14
    (c) 16
    (d) 17

38. In a village, 25% people have mobile, 15% have laptop, 65% have neither mobile nor laptop. 2000 people have both mobile and laptop. Consider the following statements :
    (1) 10% people have both mobile and laptop.
    (2) 35% people have either a mobile or a laptop.
    (3) 40,000 people live in town.
    Which of these statements are correct ?
    (a) 1 and 2
    (b) 1 and 3
    (c) 2 and 3
    (d) All the three, 1, 2, 3

39. If $n(A) = p$, $n(B) = q$, then number of elements in $A \times B$ is :
    (a) $p + q + 1$
    (b) pq
    (c) $p + q$
    (d) None of these

40. $A = \{x : x \neq x\}$ represents :
    (a) $\{ x \}$
    (b) $\{ 1 \}$
    (c) $\{ 0 \}$
    (d) $\{ \}$

41. In a class of 55 students, 23 study music, 24 psychology and 19 computers, 12 study music and psychology, 9 study music and computers, 7 study psychology and computers and 4 study all the 3. Number of students who have only one of the three subjects is :
    (a) 6
    (b) 7
    (c) 9
    (d) 22

42. The finite sets have m and n elements, the total number of subsets of the first set is 56 more than number of subsets of 2nd set, then m and n are :
    (a) 7, 6
    (b) 6, 3
    (c) 5, 1
    (d) 8, 7

43. Let A and B be non-empty subsets of X such that A $\not\subset$ B. Then :

(a) A is a subset of B'

(b) B $\subset$ A

(c) A and B are disjoint

(d) A $\cap$ B' $\neq \phi$

44. Let R be a relation on N $\times$ N defined by (a, b) R(c, d) iff ad (b + c) = bc (a + d), then R is :

(a) reflexive only

(b) symmetric only

(c) transitive only

(d) an equivalence ralation

45. If A, B, C are non-empty sets, then

(A – B) $\cup$ (B – A) =

(a) (A $\cap$ B) $\cup$ (A $\cup$ B)

(b) (A $\cup$ B) – (A $\cap$ B)

(c) A – (A $\cap$ B)

(d) (A $\cup$ B) – B

46. If A = {x $\in$ R |0 < 1} & B = (x $\in$ R| – 1 < x < 1}, then A $\times$ B is the set

(a) of all points lying inside the rectangle having vertices at (1, 1), (0, 1), (0, – 1) and (1, – 1)

(b) of all points lying inside the rectangle having vertices at (1, 0), (1, 1), (0, 1) and (0, 0)

(c) of all points lying on the sides of the rectangle whose vertices are at (1, 1) (0, 1), (0, –1) and (1, –1)

(d) none of these.

47. If X = {4^n – 3n – 1 | n $\in$ N} and

Y = {9 (n – 1) | n f $\in$ N} then X $\cup$ Y is equal to

(a) X

(b) Y

(c) N

(d) none of these.

48. Let A and B be two non-empty subsets of a set X such that A is not a subset of B, then

(a) A is a subset of complement of B

(b) B is a subset of A

(c) A and B are disjoint

(d) A and the complement of B are non-disjoint

49. Let N denote the set of natural numbers and R a relation of N $\times$ N. Which of the following is not an equivalence relation on N?

(a) (a, b) R (c, d) $\Leftrightarrow$ ad (b + c) = bc (a + b)

(b) (a, b) R (c, d) $\Leftrightarrow$ a + d = b + c

(c) (a, b) R (c, d) $\Leftrightarrow$ ad = bc

(d) none of these.

50. Which of the following is not an equivalence relation of Z ?

(a) aRb $\Leftrightarrow$ a + b is an even integer

(b) aRb $\Leftrightarrow$ a – b is an even integer

(c) aRb $\Leftrightarrow$ a < b

(d) aRb $\Leftrightarrow$ a = b

51. The minimum number of elements that must be added to the relation R = {(1, 2), (2, 3)} on the set N so that it is an equivalence relation is :

(a) 4 (b) 7

(c) 6 (d) 5

52. If R is the largest equivalence relation on a set A and S is any relation on A, then :

(a) R $\subset$ S (b) S $\subset$ R

(c) R = S (d) none of these.

53. The relation R defined on the set A = {1, 2, 3, 4, 5} by R = {(x, y) : | x^2 – y^2 | < 16} is given by :

(a) R_1 = {(1, 1), (2, 1), (3, 1), (4, 1), (2, 3)}

(b) R_2 = {(2, 2), (3, 2), (4, 2), (2, 4)}

(c) R = {(3, 3), (4, 3), (5, 4), (3, 4)}

(d) none of these.

54. Let A be the set of all determinants of order 3 with entries 0 or 1 only, B the subset of A consisting of all determinants with value a, and C the subset consisting of all determinants with value – 1. Then if n (B) and n (C) denote the number of elements in B and C respectively, we have :

(a) C = ϕ (b) n (B) = n (C)

(c) A = B $\cup$ C (d) n (B) = 2n (C).

55. The solution of 8x $\equiv$ 6 (mod 14) is :

(a) [8], [6] (b) [6], [14]

(c) [6], [13] (d) [8], [14], [16].

56. The relation R: → A B, where A = {1, 2, 3, 4, 5} and B = {a, v, x, y, z} is a function of R is given by :

(a) {(1, u), (2, v), (3, v), (4, v)}

(b) {(1, u), (1, u), (2, x), (3, y), (5, z)}

(c) {(1, u), (2, v), (3, x), (4, z), (5, 4)}

(d) {(1, 4), (2, x), (2, y), (3, z), (4, v), (5, 4)}.

57. Which of the following is not correct ?

(a) $A \subseteq A^c$ if and only if A = ϕ

(b) $A^c \subseteq A$ if and only if A = X where X is a universal set

(c) If $A \cup B = A \cup C$ then B = C

(d) A = B is equivalent to $A \cup C = B \cup C$ and $A \cap C = B \cap C$

58. The set $(A \cup B \cup C) \cap (A \cap B^c \cap C^c)^c \cap C^c$ is equal to

(a) $B \cap C^c$ (b) $A \cap C$

(c) $B \cap C^c$ (d) none of these.

59. If A is set of all regular polygons and B is a set of all quadrilaterals, then $A \cap B$ is a set of all :

(a) squares   (b) rectangles

(c) rhombuses   (d) parallelograms.

60. If $P \subset Q$, then which of the following is true ?

(a) $P \cup Q = P$ (b) $P \cup Q = \phi$

(c) $P \cup Q = Q$ (d) $P \cap Q = Q$.

61. Given that :

R = {All right triangles} and

E = {All equilateral triangles} n (E ∩ R) is :

(a) 3   (b) 0

(c) 1   (d) 2.

62. $(A \cup B)'$ is equal to :

(a) $A' \cup B'$ (b) $A \cup B'$

(c) $A' \cap B'$ (d) $A \cap B$.

63. If $P \subset Q$ and n (P) = 5 and n (Q) = 8, then n (P ∪ Q) is :

(a) 13   (b) 8

(c) 0   (d) 3.

64. Let sets A and B be two disjoint subsets of a universal set U. Then $(A \cup B) \cup B' =$

(a) A   (b) B

(c) ϕ (d) none of these

65. Given the set A = {1, 2, 3}, B = {3, 4}, C = {4, 5, 6}, then $A \cup (B \cap C)$ is :

(a) {3}   (b) {1, 2, 3, 4}

(c) {1, 2, 5, 6}   (d) {1, 2, 3, 4, 5, 6}.

66. Let A = {x : x ∈ R, x ≥ 2}

and B = {x : x ∈ R, x < 4}. Then $A \cup B =$

(a) {x : x ∈ R, 2 < x < 4}

(b) {x : x ∈ R, 2 ≤ x < 4}

(c) B

(d) none of these.

67. If X and Y are two sets, then $X \cap (X \cup Y)$ equals :

(a) X   (b) Y

(c) ϕ (d) none of these

68. If A = {ϕ {ϕ}}, then the power set P (A) of A is :

(a) A   (b) {ϕ {ϕ}, A}

(c) {ϕ}, {ϕ}, {{ϕ}}   (d) none of these.

69. If a set A has n elements then the number of elements in the power set of A is :

(a) n^2 (b) 2^n

(c) 2^{2n} (d) 2^{n+1}.

70. A relation R on a set A is called an equivalence relation if :

(a) it is transitive

(b) it is reflexive

(c) it is symmetric

(d) it is reflexive, symmetric and transitive

71. A relation from set A to B is :

(a) a subset of A × B

(b) a set equivalent to A × B

(c) a set equal to A × B

(d) a universal set of A × B.

72. If A is any set, then :

(a) $A \cap A' = X$

(b) $A \cup A' = \phi$

(c) $A \cup A' = X$

(d) none of these.

73. If $A \subseteq B$, then $B \cup A$ is equal to :

(a) $B \cap A$

(b) A

(c) B

(d) none of these.

74. If A, B and C are any three sets, then

$A \times B (B \cap C)$ is equal to :

(a) $(A \cap B) \times (A \cup C)$

(b) $(A \cup B)(A \cup C)$

(c) $(A \times B) \cap (A \times C)$

(d) $(A \times B) \cup (A \times C)$.

75. Which of the following statements is true ?

(a) $\{3, 5\} \in \{1, 3, 5\}$

(b) $\{3\} \in (1, 3, 5)$

(c) $3 \in \{1, 3, 5\}$

(d) $3 \subseteq \{1, 3, 5\}$

76. If A, B, C be three sets such that :

(a) $A = B = C$

(b) $A = C$

(c) $B = C$

(d) $A = B$.

77. If $Q = \{x : x = \dfrac{1}{y}$, where $y \in N\}$, then :

(a) $\dfrac{2}{3} \in Q$

(b) $2 \in Q$

(c) $0 \in Q$

(d) $1 \in Q$.

78. Let $O(A) = m$, $O(B) = n$. Then the number of relations from A to B is :

(a) 2^{nm}

(b) 2^{m+n}

(c) $m + n$

(d) nm.

79. Let $X = \{1, 2, 3, 4, 5\}$. The number of different ordered pairs (Y, Z) that can be formed such that $Y \subseteq X$, $Z \subseteq X$ and $Y \cap Z$ is empty, is

[AIEEE - 2012]

(a) 5^2

(b) 3^5

(c) 2^5

(d) 5^3

80. Let R be the set of real numbers. **[AIEEE - 2011]**

Statement 1: $A = \{(x, y) \in R \times R : y - x$ is an integer$\}$ is an equivalence relation on R.

Statement 2: $B = \{(x, y) \in R \times R : x = \alpha y$ for some rational number $\alpha]$ is an equivalence relation on R.

(a) Statement 1 is false, statement 2 is true.

(b) Statement 1 is true, statement 2 is true; statement 2 is a correct explanation for statement 1.

(c) Statement 1 is true, statement 2 is true; statement 2 is not a correct explanation for statement 1.

(d) Statement 1 is true, statement 2 is false.

81. Consider the following relations:**[AIEEE - 2010]**

$R = \{(x, y) \,|\, x, y$ are real numbers and $x = wy$ for some rational number w$\}$;

$S =$

$\left\{ \left(\dfrac{m}{n}, \dfrac{p}{q}\right) \,\middle|\, m, n, p \text{ and } q \text{ are integers such that } n, q \neq 0 \text{ and } qm = pn \right\}.$

Then

(a) neither R nor S is an equivalence relation

(b) S is an equivalence relation but R is not an equivalence relation

(c) R and S both are equivalence relations

(d) R is an equivalence relation but S is not an equivalence relation

82. If A, B & C are three sets such that $A \cap B = A \cap C$ and $A \cup B = A \cup C$, then **[AIEEE - 2009]**

(a) $A = B$

(b) $A = C$

(c) $B = C$

(d) $A \cap B = \phi$

83. Let R be the real line. Consider the following subsets of the plane $R \times R$. **[AIEEE - 2008]**

$S = \{(x, y) : y = x + 1$ and $0 < x < 2\}$, $T = \{(x, y) : x - y$ is an integer$\}$. Which one of the following is true?

(a) neither S nor T is an equivalence relation on R.

(b) both S and T are equivalence relations on R.

(c) S is an equivalence relation on R, but T is not.

(d) T is an equivalence relation on R, but S is not.

84. The set $S = \{1, 2, 3, \ldots, 12)$ is to be partitioned into three sets A, B, C of equal size. Thus, $A \cup B \cup C = S$, $A \cap B = B \cap C = A \cap C = \phi$. The number of ways to partition S is

[AIEEE - 2007]

(a) $\dfrac{12!}{3! \, (4!)^3}$

(b) $\dfrac{12!}{3! \, (3!)^4}$

(c) $\dfrac{12!}{(4!)^4}$

(d) $\dfrac{12!}{(3!)^4}$

85. Let W denote the words in the English dictionary. Define the relation R by :

[AIEEE - 2006]

R = {x, y) ∈ W × W | the words x and y have at least one letter in common}. Then R is

(a) not reflexive, symmetric and transitive

(b) reflexive, symmetric and not transitive

(c) reflexive, symmetric and transitive

(d) reflexive, not symmetric and transitive

86. Let R = {(3, 3), (6, 6), (9, 9), (12, 12), (6, 12), (3, 9), (3, 12), (3, 6)} be a relation on the set A = {3, 6, 9, 12}

The relation is   [AIEEE - 2005]

(a) reflexive and transitive only

(b) reflexive only

(c) an equivalence relation

(d) reflexive and symmetric only

ANSWER KEY

1. (b)	2. (b)	3. (a)	4. (d)	5. (c)	6. (a)	7. (d)	8. (c)	9. (c)	10. (a)
11. (c)	12. (a)	13. (a)	14. (a)	15. (b)	16. (a)	17. (d)	18. (a)	19. (d)	20. (d)
21. (d)	22. (a)	23. (a)	24. (a)	25. (d)	26. (b)	27. (a)	28. (b)	29. (d)	30. (d)
31. (b)	32. (b)	33. (c)	34. (b)	35. (a)	36. (d)	37. (a)	38. (c)	39. (b)	40. (d)
41. (d)	42. (b)	43. (d)	44. (d)	45. (b)	46. (a)	47. (b)	48. (d)	49. (d)	50. (c)
51. (b)	52. (b)	53. (d)	54. (b)	55. (c)	56. (c)	57. (c)	58. (c)	59. (a)	60. (c)
61. (b)	62. (c)	63. (b)	64. (a)	65. (b)	66. (b)	67. (c)	68. (c)	69. (b)	70. (d)
71. (a)	72. (c)	73. (c)	74. (c)	75. (c)	76. (c)	77. (d)	78. (a)	79. (b)	80. (d)
81. (b)	82. (c)	83. (d)	84. (c)	85. (b)	86. (a)				

❑❑❑

Chapter 2

QUADRATIC EQUATIONS AND INEQUATIONS

MULTIPLE CHOICE QUESTIONS

1. If $a + b + c = 0$ and a, b, c, are rational, then the roots of the equation $(b + c - a) x^2 + (c + a - b) x + (a + b - c) = 0$ are :

   (a) rational
   (b) irrational
   (c) imaginary
   (d) equal

2. If the equations $ax + by = 1$, $cx^2 + dy^2 = 1$ have only one solution, then :

   (a) $\dfrac{a^2}{c} + \dfrac{b^2}{d} = 1$
   (b) $x = \dfrac{a}{c}$

   (c) $y = \dfrac{b}{d}$
   (d) all of these

3. If α is a root of $4x^2 + 2x - 1 = 0$, then the other root is :

   (a) $3\alpha^3 - 4\alpha$
   (b) $4\alpha^3 - 3\alpha$

   (c) $3\alpha^3 + 4\alpha$
   (d) $4\alpha^3 + 3\alpha$

4. If the roots of the equation

   $(b - c) x^2 + (c - a) x + c (a - b) = 0$

   are equal, then a, b, c are in :

   (a) A.P.
   (b) G.P.

   (c) H.P.
   (d) None of these

5. If α, β are the roots of the equation $\lambda(x^2 - x) + x + 5 = 0$ and if λ_1 and λ_2 are two values of λ for which the roots α, β are related by : $\dfrac{\alpha}{\beta} + \dfrac{\beta}{\alpha} = \dfrac{4}{5}$, then the value of $\dfrac{\lambda_1}{\lambda_2} + \dfrac{\lambda_2}{\lambda_1}$ is :

   (a) 254
   (b) 246

   (c) 225
   (d) None of these

6. If r is the ratio of the roots of the equation $ax^2 + bx + c = 0$, then $\dfrac{(r + 1)^2}{r} =$

   (a) $\dfrac{a^2}{bc}$
   (b) $\dfrac{b^2}{ca}$

   (c) $\dfrac{c^2}{ab}$
   (d) None of these

7. If the roots of the equation $x^2 + a^2 = 8x + 6a$ are real, then :

   (a) $a \in (-\infty, -2]$
   (b) $a \in [-2, 8]$

   (c) $a \in [8, \infty)$
   (d) None of these

8. If one root of $ax^2 + bx + c = 0$ is n^{th} power of the other, then $(a^n c)^k + (ac^n)^k + b = 0$, where k is equal to :

   (a) $\dfrac{1}{n}$
   (b) $\dfrac{1}{n + 1}$

   (c) $\dfrac{2}{n + 1}$
   (d) None of these

9. If the ratio of the roots of $lx^2 + nx + n = 0$ is $p : q$, then :

   (a) $\sqrt{\dfrac{q}{p}} + \sqrt{\dfrac{p}{q}} + \sqrt{\dfrac{l}{n}} = 0$

   (b) $\sqrt{\dfrac{p}{q}} + \sqrt{\dfrac{q}{p}} + \sqrt{\dfrac{n}{l}} = 0$

   (c) $\sqrt{\dfrac{q}{p}} + \sqrt{\dfrac{p}{q}} + \sqrt{\dfrac{l}{n}} = 1$

   (d) $\sqrt{\dfrac{p}{q}} + \sqrt{\dfrac{q}{p}} + \sqrt{\dfrac{n}{l}} = 1$

10. The number of real solutions of the equation $|x|^2 - 3|x| + 2 = 0$ is :

    (a) 4
    (b) 3

    (c) 1
    (d) 2

11. If α, β are irrational roots of $ax^2 + bx + c = 0$ $(a, b, c, \in Q)$, then :

    (a) $\alpha = \beta$

    (b) $\alpha\beta = 1$

    (c) α and β are conjugate roots

    (d) $\alpha^2 + \beta^2 = 1$

12. If the difference of the roots of $x^2 - px + q = 0$ is unity, then :

    (a) $p^2 + 4q = 1$

    (b) $p^2 - 4q = 1$

    (c) $p^2 + 4q^2 = (1 + 2q)^2$

    (d) $q^2 + 4p^2 = (1 + 2p)^2$

13. If one root of the equation $(l - m) x^2 + lx + 1 = 0$ is double of the other and if l is real, then :

(a) $m < \dfrac{9}{8}$ (b) $m > \dfrac{9}{8}$

(c) $m \le \dfrac{9}{8}$ (d) $m \ge \dfrac{9}{8}$

14. If one root of the equation $x^2 + px + q = 0$ is the square of the other, $p^3 + q^2 + q = kpq$, where $k =$

(a) 1   (b) 2

(c) 3   (d) None of these

15. The equation

$\sqrt{x + 3 - 4\sqrt{x - 1}} + \sqrt{x + 8 - 6\sqrt{x - 1}} = 1$ has :

(a) no solution

(b) one solution

(c) two solutions

(d) more than two solutions

16. If α and β are the roots of the equation $x^2 + px + q = 0$, then the value of $(\omega\alpha + \omega^2\beta)(\omega^2\alpha + \omega\beta)$, where ω is an imaginary cube root of unity, is :

(a) $q^2 - 3p$ (b) $p^2 - 3q$

(c) $p^2 + 3q$ (d) $q^2 + 3p$

17. In a quadratic equation with coefficient of x^2 as 1, a student reads the coefficient 16 of x wrongly as 19 and obtain the roots as -15 and -4. The correct roots are :

(a) 6, 10   (b) $-6, -10$

(c) $-7, -9$ (d) None of these

18. If the roots of the equation $ax^2 + bx + c = 0$, are of the form $\dfrac{\alpha}{\alpha - 1}$ and $\dfrac{\alpha + 1}{\alpha}$, then the value of $(a + b + c)^2$ is:

(a) $b^2 - 2ac$ (b) $2b^2 - ac$

(c) $b^2 - 4ac$ (d) $4b^2 - 2ac$

19. The equation $125^x + 45^x = 2 \cdot 27^x$ has :

(a) no solution

(b) one solution

(c) two solutions

(d) more than two solutions

20. If α and β are roots of the equation :

$A(x^2 + m^2) + A mx + c m^2 x^2 = 0$, then

$A(\alpha^2 + \beta^2) + A \alpha\beta + c \alpha^2\beta^2 =$

(a) 0   (b) 1

(c) -1 (d) None of these

21. The number of real roots of the equation :

$| 1 + a_1 x + a_2 x^2 + \ldots + a_n x^n |^n = 0$

where $| x | < \dfrac{1}{3}$ and $| a_n | < 2$, is :

(a) n if n is even

(b) 0 for any natural number n

(c) $-n$ if n is odd

(d) None of these

22. The equations $ax^2 + bx + c = 0$ and $x^2 + 2x + 3 = 0$ have a common root. Then $a : b : c =$

(a) $2 : 4 : 5$ (b) $1 : 3 : 4$

(c) $1 : 2 : 3$ (d) None of these

23. If $f(x) = 2x^3 + mx^2 - 13x + n$ and 2, 3 are roots of the equation $f(x) = 0$, then the values of m and n are :

(a) $-5, -30$ (b) $-5, 30$

(c) $5, 30$ (d) None of these

24. If $\sin\theta$ and $\cos\theta$ are the roots of the equation $ax^2 + bx + c = 0$, then :

(a) $(a - c)^2 = b^2 - c^2$ (b) $(a - c)^2 = b^2 + c^2$

(c) $(a + c)^2 = b^2 - c^2$ (d) $(a + c)^2 = b^2 + c^2$

25. If a, b are roots of equation $x^2 + px + 1 = 0$, and c, d are the roots of the equation $x^2 + qx + 1 = 0$, then $(a - c)(b - c)(a + d)(b + d) =$

(a) $p^2 - q^2$ (b) $q^2 - p^2$

(c) $p^2 + q^2$ (d) $2(p^2 - q^2)$

26. If α, β are roots of the equation $x^2 - px + q = 0$ and $\alpha > 0, \beta > 0$, then the value of $\alpha^{1/4} + \beta^{1/4}$ is $(p + 6\sqrt{q} + 4q^{1/4}\sqrt{p + 2\sqrt{q}})^k$, where k is equal to :

(a) 1   (b) 1/2

(c) 1/3   (d) 1/4

27. The solutions of the equation $(3 | x | - 3)^2 = | x | + 7$ which belongs to the domain of definition of the function $y = \sqrt{x(x - 3)}$, are given by :

(a) $\dfrac{1}{9}, -2$ (b) $\dfrac{-1}{9}, 2$

(c) $\pm\dfrac{1}{9}, \pm 2$ (d) $-\dfrac{1}{9}, -2$

28. The roots of the equation $2^{x+2} \cdot 3^{\frac{3x}{x-1}} = 9$, are given by:

   (a) $\log_2\left(\frac{2}{3}\right), -2$ (b) $3, -3$

   (c) $-2, -\frac{\log 3}{\log 2}$ (d) $1 - \log_2 3, 2$

29. In copying a quadratic equation of the form $x^2 + px + q = 0$, a student wrote the coefficient of x incorrectly and the roots were found to be 3 and 10; another student wrote the same equation, but he wrote the constant term incorrectly and thus he found the roots to be 4 and 7. The roots of the correct equation are :

   (a) 5, 6   (b) 4, 6

   (c) 4, 5   (d) None of these

30. The number of real roots of the equation $\left| x^2 + 4|x| + 3 \right| + 2x - 11 = 0$ is :

   (a) 1   (b) 2

   (c) 3   (d) None of these

31. If the roots of the equation $x^2 + px + q = 0$ differ from the roots of the equation $x^2 + qx + p = 0$ by the same quantity, then :

   (a) $p + q + 1 = 0$ (b) $p + q + 2 = 0$

   (c) $p + q + 4 = 0$ (d) None of the these

32. If α, β are the roots of $x^2 + px + q = 0$ and

   $x^{2n} + p^n x^n + q^n = 0$ and if $\frac{\alpha}{\beta}, \frac{\beta}{\alpha}$ are the roots of

   $x^n + 1 + (x+1)^n = 0$, then n must be :

   (a) even integer

   (b) odd integer

   (c) rational but not integer

   (d) None of these

33. $7^{\log_7 (x^2 - 4x + 5)} = x - 1$, x may have values :

   (a) 2, 3   (b) 7

   (c) $-2, -3$ (d) 2, -3

34. For the equation $|x^2| + |x| - 6 = 0$, the roots are :

   (a) real and equal   (b) real with sum 0

   (c) real with sum 1   (d) real with product 0

35. If α and β are the roots of the equation

   $x^2 - p(x+1) - q = 0$, then the value of

   $\frac{\alpha^2 + 2\alpha + 1}{\alpha^2 + 2\alpha + q} + \frac{\beta^2 + 2\beta + 1}{\beta^2 + 2\beta + q}$ is :

   (a) 1   (b) 2

   (c) 3   (d) 0

36. The sum of the real roots of the equation $|x-2|^2 + |x-2| - 2 = 0$ is :

   (a) 2   (b) 6

   (c) 4   (d) 8

37. If α, β are roots of the equation $ax^2 + bx + c = 0$ and $S_n = \alpha^n + \beta^n$, then $aS_{n+1} + bS_n + cS_{n-1}$ is equal to :

   (a) 0   (b) abc

   (c) $a + b + c$ (d) None of these

38. If α, β are the roots of $x^2 - 2px + q = 0$ and γ, δ are roots of $x^2 - 2rx + s = 0$ and $\alpha, \beta, \gamma, \delta$ are in A.P., then :

   (a) $p - q = r^2 - s^2$ (b) $s - q = r^2 - p^2$

   (c) $r - s = p^2 - q^2$ (d) None of these

39. The values of a for which the equation $2x^2 - 2(2a+1)x + a(a-1) = 0$ has roots α and β satisfying the condition $\alpha < a < \beta$, are :

   (a) $(-3, 0)$ (b) $(0, \infty)$

   (c) $(-\infty, -3) \cup (0, \infty)$ (d) None of these

40. If α, β are roots of $x^2 - px + q = 0$; γ, δ are roots of $x^2 - rx + s = 0$ and $\alpha, \beta, \gamma, \delta$ are in G.P., then :

   (a) $p^2 s = r^2 q$ (b) $p^2 q = r^2 s$

   (c) $p^2 r = s^2 q$ (d) None of these

41. If α and β are the values of x obtained from the equation $m^2(x^2 - x) + 2mx + 3 = 0$ and if m_1 and m_2 are the two values of m for which α and β are connected by the relation $\frac{\alpha}{\beta} + \frac{\beta}{\alpha} = \frac{4}{3}$, then the value of $\frac{m_1^2}{m_2} + \frac{m_2^2}{m_1}$ is :

   (a) $\frac{68}{3}$ (b) $-\frac{68}{3}$

   (c) $\frac{29}{3}$ (d) None of these

42. If a, b, c $\in$ R and the equations $ax^2 + bx + c = 0$ and $x^3 + 3x^2 + 3x + 2 = 0$ have two roots in common, then :

(a) $a = b \neq c$ (b) $a = b = -c$

(c) $a = b = c$ (d) None of these

43. If one of the roots of equation $ax^2 + bx + c = 0$ is reciprocal of one of the roots of $a'x^2 + b'x + c' = 0$, then :

(a) $(aa' - cc')^2 = (bc' - ab')(b'c - a'b)$

(b) $(bb' - cc')^2 = (ab' - bc')(b'c - a'b)$

(c) $(aa' - bb')^2 = (ac' - a'c)(ab' - a'b)$

(d) None of these

44. The equation $x^{\left(\frac{3}{4}(\log_2 x)^2 + \log_2 x - \frac{5}{4}\right)} = \sqrt{2}$ has :

(a) exactly one real solution

(b) exactly two real solutions

(c) exactly three real solutions

(d) no real solution.

45. If $f(x) = x - [x]$, $x (\neq 0) \in$ R, where $[x]$ is the greatest integer less than or equal to x, then the number of solutions of $f(x) + f\left(\frac{1}{x}\right) = 1$ are :

(a) 0   (b) 1

(c) infinite   (d) 2

46. The quadratic equation with rational coefficients, one of whose roots is $\dfrac{1}{2 + \sqrt{5}}$, is :

(a) $x^2 + 4x - 1 = 0$ (b) $x^2 - 4x + 1 = 0$

(c) $x^2 - 4x - 1 = 0$ (d) None of these

47. If $(\log_5 x)^2 + \log_5 x < 2$, then x belongs to the interval :

(a) $\left(\dfrac{1}{25}, 5\right)$ (b) $\left(\dfrac{1}{5}, \dfrac{1}{\sqrt{5}}\right)$

(c) $(1, \infty)$ (d) None of these

48. The number of solutions of the equation $\sin(e^x) = 5^x + 5^{-x}$ is :

(a) 0   (b) 1

(c) 2   (d) infinite

49. If x_1, x_2 are roots of equation $ax^2 + bx + c = 0$, then the value of $(ax_1 + b)^{-2} + (ax_2 + b)^{-2}$ is :

(a) $\dfrac{b^2 - 4ac}{a^2c^2}$ (b) $\dfrac{b^2 - ac}{a^2c^2}$

(c) $\dfrac{b^2 - 2ac}{a^2c^2}$ (d) None of these

50. If α and β are the roots of the equation $ax^2 + bx + c = 0$, then the quadratic equation whose roots are $\dfrac{1}{a\alpha + b}$ and $\dfrac{1}{a\beta + b}$ is :

(a) $acx^2 - bx + 1 = 0$ (b) $abx^2 - cx + 1 = 0$

(c) $bcx^2 - ax + 1 = 0$ (d) None of these

51. Let $f(x) = 1 + 2x + 3x^2 + ... + (n + 1) x^n$, where n is even. Then the number of real roots of the equation $f(x) = 0$ is :

(a) 0   (b) 1

(c) n   (d) None of these

52. If c, d are the roots of the equation $(x - a)(x - b) - k = 0$, then a, b are the roots of the equation :

(a) $(x - c)(x - d) - k = 0$

(b) $(x - c)(x - d) + k = 0$

(c) $(x - c)(x - d) + 2k = 0$

(d) None of these

53. If α, β are roots of the equation $x^2 + px + q = 0$ and γ, δ are roots of $x^2 + rx + s = 0$, then the value of $(\alpha - \gamma)(\alpha - \delta)(\beta - \gamma)(\beta - \delta)$ is :

(a) $q^2 + s^2 - pr(q + s) + s(p^2 - 2q) - qr^2$

(b) $q^2 + s^2 - pr(q + s) + s(p^2 - 2q) + qr^2$

(c) $q^2 + s^2 + pr(q + s) + s(p^2 - 2q) + qr^2$

(d) None of these

54. The value of greatest negative integer satisfying $x^2 - 4x - 77 < 0$ and $x^2 > 4$ is :

(a) -4 (b) -6

(c) -7 (d) None of these

55. If the equations $k(6x^2 + 3) + rx + 2x^2 - 1 = 0$ and $6k(2x^2 + 1) + px + 4x^2 - 2 = 0$ have both the roots common, then the value of $2r - p$ is :

(a) 0   (b) 1

(c) -1 (d) None of these

56. If $x = 2 + 2^{2/3} + 2^{1/3}$ then value of $x^3 - 6x^2 + 6x$ is :

(a) 3   (b) 2

(c) 1   (d) None of these

57. If $x^2 + px + 1$ is a factor of $ax^3 + bx + c$, then :

(a) $a^2 + c^2 = -ab$ (b) $a^2 - c^2 = -ab$

(c) $a^2 - c^2 = ab$ (d) None of these

58. If $(a^2 - 1) x^2 + (a - 1) x + a^2 - 4a + 3 = 0$ is an identity in x, then the value of a is :

(a) 1   (b) 3

(c) −1   (d) −3

59. Both the roots of the equation

$(x-b)(x-c) + (x-a)(x-c) + (x-a)(x-b) = 0$

are always :

(a) positive   (b) negative

(c) real   (d) None of these

60. If one root of $x^2 + px + q = 0$ is $5 - 3i$, then the real values of p and q are :

(a) $p = -10, q = -34$ (b) $p = -10, q = 34$

(c) $p = 10, q = -34$ (d) None of these

61. If one root of the equation $x^2 + px + 12 = 0$ is 4, while the equation $x^2 + px + q = 0$ has equal roots, then the value of q is :

(a) 49/4   (b) 4/49

(c) 4   (d) None of these

62. The roots of the equation

$$\left(x + \frac{1}{x}\right)^2 = 4 + \frac{3}{2}\left(x - \frac{1}{x}\right)$$ are :

(a) $\pm 1, 2, \dfrac{1}{2}$ (b) $\pm 1, 2, -\dfrac{1}{2}$

(c) $\pm 1, -2, -\dfrac{1}{2}$ (d) None of these

63. The roots of the equation $3^{2x+1} + 3^2 = 3^{x+3} + 3^x$ are :

(a) 1, −2   (b) 1, 2

(c) −1, 2   (d) −1, −2

64. The rational values of a and b in $ax^2 + bx + 1 = 0$ if $\dfrac{1}{4 + \sqrt{3}}$ is a root, are :

(a) $a = 13, b = -8$ (b) $a = -13, b = 8$

(c) $a = 13, b = 8$ (d) $a = -13, b = -8$

65. The quadratic equation whose roots are cubes of the roots of $x^2 + bx + c = 0$ is :

(a) $x^2 + b(b^2 - 3c)x - c^3 = 0$

(b) $x^2 + b(b^2 - 3c)x + c^3 = 0$

(c) $x^2 - b(b^2 - 3c)x + c^3 = 0$

(d) None of these

66. The roots of the equation

$(5 + 2\sqrt{6})^{x^2 - 3} + (5 - 2\sqrt{6})^{x^2 - 3} = 10$ are :

(a) $\pm 2, \pm\sqrt{3}$ (b) $\pm\sqrt{2}, \pm 3$

(c) $\pm 2, \pm\sqrt{2}$ (d) None of these

67. A car travels 25 km an hour faster than a bus for a journey of 500 km. If the bus takes 10 hours more than the car, then the speed of the car and the bus is :

(a) 25 km/hr, 40 km/hr

(b) 25 km/hr, 50 km/hr

(c) 25 km/hr, 60 km/hr

(d) None of these

68. The values of a, for which the quadratic equation $3x^2 + 2(a^2 + 1)x + (a^2 - 3a + 2) = 0$ possesses roots of opposite sign, are :

(a) $1 < a < 2$ (b) $a \in (2, \infty)$

(c) $1 < a < 3$ (d) None of these

69. Solution of the equation

$\sqrt{x + 3 - 4\sqrt{x - 1}} + \sqrt{x + 8 - 6\sqrt{x - 1}} = 1$ is :

(a) $x \in [2, 3]$ (b) $x \in [2, 5]$

(c) $x \in (5, 10)$ (d) $x \in [5, 10]$

70. If tan A and tan B are roots of $x^2 - px + q = 0$, then the value of $\sin^2(A + B)$ is :

(a) $\dfrac{p^2}{p^2 + q^2}$ (b) $\dfrac{p^2}{p^2 + (1 - q)^2}$

(c) $\dfrac{q^2}{p^2 + (1 - q)^2}$ (d) $\dfrac{p^2}{(p + q)^2}$

71. The quadratic equation whose roots are the reciprocals of the squares of the roots of $ax^2 + bx + c = 0$ is :

(a) $c^2x^2 - (b^2 - 2ca)x + a^2 = 0$

(b) $c^2x^2 + (b^2 - 2ca)x + a^2 = 0$

(c) $c^2x^2 - (b^2 - 2ca)x - a^2 = 0$

(d) None of these

72. If one root of the equation $px^2 - 14x + 8 = 0$ is six times the other, then p is equal to :

(a) 2　　　　　　　　(b) 3

(c) 1　　　　　　　　(d) None of these

73. Root of the equation $3^{x-1} + 3^{1-x} = 2$ is :

(a) 1　　　　　　　　(b) 2

(c) 0　　　　　　　　(d) −1

74. Solution of the equation

$\sqrt{x-2} + \sqrt{4-x} = \sqrt{6-x}$ is :

(a) $x = 4 - \dfrac{4}{\sqrt{5}}$　　(b) $x = 4 + \dfrac{4}{\sqrt{5}}$

(c) $x = 4 - \dfrac{2}{\sqrt{5}}$　　(d) $x = 4 + \dfrac{2}{\sqrt{5}}$

75. If $\alpha \neq \beta$, but $\alpha^2 = 5\alpha - 3$, $\beta^2 = 5\beta - 3$, then the equation whose roots are $\dfrac{\alpha}{\beta}$ and $\dfrac{\beta}{\alpha}$ is :

(a) $x^2 - 5x - 3 = 0$　　(b) $3x^2 - 19x + 3 = 0$

(c) $3x^2 + 12x + 3 = 0$　　(d) None of these

76. For real values of x, the expression $\dfrac{x^2 - 3x + 4}{x^2 + 3x + 4}$ lies between :

(a) $-\dfrac{1}{7}$ and 7　　(b) $\dfrac{1}{7}$ and 7

(c) $\dfrac{1}{3}$ and 3　　(d) None of these

77. If x is real, then the expression $\dfrac{x^2 + 34x - 71}{x^2 + 2x - 7}$

(a) lies between 4 and 7

(b) lies between 5 and 9

(c) has no value between 4 and 7

(d) has no value between 5 and 9

78. If x is real, then the maximum value of $3 - 6x - 8x^2$ is :

(a) $\dfrac{17}{8}$　　　　(b) $\dfrac{33}{8}$

(c) $\dfrac{21}{8}$　　　　(d) None of these

79. If α, β are roots of $x^2 - px + q = 0$ and α_1, β_1 are roots of the equation $x^2 - qx + p = 0$, then the equation whose roots are

$\dfrac{1}{\alpha_1 \beta} + \dfrac{1}{\alpha \beta_1}$ and $\dfrac{1}{\alpha \alpha_1} + \dfrac{1}{\beta \beta_1}$ is :

(a) $p^2 q^2 x^2 - p^2 q^2 x + p^3 + q^3 + 4pq = 0$

(b) $p^2 q^2 x^2 + p^2 q^2 x + p^3 + q^3 - 4pq = 0$

(c) $p^2 q^2 x^2 - p^2 q^2 x + p^3 + q^3 - 4pq = 0$

(d) None of these

80. The number of real solutions of the equation $27^{1/x} + 12^{1/x} = 2 . 8^{1/x}$ is :

(a) one　　　　　　(b) two

(c) infinite　　　　　(d) zero

81. If α, β are roots of the equation $x^2 + px + p^2 + q = 0$, then the value of $\alpha^2 + \alpha\beta + \beta^2 + q$ is :

(a) 0　　　　　　　　(b) 1

(c) q　　　　　　　　(d) 2q

82. If a, b, c are rational and $ax^2 + bx + c = 0$ and $3x^2 + x - 5 = 0$ have a common root, then $3a + b + 2c =$

(a) 0　　　　　　　　(b) 1

(c) 2　　　　　　　　(d) None of these

83. If one root of $x^2 + px + q = 0$ is also the root of the equation $x^2 + mx + n = 0$, then the other root of the first equation will satisfy the equation :

(a) $nx^2 + mqx + q^2 = 0$

(b) $mx^2 + nqx + q^2 = 0$

(c) $mx^2 - mqx + q^2 = 0$

(d) None of these

84. Expression $x^2 + 2(a + b + c)x + 3(bc + ca + ab)$ will be a perfect square if :

(a) $a + b + c = 0$　　(b) $ac + bc + ab = 0$

(c) $a = b = c$　　　　(d) None of these

85. If $x^2 + y^2 + z^2 + k(yz + zx + xy)$ has rational factors, then k is equal to :

(a) 1　　　　　　　　(b) 2

(c) −1　　　　　　　(d) None of these

86. For all real values of x, $\left| \dfrac{12x}{4x^2 + 9} \right|$:

(a) ≤ 1　　　　　　(b) ≤ 2

(c) > 1　　　　　　(d) > 2

87. If $x^2 - 3x + 2$ is one of the factors of the expression $x^4 - px^2 + q$, then :

(a) $p = 4, q = 5$　　(b) $p = 5, q = 4$

(c) $p = -5, q = -4$　　(d) None of these

88. If the roots of the equation

$(a^2 + b^2) t^2 - 2 (ac + bd) t + (c^2 + d^2) = 0$ are equal, then :

(a) $ab = cd$ (b) $ac = bd$

(c) $ad + bc = 0$ (d) $\dfrac{a}{b} = \dfrac{c}{d}$

89. The number of real solutions of the equation

$x^2 - 3 |x| + 2 = 0$ are :

(a) 2   (b) 3

(c) 4   (d) 1

90. If $(2 + i\sqrt{3})$ is a root of equation $x^2 + px + q = 0$, where p and q are real, then (p, q) equals :

(a) (4, 7)   (b) (−4, −7)

(c) (−4, 7)   (d) (4, −7)

91. Let α, β be the roots of the quadratic equation $x^2 + px + p^3 = 0$ $(p \neq 0)$. If (α, β) is a point on the parabola $y^2 = x$, then the roots of the quadratic equation are :

(a) 4, −2   (b) −4, −2

(c) 4, 2   (d) −4, 2

92. Let α, β be the roots of the equation $(x - a) (x - b) = c$, $c \neq 0$. The roots of the equation $(x - \alpha) (x - \beta) + c = 0$ are:

(a) a, c   (b) b, c

(c) a, b   (d) a + c, b + c

93. If the roots of the equation $x^2 - 2ax + a^2 + a - 3 = 0$ are real and less than 3, then :

(a) $a < 2$ (b) $2 \leq a \leq 3$

(c) $3 \leq a \leq 4$ (d) $a > 4$

94. For all real x, the minimum value of $\dfrac{1 - x + x^2}{1 + x + x^2}$

is :

(a) 0   (b) $\dfrac{1}{3}$

(c) 1   (d) 3

95. Given that, for all real x, the expression $\dfrac{x^2 - 2x + 4}{x^2 + 2x + 4}$ lies between $\dfrac{1}{3}$ and 3. The values between which the expression $\dfrac{9 \cdot 3^{2x} + 6 \cdot 3^x + 4}{9 \cdot 3^{2x} - 6 \cdot 3^x + 4}$

lies are :

(a) 0 and 2   (b) −1 and 1

(c) −2 and 0   (d) $\dfrac{1}{3}$ and 3

96. The numerical difference between the roots of $x^2 - 7x - 9 = 0$ is :

(a) $\sqrt{85}$ (b) $9\sqrt{7}$

(c) $2\sqrt{85}$ (d) 5

97. The value of $x^2 + 2bx + c$ is positive if :

(a) $b^2 < c$ (b) $c^2 < b$

(c) $b^2 - 4ac < 0$ (d) $b^2 - 4ac > 0$

98. If $\sin \alpha$ and $\cos \alpha$ are the roots of the equation $px^2 + qx + r = 0$, then :

(a) $p^2 + q^2 - 2pr = 0$ (b) $(p - r)^2 = q^2 + r^2$

(c) $p^2 - q^2 + 2pr = 0$ (d) $(p + r)^2 = q^2 - r^2$

99. If the sum of the roots of the equation $ax^2 + 2x + 3a = 0$, is equal to their product, then value of a is :

(a) $\dfrac{-2}{3}$ (b) −3

(c) 4   (d) None of these

100. The value of k for which the number 3 lies between the roots of the equation $x^2 + (1 - 2k) x + (k^2 - k - 2) = 0$ is given by :

(a) $2 < k < 5$ (b) $k < 2$

(c) $2 < k < 3$ (d) $k > 5$

101. The solutions of the equation $2x^2 + 3x - 9 \leq 0$ are given by :

(a) $-3 \leq x \leq -\dfrac{3}{2}$ (b) $-3 \leq x \leq \dfrac{3}{2}$

(c) $\dfrac{3}{2} \leq x \leq 3$ (d) None of these

102. The roots of the equation $x^2 + 2 (3a + 5) x + 2 (9a^2 + 25) = 0$ are real, when 'a' equals :

(a) $\dfrac{-5}{3}$ (b) $\dfrac{3}{5}$

(c) $\dfrac{5}{3}$ (d) $\dfrac{-3}{5}$

103. The value of λ for which the quadratic equation $3x^2 + 2 (\lambda^2 + 1) x + (\lambda^2 - 3\lambda + 2) = 0$ has roots of opposite signs, lies in the interval :

(a) (1, 2)   (b) $\left(\dfrac{3}{2}, 2\right)$

(c) $(-\infty, 1)$ (d) $(-\infty, 0)$

104. The greatest and the least values of the expression $\dfrac{x^2 + 2x + 1}{x^2 + 2x + 7}$ for all real values of x, are respectively :

    (a) 1, 0
    (b) 2, 3
    (c) 1, 2
    (d) 2, 0

105. If the roots of $x^2 - bx + c = 0$ are two consecutive integers, then $b^2 - 4ac$ is :

    (a) 1
    (b) 0
    (c) 2
    (d) None of these

106. The condition that the equation $ax^2 + bx + c = 0$, has both the roots positive is that :

    (a) a and b are of the same sign.
    (b) a, b and c are of the same sign.
    (c) a and c are of the same sign opposite to that of b.
    (d) b and c have the same sign opposite to that of a.

107. If $f(x) = 2x^3 + mx^2 - 13x + n$ and 2, 3 are roots of the equation $f(x) = 0$, then the values of m and n are :

    (a) 5, 30
    (b) –5, –30
    (c) –5, 30
    (d) None of these

108. For $a > 0$, the roots of the equation $\log_{ax} a + \log_x a^2 + \log_{a^2 x} a^3 = 0$ are given by :

    (a) $a^{-3/2}, a^{-1/3}$
    (b) $a^{-4/3}, a^{-1/2}$
    (c) $a^{-4/3}, a^{-1/4}$
    (d) a^{-1}, a

109. Let a, b and c be real numbers such that $4a + 2b + c = 0$ and $ab > 0$. Then the quadratic equation $ax^2 + bx + c = 0$ has :

    (a) purely imaginary roots
    (b) only one root
    (c) real roots
    (d) complex roots

110. The value of k for which $1 + \sqrt{2}$ is one of the roots of $x^2 - 2x + k = 0$ is :

    (a) –1
    (b) 1
    (c) $\sqrt{2}$
    (d) $-\sqrt{2}$

111. If the equation $y = \lambda x + a\sqrt{1 + \lambda^2}$, regarded as a quadratic in λ, has equal roots, then $x^2 + y^2$ is equal to :

    (a) $-a^2$
    (b) a^2
    (c) 0
    (d) None of these

112. If the roots of $(b - c) x^2 + (c - a) x + (a - b) = 0$ are equal, then $a + c =$

    (a) b^2
    (b) b
    (c) 2b
    (d) 3b

113. If $(7 - 4\sqrt{3})^{x^2 - 4x + 3} + (7 + 4\sqrt{3})^{x^2 - 4x + 3} = 14$, then the value of x is given by :

    (a) $2, 2 \pm \sqrt{2}$
    (b) $2 \pm \sqrt{3}, 3$
    (c) $3 \pm \sqrt{2}, 2$
    (d) None of these

114. The roots of the equation $4^x - 3 \cdot 2^{x+3} + 128 = 0$ are :

    (a) 4 and 5
    (b) 3 and 4
    (c) 2 and 3
    (d) 1 and 2

115. The number of roots of the equation $\dfrac{(x + 2)(x - 5)}{(x - 3)(x + 6)} = \dfrac{(x - 2)}{(x + 4)}$ is :

    (a) 0
    (b) 1
    (c) 2
    (d) 3

116. The number of negative integral solutions of $x^2 \cdot 2^{x+1} + 2^{|x-3|+2} = x^2 \cdot 2^{(|x-3|+4)} + 2^{x-1}$ is :

    (a) 4
    (b) 2
    (c) 1
    (d) 0

117. If α, β are the roots of quadratic equation $x^2 + bx - c = 0$, then the equation whose roots are b and c is :

    (a) $x^2 + (\alpha\beta + \alpha + \beta) x - \alpha\beta (\alpha + \beta) = 0$
    (b) $x^2 + [(\alpha + \beta) + \alpha\beta] x + \alpha\beta (\alpha + \beta) = 0$
    (c) $x^2 - [(\alpha + \beta) + \alpha\beta] x - \alpha\beta (\alpha + \beta) = 0$
    (d) $x^2 + ax - \beta = 0$

118. If the roots of the equation $ax^2 + bx + c = 0$ are in the ratio m : n, then $\sqrt{\dfrac{m}{n}} + \sqrt{\dfrac{n}{m}} + \dfrac{b}{\sqrt{ac}} =$

    (a) 0
    (b) 1
    (c) –1
    (d) None of these

119. The values of k for which the quadratic equation $kx^2 + 1 = kx + 3x - 11x^2$ has real and equal roots are :
(a) $\{-11, -3\}$ (b) $\{5, 7\}$
(c) $\{5, -7\}$ (d) None of these

120. If the roots of the equation $\dfrac{1}{x+p} + \dfrac{1}{x+q} = \dfrac{1}{r}$ are equal in magnitude but opposite in sign, then (p + q) equals :
(a) 2r (b) r
(c) $-2r$ (d) None of these

121. If roots of $ax^2 + bx + c = 0$ are α, β and roots of $Ax^2 + Bx + C = 0$ are $\alpha + k$, $\beta + k$ then, $(B^2 - 4AC)/(b^2 - 4ac)$ is equal to :
(a) a/A (b) A/a
(c) $(a/A)^2$ (d) $(A/a)^2$

122. If the sum of squares of the roots of the equation $x^2 - (a - 2)\,x - (a + 1) = 0$ is least, then the value of a is:
(a) 0 (b) 2
(c) -1 (d) 1

123. If one root of the equation $ax^2 - bx + c = 0$ is square of the other, then :
(a) $b^2 - 4ac = 0$ (b) $ac\,(a + c + 3b) = b^2$
(c) $ac = b^3$ (d) None of these

124. If the roots of $10x^3 - cx^2 - 54x - 27 = 0$ are in harmonic progression, then the roots are :
(a) $\dfrac{-3}{5}, \dfrac{-3}{2}, 3$ (b) $\dfrac{3}{5}, \dfrac{-3}{2}, 3$
(c) $\dfrac{-3}{5}, \dfrac{3}{2}, 3$ (d) None of these

125. Let $2\sin^2 x + 3\sin x - 2 > 0$ and $x^2 - x - 2 < 0$ (x is measured in radians). Then x lies in the interval :
(a) $\left(\dfrac{\pi}{6}, \dfrac{5\pi}{6}\right)$ (b) $\left(-1, \dfrac{5\pi}{6}\right)$
(c) $(-1, 2)$ (d) $\left(\dfrac{\pi}{6}, 2\right)$

126. If p and q are roots of equation $x^3 + px + q = 0$, then :
(a) $p = 1$ (b) $p = 1$ or 0
(c) $p = -2$ (d) $p = -2$ or 0

127. If α and β ($\alpha < \beta$), are the roots of the equation $x^2 + bx + c = 0$, where $c < 0 < b$, then :
(a) $0 < \alpha < \beta$ (b) $\alpha < 0 < \beta < |\alpha|$
(c) $\alpha < \beta < 0$ (d) $\alpha < 0 < |\alpha| < \beta$

128. Let α, β be roots of $x^2 - x + p = 0$ and γ, δ be the roots of $x^2 - 4x + q = 0$. If $\alpha, \beta, \gamma, \delta$ are in G.P., then the integral values of p and q respectively, are :
(a) $-2, -32$ (b) $-2, 3$
(c) $-6, 3$ (d) $-6, -32$

129. If α and β are the roots of $x^2 + px + q = 0$ and α^4 and β^4 are the roots of $x^2 - rx + s = 0$, then the equation $x^2 - 4qx + 2q^2 - r = 0$ has always :
(a) two real roots
(b) two positive roots
(c) two negative roots
(d) one positive and one negative root.

130. If roots of the equation $x^2 - 2ax + a^2 + a - 3 = 0$ are real less than 3, then :
(a) $a < 2$ (b) $2 \leq a \leq 3$
(c) $3 < a \leq 4$ (d) $a > 4$

131. The equation $\sqrt{x+1} - \sqrt{x-1} = \sqrt{4x-1}$ has :
(a) no solution
(b) one solution
(c) two solutions
(d) more than two solutions

132. If α, β are roots of the equation $ax^2 + bx + c = 0$, $(a \neq 0)$ and $\alpha + \delta$, $\beta + \delta$ are the roots of $Ax^2 + Bx + C = 0$, $(A \neq 0)$ for some constant δ, then :
(a) $\dfrac{b^2 - 4ac}{a^2} = \dfrac{B^2 - 4AC}{A^2}$
(b) $\dfrac{b^2 - 2ac}{a^2} = \dfrac{B^2 - 2AC}{A^2}$
(c) $\dfrac{b^2 - 8ac}{a^2} = \dfrac{B^2 - 8AC}{A^2}$
(d) None of these

133. Let p and q be the roots of the equation $x^2 - 2x + A = 0$ and let r & s be the roots of the equation $x^2 - 18x + B = 0$. If $p < q < r < s$ are in A.P., then values of A and B are :
(a) $-3, 77$ (b) $3, -77$
(c) $3, 77$ (d) None of these

134. The equation formed by decreasing each root of $ax^2 + bx + c = 0$ by 1 is $2x^2 + 8x + 2 = 0$, then :
(a) $a = -b$ (b) $b = -c$
(c) $c = -a$ (d) $b = a + c$

135. If $x = \sqrt{7 + 4\sqrt{3}}$, then $x + \dfrac{1}{x} =$
(a) 4 (b) 6
(c) 3 (d) 2

136. The value of x satisfying
$x = \sqrt{6 + \sqrt{6 + \sqrt{6 + \ldots \ldots \infty}}}$ is :
(a) $3, -2$ (b) -2
(c) 3 (d) None of these

137. The number of solutions of $| [x] - 2x | = 4$, where [x] is the greatest integer $\le x$, is :
(a) 2 (b) 4
(c) 1 (d) infinite

138. If $px^2 + qx + r = 0$ has no real roots and p, q, r, are real such that $p + r > 0$ then :
(a) $p - q + r < 0$ (b) $p - q + r > 0$
(c) $p + r = q$ (d) All of these

139. The number of values of k for which $[x^2 - (k - 2) x + k^2] [x^2 + kx + (2k - 1)]$ is a perfect square is :
(a) 1 (b) 2
(c) 0 (d) None of these

140. If all real values of x obtained from the equation $4^x - (a - 3) 2^x + a - 4 = 0$ are non-positive then :
(a) $a \in (4, 5]$ (b) $a \in (0, 4)$
(c) $a \in (4, +\infty)$ (d) None of these

141. Let a, b, c be real numbers and $a \ne 0$. If α is a root of $a^2x^2 + bx + c = 0$, β is a root of $a^2x^2 - bx - c = 0$, and $0 < \alpha < \beta$, then the equation $a^2x^2 + 2bx + 2c = 0$ has a root γ that always satisfies :
(a) $\gamma = \dfrac{1}{2}(\alpha + \beta)$ (b) $\gamma = \alpha + \dfrac{\beta}{2}$
(c) $\gamma = \alpha$ (d) $\alpha < \gamma < \beta$

142. If the absolute value of the difference of roots of the equation $x^2 + px + 1 = 0$ exceeds $\sqrt{3p}$ then :
(a) $p < -1$ or $p > 4$ (b) $p > 4$
(c) $-1 < p < 4$ (d) $0 \le p < 4$

143. If the product of the roots of the equation $x^2 - 5x + 4^{\log_2 \lambda} = 0$ is 8 then λ is :
(a) $\pm 2\sqrt{2}$ (b) $2\sqrt{2}$
(c) 3 (d) None of these

144. If a, b, c, d are four consecutive terms of an increasing A.P., then the roots of the equation $(x - a) (x - c) + 2 (x - b) (x - d) = 0$ are
(a) real and distinct (b) non-real complex
(c) real and equal (d) integers

145. If $a.3^{\tan x} + a \cdot 3^{-\tan x} - 2 = 0$ has real solutions, $x \ne \dfrac{\pi}{2}, 0 \le x \le \pi$, then the set of possible values of the parameter 'a' is :
(a) $[-1, 1]$ (b) $[-1, 0)$
(c) $[0, 1]$ (d) $(0, +\infty)$

146. Let R = the set of real numbers, Z = the set of integers, N = the set of natural numbers. If S is the solution set of the equation $(x)^2 + [x]^2 = (x - 1)^2 + [x + 1]^2$, where (x) = the least integer greater than or equal to x and [x] = the greatest integer less than or equal to x, then :
(a) $S = R$ (b) $S = R - Z$
(c) $S = R - N$ (d) None of these

147. If $[x]^2 = [x + 2]$, where [x] = the greatest integer less than or equal to x, then x must be such that :
(a) $x = 2, -1$ (b) $x \in [2, 3)$
(c) $x \in [-1, 0)$ (d) None of these

148. The solution set of $(x)^2 + (x + 1)^2 = 25$, where (x) is the least integer greater than or equal to x is :
(a) $(2, 4)$ (b) $(-5, -4] \cup (2, 3]$
(c) $[-4, -3) \cup [3, 4)$ (d) None of these

149. For the equation $| x^2 - 2x - 3 | = b$, which statement or statements are true ?
(a) For $b < 0$, there are no solutions.
(b) For $b = 0$, there are three solutions.
(c) For $0 < b < 1$, there are four solutions.
(d) For $b = 1$, there are two solutions.

150. The solution of $\left|\dfrac{x}{x-1}\right| + |x| = \dfrac{x^2}{|x-1|}$ is :

(a) $x \geq 0$ (b) $x > 0$

(c) $x \in (1, \infty)$ (d) None of these

151. If '1' lies between the roots of the equation $-x^2 - ax + a = 0$, then set of possible values of 'a' is :

(a) ϕ (b) $[0, 4]$

(c) $(0, 4)$ (d) $(-4, 4)$

152. The equation $x^2 + ax + b^2 = 0$ has two roots each of which exceeds a number c, then :

(a) $a^2 < 4b^2$ (b) $c^2 + ac + b^2 > 0$

(c) $-\dfrac{a}{2} < c$ (d) None of these

153. The system $y^{(x^2 + 7x + 12)} = 1$ and $x + y = 6$, $y > 0$ has :

(a) no solution

(b) one solution

(c) two solutions

(d) more than 2 solutions

154. The least integral value of 'a' for which :

$(a - 2) x^2 + 8x + a + 4 > 0$ for all x is :

(a) $a = 4$ (b) $a = 3$

(c) $a = 5$ (d) $a = 2$

155. Let $f(x) = ax^2 + bx + c$; $a, b, c \in R$, $a \neq 0$, satisfying $f(1) + f(2) = 0$. Then the quadratic equation $f(x) = 0$ has :

(a) no real roots

(b) 1 and 2 as real roots

(c) two equal roots

(d) two distinct real roots

156. The constant term of the quadratic expression

$\displaystyle\sum_{k=2}^{n} \left(x - \dfrac{1}{k-1}\right)\left(x - \dfrac{1}{k}\right)$, as $n \to \infty$ is :

(a) -1 (b) 0

(c) 1 (d) None of these

157. If b is harmonic mean of a and c, and α, β are roots of the equation $a(b - c)x^2 + b(c - a)x + c(a - b) = 0$, then :

(a) $\alpha + \beta = 3$ (b) $\alpha + \beta = 1/2$

(c) $\alpha\beta = 2$ (d) $\alpha = 1$, $\beta = 1$

158. If the roots of $x^2 + x + a = 0$ exceed a, then :

(a) $2 < a < 3$ (b) $a > 3$

(c) $-3 < a < 3$ (d) $a < -2$

159. If roots of the equation $x^2 - \alpha x - \beta x + 1 - k + \alpha\beta = 0$ are γ & δ, then roots of $x^2 - \gamma x - \delta x - 1 + k + \gamma\delta = 0$ are :

(a) $\alpha + 1$, $\beta + 1$ (b) α, β

(c) $\alpha - 1$, $\beta - 1$ (d) $\alpha + k$, $\beta + k$

160. If roots of equation $x^2 + 2(m - 1)x + m + 5 = 0$ are equal in magnitude but opposite in sign, then m is equal to :

(a) 1

(b) -5

(c) No such value of 'm' exists

(d) None of these

161. If α, β, γ are the roots of $x^3 + 64 = 0$, then the equation whose roots are $\left(\dfrac{\alpha}{\beta}\right)^2$ and $\left(\dfrac{\alpha}{\gamma}\right)^2$ is :

(a) $x^2 - 4x + 16 = 0$ (b) $x^2 + 4x + 16 = 0$

(c) $x^2 - x + 1 = 0$ (d) $x^2 + x + 1 = 0$

162. The adjoining figure shows the graph of $y = ax^2 + bx + c$. Then :

(a) $a > 0$

(b) a and c are of opposite sign

(c) $c > 0$

(d) a and b are of opposite sign

163. If $2^{\log_2 (x^2 - 5x - 3)} = 2 - x$, then the set of values of x is :

(a) $\{-1, 5\}$ (b) $\{-1\}$

(c) $\{5\}$ (d) $\{\ \}$

164. If $-a^2 x^2 + 2x + 3a^2 \geq 0$ for all $x \in (2, 4)$, then the value of 'a' lies in the interval :

(a) $\left(-\dfrac{1}{\sqrt{3}}, \dfrac{1}{\sqrt{3}}\right)$ (b) $\left(-\dfrac{2}{\sqrt{7}}, \dfrac{2}{\sqrt{7}}\right)$

(c) $\left(-\dfrac{4}{7}, \dfrac{4}{7}\right)$ (d) $\left(-\dfrac{2\sqrt{2}}{\sqrt{13}}, \dfrac{2\sqrt{2}}{\sqrt{13}}\right)$

165. If the roots of the equation

$a (b - c) x^2 + b (c - a) x + c (a - b) = 0$ are equal, then :

(a) a, b, c are in A.P.   (b) a, b, c are in G.P.

(c) a, b, c are in H.P.   (d) None of these

166. If $F (x) = x^4 + 9x^3 + 35x^2 - x + 4$, then $F (-5 + 2\sqrt{-4})$ is equal to :

(a) −160   (b) 160

(c) 0   (d) None of these

167. The value of 'a' for which exactly one root of the equation $e^a x^2 - e^{2a} x + e^a - 1 = 0$ lies between 1 and 2 are given by :

(a) $ln \dfrac{(5 - \sqrt{17})}{4} < a < ln \dfrac{(5 + \sqrt{17})}{4}$

(b) $0 < a < 100$

(c) $ln \dfrac{5}{4} < a < ln \dfrac{10}{3}$

(d) None of these

168. If tan A and tan B are the roots of the quadratic equation $x^2 - ax + b = 0$, then the value of $\sin^2 (A + B)$ is :

(a) $\dfrac{a^2}{a^2 + (1 - b)^2}$ (b) $\dfrac{a^2}{a^2 + b^2}$

(c) $\dfrac{a^2}{(b + c)^2}$ (d) $\dfrac{a^2}{b^2 (1 - a)^2}$

169. The number of solutions of the equation

$x + \sqrt{x + 2} = 0$ is :

(a) 0   (b) 1

(c) 2   (d) 4

170. If the quadratic equations $ax^2 + 2cx + b = 0$ and $ax^2 + 2bx + c = 0$, have a common root, then $a + 4b + 4c =$

(a) −2   (b) −1

(c) 0   (d) 1

171. If $2a + 3b + 6c = 0$, a, b, c $\in$ R, then the quadratic equation $ax^2 + bx + c = 0$ has :

(a) at least one root in $[0, 1]$

(b) at least one root in $[2, 3]$

(c) at least one root in $[3, 4]$

(d) None of these

172. For the equation $| x |^2 + | x | - 6 = 0$, sum of the roots is :

(a) −1   (b) 0

(c) 2   (d) None of these

173. If $ax^2 + bx + 10 = 0$ does not have two distinct real roots, then the least value of $5a + b$ is :

(a) −3   (b) 2

(c) 3   (d) None of these

174. The number of solutions of the equation

$x^3 + x^2 + 20x + 2 \cos x = 0$, $x \in [0, 2\pi]$ are :

(a) 1   (b) 2

(c) 3   (d) None of these

175. Let $\alpha + i\beta$; α, $\beta \in$ R be a root of the equation $x^3 + qx + r = 0$; q, r $\in$ R. The cubic equation independent of α and β whose one root is 2α, is

(a) $x^3 + qx - r = 0$ (b) $x^3 + qx + r = 0$

(c) $x^3 - qx - r = 0$ (d) $x^3 - qx + r = 0$

176. If the expression $a^2 (b^2 - c^2) x^2 + b^2 (c^2 - a^2) x + c^2 (a^2 - b^2)$ is a perfect square then :

(a) a, b, c are in A.P.

(b) a^2, b^2, c^2 are in A.P.

(c) a^2, b^2, c^2 are in H.P.

(d) a^2, b^2, c^2 are in G.P.

177. The necessary and sufficient condition for the equation $(1 - a^2) x^2 + 2ax - 1 = 0$ to have roots lying in the interval $(0, 1)$ is :

(a) $a > 0$ (b) $a < 0$

(c) $a > 2$ (d) None of these

178. If the two equations $a_1 x^2 + b_1 x + c_1 = 0$ and $a_2 x^2 + b_2 x + c_2 = 0$ have common roots, then the value of $(a_1 b_2 - a_2 b_1) (b_1 c_2 - b_2 c_1)$ is :

(a) $- (a_1 c_2 - a_2 c_1)^2$ (b) $(a_1 a_2 - c_1 c_2)^2$

(c) $(a_1 c_1 - a_2 c_2)^2$ (d) $(a_1 c_2 - c_1 a_2)^2$

179. If roots of the equation $\dfrac{l}{x + l + k} + \dfrac{b}{x + b + k} = 2$ are equal in magnitude, but in opposite in sign, then the value of k is :

(a) 0   (b) $-\dfrac{(l + b)}{4}$

(c) $\dfrac{(l + b)}{4}$ (d) $\dfrac{(l + b)}{2}$

180. The real roots of the equation $x^2 + 5|x| + 4 = 0$ are :

(a) $\{-1, 4\}$ (b) $\{1, 4\}$

(c) $\{-4, 4\}$ (d) None of these

181. If a, b, c are positive real numbers, then both the roots of equation $ax^2 + bx + c = 0$

(a) are always real and +ve

(b) have −ve real parts

(c) are real and negative

(d) None of these

182. The maximum number of real roots of the equation $x^{2n} - 1 = 0$ is :

(a) 3   (b) n

(c) 2   (d) 2n

183. If α, β are the roots of $ax^2 + bx + c = 0$, then $\dfrac{1}{\alpha}, \dfrac{1}{\beta}$ are the roots of :

(a) $ax^2 + cx + a = 0$ (b) $cx^2 + bx + a = 0$

(c) $bx^2 + ax + a = 0$ (d) $cx^2 + ax + b = 0$

184. Let $P_n(x) = 1 + 2x + 3x^2 + ... + (n + 1)x^n$ be a polynomial such that n is even. Then the number of real roots of $P_n(x) = 0$ is :

(a) 1   (b) n

(c) 0   (d) None of these

185. If α, β are the roots of $x^2 - 3x + 1 = 0$, then the equation whose roots are $\dfrac{1}{\alpha - 2} \cdot \dfrac{1}{\beta - 2}$ is :

(a) $x^2 + x - 1 = 0$ (b) $x^2 + x + 1 = 0$

(c) $x^2 - x - 1 = 0$ (d) None of these

186. If α, β are roots of the equation $x^2 - 5x - 3 = 0$, then the equation whose roots are $\dfrac{1}{2\alpha - 3}, \dfrac{1}{2\beta - 3}$ will be :

(a) $33x^2 + 4x + 1 = 0$ (b) $33x^2 - 4x - 1 = 0$

(c) $33x^2 - 4x + 1 = 0$ (d) $33x^2 + 4x - 1 = 0$

187. If the equation $4x^2 + 3x + 7 = 0$ has roots α and β, then $\dfrac{1}{\alpha} + \dfrac{1}{\beta}$ is equal to :

(a) $\dfrac{3}{7}$ (b) $-\dfrac{3}{7}$

(c) $\dfrac{2}{7}$ (d) $\dfrac{7}{3}$

188. If ratio of the roots of equation $x^2 + x + 1 = 0$ are m, n then :

(a) $m + n + 1 = 0$

(b) $\sqrt{m} + \sqrt{n} + 1 = 0$

(c) $\sqrt{\dfrac{m}{n}} + \sqrt{\dfrac{n}{m}} + 1 = 0$

(d) $(m + n)^2 = mn$

189. If α, β are the roots of $9x^2 + 6x + 1 = 0$, then the equation with the roots $\dfrac{1}{\alpha}, \dfrac{1}{\beta}$ is :

(a) $2x^2 + 3x + 18 = 0$ (b) $x^2 + 6x - 9 = 0$

(c) $x^2 + 6x + 9 = 0$ (d) $x^2 - 6x + 9 = 0$

190. The equation $e^{\sin x} - e^{-\sin x} - 4 = 0$ has :

[AIEEE - 2012]

(a) infinite number of real roots

(b) no real roots

(c) exactly one real root

(d) exactly four real roots

191. If the roots of the equation $bx^2 + cx + a = 0$ are imaginary, then for all real values of x, the expression $3b^2x^2 + 6bcx + 2c^2$ is

AIEEE - 2009]

(a) greater than 4ab   (b) less than 4ab

(c) greater than − 4ab (d) less than − 4ab

192. Suppose the cube $x^3 - px + q$ has three distinct real roots, where $p > 0$ and $q > 0$. Then which one of the following holds ?   **[AIEEE - 2008]**

(a) The cubic has minima at $\sqrt{p/3}$ and maxima at $-\sqrt{p/3}$

(b) The cubic has minima at $-\sqrt{p/3}$ and maxima at $\sqrt{p/3}$

(c) The cubic has minima at both $\sqrt{p/3}$ and $-\sqrt{p/3}$

(d) The cubic has maxima at both $\sqrt{p/3}$ and $-\sqrt{p/3}$

193. How many real solutions does the equation $x^7 + 14x^5 + 16x^3 + 30x - 560 = 0$ have ?

[AIEEE - 2008]

(a) 7   (b) 1

(c) 3   (d) 5

194. If the roots of the quadratic equation $x^2 + px + q = 0$ are $\tan 30°$ and $\tan 15°$, respectively then the value of $2 + q - p$ is **[AIEEE - 2006]**

(a) 2   (b) 3
(c) 0   (d) 1

195. All the values of m for which both roots of the equation $x^2 - 2mx + m^2 - 1 = 0$ are greater than -2 but less than 4, lie in the interval **[AIEEE - 2006]**

(a) $-2 < m < 0$ (b) $m > 3$
(c) $-1 < m < 3$ (d) $1 < m < 4$

196. If x is real, the maximum value of $\dfrac{3x^2 + 9x + 17}{3x^2 + 9x + 7}$ is : **[AIEEE - 2006]**

(a) 1/4   (b) 41
(c) 1   (d) 17/7

197 In a triangle PQR, $\angle R = \dfrac{\pi}{2}$. If $\tan\left(\dfrac{P}{2}\right)$ and $\tan\left(\dfrac{Q}{2}\right)$ are roots of $ax^2 + bx + c = 0$, $a \neq 0$ then : **[AIEEE - 2005]**

(a) $a = b + c$ (b) $c = a + b$
(c) $b = c$ (d) $b = a + c$

198. The value of α for which the sum of the squares of roots of the equation $x^2 - (a - 2)x - a - 1 = 0$ assume the least value is **[AIEEE - 2005]**

(a) 1   (b) 0
(c) 3   (d) 2

199. If roots of the equation $x^2 - bx + c = 0$ are two consecutive integers, then $b^2 - 4c$ equals : **[AIEEE - 2005]**

(a) -2 (b) 3
(c) 2   (d) 1

200. Let α and β be the roots of the equation $x^2 - 6x - 2 = 0$ with $\alpha > \beta$. If $a_n = \alpha^n - \beta^n$ for $n \geq 1$, then the value of $\dfrac{a_{10} - 2a_8}{2a_9}$ is

(a) 1   (b) 2
(c) 3   (d) 4

ANSWER KEY

1. (a)	2. (d)	3. (b)	4. (a)	5. (a)	6. (b)	7. (b)	8. (b)	9. (b)	10. (a)
11. (c)	12. (c)	13. (c)	14. (c)	15. (d)	16. (b)	17. (b)	18. (c)	19. (b)	20. (a)
21. (b)	22. (c)	23. (b)	24. (d)	25. (b)	26. (d)	27. (d)	28. (c)	29. (a)	30. (b)
31. (c)	32. (a)	33. (a)	34. (b)	35. (a)	36. (c)	37. (a)	38. (b)	39. (c)	40. (a)
41. (b)	42. (c)	43. (a)	44. (c)	45. (c)	46. (a)	47. (a)	48. (a)	49. (c)	50. (a)
51. (a)	52. (b)	53. (b)	54. (c)	55. (a)	56. (b)	57. (c)	58. (a)	59. (c)	60. (b)
61. (a)	62. (b)	63. (c)	64. (a)	65. (b)	66. (c)	67. (b)	68. (a)	69. (d)	70. (b)
71. (a)	72. (b)	73. (a)	74. (a)	75. (b)	76. (b)	77. (d)	78. (b)	79. (c)	80. (d)
81. (a)	82. (a)	83. (a)	84. (c)	85. (b)	86. (a)	87. (b)	88. (d)	89. (c)	90. (c)
91. (a)	92. (c)	93. (a)	94. (b)	95. (d)	96. (a)	97. (a)	98. (c)	99. (a)	100.(a)
101. (b)	102.(c)	103.(a)	104.(a)	105.(a)	106.(c)	107.(c)	108.(b)	109.(c)	110.(a)
111. (b)	112.(c)	113.(a)	114.(b)	115.(b)	116.(d)	117.(b)	118.(a)	119.(c)	120.(a)
121. (d)	122.(d)	123.(b)	124.(a)	125.(d)	126.(b)	127.(b)	128.(a)	129.(a)	130.(a)
131. (a)	132.(a)	133.(a)	134.(b)	135.(a)	136.(c)	137.(b)	138. (d)	139.(a)	140.(a)
141. (d)	142.(b)	143.(b)	144.(a)	145.(c)	146.(b)	147.(d)	148.(b)	149.(a)	150.(c)
151. (a)	152.(b)	153.(d)	154.(c)	155.(a)	156.(c)	157.(d)	158.(d)	159.(b)	160.(c)
161. (d)	162.(d)	163.(b)	164.(d)	165.(b)	166.(d)	167.(a)	168.(a)	169.(a)	170.(c)
171. (a)	172.(b)	173.(b)	174.(d)	175.(a)	176.(c)	177.(c)	178.(d)	179.(b)	180.(d)
181. (b)	182.(c)	183.(b)	184.(c)	185.(c)	186.(d)	187.(b)	188.(d)	189.(c)	190.(b)
191. (c)	192.(a)	193.(b)	194.(b)	195.(c)	196.(b)	197.(b)	198.(a)	199.(d)	200.(c)

❏❏❏

Chapter 3

TRIGONOMETRIC RATIOS AND IDENTITIES

MULTIPLE CHOICE QUESTIONS

1. The value of the expression

   $3 (\sin x - \cos x)^4 + 4 (\sin^6 x + \cos^6 x)$

   $+ 6 (\sin x + \cos x)^2 = 13$ is :

   (a) 10   (b) 12

   (c) 13   (d) None of these

2. The expression

   $\dfrac{1}{\tan 3A - \tan A} - \dfrac{1}{\cot 3A - \cot A}$ is equal to :

   (a) cot 2A   (b) tan 2A

   (c) cot 3A   (d) tan 3A

3. If $\operatorname{cosec} \theta = x + \dfrac{1}{4x}$, then the value of

   $\operatorname{cosec} \theta + \cot \theta$ is:

   (a) 2x   (b) $-2x$

   (c) $\dfrac{1}{2x}$ (d) $-\dfrac{1}{2x}$

4. If $3 \sin \theta + 5 \cos \theta = 5$, then the value of

   $5 \sin \theta - 3 \cos \theta$ is :

   (a) 4   (b) -3

   (c) 5   (d) -5

5. If $\cos (\alpha + \beta) \sin (\gamma + \delta) = \cos (\alpha - \beta) \sin (\gamma - \delta)$,

   then $\cot \alpha \cot \beta \cot \gamma =$

   (a) cot δ   (b) $-$ cot δ

   (c) tan δ   (d) $-$ tan δ

6. If $\tan^2 \theta = 1 - e^2$, then $\sec \theta + \tan^3 \theta \operatorname{cosec} \theta =$

   (a) $(1 - e^2)^{3/2}$ (b) $(2 - e^2)^{1/2}$

   (c) $(2 - e^2)^{3/2}$ (d) None of these

7. The value of the expression

   $2 \sin^2\beta + 4 \cos (\alpha + \beta) \sin \alpha \sin \beta + \cos 2 (\alpha + \beta)$

   is :

   (a) sin α   (b) sin 2α

   (c) cos α   (d) cos 2α

8. If $a \sec \theta + b \tan \theta + c = 0$ and

   $p \sec \theta + q \tan \theta + r = 0$, then :

   (a) $(br - qc)^2 - (aq - pb)^2 = (pc - ar)^2$

   (b) $(br - qc)^2 - (pc - ar)^2 = (aq - pb)^2$

   (c) $(pc - ar)^2 - (br - qc)^2 = (aq - pb)^2$

   (d) None of these

9. The value of the expression

   $\cos^2 (A - B) + \cos^2 B - 2 \cos (A - B) \cos A \cos B$

   is :

   (a) $\cos^2 A$ (b) $\cos^2 B$

   (c) $\sin^2 A$ (d) $\sin^2 B$

10. If $\operatorname{cosec} \theta - \sin \theta = m$ and $\sec \theta - \cos \theta = n$, then :

    (a) $(m^2n)^{1/3} + (mn^2)^{1/3} = 1$

    (b) $(m^2n)^{2/3} + (mn^2)^{2/3} = 1$

    (c) $(m^2n)^{4/3} + (mn^2)^{4/3} = 1$

    (d) None of these

11. The equation $\sec^2 \theta = \dfrac{4xy}{(x + y)^2}$ is possible for real

    values of x and y only if :

    (a) $x + y = 2xy$ (b) $x + y = -2xy$

    (c) $x + y = 1$ (d) $x = y$

12. If $\cos 2\alpha = \dfrac{3 \cos 2\beta - 1}{3 - \cos 2\beta}$, then $\dfrac{\tan \alpha}{\tan \beta} =$

    (a) 1   (b) -1

    (c) $\sqrt{2}$ (d) $\sqrt{3}$

13. The value of $\tan 1° \tan 2° .... \tan 89°$ is :

    (a) 0   (b) 1

    (c) -1 (d) None of these

14. The value of

    $\cos^4 \dfrac{\pi}{8} + \cos^4 \dfrac{3\pi}{8} + \cos^4 \dfrac{5\pi}{8} + \cos^4 \dfrac{7\pi}{8}$ is :

    (a) $\dfrac{1}{2}$ (b) $\dfrac{3}{2}$

    (c) $\dfrac{5}{2}$ (d) None of these

15. If $\sin x + \sin^2 x = 1$, then $\cos^8 x + 2\cos^6 x + \cos^4 x =$

   (a) 0   (b) – 1

   (c) 2   (d) 1

16. The value of

   $\cos^2 \dfrac{\pi}{16} + \cos^2 \dfrac{3\pi}{16} + \cos^2 \dfrac{5\pi}{16} + \cos^2 \dfrac{7\pi}{16}$ is :

   (a) 1   (b) 2

   (c) 3   (d) None of these

17. $\tan \theta \tan (\theta + 60°) + \tan \theta \tan (\theta - 60°)$

   $+ \tan (\theta + 60°) \tan (\theta - 60°) + 3 =$:

   (a) 0   (b) 1

   (c) – 1   (d) None of these

18. If $A + B = 45°$, then $(1 + \tan A)(1 + \tan B) =$

   (a) 1   (b) – 1

   (c) 2   (d) None of these

19. $\tan A + \tan (60° + A) - \tan (60° - A) =$:

   (a) $\tan 3A$ (b) $2 \tan 3A$

   (c) $3 \tan 3A$ (d) None of these

20. If $\tan \beta = \dfrac{n \sin \alpha \cos \alpha}{1 - n \sin^2 \alpha}$, then $\tan (\alpha - \beta) =$

   (a) $(1 - n) \tan \beta$ (b) $(1 - n) \tan \alpha$

   (c) $(n - 1) \tan \beta$ (d) None of these

21. If $p \sin \theta + q \cos \theta = a$ and $p \cos \theta - q \sin \theta = b$,

   then $\dfrac{p + a}{q + b} + \dfrac{q - b}{p - a}$ is equal to :

   (a) 1   (b) 2

   (c) 0   (d) None of these

22. If $\cos (\beta - \gamma) + \cos (\gamma - \alpha) + \cos (\alpha - \beta) = -\dfrac{3}{2}$,

   then :

   (a) $\cos \alpha + \cos \beta + \cos \gamma = 1$

   (b) $\cos \alpha + \cos \beta + \cos \gamma = - 1$

   (c) $\sin \alpha + \sin \beta + \sin \gamma = 1$

   (d) $\sin \alpha + \sin \beta + \sin \gamma = 0$

23. If $3 \tan \theta \tan \phi = 1$, then $\dfrac{\cos (\theta - \phi)}{\cos (\theta + \phi)} =$

   (a) $\dfrac{1}{2}$ (b) 2

   (c) $\dfrac{1}{3}$ (d) 3

24. If three angles A, B and C are such that

   $\cot B = \dfrac{\sin A - \sin C}{\cos C - \cos A}$, then A, B and C are in :

   (a) A.P.   (b) G.P.

   (c) H.P.   (d) None of these

25. If $\sin A = \dfrac{3}{5}$, $\tan B = \dfrac{1}{2}$ and $\dfrac{\pi}{2} < A < \pi < B < \dfrac{3\pi}{2}$,

   then the value of $8 \tan A - \sqrt{5} \sec B$ is :

   (a) $\dfrac{5}{2}$ (b) $-\dfrac{5}{2}$

   (c) $-\dfrac{7}{2}$ (d) $\dfrac{7}{2}$

26. The value of $5 \cos \theta + 3 \cos \left(\theta + \dfrac{\pi}{3}\right) + 3$ lies

   between :

   (a) – 2 and 10   (b) – 3 and 10

   (c) – 4 and 10   (d) None of these

27. The value of $\cos \dfrac{2\pi}{7} + \cos \dfrac{4\pi}{7} + \cos \dfrac{6\pi}{7}$ is :

   (a) 0   (b) 1

   (c) $\dfrac{1}{2}$ (d) $-\dfrac{1}{2}$

28. The value of $\sin 20° \sin 40° \sin 80°$ is :

   (a) $\dfrac{\sqrt{3}}{8}$ (b) $\dfrac{1}{8}$

   (c) $\dfrac{1}{16}$ (d) None of these

29. $\cos^2 73° + \cos^2 47° + \cos 73° \cos 47° =$:

   (a) $\dfrac{1}{4}$ (b) $-\dfrac{1}{4}$

   (c) $\dfrac{3}{4}$ (d) None of these

30. If $\alpha + \beta = 90°$, then the maximum value of $\sin \alpha \sin \beta =$

   (a) 1   (b) $\dfrac{1}{2}$

   (c) $\dfrac{3}{2}$ (d) None of these

31. If in a $\triangle ABC$, $\cos A = \dfrac{\sin B}{2 \sin C}$, then it is :

   (a) an isosceles triangle

   (b) an equilateral triangle

   (c) a right angled triangle

   (d) None of these

32. If $\sin \theta = n \sin (\theta + 2\alpha)$, then $\tan (\theta + \alpha) =$

(a) $\dfrac{1-n}{1+n} \tan \alpha$ (b) $\dfrac{n+1}{n-1} \tan \alpha$

(c) $\dfrac{1+n}{1-n} \tan \alpha$ (d) None of these

33. The value of $\cos \dfrac{2\pi}{15} \cos \dfrac{4\pi}{15} \cos \dfrac{8\pi}{15} \cos \dfrac{14\pi}{15}$ is :

(a) $\dfrac{1}{4}$ (b) $\dfrac{1}{8}$

(c) $\dfrac{1}{16}$ (d) None of these

34. If $\dfrac{\sin (\theta + \alpha)}{\cos (\theta - \alpha)} = \dfrac{i-m}{1+m}$, then

$$\tan \left(\dfrac{\theta}{4} - \theta\right) \cdot \tan \left(\dfrac{\pi}{4} - \alpha\right) =$$

(a) $\dfrac{1}{m}$ (b) $-\dfrac{1}{m}$

(c) m (d) None of these

35. If $\cot \alpha \cot \beta = 2$, then $\dfrac{\cos (\alpha + \beta)}{\cos (\alpha - \beta)} =$

(a) $\dfrac{1}{3}$ (b) $-\dfrac{1}{3}$

(c) $\dfrac{1}{2}$ (d) $-\dfrac{1}{2}$

36. $\cos \dfrac{\pi}{15} \cos \dfrac{2\pi}{15} \cos \dfrac{3\pi}{15} \cos \dfrac{4\pi}{15} \cos \dfrac{5\pi}{15} \cos \dfrac{6\pi}{15} \cos \dfrac{7\pi}{15} =$:

(a) $\dfrac{1}{128}$ (b) $\dfrac{1}{64}$

(c) $\dfrac{1}{16}$ (d) None of these

37. The value of $\sqrt{3} \operatorname{cosec} 20° - \sec 20°$ is :

(a) 4   (b) 12

(c) -2 (d) None of these

38. $\sin \dfrac{\pi}{10} \cdot \sin \dfrac{13\pi}{10}$ is equal to :

(a) $\dfrac{1}{2}$ (b) $-\dfrac{1}{2}$

(c) $-\dfrac{1}{4}$ (d) 1

39. The value of

$\cot \alpha - \tan \alpha - 2 \tan 2\alpha - 4 \tan 4\,\alpha - 8 \cot 8\alpha$ is

(a) 0   (b) 1

(c) -1 (d) None of these

40. If $\cos \alpha + \cos \beta + \cos \gamma + \cos (\alpha + \beta + \gamma)$

$$= k \cos \left(\dfrac{\alpha + \beta}{2}\right) \cos \left(\dfrac{\beta + \gamma}{2}\right) \cos \left(\dfrac{\gamma + \alpha}{2}\right),$$

then k is equal to :

(a) 1   (b) 2

(c) 4   (d) None of these

41. The value of

$$\left(1 + \cos \dfrac{\pi}{10}\right)\left(1 + \cos \dfrac{3\pi}{10}\right)\left(1 + \cos \dfrac{7\pi}{10}\right)\left(1 + \cos \dfrac{9\pi}{10}\right) \text{ is :}$$

(a) $\dfrac{1}{8}$ (b) $\dfrac{1}{16}$

(c) $\dfrac{1}{32}$ (d) None of these

42. The value of

$$\cos^2 \theta + \cos^2 \left(\dfrac{2\pi}{3} - \theta\right) + \cos^2 \left(\dfrac{2\pi}{3} + \theta\right) = :$$

(a) $\dfrac{1}{2}$ (b) $-\dfrac{1}{2}$

(c) 1   (d) $\dfrac{3}{2}$

43. If $b \sin \beta = a \sin (2\alpha + \beta)$, then $\dfrac{\cot (\alpha + \beta)}{\cot \alpha} =$

(a) $\dfrac{b-a}{b+a}$ (b) $\dfrac{b+a}{b-a}$

(c) $\dfrac{a-b}{a+b}$ (d) None of these

44. The value of

$$\left(1 + \cos \dfrac{\pi}{8}\right)\left(1 + \cos \dfrac{3\pi}{8}\right)\left(1 + \cos \dfrac{7\pi}{8}\right)\left(1 + \cos \dfrac{9\pi}{8}\right) \text{ is}$$

:

(a) $\dfrac{1}{4}$ (b) $\dfrac{1}{8}$

(c) $\dfrac{1}{16}$ (d) None of these

45. If $\tan \alpha = \dfrac{1}{3}$ and $\tan \dfrac{\beta}{2} = \dfrac{1}{2}$, then $\tan (\alpha + \beta) =$

(a) 1   (b) -1

(c) 2   (d) 3

46. $\sin^3 \alpha + \sin^3 \left(\dfrac{2\pi}{3} + \alpha \right) + \sin^3 \left(\dfrac{4\pi}{3} + \alpha \right) =$

(a) $\dfrac{3}{4} \sin 3\alpha$ (b) $-\dfrac{3}{4} \sin 3\alpha$

(c) $\dfrac{4}{3} \sin 3\alpha$ (d) $-\dfrac{4}{3} \sin 3\alpha$

47. If $2 \tan \alpha = 3 \tan \beta$, then $\tan (\alpha - \beta) =$

(a) $\dfrac{\sin 2\beta}{5 - \cos 2\beta}$ (b) $\dfrac{\cos 2\beta}{5 - \cos 2\beta}$

(c) $\dfrac{\sin 2\beta}{5 + \cos 2\beta}$ (d) None of these

48. In a $\triangle ABC$, if $\sin 2A = \sin 2B + \sin 2C$, then :

(a) $A = 90°$ or $B = 90°$ (b) $A = 90°$ or $C = 90°$

(c) $B = 90°$ or $C = 90°$ (d) None of these

49. For $\theta = \dfrac{\pi}{2^n + 1}$, the value of

$\cos \theta \cdot \cos 2\theta \cdot \cos 2^2\theta \dots \cos 2^{n-1} \theta =$

(a) 1 (b) $\dfrac{1}{2^n}$

(c) 2^n (d) None of these

50. If $\tan A - \tan B = x$ and $\cot B - \cot A = y$, then $\cot (A - B)$:

(a) $\dfrac{1}{x} - \dfrac{1}{y}$ (b) $\dfrac{1}{x} + \dfrac{1}{y}$

(c) $\dfrac{1}{y} - \dfrac{1}{x}$ (d) None of these

51. $\tan 6° \cdot \tan 42° \cdot \tan 66° \cdot \tan 78° = :$

(a) $\dfrac{3}{2}$ (b) 1

(c) -1 (d) None of these

52. If α and β are acute angles and

$\cos 2\alpha = \dfrac{3 \cos 2\beta - 1}{3 - \cos 2\beta}$ then $\tan \alpha =$

(a) $\tan \beta$ (b) $2 \tan \beta$

(c) $\sqrt{2} \tan \beta$ (d) None of these

53. If α and β are solutions of $a \cos \theta + b \sin \theta = c$, then :

(a) $\sin \alpha + \sin \beta = \dfrac{2bc}{a^2 + b^2}$

(b) $\sin \alpha + \sin \beta = \dfrac{2ac}{b^2 + c^2}$

(c) $\sin \alpha \cdot \sin \beta = \dfrac{a^2 - b^2}{b^2 + c^2}$

(d) None of these

54. The value of $\sin 47° + \sin 61° - \sin 11° - \sin 25°$ is :

(a) $\sin 7°$ (b) $\cos 7°$

(c) $\sin 14°$ (d) $\cos 14°$

55. If $\tan \theta = \dfrac{\tan \alpha + \tan \beta}{1 + \tan \alpha \tan \beta}$, then $\sin 2\theta =$

(a) $\dfrac{\sin 2\alpha - \sin 2\beta}{1 + \sin 2\alpha \sin 2\beta}$ (b) $\dfrac{\sin 2\alpha - \sin 2\beta}{1 - \sin 2\alpha \sin 2\beta}$

(c) $\dfrac{\sin 2\alpha + \sin 2\beta}{1 + \sin 2\alpha \sin 2\beta}$ (d) None of these

56. If $\sec (\phi + \alpha) + \sec (\phi - \alpha) = 2 \sec \phi$, then $\cos \phi =$

(a) $\pm \sqrt{4 \cos^2 \dfrac{\alpha}{2}}$ (b) $\pm \sqrt{2 \cos^2 \dfrac{\alpha}{2}}$

(c) $\pm \sqrt{\cos^2 \dfrac{\alpha}{2}}$ (d) None of these

57. The value of $\dfrac{1}{\sin 10°} - \dfrac{\sqrt{3}}{\cos 10°}$ is :

(a) 1 (b) 2

(c) 4 (d) None of these

58. If $\tan \dfrac{\theta}{2} = \sqrt{\dfrac{1 - e}{1 + e}} \tan \dfrac{\phi}{2}$, then $\cos \phi =$

(a) $\dfrac{\cos \theta + e}{1 - e \cos \theta}$ (b) $\dfrac{\cos \theta - e}{1 + e \cos \theta}$

(c) $\dfrac{\cos \theta - e}{1 - e \cos \theta}$ (d) None of these

59. If $A + B + C = \pi$, then $\Sigma \tan \dfrac{A}{2} \tan \dfrac{B}{2} =$

(a) 1 (b) -1

(c) 2 (d) None of these

60. If $\cos \theta = \dfrac{a \cos \phi + b}{a + b \cos \phi}$, then $\tan \dfrac{\theta}{2} =$

(a) $\sqrt{\dfrac{a + b}{a - b}} \tan \dfrac{\phi}{2}$ (b) $\sqrt{\dfrac{a + b}{a - b}} \cot \dfrac{\phi}{2}$

(c) $\sqrt{\dfrac{a - b}{a + b}} \tan \dfrac{\phi}{2}$ (d) None of these

61. If $A + B + C = \pi$, then

$\dfrac{\cos A}{\sin B \sin C} + \dfrac{\cos B}{\sin A \sin C} + \dfrac{\cos C}{\sin A \sin B} =$

(a) 1 (b) 2

(c) -1 (d) -2

62. If sin (y + z − x), sin (z + x − y) and

sin (x + y − z) are in A.P., then tan x tan y and

tan z are in :

(a) A.P. (b) G..P.

(c) H.P. (d) None of these

63. If A + B + C = 180°, then Σ cot A cot B =

(a) 1 (b) − 1

(c) 2 (d) None of these

64. If A + B + C = 2S and

sin (S − A) + sin (S − B) + sin (S − C) − sin S

$= k \sin \dfrac{A}{2} \sin \dfrac{B}{2} \sin \dfrac{C}{2}$, then k =

(a) 1 (b) 2

(c) 4 (d) None of these

65. If x + y + z = xyz, then $\dfrac{2x}{1-x^2} + \dfrac{2y}{1-y^2} + \dfrac{2z}{1-z^2}$

$= \dfrac{kxyz}{(1-x^2)(1-y^2)(1-z^2)}$ where k =

(a) 2 (b) 4

(c) 8 (d) None of these

66. The smallest positive value of x for which

tan (x + 100°) = tan (x + 50°) tan x tan (x − 50°)

is :

(a) 30° (b) 45°

(c) 55° (d) None of these

67. Which of the following is correct ?

(a) sin 1° > sin 1 (b) sin 1° < sin 1

(c) sin 1° = sin 1 (d) $\sin 1° = \dfrac{\pi}{180} \sin 1$

68. The value of $\tan^2 \dfrac{\pi}{16} + \tan^2 \dfrac{2\pi}{16} + \dots + \tan^2 \dfrac{7\pi}{16}$ is :

(a) 5 (b) 25

(c) 35 (d) None of these

69. $\sin \theta = -\dfrac{4}{5}$ and θ lies in third quadrant, then the

value of $\cos \dfrac{\theta}{2}$ is :

(a) $\dfrac{1}{5}$ (b) $-\dfrac{1}{\sqrt{10}}$

(c) $-\dfrac{1}{\sqrt{5}}$ (d) $\dfrac{1}{\sqrt{10}}$

70. The value of $\tan \dfrac{\pi}{7} \cdot \tan \dfrac{2\pi}{7} \cdot \tan \dfrac{3\pi}{7}$ is :

(a) $\sqrt{7}$ (b) 7

(c) $-\sqrt{7}$ (d) None of these

71. If $\dfrac{\sin^4 \alpha}{a} + \dfrac{\cos^4 \alpha}{b} = \dfrac{1}{a+b}$, then $\dfrac{\sin^8 \alpha}{a^3} + \dfrac{\cos^8 \alpha}{b^3} =$

(a) $\dfrac{1}{a+b}$ (b) $\dfrac{1}{(a+b)^2}$

(c) $\dfrac{1}{(a+b)^3}$ (d) None of these

72. The values of a and b such that

$a \le 3 \cos x + 5 \sin \left(x - \dfrac{\pi}{4} \right) \le b$ for all x, are :

(a) $-\sqrt{34 - 15\sqrt{2}}, \sqrt{34 - 15\sqrt{2}}$

(b) $-\sqrt{17 - 15\sqrt{2}}, \sqrt{17 - 15\sqrt{2}}$

(c) $-\sqrt{36 - 15\sqrt{2}}, \sqrt{36 - 15\sqrt{2}}$

(d) None of these

73. If the angle A of a triangle ABC is given by the

equation 5 cos A + 3 = 0, then sin A and tan A

are the roots of the equation :

(a) $15x^2 - 8x - 16 = 0$

(b) $15x^2 - 8\sqrt{2}\, x + 16 = 0$

(c) $15x^2 - 8x + 16 = 0$

(d) $15x^2 + 8x - 16 = 0$

74. $\dfrac{\sec^2\theta - \tan\theta}{\sec^2\theta + \tan\theta}$ lies between :

(a) $\dfrac{1}{2}$ and 2 (b) $\dfrac{1}{3}$ and 3

(c) $\dfrac{1}{4}$ and 4 (d) None of these

75. The inequality $2^{\sin\theta} + 2^{\cos\theta} \ge 2^{\left(1 - \frac{1}{\sqrt{2}}\right)}$ holds for :

(a) $0 \le \theta < \pi$ (b) $\pi \le \theta < 2\pi$

(c) for all real θ (d) None of these

76. The value of $\dfrac{\tan x}{\tan 3x}$, wherever defined, never lies

between :

(a) $\dfrac{1}{2}$ and 2 (b) $\dfrac{1}{3}$ and 3

(c) $\dfrac{1}{4}$ and 4 (d) None of these

77. If $\cos 2B = \dfrac{\cos(A+C)}{\cos(A-C)}$, than $\tan A$, $\tan B$, $\tan C$ are in

(a) A.P.   (b) G.P.

(c) H.P.   (d) None of these

78. If $\sin x + \sin^2 x + \sin^3 x = 1$, then

$\cos^6 x - 4\cos^4 x + 8\cos^2 x =$

(a) 2   (b) 1

(c) 3   (d) 4

79. $\sin^6 x + \cos^6 x$ lies between :

(a) $\dfrac{1}{4}$ and 1   (b) $\dfrac{1}{4}$ and 2

(c) 0 and 1   (d) None of these

80. If $e^{-\pi/2} < \theta < \dfrac{\pi}{2}$, then :

(a) $\cos \log \theta < \log \cos \theta$

(b) $\cos \log \theta > \log \cos \theta$

(c) $\cos \log \theta \le \log \cos \theta$

(d) None of these

81. If $y = 4\sin^2 \theta - \cos 2\theta$, then y lies in the interval :

(a) $(-1, 5)$ (b) $[-1, 5]$

(c) $(-\infty, -1) \cup (5, \infty)$ (d) None of these

82. The minimum value of the expression

$\sin \alpha + \sin \beta + \sin \gamma$, where α, β, γ are real numbers satisfying $\alpha + \beta + \gamma = \pi$, is :

(a) -3 (b) negative

(c) positive   (d) zero

83. If $\sin \alpha$ and $\cos \alpha$ are the roots of the equation

$px^2 + qx + r = 0$, then :

(a) $p^2 + q^2 - 2pr = 0$ (b) $(p-r)^2 = q^2 + r^2$

(c) $p^2 - q^2 + 2pr = 0$ (d) $(p+r)^2 = q^2 - r^2$

84. The greatest value of $\cos(xe^{|x|} + 7x^2 - 3x)$, $x \in [-1, \infty)$ is :

(a) 0   (b) 1

(c) -1 (d) None of these

85. In a $\triangle ABC$, if angle C is obtuse, then :

(a) $\tan A \tan B < 1$ (b) $\tan A \tan B \le 1$

(c) $\tan A \tan B > 1$ (d) None of these

86. $\log \tan 1° + \log \tan 2° + ... + \log \tan 89° =$

(a) 1   (b) 0

(c) $\dfrac{\pi}{4}$ (d) None of these

87. If $\tan \dfrac{\alpha}{2}$ and $\tan \dfrac{\beta}{2}$ are the roots of the equation

$4x^2 - 16x + 15 = 0$ then $\sin(\alpha + \beta)$ is equal to :

(a) $-\dfrac{352}{377}$ (b) $\dfrac{352}{377}$

(c) 1   (d) None of these

88. If $\tan \dfrac{\pi}{9}$, x and $\tan \dfrac{5\pi}{18}$ are in A.P.; y and $\tan \dfrac{\pi}{9}$;

y and $\tan \dfrac{7\pi}{18}$ are also in A.P., then :

(a) $2x = y$ (b) $x > y$

(c) $x = y$ (d) None of these

89. If x_1, x_2, x_3, ..., x_n are in A.P. whose common difference is α, then the value of :

$\sin \alpha \,[\sec x_1 \sec x_2 + \sec x_2 \sec x_3 + ...$

$+ \sec x_{n-1} \sec x_n]$ is equal to :

(a) $\dfrac{\sin n\alpha}{\cos x_1 \cos x_n}$ (b) $\dfrac{\sin (n-1)\alpha}{\cos x_1 \cos x_n}$

(c) $\dfrac{\sin (n+1)\alpha}{\cos x_1 \cos x_n}$ (d) None of these

90. The ratio of the greatest value of

$2 - \cos x + \sin^2 x$ to its least value is :

(a) $\dfrac{1}{4}$ (b) $\dfrac{9}{4}$

(c) $\dfrac{13}{4}$ (d) None of these

91. Which of the following is a rational number ?

(a) $\sin 15°$ (b) $\cos 15°$

(c) $\sin 15° \cos 15°$ (d) $\sin 15° \cos 75°$

92. If $f_n(\theta) = \tan \dfrac{\theta}{2} \cdot (1 + \sec \theta) \cdot (1 + \sec 2\theta) \cdot$

$(1 + \sec 4\theta) ... (1 + \sec 2^n \theta)$, then :

(a) $f_2\left(\dfrac{\pi}{16}\right) = 1$ (b) $f_3\left(\dfrac{\pi}{32}\right) = 1$

(c) $f_4\left(\dfrac{\pi}{64}\right) = 1$ (d) All of these

93. Let $f(\theta) = \sin\theta (\sin\theta + \sin 3\theta)$. Then $f(\theta)$:

   (a) ≥ 0 only when $\theta \geq 0$

   (b) ≤ 0 for all real θ

   (c) ≥ 0 for all real θ

   (d) ≤ 0 only when $\theta \leq 0$

94. For $m \neq n$, if $\tan m\theta = \tan n\theta$, then the different values of θ are in :

   (a) A.P.   (b) H.P.

   (c) G.P.   (d) None of these

95. If $\tan(\pi\cos\theta) = \cot(\pi\sin\theta)$, $0 < \theta < \dfrac{3\pi}{4}$, then $\sin\left(\theta + \dfrac{\pi}{4}\right)$ equals :

   (a) $\dfrac{1}{\sqrt{2}}$ (b) $\dfrac{1}{2}$

   (c) $\dfrac{1}{2\sqrt{2}}$ (d) $\sqrt{2}$

96. The value of $\cos^2\theta + \sec^2\theta$ is always :

   (a) equal to 1

   (b) less than 1

   (c) greater than or equal to 2

   (d) greater than 1 but less than 2

97. $\sin^6 A + \cos^6 A + 3\sin^2 A \cos^2 A =$

   (a) 0   (b) 1

   (c) 2   (d) 3

98. In ΔABC, the line joining the circumcentre to the incentre is parallel to BC, then $\cos B + \cos C$ is equal to :

   (a) $\dfrac{3}{2}$ (b) 1

   (c) $\dfrac{3}{4}$ (d) $\dfrac{1}{2}$

99. If $\tan^2\theta = \dfrac{3}{4}$, then $\sec\theta + \tan^3\theta \; \text{cosec}\,\theta = $:

   (a) $\dfrac{\sqrt{7}}{4}$ (b) $\dfrac{7}{4}$

   (c) $\left(\dfrac{7}{4}\right)^{3/2}$ (d) $\dfrac{7\sqrt{7}}{2}$

100. If $\cos(x - y)$, $\cos x$ and $\cos(x + y)$ are in H.P. Then $\cos x \sec\dfrac{y}{2} =$

   (a) $\sqrt{2}$ (b) $\sqrt{3}$

   (c) $\sqrt{5}$ (d) None of these.

101. If $\dfrac{2\sin\alpha}{1 + \cos\alpha + \sin\alpha} = x$ then $\dfrac{1 - \cos\alpha + \sin\alpha}{1 + \sin\alpha}$ is equal to :

   (a) $\dfrac{1}{x}$ (b) x

   (c) $1 - x$ (d) $1 + x$.

102. Given that $(1 + \sqrt{1 + x})\tan x = (1 + \sqrt{1 - x})$, then $\sin 4x$ is equal to :

   (a) $4x$ (b) $2x$

   (c) x (d) None of these.

103. If $\cos\alpha = \dfrac{2\cos\beta - 1}{2 - \cos\beta}$ $(0 < \alpha, \beta < \pi)$, then $\dfrac{\tan\dfrac{\alpha}{2}}{\tan\dfrac{\beta}{2}}$ is equal to :

   (a) 1   (b) $\sqrt{2}$

   (c) $\sqrt{3}$ (d) $\dfrac{1}{\sqrt{3}}$

104. The value of the determinant

$$\begin{vmatrix} \sin^2 13° & \sin^2 77° & \tan 135° \\ \sin^2 77° & \tan 135° & \sin^2 13° \\ \tan 135° & \sin^2 13° & \sin^2 77° \end{vmatrix}$$ is equal to :

   (a) -1 (b) 0

   (c) 1   (d) 2.

105. The numbers $3^{2\sin 2a - 1}$, 14 and $3^{4 - 2\sin 2a}$ form first three terms of an AP, its fifth term is given by :

   (a) -25 (b) -12

   (c) 40   (d) 53.

106. If $\tan\alpha$, $\tan\beta$, $\tan\gamma$ are the roots of the equation $x^3 - px^2 - r = 0$, then the value of $(1 + \tan^2\alpha)(1 + \tan^2\beta)(1 + \tan^2\gamma)$ is equal to :

   (a) $(p - r)^2$ (b) $1 + (p - r)^2$

   (c) $1 - (p - r)^2$ (d) None of these.

107. If $0.\ddot{2}\ddot{7}$, x and $0.\ddot{7}\ddot{2}$ are in H.P., then x is :

(a) rational　　　　　　(b) irrational

(c) integer　　　　　　(d) None of these.

108. If $\dfrac{\cos x}{a} = \dfrac{\cos (x + \theta)}{b} = \dfrac{\cos (x + 2\theta)}{c} = \dfrac{\cos (x + 3\theta)}{d}$

then $\dfrac{a + c}{b + d}$ is equal to :

(a) $\dfrac{a}{d}$　　　　　　(b) $\dfrac{c}{b}$

(c) $\dfrac{b}{c}$　　　　　　(d) $\dfrac{d}{a}$

109. If $\alpha, \beta, \gamma, \delta$ are the smallest positive angles in ascending order of magnitude which have their sines equal to the positive quantity k, then the value of

$4 \sin \dfrac{\alpha}{2} + 3 \sin \dfrac{\beta}{2} + 2 \sin \dfrac{\gamma}{2} + \sin \dfrac{\delta}{2}$ is equal to :

(a) $2\sqrt{1 - k}$　　　　(b) $2\sqrt{1 + k}$

(c) $2\sqrt{k}$　　　　　　(d) None of these.

110. In the right angled triangle, the hypotenuse is four times as long as the perpendicular drawn to it from the opposite vertex. One of the acute angle is :

(a) 15°　　　　　　(b) 30°

(c) 45°　　　　　　(d) None of these.

111. The equation a sin x + b cos x = c, where $|c| > \sqrt{a^2 + b^2}$ has :

(a) a unique solution

(b) infinite number of solutions

(c) no solution

(d) None of these.

112. Suppose that $\sin^3 x \sin 3x = \sum\limits_{m=0}^{n} c_m \cos mx$ is an identity in x, where $c_1, c_1, ..., c_n$ are constants and $c_n \neq 0$. Then the value of n is :

(a) 4　　　　　　(b) 5

(c) 6　　　　　　(d) 8.

113. If $\tan \theta = n \tan \phi$ then maximum value of $\tan^2 (\theta - \phi)$ is :

(a) $\dfrac{(n + 1)^2}{4n}$　　　　(b) $\dfrac{(n - 1)^2}{4n}$

(c) $\dfrac{(2n + 1)^2}{4n}$　　　(d) $\dfrac{(2n - 1)^2}{4n}$

114. If a, b and c are sides of a triangle such that $b \cdot c = k^2$, then :

(a) $a < 2k \sin (A/2)$　　(b) $a > 2k \sin (A/2)$

(c) $a > 2k \sin A$　　　(d) $a < 2k \sin (A/4)$

115. If $\cos (\theta - \alpha) = a$, $\cos (\theta - \beta) = b$, then $\sin^2 (\alpha - \theta) + 2ab \cos (\alpha - \beta) =$

(a) $a^2 + b^2$　　　　(b) $a^2 - b^2$

(c) $b^2 - a^2$　　　　(d) $-a^2 - b^2$

116. If $\sin 2A = \dfrac{1}{2}$ and $\sin 2B = \dfrac{1}{2}$, then which one of the following is false ?

(a) sin (A + B) may be 0.

(b) cos (A – B) may be zero.

(c) sin (A + B) or cos (A – B) is zero.

(d) sin (A + B) = 0.

117. If $\tan x = \dfrac{2b}{a - c}$, $a \neq c$ and

$y = a \cos^2 x + 2b \sin x \cos x + c \sin^2 x$

$z = a \sin^2 x - 2b \sin x \cos x + c \cos^2 x$, then :

(a) $y = z$

(b) $y + z = a - c$

(c) $y - z = a - c$

(d) $(y - z) = (a - c)^2 + 4b^2$.

118. If $\cos x + \sin x = a$, $\left(-\dfrac{\pi}{2} < x < \dfrac{\pi}{4}\right)$ then cos 2x =

(a) $a\sqrt{2 - a^2}$　　　　(b) $a\sqrt{a^2 - 2}$

(c) $a^2\sqrt{a - 2}$　　　　(d) $a^2\sqrt{2 - a}$

119. If an angle α is divided into two parts A and B such that A – B = x and tan A : tan B = K : 1, then the value of sin x is :

(a) $\dfrac{K + 1}{K - 1} \sin \alpha$　　　(b) $\dfrac{K}{K + 1} \sin \alpha$

(c) $\dfrac{K - 1}{K + 1} \sin \alpha$　　　(d) None of these.

120. Ratio of the greatest value of $2 - \cos x + \sin^2 x$ to its least value is :

(a) $\dfrac{7}{4}$　　　　　　(b) $\dfrac{11}{4}$

(c) $\dfrac{13}{4}$　　　　　　(d) none of these.

121. $\tan^6 \dfrac{\pi}{9} - 33 \tan^4 \dfrac{\pi}{9} + 27 \tan^2 \dfrac{\pi}{9} =$

(a) 0　　　　　　(b) $\sqrt{3}$

(c) 3　　　　　　(d) 9.

122. If $\tan \alpha$ is an integral solution of the equation $4x^2 - 16x + 15 < 0$ and $\cos \beta$ in the slope of the bisector of the angle in the first quadrant between the x and y axis, then the value of $\sin(\alpha + \beta) \times \sin(\alpha - \beta)$ is :

(a) $\dfrac{1}{5}$ (b) $\dfrac{2}{5}$

(c) $\dfrac{4}{5}$ (d) None of these.

123. If $4n\alpha = \pi$, then the value of

$\tan\alpha \tan 2\alpha \tan 3\alpha ... \tan(2n-2)\alpha \tan(2n-1)\alpha$

is :

(a) 0   (b) 1

(c) −1   (d) None of these.

124. If $A_1 A_2 A_3 A_4 A_5$ is a regular pentagon inscribed in a unit circle, then $(A_1 A_2)(A_1 A_3)$ is equal to :

(a) 1   (b) 3

(c) 4   (d) 5.

125. If $[y] = [\sin x]$ and $y = \cos x$ are two given equations, then the number of solutions is :

(a) 2   (b) 4

(c) Infinitely many   (d) None of these.

126. Let A and B denote the statements

[AIEEE - 2009]

A: $\cos\alpha + \cos\beta + \cos\gamma = 0$

B: $\sin\alpha + \sin\beta + \sin\gamma = 0$

If $\cos(\beta - \gamma) + \cos(\gamma - \alpha) + \cos(\alpha - \beta) = -\dfrac{3}{2}$,

then

(a) A is true and B is false

(b) A is false and B is true

(c) both A and B are true

(d) both A and B are false

127. The minimum value of $3\cos x + 4\sin x + 5$ is :

(a) 5   (b) 10

(c) 0   (d) 7.

128. The values of θ $(0 < \theta < 360°)$ satisfying $\csc\theta + 2 = 0$ are :

(a) $210°, 300°$ (b) $240°, 300°$

(c) $210°, 240°$ (d) $210°, 330°$.

129. The value of $\sin 18°$ is :

(a) $\dfrac{\sqrt{3}+1}{4}$ (b) $\dfrac{\sqrt{3}-1}{4}$

(c) $\dfrac{\sqrt{5}-1}{4}$ (d) $\dfrac{\sqrt{5}+1}{4}$

130. If $\sin\beta$ is the G.M. between $\sin\alpha$ and $\cos\alpha$, then $\cos 2\beta =$

(a) $2\sin^2\left(\dfrac{\pi}{4} - \alpha\right)$ (b) $2\cos^2\left(\dfrac{\pi}{4} - \alpha\right)$

(c) $2\sin^2\left(\dfrac{\pi}{4} + \alpha\right)$ (d) None of these.

131. The minimum value of $\sin\theta + \cos\theta$ will be :

(a) 0   (b) − 1

(c) $\dfrac{1}{\sqrt{2}}$ (d) $-\sqrt{2}$

132. If $0° < \theta < 180°$ then

$\sqrt{2 + \sqrt{2 + \sqrt{2 + ... + \sqrt{2(1 + \cos\theta)}}}}$,

there being n number of 2's, is equal to :

(a) $2\cos\dfrac{\theta}{2^n}$ (b) $2\cos\dfrac{\theta}{2^{n-1}}$

(c) $2\cos\dfrac{\theta}{2^{n+1}}$ (d) None of these.

133. If $\alpha + \beta + \gamma = \dfrac{\pi}{2}$, then the value of

$\tan\alpha \tan\beta + \tan\beta \tan\gamma + \tan\gamma \tan\alpha$ will be :

(a) 1   (b) $\dfrac{1}{2}$

(c) $\dfrac{3}{2}$ (d) 2

134. If $\tan\alpha = \sqrt{a}$, where a is a rational number which is not a perfect square, then which of the following is a rational number ?

(a) $\sin 2\alpha$ (b) $\tan 2\alpha$

(c) $\cos 2\alpha$ (d) None of these.

135. The maximum value of $a\cos x + b\sin x$ is

(a) $a + b$ (b) $a - b$

(c) $|a| + |b|$ (d) $\sqrt{a^2 + b^2}$

136. If n is an odd integer, & $\sin(n\theta) = \sum\limits_{r=0}^{n} b_r \sin^r\theta$

for all real θ, then

(a) $b_0 = 1, b_1 = 3$

(b) $b_0 = 0, b_1 = n$

(c) $b_0 = -1, b_1 = n$

(d) $b_0 = 0, b_1 = n^2 - 3n - 3$.

137. The maximum value of $12\sin\theta - 9\sin^2\theta$ is :

(a) 4   (b) 5

(c) 3   (d) None of these.

138. If the solutions for θ from the equation

$\sin^2 \theta - 2 \sin \theta + \lambda = 0$ lie in

$\bigcup_{n \in Z} \left(2n\pi - \dfrac{\pi}{6}, \overline{2n+1}\,\pi + \dfrac{\pi}{6} \right)$

then the set of possible values of λ is :

(a) $\left(-\dfrac{5}{4}, 1 \right]$ (b) $(-\infty, 1]$

(c) $\left(-\dfrac{5}{4}, +\infty \right]$ (d) {1}

139. If $\sin \alpha + \sin \beta + \sin \gamma = 0 = \cos \alpha + \cos \beta + \cos \gamma$, then $\sin^2 \alpha + \sin^2 \beta + \sin^2 \gamma$ is equal to :

(a) $\dfrac{2}{3}$ (b) $-\dfrac{3}{2}$

(c) $\dfrac{3}{2}$ (d) 0.

140. If $\tan x + \tan \left(x + \dfrac{\pi}{3} \right) + \tan \left(x + \dfrac{2\pi}{3} \right) = 3$, then :

(a) tan x = 1   (b) tan 2x = 1
(c) tan 3x = 1   (d) None of these.

141. If $\cos (\theta - \alpha) = a$ and $\sin (\theta - \beta) = b, (0 < \theta - \alpha,$ $\theta - \beta < \dfrac{\pi}{2})$, then $\cos^2 (\alpha - \beta) + 2ab \sin (\alpha - \beta)$ is equal to :

(a) $4 a^2 b^2$ (b) $a^2 - b^2$
(c) $a^2 + b^2$ (d) $- a^2 b^2$.

142. If $\tan \theta_1, \tan \theta_2, \tan \theta_3$ and $\tan \theta_4$ are the roots of the equation

$x^4 - x^3 \sin 2\beta + x^2 \cos 2\beta - x \cos \beta - \sin \beta = 0$, then $\tan (\theta_1 + \theta_2 + \theta_3 + \theta_4)$ is equal to

(a) sin β   (b) cos β
(c) tan β   (d) cot β

143. In a Δ PQR, if 3 sin P + 4 cos Q = 6 and 4 sin Q + 3 cos P = 1, then the angle R is equal to :

(a) $\dfrac{5\pi}{6}$ (b) $\dfrac{\pi}{6}$ [AIEEE - 2012]

(c) $\dfrac{\pi}{4}$ (d) $\dfrac{3\pi}{4}$

144. Let an object be placed at some height h cm and let P and Q be two points of observation which are at a distance 10 cm apart on a line inclined at an angle 15° to the horizontal. If the angles of elevation of the object from P and Q are 30° and 60° respectively, then h is

(a) $5\sqrt{2}$ (b) $\dfrac{5}{\sqrt{2}}$

(c) $5\sqrt{6}$ (d) $5\sqrt{3}$

145. In a Δ PQR , if 3 sin P + 4 cos Q = 6 and 4 sin Q + 3 cos P = 1, then the angle R is equal to

(a) $\dfrac{\pi}{4}$ (b) $\dfrac{3\pi}{4}$

(c) $\dfrac{5\pi}{6}$ (d) $\dfrac{\pi}{6}$

ANSWER KEY

1. (c)	2. (a)	3. (a)	4. (b)	5. (a)	6. (c)	7. (d)	8. (b)	9. (c)	10. (b)
11. (d)	12. (c)	13. (b)	14. (b)	15. (d)	16. (b)	17. (a)	18. (c)	19. (c)	20. (b)
21. (c)	22. (d)	23. (b)	24. (a)	25. (c)	26. (c)	27. (d)	28. (a)	29. (c)	30. (b)
31. (a)	32. (c)	33. (c)	34. (c)	35. (a)	36. (a)	37. (a)	38. (c)	39. (a)	40. (c)
41. (b)	42. (d)	43. (a)	44. (b)	45. (d)	46. (b)	47. (a)	48. (c)	49. (b)	50. (b)
51. (b)	52. (c)	53. (a)	54. (b)	55. (c)	56. (b)	57. (c)	58. (c)	59. (a)	60. (c)
61. (b)	62. (a)	63. (a)	64. (c)	65. (c)	66. (a)	67. (b)	68. (c)	69. (c)	70. (a)
71. (c)	72. (a)	73. (d)	74. (b)	75. (c)	76. (b)	77. (b)	78. (d)	79. (a)	80. (b)
81. (b)	82. (c)	83. (c)	84. (b)	85. (a)	86. (b)	87. (a)	88. (a)	89. (b)	90. (c)
91. (c)	92. (d)	93. (c)	94. (a)	95. (c)	96. (c)	97. (b)	98. (b)	99. (c)	100. (a)
101. (b)	102. (c)	103. (c)	104. (b)	105. (d)	106. (b)	107. (a)	108. (c)	109. (b)	110. (a)
111. (c)	112. (c)	113. (b)	114. (b)	115. (a)	116. (d)	117. (c)	118. (a)	119. (c)	120. (c)
121. (c)	122. (c)	123. (b)	124. (d)	125. (c)	126. (c)	127. (c)	128. (d)	129. (c)	130. (a)
131. (d)	132. (a)	133. (a)	134. (c)	135. (d)	136. (b)	137. (a)	138. (a)	139. (c)	140. (c)
141. (c)	142. (d)	143. (b)	144. (a)	145. (d)					

TRIGONOMETRIC EQUATIONS

MULTIPLE CHOICE QUESTIONS

1. The general solution of the equation :
$7 \cos^2\theta + 3 \sin^2\theta = 4$ is :

(a) $\theta = 2n\pi \pm \dfrac{\pi}{3}$

(b) $\theta = n\pi \pm \dfrac{2\pi}{3}$

(c) $\theta = n\pi \pm \dfrac{\pi}{3}$

(d) None of these

2. The general solution of the equation :
$2 \sin^2 x + \sqrt{3} \cos x + 1 = 0$ is

(a) $x = 2n\pi \pm \dfrac{7\pi}{6}$

(b) $x = 2n\pi \pm \dfrac{5\pi}{3}$

(c) $x = 2n\pi \pm \dfrac{5\pi}{6}$

(d) None of these

3. The solution of the equation :
$\sin 2x + \sin 4x = 2 \sin 3x$ is :

(a) $x = \dfrac{2n\pi}{3}$

(b) $x = n\pi$

(c) $x = 2n\pi$

(d) None of these

4. The general value of θ satisfying the equation
$3 \tan (\theta - 15°) = \tan (\theta + 15°)$, is :

(a) $n\pi + (-1)^n \dfrac{\pi}{4}$

(b) $\dfrac{n\pi}{2} + (-1)^n \dfrac{\pi}{4}$

(c) $\dfrac{n\pi}{2} + (-1)^n \dfrac{\pi}{6}$

(d) None of these

5. The values of θ satisfying $\sin^2\theta - \cos\theta = \dfrac{1}{4}$ in
the interval $0 \le \theta \le 2\pi$, are :

(a) $\dfrac{\pi}{3}, \dfrac{4\pi}{3}$

(b) $\dfrac{\pi}{3}, \dfrac{7\pi}{3}$

(c) $\dfrac{\pi}{3}, \dfrac{5\pi}{3}$

(d) $\dfrac{\pi}{6}, \dfrac{5\pi}{6}$

6. The general solution of the equation
$\cos x + \cos 2x + \cos 3x = 0$ is :

(a) $x = (2n + 1) \dfrac{\pi}{3}$

(b) $x = (2n) \dfrac{\pi}{4}$

(c) $x = 2n\pi \pm \dfrac{2\pi}{3}$

(d) $x = 2n\pi \pm \dfrac{3\pi}{4}$

7. The general value of θ, satisfying the equation
$2 \cos 2\theta + \sqrt{2} \sin\theta = 2$, is :

(a) $\dfrac{2n\pi}{3}$

(b) $n\pi + (-1)^n \dfrac{\pi}{3}$

(c) $n\pi + (-1)^n \dfrac{\pi}{6}$

(d) None of these

8. The solution set of $2 \sin^2\theta = 3 \cos\theta$, in the
interval $0 \le \theta \le 2\pi$, is :

(a) $\left\{\dfrac{\pi}{3}\right\}$

(b) $\left\{\dfrac{\pi}{3}, \dfrac{5\pi}{3}, \cos^{-1}(-2)\right\}$

(c) $\left\{\dfrac{\pi}{3}, \dfrac{5\pi}{3}\right\}$

(d) None of these

9. The general solution of equation :
$\cos\theta + \cos 3\theta - 2\cos 2\theta = 0$ is :

(a) $\theta = (2n + 1) \dfrac{\pi}{4}$

(b) $\theta = (2n + 1)\pi$

(c) $\theta = n\pi$

(d) None of these

10. The general solution of $8 \tan^2 \dfrac{x}{2} = 1 + \sec x$ is :

(a) $x = 2n\pi \pm \cos^{-1}\left(\dfrac{-1}{3}\right)$

(b) $x = 2n\pi \pm \dfrac{\pi}{6}$

(c) $x = 2n\pi \pm \cos^{-1}\left(\dfrac{1}{3}\right)$

(d) None of these

11. If $4 \cos^2\theta + \sqrt{3} = 2 (\sqrt{3} + 1) \cos\theta$, then $\theta =$

(a) $2n\pi \pm \dfrac{2\pi}{3}$

(b) $2n\pi \pm \dfrac{\pi}{4}$

(c) $2n\pi \pm \dfrac{\pi}{6}$

(d) None of these

12. The solution of the equation $\cos^2\theta + \sin\theta + 1 = 0$,
lies in the interval :

(a) $\left(\dfrac{-\pi}{4}, \dfrac{\pi}{4}\right)$

(b) $\left(\dfrac{\pi}{4}, \dfrac{3\pi}{4}\right)$

(c) $\left(\dfrac{3\pi}{4}, \dfrac{5\pi}{4}\right)$

(d) $\left(\dfrac{5\pi}{4}, \dfrac{7\pi}{4}\right)$

13. The general solution of the equation :

$\sin x + \cos x = \sqrt{2} \cos A$ is :

(a) $x = 2n\pi + \dfrac{\pi}{4} \pm A$ (b) $x = 2n\pi + \dfrac{\pi}{3} \pm A$

(c) $x = 2n\pi + \dfrac{\pi}{6} \pm A$ (d) None of these

14. The value of θ, lying between $\theta = 0$ and $\theta = \dfrac{\pi}{2}$ and satisfying the equation

$$\begin{vmatrix} 1 + \cos^2 \theta & \sin^2 \theta & 4 \sin 4\theta \\ \cos^2 \theta & 1 + \sin^2 \theta & 4 \sin 4\theta \\ \cos^2 \theta & \sin^2 \theta & 1 + 4 \sin 4\theta \end{vmatrix} = 0 \text{ is :}$$

(a) $\dfrac{11\pi}{24}$ (b) $\dfrac{9\pi}{24}$

(c) $\dfrac{5\pi}{24}$ (d) None of these

15. The general solution of the equation :

$\cos \theta \cos 2\theta \cos 3\theta = \dfrac{1}{4}$ is :

(a) $\theta = (2n + 1) \dfrac{\pi}{4}$ (b) $\theta = \dfrac{n\pi}{8}$

(c) $\theta = n\pi \pm \dfrac{\pi}{3}$ (d) None of these

16. The general solution of the equation

$\tan^2 x + (1 - \sqrt{3}) \tan x - \sqrt{3} = 0$ is :

(a) $n\pi + \dfrac{\pi}{4}$ (b) $n\pi - \dfrac{\pi}{4}$

(c) $2n\pi + \dfrac{\pi}{3}$ (d) $n\pi - \dfrac{\pi}{3}$

17. The solution of the equation $\tan 2\theta \tan \theta = 1$ is :

(a) $\theta = \dfrac{n\pi}{3} + \dfrac{\pi}{6}$ (b) $\theta = \dfrac{n\pi}{3} + \dfrac{\pi}{4}$

(c) $\theta = \dfrac{n\pi}{3} - \dfrac{\pi}{6}$ (d) None of these

18. Number of solutions of the equation

$\tan x + \sec x = 2 \cos x$, lying in the interval $[0, 2\pi]$, is :

(a) 0   (b) 1

(c) 2   (d) 3

19. The solution of the equation

$\tan x + \tan 2x + \tan 3x = 0$ is :

(a) $x = \dfrac{n\pi}{3}$ (b) $x = n\pi + \tan^{-1} \dfrac{1}{\sqrt{2}}$

(c) $x = n\pi - \tan^{-1} \dfrac{1}{\sqrt{2}}$ (d) All of these

20. The solution set of the equation

$5 \cos 2\theta + 2 \cos^2 \dfrac{\theta}{2} + 1 = 0$, in the interval $-\pi < \theta < \pi$, is :

(a) $\left\{ \dfrac{\pi}{6}, \pi - \cos^{-1}\left(\dfrac{3}{5}\right) \right\}$ (b) $\left\{ \dfrac{\pi}{3}, \pi - \cos^{-1}\left(\dfrac{3}{5}\right) \right\}$

(b) $\left\{ \dfrac{\pi}{4}, \pi - \cos^{-1}\left(\dfrac{3}{5}\right) \right\}$ (d) None of these

21. The general solution of the equation :

$\tan \theta + \tan 2\theta + \sqrt{3} \tan \theta \tan 2\theta = \sqrt{3}$ is :

(a) $\theta = (3n + 1) \dfrac{\pi}{9}$ (b) $\theta = \dfrac{n\pi}{9}$

(c) $\theta = (3n - 1) \dfrac{\pi}{9}$ (d) None of these

22. The general value of θ satisfying the equation

$\cot \theta - \tan \theta - \cos \theta + \sin \theta = 0$ is :

(a) $n\pi - \dfrac{\pi}{4}$ (b) $n\pi + \dfrac{\pi}{4}$

(c) $\dfrac{n\pi}{2} + \dfrac{1}{2} (-1)^n \sin^{-1} (2 - 2\sqrt{2})$

(d) None of these

23. The general solution of $4 \sin^4 x + \cos^4 x = 1$ is :

(a) $(2n + 1) \dfrac{\pi}{2}$ (b) $2n\pi$

(c) $n\pi \pm \sin^{-1} \sqrt{\dfrac{2}{5}}$ (d) None of these

24. The most general value of θ which satisfies both the equations $\sin \theta = -\dfrac{1}{2}$ and $\tan \theta = \dfrac{1}{\sqrt{3}}$, is :

(a) $2n\pi + \dfrac{\pi}{6}$ (b) $2n\pi + \dfrac{7\pi}{6}$

(c) $2n\pi + \dfrac{11\pi}{6}$ (d) None of these

25. The solution of the equation

$2 \sin^2 x - 5 \sin x \cos x - 8 \cos^2 x = -2$ is :

(a) $2n\pi + \tan^{-1} 2$ (b) $n\pi - \tan^{-1} 2$

(c) $n\pi + \tan^{-1}\left(-\dfrac{3}{4}\right)$ (d) None of these

26. General solution of the equation

$(\sqrt{3} - 1) \sin \theta + (\sqrt{3} + 1) \cos \theta = 2$ is :

(a) $2n\pi \pm \dfrac{\pi}{4} + \dfrac{\pi}{12}$ (b) $n\pi + (-1)^n \dfrac{\pi}{4} + \dfrac{\pi}{12}$

(c) $2n\pi \pm \dfrac{\pi}{4} - \dfrac{\pi}{12}$ (d) $n\pi + (-1)^n \dfrac{\pi}{4} - \dfrac{\pi}{12}$

27. Solution of the equation

$(1 - \tan \theta)(1 + \sin 2\theta) = 1 + \tan \theta$ is :

(a) $\theta = n\pi$ (b) $\theta = n\pi + \dfrac{\pi}{4}$

(c) $\theta = 2n\pi - \dfrac{\pi}{4}$ (d) None of these

28. The general solution of the equation

$\cos x + \sqrt{3} \sin x = 2 \cos 2x$ is :

(a) $x = 2n\pi + \dfrac{\pi}{3}$ (b) $x = -\left(2n\pi + \dfrac{\pi}{3}\right)$

(c) $x = \dfrac{2n\pi}{3} - \dfrac{\pi}{9}$ (d) $x = 2n\pi + \dfrac{\pi}{9}$

29. The solution of the equation $1 + \sin^2 ax = \cos x$, where a is irrational, is :

(a) $x = 0$ (b) $x = \dfrac{n\pi}{12}$

(c) $x = 2n\pi$ (d) None of these

30. The general solution of the equation :

$\tan \theta + \tan 4\theta + \tan 7\theta = \tan \theta \tan 4\theta \tan 7\theta$ is :

(a) $\theta = \dfrac{n\pi}{4}$ (b) $\theta = \dfrac{n\pi}{12}$

(c) $\theta = \dfrac{n\pi}{6}$ (d) None of these

31. The solution of the equation $e^{\sin x} - e^{-\sin x} - 4 = 0$ is :

(a) $x = 0$

(b) $x = \sin^{-1} \left[\log (2 - \sqrt{5})\right]$

(c) No real solution

(d) None of these

32. Number of solutions of the equation

$\tan \theta + \sec \theta = \sqrt{3}$ in the interval $[0, 2\pi]$ is :

(a) 0   (b) 1

(c) 2   (d) 3

33. Common roots of equations $2 \sin^2 x + \sin^2 2x = 2$ and $\sin 2x = \cos 2x = \tan x$ are :

(a) $(2n - 1) \dfrac{\pi}{2}$ (b) $(2n + 1) \dfrac{\pi}{2}$

(c) $(2n + 1) \dfrac{\pi}{4}$ (d) None of these

34. If $\tan (\cot x) = \cot (\tan x)$, then :

(a) $\sin 2x = \dfrac{2}{(2n + 1) \pi}$ (b) $\sin x = \dfrac{4}{(2n + 1) \pi}$

(c) $\sin 2x = \dfrac{4}{(2n + 1) \pi}$ (d) None of these

35. Solution of the system of equations $2^{\sin x + \cos y} = 1$, $16^{\sin^2 x + \cos^2 y} = 4$ is :

(a) $x = n\pi + (-1)^n \dfrac{\pi}{6}$, $y = n\pi \pm \dfrac{2\pi}{3}$

(b) $x = n\pi + (-1)^n \dfrac{\pi}{6}$, $y = 2n\pi \pm \dfrac{\pi}{3}$

(c) $x = n\pi - (-1)^n \dfrac{\pi}{6}$, $y = 2n\pi \pm \dfrac{2\pi}{3}$

(d) $x = n\pi - (-1)^n \dfrac{\pi}{6}$, $y = 2n\pi \pm \dfrac{\pi}{3}$

36. Solution of the equation

$3^{\sin 2x + 2\cos^2 x} + 3^{1 - \sin 2x + 2\sin^2 x} = 28$ is :

(a) $x = n\pi$ (b) $x = (2n + 1) \dfrac{\pi}{3}$

(c) $x = n\pi - \dfrac{\pi}{4}$ (d) None of these

37. $2 \sec 2\alpha = \tan \beta + \cot \beta$, then one of the values of $\alpha + \beta$ is :

(a) $\dfrac{\pi}{4}$ (b) $\dfrac{\pi}{2}$

(c) π (d) $n\pi - \dfrac{\pi}{4}, n \in I$

38. The equation $(\cos p - 1) x^2 + (\cos p) x + \sin p = 0$ in the variable x has a real root. Then p can take any value in the interval :

(a) $(0, \pi)$ (b) $\left(\dfrac{-\pi}{2}, \dfrac{\pi}{2}\right)$

(c) $(-\pi, 0)$ (d) $(0, 2\pi)$

39. The number of solutions in $0 \le x \le \dfrac{x}{2}$, of the equation $\cos 3x \tan 5x = \sin 7x$, is :

(a) 5   (b) 7

(c) 6   (d) None of these

40. The number of points of intersection of $2y = 1$ and $y = \sin x$, $-2\pi \le x \le 2\pi$, is :

(a) 2   (b) 3

(c) 4   (d) 1

41. The general value of θ, obtained from the equation $\cos 2\theta = \sin \alpha$, is :

(a) $\theta = n\pi \pm \left(\dfrac{\pi}{4} - \dfrac{\alpha}{2} \right)$ (b) $\theta = \dfrac{n\pi + (-1)^n \pi}{2}$

(c) $\theta = 2n\pi \pm \left(\dfrac{\pi}{2} - \alpha \right)$ (d) $2\theta = \dfrac{\pi}{2} - \alpha$

42. For $m \ne n$, if $\tan m\theta = \tan n\theta$, then the different values of θ are in :

(a) A. P.

(b) H. P.

(c) G. P.

(d) No particular sequence

43. The equation $2 \cos^2 \left(\dfrac{x}{2} \right) \cdot \sin^2 x = x^2 + \dfrac{1}{x^2}$, where $0 \le x \le \dfrac{\pi}{2}$, has :

(a) one real solution

(b) no solution

(c) more than one real solution

(d) None of these

44. The number of the solutions of the equation $\cos (\pi \sqrt{x-4}) \cos (\pi \sqrt{x}) = 1$ is

(a) > 2 (b) 2

(c) 1   (d) 0

45. The solution of $(2 \cos x - 1)(3 + 2 \cos x) = 0$ in the interval $0 \le x \le 2\pi$ is :

(a) $\dfrac{\pi}{3}$ (b) $\dfrac{\pi}{3}, \dfrac{5\pi}{3}$

(c) $\dfrac{\pi}{3}, \dfrac{5\pi}{3}, \cos^{-1} \left(\dfrac{-3}{2} \right)$ (d) None of these

46. The smallest positive angle which satisfies the equation $2 \sin^2 \theta + \sqrt{3} \cos \theta + 1 = 0$ is :

(a) $\dfrac{5\pi}{6}$ (b) $\dfrac{2\pi}{3}$

(c) $\dfrac{\pi}{3}$ (d) $\dfrac{\pi}{6}$

47. The number of solutions of the equation $3 \sin^2 x - 7 \sin x + 2 = 0$, in the interval $[0, 5\pi]$ is

(a) 0   (b) 5

(c) 6   (d) 10

48. The real roots of the equation $\cos^7 x + \sin^4 x = 1$, in the interval $(-\pi, \pi)$, are :

(a) $0, \dfrac{\pi}{3}, -\dfrac{\pi}{3}$ (b) $0, \dfrac{\pi}{4}, -\dfrac{\pi}{4}$

(c) $0, \dfrac{\pi}{2}, -\dfrac{\pi}{2}$ (d) None of these

49. The equation $\sin^4 x + \cos^4 x = a$ has a solution for :

(a) $a = 1$ (b) $a = \dfrac{1}{2}$

(c) $\dfrac{1}{2} < a < 1$ (d) All the above

50. The number of real solutions of the equation $\sin (e^x) = 5^x + 5^{-x}$ is :

(a) 0   (b) 1

(c) 2   (d) infinitely many

51. $\triangle ABC$ is a triangle such that $\sin (2A + B) = \sin (C - A) = -\sin (B + 2C) = \dfrac{1}{2}$.
If A, B and C are in A.P., then the values of A, B and C are :

(a) $45°, 60°, 75°$ (b) $30°, 60°, 90°$

(c) $20°, 60°, 100°$ (d) None of these

52. The general solution of the equation $\sin x - 3 \sin 2x + \sin 3x = \cos x - 3 \cos 2x + \cos 3x$ is :

(a) $n\pi + \dfrac{\pi}{8}$ (b) $\dfrac{n\pi}{2} + \dfrac{\pi}{8}$

(c) $(-1)^n \dfrac{n\pi}{2} + \dfrac{\pi}{8}$ (d) $2n\pi + \cos^{-1} \left(\dfrac{3}{2} \right)$

53. Solution of the equation $4\sin^4 x + \cos^4 x = 1$ is :

(a) $x = n\pi$

(b) $x = 2n\pi \pm \cos^{-1}\left(\sqrt{\dfrac{3}{5}}\right)$

(c) $x = (2n + 1)\dfrac{\pi}{2}$

(d) None of these

54. The values of α for which the equation

$\sin^4 x + \cos^4 x + \sin 2x + \alpha = 0$ may be valid, are :

(a) $-\dfrac{3}{2} \le \alpha \le 1$ (b) $0 \le \alpha \le \dfrac{1}{2}$

(c) $-\dfrac{3}{2} \le \alpha \le \dfrac{1}{2}$ (d) None of these

55. Solution of the equation $\sec\theta - \operatorname{cosec}\theta = 4/3$ is

(a) $\theta = \dfrac{n\pi}{2} + \dfrac{(-1)^n}{2}\sin^{-1}\left(\dfrac{3}{4}\right)$

(b) $\theta = n\pi + (-1)^n \sin^{-1}\left(\dfrac{3}{4}\right)$

(c) $\theta = n\pi \pm \sin^{-1}\left(\dfrac{3}{4}\right)$

(d) None of these

56. The smallest positive values of x and y, satisfying $x - y = \dfrac{\pi}{4}$ and $\cot x + \cot y = 2$, are :

(a) $x = \dfrac{\pi}{6}, y = \dfrac{5\pi}{12}$ (b) $x = \dfrac{5\pi}{12}, y = \dfrac{\pi}{6}$

(c) $x = \dfrac{\pi}{3}, y = \dfrac{7\pi}{12}$ (d) None of these

57. Let $2\sin^2 x + 3\sin x - 2 > 0$ and $x^2 - x - 2 < 0$ (x is measured in radians). Then x lies in the interval

(a) $\left(\dfrac{\pi}{6}, \dfrac{5\pi}{6}\right)$ (b) $\left(-1, \dfrac{5\pi}{6}\right)$

(c) $(-1, 2)$ (d) $\left(\dfrac{\pi}{6}, 2\right)$

58. Let n be a positive integer such that :

$\sin\dfrac{\pi}{2n} + \cos\dfrac{\pi}{2n} = \dfrac{\sqrt{n}}{2}$, then :

(a) $6 \le n \le 8$ (b) $4 < n \le 8$

(c) $4 \le n < 8$ (d) $4 < n < 8$

59. The number of points of intersection of the two curves $y = 2\sin x$ and $y = 5x^2 + 2x + 3$ is :

(a) 0   (b) 1

(c) 2   (d) ∞

60. The number of distinct values of θ satisfying $0 \le \theta \le \pi$ and satisfying the equation $\sin\theta + \sin 5\theta = \sin 3\theta$, is :

(a) 6   (b) 7

(c) 8   (d) 9

61. The number of all possible triplets (a_1, a_2, a_3) such that $a_1 + a_2\cos 2x + a_3\sin^2 x = 0$ for all x is :

(a) 0   (b) 1

(c) 3   (d) infinite

62. The equation $\sin^4 x - (k + 2)\sin^2 x - (k + 3) = 0$ possesses a solution if :

(a) $k > -3$

(b) $k < -2$

(c) $-3 \le k \le -2$

(d) k is any positive integer

63. The least difference between the roots, in the first quadrant $\left(0 \le x \le \dfrac{\pi}{2}\right)$, of the equation

$4\cos x\,(2 - 3\sin^2 x) + (\cos 2x + 1) = 0$, is :

(a) $\dfrac{\pi}{6}$ (b) $\dfrac{\pi}{4}$

(c) $\dfrac{\pi}{3}$ (d) $\dfrac{\pi}{2}$

64. If α and β are two distinct values of θ lying between 0 and 2π, satisfying the equation $3\cos\theta + 4\sin\theta = 2$, then the value of $\sin(\alpha + \beta)$ is :

(a) $\dfrac{12}{25}$ (b) $\dfrac{24}{25}$

(c) $\dfrac{13}{25}$ (d) None of these

65. The solution of the equation

$\sin x + \sin\dfrac{\pi}{8}\sqrt{[(1 - \cos x)^2 + \sin^2 x]} = 0$

in the interval $\left[\dfrac{5\pi}{2}, \dfrac{7\pi}{2}\right]$, is :

(a) $x = \dfrac{11\pi}{4}$ (b) $x = \dfrac{13\pi}{4}$

(c) $x = \dfrac{7\pi}{4}$ (d) None of these

66. The solution of the equation

$\dfrac{\sqrt{3}}{2}\sin x - \cos x = \cos^2 x$ is :

(a) $x = (2n + 1)\,\pi$

(b) $x = n\pi \pm \dfrac{\pi}{3}$

(c) $x = 2n\pi \pm \dfrac{\pi}{6}$

(d) None of these

67. Solution of the equation

$\sin^3\theta + \sin\theta\cos\theta + \cos^3\theta = 1$ is :

(a) $\theta = 2n\pi + \dfrac{\pi}{4}$

(b) $\theta = 2n\pi - \dfrac{\pi}{4}$

(c) $\theta = 2n\pi + \dfrac{\pi}{2}$

(d) $\theta = 2n\pi - \dfrac{\pi}{2}$

68. The values of x in $(-\pi, \pi)$ which satisfy the equation

$8^{1 + |\cos x| + \cos^2 x + |\cos^3 x| + \dots \text{ to infinity}} = 4^3$ are

(a) $\pm\dfrac{\pi}{4}$

(b) $\pm\dfrac{\pi}{6}$

(c) $\pm\dfrac{2\pi}{3}$

(d) None of these

69. Solution of the equation $|\cos x|^{\sin^2 x - \frac{3}{2}\sin x + \frac{1}{2}} = 1$ is

(a) $x = 2n\pi$

(b) $x = (2n \pm 1)\,\pi$

(c) $x = n\pi + (-1)^n\dfrac{\pi}{6}$

(d) None of these

70. Solution of the equation

$\tan\theta + \tan\left(\theta + \dfrac{\pi}{3}\right) + \tan\left(\theta + \dfrac{2\pi}{3}\right) = 3$ is :

(a) $\theta = \dfrac{n\pi}{3} + \dfrac{\pi}{6}$

(b) $\theta = \dfrac{n\pi}{3} - \dfrac{\pi}{12}$

(c) $\theta = \dfrac{n\pi}{3} + \dfrac{\pi}{12}$

(d) None of these

71. Solution of equation $3\tan(\theta - 15°) = \tan(\theta + 15°)$ is :

(a) $\theta = n\pi - \dfrac{\pi}{3}$

(b) $\theta = n\pi + \dfrac{\pi}{3}$

(c) $\theta = n\pi - \dfrac{\pi}{4}$

(d) $\theta = n\pi + \dfrac{\pi}{4}$

72. Solution of equation $4\cot 2\theta = \cot^2\theta - \tan^2\theta$ is :

(a) $\theta = n\pi \pm \dfrac{\pi}{2}$

(b) $\theta = n\pi \pm \dfrac{\pi}{3}$

(c) $\theta = n\pi \pm \dfrac{\pi}{4}$

(d) None of these

73. Solution of equation $\tan 3\theta + \tan\theta = 2\tan 2\theta$ is :

(a) $\theta = \dfrac{n\pi}{2}$

(b) $\theta = \dfrac{n\pi}{3}$

(c) $\theta = n\pi$

(d) None of these

74. The number of solutions of the equation

$\sin x + 2\sin 2x = 3 + \sin 3x$ in the interval $0 \le x \le \pi$, is :

(a) 0

(b) 1

(c) 2

(d) 3

75. The values of k for which the equation

$\sin x + \cos(k + x) + \cos(k - x) = 2$ has real solutions, are :

(a) $n\pi - \dfrac{\pi}{2} \le k \le n\pi + \dfrac{\pi}{2}$

(b) $n\pi - \dfrac{\pi}{6} \le k \le n\pi + \dfrac{\pi}{6}$

(c) $n\pi - \dfrac{\pi}{4} \le k \le n\pi + \dfrac{\pi}{4}$

(d) None of these

76. The equation $\cos 2x + a\sin x = 2a - 7$ has a solution for :

(a) all a

(b) $a > 6$

(c) $a < 2$

(d) $a \in [2, 6]$

77. The equation $a\sin x + b\cos x = c$ where $|c| > \sqrt{a^2 + b^2}$, has :

(a) one solution

(b) two solutions

(c) no solution

(d) infinite number of solutions

78. The most general values of θ for which

$\sin\theta - \cos\theta - \min_{a \in R}\{1,\ a^2 - 6a + 10\}$ are

given by

(a) $n\pi + (-1)^n\dfrac{\pi}{4} - \dfrac{\pi}{4}$

(b) $n\pi + (-1)^n\dfrac{\pi}{4} + \dfrac{\pi}{4}$

(c) $2n\pi + \dfrac{\pi}{4}$

(d) None of these

79. The general solution of the equation

$\sin^{50}x - \cos^{50}x = 1$ is :

(a) $2n\pi + \dfrac{\pi}{2}$

(b) $2n\pi + \dfrac{\pi}{3}$

(c) $n\pi + \dfrac{\pi}{2}$

(d) $n\pi + \dfrac{\pi}{3}$

80. The set of all x in $(-\pi, \pi)$ satisfying $|4 \sin x - 1| < \sqrt{5}$ is given by :

(a) $\left(-\dfrac{\pi}{10}, \dfrac{3\pi}{10}\right)$ (b) $\left(-\dfrac{\pi}{10}, \pi\right)$

(c) $(-\pi, \pi)$ (d) $\left(-\pi, \dfrac{\pi}{10}\right)$

81. The number of solutions of the equation $\sin 2x + \cos 2x + \sin x + \cos x + 1 = 0$ between $x = 0$ and $x = \dfrac{\pi}{2}$ is :

(a) 0   (b) 1

(c) 2   (d) None of these

82. The least positive non-integral solution of the equation $\sin \pi (x^2 + x) = \sin \pi x^2$ is :

(a) rational

(b) irrational of the form $\sqrt{p}$

(c) irrational of the form $\dfrac{\sqrt{p} - 1}{4}$, where p is an odd integer.

(d) irrational of the form $\dfrac{\sqrt{p} + 1}{4}$, where p is an even integer.

83. The smallest positive angle satisfying the equation $\sin^2 \theta - 2 \cos \theta + \dfrac{1}{4} = 0$ is :

(a) $\dfrac{\pi}{2}$ (b) $\dfrac{\pi}{3}$

(c) $\dfrac{\pi}{4}$ (d) $\dfrac{\pi}{6}$

84. Let n be an odd integer. If $\sin n\theta = \sum\limits_{r=0}^{n} b_r \sin^r \theta$, for every value of θ, then :

(a) $b_0 = 1, b_1 = 3$ (b) $b_0 = 0, b_1 = n$

(c) $b_0 = -1, b_1 = n$ (d) $b_0 = 0, b_1 = n^2 - n + 3$

85. Number of ordered pairs (a, x) satisfying the equation $\sec^2 (a + 2) x + a^2 - 1 = 0; -\pi < x < \pi$ is

(a) 2   (b) 1

(c) 3   (d) infinite

86. The number of solutions of the equation $\tan \theta = \tan 3\theta, \tan \theta \neq 0, \pi \in [-\pi, \pi]$, is :

(a) 0   (b) 1

(c) 2   (d) infinite

87. In the interval $\left[-\dfrac{\pi}{2}, \dfrac{\pi}{2}\right]$, the equation $\log_{\sin \theta} (\cos 2\theta) = 2$ has :

(a) no solution

(b) a unique solution

(c) two solutions

(d) infinitely many solutions

88. A solution of the equation : $(1 - \tan \theta)(1 + \tan \theta) \sec^2 \theta + 2 \tan^2 \theta = 0 \cdot$ $\left(-\dfrac{\pi}{2} \leq \theta \leq \dfrac{\pi}{2}\right)$

(a) $\theta = 0$ (b) $\theta = \dfrac{\pi}{3}$

(c) $\theta = \dfrac{\pi}{6}$ (d) None of these

89. If $x \neq \dfrac{n\pi}{2}$ and $(\cos x)^{\sin^2 x - 3 \sin x + 2} = 1$, then all solutions of x are given by :

(a) $2n\pi + \dfrac{\pi}{2}$ (b) $(2n + 1) \pi - \dfrac{\pi}{2}$

(c) $n\pi + (-1)^n \dfrac{\pi}{2}$ (d) None of these

90. The number of solutions of the equation $1 + \sin x \sin^2 \dfrac{x}{2} = 0$ in $[-\pi, \pi]$ is :

(a) zero   (b) 1

(c) 3   (d) None of these

91. The most general value of θ satisfying the equation $(1 + 2 \sin \theta)^2 + (\sqrt{3} \tan \theta - 1)^2 = 0$ is given by :

(a) $n\pi \pm \dfrac{\pi}{6}$ (b) $n\pi + (-1)^n \dfrac{7\pi}{6}$

(c) $2n\pi + \dfrac{7\pi}{6}$ (d) $2n\pi + \dfrac{11\pi}{6}$

92. The general solution of the equation $\cos x \cos 6x = -1$ is :

(a) $x = (2n + 1) \pi, n \in I$

(b) $x = 2n\pi, n \in I$

(c) $x = (2n - 1) \dfrac{\pi}{2}, n \in I$

(d) None of these

93. If the equation $2 \cos x + \cos 2\lambda x = 3$ has only one solution, then λ is :

(a) 1

(b) a rational number

(c) an irrational number

(d) None of these

94. Number of solutions of the equation $|\cos x| = 2 [x]$ are :

(a) zero

(b) 1

(c) 2

(d) Infinitely many

95. If $|\tan x| \le 1$ and $x \in [-\pi, \pi]$ then the solution set for x is :

(a) $\left[-\pi - \dfrac{3\pi}{4}\right] \cup \left[-\dfrac{\pi}{4}, \dfrac{\pi}{4}\right] \cup \left[\dfrac{3\pi}{4}, \pi\right]$

(b) $\left[-\dfrac{\pi}{4}, \dfrac{\pi}{4}\right] \cup \left[\dfrac{3\pi}{4}, \pi\right]$

(c) $\left[-\dfrac{\pi}{4}, \dfrac{\pi}{4}\right]$

(d) None of these

96. The general solution of the equation $\sin^{100} x - \cos^{100} x = 1$ is :

(a) $2n\pi - \dfrac{\pi}{2}$

(b) $n\pi + \dfrac{\pi}{2}$

(c) $2n\pi + \dfrac{\pi}{2}$

(d) None of these

97. The general solution of the equation

$\dfrac{1 - \sin x + \ldots + (-1)^n \sin^n x + \ldots}{1 + \sin x + \ldots + \sin^n x + \ldots} = \dfrac{1 - \cos 2x}{1 + \cos 2x}$ is :

(a) $(-1)^n \left(\dfrac{\pi}{3}\right) + n\pi$

(b) $(-1)^n \left(\dfrac{\pi}{6}\right) + n\pi$

(c) $(-1)^{n+1} \left(\dfrac{\pi}{6}\right) + n\pi$

(d) $(-1)^{n-1} \left(\dfrac{\pi}{3}\right) + n\pi, (n \in I)$

98. The solution of the inequality

$\log_{1/2} \sin x > \log_{1/2} \cos x$ in $[0, 2\pi]$ is :

(a) $\left(0, \dfrac{\pi}{2}\right)$

(b) $\left(-\dfrac{\pi}{4}, \dfrac{\pi}{4}\right)$

(c) $\left(0, \dfrac{\pi}{4}\right)$

(d) None of these

99. A solution of the equation $\log_2 \sin x - \log_2 \cos x - \log_2 (1 - \tan x) - \log_2 (1 + \tan x) + 1 = 0$ is given by :

(a) $\tan x = -1$

(b) $\tan x = 1$

(c) $\tan 2x = -1$

(d) $\tan 2x = 1$

100. The number of solutions of the equation $2 \cos x = [\sin x]$ in $[-2\pi, 2\pi]$ is :

(a) One

(b) Four

(c) Six

(d) Eight

101. If $x \in (0, 1)$, then the greatest root of the equation $\sin 2\pi x = \sqrt{2} \cos \pi x$ is :

(a) $\dfrac{\sqrt{3}}{2}$

(b) $\dfrac{3}{4}$

(c) $\dfrac{\sqrt{3}}{4}$

(d) None of these

102. $\cos x - 3 \cos x + 1 = \dfrac{1}{(\cot 2x - \cot x) \sin (x - \pi)}$ holds :

(a) if $\cos x = 0$

(b) if $\cos x = 1$

(c) if $\cos x = 5/2$

(d) for no real value of x

103. If the equation $\sin \theta (\sin \theta + 2 \cos \theta) = a$ has real solution then the shortest interval containing 'a' is :

(a) $\left[\dfrac{1 - \sqrt{5}}{2}, \dfrac{1 + \sqrt{5}}{2}\right]$

(b) $\left(\dfrac{\sqrt{5} - 1}{2}, \dfrac{\sqrt{5} + 1}{2}\right)$

(c) $\left(-\dfrac{1}{2}, \dfrac{1}{2}\right)$

(d) None of these

104. The number of solutions of $\tan (5\pi \cos \alpha) = \cot (5\pi \sin \alpha)$, for $\alpha \in (0, 2\pi)$, is :

(a) 6

(b) 8

(c) 12

(d) 14

105. The number of solutions of the equation $\sin^3 x \cos x + \sin^2 x \cos^2 x + \sin x \cos^3 x = 1$ in the interval $[0, 2\pi]$ are :

(a) zero

(b) one

(c) two

(d) three

106. If $[y] = [\sin x]$ and $y = \cos x$ are two given equations, then the number of solutions is ([.] denotes the greatest interger function)

(a) 2

(b) 3

(c) 4

(d) Infinitely many solutions

107. $\tan (p\,\pi/4) = \cot (q\,\pi/4)$ if :

(a) $p + q = 0$

(b) $p + q = 2n + 1$

(c) $p + q = 2n$

(d) $p + q = 2(2n + 1)$

where n is any integer.

108. If $\sin x = \cos y$, $\sqrt{6} \sin y = \tan z$ and $2 \sin z = \sqrt{3} \cos x$; u, v, w, denote respectively $\sin^2 x$, $\sin^2 y$, $\sin^2 z$, then the value of the triplet (u, v, w) is :

(a) (1, 0, 0)

(b) (0, 1, 0)

(c) (1/2, 1/2, 3/4)

(d) (1/2, 3/4, 1/2)

109. From the identity $\sin 3x = 3 \sin x - 4 \sin^3 x$ it follows that if x is real and $|x| < 1$, then :

(a) $(3x - 4x^3) > 1$

(b) $(3x - 4x^3) \le 1$

(c) $(3x - 4x^3) < 1$

(d) nothing can be said about $3x - 4x^3$

110. If $\tan p\theta - \tan q\theta = 0$, then the values of θ form a series in :

(a) A. P.

(b) G. P.

(c) H. P.

(d) None of these

111. The number of pairs (x, y), satisfying the equations $\sin x + \sin y = \sin (x + y)$ and $|x| + |y| = 1$, is

(a) 2

(b) 4

(c) 6

(d) infinite

112. If a is any real number, then the number of roots of $\cot x - \tan x = a$ in the first quadrant is (are) :

(a) 2

(b) 0

(c) 1

(d) None of these

113. If $\tan \theta = \sqrt{3}$, then the value of θ is :

(a) $n\pi + \dfrac{\pi}{6}$

(b) $n\pi + \dfrac{\pi}{3}$

(c) $2n\pi \pm \dfrac{\pi}{6}$

(d) $2n\pi + \dfrac{\pi}{3}$

114. If $\sin \theta = 1$, then the standard value of θ will be

(a) $n\pi + (-1)^n \dfrac{\pi}{2}$

(b) $n\pi \pm \dfrac{\pi}{2}$

(c) $2n\pi \pm \dfrac{\pi}{2}$

(d) $2n\pi + \dfrac{\pi}{2}$

115. If $A = \sin^2 x + \cos^4 x$, then for all real x

[AIEEE - 2011]

(a) $\dfrac{3}{4} \le A \le \dfrac{13}{16}$

(b) $\dfrac{3}{4} \le A \le 1$

(c) $\dfrac{13}{16} \le A \le 1$

(d) $1 \le A \le 2$

116. The number of values of x in the interval $[0, 3\pi]$ satisfying the equation $2 \sin^2 x + 5 \sin x - 3 = 0$ is :

[AIEEE - 2006]

(a) 4

(b) 6

(c) 1

(d) 2

ANSWER KEY

1. (a)	2. (c)	3. (c)	4. (b)	5. (c)	6. (c)	7. (c)	8. (c)	9. (a)	10. (c)
11. (c)	12. (d)	13. (a)	14. (a)	15. (c)	16. (b)	17. (a)	18. (c)	19. (d)	20. (b)
21. (a)	22. (c)	23. (c)	24. (b)	25. (c)	26. (a)	27. (a)	28. (b)	29. (a)	30. (b)
31. (c)	32. (b)	33. (c)	34. (c)	35. (d)	36. (c)	37. (a)	38. (a)	39. (c)	40. (c)
41. (a)	42. (a)	43. (b)	44. (c)	45. (b)	46. (a)	47. (c)	48. (c)	49. (d)	50. (a)
51. (a)	52. (b)	53. (b)	54. (c)	55. (a)	56. (b)	57. (d)	58. (d)	59. (a)	60. (a)
61. (d)	62. (c)	63. (a)	64. (b)	65. (b)	66. (a)	67. (c)	68. (c)	69. (d)	70. (c)
71. (d)	72. (c)	73. (c)	74. (a)	75. (b)	76. (d)	77. (c)	78. (b)	79. (c)	80. (a)
81. (a)	82. (c)	83. (b)	84. (b)	85. (c)	86. (a)	87. (b)	88. (b)	89. (d)	90. (a)
91. (c)	92. (a)	93. (c)	94. (a)	95. (a)	96. (b)	97. (b)	98. (c)	99. (d)	100. (d)
101. (b)	102. (d)	103. (a)	104. (d)	105. (a)	106. (d)	107. (d)	108. (a)	109. (d)	110. (c)
111. (c)	112. (c)	113. (b)	114. (a)	115. (b)	116. (a)				

❑❑❑

INVERSE TRIGONOMETRIC FUNCTIONS

MULTIPLE CHOICE QUESTIONS

1. The value of $\sin\left[\dfrac{\pi}{3} - \sin^{-1}\left(-\dfrac{1}{2}\right)\right]$ is :

   (a) 1   (b) –1

   (c) 0   (d) $\dfrac{1}{2}$

2. The principal value of $\cot^{-1}(-1)$ is :

   (a) $\dfrac{\pi}{4}$ (b) $-\dfrac{\pi}{4}$

   (c) $\dfrac{3\pi}{4}$ (d) None of these

3. The value of $\cos^{-1}\left(\cos\dfrac{7\pi}{6}\right)$ is

   (a) $\dfrac{\pi}{6}$ (b) $-\dfrac{\pi}{6}$

   (c) $\dfrac{7\pi}{6}$ (d) $\dfrac{5\pi}{6}$

4. The principal value of $\sin^{-1}\left(-\dfrac{\sqrt{3}}{2}\right)$ is :

   (a) $-\dfrac{2\pi}{3}$ (b) $-\dfrac{\pi}{3}$

   (c) $\dfrac{4\pi}{3}$ (d) $\dfrac{5\pi}{3}$

5. The value of $\sin\left[\arccos\left(-\dfrac{1}{2}\right)\right]$ is :

   (a) $\dfrac{1}{\sqrt{2}}$ (b) 1

   (c) $\dfrac{\sqrt{3}}{2}$ (d) None of these

6. The value of $\cos\left[\cos^{-1}\left(-\dfrac{\sqrt{3}}{2}\right) + \dfrac{\pi}{6}\right]$ is :

   (a) 1   (b) –1

   (c) 0   (d) None of these

7. The value of $\sin\left[\tan^{-1}(-\sqrt{3}) + \cos^{-1}\left(-\dfrac{\sqrt{3}}{2}\right)\right]$ is :

   (a) 1   (b) –1

   (c) 0   (d) None of these

8. The value of $\tan^{-1}\left[\tan\left(\dfrac{3\pi}{4}\right)\right]$ is

   (a) $\dfrac{\pi}{3}$ (b) $-\dfrac{\pi}{3}$

   (c) $\dfrac{\pi}{4}$ (d) $-\dfrac{\pi}{4}$

9. The principal value of $\sin^{-1}\left[\sin\left(\dfrac{2\pi}{3}\right)\right]$ is :

   (a) $-\dfrac{2\pi}{3}$ (b) $\dfrac{2\pi}{3}$

   (c) $\dfrac{4\pi}{3}$ (d) None of these

10. The value of $\tan\left(\dfrac{1}{2}\cos^{-1}\dfrac{\sqrt{5}}{3}\right)$ is :

    (a) $\dfrac{3-\sqrt{5}}{2}$ (b) $\dfrac{3+\sqrt{5}}{2}$

    (c) $\dfrac{\sqrt{5}-3}{2}$ (d) None of these

11. $\tan(\cos^{-1}x)$ is equal to :

    (a) $\dfrac{\sqrt{1-x^2}}{x}$ (b) $\dfrac{x}{\sqrt{1+x^2}}$

    (c) $\dfrac{\sqrt{1+x^2}}{x}$ (d) $\dfrac{x}{\sqrt{1-x^2}}$

12. The value of $\sin[\cot^{-1}\{\tan(\cos^{-1}x)\}]$ is :

    (a) $\dfrac{\sqrt{1-x^2}}{x}$ (b) $\dfrac{x}{\sqrt{1-x^2}}$

    (c) x (d) None of these

13. The value of $\tan\left[2\tan^{-1}\left(\dfrac{1}{5}\right) - \dfrac{\pi}{4}\right]$ is :

    (a) $\dfrac{7}{17}$ (b) $-\dfrac{7}{17}$

    (c) $\dfrac{2}{3}$ (d) $-\dfrac{2}{3}$

14. If $\sin^{-1} x = \frac{\pi}{5}$ for some $x \in (-1, 1)$, then the value of $\cos^{-1}x$ is :

(a) $\frac{3\pi}{10}$

(b) $\frac{5\pi}{10}$

(c) $\frac{7\pi}{10}$

(d) $\frac{9\pi}{10}$

15. In a ΔABC, if $A = \tan^{-1} 2$ and $B = \tan^{-1} 3$, then $C = :$

(a) $\frac{\pi}{3}$

(b) $\frac{\pi}{4}$

(c) $\frac{\pi}{6}$

(d) None of these

16. $\tan^{-1}\left(\frac{x}{y}\right) - \tan^{-1}\left(\frac{x-y}{x+y}\right)$ is :

(a) $\frac{\pi}{2}$

(b) $\frac{\pi}{3}$

(c) $\frac{\pi}{4}$

(d) $\frac{\pi}{4}$ or $-\frac{3\pi}{4}$

17. $\sin^{-1}\frac{4}{5} + \sin^{-1}\frac{5}{13} + \sin^{-1}\frac{16}{65}$ is equal to :

(a) $\frac{\pi}{3}$

(b) $\frac{\pi}{6}$

(c) $\frac{\pi}{4}$

(d) $\frac{\pi}{2}$

18. $\sin^{-1}\frac{12}{13} + \cos^{-1}\frac{4}{5} + \tan^{-1}\frac{63}{16}$ is equal to :

(a) π

(b) $\frac{\pi}{2}$

(c) $\frac{\pi}{3}$

(d) 0

19. $4 \tan^{-1}\frac{1}{5} - \tan^{-1}\frac{1}{70} + \tan^{-1}\frac{1}{99} =$

(a) $\frac{\pi}{4}$

(b) $\frac{\pi}{2}$

(c) $\frac{\pi}{3}$

(d) $\frac{\pi}{6}$

20. If $\sin^{-1} x + \sin^{-1} y = \frac{2\pi}{3}$, then $\cos^{-1} x + \cos^{-1} y =$

(a) $\frac{2\pi}{3}$

(b) $\frac{\pi}{3}$

(c) $\frac{\pi}{6}$

(d) π

21. The value of $\cos (2 \cos^{-1} x + \sin^{-1} x)$ at $x = \frac{1}{5}$ is :

(a) $\frac{2\sqrt{6}}{5}$

(b) $-\frac{2\sqrt{6}}{5}$

(c) $\frac{3\sqrt{6}}{5}$

(d) None of these

22. If $\cos^{-1} x + \cos^{-1} y + \cos^{-1} z = \pi$, then $x^2 + y^2 + z^2 + 2xyz =$

(a) 0

(b) 1

(c) -1

(d) None of these

23. If $\sin^{-1}\frac{1}{3} + \sin^{-1}\frac{2}{3} = \sin^{-1} x$, then value of x is :

(a) 0

(b) $\frac{(\sqrt{5} - 4\sqrt{2})}{9}$

(c) $\frac{(\sqrt{5} + 4\sqrt{2})}{9}$

(d) $\frac{\pi}{2}$

24. $2 \tan^{-1}\frac{1}{5} + \sec^{-1}\frac{5\sqrt{2}}{7} + 2 \tan^{-1}\frac{1}{8} =$

(a) $\frac{\pi}{2}$

(b) $\frac{\pi}{4}$

(c) $\frac{\pi}{6}$

(d) None of these

25. If $\cos^{-1}\frac{x}{2} + \cos^{-1}\frac{y}{3} = \theta$, then $9x^2 - 12xy \cos \theta + 4y^2 =$

(a) $36 \sin^2 \theta$

(b) $36 \cos^2 \theta$

(c) $18 \sin^2 \theta$

(d) None of these

26. If $r = x + y + z$, then
$$\tan^{-1}\sqrt{\frac{xr}{yz}} + \tan^{-1}\sqrt{\frac{yr}{zx}} + \tan^{-1}\sqrt{\frac{zr}{xy}} =$$

(a) π

(b) 2π

(c) $\frac{\pi}{2}$

(d) None of these

27. $\cot\left(\frac{\pi}{4} - 2 \cot^{-1} 3\right) =$

(a) 1

(b) 7

(c) 4

(d) None of these

28. If $\sin^{-1}\frac{2a}{1 + a^2} + \sin^{-1}\frac{2b}{1 + b^2} = 2 \tan^{-1} x$, then :

(a) $x = \frac{a + b}{1 - ab}$

(b) $x = \frac{a - b}{1 + ab}$

(c) $x = \frac{b - a}{1 + ab}$

(d) None of these

29. $\tan\left[\cos^{-1}\dfrac{4}{5}+\tan^{-1}\dfrac{2}{3}\right]=$

    (a) $\dfrac{13}{6}$ (b) $\dfrac{17}{6}$

    (c) $-\dfrac{13}{6}$ (d) $-\dfrac{17}{6}$

30. $\sin\left[\tan^{-1}\dfrac{1-x^2}{2x}+\cos^{-1}\dfrac{1-x^2}{1+x^2}\right]=$

    (a) 1   (b) 0

    (c) -1 (d) None of these

31. The value of $\sin^{-1}(\sin 10)$ is :

    (a) $3\pi-10$ (b) $10-3\pi$

    (c) 10 (d) None of these

32. $\tan\left[\dfrac{1}{2}\sin^{-1}\left(\dfrac{2x}{1+x^2}\right)+\dfrac{1}{2}\cos^{-1}\left(\dfrac{1-x^2}{1+x^2}\right)\right]=$

    (a) ∞ (b) 1

    (c) $\dfrac{2x}{1-x^2}$ (d) $\dfrac{2x}{1+x^2}$

33. $\tan\left(\dfrac{\pi}{4}+\dfrac{1}{2}\cos^{-1}\dfrac{a}{b}\right)+\tan\left(\dfrac{\pi}{4}-\dfrac{1}{2}\cos^{-1}\dfrac{a}{b}\right)=$

    (a) $\dfrac{2a}{b}$ (b) $\dfrac{a}{b}$

    (c) $\dfrac{b}{a}$ (d) $\dfrac{2b}{a}$

34. If $\tan^{-1}\dfrac{\sqrt{1+x^2}-\sqrt{1-x^2}}{\sqrt{1+x^2}+\sqrt{1-x^2}}=\alpha$, then $x^2=$

    (a) $\sin 2\alpha$ (b) $\sin\alpha$

    (c) $\cos 2\alpha$ (d) $\cos\alpha$

35. If $\dfrac{m\tan(\alpha-\theta)}{\cos^2\theta}=\dfrac{n\tan\theta}{\cos^2(\alpha-\theta)}$, then

    $\theta=\dfrac{1}{2}(\alpha-\tan^{-1}y)$, where $y=$

    (a) $\dfrac{m+n}{m-n}\tan\alpha$ (b) $\dfrac{n+m}{n-m}\tan\alpha$

    (c) $\dfrac{n-m}{n+m}\tan\alpha$ (d) None of these

36. $2\tan^{-1}\left(\sqrt{\dfrac{a-b}{a+b}}\tan\dfrac{\theta}{2}\right)=$

    (a) $\cos^{-1}\left(\dfrac{a+b\cos\theta}{a\cos\theta+b}\right)$ (b) $\cos^{-1}\left(\dfrac{a\cos\theta+b}{a+b\cos\theta}\right)$

    (c) $\cos^{-1}\left(\dfrac{a-b\cos\theta}{a\cos\theta+b}\right)$ (d) None of these

37. $2\tan^{-1}\left(\tan\dfrac{\theta}{2}\tan\dfrac{\phi}{2}\right)=$

    (a) $\cos^{-1}\left(\dfrac{\cos\theta+\cos\phi}{1+\cos\theta\cos\phi}\right)$

    (b) $\cos^{-1}\left(\dfrac{\cos\theta-\cos\phi}{1+\cos\theta\cos\phi}\right)$

    (c) $\cos^{-1}\left(\dfrac{\cos\theta+\cos\phi}{1-\cos\theta\cos\phi}\right)$

    (d) None of these

38. If $\tan^{-1}\dfrac{1}{1+2x}+\tan^{-1}\dfrac{1}{4x+1}=\tan^{-1}\dfrac{2}{x^2}$, then $x=$

    (a) 0   (b) 3

    (c) $-\dfrac{2}{3}$ (d) All of these

39. Solution of the equation $\cos^{-1}\sqrt{3}x+\cos^{-1}x=\dfrac{\pi}{2}$ is :

    (a) $x=-\dfrac{1}{2}$ (b) $x=\dfrac{1}{2}$

    (c) $x=1$ (d) $x=-1$

40. Solution of the equation $\sin^{-1}x+\sin^{-1}2x=\dfrac{\pi}{3}$ is :

    (a) $x=\dfrac{\sqrt{3}}{2\sqrt{7}}$ (b) $x=-\dfrac{\sqrt{3}}{2\sqrt{7}}$

    (c) $x=\pm\dfrac{1}{\sqrt{2}}$ (d) None of these

41. If $\cos^{-1}\left(\dfrac{1-a^2}{1+a^2}\right)-\cos^{-1}\left(\dfrac{1-b^2}{1+b^2}\right)=2\tan^{-1}x$,

    then $x=$

    (a) $\dfrac{a-b}{1+ab}$ (b) $\dfrac{b-a}{1+ba}$

    (c) $\dfrac{a+b}{1-ab}$ (d) None of these

42. Solution of equation $\cot^{-1}x+\sin^{-1}\dfrac{1}{\sqrt{5}}=\dfrac{\pi}{4}$ is :

    (a) $x=3$ (b) $x=\dfrac{1}{\sqrt{5}}$

    (c) $x=0$ (d) None of these

43. Solution of the equation

$\tan(\cos^{-1} x) = \sin\left(\cot^{-1}\dfrac{1}{2}\right)$ is :

(a) $x = \pm\dfrac{\sqrt{7}}{3}$

(b) $x = \pm\dfrac{\sqrt{5}}{3}$

(c) $x = \pm\dfrac{3\sqrt{5}}{2}$

(d) None of these

44. $\cot^{-1}\dfrac{xy+1}{x-y} + \cot^{-1}\dfrac{yz+1}{y-z} + \cot^{-1}\dfrac{xz+1}{x-z} =$

(a) 1

(b) −1

(c) 0

(d) None of these

45. $2\tan^{-1}\left[\tan\dfrac{\alpha}{2}\tan\left(\dfrac{\pi}{4}-\dfrac{\beta}{2}\right)\right] =$

(a) $\tan^{-1}\left(\dfrac{\sin\beta\,\cos\alpha}{\sin\beta+\cos\alpha}\right)$

(b) $\tan^{-1}\left(\dfrac{\sin\beta\,\cos\alpha}{\sin\alpha+\cos\beta}\right)$

(c) $\tan^{-1}\left(\dfrac{\sin\alpha\,\cos\beta}{\sin\alpha+\cos\beta}\right)$

(d) $\tan^{-1}\left(\dfrac{\sin\alpha\,\cos\beta}{\sin\beta+\cos\alpha}\right)$

46. If $\cos^{-1}\dfrac{3}{5} - \sin^{-1}\dfrac{4}{5} = \cos^{-1} x$, then $x = :$

(a) 0

(b) 1

(c) −1

(d) None of these

47. Solution of the equation

$\sin^{-1}\dfrac{3x}{5} + \sin^{-1}\dfrac{4x}{5} = \sin^{-1} x$ is :

(a) $x = 0$

(b) $x = 1$

(c) $x = -1$

(d) All of these

48. $\tan^{-1}\left(\dfrac{a_1 x - y}{a_1 y + x}\right) + \tan^{-1}\left(\dfrac{a_2 - a_1}{a_1 a_2 + 1}\right) + \tan^{-1}\left(\dfrac{a_3 - a_2}{a_2 a_3 - 1}\right)$

$+ \ldots + \tan^{-1}\left(\dfrac{a_n - a_{n-1}}{a_{n-1}\,a_n + 1}\right) + \tan^{-1}\dfrac{1}{a_n} =$

(a) $\tan^{-1} xy$

(b) $\tan^{-1}\dfrac{x}{y}$

(c) $\tan^{-1}\dfrac{y}{x}$

(d) None of these

49. If $f(x) = 2\tan^{-1} x + \sin^{-1}\dfrac{2x}{1+x^2}$, then for $x \geq 1$,

$f(x)$ is equal to :

(a) π

(b) 2π

(c) $\dfrac{\pi}{2}$

(d) None of these

50. $\tan^{-1}\sqrt{\dfrac{a}{bc}(a+b+c)} + \tan^{-1}\sqrt{\dfrac{b}{ca}(a+b+c)}$

$+ \tan^{-1}\sqrt{\dfrac{c}{ab}(a+b+c)} =$

(a) $\dfrac{\pi}{2}$

(b) π

(c) 0

(d) None of these

51. The value of $\cot^{-1}\left[\dfrac{\sqrt{1-\sin x}+\sqrt{1+\sin x}}{\sqrt{1-\sin x}-\sqrt{1+\sin x}}\right]$ is :

(a) $\pi - x$

(b) $2\pi - x$

(c) $\dfrac{x}{2}$

(d) $\pi - \dfrac{x}{2}$

52. If $\tan\theta + \tan\left(\dfrac{\pi}{3}+\theta\right) + \tan\left(-\dfrac{\pi}{3}+\theta\right) = a\tan 3\theta$,

then $a =$

(a) $\dfrac{1}{3}$

(b) 1

(c) 3

(d) None of these

53. If $a_1,\ a_2,\ a_3,\ \ldots\ a_n$ are in A.P. with common difference d, then :

$\tan\left[\tan^{-1}\left(\dfrac{d}{1+a_1 a_2}\right) + \tan^{-1}\left(\dfrac{d}{1+a_2 a_3}\right)\right.$

$\left. + \ldots + \tan^{-1}\left(\dfrac{d}{1+a_{n-1}\,a_n}\right)\right]$ is equal to :

(a) $\dfrac{(n-1)\,d}{1+a_1 a_n}$

(b) $\dfrac{nd}{1+a_1 a_n}$

(c) $\dfrac{a_n - a_1}{a_n + a_1}$

(d) $\dfrac{(n-1)\,d}{a_1 + a_n}$

54. If θ and ϕ are the roots of the equation

$8x^2 + 22x + 5 = 0$, then :

(a) both $\sin^{-1}\theta$ and $\sin^{-1}\phi$ are real.

(b) both $\sec^{-1}\theta$ and $\sec^{-1}\phi$ are real.

(c) both $\tan^{-1}\theta$ and $\tan^{-1}\phi$ are real.

(d) None of these.

55. Let $f(x) = \cot^{-1} x + \operatorname{cosec}^{-1} x$. Then $f(x)$ is real for :

(a) $x \in [-1,\ 1]$

(b) $x \in (-\infty,\ -1] \cup [1,\ \infty)$

(c) $x \in (-\infty,\ \infty)$

(d) None of these

56. $\sec^{-1}(\sin x)$ is real if :

(a) $x \in (-\infty, \infty)$

(b) $x \in [-1, 1]$

(c) $x = (2n + 1)\dfrac{n}{2}, n \in I$

(d) $x = n\pi, n \in Z$

57. If $\sin^{-1}\alpha + \sin^{-1}\beta + \sin^{-1}\gamma = \dfrac{3\pi}{2}$ then $\alpha\beta + \alpha\gamma + \beta\gamma$

is equal to :

(a) 1

(b) 0

(c) 3

(d) -3

58. If $\displaystyle\sum_{i=1}^{2n} \cos^{-1} x_i = 0$, then $\displaystyle\sum_{i=1}^{2n} x_i$ is :

(a) n

(b) $2n$

(c) $\dfrac{n(n+1)}{2}$

(d) None of these

59. If $\displaystyle\sum_{i=1}^{20} \sin^{-1} x_i = 10\pi$, then $\displaystyle\sum_{i=1}^{20} x_i$ is equal to :

(a) 20

(b) 10

(c) 0

(d) None of these

60. The value of $\cot^{-1}3 + \sec^{-1}\dfrac{\sqrt{5}}{2}$ is :

(a) $\dfrac{\pi}{4}$

(b) $\dfrac{\pi}{3}$

(c) $\dfrac{\pi}{2}$

(d) None of these

61. The value of $\sin^2\left(\cos^{-1}\dfrac{1}{2}\right) + \cos^2\left(\sin^{-1}\dfrac{1}{3}\right)$ is :

(a) $\dfrac{17}{36}$

(b) $\dfrac{59}{36}$

(c) $\dfrac{36}{59}$

(d) None of these

62. If $\tan^{-1}\dfrac{x}{\pi} < \dfrac{\pi}{3}$, $x \in N$, then the maximum integral

value of x is :

(a) 2

(b) 5

(c) 7

(d) None of these

63. If we consider only the principal values of the inverse trigonometric functions, then the value of $\tan\left(\cos^{-1}\dfrac{1}{5\sqrt{2}} - \sin^{-1}\dfrac{4}{\sqrt{17}}\right)$ is :

(a) $\dfrac{\sqrt{29}}{3}$

(b) $\dfrac{29}{3}$

(c) $\dfrac{\sqrt{3}}{29}$

(d) $\dfrac{3}{29}$

64. If $\sin^{-1}\left(x - \dfrac{x^2}{2} + \dfrac{x^3}{4} - \ldots\right) + \cos^{-1}\left(x^2 - \dfrac{x^4}{2} + \dfrac{x^6}{4} - \ldots\right)$

$= \dfrac{\pi}{2}$ for $0 < |x| < \sqrt{2}$, then x equals :

(a) $\dfrac{1}{2}$

(b) 1

(c) $-\dfrac{1}{2}$

(d) -1

65. The number of real solutions of

$\tan^{-1}\sqrt{x(x+1)} + \sin^{-1}\sqrt{x^2 + x + 1} = \dfrac{\pi}{2}$ is :

(a) zero

(b) one

(c) two

(d) infinite

66. Solution of the equation

$\sin\left[2\cos^{-1}\left\{\cot\left(2\tan^{-1}x\right)\right\}\right] = 0$ is :

(a) $x = \pm 1$

(b) $1 \pm \sqrt{2}$

(c) $-(1 \pm \sqrt{2})$

(d) All of these

67. The positive integral solution of the equation

$\tan^{-1}x + \cos^{-1}\left(\dfrac{y}{\sqrt{1 + y^2}}\right) = \sin^{-1}\left(\dfrac{3}{\sqrt{10}}\right)$ is :

(a) $x = 1, y = 2$

(b) $x = 2, y = 1$

(c) $x = 3, y = 2$

(d) $x = -2, y = -1$

68. The value of $3\tan^{-1}\dfrac{1}{2} + 2\tan^{-1}\dfrac{1}{5} + \sin^{-1}\dfrac{142}{65\sqrt{5}}$ is :

(a) $\dfrac{\pi}{4}$

(b) $\dfrac{\pi}{2}$

(c) π

(d) None of these

69. The value of $\tan\left(\cos^{-1}\dfrac{4}{5} + \tan^{-1}\dfrac{2}{3}\right)$ is :

(a) $\dfrac{16}{7}$

(b) $\dfrac{6}{17}$

(c) $\dfrac{7}{16}$

(d) None of these

70. The principal value of $\sin^{-1}\left(\sin\dfrac{5\pi}{3}\right)$ is :

(a) $\dfrac{4\pi}{3}$

(b) $-\dfrac{\pi}{3}$

(c) $-\dfrac{5\pi}{3}$

(d) $\dfrac{5\pi}{3}$

71. If $\sin^{-1} x = \dfrac{\pi}{5}$ for some $x \in [-1, 1]$, then the value of $\cos^{-1} x$ is :

(a) $\dfrac{9\pi}{10}$ (b) $\dfrac{7\pi}{10}$

(c) $\dfrac{5\pi}{10}$ (d) $\dfrac{3\pi}{10}$

72. $\tan^{-1} \dfrac{1}{5} + \tan^{-1} \dfrac{1}{7} + \tan^{-1} \dfrac{1}{3} + \tan^{-1} \dfrac{1}{8} =$

(a) $\dfrac{\pi}{3}$ (b) $\dfrac{\pi}{4}$

(c) $\dfrac{\pi}{2}$ (d) π

73. The value of $\tan^{-1} \dfrac{1}{2} + \tan^{-1} \dfrac{1}{3}$ is :

(a) $\dfrac{\pi}{4}$ (b) $\dfrac{\pi}{6}$

(c) $\dfrac{\pi}{3}$ (d) 0

74. $\tan (\cot^{-1} x)$ is equal to :

(a) $\dfrac{\pi}{2} - x$ (b) $\cot (\tan^{-1} x)$

(c) $\tan x$ (d) None of these

75. $\cos^{-1} \left(\dfrac{1}{2}\right) + 2 \sin^{-1} \left(\dfrac{1}{2}\right)$ is equal to :

(a) $\dfrac{\pi}{6}$ (b) $\dfrac{\pi}{3}$

(c) $\dfrac{2\pi}{3}$ (d) $\dfrac{\pi}{4}$

76. If $\sin^{-1} x + \sin^{-1} y + \sin^{-1} z = \pi$, then

$x^4 + y^4 + z^4 + 4x^2 y^2 z^2 = k (x^2 y^2 + y^2 z^2 + z^2 x^2)$, where $k =$

(a) 1 (b) 2

(c) 4 (d) None of these

77. If $\sin^{-1} \dfrac{2a}{1 + a^2} + \sin^{-1} \dfrac{2b}{1 + b^2} = 2 \tan^{-1} x$, then x is equal to :

(a) $\dfrac{a - b}{1 + ab}$ (b) $\dfrac{b}{1 + ab}$

(c) $\dfrac{b}{1 - ab}$ (d) $\dfrac{a + b}{1 - ab}$

78. $\tan^{-1} \dfrac{1}{3} + \tan^{-1} \dfrac{1}{7} + \tan^{-1} \dfrac{1}{18} + \ldots\ldots$

$+ \tan^{-1} \left(\dfrac{1}{n^2 + n + 1}\right) + \ldots$ to ∞ is equal to :

(a) $\dfrac{\pi}{2}$ (b) $\dfrac{\pi}{4}$

(c) $\dfrac{2\pi}{3}$ (d) 0

79. If $\tan^{-1} x + 2 \cot^{-1} x = \dfrac{2\pi}{3}$, then $x =$

(a) 3 (b) $\sqrt{3}$

(c) $\sqrt{2}$ (d) $\dfrac{\sqrt{3} - 1}{\sqrt{3} + 1}$

80. The value of $\tan^{-1} \dfrac{a}{b} - \tan^{-1} \dfrac{a - b}{a + b}$ is :

(a) $\dfrac{\pi}{3}$ (b) $\dfrac{\pi}{4}$

(c) $\dfrac{\pi}{6}$ (d) 0

81. If $\tan^{-1}(x + 1) + \tan^{-1} (x - 1) = \tan^{-1} \left(\dfrac{8}{31}\right)$, then $x =$

(a) $\dfrac{1}{2}$ (b) $-\dfrac{1}{2}$

(c) $\dfrac{1}{4}$ (d) 1

82. $\tan^{-1} \left(\dfrac{x}{y}\right) - \tan^{-1} \left(\dfrac{x - y}{x + y}\right)$ is :

(a) $\dfrac{\pi}{4}$ (b) $\dfrac{\pi}{3}$

(c) $\dfrac{\pi}{2}$ (d) $\dfrac{\pi}{4}$ or $-\dfrac{3\pi}{4}$

83. $3 \tan^{-1} a$ is equal to :

(a) $\tan^{-1} \dfrac{3a + a^3}{1 + 3a^2}$ (b) $\tan^{-1} \dfrac{3a - a^3}{1 + 3a^2}$

(c) $\tan^{-1} \dfrac{3a + a^3}{1 - 3a^2}$ (d) $\tan^{-1} \dfrac{3a - a^3}{1 - 3a^2}$

84. If $\tan^{-1} 3 + \tan^{-1} x = \tan^{-1} 8$, then $x =$

(a) 5 (b) $\dfrac{1}{5}$

(c) $\dfrac{5}{14}$ (d) $\dfrac{14}{5}$

85. The number of triplets (x, y, z) satisfying
$\sin^{-1} x + \cos^{-1} y + \sin^{-1} z = 2\pi$, is

    (a) 0   (b) 2

    (c) 1   (d) Infinite

86. If $\alpha = \tan^{-1} x + \tan^{-1} y$ and $\beta = \tan^{-1}\left(\dfrac{x+y}{1-xy}\right)$;

    $x < 0,\ y < 0,\ xy > 1$ then :

    (a) $\alpha - \beta = \pi$ (b) $\alpha + \beta = \pi$

    (c) $\alpha + \beta = -\pi$ (d) $\beta - \alpha = \pi$.

87. $\cos^{-1}\left\{\dfrac{1}{2}x^2 + \sqrt{1-x^2} \cdot \sqrt{1-\dfrac{x^2}{4}}\right\} = \cos^{-1}\dfrac{x}{2} - \cos^{-1} x$

    holds for :

    (a) $|x| \leq 1$ (b) $x \in R$

    (c) $0 \leq x \leq 1$ (d) $-1 \leq x \leq 0$.

88. The value of x that satisfies $\tan^{-1}(\tan 3) = \tan^2 x$
    is :

    (a) $\dfrac{\pi}{3}$ (b) $-\dfrac{\pi}{3}$

    (c) $\sqrt{\tan^{-1} 3}$ (d) none of these.

89. If $2\tan^{-1} x + \sin^{-1}\dfrac{2x}{1+x^2}$ is independent of x,

    then :

    (a) $x \in [1, +\infty]$ (b) $x \in [-1, 1]$

    (c) $x \in [-\infty, -1]$ (d) none of these.

90. If $\alpha \leq \sin^{-1} x + \cos^{-1} x + \tan^{-1} x \leq \beta$ then :

    (a) $\alpha = \dfrac{\pi}{4}, \beta = \dfrac{3\pi}{4}$ (b) $\alpha = -\pi, \beta = 2\pi$

    (c) $\alpha = 0, \beta = \pi$ (d) none of these.

91. The number of real solutions of the equation
    $\sqrt{1 + \cos 2x} = \sqrt{2}\sin^{-1}(\sin x)$, $-\pi \leq x \leq \pi$ is :

    (a) 0   (b) 1

    (c) 2   (d) infinite.

92. The number of real solution of (x, y), where
    $|y| = \sin x$,
    $y = \cos^{-1}(\cos x)$, $-2\pi \leq x \leq 2\pi$, is

    (a) 2   (b) 1

    (c) 3   (d) 4.

93. $\tan^{-1}\dfrac{1}{4} + \tan^{-1}\dfrac{5}{3}$ equals :

    (a) $\tan^{-1} 4 + \tan^{-1}\dfrac{3}{5}$

    (b) $2\left\{\tan^{-1}\dfrac{1}{4} + \tan^{-1}\dfrac{3}{4}\right\}$

    (c) $3\left\{\tan^{-1}\dfrac{1}{4} + \tan^{-1}\dfrac{3}{4}\right\}$

    (d) none of these.

94. Let $f(x) = \sin^{-1} x + \cos^{-1} x$. Then $\dfrac{\pi}{2}$ is equal to :

    (a) $f\left(-\dfrac{1}{2}\right)$ (b) $f(k^2 - 2k + 3), k \in R$

    (c) $f\left(\dfrac{1}{1+k^2}\right), k \in R$ (d) $f(-2)$.

95. If $-1 < x < 0$ then $\sin^{-1} x$ equals :

    (a) $\pi - \sin^{-1}\sqrt{1-x^2}$ (b) $\tan^{-1}\dfrac{x}{\sqrt{1-x^2}}$

    (c) $-\cot^{-1}\left(\dfrac{\sqrt{1-x^2}}{x}\right)$ (d) none of these.

96. If $f(x) = \cos^{-1} x + \cos^{-1}\left\{\dfrac{x}{2} + \dfrac{1}{2}\sqrt{3 - 3x^2}\right\}$, then

    (a) $f\left(\dfrac{2}{3}\right) = \dfrac{\pi}{3}$

    (b) $f\left(\dfrac{2}{3}\right) = 2\cos^{-1}\dfrac{2}{3} - \dfrac{\pi}{3}$

    (c) $f\left(\dfrac{1}{3}\right) = \dfrac{\pi}{3}$

    (d) $f\left(\dfrac{1}{3}\right) = 2\cos^{-1}\dfrac{1}{3} - \dfrac{\pi}{3}$

97. The value of

    $\sin^{-1}\left\{\cot\left(\sin^{-1}\sqrt{\dfrac{2-\sqrt{3}}{4}} + \cos^{-1}\dfrac{\sqrt{12}}{4} + \sec^{-1}\sqrt{2}\right)\right\}$ is

    (a) 0   (b) $\dfrac{\pi}{4}$

    (c) $\dfrac{\pi}{6}$ (d) $\dfrac{\pi}{2}$

98. α, β and γ are three angles given by
    $\alpha = 2\tan^{-1}(\sqrt{2} - 1), \beta = 3\sin^{-1}\dfrac{1}{\sqrt{2}} + \sin^{-1}\left(-\dfrac{1}{2}\right)$

    and $\gamma = \cos^{-1}\dfrac{1}{3}$. Then

    (a) $\alpha > \beta$ (b) $\beta > \gamma$

    (c) $\alpha < \gamma$ (d) none of these.

99. The value of $\tan\left\{\cos^{-1}\left(-\dfrac{2}{7}\right) - \dfrac{\pi}{2}\right\}$ is

(a) $\dfrac{2}{3\sqrt{5}}$ (b) $\dfrac{3}{2\sqrt{5}}$

(c) $\dfrac{1}{2\sqrt{5}}$ (d) none of these.

100. The inequality $\sin^{-1}(\sin 5) > x^2 - 4x$ holds if

(a) $x = 2 - \sqrt{9 - 2\pi}$

(b) $x = 2 + \sqrt{9 - 2\pi}$

(c) $x \in (2 - \sqrt{9 - 2\pi}, 2 + \sqrt{9 - 2\pi})$

(d) $x > 2 + \sqrt{9 - 2\pi}$

101. The set of values of x satisfying $|\sin^{-1} x| < |\cos^{-1} x|$ is

(a) $\left[-1, \dfrac{1}{\sqrt{2}}\right)$

(b) $\left[-1, \dfrac{1}{\sqrt{2}}\right] \cup \left[\dfrac{1}{\sqrt{2}}, 1\right]$

(c) $\left(-1, \dfrac{1}{\sqrt{2}}\right)$

(d) none of these.

102. If a, b are positive quantities and if

$a_1 = \dfrac{a+b}{2}$, $b_1 = \sqrt{a_1 b}$, $a_2 = \dfrac{a_1 + b_1}{2}$, $b_2 = \sqrt{a_2 b_1}$

and so on, then

(a) $a_\infty = \dfrac{\sqrt{b^2 - a^2}}{\cos^{-1}\left(\frac{a}{b}\right)}$ (b) $b_\infty = \dfrac{\sqrt{(b^2 - a^2)}}{\cos^{-1}\left(\frac{a}{b}\right)}$

(c) $b_\infty = \dfrac{\sqrt{(a^2 - b^2)}}{\cos^{-1}\left(\frac{b}{a}\right)}$ (d) none of these.

103. If $\tan^{-1}\dfrac{x+1}{x-1} + \tan^{-1}\dfrac{x-1}{x} = \tan^{-1}(-7) - \pi$

then x =

(a) 2   (b) 3

(c) 4   (d) none of these.

104. Sum of infinite terms of the series

$\cot^{-1}\left(1^2 + \frac{3}{4}\right) + \cot^{-1}\left(2^2 + \frac{3}{4}\right) + \cot^{-1}\left(3^2 + \frac{3}{4}\right) + \dots$ is :

(a) $\dfrac{\pi}{4}$ (b) $\tan^{-1} 2$

(c) $\tan^{-1} 3$ (d) none of these.

105. The formula $2 \tan^{-1} x = \tan^{-1}\dfrac{2x}{1 - x^2}$ holds only for

(a) $x \in (-\infty, \infty)$ (b) $x \in [-1, 1]$

(c) $|x| < 1$ (d) $x \in (1, \infty)$.

106. If $[\sin^{-1} \cos^{-1} \sin^{-1} \sin^{-1} x] = 1$, where $[\cdot]$ denotes the greatest integer function, then x is given by the interval

(a) [tan sin cos 1, tan sin cos sin 1]

(b) (tan sin cos 1, tan sin cos sin 1]

(c) $[-1, 1]$

(d) [sin cos tan 1, sin cos sin tan 1].

107. $\tan^{-1} x + \tan^{-1} y$, where $x < 0$, $y < 0$, $xy = 1$, is equal to

(a) $\dfrac{\pi}{2}$ (b) $-\dfrac{\pi}{2}$

(c) $-x + \tan^{-1}\left(\dfrac{x+y}{1-xy}\right)$ (d) $x + \tan^{-1}\left(\dfrac{x+y}{1-xy}\right)$

108. Indicate the relation which is true

(a) $\tan |\tan^{-1} x| = |x|$ (b) $\cot |\cot^{-1} x| = x$

(c) $\tan^{-1} |\tan x| = |x|$ (d) $\sin |\sin^{-1} x| = |x|$.

109. $\cot^{-1}(\cot x) = x$ holds for

(a) $x \in [0, \pi]$ (b) $x \in (0, \pi)$

(c) $x \in [-1, 1]$ (d) $x \in (-1, 1]$.

110. If $\tan^{-1}\dfrac{\sqrt{1 + x^2}}{x} = 4$, then

(a) $x = \tan 2$ (b) $x = \tan 4$

(c) $x = \tan\left(\dfrac{1}{4}\right)$ (d) $x = \tan 8$.

111. At $x = -\dfrac{1}{3}$, the value is real for

(a) $\cos^{-1} x$ (b) $\tan^{-1} x$

(c) $\operatorname{cosec}^{-1} 2x$ (d) none of these.

112. The equation $2\cos^{-1} x = \sin^{-1}(2x\sqrt{1 - x^2})$ is valid for all values of x satisfying

(a) $-1 \le x \le 1$ (b) $0 \le x \le 1$

(c) $0 \le x \le \dfrac{1}{\sqrt{2}}$ (d) $\dfrac{1}{\sqrt{2}} \le x \le 1$

113. Which of the following is not the value of $2 \tan^{-1} x$?

(a) $\tan^{-1}\left(\dfrac{2x}{1+x^2}\right)$ (b) $\tan^{-1}\left(\dfrac{2x}{1-x^2}\right)$

(c) $\cos^{-1}\left(\dfrac{1-x^2}{1+x^2}\right)$ (d) $\sin^{-1}\left(\dfrac{2x^2}{1+x^2}\right)$

[BIT (Mesra) 2000]

114. If $u = \cot^{-1}\sqrt{\cot \alpha} - \tan^{-1}\sqrt{\tan \alpha}$, then $\tan\left(\dfrac{\pi}{4} - \dfrac{u}{2}\right)$ is equal to

(a) $\sqrt{\tan \alpha}$ (b) $\sqrt{\cot \alpha}$

(c) $\tan \alpha$ (d) $\cot \alpha$.

115. The principal value of $\sin^{-1}\left(-\dfrac{\sqrt{3}}{2}\right)$ is

(a) $\dfrac{4\pi}{3}$ (b) $\dfrac{5\pi}{3}$

(c) $-\dfrac{2\pi}{3}$ (d) $-\dfrac{\pi}{3}$

116. $\cot^{-1}\sqrt{\dfrac{a-x}{a-b}} = \sin^{-1}\sqrt{\dfrac{x-b}{a-b}}$ is possible if

(a) $a > x > b$

(b) $a < x < b$

(c) $a = x = b$

(d) $a > b$ and x, takes any value.

117. If $\tan^{-1} y = 4 \tan^{-1} x$, then y is infinite if

(a) $x^2 = 3 + 2\sqrt{2}$ (b) $x^2 = 3 - 2\sqrt{2}$

(c) $x^4 = 6x^2 - 1$ (d) $x^4 = 6x^2 + 1$

118. $3 \cos^{-1} x - \pi x - \dfrac{\pi}{2} = 0$ has

(a) one solution

(b) one and only one solution

(c) no solution

(d) more than one solution.

119. If $\cos^{-1} x = \tan^{-1} x$ then

(a) $x^2 = \dfrac{\sqrt{5}-1}{2}$

(b) $x^2 = \dfrac{\sqrt{5}+1}{2}$

(c) $\sin(\cos^{-1} x) = \dfrac{\sqrt{5}+1}{2}$

(d) $\tan(\cos^{-1} x) = \dfrac{\sqrt{5}-1}{2}$

120. An integral solution of the equation $\tan^{-1} x + \tan^{-1}\left(\dfrac{1}{y}\right) = \tan^{-1} 3$ is

(a) $(2, 7)$ (b) $(4, -13)$

(c) $(5, -8)$ (d) $(1, 2)$

(e) all of these.

121. The value of $\cot\left(\text{cosec}^{-1}\dfrac{5}{3} + \tan^{-1}\dfrac{2}{3}\right)$ is :

[AIEEE - 2008]

(a) $\dfrac{6}{17}$ (b) $\dfrac{3}{17}$

(c) $\dfrac{4}{17}$ (d) $\dfrac{5}{17}$

122. If $\sin^{-1}\left(\dfrac{x}{5}\right) + \text{cosec}^{-1}\left(\dfrac{5}{4}\right) = \dfrac{\pi}{2}$, then a value of x is :   **[AIEEE - 2007]**

(a) 1   (b) 3

(c) 4   (d) 5

123. Let $f : (-1, 1) \to B$, be a function defined by $f(x) = \tan^{-1}\dfrac{2x}{1-x^2}$, then f is both one-one and onto when B is the interval **[AIEEE - 2005]**

(a) $\left(0, \dfrac{\pi}{2}\right)$ (b) $\left[0, \dfrac{\pi}{2}\right)$

(c) $\left[-\dfrac{\pi}{2}, \dfrac{\pi}{2}\right]$ (d) $\left(-\dfrac{\pi}{2}, \dfrac{\pi}{2}\right)$

ANSWER KEY

1. (a)	2. (c)	3. (d)	4. (b)	5. (c)	6. (b)	7. (a)	8. (d)	9. (d)	10. (a)
11. (a)	12. (c)	13. (b)	14. (a)	15. (b)	16. (c)	17. (d)	18. (a)	19. (a)	20. (b)
21. (b)	22. (b)	23. (c)	24. (b)	25. (a)	26. (a)	27. (b)	28. (a)	29. (b)	30. (a)

31. (a)	**32.** (c)	**33.** (d)	**34.** (a)	**35.** (c)	**36.** (d)	**37.** (a)	**38.** (d)	**39.** (b)	**40.** (a)
41. (a)	**42.** (a)	**43.** (b)	**44.** (c)	**45.** (d)	**46.** (b)	**47.** (d)	**48.** (b)	**49.** (a)	**50.** (b)
51. (d)	**52.** (c)	**53.** (a)	**54.** (c)	**55.** (b)	**56.** (c)	**57.** (c)	**58.** (b)	**59.** (a)	**60.** (a)
61. (b)	**62.** (b)	**63.** (d)	**64.** (b)	**65.** (c)	**66.** (d)	**67.** (a)	**68.** (c)	**69.** (d)	**70.** (b)
71. (d)	**72.** (b)	**73.** (a)	**74.** (b)	**75.** (c)	**76.** (b)	**77.** (d)	**78.** (b)	**79.** (b)	**80.** (b)
81. (c)	**82.** (a)	**83.** (d)	**84.** (b)	**85.** (c)	**86.** (d)	**87.** (c)	**88.** (d)	**89.** (ac)	**90.** (c)
91. (c)	**92.** (c)	**93.** (d)	**94.** (a)	**95.** (b)	**96.** (ad)	**97.** (a)	**98.** (bc)	**99.** (a)	**100.** (c)
101. (a)	**102.** (b)	**103.** (a)	**104.** (b)	**105.** (c)	**106.** (a)	**107.** (b)	**108.** (abd)	**109.** (b)	**110.** (d)
111. (ab)	**112.** (d)	**113.** (a)	**114.** (a)	**115.** (d)	**116.** (ab)	**117.** (b)	**118.** (b)	**119.** (a)	**120.** (e)
121. (a)	**122.** (b)	**123.** (d)							

Chapter 6

PROPERTIES AND SOLUTION OF TRIANGLE

MULTIPLE CHOICE QUESTIONS

1. In ΔABC, if $a = 25, b = 52$ and $c = 63$, then :

   (a) $\tan \dfrac{A}{2} = -\dfrac{1}{5}$ (b) $\tan \dfrac{B}{2} = \dfrac{1}{2}$

   (c) $\tan \dfrac{C}{2} = \dfrac{9}{7}$ (d) All of these.

2. In ΔABC, $\dfrac{\cos^2 \dfrac{A}{2}}{a} + \dfrac{\cos^2 \dfrac{B}{2}}{b} + \dfrac{\cos^2 \dfrac{C}{2}}{c} =$

   (a) $\dfrac{s^2}{2abc}$ (b) $\dfrac{s^2}{abc}$

   (c) $\dfrac{s^2}{3abc}$ (d) None of these

3. If $b + c = 3a$, then $\cot \dfrac{B}{2} \cot \dfrac{C}{2} =$

   (a) 3   (b) 1

   (c) 4   (d) 2.

4. In ΔABC, $a = 18, b = 24, c = 30$, then $\sin A =$

   (a) $\dfrac{1}{5}$ (b) $\dfrac{3}{5}$

   (c) $\dfrac{2}{5}$ (d) None of these.

5. In any ΔABC, $1 - \tan \dfrac{B}{2} \tan \dfrac{C}{2} =$

   (a) $\dfrac{a}{a + b + c}$ (b) $\dfrac{2a}{a + b + c}$

   (c) $\dfrac{3a}{a + b + c}$ (d) None of these.

6. In ΔABC, $b \cos^2 \dfrac{C}{2} + c \cos^2 \dfrac{B}{2} =$

   (a) 3s   (b) 2s

   (c) s   (d) None of these.

7. In any ΔABC, $2 \left[a \sin^2 \dfrac{C}{2} + c \sin^2 \dfrac{A}{2} \right] =$

   (a) $c + a - b$ (b) $b + a - c$

   (c) $a + b - c$ (d) None of these.

8. In any ΔABC, $(a + b + c) \left(\tan \dfrac{A}{2} + \tan \dfrac{B}{2} \right) =$

   (a) $2c \cot \dfrac{C}{2}$ (b) $2c \tan \dfrac{C}{2}$

   (c) $c \cot \dfrac{C}{2}$ (d) None of these.

9. In any ΔABC, $2a \cos \dfrac{B}{2} \cos \dfrac{C}{2} =$

   (a) $(a + b + c) \cos \dfrac{A}{2}$

   (b) $(a + b + c) \sin \dfrac{A}{2}$

   (c) $2(a + b + c) \cos \dfrac{A}{2}$

   (d) None of these.

10. In any ΔABC, if $(a + b + c)(b + c - a) = 3bc$, then $A =$

    (a) $60°$ (b) $45°$

    (c) $30°$ (d) None of these.

11. In any ΔABC,

    $4 \left[bc \cos^2 \dfrac{A}{2} + ca \cos^2 \dfrac{B}{2} + ab \cos^2 \dfrac{C}{2} \right] =$

    (a) $(a + b + c)^2$ (b) $a + b + c$

    (c) $2(a + b + c)^2$ (d) None of these.

12. In any ΔABC, $(a + b - c) \cot \dfrac{B}{2} =$

    (a) $(a - b + c) \cot \dfrac{C}{2}$ (b) $2(a + b + c) \cot \dfrac{C}{2}$

    (c) $(a + b + c) \tan \dfrac{C}{2}$ (d) None of these.

13. In any ΔABC,

    $(b - c) \cot \dfrac{A}{2} + (c - a) \cot \dfrac{B}{2} + (a - b) \cot \dfrac{C}{2} =$

    (a) 1   (b) -1

    (c) 0   (d) None of these.

14. If the cotangents of half the angles of a triangle are in A.P., then its sides are in :

(a) A.P.　　　　　　　(b) G.P.

(c) H.P.　　　　　　　(d) None of these.

15. In a triangle ABC, tan A, tan B, tan C are in H.P. if a^2, b^2, c^2 are in :

(a) A.P.　　　　　　　(b) G.P.

(c) H.P.　　　　　　　(d) None of these.

16. In a $\triangle$ABC, if $3 \tan \frac{A}{2} \tan \frac{C}{2} = 1$, then sides a, b, c are in :

(a) A.P.　　　　　　　(b) G.P.

(c) H.P.　　　　　　　(d) None of these.

17. If $a \cos^2 \frac{C}{2} + c \cos^2 \frac{A}{2} = \frac{3b}{2}$, then the sides of the triangle are in :

(a) G.P.　　　　　　　(b) A.P.

(c) H.P.　　　　　　　(d) None of these.

18. In a $\triangle$ABC, $2 \sin \frac{A}{2} \sin \frac{C}{2} = \sin \frac{B}{2}$, if a,b,c are in :

(a) H.P.　　　　　　　(b) G.P.

(c) A.P.　　　　　　　(d) None of these.

19. The area of the $\triangle$ ABC, where $a = \sqrt{2}$, $b = \sqrt{3}$, $c = \sqrt{5}$, is :

(a) $\frac{1}{2}\sqrt{6}$　　　　　(b) $\frac{1}{2}\sqrt{9}$

(c) $\frac{1}{2}\sqrt{7}$　　　　　(d) None of these.

20. In any $\triangle$ABC

$4\Delta (\cot A + \cot B + \cot C) =$

(a) $3 (a^2 + b^2 + c^2)$　　　(b) $2 (a^2 + b^2 + c^2)$

(c) $a^2 + b^2 + c^2$　　　　(d) None of these.

21. In any $\triangle$ABC, $abc \, s \sin \frac{A}{2} \sin \frac{B}{2} \sin \frac{C}{2} =$

(a) Δ^3　　　　　　(b) $3\Delta^2$

(c) Δ^2　　　　　　(d) None of these.

22. In any $\triangle$ABC, $4\Delta \cot A =$

(a) $2 (b^2 + c^2 - a^2)$　　　(b) $a^2 + b^2 + c^2$

(c) $b^2 + c^2 - a^2$　　　　(d) None of these.

23. In any $\triangle$ABC, $\frac{2abc}{a + b + c} \cos \frac{A}{2} \cos \frac{B}{2} \cos \frac{C}{2} =$

(a) Δ　　　　　　　(b) 2Δ

(c) 3Δ　　　　　　(d) None of these.

24. In any $\triangle$ABC, $\Delta \left[\cot \frac{A}{2} + \cot \frac{B}{2} + \cot \frac{C}{2} \right] =$

(a) s^2　　　　　　　(b) $2s^2$

(c) $3s^2$　　　　　　(d) None of these.

25. In any $\triangle$ABC, $s^2 \tan \frac{A}{2} \tan \frac{B}{2} \tan \frac{C}{2} =$

(a) Δ　　　　　　　(b) 2Δ

(c) 3Δ　　　　　　(d) None of these.

26. In any $\triangle$ABC, $a \cos A + b \cos B + c \cos C =$

(a) $\frac{4\Delta^2}{abc}$　　　　　(b) $\frac{2\Delta^2}{abc}$

(c) $\frac{8\Delta^2}{abc}$　　　　　(d) None of these.

27. In any $\triangle$ABC, if $a = 18$, $b = 24$, $c = 30$, then r =

(a) 6　　　　　　　　(b) 9

(c) 12　　　　　　　(d) None of these.

28. If $a = 13$ cm, $b = 14$ cm, $c = 15$ cm, then R =

(a) $7\frac{1}{8}$ cm　　　　　(b) $8\frac{1}{8}$ cm

(c) $6\frac{1}{8}$ cm　　　　　(d) None of these.

29. In any $\triangle$ABC, $2R^2 \sin A \sin B \sin C =$

(a) 2Δ　　　　　　(b) 3Δ

(c) Δ　　　　　　　(d) None of these.

30. In any $\triangle$ABC, $\frac{1}{ab} + \frac{1}{bc} + \frac{1}{ca} =$

(a) $\frac{1}{Rr}$　　　　　　(b) $\frac{1}{2Rr}$

(c) $\frac{1}{3Rr}$　　　　　(d) None of these.

31. In any $\triangle$ABC, $Rr (\sin A + \sin B + \sin C) =$

(a) Δ　　　　　　　(b) 2Δ

(c) 3Δ　　　　　　(d) None of these.

32. In any $\triangle$ABC, $4R \sin \frac{A}{2} \sin \frac{B}{2} \sin \frac{C}{2} =$

(a) $2r$　　　　　　　(b) r

(c) $3r$　　　　　　　(d) None of these.

33. In any $\triangle ABC$, $\dfrac{1}{s-a} + \dfrac{1}{s-b} + \dfrac{1}{s-c} - \dfrac{1}{s} =$

(a) $\dfrac{2R}{\Delta}$

(b) $\dfrac{3R}{\Delta}$

(c) $\dfrac{4R}{\Delta}$

(d) None of these

34. In any $\triangle ABC$, $4\left(\dfrac{s}{a}-1\right)\left(\dfrac{s}{b}-1\right)\left(\dfrac{s}{c}-1\right) =$

(a) $\dfrac{r}{R}$

(b) $\dfrac{2r}{R}$

(c) $\dfrac{3r}{R}$

(d) None of these.

35. In any $\triangle ABC$, $a \cot A + b \cot B + c \cot C =$

(a) $(R+r)$

(b) $2(R+r)$

(c) $3(R+r)$

(d) None of these.

36. In any $\triangle ABC$, $4Rr \cos\dfrac{A}{2}\cos\dfrac{B}{2}\cos\dfrac{C}{2} =$

(a) 3Δ

(b) Δ

(c) 2Δ

(d) None of these.

37. In any $\triangle ABC$, $r_1 + r_2 + r_3 - r =$

(a) R

(b) $2R$

(c) $4R$

(d) None of these.

38. In any $\triangle ABC$, $\dfrac{1}{r_1} + \dfrac{1}{r_2} + \dfrac{1}{r_3} =$

(a) $\dfrac{3}{r}$

(b) $\dfrac{1}{r}$

(c) $\dfrac{2}{r}$

(d) None of these.

39. If $\triangle ABC$ is a triangle right angled at C, then $R + r =$

(a) $\dfrac{1}{2}(a+b)$

(b) $\dfrac{1}{3}(a+b)$

(c) $\dfrac{1}{4}(a+b)$

(d) None of these.

40. If p_1, p_2, p_3 are the perpendiculars from the angular points of a triangle on the opposite sides, then : $\dfrac{1}{p_1} + \dfrac{1}{p_2} + \dfrac{1}{p_3} =$

(a) $\dfrac{1}{r}$

(b) $\dfrac{2}{r}$

(c) $\dfrac{3}{r}$

(d) None of these.

41. If A, A_1, A_2, A_3 are the areas of the incircle and excircles, then $\dfrac{1}{\sqrt{A_1}} + \dfrac{1}{\sqrt{A_2}} + \dfrac{1}{\sqrt{A_3}} =$

(a) $\dfrac{1}{\sqrt{A}}$

(b) $\dfrac{2}{\sqrt{A}}$

(c) $\dfrac{3}{\sqrt{A}}$

(d) None of these.

42. In a $\triangle ABC$, r_1, r_2, r_3 are in H.P. if a, b, c are in :

(a) A.P.

(b) G.P.

(c) H.P.

(d) None of these.

43. In a $\triangle ABC$, if $\cos B = \dfrac{\sin A}{2 \sin C}$, then the triangle is :

(a) equilateral

(b) isosceles

(c) right angled

(d) None of these.

44. Let D be the middle point of BC in a $\triangle ABC$. If $AD \perp BC$, then $\cos A \cos C =$

(a) $\dfrac{c^2 - a^2}{ac}$

(b) $\dfrac{4(c^2 - a^2)}{3ac}$

(c) $\dfrac{2(c^2 - a^2)}{3ac}$

(d) None of these.

45. In a $\triangle ABC$, if $\dfrac{\cos A}{a} = \dfrac{\cos B}{b} = \dfrac{\cos C}{c}$ and the side $a = 2$, then the area of the triangle is :

(a) 1

(b) 2

(c) $\dfrac{\sqrt{3}}{2}$

(d) $\sqrt{3}$

46. If in a $\triangle ABC$, $\dfrac{2\cos A}{a} + \dfrac{\cos B}{b} + \dfrac{2\cos C}{c} = \dfrac{a}{bc} + \dfrac{b}{ca}$, then the triangle is :

(a) right angled

(b) isosceles

(c) equilateral

(d) None of these.

47. If in a $\triangle ABC$, $\cos A + \cos B + \cos C = \dfrac{3}{2}$, then the triangle is :

(a) equilateral

(b) isosceles

(c) right angled

(d) None of these.

48. In any $\triangle ABC$, if $\dfrac{1}{a+c} + \dfrac{1}{b+c} = \dfrac{3}{a+b+c}$, then:

(a) $A = 60°$

(b) $C = 60°$

(c) $B = 60°$

(d) None of these.

49. In any $\triangle ABC$, $2\left(a\sin^2\dfrac{C}{2} + c\sin^2\dfrac{A}{2}\right) =$

(a) $a + c - b$ (b) $a + b - c$

(c) $a + c - 2b$ (d) None of these.

50. In any $\triangle ABC$, $a\,(b\cos C + c\cos B) =$

(a) $2\,(b^2 - c^2)$ (b) $b^2 - c^2$

(c) $3\,(b^2 - c^2)$ (d) None of these.

51. In any $\triangle ABC$,

$2\,(bc\cos A + ca\cos B + ab\cos C) =$

(a) $a^2 + b^2 + c^2$ (b) $\dfrac{a^2 + b^2 + c^2}{2}$

(c) $3\,(a^2 + b^2 + c^2)$ (d) None of these.

52. If in a $\triangle ABC$, $\angle B = 90°$, then, $\sqrt{\dfrac{b - c}{b + c}} =$

(a) $\tan\dfrac{A}{2}$ (b) $2\tan\dfrac{A}{2}$

(c) $3\tan\dfrac{A}{2}$ (d) None of these.

53. In any $\triangle ABC$, if $a\cos A = b\cos B$, then $\triangle ABC$ is :

(a) right angled   (b) equilateral

(c) isosceles   (d) None of these.

54. In a triangle, $A = 45°$, $B = 75°$, $C = 60°$, then $a + c\sqrt{2} =$

(a) $3b$ (b) $2b$

(c) b (d) None of these.

55. In a $\triangle ABC$, $a = 5$, $b = 7$ and $\sin A = \dfrac{3}{4}$, how many such triangles are possible ?

(a) 1   (b) 0

(c) 2   (d) infinite.

56. In any $\triangle ABC$,

$a^3\cos(B - C) + b^3\cos(C - A) + c^3\cos(A - B) =$

(a) $3abc$ (b) $2abc$

(c) abc (d) None of these.

57. In a $\triangle ABC$, if :

$\tan\dfrac{1}{2}A = \dfrac{5}{6}$ and $\tan\dfrac{1}{2}B = \dfrac{20}{37}$, then $a + c =$

(a) b (b) $2b$

(c) $3b$ (d) None of these.

58. The greatest angle of triangle whose sides are $x^2 + x + 1$, $2x + 1$ and $x^2 - 1$, is :

(a) $60°$ (b) $90°$

(c) $120°$ (d) None of these.

59. If in $\triangle ABC$,

$a\tan A + b\tan B = (a + b)\tan\dfrac{1}{2}(A + B)$, then :

(a) $A = B$ (b) $A = 2B$

(c) $2A = B$ (d) None of these.

60. If in $\triangle ABC$, $\cos A + 2\cos B + \cos C = 2$, then the sides of the triangle are in :

(a) A.P.   (b) G.P.

(c) H.P.   (d) None of these.

61. If a, b, c are H.P., then $\sin^2\dfrac{A}{2}$, $\sin^2\dfrac{B}{2}$, $\sin^2\dfrac{C}{2}$ are in :

(a) A.P.   (b) G.P.

(c) H.P.   (d) None of these.

62. If in a $\triangle ABC$, $\dfrac{\tan A}{1} = \dfrac{\tan B}{2} = \dfrac{\tan C}{3}$, then :

(a) $6\sqrt{2}\,a = 3\sqrt{5}\,b = 2\sqrt{10}\,c$

(b) $3\sqrt{2}\,a = 4\sqrt{5}\,b = 7\sqrt{10}\,c$

(c) $6\sqrt{2}\,a = 4\sqrt{5}\,b = 2\sqrt{10}\,c$

(d) None of these.

63. In a $\triangle ABC$, angle A is greater than angle B. If the measures of angles A and B satisfy the equation $3\sin x - 4\sin^3 x - k = 0$, $0 < k < 1$, then the measure of angle C is :

(a) $\dfrac{\pi}{3}$ (b) $\dfrac{\pi}{2}$

(c) $\dfrac{2\pi}{3}$ (d) $\dfrac{5\pi}{6}$

64. In any $\triangle ABC$, if $\tan\theta = \dfrac{2\sqrt{ab}}{a - b}\sin\dfrac{C}{2}$ then $C =$

(a) $(a - b)\cos\theta$ (b) $(a - b)\sec\theta$

(c) $(a - b)\csc\theta$ (d) None of these.

65. In a $\triangle ABC$, if $\cot A + \cot B + \cot C = \sqrt{3}$, then the triangle is :

(a) equilateral   (b) right angled

(c) isosceles   (d) None of these.

66. If the sides of a triangle are in A.P. and its area is $\dfrac{3}{5}^{th}$ of an equilateral triangle of the same perimeter, then the sides are in the ratio :

(a) $2 : 5 : 7$ (b) $3 : 5 : 7$

(c) $4 : 5 : 7$ (d) None of these.

67. If Δ denotes the area of any triangle and s its semiperimeter, then :

(a) $\Delta < \dfrac{s^2}{2}$ (b) $\Delta > \dfrac{s^2}{4}$

(c) $\Delta < \dfrac{s^2}{4}$ (d) None of these.

68. In any ΔABC, if $b + c = 3a$, then the value of $\cot \dfrac{1}{2} B \cot \dfrac{1}{2} C$ is :

(a) 1 (b) 2

(c) $\sqrt{3}$ (d) 3.

69. The perimeter of a ΔABC is 6 times the arithmetic mean of the sines of its angles. If the side a is 1, then the angle A is :

(a) $\dfrac{\pi}{6}$ (b) $\dfrac{\pi}{3}$

(c) $\dfrac{\pi}{2}$ (d) π

70. If in ΔABC, $3 \sin A = 6 \sin B = 2\sqrt{3} \sin C$, then angle A is :

(a) $0°$ (b) $30°$

(c) $60°$ (d) $90°$

71. If the radius of the incircle of a triangle with its sides 5k, 6k and 5k is 6, then k is equal to :

(a) 3 (b) 4

(c) 5 (d) 6

72. If the radius of the circumcircle of an isosceles ΔPQR is equal to PQ ($= PR$), then the angle P is :

(a) $\dfrac{\pi}{6}$ (b) $\dfrac{\pi}{3}$

(c) $\dfrac{\pi}{2}$ (d) $\dfrac{2\pi}{3}$

73. If a circle is inscribed in an equilateral triangle of side a, then area of the square inscribed in the circle is :

(a) $\dfrac{a^3}{6}$ (b) $\dfrac{a^2}{3}$

(c) $\dfrac{2a^2}{5}$ (d) $\dfrac{2a^2}{3}$

74. The area of the circle and the area of the regular polygon of n sides and of perimeter equal to that of circle are in the ratio of :

(a) $\tan\left(\dfrac{\pi}{n}\right) : \dfrac{\pi}{n}$ (b) $\cos\left(\dfrac{\pi}{n}\right) : \dfrac{\pi}{n}$

(c) $\sin\left(\dfrac{\pi}{n}\right) : \dfrac{\pi}{n}$ (d) $\cot\left(\dfrac{\pi}{n}\right) : \dfrac{\pi}{n}$

75. Let the angles A, B, C of ΔABC be in A.P. and let $b : c = \sqrt{3} : \sqrt{2}$. Then angle A is :

(a) $75°$ (b) $45°$

(c) $60°$ (d) None of these.

76. If in a ΔABC, AD, BE and CF are the altitudes and R is the circum radius, then the radius of the circle DEF is :

(a) $\dfrac{R}{2}$ (b) $2R$

(c) R (d) None of these.

77. If D is the mid point of the side BC of a ΔABC and AD is perpendicular to AC, then :

(a) $b^2 = a^2 - c^2$ (b) $a^2 + b^2 = 5c^2$

(c) $3b^2 = a^2 - c^2$ (d) $3a^2 = b^2 - 3c^2$.

78. The angle A of ΔABC, in which $(a + b + c)(b + c - a) = 3bc$, is :

(a) $30°$ (b) $45°$

(c) $60°$ (d) $120°$.

79. $\cos^2 \dfrac{A}{2} + \cos^2 \dfrac{B}{2} + \cos^2 \dfrac{C}{2} =$

(a) $2 - \dfrac{r}{R}$ (b) $2 - \dfrac{r}{2R}$

(c) $2 + \dfrac{r}{2R}$ (d) None of these.

80. In a ΔABC, $a = 2b$ and $\angle A = 3\angle B$, then angle A is :

(a) $90°$ (b) $60°$

(c) $30°$ (d) None of these.

81. If $\sin (A + B + C) = 1$, $\tan (A - B) = \dfrac{1}{\sqrt{3}}$ and $\sec (A + C) = 2$, then :

(a) $A = 90°, B = 60°, C = 30°$

(b) $A = 120°, B = 60°, C = 0°$

(c) $A = 60°, B = 30°, C = 0°$

(d) None of these.

82. The value of $\dfrac{3 + \cot 76° \cot 16°}{\cot 76° + \cot 16°}$ is :

(a) $\cot 60°$ (b) $\tan 2°$

(c) $\tan 44°$ (d) $\cot 44°$

83. If H is the orthocentre of $\triangle ABC$, then AH is equal to :

(a) $c \cot A$ (b) $b \cot A$

(c) $a \cot B$ (d) $a \cot A$

84. In a right angled triangle, the hypotenuse is four times as long as the perpendicular drawn to it from the opposite vertex. One of the acute angle is :

(a) $45°$ (b) $30°$

(c) $15°$ (d) None of these

85. In an equilateral triangle, $r : R : r_1 =$

(a) $1 : 2 : 3$ (b) $3 : 2 : 1$

(c) $3 : 1 : 2$ (d) None of these.

86. If in $\triangle ABC$,

$a \tan A + b \tan B = (a + b) \tan \dfrac{(A + B)}{2}$, then :

(a) $B = C$ (b) $A = B$

(c) $C = A$ (d) $A = B = C$.

87. $\triangle ABC$ is right angled at C, then $\tan A + \tan B =$

(a) $\dfrac{b^2}{ac}$ (b) $a + b$

(c) $\dfrac{a^2}{bc}$ (d) $\dfrac{c^2}{ab}$

88. If, in a $\triangle ABC$, $(a + b + c)(b + c - a) = \lambda\, bc$, then :

(a) $\lambda < 0$ (b) $\lambda > 4$

(c) $\lambda > 0$ (d) $0 < \lambda < 4$

89. In a $\triangle ABC$, $\angle A = \dfrac{\pi}{2}$, then $\cos^2 B + \cos^2 C$ equals :

(a) -2 (b) -1

(c) 1 (d) zero

90. If the sides of a right angled triangle are in A.P., then tangents of the acute angled triangle are :

(a) $\sqrt{\sqrt{3} + \dfrac{1}{2}}, \sqrt{\sqrt{3} - \dfrac{1}{2}}$

(b) $\sqrt{\sqrt{5} - \dfrac{1}{2}}, \sqrt{\sqrt{5} + \dfrac{1}{2}}$

(c) $\sqrt{3}, \dfrac{1}{\sqrt{3}}$

(d) $\dfrac{3}{4}, \dfrac{4}{3}$

91. With usual notations, in a $\triangle ABC$,

$\dfrac{b^2 - c^2}{a \sec C} + \dfrac{c^2 - a^2}{b \sec C} + \dfrac{a^2 - b^2}{c \sec C} =$

(a) 1 (b) 0

(c) abc (d) None of these.

92. In a $\triangle ABC$, $\angle B = \dfrac{\pi}{3}$ and $\angle C = \dfrac{\pi}{4}$ and D divides BC internally in the ratio $1 : 3$. Then $\dfrac{\sin \angle BAD}{\sin \angle CAD}$ equals :

(a) $\dfrac{\sqrt{2}}{3}$ (b) $\dfrac{1}{\sqrt{3}}$

(c) $\dfrac{1}{\sqrt{6}}$ (d) $\dfrac{1}{3}$

93. The radii r_1, r_2, r_3 of escribed circles of the $\triangle ABC$ are in H.P. If its area is 24 sq. cm and its perimeter is 24 cm, then the lengths of its sides are :

(a) $4, 6, 8$ (b) $3, 9, 11$

(c) $6, 8, 10$ (d) None of these.

94. The sides of a triangle inscribed in a given circle subtend angles α, β, γ at the centre. Then the minimum value of the A.M. of

$\cos\left(\alpha + \dfrac{\pi}{2}\right), \cos\left(\beta + \dfrac{\pi}{2}\right), \cos\left(\gamma + \dfrac{\pi}{2}\right)$, is :

(a) $-\dfrac{\sqrt{3}}{2}$ (b) $\dfrac{\sqrt{3}}{2}$

(c) $\dfrac{1}{\sqrt{2}}$ (d) None of these.

95. If in a $\triangle ABC$, $a = 6$, $b = 3$ and $\cos(A - B) = \dfrac{4}{5}$, then its area is :

(a) 8 sq. units   (b) 9 sq. units

(c) 6 sq. units   (d) None of these.

96. A cyclic quadrilateral ABCD of area $\dfrac{3\sqrt{3}}{4}$ is inscribed in a unit circle. If one of its sides AB = 1 and the diagonal BD = $\sqrt{3}$, then the lengths of the other sides are :

(a) $2, 1, 1$ (b) $2, 1, 2$

(c) $3, 1, 2$ (d) None of these.

97. If the two angles on the base of a triangle are $22\frac{1°}{2}$ and $112\frac{1°}{2}$ then the ratio of the height of the triangle to the length of the base is :

   (a) 1 : 2   (b) 2 : 1

   (c) 2 : 3   (d) 1 : 1.

98. If the perpendicular AD divides the base of the $\triangle ABC$ such that BD, CD and AD are in ratio 2 : 3 : 6, then angle A is equal to :

   (a) $\frac{\pi}{2}$ (b) $\frac{\pi}{3}$

   (c) $\frac{\pi}{4}$ (d) $\frac{\pi}{6}$

99. In any $\triangle ABC$,
   cosec A (sin B cos C + cos B sin C) =

   (a) $\frac{c}{a}$ (b) $\frac{a}{c}$

   (c) 1   (d) None of these.

100. If the angles of a triangle are in the ratio of 2 : 3 : 7, then the sides are in the ratio of :

   (a) $\sqrt{2} : 2 : (\sqrt{3}+1)$ (b) $2 : \sqrt{2} : (\sqrt{3}+1)$
   (c) $\sqrt{2} : (\sqrt{3}+1) : 2$ (d) $2 : (\sqrt{3}+1) : \sqrt{2}$

101. In a $\triangle ABC$, $2ac \sin \frac{1}{2}(A - B + C)$ =

   (a) $a^2 + b^2 - c^2$ (b) $c^2 + a^2 - b^2$
   (c) $b^2 - c^2 - a^2$ (d) $c^2 - a^2 - b^2$.

102. In a $\triangle PQR$, $\angle R = \frac{\pi}{2}$. If $\tan \frac{P}{2}$ and $\tan \frac{Q}{2}$ are the roots of the equation $ax^2 + bx + c = 0$ $(a \neq 0)$ then :

   (a) $a + b = c$ (b) $b + c = a$
   (c) $c + a = b$ (d) $b = c$.

103. In a $\triangle ABC$, AD is altitude from A. Given b > c, $\angle C = 23°$ and $AD = \frac{abc}{b^2 - c^2}$ then $\angle B$ =

   (a) 113°   (b) 46°
   (c) 79°   (d) None of these.

104. The sides of a triangle are three consecutive natural numbers and its largest angle is twice the smallest one. Then the sides of the triangle are :

   (a) 2, 3, 4   (b) 2, 5, 6
   (c) 4, 5, 6   (d) None of these.

105. If, in a $\triangle ABC$, $m \angle A = \frac{\pi}{3}$ and AD is a median then:

   (a) $2 AD^2 = c^2 + b^2 + bc$
   (b) $4 AD^2 = c^2 + b^2 + bc$
   (c) $6 AD^2 = c^2 + b^2 + bc$
   (d) None of these.

106. In a $\triangle ABC$, let $\angle C = \frac{\pi}{2}$. If r is the inradius and R is the circumradius of the triangle, then $2(r + R)$ is equal to:

   (a) $a + b$ (b) $b + c$
   (c) $c + a$ (d) $a + b + c$.

107. If in a $\triangle ABC$, $\tan A + \tan B + \tan C > 0$, then the triangle is :

   (a) acute angled   (b) obtuse angled
   (c) right angled   (d) nothing can be said.

108. The radius of the circle passing through the centre of incircle of $\triangle ABC$ and through the end points of BC is given by :

   (a) $\frac{a}{2} \cos A$ (b) $\frac{a}{2} \sec \frac{A}{2}$

   (c) $\frac{a}{2} \sin A$ (d) $a \sec \frac{A}{2}$

109. In the $\triangle ABC$, $\angle A = 90°$ and c, sin B, cos B are rational numbers then :

   (a) a is irrational   (b) b is rational
   (c) b is irrational   (d) None of these.

110. In the $\triangle ABC$, if $r_1 > r_2 > r_3$, then :

   (a) $a > b > c$ (b) $a < b < c$
   (c) $a > b$ and $b < c$ (d) $a < b$ and $b > c$.

111. In a $\triangle ABC$, $\sqrt{a} + \sqrt{b} - \sqrt{c}$ is :

   (a) always positive
   (b) always negative
   (c) positive only when c is the smallest side
   (d) positive only when $a = b$.

112. If in a $\triangle ABC$, $c = 3b$ and $C - B = 90°$, then tan B equals (The symbols have their usual meanings) :

   (a) $2 + \sqrt{3}$ (b) $2 - \sqrt{3}$
   (c) 3   (d) 1/3.

113. If A is the area and 2s is the sum of three sides of a triangle, then :

(a) $A \le \dfrac{s^2}{3\sqrt{3}}$ (b) $A \le \dfrac{s^2}{2}$

(c) $A > \dfrac{s^2}{\sqrt{3}}$ (d) None of these.

114. If P is a point on the altitude AD of the $\triangle ABC$ such that $\angle CBP = \dfrac{B}{3}$ then AP is equal to :

(a) $2a \sin \dfrac{C}{3}$ (b) $2b \sin \dfrac{A}{3}$

(c) $2c \sin \dfrac{B}{3}$ (d) $2c \sin \dfrac{C}{3}$

115. If in an obtuse angled triangle, the obtuse angle is $\dfrac{3\pi}{4}$ and the other two angles are equal to two values of θ satisfying $a \tan \theta + b \sec \theta = c$, when $|b| \le \sqrt{a^2 + b^2}$, then $a^2 - c^2$ is equal to :

(a) ac (b) 2ac

(c) $\dfrac{a}{c}$ (d) None of these.

116. If $\tan \alpha$ and $\tan \beta$ are the roots of the equation $x^2 + px + q = 0$ then the value of the expression $\sin^2 (\alpha + \beta) + p \cos (\alpha + \beta) \sin (\alpha + \beta) + q \cos^2 (\alpha + \beta)$ is equal to :

(a) $p + q$ (b) $\dfrac{p + q}{q}$

(c) q (d) $\dfrac{p}{p + q}$

117. In a right angled $\triangle ABC$ right angled at C, bisector of angle 'C' divides AB in the ratio $p : q$. If $\cot \dfrac{A - B}{2} = k$ then $p : q$ is :

(a) $\dfrac{1 + k}{1 - k}$ (b) $\dfrac{k - 1}{1 + k}$

(c) $\dfrac{1}{1 + k}$ (d) $k - 1$.

118. If in a $\triangle ABC$, CD is the angle bisector of the angle ACB, then CD is equal to :

(a) $\dfrac{a + b}{2ab} \cos \dfrac{C}{2}$ (b) $\dfrac{a + b}{ab} \cos \dfrac{C}{2}$

(c) $\dfrac{2ab}{a + b} \cos \dfrac{C}{2}$ (d) $\dfrac{b \sin A}{\sin \left(B + \dfrac{C}{2}\right)}$

119. If r_1, r_2, r_3 are the radii of escribed circles of a $\triangle ABC$ and if r is the radius of its incircle, then $r_1 r_2 r_3 - r (r_1 r_2 + r_2 r_3 + r_3 r_1)$ is equal to :

(a) 0 (b) 1

(c) 2 (d) 3.

120. In any $\triangle ABC$, $\left(\dfrac{\sin^2 A + \sin A + 1}{\sin A}\right) \times \left(\dfrac{\sin^2 B + \sin B + 1}{\sin B}\right) \times \left(\dfrac{\sin^2 C + \sin C + 1}{\sin C}\right)$

is always greater than :

(a) 9 (b) 3

(c) 27 (d) None of these.

121. If in a $\triangle ABC$, $a^2 \cos^2 A = b^2 + c^2$ then :

(a) $A < \dfrac{\pi}{4}$ (b) $\dfrac{\pi}{4} < A < \dfrac{\pi}{2}$

(c) $A > \dfrac{\pi}{2}$ (d) $A = \dfrac{\pi}{2}$

122. If A is the area and 2s the sum of three sides of a triangle then :

(a) $A \le \dfrac{s^2}{3\sqrt{3}}$ (b) $A \le \dfrac{s^2}{2}$

(c) $A > \dfrac{s^2}{\sqrt{3}}$ (d) None of these.

123. In a $\triangle ABC$, the sides a, b, c are the roots of the equation $x^3 - 11x^2 + 38x - 40 = 0$. Then $\dfrac{\cos A}{a} + \dfrac{\cos B}{b} + \dfrac{\cos C}{c}$ is equal to :

(a) 1 (b) $\dfrac{3}{4}$

(c) $\dfrac{9}{16}$ (d) None of these.

124. If in a $\triangle ABC$, $\angle B = 90°$ then $\tan^2 \dfrac{A}{2}$ is :

(a) $\dfrac{b - c}{b + c}$ (b) $\dfrac{b + c}{b - c}$

(c) $\dfrac{b - c}{a}$ (d) None of these.

125. In a triangle $a^2 + b^2 + c^2 = ca + ab \sqrt{3}$. Then the triangle is :

(a) equilateral

(b) right angled and isosceles

(c) right angled with $A = 90°$, $B = 60°$, $C = 30°$

(d) None of these.

126. In a ∆ABC, I is the incentre. Then the ratio IA : IB : IC is equal to :

(a) $\operatorname{cosec} \dfrac{A}{2} : \operatorname{cosec} \dfrac{B}{2} : \operatorname{cosec} \dfrac{C}{2}$

(b) $\sin \dfrac{A}{2} : \sin \dfrac{B}{2} : \sin \dfrac{C}{2}$

(c) $\sec \dfrac{A}{2} : \sec \dfrac{B}{2} : \sec \dfrac{C}{2}$

(d) None of these.

127. Three equal circles each of radius r touch one another. The radius of the circle touching the three given circles internally is :

(a) $(2 + \sqrt{3})\, r$

(b) $\dfrac{2 + \sqrt{3}}{\sqrt{3}}\, r$

(c) $\dfrac{2 - \sqrt{3}}{\sqrt{3}}\, r$

(d) $(2 - \sqrt{3})\, r$

128. sin A, sin B and sin C are in A.P. for the ∆ABC. Then :

(a) the altitudes are in A.P.

(b) the altitudes are in H.P.

(c) the medians are in G.P.

(d) the medians are in A.P.

129. In a ∆ABC, AD, BE and CF are the altitudes and R is the circumradius, then radius of the circle DEF is :

(a) 2R

(b) R

(c) R/2

(d) None of these.

130. In a ∆ABC, ∠A < ∠B. If sin A and sin B satisfy the equation $3 \sin x - 4 \sin^3 x - k = 0$, $0 < k < 1$, then ∠C is:

(a) $\dfrac{\pi}{3}$

(b) $\dfrac{\pi}{2}$

(c) $\dfrac{2\pi}{3}$

(d) $\dfrac{5\pi}{6}$

131. In any ∆ABC,

(a) $b^2 = c^2 + a^2 - 2ca \sin B$

(b) $b^2 = c^2 + a^2 - 2ca \cos B$

(c) $b^2 = c^2 + a^2 + 2ca \cos B$

(d) $b^2 = c^2 + a^2 + 2ca \tan B$.

132. Two angles of a triangle are $\dfrac{\pi}{6}$ and $\dfrac{\pi}{4}$, the length of the included side is $(\sqrt{3} + 1)$ cm. The area of the triangle is :

(a) $\dfrac{\sqrt{3} - 1}{2}$ cm²

(b) $\dfrac{\sqrt{3}}{2}$ cm²

(c) $\dfrac{\sqrt{3} + 1}{2}$ cm²

(d) None of these.

133. In ∆ABC, $\tan\left(\dfrac{B - C}{2}\right)$ is equal to :

(a) $\left(\dfrac{b - c}{b + c}\right) \cot \dfrac{A}{2}$

(b) $\left(\dfrac{b - c}{b + c}\right) \tan \dfrac{A}{2}$

(c) $\left(\dfrac{b + c}{b - c}\right) \cot \dfrac{A}{2}$

(d) $\left(\dfrac{b + c}{b - c}\right) \tan \dfrac{A}{2}$

134. In a ∆ABC, B = 90°, AC = h and length of the perpendicular from B to AC is p such that h = 4p. If AB < BC, then ∠C has the measure :

(a) $\dfrac{5\pi}{12}$

(b) $\dfrac{\pi}{6}$

(c) $\dfrac{\pi}{12}$

(d) None of these.

135. Value of $\cot \dfrac{A}{2}$ is :

(a) $\sqrt{\dfrac{s(s - a)}{(s - b)\,(s - c)}}$

(b) $\sqrt{s(s - a)\,(s - b)\,(s - c)}$

(c) $\sqrt{\dfrac{(s - b)\,(s - c)}{s(s - a)}}$

(d) $\sqrt{\dfrac{s(s - b)\,(s - c)}{(s - a)}}$

136. If O is a point inside the ∆ABC such that

$\angle OBC = \dfrac{A}{2}$, $\angle OCA = \dfrac{B}{2}$, $\angle OAB = \dfrac{C}{2}$ then,

$\dfrac{\sin\left(\dfrac{A - C}{2}\right) \sin\left(\dfrac{B - A}{2}\right) \sin\left(\dfrac{C - B}{2}\right)}{\sin \dfrac{A}{2} \sin \dfrac{B}{2} \sin \dfrac{C}{2}}$ is equal to :

(a) $\cos \dfrac{A}{2} \cos \dfrac{B}{2} \cos \dfrac{C}{2}$

(b) sin A sin B sin C

(c) 1

(d) cos A cos B cos C.

137. In ΔABC, $a = 13$, $b = 14$, $c = 15$, then the value of R is:

  (a) 7.125   (b) 8.125

  (c) 6.715   (d) 4.

138. If the sides of a triangle are 3, 5, 6, then the ratio r : R will be :

  (a) 8 : 25   (b) 7 : 25

  (c) 16 : 45   (d) 24 : 25.

139. If in a ΔABC, cot A, cot B, cot C are in A.P. then :

  (a) $a^2 = b^2 = c^2$

  (b) $a^2 + b^2 = c^2$

  (c) a^2, b^2, c^2, are in A.P.

  (d) None of these

140. For a regular polygon, let r and R be the radii of the inscribed and the circumscribed circles. A false statement among the following is :

[AIEEE - 2010]

  (a) There is a regular polygon with $\dfrac{r}{R} = \dfrac{1}{\sqrt{2}}$

  (b) There is a regular polygon with $\dfrac{r}{R} = \dfrac{2}{3}$

  (c) There is a regular polygon with $\dfrac{r}{R} = \dfrac{\sqrt{3}}{2}$

  (d) There is a regular polygon with $\dfrac{r}{R} = \dfrac{1}{2}$

ANSWER KEY

1. (d)	**2.** (b)	**3.** (d)	**4.** (b)	**5.** (b)	**6.** (c)	**7.** (a)	**8.** (a)	**9.** (b)	**10.** (a)
11. (a)	**12.** (a)	**13.** (c)	**14.** (a)	**15.** (a)	**16.** (a)	**17.** (b)	**18.** (c)	**19.** (a)	**20.** (c)
21. (c)	**22.** (c)	**23.** (a)	**24.** (a)	**25.** (a)	**26.** (c)	**27.** (a)	**28.** (b)	**29.** (c)	**30.** (b)
31. (a)	**32.** (b)	**33.** (c)	**34.** (a)	**35.** (b)	**36.** (b)	**37.** (c)	**38.** (b)	**39.** (a)	**40.** (a)
41. (a)	**42.** (a)	**43.** (b)	**44.** (c)	**45.** (d)	**46.** (a)	**47.** (a)	**48.** (b)	**49.** (a)	**50.** (b)
51. (a)	**52.** (a)	**53.** (a)	**54.** (b)	**55.** (b)	**56.** (a)	**57.** (b)	**58.** (c)	**59.** (a)	**60.** (a)
61. (c)	**62.** (a)	**63.** (c)	**64.** (b)	**65.** (a)	**66.** (b)	**67.** (c)	**68.** (b)	**69.** (a)	**70.** (d)
71. (b)	**72.** (d)	**73.** (a)	**74.** (a)	**75.** (a)	**76.** (a)	**77.** (c)	**78.** (c)	**79.** (d)	**80.** (a)
81. (c)	**82.** (d)	**83.** (d)	**84.** (c)	**85.** (a)	**86.** (b)	**87.** (d)	**88.** (d)	**89.** (c)	**90.** (d)
91. (b)	**92.** (c)	**93.** (c)	**94.** (a)	**95.** (b)	**96.** (a)	**97.** (a)	**98.** (c)	**99.** (c)	**100.** (a)
101. (b)	**102.** (a)	**103.** (a)	**104.** (c)	**105.** (b)	**106.** (a)	**107.** (a)	**108.** (b)	**109.** (b)	**110.** (a)
111. (a)	**112.** (d)	**113.** (a)	**114.** (c)	**115.** (b)	**116.** (c)	**117.** (b)	**118.** (d)	**119.** (a)	**120.** (c)
121. (c)	**122.** (a)	**123.** (c)	**124.** (a)	**125.** (c)	**126.** (a)	**127.** (b)	**128.** (b)	**129.** (c)	**130.** (c)
131. (b)	**132.** (c)	**133.** (a)	**134.** (c)	**135.** (a)	**136.** (c)	**137.** (b)	**138.** (c)	**139.** (c)	**140.** (b)

❑❑❑

HEIGHTS AND DISTANCES

MULTIPLE CHOICE QUESTIONS

1. A person, standing on the bank of river, observes that the angle subtended by a tree on the opposite bank is 60°. When he retreats 40 m from the bank, he finds the angle to be 30°. The height of the tree and the breadth of the river are :

   (a) $10\sqrt{3}$ m, 10 m (b) $20\sqrt{3}$ m, 10 m

   (c) $20\sqrt{3}$ m, 20 m (d) None of these.

2. At a point A, the angle of elevation of a tower is such that its tangent is $\frac{5}{12}$. On walking 120 m nearer the tower, the tangent of the angle of elevation is $\frac{3}{4}$. The height of the tower is :

   (a) 225 metres (b) 200 metres

   (c) 230 metres (d) None of these.

3. A chimney is such that on walking towards it 50 m in a horizontal line through its base, the angular elevation of its top changes from 30° to 45°. The height of the chimney is :

   (a) $15(\sqrt{3}+1)$ m (b) $25(\sqrt{3}+1)$ m

   (c) $30(\sqrt{3}+1)$ m (d) None of these.

4. An observer on the top of a cliff 200 m above the sea level, observes the angles of depression of two ships on opposite sides of the cliff to be 45° and 30° respectively. The distance between the ships if the line joining them passes through the base of cliff, is :

   (a) $100(\sqrt{3}+1)$ m (b) $200(\sqrt{3}+1)$ m

   (c) $150(\sqrt{3}+1)$ m (d) None of these.

5. If upper part of a tree broken over by the wind makes an angle of 30° with the ground, and the distance from the root to the point where the top of the tree touches the ground is 10 m, then the height of the tree is :

   (a) $20\sqrt{3}$ m (b) $10\sqrt{3}$ m

   (c) $15\sqrt{3}$ m (d) None of these.

6. At the foot of the mountain, the elevation of its summit is 45°; after ascending 1000 m towards the mountain up a slope of 30° inclination, the elevation is found to be 60°. The height of the mountain is :

   (a) $\frac{\sqrt{3}+1}{2}$ m (b) $\frac{\sqrt{3}-1}{2}$ m

   (c) $\frac{\sqrt{3}+1}{2\sqrt{3}}$ m (d) None of these.

7. The angle of elevation of the top of a vertical tower from two points distant a and b from the base and in the same line with it, are complementary. If θ is the angle subtended at the top of the tower by the line joining these points, then sin θ =

   (a) $\frac{a-b}{\sqrt{2}\,(a+b)}$ (b) $\frac{a+b}{a-b}$

   (c) $\frac{a-b}{a+b}$ (d) None of these.

8. An aeroplane flying horizontally 1 km above the ground is observed at an elevation of 60°. If after 10 seconds the elevation is observed to be 30°, the uniform speed per hour of the aeroplane is :

   (a) $120\sqrt{3}$ km/hour (b) $240\sqrt{3}$ km/hour

   (c) $250\sqrt{3}$ km/hour (d) None of these.

9. The angle of elevation of a cloud at a point P, which is at height h above the level of water in a lake, is α and the angle of depression of its image in the lake at P is β. The height of the cloud above the surface of the lake is :

   (a) $\frac{h\sin(\alpha+\beta)}{\sin(\beta-\alpha)}$ (b) $\frac{h\sin(\alpha-\beta)}{\sin(\alpha+\beta)}$

   (c) $\frac{h\cos(\alpha+\beta)}{\sin(\beta-\alpha)}$ (d) None of these.

10. The longer side of a parallelogram is 10 cm and the shorter is 6 cm. If the longer diagonal makes an angle 30° with the longer side, the length of the longer diagonal is :

(a) $5\sqrt{3} + \sqrt{11}$ (b) $4\sqrt{3} + \sqrt{11}$

(c) $5\sqrt{3} + \sqrt{13}$ (d) None of these.

11. A tower subtends an angle α at a point on the same level as the root of the tower and at a second point, h metres above the first, the angle of depression of the foot of the tower is β. The height of the tower is :

(a) $b \cot \alpha \tan \beta$ (b) $b \tan \alpha \tan \beta$

(c) $b \tan \alpha \cot \beta$ (d) None of these.

12. Two stations due south of a tower, which leans towards the north, are at distances a and b from its foot. If α, β are the elevations of the top of the tower from these stations, then the inclination of the tower to the horizontal is :

(a) $\tan^{-1}\left(\dfrac{b \cot \alpha - a \cot \beta}{b - a}\right)$

(b) $\cot^{-1}\left(\dfrac{b \cot \alpha - a \cot \beta}{b - a}\right)$

(c) $\cot^{-1}\left(\dfrac{a \cot \alpha - b \cot \beta}{a + b}\right)$

(d) None of these.

13. The angle of elevation of a tower from a point A due south of it is x and from a point B due east of A is y. If AB = l, then the height h of the tower is given by :

(a) $\dfrac{l}{\sqrt{\cot^2 y - \cot^2 x}}$ (b) $\dfrac{l}{\sqrt{\tan^2 y - \tan^2 x}}$

(c) $\dfrac{2l}{\sqrt{\cot^2 y - \cot^2 x}}$ (d) None of these.

14. The elevation of a tower at a station A due north of it is α and at a station B due west of A is β. Its altitude is :

(a) $\dfrac{AB \cos \alpha \cos \beta}{\sqrt{\cos^2 \alpha - \cos^2 \beta}}$ (b) $\dfrac{AB \sin \alpha \sin \beta}{\sqrt{\sin^2 \beta - \sin^2 \alpha}}$

(c) $\dfrac{AB \sin \alpha \sin \beta}{\sqrt{\sin^2 \alpha - \sin^2 \beta}}$ (d) None of these.

15. A statue standing on a column subtends equal angles at two points A and B which are 18 m and 22 m away from the foot of the column. If the tangent of the angles be 10, the heights of the statue and the column are :

(a) 18 m, 4 m   (b) 4 m, 18 m

(c) 6 m, 12 m   (d) None of these.

16. An object is observed from three points A, B, C in the same horizontal line passing through the base of the object. The angle of elevation at B is twice and at C is thrice that at A. If AB = a, BC = b, the height of the object is :

(a) $\dfrac{a}{b}\sqrt{(a + b)(a - 3b)}$

(b) $\dfrac{a}{3b}\sqrt{(a + b)(3b - a)}$

(c) $\dfrac{a}{2b}\sqrt{(a + b)(3b - a)}$

(d) None of these.

17. The pole stands vertically on the centre of a square. When α is the elevation of the sun, its shadow just reaches the side of a square and is at a distance x and y from the ends of that side. The height of the pole is :

(a) $\sqrt{\dfrac{x^2 + y^2}{2}} \tan \alpha$ (b) $\sqrt{\dfrac{x^2 + y^2}{2}} \cot \alpha$

(c) $\sqrt{\dfrac{x^2 - y^2}{2}} \tan \alpha$ (d) None of these.

18. A ladder rests against a vertical wall at an angle α to the horizontal. If its foot is pulled away from the wall through a distance 'a' so that it slides a distance 'b' down the wall making an angle β with the horizontal, then a =

(a) $b \tan \dfrac{\alpha - \beta}{2}$ (b) $b \tan \dfrac{\alpha + \beta}{2}$

(c) $b \cot \dfrac{\alpha - \beta}{2}$ (d) None of these.

19. A balloon moving in a straight line passes vertically above two points A and B on a horizontal plane 1000 m apart. When above A it has an altitude 60° as seen from B, and when above B, 30° as seen from A. The distance from A of the point at which it will strike the plane is :

(a) 1500 metres   (b) 1000 metres

(c) 2000 metres   (d) None of these.

20. AB is a vertical pole. The end A is on the level ground. C is the middle point of AB. P is the point on the level ground. The portion CB subtends an angle β at P. If AP = nAB, then tan β =

(a) $\dfrac{3n}{n^2 + 1}$

(b) $\dfrac{n}{2n^2 + 3}$

(c) $\dfrac{n}{2n^2 + 1}$

(d) None of these.

21. The angular depressions of the top and the foot of a chimney as seen from the top of a second chimney, which is 150 metres high and standing on the same level as the first, are θ and ϕ respectively. The distance between their tops when tan $\theta = \dfrac{4}{3}$ and tan $\phi = \dfrac{5}{2}$ is :

(a) 100 metres

(b) 150 metres

(c) 230 metres

(d) None of these.

22. A man observes that when he moves up a distance c metres on a slope, the angle of depression of a point on the horizontal plane from the base of the slope is 30° and when he moves up further a distance c metres, the angle of depression of that point is 45°. The angle of inclination of the slope with the horizontal is :

(a) 60°

(b) 45°

(c) 75°

(d) 30°

23. The angle of elevation of the top of an incomplete vertical pillar at a horizontal distance of 100 metres from its base is 45°. If the angle of elevation of the top of the complete pillar at the same point is to be 60°, then the height of the incomplete pillar is to be increased by :

(a) $50\sqrt{2}$ m

(b) 100 m

(c) $100(\sqrt{3} - 1)$ m

(d) $100(\sqrt{3} + 1)$ m

24. ABC is a triangular park with AB = AC = 100 metres. A clock tower is situated at the mid point of BC. The angles of elevation of the top of the tower at A and B are $\cot^{-1}(3.2)$ and $\text{cosec}^{-1}(2.6)$ respectively. The height of the tower in metres is :

(a) $\dfrac{25}{2}$

(b) 25

(c) 50

(d) None of these.

25. If a flagstaff 6 metres high placed on the top of a tower throws a shadow of $2\sqrt{3}$ m along the ground, then the angle (in degrees) that the sun makes with the ground is :

(a) 30°

(b) 60°

(c) 45°

(d) None of these.

26. The angle of elevation of the top of a tower from the top and bottom of a building of height 'a' are 30° and 45° respectively. If the tower and the building stand at the same level, the height of the tower is :

(a) $\dfrac{a(3 + \sqrt{3})}{2}$

(b) $a(\sqrt{3} + 1)$

(c) $a\sqrt{3}$

(d) $a(\sqrt{3} - 1)$

27. From the bottom of a pole of height h, the angle of elevation of the top of a tower is α. The pole subtends an angle β at the top of a tower. The height of the tower is :

(a) $\dfrac{h \sin \alpha \sin (\alpha - \beta)}{\sin \beta}$

(b) $\dfrac{h \sin \alpha \cos (\alpha + \beta)}{\cos \beta}$

(c) $\dfrac{h \sin \alpha \cos (\alpha - \beta)}{\sin \beta}$

(d) $\dfrac{h \sin \alpha \sin (\alpha + \beta)}{\cos \beta}$

28. A tower of height b subtends an angle at a point O on the level of the foot of the tower and at a distance 'a' from the foot of the tower. If the pole mounted on the tower also subtends an equal angle at O, the height of the pole is :

(a) $b \left(\dfrac{a^2 - b^2}{a^2 + b^2} \right)$

(b) $b \left(\dfrac{a^2 + b^2}{a^2 - b^2} \right)$

(c) $a \left(\dfrac{a^2 - b^2}{a^2 + b^2} \right)$

(d) $a \left(\dfrac{a^2 + b^2}{a^2 - b^2} \right)$

29. A person standing on the bank of a river finds that the angle of elevation of the top of a tower on the opposite bank is 45°. Then which of the following statements is correct ?

(a) Breadth of the river is twice the height of the tower.

(b) Breadth of the river and the height of the tower are the same.

(c) Breadth of the river is half of the height of the tower.

(d) None of these.

30. The length of the shadows of a vertical pole of height h, thrown by the sun's rays at three different moments are h, 2h and 3h. The sum of the angles of elevation of the rays at these three moments is equal to :

(a) $\frac{\pi}{2}$ (b) $\frac{\pi}{3}$

(c) $\frac{\pi}{4}$ (d) $\frac{\pi}{6}$

31. From the top of a cliff 300 metres high, the top of a tower was observed at an angle of depression 30° and from the foot of the tower the top of the cliff was observed at an angle of elevation 45°. The height of the tower is :

(a) $50(3 - \sqrt{3})$ m   (b) $200(3 - \sqrt{3})$ m

(c) $100(3 - \sqrt{3})$ m   (d) None of these.

32. The horizontal distance between two towers is 60 m. The angular elevation of the top of the taller tower as seen from the top of the shorter one is 30°. If the height of the taller tower is 150 m, the height of the shorter one is :

(a) 116 m   (b) 200 m

(c) 216 m   (d) None of these.

33. AB is a vertical pole and C is its middle point. The end A is on the level ground and P is any point on the level ground other than A. The portion CB subtends an angle β at P. If AP : AB = 2 : 1, then β =

(a) $\tan^{-1} \frac{4}{9}$ (b) $\tan^{-1} \frac{1}{9}$

(c) $\tan^{-1} \frac{5}{9}$ (d) $\tan^{-1} \frac{2}{9}$.

34. An aeroplane flying at a height of 300 metres above the ground passes vertically above another plane at an instant when the angle of elevation of the two planes from the same point on the ground are 60° and 45° respectively. Then the height of the lower plane from the ground is (in metres) :

(a) $100\sqrt{3}$ (b) $\frac{100}{\sqrt{3}}$

(c) 50   (d) $150(\sqrt{3} + 1)$

35. A circular ring of radius 3 cm is suspended horizontally from a point 4 cm vertically above the centre by 4 strings attached at equal interval to its circumference. If the angle between two consecutive strings is θ, then cos θ is :

(a) $\frac{4}{5}$ (b) $\frac{4}{25}$

(c) $\frac{16}{25}$ (d) None of these.

36. A rocket of height h is fired vertically upwards. Its velocity at time t seconds is $(2t + 3)$ m/s. If the angle of elevation of the top of the rocket from a point on the ground after 1 second of firing is $\frac{\pi}{6}$ and after 3 seconds it is $\frac{\pi}{3}$, then the distance of the point from the rocket is:

(a) $14\sqrt{3}$ metres   (b) $7\sqrt{3}$ metres

(c) $2\sqrt{3}$ metres

(d) cannot be found without the value of h.

37. A vertical lamp post, 6 m high, stands at a distance of 2 m from a wall, 4 m high. A 1.5 m tall man starts to walk away from the wall on the other side of the wall, in line with the lamp-post. The maximum distance to which the man can walk remaining in the shadow is :

(a) $\frac{5}{2}$ m   (b) $\frac{3}{2}$ m

(c) 4 m   (d) None of these.

38. The angles of elevation of the top of a T.V. tower from three points A, B, C in a straight line, (in the horizontal plane) through the foot of the tower are α, 2α, 3α respectively. If AB = a, the height of the tower is :

(a) a tan α   (b) a sin α

(c) a sin 2α   (d) a sin 3α

39. Two rays are drawn through a point A at an angle of 30°. A point B is taken on one of them at distance a from the point A. A perpendicular is drawn from the point B to the other ray, another perpendicular is drawn from its foot to AB, and so on. Then the length of the resulting infinite polygonal line is :

(a) $2\sqrt{3}a$ (b) $a(2 + \sqrt{3})$

(c) $a(2 - \sqrt{3})$ (d) None of these.

40. The angle of elevation of the top of the tower from a point A due south of it, is $\tan^{-1}(6)$ and that from B due east of it, is $\tan^{-1}(7.5)$. If h is the height of the tower, then $AB = \lambda h$, where $\lambda^2 =$

(a) $\dfrac{21}{700}$ (b) $\dfrac{42}{1300}$

(c) $\dfrac{41}{900}$ (d) None of these.

41. A tower and a flag staff on its top subtend equal angles at the observer's eye. If the heights of flag-staff, tower and the eye of the observer are respectively a, b and h, then the distance of the observer's eye from the base of the tower is :

(a) $a\sqrt{\dfrac{a+b-2h}{a+b}}$ (b) $b\sqrt{\dfrac{a+b-2h}{a-b}}$

(c) $a\sqrt{\dfrac{a-h}{a+b}}$ (d) None of these.

42. ABC is a triangular park with $AB = AC = 100$ m. A clock tower is situated at the mid point of BC. The angle of elevation of the top of the tower at A and B are $\cot^{-1}(3.2)$ and $\text{cosec}^{-1}(2.6)$ respectively. The height of the tower is :

(a) 16 m   (b) 25 m

(c) 50 m   (d) None of these.

43. A statue situated at any tower makes an angle α with two points which are at the distance of 18 m and 22 m from the tower if $\tan\alpha = \dfrac{1}{10}$, then the height of the statue will be :

(a) 2.5 m   (b) 4 m

(c) 8 m   (d) 5 m.

44. ABCD is a rectangular plot. A vertical tower at D subtends angles α, β, γ at A, B, C respectively, then :

(a) $\cot^2\alpha = \cot^2\beta - \cot^2\gamma$

(b) $\cot^2\beta = \cot^2\alpha - \cot^2\gamma$

(c) $\cot^2\gamma = \cot^2\alpha - \cot^2\beta$

(d) $\cot^2\alpha + \cot^2\beta + \cot^2\gamma = 0$.

45. AB is a vertical pole with B at the ground level and A at the top. A man finds that the angle of elevation of the point A from a certain point C on the ground is 60°. He moves away from the pole along the line BC to a point D such that $CD = 7$ m. From D the angle of elevation of the point A is 45°. Then the height of the pole is :

[**AIEEE – 2008**]

(a) $\dfrac{7\sqrt{3}}{2} \cdot \dfrac{1}{\sqrt{3}-1}$ m   (b) $\dfrac{7\sqrt{3}}{2} \cdot (\sqrt{3}+1)$ m

(c) $\dfrac{7\sqrt{3}}{2} \cdot (\sqrt{3}-1)$ m   (d) $\dfrac{7\sqrt{3}}{2} \cdot \dfrac{1}{\sqrt{3}+1}$

46. A tower stands at the centre of a circular park. A and B are two points on the boundary of the park such that $AB (= a)$ subtends an angle of 60° at the foot of the tower and the angle of elevation of the top of the tower from A or B is 30°. The height of the tower is :   [**AIEEE – 2007**]

(a) $\dfrac{2a}{\sqrt{3}}$ (b) $2a\sqrt{3}$

(c) $\dfrac{a}{\sqrt{3}}$ (d) $a\sqrt{3}$

ANSWER KEY

1. (c)	2. (a)	3. (b)	4. (b)	5. (b)	6. (a)	7. (c)	8. (b)	9. (a)	10. (a)
11. (c)	12. (b)	13. (a)	14. (c)	15. (b)	16. (c)	17. (a)	18. (b)	19. (a)	20. (c)
21. (a)	22. (c)	23. (c)	24. (b)	25. (b)	26. (a)	27. (c)	28. (b)	29. (b)	30. (a)
31. (c)	32. (a)	33. (d)	34. (a)	35. (c)	36. (b)	37. (a)	38. (c)	39. (b)	40. (c)
41. (b)	42. (b)	43. (b)	44. (a)	45. (b)	46. (c)				

Chapter 8

COMPLEX NUMBERS

MULTIPLE CHOICE QUESTIONS

1. $i^{n+1} + i^{n+2} + i^{n+3} + i^{n+4} =$
   - (a) 1
   - (b) −1
   - (c) 0
   - (d) 4

2. The value of $\dfrac{i^{256} + i^{258} + i^{260} + i^{262} + i^{262}}{i^{562} + i^{564} + i^{566} + i^{568} + i^{570}} - 1$ is :
   - (a) 1
   - (b) −2
   - (c) 2
   - (d) −1

3. The value of $\left[i^{23} + \left(\dfrac{1}{i} \right)^{37} \right]^2$ is :
   - (a) 4
   - (b) −4
   - (c) 2
   - (d) −2

4. The value of $\left(\dfrac{1-i}{1+i} \right)^2 + \left(\dfrac{1+i}{1-i} \right)^2$ is :
   - (a) 2i
   - (b) −2i
   - (c) 2
   - (d) −2

5. If $n \in N$, then $\dfrac{i^{4n+1} - i^{4n-1}}{2} =$
   - (a) 1
   - (b) i
   - (c) −1
   - (d) −i

6. The least positive integral value of n for which $\left(\dfrac{2i}{1+i} \right)^n$ is a natural number is :
   - (a) 2
   - (b) 4
   - (c) 8
   - (d) 16

7. For $n \in N$, $(1-i)^n \left(1 - \dfrac{1}{i} \right)^n$ equals :
   - (a) 0
   - (b) $2i^n$
   - (c) 2^n
   - (d) 4^n

8. If $\dfrac{(1+i) x - 2i}{3+i} + \dfrac{(2-3i) y + i}{3-i} = i$, then $(x, y) =$
   - (a) (3, −1)
   - (b) (−3, 1)
   - (c) (3, 1)
   - (d) (−3, −1)

9. If $\sqrt[3]{(x+iy)} = a + bi$, then $\dfrac{x}{a} + \dfrac{y}{b} =$
   - (a) $2(a^2 - b^2)$
   - (b) $8(a^2 - b^2)$
   - (c) $4(a^2 - b^2)$
   - (d) $4(a^2 + b^2)$

10. The value of $\dfrac{1-2i}{2+i} + \dfrac{4-i}{3+2i}$ is a + bi, then (a, b) is :
    - (a) $\left(\dfrac{24}{13}, \dfrac{10}{13} \right)$
    - (b) $\left(\dfrac{24}{13}, \dfrac{-10}{13} \right)$
    - (c) $\left(\dfrac{10}{13}, \dfrac{24}{13} \right)$
    - (d) $\left(\dfrac{10}{13}, \dfrac{-24}{13} \right)$

11. If $\dfrac{1-ix}{1+ix} = p - qi$, p, q are real and $p^2 + q^2 = 1$, then x =
    - (a) $\dfrac{2p}{(1+p)^2 + q^2}$
    - (b) $\dfrac{2q}{(1+p)^2 + q^2}$
    - (c) $\dfrac{2p}{(1+q)^2 + p^2}$
    - (d) $\dfrac{2q}{(1+q)^2 + p^2}$

12. $\left| \dfrac{(3+2i)^2}{4-3i} \right| =$
    - (a) $\dfrac{11}{5}$
    - (b) $\dfrac{9}{5}$
    - (c) $\dfrac{7}{5}$
    - (d) $\dfrac{13}{5}$

13. If $(\sqrt{3} - i)^n = 2^n$, $n \in Z$, then n should be a multiple of :
    - (a) 3 and 4
    - (b) either 3 or 4
    - (c) 6
    - (d) only 3

14. The multiplicative inverse of $(2 + 3i)^2$ is :
    - (a) $\dfrac{5}{13} + \dfrac{12}{13} i$
    - (b) $\dfrac{-5}{13} - \dfrac{12}{13} i$
    - (c) $\dfrac{-5}{169} + \dfrac{12}{169} i$
    - (d) $\dfrac{-5}{169} - \dfrac{12}{169} i$

15. If $z = x + iy$; $x, y \in R$, then $|x| + |y| \le k |z| \Rightarrow k =$

(a) $\sqrt{2}$ (b) 1

(c) $\sqrt{3}$ (d) 2

16. If $x + iy = \dfrac{u + iv}{u - iv}$, then the value of $x^2 + y^2$ is :

(a) -1 (b) 1

(c) 0   (d) None of these

17. If $\dfrac{(a + i)^2}{2a - i} = p + iq$ then $p^2 + q^2$ is :

(a) $\dfrac{(a^2 + 1)^2}{2a^2 + 1}$ (b) $\dfrac{(a^2 + 1)^2}{2a^2 - 1}$

(c) $\dfrac{(a^2 + 1)^2}{4a^2 + 1}$ (d) None of these

18. Square roots of $7 - 24i$ are :

(a) $\pm (3 + 4i)$ (b) $\pm (3 - 4i)$

(c) $\pm (4 + 3i)$ (d) $\pm (3i - 4)$

19. $\sqrt{-2 + 2\sqrt{3}i} = \pm (a + bi)$ then :

(a) $a = 1, b = \sqrt{3}$ (b) $a = 1, b = -\sqrt{3}$

(c) $a = -1, b = \sqrt{3}$ (d) None of these

20. $\dfrac{(1 + 2i)}{1 - i}$ lies in which quadrant of argand plane :

(a) 1st (b) 2nd

(c) 3rd (d) 4th

21. The conjugate complex number of $\dfrac{3 + 2i}{(1 + i)^2}$ is :

(a) $\dfrac{3}{2} + i$ (b) $1 + \dfrac{3}{2}i$

(c) $1 - \dfrac{3}{2}i$ (d) $\dfrac{3}{2} - i$

22. The value of $i^{\,i}$ is :

(a) ω (b) $\dfrac{\pi}{2}$

(c) $-\omega^2$ (d) None of these

23. $|z - 4| < |z - 2|$ represents the region given by :

(a) Re $(z) > 3$ (b) Re $(z) > 0$

(c) Re $(z) < 0$ (d) None of these

24. If $(1 + i)(1 + 2i)(1 + 3i) \ldots (1 + ni) = a + ib$, then $2 \times 5 \times 10 \times \ldots \times (1 + n^2)$ is :

(a) $a - bi$ (b) $a^2 - b^2$

(c) $a^2 + b^2$ (d) $|a + ib|$

25. If $z = \dfrac{1 - \sqrt{3}i}{1 + \sqrt{3}i}$, then arg $(z) =$

(a) $\dfrac{\pi}{3}$ (b) $\dfrac{2\pi}{3}$

(c) $\dfrac{4\pi}{3}$ (d) $\dfrac{-2\pi}{3}$

26. The smallest positive integer n such that $(1+i)^{2n} = (1 - i)^{2n}$ is :

(a) 2   (b) 4

(c) 8   (d) 12

27. The complex number z which satisfies $\left|\dfrac{z - 5i}{z + 5i}\right| = 1$ lies on :

(a) x-axis

(b) the line $y = 5$

(c) a circle through origin

(d) None of these

28. If $\left|\dfrac{z + 4 - i}{z + 3 + 2i}\right| = 1$, then locus of z is :

(a) $x^2 + y^2 = 1$

(b) x-axis

(c) y-axis

(d) perpendicular bisector of line segment joining $-4 + i$ and $-3 - 2i$

29. The locus of z such that $|z - ai| = |z + ai|$ for any real a is :

(a) x-axis

(b) y-axis

(c) a straight line other than co-ordinate axes

(d) a circle

30. The locus of z such that $\left|\dfrac{z-3}{z+3}\right| = 2$ is :

  (a) a straight line   (b) a point

  (c) a circle   (d) can't say

31. The locus of z such that $\left|\dfrac{1-iz}{z-i}\right| = 1$ is :

  (a) a circle   (b) x-axis

  (c) y-axis   (d) None of these

32. The equation $|z-1|^2 + |z+1|^2 = 4$ represents ...... on the argand plane.

  (a) an ellipse

  (b) a hyperbola

  (c) a circle with centre at origin and radius 2

  (d) a circle with centre at origin and radius 1

33. For any complex number z, the minimum value of $|z| + |z-1|$ is :

  (a) 0   (b) $\dfrac{1}{2}$

  (c) 1   (d) $\dfrac{3}{2}$

34. If $z = 1 + i\tan\alpha$ and $\pi < \alpha < \dfrac{3\pi}{2}$, then $|z|$ is equal to :

  (a) $\sec\alpha$ (b) $-\sec\alpha$

  (c) $\csc\alpha$ (d) $|\sec\alpha|$

35. If z is such that $|z| - z = 1 + 2i$, then z is :

  (a) $\dfrac{3}{2} - 2i$ (b) $\dfrac{3}{2} + 2i$

  (c) $2 - \dfrac{3}{2}i$ (d) $2 + \dfrac{3}{2}i$

36. The imaginary part of $\dfrac{2z+1}{iz+1}$ is -2, then locus of z is :

  (a) a circle   (b) a straight line

  (c) a parabola   (d) None of these

37. If α, β are complex cube roots of 1, then $\alpha^3 + \beta^3 + (\alpha\beta)^{-2} =$

  (a) 0   (b) 3

  (c) -3 (d) None of these

38. If ω is a complex cube root of 1, then

$(1 - \omega + \omega^2) \cdot (1 - \omega^2 + \omega^4) \cdot (1 - \omega^4 + \omega^8) \cdot$
$(1 - \omega^8 + \omega^{16}) =$

  (a) 12   (b) 14

  (c) 16   (d) 18

39. $p, q, r \in N$ and ω is an imaginary cube root of 1 and $f(x) = x^{3p} + x^{3q+1} + x^{3r+2}$, then $f(\omega) =$

  (a) ω (b) $-\omega^2$

  (c) 0   (d) None of these

40. If α, β, γ are the cube roots of a real number p, then for non-zero x, y, z, $\dfrac{x\alpha + y\beta + z\gamma}{x\beta + y\gamma + z\alpha} =$

  (a) $\dfrac{-1+\sqrt{3}i}{2}$ (b) $\dfrac{1-\sqrt{3}i}{2}$

  (c) $\dfrac{1+\sqrt{3}i}{2}$ (d) None of these

41. The value of $\left(\dfrac{-1+i\sqrt{3}}{2}\right)^{3n} + \left(\dfrac{-1-i\sqrt{3}}{2}\right)^{3n}$ is :

  (a) 0   (b) 1

  (c) 2   (d) 3

42. The product of the 4 values of $\left(\cos\dfrac{\pi}{3} + i\sin\dfrac{\pi}{3}\right)^{3/4}$ is :

  (a) 1   (b) -1

  (c) $\dfrac{3\sqrt{3}}{8}$ (d) $\dfrac{1}{8}$

43. If $z_r = \cos\left(\dfrac{\pi}{3^r}\right) + i\sin\left(\dfrac{\pi}{3^r}\right)$ where $r \in N$, then

$z_1 \cdot z_2 \cdot z_3 \cdots\cdots \infty =$

  (a) 1   (b) -1

  (c) $-i$ (d) i

44. If $(1+i)z = (1-i)\bar{z}$, then $z =$

  (a) $\alpha(1-i), \alpha \in R$ (b) $\alpha(1+i), \alpha \in R$

  (c) $\dfrac{\alpha}{1+i}, \alpha \in R^+$ (d) None of these

45. If $x = \omega - \omega^2 - 1$, then the value of $x^4 + x^3 - x^2 - 10x - 7$ is :

  (a) ω (b) 1

  (c) -1 (d) 5

46. If the cube roots of unity are 1, ω, ω^2, then the value of $(1 + \omega)(1 + \omega^2)(1 + \omega^4)(1 + \omega^8)$ ...... upto 2n factors is :

(a) 0   (b) 1

(c) −1   (d) None of these

47. If $z_k = \left(\sin\dfrac{2\pi k}{11} - i\cos\dfrac{2\pi k}{11}\right)$, then the value of

$z_1 + z_2 + z_3 + ... + z_{10} =$

(a) 1   (b) −1

(c) i   (d) −i

48. If amp $(z^{1/3}) = \dfrac{1}{2}$ amp $(z^2 + z\bar{z}^{1/3})$ then the value of $|z|$ is :

(a) 1   (b) 2

(c) 4   (d) 0

49. If $1, \alpha, \alpha^2, ... \alpha^{n-1}$ are n n^{th} roots of unity, then $(1 - \alpha)(1 - \alpha^2) ..... (1 - \alpha^{n-1}) =$

(a) 0   (b) 1

(c) n   (d) n^2

50. The vertices A, B, C of parallelogram ABCD are the complex numbers z_1, z_2 and z_3, then the vertex D is :

(a) $\dfrac{1}{2}(z_1 + z_2)$ (b) $\dfrac{1}{4}(z_1 + z_2 + z_3 + z_4)$

(c) $z_1 + z_3 - z_2$ (d) $\dfrac{1}{2}(z_1 + z_2 + z_3)$

51. The complex numbers z_1, z_2, z_3, and z_4 taken in order in the argand plane will represent parallelogram if and only if :

(a) $z_1 + z_4 = z_2 + z_3$ (b) $z_1 + z_3 = z_2 + z_4$

(c) $z_1 + z_2 = z_3 + z_4$ (d) $z_1 + z_2 + z_3 + z_4 = 0$

52. The value of $\{\sin(\log i^i)\}^3 + \{\cos(\log i^i)\}^3$ is :

(a) 1   (b) −1

(c) 2   (d) 2i

53. The value of

$\dfrac{(\cos 2\theta + i\sin 2\theta)^{-7}(\cos 3\theta - i\sin 3\theta)^5}{(\cos 4\theta - i\sin 4\theta)^{-12}(\cos 5\theta - i\sin 5\theta)^6}$ is :

(a) $\cos 33\theta - i\sin 33\theta$ (b) $\cos 47\theta - i\sin 47\theta$

(c) $\cos 33\theta + i\sin 33\theta$ (d) $\cos 47\theta + i\sin 47\theta$

54. If $z = \dfrac{q + ir}{1 + p}$, then $\dfrac{p + iq}{1 + r} = \dfrac{1 + iz}{1 - iz}$ if :

(a) $p^2 + q^2 + r^2 = 1$ (b) $p^2 + q^2 + r^2 = 2$

(c) $p^2 + q^2 - r^2 = 1$ (d) $p^2 + q^2 - r^2 = 2$

55. If $\dfrac{3}{2 + \cos\theta + i\sin\theta} = p + qi$, then $p^2 + q^2 =$

(a) $2p - 3$ (b) $2p + 3$

(c) $4p + 3$ (d) $4p - 3$

56. If $\sqrt[3]{p + qi} = \alpha + \beta i$, then $\sqrt[3]{p - qi} =$

(a) $\alpha - \beta i$ (b) $\alpha + \beta i$

(c) $\beta + \alpha i$ (d) $\beta - \alpha i$

57. If z_1 and z_2 both satisfy the relation

$z + \bar{z} = 2|z - 1|$ and $\arg(z_1 - z_2) = \dfrac{\pi}{4}$,

then Im $(z_1 + z_2) =$

(a) 0   (b) 1

(c) 2   (d) −1

58. If $1, \omega, \omega^2$ are cube roots of 1, then the value of $(3 + 3\omega + 5\omega^2)^6 - (2 + 6\omega + 2\omega^2)^3$ is :

(a) 0   (b) 1

(c) −1   (d) 2

59. If ω is an imaginary cube root of unity, then the value of $(1 - \omega)(1 - \omega^2)(1 - \omega^4)(1 - \omega^5)$ is :

(a) 3   (b) 9

(c) 18   (d) None of these

60. If n is a positive integer, then

$\left(\dfrac{-1 + i\sqrt{3}}{2}\right)^n + \left(\dfrac{-1 - i\sqrt{3}}{2}\right)^n$ is equal to :

(a) −1 if n is a multiple of 3

(b) 2 if n is not a multiple of 3

(c) 1 if n is not a multiple of 3

(d) 2 if n is a multiple of 3

61. In a G.P., the first term is $\sqrt{3} - i$ and the common ratio is $\dfrac{1}{2}(\sqrt{3} - i)$, then the absolute value of its nth term is:

(a) 2^n (b) 4^n

(c) 2   (d) 2^{n-1}

62. If $z = \cos\theta + i\sin\theta$, then $\arg(z^2 + \bar{z})$ is :

(a) θ

(b) $\dfrac{3\theta}{2}$

(c) $\dfrac{\theta}{2}$

(d) None of these

63. The value of $\sqrt{-1 - \sqrt{-1 - \sqrt{-1 - \sqrt{-1} \ldots \infty}}}$ is :

(a) 1

(b) -1

(c) ω

(d) i

64. If $z = \dfrac{1 + 7i}{(2 - i)^2}$, then the polar form of z is :

(a) $\sqrt{2}\left(\cos\left(\dfrac{-\pi}{4}\right) + i\sin\left(\dfrac{-\pi}{4}\right)\right)$

(b) $\sqrt{2}\left(\cos\dfrac{\pi}{4} + i\sin\dfrac{\pi}{4}\right)$

(c) $\sqrt{2}\left(\cos\dfrac{5\pi}{4} + i\sin\dfrac{5\pi}{4}\right)$

(d) $\sqrt{2}\left(\cos\dfrac{3\pi}{4} + i\sin\dfrac{3\pi}{4}\right)$

65. If z is a complex number lying on the circle $|z| = 1$, then $z =$

(a) $\dfrac{1 + i\tan\left(\dfrac{\arg z}{2}\right)}{1 - i\tan\left(\dfrac{\arg z}{2}\right)}$

(b) $\dfrac{1 - i\tan(\arg z)}{1 + i\tan(\arg z)}$

(c) $\dfrac{1 - i\tan\left(\dfrac{\arg z}{2}\right)}{1 + i\tan\left(\dfrac{\arg z}{2}\right)}$

(d) None of these

66. If $x = a + b$, $y = a\omega + b\omega^2$, $z = a\omega^2 + b\omega$, where ω is cube root of unity, then $xyz =$

(a) $2(a^3 - b^3)$

(b) $2(a^3 + b^3)$

(c) $a^3 - b^3$

(d) $a^3 + b^3$

67. If $x = a + b$, $y = a\omega + b\omega^2$, $z = a\omega^2 + b\omega$, where ω is a complex cube root of unity, then $x^3 + y^3 + z^3 =$

(a) $3(a^3 - b^3)$

(b) $3(a^3 + b^3)$

(c) $a^3 - b^3$

(d) $a^3 + b^3$

68. Common roots of equations $z^3 + 2z^2 + 2z + 1 = 0$ and $z^{2011} + z^{-2011} + 1 = 0$ are :

(a) $-1, \omega$

(b) $-1, \omega^2$

(c) ω, ω^2

(d) $1, -1$

69. The region of argand plane defined by $|z + 1| + |z - 1| \le 4$ is :

(a) interior and boundary of circle

(b) interior and boundary of ellipse

(c) interior and boundary of parabola

(d) None of these

70. If $z = x + iy$ is such that $\mathrm{amp}\,(z - 1) = \mathrm{amp}\,(z + 3i)$, then $(x - 1) : y$ is :

(a) $1 : 3$

(b) $-1 : 3$

(c) $2 : 1$

(d) None of these

71. If complex numbers z_1 and z_2 are such that $|z_1 + z_2| = |z_1 - z_2|$ then $\mathrm{amp}\,z_1 \sim \mathrm{amp}\,z_2 =$

(a) $\dfrac{\pi}{4}$

(b) π

(c) $\dfrac{\pi}{2}$

(d) None of these

72. If $n > 1$, then the roots of $z^n = (z + 1)^n$ lie on a :

(a) circle

(b) parabola

(c) line

(d) None of these

73. If z satisfies $\log_{1/2}\left(\dfrac{|z - 1| + 4}{3|z - 1| - 2}\right) > 1$, where $|z - 1| \ne 2/3$, then z represents :

(a) a circle

(b) interior of a circle

(c) exterior of a circle

(d) None of these

74. If z satisfies $z^2 + z + 1 = 0$ and n is not a multiple of 3, then $z^n + z^{2n} =$

(a) 0

(b) -1

(c) 2

(d) -2

75. If $1, \alpha_1, \alpha_2, \alpha_3, \alpha_4$, are the zeros of $x^5 - 1 = 0$, then $\dfrac{\omega - \alpha_1}{\omega^2 - \alpha_1} \cdot \dfrac{\omega - \alpha_2}{\omega^2 - \alpha_2} \cdot \dfrac{\omega - \alpha_3}{\omega^2 - \alpha_3} \cdot \dfrac{\omega - \alpha_4}{\omega^2 - \alpha_4} =$

(a) 1

(b) ω

(c) ω^2

(d) None of these

76. The complex number z satisfying
    $|z| - 4 = |z - i| - |z + 5i| = 0$ is :
    (a) $\sqrt{3} - i$ (b) $2\sqrt{3} + 2i$
    (c) $-2\sqrt{3} - 2i$ (d) 0

77. If $z = \dfrac{(1 + \cos\theta + i\sin\theta)^5}{(\cos\theta + i\sin\theta)^3}$ then $|z|$ and amp z
    (principle value) are :
    (a) $32\cos^5\dfrac{\theta}{2}, \dfrac{-\theta}{2}$ (b) $32\cos^5\dfrac{\theta}{2}, \dfrac{\theta}{2}$
    (c) $16\cos^4\dfrac{\theta}{2}, \dfrac{-\theta}{2}$ (d) None of these

78. If $z = \cos\theta + i\sin\theta$, then :
    (a) $z^n + z^{-n} = 2\cos n\theta$ (b) $z^n + z^{-n} = 2^n\cos n\theta$
    (c) $z^n - z^{-n} = 2i\sin^n\theta$ (d) $z^n - z^{-n} = (2i)^n\sin n\theta$

79. If $z = \cos\theta + i\sin\theta$, then $\dfrac{z^n - 1}{z^n + 1} =$
    (a) $i\cot\dfrac{n\theta}{2}$ (b) $i\tan\dfrac{n\theta}{2}$
    (c) $\cot\dfrac{n\theta}{2}$ (d) $\tan\dfrac{n\theta}{2}$

80. If $\left(\dfrac{3}{2} + i\dfrac{\sqrt{3}}{2}\right)^{50} = 3^{25}(x + iy)$ then $(x, y) =$
    (a) $(0, 3)$ (b) $\left(\dfrac{1}{2}, \dfrac{\sqrt{3}}{2}\right)$
    (c) $(-3, 0)$ (d) $(0, -3)$

81. If $n \in I$, then
    $(1 + \cos\theta + i\sin\theta)^n + (1 + \cos\theta - i\sin\theta)^n =$
    (a) $2^n\cos^n\dfrac{\theta}{2}\sin\dfrac{n\theta}{2}$ (b) $2^{n+1}\cos^n\dfrac{\theta}{2}\sin\dfrac{n\theta}{2}$
    (c) $2^n\cos^n\dfrac{\theta}{2}\cos\dfrac{n\theta}{2}$ (d) $2^{n+1}\cos^n\dfrac{\theta}{2}\cos\dfrac{n\theta}{2}$

82. If $z_r = \cos\dfrac{\pi}{2^r} + i\sin\dfrac{\pi}{2^r}$, then $z_1 \cdot z_2 \cdot z_3 \cdot \ldots \infty =$
    (a) 1   (b) 0
    (c) -1 (d) None of these

83. If $\cos\alpha + 2\cos\beta + 3\cos\gamma = \sin\alpha + 2\sin\beta + 3\sin\gamma = 0$, then
    (a) $\cos 3\alpha + 8\cos 3\beta + 27\cos 3\gamma = 9\cos(\alpha + \beta + \gamma)$
    (b) $\sin 3\alpha + 8\sin 3\beta + 27\sin 3\gamma = 9\sin(\alpha + \beta + \gamma)$
    (c) $\cos 3\alpha + 8\cos 3\beta + 27\cos 3\gamma = 18\cos(\alpha + \beta + \gamma)$
    (d) None of these

84. If α, β are roots of $x^2 - 2x + 2 = 0$, then $\alpha^n + \beta^n =$
    (a) $2^{\frac{n}{2}-1}\cos\dfrac{n\pi}{4}$ (b) $2^{\frac{n}{2}}\cos\dfrac{n\pi}{4}$
    (c) $2^{\frac{n}{2}+1}\cos\dfrac{n\pi}{4}$ (d) None of these

85. If n is a positive integer and $(1 + z)^n = c_0 + c_1 z + c_2 z^2 + \ldots + c_n z^n$, then
    (a) $c_0 - c_2 + c_4 - \ldots = 2^{n/2}\cos\dfrac{n\pi}{4}$
    (b) $c_1 + c_3 + c_5 + \ldots = 2^{n/2}\sin\dfrac{n\pi}{4}$
    (c) $c_0 - c_2 + c_4 - \ldots = 2^{\frac{n}{2}+1}\cos\dfrac{n\pi}{4}$
    (d) $c_1 - c_3 + c_5 - \ldots = 2^{\frac{n}{2}+1}\sin\dfrac{n\pi}{4}$

86. If $f(x) = x^4 - 8x^3 + 4x^2 + 4x + 39$ and $f(3 + 2i) = p + iq$, then $\dfrac{p}{q} =$
    (a) $\dfrac{-1}{4}$ (b) $\dfrac{1}{8}$
    (c) $\dfrac{-1}{8}$ (d) $\dfrac{1}{4}$

87. If $|z - 25i| \leq 15$, then the least value of amp (z) is :
    (a) $\tan^{-1}\dfrac{4}{3}$ (b) $\pi - \tan^{-1}\dfrac{4}{3}$
    (c) $-\pi + \tan^{-1}\dfrac{4}{3}$ (d) None of these

88. If $|z - 4 + 3i| \leq 2$, then the minimum and maximum value of $|z|$ are :
    (a) 3, 7   (b) 3, 9
    (c) 4, 7   (d) None of these

89. The equation $|z - i| + |z + i| = k$ represents an ellipse if $k =$
    (a) 1   (b) 2
    (c) 4   (d) None of these

90. If ω is a complex cube root of 1 and $|z - \omega|^2 + |z - \omega^2|^2 = \lambda$ be the equation of a circle with ω, ω^2 as ends of a diameter then $\lambda =$
    (a) 2   (b) $\sqrt{2}$
    (c) 3   (d) 4

91. The equation $|z + i| + |z - i| = k$ represents a hyperbola if :

(a) $0 < k < 2$ (b) $-2 < k < 2$

(c) $k > 2$ (d) None of these

92. The equation $|z - z_1|^2 + |z - z_2|^2 = k$ represents a circle if :

(a) $k \geq \dfrac{1}{2}|z_1 - z_2|^2$ (b) $k < \dfrac{1}{2}|z_1 - z_2|^2$

(c) $k < |z_1 - z_2|^2$ (d) $k = |z_1 - z_2|^2$

93. If z_1 and z_2 are two complex numbers such that $|z_1| = |z_2|$ and $\arg z_1 + \arg z_2 = \pi$, then $z_1 =$

(a) z_2 (b) $-z_2$

(c) $\bar{z}_2$ (d) $-\bar{z}_2$

94. If $z = x + iy$ lies in IIIrd quadrant, then $\dfrac{\bar{z}}{z}$ also lies in IIIrd quadrant if :

(a) $y > x > 0$ (b) $y < x < 0$

(c) $x < y < 0$ (d) $x > y > 0$

95. The values of $(16)^{3/4}$ are :

(a) $\pm 8, \pm 8i$ (b) $\pm 4, \pm 4i$

(c) $\pm 1, \pm 1i$ (d) None of these

96. The solution of the equation $|z| = z + 1 + 2i$ is :

(a) $3 - 2i$ (b) $2 - \dfrac{3}{2}i$

(c) $\dfrac{3}{2} + 2i$ (d) $\dfrac{3}{2} - 2i$

97. $\tan\left[i \log \dfrac{a - bi}{a + bi}\right] =$

(a) $\dfrac{2ab}{a^2 + b^2}$ (b) $\dfrac{a^2 - b^2}{2ab}$

(c) $\dfrac{2ab}{a^2 - b^2}$ (d) ab

98. If the area of Δ on the argand plane, whose vertices are $-z, iz, z - iz$, is 600 sq. units, then $|z| =$

(a) 30   (b) 10

(c) 20   (d) None of these

99. If $|z + \bar{z}| + |z - \bar{z}| = 8$, then z lies on :

(a) a straight line   (b) a circle

(c) a square   (d) None of these

100. The complex numbers $1 - 3i$, $4 + 3i$ and $3 + i$ are the vertices of :

(a) a right angled triangle

(b) an isosceles triangle

(c) an equilateral triangle

(d) None of these

101. If $z^2 - 2z \cos \theta + 1 = 0$, then $z^2 + z^{-2} =$

(a) $2 \cos 2\theta$ (b) $2 \cos \theta$

(c) $2 \sin 2\theta$ (d) $2 \sin \theta$

102. $e^{2mi \cot^{-1} p} \cdot \left(\dfrac{pi + 1}{pi - 1}\right)^m =$

(a) 0   (b) -1

(c) 1   (d) None of these

103. If $f(x) = i^x + i^{-x}$, where $i = \sqrt{-1}$ and $x \in N$, then the total number of distinct values of $f(x)$ is :

(a) 4   (b) 3

(c) 2   (d) 1

104. The roots of the equation $z^4 + 1 = 0$ are :

(a) $(\pm 1, \pm i)$ (b) $(\pm 2, \pm 2i)$

(c) $\dfrac{1}{\sqrt{2}}(\pm 1, \pm i)$ (d) None of these

105. The quadratic equation whose one root is square root of $-47 + 8\sqrt{-3}$ is :

(a) $x^2 - 2x + 49 = 0$ (b) $x^2 - 2x - 49 = 0$

(c) $x^2 + 2x - 49 = 0$ (d) None of these

106. The principal value of the amplitude of $(1 + i)$ is

(a) $\dfrac{\pi}{4}$ (b) π

(c) $\dfrac{\pi}{12}$ (d) $\dfrac{3\pi}{4}$

107. The equation $z^2 = \bar{z}$ has :

(a) infinite number of solutions

(b) four solutions

(c) two solutions

(d) no solution

108. If z_1 and z_2 are complex numbers such that $z_1 + z_2$ is a real number, then :

(a) $z_1 = -\bar{z}_2$

(b) $z_2 = \bar{z}_1$

(c) $\bar{z}_1$ and $\bar{z}_2$ are any two complex numbers

(d) $z_1 = \bar{z}_1, z_2 = \bar{z}_2$

109. If $\alpha + i\beta = \tan^{-1}z$, where α is a constant and $z = x + iy$, then the locus of z is :

(a) $x^2 + y^2 + 2x \sin \alpha = 1$

(b) $x^2 + y^2 + 2y \tan 2\alpha = 1$

(c) $\cot 2\alpha (x^2 + y^2) = 1 + x$

(d) $x^2 + y^2 + 2x \cot 2\alpha = 1$

110. If $\left|\dfrac{z-2}{z-3}\right| = 2$ represents a circle, then its radius is :

(a) $\dfrac{1}{3}$

(b) $\dfrac{2}{3}$

(c) $\dfrac{3}{4}$

(d) 1

111. If $x^2 + x + 1 = 0$, then the value of

$$\left(x + \frac{1}{x}\right)^2 + \left(x^2 + \frac{1}{x^2}\right)^2 + \dots \left(x^{27} + \frac{1}{x^{27}}\right)^2 =$$

(a) 27

(b) 45

(c) 54

(d) 72

112. The locus of z satisfying the condition $\arg\left(\dfrac{z-1}{z+1}\right) = \dfrac{\pi}{3}$ is :

(a) a straight line

(b) a circle

(c) a parabola

(d) None of these

113. The maximum value of $|z|$ such that $\left|z - \dfrac{4}{z}\right| = 2$ is :

(a) $\sqrt{5} + 1$

(b) $\sqrt{5}$

(c) $\sqrt{5} - 1$

(d) $\sqrt{5} + 2$

114. If $\dfrac{z-1}{z+1}$ is purely imaginary, then :

(a) $|z| = 1$

(b) $|z| > 1$

(c) $|z| < 1$

(d) None of these

115. If $|z - i| < 1$, then $|z + 12 - 6i|$ is :

(a) less than 14

(b) less than 11

(c) greater than 14

(d) equal to 14

116. $\sqrt{i} - \sqrt{-i} =$

(a) i

(b) $\dfrac{1}{i\sqrt{2}}$

(c) 0

(d) $-i\sqrt{2}$

117. If $\operatorname{Re}\left(\dfrac{z + 2i}{z + 4}\right) = 0$, then z lies on a circle with centre :

(a) $(2, 1)$

(b) $(2, -1)$

(c) $(-2, 1)$

(d) $(-2, -1)$

118. If $\operatorname{Im}\left(\dfrac{z + 2i}{z + 2}\right) = 0$, then z lies on :

(a) $x^2 + y^2 + 2x + 2y = 0$

(b) $x + y + 2 = 0$

(c) $x^2 + y^2 - 2x = 0$

(d) None of these

119. If $\dfrac{z-2}{z+2}$ with $z \neq -2$ is purely imaginary, then $|z|$ is equal to :

(a) 1

(b) 2

(c) 3

(d) 4

120. The number of solutions of the equation $z^2 + |z|^2 = 0$, where $z \in C$ is :

(a) 1

(b) 2

(c) 3

(d) infinitely many

121. If α is an imaginary n^{th} root of unity, then :

$1 + \alpha + \alpha^2 + \alpha^3 \ldots + \alpha^{n-1} =$

(a) 0   (b) 1

(c) 2   (d) –1

122. The complex number z for which $\arg \left(\dfrac{3z - 6 - 3i}{2z - 8 - 6i}\right) = \dfrac{\pi}{4}$ and $|z - 3 + i| = 3$ is :

(a) $\left(4 - \dfrac{4}{\sqrt{5}}\right) + i\left(1 - \dfrac{2}{\sqrt{5}}\right)$

(b) $\left(4 + \dfrac{4}{\sqrt{5}}\right) - i\left(1 + \dfrac{2}{\sqrt{5}}\right)$

(c) $\left(4 + \dfrac{4}{\sqrt{5}}\right) + i\left(1 - \dfrac{2}{\sqrt{5}}\right)$

(d) None of these

123. The complex number z for which $\left|\dfrac{z - 12}{z - 81}\right| = \dfrac{5}{3}$ and $\left|\dfrac{z - 4}{z - 8}\right| = 1$ is :

(a) $8 + 6i$ (b) $6 + 17i$

(c) $6 - 8i$ (d) $6 - 17i$

124. If z_1 and z_2 are complex numbers such that

$\text{Re } (z_1 + z_2) = 0$ and $\text{Im } (z_1 . z_2) = 0$ then :

(a) $z_1 = z_2$ (b) $z_1 = \bar{z}_2$

(c) $z_1 = -\bar{z}_2$ (d) None of these

125. If $z \neq 1$ and $\dfrac{z^2}{z - 1}$ is real, then the point represented by the complex number z lies :

[AIEEE - 2012]

(a) either on the real axis or on a circle passing through the origin

(b) on a circle with centre at the origin

(c) either on the real axis or on a circle not passing through the origin

(d) on the imaginary axis

126. Let α, β be real and z be a complex number. If $z^2 + az + \beta = 0$ has two distinct roots on the line $\text{Re } (z) = 1$, then it is necessary that :

[AIEEE - 2011]

(a) $\beta \in (1, \infty)$ (b) $\beta \in (0, 1)$

(c) $\beta \in (-1, 0)$ (d) $|\beta| = 1$

127. If $\omega (\neq 1)$ is a cube root of unity, and $(1 + \omega)^7 = A + B\omega$. Then (A, B) equals :   **[AIEEE - 2011]**

(a) $(-1, 1)$ (b) $(0, 1)$

(c) $(1, 1)$ (d) $(1, 0)$

128. If α and β are the roots of the equation $x^2 - x + 1 = 0$, then $\alpha^{2009} + \beta^{2009} =$

[AIEEE - 2010]

(a) –1   (b) 1

(c) 2   (d) –2

129. The number of complex numbers z such that

$|z - 1| = |z + 1| = |z - i|$ equals : **[AIEEE - 2010]**

(a) 1   (b) 2

(c) ∞ (d) 0

130. If $\left|z - \dfrac{4}{z}\right| = 2$, then the maximum value of $|z|$ is equal to: **[AIEEE - 2009]**

(a) $\sqrt{3} + 1$ (b) $\sqrt{5} + 1$

(c) 2   (d) $2 + \sqrt{2}$

131. The conjugate of complex number is $\dfrac{-1}{1 - i}$. Then the complex number is :   **[AIEEE - 2008]**

(a) $\dfrac{-1}{i - 1}$ (b) $\dfrac{1}{i - 1}$

(c) $\dfrac{-1}{i + 1}$ (d) $\dfrac{1}{i - 1}$

132. If $|z + 4| \leq 3$, then the maximum value of $|z + 1|$ is :   **[AIEEE - 2007]**

(a) 4   (b) 10

(c) 6   (d) 0

133. The value of $\sum_{k=1}^{10} \left(\sin\dfrac{2k\pi}{11} + i\cos\dfrac{2k\pi}{11}\right)$ is :

(a) i   (b) 1   **[AIEEE - 2006]**

(c) −1   (d) −i

134. If the cube roots of unity are 1, ω, ω^2, then the roots of the equation $(x - 1)^3 + 8 = 0$, are

[AIEEE - 2005]

(a) $-1, -1 + 2\omega, -1 - 2\omega^2$

(b) $-1, -1, -1$

(c) $-1, 1 - 2\omega, 1 - 2\omega^2$

(d) $-1, 1 + 2\omega, 1 + 2\omega^2$

135. If z_1 and z_2 are two non-zero complex numbers such that $|z_1 + z_2| = |z_1| + |z_2|$, then arg z_1 − arg z_2 is equal to :

(a) $\dfrac{\pi}{2}$ (b) $-\pi$

(c) 0   (d) $-\dfrac{\pi}{2}$ **[AIEEE - 2005]**

136. If $\omega = \dfrac{z}{z - \dfrac{1}{3}i}$ and $|\omega| = 1$, then z lies on :

[AIEEE - 2005]

(a) an ellipse   (a) a circle

(c) a straight line   (d) a parabola

137. If z is a complex number of unit modulus and argument θ, then argument $\left(\dfrac{1 + z}{1 + \bar{z}}\right)$ equals

(a) $\pi - \theta$ (b) $-\theta$

(c) $\dfrac{\pi}{2} - \theta$ (d) θ

138. Let $z = x + yi$ be a complex number where x and y are integers. Then area of the rectangle whose vertices are roots of the equation $z\bar{z}^3 + \bar{z}z^3 = 350$ is

(a) 48   (b) 32

(c) 40   (d) 80

ANSWER KEY

1. (c)	2. (b)	3. (c)	4. (d)	5. (b)	6. (c)	7. (c)	8. (a)	9. (c)	10. (d)
11. (b)	12. (d)	13. (a)	14. (d)	15. (a)	16. (b)	17. (c)	18. (d)	19. (a)	20. (b)
21. (b)	22. (d)	23. (a)	24. (c)	25. (d)	26. (a)	27. (a)	28. (d)	29. (a)	30. (c)
31. (b)	32. (d)	33. (c)	34. (b)	35. (a)	36. (b)	37. (b)	38. (c)	39. (c)	40. (a)
41. (c)	42. (a)	43. (d)	44. (a)	45. (d)	46. (b)	47. (c)	48. (a)	49. (c)	50. (c)
51. (b)	52. (b)	53. (b)	54. (a)	55. (d)	56. (a)	57. (c)	58. (a)	59. (b)	60. (d)
61. (c)	62. (c)	63. (c)	64. (d)	65. (a)	66. (d)	67. (b)	68. (c)	69. (b)	70. (a)
71. (c)	72. (c)	73. (c)	74. (b)	75. (b)	76. (c)	77. (a)	78. (a)	79. (b)	80. (b)
81. (d)	82. (c)	83. (c)	84. (c)	85. (a)	86. (c)	87. (a)	88. (a)	89. (c)	90. (c)
91. (b)	92. (a)	93. (d)	94. (c)	95. (a)	96. (d)	97. (c)	98. (c)	99. (c)	100. (d)
101. (a)	102. (c)	103. (b)	104. (c)	105. (a)	106. (a)	107. (b)	108. (b)	109. (d)	110. (b)
111. (c)	112. (b)	113. (a)	114. (b)	115. (a)	116. (d)	117. (d)	118. (b)	119. (b)	120. (d)
121. (a)	122. (c)	123. (b)	124. (c)	125. (a)	126. (a)	127. (c)	128. (b)	129. (a)	130. (b)
131. (c)	132. (c)	133. (d)	134. (c)	135. (c)	136. (c)	137. (d)	138. (a)		

SEQUENCES AND SERIES

MULTIPLE CHOICE QUESTIONS

1. The number of numbers lying between 100 and 500 that are divisible by 7, but not by 21 is :

   (a) 57
   (b) 19
   (c) 38
   (d) None of these.

2. In the following two A.P.s, 2, 5, 8, 11, ... to 60 terms and 3, 5, 7, 9, ... to 50 terms, the number of terms that are identical is :

   (a) 17
   (b) 15
   (c) 19
   (d) None of these.

3. In the series 3, 7, 11, 15, ... and 2, 5, 8, ... each continued to 100 terms, the number of terms that are identical is :

   (a) 21
   (b) 27
   (c) 25
   (d) None of these.

4. If a_1, a_2, a_3, ..., a_n are in A.P., where $a_i > 0$ for all i, then:

   $$\frac{1}{\sqrt{a_1} + \sqrt{a_2}} + \frac{1}{\sqrt{a_2} + \sqrt{a_3}} + ... + \frac{1}{\sqrt{a_{n-1}} + \sqrt{a_n}} =$$

   (a) $\dfrac{n-1}{\sqrt{a_1} + \sqrt{a_n}}$
   (b) $\dfrac{n-3}{\sqrt{a_1} + \sqrt{a_n}}$
   (c) $\dfrac{n}{\sqrt{a_1} + \sqrt{a_n}}$
   (d) None of these.

5. If a, b, c are the pth, q^{th} and r^{th} terms respectively of an A.P., then $a(q-r) + b(r-p) + c(p-q) =$

   (a) a
   (b) 0
   (c) b
   (d) c.

6. The sum of first 24 terms of the A.P. $a_1, a_2, a_3, ...$ if it is known that $a_1 + a_5 + a_{10} + a_{15} + a_{20} + a_{24} = 225$, is :

   (a) 865
   (b) 900
   (c) 930
   (d) None of these.

7. If $a_1, a_2, a_3, ...$are in A.P. and

   $$a_1^2 - a_2^2 + a_3^2 - a_4^2 + ... + a_{2k-1}^2 - a_{2k}^2 = A(a_1^2 - a_{2k}^2),$$

   then A is equal to :

   (a) $\dfrac{k}{2k-1}$
   (b) $\dfrac{k}{2k+1}$
   (c) $\dfrac{k-1}{2k+1}$
   (d) None of these.

8. The maximum sum of the series

   $$20 + 19\frac{1}{3} + 18\frac{2}{3} + 18 + ... \text{ is :}$$

   (a) 310
   (b) 290
   (c) 320
   (d) None of these.

9. The sum of all natural numbers less than 200, that are divisible neither by 3 nor by 5, is :

   (a) 10730
   (b) 10732
   (c) 15375
   (d) None of these.

10. If the 12th term of an A.P. is -13 and the sum of the first four terms is 24, then the sum of first 10 terms is :

    (a) 20
    (b) 35
    (c) 0
    (d) None of these.

11. The sum of n terms of the sequence

    $\log a, \ \log ar, \log ar^2, ...$is :

    (a) $\dfrac{n}{2} \log a^2 r^{n-1}$
    (b) $n \log a^2 r^{n-1}$
    (c) $\dfrac{3n}{2} \log a^2 r^{n-1}$
    (d) None of these.

12. The interior angles of a polygon are in A.P. If the smallest angle is 120° and the common difference is 5, then the number of sides of the polygon is :

    (a) 16
    (b) 8
    (c) 9
    (d) None of these.

13. If $x^{18} = y^{21} = z^{28}$, then 3, $3 \log_y x$, $3 \log_z y$, $7 \log_x z$ are in:

    (a) A.P.
    (b) G.P.
    (c) H.P.
    (d) None of these.

14. The sum of all two digit numbers which when divided by 4, yield unity as remainder is :

    (a) 1100   (b) 1200

    (c) 1210   (d) None of these.

15. Let S_n denotes the sum of n terms of an A.P. whose first term is a. If the common difference $d = S_n - k S_{n-1} + S_{n-2}$ then k =

    (a) 1   (b) 2

    (c) 3   (d) None of these.

16. If S_1, S_2, S_3 are the sum of n, 2n, 3n terms of an A.P., then $3 (S_2 - S_1) =$

    (a) S_3 (b) $2S_3$

    (c) $4S_3$ (d) None of these.

17. The pth term of an A.P. is a and the qth term is b. If the sum of its (p + q) terms is

    $$k \left[a + b + \frac{a-b}{p-q} \right]$$ then k is equal to :

    (a) $\frac{p-q}{2}$ (b) $p - q$

    (c) $p + q$ (d) $\frac{p+q}{2}$

18. If the sum of first n terms of an A.P. (having first term a) is zero, then the sum of next m terms is :

    (a) $\frac{am (m+n)}{n-1}$ (b) $-\frac{am (m+n)}{n-1}$

    (c) $\frac{an (m+n)}{n-1}$ (d) None of these.

19. If $5^{1+x} + 5^{1-x}$, $\frac{a}{2}$ and $25^x + 25^{-x}$ are three consecutive terms of an A.P., then the values of a are given by :

    (a) $a \geq 12$ (b) $a > 12$

    (c) $a < 12$ (d) $a \leq 12$.

20. The sum of two numbers is $2\frac{1}{6}$. If an even number of arithmetic means are inserted between them and their sum exceeds their number by 1, then number of means inserted is :

    (a) 12   (b) 8

    (c) 6   (d) None of these.

21. In an A.P. of even number of terms, the sum of the odd terms is 24, while that of even terms is 30. If the last term exceeds the first by 10.5, then the number of terms is :

    (a) 8   (b) 6

    (c) 10   (d) None of these.

22. If there are (2n + 1) terms in A.P., then the ratio of the sum of odd terms and the sum of even terms is :

    (a) n : (n + 1)   (b) (n + 1) : n

    (c) (n – 1) : n   (d) None of these.

23. If the ratio of the sum of n terms of two A.P.s is (3n – 13) : (5n + 21), then the ratio of 24th terms of the two progressions is :

    (a) 2 : 3   (b) 2 : 1

    (c) 1 : 2   (d) none of these.

24. If S_1, S_2, S_3, ..., S_p are the sums, each of n terms of p A.P.s whose first terms are 1, 2, 3, ...and common differences are 1, 3, 5, 7, ... respectively, then $S_1 + S_2 + S_3 + ... + S_p =$

    (a) $\frac{np (np + 1)}{2}$ (b) $\frac{np (np - 1)}{2}$

    (c) $\frac{3np (np + 1)}{2}$ (d) None of these.

25. If the series of natural numbers is divided into groups (1); (2, 3, 4); (5, 6, 7, 8, 9); ... and so on, then the sum of the numbers in the nth group is:

    (a) $n^3 + (n + 1)^3$ (b) $n^2 + (n + 1)^2$

    (c) $(n - 1)^2 + n^2$ (d) $(n - 1)^3 + n^3$.

26. If a is the first term, d the common difference and S_k the sum of k terms of an A.P., then for $\frac{S_{kx}}{S_k}$ to be independent of x :

    (a) a = 2d   (b) a = d

    (c) 2a = d   (d) None of these.

27. Let a_1, a_2, a_3, ..., a_n be in A.P.

    If $\frac{1}{a_1 a_n} + \frac{1}{a_2 a_{n-1}} + ... + \frac{1}{a_n a_1}$

    $= \frac{k}{a_1 + a_n} \left(\frac{1}{a_1} + \frac{1}{a_2} + ... + \frac{1}{a_n} \right)$, then k is equal to :

    (a) 1   (b) 2

    (c) 3   (d) None of these.

28. The digits of a positive integer having three digits are in A.P. and their sum is 15. If the number obtained by reversing the digits is 594 less than the original number, then the number is

(a) 352   (b) 652

(c) 852   (d) None of these.

29. If a, b, c are three consecutive terms of an A.P., then k^a, k^b, k^c are three consecutive terms of :

(a) an A.P.   (b) a G.P.

(c) an H.P.   (d) None of these.

30. If p^{th}, q^{th} and r^{th} terms of a G.P. are themselves in G.P., then p, q, r are in :

(a) A.P.   (b) G.P.

(c) H.P.   (d) None of these.

31. If $\dfrac{1}{x+y}, \dfrac{1}{2y}, \dfrac{1}{y+z}$ are the three consecutive terms of an A.P., then x, y, z are the three consecutive terms of:

(a) an A.P.   (b) a G.P.

(c) an H.P.   (d) None of these.

32. If the common ratio, the last term and the sum of a G.P. are 3, 486 and 728 respectively, then the first term and the number of terms are :

(a) 2, 5   (b) 3, 6

(c) 2, 6   (d) None of these.

33. If the sum of the n terms of a G.P. is S, their product is P and the sum of their reciprocals is R, then $\left(\dfrac{S}{R}\right)^n =$

(a) P   (b) P^2

(c) $2P^2$ (d) None of these.

34. The sum of 50 terms of the sequence

7, 7.7, 7.77, 7.777, ...is :

(a) $\dfrac{8}{81}\left\{4490 + \dfrac{1}{10^{49}}\right\}$ (b) $\dfrac{7}{81}\left\{4490 + \dfrac{1}{10^{49}}\right\}$

(c) $\dfrac{5}{81}\left\{4490 + \dfrac{1}{10^{49}}\right\}$ (d) none of these.

35. Sum of the series $(1 + x) + (1 + x + x^2) + (1 + x + x^2 + x^3) + ...$ upto n terms is :

(a) $\dfrac{1}{1-x}\left[n - \dfrac{x^2(1-x^n)}{1-x}\right]$

(b) $\dfrac{1}{1-x}\left[n - \dfrac{x^3(1-x^n)}{1-x}\right]$

(c) $\dfrac{1}{1-x}\left[n - \dfrac{x(1-x^n)}{1-x}\right]$

(d) None of these.

36. The sum of an infinite G.P., whose first term is 28 and fourth term is $\dfrac{4}{49}$, is :

(a) $\dfrac{98}{3}$ (b) $\dfrac{49}{3}$

(c) $\dfrac{78}{3}$ (d) None of these.

37. The product $9^{1/3} \cdot 9^{1/9} \cdot 9^{1/27} ...$ to infinity is :

(a) 9   (b) 3

(c) 81   (d) None of these.

38. Let a be the first term and b be the nth term of a G.P. If P is the product of n terms, then $P^2 =$

(a) ab   (b) $(ab)^n$

(c) $(ab)^{n/2}$ (d) None of these.

39. If every even term of a series is a times the term before it and every odd term is c times the term before it, the first term being unity, then the sum of 2n terms of the series is :

(a) $\dfrac{(1-a)(1-c^n a^n)}{1-ca}$

(b) $\dfrac{(1+a)(1-c^{n-1} a^{n-1})}{1-ca}$

(c) $\dfrac{(1-a)(1-c^{n-2} a^{n-2})}{1-ca}$

(d) None of these.

40. If $a_1, a_2, a_3, ...$ are in A.P. such that $a_i \neq 0$ and

$S = \dfrac{1}{a_1 a_2} + \dfrac{1}{a_2 a_3} + ... + \dfrac{1}{a_n a_{n+1}}$ then $\displaystyle\lim_{n\to\infty} S =$

(a) $\dfrac{1}{a_1 (a_2 - a_1)}$ (b) $\dfrac{1}{a_2 (a_2 - a_1)}$

(c) $\dfrac{1}{a_1 (a_1 + a_2)}$ (d) $\dfrac{1}{a_2 (a_1 + a_2)}$

41. If $S_1, S_2, S_3, ... S_p$ are the sums of the infinite geometric series whose first terms are 1, 2, 3, ..., p and whose common ratios are $\frac{1}{2}, \frac{1}{3}, \frac{1}{4}, ... , \frac{1}{p+1}$ respectively, then $S_1 + S_2 + S_3 ... + S_p =$

(a) $\frac{p(p+1)}{2}$

(b) $\frac{p(p+2)}{2}$

(c) $\frac{p(p+3)}{2}$

(d) None of these.

42. The sum to infinity of the series $1 + (1 + a) r + (1 + a + a^2) r^2 + ...$ where $0 < a < 1$ and $0 < r < 1$ is :

(a) $\frac{1}{(1-r)(1-ar)}$

(b) $\frac{1}{(1+r)(1-ar)}$

(c) $\frac{1}{(1-r)(1+ar)}$

(d) None of these.

43. Representation of the decimal $24.28\overline{137}$ as a common fraction is :

(a) $\frac{2425609}{99900}$

(b) $\frac{2325709}{99900}$

(c) $\frac{2425709}{99900}$

(d) None of these.

44. The sum to n terms of the series $\frac{1}{2} + \frac{3}{4} + \frac{7}{8} + \frac{15}{16} + ...$ is given by :

(a) $2^n - 1$

(b) $2^n - n - 1$

(c) $2^{-n} + n - 1$

(d) $1 - 2^{-n}$.

45. If two geometric means g_1 and g_2 and one arithmetic mean A are inserted between two numbers, then : $\frac{g_1^2}{g_2} + \frac{g_2^2}{g_1} =$

(a) 4A

(b) 3A

(c) 2A

(d) A.

46. If, in a G.P. of 3n terms, S_1 denotes the sum of the first n terms, S_2 the sum of the second block of n terms and S_3 the sum of the last n terms, then S_1, S_2, S_3 are in :

(a) A.P.

(b) G.P.

(c) H.P.

(d) None of these.

47. If $a^{1/x} = b^{1/y} = c^{1/z}$ and a, b, c are in G.P., then x, y, z are in :

(a) A.P.

(b) G.P.

(c) H.P.

(d) None of these.

48. If H is the harmonic mean between a and b, then $\frac{H+a}{H-a} + \frac{H+b}{H-b} =$

(a) 1

(b) 2

(c) − 1

(d) − 2.

49. If a, b, c are in A.P., p, q, r are in H.P. and ap, bq, cr are in G.P., then :

(a) $\frac{p}{r} + \frac{r}{p} = \frac{c}{a} + \frac{a}{c}$

(b) $\frac{p}{q} + \frac{q}{p} = \frac{c}{a} + \frac{a}{c}$

(c) $\frac{p}{r} + \frac{r}{p} = \frac{b}{c} + \frac{c}{b}$

(d) None of these.

50. If $x_1, x_2, x_3, .., x_n$ are in H.P. then $x_1 x_2 + x_2 x_3 + ... + x_{n-1} x_n$ is equal to :

(a) $nx_1 x_n$

(b) $(n-1) x_1 x_n$

(c) $(n-2) x_1 x_n$

(d) None of these.

51. If roots of the equation $x^3 - 12x^2 + 39x - 28 = 0$ are in A.P., then their common difference is :

(a) ± 1

(b) ± 2

(c) ± 3

(d) ± 4

52. If a, b, c are in H.P. then $\frac{a}{b+c}, \frac{b}{c+a}, \frac{c}{a+b}$ are in :

(a) A.P.

(b) G.P.

(c) H.P.

(d) None of these.

53. Let a_n be the nth term of the G.P. of positive numbers. Let $\sum_{n=1}^{100} a_{2n} = \alpha$ and $\sum_{n=1}^{100} a_{2n-1} = \beta$, such that $\alpha \neq \beta$, then the common ratio is :

(a) $\frac{\alpha}{\beta}$

(b) $\frac{\beta}{\alpha}$

(c) $\sqrt{\frac{\alpha}{\beta}}$

(d) $\sqrt{\frac{\beta}{\alpha}}$

54. If three positive numbers a, b, c are in H.P., then $a^n + c^n$:

(a) $> 2b^n$

(b) $= 2b^n$

(c) $< 2b^n$

(d) $> b^n$.

55. If x, 2x + 2, 3x + 3, ...are in G.P., then the fourth term is:

(a) 27   (b) – 27

(c) 13.5   (d) – 13.5

56. If the A.M. and G.M. of the roots of a quadratic equation in x are p and q respectively, then its equation is :

(a) $x^2 – 2px + q^2 = 0$ (b) $x^2 + 2px + q^2 = 0$

(c) $x^2 – px + q = 0$ (d) $x^2 – 2px + q = 0$.

57. $2^{1/4} \cdot 4^{1/8} \cdot 8^{1/16} \cdot 16^{1/32}$ ... is equal to :

(a) 1   (b) 2

(c) $\dfrac{3}{2}$ (d) $\dfrac{5}{2}$

58. The value of x in $(-\pi, \pi)$ which satisfies the equation $8^{(1 + |\cos x| + |\cos^2 x| + |\cos^3 x| + ... \infty)} = 4^3$ is :

(a) $\dfrac{\pi}{3}$ (b) $-\dfrac{\pi}{3}$

(c) $\dfrac{2\pi}{3}$ (d) All of these.

59. $\log_3 2$, $\log_6 2$, $\log_{12} 2$ are in :

(a) A.P.   (b) G.P.

(c) H.P.   (d) None of these.

60. The sum of first n terms of the series

$\dfrac{1}{2} + \dfrac{3}{4} + \dfrac{7}{8} + \dfrac{15}{16} + ...$ is :

(a) $2^n – 1$ (b) $1 – 2^{-n}$

(c) $2^{-n} – n + 1$ (d) $2^{-n} + n – 1$.

61. If a, b, c, d are four unequal positive numbers in H.P. then :

(a) $a + d > b + c$ (b) $a + c > b + d$

(c) $b + c > a + d$ (d) None of these.

62. If x > 1, y > 1, z > 1 are in G.P., then

$\dfrac{1}{1 + \ln x}, \dfrac{1}{1 + \ln y}, \dfrac{1}{1 + \ln z}$ are in :

(a) A. P.   (b) G. P.

(c) H. P.   (d) None of these.

63. If x, 1, z are in A.P. and x, 2, z are in G.P. then x, 4, z are in :

(a) A.P.   (b) G.P.

(c) H.P.   (d) None of these.

64. If a, b, c are in G.P., then the equation $ax^2 + 2bx + c = 0$ and $dx^2 + 2 ex + f = 0$ have a common root, if $\dfrac{d}{a}, \dfrac{e}{b}$ and $\dfrac{f}{c}$ are in :

(a) A. P.   (b) G. P.

(c) H. P.   (d) None of these.

65. If the sum to infinity of the series

$3 + 5r + 7r^2 + ...$ is $\dfrac{49}{9}$, then r is equal to :

(a) $\dfrac{1}{4}$ (b) $\dfrac{1}{3}$

(c) $\dfrac{1}{2}$ (d) None of these.

66. Sum upto 16 terms of the series

$\dfrac{1^3}{1} + \dfrac{1^3 + 2^3}{1 + 3} + \dfrac{1^3 + 2^3 + 3^3}{1 + 3 + 5} + ...$ is :

(a) 450   (b) 456

(c) 446   (d) None of these.

67. Sum to 20 terms of the series $1.3^2 + 2.5^2 + 3.7^2 +$ ... is :

(a) 178090   (b) 168090

(c) 188090   (d) None of these.

68. Sum to n terms of the series $2 + 5 + 14 + 41 + ...$ is :

(a) $\dfrac{n}{2} + \dfrac{1}{4}(3^n – 1)$ (b) $\dfrac{n}{2} + \dfrac{3}{4}(3^n – 1)$

(c) $\dfrac{n}{2} + \dfrac{1}{2}(3^n – 1)$ (d) None of these.

69. Sum to infinity of the series

$1 + 2^2x + 3^2x^2 + 4^2x^3 + ...$ to ∞, $|x| < 1$ is :

(a) $\dfrac{1 + x}{(1 – x)^3}$ (b) $\dfrac{1 – x}{(1 + x)^3}$

(c) $\dfrac{2 + x}{(1 – x)^3}$ (d) None of these.

70. If $\dfrac{b + c – 2a}{a}, \dfrac{c + a – 2b}{b}, \dfrac{a + b – 2c}{c}$ are in A.P., then a, b, c are in :

(a) A.P.   (b) G.P.

(c) H.P.   (d) None of these.

71. If the sides of a right angled triangle are in G.P., then the cosine of the greater acute angle is :

(a) $\dfrac{1}{1+\sqrt{5}}$

(b) $\dfrac{1}{1-\sqrt{5}}$

(c) $\dfrac{1+\sqrt{5}}{2}$

(d) none of these.

72. The coefficients of x^{99} and x^{98} in the polynomial

$(x-1)(x-2)(x-3)...(x-100)$ are :

(a) -5050 and 12482075

(b) -4050 and 12582075

(c) -5050 and 12582075

(d) None of these.

73. The sum upto n terms of the series

$\dfrac{1}{1+1^2+1^4}+\dfrac{2}{1+2^2+2^4}+\dfrac{3}{1+3^2+3^4}+\,......$ is :

(a) $\dfrac{n(n+1)}{2(n^2+n+1)}$

(b) $\dfrac{n(n+1)}{3(n^2+n+1)}$

(c) $\dfrac{n(n+1)}{n^2+n+1}$

(d) None of these.

74. If $a+b+c=3$ and $a>0, b>0, c>0$, then the greatest value of $a^2b^3c^2$ is :

(a) $\dfrac{3^{10}\cdot 2^4}{7^7}$

(b) $\dfrac{3^9\cdot 2^4}{7^7}$

(c) $\dfrac{3^8\cdot 2^4}{7^7}$

(d) None of these.

75. The largest term of the sequence

$\dfrac{1}{503},\dfrac{4}{524},\dfrac{9}{581},\dfrac{16}{692},\,...$ is :

(a) $\dfrac{16}{692}$

(b) $\dfrac{4}{524}$

(c) $\dfrac{49}{1529}$

(d) None of these.

76. The consecutive numbers of a three digit number form a G.P. If we subtract 792 from this number, we get a number consisting of the same digits written in the reverse order and if we increase the second digit of the required number by 2, the resulting digits form an A.P. The number is :

(a) 139

(b) 193

(c) 931

(d) None of these.

77. If a, b, c are digits, then the rational number represented by $0\cdot cababab\,...$ is :

(a) $\dfrac{99c+ab}{990}$

(b) $\dfrac{99c+10a+b}{99}$

(c) $\dfrac{99c+10a+b}{990}$

(d) None of these.

78. If $\Sigma\, n = 210$, then $\Sigma\, n^2 =$

(a) 2870

(b) 2160

(c) 2970

(d) None of these.

79. If $a_1, a_2, a_3, ..., a_n$ are in H.P., then

$\dfrac{a_1}{a_2+a_3+...+a_n},\ \dfrac{a_2}{a_1+a_3+...+a_n},\ ......$

$\dfrac{a_n}{a_1+a_2+...+a_{n-1}}$ are in :

(a) A.P.

(b) G.P.

(c) H.P.

(d) None of these.

80. If $a_1=0$ and $a_1, a_2, a_3, ..., a_n$ are real numbers such that $|a_i|=|a_{i-1}+1|$ for all i, then the A.M. of the numbers $a_1, a_2, ..., a_n$ has value x where :

(a) $x \le -\dfrac{1}{2}$

(b) $x \ge -\dfrac{1}{2}$

(c) $x < -\dfrac{1}{2}$

(d) None of these.

81. If a, $a_1, a_2, a_3, ..., a_{2n}$, b are in A.P. and a, $g_1, g_2, ..., g_{2n}$, b are in G.P. and h is the H.M. of a and b,

then $\dfrac{a_1+a_{2n}}{g_1g_{2n}}+\dfrac{a_2+a_{2n-1}}{g_2g_{2n-1}}+...+\dfrac{a_n+a_{n+1}}{g_ng_{n+1}}$ is equal to :

(a) $2nh$

(b) $\dfrac{n}{h}$

(c) nh

(d) $\dfrac{2n}{h}$

82. If 0.272727..., x and 0.727272...are in H.P., then x must be :

(a) rational

(b) integer

(c) irrational

(d) None of these.

83. $\displaystyle\sum_{i=1}^{n}\sum_{j=1}^{i}\sum_{k=1}^{j} 1 =$

(a) $\dfrac{n(n+1)(2n+1)}{6}$

(b) $\dfrac{n(n+1)}{2}$

(c) $\left(\dfrac{n(n+1)}{2}\right)^2$

(d) $\dfrac{n(n+1)(n+2)}{6}$

84. If $T_n = n \times (n!)$, then $\sum\limits_{n=1}^{20} T_n$ is equal to :

    (a) $(21)! - 1$ (b) $(20)! - 1$

    (c) $(21)! + 1$ (d) None of these.

85. The sum of the products of the 2n numbers
    $\pm 1, \pm 2, \pm 3, ..., \pm n$ taking two at a time is :

    (a) $-\dfrac{n(n+1)}{2}$ (b) $\dfrac{n(n+1)(2n+1)}{6}$

    (c) $-\dfrac{n(n+1)(2n+1)}{6}$ (d) None of these.

86. The coefficient of x^n in the product
    $(1-x)(1-2x)(1-2^2 \cdot x)(1-2^3 \cdot x) ....$
    $(1-2^n \cdot x)$ is equal to :

    (a) $(1-2^{n+1}) \cdot 2^{\frac{n(n-1)}{2}}$

    (b) $(2^{n+1}-1) \cdot 2^{\frac{n(n-1)}{2}}$

    (c) $(1-2^n) \cdot 2^{\frac{n(n-1)}{2}}$

    (d) None of these.

87. The largest value of the positive integer k for which $n^k + 1$ divides $1 + n + n^2 + ... + n^{127}$ is divisible by :

    (a) 8 (b) 16

    (c) 32 (d) 64

88. $\lim\limits_{n \to \infty} (1 + 3^{-1})(1 + 3^{-2})(1 + 3^{-4})(1 + 3^{-8}) ......$
    $(1 + 3^{-2^n})$ is equal to :

    (a) 1 (b) $\dfrac{1}{2}$

    (c) $\dfrac{3}{2}$ (d) None of these.

89. If x_1, x_2, x_3 as well as y_1, y_2, y_3 are in G.P. with the same common ratio, then the points (x_1, y_1), (x_2, y_2) and (x_3, y_3) :

    (a) lie on a straight line

    (b) lie on an ellipse

    (c) lie on a circle

    (d) are vertices of a triangle.

90. For a positive integer n,
    let $a(n) = 1 + \dfrac{1}{2} + \dfrac{1}{3} + \dfrac{1}{4} + ... + \dfrac{1}{(2^n) - 1}$. Then

    (a) $a(100) \le 100$ (b) $a(100) > 100$

    (c) $a(200) \le 100$ (d) $a(200) > 100$.

91. The real numbers x_1, x_2, x_3 satisfying the equation $x^3 - x^2 + \beta x + \gamma = 0$ are in A.P. The intervals in which β and γ lie are :

    (a) $\left(-\infty, \dfrac{1}{3}\right], \left[-\dfrac{1}{27}, \infty\right)$

    (b) $\left(-8, \dfrac{1}{3}\right), \left[-\dfrac{1}{27}, \infty\right)$

    (c) $\left(-\infty, \dfrac{1}{3}\right], \left(-\dfrac{1}{27}, \infty\right)$

    (d) None of these.

92. The determinant
    $$\begin{vmatrix} xp+y & x & y \\ yp+z & y & z \\ 0 & xp+y & yp+z \end{vmatrix} = 0 \text{ if :}$$

    (a) x, y, z are in A.P. (b) x, y, z are in G.P.

    (c) x, y, z are in H.P. (d) xy, yz, zx are in A.P.

93. Let x be the arithmetic mean and y, z be two geometric means between any two positive numbers. Then $\dfrac{y^3 + z^3}{xyz} =$

    (a) 2 (b) 1

    (c) 3 (d) 4.

94. Let T_r be the rth term of an A.P., for r = 1, 2, 3, ... If for some positive integers m, n we have $T_m = \dfrac{1}{n}$ and $T_n = \dfrac{1}{m}$. Then T_{mn} equals :

    (a) $\dfrac{1}{mn}$ (b) $\dfrac{1}{m} + \dfrac{1}{n}$

    (c) 1 (d) 0.

95. H.M. between the roots of the equation $x^2 - 10x + 11 = 0$ is :

    (a) $\dfrac{1}{5}$ (b) $\dfrac{5}{21}$

    (c) $\dfrac{21}{20}$ (d) $\dfrac{11}{5}$

96. If A.M. of a and b is $\dfrac{a^{n+1}+b^{n+1}}{a^n+b^n}$ then n =

(a) -1 (b) 2

(c) 1   (d) 0.

97. If the ratio of the sums of m and n terms of an A.P. is $m^2 : n^2$, then the ratio of its mth and n^{th} terms is :

(a) $m-1:n-1$ (b) $2m+1:2n+1$

(c) $2m-1:2n-1$ (d) None of these.

98. If the sum of the first n terms of a series is $5n^2 + 2n$, then its second term is :

(a) 7   (b) 17

(c) 24   (d) 42

99. If the 7th term of an H.P. is 8 and 8th term is 7, then its 15th term is :

(a) 16   (b) 14

(c) $\dfrac{27}{14}$ (d) $\dfrac{56}{15}$

100. If the 7th term of an H.P. is $\dfrac{1}{10}$ and the 12th term is $\dfrac{1}{25}$, then the 20th term is :

(a) $\dfrac{1}{37}$ (b) $\dfrac{1}{41}$

(c) $\dfrac{1}{45}$ (d) $\dfrac{1}{49}$

101. If log 2, log $(2^x - 1)$ and log $(2^x + 3)$ are in A.P. then x =

(a) $\dfrac{5}{2}$ (b) $\log_2 5$

(c) $\log_3 2$ (d) $\dfrac{3}{2}$

102. Let the harmonic mean and the geometric mean of two positive numbers be in the ratio 4 : 5. The two numbers are in the ratio :

(a) $1:1$ (b) $2:1$

(c) $3:1$ (d) $4:1$

103. The product of n positive numbers is unity, their sum is :

(a) a positive integer   (b) equal to $\dfrac{n+1}{n}$

(c) divisible by n   (d) never less than n.

104. In an A.P. of 81 terms, the 41th term is 10. Then the sum of series is :

(a) 10×41 (b) $\dfrac{10 \times 41}{2}$

(c) 10×81 (d) 41×81.

105. If a, b, c are in G.P.; then the equations $ax^2 + 2bx + c = 0$ and $dx^2 + 2ex + f = 0$ have a common root if $\dfrac{d}{a}, \dfrac{e}{b}, \dfrac{f}{c}$ are in :

(a) G.P.   (b) A.P.

(c) H.P.   (d) None of these.

106. Every term of a G.P. is positive and also every term is the sum of two preceding terms. Then the common ratio of the G.P. is :

(a) $\dfrac{1-\sqrt{5}}{2}$ (b) $\dfrac{\sqrt{5}+1}{2}$

(c) $\dfrac{\sqrt{5}-1}{2}$ (d) 1.

107. If $A = 1 + r^a + r^{2a} + r^{3a} + ... \infty$ and $B = 1 + r^b + r^{2b} + r^{3b} + ... \infty$, then $\dfrac{a}{b}$ is equal to :

(a) $\log_B A$ (b) $\log_{1-B}(1-A)$

(c) $\log_{\frac{B-1}{B}}\left(\dfrac{A-1}{A}\right)$ (d) None of these.

108. The 9th term of an A.P. is 499 and 499th term is 9. The term which is equal to zero is :

(a) 501th (b) 502th

(c) 508th (d) None of these.

109. cos x = b. For what b do the roots of the equation form an A.P. ?

(a) $\dfrac{\sqrt{3}}{2}$ (b) $\dfrac{1}{2}$

(c) -1 (d) None of these.

110. The sum of first n terms of the series $1^2 + 2.2^2 + 3^2 + 2.4^2 + 5^2 + 5.6^2 + ...$ is $\dfrac{n(n+1)^2}{2}$ when n is even. When n is odd, the sum is :

(a) $\dfrac{n^2(n+1)}{2}$ (b) $\dfrac{n(n+1)^2}{2}$

(c) $\left[\dfrac{n(n+1)}{2}\right]^2$ (d) $\dfrac{n(n+1)}{2}$

111. If $\dfrac{a+b}{1-ab}$, b, $\dfrac{b+c}{1-bc}$ are in A.P., then a, $\dfrac{1}{b}$, c are in :

    (a) H.P. (b) A.P.

    (c) G.P. (d) None of these.

112. The sum of the series $\sqrt{2}+\sqrt{6}+\sqrt{18}+\ldots$ is

    (a) $242(\sqrt{3}-1)$ (b) $\dfrac{121}{\sqrt{3}-1}$

    (c) $243(\sqrt{3}+1)$ (d) $121(\sqrt{6}+\sqrt{2})$

113. The next term of the sequence 1, 5, 14, 30, 55, ... is :

    (a) 91 (b) 85

    (c) 90 (d) 95.

114. The sum of the squares of three distinct real numbers which are in G.P. is s^2. If their sum is αs, then

    (a) $\dfrac{1}{3}<\alpha^2<1$ (b) $\dfrac{1}{3}<\alpha<1$

    (c) $\dfrac{1}{3}\le\alpha^2\le 3$ (d) $1<\alpha<3$

115. A person purchases one kg of tomatoes from each of the 4 places at the rate of 1 kg, 2 kg, 3 kg and 4 kg per rupee respectively. On the average he has purchased x kg of tomatoes per rupee, then the value of x is :

    (a) 2 (b) 2.5

    (c) 1.92 (d) None of these.

116. The sum of the series

    $1+2\cdot 2+3\cdot 2^2+4\cdot 2^3+5\cdot 2^4+\ldots+100\cdot 2^{99}$ is :

    (a) $99\cdot 2^{100}+1$ (b) $100\cdot 2^{100}$

    (c) $99\cdot 2^{100}$ (d) $99\cdot 2^{100}+1$.

117. If $b+c$, $c+a$, $a+b$ are in H.P., then a^2, b^2, c^2 will be in :

    (a) G.P. (b) H.P.

    (c) A.P. (d) None of these.

118. If the A.M. of the root of a quadratic equation is $\dfrac{8}{5}$ and A.M. of their reciprocals is $\dfrac{8}{7}$, then the quadratic equation is :

    (a) $5x^2-8x+7=0$ (b) $5x^2-16x+7=0$

    (c) $7x^2-16x+5=0$ (d) $7x^2+16x+5=0$

119. The number of terms common to two A.P.s 3, 7, 11, ..., 407 and 2, 9, 16, ..., 709 is :

    (a) 21 (b) 28

    (c) 14 (d) None of these.

120. Sum of all terms of a G.P. is 5 times the sum of odd terms. The common ratio is :

    (a) 5 (b) 4

    (c) 3 (d) 2.

121. If a, b, c are in A.P., a, mb, c are in G.P. then a, m^2b, c are in :

    (a) H.P. (b) G.P.

    (c) A.P. (d) None of these.

122. If $\log_3 2$, $\log_3(2^x-5)$ and $\log_3\left(2^x-\dfrac{7}{2}\right)$ are in A.P., then the value of x is :

    (a) 3 (b) 2

    (c) 4 (d) 5

123. If a, b, c are in A.P., then 3^a, 3^b, 3^c are in :

    (a) G.P. (b) H.P.

    (c) A.P. (d) None of these.

124. The product $(32)\,(32)^{1/6}\,(32)^{1/36}\,\ldots\ldots\,\infty$ is equal to :

    (a) 64 (b) 16

    (c) 32 (d) 0.

125. If each term of a G.P. is positive and each term is the sum of its two succeeding terms, then the common ratio of G.P., is :

    (a) $-\dfrac{(\sqrt{5}+1)}{2}$ (b) $\dfrac{1-\sqrt{5}}{2}$

    (c) $\dfrac{\sqrt{5}-1}{2}$ (d) $\dfrac{\sqrt{5}+1}{2}$

126. Given that α, γ are roots of the equation $Ax^2-4x+1=0$, and β, δ the roots of the equation $Bx^2-6x+1=0$, the values of A and B such that α, β, γ and δ are in H.P. are:

    (a) $A=3$, $B=8$ (b) $A=-3$, $B=8$

    (c) $A=3$, $B=-8$ (d) None of these.

127. a, b, c are the first three terms of a geometric series. If the harmonic mean of a and b is 12 and that of b and c is 36, then the first five terms of the series are :

(a) 9, 16, 27, 41, 58   (b) 8, 24, 72, 216, 648

(c) 4, 22, 38, 46   (d) None of these.

128. The sum of n terms of $1.2.3 + 2.3.4 + \ldots\ldots$ will be :

(a) $\dfrac{n\,(n+1)\,(n+2)\,(n+3)}{4}$

(b) $\dfrac{2n\,(n+1)\,(n+2)\,(n+3)}{3}$

(c) $\dfrac{(n+1)\,(n+2)\,(n+3)}{4}$

(d) $\dfrac{n\,(n-1)\,(n-2)\,(n-3)}{4}$

129. The sum of all the numbers of the form n^3 which lie between 100 and 10,000 is :

(a) 43261   (b) 53261

(c) 63261   (d) None of these.

130. The sum of an infinite geometric series is 2 and the sum of the geometric series made from the cubes of this infinite series is 24. Then the series is :

(a) $3 + \dfrac{3}{2} - \dfrac{3}{4} + \dfrac{3}{8} \ldots$

(b) $3 + \dfrac{3}{2} + \dfrac{3}{4} + \dfrac{3}{8} + \ldots$

(c) $3 - \dfrac{3}{2} + \dfrac{3}{4} - \dfrac{3}{8} + \ldots$

(d) None the these

131. a, b, c are three distinct real numbers and they are in a G.P. If $a + b + c = xb$ then :

(a) $x < -1$ or $x > 3$ (b) $x < -3$ or $x > 2$

(c) $x < -4$ or $x > 3$ (d) None of these.

132. The largest interval for which the series $1 + (x - 1) + (x - 1)^2 + \ldots$ to ∞ may be summed, is :

(a) $0 < x < 1$ (b) $0 < x < 2$

(c) $-1 < x < 1$ (d) $-2 < x < 2$.

133. If $(1.05)^{50} = 11.658$, then $\sum\limits_{n=1}^{49} (1.05)^n$ equals :

(a) 208.34   (b) 212.12

(c) 212.16   (d) 213.16.

134. If $\sum\limits_{n=1}^{\infty} a^{n-1} = x$, $\sum\limits_{n=1}^{\infty} b^{n-1} = y$, $a < 1$, $b < 1$, then $\sum\limits_{n=1}^{\infty} (ab)^{n-1}$ equals :

(a) xy   (b) $\dfrac{1}{1-xy}$

(c) $\dfrac{x+y-1}{xy}$ (d) $\dfrac{xy}{x+y-1}$

135. If p, q, r are the three positive real numbers in A.P., then the roots of the quadratic equation $px^2 + qx + r = 0$ are all real for :

(a) $\left|\left(\dfrac{r}{p}\right) - 7\right| \geq 4\sqrt{3}$ (b) $\left|\dfrac{p}{r} - 7\right| < 4\sqrt{3}$

(c) all p and r   (d) no p and r.

136. The sum to inifinity of the series,

$$1 + 2\left(1 - \dfrac{1}{n}\right) + 3\left(1 - \dfrac{1}{n}\right)^2 + \ldots \text{ is}$$

(a) n^2 (b) $n\,(n+1)$

(c) $n\left(1 + \dfrac{1}{n}\right)^2$ (d) None of these.

137. The cubes of the natural numbers are grouped as 1^3, $(2^3, 3^3)$, $(4^3, 5^3, 6^3)$ $\ldots\ldots$ then the sum of the numbers in the nth group is :

(a) $\dfrac{1}{8} n^3 (n^2 + 1)\,(n^2 + 3)$

(b) $\dfrac{1}{16} n^3 (n^2 + 16)\,(n^2 + 12)$

(c) $\dfrac{n^3}{12}\,(n^2 + 2)\,(n^2 + 4)$

(d) None of these.

138. Let a_1, a_2, a_3, … be in an A.P. with common difference not a multiple of 3. Then maximum number of consecutive terms so that all are primes is :

(a) 2   (b) 3

(c) 5   (d) infinite

139. If b_1, b_2, b_3 ($b_1 > 0$) are three successive terms of a G.P. with common ratio r, the value of r for which the inequality $b_3 > 4b_2 - 3b_1$ holds is given by :

(a) $r > 3$ (b) $r < 1$

(c) $r = 3.5$ (d) $r = 5.2$.

140. If $< a_n >$ and $< b_n >$ are two sequences given by $a_n = (x)^{1/2^n} + (y)^{1/2^n}$ and $b_n = (x)^{1/2^n} - (y)^{1/2^n}$ for all $n \in N$ then $a_1\, a_2\, a_3 ... a_n$ is :

(a) $\dfrac{x + y}{b_n}$ (b) $\dfrac{x - y}{b_n}$

(c) $\dfrac{x^2 + y^2}{b_n}$ (d) $\dfrac{x^2 - y^2}{b_n}$

141. If x, $|x + 1|$, $|x - 1|$ are first three terms of an A.P., its sum upto 20 terms is :

(a) 90 or 175   (b) 180 or 350

(c) 360 or 700   (d) 720 or 1400.

142. Let $\displaystyle\sum_{r=1}^{n} r^4 = f(n)$. Then $\displaystyle\sum_{r=1}^{n} (2r - 1)^4$ is equal to :

(a) $f(2n) - 16f(n)$ for all $n \in N$

(b) $f(n) - 16f\left(\dfrac{n-1}{2}\right)$ when n is odd

(c) $f(n) - 16f\left(\dfrac{n}{2}\right)$ when n is even

(d) None of these.

143. A_r ; $r = 1, 2, 3, ...n$ are n points on the parabola $y^2 = 4x$ in the first quadrant. If $A_r = (x_r, y_r)$, where $x_1, x_2, x_3, ... x_n$ are in G.P. and $x_1 = 1$, $x_2 = 2$, then y_n is equal to :

(a) $-2^{\frac{n+1}{2}}$ (b) 2^{n+1}

(c) $(\sqrt{2})^{n+1}$ (d) $2^{n/2}$

144. The sum of the series :

$\dfrac{1}{\log_2 4} + \dfrac{1}{\log_4 4} + \dfrac{1}{\log_8 4} + ... + \dfrac{1}{\log_{2^n} 4}$ is :

(a) $\dfrac{n(n+1)}{2}$ (b) $\dfrac{n(n+1)(2n+1)}{12}$

(c) $\dfrac{1}{n(n+1)}$ (d) $\dfrac{n(n+1)}{4}$

145. If S_r denotes the sum of the first r terms of an A.P., then $\dfrac{S_{3r} - S_{r-1}}{S_{2r} - S_{2r-1}}$ is equal to :

(a) $2r - 1$ (b) $2r + 1$

(c) $4r + 1$ (d) $2r + 3$.

146. If $\dfrac{a + be^y}{a - be^y} = \dfrac{b + ce^y}{b - ce^y} = \dfrac{c + de^y}{c - de^y}$, then a, b, c, d are in :

(a) A. P.   (b) G. P.

(c) H. P.   (d) None of these.

147. If $(1^2 - a_1) + (2^2 - a_2) + (3^2 - a_3) + ... + (n^2 - a_n)$ $= \dfrac{1}{3} n (n^2 - 1)$, then a_n is given by :

(a) n (b) $n + 1$

(c) $n - 1$ (d) $\dfrac{n}{2}$

148. The sum of n terms of the series

$1 + 2\left(1 + \dfrac{2}{n}\right) + 3\left(1 + \dfrac{2}{n}\right)^2 + 4\left(1 + \dfrac{2}{n}\right)^3 + ...$ is :

(a) $\dfrac{n^2}{4}$ (b) $\dfrac{n^2}{4} + n$

(c) $\dfrac{n^2}{2} - n$ (d) None of these.

149. If x, y, z are in H.P. $(z > y > x)$ then, $\log (x + z) + \log (z - 2y + x) =$

(a) $2 \log (z - x)$ (b) $2 \log (y - z)$

(c) $4 \log (x - z)$ (d) $\log (y - z)$.

150. The sum of the series $3 + 33 + 333 + ...$ n terms is :

(a) $\dfrac{1}{27} (10^{n+1} - 9n - 10)$

(b) $\dfrac{1}{27} (10^{n+1} + 10n - 9)$

(c) $\dfrac{1}{27} (10^{n+1} + 9n - 28)$

(d) None of these.

151. If G.M. is 4 and A.M. is 5, then H.M. will be :

(a) $\dfrac{5}{16}$ (b) $\dfrac{16}{5}$

(c) $\dfrac{17}{8}$ (d) $\dfrac{25}{15}$

152. If $\dfrac{1}{q+r} \cdot \dfrac{1}{r+p} \cdot \dfrac{1}{p+q}$ are in A.P. then :

(a) p, q, r are in A.P.

(b) p^2, q^2, r^2 are in A.P.

(c) $\dfrac{1}{p}, \dfrac{1}{q}, \dfrac{1}{r}$ are in A.P.

(d) p, q, r are in G.P.

153. In a G.P., second term is 2 and sum of infinte terms is 8, then its first term will be :

(a) 8   (b) 6

(c) 4   (d) 2

154. The value of $2.\overline{357}$ is :

(a) $\dfrac{2355}{997}$ (b) $\dfrac{2355}{999}$

(c) $\dfrac{2379}{999}$ (d) None of these.

155. If in an A.P. sum of n terms is $3n^2 - n$ and common difference is 6, then first term will be :

(a) 1   (b) 2

(c) 3   (d) 4

156. If in an infinite G.P. every term is 10 times the sum of next terms, then common ratio of the G.P. is :

(a) $\dfrac{1}{2}$ (b) $\dfrac{1}{10}$

(c) $\dfrac{1}{11}$ (d) $\dfrac{10}{11}$

157. If a, b, c are in H.P., then :

(a) $a^2 + c^2 = 2b^2$ (b) $a^2 + c^2 < 2b^2$

(c) $a^2 + c^2 > 2b^2$ (d) $a^2 + c^2 < b^2$.

158. If in an A.P., sum of p terms is q and sum of q terms is p, then sum of (p + q) terms will be :

(a) $-(p + q)$ (b) 0

(c) $p + q + 1$ (d) $p - q$

159. If sum of the terms of any A.P. is 36, with first term 1 and last term 11, then number of terms are :

(a) 10   (b) 6

(c) 12   (d) 3.

160. If $\dfrac{a}{b+c}, \dfrac{b}{c+a}, \dfrac{c}{a+b}$ are in H.P., then a, b, c are in :

(a) G.P.   (b) A.P.

(c) H.P.   (d) None of these.

161. **Statement 1:** The sum of the series $1 + (1 + 2 + 4) + (4 + 6 + 9) + (9 + 12 + 16) + ... + (361 + 380 + 400)$ is 8000.   **[AIEEE - 2012]**

Statement 2: $\displaystyle\sum_{k=1}^{n} [k^3 - (k-1)^3] = n^3$ for any natural number n.

(a) Statement 1 is false, statement 2 is true.

(b) Statement 1 is true, statement 2 is true; statement 2 is a correct explanation for statement 1.

(c) Statement 1 is true, statement 2 is true; statement 2 is not a correct explanation for statement 1.

(d) Statement 1 is true, statement 2 is false.

162. If 100 times the 100th term of an AP with non-zero common difference equals the 50 times its 50th term, then the 150th term of this AP is :   **[AIEEE - 2012]**

(a) -150 (b) 150 times its 50th term

(c) 150   (d) zero

163. A man saves ₹ 200 in each of the first three months of his service. In each of the subsequent months his saving increases by ₹ 40 more than the saving of immediately previous month. His total saving from the start of service will be ₹ 11040 after :   **[AIEEE - 2011]**

(a) 21 months   (b) 18 months

(c) 19 months   (d) 20 months

164. A person is to count 4500 currency notes. Let a_n denote the number of notes he counts in the nth minute. If $a_1 = a_2 = \ldots\ldots = a_{10} = 150$ and a_{10}, $a_{11}, \ldots\ldots$ are in A.P. with common difference -2, then the time taken by him to count all the notes is :   **[AIEEE - 2010]**

(a) 34 minutes   (b) 125 minutes

(c) 135 minutes   (d) 24 minutes

165. The sum to the infinity of the series

$$1 + \frac{2}{3} + \frac{6}{3^2} + \frac{10}{3^3} + \frac{14}{3^4} + \ldots \text{ is}$$ **[AIEEE - 2009]**

(a) 2   (b) 3

(c) 4   (d) 6

166. **Statement 1:** For every natural number $n \geq 2$,

$$\frac{1}{\sqrt{1}} + \frac{1}{\sqrt{2}} + \ldots + \frac{1}{\sqrt{n}} > \sqrt{n}$$ **[AIEEE - 2008]**

Statement 2: For every natural number,

$n \geq 2, \sqrt{n(n + 1)} < n + 1.$

(a) Statement 1 is false, statement 2 is true.

(b) Statement 1 is true, statement 2 is true; statement 2 is a correct explanation for statement 1.

(c) Statement 1 is true, statement 2 is true; statement 2 is not a correct explanation for statement 1.

(d) Statement 1 is true, statement 2 is false.

167. The first two terms of a geometric progression add upto 12. The sum of the third and the fourth terms is 48. If the terms of the geometric progression are alternately positive and negative, then the first term is : **[AIEEE - 2008]**

(a) –4   (b) –12

(c) 12   (d) 4

168. In a geometric progression consisting of positive terms, each term equals the sum of the next two terms. Then the common ratio of this progression equals : **[AIEEE - 2007]**

(a) $\frac{1}{2}(1 - \sqrt{5})$ (b) $\frac{1}{2}\sqrt{5}$

(c) $\sqrt{5}$ (d) $\frac{1}{2}(\sqrt{5} - 1)$

169. If p and q are positive real numbers such that $p^2 + q^2 = 1$, then the maximum value of $(p + q)$ is : **[AIEEE - 2007]**

(a) 2   (b) 1/2

(c) $\frac{1}{\sqrt{2}}$ (d) $\sqrt{2}$

170. Let $a_1, a_2, a_3, \ldots$ be terms of an A.P. If

$$\frac{a_1 + a_2 + \ldots + a_p}{a_1 + a_2 + \ldots + a_q} = \frac{p^2}{q^2}, p \neq q, \text{ then } \frac{a_6}{a_{21}} \text{ equals :}$$

[AIEEE - 2006]

(a) $\frac{41}{11}$ (b) $\frac{7}{2}$

(c) $\frac{2}{7}$ (d) $\frac{11}{41}$

ANSWER KEY

1. (c)	2. (a)	3. (c)	4. (a)	5. (b)	6. (b)	7. (a)	8. (a)	9. (b)	10. (c)
11. (a)	12. (c)	13. (a)	14. (c)	15. (b)	16. (a)	17. (d)	18. (b)	19. (a)	20. (a)
21. (a)	22. (b)	23. (c)	24. (a)	25. (d)	26. (c)	27. (b)	28. (c)	29. (b)	30. (a)
31. (b)	32. (c)	33. (b)	34. (b)	35. (a)	36. (a)	37. (b)	38. (b)	39. (d)	40. (a)
41. (c)	42. (a)	43. (c)	44. (c)	45. (c)	46. (b)	47. (a)	48. (b)	49. (a)	50. (b)
51. (c)	52. (c)	53. (a)	54. (a)	55. (d)	56. (a)	57. (b)	58. (d)	59. (c)	60. (d)
61. (a)	62. (c)	63. (c)	64. (a)	65. (a)	66. (c)	67. (c)	68. (b)	69. (a)	70. (c)
71. (a)	72. (c)	73. (a)	74. (a)	75. (c)	76. (c)	77. (c)	78. (a)	79. (c)	80. (b)
81. (d)	82. (a)	83. (d)	84. (a)	85. (c)	86. (a)	87. (d)	88. (c)	89. (a)	90. (d)
91. (a)	92. (b)	93. (a)	94. (c)	95. (d)	96. (d)	97. (c)	98. (b)	99. (d)	100. (d)
101. (b)	102. (d)	103. (d)	104. (c)	105. (b)	106. (b)	107. (c)	108. (c)	109. (c)	110. (a)
111. (a)	112. (d)	113. (a)	114. (c)	115. (c)	116. (d)	117. (c)	118. (b)	119. (c)	120. (b)
121. (a)	122. (a)	123. (a)	124. (a)	125. (c)	126. (a)	127. (b)	128. (a)	129. (b)	130. (c)
131. (a)	132. (b)	133. (c)	134. (d)	135. (a)	136. (a)	137. (a)	138. (b)	139. (c)	140. (b)
141. (b)	142. (a)	143. (c)	144. (d)	145. (b)	146. (b)	147. (a)	148. (d)	149. (a)	150. (a)
151. (b)	152. (b)	153. (c)	154. (b)	155. (b)	156. (c)	157. (c)	158. (a)	159. (b)	160. (b)
161. (b)	162. (d)	163. (a)	164. (a)	165. (b)	166. (c)	167. (b)	168. (d)	169. (d)	170. (d)

❏❏❏

Chapter 10

PERMUTATIONS AND COMBINATIONS

MULTIPLE CHOICE QUESTIONS

1. If $^{56}P_{r+6} : {}^{54}P_{r+3} = 30800 : 1$, then r is equal to :
   (a) 39
   (b) 40
   (c) 41
   (d) None of these

2. If $^{2n}C_3 : {}^nC_2 = 44 : 3$, then n is equal to :
   (a) 6
   (b) 5
   (c) 4
   (d) None of these

3. If $^{10}P_r = 5040$, then the value of r is :
   (a) 3
   (b) 4
   (c) 5
   (d) None of these

4. If $^{n+2}C_8 : {}^{n-2}P_4 = 57 : 16$, then n is equal to :
   (a) 19
   (b) 20
   (c) 21
   (d) None of these

5. $\sum_{k=m}^{n} {}^kC_r = a({}^{n+1}C_{r+1} - {}^mC_{r+1})$, then a is equal to :
   (a) 1
   (b) m
   (c) n
   (d) None of these

6. $^{n-1}P_r + r \cdot {}^{n-1}P_{r-1} =$
   (a) $^{n+1}P_r$
   (b) ^nP_r
   (c) $r \cdot {}^nP_r$
   (d) None of these

7. If ^nP_r $^nP_{r+1}$ and $^nC_r = {}^nC_{r-1}$, then the values of n and r are:
   (a) 4, 3
   (b) 3, 2
   (c) 4, 2
   (d) None of these

8. If $^{n-1}C_3 + {}^{n-1}C_4 > {}^nC_3$, then :
   (a) n > 5
   (b) n > 6
   (c) n > 7
   (d) None of these

9. If $^nC_{r-1} = 36$, $^nC_r = 84$ and $^nC_{r+1} = 126$, then r is equal   to :
   (a) 1
   (b) 2
   (c) 3
   (d) None of these

10. $\sum_{r=0}^{n} \frac{^nP_r}{r!} =$
    (a) $2^n - 1$
    (b) 2^n
    (c) 2^{n-1}
    (d) $2^n + 1$

11. If $^{12}P_r = {}^{11}P_6 + 6 \cdot {}^{11}P_5$, then r is equal to :
    (a) 5
    (b) 6
    (c) 7
    (d) None of these

12. $^1P_1 + 2 \cdot {}^2P_2 + 3 \cdot {}^3P_3 + ... + n \cdot {}^nP_n =$
    (a) $^{n+1}P_{n+1}$
    (b) $^{n+1}P_{n+1} - 1$
    (c) $^{n+1}P_{n+1} - 2$
    (d) None of these

13. If $^nC_{12} = {}^nC_8$, then $^nC_{17}$ is equal to :
    (a) 1040
    (b) 1140
    (c) 1240
    (d) None of these

14. $^{47}C_4 + \sum_{j=1}^{5} {}^{52-j}C_3 =$
    (a) $^{52}C_4$
    (b) $^{51}C_4$
    (c) $^{52}C_3$
    (d) None of these

15. $^{15}C_8 + {}^{15}C_9 - {}^{15}C_6 - {}^{15}C_7 =$
    (a) 8
    (b) 0
    (c) 6
    (d) None of these

16. If $^{28}C_{2r} : {}^{24}C_{2r-4} = 225 : 11$, then ...
    (a) r = 24
    (b) r = 14
    (c) r = 7
    (d) None of these

17. If $3 \cdot {}^{x+1}C_2 + {}^2P_2 \cdot x = 4 \cdot {}^xP_2$, $x \in N$, then x is equal to :
    (a) 2
    (b) 3
    (c) 4
    (d) None of these

18. The number of positive terms in the sequence $x_n = \frac{195}{4 \, {}^nP_n} - \frac{^{n+3}P_3}{^{n+1}P_{n+1}}$, $n \in N$ is :
    (a) 2
    (b) 3
    (c) 4
    (d) None of these

19. The number of numbers that can formed with the help of the digits 1, 2, 3, 4, 3, 2, 1 so that odd digits always occupy odd places is :
    (a) 24
    (b) 18
    (c) 12
    (d) 30

10.1

20. All the letters of the word EAMCET' are arranged in all possible ways. The number of such arrangements in which two vowels are not adjacent to each other is :

(a) 360   (b) 114

(c) 72   (d) 54

21. A gentleman invites 13 guests to a dinner and places 8 of them at one table and remaining 5 at the other, the tables being round. The number of ways he can arrange the guests is :

(a) $\dfrac{11!}{40}$ (b) 9!

(c) $\dfrac{12!}{40}$ (d) $\dfrac{13!}{40}$

22. The chief ministers of 11 states of India meet to discuss the language problem. The number of ways they can seat themselves at a round table so that the Punjab and Madras Chief Ministers sit together is :

(a) 725760   (b) 725748

(c) 725778   (d) None of these

23. The number of ways in which n things of which r are alike, can be arranged in a circular order, is :

(a) $\dfrac{n!}{r!}$ (b) $\dfrac{(n-1)!}{r!}$

(c) $\dfrac{n!}{(r-1)!}$ (d) None of these

24. The number of ways in which 6 different beads can be string into a necklace is :

(a) 60   (b) 48

(c) 72   (d) None of these

25. There are 4 candidates for the post of a lecturer in Mathematics and one is to be selected by votes of 5 men. The number of ways in which the votes can be given is :

(a) 1048   (b) 1024

(c) 1072   (d) None of these

26. The number of numbers, greater than 4,00,000 that can be formed by using the digits 0, 2, 2, 4, 4, 5 is :

(a) 30   (b) 48

(c) 50   (d) None of these

27. The number of numbers greater than 50,000 that can be formed by using the digits 3, 5, 6, 6, 7, 9 is :

(a) 36   (b) 48

(c) 54   (d) None of these

28. 7 candidates are to take examination, 2 in mathematics and remaining in different subjects. The number of ways in which they can be seated in a row so that the two examinees in Mathematics may not sit together, is :

(a) 5400   (b) 4800

(c) 3600   (d) None of these

29. The number of ways in which the letters of the word "STRANGE" can be arranged so that the vowels may appear in the odd places, is :

(a) 1440   (b) 1470

(c) 1370   (d) None of these

30. The total number of 8-digit numbers which have all different digits is :

(a) 3265920   (b) 3265860

(c) 3268620   (d) None of these

31. Ten different letters of an alphabet are given. Words with five letters are formed from these given letters. Then the number of words which have at least one letter repeated is :

(a) 69760   (b) 30240

(c) 99748   (d) None of these

32. The sum of the digits in the unit place of all the numbers formed with the help of 3, 4, 5, 6 taken all at a time is :

(a) 432   (b) 108

(c) 36   (d) 18

33. If there are 12 persons in a party, and if each of them shakes hands with each other, then number of handshakes happen in the party is :

(a) 66   (b) 48

(c) 72   (d) None of these

34. The number of ways in which a committee of 5 can be chosen from 10 candidates so as to exclude the youngest if it includes the oldest, is:

(a) 196   (b) 178

(c) 202   (d) None of these

35. Three boys and three girls are to be seated around a table, in a circle. Among them, the boy X does not want any girl neighbour and the girl Y does not want any boy neighbour. The number of such arrangements possible is :

(a) 4   (b) 6

(c) 8   (d) None of these

36. The 'number of ways in which the letters of the word "VOWEL" can be arranged so that the letters O, E occupy only even places is :

(a) 12   (b) 18

(c) 24   (d) None of these

37. The number of ways in which the letters of the word 'FRACTION' be arranged so that no two vowels are together, is :

(a) 17330   (b) 14400

(c) 16440   (d) None of these

38. The number of words that can be formed from the letters of the word DAUGHTER so that the vowels always come together, is :

(a) 4320   (b) 3470

(c) 5230   (d) None of these

39. In an examination there are three multiple choice questions and each question has 4 choices. Number of ways in which a student can fail to get all answers correct is :

(a) 11   (b) 12

(c) 27   (d) 63

40. There are 10 lamps in a hall. Each one of them can be switched on independently. The number of ways in which the hall can be illuminated is :

(a) 10^2 (b) 18

(c) 2^{10} (d) 1023

41. 12 persons are to be arranged to a round table. If two particular persons among them are not to be side by side, the total number of arrangements is :

(a) 9 (10)!   (b) 2 (10)!

(c) 45 (8)!   (d) 10!

42. Among 20 members of a cricket club, there are two wicket keepers and 5 bowlers. The number of ways in which the eleven can be chosen so as to include only one of the wicket-keepers and atleast three bowlers is :

(a) 54054   (b) 48034

(c) 56038   (d) None of these

43. The number of ways in which a committee of 3 ladies and 4 gentlemen can be appointed from a meeting consisting of 8 ladies and 7 gentlemen, if Mrs. X refuses to serve in a committee if Mr. Y is a member is :

(a) 1960   (b) 1540

(c) 3240   (d) None of these

44. 4 letter lock consists of three rings each marked with 10 different letters, the number of ways in which it is possible to make an unsuccessful attempt to open the lock, is :

(a) 899   (b) 999

(c) 479   (d) None of these

45. There are stalls for 10 animals in a ship. The number of ways the shipload can be made if there are cows, calves and horses to be transported, animals of each kind being not less than 10, is :

(a) 59049   (b) 49049

(c) 69049   (d) None of these

46. The number of even numbers greater than 100 that can be formed by the digits 0, 1, 2, 3 (no digit being repeated) is :

(a) 20   (b) 30

(c) 40   (d) None of these

47. The number of arrangements which can be made out of the letters of the word ALGEBRA, without changing the relative order (positions) of vowels and consonants, is :

(a) 72   (b) 54

(c) 36   (d) None of these

48. The number of arrangements of the letters of the word "pencil" so that e always comes earlier than i, is :

(a) 290   (b) 340

(c) 360   (d) None of these

49. A bag contains 4 red, 2 white and 2 blue marbles. 3 marbles are drawn at random. The number of ways of selecting at least 1 white marble in this selection, is :

(a) 64   (b) 32

(c) 72   (d) None of these

50. The number of ways in which two 10-paise, two 20-paise, three 25-paise and one 50-paise coins can be distributed among 8 children so that each child gets only one coin, is :

(a) 1720   (b) 1680

(c) 1570   (d) None of these

51. When a group photograph is taken, all the seven teachers should be in the first row and all the twenty students should be in the second row. If the two corners of the second row are reserved for the two tallest students, interchangeable only between them, and if the middle seat of the front row is reserved for the principal, the number of such possible 'arrangements' is :

(a) $720 \times 18!$ (b) $1370 \times 18!$

(c) $1440 \times 18!$ (d) None of these

52. The number of divisors of 9600 including 1 and 9600 are :

(a) 60   (b) 58

(c) 48   (d) 46

53. The number of parallelograms that can be formed from a set of four parallel lines intersecting another set of three parallel lines is

(a) 6   (b) 18

(c) 12   (d) 9

54. A question paper contains 12 questions, divided into three parts (a), (b), (c). Part (a) contains 6 questions and parts (b), (c) 3 questions each. A candidate is required to attempt 6 questions selecting at least 2 questions from part (a), one from (b) and one from (c). The number of ways in which a candidate can select 6 questions is :

(a) 780   (b) 640

(c) 720   (d) None of these

55. In a village there are 87 families, of which 52 families have at most 2 children. In a rural development programme, 20 families are to be chosen for assistance, of which at least 18 families must have at most 2 children. The number of ways in which the choice can be made is :

(a) $C(52, 18) \times C(35, 2) + C(52, 19) \times C(35, 1)$
$+ C(52, 20)$

(b) $C(52, 18) \times C(35, 2) + C(52, 19) \times C(35, 1)$

(c) $C(52, 18) \times C(35, 2) + C(52, 20)$

(d) None of these

56. The number of diagonals that can be drawn by joining the vertices of an octagon is :

(a) 28   (b) 48

(c) 20   (d) None of these

57. The total number of ways of selecting five letters from the letters of the word INDEPENDENT, is

(a) 4200   (b) 3320

(c) 3840   (d) None of these

58. In a football championship, there were played 153 matches. Every two teams played one match with each other. The number of teams, participating in the championship are :

(a) 14   (b) 22

(c) 18   (d) None of these

59. The number of ways in which a team of eleven players can be selected from 22 players including 2 of them and excluding 4 of them is :

(a) $^{16}C_{11}$ (b) $^{16}C_5$

(c) $^{16}C_9$ (d) $^{20}C_9$

60. A candidate is required to answer 7 questions out of 12 questions which are divided into two groups each containing 6 questions. He is not permitted to attempt more than 5 questions from each group. The number of ways in which he can choose the 7 questions is :

(a) 780   (b) 640

(c) 820   (d) None of these

61. In how many ways can 6 persons be selected from 4 officers and 8 constables, if at least one officer is to be included :

(a) 224   (b) 672

(c) 896   (d) None of these

62. From a class of 12 boys and 10 girls, 10 students are to be chosen for a competition, at least including 4 boys and 4 girls. The two girls who won the prizes last year should be included. The number of ways in which the selection can be made is :

(a) 10320   (b) 11470

(c) 104874   (d) None of these

63. A boy has 3 Library tickets and 8 books of his interest in the library. Out of these 8, he does not want to borrow Maths part II, unless Maths part I is also borrowed. The number of ways in which he can choose the three books to be borrowed is :

(a) 41   (b) 32

(c) 51   (d) None of these

64. $^{n+1}C_{r+1} : {}^nC_r : {}^{n-1}C_{r-1} = 11 : 6 : 3$, then the values of n and r are :

(a) 10, 5   (b) 11, 4

(c) 9, 5   (d) None of these

65. If $\dfrac{{}^nP_{r-1}}{a} = \dfrac{{}^nP_r}{b} = \dfrac{{}^nP_{r+1}}{c}$, then

(a) $a^2 = b\,(a + c)$ (b) $b^2 = a\,(b + c)$

(c) $c^2 = b\,(c + a)$ (d) None of these

66. Eleven animals of circus have to be placed in eleven cages one in each cage. If 4 of the cages are too small for 6 of the animals, then the number of ways of caging the animals is :

(a) 304800   (b) 504800

(c) 604800   (d) None of these

67. A person wishes to make up as many different parties as he can out of 20 friends, each party consisting of the same number. The number of persons he should invite at a time is :

(a) 8   (b) 10

(c) 12   (d) None of these

68. The sum of five digit numbers which can be formed with the digits 3, 4, 5, 6, 7 using each digit only once in each arrangement, is :

(a) 5666600   (b) 666660

(c) 7666600   (d) None of these

69. The sum of all numbers greater than 1000 formed by using the digits 0, 1, 2, 3, no digit being repeated in any number, is :

(a) 38664   (b) 48664

(c) 58664   (d) None of these

70. The rank of the word 'MOTHER' when its letters are arranged as in a dictionary is :

(a) 209   (b) 309

(c) 350   (d) 308

71. The number of four digit numbers that can be formed from the digits 0, 1, 2, 3, 4, 5 with atleast one digit repeated is :

(a) 420   (b) 560

(c) 780   (d) None of these

72. The number of odd numbers lying between 40000 and 70000 that can be made from the digits 0, 1, 2, 4, 5, 7 if digits can be repeated in the same number is :

(a) 864   (b) 932

(c) 766   (d) None of these

73. In a network of railways, a small island has 15 stations. The number of different types of tickets to be printed for each class, if every station must have tickets for other station, is :

(a) 230   (b) 210

(c) 340   (d) None of these

74. There are 10 concurrent lines and another line parallel to one of them. The number of different triangles that will be formed by the 11 lines, is :

(a) 45   (b) 36

(c) 55   (d) 66

75. If each of 10 points on a straight line be joined to each of 10 points on a parallel line then the total number of triangles that can be formed with the given points as vertices, is :

(a) 860   (b) 900

(c) 920   (d) None of these

76. A father with 8 children takes them 3 at a time to the zoological garden, as often as he can without taking the same 3 children together more than once. Then :

(a) Number of times he will go is 56.

(b) Number of times each child will go is 21.

(c) Number of times a particular child will not go is 35.

(d) All of these

77. In an examination, a candidate has to pass in each of the papers to be successful. If the total number of ways to fail is 63, how many papers are there in the examination?

(a) 6   (b) 8

(c) 14   (d) None of these

78. Given five different green dyes, four different blue dyes and three different red dyes. The number of combinations of dyes that can be chosen, taking at least one green and one blue dye, is :

(a) 3720   (b) 4260

(c) 5340   (d) None of these

79. The number of ways in which 52 different cards can be divided equally among four players in order, is :

(a) $\dfrac{52!}{(13!)^3}$ (b) $\dfrac{52!}{(13!)^4}$

(c) $\dfrac{52!}{(13!)^2}$ (d) None of these

80. From 17 consonants and 5 vowels, the number of words containing 3 consonants and 2 vowels that can be made if all the letters are different, is :

(a) 816000   (b) 736000

(c) 926000   (d) None of these

81. A boat is to be manned by eight men of whom 2 can only row on bow side and 1 can only row on stroke side; the number of ways in which the crew can be arranged is :

(a) 4360   (b) 5760

(c) 5930   (d) None of these

82. A table has provision for 7 seats, 4 being on one side facing the window and 3 being on the opposite side. The number of ways in which 7 people can be seated at the table if 2 people, X and Y, must sit on the same side, is :

(a) 3260   (b) 2160

(c) 3350   (d) None of these

83. The number of ways in which 2 young men, 1 old man and 1 lady can sit for a trip in a four-sitter car (two seats in the front and two in the back) so that the old man always sits in the back seat, it is being given that the two young men only can drive the car, is :

(a) 8   (b) 12

(c) 16   (d) None of these

84. The number of ways in which p positive and n negative signs may be placed in a row so that no two negative signs shall be together is :

(a) $^{p+1}C_n$ (b) $^{p}C_n$

(c) $^{p-1}C_n$ (d) None of these

85. There are four oranges, five apples and six mangoes in a fruit basket. The number of ways in which a person can make a selection of fruits among the fruits in the basket, is :

(a) 210   (b) 330

(c) 209   (d) None of these

86. The number of proper divisors of 1260, is :

(a) 42   (b) 26

(c) 34   (d) None of these

87. The number of factors of 4200 is :

(a) 42   (b) 46

(c) 54   (d) None of these

88. The number of proper divisors of 2520 is :

(a) 46   (b) 52

(c) 64   (d) None of these

89. Four boys picked 30 apples. The number of ways in which they can divide them if all the apples are identical, is :

(a) 5630   (b) 4260

(c) 5456   (d) None of these

90. A family consists of grandfather, 5 sons and daughters and 8 grandchildren. They are to be seated in a row for dinner. The grandchildren wish to occupy the 4 seats at each end and the grandfather refuses to have a grand child on either side of him. The number of ways in which the family can be made to sit is

(a) 11360   (b) 11520

(c) 21530   (d) None of these

91. The number of ways in which a mixed doubles game in tennis can be arranged from 5 married couples, if no husband and wife play in the same game, is :

(a) 46   (b) 54

(c) 60   (d) None of these

92. The number of seven letter words that can be formed by using the letters of the word SUCCESS so that the two C are together but no two S are together is :

(a) 24   (b) 36

(c) 54   (d) None of these

93. The number of zeroes at the end of 100! is :

(a) 36   (b) 18

(c) 24   (d) None of these

94. The largest integer n such that 33! is divisible by 2^n is :

(a) 30   (b) 31

(c) 32   (d) None of these

95. The number of non-negative integral solutions of $x_1 + x_2 + x_3 + 4x_4 = 20$ is:

(a) 436   (b) 536

(c) 602   (d) None of these

96. If 7 points out of 12 are in the same straight line, then the number of triangles formed is :

(a) 19   (b) 185

(c) 201   (d) None of these

97. In a certain test, a_i students gave wrong answers to at least i questions where i = 1, 2, 3, ..., k. No student gave more than k wrong answers. The total number of wrong answers given is :

(a) $a_1 + a_2 + ... + a_k$ (b) $a_1 + a_2 + ... + a_{k-1}$

(c) $a_1 + a_2 + ... + a_{k+1}$ (d) None of these

98. The number of ordered triplets of positive integers which are solutions of the equation x + y + z = 100 is :

(a) 5081   (b) 6005

(c) 4851   (d) None of these

99. In a class tournament where the participants were to play one game with another, two class players fell ill, having played 3 games, each. If the total number of games played is 84, the number of participants at the beginning was :

(a) 22   (b) 15

(c) 17   (d) None of these

100. The number of ways in which 10 examination papers can be arranged so that the best and the worst papers never come together, is :

(a) 9.9!   (b) 8.9!

(c) 4.9!   (d) None of these

101. The number of words that can be formed with the letters of the word 'Pataliputra' without changing the relative order of the vowels and consonants, is :

(a) 3600   (b) 4200

(c) 3680   (d) None of these

102. On a new year day every student of a class sends a card to every other student. The postman delivers 600 cards. The number of students in the class are :

(a) 42   (b) 34

(c) 25   (d) None of these

103. Out of 18 points in a plane, no three are in the same straight line except five points which are collinear. The number of straight lines that can be formed by joining them is :

(a) 143   (b) 144

(c) 153   (d) None of these

104. The number of ways in which r letters can be posted in n letterboxes in a town is :

(a) n^r (b) r^n

(c) ^nP_r (d) ^nC_r

105. The number of lines drawn through 6 points lying on a circle is :

(a) 12   (b) 15

(c) 24   (d) 30

106. The least positive integral value of n which satisfies the inequality $^{10}C_{n-1} > 2 \cdot {}^{10}C_n$ is ...

(a) 7   (b) 8

(c) 9   (d) 10

107. The maximum number of points into which 4 circles and 4 straight lines intersect is :

(a) 26   (b) 50

(c) 56   (d) 72

108. There are n seats round a table numbered 1, 2, 3, ... n. The number of ways in which m ($\leq$ n) persons can take seats is :

(a) ^nP_m (b) $^nC_m \times (m-1)!$

(c) $\frac{1}{2} \cdot {}^nP_m$ (d) $^{n-1}P_m$

109. The straight lines I_1, I_2, I_3 are parallel and lie in the same plane. A total number of m points are taken on I_1, n points on I_2, k points on I_3. The maximum number of triangles formed with vertices at these points are :

(a) $^{m+n+k}C_3$

(b) $^{m+n+k}C_3 - {}^mC_3 - {}^nC_3 - {}^kC_3$

(c) $^mC_3 + {}^nC_3 + {}^kC_3$

(d) None of these

110. The maximum number of points of intersection of 8 straight lines is :

(a) 56   (b) 28

(c) 16   (d) 8

111. The total number of numbers greater than 100 and divisible by 5, that can be formed from the digits 3, 4, 5, 6 if no digit is repeated is :

(a) 24   (b) 48

(c) 36   (d) 12

112. The number of ways in which 9 students can be equally distributed among 3 sections is :

(a) $\frac{9!}{3(3!)^2}$ (b) $\frac{9!}{(3!)^3}$

(c) 9!   (d) None of these

113. The value of $(^7C_0 + {}^7C_1) + (^7C_1 + {}^7C_2) + \ldots\ldots + (^7C_6 + {}^7C_7)$ is :

(a) $2^8 - 2$ (b) $2^8 - 1$

(c) $2^8 + 1$ (d) 2^8

114. A polygon has 44 diagonals. The number of its sides are :

(a) 13   (b) 12

(c) 11   (d) 10

115. If $^{n+2}C_8 : {}^{n-2}P_4 = \frac{57}{16}$, then n is equal to :

(a) 19   (b) 21

(c) 20   (d) 5

116. If eight persons are to address a meeting then the number of ways in which a specified speaker is to speak before another specified speaker, is :

(a) 40320   (b) 2520

(c) 20160   (d) None of these

117. If $^nC_4, {}^nC_5, {}^nC_6$ are in A.P., then the value of n is:

(a) 11   (b) 17

(c) 8   (d) 14 or 7

118. How many different arrangements can be made out of the letters in the expansion $A^2 B^3 C^4$, when written in full :

(a) $\frac{9!}{2! + 3! + 4!}$ (b) $\frac{9!}{2! \, 3! \, 4!}$

(c) $2! + 3! + 4! \, (2! \, 3! \, 4!)$ (d) $2! \, 3! - 4$

119. If C (10, 4) + C (10, 5) = C (11, r), then r equals

(a) 6   (b) 5

(c) 4   (d) 3

120. The number of ways in which 5 boys and 5 girls can sit in a row so that all girls sit together is :

(a) 12600   (b) 7200

(c) 86400   (d) 14400

121. Given five line segments of length 2, 3, 4, 5, 6, units. Then the number of triangles that can be formed by joining these lines is :

(a) $^5C_3 - 3$ (b) $^5C_3 - 1$

(c) $^5C_3$ (d) $^5C_3 - 2$

122. Among 14 players, 5 are bowlers. In how many ways a team of 11 may be formed with at least 4 bowlers :

(a) 265　　　　　　　　(b) 263

(c) 264　　　　　　　　(d) 275

123. How many different nine digit numbers can be formed from the number 22 33 55 8 88 by rearranging its digits so that the odd digits occupy even positions :

(a) 16　　　　　　　　(b) 36

(c) 60　　　　　　　　(d) 180

124. An n-digit number is a positive number with exactly n digits. Nine hundred distinct n-digit numbers are to be formed using only the three digits 2, 5 and 7. The smallest value of n for which this is possible is :

(a) 6　　　　　　　　(b) 7

(c) 8　　　　　　　　(d) 9

125. For any positive integers m, n with $(n \geq m)$, let $\binom{n}{m} = {}^nC_m$, then $\binom{n}{m} + \binom{n-1}{m} + \binom{n-2}{m} + \ldots + \binom{m}{m} =$

(a) $\binom{n+1}{m}$　　　　(b) $\binom{n+1}{m+1}$

(c) $\binom{n}{m+1}$　　　　(d) None of these

126. There are four balls of different colours and four boxes of colours, same as those of the balls. The number of ways in which the balls, one each in a box, could be placed such that a ball does not go to a box of its own colour is :

(a) 9　　　　　　　　(b) 13

(c) 8　　　　　　　　(d) None of these

127. A five digit number divisible by 3 is to be formed using the numerals 0, 1, 2, 3, 4 and 5 without repetition. The total number of ways this can be done is :

(a) 216　　　　　　　(b) 600

(c) 240　　　　　　　(d) 3125

128. The total number of ways in which six '+' and four '−' signs can be arranged in a line such that no two '−' signs occur together is :

(a) 26　　　　　　　　(b) 35

(c) 34　　　　　　　　(d) None of these

129. A student is allowed to select almost n books from a collection of $(2n + 1)$ books. If the total number of ways in which he can select at least one book is 63, the value of n is :

(a) 1　　　　　　　　(b) 2

(c) 3　　　　　　　　(d) None of these

130. A box contains two white balls, three black balls and four red balls. The number of ways in which three balls can be drawn from the box if atleast one black ball is to be included in the draw, is :

(a) 32　　　　　　　　(b) 64

(c) 128　　　　　　　(d) None of these

131. A man has 7 relatives, 4 of them are ladies and 3 gentlemen. His wife has also 7 relatives, 3 of them are ladies and 4 gentlemen. The number of ways in which they can invite a dinner party of 3 ladies and 3 gentlemen so that there are 3 of the man's relatives and 3 of the wife's relatives, is :

(a) 485　　　　　　　(b) 463

(c) 265　　　　　　　(d) None of these

132. Sita has 5 coins each of different denomination. The number of different sums of money she can form is :

(a) 32　　　　　　　　(b) 25

(c) 31　　　　　　　　(d) None of these

133. The number of ways in which the six faces of a cube be painted with six different colours is :

(a) 6　　　　　　　　(b) 6!

(c) ${}^6C_2$　　　　　　(d) None of these

134. Out of 6 boys and 4 girls, a group of 7 is to be formed. In how many ways can this be done, if the group is to have a majority of boys ?

(a) 120　　　　　　　(b) 90

(c) 100　　　　　　　(d) 180

135. There are 5 roads leading to a town from a village. The number of different ways in which a villager can go to the town and return back, is :

(a) 25 (b) 20

(c) 10 (d) 5

136. Two straight lines intersect at a point O. Points $A_1, A_2, ..., A_n$ are taken on one line and points $B_1, B_2, ..., B_n$ on the other. If the point O is not to be used, the number of triangles that can be drawn using these points as vertices, is :

(a) $n(n-1)$ (b) $n(n-1)^2$

(c) $n^2(n-1)$ (d) $n^2(n-1)^2$

137. We are required to form different words with the help of the letters of the word INTEGER. Let m_1 be the number of words in which I and N are never together and m_2 be the number of words which begin with I and end with R, then m_1/m_2 is given by :

(a) 42 (b) 30

(c) 6 (d) 1/30

138. If a denotes the number of permutations of $x + 2$ things taken all at a time, b the number of permutations of x things taken 11 at a time and c the number of permutations of $x - 11$ things taken all at a time such that $a = 182bc$, then the value of x is :

(a) 15 (b) 12

(c) 10 (d) 18

139. The number of different 7 digit numbers that can be written using only the three digits 1, 2 and 3 with the condition that the digit 2 occurs twice in each number is :

(a) $^7P_2 \, 2^5$ (b) $^7C_2 \, 2^5$

(c) $^7C_2 \, 5^2$ (d) None of these

140. A set contains $(2n + 1)$ elements. If the number of subsets of this set which contain at most n elements is 4096, then the value of n is:

(a) 6 (b) 15

(c) 21 (d) None of these

141. Let p be a prime number such that $p \geq 11$.

Let $n = p! + 1$.

The number of primes in the list

$n + 1, n + 2, n + 3, ..., n + p - 1$, is:

(a) $p - 1$ (b) 2

(c) 1 (d) None of these

142. Five distinct letters are to be transmitted through a communication channel. A total number of 15 blanks is to be inserted between these letters with at least three between every two. The number of ways in which this can be done is :

(a) 1200 (b) 1800

(c) 2400 (d) 3000

143. The tens digit of $1! + 2! + 3! + ... + 49!$ is :

(a) 1 (b) 2

(c) 3 (d) 4

144. Let A = {x | x is a prime number and x < 30}. The number of different rational numbers whose numerator and denominator belong to A is :

(a) 90 (b) 180

(c) 91 (d) None of these

145. Let S be the set of all functions from the set A to the set A. If n (A) = k then n (S) is:

(a) k! (b) k^k

(c) $2^k - 1$ (d) 2^k

146. The number of numbers of 9 different non-zero digits such that all the digits in the first four places are less than the digit in the middle and all the digits in the last four places are greater than that in the middle is :

(a) 2 (4!) (b) $(4!)^2$

(c) 8! (d) None of these

147. ABCD is a quadrilateral. 3, 4, 5 and 6 points are marked on the sides AB, BC, CD and DA respectively. The number of triangles with vertices on different sides is :

(a) 270 (b) 220

(c) 282 (d) None of these

148. There are 10 points in a plane of which no three points are collinear and 4 points are concyclic. The number of different circles that can be drawn through at least 3 of these points is :
(a) 116 (b) 120
(c) 117 (d) None of these

149. The number of 7 digit numbers, the sum of whose digits is even, is :
(a) 35×10^5 (b) 45×10^5
(c) 50×10^5 (d) None of these

150. The number of ways of choosing m coupons out of an unlimited number of coupons bearing the letters A, B and C so that they cannot be used to spell the word BAC, is :
(a) $3(2^m - 1)$ (b) $3(2^{m-1} - 1)$
(c) $3(2^m + 1)$ (d) None of these

151. Six "X"s have to be placed in squares of the figure given below, such that each row contains at least one X. The number of different ways in which this can be done is :

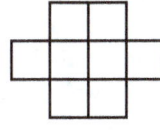

Fig.
(a) 26 (b) 28
(c) 18 (d) None of these

152. The number of ways in which 30 marks can be allotted to 8 questions if each question carries at least 2 marks, is :
(a) 115280 (b) 117280
(c) 116280 (d) None of these

153. In an examination the maximum marks for each of the three papers are 50 each. Maximum marks for fourth paper are 100. The number of ways in which the candidate can score 60% marks in aggregate is
(a) 110256 (b) 110456
(c) 110556 (d) None of these

154. The number of integers between 1 and 1000000 that have the sum of the digits 18, is:
(a) 25927 (b) 25827
(c) 24927 (d) None of these

155. The number of non-negative integral solutions to the system of equations $x + y + z + u + t = 20$ and $x + y + z = 5$ is :
(a) 336 (b) 346
(c) 246 (d) None of these

156. The number of positive integral solutions of the inequality $3x + y + z \leq 30$, is :
(a) 1115 (b) 1215
(c) 1315 (d) None of these

157. The sides AB, BC and CA of a triangle ABC have 3, 4 and 5 interior points respectively on them. The number of triangles that can be constructed using these interior points as vertices, is :
(a) 205 (b) 208
(c) 220 (d) 380

158. The number of words that can be made by writing downthe letters of the word CALCULATE such that each word starts and ends with a consonant, is :
(a) $\dfrac{5(7)!}{2}$ (b) $\dfrac{3(7)!}{2}$
(c) $2(7!)$ (d) None of these

159. The letters of the word SURITI are written in all possible orders and these words are written out as in dictionary. Then the rank of the word SURITI is :
(a) 236 (b) 245
(c) 307 (d) 315

160. Number of ways of distributing 10 identical objects among 8 persons (one or many persons may not be getting any object) is :
(a) 8^{10} (b) 10^8
(c) $^{17}C_7$ (d) $^{10}C_8$

161. For $2 \leq r \leq n$, $\dbinom{n}{r} + 2\dbinom{n}{r-1} + \dbinom{n}{r-2} =$
(a) $\dbinom{n+1}{r-1}$ (b) $2\dbinom{n+1}{r+1}$
(c) $\dbinom{n+r}{r}$ (d) $\dbinom{n+2}{r}$

162. Number of ways in which 3 boys and 3 girls (all are of different heights) can be arranged in a line so that boys as well as girls among themselves are in decreasing order of height (from left to right) is :

(a) 1 (b)   6 !

(c) 20   (d) None of these

163. The total number of ways in which 2n persons can be divided into n couples is :

(a) $\dfrac{2n!}{n!\,n!}$ (b) $\dfrac{2n!}{(2!)^n}$

(c) $\dfrac{2n!}{n!\,(2!)^n}$ (d) None of these

164. Seven different coins are to be divided amongst three persons. If no two of the persons receive the same number of coins but each receives at least one coin and none is left over, then the number of ways in which the coins can be distributed are :

(a) 420   (b) 630

(c) 710   (d) None of these

165. In a plane there are 37 straight lines, of which 13 pass through the point A and 11 pass through the point B. Besides, no three lines pass through one point, no lines pass through both points A and B, and no two are parallel, then the number of intersection points the lines have is equal to :

(a) 535   (b) 601

(c) 728   (d) 963

166. The number of integral solutions of $x_1 + x_2 + x_3 = 0$ with $x_i \geq 5$ is :

(a) $^{15}C_2$ (b) $^{16}C_2$

(c) $^{17}C_2$ (d) $^{18}C_2$

167. If the (n + 1) numbers a, b, c, d, ..., be all different and
each of them a prime number, then the number of different factors (other than 1) of $a^m \cdot b \cdot c \cdot d \ldots$ is :

(a) $m - 2^n$ (b) $(m + 1)\,2^n$

(c) $(m + 1)\,2^n - 1$ (d) None of these

168. The number of triangles whose vertices are at the vertices of an octagon but none of whose sides happen to come from the sides of the octagon is :

(a) 24   (b) 52

(c) 48   (d) 16

169. The number of different permutations of 4 letters of the word EARTHQUAKE is :

(a) 2140   (b) 2190

(c) 2240   (d) None of these

170. If a, b, c, d are odd natural numbers such that $a + b + c + d = 20$ then the number of values of the ordered quadruplet (a, b, c, d) is :

(a) 165   (b) 310

(c) 295   (d) 398

171. There are three teams each of a chairman, a supervisor and a worker of three different companies. There are nine bonus of different denominations to be paid to these nine persons in all. In how many ways can this be done if due respect to superiority is given in every team :

(a) 865   (b) 129

(c) 1680   (d) None of these

172. The number of ways in which we can choose 2 distinct integers from 1 to 100 such that difference between them is at most 10 is :

(a) $^{10}C_2$ (b) 72

(c) $^{100}C_2 - {}^{90}C_2$ (d) None of these

173. The number of ways in which 30 coins of one rupee each be given to six persons so that none of them receives less than 4 rupees is :

(a) 231   (b) 462

(c) 693   (d) 924

174. The minimum number of marks required for clearing a certain paper is 210 out of 300. The paper consists of '3' sections each of Physics, Chemistry and Maths. Each section has 100 as maximum marks. Assuming there is no negative marking and marks obtained in each section are integers, the number of ways in which a student can qualify the examination are : (Assuming no cut-off limit)

(a) $^{210}C_3 - {}^{90}C_3$ (b) $^{93}C_3$

(c) $^{213}C_3$ (d) $(210)^3$

175. A die is rolled 216 times. The number of ways in which each of the six faces appear equal number of times, is :

(a) $\dfrac{(216)!}{(6)^5}$

(b) $\dfrac{(216)!}{(6!)^{36}}$

(c) $\dfrac{(216)!}{(36!)^6}$

(d) None of these

176. The sum of divisors of $2^6 \cdot 5^3 \cdot 7^4 \cdot 11$ is :

(a) $41^5 - 1$

(b) $31^5 - 1$

(c) 11^5

(d) None of these

177. If two numbers are selected from numbers 1 to 25, then the number of ways that their difference does not exceed 10 is :

(a) 105

(b) 195

(c) $^{15}C_2$

(d) None of these

178. A is a set containing n elements. A subset P of A is chosen. The set A is reconstructed by replacing the elements of P. A subset Q of A is again chosen. The number of ways of choosing P and Q so that $P \cap Q = \phi$ is:

(a) $2^{2n} - {}^{2n}C_n$

(b) 2^n

(c) $2^n - 1$

(d) 3^n

179. Number of ways arranging letters of the word ALTERNATIVE such that no two vowels are together is :

(a) $6! \times 5! \times \dfrac{1}{2!}$

(b) $\dfrac{6!}{2!}\, {}^7P_5$

(c) $\dfrac{7!6!}{(2!)^4}$

(d) None of these

180. The greatest common divisor of :

$^{31}C_{16}, {}^{31}C_{17}, {}^{31}C_{18}, \ldots, {}^{31}C_{30}$, is

(a) $^{31}C_{16}$

(b) 31

(c) 465

(d) None of these

181. Value of $\dfrac{^{10}C_r}{^{11}C_r}$, when numerator and denominator takes its greatest value is :

(a) $\dfrac{6}{11}$

(b) $\dfrac{5}{11}$

(c) $\dfrac{10}{6}$

(d) $\dfrac{10}{5}$

182. The number of ways in which 12 dice can be thrown so that each face occurs exactly twice is

(a) 6^6

(b) 2^6

(c) $\dfrac{6^{12}}{12!}$

(d) None of these

183. The number of subsets of $\{1, 2, 3, \ldots n\}$ having least element m and greatest element k, $(1 \le m < k \le n)$ is :

(a) $2^{n-(k-m)}$

(b) 2^{k-m-2}

(c) 2^{k-m-1}

(d) 2^{k-m+1}

184. The number of ways in which 31 seats of state legislature can be divided among three political parties so that any two will ensure them of a majority is :

(a) 120

(b) 121

(c) 528

(d) 408

185. The number of divisors of a number 38808 (excluding 1 and the number itself) is :

(a) 70

(b) 72

(c) 71

(d) None of these

186. The number of ways in which 10 candidates A_1, A_2, ... A_{10} can be ranked so that A_1 is always above A_2 is :

(a) $^{10}C_2$

(b) 90

(c) $\dfrac{10!}{2!}$

(d) None of these

187. The number of different signals that can be transmitted by arranging 3 red, 2 yellow and 2 green flags on a pole is :

(a) 210

(b) 186

(c) 172

(d) None of these

188. Let p, q $\in \{1, 2, 3, 4\}$. The number of equations of the form $px^2 + qx + 1 = 0$ having real roots is

(a) 15

(b) 9

(c) 7 (d) 8

189. A lady gives a dinner party for six guests. The number of ways in which they may be selected from among ten friends if two of the friends will not attend the party together, is :

(a) 164

(b) 112

(c) 140

(d) None of these

190. 66 games were played in a tournament where each placed one against the rest. The number of players are :

(a) 11   (b) 13

(c) 12   (d) 14

191. The number of ways in which 7 persons can sit around a table so that all shall not have the same neighbours in any two arrangements is

(a) 360   (b) 720

(c) 270   (d) 180

192. A class is composed of two brothers and six other boys. In how many ways can all the boys be seated at a round table so that the two brothers are not seated besides each other ?

(a) 4320   (b) 3600

(c) 720   (d) 1440

193. The number of words which can be formed by using all letters of the word "MISSISIPI" is :

(a) 2520   (b) 1520

(c) 6705   (d) 5067

194. Four digit numbers are formed by using all possible arrangements of the digits 1, 2, 4, 6. Then sum of all such numbers will be :

(a) 14443   (b) 86658

(c) 43329   (d) 28836

195. The number of ways in which we can select three numbers from 1 to 30 so as to exclude every selection of three consultative numbers is

(a) 4032   (b) 4040

(c) 4048   (d) 4060

196. The straight lines I_1, I_2, I_3 are parallel and lie in the same plane. A total number of m points on I_1 : n points on I_2 : k points on I_3, the maximum number of triangles formed with vertices at these points are :

(a) $^{m+n+k}C_3$

(b) $^{m+n+k}C_3 - {}^mC_3 - {}^nC_3 - {}^kC_3$

(c) $^mC_3 + {}^nC_3 + {}^kC_3$

(d) None of these

197. Assuming the balls to be identical except for difference in colours, the number of ways in which one or more balls can be selected from 10 white, 9 green and 7 black balls is :

[AIEEE - 2012]

(a) 880   (b) 629

(c) 630   (d) 879

198. Statement 1 : The number of ways of distributing 10 identical balls in 4 distinct boxes such that no box is empty is $^9C_3$.

[AIEEE - 2011]

Statement 2: The number of ways of choosing any 3 places from 9 different places is $^9C_3$.

(a) Statement 1 is false, statement 2 is true.

(b) Statement 1 is true, statement 2 is true; statement 2 is the correct explanation for statement 1.

(c) Statement 1 is true, statement 2 is true; statement 2 is not a correct explanation for statement 1.

(d) Statement 1 is true, statement 2 is false.

199. Let $S_1 = \sum\limits_{j=1}^{10} j(j-1)\ {}^{10}C_j$, $S_2 = \sum\limits_{j=1}^{10} j\ {}^{10}C_j$

and $S_3 = \sum\limits_{j=1}^{10} j^2\ {}^{10}C_j$ **[AIEEE - 2010]**

Statement 1: $S_3 = 55 \times 2^9$

Statement 2: $S_1 = 90 \times 2^8$ and $S_2 = 10 \times 2^8$

(a) Statement 1 is true, statement 2 is true; statement 2 is not the correct explanation for statement 1.

(b) Statement 1 is true, statement 2 is false.

(c) Statement 1 is false, statement 2 is true.

(d) Statement 1 is true, statement 2 is true; statement 2 is the correct explanation for statement 1.

200. There are two urns. Urn A has 3 distinct red balls and urn B has 9 distinct blue balls. From each urn two balls are taken out at random and then transferred to the other. The number of ways in which this can be done is:

[AIEEE - 2010]

(a) 36   (b) 66

(c) 108   (d) 3

201. From 6 different novels and 3 different dictionaries, 4 novels and 1 dictionary are to be selected and arranged in a row on the shelf so that the dictionary is always in the middle. Then the number of such arrangements is

[AIEEE - 2009]

(a) less than 500

(b) at least 500 but less than 750

(c) at least 750 but less than 1000

(d) at least 1000

202. In a shop there are five types of ice-creams available. A child buys six ice-creams.

[AIEEE - 2008]

Statement 1: The number of different ways the child can buy the six ice-creams is $^{10}C_5$.

Statement 2: The number of different ways the child can buy the six ice-creams is equal to the number of different ways of arranging 6 A's and 4 B's in a row.

(a) Statement 1 is false, statement 2 is true.

(b) Statement 1 is true, statement 2 is true; statement 2 is a correct explanation for statement 1.

(c) Statement 1 is true, statement 2 is a true; statement 2 is not a correct explanation for statement 1.

(d) Statement 1 is true, statement 2 is false.

203. At an election, a voter may vote for any number of candidates, not greater than the number to be elected. There are 10 candidates and 4 are to be elected. If a voter votes for at least one candidate, then the number of ways in which he can vote is :   **[AIEEE - 2006]**

(a) 5040   (b) 6210

(c) 385   (d) 1110

204. If the letters of word SACHIN are arranged in all possible ways and these words are written out as in dictionary, then the word SACHIN appears at serial number.   **[AIEEE - 2005]**

(a) 601   (b) 600

(c) 603   (d) 602

205. The value of $^{50}C_4 + 6\sum\limits_{r=1}^{6}{}^{56-r}C_3$ is :

[AIEEE - 2005]

(a) $^{55}C_4$ (b) $^{55}C_3$

(c) $^{56}C_3$ (d) $^{56}C_4$

206. The words; with or without meanings; of length upto 3 are formed by using the letters of the word MANGO. Repetition of letters is allowed. The words are then arranged in alphabetic order so as to form a small dictionary. Then the number of words between two words GOA and NM is

(a) 47   (b) 48

(c) 49   (d) 50

207. The sum of all possible 5 digit numbers formed by using the digits 1, 1, 2, 2, 4 is

(a) 565450   (b) 666660

(c) 654600   (d) 654640

ANSWER KEY

1. (c)	2. (a)	3. (b)	4. (a)	5. (a)	6. (b)	7. (b)	8. (c)	9. (c)	10. (b)
11. (b)	12. (b)	13. (b)	14. (a)	15. (b)	16. (c)	17. (b)	18. (c)	19. (b)	20. (c)
21. (d)	22. (a)	23. (b)	24. (a)	25. (b)	26. (d)	27. (b)	28. (c)	29. (a)	30. (a)
31. (a)	32. (b)	33. (a)	34. (a)	35. (a)	36. (a)	37. (b)	38. (a)	39. (d)	40. (d)
41. (a)	42. (a)	43. (b)	44. (b)	45. (a)	46. (a)	47. (a)	48. (c)	49. (a)	50. (b)
51. (c)	52. (c)	53. (b)	54. (c)	55. (a)	56. (c)	57. (b)	58. (c)	59. (c)	60. (a)

61. (c)	**62.** (c)	**63.** (a)	**64.** (a)	**65.** (b)	**66.** (c)	**67.** (b)	**68.** (b)	**69.** (a)	**70.** (b)
71. (c)	**72.** (a)	**73.** (b)	**74.** (b)	**75.** (b)	**76.** (d)	**77.** (a)	**78.** (a)	**79.** (b)	**80.** (a)
81. (b)	**82.** (b)	**83.** (a)	**84.** (a)	**85.** (c)	**86.** (c)	**87.** (b)	**88.** (a)	**89.** (c)	**90.** (b)
91. (c)	**92.** (a)	**93.** (c)	**94.** (b)	**95.** (b)	**96.** (b)	**97.** (a)	**98.** (c)	**99.** (b)	**100.** (b)
101. (a)	**102.** (c)	**103.** (b)	**104.** (a)	**105.** (b)	**106.** (b)	**107.** (b)	**108.** (a)	**109.** (b)	**110.** (b)
111. (d)	**112.** (b)	**113.** (a)	**114.** (c)	**115.** (a)	**116.** (c)	**117.** (d)	**118.** (b)	**119.** (b)	**120.** (c)
121. (a)	**122.** (c)	**123.** (c)	**124.** (b)	**125.** (b)	**126.** (a)	**127.** (a)	**128.** (b)	**129.** (c)	**130.** (b)
131. (a)	**132.** (c)	**133.** (d)	**134.** (c)	**135.** (a)	**136.** (c)	**137.** (b)	**138.** (b)	**139.** (b)	**140.** (a)
141. (d)	**142.** (c)	**143.** (a)	**144.** (c)	**145.** (b)	**146.** (b)	**147.** (d)	**148.** (c)	**149.** (b)	**150.** (a)
151. (a)	**152.** (c)	**153.** (c)	**154.** (a)	**155.** (a)	**156.** (b)	**157.** (a)	**158.** (a)	**159.** (a)	**160.** (c)
161. (d)	**162.** (c)	**163.** (c)	**164.** (b)	**165.** (a)	**166.** (c)	**167.** (c)	**168.** (d)	**169.** (b)	**170.** (a)
171. (c)	**172.** (c)	**173.** (b)	**174.** (b)	**175.** (c)	**176.** (d)	**177.** (b)	**178.** (d)	**179.** (c)	**180.** (b)
181. (a)	**182.** (d)	**183.** (c)	**184.** (a)	**185.** (a)	**186.** (c)	**187.** (a)	**188.** (c)	**189.** (c)	**190.** (c)
191. (a)	**192.** (b)	**193.** (a)	**194.** (b)	**195.** (a)	**196.** (b)	**197.** (a)	**198.** (c)	**199.** (b)	**200.** (c)
201. (d)	**202.** (a)	**203.** (c)	**204.** (a)	**205.** (d)	**206.** (b)	**207.** (b)			

❑❑❑

Chapter 11

BINOMIAL THEOREM

MULTIPLE CHOICE QUESTIONS

1. In the expansion of $\left(3x - \dfrac{1}{x^2}\right)^{10}$, the 5th term from the end is :

   (a) $\dfrac{16486}{x^8}$

   (b) $\dfrac{17010}{x^8}$

   (c) $\dfrac{13486}{x^8}$

   (d) None of these

2. The 8th term of $\left(3x + \dfrac{2}{3x^2}\right)^{12}$, when expanded in ascending power of x, is :

   (a) $\dfrac{228096}{x^3}$

   (b) $\dfrac{228096}{x^9}$

   (c) $\dfrac{328179}{x^9}$

   (d) None of these.

3. If A is the sum of the odd terms and B the sum of even terms in the expansion of $(x + a)^n$, then $A^2 - B^2 =$

   (a) $(x^2 + a^2)^n$

   (b) $(x^2 - a^2)^n$

   (c) $2(x^2 - a^2)^n$

   (d) None of these.

4. The term independent of x in $\left(\dfrac{3}{2}x^2 - \dfrac{1}{3x}\right)^9$ is :

   (a) $\dfrac{7}{18}$

   (b) $\dfrac{18}{7}$

   (c) $\dfrac{7}{29}$

   (d) None of these

5. The term independent of x in
   $$\left[\sqrt{\left(\dfrac{x}{3}\right)} + \sqrt{\left(\dfrac{3}{3x^2}\right)}\right]^{10}$$ is :

   (a) None

   (b) $^{10}C_1$

   (c) $\dfrac{5}{12}$

   (d) 1

6. The 13th term of $\left(9x - \dfrac{1}{3\sqrt{x}}\right)^{18}$ is :

   (a) 17682

   (b) 18564

   (c) $18564\, x^6$

   (d) None of these

7. The coefficient of $\dfrac{1}{y^2}$ in $\left(y + \dfrac{c^3}{y^2}\right)^{10}$ is :

   (a) $187\, c^{12}$

   (b) $\dfrac{210}{c^{12}}$

   (c) $\dfrac{c^{12}}{210}$

   (d) $210C^{12}$

8. The $(n + 1)^{th}$ term from the end in the expansion of $\left(2x - \dfrac{1}{x}\right)^{3n}$ is :

   (a) $\dfrac{3n!}{2n!\, n!}\, 2^n \cdot x^{-n}$

   (b) $\dfrac{3n!}{2n!\, n!}\, 2^{2n} \cdot x^{-2n}$

   (c) $\dfrac{3n!}{2n!\, n!}\, 2^n \cdot x^n$

   (d) None of these

9. If the rth term in the expansion of $\left(\dfrac{x}{3} - \dfrac{2}{x^2}\right)^{10}$ contains x^4, then r is equal to :

   (a) 2

   (b) 3

   (c) 4

   (d) 5.

10. The 7th term in $\left(\dfrac{1}{y} + y^2\right)^{10}$, when expanded in descending power of y, is :

    (a) $\dfrac{210}{y^2}$

    (b) $\dfrac{y^2}{210}$

    (c) $210\, y^2$

    (d) None of these

11. The term independent of x in $(1 + x)^m \left(1 + \dfrac{1}{x}\right)^n$ is

    (a) $^{m+n}C_m$

    (b) $^{m+n}C_n$

    (c) $^{m+n}C_{m-n}$

    (d) None of these.

12. The greatest term (numerically) in the expansion of $(2 + 3x)^9$, when $x = \dfrac{3}{2}$, is :

    (a) $\dfrac{5 \times 3^{11}}{2}$

    (b) $\dfrac{5 \times 3^{13}}{2}$

    (c) $\dfrac{7 \times 3^{13}}{2}$

    (d) None of these

13. The greatest term (numerically) in the expansion of $(3-5x)^{11}$ when $x = \dfrac{1}{5}$ is :

(a) 55×3^9 (b) 46×3^9

(c) 55×3^6 (d) None of these

14. The coefficient of x^{53} in the expansion of :

$$\sum_{m=0}^{100} {}^{100}C_m (x-3)^{100-m} \cdot 2^m \text{ is :}$$

(a) ${}^{100}C_{47}$ (b) ${}^{100}C_{53}$

(c) $-{}^{100}C_{53}$ (d) $-{}^{100}C_{100}$

15. If, in the expansion of $\left(\sqrt[3]{2} + \dfrac{1}{\sqrt[3]{3}}\right)^n$, the ratio of the 7th term from the beginning to the seventh term from the end is equal to $\dfrac{1}{6}$, then n is equal to :

(a) 3   (b) 6

(c) 9   (d) None of these

16. If the binomial coefficient of the third term in the expansion of $\left(9x - \dfrac{1}{\sqrt{3x}}\right)^m$ is 105, then the third term in the expansion is :

(a) $35 \cdot 9^{13} \cdot x^{12}$ (b) $24 \cdot 9^{13} \cdot x^{12}$

(c) $35 \cdot 9^{13} \cdot x^9$ (d) None of these

17. The coefficient of x^{-1} in the expansion of $(1 + 3x^2 + x^4)\left(1 + \dfrac{1}{x}\right)^8$ is :

(a) 176   (b) 232

(c) 216   (d) None of these

18. The sum of the coefficients in the expansion of $(1 + 5x - 7x^3)^{3165}$ is :

(a) 1   (b) 2^{3165}

(c) 2^{3164} (d) -1

19. The number of non-zero terms in the expansion of $(1 + 3\sqrt{2}x)^9 + (1 - 3\sqrt{2}x)^9$ is :

(a) 9   (b) 0

(c) 5   (d) 10

20. The coefficient of x^{30} in the expansion of $(1 + 3x + 3x^2 + x^3)^{15}$ is :

(a) ${}^{45}C_{15}$ (b) ${}^{45}C_{25}$

(c) ${}^{45}C_{30}$ (d) $.^{15}C_{11}$

21. The term independent of x in the expansion of $(1 + x + 2x^3)\left(\dfrac{3}{2}x^2 - \dfrac{1}{3x}\right)^9$ is :

(a) $\dfrac{17}{54}$ (b) $\dfrac{54}{17}$

(c) $\dfrac{21}{54}$ (d) None of these

22. If the fourth term in the expansion of $\left(px + \dfrac{1}{x}\right)^n$ is independent of x, then the value of term is :

(a) $5p^3$ (b) $10p^3$

(c) $20p^3$ (d) None of these

23. The ratio of the coefficient of x^{10} in $(1 - x^2)^{10}$ and the term independent of x in $\left(x - \dfrac{2}{x}\right)^{10}$ is :

(a) $1 : 16$ (b) $1 : 32$

(c) $1 : 64$ (d) None of these

24. The relation between a and b, so that the coefficients of x^7 in $\left(ax^2 + \dfrac{1}{bx}\right)^{11}$ and x^{-7} in $\left(ax - \dfrac{1}{bx^2}\right)^{11}$ are equal, is

(a) $ab = -1$ (b) $ab = 1$

(c) $ab = 2$ (d) None of these

25. If the coefficients of $(2r + 1)^{th}$ term and $(r + 2)^{th}$ term in the expansion of $(1 + x)^{43}$ are equal, then $r =$

(a) 14   (b) 16

(c) 10   (d) None of these

26. If the greatest term in the expansion of $(1 + x)^{2n}$ has also the greatest coefficient, then x lies between :

(a) $\dfrac{n}{n+1}$ and $\dfrac{n+1}{n}$ (b) $\dfrac{n}{n+2}$ and $\dfrac{n+2}{n}$

(c) $\dfrac{n}{n+3}$ and $\dfrac{n+3}{n}$ (d) None of these

27. If the coefficients of x^{r-1}, x^r, x^{r+1} in the binomial expansion of $(1 + x)^n$ are in A.P., then $n^2 - (4r + 1) n + kr - 2 = 0$, where k =

(a) r + 1
(b) 2r + 1
(c) 4r
(d) None of these

28. The two consecutive terms in the expansion of $(3x + 2)^{74}$, whose coefficients are equal, are :

(a) 20th and 21st
(b) 30th and 31st
(c) 40th and 41st
(d) None of these

29. If the sum of the coefficients in the expansion of $(\alpha x^2 - 2x + 1)^{35}$ is equal to the sum of the coefficients in the expansion of $(x - \alpha y)^{35}$, then α is equal to :

(a) 3
(b) 2
(c) 1
(d) – 2

30. In the expansion of $(3^{-x/4} + 3^{5x/4})^n$, the sum of the binomial coefficients is 64 and the term with the greatest binomial coefficient exceeds the third by $(n – 1)$. The value of x is :

(a) 1
(b) 2
(c) 0
(d) None of these

31. Which term in the expansion of the binomial

$$\left[\sqrt[3]{\left(\frac{a}{\sqrt{b}}\right)} + \sqrt{\left(\frac{b}{\sqrt[3]{a}}\right)} \right]^{21}$$

contains a and b to one and the same power ?

(a) 5th
(b) 8th
(c) 10th
(d) None of these

32. If three consecutive coefficients in the expansion of $(1 + x)^n$ are 165, 330 and 462, then n is equal to :

(a) 10
(b) 11
(c) 12
(d) None of these

33. If 7^{103} is divided by 25, then the remainder is :

(a) 20
(b) 16
(c) 18
(d) 15.

34. If a, b, c and d are any four consecutive coefficients of any binomial expansion, then $\dfrac{a + b}{a}$, $\dfrac{b + c}{b}$, $\dfrac{c + d}{c}$ are in :

(a) A.P.
(b) G.P.
(c) H.P.
(d) None of these

35. If $(1 + x)^n = C_0 + C_1 x + C_2 x^2 + ... + C_n x^n$, then $C_0 + 3 \cdot C_1 + 5 \cdot C_2 + ... + (2n + 1) \cdot C_n$ is equal to :

(a) $n2^n$
(b) $n2^{n-1}$
(c) $(n + 1) 2^n$
(d) None of these

36. If n is a positive integer greater than 1, then $a - {}^nC_1 (a – 1) + {}^nC_2 (a – 2) - ... + (– 1)^n (a – n)$ is equal to :

(a) n
(b) a
(c) 0
(d) None of these

37. The sum of rational terms in the expansion of $(\sqrt{2} + 3^{1/15})^{10}$ is :

(a) 31
(b) 41
(c) 51
(d) None of these

38. The fractional part of $\dfrac{2^{4n}}{15}$ is :

(a) $\dfrac{1}{15}$
(b) $\dfrac{2}{15}$
(c) $\dfrac{4}{15}$
(d) None of these

39. In the expansion of $(x + a)^n$ if the sum of odd terms is P and the sum of even terms is θ, then $4 PQ =$

(a) $(x + a)^n - (x - a)^n$
(b) $(x + a)^n + (x - a)^n$
(c) $(x + a)^{2n} - (x - a)^{2n}$
(d) None of these

40. If the 3rd, 4th and 5th terms in the expansion of $(x + a)^n$ are respectively 84, 280 and 560, then the values of x, a and n are :

(a) 1, 2 and 5
(b) 2, 2 and 7
(c) 1, 2 and 7
(d) 2, 3 and 7

41. If $(1 + x)^n = C_0 + C_1 x + C_2 x^2 + ... + C_n x^n$, then

$$\sum_{k=1}^{n} k^2 \cdot C_k =$$

(a) $n (n - 1) 2^{n-1}$
(b) $n (n + 1) 2^{n-2}$
(c) $(n + 1) (n + 2) 2^{n-1}$
(d) None of these

42. If $(1 + x)^n = C_0 + C_1 x + C_2 x^2 + ... + C_n x^n$, then $1 - (1 + x) C_1 + (1 + 2x) C_2 - (1 + 3x) C_3 + ... =$

(a) 0
(b) 1
(c) 2
(d) None of these

43. If $(1 + x)^n = C_0 + C_1 x + C_2 x^2 + ... + C_n x^n$, and if $a_0, a_1, a_2, ... a_n$ is a set of numbers in A.P., then $a_0 - {}^nC_1 \cdot a_1 + {}^nC_2 \cdot a_2 - ... + (-1)^n \cdot {}^nC_n \cdot a_n =$

(a) 0   (b) 1

(c) -1 (d) None of these

44. If $C_0, C_1, C_2 ..., C_n$ are the coefficients of the expansion of $(1 + x)^n$, then the value of $\sum_0^n \dfrac{C_k}{k + 1}$ is :

(a) 0   (b) $\dfrac{2^n - 1}{n}$

(c) $\dfrac{2^{n+1} - 1}{n + 1}$ (d) None of these

45. If $C_0, C_1, C_2, ..., C_n$ are the coefficients in the expansion of $(1 + x)^n$, then $\dfrac{2^2 \cdot C_0}{1 \cdot 2} + \dfrac{2^3 \cdot C_1}{2 \cdot 3} + ... + \dfrac{2^{n+2} \cdot C_n}{(n + 1)(n + 2)}$ is equal to:

(a) $\dfrac{3^{n+1} - 2n - 5}{(n + 1)(n + 2)}$ (b) $\dfrac{3^{n+2} - 2n - 5}{(n + 1)(n + 2)}$

(c) $\dfrac{3^{n+2} + 2n - 5}{(n + 1)(n + 2)}$ (d) None of these

46. The value of $\dfrac{(18^3 + 7^3 + 3 \cdot 18 \cdot 7 \cdot 25)}{\left[\begin{array}{c} 3^6 + 6 \cdot 243 \cdot 2 + 15 \cdot 81 \cdot 4 + 20 \cdot 27 \cdot 8 \\ + 15 \cdot 9 \cdot 16 + 6 \cdot 3 \cdot 32 + 64 \end{array} \right]}$ is :

(a) 0   (b) 1

(c) 2   (d) None of these

47. The integral part of $(\sqrt{2} + 1)^6$ is :

(a) 198   (b) 196

(c) 197   (d) 199.

48. Larger of $99^{50} + 100^{50}$ and 101^{50} is :

(a) 101^{50} (b) $99^{50} + 100^{50}$

(c) both are equal   (d) None of these

49. For all $n \in N$, the integer just above $(\sqrt{3} + 1)^{2n}$ is divisible by

(a) 2^{n+1} (b) $2^n + 1$

(c) $2^{n+1} + 1$ (d) None of these

50. The sum of the series $\sum_{r = 0}^n (-1)^r \cdot {}^nC_r \left[\dfrac{1}{2^r} + \dfrac{3^r}{2^{2r}} + \dfrac{7^r}{2^{3r}} + \dfrac{15^r}{2^{4r}} + ... \text{ to m terms} \right]$ is :

(a) $\dfrac{1 - \dfrac{1}{2^{mn}}}{2^m - 1}$ (b) $\dfrac{1 - \dfrac{1}{2^{mn}}}{2^n - 1}$

(c) $\dfrac{1 - \dfrac{1}{2^m}}{2^n - 1}$ (d) None of these

51. ${}^nC_0 - \dfrac{{}^nC_1}{2} + \dfrac{{}^nC_2}{3} - ... + (-1)^n \dfrac{{}^nC_n}{n + 1} =$

(a) $\dfrac{1}{n - 1}$ (b) $\dfrac{1}{n}$

(c) $\dfrac{1}{n + 1}$ (d) None of these

52. For all $n \in N$, $2^{4n} - 15n - 1$ is divisible by :

(a) 225   (b) 125

(c) 325   (d) None of these

53. When 5^{99} is divided by 13, the remainder is :

(a) 8   (b) 9

(c) 10   (d) None of these

54. If $(2 + \sqrt{3})^n = I + f$, where I and n are positive integers and $0 < f < 1$, then $(1 - f)(I + f) =$

(a) 1   (b) 2

(c) -1 (d) None of these

55. The coefficient of x^{50} in the expression $(1+x)^{1000} + 2x(1 + x)^{999} + 3x^2(1 + x)^{998} + ... + 1001 x^{1000}$ is :

(a) ${}^{1000}C_{50}$ (b) ${}^{1001}C_{50}$

(c) ${}^{1002}C_{50}$ (d) None of these

56. The last digit of the number $(32)^{32}$ is :

(a) 4   (b) 6

(c) 8   (d) None of these

57. If n is an even positive integer and $k = \dfrac{3n}{2}$, then $\sum_{r = 1}^k (-3)^{r-1} \cdot {}^{3n}C_{2r-1} =$

(a) 1   (b) -1

(c) 0   (d) 2

58. If a and d are two complex numbers, then the sum to (n + 1) terms of the series

$aC_0 - (a + d) C_1 + (a + 2d) C_2 - (a + 3d) C_3 + ...$

is :

(a) a
(b) d
(c) 0
(d) None of these

59. If $(1 + x)^n = C_0 + C_1 x + C_2 x^2 + ... + C_n x^n$, then

$2C_0 + 2^2 \cdot \dfrac{C_1}{2} + 2^3 \cdot \dfrac{C_2}{3} + ... + 2^{n+1} \dfrac{C_n}{n + 1} =$

(a) $\dfrac{3^{n+1} - 1}{n + 1}$
(b) $\dfrac{3^n - 1}{n}$

(c) $\dfrac{3^{n+2} - 1}{n + 2}$
(d) None of these

60. $\displaystyle\sum_{k = 0}^{n} \dfrac{{}^nC_k}{(k + 1)(k + 2)} =$

(a) $\dfrac{2^{n+1} - n - 3}{(n + 1)(n + 2)}$
(b) $\dfrac{2^{n+2} - n - 3}{(n + 1)(n + 2)}$

(c) $\dfrac{2^{n+2} - n + 3}{(n + 1)(n + 2)}$
(d) None of these.

61. If $(1 + x)^n = C_0 + C_1 x + C_2 x^2 + ... + C_n x^n$, then

$C_0^2 + C_1^2 + C_2^2 + ... + C_n^2 =$

(a) $\dfrac{(2n)!}{(n!)^2}$
(b) $\dfrac{(2n)!}{(n - 1)!(n + 1)!}$

(c) $\dfrac{(2n)!}{(n - 2)!(n + 2)!}$
(d) None of these

62. If $(1 + x)^n = C_0 + C_1 x + C_2 x^2 + ... + C_n x^n$, then

$C_0C_1 + C_1C_2 + C_2C_3 + ... + C_{n-1} C_n =$

(a) $\dfrac{(2n!)!}{(n!)^2}$
(b) $\dfrac{(2n)!}{(n - 1)!(n + 1)!}$

(c) $\dfrac{(2n)!}{(n - 2)!(n + 2)!}$
(d) None of these.

63. If $(1 + x)^n = C_0 + C_1 x + C_2 x^2 + ... + C_n x^n$, then

$C_0C_2 + C_1C_3 + C_2C_4 + ... + C_{n-2} C_n =$

(a) $\dfrac{(2n)!}{(n!)^2}$
(b) $\dfrac{(2n)!}{(n - 1)!(n + 1)!}$

(c) $\dfrac{(2n)!}{(n - 2)!(n + 2)!}$
(d) None of these

64. If $(1 + x)^n = C_0 + C_1 x + C_2 x^2 + ... + C_n x^n$, then

$C_0C_r + C_1C_{r+1} + C_2C_{r+2} + ... + C_{n-r} C_n =$

(a) $\dfrac{(2n)!}{(n!)^2}$
(b) $\dfrac{(2n)!}{(n - r)!(n + r)!}$

(c) $\dfrac{(2n)!}{[(n - 1)!]^2}$
(d) None of these

65. The value of the sum of the series

${}^{14}C_0 \cdot {}^{15}C_1 + {}^{14}C_1 \cdot {}^{15}C_2 + {}^{14}C_2 \cdot {}^{15}C_3 + ...$

$+ {}^{14}C_{14} \cdot {}^{15}C_{15}$ is :

(a) ${}^{29}C_{12}$
(b) ${}^{29}C_{10}$

(c) ${}^{29}C_{14}$
(d) ${}^{29}C_{16}$.

66. If $(1 + x)^n = C_0 + C_1 x + C_2 x^2 + ... + C_n x^n$, then for n even, $C_0^2 - C_1^2 + C_2^2 - ... + (-1)^n C_n^2$ is equal to :

(a) 0
(b) $(-1)^{n/2} \cdot {}^nC_{n/2}$

(c) ${}^nC_{n/2}$
(d) None of these

67. If $(1 + x)^{15} = C_0 + C_1 x + C_2 x^2 + ... + C_{15} x^{15}$, then

$({}^{15}C_0)^2 - ({}^{15}C_1)^2 + ({}^{15}C_2)^2 - ({}^{15}C_3)^2 + ... - ({}^{15}C_{15})^2$

is equal to :

(a) 0
(b) 1

(c) – 1
(d) None of these

68. ${}^mC_r + {}^mC_{r-1} \cdot {}^nC_1 + {}^mC_{r-2} \cdot {}^nC_2 + ... + {}^mC_1 \cdot {}^nC_{r-1} + {}^nC_r =$

(a) ${}^{m+n}C_{r-1}$
(b) ${}^{m+n}C_r$

(c) ${}^{m+n}C_{r+1}$
(d) None of these

69. If n is a positive integer and $C_k = {}^nC_k$, then the

value of $\displaystyle\sum_{k = 1}^{n} k^3 \left(\dfrac{C_k}{C_{k-1}}\right)^2$ is :

(a) $\dfrac{n(n + 2)(n + 1)^2}{12}$
(b) $\dfrac{n(n + 1)(n + 2)^2}{12}$

(c) $\dfrac{n(n + 1)(n + 2)}{12}$
(d) None of these

70. If $a_0, a_1, a_2, ..., a_{2n}$ are the coefficients in the expansion of $(1 + x + x^2)^n$ in ascending powers of x, then :

$a_0^2 - a_1^2 + a_2^2 - a_3^2 + ... - a_{2n-1}^2 + a_{2n}^2 =$

(a) a_{2n}
(b) a_n

(c) a_0
(d) None of these.

71. If T_0, T_1, T_2, ...T_n represent the terms in the expansion of $(x + a)^n$, then

$(T_0 - T_2 + T_4 - ...)^2 + (T_1 - T_3 + T_5 - ...)^2 =$

(a) $(x^2 - a^2)^n$ (b) $(x^2 - a^2)^{2n}$

(c) $(x^2 + a^2)^{2n}$ (d) $(x^2 + a^2)^n$

72. If $(1 + x)^n = C_0 + C_1 x + C_2 x^2 + ... + C_n x^n$, then

$(C_0 + C_1)(C_1 + C_2) ... (C_{n-1} + C_n) = K \cdot C_1 C_2 C_3$ ...... C_n, where $k =$

(a) $\dfrac{(n + 1)^n}{n!}$ (b) $\dfrac{n^2}{(n - 1)!}$

(c) $\dfrac{(n + 1)^n}{(n - 1)!}$ (d) None of these

73. $\dfrac{C_1}{C_0} + 2\dfrac{C_2}{C_1} + 3\dfrac{C_3}{C_2} + ... + n\dfrac{C_n}{C_{n-1}} =$

(a) $\dfrac{n(n - 1)}{2}$ (b) $\dfrac{n(n + 1)}{2}$

(c) $\dfrac{(n + 1)(n + 2)}{2}$ (d) None of these

74. If $S_n = 1 + q + q^2 + q^3 + ... + q^n$ and

$S'_n = 1 + \left(\dfrac{q + 1}{2}\right) + \left(\dfrac{q + 1}{2}\right)^2 + ... \left(\dfrac{q + 1}{2}\right)^n$, $q \neq 1$

then

$^{n+1}C_1 + {}^{n+1}C_2 \cdot S_1 + {}^{n+1}C_3 \cdot S_2 + ... + {}^{n+1}C_{n+1} \cdot S_n =$

(a) $2^{n-1} \cdot S'_n$ (b) $2^n \cdot S'_n$

(c) $2^{n+1} \cdot S'_n$ (d) None of these

75. $^nC_n + {}^{n+1}C_n + {}^{n+2}C_n + ... + {}^{n+k}C_n =$

(a) $^{n+k-1}C_{n+1}$ (b) $^{n+k}C_{n+1}$

(c) $^{n+k+1}C_{n+1}$ (d) None of these

76. The last three digits of 17^{256} are :

(a) 681 (b) 816

(c) 186 (d) 168

77. If $32^{32^{32}}$ is divided by 7, then the remainder is :

(a) 1 (b) 2

(c) 3 (d) 4

78. The sum of the coefficients in the expansion of $(7x - 8y)^{149}$ is :

(a) 1 (b) -1

(c) 0 (d) None of these

79. If $(1 + x)^n = C_0 + C_1 x + C_2 x^2 + ... + C_n x^n$, then

$C_0^2 + \dfrac{C_1^2}{2} + \dfrac{C_2^2}{3} + ... + \dfrac{C_n^2}{n + 1} =$

(a) $\dfrac{(2n + 1)!}{[(n + 1)!]^2}$ (b) $\dfrac{(2n)!}{(n!)^2}$

(c) $\dfrac{(2n - 1)!}{[(n - 1)!]^2}$ (d) None of these

80. If $(1 + x)^n = C_0 + C_1 x + C_2 x^2 + ... + C_n x^n$, then

$\displaystyle\sum_{0 \leq i \leq j \leq n}\sum (C_i + C_j)^2 =$

(a) $(n - 1) \cdot {}^{2n}C_n + 2^{2n}$

(b) $n \cdot {}^{2n}C_n + 2^{2n}$

(c) $(n + 1) \cdot {}^{2n}C_n + 2^{2n}$

(d) None of these

81. If n is an even positive integer, then

$\dfrac{1}{1!(n - 1)!} + \dfrac{1}{3!(n - 3)!} + \dfrac{1}{5!(n - 5)!} + ... + \dfrac{1}{(n - 1)! \, 1!} =$

(a) $\dfrac{2^{n-1}}{(n - 1)!}$ (b) $\dfrac{2^{n-1}}{n!}$

(c) $\dfrac{2^n}{n!}$ (d) None of these

82. The total number of terms in the expansion of $(a + b + c + d)^n$, $n \in N$ is :

(a) $\dfrac{n(n + 1)(n + 2)}{6}$

(b) $\dfrac{n(n + 1)(n + 2)(n + 3)}{6}$

(c) $\dfrac{(n + 1)(n + 2)(n + 3)}{6}$

(d) None of these

83. The greatest coefficient in the expansion of $(x + y + z + w)^{15}$ is :

(a) $\dfrac{15!}{3!(4!)^3}$ (b) $\dfrac{15!}{(3!)^3 4!}$

(c) $\dfrac{15!}{2!(4!)^2}$ (d) None of these

84. The coefficient of $x^3 y^4 z^2$ in the expansion of $(2x - 3y + 4z)^9$ is :

(a) 12063600 (b) 13063600

(c) 11063600 (d) None of these

85. The coefficient of x^r in the expansion of $(1-4x)^{-1/2}$ is:

(a) $\dfrac{2r!}{(r!)^2}$

(b) $\dfrac{2r!}{(r!)^2} \cdot 2^r$

(c) $\dfrac{2r!}{(r!)^2} \cdot 2^{2r}$

(d) None of these

86. $1 - \dfrac{1}{2} \cdot \dfrac{1}{2} + \dfrac{1\cdot 3}{2\cdot 4} \cdot \dfrac{1}{2^2} - \dfrac{1\cdot 3\cdot 5}{2\cdot 4\cdot 6} \cdot \dfrac{1}{2^3} + \dfrac{1\cdot 3\cdot 5\cdot 7}{2\cdot 4\cdot 6\cdot 8} \cdot \dfrac{1}{2^4} \cdots =$

(a) $\dfrac{1}{\sqrt{3}}$

(b) $\sqrt{\dfrac{2}{3}}$

(c) 1

(d) $\sqrt{\dfrac{4}{3}}$

87. The coefficient of x^n in the expansion of

$\dfrac{x}{(x-a)(x-b)}$ in ascending power of x is :

(a) $\dfrac{a^n - b^n}{ab(a-b)}$

(b) $\dfrac{b^n - a^n}{ab(a-b)}$

(c) $\dfrac{a^n - b^n}{a^n b^n (a-b)}$

(d) None of these

88. The coefficient of x^r in the expansion of $\dfrac{(1+4x^2+x^4)}{(1-x)^4}$ is :

(a) $r(r^2 + 3)$

(b) $r(r^2 + 2)$

(c) $r(r^2 - 3)$

(d) None of these

89. The approximate value of $(7.995)^{1/3}$ correct to four decimal places is :

(a) 1.9995

(b) 1.9996

(c) 1.9990

(d) 1.9991

90. The approximate value of $\dfrac{1}{\sqrt{23}}$ correct to four decimal places is :

(a) 0.2084

(b) 0.2085

(c) 0.2086

(d) None of these.

91. If x is so small that its square and higher powers may be neglected, then the value of $\dfrac{(8+3x)^{2/3}}{(2+3x)(4-5x)^{1/2}}$ is :

(a) $1 - \dfrac{3}{2}x$

(b) $1 + \dfrac{5}{8}x$

(c) $1 - \dfrac{5}{8}x$

(d) None of these

92. If c is a quantity so small that c^3 may be neglected in comparison with l^3, then $\sqrt{\dfrac{l}{l+c}} + \sqrt{\dfrac{l}{l-c}}$ is very nearly equal to :

(a) $2 + \dfrac{3c^2}{4l^2}$

(b) $2 + \dfrac{3l^2}{4c^2}$

(c) $2 + \dfrac{4c^2}{3l^2}$

(d) None of these

93. If x is so small that its cube and higher powers may be neglected, then the value of

$\dfrac{3\left(x+\dfrac{4}{9}\right)^{1/2} \cdot \left(1-\dfrac{3x^2}{4}\right)^{1/2}}{2\left(1+\dfrac{9x}{16}\right)^2}$ is :

(a) $1 + \dfrac{307}{256}x^2$

(b) $1 + \dfrac{256}{307}x^2$

(c) $1 - \dfrac{307}{256}x^2$

(d) None of these

94. The coefficient of x^6 in the expansion of $(1-2x)^{-5/2}$ is:

(a) $\dfrac{15021}{16}$

(b) $\dfrac{15015}{8}$

(c) $\dfrac{15015}{16}$

(d) None of these

95. If the binomial expansion of $(a+bx)^{-2}$ is $\dfrac{1}{4} - 3x + \ldots$, then the values of a and b are :

(a) 2, 12

(b) 2, 10

(c) 1, 12

(d) None of these

96. The two values of the rational exponent m such that in the binomial expansion of $(1-x)^m$, the coefficient of x^2 is 3, are :

(a) $-3, 2$

(b) $3, 2$

(c) $3, -2$

(d) $-3, -2$

97. If $\dfrac{(1-3x)^{1/2} + (1-x)^{5/3}}{\sqrt{4-x}}$ is approximately equal to a + bx for all small values of x, then :

(a) $a = 1, b = -\dfrac{35}{24}$

(b) $a = -\dfrac{35}{24}, b = 1$

(c) $a = 1, b = \dfrac{35}{24}$

(d) None of these

98. If x is nearly equal to 1, then the approximate value of $\dfrac{mx^m - nx^n}{m - n}$ is :

(a) x^m (b) x^n

(c) x^{m+n} (d) None of these

99. If p is nearly equal to q and $n > 1$, then $\dfrac{(n+1)p + (n-1)q}{(n-1)p + (n+1)q} =$

(a) $\left(\dfrac{p}{q}\right)^n$ (b) $\left(\dfrac{q}{p}\right)^n$

(c) $\left(\dfrac{q}{p}\right)^{1/n}$ (d) None of these

100. If x is nearly equal to one, then the approximate value of $\dfrac{ax^b - bx^a}{x^b - x^a}$ is :

(a) $\dfrac{1}{x-1}$ (b) $\dfrac{1}{1-x}$

(c) $x - 1$ (d) $1 - x$

101. If n and N are nearly equal, then the approximate value of $\dfrac{N}{N+n} + \dfrac{n+N}{4n}$ is :

(a) $\left(\dfrac{N}{n}\right)^{1/2}$ (b) $\left(\dfrac{n}{N}\right)^{1/2}$

(c) $\left(\dfrac{N}{n}\right)^{3/2}$ (d) $\left(\dfrac{n}{N}\right)^{3/2}$

102. The approximate value of $\sqrt[3]{999}$ to three places of decimal is :

(a) 9.992   (b) 9.997

(c) 9.999   (d) None of these

103. If the expansion of $\left(x - \dfrac{1}{x^2}\right)^{2n}$ contains a term independent of x, then n is a multiple of :

(a) 5   (b) 2

(c) 3   (d) None of these

104. The expression $[x + (x^3 - 1)^{1/2}]^5 + [x - (x^3 - 1)^{1/2}]^5$ is a polynomial of degree :

(a) 5   (b) 6

(c) 7   (d) 8

105. $7^9 + 9^7$ is divisible by :

(a) 16   (b) 24

(c) 64   (d) 72

106. If x is very small in magnitude when compared with a, then the approximate value of $\left(\dfrac{a}{a+x}\right)^{1/2} + \left(\dfrac{a}{a-x}\right)^{1/2}$ is:

(a) $2 + \dfrac{3x^2}{4a^2}$ (b) $2 - \dfrac{3x^2}{4a^2}$

(c) $2 + \dfrac{4x^2}{3a^2}$ (d) None of these

107. If x is so small that x^3 can be neglected in comparison with y^3 such that $\sqrt{\dfrac{y}{y+x}} + \sqrt{\dfrac{y}{y-x}} = 2 + k \cdot \dfrac{x^2}{y^2}$ nearly, then the value of k is :

(a) $\dfrac{4}{3}$ (b) $\dfrac{3}{4}$

(c) $\dfrac{1}{4}$ (d) None of these

108. If $(1 + 2x + x^2)^n = \displaystyle\sum_{r=0}^{2n} a_r x^r$, then $a_r =$

(a) $(^nC_r)^2$ (b) $^nC_r \cdot {}^nC_{r+1}$

(c) $^{2n}C_r$ (d) $^{2n}C_{r+1}$

109. If $x = \dfrac{1}{3}$, then the greatest term in the expansion of $(1 + 4x)^8$ is the

(a) 3rd term   (b) 6th term

(c) 5th term   (d) 4th term

110. The expansion of $(8 - 3x)^{3/2}$ in terms of powers of x is valid only if :

(a) $x > \dfrac{8}{3}$ (b) $|x| < \dfrac{8}{3}$

(c) $x < \dfrac{3}{8}$ (d) $x < \dfrac{8}{3}$

111. The largest coefficient in the expansion of $(1 + x)^{24}$ is :

(a) $^{24}C_{13}$ (b) $^{24}C_{11}$

(c) $^{24}C_{24}$ (d) $^{24}C_{12}$

112. The coefficient of x^6 in the expansion of $(1 + x + x^2)^{-3}$ is:

(a) 6   (b) 5

(c) 4   (d) 3

113. The sum of the series $\sum\limits_{r=0}^{10} {}^{20}C_r$ is :

(a) $2^{19} - \frac{1}{2} \cdot {}^{20}C_{10}$ (b) $2^{19} + \frac{1}{2} \cdot {}^{20}C_{10}$

(c) 2^{19} (d) 2^{20}

114. The binomial coefficient of the 4th term in the expansion of $(x - q)^5$ is :

(a) 15   (b) 20

(c) 10   (d) 5

115. If $(1 - x + x^2)^n = a_0 + a_1 x + a_2 x^2 + ... + a_{2n} x^{2n}$, then $a_0 + a_2 + a_4 + ... + a_{2n}$ is equal to :

(a) $3n^2 + \frac{1}{2}$ (b) $\frac{1 - 3^n}{2}$

(c) $\frac{3^n - 1}{2}$ (d) $\frac{3^n + 1}{2}$

116. The coefficient of x^{17} in the expansion of $(x - 1) (x - 2) (x - 3) ...(x - 18)$ is :

(a) $\frac{171}{2}$ (b) 342

(c) -171 (d) 684

117. If $|x| < 1$, then $1 + n \left(\frac{2x}{1+x}\right) + \frac{n(n+1)}{2!} \left(\frac{2x}{1+x}\right)^2$ + ... is equal to :

(a) $\left(\frac{1-x}{1+x}\right)^n$ (b) $\left(\frac{1+x}{1-x}\right)^n$

(c) $\left(\frac{1+x}{2x}\right)^n$ (d) $\left(\frac{2x}{1+x}\right)^n$

118. If, in the expansion of $(1 + x)^m (1 - x)^n$, the coefficient of x and x^2 are 3 and -6 respectively, then m is :

(a) 6   (b) 9

(c) 12   (d) 24

119. Let n and k be positive integers such that $n \geq \frac{k(k+1)}{2}$. The number of solutions $(x_1, x_2, ..., x_k)$, $x_1 \geq 1$, $x_2 \geq 2$, ..., $x_k \geq k$, all integers, satisfying $x_1 + x_2 + ... + x_k = n$, is :

(a) ${}^m C_{k-1}$ (b) ${}^m C_k$

(c) ${}^m C_{k+1}$ (d) None of these

where m $= \frac{1}{2} (2n - k^2 + k - 2)$

120. For $n > 2$,
$C_0 - 2^2 \cdot C_1 + 3^2 \cdot C_2 - ... + (-1)^n (n + 1)^2 C_n =$

(a) 0   (b) 1

(c) -1 (d) None of these

121. Let $R = (5\sqrt{5} + 11)^{2n+1}$ and $f = R - [R]$ where [ ] denotes the greatest integer function. Then R f =

(a) 2^{2n+1} (b) 2^{4n+1}

(c) 4^{2n+1} (d) None of these

122. If C_r stands for ${}^n C_r$, then the sum of the series

$$\frac{2 \left(\frac{n}{2}\right)! \left(\frac{n}{2}\right)!}{n!} \times [C_0^2 - 2 \cdot C_1^2 + 3 \cdot C_2^2 + ... + (-1)^n (n+1) C_n^2],$$

where n is an even positive integer, is equal to :

(a) $(-1)^n n$ (b) $(-1)^{n/2} (n + 1)$

(c) $(-1)^n (n + 2)$ (d) None of these

123. The integral part of $(8 + 3\sqrt{7})^n$ is :

(a) an even integer   (b) an odd integer

(c) zero   (d) Nothing can be said.

124. If $(1 + ax)^n = 1 + 8x + 24x^2 + ...$, then the values of a and n are equal to :

(a) 1, 2   (b) 3, 6

(c) 2, 3   (d) 2, 4

125. If n is a positive integer, then $2 \cdot 4^{2n+1} + 3^{3n+1}$ is divisible by :

(a) 27   (b) 11

(c) 9   (d) 2

126. Given positive integers $r > 1$, $n > 2$ and the coefficient of (3r) and $(r + 2)^{th}$ terms in the expansion of $(1 + x)^{2n}$ are equal, then :

(a) $n = 2r$ (b) $n = 2r + 1$

(c) $n = 3r$ (d) None of these

127. Coefficient of x^r in the expansion of $(1 - 2x)^{-1/2}$ is :

(a) $\frac{2r!}{(r!)^2 \cdot 2^{2r}}$ (b) $\frac{2r!}{2^r (r + 1) ! (r - 1)!}$

(c) $\frac{2r!}{(r!)^2}$ (d) $\frac{2r!}{(r!)^2 \cdot 2^r}$

128. The value of $\frac{C_1}{2} + \frac{C_3}{4} + \frac{C_5}{6} + \dots$ is equal to :

(a) $\frac{2^n + 1}{n + 1}$ (b) $\frac{2^n - 1}{n + 1}$

(c) $\frac{2^n + 1}{n - 1}$ (d) $\frac{2^n}{n + 1}$

129. The sum to $(n + 1)$ terms of the series

$\frac{C_0}{2} - \frac{C_1}{3} + \frac{C_2}{4} - \frac{C_3}{5} + \dots$ is :

(a) $\frac{1}{n(n + 1)}$ (b) $\frac{1}{n + 2}$

(c) $\frac{1}{n + 1}$ (d) None of these

130. If $\frac{1}{1 - 2x + x^2} = 1 + a_1 x + a_2 x^2 + \dots$ then the value of a_r is :

(a) $2r$ (b) $r + 1$

(c) r (d) $r - 1$

131. If the sum of the coefficients in the expansion of $(\alpha^2 x^2 + 2\alpha x + 1)^{51}$ vanishes, then α is equal to :

(a) -2 (b) 2

(c) 1 (d) -1.

132. The value of $2C_0 + \frac{2^2}{2} C_1 + \frac{2^3}{3} C_2 + \dots + \frac{2^{11}}{11} C_{10}$ is :

(a) $\frac{11^2 - 1}{11}$ (b) $\frac{11^3 - 1}{11}$

(c) $\frac{2^{11} - 1}{11}$ (d) $\frac{3^{11} - 1}{11}$

133. $1 + \frac{2nx}{1 + x} + \frac{n(n + 1)}{2!} + \dots \infty$ equals :

(a) $\left(\frac{1 + x}{1 - x}\right)^n$ (b) $\left(\frac{1 + x}{1 - x}\right)^{2n}$

(c) $\left(\frac{1 - x}{1 + x}\right)^n$ (d) None of these

134. Sum of the infinite series

$1 + \frac{2}{3} \cdot \frac{1}{2} + \frac{2}{3} \cdot \frac{5}{6} \cdot \frac{1}{2^2} + \frac{2}{3} \cdot \frac{5}{6} \cdot \frac{8}{9} \cdot \frac{1}{2^3} + \dots \infty$ is

(a) $2^{1/3}$ (b) $4^{1/3}$

(c) $8^{1/3}$ (d) None of these

135. The middle term in the expansion of $\left(x + \frac{1}{2x}\right)^{2n}$ is

(a) $\frac{1 \cdot 3 \cdot 5 \dots (2n - 1)}{n!}$ (b) $\frac{1 \cdot 3 \cdot 5 \dots (2n - 1)}{n!}$

(c) $\frac{1 \cdot 3 \cdot 5 \dots (2n + 1)}{n!}$ (d) None of these

136. The number of terms in the expansion of $(\sqrt{5} + \sqrt[4]{11})^{124}$ which are integers, is equal to :

(a) 0 (b) 30

(c) 31 (d) 32

137. The value of $\left\{\frac{5^{2n}}{24}\right\}$, $n \in N$ where $\{\ \}$ denotes the fractional part of x, is :

(a) $\frac{5}{24}$ (b) $\frac{9}{24}$

(c) $\frac{1}{24}$ (d) None of these

138. If the second term in the expansion of $\left(\sqrt[13]{a} + \frac{a}{\sqrt{a^{-1}}}\right)^n$ is $14 \, a^{5/2}$, then the value of $\frac{{}^nC_3}{{}^nC_2}$ is :

(a) 8 (b) 12

(c) 4 (d) None of these

139. The number of irrational terms in the expansion of $(4^{1/5} + 7^{1/10})^{45}$ is :

(a) 40 (b) 5

(c) 41 (d) None of these

140. Let $n \in N$ and $n < (\sqrt{2} + 1)^6$. Then the greatest value of n is :

(a) 198 (b) 196

(c) 197 (d) 199

141. The coefficient of x in the expansion of $[\sqrt{1 + x^2} - x]^{-1}$ in ascending powers of x, when $|x| < 1$, is :

(a) 0 (b) $\frac{1}{2}$

(c) $-\frac{1}{2}$ (d) 1

142. The greatest integer which divides the number $(100)^{100} - 1$ is :

  (a) 100   (b) 1000

  (c) 10000   (d) 100000

143. If A and B are coefficients of x^n in the expansions of $(1 + x)^{2n}$ and $(1 + x)^{2n-1}$ respectively, then :

  (a) $A = B$ (b) $2A = B$

  (c) $A = 2B$ (d) None of these

144. In the expansion of $(1 + x + x^3 + x^4)^{10}$, then coefficient of x^4 is :

  (a) $^{40}C_4$ (b) 210

  (c) 310   (d) None of these

145. If $(1 + x)^n = C_0 + C_1 x + C_2 x^2 + ... + C_n x^n$, then the value of $C_1 - 2 C_2 + 3 C_3 + ... + (-1)^{n-1} n C_n$ is :

  (a) 1   (b) 0

  (c) -1 (d) None of these

146. If $0 \le r \le n$, then the coefficient of x^r in the expansion of $P = 1 + (1 + x) + (1 + x)^2 + ... + (1 + x)^n$ is :

  (a) ^nC_r (b) $^{n+1}C_{r+1}$

  (c) $^nC_{r+1}$ (d) None of these

147. If $(1 + x)^n = C_0 + C_1 x + C_2 x^2 + ... + C_n x^n$, then the value of $\dfrac{C_0}{2} + \dfrac{C_1}{3} + \dfrac{C_2}{4} + ... + \dfrac{C_n}{n+2}$ is

  (a) $\dfrac{2^{n+1}}{(n+1)(n+2)}$ (b) $\dfrac{n \cdot 2^{n+1}}{(n+1)(n+2)}$

  (c) $\dfrac{n \cdot 2^{n+1} + 1}{(n+1)(n+2)}$ (d) None of these

148. If x is so small that its second and higher powers can be neglected, then coefficient of x in the expansion of $(1 + 4x)^{-5/4} \cdot (1 + 2x)^{1/2}$ is :

  (a) 0   (b) 2

  (c) 4   (d) -4

149. In the binomial expansion of $(a - b)^n$, $n \ge 5$, the sum of the 5th and 6th terms is zero. Then $\dfrac{a}{b}$ is equal to :

  (a) $\dfrac{1}{6}(n-5)$ (b) $\dfrac{1}{5}(n-4)$

  (c) $\dfrac{5}{n-4}$ (d) $\dfrac{6}{n-5}$

150. For $n \in N$, the value of $^nC_1 \cdot x (1-x)^{n-1} + 2 \cdot {}^nC_2 x^2 (1-x)^{n-2} + 3 \cdot {}^nC_3 x^3 (1-x)^{n-3} + ... + n \cdot {}^nC_n x^n =$

  (a) 0   (b) nx

  (c) $nx (2-x)^2$ (d) $\dfrac{n(n+1)}{2} x$

151. If $A = {}^{2n}C_0 \cdot {}^{2n}C_1 + {}^{2n}C_1 \, {}^{2n-1}C_1 + {}^{2n}C_2 \, {}^{2n-2}C_1 + ...$, then A is :

  (a) 0   (b) 2^n

  (c) $n \, 2^{2n}$ (d) 1

152. The first integral term in the expansion of $(\sqrt{3} + \sqrt[3]{2})^9$, is its :

  (a) 2nd term   (b) 3rd term

  (c) 4th term   (d) 5th term

153. The number of distinct terms in the expansion of $(x + 2y - 3z + 5w - 7u)^n$ is :

  (a) $n + 1$ (b) $^{n+4}C_4$

  (c) $n + 3$ (d) None of these

154. The greatest value of the term independent of x in the expansion of $(x \sin \alpha - x^{-1} \cos \alpha)^{10}$, $\alpha \in R$ is :

  (a) 2^5 (b) $\dfrac{10!}{(5!)^2}$

  (c) $\dfrac{1}{25} \cdot \dfrac{10!}{(5!)^2}$ (d) None of these

155. If n is a positive integer and $(3\sqrt{3} + 5)^{2n+1} = \alpha + \beta$, where α is an integer and $0 < \beta < 1$, then

  (a) α is an even integer

  (b) $(\alpha + \beta)^2$ is divisible by 2^{2n+1}

  (c) α is an odd integer

  (d) None of these

156. If $(1 + x + 2x^2)^{20} = a_0 + a_1 x + a_2 x^2 + ... + a_{40} x^{40}$ then $a_0 + a_2 + a_4 + ... + a_{38}$ equals :

  (a) $2^{19} (2^{20} + 1)$ (b) $2^{19} (2^{20} - 1)$

  (c) $2^{20} (2^{19} - 1)$ (d) None of these

157. For $1 \le r \le n$, the value of $^nC_r + {}^{n-1}C_r + {}^{n-2}C_r + ... + {}^rC_r$ is :

  (a) $^nC_{r+1}$ (b) $^{n+1}C_r$

  (c) $^{n+1}C_{r+1}$ (d) None of these

158. The coefficient of x^n in the polynomial

$(x + {}^{2n+1}C_0) (x + {}^{2n+1}C_1) (x + {}^{2n+1}C_2) \ldots\ldots$

$(x + {}^{2n+1}C_n)$ is :

(a) 2^{n+1} (b) $2^{2n+1} - 1$

(c) 2^{2n} (d) None of these

159. If sum of the coefficients in the expansion of

$(\alpha x^2 - 2x + 1)^{35}$ is equal to sum of coefficients in the expansion of $(x - \alpha y)^{35}$ then $\alpha =$

(a) 0   (b) 1

(c) any real number   (d) None of these

160. If the fourth term of $\left(\sqrt{x^{\left(\frac{1}{1+ln\,x}\right)}} + \sqrt[12]{x} \right)^6$ is

equal to 200 and $x > 1$, then x is equal to :

(a) $10\sqrt{2}$ (b) 10

(c) 10^4 (d) None of these

161. The remainder of 7^{103} when divided by 25 is :

(a) 7   (b) 14

(c) 18   (d) 1

162. The sum of the last ten coefficients in the expansion of $(1 + x)^{19}$ when expanded in ascending powers of x is :

(a) 2^{18} (b) 2^{19}

(c) $2^{18} - {}^{19}C_{10}$ (d) None of these

163. If $(1 + x)^n = C_0 + C_1 x + C_2 x^2 + \ldots + C_n x^n$ then

$\underset{0 \le i \le j \le n}{\sum\sum} (c_i - c_j)^2 =$

(a) $(n + 1)\, {}^{2n}C_n - 2^{2n}$

(b) $(n + 1)^2 \times {}^{2n}C_n - 2^n$

(c) $(n + 1) \times {}^{2n}C_n + 2^n$

(d) None of these

164. The last two digits of the number 3^{400} are :

(a) 39   (b) 29

(c) 01   (d) 43

165. If n is an even integer and a, b, c are distinct numbers, then number of distinct terms in the expansion of $(a + b + c)^n + (a + b - c)^n$ is

(a) $\left(\frac{n+2}{2}\right)^2$ (b) $n + 2$

(c) $\frac{n+4}{2}$ (d) None of these

166. $99^{50} - 99 \cdot 98^{50} + \frac{99.98}{1.2} (97)^{50} + \ldots + 99 =$

(a) -1 (b) -2

(c) -3 (d) 0

167. The sum upto $(n + 1)$ terms of the series

$\frac{C_0}{2} - \frac{C_1}{3} + \frac{C_2}{4} - \frac{C_3}{5} + \ldots$

(a) $\frac{1}{n+1}$ (b) $\frac{1}{n+2}$

(c) $\frac{n+4}{2}$ (d) None of these

168. If $n > 3$, then $\Sigma (-1)^r (n - r + 1) (n - r + 2) C_r =$

(a) 4   (b) 3

(c) 0   (d) 1

169. The coefficient of $\lambda^n \mu^n$ in the expansion of

$(1 + \lambda)^n (1 + \mu)^n (\lambda + \mu)^n$ is

(a) $\sum_{r=0}^{n} ({}^nC_r)^2$ (b) $\sum_{r=0}^{n} ({}^nC_{r+2})^2$

(c) $\sum_{r=0}^{n} ({}^nC_{r+3})^2$ (d) $\sum_{r=0}^{n} ({}^nC_r)^3$

170. The coefficient of x^r ($0 \le r \le (n-1)$) in the expansion of

$(x + 3)^{n-1} + (x + 3)^{n-2} (x + 2) +$

$(x + 3)^{n-3} (x + 2)^2 + \ldots + (x + 2)^{n-1}$ is

(a) ${}^nC_r (3^r - 2^n)$ (b) ${}^nC_r (3^{n-r} - 2^{n-r})$

(c) ${}^nC_r (3^r + 2^{n-r})$ (d) None of these

171. If n is even positive integer, then the condition that the greatest term in the expansion of $(1 + x)^n$ may have the greatest coefficient also is

(a) $\frac{n}{n+2} < x < \frac{n+2}{n}$ (b) $\frac{n+1}{n} < x < \frac{n}{n+1}$

(c) $\frac{n}{n+4} < x < \frac{n+4}{n}$ (d) None of these

172. Let n be an odd natural number greater than 1. Then the number of zeros at the end of the sum $99^n + 1$ is :

(a) 3   (b) 4

(c) 2   (d) None of these

173. The coefficient of the term independent of x in the expansion of $(1 + x + 2x^3) \left(\frac{3}{2}x^2 - \frac{1}{3x}\right)^9$ is :

(a) 1/3

(b) 19/54

(c) 17/54

(d) 1/4

174. The coefficient of x^{203} in the expansion of $(x - 1) (x^2 - 2) (x^3 - 3)...(x^{20} - 20)$ is :

(a) 35

(b) 21

(c) 13

(d) 15

175. If $(1 + x)^{10} = a_0 + a_1 x + a_2 x^2 + ... + a_{10} x^{10}$ then $(a_0 - a_2 + a_4 - a_6 + a_8 - a_{10})^2 + (a_1 - a_3 + a_5 - a_7 + a_9)^2$ is equal to :

(a) 3^{10}

(b) 2^{10}

(c) 2^9

(d) None of these

176. If the 4th term in the expansion of $\left(x + \frac{\alpha}{2x}\right)^n$ is 20, then the respective values of α and n are :

(a) 2, 7

(b) 5, 8

(c) 3, 6

(d) 2, 6

177. The last term in the binomial expansion of $\left(\sqrt[3]{2} - \frac{1}{\sqrt{2}}\right)^n$ is $\left(\frac{1}{3 \cdot \sqrt[3]{9}}\right)^{\log_3 8}$. Then the 5th term from the beginning is :

(a) $^{10}C_6$

(b) $2 \cdot {}^{10}C_4$

(c) $\frac{1}{2} \cdot {}^{10}C_4$

(d) None of these

178. The number of real negative terms in the binomial expansion of $(1 + ix)^{4n - 2}$, $n \in N$, $x > 0$ is :

(a) n

(b) n + 1

(c) n - 1

(d) 2n

179. The expansion $\left(\sqrt{2x^2 + 1} + \sqrt{2x^2 - 1}\right)^6 + \left(\frac{2}{\sqrt{2x^2 + 1} + \sqrt{2x^2 - 1}}\right)^6$ is a polynomial of degree :

(a) 5

(b) 6

(c) 7

(d) 8

180. If n is a positive integer, then $(\sqrt{3} + 1)^{2n} - (\sqrt{3} - 1)^{2n}$ is   [AIEEE - 2012]

(a) an irrational number

(b) an odd positive integer

(c) an even positive integer

(d) a rational number other than positive integers

181. The coefficient of x^7 in the expansion of $(1 - x - x^2 + x^3)^6$ is :   [AIEEE - 2011]

(a) 132

(b) 144

(c) -132

(d) -144

182. The remainder left out when $8^{2n} - (62)^{2n+1}$ is divided by 9 is :   [AIEEE - 2009]

(a) 0

(b) 2

(c) 7

(d) 8

183. Statement 1: $\sum\limits_{r = 0}^{n} (r + 1) \, {}^nC_r = (n + 2) \, 2^{n-1}$

Statement 2 : $\sum\limits_{r = 0}^{n} (r + 1) \, {}^nC_r x^r = (1 + x)^n + nx(1 + x)^{n-1}$ [AIEEE - 2008]

(a) Statement 1 is false, statement 2 is true.

(b) Statement 1 is true, statement 2 is true; statement 2 is a correct explanation for statement 1.

(c) Statement 1 is true, statement 2 is true; statement 2 is not a correct explanation for statement 1.

(d) Statement 1 is true, statement 2 is false.

184. In the binomial expansion of $(a - b)^n$, $n \geq 5$, the sum of 5th and 6th terms is zero, then $\frac{a}{b}$ equals :   [AIEEE - 2007]

(a) $\frac{5}{n - 4}$

(b) $\frac{6}{n - 5}$

(c) $\frac{n - 5}{6}$

(d) $\frac{n - 4}{5}$

185. The sum of the series   [AIEEE - 2007] $^{20}C_0 - {}^{20}C_1 + {}^{20}C_2 - {}^{20}C_3 + ... - ... + {}^{20}C_{10}$ is :

(a) $- {}^{20}C_{10}$

(b) $\frac{1}{2} {}^{20}C_{10}$

(c) 0

(d) $^{20}C_{10}$

186. If the expansion in powers of x of the function $\dfrac{1}{(1-ax)(1-bx)}$ is : **[AIEEE - 2006]**

$a_0 + a_1 x + a_2 x^2 + a_3 x^3 + \ldots$, then a_n is

(a) $\dfrac{b^n - a^n}{b - a}$

(b) $\dfrac{a^n - b^n}{b - a}$

(c) $\dfrac{a^{n+1} - b^{n+1}}{b - a}$

(d) $\dfrac{b^{n+1} - a^{n+1}}{b - a}$

187. For natural numbers m, n if

$(1 - y)^m (1 + y)^n = 1 + a_1 y + a_2 y^2 + \ldots$,

and $a_1 = a_2 = 10$, then (m, n) is :

(a) (20, 45)

(b) (35, 20)

(c) (45, 35)

(d) (35, 45)

188. If the coefficients of rth, $(r + 1)^{th}$ and $(r + 2)^{th}$ terms in the binomial expansion of $(1 + y)^m$ are in A.P., then m and r satisfy the equation **[AIEEE - 2005]**

(a) $m^2 - m(4r - 1) + 4r^2 - 2 = 0$

(b) $m^2 - m(4r + 1) + 4r^2 + 2 = 0$

(c) $m^2 - m(4r + 1) + 4r^2 - 2 = 0$

(d) $m^2 - m(4r - 1) + 4r^2 + 2 = 0$

189. If the coefficient of x^7 in $\left[ax^2 + \left(\dfrac{1}{bx}\right)\right]^{11}$ equals the coefficient of x^{-7} in, $\left[ax^2 - \left(\dfrac{1}{bx}\right)\right]^{11}$ then a and b satisfy the relation **[AIEEE - 2005]**

(a) $a - b = 1$

(b) $a + b = 1$

(c) $\dfrac{a}{b} = 1$

(d) $ab = 1$

190. If x is [AIEEE - 2006] and higher powers of x may be neglected, then $\dfrac{(1 + x)^{3/2} - \left(1 + \dfrac{1}{2}x\right)^3}{(1 - x)^{1/2}}$ may be approximated as : **[AIEEE - 2005]**

(a) $1 - \dfrac{3}{8}x^2$

(b) $3x + \dfrac{3}{8}x^2$

(c) $-\dfrac{3}{8}x^2$

(d) $\dfrac{x}{2} - \dfrac{3}{8}x^2$

ANSWER KEY

1. (b)	2. (a)	3. (b)	4. (a)	5. (a)	6. (b)	7. (d)	8. (a)	9. (b)	10. (c)
11. (b)	12. (c)	13. (a)	14. (c)	15. (c)	16. (a)	17. (b)	18. (d)	19. (c)	20. (c)
21. (a)	22. (c)	23. (b)	24. (b)	25. (a)	26. (a)	27. (c)	28. (b)	29. (c)	30. (c)
31. (c)	32. (b)	33. (c)	34. (c)	35. (c)	36. (c)	37. (b)	38. (a)	39. (c)	40. (c)
41. (b)	42. (a)	43. (a)	44. (c)	45. (b)	46. (b)	47. (c)	48. (a)	49. (a)	50. (b)
51. (c)	52. (a)	53. (a)	54. (a)	55. (c)	56. (b)	57. (c)	58. (c)	59. (a)	60. (b)
61. (a)	62. (b)	63. (c)	64. (b)	65. (c)	66. (b)	67. (a)	68. (b)	69. (a)	70. (b)
71. (d)	72. (a)	73. (b)	74. (b)	75. (c)	76. (a)	77. (d)	78. (b)	79. (a)	80. (a)
81. (b)	82. (c)	83. (a)	84. (b)	85. (a)	86. (b)	87. (c)	88. (a)	89. (b)	90. (b)
91. (c)	92. (a)	93. (c)	94. (c)	95. (a)	96. (c)	97. (a)	98. (c)	99. (c)	100. (b)
101. (a)	102. (b)	103. (c)	104. (c)	105. (c)	106. (a)	107. (b)	108. (c)	109. (b)	110. (b)
111. (d)	112. (d)	113. (b)	114. (c)	115. (d)	116. (c)	117. (b)	118. (c)	119. (a)	120. (a)
121. (c)	122. (d)	123. (b)	124. (d)	125. (b)	126. (a)	127. (d)	128. (b)	129. (d)	130. (b)
131. (c)	132. (d)	133. (a)	134. (b)	135. (b)	136. (d)	137. (c)	138. (b)	139. (c)	140. (c)
141. (d)	142. (c)	143. (c)	144. (d)	145. (b)	146. (b)	147. (c)	148. (d)	149. (b)	150. (b)
151. (c)	152. (c)	153. (b)	154. (c)	155. (a)	156. (b)	157. (c)	158. (a)	159. (b)	160. (a)
161. (c)	162. (a)	163. (a)	164. (c)	165. (a)	166. (d)	167. (d)	168. (c)	169. (d)	170. (b)
171. (a)	172. (c)	173. (b)	174. (c)	175. (b)	176. (d)	177. (a)	178. (a)	179. (b)	180. (a)
181. (d)	182. (b)	183. (b)	184. (d)	185. (b)	186. (d)	187. (d)	188. (c)	189. (d)	190. (c)

Chapter 12

EXPONENTIAL AND LOGARITHMIC SERIES

MULTIPLE CHOICE QUESTIONS

1. The sum of the series $\frac{2}{1!} + \frac{4}{3!} + \frac{6}{5!} + \ldots \infty$ is :

   (a) e   (b) 2e

   (c) 3e   (d) 4e

2. The sum of the series $\frac{1}{0!} + \frac{3}{2!} + \frac{5}{4!} + \frac{7}{6!} + \ldots \infty$ is :

   (a) e   (b) 2e

   (c) 3e   (d) None of these

3. The value of

   $\left(1 + \frac{1}{2!} + \frac{1}{4!} + \ldots\right)^2 - \left(1 + \frac{1}{3!} + \frac{1}{5!} + \ldots\right)^2$ is :

   (a) 2   (b) −2

   (c) 1   (d) −1

4. The coefficient of x^{12} in the expansion of e^{2x} is :

   (a) $\frac{2^{12}}{12!}$ (b) $\frac{2^{11}}{12!}$

   (c) $\frac{2^{10}}{12!}$ (d) None of these

5. The value of $\dfrac{1 + \frac{2^2}{2!} + \frac{2^4}{3!} + \frac{2^6}{4!} + \ldots}{1 + \frac{1}{2!} + \frac{2}{3!} + \frac{2^2}{4!} + \ldots}$ is :

   (a) $\frac{1}{2}(e^2 - 1)$ (b) $e^2 - 1$

   (c) $\frac{1}{4}(e^2 - 1)$ (d) None of these

6. The coefficient of x^n in the expansion of $\frac{a - bx}{e^x}$ is

   (a) $\frac{(-1)^n}{n!}(a - bn)$ (b) $\frac{(-1)^n}{n!}(a + bn)$

   (c) $\frac{(-1)^n}{n!}(b + an)$ (d) None of these

7. The coefficient of x^n in the series :

   $\frac{1 + x}{1!} + \frac{(1 + x)^2}{2!} + \frac{(1 + x)^3}{3!} + \ldots$ is :

   (a) $\frac{2e}{n!}$ (b) $\frac{4e}{n!}$

   (c) $\frac{e}{n!}$ (d) None of these

8. The coefficient of x^n in the expansion of

   $\left[1 + \frac{a + bx}{1!} + \frac{(a + bx)^2}{2!} + \frac{(a + bx)^3}{3!} + \ldots\right]$ is :

   (a) $\frac{e^a b^n}{n!}$ (b) $\frac{e^a \cdot b^n}{(n - 1)!}$

   (c) $\frac{e^b \cdot a^n}{n!}$ (d) None of these

9. $\sum\limits_{n=1}^{\infty} \dfrac{c(n, 0) + c(n, 1) + \ldots + c(n, n)}{P(n, n)}$ is equal to :

   (a) e^2 (b) $e^2 + 1$

   (c) $e^2 - 1$ (d) None of these

10. The sum of the series $2\left(\frac{1}{3!} + \frac{2}{5!} + \frac{3}{7!} + \ldots \infty\right)$ is

    (a) e   (b) e^{-1}

    (c) 2e   (d) $2e^{-1}$

11. The sum of the series $1 + \frac{2^2}{2!} + \frac{3^2}{3!} + \frac{4^2}{4!} + \ldots \infty$ is

    (a) e   (b) 2e

    (c) 3e   (d) None of these

12. The sum of the series $1 + \frac{2^3}{2!} + \frac{3^3}{3!} + \frac{4^3}{4!} + \ldots \infty$ is

    (a) 5e   (b) 4e

    (c) 2e   (d) e

13. The sum of the series

    $1 + \frac{1 + 2}{2!} + \frac{1 + 2 + 3}{3!} + \frac{1 + 2 + 3 + 4}{4!} + \ldots \infty$ is :

    (a) e   (b) $\frac{1}{2}e$

    (c) $\frac{3}{2}e$ (d) None of these

14. The coefficient of x^n in the expansion of $\dfrac{(a + bx + cx^2)}{e^x}$ is :

(a) $\dfrac{(-1)^n}{n!} [cn^2 - (b + c) n + a]$

(b) $\dfrac{(-1)^n}{n!} [cn^2 + (b + c) n + a]$

(c) $\dfrac{(-1)^n}{n!} [cn^2 - (b + c) n - a]$

(d) None of these

15. The sum of series $\dfrac{1}{1\cdot 2} + \dfrac{1\cdot 3}{1\cdot 2\cdot 3\cdot 4} + \dfrac{1\cdot 3\cdot 5}{1\cdot 2\cdot 3\cdot 4\cdot 5\cdot 6} + \dots$ is

(a) $\sqrt{e}$

(b) $\sqrt{e} - 1$

(c) $\sqrt{e} - 2$

(d) None of these

16. The sum of series $\dfrac{1\cdot 3}{1!} + \dfrac{2\cdot 4}{2!} + \dfrac{3\cdot 5}{3!} + \dfrac{4\cdot 6}{4!} + \dots \infty$ is

(a) e

(b) $2e$

(c) $3e$

(d) $4e$

17. The sum of the series
$\dfrac{4}{1!} + \dfrac{11}{2!} + \dfrac{22}{3!} + \dfrac{37}{4!} + \dfrac{56}{5!} + \dots \infty$ is :

(a) $6e$

(b) $6e - 1$

(c) $6e - 2$

(d) None of these

18. The sum of the series
$1 + \dfrac{1^2 + 2^2}{2!} + \dfrac{1^2 + 2^2 + 3^2}{3!} + \dfrac{1^2 + 2^2 + 3^2 + 4^2}{4!} + \dots \infty$ is :

(a) $\dfrac{5e}{6}$

(b) $\dfrac{11e}{6}$

(c) $\dfrac{17e}{6}$

(d) None of these

19. The sum of the series $1 + \dfrac{1}{2!} + \dfrac{1\cdot 3}{4!} + \dfrac{1\cdot 3\cdot 5}{6!} + \dots$ is

(a) $\sqrt{e}$

(b) $e^{3/2}$

(c) $e^{-1/2}$

(d) e

20. $\displaystyle\sum_{n=1}^{\infty} \dfrac{n^2}{(n+1)!} =$

(a) e

(b) $e - 1$

(c) $1 - e$

(d) None of these

21. The sum of the series $1 + \dfrac{1}{3}\left(\dfrac{1}{2}\right)^2 + \dfrac{1}{5}\left(\dfrac{1}{2}\right)^4 + \dots \infty$
is :

(a) $\log 3$

(b) $2 \log 3$

(c) $\log \dfrac{3}{2}$

(d) None of these

22. The sum of the series
$3 \log 2 + \dfrac{1}{4} - \dfrac{1}{2}\left(\dfrac{1}{4}\right)^2 + \dfrac{1}{3}\left(\dfrac{1}{4}\right)^3 \dots$ is equal to :

(a) $\log 3$

(b) $\log 5$

(c) $\log 10$

(d) None of these

23. The sum of the series
$2\left[\dfrac{1}{2n+1} + \dfrac{1}{3(2n+1)^3} + \dfrac{1}{5(2n+1)^5} + \dots\right]$ is :

(a) $\log \dfrac{n}{n+1}$

(b) $\log \dfrac{n+1}{n}$

(c) $\log n$

(d) None of these

24. The sum of the series
$\dfrac{n-1}{n+1} + \dfrac{1}{2} \cdot \dfrac{n^2 - 1}{(n+1)^2} + \dfrac{1}{3} \cdot \dfrac{n^3 - 1}{(n+1)^3} + \dots \infty$ is :

(a) $\log (n + 1)$

(b) $\log (n - 1)$

(c) $\log n$

(d) None of these

25. If α, β are roots of the equation $x^2 - px + q = 0$, then $(\alpha + \beta)\, x - \dfrac{\alpha^2 + \beta^2}{2} x^2 + \dfrac{\alpha^3 + \beta^3}{3} x^3 \dots$ is equal to :

(a) $\log (1 + px + qx^2)$ (b) $\log (1 - px + qx^2)$
(c) $\log (1 + px - qx^2)$ (d) None of these

26. $\log (1 + x)^{1+x} (1 - x)^{1-x} =$

(a) $\dfrac{x^2}{1\cdot 2} + \dfrac{x^4}{3\cdot 4} + \dfrac{x^6}{5\cdot 6} + \dots$

(b) $2\left[\dfrac{x^2}{1\cdot 2} + \dfrac{x^4}{3\cdot 4} + \dfrac{x^6}{5\cdot 6} + \dots\right]$

(c) $\dfrac{x^2}{1\cdot 2} + \dfrac{x^4}{2\cdot 3} + \dfrac{x^6}{3\cdot 4} + \dots$

(d) None of these

27. The sum of the series
$1 + \left(\dfrac{1}{2} + \dfrac{1}{3}\right)\dfrac{1}{4} + \left(\dfrac{1}{4} + \dfrac{1}{5}\right)\dfrac{1}{4^2} + \left(\dfrac{1}{6} + \dfrac{1}{7}\right)\dfrac{1}{4^3} + \dots \infty$ is

(a) $\log 3$

(b) $\log 4$

(c) $\log 12$

(d) $\log \sqrt{12}$

28. The product of the following series

$$\left(1 + \frac{1}{1!} + \frac{1}{2!} + \ldots\right)\left(1 - \frac{1}{1!} + \frac{1}{2!} - \frac{1}{3!} + \ldots\right) \text{ is}$$

(a) 1   (b) e^{-2}

(c) e^2 (d) -1

29. The sum of the series $9 + \frac{16}{2!} + \frac{27}{3!} + \frac{42}{4!} + \ldots \infty$ is

(a) $9e - 6$ (b) $11e - 6$

(c) $13e - 6$ (d) None of these

30. The sum of the series $1 + \frac{3}{2!} + \frac{7}{3!} + \frac{15}{4!} + \ldots \infty$ is

(a) $e(e + 1)$ (b) $e(1 - e)$

(c) $e(e - 1)$ (d) $3e$

31. The value of $(1 + 3) \log_e 3 + \frac{(1 + 3^2)}{2!}(\log_e 3)^2$

$+ \frac{(1 + 3^3)}{3!}(\log_e 3)^3 + \ldots \infty$ is

(a) 18   (b) 28

(c) 36   (d) None of these

32. $1 + \frac{2}{1 \cdot 2 \cdot 3} + \frac{2}{3 \cdot 4 \cdot 5} + \frac{2}{5 \cdot 6 \cdot 7} + \ldots \infty =$

(a) $2 \log_e 4$ (b) $2 \log_e 2$

(c) $2 \log_e 3$ (d) None of these

33. If $e^{e^x} = a_0 + a_1 x + a_2 x^2 + \ldots$ then :

(a) $a_0 = e$ (b) $a_1 = e$

(c) $a_2 = e$ (d) All of these

34. If $f = \frac{x}{1 + x^2} + \frac{1}{3}\left(\frac{x}{1 + x^2}\right)^3 + \frac{1}{5}\left(\frac{x}{1 + x^2}\right)^5 + \ldots \infty$

and $g = x - \frac{2}{3}x^3 + \frac{1}{5}x^5 + \frac{1}{7}x^7 - \frac{2}{9}x^9 + \ldots \infty$, then

(a) $f \equiv g$ (b) $2f \equiv g$

(c) $f \equiv 2g$ (d) None of these

35. The value $1 + \frac{1 + a}{2!} + \frac{1 + a + a^2}{3!} + \ldots \infty$ is :

(a) $\frac{e - e^a}{a - 1}$ (b) $\frac{e^a - e}{a - 1}$

(c) $\frac{e^{a-1} - e}{a - 1}$ (d) None of these

36. If $y = -\left(x^3 + \frac{x^6}{2} + \frac{x^9}{3} + \ldots\right)$, then :

(a) $x^3 = 1 - e^y$ (b) $x = \log(1 + y)$

(c) $x^3 = e^y$ (d) $x = 1 + e^y$

37. The sum of $\frac{1^2 \cdot 2}{1!} + \frac{2^2 \cdot 3}{2!} + \frac{3^2 \cdot 4}{3!} + \frac{4^2 \cdot 5}{4!} + \ldots$ is :

(a) $5e$ (b) $3e$

(c) $7e$ (d) $2e$

38. $\frac{1}{n!} + \frac{1}{2!(n - 2)!} + \frac{1}{4!(n - 4)!} + \ldots \infty$ is :

(a) $\frac{2^{n-1}}{n!}$ (b) $\frac{2^n}{(n + 1)!}$

(c) $\frac{2^n}{n!}$ (d) $\frac{2^{n-2}}{(n - 1)!}$

39. $\frac{1}{2}x^2 + \frac{2}{3}x^3 + \frac{3}{4}x^4 + \frac{4}{5}x^5 + \ldots$ is :

(a) $-\frac{x}{1 + x} + \log(1 + x)$

(b) $\frac{x}{1 + x} + \log(1 + x)$

(c) $\frac{x}{1 + x} + \log(1 - x)$

(d) None of these

40. If S_n denotes the sum of the products of the first n natural numbers taken two at a time, then

$\sum_{n=0}^{\infty} \frac{S_n}{(n + 1)!}$ is equal to :

(a) $\frac{13e}{24}$ (b) $\frac{11e}{24}$

(c) $\frac{11e}{12}$ (d) None of these

41. The value of

$(x + y)(x - y) + \frac{1}{2!}(x + y)(x - y)(x^2 + y^2)$

$+ \frac{1}{3!}(x + y)(x - y)(x^4 + y^4 + x^2 y^2) + \ldots \infty$ is :

(a) $e^{x^2} + e^{y^2}$ (b) $e^{x^2 - y^2}$

(c) $e^{x^2} - e^{y^2}$ (d) None of these

42. The value of

$\frac{1}{1 \cdot 2 \cdot 3 \cdot 4} + \frac{4}{3 \cdot 4 \cdot 5 \cdot 6} + \frac{9}{5 \cdot 6 \cdot 7 \cdot 8} + \frac{16}{7 \cdot 8 \cdot 9 \cdot 10} + \ldots \infty$ is :

(a) $\frac{1}{6} \log 2 - \frac{1}{24}$ (b) $\frac{5}{2} - \log 2$

(c) $\frac{3}{2} - \log 2$ (d) None of these

43. If $a = \sum\limits_{n=1}^{\infty} \dfrac{2n}{(2n-1)!}$, $b = \sum\limits_{n=1}^{\infty} \dfrac{2n}{(2n+1)!}$, then ab equals :

(a) $\dfrac{e+1}{e-1}$ (b) $\dfrac{e-1}{e+1}$

(c) e^2 (d) 1

44. If $S = \dfrac{y - 1 - \frac{1}{2}(y-1)^2 + \frac{1}{3}(y-1)^3 \dots}{a - 1 - \frac{1}{2}(a-1)^2 + \frac{1}{3}(a-1)^3 \dots}$, then S is equal to :

(a) $\log_a y$ (b) $\log_y a$

(c) $\log_e a$ (d) $\log_c y$

45. The sum of the series

$\log_4 2 - \log_8 2 + \log_{16} 2 - \dots \infty$ is :

(a) e^2 (b) $\log_e 2 + 1$

(c) $\log_e 2 - 1$ (d) $1 - \log_e 2$

46. If $S = \dfrac{1}{1 \cdot 2} - \dfrac{1}{2 \cdot 3} + \dfrac{1}{3 \cdot 4} - \dfrac{1}{4 \cdot 5} + \dots \infty$, then $e^S =$

(a) $\log_e \left(\dfrac{4}{e}\right)$ (b) $\dfrac{4}{e}$

(c) $\log_e \left(\dfrac{e}{4}\right)$ (d) $\dfrac{e}{4}$

47. The coefficient of x^n in the expansion of $\dfrac{e^{7x} + e^x}{e^{3x}}$ is :

(a) $\dfrac{4^{n-1} + (-2)^n}{n!}$ (b) $\dfrac{4^{n-1} + 2^n}{n!}$

(c) $\dfrac{4^{n-1} + (-2)^{n-1}}{n!}$ (d) $\dfrac{4^n + (-2)^n}{n!}$

48. $1 + \dfrac{(\log_e n)^2}{2!} + \dfrac{(\log_e n)^4}{4!} + \dots =$

(a) n (b) $\dfrac{1}{n}$

(c) $\dfrac{1}{2}(n + n^{-1})$ (d) $\dfrac{1}{2}(e^n + e^{-n})$

49. The expansion of $\left(1 + \dfrac{x^2}{2!} + \dfrac{x^4}{4!} + \dots\right)^2$ in ascending powers of x is :

(a) $1 + \dfrac{x^2}{2!} + \dfrac{x^4}{4!} + \dfrac{x^6}{6!} + \dots$

(b) $1 + \dfrac{2^2 x^2}{2!} + \dfrac{2^4 x^4}{4!} + \dots$

(c) $1 + \dfrac{2x^2}{2!} + \dfrac{2^3 x^4}{4!} + \dfrac{2^5 x^6}{6!} + \dots$

(d) None of these

50. If $e^x = y + \sqrt{1 + y^2}$, then the value of y is :

(a) $e^x - e^{-x}$ (b) $\dfrac{1}{2}(e^x - e^{-x})$

(c) $e^x + e^{-x}$ (d) $\dfrac{1}{2}(e^x + e^{-x})$

51. If $\dfrac{e^{5x} + e^x}{e^{3x}}$ is expanded in a series of ascending powers of x and n is an odd natural number, then the coefficient of x^n is :

(a) $\dfrac{2^n}{n!}$ (b) $\dfrac{2^{n+1}}{(2n)!}$

(c) $\dfrac{2^{2n}}{(2n)!}$ (d) None of these

52. If $x = 1 + 2 + \dfrac{4}{2!} + \dfrac{8}{3!} + \dfrac{16}{4!} + \dots$, then x^{-1} is equal to :

(a) e^{-2} (b) e^2

(c) $e^{1/2}$ (d) None of these

53. The sum of the series $\dfrac{12}{1!} + \dfrac{28}{3!} + \dfrac{50}{4!} + \dfrac{78}{5!} + \dots$ is :

(a) e (b) $3e$

(c) $4e$ (d) $5e$

54. If $a = \sum\limits_{n=0}^{\infty} \dfrac{x^{3n}}{(3n)!}$, $b = \sum\limits_{n=1}^{\infty} \dfrac{x^{3n-2}}{(3n-2)!}$

and $c = \sum\limits_{n=1}^{\infty} \dfrac{x^{3n-1}}{(3n-1)!}$, then the value of

$a^3 + b^3 + c^3 - 3abc$ is :

(a) 1   (b) 0

(c) -1 (d) -2

55. $\sum_{n=0}^{\infty} \dfrac{(\log_e x)^n}{n!}$ is equal to :

(a) $\log_e x$ (b) x

(c) $\log_x e$ (d) None of these

56. If $S = \sum_{n=0}^{\infty} \dfrac{(\log x)^{2n}}{(2n)!}$, then S equals :

(a) $x + x^{-1}$ (b) $x - x^{-1}$

(c) $\dfrac{1}{2}(x + x^{-1})$ (d) None of these

57. $e^{x-1-\frac{1}{2}(x-1)^2+\frac{1}{3}(x-1)^3-\frac{1}{4}(x-1)^4+\dots}$ is equal to :

(a) $\log(x-1)$ (b) $\log x$

(c) x (d) None of these

58. The coefficient of x^n, when n is a multiple of 3, in the expansion of $\log(1 + x + x^2)$ is :

(a) $\dfrac{-2}{n}$ (b) $\dfrac{2}{n}$

(c) $\dfrac{1}{n}$ (d) None of these

59. The coefficient of x^n in the expansion of $\log(1 + x + x^2)$, when n is not a multiple of 3, is :

(a) $\dfrac{-2}{n}$ (b) $\dfrac{1}{n}$

(c) $\dfrac{2}{n}$ (d) None of these

60. The coefficient of x^n in the expansion of $\log_e\left(\dfrac{1}{1 + x + x^2 + x^3}\right)$; when n is odd, is :

(a) $\dfrac{-2}{n}$ (b) $\dfrac{-1}{n}$

(c) $\dfrac{1}{n}$ (d) None of these

61. The sum of the series $2\{7^{-1} + 3^{-1} \cdot 7^{-3} + 5^{-1} \cdot 7^{-5} + \dots\}$ is :

(a) $\log_e\left(\dfrac{4}{3}\right)$ (b) $\log_e\left(\dfrac{3}{4}\right)$

(c) $2\log_e\left(\dfrac{3}{4}\right)$ (d) $2\log_e\left(\dfrac{4}{3}\right)$

62. If x, y, z are three consecutive positive integers, then

$\dfrac{1}{2}\log_e x + \dfrac{1}{2}\log_e z + \dfrac{1}{2xz+1} + \dfrac{1}{3}\left(\dfrac{1}{2xz+1}\right)^3 + \dots$

(a) $\log_e x$ (b) $\log_e y$

(c) $\log_e z$ (d) None of these

63. $\dfrac{9}{1!} + \dfrac{19}{2!} + \dfrac{35}{3!} + \dfrac{57}{4!} + \dfrac{85}{5!} + \dots =$

(a) $16e - 5$ (b) $7e - 3$

(c) $12e - 5$ (d) None of these

64. The sum of the series $\dfrac{1}{2!} - \dfrac{1}{3!} + \dfrac{1}{4!} - \dots$ upto infinity is **[AIEEE - 2007]**

(a) e^{-2} (b) e^{-1}

(c) $e^{-1/2}$ (d) $e^{1/2}$

ANSWER KEY

1. (a)	**2.** (a)	**3.** (c)	**4.** (a)	**5.** (b)	**6.** (b)	**7.** (c)	**8.** (a)	**9.** (c)	**10.** (b)
11. (b)	**12.** (a)	**13.** (c)	**14.** (a)	**15.** (b)	**16.** (d)	**17.** (b)	**18.** (c)	**19.** (a)	**20.** (b)
21. (a)	**22.** (c)	**23.** (b)	**24.** (c)	**25.** (a)	**26.** (b)	**27.** (d)	**28.** (a)	**29.** (b)	**30.** (c)
31. (b)	**32.** (b)	**33.** (d)	**34.** (a)	**35.** (b)	**36.** (a)	**37.** (c)	**38.** (a)	**39.** (c)	**40.** (b)
41. (c)	**42.** (a)	**43.** (d)	**44.** (a)	**45.** (d)	**46.** (b)	**47.** (d)	**48.** (c)	**49.** (c)	**50.** (b)
51. (d)	**52.** (a)	**53.** (d)	**54.** (a)	**55.** (b)	**56.** (c)	**57.** (d)	**58.** (a)	**59.** (b)	**60.** (b)
61. (a)	**62.** (b)	**63.** (c)	**64.** (b)						

Chapter 13

CO-ORDINATE GEOMETRY AND STRAIGHT LINES

MULTIPLE CHOICE QUESTIONS

1. The vertices of $\triangle ABC$ are A $(2, -1)$, B $(7, -5)$ and C $(5, 9)$. The length of median AD is :

   (a) 3

   (b) 4

   (c) 5

   (d) None of these

2. A point moves such that sum of its distances from $(1, 0)$ and $(-1, 0)$ is 4. The equation of its locus is :

   (a) $\dfrac{x^2}{4} + \dfrac{y^2}{3} = 1$

   (b) $4x^2 + 3y^2 = 12$

   (c) $4x^2 + 3y^2 = 1$

   (d) None of these

3. The ends of a rod of length 3 m move on the two co-ordinate axes. The locus of point on the rod which divides it in the ratio 1 : 2 is :

   (a) $\dfrac{x^2}{1} + \dfrac{y^2}{4} = 1$

   (b) $\dfrac{x^2}{4} + \dfrac{y^2}{1} = 1$

   (c) $\dfrac{x^2}{1} - \dfrac{y^2}{4} = 1$

   (d) $\dfrac{x^2}{4} - \dfrac{y^2}{1} = 1$

4. The distance between two parallel lines is 1. A point P lies between these lines at a distance 'd' from one of them. The length of a side of equilateral $\triangle PQR$, where Q lies on one parallel line and R on the other, is :

   (a) $\dfrac{2}{\sqrt{3}}\sqrt{d^2 + d + 1}$

   (b) $\dfrac{2}{\sqrt{3}}\sqrt{d^2 - d + 1}$

   (c) $\dfrac{1}{\sqrt{3}}\sqrt{d^2 + d + 1}$

   (d) $\dfrac{1}{\sqrt{3}}\sqrt{d^2 - d + 1}$

5. If the point $(1, 3)$ is equidistant from $(6, -1)$ and $(x, 8)$ then the value of x is :

   (a) 3

   (b) – 3

   (c) – 5

   (d) None of these

6. Co-ordinates of two points A and B are $(3, 4)$ and $(5, -2)$ respectively. If PA = PB and area of $\triangle PAB = 10$, then the co-ordinates of P are :

   (a) $(1, 0)$

   (b) $(7, -2)$

   (c) $(13, -4)$

   (d) None of these

7. If all the vertices of a triangle have integral co-ordinates, then the triangle will not be :

   (a) right angled

   (b) equilateral

   (c) isosceles

   (d) None of these

8. If A $(a + b, b - a)$, B $(a - b, a + b)$ and P (x, y) be such that PA = PB, then :

   (a) $ax = by$

   (b) $bx = ay$

   (c) $ax = -by$

   (d) $bx = -ay$

9. If B (x_1, y_1) and C (x_2, y_2) are such that $x_1 < x_2$, $y_1 > y_2$ and x_1, x_2 are zeros of $x^2 + 4x + 3 = 0$ and y_1, y_2 are zeros of $y^2 - y - 6 = 0$ and A $(3, -5)$ then, equation of bisector of interior angle A of $\triangle ABC$ is :

   (a) $x + y = 2$

   (b) $x + y = -2$

   (c) $x - y = 8$

   (d) None of these

10. The area of triangle formed by the lines $x + 2y - 2 = 0$, $x - y + 1 = 0$ and $2x + y = 7$ is :

    (a) 3

    (b) 4

    (c) 5

    (d) 6

11. The area of a triangle is 5 sq. units. Two of its vertices are $(2, 1)$ and $(3, -2)$. The third vertex lies on the line $x - y + 3 = 0$. The co-ordinates of 3rd vertex are :

    (a) $\left(\dfrac{7}{2}, \dfrac{13}{2}\right)$

    (b) $\left(\dfrac{3}{2}, \dfrac{3}{2}\right)$

    (c) $\left(\dfrac{7}{2}, \dfrac{3}{2}\right)$

    (d) $\left(\dfrac{-3}{2}, \dfrac{13}{2}\right)$

12. $(k, 2 - 2k)$, $(-k + 1, 2k)$ and $(-4 - k, 6 - 2k)$ are collinear. The value of 3k is :

    (a) – 1

    (b) $\dfrac{1}{2}$

    (c) $\dfrac{5}{2}$

    (d) – 3

13. If α, β, γ are the zeros of the equation $x^3 - 3x^2 + 21x - 7 = 0$, then the centroid of triangle with vertices $\left(\alpha, \frac{1}{\alpha}\right)$, $\left(\beta, \frac{1}{\beta}\right)$ and $\left(\gamma, \frac{1}{\gamma}\right)$ is :

(a) $\left(-1, \frac{21}{7}\right)$ (b) $\left(+1, \frac{-21}{7}\right)$

(c) $(1, 1)$ (d) None of these

14. The area of quadrilateral whose vertices are $(1, 1)$, $(7, -3)$, $(12, 2)$ and $(7, 21)$, taken in order, is :

(a) 82   (b) 132

(c) 282   (d) 364

15. The points $(3, 3)$, $(a, 0)$ and $(0, b)$ are collinear if :

(a) $\frac{1}{a} + \frac{1}{b} = \frac{1}{3}$ (b) $\frac{1}{a} - \frac{1}{b} = -\frac{1}{3}$

(c) $\frac{1}{a} - \frac{1}{b} = \frac{1}{3}$ (d) None of these

16. If the centroid of a triangle is origin and two of its vertices are $(3, -1)$ and $(4, 5)$, then the area of triangle is :

(a) $\frac{19}{2}$ (b) $\frac{19}{6}$

(c) $\frac{57}{2}$ (d) $\frac{57}{6}$

17. The circum radius of triangle having vertices $A(5, -1)$, $B(-1, 5)$ and $C(6, 6)$ is :

(a) $\frac{25\sqrt{2}}{8}$ (b) $\frac{17\sqrt{2}}{8}$

(c) $\frac{21\sqrt{2}}{8}$ (d) $\frac{5}{2}$

18. The incentre of triangle with vertices $(1, \sqrt{3})$, $(0, 0)$ and $(2, 0)$ is :

(a) $\left(1, \frac{\sqrt{3}}{2}\right)$ (b) $\left(1, \frac{1}{\sqrt{3}}\right)$

(c) $\left(\frac{2}{3}, \frac{\sqrt{3}}{2}\right)$ (d) None of these

19. The angles A, B, C of $\triangle ABC$ are in A.P. If $AB = 6$, $BC = 7$, then AC is :

(a) 3   (b) $\sqrt{5}$

(c) $\sqrt{41}$ (d) $\sqrt{43}$

20. The co-ordinates of incentre of triangle whose sides are $3x - 4y = 0$, $5x + 12y = 0$ and $y = 15$ are :

(a) $(1, 8)$ (b) $(-1, 8)$

(c) $(1, -8)$ (d) $(-1, -8)$

21. The orthocentre of triangle whose vertices are $(2, -1)$, $(-1, 3)$ and origin is :

(a) $(4, -3)$ (b) $(2, -3)$

(c) $(-1, 7)$ (d) $(-4, -3)$

22. Three vertices of a parallelogram taken in order are $(-3, 5)$, $(2, -4)$ and $(1, 7)$. Its fourth vertex is :

(a) $(1, -1)$ (b) $(-4, 16)$

(c) $(-2, -6)$ (d) $(0, 0)$

23. The orthocentre of triangle whose sides are $3x - 2y = 6$, $3x + 4y = -12$ and $3x - 8y + 12 = 0$ is

(a) $\left(\frac{1}{6}, \frac{23}{9}\right)$ (b) $\left(\frac{-1}{6}, \frac{-23}{9}\right)$

(c) $\left(\frac{-1}{6}, \frac{23}{9}\right)$ (d) $(1, 5)$

24. Two vertices of a triangle with orthocentre as origin are $(3, -1)$ and $(-2, 3)$. The third vertex of the triangle is :

(a) $\left(\frac{-36}{7}, \frac{-45}{7}\right)$ (b) $(36, -45)$

(c) $\left(\frac{6}{7}, \frac{-9}{7}\right)$ (d) None of these

25. The circumcentre of a triangle with vertices $(6, 2)$, $(5, 3)$ and $(-1, -5)$ is :

(a) $(5, 0)$ (b) $(0, -5)$

(c) $(\sqrt{5}, \sqrt{5})$ (d) $(2, -1)$

26. Two sides of a triangle are $3x - 2y + 6 = 0$ and $4x + 5y = 20$. If its orthocentre is $(1, 1)$, then its third side is :

(a) $26x + 122y - 1675 = 0$

(b) $26x - 122y + 1675 = 0$

(c) $26x - 122y - 1675 = 0$

(d) $26x + 122y + 1675 = 0$

27. If orthocentre and circumcentre of a triangle are (1, 1) and $\left(\frac{3}{2}, \frac{3}{4}\right)$, then the centroid of the triangle is :

(a) $\left(\frac{4}{3}, -\frac{5}{6}\right)$ (b) $\left(\frac{4}{3}, \frac{5}{6}\right)$

(c) $\left(-\frac{4}{3}, \frac{5}{6}\right)$ (d) $\left(-\frac{4}{3}, -\frac{5}{6}\right)$

28. If one vertex of a triangle is (2, 1) and the midpoints of two sides through it are (–2, 2) and (0, 3), then the centroid of the triangle is :

(a) (–2, 3)   (b) (0, 0)

(c) (0, 2)   (d) None of these

29. A and B are two fixed points. The locus of P such that $\angle APB = 90°$ is :

(a) $x^2 - y^2 = a^2$ (b) $\frac{x^2}{a^2} + \frac{y^2}{b^2} = 1$

(c) $x^2 + y^2 = a^2$ (d) None of these

30. If four points A (p, 0), B (q, 0), C (r, 0) and D (s, 0) are such that the sum of the ratios in which C and D divide AB is zero and p, q are zeros of $ax^2 + 2hx + b = 0$ and r, s are zeros of $fx^2 + 2cx + g = 0$ then :

(a) $ag + fb = 2hc$ (b) $ag + fb = hc$

(c) $ag - fb = 2hc$ (d) $ag - fb = hc$

31. The incentre of triangle whose sides are $4x + 3y + 10 = 0$, $7x + 24y - 50 = 0$ and $5x - 12y + 26 = 0$ is :

(a) (0, 0)   (b) (1, –1)

(c) (–1, 1)   (d) (0, –1)

32. In order to remove first degree terms from the equation $2x^2 + 7y^2 + 8x - 14y + 4 = 0$, the origin should be shifted to :

(a) (–2, 1)   (b) (1, 2)

(c) (2, 1)   (d) (1, –2)

33. When origin is shifted to (1, 1), the co-ordinates of a point P become (cos α, cos β). The original co-ordinates of P were :

(a) $\left(2 \sin^2 \frac{\alpha}{2}, 2 \sin^2 \frac{\beta}{2}\right)$ (b) $\left(2 \sin \frac{\alpha}{2}, 2 \sin \frac{\beta}{2}\right)$

(c) $\left(2 \cos^2 \frac{\alpha}{2}, 2 \cos^2 \frac{\beta}{2}\right)$ (d) $\left(2 \cos \frac{\alpha}{2}, 2 \cos \frac{\beta}{2}\right)$

34. If the equation $2x^2 + y^2 - 4x - 4y = 0$ is transformed to $2X^2 + Y^2 - 8X - 8Y + 18 = 0$ by shifting origin to P, keeping the axes parallel to the original axes, then co-ordinates of P are :

(a) (1, 2)   (b) (–1, –2)

(c) (1, –2)   (d) (–1, 2)

35. A line through (2, 0) with slope $\frac{1}{\sqrt{3}}$ is rotated about (2, 0) in clockwise direction through an angle of 15°. The equation of the line in new position is :

(a) $(2 - \sqrt{3}) x - y - 4 + 2\sqrt{3} = 0$

(b) $(2 - \sqrt{3}) x - y + 4 + 2\sqrt{3} = 0$

(c) $(2 - \sqrt{3}) x + y - 4 + 2\sqrt{3} = 0$

(d) None of these

36. The equation of a line passing through A (–5, 4) and the portion of which is intercepted between the co-ordinate axes being divided at (–5, 4) in the ratio 1 : 2 is :

(a) $8x + 5y = 60$ (b) $8x - 5y = 60$

(c) $-8x + 5y = 60$ (d) $8x + 5y = -60$

37. The point on the line $x + y = 4$ that lies at a unit distance from the line $4x + 3y - 10 = 0$ is :

(a) (3, 1)   (b) (–6, 10)

(c) (1, 3)   (d) (5, –1)

38. Two vertices of a triangle are (3, –2) and (2, –3), its centroid lies on the line $3x - y - 8 = 0$ and its area is 1.5 square units. Its third vertex is :

(a) (–2, –10)   (b) (–1, 1)

(c) (–2, 10)   (d) (–1, –1)

39. The vertices of ΔABC are A (5, 2), B (6, 5), C (2, 3). The equation of bisector of $\angle BAC$ of ΔABC is :

(a) $2x + y + 12 = 0$ (b) $x + 2y - 12 = 0$

(c) $x + y + 12 = 0$ (d) $2x + y - 12 = 0$

40. A rectangle has the ends of one of its diagonals as (1, 2) and (5, 5). Its other diagonal is x = 3. The other two vertices of the rectangle are :

(a) (3, –1), (3, –6)   (b) (3, 1), (3, 6)

(c) (3, 1), (3, 5)   (d) (3, 0), (3, 2)

41. The co-ordinates of a point P, lying on the line $3x + 2y + 10 = 0$, such that |PA − PB| is maximum where A (4, 2) and B (2, 4) are :

(a) (−22, 28)   (b) (22, 28)

(c) (22, −28)   (d) (−22, −28)

42. The angle made with x-axis by a line drawn through (1, 2), so that it intersects $x + y = 4$ at a distance of $\sqrt{\dfrac{2}{3}}$ from (1, 2) is :

(a) 105°   (b) 75°

(c) 60°   (d) 90°

43. The equation of a straight line passing through origin and the mid point of the intercept of the line $2x + y = 4$ between the axes is :

(a) $x + 2y = 0$ (b) $x + y = 0$

(c) $2x − y = 0$ (d) $y = x$

44. The equation of a straight line which makes a triangle of area $96\sqrt{3}$ with the co-ordinate axes and perpendicular from the origin to it makes an angle of 30° with positive direction of y-axis is :

(a) $x − y\sqrt{3} = 24$ (b) $y + x\sqrt{3} = 24$

(c) $y − x\sqrt{3} = 24$ (d) $x + y\sqrt{3} = 24$

45. The co-ordinates of the points at distance of $4\sqrt{2}$ units from the point (−2, 3) in the direction making an angle of 45° with positive direction of x-axis are :

(a) (2, 7), (−6, −1)   (b) (2, 7), (6, −1)

(c) (2, −7), (−6, −1)   (d) None of these

46. The ends of a diagonal of a square are (1, 1) and (−2, −1), the equation of the other diagonal is :

(a) $4x + 6y + 3 = 0$ (b) $6x + 4y + 3 = 0$

(c) $6x − 4y + 3 = 0$ (d) None of these

47. A and B are fixed points. The vertex C of ΔABC is variable such that cot A + cot B = constant. The locus of C is :

(a) a line ⊥ AB

(b) a line ∥ AB

(c) a line inclined at an angle A − B to AB

(d) None of these

48. The equation of straight line passing through (1, −2) and parallel to the line $8x − 4y + 17 = 0$ is :

(a) $2x − y − 4 = 0$ (b) $2x + y − 4 = 0$

(c) $2x − y + 4 = 0$ (d) None of these

49. The equation of straight line passing through (2, −4) and ⊥ to the line $5x − 8y + 17 = 0$ is :

(a) $8x − 5y + 9 = 0$ (b) $8x + 5y + 4 = 0$

(c) $8x + 5y − 4 = 0$ (d) None of these

50. The equation of a straight line having x-intercept −2 and perpendicular to the line $3x + 2y + 18 = 0$ is :

(a) $2x + 3y = 7$ (b) $2x − 3y + 18 = 0$

(c) $2x − 3y − 18 = 0$ (d) $2x − 3y + 4 = 0$

51. The equation of perpendicular bisector of the line segment joining (−1, 2) and (5, −4) is :

(a) $2x + 3y = 5$ (b) $x − y = 3$

(c) $x + y = 2$ (d) $3x − 4y − 10 = 0$

52. If x_1, x_2, x_3 as well as y_1, y_2, y_3 are in G.P. with same common ratio, then P (x_1, y_1), Q (x_2, y_2), R (x_3, y_3) :

(a) lie on a circle

(b) lie on a straight line

(c) lie on an ellipse

(d) are vertices of a right angled triangle.

53. The vertices B and C of ΔABC lie on the line $3y = 4x$ and x-axis respectively and BC passes through the point $\left(\dfrac{2}{3}, \dfrac{2}{3}\right)$. If ABOC is a rhombus, O being origin, the equation of line BC is :

(a) $2x − y = 2$ (b) $x − 2y = 2$

(c) $2x + y = 2$ (d) None of these

54. The equation of line through (3, 2) and making angle of 45° with the line $x − 2y = 3$ is :

(a) $x + 3y = 7$ (b) $x + 3y = 9$

(c) $x − 3y = 7$ (d) $x − 3y = 9$

55. A vertex and the opposite side of an equilateral triangle are (2, 3) and x + y = 2 respectively. The equation of other sides of triangle are :

(a) $(2 + \sqrt{3}) x + y - 2\sqrt{3} - 1 = 0$ and
$(2 - \sqrt{3}) x + y + 2\sqrt{3} - 1 = 0$

(b) $(2 + \sqrt{3}) x - y + 2\sqrt{3} + 1 = 0$ and
$(2 - \sqrt{3}) x + y + 2\sqrt{3} + 1 = 0$

(c) $(2 + \sqrt{3}) x - y - 2\sqrt{3} - 1 = 0$ and
$(2 - \sqrt{3}) x - y + 2\sqrt{3} - 1 = 0$

(d) None of these

56. Two sides of a parallelogram are 4x + 5y = 0 and 7x + 2y = 0. If one of its diagonal is 11x + 7y = 9, then the equation of the other diagonal is :

(a) y = 3x   (b) y = x

(c) y = 2x   (d) y = 4x

57. Let PS be the median of the triangle with vertices P (2, 2), Q (6, –1), R (7, 3). The equation of the line passing through (1, –1) and parallel to PS is :

(a) 2x – 9y – 7 = 0   (b) 2x – 9y – 11 = 0

(c) 2x + 9y – 11 = 0   (d) 2x + 9y + 7 = 0

58. The image of point (–8, 12) w.r.t. the line mirror 4x + 7y + 13 = 0 is :

(a) (16, –2)   (b) (16, 2)

(c) (–16, –2)   (d) (–16, 2)

59. The image of (3, 5) with respect to the line y = x is Q and the image of Q in x-axis is R (a, b), then (a, b) is :

(a) (–5, –3)   (b) (5, 3)

(c) (5, –3)   (d) (–5, 3)

60. A ray moving along the line x – 2y – 3 = 0 when reaches the line 3x – 2y – 5 = 0 and gets reflected from it. The reflected ray moves along :

(a) 29x + 2y – 31 = 0 (b) 29x – 2y – 31 = 0

(c) 2x – 29y – 31 = 0 (d) 2x + 29y + 31 = 0

61. The line passing through the intersection of the lines 5x – y – 9 = 0 and x + 6y – 8 = 0 and the point (2, –2) is :

(a) y = 2   (b) x = 2

(c) y = –2   (d) x = –2

62. The number of integral values of m, for which the x-coordinate of the point of intersection of the lines 3x + 4y = 9 and y = mx + 1 is also an integer is :

(a) 0   (b) 1

(c) 2   (d) 4

63. A straight line through the origin meets the parallel lines 4x + 2y = 9 and 2x + y + 6 = 0 at points P and Q respectively. The ratio in which O divides PQ is :

(a) 3 : 4   (b) 2 : 1

(c) 1 : 2   (d) Not a constant

64. The equation of line passing through the intersection of x + 2y + 1 = 0 & 5x + 3y – 2 = 0 and parallel to the line 3x + 4y = 17 is :

(a) 3x + 4y = 9   (b) 3x + 4y = –1

(c) 6x + 8y + 2 = 0 (d) 4x + 3y = –2

65. The equation of straight line passing through the intersection of the lines 3x + y + 2 = 0 and 4x – 3y = 6 and perpendicular to the line 2x + 7y = 17 is :

(a) 7x = 2y + 4   (b) 7x – 2y = 1

(c) 7x – 2y + 4 = 0 (d) 7x = 2y – 9

66. The distance of the point (1, 2) from the line, through the intersection of the lines x + 2y = 5 and x – 3y = 7 and having slope 5, is :

(a) $\dfrac{132}{\sqrt{650}}$ (b) $\dfrac{16}{\sqrt{650}}$

(c) $\dfrac{64}{\sqrt{650}}$ (d) $\dfrac{1}{\sqrt{650}}$

67. If vertices of a variable triangle are (3, 4), (5 sin θ, – 5 cos θ) and (5 cos θ, 5 sin θ), then locus of the orthocentre of this triangle is :

(a) $(x + y - 1)^2 + (x - y - 7)^2 = 100$

(b) $(x + y - 7)^2 + (x + y - 1)^2 = 100$

(c) $(x + y - 7)^2 + (x - y + 1)^2 = 100$

(d) $(x + y - 7)^2 + (x - y - 1)^2 = 100$

68. The line (a + 2b) x + (a + 3b) y = a + b passes through a fixed point (h, k) for all values of a and b. Then (h, k) is :

(a) (2, –1)   (b) (1, –2)

(c) (1, 2)   (d) (2, 1)

69. If the lines $ax + y + 1 = 0$, $x + by + 1 = 0$ and $x + y + c = 0$ are concurrent and $a \neq b \neq c$ and $a \neq 1$, $b \neq 1$, $c \neq 1$, then the value of $\dfrac{1}{1-a} + \dfrac{1}{1-b} + \dfrac{1}{1-c}$ is :

(a) 0   (b) 2

(c) –1   (d) 1

70. The distance between the lines $7x + 24y - 5 = 0$ and $7x + 24y + 20 = 0$ is :

(a) 1   (b) 2

(c) 3   (d) 4

71. Set of values of α for which the point $(\alpha, \alpha^2 - 2)$ lies in the interior of triangle whose sides are $x + y = 1$, $y = x + 1$ and $y = -1$ is :

(a) $(-2, 1)$ (b) $\left(\dfrac{1-\sqrt{13}}{2}, -1\right)$

(c) $(-1, 1)$ (d) $\left(\dfrac{\sqrt{13}-1}{2}, \dfrac{\sqrt{13}+1}{2}\right)$

72. The lengths of perpendiculars from the origin to the lines $x \sec \theta + y \csc \theta = a$ and $x \cos \theta - y \sin \theta = a \cos 2\theta$ are P_1 and P_2 respectively, then $4P_1^2 + P_2^2 =$

(a) $4a^2$ (b) $2a^2$

(c) a^2 (d) 1

73. The equation of angle bisector bisecting obtuse angle between the lines $4x + 3y - 6 = 0$ and $5x + 12y + 9 = 0$ is :

(a) $7x + 9y - 3 = 0$ (b) $9x - 7y - 41 = 0$

(c) $7x + 9y + 3 = 0$ (d) None of these

74. The equation of angle bisector bisecting the acute angle between the lines $3x + 4y - 11 = 0$ and $12x - 5y - 2 = 0$ is :

(a) $11x + 3y - 17 = 0$ (b) $3x + 11y + 17 = 0$

(c) $11x + 3y + 17 = 0$ (d) None of these

75. The diagonals of a parallelogram ABCD are along the lines $2x - 3y + 5 = 0$ & $6x + 4y - 9 = 0$, then PQRS must be :

(a) Rectangle   (b) Rhombus

(c) Square   (d) Cyclic quadrilateral

76. If $d(x, y)$ is defined as $d(x, y) = $ maximum of $|x|$ or $|y|$, then the locus of point (x, y) where $d(x, y) = 1$ is :

(a) a circle   (b) a triangle

(c) a straight line   (d) a square

77. If $A(1, 0)$, $B(-1, 0)$, $C(2, 0)$ are three given points, then the locus of point S satisfying the relation $SB^2 + SC^2 = 2SA^2$ is :

(a) a straight line parallel to x-axis

(b) a straight line parallel to y-axis

(c) a circle with centre $(0, 0)$

(d) a circle passing through $(0, 0)$

78. If $p + q + r = 0$, then the line $3px + qy + 2r = 0$ passes through a fixed point with co-ordinates :

(a) $\left(2, -\dfrac{2}{3}\right)$ (b) $(-2, 1)$

(c) $\left(-2, \dfrac{2}{3}\right)$ (d) $\left(\dfrac{2}{3}, 2\right)$

79. The area of the region enclosed by $2|x| + 3|y| \leq 6$ is :

(a) 10   (b) 12

(c) 14   (d) 20

80. The centroid and circumcentre of a triangle are $(3, 3)$ & $(6, 2)$ respectively, then the orthocentre is :

(a) $(-3, 5)$ (b) $(-4, 2)$

(c) $(6, 2)$ (d) $(3, 3)$

81. If $A(1, 2)$, $B(3, 4)$ and $C(x, y)$ are such that $(x - 1)(x - 3) + (y - 2)(y - 4) = 0$ and area of $\triangle ABC$ is $\dfrac{3}{2}$ sq. units; then maximum number of positions of C in xy-plane is :

(a) 2   (b) 4

(c) 8   (d) 0

82. If a, b, c are in A.P., then the line $ax + by + c = 0$ will always pass through a fixed point with co-ordinates :

(a) $(1, 2)$ (b) $(1, -2)$

(c) $(2, 1)$ (d) $(2, -1)$

83. If a, b, c are in H.P., then the line $\dfrac{3x}{a} + \dfrac{2y}{b} + \dfrac{1}{c} = 0$ always passes through a fixed point whose co-ordinates are :

(a) $(2, -1)$
(b) $(1, -2)$
(c) $\left(\dfrac{1}{3}, -1\right)$
(d) $\left(-\dfrac{1}{3}, +1\right)$

84. The equation of a straight line passing through $(-5, 4)$ and making an intercept of $\sqrt{2}$ units between the lines $x + y + 1 = 0$ & $2x + 2y - 2 = 0$ is :

(a) $x - y + 9 = 0$
(b) $x + y - 2 = 0$
(c) $2x + y + 1 = 0$
(d) $2x - y + 1 = 0$

85. The sum of distance of a point from two perpendicular lines in a plane is 2 units, then its locus is :

(a) a triangle
(b) a straight line
(c) a square
(d) a circle

86. The vertices of a quadrilateral, taken in order are $(-2, 4)$, $(-1, 2)$, $(1, 2)$ and $(2, 4)$. The equation of the line through $(-1, 2)$ and dividing the quadrilateral into two parts equal in area is :

(a) $x + y + 3 = 0$
(b) $x = -1$
(c) $y = 2$
(d) $x - y + 3 = 0$

87. Two sides of a rhombus ABCD are parallel to the lines $y - x - 2 = 0$ and $y - 7x = 3$. If its diagonals intersect at $(1, 2)$ and the vertex A lies on y-axis and not on x-axis, then the possible co-ordinates of A are :

(a) $(0, 0)$
(b) $\left(0, \dfrac{5}{2}\right)$
(c) $(0, 3)$
(d) $\left(0, \dfrac{2}{5}\right)$

88. The new co-ordinates of $(2, 7)$, when origin is shifted to $(1, -2)$, keeping the axes parallel to the co-ordinate axes, are :

(a) $(9, 1)$
(b) $(3, 5)$
(c) $(3, 9)$
(d) $(1, 9)$

89. The distance of the point $(2, 3)$ from the line $3x + 2y - 17 = 0$ measured parallel to the line $2x - 2y = 17$ is :

(a) $\sqrt{2}$
(b) $2\sqrt{2}$
(c) $3\sqrt{2}$
(d) 2

90. The limiting position of point of intersection of the lines $3x + 4y = 1$ and $(c+1)x + 3c^2y - 2 = 0$ as c tends to 1 is :

(a) $(3, 4)$
(b) $(2, 3)$
(c) $(-5, 4)$
(d) Does not exist

91. The sides of a quadrilateral are given by $x^2 - 2x = 0$ and $y^2 - 3y = 0$. The equation of the line parallel to $x - 4y = 17$ that divides the quadrilateral into two parts equal in area is :

(a) $4y = x + 1$
(b) $4y = x - 1$
(c) $x - 4y = 5$
(d) $x - 4y + 5 = 0$

92. The point $(1, \beta)$ lies on or inside the triangle whose sides are $y = x$, x-axis and $x + y = 8$ if :

(a) $0 < \beta < 1$
(b) $0 \le \beta \le 1$
(c) $0 < \beta < 8$
(d) None of these

93. If B (x_1, y_1) and C (x_2, y_2) are such that $x_1 < x_2$, $y_1 > y_2$ and x_1, x_2 are zeros of $x^2 + 4x + 3 = 0$ and y_1, y_2, are zeros of $y^2 - y - 6 = 0$ and A $(3, -5)$, then the length of bisector of $\angle$ A of Δ ABC is :

(a) $\dfrac{7\sqrt{2}}{3}$
(b) $\dfrac{14\sqrt{2}}{3}$
(c) $\dfrac{5\sqrt{2}}{3}$
(d) $\dfrac{8}{3}$

94. The equation of a line through $(1, 2)$ which is at maximum distance from $(3, 1)$ is :

(a) $y = 2x$
(b) $x = 2y$
(c) $2x + y = 0$
(d) $x + 2y = 0$

95. Points with both co-ordinates as integer are called integral points. The number of integral points exactly in the interior of triangle with vertices $(0, 0)$, $(0, 21)$ and $(21, 0)$ is :

(a) 133
(b) 190
(c) 233
(d) 105

96. If the line $2x + y = k$ passes through the point which divides the line segment joining the points $(1, 1)$ and $(2, 4)$ in the ratio $3 : 2$, then k equals :

[AIEEE - 2012]

(a) $\dfrac{29}{5}$
(b) 5
(c) 6
(d) $\dfrac{11}{5}$

97. A line is drawn through the point (1, 2) to meet the coordinate axes at P and Q such that it forms a triangle OPQ, where O is the origin. If the area of the triangle OPQ is least, then the slope of the line PQ is : **[AIEEE - 2012]**

(a) $-\dfrac{1}{4}$

(b) -4

(c) -2

(d) $-\dfrac{1}{2}$

98. The lines $L_1 : y - x = 0$ and $L_2 : 2x + y = 0$ intersect the line $L_3 : y + 2 = 0$ at P and Q respectively. The bisector of the acute angle between L_1 and L_2 intersects L_3 at R.

[AIEEE - 2011]

Statement 1 : The ratio PR : RQ equals $2\sqrt{2} : \sqrt{5}$.

Statement 2 : In any triangle, bisector of an angle divides the triangle into two similar triangles.

(a) Statement 1 is true, statement 2 is false.

(b) Statement 1 is true, statement 2 is true; statement 2 is the correct explanation of statement 1.

(c) Statement 1 is true, statement 2 is true; statement 2 is not a correct explanation of statement 1.

(d) Statement 1 is false, statement 2 is true.

99. The line L given by $\dfrac{x}{5} + \dfrac{y}{b} = 1$ passes through the point (13, 32). The line K is parallel to L and has the equation $\dfrac{x}{c} + \dfrac{y}{3} = 1$. Then the distance between L and K is : **[AIEEE - 2010]**

(a) $\sqrt{17}$

(b) $\dfrac{17}{\sqrt{15}}$

(c) $\dfrac{23}{\sqrt{17}}$

(d) $\dfrac{23}{\sqrt{15}}$

100. The lines $p(p^2 + 1) x - y + q = 0$ and $(p^2 + 1)^2 x + (p^2 + 1) y + 2q = 0$ are perpendicular to a common line for : **[AIEEE - 2009]**

(a) no value of p

(b) exactly one value of p

(c) exactly two values of p

(d) more than two values of p

101. Three distinct points A, B and C are given in the 2-dimensional coordinate plane such that ratio of the distance of any one of them from the point (1, 0) to the distance from the point (–1, 0) is equal to $\dfrac{1}{3}$. Then the circumcentre of the triangle ABC is at the point : **[AIEEE - 2009]**

(a) (0, 0)

(b) $\left(\dfrac{5}{4}, 0\right)$

(c) $\left(\dfrac{5}{2}, 0\right)$

(d) $\left(\dfrac{5}{3}, 0\right)$

102. The perpendicular bisector of the line segment joining P (1, 4) and Q (k, 3) has y-intercept – 4. Then a possible value of k is : **[AIEEE - 2008]**

(a) 1

(b) 2

(c) –2

(d) –4

103. A straight line through the point A(3, 4) is such that its intercept between the axes is bisected at A. Its equation is : **[AIEEE - 2006]**

(a) x + y = 7

(b) 3x – 4y + 7 = 0

(c) 4x + 3y = 24

(d) 3x + 4y = 25

ANSWER KEY

1. (c)	2. (a)	3. (b)	4. (b)	5. (b)	6. (a)	7. (b)	8. (b)	9. (b)	
10. (d)	11. (a)	12. (d)	13. (c)	14. (b)	15. (a)	16. (c)	17. (a)	18. (b)	19. (d)
20. (b)	21. (d)	22. (b)	23. (b)	24. (a)	25. (d)	26. (c)	27. (b)	28. (a)	29. (c)
30. (a)	31. (a)	32. (a)	33. (c)	34. (b)	35. (a)	36. (c)	37. (a)	38. (a)	39. (d)
40. (b)	41. (a)	42. (b)	43. (c)	44. (d)	45. (a)	46. (b)	47. (b)	48. (a)	49. (b)
50. (d)	51. (b)	52. (b)	53. (c)	54. (b)	55. (c)	56. (b)	57. (d)	58. (c)	59. (c)
60. (b)	61. (b)	62. (c)	63. (a)	64. (c)	65. (a)	66. (a)	67. (c)	68. (a)	69. (d)
70. (a)	71. (b)	72. (c)	73. (b)	74. (a)	75. (b)	76. (d)	77. (b)	78. (d)	79. (b)
80. (a)	81. (b)	82. (b)	83. (c)	84. (a)	85. (c)	86. (d)	87. (b)	88. (d)	89. (a)
90. (c)	91. (d)	92. (b)	93. (b)	94. (a)	95. (b)	96. (c)	97. (c)	98. (d)	99. (c)
100. (b)	101. (b)	102. (d)	103. (c)						

CIRCLE

MULTIPLE CHOICE QUESTIONS

1. A square is inscribed in the circle $x^2 + y^2 - 2x + 4y + 3 = 0$ and its sides are parallel to x and y-axis. One vertex of the square can be :
   (a) $(1 + \sqrt{2}, -2)$ (b) $(1 - \sqrt{2}, -2)$
   (c) $(1, -2 + \sqrt{2})$ (d) None of these

2. The locus of the centre of a circle of radius 1 unit which rolls on the outside of the circle $x^2 + y^2 + 3x - 6y - 9 = 0$ is :
   (a) $x^2 + y^2 + 3x - 6y + 5 = 0$
   (b) $x^2 + y^2 + 3x - 6y - 19 = 0$
   (c) $4x^2 + 4y^2 + 12x - 24y + 29 = 0$
   (d) None of these

3. A circle has $(0, 1)$ and (a, b) as end points of its diameter. The abcissa of the points where this circle cuts x-axis; are zeros of :
   (a) $x^2 - ax + b = 0$ (b) $x^2 + ax - b = 0$
   (c) $x^2 + ax + b = 0$ (d) $x^2 - ax - b = 0$

4. The points $(2k, 3k)$, $(1, 0)$, $(0, 1)$ and $(0, 0)$ are concyclic for :
   (a) all integral values of k
   (b) $0 < k < 1$
   (c) $k < 0$
   (d) For two values of k

5. A square is inscribed in the circle $x^2 + y^2 - 2x + 4y - 93 = 0$ with its sides parallel to x and y-axis. The co-ordinates of its vertices are :
   (a) $(-6, -9), (-6, 5), (8, 9), (8, 5)$
   (b) $(-6, -9), (-6, 5), (8, -9), (8, -5)$
   (c) $(-6, -9), (-6, 5), (8, -9), (8, 5)$
   (d) $(-6, 9), (-6, -5), (8, -9), (8, 5)$

6. The equation of circle passing through $(3, -6)$ and touching both the axes is :
   (a) $x^2 + y^2 - 6x + 6y + 9 = 0$
   (b) $x^2 + y^2 + 30x - 30y + 225 = 0$
   (c) $x^2 + y^2 - 15x + 15y + 225 = 0$
   (d) $x^2 + y^2 + 6x - 6y + 36 = 0$

7. The centre of a circle passing through $(0, 0)$, $(1, 0)$ and touching the circle $x^2 + y^2 = 9$ is :
   (a) $\left(\frac{3}{2}, \frac{1}{2}\right)$ (b) $\left(\frac{1}{2}, \frac{3}{2}\right)$
   (c) $\left(\frac{1}{2}, \frac{1}{2}\right)$ (d) $\left(\frac{1}{2}, -\sqrt{2}\right)$

8. One of the diameters of the circle $x^2 + y^2 - 12x + 4y + 6 = 0$ is :
   (a) $x + y = 0$ (b) $x - y = 0$
   (c) $x + 3y = 0$ (d) $3x + y = 0$

9. The length of common chord cut off by $y = 2x + 1$ from the circle $x^2 + y^2 = 2$ is :
   (a) $\frac{6}{\sqrt{5}}$ (b) $\frac{\sqrt{5}}{6}$
   (c) $\frac{6}{5}$ (d) $\frac{5}{6}$

10. Area of the circle in which a chord of length $\sqrt{2}$ makes an angle of $\pi/2$ at the centre is :
    (a) $\pi/2$ (b) 2π
    (c) π (d) $\pi/4$

11. The co-ordinates of the mid-point of the chord cut off by $2x - 5y + 18 = 0$ by the circle $x^2 + y^2 - 6x + 2y - 54 = 0$ are :
    (a) $(2, 4)$ (b) $(1, 4)$
    (c) $(4, 1)$ (d) $(1, 1)$

12. Equation of the circle whose centre lies on $3x + 4y = 7$ and passes through $(1, -2)$ and $(4, -3)$ is :
    (a) $x^2 + y^2 - 94x - 18y + 55 = 0$
    (b) $x^2 + y^2 - 94x + 18y + 55 = 0$
    (c) $15x^2 + 15y^2 - 94x + 18y + 55 = 0$
    (d) $15x^2 + 15y^2 + 94x + 18y + 55 = 0$

13. Equation of circle with centre on y –axis and passing through origin and (2, 3) is :
    (a) $x^2 + y^2 + 13y = 0$
    (b) $x^2 + y^2 + 13x + 3 = 0$
    (c) $6x^2 + 6y^2 - 13x = 0$
    (d) $3x^2 + 3y^2 - 13y = 0$

14. The equations of circles which touch both the axes and the line x = a are :
    (a) $x^2 + y^2 \pm ax \pm ay + \dfrac{a^2}{4} = 0$
    (b) $x^2 + y^2 + ax \pm ay + \dfrac{a^2}{4} = 0$
    (c) $x^2 + y^2 - ax \pm ay + \dfrac{a^2}{4} = 0$
    (d) None of these

15. If a circle passes through the point of intersection of co-ordinate axes with lines $\lambda x - y + 1 = 0$ and $x - 2y + 3 = 0$, then the value of λ is :
    (a) 2/3 (b) 3
    (c) 6 (d) 1/3

16. If the points (2, 0), (0, 1), (4, 5) and (0, c) are concyclic, then the value of c is :
    (a) 1 (b) 14/3
    (c) 5 (d) None of these

17. If P (x_1, y_1) and Q (x_2, y_2) are such that the zeros of $x^2 + ax - b^2 = 0$ are x_1 and x_2 and the zeros of $y^2 + py - q^2 = 0$ are y_1 and y_2, then the equation of circle with PQ as diameter is :
    (a) $x^2 + y^2 + ax + py - b^2 - q^2 = 0$
    (b) $x^2 + y^2 - ax - py + b^2 + q^2 = 0$
    (c) $x^2 + y^2 - ax - py - b^2 - q^2 = 0$
    (d) $x^2 + y^2 + ax + py + b^2 + q^2 = 0$

18. If (i) x = 0
    (ii) y = 0
    (iii) $(h^2 - r^2) x - 2rhy = 0$
    (iv) $(h^2 - r^2) x + 2rhy = 0$,
    then the equations of tangents from (0, 0) to the circle $x^2 + y^2 - 2rx - 2hy + h^2 = 0$ are :
    (a) (i) and (ii) (b) (i) and (iii)
    (c) (i) and (iv) (d) (iii) and (iv)

19. If the circles $(x - 1)^2 + (y - 3)^2 = r^2$ and $x^2 + y^2 - 8x + 2y + 8 = 0$ intersect in two distinct points, then :
    (a) $r \in (2, 8)$ (b) $r < 2$
    (c) $r = 2$ (d) $r > 2$

20. If from any point on the circle $x^2 + y^2 + 2gx + 2fy + c = 0$ tangents are drawn to the circle $x^2 + y^2 + 2gx + 2fy + c \sin^2 \alpha + (g^2 + f^2) \cos^2 \alpha = 0$, then the angle between the tangents is :
    (a) α (b) 2α
    (c) $\alpha/2$ (d) None of these

21. The equation of circle passing through (1, – 3) and the point of intersection of the circles $x^2 + y^2 - 6x + 8y - 16 = 0$ and $x^2 + y^2 + 4x - 2y - 8 = 0$ is :
    (a) $3x^2 + 3y^2 - 5x + 7y - 19 = 0$
    (b) $x^2 + y^2 - 4x + 6y + 24 = 0$
    (c) $2x^2 + 2y^2 + 3x + y - 20 = 0$
    (d) None of these

22. The lines $2x + 3y + 4 = 0$ and $3x - y - 5 = 0$ are diameters of a circle of area 154 sq. units, then the equation of circle is :
    (a) $x^2 + y^2 - 2x - 4y + 44 = 0$
    (b) $x^2 + y^2 - 2x + 4y + 44 = 0$
    (c) $x^2 + y^2 + 2x - 4y - 44 = 0$
    (d) $x^2 + y^2 - 2x + 4y - 44 = 0$

23. The angle subtended by the common chord of the circles $x^2 + y^2 - 4x - 4y = 0$ and $x^2 + y^2 = 16$ at the origin is :
    (a) $\pi/2$ (b) $\pi/3$
    (c) $\pi/4$ (d) $\pi/6$

24. Equation of circle with common chord of the circles $x^2 + y^2 + 3x + 2y + 1 = 0$ and $x^2 + y^2 + 3x + 4y + 2 = 0$ as diameter is :
    (a) $2x^2 + 2y^2 + 6x + 2y + 1 = 0$
    (b) $x^2 + y^2 + 8x + 10y + 2 = 0$
    (c) $x^2 + y^2 - 5x + 4y + 7 = 0$
    (d) None of these

25. The tangents to $x^2 + y^2 = a^2$ having inclinations of α and β with positive direction of x-axis intersect at P. If $\dfrac{1}{\tan \alpha} + \dfrac{1}{\tan \beta} = 0$, then the locus of P is :

(a) $x + y = 0$
(b) $x = y$
(c) $xy = 0$
(d) None of these

26. Equation of circle touching $x^2 + y^2 = 1$ and having centre at (4, 3) is

(a) $x^2 + y^2 - 8x - 6y - 9 = 0$
(b) $x^2 + y^2 - 8x - 6y - 11 = 0$
(c) $x^2 + y^2 - 6x - 8y - 11 = 0$
(d) $x^2 + y^2 - 6x - 8y - 9 = 0$

27. The length of tangent from any point on the circle $15x^2 + 15 y^2 - 48x + 64y = 0$ to the circles $5x^2 + 5y^2 - 24x + 32y + 75 = 0$ and $5x^2 + 5y^2 - 48x + 64y + 300 = 0$ are in ratio

(a) $3 : 4$
(b) $2 : 3$
(c) $1 : 2$
(d) $2 : 1$

28. The number of common tangents that can be drawn to the circles $x^2 + y^2 - 4x - 6y - 3 = 0$ and $x^2 + y^2 + 2x + 2y + 1 = 0$ is :

(a) 1
(b) 2
(c) 3
(d) 4

29. If $3x + 2y = 0$ is a tangent to the circle with centre (1, 2), then the equation of other tangent to the circle from (0, 0) is :

(a) $2x - 3y = 0$
(b) $x = y$
(c) $18 x - y = 0$
(d) $x - 18y = 0$

30. The condition that the chord $x \cos \alpha + y \sin \alpha - p = 0$ of $x^2 + y^2 = a^2$ may subtend a right angle at the centre of the circle is :

(a) $p = 2a$
(b) $a^2 = 2p^2$
(c) $p^2 = 2a^2$
(d) $a = 2p$

31. If the distances of the centres of the circles $x^2 + y^2 + 2g_1x - c^2 = 0$, $x^2 + y^2 + 2g_2x - c^2 = 0$ and $x^2 + y^2 + 2g_3x - c^2 = 0$ from the origin are in G.P., then the lengths of the tangents drawn to them from any point on the circle $x^2 + y^2 = c^2$ are in :

(a) A.P.
(b) G.P.
(c) H.P.
(d) A.G.P.

32. The locus of centre of circles which touch both the circles $x^2 + y^2 = a^2$ and $x^2 + y^2 = 4ax$ externally is :

(a) $12 (x - a)^2 - 4y^2 = 3a^2$
(b) $9 (x - a)^2 - 5y^2 = 2a^2$
(c) $8x^2 - 3 (y - a)^2 = 9a^2$
(d) None of these

33. P is a point on $x^2 + y^2 = 9$ and Q is any point on $7x + y + 3 = 0$. If perpendicular bisector of PQ is $y = x + 1$, then co-ordinates of P may be :

(a) (2, 0)
(b) (0, 3)
(c) $\left(\dfrac{72}{25}, \dfrac{-21}{25}\right)$
(d) $\left(\dfrac{-72}{25}, \dfrac{21}{25}\right)$

34. The point on circle $x^2 + y^2 - 12x - 4y + 30 = 0$ which is at maximum distance from origin is :

(a) (8, 5)
(b) (9, 3)
(c) (12, 4)
(d) None of these

35. Equation of circle having area 25π sq. units and touching the circle $x^2 + y^2 - 2x - 4y - 20 = 0$ at (5, 5) is :

(a) $x^2 + y^2 + 18x - 16y + 120 = 0$
(b) $x^2 + y^2 + 18x + 16y + 120 = 0$
(c) $x^2 + y^2 - 18x - 16y + 120 = 0$
(d) $x^2 + y^2 - 18x + 16y + 120 = 0$

36. Circles $x^2 + y^2 + x + y = 0$ and $x^2 + y^2 + x - y = 0$ intersect at an angle of :

(a) $\pi/6$
(b) $\pi/4$
(c) $\pi/3$
(d) $\pi/2$

37. The locus of points, tangents from which to the circles $3x^2 + 3y^2 + 2x + 4y - 6 = 0$ and $x^2 + y^2 - 5x - 3 = 0$ are equal, is given by :

(a) $17x + 4y + 3 = 0$
(b) $x^2 + y^2 + \dfrac{7}{2}x + 2y - \dfrac{3}{2} = 0$
(c) $13x - 4y + 15 = 0$
(d) $4x^2 + 4y^2 - 3x + 4y - 9 = 0$

38. The equation of circle having radius 3 and touching $x^2 + y^2 - 4x - 6y - 12 = 0$ at $(-1, -1)$ is :

(a) $5x^2 + 5y^2 - 8x - 14y - 32 = 0$

(b) $5x^2 + 5y^2 - 8x + 14y - 4 = 0$

(c) $5x^2 + 5y^2 + 8x + 14y + 12 = 0$

(d) $5x^2 + 5y^2 + 8x - 14y - 16 = 0$

39. AB is diameter of a circle and C is any point on the circumference of the circle, then :

(a) Area of $\triangle$ ABC is minimum when it is isosceles.

(b) Area of $\triangle$ ABC is maximum when it is isosceles.

(c) Perimeter of $\triangle$ ABC is maximum when it is isosceles.

(d) None of these

40. The pole of the straight line $9x + y = 28$ w.r.t. the circle $2x^2 + 2y^2 - 3x + 5y - 7 = 0$ is :

(a) $(-3, 1)$ (b) $(3, -1)$

(c) $(1, 3)$ (d) $(3, 1)$

41. If the chord of contact of tangents drawn from a point on the circle $x^2 + y^2 = a^2$ to the circle $x^2 + y^2 = b^2$ touches the circle $x^2 + y^2 = c^2$, then a, b, c are in :

(a) A.P. (b) G.P.

(c) H.P. (d) A.G.P.

42. The straight line $2y = x + 1$ intersects the circle $x^2 + y^2 = 25$ at P and Q. The point of intersection of tangents to the circle, at P and Q, is :

(a) $(25, -50)$ (b) $(25, 50)$

(c) $(-25, 50)$ (d) $(-25, -50)$

43. The chord of contact of tangents drawn from (h, k) to the circle $x^2 + y^2 = a^2$ subtend a right angle at the centre, then $h^2 + k^2 =$

(a) a^2 (b) $a^2/2$

(c) $-a^2$ (d) $2a^2$

44. The equation of circle which cuts the three circles $x^2 + y^2 - 3x - 6y + 14 = 0$, $x^2 + y^2 - x - 4y + 8 = 0$ and $x^2 + y^2 + 2x - 6y + 9 = 0$ orthogonally is :

(a) $x^2 + y^2 - 2x - 4y + 1 = 0$

(b) $x^2 + y^2 - 2x + 4y + 1 = 0$

(c) $x^2 + y^2 - 2x - 4y - 1 = 0$

(d) $x^2 + y^2 + 2x + 4y - 1 = 0$

45. The equation of circle through (2a, 0) and whose radical axis with the circle $x^2 + y^2 = a^2$ is $2x - a = 0$, is :

(a) $x^2 + y^2 + 2ax = 0$ (b) $x^2 + y^2 - 2ax = 0$

(c) $x^2 + y^2 + ax = 0$ (d) $x^2 + y^2 - ax = 0$

46. If the circle $x^2 + y^2 + 2g_1 x + 2f_1 y + c_1 = 0$ bisects the circumference of the circle, $x^2 + y^2 + 2g_2 x + 2f_2 y + c_2 = 0$, then :

(a) $2g_1(g_1 - g_2) + 2f_1(f_1 - f_2) = c_1 - c_2$

(b) $2g_2(g_1 - g_2) + 2f_2(f_1 - f_2) = c_1 - c_2$

(c) $2g_2(g_1 - g_2) + 2f_2(f_1 - f_2) = c_2 - c_1$

(d) $2g_1(g_1 - g_2) + 2f_1(f_1 - f_2) = c_2 - c_1$

47. The equation of circle on the common chord of the circles $x^2 + y^2 - 2ax = 0$ and $x^2 + y^2 + 2by = 0$ as diameter is :

(a) $x^2 + y^2 - 2ab^2 x - 2a^2 by = 0$

(b) $x^2 + y^2 - bx - ay = 0$

(c) $(a^2 + b^2)(x^2 + y^2) = 2ab(bx - ay)$

(d) $(a^2 + b^2)(x^2 + y^2) = 2(bx + ay)$

48. $(1, -2)$ is the mid-point of chord AB of circle $x^2 + y^2 = 9$. Equation of AB is :

(a) $x - 2y = 4$ (b) $x - 2y = 9$

(c) $x - 2y + 5 = 0$ (d) $x - 2y = 5$

49. The equation of image of the circle $x^2 + y^2 + 16x - 24y + 183 = 0$ in the line mirror $4x + 7y + 13 = 0$ is :

(a) $x^2 + y^2 + 32x + 4y + 235 = 0$

(b) $x^2 + y^2 + 32x - 4y - 235 = 0$

(c) $x^2 + y^2 + 32x + 4y - 235 = 0$

(d) $x^2 + y^2 + 32x - 4y + 235 = 0$

50. Number of tangents that can be drawn from (1, 2) to $x^2 + y^2 = 5$ is :

(a) 1 (b) 2

(c) 3 (d) 0

51. Equation of circle passing through origin and making intercepts of 3 and 4 units on positive side of x and y-axis respectively is :

(a) $x^2 + y^2 - 3x + 4y = 0$

(b) $x^2 + y^2 + 3x = 4y$

(c) $x^2 + y^2 = 3x + 4y$

(d) $x^2 + y^2 + 3x + 4y = 0$

52. The equation of chord of the circle $x^2 + y^2 = 4x$ with mid-point $(1, 0)$ is :

(a) $x = 2$ (b) $x = 1$

(c) $y = 2$ (d) $y = 1$

53. Circles $x^2 + y^2 = 5$ and $x^2 + y^2 - 2x - 4y - 15 = 0$

(a) touch each other internally

(b) touch each other externally

(c) cut each other orthogonally

(d) do not intersect

54. If $x^2 + y^2 - 4x - k = 0$ is a circle passing through the intersection of the circles $x^2 + y^2 = 4$ and $x^2 + y^2 - 2x - 4 = 0$, then k =

(a) -4 (b) 0

(c) -8 (d) 4

55. $y = x$ touches the circle $x^2 + y^2 + 2gx + 2fy + c = 0$ at P and $OP = 6\sqrt{2}$ where O is origin, then c =

(a) 36 (b) 72

(c) 144 (d) None of these

56. The number of common tangents to the circles $x^2 + y^2 - 2x - 1 = 0$ and $x^2 + y^2 - 2y - 7 = 0$ is :

(a) 1 (b) 2

(c) 3 (d) 4

57. The length of common chord of the circles $x^2 + y^2 + 4x + 1 = 0$ and $x^2 + y^2 + 4y - 1 = 0$ is :

(a) $2\sqrt{15}$ (b) $\sqrt{15}$

(c) $\sqrt{\dfrac{15}{2}}$ (d) $\dfrac{\sqrt{15}}{4}$

58. If the radical axis of the circles $x^2 + y^2 + 2gx + 2fy + c = 0$ and $2x^2 + 2y^2 + 3x + 8y + 2c = 0$ is tangent to the circle $x^2 + y^2 + 2x + 2y + 1 = 0$, then

(a) $g = 3/4$ and $f \neq 2$

(b) $g \neq 3/4$ and $f = 2$

(c) $g = 3/4$ or $f = 2$

(d) None of these

59. If a circle cuts the circle $x^2 + y^2 = 4$ orthogonally and passes through $(1, 2)$ then the locus of its centre is given by :

(a) $2x + 4y - 9 = 0$ (b) $2x + 4y + 9 = 0$

(c) $2x - 4y + 9 = 0$ (d) None of these

60. The radius of a circle which has $3x - 4y + 4 = 0$ and $6x - 8y = 7$ as tangents is :

(a) $1/4$ (b) $1/2$

(c) $3/4$ (d) None of these

61. $x - 4y + 7 = 0$ is the diameter of a circle circumscribing rectangle ABCD. If A and B are $(-3, 4)$ and $(5, 4)$, then area of rectangle ABCD is :

(a) 16 sq. units   (b) 32 sq. units

(c) 24 sq. units   (d) None of these

62. The area of triangle formed by the positive x-axis and the normal and tangent to the circle $x^2 + y^2 = 4$ at $(1, \sqrt{3})$ in sq. units is :

(a) $\sqrt{6}$ (b) $2\sqrt{3}$

(c) $3\sqrt{2}$ (d) None of these

63. Tangent at any point P on the circle $x^2 + y^2 = 4$ intersects the co-ordinate axes in A and B. Then :

(a) PA = PB

(b) Locus of mid-point of AB is $x^2 + y^2 = x^2 y^2$

(c) AB = constant

(d) None of these

64. A chord of the circle $x^2 + y^2 - 2x = 0$ passes through origin. The locus of mid-point of the chord is :

(a) $x^2 + y^2 - 2x + y = 0$

(b) $x^2 + y^2 - x = 0$

(c) $x^2 + y^2 + 2x + y = 0$

(d) $x^2 + y^2 + x + y = 0$

65. The equation of a circle passing through the intersection of circles $x^2 + y^2 - 2x - 4y + 1 = 0$ and $x^2 + y^2 - 4x - 2y + 4 = 0$ and having a diameter along $x + 2y - 3 = 0$ is :

(a) $x^2 + y^2 + 2x - 4y + 4 = 0$

(b) $x^2 + y^2 - 2x - 2y + 1 = 0$

(c) $x^2 + y^2 - 3x + 4 = 0$

(d) $x^2 + y^2 - 6x + 7 = 0$

66. The tangents from the origin to the circle $x^2 + y^2 - 14x + 2y + 25 = 0$ are inclined to each other at:

(a) $\pi/8$ (b) $\pi/6$

(c) $\pi/2$ (d) $\pi/3$

67. Equation of family of circles passing through (2, 0), cutting intercept of 5 units on x-axis and centre in first quadrant is :

(a) $x^2 + y^2 - 2kx - 9y + 14 = 0$

(b) $x^2 + y^2 - 9x - 2ky + 14 = 0$

(c) $x^2 + y^2 - 9x + 2ky + 14 = 0$

(d) $3x^2 + 3y^2 + 27x - 2ky + 42 = 0$

68. Equation of the circle touching both the axes and the line $4x + 3y = 6$ in the first quadrant and lying below it is :

(a) $4x^2 + 4y^2 - 4x - 4y + 1 = 0$

(b) $4x^2 + 4y^2 - 4x - 24y + 1 = 0$

(c) $x^2 + y^2 - 6x - 6y + 9 = 0$

(d) $x^2 + y^2 - 6x - y + 9 = 0$

69. Circles $x^2 + y^2 - 10x + 16 = 0$ and $x^2 + y^2 = r^2$ intersect at two distinct real points then :

(a) $r < 2$ (b) $r > 8$

(c) $2 \le r \le 8$ (d) $2 < r < 8$

70. The radical centre of three circles on the three sides of a triangle as diameter is :

(a) the centroid   (b) the incentre

(c) the orthocentre   (d) the circumcentre

71. A circle touches x-axis and also touches the circle with centre (0, 3) and radius 2. The locus of the centre of the circle is :

(a) a circle   (b) a parabola

(c) an ellipse   (d) a hyperbola

72. The equation of a unit circle concentric with $x^2 + y^2 - 8x + 4y - 17 = 0$ is

(a) $x^2 + y^2 - 8x + 4y + 8 = 0$

(b) $x^2 + y^2 - 8x + 4y + 19 = 0$

(c) $x^2 + y^2 - 8x + 4y - 8 = 0$

(d) $x^2 + y^2 - 8x + 4y - 28 = 0$

73. The length of tangent from (–1, –3) to the circle $x^2 + y^2 - 2x - y - 7 = 0$ is :

(a) $2\sqrt{2}$ (b) 2

(c) 4   (d) 8

74. The circles $x^2 + y^2 - 2x + 6y + 6 = 0$ and $x^2 + y^2 - 5x + 6y + 15 = 0$ touch. The equation of their common tangent is :

(a) $7x - 12y - 21 = 0$ (b) $7x + 12y + 21 = 0$

(c) $x = 3$ (d) $y = 6$

75. If the circle $x^2 + y^2 + 4x + 22y + c = 0$ bisects the circumference of the circle $x^2 + y^2 - 2x + 8y - d = 0$, the $c + d$ equals

(a) 60   (b) 50

(c) 40   (d) 56.

76. The maximum number of points with rational co-ordinates on a circle whose centre is $(\sqrt{3}, 0)$ is

(a) 1   (b) 2

(c) 4   (d) infinite.

77. Tangents are drawn from a point on the circle $x^2 + y^2 = r_1^2$. If the chord of contact touches the circle $x^2 + y^2 = r_3^2$ then r_1, r_2, r_3 are in

(a) A.P.   (b) G.P.

(c) H.P.   (d) none of these.

78. C_1 is a circle of radius 1 touching the x-axis and the y-axis. C_2 is another circle of radius > 1 and touching the axes as well as the circle C_1. Then the radius of C_2 is

(a) $3 - 2\sqrt{2}$ (b) $3 + 2\sqrt{2}$

(c) $3 + 2\sqrt{3}$ (d) none of these.

79. If the chords of contact of tangents from three points A, B, C to the circle $x^2 + y^2 = a^2$ are concurrent then A, B, C will

(a) be concyclic   (b) be collinear

(c) form a triangle   (d) none of these

80. If p and q be the longest distance and the shortest distance respectively of the point (– 7, 2) from any point (α, β) on the curve whose equation is $x^2 + y^2 - 10x - 14y - 51 = 0$ then G.M. of p and q is equal to

(a) $2\sqrt{11}$ (b) $5\sqrt{5}$

(c) 13   (d) none of these.

81. If the circle $x^2 + y^2 = a^2$ cuts off a length $2l$ from the straight line $y = mx + c$ then

(a) $c^2 = (1 + m^2)(a^2 - l^2)$

(b) $c^2 = (1 - m^2)(a^2 + l^2)$

(c) $c^2 = (1 + m^2)(a^2 + l^2)$

(d) $c^2 = (1 - m^2)(a^2 - l^2)$.

82. For each $k \in N$, let C_k denote the circle whose equation is $x^2 + y^2 = k^2$. On the circle C_k, a particle moves k units in the anticlockwise direction. After completing its motion on C_k, the particle moves to C_{k+1} in the radical direction. The motion of the particle continues in this manner. The particle starts at $(1, 0)$. If the particle crosses the positive direction of the x-axis for the first time on the circle C_n then n is

(a) 7   (b) 6

(c) 2   (d) none of these.

83. The equation of a circle passing through two points $(1, 1)$ and $(2, 2)$ having the radius 4 times the radius of smallest circle passing through above two points is :

(a) $x^2 + y^2 + (\sqrt{15} - 3)x - (\sqrt{15} + 3)y + 4 = 0$

(b) $x^2 + y^2 - 3x - 3y + 4 = 0$

(c) $x^2 + y^2 - (\sqrt{15} + 3)x - (\sqrt{15} + 3)y + 4 = 0$

(d) $x^2 + y^2 - 6x - 6y + 4 = 0$.

84. Equation of chord of the circle $x^2 + y^2 = 25$ of length 8 that passes through the point $(2\sqrt{3}, 2)$ and makes an acute angle with the positive direction of the x-axis is :

(a) $(4\sqrt{3} - 3\sqrt{7})x + 3y = 18 - 6\sqrt{21}$

(b) $(4\sqrt{3} + 3\sqrt{7})x - 3y = 18 + 6\sqrt{21}$

(c) $(4\sqrt{3} + 3\sqrt{7})x - 3y + 18 + 6\sqrt{21} = 0$

(d) none of these.

85. The straight line $y = x + c$ is non intersecting to the circle $x^2 + y^2 - 8x - 8y + 23 = 0$ if

(a) $c \in [4, 4]$ (b) $c \in [-4, 4]$

(c) $c \notin [-3\sqrt{2}, 3\sqrt{2}]$ (d) none of these.

86. The number of points with integral coordinates that are interior of the circle $x^2 + y^2 = 16$ is :

(a) 43   (b) 49

(c) 45   (d) 51.

87. The distance of the chord of contact of tangents from the origin to the circle $x^2 + y^2 + 2gx + 2fy + c = 0$ from the point (g, f) is :

(a) $\sqrt{g^2 + f^2}$ (b) $\dfrac{\sqrt{g^2 + f^2} - c}{2}$

(c) $\dfrac{g^2 + f^2 + c}{2\sqrt{g^2 + f^2}}$ (d) $\dfrac{\sqrt{g^2 + f^2} + c}{2\sqrt{g^2 + f^2}}$

88. The range of values of r for which the point $\left(-5 + \dfrac{r}{\sqrt{2}}, -3 + \dfrac{4}{\sqrt{2}}\right)$ is an interior point of the major segment of circle $x^2 + y^2 = 16$, cut off by the line $x + y = 2$, is :

(a) $(\infty, 5\sqrt{2})$

(b) $(4\sqrt{2} - \sqrt{14}, 5\sqrt{2})$

(c) $(4\sqrt{2} - \sqrt{14}, 4\sqrt{2} + \sqrt{14})$

(d) none of these.

89. Centre of a circle which is orthogonal to the circles $c_1 : x^2 + y^2 = 25$ and $c_2 : (x - 7)^2 + (y - 5)^2 = 4$ and which has the least radius is :

(a) $\left(5, \dfrac{25}{7}\right)$ (b) $(5, 7)$

(c) $(7, 12)$ (d) none of these.

90. If the points A $(1, 4)$ and B are symmetrical about the tangent to the circle $x^2 + y^2 - x + y = 0$ at the origin then co-ordinates of B are :

(a) $(1, 2)$ (b) $(\sqrt{2}, 1)$

(c) $(4, 1)$ (d) none of these.

91. AB is the intercept of the tangent to the circle $x^2 + y^2 = p^2$ between the coordinate axes. The locus of the vertex C of the rectangle OACB is :

(a) $\dfrac{1}{x^2} + \dfrac{1}{y^2} = \dfrac{1}{p^2}$ (b) $\dfrac{1}{x^2} + \dfrac{1}{y^2} = p^2$

(c) $x^2 + y^2 = \dfrac{1}{p^2}$ (d) none of these.

92. Equations of two circles are $x^2 + y^2 + 2\lambda x + 5 = 0$ and $x^2 + y^2 + 2\lambda y + 5 = 0$. P is any point on the line $x - y = 0$. If PA and PB are the lengths of the tangents from P to the two circles and PA = 3, then PB is equal to:

(a) 15   (b) 6

(c) 3   (d) none of these.

93. The locus of the point, the chord of contact of tangents from which to the circle $x^2 + y^2 = a^2$ subtends a right angle at the centre is a circle of radius :

    (a) 2a
    (b) a/2
    (c) $\sqrt{2}$ a
    (d) a^2.

94. The equation of the locus of the middle point of a chord of the circle $x^2 + y^2 = 2 (x + y)$ such that pair of lines joining the origin to the point of intersection of the chord and the circle are equally inclined to the x-axis is:

    (a) $x + y = 2$
    (b) $x - y = 2$
    (c) $2x - y = 1$
    (d) none of these.

95. If the squares of the lengths of the tangents from a point P to the circles

    $x^2 + y^2 = a^2$, $x^2 + y^2 = b^2$ and $x^2 + y^2 = c^2$ are in A.P. then a^2, b^2, c^2 are in :

    (a) A.P.
    (b) G.P.
    (c) H.P.
    (d) none of these.

96. The equation of largest circle passing through points (1, 1) and (2, 2) and always lying in first quadrant is :

    (a) $x^2 + y^2 - 4x - 2y + 4 = 0$
    (b) $x^2 + y^2 - 2x + 4y + 4 = 0$
    (c) $x^2 + y^2 - 3x - 3y + 4 = 0$
    (d) $x^2 + y^2 - 5x - y + 4 = 0$.

97. If a line is drawn through fixed point P (α, β) to cut circle $x^2 + y^2 = r^2$ at A and B, then PA $\times$ PB is equal to :

    (a) $(\alpha + \beta)^2 - r^2$
    (b) $\alpha^2 + \beta^2 + r^2$
    (c) $(\alpha + \beta)^2 + r^2$
    (d) $\alpha^2 + \beta^2 - r^2$.

98. If one of the circles $x^2 + y^2 + 2ax + c = 0$ and $x^2 + y^2 + 2bx + c = 0$ lies within the other, then

    (a) $ab > 0, c > 0$
    (b) $ab > 0, c < 0$
    (c) $ab < 0, c > 0$
    (d) none of these.

99. From a point A(1, 1) on the circle $x^2 + y^2 - 4x - 4y + 6 = 0$ two equal chords AB and AC of length 2 units are drawn. The equation of chord BC is :

    (a) $4x + 3y = 12$
    (b) $x + y = 4$
    (c) $3x + 4y = 4$
    (d) $x + y = 6$.

100. Two equal circles with their centres on x and y axes will possess the radical of chord BC is :

    (a) $ax - bx - \dfrac{a^2 + b^2}{4} = 0$
    (b) $2gx - 2 fy + g^2 - f^2 = 0$
    (c) $g^2x - f^2y - g^4 - f^4 = 0$
    (d) $2g^2x - 2 f^2y - g^4 - f^4 = 0$.

101. The condition for the line

     $(x + g) \cos \theta + (y + f) \sin \theta = k$

     to be a tangent to the circle is

     $x^2 + y^2 + 2gx + 2fy + c = 0$, is :

     (a) $g^2 + f^2 = c + k^2$
     (b) $g^2 + f^2 = c^2 + k$
     (c) $g^2 + f^2 = c^2 + k^2$
     (d) none of these.

102. The circle $x^2 + y^2 = 4$ cuts the line joining the points A(1, 0) and B(3, 4) in two points P and Q. Let $\dfrac{BP}{PA} = \alpha$ and $\dfrac{BQ}{QA} = \beta$. Then a and b are roots of the quadratic equation

     (a) $3x^2 + 2x - 21 = 0$
     (b) $3x^2 + 2x + 21 = 0$
     (c) $3x^2 - 2x - 21 = 0$
     (d) none of these.

103. The length of the chord of the circle $x^2 + y^2 = 25$ joining the points the tangents at which intersects at an angle of 120° is :

     (a) 5/2
     (b) 5
     (c) 10
     (d) none of these.

104. The circle passing through the distinct points (1, t), (t, 1) and (t, t) for all values of t, passes through the point :

     (a) (1, 1)
     (b) (– 1, – 1)
     (c) (1, – 1)
     (d) (– 1, 1).

105. C_1 and C_2 are the two concentric circles with radii r_1 and r_2 given that $r_1 < r_2$, if the tangents drawn from any point C_2 to C_1 meets again C_2 at the ends of its diameter then :

     (a) $r_2 = 2r_1$
     (b) $r_2 = \sqrt{2}r_1$
     (c) $r_2^2 < 2r_1^2$
     (d) none of these.

106. If the distance from the origin of the centres of three circles $x^2 + y^2 + 2\lambda_i x = c^2$ (i = 1, 2, 3) ($\lambda_i > 0 \ \forall$ i) are in G.P., the lengths of the tangents drawn to them from any point on the circle $x^2 + y^2 = c^2$ are in :

(a) A.P. (b) G.P.

(c) H.P. (d) none of these.

107. The maximum number of rational points may lie on the circle whose centre is $(\sqrt{3}, \sqrt{3})$ where rational point is the point whose both the co-ordinates are rational numbers :

(a) 1 (b) 2

(c) 3 (d) 0.

108. If two circles are drawn through the points (a, 5a) and (4a, a) to touch the axis of y, then they intersect at an angle :

(a) $\tan^{-1}\left(\dfrac{29}{9}\right)$ (b) $\tan^{-1}\left(\dfrac{40}{9}\right)$

(c) $\tan^{-1}\left(\dfrac{35}{9}\right)$ (d) none of these.

109. The tangents PA and PB are drawn from any point P of the circle $x^2 + y^2 = 2a^2$ to the circle $x^2 + y^2 = a^2$ the chord of contact AB on extending meets again the first circle at the point A' and B' then the locus of the point of intersection of tangents at A' and B' may be given as:

(a) $x^2 + y^2 = 3a^2$ (b) $x^2 + y^2 = 4a^2$

(c) $x^2 + y^2 = 6a^2$ (d) none of these.

110. The circle $x^2 + y^2 = 1$ cuts the x-axis at P and Q, another circle with centre at Q and variable radius intersects the first circle at R above the x-axis and the line segment PQ at S. The maximum area of the triangle QSR is :

(a) $\dfrac{2\sqrt{3}}{9}$ (b) $\dfrac{\sqrt{3}}{9}$

(c) $\dfrac{4\sqrt{3}}{9}$ (d) none of these.

111. The number of common tangents to the circle $x^2 + y^2 = |x|$ is :

(a) 2 (b) 1

(c) 3 (d) 4.

112. The circle $x^2 + y^2 - 4k - 4y + 4 = 0$ is inscribed in a triangle which has two of its sides along the coordinate axes.

If the locus of the circumcentre of the triangle is $x - y - xy + k (x^2 + y^2)^{1/2} = 0$, then k =

(a) 1 (b) – 1

(c) 2 (d) none of these.

113. Let P be any point on $x^2 + y^2 = 5$, Q be a point on line $7x + y + 3 = 0$. Line $x - y + 1 = 0$ is perpendicular bisector of PQ, if P is :

(a) (2, 1) (b) (1, 2)

(c) (1, – 2) (d) none of these.

114. The length of the common chord of the circles

$$x^2 + y^2 + 2x + 3y + 1 = 0$$

and $\quad x^2 + y^2 + 4x + 3y + 2 = 0$, is :

[PET (MP) 2000]

(a) $\dfrac{a}{2}$ (b) $2\sqrt{2}$

(c) $3\sqrt{2}$ (d) $\dfrac{3}{2}$

115. The circle $x^2 + y^2 = 4$ cuts the circle $x^2 + y^2 + 2x + 3y - 5 = 0$ in A and B, then centre of the circle with AB as diameter is :

(a) (0, 0) (b) $\left(\dfrac{2}{13}, \dfrac{2}{13}\right)$

(c) $\left(\dfrac{4}{13}, \dfrac{6}{13}\right)$ (d) (2, – 1).

116. The gradient of the radical axis of the circles

$$x^2 + y^2 - 3x - 4y + 5 = 0$$

and $\ 3x^2 + 3y^2 - 7x + 8y + 11 = 0$ is :

[PET (MP) 2000]

(a) $\dfrac{1}{3}$ (b) $-\dfrac{1}{10}$

(c) $-\dfrac{1}{2}$ (d) $-\dfrac{2}{3}$

117. If the circle $x^2 + y^2 + 2gx + 2fy + c = 0$ passes through all the four quadrants, then :

(a) g = f (b) g = – f

(c) c > 0 (d) c < 0.

118. If a circle whose centre is $(-1, 1)$ touches the straight line $x + 2y + 12 = 0$, then the coordinates of the point of contact are :

(a) $\left(-\dfrac{7}{2}, -4\right)$ (b) $\left(-\dfrac{18}{5}, -\dfrac{21}{5}\right)$

(c) $(2, -7)$ (d) $(-2, -5)$.

119. The locus of the centre of the circle
$(x \cos \alpha + y \sin \alpha - a)^2 + (x \sin \alpha - y \cos \alpha - b)^2$
$= a + b$, where α is a parameter, is a :

(a) line   (b) circle

(c) parabola   (d) hyperbola.

120. The equation of the circle in the first quadrant which touches each axis at a distance 5 from the origin is :

(a) $x^2 + y^2 + 5x + 5y + 25 = 0$

(b) $x^2 + y^2 - 10x - 10y + 25 = 0$

(c) $x^2 + y^2 - 5x - 5y + 25 = 0$

(d) $x^2 + y^2 + 10x + 10y + 25 = 0$.

121. The points $(\sin \theta, \cos \theta)$, θ being any real number, lie inside circle
$x^2 + y^2 - 2x - 2y + k = 0$, if :

(a) $k < 1 + 2\sqrt{2}$ (b) $k > 2\sqrt{2} - 1$

(c) $k > -1 - 2\sqrt{2}$ (d) $k > 1 + 2\sqrt{2}$

122. The equation of radical axis of the circles
$$x^2 + y^2 + x - y + 2 = 0$$
and $3x^2 + 3y^2 - 4x - 12 = 0$ will be

[PET (Raj.) 2000]

(a) $2x^2 + 2y^2 - 5x + y - 14 = 0$

(b) $7x - 3y + 18 = 0$

(c) $5x - y + 14 = 0$

(d) none of these.

123. The radical axis of the circles
$$x^2 + y^2 + 2gx + 2fy + c = 0$$
and $2x^2 + 2y^2 + 3x + 2y + 2c = 0$
touches the circle $x^2 + y^2 + 2x + 2y + 1 = 0$ if

(a) $g = \dfrac{4}{3}$ and $f = 2$ (b) $g = \dfrac{4}{3}$ or $f = \dfrac{1}{2}$

(c) $g = \dfrac{4}{3}$ or $f = 2$ (d) $g = \dfrac{4}{3}$ or $f = \dfrac{1}{2}$

124. The number of common tangents to the circles $x^2 + y^2 - 4x - 4y - 10 = 0$ and $x^2 + y^2 = 2$ is :

(a) 1   (b) 2

(c) 3   (d) 4.

125. A circle circumscribing an equilateral triangle with centroid at $(0, 0)$ of side a is drawn and a square is drawn touching its four sides to circle. The equation of circle circumscribing the square is :

(a) $x^2 + y^2 = 2a^2$ (b) $3x^2 + 3y^2 = 2a^2$

(c) $5x^2 + 5y^2 = 3a^2$ (d) none of these.

126. The equation $x^2 + y^2 + 4x + 6y + 13 = 0$ represents :

(a) a circle

(b) a pair of two distinct straight lines

(c) a pair of coincident straight lines

(d) a point.

127. The equation of the circle touching the pair of lines $7x^2 - 18xy + 7y^2 = 0$ and the circle $x^2 + y^2 - 8x - 8y = 0$ and contained in the given circle, is :

(a) $x^2 + y^2 - 12x - 12y + 64 = 0$

(b) $x^2 + y^2 + 12x + 12y + 64 = 0$

(c) $x^2 + y^2 - 12x - 12y - 64 = 0$

(d) none of these.

128. From the origin, chords are drawn to the circle $(x - 1)^2 + y^2 = 1$. The equation of the locus of the mid-points of these chords is :

(a) $x^2 + y^2 - x = 0$ (b) $x^2 + y^2 + x = 0$

(c) $x^2 + y^2 - 2x = 0$ (d) None of these

129. Let $x^2 + y^2 - 4x - 2y - 11 = 0$ be a circle. A pair of tangents from the point $(4, 5)$ with a pair of radii form a quadrilateral of area :

(a) 8 sq. units   (b) 16 sq. units

(c) 4 sq. units   (d) none of these.

130. The lines $3x - 4y - 4 = 0$ and $6x - 8y - 7 = 0$ are tangents to the same circle. The radius of the circle is :

(a) $\dfrac{4}{3}$ (b) $\dfrac{3}{4}$

(c) 4   (d) none of these.

131. In coaxial system of circles $x^2 + y^2 + 2gx + c = 0$, where g is a parameter, if $c > 0$ then the circles are of :

(a) orthogonal type

(b) non-intersecting type

(c) touching type

(d) intersecting type.

132. The circle $x^2 + y^2 - 8x - 4y + 4 = 0$ touches

(a) neither of the two axes

(b) x-axis

(c) y-axis

(d) both x and y-axis.

133. The locus of the centre of a circle which touches externally the given two circles is :

(a) hyperbola   (b) circle

(c) parabola   (d) ellipse.

134. The radical centre of the three circles described on the three sides of a triangle as diameter is :

(a) the circumcentre   (b) the incentre

(c) the centroid   (d) the orthocentre.

135. The cut points of circle $x^2 + y^2 = 25$ and

$x^2 + y^2 - 8x + 9 = 0$ are :

(a) $(4, 3)$ and $(4, -3)$ (b) $(4, -3)$ and $(3, 4)$

(c) $(-4, 3)$ and $(4, 3)$ (d) $(4, 3)$ and $(3, 4)$.

136. The point of intersection of the common chords of three circles described on the three sides of a triangle as diameter is :

(a) orthocentre   (b) centroid

(c) circumcentre   (d) incentre.

137. A circle passing through the origin has its centre (α, β), then the equation of tangent at the origin is : **[PET (Raj.) 2000]**

(a) $\alpha x - \beta y = 0$ (b) $\alpha x + \beta y = 0$

(c) $y = 0$ (d) none of these.

138. The equation of the circle passing through $(2a, 0)$ and whose radical axis w.r.t. the circle $x^2 + y^2 = a^2$ is $x = \dfrac{a}{2}$, is

(a) $x^2 + y^2 + 2ay = 0$

(b) $x^2 + y^2 + 2ax = 0$

(c) $x^2 + y^2 = a^2 - l^2$

(d) $2x^2 + 2y^2 = a^2 - l^2$.

139. The locus of the middle point of the chord of length $2l$ to the circle $x^2 + y^2 = a^2$ is :

(a) $x^2 + y^2 = l^2 + a^2$ (b) $x^2 + 2y^2 = l^2 + a^2$

(c) $x^2 + y^2 = a^2 - l^2$ (d) $2x^2 + 2y^2 = a^2 - l^2$

140. If $3x - 4y + 4 = 0$ and $6x + 8y - 7 = 0$ are tangents to the same circle, then the radius of the circle is :

(a) $\dfrac{3}{2}$ (b) $\dfrac{3}{4}$

(c) $\dfrac{11}{10}$ (d) $\dfrac{1}{10}$

141. The equation of normal to the circle

$x^2 + y^2 + 6x + 4y - 3 = 0$ at $(1, 1)$ is :

[EAMCET (2001)]

(a) $y + 1 = 0$ (b) $y + 4 = 0$

(c) $y + 2 = 0$ (d) $y = 0$.

142. The length of the diameter of the circle which touches the x-axis at the point $(1, 0)$ and passes through the point $(2, 3)$ is : **[AIEEE - 2012]**

(a) $\dfrac{10}{3}$ (b) $\dfrac{3}{5}$

(c) $\dfrac{6}{5}$ (d) $\dfrac{5}{3}$

143. The two circles $x^2 + y^2 = ax$ and $x^2 + y^2 = c^2$ $(c > 0)$ touch each other, if : **[AIEEE - 2011]**

(a) $|a| = 2c$ (b) $2|a| = c$

(c) $|a| = c$ (d) $a = 2c$

144. The circle $x^2 + y^2 = 4x + 8y + 5$ intersects the line $3x - 4y = m$ at two distinct points if :

[AIEEE - 2010]

(a) $-35 < m < 15$ (b) $15 < m < 65$

(c) $35 < m < 85$ (d) $-85 < m < -35$

145. If P and Q are the points of intersection of the circles $x^2 + y^2 + 3x + 7y + 2p - 5 = 0$ and $x^2 + y^2 + 2x + 2y - p^2 = 0$, then there is a circle passing through P, Q and (1, 1) for :

[AIEEE - 2009]

(a) all values of p

(b) all except one value of p

(c) all except two values of p

(d) exactly one value of p

146. The point diametrically opposite to the point P(1, 0) on the circle $x^2 + y^2 + 2x + 4y - 3 = 0$ is :   **[AIEEE - 2008]**

(a) (3, –4)   (b) (–3, 4)

(c) (–3, –4)   (d) (3, 4)

147. Consider a family of circles which are passing through the point (–1, 1) and are tangent to x-axis. If (h, k) are the co-ordinates of the centre of the circles, then the set of values of k is given by the interval :   **[AIEEE - 2007]**

(a) $0 < k < 1/2$ (b) $k \geq 1/2$

(c) $-1/2 \leq k \leq 1/2$ (d) $k \leq 1/2$

148. The circle $x^2 + y^2 - 8x = 0$ and hyperbola $\dfrac{x^2}{9} - \dfrac{y^2}{4} = 1$ intersect at the points A and B. Then the equation of the circle with AB as diameter is

(a) $x^2 + y^2 - 12x + 24 = 0$

(b) $x^2 + y^2 + 12x + 24 = 0$

(c) $x^2 + y^2 + 24x - 12 = 0$

(d) $x^2 + y^2 - 24x - 12 = 0$

ANSWER KEY

1. (d)	**2.** (b)	**3.** (a)	**4.** (d)	**5.** (c)	**6.** (a)	**7.** (d)	**8.** (c)	**9.** (a)	**10.** (c)
11. (b)	**12.** (c)	**13.** (d)	**14.** (c)	**15.** (d)	**16.** (b)	**17.** (a)	**18.** (b)	**19.** (a)	**20.** (b)
21. (c)	**22.** (d)	**23.** (a)	**24.** (a)	**25.** (c)	**26.** (b)	**27.** (c)	**28.** (c)	**29.** (d)	**30.** (b)
31. (b)	**32.** (a)	**33.** (d)	**34.** (b)	**35.** (c)	**36.** (d)	**37.** (a)	**38.** (a)	**39.** (b)	**40.** (b)
41. (b)	**42.** (c)	**43.** (d)	**44.** (a)	**45.** (b)	**46.** (b)	**47.** (c)	**48.** (d)	**49.** (a)	**50.** (a)
51. (c)	**52.** (b)	**53.** (a)	**54.** (d)	**55.** (b)	**56.** (a)	**57.** (c)	**58.** (c)	**59.** (a)	**60.** (c)
61. (b)	**62.** (b)	**63.** (b)	**64.** (b)	**65.** (d)	**66.** (c)	**67.** (b)	**68.** (a)	**69.** (d)	**70.** (c)
71. (b)	**72.** (b)	**73.** (a)	**74.** (c)	**75.** (b)	**76.** (b)	**77.** (b)	**78.** (b)	**79.** (b)	**80.** (a)
81. (a)	**82.** (a)	**83.** (a)	**84.** (b)	**85.** (c)	**86.** (c)	**87.** (c)	**88.** (b)	**89.** (d)	**90.** (c)
91. (a)	**92.** (c)	**93.** (c)	**94.** (a)	**95.** (a)	**96.** (a)	**97.** (d)	**98.** (a)	**99.** (b)	**100.** (b)
101. (a)	**102.** (a)	**103.** (b)	**104.** (a)	**105.** (b)	**106.** (b)	**107.** (b)	**108.** (b)	**109.** (b)	**110.** (c)
111. (c)	**112.** (a)	**113.** (d)	**114.** (b)	**115.** (b)	**116.** (b)	**117.** (d)	**118.** (d)	**119.** (b)	**120.** (b)
121. (c)	**122.** (b)	**123.** (b)	**124.** (a)	**125.** (b)	**126.** (a)	**127.** (a)	**128.** (a)	**129.** (c)	**130.** (b)
131. (b)	**132.** (c)	**133.** (a)	**134.** (a)	**135.** (a)	**136.** (a)	**137.** (b)	**138.** (c)	**139.** (a)	**140.** (b)
141. (c)	**142.** (a)	**143.** (c)	**144.** (a)	**145.** (a)	**146.** (c)	**147.** (b)	**148.** (a)		

PARABOLA

MULTIPLE CHOICE QUESTIONS

1. The focal distance of a point on the parabola $y^2 = 8x$ is 4. Its co-ordinates are :

   (a) $(2, 2)$ (b) $(2, -4)$

   (c) $(-2, 4)$ (d) $(-2, -2)$

2. The equation of parabola with focus $(3, -4)$ and directrix $x + y - 2 = 0$ is :

   (a) $x^2 - 2xy + y^2 + 8x - 20y + 46 = 0$

   (b) $x^2 + 2xy + y^2 - 8x + 20y + 46 = 0$

   (c) $x^2 - 2xy + y^2 - 8x + 20y + 46 = 0$

   (d) None of these

3. The equation of parabola with vertex $(2, 1)$ and focus $(1, -1)$ is :

   (a) $4x^2 - 4xy + y^2 + 8x + 46y - 71 = 0$

   (b) $x^2 - 4xy + 4y^2 + 4x + 23y - 84 = 0$

   (c) $4x^2 - 4xy + y^2 + 8x - 46y + 71 = 0$

   (d) None of these

4. The equation of tangent to the parabola $y^2 = 6x$, at the point whose ordinate is 6, is :

   (a) $2x - y + 6 = 0$ (b) $x - 2y + 6 = 0$

   (c) $x + 2y + 6 = 0$ (d) None of these

5. The normal to the parabola $y^2 = 8x$ at $(2, 4)$ meets the parabola again at :

   (a) $(18, 12)$ (b) $(18, -12)$

   (c) $(-18, 12)$ (d) None of these

6. The tangent to the parabola $y^2 = 16x$, inclined at an angle of $60°$ to x-axis is :

   (a) $3x + \sqrt{3}y + 4 = 0$ (b) $\sqrt{3}x - y + 4 = 0$

   (c) $3x - \sqrt{3}y + 4 = 0$ (d) None of these

7. Th equation of tangent to $y^2 = 16x$ perpendicular to $4x - 2y = 17$ is :

   (a) $2x + y + 2 = 0$ (b) $x + 2y + 2 = 0$

   (c) $x + 2y - 16 = 0$ (d) $x + 2y + 16 = 0$

8. If a tangent to the parabola $y^2 = 8x$ makes an angle of $45°$ with the line $y = 3x + 17$, then the point of contact can be :

   (a) $(-1/2, -2)$ (b) $(-1/2, 2)$

   (c) $(8, -8)$ (d) $(8, 8)$

9. The ortho centre of triangle formed by three tangents to a parabola lies on the :

   (a) axis   (b) tangent at vertex

   (c) directrix   (d) None of these

10. The equation of normal to the parabola $y^2 = 4x$, which is parallel to $y - 2x + 17 = 0$ is :

    (a) $y - 2x - 17 = 0$ (b) $2x - y = 12$

    (c) $4x - 2y - 12 = 0$ (d) None of these

11. The condition that the line $\dfrac{x}{p} + \dfrac{y}{q} = 1$ to be a normal to the parabola $y^2 = 4ax$ is :

    (a) $p^3 - 2ap^2 = aq^2$ (b) $q^3 - 2ap^2 = aq^2$

    (c) $p^3 - ap^2 = 2aq^2$ (d) None of these

12. $y = mx + c$ touches $y^2 = 4a(x + a)$ if :

    (a) $c = am - \dfrac{a}{m}$ (b) $c = m - \dfrac{a}{m}$

    (c) $c = am + \dfrac{a}{m}$ (d) $c = am + a$

13. The equation $\lambda x^2 + 4xy + y^2 + \lambda x + 3y + 2 = 0$ represents a parabola if $\lambda =$

    (a) 0 (b) 4

    (c) -4 (d) 8

14. A straight line touches $x^2 + y^2 = 2a^2$ and $y^2 = 8ax$. The equation of the line is :

    (a) $y = x + 2a$ (b) $y = x - 2a$

    (c) $y = -x + 2a$ (d) None of these

15. The equation of common tangent to the parabolas $y^2 = 4ax$ and $x^2 = 4by$ is :

    (a) $xb^{1/3} + ya^{1/3} + a^{2/3}b^{2/3} = 0$

    (b) $xa^{1/3} + yb^{1/3} - a^{2/3}b^{2/3} = 0$

    (c) $xa^{1/3} + yb^{1/3} + a^{2/3}b^{2/3} = 0$

    (d) None of these

16. The equation(s) of normal to the parabola $y^2 = 4x$, which passes through $(3, 0)$ is :
    (a) $y = 0$
    (b) $y = x - 3$
    (c) $y = -x + 3$
    (d) All of these

17. The locus of the point such that two of the normals drawn through it to the parabola $y^2 = 4ax$ are perpendicular to each other is :
    (a) $y^2 = 2a (x + 3a)$
    (b) $y^2 = a (x - 3a)$
    (c) $y^2 = 2a (x - 3a)$
    (d) $y^2 = a (x + 3a)$

18. If the three normals drawn from a point to a parabola $y^2 = 4ax$ are such that the sum of the three angles made by them with the x-axis is constant, then the point lies on the :
    (a) parabola
    (b) straight line
    (c) circle
    (d) None of these

19. If the normals at P, Q, R of the parabola $y^2 = 4ax$ meet in (h, k), then the centroid of triangle PQR lies on :
    (a) axis
    (b) directrix
    (c) tangent at the vertex
    (d) None of these

20. The locus of points such that two of the three normals drawn from them to the parabola $y^2 = 4ax$ coincide is :
    (a) $27ay^2 = 4 (x + 2a)^3$
    (b) $27y^2 = 4a (x - 2a)^3$
    (c) $27ay^2 = 4 (x - 2a)^3$
    (d) None of these

21. If three normals from a point to the parabola $y^2 = 4ax$ cut the x-axis in points whose distances from the vertex are in A.P., then the point lies on the curve :
    (a) $27ay^2 = 2 (x + 2a)^3$
    (b) $27ay^2 = 4 (x - 2a)^3$
    (c) $27ay^2 = 2 (x - 2a)^3$
    (d) None of these

22. The point of intersection of two perpendicular tangents to a parabola lies on the :
    (a) axis
    (b) directrix
    (c) tangent at the vertex
    (d) None of these

23. The angle between two tangents drawn from the point $(1, 4)$ to the parabola $y^2 = 12x$ is :
    (a) $\tan^{-1} 2$
    (b) $\tan^{-1} 1/2$
    (c) $\tan^{-1} 1/3$
    (d) None of these

24. If two tangents to the parabola $y^2 = 4ax$ make angles θ_1 and θ_2 with x-axis where $\tan^2 \theta_1 + \tan^2 \theta_2 = c$, then the locus of their point of intersection is :
    (a) $y^2 - ax + 2cx^2 = 0$
    (b) $y^2 + 2ax = cx^2$
    (c) $y^2 - 2ax = cx^2$
    (d) None of these

25. The pole of the line $2x = y$ w.r.t. the parabola $y^2 = 2x$ is:
    (a) $(0, 1/2)$
    (b) $(0, -1/2)$
    (c) $(1/2, 0)$
    (d) None of these

26. If the polar of any point w.r.t. the parabola $y^2 = 4ax$, touches the circle $x^2 + y^2 = 4a^2$, then the locus of the point is the curve
    (a) $x^2 - y^2 = 3a^2$
    (b) $x^2 - y^2 = 4a^2$
    (c) $x^2 - y^2 = 2a^2$
    (d) $x^2 - y^2 = a^2$

27. If the line $x - 1 = 0$ is the directrix of the parabola $y^2 - kx + 8 = 0$, then one of the value of k is :
    (a) $\dfrac{1}{8}$
    (b) 8
    (c) 4
    (d) $\dfrac{1}{4}$

28. Chords of the parabola $y^2 = 4ax$ are drawn at fixed distance a from the focus. The locus of their poles w.r.t. the parabola is :
    (a) $y^2 = 4x (2a + x)$
    (b) $y^2 = 2x (2a + x)$
    (c) $y^2 = 4x (2a - x)$
    (d) None of these

29. The locus of the mid points of chords of the parabola $y^2 = 4ax$, which pass through a fixed point (h, k) is given by :

(a) $y^2 - 2ax + ky + 2ah = 0$

(b) $y^2 - 2ax - ky - 2ah = 0$

(c) $y^2 - 2ax - ky + 2ah = 0$

(d) None of these

30. If the point $(at^2, 2at)$ is one extremity of a focal chord of the parabola $y^2 = 4ax$, then the length of the chord is :

(a) $2at\left(t - \dfrac{1}{t}\right)^2$ (b) $a\left(t + \dfrac{1}{t}\right)^2$

(c) $a\left(t - \dfrac{1}{t}\right)^2$ (d) None of these

31. The locus of mid points of the chords of the parabola $y^2 = 4ax$ which subtend a right angle at the vertex is :

(a) $y^2 = 2a(x + 4a)$ (b) $y^2 = 2a(x - 4a)$

(c) $y^2 = a(x - 4a)$ (d) None of these

32. The locus of mid-points of the focal chords of the parabola $y^2 = 4ax$ is another parabola whose vertex is :

(a) (a, 0)   (b) (−a, 0)

(c) (0, a)   (d) None of these

33. A tangent to the parabola $y^2 + 4bx = 0$ meets the parabola $y^2 = 4ax$ at P and Q. The locus of mid-point of PQ is :

(a) $y^2(2a + b) = 4a^2x$ (b) $y^2(2a + b) = 2a^2x$

(c) $y^2(2a - b) = 4a^2x$ (d) None of these

34. If PNP' is a double ordinate of the parabola $y^2 = 4ax$, then the locus of the point of intersection of the normal of P and the line parallel to the axis through P' is given by :

(a) $y^2 = 4a(x - 4a)$ (b) $y^2 = a(x - 4a)$

(c) $y^2 = 2a(x - 4a)$ (d) None of these

35. The length of the side of an equilateral triangle, inscribed in $y^2 = 8x$, so that one angular point is at the vertex x, is :

(a) $4\sqrt{3}$ (b) $8\sqrt{3}$

(c) $16\sqrt{3}$ (d) None of these

36. The equation of parabola, whose extremities of latus rectum are (1, 2) and (1, −4) is :

(a) $(y + 1)^2 = 3(2x + 3)$

(b) $(y + 1)^2 = -3(2x + 3)$

(c) $(y + 1)^2 = -3(2x - 3)$

(d) $(y + 1)^2 = -3(2x - 5)$

37. The equation of parabola with focus (0, 0) and tangent at vertex as $x - y + 1 = 0$, is :

(a) $x^2 + y^2 + 2xy - 4x + 4y - 4 = 0$

(b) $x^2 + y^2 + 2xy + 4x + 4y - 4 = 0$

(c) $x^2 + y^2 + 2xy - 4x + 4y + 4 = 0$

(d) None of these

38. The focus and vertex of the parabola $9y^2 - 16x - 12y - 57 = 0$ are respectively given by :

(a) $\left(\dfrac{485}{144}, \dfrac{-2}{3}\right), \left(\dfrac{61}{16}, \dfrac{-2}{3}\right)$

(b) $\left(\dfrac{-485}{144}, \dfrac{-2}{3}\right), \left(\dfrac{-61}{16}, \dfrac{-2}{3}\right)$

(c) $\left(\dfrac{485}{144}, \dfrac{2}{3}\right), \left(\dfrac{61}{16}, \dfrac{2}{3}\right)$

(d) $\left(\dfrac{-485}{144}, \dfrac{2}{3}\right), \left(\dfrac{-61}{16}, \dfrac{2}{3}\right)$

39. For the parabola $x^2 + 4x + 4y + 16 = 0$, the equation of axis and directrix are respectively given by :

(a) $x + 2 = 0, y - 2 = 0$

(b) $x - 2 = 0, y + 2 = 0$

(c) $x + 2 = 0, y + 2 = 0$

(d) None of these

40. The locus of the mid-point of the line joining the focus to any point on the parabola $y^2 = 4ax$ is another parabola with directrix :

(a) $x + a = 0$ (b) $x = 0$

(c) $2x + a = 0$ (d) $2x - a = 0$

41. The equation of the parabola having axis parallel to y-axis and which passes through the points (0, 4), (1, 9) and (4, 5) is :

(a) $12y = -19x^2 + 79x + 48$

(b) $12y = -19x^2 + 79x - 48$

(c) $12y = 19x^2 + 79x + 48$

(d) $12y = 19x^2 - 79x + 48$

42. The radius of the smaller of the two circles that touch the parabola $75y^2 = 64(5x - 3)$ at $(6/5, 8/5)$ and x-axis is :

(a) 1   (b) 2

(c) 4   (d) None of these

43. Consider a curve $ax^2 + 2hxy + by^2 = 1$ and a point P not on the curve. A line drawn from the point P intersects the curve at points Q and R. If the product PQ. PR is independent of the slope of the line, then the curve is :

(a) parabola   (b) ellipse

(c) circle   (d) None of these

44. Through the vertex O of a parabola $y^2 = 4x$, chords OP and OQ are drawn at right angles to one another. The locus of mid point of PQ is :

(a) $y^2 = 2x + 8$ (b) $y^2 = x + 8$

(c) $y^2 = 2x - 8$ (d) None of these

45. The locus of point of intersection of two normals to the parabola $x^2 = 8y$, which are at right angles to each other is :

(a) $x^2 = 2(y - 6)$ (b) $x^2 + 2(y - 6) = 0$

(c) $x^2 = 2(y + 6)$ (d) None of these

46. Three normals are drawn from $(14, 7)$ to the parabola $y^2 - 16x - 8y = 0$. The feet of normals are :

(a) $(0, 0), (8, 16), (3, -4)$

(b) $(0, 0), (-8, 16), (3, -4)$

(c) $(0, 0), (8, -16), (3, -4)$

(d) None of these

47. A ray of light coming along the line $y = b$ from positive direction of x-axis strikes a concave mirror whose intersection with xy–plane is $y^2 = 4ax$. If a and b are positive, then the reflected ray is :

(a) $y - 2at = \dfrac{2t}{1 + t^2}(x - at^2)$

(b) $y - 2at = \dfrac{2t}{t^2 - 1}(x - at^2)$

(c) $y - 2at = \dfrac{2t}{1 - t^2}(x - at^2)$

(d) None of these

48. The normal chord to a parabola $y^2 = 4ax$ at the point whose ordinate is equal to abcissa subtends an angle θ at the focus where θ is :

(a) $\dfrac{\pi}{6}$ (b) $\dfrac{\pi}{4}$

(c) $\dfrac{\pi}{3}$ (d) $\dfrac{\pi}{2}$

49. Points A, B, C lie on the parabola $y^2 = 4ax$. The tangents to the parabola, at A, B, C taken in pairs intersect at P, Q, R. The ratio of areas of $\triangle$ ABC and $\triangle$PQR is :

(a) $2 : 1$ (b) $1 : 2$

(c) $3 : 1$ (d) None of these

50. If the ordinates of P and Q on the parabola $y^2 = 12x$ are in the ratio $1 : 2$, then the locus of point of intersection of the normals to the parabola at P and Q is :

(a) $343y^2 = 12(x - 6)^3$

(b) $343y^2 = 12(x + 6)^3$

(c) $343y^2 = -12(x - 6)^3$

(d) None of these

51. The locus of point through which pass three normals to the parabola $y^2 = 4ax$ such that two of them make angles α and β with x-axis and $\tan \alpha$. $\tan \beta = 2$ is :

(a) $y^2 = 2ax$ (b) $y^2 = 4ax$

(c) $y^2 = ax$ (d) $y^2 = -2ax$

52. From a point A, common tangents are drawn to $2x^2 + 2y^2 = a^2$ and $y^2 = 4ax$. The area of the quadrilateral, formed by the common tangents, the chord of contact of the circle and the chord of contact of the parabola, is :

(a) $\dfrac{21a^2}{4}$ (b) $\dfrac{15a^2}{4}$

(c) $\dfrac{9a^2}{4}$ (d) None of these

53. The number of points with integral co-ordinates that lie in the interior of the region common to the circle $x^2 + y^2 = 16$ and the parabola $y^2 = 4x$ is :

(a) 13   (b) 10

(c) 16   (d) None of these

54. The parametric equation $x = t^2 + t + 1, y = t^2 - t + 1$ represents :

(a) a pair of straight lines

(b) a parabola

(c) an ellipse

(d) a hyperbola

55. If $(4, 0)$ is vertex and y-axis is directrix of a parabola, then its focus is :

(a) $(4, 0)$ (b) $(0, 4)$

(c) $(8, 0)$ (d) $(0, 8)$

56. The focus of the parabola $x^2 - 2x - y + 2 = 0$ is :

(a) $(1, 0)$ (b) $(1, 5/4)$

(c) $(5/4, 1)$ (d) $(0, 5/4)$

57. The equation of parabola with vertex $(-3, -2)$, passing through $(1, 2)$ and axis horizontal, is :

(a) $y^2 + 4y - 4x + 8 = 0$

(b) $y^2 + 4x + 4y - 8 = 0$

(c) $y^2 + 4y - 4x - 8 = 0$

(d) None of these

58. The locus of a point that divides a chord parallel to $2x - y = 17$, of the parabola $y^2 = 4x$, internally in the ratio $1 : 2$ is a parabola. The vertex of this parabola is :

(a) $\left(\dfrac{2}{9}, \dfrac{8}{9}\right)$ (b) $\left(\dfrac{8}{9}, \dfrac{2}{9}\right)$

(c) $\left(\dfrac{-2}{9}, \dfrac{-8}{9}\right)$ (d) None of these

59. If tangents are drawn from any point on the line $x = -4a$ to the parabola $y^2 = 4ax$, then their chord of contact subtends an angle θ at the vertex, where θ is :

(a) $\dfrac{\pi}{2}$ (b) $\dfrac{\pi}{3}$

(c) $\dfrac{\pi}{4}$ (d) None of these

60. Axis of the parabola $x^2 - 3y - 6x + 6 = 0$ is :

(a) $x + 3 = 0$ (b) $y + 1 = 0$

(c) $x = 3$ (d) $y = 1$

61. The angle subtended by the double ordinate of length 2a of the parabola $y^2 = ax$, at the vertex is

(a) $\dfrac{\pi}{4}$ (b) $\dfrac{\pi}{3}$

(c) $\dfrac{\pi}{2}$ (d) None of these

62. If a variable circle is described to pass through $(a, 0)$ and touch the line $x + y = 0$, then the locus of center of the circle is :

(a) a parabola

(b) an ellipse

(c) a pair of straight lines

(d) None of these

63. If $\left(\dfrac{a}{b}\right)^{1/3} + \left(\dfrac{b}{a}\right)^{1/3} = \dfrac{\sqrt{3}}{2}$, then the angle of intersection of the parabolas $y^2 = 4ax$ and $x^2 = 4by$ at a point other than origin is :

(a) $\dfrac{\pi}{4}$ (b) $\dfrac{\pi}{3}$

(c) $\dfrac{\pi}{2}$ (d) None of these

64. The line $y = mx + 1$ is a tangent to the parabola $y^2 = 4x$ if m =

(a) 1   (b) 2

(c) 3   (d) 4

65. AB is a chord of a parabola $y^2 = 4ax$ with vertex at A. BC is drawn perpendicular to AB meeting the axis at C. The projection of BC on the axis of the parabola is :

(a) a   (b) 2a

(c) 4a   (d) 8a

66. The line $x - y + 2 = 0$ touches $y^2 = 8x$ at :

(a) $(2, -4)$ (b) $(2, 4)$

(c) $(1, 2\sqrt{2})$ (d) $(4, -4\sqrt{2})$

67. Two tangents are drawn from $(-2, -1)$ to $y^2 = 4x$. The angle between them, α, is given by $\tan \alpha =$

(a) 2   (b) $\dfrac{1}{2}$

(c) 3   (d) $\dfrac{1}{3}$

68. If the points $(at^2, 2at)$ and $(au^2, 2au)$ are extremities of focal chord of $y^2 = 4ax$, then :

(a) $tu = -1$ (b) $tu = 1$

(c) $t = -u$ (d) $t = u$

69. The equation of tangent to $y^2 = 16x$ which is perpendicular to $y = 3x + 17$ is :

(a) $y + 4 = 3x$ (b) $3y + 36 = x$

(c) $3y + x = 36$ (d) $3y + x + 36 = 0$

70. If the parabola $y^2 = 4ax$ passes through $(1, -2)$, then the tangent at this point is :

(a) $x + y = 1$ (b) $x - y = 1$

(c) $x + y + 1 = 0$ (d) None of these

71. The length of latus rectum of the parabola
$4y^2 + 2x - 20y + 17 = 0$ is :

(a) 3   (b) 6

(c) 9   (d) 1/2

72. The line $y = mx + c$ touches $x^2 = 4ay$ if :

(a) $\dfrac{c}{a} + m = 0$ (b) $cm + a = 0$

(c) $\dfrac{c}{a} + m^2 = 0$ (d) $a - cm^2 = 0$

73. The centroid to the triangle formed by joining the feet at the normals drawn from any point to the parabola $y^2 = 4ax$, lies on :

(a) axis   (b) directrix

(c) latus rectum   (d) tangent to vertex

74. If a chord is normal to the parabola at one end and subtends a right angle at the vertex, then slope of the chord is :

(a) 1   (b) −2

(c) $\sqrt{2}$ (d) $\dfrac{1}{\sqrt{2}}$

75. If the vertex is $(3, 0)$, and the extremities of the latus rectum are $(4, 3)$ and $(4, -3)$, then the equation of the parabola is :

(a) $y^2 = 4(x - 3)$ (b) $y^2 = -4(x - 3)$

(c) $y^2 = 9(x - 3)$ (d) None of these

76. Co-ordinates of any point on the parabola, whose focus is $\left(-\dfrac{3}{2}, 3\right)$ and the directrix is $2x + 5 = 0$ is given by :

(a) $(2t^2 - 2, 2t + 3)$ (b) $(2t^2 + 2, 2t - 3)$

(c) $(2t^2 - 2, 2t - 3)$ (d) None of these

77. The conic represented by $\sqrt{ax} + \sqrt{by} = 1$ is :

(a) ellipse   (b) hyperbola

(c) parabola   (d) None of these

78. If the point $(a, -1)$ is exterior to both the parabolas $y^2 = |x|$, then :

(a) $a \in (0, 2)$ (b) $a \in (-1, 1)$

(c) $a \in (-2, 0)$ (d) None of these

79. The length of latus rectum of the parabola
$25 [(x - 2)^2 + (y - 4)^2] = (4x - 3y + 12)^2$ is :

(a) $\dfrac{8}{5}$ (b) $\dfrac{12}{5}$

(c) $\dfrac{16}{5}$ (d) None of these

80. If the parabola $x^2 = ay$ makes an intercept of length $\sqrt{40}$ on the line $y = 2x + 1$, then $a =$

(a) 1   (b) −1

(c) 2   (d) 3

81. A ray of light is coming along the line which is parallel to y-axis and strikes a concave mirror whose intersection with the xy-plane is a parabola $(x - 4)^2 = 4(y + 2)$. After reflection the ray must pass through the point :

(a) $(-4, 1)$ (b) $(4, -1)$

(c) $(0, 1)$ (d) None of these

82. With respect to the parabola $y^2 = 2x$ the points $P(4, 2)$ and $Q(1, 4)$ are such that :

(a) P and Q both lie inside the parabola

(b) P and Q both lie outside the parabola

(c) P lies inside and Q outside the parabola

(d) P lies outside and Q inside the parabola

83. A circle has its centre at the vertex of $x^2 = 4y$ and the circle cuts the parabola at the ends of its latus rectum. The equation of circle is :

(a) $x^2 + y^2 = 5$ (b) $x^2 + y^2 = 4$

(c) $x^2 + y^2 = 1$ (d) None of these

84. The parametric representation $(3 + t^2, 3t - 2)$ represents a parabola with :

(a) focus $(-3, -2)$ (b) directrix $x + 5 = 0$

(c) vertex $(3, -2)$ (d) All of these

85. The normals to the parabola $y^2 = x$ are drawn through $(c, 0)$ then :

(a) $c = \dfrac{1}{4}$ (b) $c = \dfrac{1}{2}$

(c) $c > \dfrac{1}{2}$ (d) None of these

86. If the line $x = 1$ is the directrix of the parabola $y^2 - kx + 8 = 0$, then one of the values of k is :

(a) 8   (b) 1/8

(c) 4   (d) 1/4

87. Consider a circle with its centre lying on the focus of the parabola $y^2 = 2px$ such that it touches the directrix of the parabola. Then a point of intersection of the circle and the parabola is :

(a) $\left(\dfrac{p}{2}, p\right)$ (b) $\left(\dfrac{p}{2}, \dfrac{-p}{2}\right)$

(c) $\left(\dfrac{-p}{2}, p\right)$ (d) $\left(\dfrac{-p}{2}, -p\right)$

88. Two perpendicular tangents to $y^2 = 4ax$ always intersect on the line :

(a) $x = -a$ (b) $x = a$

(c) $x = -2a$ (d) $x = -4a$

89. Focus of the parabola $(y - 2)^2 = 20(x + 3)$ is :

(a) $(3, -2)$ (b) $(-3, 2)$

(c) $(2, 2)$ (d) $(2, -3)$

90. If b and c are lengths of the segments of any focal chord of a parabola $y^2 = 4ax$, then the length of the semi latus rectum is :

(a) $\dfrac{b + c}{2}$ (b) $\dfrac{2bc}{b + c}$

(c) $\dfrac{bc}{b + c}$ (d) $\sqrt{bc}$

91. If t is the parameter for one end of a focal chord of the parabola $y^2 = 4ax$, then its length is :

(a) $a\left(t - \dfrac{1}{t}\right)$ (b) $a\left(t + \dfrac{1}{t}\right)$

(c) $a\left(t - \dfrac{1}{t}\right)^2$ (d) $a\left(t + \dfrac{1}{t}\right)^2$

92. The locus of a point whose sum of the distances from the origin and the line $x - 2 = 0$ is 4 units, is

(a) $y^2 + 12(x - 3) = 0$ (b) $y^2 = 12(x - 3)$

(c) $x^2 = 12(y - 3)$ (d) $x^2 + 12(y - 3) = 0$

93. If M is the foot of perpendicular from a point P on a parabola to its directrix and SPM is an equilateral triangle, where S is the focus, then SP =

(a) a (b) $2a$

(c) $3a$ (d) $4a$

94. The axis of the parabola $9y^2 - 16x - 12y - 57 = 0$ is :

(a) $3y - 2 = 0$ (b) $x + 3y = 3$

(c) $2x - 3 = 0$ (d) $y - 3 = 0$

95. The equation of the directrix of parabola $5y^2 = 4x$ is :

(a) $4x - 1 = 0$ (b) $4x + 1 = 0$

(c) $5x - 1 = 0$ (d) $5x + 1 = 0$

96. The co-ordinates of the focus of the parabola $y^2 - 4y - 6x + 13 = 0$ are :

(a) $(3/2, 2)$ (b) $(3, 2)$

(c) $(2, 3/2)$ (d) None of these

97. The equation of common tangent touching the circle $(x - 3)^2 + y^2 = 9$ and parabola $y^2 = 4x$ above the x-axis is :

(a) $\sqrt{3}y + x + 3 = 0$ (b) $\sqrt{3}y = 3x + 1$

(c) $\sqrt{3}y = x + 3$ (d) $\sqrt{3}y + 3x + 1 = 0$

98. The equation of directrix of the parabola $y^2 + 4y + 4x - 2 = 0$ is :

(a) $x + 1 = 0$ (b) $x = 1$

(c) $2x + 3 = 0$ (d) $2x - 5 = 0$

99. The mirror image of the directrix of the parabola $y^2 = 4x + 4$ in the line mirror $x + 2y = 3$ is :

(a) $x + 2 = 0$ (b) $3x + 4y = 16$

(c) $3x - 4y + 16 = 0$ (d) None of these

100. The maximum number of common chords of a circle and a parabola can be :

(a) 2   (b) 4

(c) 6   (d) 8

101. The shortest distance between line $y - x = 1$ and curve $x = y^2$ is   [AIEEE - 2011]

(a) $\dfrac{4}{\sqrt{3}}$

(b) $\dfrac{\sqrt{3}}{4}$

(c) $\dfrac{3\sqrt{2}}{8}$

(d) $\dfrac{8}{3\sqrt{2}}$

102. If two tangents drawn from a point P to the parabola $y^2 = 4x$ are at right angles, then the locus of P is :   [AIEEE - 2010]

(a) $2x + 1 = 0$

(b) $x = -1$

(c) $2x - 1 = 0$

(d) $x = 1$

103. The shortest distance between the line $y - x = 1$ and the curve $x = y^2$ is :   [AIEEE - 2009]

(a) $\dfrac{3\sqrt{2}}{8}$

(b) $\dfrac{2\sqrt{3}}{8}$

(c) $\dfrac{3\sqrt{2}}{5}$

(d) $\dfrac{3}{4}$

104. A parabola has the origin as its focus and the line $x = 2$ as the directrix. Then the vertex of the parabola is at :   [AIEEE - 2008]

(a) $(0, 2)$

(b) $(1, 0)$

(c) $(0, 1)$

(d) $(2, 0)$

105. The equation of a tangent to the parabola $y^2 = 8x$ is $y = x + 2$. The point on this line from which the other tangent to the parabola is perpendicular to the given tangent is :   [AIEEE - 2007]

(a) $(-1, 1)$

(b) $(0, 2)$

(c) $(2, 4)$

(d) $(-2, 0)$

106. The locus of the vertices of the family of parabolas $y = \dfrac{a^3 x^2}{3} + \dfrac{a^2 x}{2} - 2a$ is :   [AIEEE - 2006]

(a) $xy = \dfrac{105}{64}$

(b) $xy = \dfrac{3}{4}$

(c) $xy = \dfrac{35}{16}$

(d) $xy = \dfrac{64}{105}$

107. Let P be the point $(1, 0)$ and Q a point on the locus $y^2 = 8x$. The locus of mid point of PQ is :   [AIEEE - 2005]

(a) $y^2 - 4x + 2 = 0$

(b) $y^2 + 4x + 2 = 0$

(c) $x^2 + 4y + 2 = 0$

(d) $x^2 - 4y + 2 = 0$

108. Let (x, y) be a point on the parabola $y^2 = 4x$. Let P be the point that divides the segment from $(0, 0)$ to (x, y) in the ratio $1 : 3$. Then the locus of P is

(a) $x^2 = y$

(b) $y^2 = 2x$

(c) $y^2 = x$

(d) $x^2 = 2y$

ANSWER KEY

1. (b)	2. (c)	3. (a)	4. (b)	5. (b)	6. (c)	7. (d)	8. (d)	9. (c)	10. (b)
11. (a)	12. (c)	13. (b)	14. (a)	15. (c)	16. (d)	17. (b)	18. (b)	19. (a)	20. (c)
21. (c)	22. (b)	23. (b)	24. (c)	25. (a)	26. (b)	27. (c)	28. (a)	29. (c)	30. (b)
31. (b)	32. (a)	33. (a)	34. (a)	35. (c)	36. (d)	37. (a)	38. (d)	39. (c)	40. (b)
41. (a)	42. (a)	43. (c)	44. (c)	45. (a)	46. (a)	47. (b)	48. (d)	49. (a)	50. (a)
51. (b)	52. (b)	53. (a)	54. (b)	55. (c)	56. (b)	57. (c)	58. (a)	59. (a)	60. (c)
61. (c)	62. (a)	63. (b)	64. (a)	65. (c)	66. (b)	67. (c)	68. (a)	69. (d)	70. (c)
71. (d)	72. (c)	73. (a)	74. (c)	75. (c)	76. (c)	77. (c)	78. (b)	79. (c)	80. (a)
81. (b)	82. (c)	83. (a)	84. (c)	85. (c)	86. (c)	87. (a)	88. (a)	89. (c)	90. (b)
91. (d)	92. (a)	93. (d)	94. (a)	95. (d)	96. (b)	97. (c)	98. (d)	99. (c)	100. (c)
101. (c)	102. (b)	103. (a)	104. (b)	105. (d)	106. (a)	107. (a)	108. (c)		

ELLIPSE

MULTIPLE CHOICE QUESTIONS

1. The equation of an ellipse is $4x^2 + y^2 - 8x + 2y + 1 = 0$. For this ellipse :

   (a) foci are $(1, \pm\sqrt{3} - 1)$

   (b) $e = \dfrac{\sqrt{3}}{2}$

   (c) directrix is $y + 1 = \pm\dfrac{4}{\sqrt{3}}$

   (d) All of these.

2. For the ellipse $12x^2 + 4y^2 + 24x - 16y + 25 = 0$:

   (a) centre is $(-1, 2)$

   (b) major and minor axes are $\sqrt{3}$ and 1

   (c) $e = \sqrt{\dfrac{2}{3}}$

   (d) All of these.

3. The equation of ellipse with centre at $(1, 2)$, focus at $(6, 2)$ and passing through $(4, 6)$ is :

   (a) $\dfrac{(x-1)^2}{45} + \dfrac{(y-2)^2}{20} = 1$

   (b) $\dfrac{(x-1)^2}{20} + \dfrac{(y-2)^2}{45} = 1$

   (c) $\dfrac{(x+1)^2}{45} + \dfrac{(y+2)^2}{20} = 1$

   (d) None of these.

4. The equation of ellipse with centre $(2, -3)$, one focus at $(3, -3)$ and one vertex at $(4, -3)$ is :

   (a) $3x^2 + 4y^2 + 12x + 24y + 36 = 0$

   (b) $3x^2 + 4y^2 - 12x + 24y + 36 = 0$

   (c) $3x^2 + 4y^2 - 12x + 24y - 36 = 0$

   (d) None of these.

5. The equation of ellipse with its axes along co-ordinate axes, latus rectum 8 and $e = \dfrac{1}{\sqrt{2}}$ is :

   (a) $x^2 + 4y^2 = 16$ (b) $x^2 + 2y^2 = 64$

   (c) $2x^2 + y^2 = 64$ (d) None of these.

6. The eccentricity of an ellipse whose latus rectum is half of its minor axis is :

   (a) $\dfrac{1}{\sqrt{2}}$ (b) $\dfrac{\sqrt{3}}{2}$

   (c) $\dfrac{1}{2}$ (d) None of these.

7. The equation of ellipse with its axes along the co-ordinate axes, length of latus rectum 4 and distance between foci $4\sqrt{2}$ is :

   (a) $x^2 + 2y^2 = 24$ (b) $2x^2 + y^2 = 16$

   (c) $2x^2 + y^2 = 24$ (d) $x^2 + 2y^2 = 16$

8. Equation of ellipse with axes along co-ordinate axes, passing through $(-3, 1)$ and $e = \sqrt{2/5}$ is :

   (a) $3x^2 + 5y^2 = 32$ (b) $3x^2 + 5y^2 = 64$

   (c) $5x^2 + 3y^2 = 32$ (d) $5x^2 + 3y^2 = 64$

9. Equation of ellipse with co-ordinate axes as its axes and passing through $(2, 2)$ and $(1, 4)$ is :

   (a) $\dfrac{x^2}{20} + \dfrac{y^2}{5} = 1$ (b) $\dfrac{x^2}{5} + \dfrac{y^2}{20} = 1$

   (c) $\dfrac{x^2}{25} + \dfrac{y^2}{16} = 1$ (d) $\dfrac{x^2}{16} + \dfrac{y^2}{25} = 1$

10. The eccentricity of the ellipse whose latus rectum is equal to distance between its foci is :

    (a) $\dfrac{\sqrt{5} - 1}{2}$ (b) $\dfrac{\sqrt{5} + 1}{2}$

    (c) $\dfrac{1 - \sqrt{5}}{2}$ (d) None of these.

11. The equation of ellipse whose focus is $(-1, 1)$, directrix $x - y + 3 = 0$ and eccentricity is $1/2$, is :

    (a) $7x^2 + 2xy + 7y^2 + 10x - 10y - 7 = 0$

    (b) $7x^2 + 2xy + 7y^2 + 10x - 10y + 7 = 0$

    (c) $7x^2 + 2xy + 7y^2 + 10x + 10y + 7 = 0$

    (d) None of these.

12. Equation of tangent to the ellipse $x^2 + 4y^2 = 25$ at the point whose ordinate is 2, is :

    (a) $3x + 8y - 25 = 0$ (b) $8x + 3y - 25 = 0$

    (c) $3x - 8y - 25 = 0$ (d) $8x - 3y + 25 = 0$

13. The equation of normal to the ellipse $\frac{x^2}{a^2} + \frac{y^2}{b^2} = 1$ at the end of latus rectum in the first quadrant is :

(a) $x + ey - ae^3 = 0$ (b) $x - ey + ae^3 = 0$

(c) $x - ey - ae^3 = 0$ (d) None of these.

14. The condition that $x \cos \alpha + y \sin \alpha = p$ may be tangent to the ellipse $\frac{x^2}{a^2} + \frac{y^2}{b^2} = 1$ is :

(a) $a^2 \cos^2 \alpha + b^2 \sin^2 \alpha = p^2$

(b) $a^2 \cos^2 \alpha + b^2 \sin^2 \alpha = 2p^2$

(c) $a^2 \sin^2 \alpha + b^2 \cos^2 \alpha = p^2$

(d) None of these.

15. The equation of tangent to the ellipse $x^2 + 3y^2 = 3$ which is perpendicular to $4y = x + 17$ is :

(a) $4x + y + 7 = 0$ (b) $4x + y - 17 = 0$

(c) $x + 4y + 7 = 0$ (d) $x + 4y - 7 = 0$

16. If any tangent to $\frac{x^2}{a^2} + \frac{y^2}{b^2} = 1$ intercepts lengths h and k on the axes, then :

(a) $\frac{a^2}{h^2} - \frac{b^2}{k^2} = 1$ (b) $\frac{a^2}{h^2} + \frac{b^2}{k^2} = 1$

(c) $\frac{a^2}{k^2} + \frac{b^2}{h^2} = 1$ (d) $\frac{a^2}{k^2} - \frac{b^2}{h^2} = 1$

17. The equations of common tangents to
$\frac{x^2}{a^2 + b^2} + \frac{y^2}{b^2} = 1$ and $\frac{x^2}{a^2} + \frac{y^2}{a^2 + b^2} = 1$ are :

(a) $ax - by \pm \sqrt{a^4 + a^2b^2 + b^4} = 0$

(b) $bx - ay \pm \sqrt{a^4 + a^2b^2 + b^4} = 0$

(c) $bx + ay \pm \sqrt{a^4 + a^2b^2 + b^4} = 0$

(d) None of these.

18. The length of chord intercepted by $x^2 + 2y^2 = 4$ on the normal at $(\sqrt{2}, 1)$ is :

(a) $\frac{3\sqrt{6}}{5}$ (b) $\frac{2\sqrt{6}}{5}$

(c) $\frac{4\sqrt{6}}{5}$ (d) $\frac{6\sqrt{6}}{5}$

19. The equation of a tangent from (1, 2) to the ellipse $x^2 + 2y^2 = 3$ is :

(a) $5x - 2y = 9$ (b) $5x + 2y = 19$

(c) $x - 2y + 3 = 0$ (d) $2x - y + 3 = 0$

20. The locus of the point of intersection of two tangents to the ellipse $\frac{x^2}{a^2} + \frac{y^2}{b^2} = 1$ which are inclined at angle θ_1 and θ_2 with major axis such that $\cot \theta_1 + \cot \theta_2$ is constant is :

(a) $2xy = k (x^2 - a^2)$ (b) $2xy = k (x^2 - b^2)$

(c) $2xy = k (y^2 - b^2)$ (d) None of these.

21. The locus of point of intersection of two tangents to $\frac{x^2}{a^2} + \frac{y^2}{b^2} = 1$ which are inclined at θ_1 and θ_2 with the major axis such that $\theta_1 + \theta_2$ is a constant is :

(a) $2xy \cot \alpha = x^2 - y^2 + b^2 - a^2$

(b) $2xy \cot \alpha = x^2 + y^2 + b^2 - a^2$

(c) $2xy \cot \alpha = x^2 - y^2 + b^2 + a^2$

(d) None of these.

22. The locus of point of intersection of two tangents to the ellipse $\frac{x^2}{a^2} + \frac{y^2}{b^2} = 1$ which are inclined at θ_1 and θ_2 with the major axis such that $\tan^2 \theta_1 + \tan^2 \theta_2$ is constant, is :

(a) $4x^2y^2 - 2 (x^2 - a^2) (y^2 - b^2) = k (x^2 - a^2)^2$

(b) $4x^2y^2 + 2 (x^2 - a^2) (y^2 - b^2) = k (x^2 - a^2)^2$

(c) $4x^2y^2 - 2 (x^2 - a^2) (y^2 - b^2) = k (x^2 + a^2)^2$

(d) None of these.

23. If θ and ϕ are eccentric angles of the ends of a focal chord of the ellipse $\frac{x^2}{a^2} + \frac{y^2}{b^2} = 1$, then :

(a) $\cos \frac{\theta - \phi}{2} = e \cos \frac{\theta + \phi}{2}$

(b) $(a^2 + b^2) \cos^2 \frac{\theta + \phi}{2} = a^2 \cos^2 \frac{\theta - \phi}{2}$

(c) $\cos \frac{\theta + \phi}{2} = e \cos \frac{\theta - \phi}{2}$

(d) None of these.

24. The distance of a point on the ellipse $\frac{x^2}{6} + \frac{y^2}{2} = 1$ from the centre is 2, then its eccentric angle is :

(a) $\pi/2$ (b) $\pi/3$

(c) $\pi/4$ (d) $\pi/6$

25. The point on $x^2 + 3y^2 = 37$ at which the normal is perpendicular to $5x + 6y = 17$ is :

(a) $(5, -2)$ (b) $(-5, 2)$

(c) $(5, -3)$ (d) $(-5, -2)$

26. The locus of mid-points of the portions of tangents to the ellipse $\frac{x^2}{a^2} + \frac{y^2}{b^2} = 1$ included between the axes is the curve :

    (a) $\frac{a^2}{x^2} + \frac{b^2}{y^2} = 2$ (b) $\frac{a^2}{x^2} + \frac{b^2}{y^2} = 4$

    (c) $\frac{a^2}{x^2} - \frac{b^2}{y^2} = 2$ (d) None of these.

27. From a point P, two tangents are drawn to the ellipse $\frac{x^2}{a^2} + \frac{y^2}{b^2} = 1$ and the line joining the points of contact is at a given distance 'd' from the centre. The locus of P is :

    (a) $\frac{x^2}{a^4} + \frac{y^2}{b^4} = \frac{1}{d^4}$ (b) $\frac{x^2}{a^4} + \frac{y^2}{b^4} = \frac{2}{d^4}$

    (c) $\frac{x^2}{a^4} + \frac{y^2}{b^4} = \frac{1}{d^2}$ (d) None of these.

28. The pole of the line $8x - 15y = 20$ w.r.t. the ellipse $4x^2 + 5y^2 = 20$ is :

    (a) $(-2, -3)$ (b) $(-2, 3)$

    (c) $(2, 3)$ (d) $(2, -3)$

29. Equation of line through $(1, 4)$ and conjugate to the line $9x + 2y = 1$ w.r.t. ellipse $3x^2 + 2y^2 = 1$ is :

    (a) $3x + 2y = 11$ (b) $3x - 2y = 11$

    (c) $2x - 3y = 11$ (d) $2x + 3y = 11$

30. The pole of $lx + my = 1$ w.r.t. the ellipse $\frac{x^2}{a^2} + \frac{y^2}{b^2} = 1$ lies on the ellipse $\frac{x^2}{4a^2} + \frac{y^2}{4b^2} = 1$ if :

    (a) $b^2l^2 + a^2m^2 = 4$ (b) $a^2l^2 + b^2m^2 = 4$

    (c) $b^2l^2 + a^2m^2 = 1$ (d) None of these.

31. The locus of the poles of the tangents to the ellipse $\frac{x^2}{a^2} + \frac{y^2}{b^2} = 1$ w.r.t. the circle $x^2 + y^2 = a^2$ is :

    (a) a straight line   (b) a parabola

    (c) an ellipse   (d) a circle

32. The locus of poles of tangents to $x^2 + y^2 = d^2$ w.r.t. the ellipse $\frac{x^2}{a^2} + \frac{y^2}{b^2} = 1$ is :

    (a) $\frac{x^2}{a^4} + \frac{y^2}{b^4} = \frac{2}{d^2}$ (b) $\frac{x^2}{a^4} + \frac{y^2}{b^4} = \frac{1}{d^2}$

    (c) $\frac{x^2}{b^4} + \frac{y^2}{a^4} = \frac{1}{d^2}$ (d) None of these.

33. If the chords of the ellipse $\frac{x^2}{a^2} + \frac{y^2}{b^2} = 1$ pass through a fixed point (h, k), then the locus of their middle points is :

    (a) parabola   (b) ellipse

    (c) hyperbola   (d) None of these

34. The locus of mid-points of the chords of the ellipse $\frac{x^2}{a^2} + \frac{y^2}{b^2} = 1$ which are at a constant distance d from the centre is :

    (a) $\left(\frac{x^2}{a^2} - \frac{y^2}{b^2}\right)^2 = d^2\left(\frac{x^2}{a^4} + \frac{y^2}{b^4}\right)$

    (b) $\left(\frac{x^2}{a^2} + \frac{y^2}{b^2}\right)^2 = d^2\left(\frac{x^2}{a^2} - \frac{y^2}{b^2}\right)$

    (c) $\left(\frac{x^2}{a^2} + \frac{y^2}{b^2}\right)^2 = d^2\left(\frac{x^2}{a^4} + \frac{y^2}{b^4}\right)$

    (d) None of these

35. The eccentricity of $x^2 + 2y^2 - 2x + 3y + 2 = 0$ is :

    (a) 0 (b) $1/2$

    (c) $1/\sqrt{2}$ (d) $\sqrt{2}$

36. The sum of focal distances from any point on $9x^2 + 16 y^2 = 144$ is :

    (a) 32 (b) 18

    (c) 16 (d) 8

37. The number of values of c such that the straight line $y = 4x + c$ touches the curve $\frac{x^2}{4} + y^2 = 1$ is :

    (a) 0 (b) 1

    (c) 2 (d) infinite

38. The radius of the circle passing through the foci of $\frac{x^2}{16} + \frac{y^2}{9} = 1$ having its centre at $(0, 3)$ is :

    (a) 4 (b) 3

    (c) $2\sqrt{3}$ (d) 3.5

39. An ellipse has OB as semi-minor axis, F, F' as its foci and $\angle FBF' = 90°$. The eccentricity of ellipse is :

    (a) $\frac{1}{2}$ (b) $\frac{1}{\sqrt{2}}$

    (c) $\sqrt{\frac{3}{2}}$ (d) $\frac{1}{3}$

40. Let P be a variable point on the ellipse $\frac{x^2}{a^2} + \frac{y^2}{b^2} = 1$ with foci F_1 and F_2. If A is area of ΔPF_1F_2, then maximum value of A is :

(a) 2 abe

(b) $\frac{1}{2}$ abe

(c) abe

(d) 4 abe

41. The equation of tangent drawn at the ends of the major axis of the ellipse $9x^2 + 5y^2 - 30y = 0$ are :

(a) $x = \pm\sqrt{5}$

(b) $y = \pm 3$

(c) $y = 0, y = 6$

(d) None of these.

42. A tangent to the ellipse $x^2 + 4y^2 = 4$ meets the ellipse $x^2 + 2y^2 = 6$ at P and Q. The angle between the tangents at P and Q to $x^2 + 2y^2 = 6$ is :

(a) $\pi/2$

(b) $\pi/3$

(c) $\pi/4$

(d) $\pi/6$

43. On the ellipse $4x^2 + 9y^2 = 1$, the points at which the tangents are parallel to the line $8x = 9y$ are :

(a) $\left(\frac{2}{5}, \frac{1}{5}\right)$

(b) $\left(\frac{2}{5}, \frac{-1}{5}\right)$

(c) $\left(\frac{-2}{5}, \frac{-1}{5}\right)$

(d) None of these.

44. Let d be the perpendicular distance from the centre of the ellipse $\frac{x^2}{a^2} + \frac{y^2}{b^2} = 1$ to the tangent drawn at point P on the ellipse. If F_1 and F_2 are the two foci of the ellipse, then

$(PF_1 - PF_2)^2 = k\left(1 - \frac{b^2}{d^2}\right)$, where k =

(a) a^2

(b) $2a^2$

(c) $3a^2$

(d) $4a^2$

45. The maximum area of isosceles triangle inscribed in the ellipse $\frac{x^2}{a^2} + \frac{y^2}{b^2} = 1$ with its vertex on one end of the major axis is :

(a) $\sqrt{3}$ ab

(b) $\frac{3\sqrt{3}}{4}$ ab

(c) $\frac{5\sqrt{3}}{4}$ ab

(d) None of these.

46. If the eccentricity of ellipse becomes zero, then it takes the form of :

(a) a parabola

(b) a straight line

(c) a circle

(d) None of these.

47. The angle between pair of tangents drawn from $(1, 2)$ to the ellipse $3x^2 + 2y^2 = 5$ is :

(a) $\tan^{-1}\left(\frac{12\sqrt{5}}{5}\right)$

(b) $\tan^{-1}\left(\frac{6\sqrt{5}}{5}\right)$

(c) $\tan^{-1}\left(\frac{3\sqrt{5}}{5}\right)$

(d) None of these.

48. The eccentricity of the ellipse which meets $\frac{x}{7} + \frac{y}{2} = 1$ on the axis of x and meets the line $\frac{x}{3} - \frac{y}{5} = 1$ on y-axis and whose axes lie along the axes of co-ordinates is :

(a) $\frac{\sqrt{6}}{7}$

(b) $\frac{2\sqrt{6}}{7}$

(c) $\frac{3\sqrt{2}}{7}$

(d) None of these.

49. If the focal distance of an end of the minor axis of an ellipse, whose axes are along the co-ordinate axes, is k and the distance between the foci is 2h, then its equation is :

(a) $\frac{x^2}{k^2} + \frac{y^2}{h^2 + k^2} = 1$

(b) $\frac{x^2}{k^2} + \frac{y^2}{h^2 - k^2} = 1$

(c) $\frac{x^2}{k^2} + \frac{y^2}{k^2 - h^2} = 1$

(d) $\frac{x^2}{k^2} + \frac{y^2}{h^2} = 1$

50. If the tangent at $\left(4\cos\theta, \frac{16}{\sqrt{11}}\sin\theta\right)$ to the ellipse $16x^2 + 11y^2 = 256$ is also a tangent to the circle $x^2 + y^2 - 2x = 15$, then $\theta =$

(a) $\pm \pi/2$

(b) $\pm \pi/3$

(c) $\pm \pi/4$

(d) $\pm \pi/6$

51. The line $2x + y = 3$ cuts the ellipse $4x^2 + y^2 = 5$ at P and Q. If θ is the angle between the normals at these points, then $\tan\theta =$

(a) 3/4

(b) 3/5

(c) 1/2

(d) 5

52. Let E be the ellipse $\frac{x^2}{9} + \frac{y^2}{4} = 1$ and C be the circle $x^2 + y^2 = 9$. Let P and Q be points $(1, 2)$ and $(2, 1)$ respectively, then :
    (a) Q lies inside C, but outside E.
    (b) Q lies outside both C and E.
    (c) P lies inside both C and E.
    (d) P lies inside C, but outside E.

53. S and T are foci of an ellipse and B is an end of the minor axis. If ΔSTB is an equilateral triangle, the eccentricity of the ellipse is :
    (a) 1/2   (b) 1/3
    (c) 1/4   (d) 2/3

54. If the polar w.r.t. the parabola $y^2 = 4ax$ touches the ellipse $\frac{x^2}{\alpha^2} + \frac{y^2}{\beta^2} = 1$, then the locus of its pole is :
    (a) $\frac{x^2}{\alpha^2} - \frac{y^2}{4a^2\,\alpha^2/\beta^2} = 1$
    (b) $\frac{x^2}{\alpha^2} + \frac{y^2\beta^2}{4a^2} = 1$
    (c) $\alpha^2 x^2 + \beta^2 y^2 = 1$
    (d) None of these

55. The locus of mid-points of focal chords of the ellipse $\frac{x^2}{a^2} + \frac{y^2}{b^2} = 1$ is :
    (a) $\frac{x^2}{a^2} + \frac{y^2}{b^2} = \frac{ex}{a}$
    (b) $\frac{x^2}{a^2} - \frac{y^2}{b^2} = \frac{ex}{a}$
    (c) $x^2 + y^2 = a^2 + b^2$
    (d) None of these.

56. The ellipse $\frac{x^2}{a^2} + \frac{y^2}{b^2} = 1$ and the straight line $y = mx + c$ intersect in real points only if :
    (a) $c \geq b$ (b) $a^2m^2 \geq c^2 - b^2$
    (c) $a^2m^2 < c^2 - b^2$ (d) $a^2m^2 > c^2 - b^2$

57. The tangent at point with eccentric angle α on $\frac{x^2}{a^2} + \frac{y^2}{b^2} = 1$ meets auxiliary circle in two points which subtend a right angle at the centre. The eccentricity of the ellipse is :
    (a) $\frac{1}{\sqrt{1 + \cos^2 \alpha}}$ (b) $\frac{1}{\sqrt{1 + \sin^2 \alpha}}$
    (c) $\sqrt{1 + \sin^2 \alpha}$ (d) $\sqrt{1 + \cos^2 \alpha}$

58. If a chord joining two points whose eccentric angles are α and β cut the major axis of the ellipse $\frac{x^2}{a^2} + \frac{y^2}{b^2} = 1$ at a distance d from the center, then $\tan \frac{\alpha}{2} \cdot \tan \frac{\beta}{2} =$
    (a) $\frac{a - d}{a + d}$ (b) $\frac{d - a}{d + a}$
    (c) $\frac{d + a}{d - a}$ (d) None of these.

59. An ellipse slides between two lines at right angles to one another. The locus of its centre is :
    (a) a parabola   (b) an ellipse
    (c) a circle   (d) None of these.

60. A variable point P on an ellipse of eccentricity e is joined to its foci SS'. The locus of the incentre of $\Delta PSS'$ is an ellipse of eccentricity :
    (a) $\sqrt{\frac{2e}{1 + e}}$ (b) $\sqrt{\frac{3e}{1 + e}}$
    (c) $\sqrt{\frac{e}{1 + e}}$ (d) None of these.

61. If the extremities of a line segment of length l move in two fixed perpendicular straight lines, then the locus of that point which divides this line segment in the ratio 1 : 2 is :
    (a) a parabola   (b) an ellipse
    (c) a hyperbola   (d) None of these.

62. If a circle of radius r is concentric with the ellipse $\frac{x^2}{a^2} + \frac{y^2}{b^2} = 1$, then the common tangent is inclined to the major axis at an angle :
    (a) $\tan^{-1}\sqrt{\frac{r^2 - b^2}{a^2 - r^2}}$ (b) $\tan^{-1}\sqrt{\frac{a^2 - r^2}{r^2 - b^2}}$
    (c) $\tan^{-1}\sqrt{\frac{r^2 - b^2}{r^2 - a^2}}$ (d) None of these.

63. If the chords of contact of tangents from two points (α, β) and (γ, δ) to the ellipse $\frac{x^2}{5} - \frac{y^2}{2} = 1$ are perpendicular, then $\frac{\alpha\gamma}{\beta\delta}$:
    (a) $\frac{4}{25}$ (b) $\frac{25}{4}$
    (c) $\frac{-4}{25}$ (d) $\frac{-25}{4}$

64. If CP and CD is a pair of semi-conjugate diameters of ellipse $\frac{x^2}{a^2}+\frac{y^2}{b^2}=1$, then $CP^2 + CD^2 =$

(a) $a^2 - b^2$ (b) $a^2 + b^2$

(c) $\frac{a^2 + b^2}{2}$ (d) None of these.

65. The area of parallelogram formed by tangents at the extremities of two conjugate diameters of the ellipse $\frac{x^2}{a^2}+\frac{y^2}{b^2}=1$ is :

(a) ab   (b) 2ab

(c) 3ab   (d) 4ab

66. P and D are the extremities of a pair of conjugate diameters of the ellipse $\frac{x^2}{a^2}+\frac{y^2}{b^2}=1$, then the locus of the middle point of PD is :

(a) $\frac{x^2}{a^2}+\frac{y^2}{b^2}=2$ (b) $\frac{x^2}{a^2}+\frac{y^2}{b^2}=\frac{1}{2}$

(c) $\frac{x^2}{a^2}+\frac{y^2}{b^2}=\frac{1}{4}$ (d) None of these

67. The orbit of earth is an ellipse with e = 1/60, with the Sun at one focus, the major axis being approximately 186×10^6 miles in length. The shortest and the longest distance of earth from Sun is :

(a) 9145×10^4 miles, 9455×10^4 miles

(b) 9147×10^4 miles, 9457×10^4 miles

(c) 9145×10^6 miles, 9455×10^6 miles

(d) None of these.

68. Statement 1: An equation of a common tangent to the parabola $y^2 = 16\sqrt{3}x$ and the ellipse $2x^2 + y^2 = 4$ is $y = 2x + 2\sqrt{3}$.   **[AIEEE - 2012]**

Statement 2: If the line $y = mx + \frac{4\sqrt{3}}{m}$, $(m \neq 0)$ is a common tangent to the parabola $y^2 = 16\sqrt{3}x$ and the ellipse $2x^2 + y^2 = 4$, then m satisfies $m^4 + 2m^2 = 24$.

(a) Statement 1 is false, statement 2 is true.

(b) Statement 1 is true, statement 2 is true; statement 2 is a correct explanation for statement 1.

(c) Statement 1 is true, statement 2 is true; statement 2 is not a correct explanation for statement 1.

(d) Statement 1 is true, statement 2 is false.

69. An ellipse is drawn by taking a diameter of the circle $(x - 1)^2 + y^2 = 1$ as its semi-minor axis and a diameter of the circle $x^2 + (y - 2)^2 = 4$ as its semi-major axis. If the centre of the ellipse is the origin and its axes are the coordinate axes, then the equation of the ellipse is :   **[AIEEE - 2012]**

(a) $4x^2 + y^2 = 4$ (b) $x^2 + 4y^2 = 8$

(c) $4x^2 + y^2 = 8$ (d) $x^2 + 4y^2 = 16$

70. Equation of the ellipse whose axes are the axes of coordinates and which passes through the point $(-3, 1)$ and has eccentricity $\sqrt{\frac{2}{5}}$ is :

         [AIEEE - 2011]

(a) $5x^2 + 3y^2 - 32 = 0$ (b) $3x^2 + 5y^2 - 32 = 0$

(c) $5x^2 + 3y^2 - 48 = 0$ (d) $3x^2 + 5y^2 - 15 = 0$

71. The ellipse $x^2 + 4y^2 = 4$ is inscribed in a rectangle aligned with the coordinate axes, which in turn is inscribed in another ellipse that passes through the point $(4, 0)$. Then the equation of the ellipse is :   **[AIEEE - 2009]**

(a) $x^2 + 16y^2 = 16$ (b) $x^2 + 12y^2 = 16$

(c) $4x^2 + 48y^2 = 48$ (d) $4x^2 + 64y^2 = 48$

72. A focus of an ellipse is at the origin. The directrix is the line x = 4 and the eccentricity is 1/2. Then the length of the semi-major axis is :

         [AIEEE - 2008]

(a) $\frac{8}{3}$ (b) $\frac{2}{3}$

(c) $\frac{4}{3}$ (d) $\frac{5}{3}$

73. In an ellipse, the distance between its foci is 6 and minor axis is 8. Then its eccentricity is :

         [AIEEE - 2006]

(a) $\frac{3}{5}$ (b) $\frac{1}{2}$

(c) $\frac{4}{5}$ (d) $\frac{1}{\sqrt{5}}$

ANSWER KEY

1. (d)	**2.** (d)	**3.** (a)	**4.** (b)	**5.** (b)	**6.** (b)	**7.** (d)	**8.** (a)	**9.** (b)	**10.** (a)
11. (b)	**12.** (a)	**13.** (c)	**14.** (a)	**15.** (a)	**16.** (b)	**17.** (a)	**18.** (d)	**19.** (c)	**20.** (c)
21. (a)	**22.** (a)	**23.** (a)	**24.** (c)	**25.** (d)	**26.** (b)	**27.** (c)	**28.** (d)	**29.** (a)	**30.** (b)
31. (c)	**32.** (b)	**33.** (b)	**34.** (c)	**35.** (c)	**36.** (d)	**37.** (c)	**38.** (a)	**39.** (b)	**40.** (c)
41. (c)	**42.** (a)	**43.** (b)	**44.** (d)	**45.** (b)	**46.** (c)	**47.** (a)	**48.** (b)	**49.** (c)	**50.** (b)
51. (b)	**52.** (d)	**53.** (a)	**54.** (a)	**55.** (a)	**56.** (b)	**57.** (b)	**58.** (b)	**59.** (c)	**60.** (a)
61. (b)	**62.** (a)	**63.** (d)	**64.** (b)	**65.** (d)	**66.** (b)	**67.** (a)	**68.** (b)	**69.** (d)	**70.** (b)
71. (b)	**72.** (a)	**73.** (a)							

HYPERBOLA

MULTIPLE CHOICE QUESTIONS

1. The equation of hyperbola with foci $(\pm 2, 0)$ and eccentricity 3/2 is :

   (a) $\dfrac{9x^2}{16} - \dfrac{9y^2}{20} = 1$

   (b) $25x^2 - 20y^2 = 80$

   (c) $\dfrac{9x^2}{20} - \dfrac{9y^2}{16} = 1$

   (d) None of these

2. The equation of hyperbola with foci $(6, 4)$ and $(-4, 4)$ and eccentricity 2 is :

   (a) $\dfrac{(x-1)^2}{25/4} - \dfrac{(y-4)^2}{75/4} = 1$

   (b) $\dfrac{(x+1)^2}{25/4} - \dfrac{(y+4)^2}{75/4} = 1$

   (c) $\dfrac{(x-1)^2}{75/4} - \dfrac{(y-4)^2}{25/4} = 1$

   (d) None of these

3. The equation of hyperbola having distance between directrices $\dfrac{4\sqrt{3}}{3}$ and passing through $(2, 1)$ is :

   (a) $3x^2 - 2y^2 = 1$

   (b) $x^2 - 2y^2 = 2$

   (c) $2x^2 - 3y^2 = 10$

   (d) None of these

4. Equation of hyperbola with directrix $2x + y = 1$, focus $(1, 2)$ and eccentricity $\sqrt{3}$ is :

   (a) $2x^2 - 7y^2 + 12\,xy - 2x + 14y = 22$

   (b) $7x^2 - 2y^2 + 12\,xy + 2x + 14y = 22$

   (c) $7x^2 - 2y^2 + 12\,xy - 2x + 14y = 22$

   (d) None of these.

5. The eccentricity of $3x^2 - y^2 = 4$ is :

   (a) $1/\sqrt{2}$

   (b) $\sqrt{2}$

   (c) 2

   (d) 1/2

6. The equation of hyperbola with its axes along co-ordinate axes and whose distance between foci is 16 and eccentricity $\sqrt{2}$, is :

   (a) $x^2 - y^2 = 4$

   (b) $x^2 - y^2 = 32$

   (c) $x^2 - y^2 = 16$

   (d) None of these.

7. Equation of hyperbola with axes along co-ordinate axes and whose latus rectum is 4 and $e = 3$, is :

   (a) $16x^2 - 2y^2 = 1$

   (b) $2x^2 - 16y^2 = 1$

   (c) $4x^2 - 16y^2 = 1$

   (d) None of these.

8. For the hyperbola $\dfrac{(x-1)^2}{9} - \dfrac{(y-2)^2}{16} = 1$:

   (a) $e = 5/3$

   (b) centre $(1, 2)$

   (c) foci $(6, 2)$ and $(-4, 2)$

   (d) All of the above are true.

9. The foci of a hyperbola coincide with the foci of the ellipse $\dfrac{x^2}{25} + \dfrac{y^2}{9} = 1$. The equation of hyperbola, if its eccentricity is 2, is :

   (a) $3x^2 - y^2 = 12$

   (b) $x^2 - 3y^2 = 12$

   (c) $4x^2 - 3y^2 = 48$

   (d) None of these.

10. The equation of tangent to the hyperbola $\dfrac{x^2}{4} - \dfrac{y^2}{3} = 1$ parallel to the line $3y = 3x + 17$ is :

    (a) $y = x - 12$

    (b) $y + x + 1 = 0$

    (c) $y = x + 1$

    (d) $x + y = 1$

11. The equation of tangent to the hyperbola $3x^2 - 4y^2 = 12$ which makes equal intercepts on the axes, is :

    (a) $y = x + 1$

    (b) $y = x - 1$

    (c) $x + y + 1 = 0$

    (d) All of these.

12. The length of the straight line $x - 3y = 1$ intercepted by the hyperbola $x^2 - 4y^2 = 1$ is :

    (a) $\dfrac{6}{\sqrt{5}}$

    (b) $\dfrac{3\sqrt{2}}{\sqrt{5}}$

    (c) $\dfrac{6\sqrt{2}}{\sqrt{5}}$

    (d) None of these.

13. Equations of tangents to $5x^2 - y^2 = 5$ from $(0, 2)$ are :

    (a) $y = \pm 2x - 3$

    (b) $y = \pm 3x - 2$

    (c) $y = \pm 2x + 3$

    (d) $y = \pm 3x + 2$

14. Two tangents are drawn to $\frac{x^2}{a^2} - \frac{y^2}{b^2} = 1$ such that the product of their slopes is c^2. The locus of their point of intersection is :

(a) $x^2 = a^2 + c^2 (y^2 + b^2)$

(b) $x^2 + a^2 = c^2 (y^2 - b^2)$

(c) $y^2 + b^2 = c^2 (x^2 - a^2)$

(d) None of these.

15. $lx + my + n = 0$ touches $\frac{x^2}{a^2} - \frac{y^2}{b^2} = 1$ if :

(a) $a^2 l^2 - b^2 m^2 = n^2$

(b) $a^2 l^2 + b^2 m^2 = n^2$

(c) $b^2 l^2 - a^2 m^2 = n^2$

(d) None of these.

16. The point at which normal to $\frac{x^2}{a^2} - \frac{y^2}{b^2} = 1$ is $3x + 4y = 7$ is :

(a) $\left(\frac{7a^2}{3(a^2 + b^2)}, \frac{7b^2}{4(a^2 + b^2)} \right)$

(b) $\left(\frac{7a^2}{3(a^2 + b^2)}, \frac{7b^2}{4(a^2 + b^2)} \right)$

(c) $\left(\frac{7a^2}{3(a^2 - b^2)}, \frac{7b^2}{4(a^2 - b^2)} \right)$

(d) None of these

17. The lines $2x + 3y + 4 = 0$ and $3x - 2y + 5 = 0$ may be conjugate w.r.t. the hyperbola $\frac{x^2}{a^2} - \frac{y^2}{b^2} = 1$ if :

(a) $3a^2 - 3b^2 = 10$

(b) $3a^2 - 3b^2 + 10 = 0$

(c) $3a^2 + 3b^2 = 10$

(d) None of these.

18. If the polars of (x_1, y_1) and (x_2, y_2) w.r.t. the hyperbola $\frac{x^2}{a^2} - \frac{y^2}{b^2} = 1$ are at right angles, then $\frac{x_1 x_2}{y_1 y_2} = $

(a) $\frac{-a^2}{b^2}$

(b) $\frac{-a^4}{b^4}$

(c) $\frac{a^2}{b^2}$

(d) $\frac{a^4}{b^4}$

19. The line $3x + 2y + 1 = 0$ meets the hyperbola $4x^2 - y^2 = 4a^2$ in the points P and Q. The co-ordinates of the point of intersection of the tangents at P and Q are

(a) $(-3a^2, 8a^2)$

(b) $(3a^2, 8a^2)$

(c) $(3a^2, -8a^2)$

(d) None of these.

20. The locus of pole of any tangent to the circle $x^2 + y^2 = 4$ w.r.t. the hyperbola $x^2 - y^2 = 4$ is the circle :

(a) $x^2 + y^2 = 4$

(b) $x^2 + y^2 = 8$

(c) $x^2 + y^2 = 16$

(d) $x^2 + y^2 = 32$

21. If the polar of a point w.r.t. $\frac{x^2}{a^2} + \frac{y^2}{b^2} = 1$ touches the hyperbola $\frac{x^2}{a^2} - \frac{y^2}{b^2} = 1$, then the locus of the point is:

(a) given hyperbola

(b) ellipse

(c) parabola

(d) circle

22. Equation of chord of the hyperbola $4x^2 - y^2 = 4$ which is bisected at the point $(2, -3)$ is :

(a) $3x - 8y = 7$

(b) $3x + 8y = 7$

(c) $8x - 3y = 7$

(d) $8x + 3y = 7$

23. The locus of the middle points of the chords of hyperbola $\frac{x^2}{9} - \frac{y^2}{4} = 1$ which passes through $(1, 2)$ is a hyperbola with the centre :

(a) $(1, 1)$

(b) $(\frac{1}{2}, \frac{1}{2})$

(c) $(1, \frac{1}{2})$

(d) $(\frac{1}{2}, 1)$

24. The locus of middle points of the normal chords of the rectangular hyperbola $x^2 - y^2 = a^2$ is :

(a) $(y^2 - x^2)^3 = 4a^2 x^2 y^2$

(b) $(y^2 - x^2)^3 = 2a^2 x^2 y^2$

(c) $(y^2 - x^2)^3 = a^2 x^2 y^2$

(d) None of these.

25. A variable chord of the hyperbola $\frac{x^2}{a^2} - \frac{y^2}{b^2} = 1$ is a tangent to the circle $x^2 + y^2 = c^2$. The locus of its middle point is :

(a) $\left(\frac{x^2}{a^2} + \frac{y^2}{b^2} \right)^2 = c^2 \left(\frac{x^2}{a^4} - \frac{y^2}{b^4} \right)$

(b) $\left(\frac{x^2}{a^2} - \frac{y^2}{b^2} \right)^2 = c^2 \left(\frac{x^2}{a^4} + \frac{y^2}{b^4} \right)$

(c) $\left(\frac{x^2}{a^4} - \frac{y^2}{b^4} \right)^2 = c^2 \left(\frac{x^2}{a^2} + \frac{y^2}{b^2} \right)$

(d) None of these.

26. A tangent to $\dfrac{x^2}{a^2} - \dfrac{y^2}{b^2} = 1$ cuts the ellipse $\dfrac{x^2}{a^2} + \dfrac{y^2}{b^2} = 1$ in P and Q. The locus of the mid-point of PQ is

    (a) $\dfrac{x^2}{a^2} + \dfrac{y^2}{b^2} = \left(\dfrac{x^2}{a^2} - \dfrac{y^2}{b^2}\right)^2$

    (b) $\dfrac{x^2}{a^2} - \dfrac{y^2}{b^2} = \left(\dfrac{x^2}{a^4} + \dfrac{y^2}{b^4}\right)^2$

    (c) $\dfrac{x^2}{a^2} - \dfrac{y^2}{b^2} = \left(\dfrac{x^2}{a^2} + \dfrac{y^2}{b^2}\right)^2$

    (d) None of these.

27. If e_1 and e_2 are the eccentricities of a hyperbola and its conjugate, then :

    (a) $e_1^2 + e_2^2 = 1$ (b) $\dfrac{1}{e_1^2} - \dfrac{1}{e_2^2} = 1$

    (c) $\dfrac{1}{e_1^2} + \dfrac{1}{e_2^2} = 1$ (d) None of these.

28. The equation of diameter which is conjugate to $y = 3x$ w.r.t. the hyperbola $\dfrac{x^2}{4} - \dfrac{y^2}{9} = 1$, is :

    (a) $4y = 3x$ (b) $4y + 3x = 0$

    (c) $3y = 4x$ (d) $3y + 4x = 0$

29. The condition for two diameters of $\dfrac{x^2}{a^2} - \dfrac{y^2}{b^2} = 1$ represented by $Ax^2 + 2Hxy + By^2 = 0$ to be conjugate is :

    (a) $Ab^2 = Ba^2$ (b) $Aa^2 = -Bb^2$

    (c) $Aa^2 = Bb^2$ (d) None of these.

30. Equation of straight line which is tangent to the parabola $y^2 = 8x$ and the hyperbola $3x^2 - y^2 = 3$ is :

    (a) $2x - y + 2 = 0$ (b) $2x + y + 2 = 0$

    (c) $2x - y + 1 = 0$ (d) $2x + y - 11 = 0$

31. The locus of the middle points of portions of the tangents to the hyperbola $\dfrac{x^2}{a^2} - \dfrac{y^2}{b^2} = 1$, intercepted between the axes is :

    (a) $4x^2y^2 = a^2y^2 - b^2x^2$

    (b) $2x^2y^2 = a^2y^2 - b^2x^2$

    (c) $x^2y^2 = a^2y^2 - b^2x^2$

    (d) None of these.

32. The area of triangle formed by the asymptotes and any tangents to the hyperbola $\dfrac{x^2}{a^2} - \dfrac{y^2}{a^2} = 1$ is :

    (a) a^2 (b) $2a^2$

    (c) $3a^2$ (d) $4a^2$

33. If the chord of contact of tangents from a point P to the hyperbola $\dfrac{x^2}{a^2} - \dfrac{y^2}{b^2} = 1$ subtends a right angle at the centre, then the locus of P is :

    (a) a parabola   (b) an ellipse

    (c) a hyperbola   (d) a circle

34. The normal to the hyperbola $xy = c^2$ at the point t meets the curve again at a point t' such that :

    (a) $t^3t' = -1$ (b) $t^2t' = -1$

    (c) $tt' = -1$ (d) None of these.

35. The equation of the hyperbola, with axes along co-ordinate axes, given that the distances of one of its vertices from the foci are 9 and 1 units, is :

    (a) $\dfrac{x^2}{16} - \dfrac{y^2}{9} = 1$ (b) $\dfrac{x^2}{9} - \dfrac{y^2}{16} = 1$

    (c) $\dfrac{x^2}{16} - \dfrac{y^2}{9} = -1$ (d) None of these.

36. The number of tangents to the hyperbola $\dfrac{x^2}{4} - \dfrac{y^2}{3} = 1$ through $(4, 1)$ is :

    (a) 0   (b) 1

    (c) 2   (d) 3

37. PN is the ordinate of a point P on the hyperbola $\dfrac{x^2}{a^2} - \dfrac{y^2}{b^2} = 1$ and AA' is its transverse axis. If Q divides AP in the ratio $a^2 : b^2$, then NQ is :

    (a) perpendicular to A'P

    (b) perpendicular to OP

    (c) parallel to A'P

    (d) parallel to OP.

38. If the normals at (x_i, y_i), $i = 1, 2, 3, 4$, on the hyperbola $xy = c^2$ meet at (h, k), then :

    (a) $x_1 + x_2 + x_3 + x_4 = h$

    (b) $x_1 + x_2 + x_3 + x_4 = k$

    (c) $y_1 + y_2 + y_3 + y_4 = h$

    (d) None of these.

39. Slope of a common tangent to $\frac{x^2}{9} - \frac{y^2}{16} = 1$ and $\frac{y^2}{9} - \frac{x^2}{16} = 1$ is :

    (a) 2
    (b) – 1
    (c) – 2
    (d) None of these.

40. The eccentricity of conjugate hyperbola of $x^2 - 3y^2 = 1$ is :

    (a) 2
    (b) $2/\sqrt{3}$
    (c) 4
    (d) 4/3

41. The parametric equation $x = a (\cos h\theta + \sin h\theta)$, $y = b (\cos h\theta - \sin h\theta)$ is :

    (a) a parabola
    (b) an ellipse
    (c) a hyperbola
    (d) a circle

42. An asymptote of $xy - 3x + 4y + 2 = 0$ is :

    (a) $x = 3$
    (b) $x = 4$
    (c) $y = -3$
    (d) $y = 3$

43. The asymptotes of a hyperbola, having centre at (1, –1), are parallel to $2x + 4y - 17 = 0$ and $4x + 2y + 17 = 0$. If the hyperbola passes through (2, 1), then its equation is :

    (a) $2x^2 + 2y^2 + 5xy + x + y - 21 = 0$
    (b) $2x^2 + 2y^2 + 5xy + x - y - 21 = 0$
    (c) $2x^2 + 2y^2 - 5xy + x - y - 21 = 0$
    (d) None of these.

44. The locus of centre of a circle which touches two given circles externally is :

    (a) a parabola
    (b) an ellipse
    (c) a hyperbola
    (d) None of these.

45. If the normal to a hyperbola $4x^2 - 9y^2 = 36$ meets x and y-axis at A and B respectively, then the locus of mid-point of AB is a hyperbola of eccentricity :

    (a) $\sqrt{13}$
    (b) $\sqrt{13}/2$
    (c) $\sqrt{13}/4$
    (d) None of these.

46. The normal chord of parabola $y^2 = 4ax$ at (x_1, x_2) subtends a right angle at the :

    (a) focus
    (b) vertex
    (c) end of the latus rectum
    (d) none of these.

47. A Δ PQR of area A is inscribed in the parabola $y^2 = 4ax$ such that the vertex P lies at the vertex of the parabola and the base QR is a focal chord. The difference of the distance of Q and R from the axis of the parabola is:

    (a) $\frac{2A}{a}$
    (b) $\frac{3A}{a}$
    (c) $\frac{3A}{2a}$
    (d) none of these.

48. Number of integral points lying inside the parabola $y^2 = 8x$ and the circle $x^2 + y^2 = 16$ are :

    (a) 15
    (b) 17
    (c) 19
    (d) 12.

49. The triangle points lying inside the parabola $y = x^2$ at the point whose abscissa is x_0 ($x_0 \in [1, 2]$), the y-axis and the straight line $y = x_0^2$ has the greatest area if $x_0 =$

    (a) 3
    (b) 2
    (c) 1
    (d) none of these.

50. The inclination of the normal with positive direction of x-axis, drawn at another end of a normal to the parabola $y^2 = 4x$ is always :

    (a) $60°$
    (b) less then $60°$
    (c) more than $60°$
    (d) less than $45°$.

51. If the normals to the parabola $y^2 = 4ax$ from a point meet the axis in A, B, C such that B is the middle point of AC, then the squares of the slopes of the normal form :

    (a) A.P
    (b) G.P
    (c) H.P
    (d) none of these.

52. The set of values of θ, for which the line $y^2 = x \sin \theta + \sin^3 \theta$ is a normal to the parabola $y^2 = 4x$, other than the x-axis, is :

    (a) R
    (b) $[- \pi/2, \pi/2]$
    (c) ϕ
    (d) none of these.

53. A line L passing through the focus of the parabola $y^2 = 4 (x - 1)$ intersects the parabola in two distinct points. If 'm' is the slope of the line L, then :

    (a) $-1 < m < 1$
    (b) $m < -1$ or $m > 1$
    (c) $m \in R$
    (d) none of these.

54. If chord passing through S(a, 0) of the parabola $y^2 = 4ax$ intersect it at P and Q, then $\dfrac{1}{SP} + \dfrac{1}{SQ}$

(a) is equal to 2/a

(b) is equal to 1/a

(c) is equal to a

(d) depends on the slope of the chord.

55. The length of a focal chord of the parabola $y^2 = 4ax$ at a distance b from the vertex is c. Then

(a) $2a^2 = bc$ (b) $a^3 = b^2c$

(c) $ac = b^2$ (d) $b^2c = 4a^3$.

56. If (h, k) is a point on the axis of the parabola

$2(x-1)^2 + 2(y-1)^2 = (x+y+2)^2$

from where three distinct normals may be drawn then

(a) $h > 2$ (b) $h < 4$

(c) $h > 8$ (d) $h < 8$.

57. The ends of line segment are P (1, 3) and Q (1, 1). R is a point on the line segment PQ such that PR : OR = 1 : λ. If R is an interior point of the parabola $y^2 = 4x$ then

(a) $\lambda \in (0, 1)$ (b) $\lambda \in \left(\dfrac{-3}{5}, 1\right)$

(c) $\lambda \in \left(\dfrac{1}{2}, \dfrac{3}{5}\right)$ (d) none of these.

58. If the normals to the parabola $y^2 = 8ax$ at the points (x_1, y_1), (x_2, y_2) and (x_3, y_3) are concurrent then

(a) $x_1 + x_2 + x_3 = 0$

(b) $y_1 + y_2 + y_3 = 0$

(c) $x_1y_1 + x_2y_2 + x_3y_3 = 0$

(d) none of these.

59. The number of points with integral coordinates that lie in the interior of the region common to the circle $x^2 + y^2 = 16$ and the parabola $y^2 = 4x$ is :

(a) 8   (b) 10

(c) 16   (d) none of these.

60. The number of points with integral coordinates (2a, a – 1) that fall in the interior of the larger segment of the circle $x^2 + y^2 = 25$ cut off by the parabola $x^2 + 4y = 0$, is :

(a) one   (b) two

(c) three   (d) none of these.

61. The number of distinct real segments that can be drawn from (0, – 2) to the parabola $y^2 = 4x$ is :

(a) one   (b) two

(c) zero   (d) none of these.

62. The radius of the circle whose centre is (–4, 0) and which cuts the parabola $y^2 = 8x$ at A and B such that its common chord AB subtends a right angle at the vertex to the parabola is equal to :

(a) 4   (b) 3

(c) $\sqrt{18}$ (d) 5.

63. The set of points on the axis of the parabola $y^2 = 4x + 8$ from which the 3 normals to the parabola are all real and different, is :

(a) $\{(k, 0) \mid k \le -2\}$ (b) $\{(k, 0) \mid k \ge -2\}$

(c) $\{(0, k) \mid k > -2\}$ (d) none of these.

64. If a normal to the parabola $y^2 = 4ax$ makes an angle ψ with its axis then it will cut the curve again at an angle

(a) $\dfrac{\psi}{2}$ (b) $\tan^{-1}(2\tan\psi)$

(c) $\tan^{-1}\left(\dfrac{1}{2}\tan\psi\right)$ (d) none of these.

65. If the distances of two points P and Q from the focus of a parabola $y^2 = 4x$ are 4 and 9 respectively then the distance of the point of intersection of tangents at P and Q from the focus is :

(a) 8   (b) 6

(c) 5   (d) 13.

66. If P and D are the extremities of a pair of conjugate diameters of the ellipse $\dfrac{x^2}{a^2} + \dfrac{y^2}{b^2} = 1$, then the locus of the foot of the perpendicular from the centre of PD is :

(a) $(x^2 + y^2)^2 = a^2x^2 + b^2y^2$

(b) $2(x^2 + y^2)^2 = a^2x^2 + b^2y^2$

(c) $4(x^2 + y^2)^2 = a^2x^2 + b^2y^2$

(d) none of these.

67. The locus of point of intersection of tangents to the parabolas $y^2 = 4(x + 1)$ and $y^2 = 8(x + 2)$ which are perpendicular to each other is :

(a) $x + 7 = 0$

(b) $x - y = 4$

(c) $x + 3 = 0$

(d) $y - x = 12$.

68. The locus of a point, the tangent from which to the ellipse $\frac{x^2}{a^2} + \frac{y^2}{b^2} = 1$ are inclined at a constant angle α, is :

(a) $(x^2 + y^2 + a^2 + b^2)^2 \tan^2 \alpha = 4a^2b^2 \left(\frac{x^2}{a^2} + \frac{y^2}{b^2} - 1\right)$

(b) $(x^2 + y^2 - a^2 - b^2)^2 \tan^2 \alpha = 2a^2b^2 \left(\frac{x^2}{a^2} + \frac{y^2}{b^2} - 1\right)$

(c) $(x^2 + y^2 - a^2 - b^2)^2 \tan^2 \alpha = 4a^2b^2 \left(\frac{x^2}{a^2} + \frac{y^2}{b^2} - 1\right)$

(d) none of these.

69. PSQ is a focal chord of a parabola whose focus is S and vertex is A. PA, OA are produced to meet the directrix in R and T. The $\angle RST$ is equal to :

(a) $90°$

(b) $60°$

(c) $45°$

(d) $30°$.

70. The area of the rectangle formed by the perpendiculars from the centre of the ellipse $\frac{x^2}{9} + \frac{y^2}{4} = 1$ to the tangent and the normal at the point whose eccentric angle is $\frac{\pi}{4}$, is :

(a) $\frac{30}{13}$

(b) $\frac{91}{5}$

(c) $\frac{5}{13}$

(d) none of these.

71. The equation of the line touching both the parabolas $y^2 = 4x$ and $x^2 = -32y$ is :

(a) $x + 2y + 4 = 0$

(b) $2x + y + 4 = 0$

(c) $x - 2y - 4 = 0$

(d) $x - 2y + 4 = 0$.

72. A man running round a race course notes that the sum of the distances of two flag-posts from him is always 10 metres and the distance between the flag-posts is 8 metres. The area of the path he encloses in square metres is :

(a) 15π

(b) 12π

(c) 18π

(d) 8π.

73. The latus rectum of the parabola whose vertex is at origin and axis is x-axis and the length of tangent drawn from $(-4, 0)$ is of 10 unit is :

(a) $9/4$

(b) 9

(c) 36

(d) 18.

74. If $(5, 12)$ and $(24, 7)$ are the foci of a conic passing through the origin, then the eccentricity of conic is :

(a) $\sqrt{386}/12$

(b) $\sqrt{386}/13$

(c) $\sqrt{386}/25$

(d) $\sqrt{386}/38$

75. Three normals to the parabola $y = x$ are drawn through a point $(c, 0)$ then :

(a) $c = 1/4$

(b) $c = 1/2$

(c) $c = 1/2$

(d) none of these.

76. An arc of a bridge is semi-elliptical with major axis horizontal. If the length of the base is 9 m and the highest part of the bridge is 3 m from the horizontal; the best approximation of the height of the arc 2m from the centre of the base is :

(a) $\frac{11}{4}$ m

(b) $\frac{8}{3}$ m

(c) $\frac{7}{2}$ m

(d) 2m.

77. If the normal at $(ap, 2ap)$ on $y^2 = 4ax$ makes $90°$ at the vertex, then :

(a) $p = -1$

(b) $c = 1/2$

(c) $c > 1/2$

(d) none of these.

78. A normal inclined at $45°$ to the x-axis is drawn to the ellipse $\frac{x^2}{a^2} + \frac{y^2}{b^2} = 1$. It cuts major and minor axes at P and Q. If C is the centre of ellipse, then area of $\triangle CPQ =$

(a) $\frac{(a^2 - b^2)^2}{a^2 + b^2}$

(b) $\frac{(a^2 - b^2)^2}{2(a^2 + b^2)}$

(c) $\frac{(a^2 - b^2)^2}{4(a^2 + b^2)}$

(d) none of these.

79. If normal at the point A $(1, 2)$ to the parabola $y^2 = 4x$ intersect the parabola again at B and the normal at B intersects the parabola at C, then the point C is :

(a) $(1, 2)$

(b) $(1, -2)$

(c) $(2, -2\sqrt{2})$

(d) none of these.

80. The eccentric angle of any point P measured from the semi-major axis CA is ϕ. If S is the focus nearest to A and $\angle ASP = \theta$, then :

(a) $\tan \dfrac{\phi}{2} = \sqrt{\dfrac{1+e}{1-e}} \tan \dfrac{\theta}{2}$

(b) $\tan \dfrac{\phi}{2} = \sqrt{\dfrac{1-e}{1+e}} \tan \dfrac{\theta}{2}$

(c) $\tan \dfrac{\theta}{2} = \sqrt{\dfrac{1+e}{1-e}} \tan \dfrac{\phi}{2}$

(d) $\tan \dfrac{\theta}{2} = \sqrt{\dfrac{1-e}{1+e}} \tan \dfrac{\phi}{2}$

81. The parabola $y^2 = \lambda x$ and $[(x-3)^2 + (y+2)^2] = (3x - 4y - 2)^2$ are equal if λ equals

(a) 1   (b) 2

(c) 4   (d) 6.

82. A straight line PQ touches the ellipse $\dfrac{x^2}{a^2} + \dfrac{y^2}{b^2} = 1$ and the circle $x^2 + y^2 = r^2$ $(b < r < a)$. RS is a focal chord of the ellipse. If RS is parallel to PQ and meets the circle in points R and S, then the length of RS is :

(a) 2a   (b) 2b

(c) a   (d) b.

83. The curve described parametrically by $x = t^2 + t$ and $y = 2t^2 - t$ represents :

(a) a pair of straight lines

(b) an ellipse

(c) a parabola

(d) a hyperbola.

84. If e is eccentricity of hyperbola $3x^2 - 4y^2 = 12$ and e' is the eccentricity of $4y^2 - 3x^2 = 12$, then e – e' is equal to :

(a) $\dfrac{7}{12}$ (b) $-\dfrac{7}{12}$

(c) $\sqrt{2}$ (d) none of these.

85. If a variable straight line $x \cos \alpha + y \sin \alpha = p$ which is a chord of the hyperbola $\dfrac{x^2}{a^2} - \dfrac{y^2}{b^2} = 1$ $(b > a)$. subtend a right angle at the centre of the hyperbola, then it always touches a fixed circle whose radius is :

(a) $\dfrac{ab}{\sqrt{a^2 - 2a}}$ (b) $\dfrac{a}{\sqrt{ab}}$

(c) $\dfrac{ab}{\sqrt{a^2 + b^2}}$ (d) $\dfrac{ab}{b\sqrt{b} + ba}$

86. The condition that a straight line with slope m will be normal to parabola $y^2 = 4ax$ as well as a tangent to rectangular hyperbola $x^2 - y^2 = a^2$ is :

(a) $m^6 + 4m^2 + 2m - 1 = 0$

(b) $m^4 + 3m^2 + 2m + 1 = 0$

(c) $m^6 - 2m^2 = 0$

(d) $m^6 + 4m^2 + 3m + 1 = 0$

87. If H $(x, y) = 0$ represents the equation of a hyperbola and A $(x, y) = 0$, C $(x, y) = 0$ represent the equations of its asymptotes and the conjugate hyperbola respectively, then for any point (α, β) in the plane ; H (α, β), A (α, β) and C (α, β) are in :

(a) A.P   (b) G..P.

(c) H.P   (d) none of these.

88. P is a point on the hyperbola $\dfrac{x^2}{a^2} - \dfrac{y^2}{b^2} = 1$, N is the foot of the $\perp$ from P on the transverse axis. The tangent to the hyperbola at P meets the transverse axis at T. If O is the centre of the hyperbola, then OT, ON is equal to :

(a) e^2 (b) a^2

(c) b^2 (d) b^2 / a^2.

89. If PN is the perpendicular from a point on a rectangular hyperbola to its asymptotes, then the locus of the mid point of PN is :

(a) circle   (b) parabola

(c) ellipse   (d) hyperbola.

90. If SY and S'Y' are drawn perpendicular from foci to any tangent to the hyperbola $\dfrac{x^2}{a^2} - \dfrac{y^2}{b^2} = 1$, then the product of these perpendiculars is :

(a) a^2 (b) b^2

(c) $a^2 + b^2$ (d) $a^2 - b^2$.

91. The coordinates of the foci of the rectangular hyperbola $xy = c^2$ are :

(a) $(\pm c, \pm c)$ (b) $\left(\pm \dfrac{c}{2}, \pm \dfrac{c}{2}\right)$

(c) $(\pm c\sqrt{2}, \pm c\sqrt{2})$ (d) none of these.

92. Let the tangent at a point P on the ellipse meet the major axis at B and the ordinate from it meet the major axis at A. If Q is a point on the line AP such that AQ = AB, then the locus of Q is :

(a) a hyperbola   (b) an ellipse

(c) a parabola   (d) a circle.

93. If a circle with centre $(3\alpha, 3\beta)$ and of variable radius cuts rectangular hyperbola $x^2 - y^2 = 9a^2$ at the points P, Q, R, S, then the locus of the centroid of the ΔPQS is :

(a) $(x - 2\alpha)^2 - (y - 2\beta)^2 = a^2$

(b) $(x - \alpha)^2 - (y - \beta)^2 = a^2$

(c) $(x - 3\alpha)^2 - (y - 3\beta)^2 = a^2$

(d) none of these.

94. The tangent at the points $(at_1^2, 2at_1)$ and $(at_2^2, 2at^2)$ on the parabola $y^2 = 4ax$ are at right angles if :

(a) $t_1 t_2 = -1$ (b) $t_1 t_2 = 1$

(c) $t_1 t_2 = 2$ (d) $t_1 t_2 = -2$.

95. A set of parallel chords of the parabola $y^2 = 4ax$ have their mid-poins on :

(a) any straight line through the vertex

(b) any straight line through the focus

(c) a straight line parallel to the axis

(d) none of these.

96. The line $y = mx + 1$ is a tangent to the parabola $y^2 = 4x$ if :   **[UPSEAT 2000]**

(a) $m = 1$ (b) $m = 2$

(c) $m = 4$ (d) $m = 3$.

97. The slope of the normal at the point $(at^2, 2at)$ of parabola $y^2 = 4ax$ is,   **[UPSEAT 2000]**

(a) $\dfrac{1}{t}$ (b) t

(c) $-t$ (d) $\dfrac{-1}{t}$

98. The equation of normal at the point $(0, 3)$ of the ellipse $9x^2 + 5y^2 = 45$ is :

(a) $y - 3 = 0$ (b) $y + 3 = 0$

(c) x-axis   (d) y-axis.

99. The eccentricity of ellipse $5x^2 + 4y^2 = 1$ is :

(a) $\dfrac{1}{2}$ (b) $\dfrac{1}{\sqrt{2}}$

(c) $\dfrac{1}{\sqrt{5}}$ (d) $\dfrac{1}{3}$

100. An ellipse has its centre at $(1, -1)$ and semi major axis $= 8$, which passes through the point $(1, 3)$. Then the equation of an ellipse is :

(a) $\dfrac{(x + 1)^2}{64} + \dfrac{(y - 1)^2}{16} = 1$

(b) $\dfrac{(x + 1)^2}{64} + \dfrac{(y + 1)^2}{16} = 1$

(c) $\dfrac{(x - 1)^2}{64} + \dfrac{(y + 1)^2}{16} = 1$

(d) $\dfrac{(x - 1)^2}{16} + \dfrac{(y + 1)^2}{64} = 1$.

101. The number of normals to the parabola $\dfrac{x^2}{a^2} + \dfrac{y^2}{b^2} = 1$ from an external point is :

(a) 2   (b) 4

(c) 6   (d) 5.

102. Equation $ax^2 + 2hxy + 2by^2 + 2gx + 2fy + c = 0$ represents a hyperbola if :

(a) $\Delta \neq 0, h^2 > ab$ (b) $\Delta \neq 0, h^2 = ab$

(c) $\Delta \neq 0, h^2 < ab$ (d) none of these.

103. Equation $ax^2 + 2hxy + by^2 + 2gx + 2fy + c = 0$ represents a rectangular hyperbola if :

(a) $\Delta \neq 0, h^2 = ab, a + b = 0$

(b) $\Delta \neq 0, h^2 < ab, a + b = 0$

(c) $\Delta \neq 0, h^2 > ab, a + b = 0$

(d) none of these.

104. Equation $\dfrac{x^2}{6 - k} + \dfrac{y^2}{4 - k} = 1$ represents

(a) an ellipse if $k > 4$

(b) an hyperbola if $4 < k > 6$

(c) an ellipse if $k > 6$

(d) none of these.

105. Equation of the normal to the hyperbola $\frac{x^2}{a^2} + \frac{y^2}{b^2} = 1$ at the point $(a \sec \theta, b \tan \theta)$ is :

(a) $\frac{ax}{\sec \theta} - \frac{by}{\tan \theta} = a - b$

(b) $\frac{ax}{\sec \theta} - \frac{by}{\tan \theta} = a^2 - b^2$

(c) $\frac{ax}{\sec \theta} - \frac{by}{\tan \theta} = a^2 + b^2$

(d) $\frac{ax}{\sec \theta} - \frac{by}{\tan \theta} = b^2 - a^2$

106. The parametric equations of the hyperbola $\frac{x^2}{a^2} - \frac{y^2}{b^2} = 1$ are :

(a) $x = a \tan \theta,\ y = b \sec \theta$

(b) $x = a \sec \theta,\ y = b \tan \theta$

(c) $x = \sqrt{2}\, a,\ y = b$

(d) none of these.

107. The eccentricity of hyperbola is :

(a) 0   (b) 1

(c) more than 1   (d) less than 1.

108. The equation of the hyperbola referred to its axes are axes of coordinates and whose distance between the foci is 16 and eccentricity is $\sqrt{2}$ is :

(a) $x^2 - y^2 = 16$ (b) $x^2 - y^2 = 32$

(c) $x^2 - 2y^2 = 16$ (d) $y^2 - x^2 = 16$.

[UPSEAT 2000]

109. For the hyperbola $\frac{x^2}{\cos^2 \alpha} - \frac{y^2}{\sin^2 \alpha} - 1$, which of the following remains constant when α varies ?

[AIEEE-2007]

(a) eccentricity   (b) directrix

(c) abscissae of vertices   (d) abscissae of foci

110. The eccentricity of the hyperbola whose length of the latus rectum is equal to 8 and the length of its conjugate axis is equal to half of the distance between its foci, is

(a) $\frac{4}{3}$ (b) $\frac{4}{\sqrt{3}}$

(c) $\frac{2}{\sqrt{3}}$ (d) $\sqrt{3}$

ANSWER KEY

1. (a)	2. (a)	3. (b)	4. (c)	5. (c)	6. (b)	7. (a)	8. (d)	9. (a)	10. (c)
11. (d)	12. (c)	13. (d)	14. (c)	15. (a)	16. (a)	17. (c)	18. (b)	19. (a)	20. (a)
21. (a)	22. (d)	23. (d)	24. (a)	25. (b)	26. (c)	27. (c)	28. (a)	29. (c)	30. (c)
31. (a)	32. (a)	33. (b)	34. (a)	35. (a)	36. (c)	37. (a)	38. (a)	39. (b)	40. (a)
41. (c)	42. (d)	43. (b)	44. (c)	45. (b)	46. (a)	47. (a)	48. (b)	49. (b)	50. (c)
51. (a)	52. (c)	53. (d)	54. (b)	55. (d)	56. (a)	57. (a)	58. (b)	59. (a)	60. (b)
61. (b)	62. (a)	63. (d)	64. (c)	65. (b)	66. (b)	67. (c)	68. (c)	69. (a)	70. (a)
71. (d)	72. (a)	73. (b)	74. (a)	75. (c)	76. (b)	77. (d)	78. (b)	79. (c)	80. (c)
81. (d)	82. (b)	83. (d)	84. (d)	85. (c)	86. (d)	87. (a)	88. (b)	89. (d)	90. (b)
91. (c)	92. (a)	93. (a)	94. (a)	95. (c)	96. (a)	97. (c)	98. (d)	99. (c)	100. (c)
101. (c)	102. (a)	103. (c)	104. (b)	105. (c)	106. (b)	107. (c)	108. (b)	109. (d)	110. (a)

Chapter 18

FUNCTIONS

MULTIPLE CHOICE QUESTIONS

1. The domain of the function $f(x) = \dfrac{1}{\sqrt{x^2 - 3x + 2}}$ is

   (a) $(-\infty, 1)$
   (b) $(-\infty, 1) \cup (2, \infty)$
   (c) $(-\infty, 1] \cup [2, \infty)$
   (d) $(2, \infty)$

2. The domain of definition of the function

   $y = \sqrt{\log_{10}\left(\dfrac{5x - x^2}{4}\right)}$ is

   (a) $[1, 4]$
   (b) $(1, 4)$
   (c) $[1, 4)$
   (d) $(1, 4]$

3. The domain of the function

   $f(x) = \sin^{-1}\left\{\log_2\left(\dfrac{1}{2} x^2\right)\right\}$ is :

   (a) $[-2, -1) \cup [1, 2]$
   (b) $(-2, -1] \cup [1, 2]$
   (c) $[-2, -1] \cup [1, 2]$
   (d) $(-2, -1) \cup (1, 2)$

4. The domain of the function

   $f(x) = \dfrac{\sqrt{9 - x^2}}{\sin^{-1}(3 - x)}$ is :

   (a) $(2, 3)$
   (b) $[2, 3)$
   (c) $(2, 3]$
   (d) None of these

5. The domain of the function $f(x) = \sqrt{2 - 2x - x^2}$ is

   (a) $[-\sqrt{3}, \sqrt{3}]$
   (b) $[-1 - \sqrt{3}, -1 + \sqrt{3}]$
   (c) $[-2, 2]$
   (d) $[-2 - \sqrt{3}, -2 + \sqrt{3}]$

6. The domain of the function

   $f(x) = \dfrac{1}{\sqrt{[x]^2 - [x] - 6}}$ is :

   (a) $(-\infty, -2) \cup [4, \infty)$
   (b) $(-\infty, -2] \cup [4, \infty)$
   (c) $(-\infty, -2) \cup (4, \infty)$
   (d) None of these

7. The domain of definition of the function

   $y = \dfrac{1}{\log_{10}(1 - x)} + \sqrt{x + 2}$ is :

   (a) $[-2, 1]$
   (b) $[-2, 1]$
   (c) $[-2, 0[\cup]0, 1[$
   (d) None of these

8. The domain of the function

   $f(x) = \sqrt{3 - x} + \cos^{-1}\left(\dfrac{3 - 2x}{5}\right)$ is :

   (a) $[-1, 3]$
   (b) $(-1, 3]$
   (c) $[-1, 3)$
   (d) None of these

9. The domain of the function

   $f(x) = \dfrac{1}{\sqrt{x^{12} - x^9 + x^4 - x + 1}}$ is :

   (a) $(-\infty, -1)$
   (b) $(1, \infty)$
   (c) $(-1, 1)$
   (d) $(-\infty, \infty)$

10. The domain of the function

    $f(x) = \sqrt{\dfrac{(x + 1)(x - 3)}{(x - 2)}}$ is given by :

    (a) $[-1, 2) \cup [3, \infty)$
    (b) $(-1, 2) \cup [3, \infty)$
    (c) $[-1, 2] \cup [3, \infty)$
    (d) None of these

11. The domain of the function

    $f(x) = \sqrt{x - 1} + \sqrt{5 - x}$ is :

    (a) $[1, \infty)$
    (b) $(-\infty, 5)$
    (c) $(1, 5)$
    (d) $[1, 5]$

12. The domain of the function

    $f(x) = \sqrt{\dfrac{\log_{0.5}(x - 2)}{x^2 - 5x - 14}}$ is :

    (a) $[3, 7)$
    (b) $(3, 7)$
    (c) $(3, 7]$
    (d) None of these

13. The domain of the function

    $f(x) = \sqrt{3 - 2^x - 2^{1-x}} + \sqrt{\sin^{-1} x}$ is :

    (a) $[0, 1]$
    (b) $(0, 1]$
    (c) $[0, 1)$
    (d) None of these

14. The domain of the function $f(x) = \dfrac{1}{\sqrt{|x| - x}}$ is :

    (a) $(0, \infty)$
    (b) $(-\infty, 0)$
    (c) $(-\infty, \infty)$
    (d) None of these

15. The domain of the function $f(x) = \log_{10} |4 - x^2|$ is :

(a) $(-\infty, \infty) \setminus \{-2, 2\}$ (b) $(0, \infty)$

(c) $(-\infty, 0)$ (d) None of these

16. The domain of the function

$f(x) = \sqrt{1 - \sqrt{1 - \sqrt{1 - x^2}}}$ is :

(a) $(-\infty, 1)$ (b) $(-1, \infty)$

(c) $[0, 1]$ (d) $[-1, 1]$

17. The domain of the function

$f(x) = \dfrac{1}{1 - x} + 2^{\sin^{-1} x} + \dfrac{1}{\sqrt{x - 2}}$ is :

(a) $(-\infty, \infty) \setminus \{1\}$ (b) $(2, \infty)$

(c) $[-1, 1)$ (d) ϕ

18. The domain of the function

$f(x) = \cos^{-1}\left(\dfrac{2 - |x|}{4}\right) + [\log(3 - x)]^{-1}$ is :

(a) $[-6, 3) \setminus \{2\}$ (b) $[-6, 2) \cup (2, 3]$

(c) $[-6, 3]$ (d) $[-6, 3)$

19. The domain of the function $f(x) = \log_2 \log_3 \log_4 x$ is :

(a) $[4, \infty)$ (b) $(4, \infty)$

(c) $(-\infty, 4)$ (d) None of these

20. The domain of the function

$f(x) = \dfrac{1}{\log_3(x - 2)} + \sqrt{5 - x}$ is :

(a) $[2, 5] \setminus \{3\}$ (b) $(2, 5] \setminus \{3\}$

(c) $[2, 5) \setminus \{3\}$ (d) $(2, 5) \setminus \{3\}$

21. The domain of the function

$f(x) = \cos^{-1}\left(\dfrac{3}{4 + 2\sin x}\right)$ is :

(a) $\left[-\dfrac{\pi}{6} + 2n\pi, \dfrac{\pi}{6} + 2n\pi\right]$

(b) $\left(-\dfrac{\pi}{6} + 2n\pi, \dfrac{\pi}{6} + 2n\pi\right)$

(c) $\left(-\dfrac{\pi}{6} + 2n\pi, \dfrac{\pi}{6} + 2n\pi\right)$

(d) $\left[-\dfrac{\pi}{6} + 2n\pi, \dfrac{\pi}{6} + 2n\pi\right]$

22. The domain of the function

$f(x) = \log_{10}(\sqrt{x - 4} + \sqrt{6 - x})$ is :

(a) $(4, 6)$ (b) $[4, 6]$

(c) $[4, 6)$ (d) None of these

23. The domain of the function

$f(x) = \log_{10} \sin(x - 3) + \sqrt{16 - x^2}$ is :

(a) $(3, 4)$ (b) $(-4, 4)$

(c) $(3, \pi + 3)$ (d) None of these

24. The domain of the function

$f(x) = \tan^{-1}\sqrt{x(x + 1)} + \sin^{-1}\sqrt{x^2 + x + 1}$ is :

(a) $[-1, 0]$ (b) $\{-1, 0\}$

(c) $(-\infty, -1] \cup [0, \infty)$ (d) $(-\infty, \infty)$

25. The domain of the function

$f(x) = \sqrt[3]{1 - 3x} + 3\cos^{-1}\left(\dfrac{2x - 1}{3}\right) + e^{3\tan x}$ is :

(a) $[-1, 2]$ (b) $(-1, 2)$

(c) $(-\infty, \infty)$ (d) None of these

26. The domain of the function $f(x) = \sqrt{x^2 - [x]^2}$, where $[x]$ denotes the greatest integer less than or equal to x, is :

(a) $(0, \infty)$ (b) $(-\infty, 0)$

(c) $(-\infty, \infty)$ (d) None of these

27. The domain of the function

$f(x) = {}^{24-x}C_{3x-1} + {}^{40-6x}C_{8x-10}$ is :

(a) $\{2, 3\}$ (b) $\{1, 2, 3\}$

(c) $\{1, 2, 3, 4\}$ (d) None of these

28. The domain of the function

$f(x) = \log_{\left[x + \frac{1}{2}\right]} |x^2 - 5x + 6|$ is :

(a) $\left[\dfrac{3}{2}, 2\right) \cup (2, 3) \cup (3, \infty)$

(b) $\left[\dfrac{3}{2}, \infty\right)$

(c) $\left[\dfrac{1}{2}, \infty\right)$

(d) None of these

29. The domain of the function

$f(x) = \underbrace{\log_2 \log_2 \log_2 \dots \log_2}_{n \text{ times}} x$ is :

(a) $(2^{n-1}, \infty)$ (b) $[2^n, \infty)$

(c) $(2^{n-2}, \infty)$ (d) None of these

30. The domain of the function $f(x) = x^{\frac{1}{\log x}}$ is :

(a) $(0, \infty)\backslash\{1\}$ (b) $(0, \infty)$

(c) $[0, \infty)$ (d) $[0, \infty)\backslash\{1\}$

31. The range of the function $y = \dfrac{x}{1 + x^2}$ is :

(a) $\left[0, \dfrac{1}{2}\right]$ (b) $\left[-\dfrac{1}{2}, \dfrac{1}{2}\right]$

(c) $\left[-\dfrac{1}{2}, 0\right]$ (d) None of these

32. The range of the function $y = \dfrac{1}{2 - \sin 3x}$ is :

(a) $\left(\dfrac{1}{3}, 1\right)$ (b) $\left[\dfrac{1}{3}, 1\right)$

(c) $\left[\dfrac{1}{3}, 1\right]$ (d) None of these

33. The range of the function $f(x) = \log_e (3x^2 - 4x + 5)$ is :

(a) $\left(-\infty, \log_e \dfrac{11}{3}\right]$

(b) $\left[\log_e \dfrac{11}{3}, \infty\right)$

(c) $\left[-\log_e \dfrac{11}{3}, \log_e \dfrac{11}{3}\right]$

(d) None of these

34. The range of the function $y = 3\sin\sqrt{\dfrac{\pi^2}{16} - x^2}$ is

(a) $\left[0, \dfrac{3}{\sqrt{2}}\right]$ (b) $\left[-\dfrac{3}{\sqrt{2}}, \dfrac{3}{\sqrt{2}}\right]$

(c) $\left[-\dfrac{3}{\sqrt{2}}, 0\right]$ (d) None of these

35. The value of the function $f(x) = \dfrac{x^2 - 3x + 2}{x^2 + x - 6}$ lies in the interval :

(a) $(-\infty, \infty) - \left\{\dfrac{1}{5}, 1\right\}$ (b) $(-\infty, \infty)$

(c) $(-\infty, \infty) - \{1\}$ (d) None of these

36. If $A = \left[x : \dfrac{\pi}{6} \le x \le \dfrac{\pi}{3}\right]$ and

$f(x) = \cos x - x(1 + x)$, then $f(A)$ is equal to :

(a) $\left[\dfrac{1}{2} - \dfrac{\pi}{3} - \dfrac{\pi^2}{9}, \dfrac{\sqrt{3}}{2} - \dfrac{\pi}{6} - \dfrac{\pi^2}{36}\right]$

(b) $\left[\dfrac{1}{2} + \dfrac{\pi}{3} - \dfrac{\pi^2}{9}, \dfrac{\sqrt{3}}{2} + \dfrac{\pi}{6} - \dfrac{\pi^2}{36}\right]$

(c) $\left(\dfrac{1}{2} - \dfrac{\pi}{3} - \dfrac{\pi^2}{9}, \dfrac{\sqrt{3}}{2} - \dfrac{\pi}{6} - \dfrac{\pi^2}{36}\right)$

(d) None of these

37. The range of the function $f(x) = \tan\sqrt{\dfrac{\pi^2}{9} - x^2}$ is

(a) $[0, \sqrt{3}]$ (b) $(0, \sqrt{3})$

(c) $(0, \sqrt{3})$ (d) $(0, \sqrt{3}]$

38. The range of the function

$f(x) = \sqrt{2 - x} + \sqrt{1 + x}$ is :

(a) $[\sqrt{3}, \sqrt{6}]$ (b) $[0, \sqrt{6}]$

(c) $(\sqrt{3}, \sqrt{6})$ (d) None of these

39. The range of the function $f(x) = \sin x - \cos x$ is :

(a) $(-\sqrt{2}, \sqrt{2})$ (b) $[-\sqrt{2}, \sqrt{2}]$

(c) $[0, \sqrt{2}]$ (d) None of these

40. The range of the function $y = \dfrac{(x + 2)}{x^2 - 8x - 4}$ is :

(a) $\left(-\infty, -\dfrac{1}{4}\right]$ (b) $R\backslash\left(-\dfrac{1}{4}, -\dfrac{1}{20}\right)$

(c) $\left[-\dfrac{1}{20}, \infty\right)$ (d) None of these

41. The range of the function

$f(x) = \sin\left[\log\left(\dfrac{\sqrt{4 - x^2}}{1 - x}\right)\right]$ is :

(a) $[0, 1]$ (b) $(-1, 0)$

(c) $[-1, 1]$ (d) $(-1, 1)$

42. The range of the function $f(x) = \dfrac{5}{3 - x^2}$ is :

(a) $(-\infty, 0) \cup \left[\dfrac{5}{3}, \infty\right)$ (b) $(-\infty, 0) \cup \left(\dfrac{5}{3}, \infty\right)$

(c) $(-\infty, 0] \cup \left[\dfrac{5}{3}, \infty\right)$ (d) None of these

43. The period of the function $f(x) = 7 \cos (3x + 5)$ is :

(a) 2π (b) $\dfrac{2\pi}{3}$

(c) $\dfrac{\pi}{3}$ (d) None of these

44. The period of function $f(x) = a \sin kx + b \cos kx$ is :

(a) $\dfrac{2\pi}{k}$ (b) $\dfrac{2\pi}{|k|}$

(c) $\dfrac{\pi}{|k|}$ (d) None of these

45. The period of the function $f(x) = \cos x^2$ is :

(a) 2π (b) π

(c) $\dfrac{\pi}{2}$ (d) None of these

46. The period of the function $f(x) = \sin \sqrt{x}$ is :

(a) π (b) 2π

(c) $\dfrac{\pi}{2}$ (d) None of these

47. The period of function $f(x) = \sin^4 2x + \cos^4 2x$ is

(a) $\dfrac{\pi}{2}$ (b) $\dfrac{\pi}{8}$

(c) $\dfrac{\pi}{4}$ (d) None of these

48. The period of the function $f(x) = \sqrt{\tan x}$ is :

(a) π (b) 2π

(c) $\dfrac{\pi}{2}$ (d) None of these

49. The period of the function $f(x) = \cos\left(\dfrac{8x + 5}{4\pi}\right)$ is :

(a) 2π (b) π

(c) π^2 (d) None of these

50. The period of the function $f(x) = x - [x]$, where $[x]$ denotes the greatest integer less than or equal to x, is :

(a) 2 (b) 1

(c) 4 (d) None of these

51. If $e^x + e^{f(x)} = e$, then range of the function of f is

(a) $(-\infty, 1]$ (b) $(-\infty, 1)$

(c) $(1, \infty)$ (d) $[1, \infty)$

52. The period of the function

$$f(x) = \cos\left(\dfrac{\pi x}{n!}\right) - \sin\left(\dfrac{\pi x}{(n+1)!}\right) \text{ is :}$$

(a) $2(n+1)!$ (b) $2(n!)$

(c) $(n+1)$ (d) not periodic

53. The function $f(x) = k \,|\cos x| + k^2\,|\sin x| + \phi(k)$ has period $\dfrac{\pi}{2}$ if k is equal to :

(a) 1 (b) 2

(c) 3 (d) None of these

54. The domain of the function

$$f(x) = \log_{\left[x + \frac{1}{2}\right]} |x^2 - x - 6|, \text{ where } [.] \text{ denotes}$$

the greatest integer function, is :

(a) $\left(\dfrac{3}{2}, 3\right) \cup (3, \infty)$ (b) $\left[\dfrac{3}{2}, 3\right) \cup (3, \infty)$

(c) $\left[\dfrac{3}{2}, \infty\right)$ (d) None of these

55. The period of the function $f(x) = 2 \sin x + 3 \cos 2x$ is :

(a) π (b) 2π

(c) $\dfrac{\pi}{2}$ (d) None of these

56. Let f be a real valued function with domain R satisfying $f(x + k) = 1 + [2 - 5 f(x) + 10 \{f(x)\}^2 - 10 \{f(x)\}^3 + 5\{f(x)\}^4 - \{f(x)\}^5]^{1/5}$ for all real x and some positive constant k, then the period of the function $f(x)$ is:

(a) k (b) $2k$

(c) non-periodic   (d) None of these

57. Let f be a real valued function with domain R satisfying $f(x + 1) + f(x - 1) = \sqrt{2}\,f(x)\ \forall\ x \in R$. Then the period of the function $f(x)$ is :

(a) 8 (b) 12

(c) non-periodic   (d) None of these

58. The period of function $f(x) = 3x + 3 - [3x + 3] + \sin\dfrac{\pi x}{2}$, where $[x]$ denotes the greatest integer $\le x$, is :

(a) 4 (b) 1

(c) 2 (d) non-periodic

59. The value of $n \in I$ for which the function

$f(x) = \dfrac{\sin nx}{\sin\left(\dfrac{x}{n}\right)}$ has 4π as its period is :

(a) 2   (b) 3

(c) 4   (d) 5

60. Which of the following functions is non-periodic ?

(a) $f(x) = \tan(3x - 2)$

(b) $f(x) = \{x\}$, the fractional part of number x

(c) $f(x) = x + \cos x$

(d) $f(x) = 1 - \dfrac{\cos^2 x}{1 + \tan x} - \dfrac{\sin^2 x}{1 + \cot x}$

61. Let f be a real valued function with domain R satisfying $0 \le f(x) \le \dfrac{1}{2}$ and for some fixed $a > 0$,

$f(x + a) = \dfrac{1}{2} - \sqrt{f(x) - (f(x))^2} \;\; \forall\, x \in R,$

then the period of the function $f(x)$ is :

(a) a   (b) 2a

(c) non-periodic   (d) None of these

62. Which of the following functions is an odd function ?

(a) $f(x) = x\left(\dfrac{e^x - 1}{e^x + 1}\right)$

(b) $f(x) = \log(x + \sqrt{1 + x^2})$

(c) $f(x) = x^2 - |x|$

(d) None of these

63. Which of the following functions is an even function ?

(a) $f(x) = \sin x + \cos x$

(b) $f(x) = \log\left(\dfrac{1 - x}{1 + x}\right)$

(c) $f(x) = \dfrac{x}{e^x - 1} + \dfrac{x}{2}$

(d) None of these

64. The function $f(x) = \sec[\log(x + \sqrt{1 + x^2})]$ is :

(a) even   (b) odd

(c) constant   (d) None of these

65. The function $f(x) = \begin{cases} x^4 \tan\dfrac{\pi x}{2}, & |x| < 1 \\ x\,|x|, & |x| \ge 1 \end{cases}$ is :

(a) an odd function   (b) an even function

(c) a periodic function (d) None of these

66. Let $f(x) = |x - 3| + |x - 4| + |x - 5|$ and $g(x) = f(x + 2)$. Then $g(x)$ is :

(a) an even function

(b) an odd function

(c) neither even nor odd

(d) a periodic function

67. If f is an even function and g is an odd function, then the function fog is :

(a) an even function   (b) an odd function

(c) neither even nor odd (d) a periodic function

68. If f is an odd function and g is an even function, then the function fog is :

(a) an even function   (b) an odd function

(c) neither even nor odd (d) a periodic function

69. Let f and g be two odd functions, then the function fog is :

(a) an even function   (b) an odd function

(c) neither even nor odd (d) a periodic function

70. The function $f : R \to R$, defined by $f(x) = [x], \; \forall\, x \in R$, is :

(a) one-one

(b) onto

(c) both one-one and onto

(d) neither one-one nor onto.

71. The interval of values of a, for which the function $f(x) = x^3 + (a + 4)\, x^2 + 6ax + 6$ is one-one, is :

(a) (2, 8)   (b) [2, 8]

(c) [2, 8)   (d) None of these

72. Let $f : R \to R$ be a function defined by $f(x) = \sin(2x - 3)$, then f is:

(a) injective   (b) surjective

(c) bijective   (d) None of these

73. Which of the following functions from I to itself are bijections ?

(a) $f(x) = x + 3$ (b) $f(x) = x^5$

(c) $f(x) = 3x + 2$ (d) $f(x) = x^2 + x$

74. The interval of values of α for which the function $f : R \to R$ defined by $f(x) = \dfrac{\alpha x^2 + 6x - 8}{\alpha + 6x - 8x^2}$ is onto, is :

(a) $[2, 14]$ (b) $(2, 14)$

(c) $[2, 14)$ (d) None of these

75. Let $A = \{x \in R \mid -1 \le x \le 1\} = B$. Then the mapping $f : A \to B$ given by $f(x) = x \mid x \mid$ is :

(a) injective but not surjective.

(b) surjective but not injective.

(c) bijective.

(d) None of these.

76. If the function $f : (-\infty, \infty) \to B$ defined by $f(x) = -x^2 + 6x - 8$ is bijective, then $B =$

(a) $[1, \infty)$ (b) $(-\infty, 1]$

(c) $(-\infty, \infty)$ (d) None of these

77. The number of bijective functions from a set A to itself when A contains 106 elements is:

(a) 106 (b) $(106)^2$

(c) $(106)!$ (d) 2^{106}

78. The number of surjections from $A = \{1, 2, ..., n\}$, $n \ge 2$ onto $B = \{a, b\}$ is :

(a) $^nP_2$ (b) $2^n - 2$

(c) $2^n - 1$ (d) None of these

79. Set A has 3 elements and set B has 4 elements. The number of injections that can be defined from A to B is :

(a) 144 (b) 12

(c) 24 (d) 64

80. If $A = \left\{ x : -\dfrac{2}{5} \le x \le \dfrac{\pi - 2}{5} \right\}$, $B = [y : -1 \le y \le 1]$ and $f(x) = \cos(5x + 2)$, then the mapping $f : A \to B$ is :

(a) one-one but not onto.

(b) onto but not one-one.

(c) both one-one and onto.

(d) neither one-one nor onto.

81. Let $f(x) = [x]^2 + [x + 1] - 3$, where $[\cdot]$ denotes the greatest integer function, then :

(a) $f(x) \ne 0$ for all real x

(b) $f(x) = 0$ for only two real values

(c) $f(x) = 0$ for infinite number of values of x

(d) None of these

82. Let $f : R \to R$ be a function defined by $f(x) = x + \sqrt{x^2}$, then f is :

(a) injective   (b) surjective

(c) bijective   (d) None of these

83. Let $f : (-\infty, 2] \to (-\infty, 2]$ be a function defined by $f(x) = 4x - x^2$. Then $f^{-1}(x)$ is :

(a) $2 - \sqrt{4 - x}$ (b) $2 + \sqrt{4 - x}$

(c) $\sqrt{4 - x}$ (d) None of these

84. If $f : R \to R$ is given by $f(x) = 3x - 5$, then $f^{-1}(x)$:

(a) is given by $\dfrac{1}{3x - 5}$.

(b) is given by $\dfrac{x + 5}{3}$

(c) does not exist because f is not one-one.

(d) does not exist because f is not onto.

85. Let $f : [-1, \infty) \to [-1, \infty)$ be given by $f(x) = (x + 1)^2 - 1$. Then $f^{-1}(x) =$

(a) $-1 + \sqrt{x + 1}$ (b) $-1 - \sqrt{x + 1}$

(c) does not exist because f is not one-one.

(d) does not exist because f is not onto.

86. Let $f : R \to R$ be given by $f(x) = (x + 1)^2 - 1$, $x \ge -1$. Then, the set of values of x for which $f(x) = f^{-1}(x)$ is given by:

(a) $\{0\}$ (b) $\{0, -1\}$

(c) $\{-1\}$ (d) None of these

87. Let f be an injective map with domain $\{x, y, z\}$ and range $\{1, 2, 3\}$ such that exactly one of the following statements is correct and the remaining are false

$f(x) = 1$, $f(y) \ne 1$, $f(z) \ne 2$.

The value of $f^{-1}(1)$ is :

(a) y   (b) x

(c) z   (d) None of these

88. The value of the parameter α, for which the function $f(x) = 1 + \alpha x$, $\alpha \neq 0$ is the inverse of itself, is :

(a) -2 (b) -1

(c) 1 (d) 2

89. The inverse of the function $f(x) = \dfrac{a^x - a^{-x}}{a^x + a^{-x}}$ is :

(a) $\dfrac{1}{2} \log_a \left(\dfrac{1-x}{1+x} \right)$ (b) $\dfrac{1}{2} \log_a \left(\dfrac{1+x}{1-x} \right)$

(c) $\log_a \left(\dfrac{1+x}{1-x} \right)$ (d) None of these

90. The inverse of the function $y = [1 - (x - 3)^4]^{1/7}$ is

(a) $3 + (1 - x^7)^{1/4}$ (b) $3 - (1 - x^7)^{1/4}$

(c) $3 - (1 + x^7)^{1/4}$ (d) None of these

91. If $f(x)$ satisfies the relation $f(x + y) = f(x) + f(y)$ for all $x, y \in R$ and $f(1) = 5$, then the value of $\sum\limits_{n=1}^{m} f(n)$ is :

(a) $\dfrac{m(m+1)}{2}$ (b) $\dfrac{3m(m+1)}{2}$

(c) $\dfrac{5m(m+1)}{2}$ (d) None of these

92. Let $f : [0, 1] \to [0, 1]$ be defined by $f(x) = \dfrac{1-x}{1+x}$, $0 \le x \le 1$ and $g : [0, 1] \to [0, 1]$ be defined by $g(x) = 4x(1 - x)$, $0 \le x \le 1$, then $(fog)(x)$ is :

(a) $\dfrac{1 + 4x - 4x^2}{1 - 4x + 4x^2}, 0 \le x \le 1$

(b) $\dfrac{1 - 4x + 4x^2}{1 + 4x - 4x^2}, 0 \le x \le 1$

(c) $\dfrac{1 + 4x + 4x^2}{1 + 4x - 4x^2}, 0 \le x \le 1$

(d) None of these

93. If $f(x) = 1 - x$, $x \in [-3, 3]$, then the domain of $f[f(x)]$ is :

(a) $[-2, 3]$ (b) $(-2, 3)$

(c) $[-2, 3)$ (d) $(-2, 3]$

94. If $f(x) = \sqrt{2 - x}$ and $g(x) = \sqrt{1 - 2x}$, then domain of $f[g(x)]$ is :

(a) $\left(-\infty, \dfrac{1}{2} \right]$ (b) $\left[\dfrac{1}{2}, \infty \right)$

(c) $\left(-\infty, -\dfrac{3}{2} \right]$ (d) None of these

95. Let f be a function with domain $[-3, 5]$ and let $g(x) = |3x + 4|$. Then the domain of $(fog)(x)$ is :

(a) $\left(-3, \dfrac{1}{3} \right)$ (b) $\left[-3, \dfrac{1}{3} \right]$

(c) $\left[-3, \dfrac{1}{3} \right)$ (d) None of these

96. If $f(x) = \dfrac{1}{1-x}$, $x \neq 0, 1$, then the graph of the function $y = f[f\{f(x)\}]$, $x > 1$ is :

(a) a straight line

(b) a circle

(c) an ellipse

(d) a pair of straight lines

97. Let $f : R \to R$ be a function defined by $f(x) = x - [x]$, where $[\cdot]$ denotes the greatest function, then $f^{-1}(x)$ is :

(a) $[x] - x$ (b) $\dfrac{1}{x - [x]}$

(c) Not defined   (d) None of these

98. If $f(x) = 64x^3 + \dfrac{1}{x^3}$ and a, b are the roots of $4x + \dfrac{1}{x} = 3$, then :

(a) $f(a) = 12$ (b) $f(b) = 11$

(c) $f(a) = f(b)$ (d) None of these

99. If $f(x) = \cos(\log x)$, then

$f(x) \cdot f(y) - \dfrac{1}{2} \left\{ f\left(\dfrac{x}{y} \right) + f(xy) \right\}$ is equal to :

(a) 2 (b) 1

(c) 0 (d) None of these

100. If $3f(x) + 5f\left(\dfrac{1}{x} \right) = \dfrac{1}{x} - 3$, $\forall x \, (\neq 0) \in R$, then $f(x) =$

(a) $\dfrac{1}{14} \left(\dfrac{3}{x} + 5x - 6 \right)$ (b) $\dfrac{1}{14} \left(-\dfrac{3}{x} + 5x - 6 \right)$

(c) $\dfrac{1}{14} \left(-\dfrac{3}{x} + 5x + 6 \right)$ (d) None of these

101. If $f(x)$ is a function satisfying $f(x) \cdot f\left(\dfrac{1}{x} \right) = f(x) + f\left(\dfrac{1}{x} \right)$ and $f(5) = 126$, then $f(4) =$

(a) 65 (b) 0

(c) -65 (d) None of these

102. If $f(x + y) = f(x) + f(y) - xy - 1$ for all $x, y \in R$ and $f(1) = 1$, then the number of solutions of $f(n) = n, n \in N$ is :

(a) one

(b) two

(c) no solution

(d) None of these

103. $f(x) = \dfrac{1}{1-x}$, $g(x) = f[f(x)]$ & $h(x) = f[f\{f(x)\}]$. Then the value of $f(x) \cdot g(x) \cdot h(x)$ is :

(a) 1

(b) −1

(c) 0

(d) None of these

104. $f(x) = \sin^2 x + \sin^2\left(x + \dfrac{\pi}{3}\right) + \cos x \cdot \cos\left(x + \dfrac{\pi}{3}\right)$ and $g(5/4) = 1$. Then $(gof)(x) =$

(a) 1

(b) −1

(c) x

(d) None of these

105. Let $f : N \to Y$ be a function defined as $f(x) = 4x + 3$, where $Y = \{y \in N : y = 4x + 3$ for some $x \in N\}$. Show that f is invertible and its inverse is :   **[AIEEE - 2008]**

(a) $g(y) = \dfrac{3y + 4}{3}$

(b) $g(y) = 4 + \dfrac{y + 3}{4}$

(c) $g(y) = \dfrac{y + 3}{4}$

(d) $g(y) = \dfrac{y - 3}{4}$

106. The image of the interval $[1, 3]$ under the mapping $f : R \to R$, given by $f(x) = 2x^3 - 24x + 107$ is :

(a) $[0, 89]$

(b) $[75, 89]$

(c) $[0, 75]$

(d) None of these

107. The largest interval lying in $\left(-\dfrac{\pi}{2}, \dfrac{\pi}{2}\right)$ for which the function

$$\left[f(x) = 4^{-x^2} + \cos^{-1}\left(\dfrac{x}{1} - 1\right) + \log(\cos x)\right]$$

is defined, is :   **[AIEEE - 2007]**

(a) $[0, \pi]$

(b) $\left(-\dfrac{\pi}{2}, \dfrac{\pi}{2}\right)$

(c) $\left[-\dfrac{\pi}{4}, \dfrac{\pi}{2}\right)$

(d) $\left[0, \dfrac{\pi}{2}\right)$

108. Let $f(x)$ be a function defined on $[-1, 1]$. If the area of the equilateral triangle with two of its vertices at $(0, 0)$ and $(x, f(x))$ is $\dfrac{\sqrt{3}}{4}$, then the function $f(x)$ is :

(a) $\sqrt{x^2 - 1}$

(b) $-\sqrt{1 + x^2}$

(c) $\pm\sqrt{1 - x^2}$

(d) $\sqrt{1 + x^2}$

109. If $f(x) = \dfrac{4^x}{4^x + 2}$, then

$f\left(\dfrac{1}{1997}\right) + f\left(\dfrac{2}{1997}\right) + \ldots + f\left(\dfrac{1996}{1997}\right)$ is equal to

(a) 1997

(b) 998

(c) 0

(d) None of these

110. If $f(x) = \dfrac{x^2 - 1}{x^2 + 1}$, for every real number x, then the minimum value of f :

(a) does not exist because f is unbounded.

(b) is not attained even though f is bounded.

(c) is equal to 1.

(d) is equal to −1.

111. The number of values of x, where the function $f(x) = \cos x + \cos(\sqrt{2}\, x)$ attains its maximum, is :

(a) 0

(b) 1

(c) 2

(d) infinite

112. The domain of definition of the function $y(x)$ given by the equation $2^x + 2^y = 2$ is :

(a) $0 < x \le 1$

(b) $0 \le x \le 1$

(c) $-\infty < x \le 0$

(d) $-\infty < x < 1$

113. The value of the natural number 'a' for which $\sum\limits_{k=1}^{n} f(a + k) = 16(2^n - 1)$, where the function f satisfies the relation $f(x + y) = f(x) \cdot f(y)$ for all natural numbers x, y and further $f(1) = 2$, is :

(a) 3

(b) 4

(c) 2

(d) None of these

114. If $f(x) = |x - 2|$ and $g(x) = f[f(x)]$, then for $x > 20$, $g'(x) =$

(a) −1

(b) 1

(c) 2

(d) None of these

115. The range of the real function $\dfrac{x+2}{x^2-8x-4}$ is :

(a) $\left(-\infty, -\dfrac{1}{4}\right] \cup \left[-\dfrac{1}{20}, \infty\right)$

(b) $\left(-\infty, -\dfrac{1}{4}\right) \cup \left(-\dfrac{1}{20}, \infty\right)$

(c) $\left(-\infty, -\dfrac{1}{4}\right] \cup \left(-\dfrac{1}{20}, \infty\right)$

(d) None of these

116. The range of the function $f(x) = \dfrac{x^2-x}{x^2+2x}$ is :

(a) $R\backslash\left\{1, -\dfrac{1}{2}\right\}$ (b) R

(c) $R\backslash\{1\}$ (d) None of these

117. The minimum value of $2^{(x^2-3)^3+27}$ is :

(a) 1 (b) 2

(c) 2^{27} (d) None of these

118. The range of the function $f(x) = |x-1|$ is :

(a) $(-\infty, 0)$ (b) $[0, \infty)$

(c) $(0, \infty)$ (d) $(-\infty, \infty)$

119. If $f(x) = 2x^3 + mx^2 - 13x + n$ and 2, 3 are roots of the equation $f(x) = 0$, then the values of m and n are :

(a) 5, 30 (b) −5, −30

(c) −5, 30 (d) None of these

120. If $f(x) = \log\left(\dfrac{1+x}{1-x}\right)$ and $g(x) = \dfrac{3x+x^3}{1+3x^2}$, then $f[g(x)]$ is equal to :

(a) $f(3x)$ (b) $[f(x)]^3$

(c) $3f(x)$ (d) $-f(x)$

121. If $2\,f(x) - 3f\left(\dfrac{1}{x}\right) = x^2$, x is not equal to zero, then f(2) is equal to :

(a) $-\dfrac{7}{4}$ (b) $\dfrac{5}{2}$

(c) -1 (d) None of these

122. The composite mapping fog of the maps $f : R \to R, f(x) = \sin x, g : R \to R, g(x) = x^2$ is :

(a) $\sin x + x^2$ (b) $(\sin x)^2$

(c) $\sin x^2$ (d) $\sin x/x^2$

123. Let $f : R \to R$ be defined by $f(x) = 3x - 4$, then $f^{-1}(x)$ is :

(a) $\dfrac{1}{3}(x+4)$ (b) $\dfrac{1}{3}(x-4)$

(c) $3x+4$ (d) Not defined

124. If $e^x = y + \sqrt{1+y^2}$, then y is equal to :

(a) $e^x + e^{-x}$ (b) $e^x - e^{-x}$

(c) $\dfrac{e^x - e^{-x}}{2}$ (d) $\dfrac{e^x + e^{-x}}{2}$

125. The range of the function $f(x) = \dfrac{1+x^2}{x^2}$ is equal to :

(a) $(0, 1)$ (b) $[0, 1]$

(c) $(1, \infty)$ (d) $[1, \infty)$

126. Let $f\left(x + \dfrac{1}{x}\right) = x^2 + \dfrac{1}{x^2}$ $(x \neq 0)$ then $f(x)$ is equal to :

(a) $x^2 - 1$ (b) $x^2 - 2$

(c) x^2 (d) None of these

127. The function
$f(x) = \cot^{-1}\left[\sqrt{(x+3)x}\right] + \cos^{-1}\left(\sqrt{x^2+3x+1}\right)$
is defined on the set S, where S is equal to :

(a) $\{-3, 0\}$ (b) $[-3, 0]$

(c) $[0, 3]$ (d) $(-3, 0)$

128. Let $f : R \to R$, $g : R \to R$ be two functions given by $f(x) = 2x - 3$, $g(x) = x^3 + 5$. Then $(fog)^{-1}(x)$ is equal to :

(a) $\left(\dfrac{x-7}{2}\right)^{1/3}$ (b) $\left(\dfrac{x+7}{2}\right)^{1/3}$

(c) $\left(x - \dfrac{7}{2}\right)^{1/3}$ (d) $\left(\dfrac{x-2}{7}\right)^{1/3}$

129. The domain of the function $y = f(x) = \dfrac{1}{\sqrt{x-1}}$ is

(a) $(-\infty, 1)$ (b) $(0, \infty)$

(c) $(1, \infty)$ (d) $(0, 1)$

130. Which of the following functions is an even function ?

(a) $f(x) = x\,\dfrac{a^x - 1}{a^x + 1}$

(b) $f(x) = \dfrac{a^x + a^{-x}}{a^x - a^{-x}}$

(c) $f(x) = \dfrac{a^x + 1}{a^x - 1}$

(d) $f(x) = \log_2\left(x + \sqrt{x^2+1}\right)$

131. Given that $y = \dfrac{2x}{x^2 + 1}$, $x \in R$, the complete set of values of y is given by :

(a) $\{y : -1 \le y \le 1\}$

(b) $\{y : -1 < y < 1\}$

(c) $\{y : y < -1\} \cup \{y : y > 1\}$

(d) $\{y : y < 1\}$

132. If x is real, then the expression $\dfrac{x^2 + 34x - 71}{x^2 + 2x - 7}$:

(a) cannot lie between 5 and 9.

(b) always lies between 5 and 9.

(c) is not real.

(d) none of these.

133. For a real number x, [x] denotes the integral part of x. The value of

$$\left[\frac{1}{2}\right] + \left[\frac{1}{2} + \frac{1}{100}\right] + \left[\frac{1}{2} + \frac{2}{100}\right] + \dots + \left[\frac{1}{2} + \frac{99}{100}\right]$$

is :

(a) 49 (b) 50

(c) 48 (d) 51

134. Let $f(x)$ be defined for all $x > 0$ and be continuous. Let $f(x)$ satisfy $f\left(\dfrac{x}{y}\right) = f(x) - f(y)$ for all x, y and $f(e) = 1$. Then :

(a) $f(x)$ is bounded.

(b) $f\left(\dfrac{1}{x}\right) \to 0$ as $x \to 0$

(c) $x\, f(x) \to 1$ as $x \to 0$.

(d) $f(x) = \log x$.

135. Let $g(x) = 1 + x - [x]$ and $f(x) = \begin{cases} -1, & x < 0 \\ 0, & x = 0 \\ 1, & x > 0 \end{cases}$

Then, for all x, $f[g(x)]$ is equal to :

(a) x (b) 1

(c) $f(x)$ (d) $g(x)$

136. The functions $f(x) = \log(x - 1) - \log(x - 2)$ and $g(x) = \log\left(\dfrac{x - 1}{x - 2}\right)$ are identical when x lies in the interval :

(a) [1, 2] (b) [2, ∞]

(c) (2, ∞) (d) (−∞, ∞)

137. For n = 1, 2, 3, ..., the value of

$$\left[\frac{n+1}{2}\right] + \left[\frac{n+2}{4}\right] + \left[\frac{n+4}{8}\right] + \left[\frac{n+8}{16}\right] + \dots =$$

(where [.] denotes the greatest integer function)

(a) $n - 1$ (b) n

(c) $n + 2$ (d) None of these

138. The domain of the function

$f(x) = \dfrac{\log_x \cos^{-1} x}{\sqrt{3 - 2 \sin x}}$ is :

(a) (0, 1) (b) [0, 1]

(c) (0, 1] (d) None of these

139. If $f(x)$ is a polynomial of degree n (>2) and $f(x) = f(k - x)$ (where k is a fixed real number), then degree of $f'(x)$ is :

(a) n (b) $n - 1$

(c) 0 (d) None of these

140. The function $f(x) = \displaystyle\int_0^x \log\left(\dfrac{1 - x}{1 + x}\right) dx$ is :

(a) an even function (b) an odd function

(c) a periodic function (d) None of these

141. If $f : (3, 4) \to (0, 1)$ is defined by $f(x) = x - [x]$, where [x] denotes the greatest integer function then $f^{-1}(x)$ is :

(a) $\dfrac{1}{x - [x]}$ (b) $[x] - x$

(c) $x - 3$ (d) $x + 3$

142. Let $f(x) = 1 - (1 - x)^2$, $x \le 1$. The number of solutions of the equation $f[f(x)] = x$ is :

(a) one (b) two

(c) zero (d) None of these

143. Let $f(x) = |x + 1|$. The number of values of $x \in [-2, 2]$ for which $f(x - 3)$, $f(x - 1)$, $f(x + 1)$ are in A.P., is :

(a) 1 (b) 2

(c) 0 (d) infinite

144. If $(x + 1)(x^{1/2} + 1) \dots (x^{1/2^2} + 1) \dots (x^{1/2^n} + 1)$ $= (x^2 - 1) f(x)$, then $f(x)$ is

(a) $\dfrac{1}{x^{1/2^{n-1}} - 1}$ (b) $\dfrac{1}{x^{1/2^n} - 1}$

(c) $x^{1/2^n} - 1$ (d) None of these

145. The range of the function f : [0, 1] → R,

f (x) = x³ − x² + 4x + 2sin⁻¹x is :

(a) [0, 4 + 2π]　　　(b) [0, 4 + π]

(c) only zero　　　(d) None of these

146. Given $f(x) = \dfrac{1}{1-x}$, g(x) = f{f(x)} and

h (x) = f [f {f (x)}].

Then the value of f (x) · g (x) · h (x) is :

(a) 1 − x　　　(b) x

(c) $\dfrac{1}{1-x}$　　　(d) None of these

147. The domain of the function $f(x) = \sqrt{5|x| - x^2 - 6}$

is :

(a) (−3, −2) ∪ (2, 3)　(b) [−3, −2) ∪ [2, 3)

(c) [−3, −2] ∪ [2, 3]　(d) None of these

148. The domain of the real valued function f (x) for

which $4^{f(x)} + 4^{1-f(x)} = 4x$, is :

(a) (−1, 1]　　　(b) [1, ∞)

(c) (−∞, 1]　　　(d) (−∞, −1]

149. Let f : R → R and g : R → R be defined by

f(x) = x + 1 and g (x) = x² − 2,

then (gof)⁻¹ ([−2, −1]) is :

(a) (−2, 0)　　　(b) [−2, 0]

(c) [−2, 0)　　　(d) None of these

150. Let f (x) be a function satisfying f ' (x) = f (x)

and f(0) = 1 and g be a function satisfying

f(x) + g(x) = x². The value of the integral

$\int\limits_{0}^{1} f(x)\, g(x)\, dx$ is :

(a) $\dfrac{1}{4}(e-7)$　　　(b) $\dfrac{1}{4}(e-2)$

(c) $\dfrac{1}{5}(e-3)$　　　(d) $e - \dfrac{e^2}{2} - \dfrac{3}{2}$

151. The function $f(x) = \begin{cases} 1, & x \text{ is rational} \\ 0, & x \text{ is irrational} \end{cases}$

(a) is periodic with period 1.

(b) is non-periodic.

(c) is periodic with indeterminate period.

(d) None of these

152. If $f(x) = \log(x + \sqrt{1 + x^2})$,

g(x) = log (1 + √1 + x²) and

h (x) = f (x) − g (x) then :

(a) $h\left(\dfrac{1}{x}\right) = 0$　　　(b) $h\left(\dfrac{1}{x}\right) = h(x)$

(c) $h\left(\dfrac{1}{x}\right) = -h(x)$　　(d) None of these

153. Let f (x) = x³ + 3x² − 33x − 33 for x > 0 and 'g'

be its inverse, then the value of 'K' such that

Kg'(2) = 1 is :

(a) − 36　　　(b) − 42

(c) 12　　　(d) All of these

154. The function $f(x) = \left(1 + \dfrac{1}{x}\right) ln \left(1 + \dfrac{1}{x}\right) - \dfrac{1}{x}$ is :

(a) positive for x > 0　　(b) negative for x > 0

(c) increasing for x > 0　(d) None of these

155. If f : R → R, f(x) = (x +1)², g(x) = x²+ 1, then

(fog) (−3) equals :

(a) 121　　　(b) 112

(c) 211　　　(d) None of these

156. The fundamental period of the function :

$f(x) = \cos\dfrac{x}{5} + \sin\dfrac{3x}{7}$ is :

(a) 14 π　　　(b) 10 π

(c) 35 π　　　(d) None of these

157. If $f(x) = \dfrac{x}{x-1} = y$, then value of f (y) is :

(a) 1　　　(b) x −1

(c) x +1　　　(d) 1− x

158. If f is a periodic function and g is a non-periodic

function then :

(a) fog is always periodic.

(b) fog is never periodic.

(c) gof is always periodic.

(d) gof is never periodic.

159. If ϕ (x) = aˣ, then {ϕ (P)}³ is equal to :

(a) ϕ (3P)　　　(b) 2ϕ (P)

(c) 6ϕ (P)　　　(d) 4ϕ (P)

160. The function $f : R \to R$, $f(x) = x^2$ is :

(a) injection but not surjection.

(b) surjection but not injection.

(c) injection as well as surjection.

(d) neither injection nor surjection.

161. If $f(x) = \dfrac{x}{x-1}$, then $\dfrac{f(a)}{f(a+1)} =$

(a) $f(-a)$

(b) $f\left(\dfrac{1}{a}\right)$

(c) $f(a^2)$

(d) $f\left(\dfrac{-a}{a-1}\right)$

162. Domain of the function

$f(x) = \sin^{-1}\left(\dfrac{1+x^2}{2x}\right) + \sqrt{16 - x^2}$ is :

(a) $[-4, -1] \cup [1, 4]$ (b) $[-1, 1]$

(c) $\{-1, 1\}$

(d) None of these

163. Let $f(x) = x$, $g(x) = \dfrac{1}{x}$ and $h(x) = f(x) \cdot g(x)$.

Then, $h(x) = 1$, if :

(a) x is an irrational number

(b) x is a real number $\neq 0$

(c) x is a real number

(d) x is a rational number

164. If $2^{\log_2 (x^2 - 5x - 3)} = 2 - x$, then the set of values of x is :

(a) $\{-1, 5\}$

(b) $\{-1\}$

(c) $\{5\}$

(d) $\{\ \}$

165. If f is any function, then $\dfrac{1}{2}[f(x) + f(-x)]$ is always :

(a) odd

(b) even

(c) neither even nor odd

(d) one-one

166. If $f(x) = \begin{cases} x, & \text{when x is an even integer} \\ 0, & \text{when x is an odd integer} \end{cases}$

then f (x) is :

(a) even

(b) odd

(c) even or odd

(d) neither even nor odd

167. The domain of the function $f(x) = \dfrac{1}{\sqrt{|x| - x}}$ is :

[AIEEE - 2011]

(a) $(-\infty, \infty) - \{0\}$

(b) $(-\infty, \infty)$

(c) $(0, \infty)$

(d) $(-\infty, 0)$

168. Let $f : R \to R$ be a continuous function defined by $f(x) = \dfrac{1}{e^x + 2e^{-x}}$ **[AIEEE - 2010]**

Statement 1: $f(c) = \dfrac{1}{3}$, for some $c \in R$.

Statement 2: $0 < f(x) \leq \dfrac{1}{2\sqrt{2}}$, for all $x \in R$

(a) Statement 1 is true, statement 2 is true; statement 2 is not a correct explanation for statement 1.

(b) Statement 1 is true, statement 2 is false.

(c) Statement 1 is false, statement 2 is true.

(d) Statement 1 is true, statement 2 is true; statement 2 is the correct explanation for statement 1.

169. For real x, let $f(x) = x^3 + 5x + 1$, then

[AIEEE - 2009]

(a) f is one-one but not onto R

(b) f is onto R but not one-one

(c) f is one-one and onto R

(d) f is neither one-one nor onto R

170. Let $f(x) = (x + 1)^2 - 1$, $x \geq -1$ **[AIEEE - 2009]**

Statement 1: The set $\{x : f(x) = f^{-1}(x)\} = \{0, -1\}$

Statement 2: f is a bijection.

(a) Statement 1 is true, statement 2 is true; statement 2 is a correct explanation for statement 1.

(b) Statement 1 is true, statement 2 is true; statement 2 is not a correct explanation for statement 1.

(c) Statement 1 is true, statement 2 is false.

(d) Statement 1 is false, statement 2 is true.

171. Let f be a function defined on [–2, 2] and is

given by $f(x) = \begin{cases} -1, & -2 \le x \le 0 \\ x-1, & 0 < x \le 2 \end{cases}$

and $g(x) = f(|x|) + |f(x)|$. Then g (x) is equal to :

(a) $\begin{cases} -x, & -2 \le x < 0 \\ 0, & 0 \le x < 1 \\ x-1, & 1 \le x \le 2 \end{cases}$

(b) $\begin{cases} -x, & -2 \le x < 0 \\ 0, & 0 \le x < 1 \\ 2(x-1), & 1 \le x \le 2 \end{cases}$

(c) $\begin{cases} -x, & -2 \le x < 0 \\ x-1, & 0 \le x \le 2 \end{cases}$

(d) None of these

172. Let f (x) = max. {(1 – x), (1 + x), 2}, $\forall$ x $\in$ R. Then :

(a) $f(x) = \begin{cases} 1+x, & x \le -1 \\ 2, & -1 < x < 1 \\ 1-x, & x \ge 1 \end{cases}$

(b) $f(x) = \begin{cases} 1-x, & x \le -1 \\ 1, & -1 < x < 1 \\ 1+x, & x \ge 1 \end{cases}$

(c) $f(x) = \begin{cases} 1-x, & x \le -1 \\ 2, & -1 < x < 1 \\ 1+x, & x \ge 1 \end{cases}$

(d) None of these

ANSWER KEY

1. (b)	2. (a)	3. (c)	4. (b)	5. (b)	6. (a)	7. (c)	8. (a)	9. (d)	10. (a)
11. (d)	12. (b)	13. (a)	14. (b)	15. (a)	16. (d)	17. (d)	18. (a)	19. (b)	20. (b)
21. (a)	22. (b)	23. (d)	24. (b)	25. (a)	26. (d)	27. (a)	28. (a)	29. (d)	30. (a)
31. (b)	32. (c)	33. (b)	34. (a)	35. (b)	36. (a)	37. (a)	38. (a)	39. (b)	40. (b)
41. (c)	42. (a)	43. (b)	44. (b)	45. (d)	46. (d)	47. (c)	48. (a)	49. (c)	50. (b)
51. (b)	52. (a)	53. (a)	54. (b)	55. (b)	56. (b)	57. (a)	58. (a)	59. (a)	60. (c)
61. (b)	62. (b)	63. (c)	64. (a)	65. (a)	66. (c)	67. (a)	68. (a)	69. (b)	70. (d)
71. (a)	72. (d)	73. (a)	74. (a)	75. (c)	76. (b)	77. (c)	78. (b)	79. (c)	80. (c)
81. (c)	82. (d)	83. (a)	84. (b)	85. (a)	86. (b)	87. (a)	88. (b)	89. (b)	90. (a)
91. (c)	92. (b)	93. (a)	94. (d)	95. (b)	96. (a)	97. (c)	98. (c)	99. (c)	100. (b)
101. (a)	102. (a)	103. (b)	104. (a)	105. (d)	106. (b)	107. (d)	108. (c)	109. (b)	110. (d)
111. (b)	112. (d)	113. (a)	114. (b)	115. (a)	116. (a)	117. (a)	118. (b)	119. (c)	120. (c)
121. (a)	122. (c)	123. (a)	124. (c)	125. (c)	126. (b)	127. (a)	128. (a)	129. (c)	130. (a)
131. (a)	132. (a)	133. (b)	134. (d)	135. (b)	136. (c)	137. (b)	138. (a)	139. (b)	140. (a)
141. (d)	142. (b)	143. (b)	144. (b)	145. (b)	146. (d)	147. (c)	148. (b)	149. (b)	150. (d)
151. (c)	152. (c)	153. (a)	154. (a)	155. (a)	156. (d)	157. (a)	158. (c)	159. (a)	160. (d)
161. (c)	162. (c)	163. (b)	164. (b)	165. (b)	166. (b)	167. (d)	168. (d)	169. (c)	170. (c)
171. (b)	172. (c)								

LIMITS

MULTIPLE CHOICE QUESTIONS

1. The value of $\lim\limits_{x\to\infty} \sqrt{x}\,(\sqrt{x+c}-\sqrt{x})$ is :

(a) $\dfrac{c}{2}$ (b) $\dfrac{c}{3}$

(c) $\dfrac{c}{4}$ (d) None of these

2. The value of $\lim\limits_{x\to 0} \dfrac{(1+x)^{1/3}-(1-x)^{1/3}}{x}$ is :

(a) $\dfrac{2}{3}$ (b) $\dfrac{1}{3}$

(c) 1 (d) None of these

3. $\lim\limits_{x\to 0} \dfrac{\sqrt[3]{8+x}-\sqrt[3]{8+x^2-x^3}}{\sqrt[3]{8+x}-\sqrt[3]{8+x^2+x^3}}$ is equal to :

(a) -1 (b) $\dfrac{1}{2}$

(c) 1 (d) None of these

4. The value of $\lim\limits_{x\to-\infty} \left[\dfrac{x^4\sin(1/x)+x^2}{1+|x|^3}\right]$ is :

(a) 1 (b) -1

(c) 0 (d) ∞

5. $\lim\limits_{x\to\infty} \left(\dfrac{3x^2+2x+1}{x^2+x+2}\right)^{\frac{6x+1}{3x+2}}$ is equal to :

(a) 3 (b) 9

(c) 1 (d) None of these

6. The value of $\lim\limits_{x\to\infty} \left[\sqrt{x+\sqrt{x+\sqrt{x}}}-\sqrt{x}\right]$ is :

(a) $\dfrac{1}{2}$ (b) 1

(c) 0 (d) None of these

7. $\lim\limits_{n\to\infty} \cos\dfrac{x}{2}\cos\dfrac{x}{2^2}\cos\dfrac{x}{2^3}\ldots\cos\dfrac{x}{2^n}$; $x\neq 0$ is equal to :

(a) 1 (b) 0

(c) -1 (d) None of these

8. In a circle of radius r, an isosceles triangle ABC is inscribed with AB = AC. If the $\triangle$ABC has perimeter $P = 2\left[\sqrt{2hr-h^2}+\sqrt{2hr}\right]$ and area A $= h\sqrt{2hr-h^2}$, where h is the altitude from A to BC, then $\lim\limits_{h\to 0^+} \dfrac{A}{P^3}$ is equal to :

(a) 128 r (b) $\dfrac{1}{128r}$

(c) $\dfrac{1}{64r}$ (d) None of these

9. $\lim\limits_{x\to 2} \dfrac{2^x+2^{3-x}-6}{2^{-x/2}-2^{1-x}}$ is equal to :

(a) 8 (b) 4

(c) 2 (d) None of these

10. $\lim\limits_{n\to\infty} \dfrac{n^k\sin^2(n!)}{n+2}$, $0<k<1$, is equal to :

(a) ∞ (b) 1

(c) 0 (d) None of these

11. $\lim\limits_{x\to 0} \dfrac{x\sqrt[3]{z^2-(z-x)^2}}{\left(\sqrt[3]{8xz-4x^2}+\sqrt[3]{8xz}\right)^4}$ is equal to :

(a) $\dfrac{z}{2^{11/3}}$ (b) $\dfrac{1}{2^{23/3}\cdot z}$

(c) $2^{21/3}z$ (d) None of these

12. $\lim\limits_{n\to\infty} \dfrac{n!}{(n+1)!-n!}$ is equal to :

(a) 0 (b) ∞

(c) 1 (d) None of these

13. $\lim\limits_{x\to\infty} \dfrac{\sqrt[2]{x^2+1}-\sqrt[3]{x^2+1}}{\sqrt[4]{x^4+1}-\sqrt[5]{x^4-1}}$ is equal to :

(a) 1 (b) -1

(c) 0 (d) None of these

14. $\lim\limits_{x \to 1} \dfrac{\sqrt{1 - \cos 2(x - 1)}}{x - 1}$:

(a) exists and it equals $\sqrt{2}$

(b) exists and it equals $-\sqrt{2}$

(c) does not exist because $(x-1) \to 0$

(d) does not exist because left hand limit is not equal to right hand limit.

15. The value of $\lim\limits_{n \to \infty} \dfrac{3^n + 2^n}{3^n - 2^n}$ is :

(a) -1 (b) 1

(c) 0 (d) ∞

16. $\lim\limits_{x \to 2} \dfrac{\sqrt{x + 7} - 3 \cdot \sqrt{2x - 3}}{\sqrt[3]{x + 6} - 2 \cdot \sqrt[3]{3x - 5}}$ is equal to :

(a) $\dfrac{34}{23}$ (b) $\dfrac{23}{17}$

(c) $\dfrac{7}{23}$ (d) $\dfrac{23}{7}$

17. $\lim\limits_{x \to 0} \dfrac{\tan^{-1} x - \sin^{-1} x}{x^3}$ is equal to :

(a) $\dfrac{1}{2}$ (b) $-\dfrac{1}{2}$

(c) 1 (d) -1

18. The value of $\lim\limits_{x \to \frac{\pi}{4}} \dfrac{2\sqrt{2} - (\cos x + \sin x)^3}{1 - \sin 2x}$ is :

(a) $\dfrac{3}{\sqrt{2}}$ (b) $\dfrac{\sqrt{2}}{3}$

(c) $\dfrac{1}{\sqrt{2}}$ (d) $\sqrt{2}$

19. The value of $\lim\limits_{h \to 0} \dfrac{\ln(1 + 2h) - 2\ln(1 + h)}{h^2}$ is :

(a) 1 (b) -1

(c) 0 (d) None of these

20. The value of $\lim\limits_{x \to 0} \log_e (\sin x)^{\tan x}$ is :

(a) 1 (b) -1

(c) 0 (d) None of these

21. The value of $\lim\limits_{x \to \infty} \left(\dfrac{1 + 3x}{2 + 3x}\right)^{\frac{1 - \sqrt{x}}{1 - x}}$ is :

(a) 0 (b) -1

(c) e (d) 1

22. $\lim\limits_{n \to \infty} [\log_{n-1}(n) \cdot \log_n (n+1) \cdot \log_{n+1} (n + 2)$

$\qquad\qquad \cdots\cdots \log_{n^{k_{-1}}}(n^k)]$

is equal to :

(a) ∞ (b) n

(c) k (d) None of these

23. The value of $\lim\limits_{x \to 0} \left(\dfrac{1 + 5x^2}{1 + 3x^2}\right)^{1/x^2}$ is :

(a) e^2 (b) e

(c) e^{-1} (d) None of these

24. The value of $\lim\limits_{n \to \infty} \left[\dfrac{1}{n} + \dfrac{e^{1/n}}{n} + \dfrac{e^{2/n}}{n} + \ldots + \dfrac{e^{(n-1)/n}}{n}\right]$ is :

(a) 1 (b) 0

(c) $e - 1$ (d) $e + 1$

25. $\lim\limits_{x \to 0} \left[\tan\left(\dfrac{\pi}{4} + x\right)\right]^{1/x}$ is equal to :

(a) e (b) e^2

(c) e^3 (d) e^{-1}

26. The value of

$\lim\limits_{x \to 1} \dfrac{x^n + x^{n-1} + x^{n-2} + \ldots + x^2 + x - n}{x - 1}$ is :

(a) $\dfrac{n(n + 1)}{2}$ (b) 0

(c) 1 (d) n

27. The value of $\lim\limits_{x \to 0} \dfrac{\displaystyle\int_0^{x^2} \cos t^2 \, dt}{x \sin x}$ is :

(a) $\dfrac{3}{2}$ (b) 1

(c) -1 (d) None of these

28. If $\Delta = \begin{vmatrix} \sin \alpha & \sin(\alpha + h) & \sin(\alpha + 2h) \\ \sin(\alpha + 2h) & \sin \alpha & \sin(\alpha + h) \\ \sin(\alpha + h) & \sin(\alpha + 2h) & \sin \alpha \end{vmatrix}$

then $\lim\limits_{h \to 0} \left(\dfrac{\Delta}{h^2}\right)$ is :

(a) $9 \sin \alpha \cos^2 \alpha$ (b) $9 \cos \alpha \sin^2 \alpha$

(c) $9 \sin \alpha \cos \alpha$ (d) $9 \sin^2 \alpha \cos^2 \alpha$

29. $\lim\limits_{x \to \infty} (\sin \sqrt{x+1} - \sin \sqrt{x})$ is equal to :

(a) 1   (b) −1

(c) 0   (d) None of these

30. $\lim\limits_{h \to 0} \dfrac{2\left[\sqrt{3}\sin\left(\frac{\pi}{6}+h\right) - \cos\left(\frac{\pi}{6}+h\right)\right]}{h\sqrt{3}\,(\sqrt{3}\cos h - \sin h)}$ is equal to :

(a) $-\dfrac{4}{3}$ (b) $\dfrac{4}{3}$

(c) $\dfrac{3}{4}$ (d) $-\dfrac{3}{4}$

31. $\lim\limits_{x \to \infty} \sqrt{\dfrac{x + \sin x}{x - \cos x}} =$

(a) 0   (b) 1

(c) −1   (d) None of these

32. The value of $\lim\limits_{x \to 0} \dfrac{\sqrt[3]{1+\sin x} - \sqrt[3]{1-\sin x}}{x}$ is :

(a) $\dfrac{2}{3}$ (b) $-\dfrac{2}{3}$

(c) $\dfrac{3}{2}$ (d) $-\dfrac{3}{2}$

33. $\lim\limits_{x \to -1} \dfrac{(1+x)(1-x^2)(1+x^3)(1-x^4)\ldots(1-x^{4n})}{[(1+x)(1-x^2)(1+x^3)(1-x^4)\ldots(1-x^{2n})]^2} =$

(a) $^{4n}C_{2n}$ (b) $^{2n}C_n$

(c) $2 \cdot {}^{4n}C_{2n}$ (d) $2 \cdot {}^{2n}C_n$

34. If $f(x) = \displaystyle\int \dfrac{2\sin x - \sin 2x}{x^3}\, dx,\ x \ne 0$, then

$\lim\limits_{x \to 0} f'(x)$ is :

(a) 0   (b) ∞

(c) −1   (d) 1

35. The value of $\lim\limits_{x \to \infty} \left[\dfrac{1^{1/x} + 2^{1/x} + 3^{1/x} + \ldots + n^{1/x}}{n}\right]^{nx}$ is :

(a) $n!$ (b) n

(c) $(n-1)!$ (d) 0

36. The values of a and b in order that

$\lim\limits_{x \to 0} \dfrac{x(1 + a\cos x) - b\sin x}{x} = 1$, are :

(a) $a = \dfrac{5}{2},\, b = -\dfrac{3}{2}$ (b) $a = -\dfrac{5}{2},\, b = \dfrac{3}{2}$

(c) $a = -\dfrac{5}{2},\, b = -\dfrac{3}{2}$ (d) None of these

37. If [x] denotes the greatest integer $\le x$, then

$\lim\limits_{n \to \infty} \dfrac{1}{n^3}\left([1^2 x] + [2^2 x] + [3^2 x] + \ldots + [n^2 x]\right)$

equals :

(a) $\dfrac{x}{6}$ (b) $\dfrac{x}{2}$

(c) $\dfrac{x}{3}$ (d) 0

38. If $f(a) = 2,\ f'(a) = 1,\ g(a) = -1,\ g'(a) = 2$, then

$\lim\limits_{x \to a} \dfrac{g(x)\,f(a) - g(a)\,f(x)}{x - a}$ is equal to :

(a) 3   (b) 5

(c) −3   (d) 0

39. The value of $\lim\limits_{x \to 0} \dfrac{(1+x)^{1/x} - e}{x}$ is :

(a) $-\dfrac{e}{2}$ (b) $\dfrac{e}{2}$

(c) $-e$ (d) e

40. $\lim\limits_{x \to 1} \dfrac{[\log(1+x) - \log 2]\,(3 \cdot 4^{x-1} - 3x)}{[(7+x)^{1/3} - (1+3x)^{1/2}]\sin \pi x}$ is equal to :

(a) $\dfrac{9}{4\pi}\log\dfrac{e}{4}$ (b) $\dfrac{9}{4\pi}\log\dfrac{4}{e}$

(c) $\dfrac{3}{\pi}\log\dfrac{4}{e}$ (d) None of these

41. The value of $\lim\limits_{x \to 0} \dfrac{\sqrt{\frac{1}{2}(1 - \cos 2x)}}{x}$ is :

(a) 1   (b) −1

(c) 0   (d) None of these

42. $\lim\limits_{x \to 0} \dfrac{e^x - e^{-x} - 2x}{x - \sin x}$ is equal to :

(a) 1   (b) −1

(c) 2   (d) 0

43. $\lim\limits_{x \to 1} \dfrac{\sqrt[3]{x^2} - 2 \cdot \sqrt[3]{x} + 1}{(x-1)^2}$ is equal to :

(a) $\dfrac{1}{9}$ (b) $\dfrac{1}{6}$

(c) $\dfrac{1}{3}$ (d) None of these

44. The value of $\lim\limits_{h \to 0} \dfrac{(a+h)^2 \sin(a+h) - a^2 \sin a}{h}$

is :

(a) $2a \sin a + a^2 \cos a$ (b) $2a \sin a - a^2 \cos a$

(c) $2a \cos a + a^2 \sin a$ (d) None of these

45. $\lim\limits_{x \to 0} \tan x \log \sin x$ is equal to :

(a) 1   (b) -1

(c) 0   (d) None of these

46. If $g(x) = -\sqrt{25 - x^2}$, then $\lim\limits_{x \to 1} \dfrac{g(x) - g(1)}{x - 1}$ is

equal to:

(a) $\dfrac{3}{\sqrt{24}}$ (b) $\dfrac{1}{\sqrt{24}}$

(c) $-\dfrac{1}{\sqrt{24}}$ (d) None of these

47. The values of constants a and b so that

$\lim\limits_{x \to \infty} \left(\dfrac{x^2 + 1}{x + 1} - ax - b \right)$ are :

(a) $a = 1, b = -1$ (b) $a = -1, b = 1$

(c) $a = 0, b = 0$ (d) $a = 2, b = -1$

48. $\lim\limits_{x \to -1} \dfrac{\sqrt{\pi} - \sqrt{\cos^{-1} x}}{\sqrt{x + 1}}$ is equal to :

(a) $\dfrac{1}{\sqrt{2\pi}}$ (b) $\dfrac{1}{\sqrt{\pi}}$

(c) $\dfrac{1}{\sqrt{2}}$ (d) None of these

49. The value of

$\lim\limits_{x \to \frac{\pi}{2}} 1 \left[1^{1/\cos^2 x} + 2^{1/\cos^2 x} + \ldots + n^{1/\cos^2 x} \right]^{\cos^2 x}$ is :

(a) 0   (b) n

(c) ∞ (d) $\dfrac{n(n+1)}{2}$

50. The value of $\lim\limits_{x \to 0} \left(\dfrac{\sin x}{x} \right)^{\dfrac{\sin x}{x - \sin x}}$ is :

(a) 1   (b) -1

(c) 0   (d) None of these

51. $\lim\limits_{n \to \infty} \left[\dfrac{\sqrt{n^2 + 1} + \sqrt{n}}{\sqrt[4]{n^3 + n} - \sqrt[4]{n}} \right]$ is equal to :

(a) 0   (b) 1

(c) -1 (d) ∞

52. $\lim\limits_{n \to \infty} \left[\dfrac{1}{1 \cdot 2} + \dfrac{1}{2 \cdot 3} + \dfrac{1}{3 \cdot 4} + \ldots + \dfrac{1}{n(n+1)} \right]$ is equal to

:

(a) 1   (b) -1

(c) 0   (d) None of these

53. The value of

$\lim\limits_{n \to \infty} \left[\dfrac{2n}{2n^2 - 1} \cos \dfrac{n+1}{2n - 1} - \dfrac{n}{1 - 2n} \cdot \dfrac{n(-1)^n}{n^2 + 1} \right]$ is :

(a) 1   (b) -1

(c) 0   (d) None of these

54. If $\lim\limits_{x \to 0} \dfrac{\sin 2x + a \sin x}{x^3}$ be finite, then the value of

a and the limit are given by :

(a) $-2, 1$ (b) $-2, -1$

(c) $2, 1$ (d) $2, -1$

55. The values of a, b and c such that

$\lim\limits_{x \to 0} \dfrac{ae^x - b \cos x + ce^{-x}}{x \sin x} = 2$ are :

(a) $a = 1, b = -2, c = 1$ (b) $a = 1, b = 2, c = -1$

(c) $a = 1, b = 2, c = 1$ (d) $a = -1, b = 2, c = 1$

56. $\lim\limits_{x \to \infty} \left(\dfrac{x + 6}{x + 1} \right)^{x+4}$ is equal to :

(a) e^{-5} (b) e^5

(c) 0   (d) None of these

57. If $f(5) = 7$ and $f'(5) = 7$, then $\lim\limits_{x \to 5} \dfrac{xf(5) - 5f(x)}{x - 5}$ is

given by :

(a) -28 (b) 28

(c) 35   (d) -35

58. If $a = \min \{x^2 + 4x + 5, x \in R\}$ and

$b = \lim\limits_{\theta \to 0} \dfrac{1 - \cos 2\theta}{\theta^2}$, then the value of

$\sum\limits_{r=0}^{n} a^r \cdot b^{n-r}$ is :

(a) $\dfrac{2^{n+1} - 1}{4 \cdot 2^n}$ (b) $2^{n+1} - 1$

(c) $\dfrac{2^{n+1} - 1}{3 \cdot 2^n}$ (d) None of these

59. $\lim\limits_{h\to 0} \dfrac{\sin(a+3h) - 3\sin(a+2h) + 3\,\sin(a+h) - \sin a}{h^3}$

is equal to :

(a) sin a   (b) – sin a

(c) cos a   (d) – cos a

60. If f (9) = 9 and f '(9) = 1, then $\lim\limits_{x\to 9} \dfrac{3 - \sqrt{f(x)}}{3 - \sqrt{x}}$ is

equal to :

(a) 0   (b) 1

(c) –1   (d) None of these

61. Let f(x) be a twice differentiable function and f "(0) = 5, then $\lim\limits_{x\to 0} \dfrac{3f(x) - 4f(3x) + f(9x)}{x^2}$ is equal to :

(a) 30   (b) 120

(c) 40   (d) None of these

62. $\lim\limits_{x\to 0} x^x$ is equal to :

(a) 0   (b) 1

(c) –1   (d) None of these

63. The value of $\lim\limits_{x\to a} \sqrt{a^2 - x^2}\,\cot \dfrac{\pi}{2}\sqrt{\dfrac{a-x}{a+x}}$ is :

(a) $\dfrac{2a}{\pi}$ (b) $-\dfrac{2a}{\pi}$

(c) $\dfrac{4a}{\pi}$ (d) $-\dfrac{4a}{\pi}$

64. The value of $\lim\limits_{x\to 3} \left[\log_a \dfrac{x-3}{\sqrt{x+6} - 3} \right]$ is :

(a) $\log_a 6$ (b) $\log_a 3$

(c) $\log_a 2$ (d) None of these

65. $\lim\limits_{x\to 2} \left[\dfrac{\sqrt[3]{10-x} - 2}{x-2} \right]$ is equal to :

(a) $\dfrac{1}{12}$ (b) $-\dfrac{1}{12}$

(c) $\dfrac{1}{6}$ (d) $-\dfrac{1}{6}$

66. The value of $\lim\limits_{x\to 0} \dfrac{3\sin x - x^2 + x^3}{\tan x + 2\sin^2 x + 5x^4}$ is :

(a) 1   (b) –1

(c) 3   (d) –3

67. The value of

$\lim\limits_{x\to 0} \dfrac{1 - \cos x + 2\sin x - \sin^3 x - x^2 + 3x^4}{\tan^3 x - 6\sin^2 x + x - 5x^3}$ is :

(a) 1   (b) 2

(c) –1   (d) –2

68. If $\lim\limits_{x\to -\infty} \left(\sqrt{x^2 - x + 1} - ax - b \right) = 0$, then the

values of a and b are given by :

(a) $a = -1, b = \dfrac{1}{2}$ (b) $a = 1, b = \dfrac{1}{2}$

(c) $a = 1, b = -\dfrac{1}{2}$ (d) None of these

69. $\lim\limits_{x\to 0} \dfrac{(1+x)^{1/x} - e + \dfrac{1}{2}\,ex}{x^2}$ is equal to :

(a) $\dfrac{9e}{11}$ (b) $\dfrac{11e}{27}$

(c) $\dfrac{11e}{24}$ (d) None of these

70. The value of $\lim\limits_{x\to 0} \dfrac{1 - \cos(1 - \cos x)}{x^4}$ is :

(a) $\dfrac{1}{4}$ (b) $\dfrac{1}{8}$

(c) $\dfrac{1}{16}$ (d) None of these

71. If f (2) = 2 and f '(2) = 1 then $\lim\limits_{x\to 2} \dfrac{2x^2 - 4f(x)}{x-2}$ is

equal to :

(a) 4   (b) –4

(c) 2   (d) –2

72. The value of $\lim\limits_{n\to \infty} \left(1 + \tan \dfrac{b}{n} \right)^n$ is :

(a) e^b (b) $e^{b/2}$

(c) e   (d) None of these

73. $\lim\limits_{x\to 3} ([x-3] + [3-x] - x)$, where [·] denotes the greatest integer function, is equal to :

(a) 4   (b) – 4

(c) 0   (d) Does not exist

74. $\lim\limits_{x\to \infty} f(x)$, where $\dfrac{2x-3}{x} < f(x) < \dfrac{2x^2 + 5x}{x^2}$, is :

(a) 1   (b) 2

(c) –1   (d) –2

75. The value of $\lim_{x \to \sqrt{2}} [x^2]$ is :

(a) 1   (b) 2

(c) 0   (d) Does not exist

76. $\lim_{n \to \infty} \dfrac{1 \cdot 2 + 2 \cdot 3 + 3 \cdot 4 + \ldots + n(n+1)}{n^3}$ is equal to :

(a) 1   (b) −1

(c) $\dfrac{1}{3}$ (d) None of these

77. $\lim_{n \to \infty} \dfrac{1}{n} \left(1 + e^{1/n} + e^{2/n} + \ldots + e^{\frac{n-1}{n}} \right)$ is equal to :

(a) e   (b) − e

(c) e − 1   (d) 1 − e

78. $\lim_{n \to \infty} \left[\dfrac{1}{1 \cdot 3} + \dfrac{1}{3 \cdot 5} + \dfrac{1}{5 \cdot 7} + \ldots + \dfrac{1}{(2n+1)(2n+3)} \right]$ is equal to :

(a) 1   (b) $\dfrac{1}{2}$

(c) $-\dfrac{1}{2}$ (d) None of these

79. $\lim_{x \to 0} \dfrac{\sqrt{x}}{\sqrt{4 - \sqrt{x}} - \sqrt{x}}$ is equal to :

(a) 0   (b) 1

(c) −1   (d) Does not exist

80. The value of

$$\lim_{n \to \infty} \dfrac{1 \cdot \sum_{1}^{n} r + 2 \cdot \sum_{1}^{n-1} r + 3 \cdot \sum_{1}^{n-2} r + \ldots + n \cdot 1}{n^4}$$ is :

(a) $\dfrac{1}{24}$ (b) $\dfrac{1}{12}$

(c) $\dfrac{1}{6}$ (d) None of these

81. $\lim_{x \to 2} \dfrac{2 - \sqrt{2 + x}}{\sqrt[3]{2} - \sqrt[3]{4 - x}}$ is equal to :

(a) $\dfrac{3}{2^{4/3}}$ (b) $-\dfrac{3}{2^{4/3}}$

(c) $\dfrac{3}{2^{3/4}}$ (d) $-\dfrac{3}{2^{3/4}}$

82. The values of a, b and c such that

$$\lim_{x \to 0} \dfrac{axe^x - b \log(1 + x) + cxe^{-x}}{x^2 \sin x} = 2 \text{ are given by :}$$

(a) a = 3, b = 12, c = 9

(b) a = −3, b = 12, c = 9

(c) a = 3, b = 12, c = −9

(d) None of these

83. $\lim_{x \to \frac{\pi}{4}} \dfrac{4\sqrt{2} - (\cos x + \sin x)^5}{1 - \sin 2x}$ is equal to :

(a) $5\sqrt{2}$ (b) $3\sqrt{2}$

(c) $\sqrt{2}$ (d) None of these

84. If α is a repeated root of $ax^2 + bx + c = 0$, then $\lim_{x \to \alpha} \dfrac{\tan(ax^2 + bx + c)}{(x - \alpha)^2}$ is :

(a) a   (b) b

(c) c   (d) 0

85. If the rth term t_r of a series is given by $t_r = \dfrac{r}{r^4 + r^2 + 1}$. Then $\lim_{n \to \infty} \sum_{r=1}^{n} t_r$ is :

(a) 1   (b) $\dfrac{1}{2}$

(c) $\dfrac{1}{3}$ (d) None of these

86. The value of $\lim_{x \to \infty} 3^x \sin\left(\dfrac{4}{3^x}\right)$ is :

(a) 4 log 3   (b) 3 log 4

(c) 4   (d) None of these

87. If $f(x) = \begin{cases} \dfrac{\tan[x]}{[x]}, & [x] \neq 0 \\ 0, & [x] = 0 \end{cases}$ where [x] denotes the greatest integer less than or equal to x, then $\lim_{x \to 0} f(x)$ is equal to :

(a) 1   (b) −1

(c) 0   (d) Does not exist

88. $\lim_{x \to 2} \dfrac{2^x - x^2}{x^x - 2^2}$ is equal to :

(a) $\dfrac{\log 2 - 1}{\log 2 + 1}$ (b) $\dfrac{\log 2 + 1}{\log 2 - 1}$

(c) 1   (d) −1

89. $\lim\limits_{x\to 2} \dfrac{\sqrt{1+\sqrt{2+x}}-\sqrt{3}}{x-2}$ is equal to :

(a) $\dfrac{1}{8\sqrt{3}}$ (b) $\dfrac{1}{\sqrt{3}}$

(c) $8\sqrt{3}$ (d) $\sqrt{3}$

90. Let $f(x) = x - [x]$ where $[x]$ denotes the greatest integer less than or equal to x and

$g(x) = \lim\limits_{n\to\infty} \dfrac{\{f(x)\}^{2n}-1}{\{f(x)\}^{2n}+1}$, then $g(x) =$

(a) 0 (b) 1

(c) −1 (d) None of these

91. $\lim\limits_{n\to\infty} \left[\dfrac{1}{1-n^2}+\dfrac{2}{1-n^2}+\ldots+\dfrac{n}{1-n^2}\right]$ is equal to :

(a) 0 (b) $-\dfrac{1}{2}$

(c) $\dfrac{1}{2}$ (d) None of these

92. $\lim\limits_{x\to 1} (1-x)\tan\left(\dfrac{\pi x}{2}\right)$ is equal to :

(a) $\dfrac{\pi}{2}$ (b) $\dfrac{2}{\pi}$

(c) $-\dfrac{\pi}{2}$ (d) $-\dfrac{2}{\pi}$

93. $\lim\limits_{x\to e} \dfrac{\log x - 1}{x-e}$ is equal to :

(a) $\dfrac{1}{e}$ (b) 1

(c) 0 (d) $\dfrac{1}{2}$

94. $\lim\limits_{h\to 0} \dfrac{2\left[\sqrt{3}\sin\left(\dfrac{\pi}{6}+h\right)-\cos\left(\dfrac{\pi}{6}+h\right)\right]}{\sqrt{3}h(\sqrt{3}\cos h - \sin h)}$ is equal to :

(a) $\dfrac{4}{3}$ (b) $-\dfrac{4}{3}$

(c) $\dfrac{2}{3}$ (d) $\dfrac{3}{4}$

95. $\lim\limits_{x\to 0} \dfrac{e^{x^2}-\cos x}{x^2}$ is :

(a) $\dfrac{1}{2}$ (b) $\dfrac{2}{3}$

(c) $\dfrac{3}{2}$ (d) 2

96. If $f(x) = \begin{cases} x\sin\dfrac{1}{x}, & x\neq 0 \\ 0, & x=0 \end{cases}$, then $\lim\limits_{x\to 0} f(x)$ equals :

(a) 1 (b) 0

(c) −1 (d) None of these

97. $\lim\limits_{x\to 0} \dfrac{x}{\tan^{-1} 2x}$ is equal to :

(a) $\dfrac{1}{2}$ (b) ∞

(c) 0 (d) 1

98. $\lim\limits_{x\to\pi/3} \dfrac{\sin\left(\dfrac{\pi}{3}-x\right)}{2\cos x - 1}$ is equal to :

(a) $\dfrac{2}{\sqrt{3}}$ (b) $\dfrac{1}{2}$

(c) $\dfrac{1}{\sqrt{3}}$ (d) $\sqrt{3}$

99. $\lim\limits_{x\to 0} \left[\left(3x+\dfrac{1}{x}\right)^2-\left(2x-\dfrac{1}{x}\right)^2\right]$ is equal to :

(a) 5 (b) 2

(c) 10 (d) 0

100. $\lim\limits_{x\to 0} \dfrac{\sin(\pi\cos^3 x)}{x^2}$ equals :

(a) $-\pi$ (b) π

(c) $\dfrac{\pi}{2}$ (d) 1

101. $\lim\limits_{x\to 0} \left[\sin^2\left(\dfrac{\pi}{2-ax}\right)\right]^{\sec^2\left(\frac{\pi}{2-bx}\right)}$ is equal to :

(a) e^{a^2/b^2} (b) e^{-a^2/b^2}

(c) e^{b^2/a^2} (d) e^{-b^2/a^2}

102. The value of $\lim\limits_{x\to 1} (\log_5 5x)^{\log_x 5}$ is :

(a) 1 (b) e

(c) −1 (d) None of these

103. $\lim\limits_{n\to\infty}(0\cdot 2)^{\log\sqrt{5}\left(\frac{1}{4}+\frac{1}{8}+\frac{1}{16}+\ldots\text{ to n terms}\right)}$ is equal to :

(a) 2 (b) 4

(c) 8 (d) 0

104. $\lim\limits_{n\to\infty} \dfrac{\cos x + \cos 3x + \cos 5x + \ldots + \cos(2n-1)x}{n}$

where $x\neq k\pi$, $k\in I$ is equal to :

(a) 1 (b) −1

(c) 0 (d) None of these

105. $\lim\limits_{x\to 2}\dfrac{2^x+2^{3-x}-6}{\sqrt{2^{-x}}-2^{1-x}} - \lim\limits_{x\to\frac{\pi}{3}}\dfrac{\tan^3 x - 3\tan x}{\cos\left(x+\dfrac{\pi}{6}\right)}$ is :

(a) less than e^3
(b) greater than e^3
(c) equal to e^3
(d) Does not exist

106. $\lim\limits_{h\to 0}\left[\dfrac{1}{h\cdot\sqrt[3]{8+h}} - \dfrac{1}{2h}\right]$ is equal to :

(a) $\dfrac{1}{12}$
(b) $-\dfrac{4}{3}$

(c) $-\dfrac{16}{3}$
(d) $-\dfrac{1}{48}$

107. $\lim\limits_{h\to 0}\dfrac{2\left[\sqrt{3}\sin\left(\dfrac{\pi}{6}+h\right)-\cos\left(\dfrac{\pi}{6}+h\right)\right]}{\sqrt{3}\,h\,(\sqrt{3}\cos h - \sin h)}$ is equal to

(a) $\dfrac{2}{3}$
(b) $\dfrac{4}{3}$

(c) $-2\sqrt{3}$
(d) $-\dfrac{4}{3}$

108. If $P_n = \dfrac{2^3-1}{2^3+1}\cdot\dfrac{3^3-1}{3^3+1}\cdot\dfrac{4^3-1}{4^3+1}\cdots\dfrac{n^3-1}{n^3+1}$, then $\lim\limits_{n\to\infty} P_n$ is equal to :

(a) $\dfrac{2}{3}$
(b) $-\dfrac{2}{3}$

(c) $\dfrac{3}{2}$
(d) None of these

109. If x is a real number in [0, 1], then the value of $f(x) = \lim\limits_{m\to\infty}\lim\limits_{n\to\infty}\{1+\cos^{2m}(n!\,\pi x)\}$ is given by :

(a) 2 or 1 according as x is rational or irrational
(b) 1 or 2 according as x is rational or irrational
(c) 1 for all x
(d) 2 or 1 for all x

110. The graph of the function y = f(x) has a unique tangent at the point (a, 0) through which the graph passes. Then $\lim\limits_{x\to a}\dfrac{\log_e\{1+6f(x)\}}{3f(x)}$ is :

(a) 1
(b) 0
(c) 2
(d) None of these

111. If $\lim\limits_{x\to a}\left[\dfrac{f(x)}{g(x)}\right]$ exists, then :

(a) $\lim\limits_{x\to a} f(x)$ must exist but $\lim\limits_{x\to a} g(x)$ need not exist

(b) both $\lim\limits_{x\to a} f(x)$ and $\lim\limits_{x\to a} g(x)$ need not exist
(c) $\lim\limits_{x\to a} f(x)$ need not exist but $\lim\limits_{x\to a} g(x)$ exists
(d) both $\lim\limits_{x\to a} f(x)$ and $\lim\limits_{x\to a} g(x)$ must exist.

112. The value of $\lim\limits_{x\to 0}\dfrac{(1-\cos 2x)\sin 5x}{x^2\sin 3x}$ is :

(a) 10/3
(b) 3/10
(c) 6/5
(d) 5/6

113. The value of $\lim\limits_{x\to 2}\dfrac{3^{x/2}-3}{3^x-9}$ is :

(a) 0
(b) 1/3
(c) 1/6
(d) *ln* 3

114. If $\lim\limits_{x\to 5}\dfrac{x^K-5^K}{x-5} = 500$, then the positive integral value of K is :

(a) 3
(b) 4
(c) 5
(d) 6

115. The value of $\lim\limits_{x\to\frac{\pi}{2}}\dfrac{\displaystyle\int_{\pi/2}^{x} t\,dt}{\sin(2x-\pi)}$ is :

(a) ∞
(b) $\dfrac{\pi}{2}$
(c) $\dfrac{\pi}{4}$
(d) $\dfrac{\pi}{8}$

116. If f(a) = 3, f '(a) = –2, g(a) = –1, g'(a) = 4, then $\lim\limits_{x\to a}\dfrac{g(x)\,f(a) - g(a)\,f(x)}{x-a} =$

(a) – 5
(b) 10
(c) – 10
(d) 5

117. $\lim\limits_{x\to\infty}\left(\sqrt{x^2+8x+3}-\sqrt{x^2+4x+3}\right) =$

(a) 0
(b) ∞
(c) 2
(d) $\dfrac{1}{2}$

118. $\lim\limits_{\theta\to\frac{\pi}{2}}\dfrac{1-\sin\theta}{\left(\dfrac{\pi}{2}-\theta\right)\cos\theta} =$

(a) 1
(b) – 1
(c) $-\dfrac{1}{2}$
(d) $\dfrac{1}{2}$

119. $\lim\limits_{x\to 0}\dfrac{\log(1+x)}{3^x-1} =$

(a) $\log_e 3$
(b) 0
(c) 1
(d) $\log_3 e$

120. If the function $f(x) = \begin{cases} \dfrac{\sin 3x}{x}, & x \neq 0 \\ \dfrac{K}{2}, & x = 0 \end{cases}$

is continuous at $x = 0$, then $K =$

(a) 3   (b) 6

(c) 9   (d) 12

121. The value of $f(0)$, so that

$$f(x) = \frac{(4^x - 1)^3}{\sin\left(\dfrac{x}{4}\right) \log\left(1 + \dfrac{x^2}{3}\right)}$$

is continuous everywhere, is :

(a) $3 (\log 4)^3$ (b) $4 (\log 4)^3$

(c) $12 (\log 4)^3$ (d) $15 (\log 4)^3$

122. If $[x]$ denotes the greatest integer $\leq x$, then

$$\lim_{n \to \infty} \frac{1}{n^3} \left\{ [1^2 x] + [2^2 x] + [3^2 x] + \ldots + [n^2 x] \right\}$$

equals :

(a) $x/2$ (b) $x/3$

(c) $x/6$ (d) 0

123. $\lim\limits_{n \to \frac{\pi}{2}} \dfrac{\left[\dfrac{x}{2}\right]}{\ln (\sin x)}$ (where $[\cdot]$ denotes the greatest integer function) :

(a) does not exist   (b) equals 1

(c) equals 0   (d) equals -1

124. The value of $\lim\limits_{x \to 0} \dfrac{(1 + x)^{1/x} - e + \dfrac{1}{2} ex}{x^2}$ is

(a) $\dfrac{11e}{24}$ (b) $-\dfrac{11e}{24}$

(c) $\dfrac{e}{24}$ (d) None of these

125. $\lim\limits_{x \to \infty} \sec^{-1}\left(\dfrac{x}{x + 1}\right)$:

(a) 0   (b) $\pi/2$

(c) π (d) Does not exist

126. $\lim\limits_{x \to 2} \left(\dfrac{\sqrt{1 - \cos\{2(x - 2)\}}}{x - 2} \right)$ **[AIEEE - 2011]**

(a) equals $\dfrac{1}{2}$ (b) does not exist

(c) equals $\sqrt{2}$ (d) equals $-\sqrt{2}$

127. Let $f : R \to R$ be a positive increasing function with $\lim\limits_{x \to \infty} \dfrac{f(3x)}{f(x)} = 1$. Then $\lim\limits_{x \to \infty} \dfrac{f(2x)}{f(x)} =$

[AIEEE - 2010]

(a) $\dfrac{2}{3}$ (b) $\dfrac{3}{2}$

(c) 3   (d) 1

128. Let α and β be the distinct roots of the equation $ax^2 + bx + c = 0$, then

$$\lim_{x \to \alpha} \frac{1 - \cos(ax^2 + bx + c)}{(x - \alpha)^2} \text{ is equal to :}$$

[AIEEE - 2005]

(a) $\dfrac{a^2}{2} (\alpha - \beta)^2$ (b) 0

(c) $-\dfrac{a^2}{2} (\alpha - \beta)^2$ (d) $\dfrac{1}{2}(\alpha - \beta)^2$

129. Let $P(x)$ be a polynomial of degree 4; having extremum at $x = 1, 2$ and $\lim\limits_{x \to 0} \left[1 + \dfrac{P(x)}{x^2} \right] = 2$. Then the value of $P(2)$ is

(a) 0   (b) 2

(c) 4   (d) 8

130. The minimum value of the sum of real numbers $a^{-5}, a^{-4}, 3a^{-3}, 1, a^8, a^{10}$, where $a > 0$ is

(a) 5   (b) 6

(c) 7   (d) 8

131. Let $f(x)$ be a polynomial of degree four having extreme values at $x = 1$ and $x = 2$.

If $\lim\limits_{x \to 0} \left[1 + \dfrac{f(x)}{x^2} \right] = 3$, then $f(2)$ is

(a) 0   (b) 4

(c) -8 (d) -4

132. Let [·] be the greatest integer function. If x is a positive real number, then the value of $\left[x + \dfrac{1}{x} \right]$ is

(a) greater than 2

(b) greater than or equal to 2

(c) sometimes less than 2

(d) greater than 1

ANSWER KEY

1. (a)	2. (a)	3. (c)	4. (b)	5. (b)	6. (a)	7. (d)	8. (b)	9. (a)	10. (c)
11. (b)	12. (a)	13. (a)	14. (d)	15. (b)	16. (a)	17. (b)	18. (a)	19. (b)	20. (c)
21. (d)	22. (c)	23. (a)	24. (c)	25. (b)	26. (a)	27. (b)	28. (a)	29. (c)	30. (b)
31. (b)	32. (a)	33. (a)	34. (d)	35. (a)	36. (c)	37. (c)	38. (b)	39. (a)	40. (b)
41. (d)	42. (c)	43. (a)	44. (a)	45. (c)	46. (b)	47. (a)	48. (a)	49. (b)	50. (d)
51. (d)	52. (a)	53. (c)	54. (b)	55. (c)	56. (b)	57. (a)	58. (b)	59. (d)	60. (b)
61. (b)	62. (b)	63. (c)	64. (a)	65. (b)	66. (c)	67. (b)	68. (a)	69. (c)	70. (b)
71. (a)	72. (a)	73. (b)	74. (b)	75. (d)	76. (c)	77. (c)	78. (b)	79. (d)	80. (a)
81. (b)	82. (a)	83. (a)	84. (a)	85. (b)	86. (c)	87. (d)	88. (a)	89. (a)	90. (c)
91. (b)	92. (b)	93. (a)	94. (a)	95. (c)	96. (b)	97. (a)	98. (c)	99. (c)	100. (b)
101. (b)	102. (b)	103. (b)	104. (c)	105. (b)	106. (d)	107. (b)	108. (a)	109. (a)	110. (c)
111. (d)	112. (a)	113. (c)	114. (b)	115. (c)	116. (b)	117. (c)	118. (d)	119. (d)	120. (b)
121. (c)	122. (b)	123. (c)	124. (a)	125. (b)	126. (b)	127. (d)	128. (a)	129. (a)	130. (d)
131. (a)	132. (b)								

Chapter 20

CONTINUITY AND DIFFERENTIABILITY

MULTIPLE CHOICE QUESTIONS

1. The interval where the function $\log(1 + x)$ is continuous, is :
   (a) $(0, \infty)$ (b) $(-\infty, -1)$
   (c) $(-1, \infty)$ (d) None of these

2. The set of points of discontinuity of the function $1/\log |x|$ is :
   (a) $\{-1, 0, 1\}$ (b) $\{0\}$
   (c) $\{0, 1\}$ (d) None of these

3. If $f(x) = \dfrac{1}{1-x}$, then the points of discontinuity of the function $f\ [f\{f(x)\}]$ are :
   (a) $\{0, -1\}$ (b) $\{0, 1\}$
   (c) $\{1, -1\}$ (d) None of these

4. The points of discontinuity of the function $f(x) = \lim\limits_{n\to\infty} (\sin x)^{2n}$, $n \in I$ are :
   (a) $n\pi$
   (b) $n\pi \pm \dfrac{\pi}{2}$
   (c) $n\pi \pm \dfrac{\pi}{4}$
   (d) continuous everywhere

5. The function $f(x) = x - [x]$, where $[x]$ denotes the greatest integer function,
   (a) is continuous everywhere.
   (b) is continuous at integral points only.
   (c) is continuous at non-integral points only.
   (d) None of these

6. The set of points of discontinuity of the function $f(x) = |\sin x|$ is :
   (a) $\{n\pi : n \in I\}$ (b) $\left\{(2n + 1)\dfrac{\pi}{2} ; n \in I\right\}$
   (c) ϕ (d) None of these

7. The set of points of discontinuity of the function $f(x) = \dfrac{|\sin x|}{\sin x}$ is
   (a) $\{0\}$ (b) $\{n\pi : n \in I\}$
   (c) ϕ (d) None of these

8. The function $f(x) = (\sin 2x)^{\tan^2 2x}$ is not defined at $x = \pi/4$. The value of $f(\pi/4)$ so that f is continuous at $x = \pi/4$ is :
   (a) $\sqrt{e}$ (b) $1/\sqrt{e}$
   (c) 2 (d) None of these

9. The points of discontinuity of the function
   $$f(x) = \begin{cases} 2\sqrt{x}, & 0 \le x \le 1 \\ 4 - 2x, & 1 < x < 2.5 \ \text{is (are)} \\ 2x - 7, & 2.5 \le x \le 4 \end{cases}$$
   (a) $x = 1, 2.5$ (b) $x = 2.5$
   (c) $x = 1, 2.5, 4$ (d) $x = 0, 4$

10. The point(s) of discontinuity of the function
    $$f(x) = \begin{cases} \dfrac{1}{5}(2x^2 + 3), & x \le 1 \\ 6 - 5x, & 1 < x < 3 \quad \text{is (are)} : \\ x - 3, & x \ge 3 \end{cases}$$
    (a) $x = 1$ (b) $x = 3$
    (c) $x = 1, 3$ (d) None of these

11. The function $f(x) = x - |x - x^2|$, $-1 \le x \le 1$ is continuous on the interval :
    (a) $[-1, 1]$ (b) $(-1, 1)$
    (c) $[-1, 1] \setminus \{0\}$ (d) $(-1, 1) \setminus \{0\}$

12. For the function $f(x) = \begin{cases} x - 1, & x < 0 \\ 1/4, & x = 0 \\ x^2, & x > 0 \end{cases}$
    $\lim\limits_{x\to0^+} f(x)$ and $\lim\limits_{x\to0^-} f(x)$ are :
    (a) $0, 1$ (b) $0, -1$
    (c) $1, -1$ (d) None of these

13. The function $f(x) \begin{cases} 2x + 3, & -3 < x < -2 \\ x + 1, & -2 \le x < 0 \\ x + 2, & 0 \le x < 1 \end{cases}$
    is continuous on the interval :
    (a) $(-3, 1)$ (b) $(-3, 1) \setminus \{-2, 0\}$
    (c) $(-3, 1) \setminus \{0\}$ (d) None of these

14. The function $f(x) = \begin{cases} \dfrac{x(e^{1/x} - e^{-1/x})}{e^{1/x} + e^{-1/x}}, & x \neq 0 \\ 0, & x = 0 \end{cases}$

is:

(a) continuous everywhere, but not differentiable at x=0.

(b) continuous and differentiable everywhere.

(c) not continuous at x = 0.

(d) None of these

15. If $f(x) = \sum_{n=0}^{\infty} \dfrac{x^n}{n!} (\log a)^n$, then at x = 0, f(x) :

(a) has no limit.

(b) is discontinuous.

(c) is continuous, but not differentiable.

(d) is differentiable.

16. If $f(x) = \dfrac{x}{1+x} + \dfrac{x}{(x+1)(2x+1)}$

$+ \dfrac{x}{(2x+1)(3x+1)} + \dots$ to ∞,

then at x = 0, f(x) :

(a) has no limit.

(b) is discontinuous.

(c) is continuous but not differentiable.

(d) is differentiable.

17. If $f(x) = x + \dfrac{x}{1+x} + \dfrac{x}{(1+x)^2} + \dots$ to ∞, then at

x = 0, f(x) :

(a) has no limit.

(b) is discontinuous.

(c) is continuous, but not differentiable.

(d) is differentiable.

18. The values of a, b and c which make the function

$f(x) = \begin{cases} \dfrac{\sin(a+1)x + \sin x}{x}, & x < 0 \\ c, & x = 0 \\ \dfrac{\sqrt{x + bx^2} - \sqrt{x}}{bx^{3/2}}, & x > 0 \end{cases}$

continuous at x = 0 are :

(a) $a = \dfrac{-3}{2}, c = \dfrac{1}{2}, b = 0$

(b) $a = \dfrac{3}{2}, c = \dfrac{1}{2}, b \neq 0$

(c) $a = \dfrac{-3}{2}, c = \dfrac{1}{2}, b \neq 0$

(d) None of these

19. The value of k which makes the function

$f(x) = \begin{cases} \dfrac{8^x - 4^x - 2^x + 1}{x^2}, & x > 0 \\ e^x \sin x + \pi x + k \log 2, & x \leq 0 \end{cases}$

continuous at x = 0, is

(a) 2 log 2 (b) log 2

(c) 3 log 2 (d) None of these

20. If $f(x) = \begin{cases} \dfrac{1 - \sin^2 x}{3 \cos^2 x}, & x < \dfrac{\pi}{2} \\ a, & x = \dfrac{\pi}{2} \\ \dfrac{b(1 - \sin x)}{(\pi - 2x)^2}, & x > \dfrac{\pi}{2} \end{cases}$.

Then f(x) is continuous at $x = \dfrac{\pi}{2}$, if :

(a) $a = \dfrac{1}{3}, b = 2$ (b) $a = \dfrac{1}{3}, b = \dfrac{8}{3}$

(c) $a = \dfrac{2}{3}, b = \dfrac{8}{3}$ (d) None of these

21. Let $f(x) = \begin{cases} x + a\sqrt{2} \sin x, & 0 \leq x \leq \dfrac{\pi}{4} \\ 2x \cot x + b, & \dfrac{\pi}{4} \leq x < \dfrac{\pi}{2} \\ a \cos 2x - b \sin x, & \dfrac{\pi}{2} \leq x \leq \pi \end{cases}$

If f(x) is continuous for $0 \leq x \leq \pi$, then :

(a) $a = \dfrac{\pi}{6}, b = \dfrac{\pi}{12}$ (b) $a = \dfrac{\pi}{6}, b = \dfrac{-\pi}{12}$

(c) $a = \dfrac{-\pi}{6}, b = \dfrac{\pi}{12}$ (d) $a = \dfrac{-\pi}{6}, b = \dfrac{-\pi}{12}$

22. Let a function $f : R \to R$ satisfy the equation $f(x + y) = f(x) + f(y)$ for all x, y. If the function f(x) is continuous at x = 0, then :

(a) f(x) = 0, continuous for all x.

(b) f(x) is continuous for all positive real x.

(c) f(x) is continuous for all x.

(d) None of these.

23. If f(x) is a continuous function and g(x) is discontinuous, then :

(a) f(x) + g(x) must be continuous.

(b) f(x) + g(x) must be discontinuous.

(c) f(x) = g(x) for all x.

(d) can't say.

24. If f(x) is continuous in [0, 1] and $f\left(\dfrac{1}{2}\right) = 2$, then

$\lim\limits_{n\to\infty} f\left(\dfrac{\sqrt{n}}{2\sqrt{n}+1}\right)$ is equal to :

(a) 0   (b) ∞

(c) 2   (d) None of these

25. Let f(x + y) = f(x) . f(y) for all x, y where f(0) ≠ 0. If f(5) = 2, and f'(0) = 3, then f'(5) is equal to :

(a) 6   (b) 0

(c) 1   (d) None of these

26. Let f(x + y) = f(x) . f(y) for all x, y where f(0) ≠ 0. If f'(0) = 2, then f(x) is equal to :

(a) Ae^x (b) Ae^{2x}

(c) 2x   (d) None of these

27. If a function f(x) is defined as

$f(x) = \begin{cases} -x, & x < 0 \\ x^2, & 0 \le x \le 1 \\ x^2 - x + 1, & x > 1 \end{cases}$ then :

(a) f(x) is differentiable at x = 0 and x = 1.

(b) f(x) is differentiable at x = 0 but not at x = 1.

(c) f(x) is differentiable at x = 1 but not at x = 0.

(d) f(x) is not differentiable at x = 0 and x = 1.

28. The function $f(x) = \dfrac{x}{1 + |x|}$ is :

(a) continuous for all x, but not differentiable at x = 0.

(b) continuous as well as differentiable for all x.

(c) neither continuous nor differentiable at x = 0.

(d) differentiable for all x, but not continuous at x = 0.

29. Let f(x) be defined in the interval [–2, 2] such that $f(x) = \begin{cases} -1, & -2 \le x \le 0 \\ x - 1, & 0 < x \le 2 \end{cases}$

and g(x) = f(|x|) + |f(x)|, then the function g(x) is differentiable in the interval :

(a) [–2, 2]   (b) [–2, 2] \ {0}

(c) [–2, 2] \ {1}   (d) [–2, 2] \ {0, 1}

30. If $f(x) = \begin{cases} x^2/2, & 0 \le x < 1 \\ 2x^2 - 3x + \dfrac{3}{2}, & 1 \le x \le 2 \end{cases}$, then

(a) f, f' and f" are continuous in [0, 2].

(b) f and f' are continuous in [0, 2], whereas f" is continuous in [0, 2] \ {1}.

(c) f, f' and f" are continuous in [0, 2] \ {1}.

(d) None of these.

31. If $f(x) = \begin{cases} \dfrac{1 - \cos x}{x \sin x}, & x \neq 0 \\ \dfrac{1}{2}, & x = 0 \end{cases}$ then f(x) is :

(a) differentiable as well as continuous at x = 0.

(b) differentiable but not continuous at x = 0.

(c) continuous but not differentiable at x = 0.

(d) neither continuous nor differentiable at x = 0.

32. If f(x) = [x – 2], then :

(a) $f'(2.5) = \dfrac{1}{2}$ and f'(5) = 3

(b) f'(2.5) = 0 and f'(5) = 3

(c) f'(2.5) = 0 and f'(5) does not exist.

(d) both f'(2.5) and f'(5) do not exist.

33. If f(x) = |x² – 5x + 6|, then :

(a) f'(2) = –1 and f'(3) = 1

(b) f'(2) = –1 and f'(3) does not exist

(c) f'(2) does not exist and f'(3) = 1

(d) both f'(2) and f'(3) do not exist

34. The function $f(x) = \sin^{-1}(\cos x)$ is :

(a) continuous as well as differentiable at

$x = n\pi + \dfrac{\pi}{2}$, $n \in I$

(b) continuous but not differentiable at

$x = n\pi + \dfrac{\pi}{2}$, $n \in I$

(c) differentiable but not continuous at

$x = n\pi + \dfrac{\pi}{2}$, $n \in I$

(d) neither differentiable nor continuous at

$x = n\pi + \dfrac{\pi}{2}$, $n \in I$

35. The function $f(x) = |\cos x|$ is :

(a) differentiable as well as continuous at

$x = n\pi + \dfrac{\pi}{2}$, $n \in I$

(b) continuous but not differentiable at

$x = n\pi + \dfrac{\pi}{2}$, $n \in I$

(c) differentiable but not continuous at

$x = n\pi + \dfrac{\pi}{2}$, $n \in I$

(d) neither differentiable nor continuous at

$x = n\pi + \dfrac{\pi}{2}$, $n \in I$

36. If $f(x) = \sqrt{1 - \sqrt{1 - x^2}}$, then at $x = 0$,

(a) $f(x)$ is differentiable as well as continuous.

(b) $f(x)$ is differentiable but not continuous.

(c) $f(x)$ is continuous but not differentiable.

(d) $f(x)$ is neither continuous nor differentiable.

37. If $f(x) = \sqrt{1 - e^{-x^2}}$, then at $x = 0$, $f(x)$ is :

(a) differentiable as well as continuous.

(b) continuous but not differentiable.

(c) differentiable but not continuous.

(d) neither differentiable nor continuous.

38. If $f(x) = \begin{cases} x^p \cos \dfrac{1}{x}, & x \neq 0 \\ 0, & x = 0 \end{cases}$, then at $x = 0$, $f(x)$

is :

(a) continuous if $p > 0$ & differentiable if $p > 1$.

(b) continuous if $p > 1$ & differentiable if $p > 0$.

(c) continuous and differentiable if $p > 0$.

(d) None of these.

39. The value of the derivative of $|x - 1| + |x - 3|$ at $x = 2$ is :

(a) -2 (b) 0

(c) 2 (d) Not defined

40. The points where the function $f(x) = [x] + |1 - x|$, $1 \le x \le 3$, where [.] denotes the greatest integer function, is not differentiable, are :

(a) $x = -1, 0, 1, 2, 3$ (b) $x = -1, 0, 2$

(c) $x = 0, 1, 2, 3$ (d) $x = -1, 0, 1, 2$

41. If $f(x) = \begin{cases} \dfrac{1}{2}(b^2 - a^2), & 0 \le x \le a, \\ \dfrac{1}{2}b^2 - \dfrac{x^2}{6} - \dfrac{a^2}{3x}, & a < x \le b \\ \dfrac{1}{3}\left(\dfrac{b^2 - a^2}{x}\right), & x > b \end{cases}$, then :

(a) both f and f' are continuous at $x = a$ and $x = b$.

(b) f is continuous but f' is not continuous at $x = a$ and $x = b$.

(c) f' is continuous but f is not continuous at $x = a$ and $x = b$.

(d) Both f and f' are not continuous at $x = a$ and $x = b$.

42. If $f(x) = \begin{cases} 3, & x < 0 \\ 2x + 1, & x \ge 0 \end{cases}$, then :

(a) both $f(x)$ and $f(|x|)$ are differentiable at $x = 0$.

(b) $f(x)$ is differentiable but $f(|x|)$ is not differentiable at $x = 0$.

(c) $f(|x|)$ is differentiable but $f(x)$ is not differentiable at $x = 0$.

(d) both $f(x)$ and $f(|x|)$ are not differentiable at $x = 0$

43. If $f(x) = \begin{cases} |2x - 3|\,[x], & x \ge 1 \\ \sin \dfrac{\pi x}{2}, & x < 1 \end{cases}$, then $f(x)$ is :

(a) differentiable as well as continuous in $[0, 2]$.

(b) continuous but not differentiable in $[0, 2]$.

(c) differentiable but not continuous in $[0, 2]$.

(d) neither differentiable nor continuous in $[0, 2]$.

44. If $f(x) = \begin{cases} 4, & -3 < x < -1 \\ 5+x, & -1 \le x < 0 \\ 5-x, & 0 \le x < 2 \\ x^2 + x - 3, & 2 \le x < 3 \end{cases}$, then f|x|

is :

(a) differentiable but not continuous in $(-3, 3)$.

(b) continuous but not differentiable in $(-3, 3)$.

(c) continuous as well as differentiable in $(-3, 3)$.

(d) neither continuous nor differentiable in $(-3, 3)$.

45. If $f(x + y) = 2 \; f(x).f(y)$ for all x, y, where $f'(0) = 3$ and $f(4) = 2$, then $f'(4)$ is equal to :

(a) 6   (b) 12

(c) 4   (d) None of these

46. If a function $f : R \rightarrow R$ is such that

$f(x + y) = f(x) . f(y)$ for all $x, y \in R$

where $f(x) = 1 + x \; \phi(x)$ and $\lim_{x \to 0} \phi(x) = 1$, then :

(a) $f'(x)$ does not exist.

(b) $f'(x) = 2f(x)$ for all x.

(c) $f'(x) = f(x)$ for all x.

(d) None of these

47. If f is a periodic function, then :

(a) f' and f'' are also periodic.

(b) f' is periodic but f'' is not periodic.

(c) f'' is periodic but f' is not periodic.

(d) None of these

48. If sgn. $f(x) = \begin{cases} \dfrac{|x|}{x}, & x \ne 0 \\ 0, & x = 0 \end{cases}$, then the function

$f(x) = sgn \; (sgn \; (x))$ is :

(a) continuous as well as differentiable at $x = 0$

(b) continuous but not differentiable at $x = 0$

(c) differentiable but not continuous at $x = 0$

(d) neither differentiable nor continuous at $x = 0$

49. If $f(x) = -1 + |x - 1|, -1 \le x \le 3$

and $g(x) = 2 - |x + 1|, -2 \le x \le 2$, then :

(a) fog is differentiable at $x = -1$ and gof is differentiable at $x = 1$.

(b) fog is differentiable at $x = -1$ and gof is not differentiable at $x = 1$.

(c) gof is differentiable at $x = 1$ and fog is differentiable at $x = -1$.

(d) None of these

50. If $f(x) = |x - 2|$ and $g(x) = f[f(x)]$, then $g'(x)$ for $x > 20$ is :

(a) 1   (b) 2

(c) -1   (d) None of these

51. If the function $y = f(x)$ is defined as $x = 2t - |t|$,

$y = t^2 + t|t|, t \in R$, then $f(x)$ is :

(a) continuous as well as differentiable in the interval $[-1, 1]$.

(b) continuous but not differentiable in the interval $[-1, 1]$.

(c) differentiable but not continuous in the interval $[-1, 1]$.

(d) None of these

52. Let $f(x) = x^3 - x^2 + x + 1$ and

$g(x) = \begin{cases} \max. \{f(t), 0 \le t \le x\}, & 0 \le x \le 1 \\ 3 - x, & 1 < x \le 2 \end{cases}$,

then $g(x)$ is :

(a) continuous as well as differentiable in $[0, 2]$.

(b) continuous but not differentiable in $[0, 2]$.

(c) differentiable but not continuous in $[0, 2]$.

(d) None of these

53. If $f(x) = |\cos x - \sin x|$, then $f'\left(\dfrac{\pi}{4}\right)$ is equal to :

(a) $\sqrt{2}$ (b) $-\sqrt{2}$

(c) 0   (d) None of these

54. If $f(x) = \begin{cases} \dfrac{1 - \cos 10x}{x^2}, & x < 0 \\ a, & x = 0 \\ \dfrac{\sqrt{x}}{\sqrt{625 + \sqrt{x}} - 25}, & x > 0 \end{cases}$, then

the value of a so that f(x) may be continuous at x = 0 is :

(a) 25   (b) 50

(c) –25   (d) None of these

55. If the function f(x) defined by

$$f(x) = \begin{cases} \dfrac{\log(1 + 3x) - \log(1 - 2x)}{x}, & x \neq 0 \\ a, & x = 0 \end{cases}$$

is continuous at x = 0, then the value of a is :

(a) 5   (b) 1

(c) –1   (d) None of these

56. If $f(x) = \int_0^x t \cos \dfrac{1}{t} \, dt$, then the number of points

of discontinuity of f(x) in the interval (0, π) is :

(a) 1   (b) 2

(c) 0   (d) None of these

57. If $f(x) = \log_{10} x$, then at x = 1

(a) f(x) is continuous as well as differentiable.

(b) f(x) is continuous but not differentiable.

(c) f(x) is differentiable but not continuous.

(d) f(x) is neither continuous nor differentiable.

58. Let f be a function defined and continuous on [2, 5]. If f(x) takes rational values for all x and f(4) = 8, then the value of f(3·7) is :

(a) 0   (b) 8

(c) –1   (d) None of these

59. Let $f(x) = \cos x$ and $g(x) = [x + 2]$, where [.] denotes the greatest integer function. Then $(gof)'\left(\dfrac{\pi}{2}\right)$ is :

(a) 1   (b) 0

(c) –1   (d) does not exist

60. Let $f(x) = |x|$ and $g(x) = [x]$, where [.] denotes the greatest integer function. Then (fog)' (–2) is :

(a) 0   (b) does not exist

(c) –1   (d) 1

61. The set of points where the function $f(x) = |x-2| \cos x$ is differentiable, is :

(a) $(-\infty, \infty)$ (b) $(-\infty, \infty) \setminus \{2\}$

(c) $(0, \infty)$ (d) None of these

62. $f(x) = \begin{cases} (x-2)^2 \sin \dfrac{1}{x-2} - |x-1|, & x \neq 2 \\ -1, & x = 2 \end{cases}$,

then the set of points where f(x) is differentiable, is :

(a) R   (b) $R \setminus \{1, 2\}$

(c) $R \setminus \{1\}$ (d) $R \setminus \{2\}$

63. Let $f(x) = \begin{cases} \dfrac{\sin(\cos x) - \cos x}{(\pi - 2x)^2}, & x \neq \dfrac{\pi}{2} \\ k, & x = \dfrac{\pi}{2} \end{cases}$

is continuous at $x = \dfrac{\pi}{2}$, then k is equal to :

(a) 0   (b) 1/2

(c) 1   (d) –1

64. The value of f(0) so that the function

$$f(x) = \dfrac{(256 - 8x)^{1/4} - 4}{16 - 4(64 - 3x)^{1/3}} \quad (x \neq 0)$$

may be continuous everywhere is given by :

(a) –1/8   (b) 1/8

(c) 1/64   (d) None of these

65. If $f(x) = \begin{cases} ax^2 + b, & 0 \leq x < 1 \\ x + 3, & 1 < x \leq 2 \\ 4, & x = 1 \end{cases}$ then the value

of (a, b) for which f(x) cannot be continuous at x = 1 is :

(a) (2, 2)   (b) (3, 1)

(c) (4, 0)   (d) (5, 2)

66. If $4x + 3|y| = 5y$, then y as a function of x is :

(a) differentiable at x = 0

(b) continuous at x = 0

(c) $\dfrac{dy}{dx} = 2$ for all x

(d) None of these

67. The function $\dfrac{\sin{(\pi \, [x - \pi])}}{4 + [x]^2}$, where [.] denotes the greatest integer function, is :

(a) continuous as well as differentiable for all x.

(b) continuous for all x but not differentiable at some x.

(c) differentiable for all x but not continuous at some x.

(d) None of these

68. Let f(x) be a function defined on the interval [3, 6] as $f(x) = \begin{cases} \log_e \, [x], & 3 \le x < 5 \\ |\log_e x|, & 5 \le x < 6 \end{cases}$, then f(x) is :

(a) continuous as well as differentiable in [3, 6].

(b) continuous in [3, 6) but not differentiable at x = 4, 5.

(c) differentiable in [3, 6) but not continuous at x = 4, 5.

(d) None of these

69. Let f(s + t) f(s) + a st + 3s² t² for all s, t ∈ R (a is a fixed constant). If f(3) = 4 and f(5) = 52, then :

(a) f ' (x) = 10x
(b) f ' (x) = –10x
(c) f(x) = 10x
(d) None of these

70. Let f(x) be a function satisfying

f(x + y) = f(x) f(y) for all, x, y ∈ R.

If f(x) = 1 + x ϕ (x) + x² ϕ (x) ψ (x),

where $\lim\limits_{x \to 0} \phi(x) = a$ and $\lim\limits_{x \to 0} \psi(x) = b$,

then f ' (x) is equal to :

(a) (a + b) f(x)
(b) af(x)
(c) bf(x)
(d) None of these

71. The value of f(0) so that the function

$f(x) = \dfrac{\sqrt[3]{1 + x} - \sqrt[4]{1 + x}}{x}$ becomes continuous

at x = 0, is :

(a) $\dfrac{1}{12}$
(b) $\dfrac{7}{12}$
(c) 0
(d) None of these

72. Let f(x) be defined for all x > 0 and be continuous. Let f(x) satisfy $f\left(\dfrac{x}{y}\right) = f(x) - f(y)$ for all x, y and f(e) = 1. Then :

(a) f(x) is bounded

(b) $f\left(\dfrac{1}{x}\right) \to 0$ as x → 0

(c) xf(x) → 1 as x → 0

(d) f(x) = *ln* x

73. Let f be a function satisfying f(x + y) = f(x) + f(y) and f(x) = x³ ϕ (x) for x and y, where ϕ (x) is a continuous function then f ' (x) is equal to :

(a) g(0)
(b) g' (x)
(c) 0
(d) None of these

74. If f(x) = [x] $\sin\left(\dfrac{\pi}{[x + 1]}\right)$, where [.] denotes the greatest integer function, then the points of discontinuity of f in the domain are :

(a) Z
(b) Z\{0}
(c) R\[–1, 0)
(d) None of these

75. If f(x) = $\cos^{-1}\left(\dfrac{2x}{1 + x^2}\right)$, then f(x) is differentiable on :

(a) (– ∞, ∞)
(b) (– ∞, ∞) \ {0}
(c) (– ∞, ∞) \ {–1, 1}
(d) None of these

76. Let f(x + y) = f(x) . f(y) for all x, y ∈ R and

f(x) = 1 + xϕ (x) log 2 where $\lim\limits_{x \to 0} \phi(x) = 1$. Then

f ' (x) is equal to :

(a) log $2^{f(x)}$
(b) log [f(x)]²
(c) log 2
(d) None of these

77. The function f(x) = $\tan \dfrac{1}{x - 5}$ has :

(a) discontinuity of the first kind at x = 5.

(b) discontinuity of the second kind at x = 5.

(c) removable discontinuity at x = 5.

(d) continuous at x = 5.

78. The values of x for which the function

$$f(x) = \begin{cases} 1 - x, & x < 1 \\ (1 - x)(2 - x), & 1 \le x \le 2 \\ 3 - x, & x > 2 \end{cases}$$

fails to be continuous or differentiable are :

(a) x = 1   (b) x = 2

(c) x = 1 and x = 2   (d) None of these

79. The set of points of continuity of the function

$$f(x) = \sqrt{\frac{1}{2} \cos x} \text{ is :}$$

(a) $\left\{ x : \frac{\pi}{4} + 2n\pi \le x \le \frac{3\pi}{4} + 2n\pi, \, n \in I \right\}$

(b) $\left\{ x : \frac{5\pi}{4} + 2n\pi \le x \le \frac{7\pi}{4} + 2n\pi, \, n \in I \right\}$

(c) $\left\{ x : \frac{\pi}{4} + 2n\pi \le x \le \frac{3\pi}{4} + 2n\pi \right\}$

$$\cup \left\{ x : \frac{5\pi}{4} + 2n\pi \le x \le \frac{7\pi}{4} + 2n\pi \right\}$$

(d) None of these

80. Let f(x) be a continuous function defined for $1 \le x \le 3$. If f(x) takes rational values for all x and f(2) = 10, then f(1.5) is equal to :

(a) 0   (b) 10

(c) not defined   (d) any constant

81. The function $f(x) = \frac{1}{u^2 + u - 2}$, where $u = \frac{1}{x - 1}$, is discontinuous at the points :

(a) $x = -2, 1, \frac{1}{2}$ (b) $x = \frac{1}{2}, 1, 2$

(c) x = 1, 0   (d) None of these

82. If $f(x) = \begin{cases} \dfrac{x(3e^{1/x} + 4)}{2 - e^{1/x}}, & x \ne 0 \\ 0, & x = 0 \end{cases}$, then f(x) is :

(a) continuous as well as differentiable at x = 0.

(b) continuous but not differentiable at x = 0.

(c) differentiable but not continuous at x = 0.

(d) None of these

83. If the function f is defined by y = f(x), where $x = 2t - |t|, y = t^2 + t | t |, t \in R$, then :

(a) f(x) is differentiable as well as continuous at x = 0.

(b) f(x) is continuous but not differentiable at x = 0.

(c) f(x) is differentiable but not continuous at x = 0.

(d) None of these

84. If $f(x) = \begin{cases} 3^x, & -1 \le x \le 1 \\ 4 - x, & 1 < x \le 4 \end{cases}$,then :

(a) f(x) is continuous as well as differentiable at x = 1.

(b) f(x) is continuous but not differentiable at x = 1.

(c) f(x) differentiable but not continuous at x = 1.

(d) None of these

85. If $f(x) = \begin{cases} x^3, & x^2 < 1 \\ x, & x^2 \ge 1 \end{cases}$, then f(x) is :

(a) continuous as well as differentiable at x = 1.

(b) differentiable but not continuous at x = 1.

(c) continuous but not differentiable at x = 1.

(d) None of these

86. Let f(x) be a function satisfying the condition f(−x) = f(x), for all real x. If f ' (0) exists, then its value is :

(a) 0   (b) 1

(c) −1   (d) None of these

87. The value of the constants a, b and c for which

$$\text{the function } f(x) = \begin{cases} (1 + ax)^{1/x}, & x < 0 \\ b, & x = 0 \\ \dfrac{(x + c)^{1/3} - 1}{(x + 1)^{1/2} - 1}, & x > 0 \end{cases}$$

may be continuous at x = 0, are :

(a) $a = \log \frac{2}{3}, b = \frac{-2}{3}, c = 1$

(b) $a = \log \frac{2}{3}, b = \frac{2}{3}, c = -1$

(c) $a = \log \frac{2}{3}, b = \frac{2}{3}, c = 1$

(d) None of these

88. If $f(x) = \begin{cases} \dfrac{x}{1+|x|}, & |x| \ge 1 \\ \dfrac{x}{1-|x|}, & |x| < 1 \end{cases}$, then $f(x)$ is :

(a) discontinuous and non-differentiable at $x = -1, 1$ and 0.

(b) discontinuous and non-differentiable at $x = -1$, whereas continuous and differentiable at $x = 0$ and $x = 1$.

(c) discontinuous and non-differentiable at $x = -1$ and $x = 1$, whereas continuous and differentiable at $x = 0$.

(d) None of these

89. The function $f(x) = [x]^2 - [x^2]$ (where [y] is the greatest integer less than or equal to y), is discontinuous at :

(a) all integers

(b) all integers except 0 and 1

(c) all integers except 0

(d) all integers except 1

90. The function $f(x) = (x^2 - 1)|x^2 - 3x + 2| + \cos(|x|)$ is not differentiable at $x =$

(a) -1 (b) 0

(c) 1 (d) 2

91. Let $f : R \to R$ be any function. Define $g : R \to R$ by $g(x) = |f(x)|$ for all x. Then g is :

(a) onto if f is onto.

(b) one-one if f is one-one.

(c) continuous if f is continuous.

(d) differentiable if f is differentiable.

92. Let $f\left(\dfrac{x+y}{2}\right) = \dfrac{f(x) + f(y)}{2}$ for all real values x and y. If $f'(0)$ exists and equals -1 and $f(0) = 1$, then $f'(2) =$

(a) -1 (b) 1

(c) 0 (d) None of these

93. Let $f : R \to R$ be a differentiable function and $f(1) = 4$. Then the value of $\displaystyle\lim_{x \to 1} \int_{4}^{f(x)} \dfrac{2t}{x-1} dt$ is :

(a) $8 f'(1)$ (b) $4 f'(1)$

(c) $2 f'(1)$ (d) $f'(1)$

94. The function $f(x) = \begin{cases} |x - 3|, & x \ge 1 \\ \dfrac{x^2}{4} - \dfrac{3x}{2} + \dfrac{13}{4}, & x < 1 \end{cases}$ is :

(a) continuous at $x = 1$ but not derivable at $x = 1$.

(b) continuous and derivable at $x = 1$.

(c) not derivable at $x = 1$.

(d) not continuous at $x = 1$.

95. Let $f(x + y) = f(x) \cdot f(y)$ and $f(x) = 1 + x\, g(x)\, G(x)$ where $\displaystyle\lim_{x \to 0} g(x) = a$ and $\displaystyle\lim_{x \to 0} G(x) = b$. Then $f'(x) = k\, f(x)$, where k is equal to :

(a) $\dfrac{a}{b}$ (b) $1 + ab$

(c) ab (d) None of these

96. If $x + 4|y| = 6y$, then y as a function of x is :

(a) not continuous at $x = 0$.

(b) not defined for all real x.

(c) $\dfrac{dy}{dx} = \dfrac{1}{2}$ for $x > 0$

(d) derivable at $x = 0$

97. Let $f(x) = \begin{cases} \dfrac{\sqrt{1+px} - \sqrt{1-px}}{x}, & -1 \le x < 0 \\ \dfrac{2x+1}{x-2}, & 0 \le x \le 1 \end{cases}$

If $f(x)$ is continuous in the interval $[-1, 1]$ then p equals :

(a) $\dfrac{1}{2}$ (b) $-\dfrac{1}{2}$

(c) -1 (d) 1

98. Let $f(x) = \begin{cases} ax^2 + 1, & x > 1 \\ x + a, & x \le 1 \end{cases}$. Then $f(x)$ is derivable at $x = 1$, if :

(a) $a = 2$ (b) $a = 1$

(c) $a = 0$ (d) $a = \dfrac{1}{2}$

99. The function $f(x) = \dfrac{x^3 + x^2 - 16x + 20}{x - 2}$ is not defined for $x = 2$. In order to make $f(x)$ continuous at $x = 2$, $f(2)$ should be defined as :

(a) 0 (b) 1

(c) 2 (d) 3

100. Let f and g be differentiable functions satisfying g'(a) = 2, g(a) = b and fog = I (identity function). Then f'(b) is equal to :

(a) 2

(b) $\frac{2}{3}$

(c) $\frac{1}{2}$

(d) None of these

101. If $f(x) = \begin{cases} x^3 \sin\frac{1}{x}, & x \neq 0 \\ 0, & x = 0 \end{cases}$, then :

(a) f(x) is differentiable only once everywhere and f'(x) is a discontinuous function.

(b) f(x) is not differentiable everywhere.

(c) f(x) is two times differentiable everywhere.

(d) f(x) is differentiable only once everywhere f'(x) is continuous everywhere.

102. Let $f(x) = \begin{cases} 1, & x \leq -1 \\ |x|, & -1 < x < 1 \\ 0, & x \geq 1 \end{cases}$, then :

(a) f is continuous at x = -1.

(b) f is differentiable at x = -1.

(c) f is continuous everywhere.

(d) f is differentiable for all x.

103. The value of b for which the function

$f(x) = \begin{cases} 5x - 4 & \text{if } 0 < x \leq 1 \\ 4x^2 + 3bx & \text{if } 1 < x < 2 \end{cases}$

is continuous at every point of its domain, is :

(a) $\frac{13}{3}$

(b) 1

(c) 0

(d) -1

104. If $f(x) = x \sin\frac{1}{x}$, x ≠ 0, then the value of the function at x = 0, so that the function is continuous at x = 0, is :

(a) 0

(b) -1

(c) 1

(d) indeterminate

105. The number of points at which the function $f(x) = \frac{1}{\log|x|}$ discontinuous, is :

(a) 4

(b) 3

(c) 2

(d) 1

106. If $\lim_{x \to a^+} f(x) = l = \lim_{x \to a^-} g(x)$ and $\lim_{x \to a^-} f(x) = m = \lim_{x \to a^+} g(x)$, then the function f(x) . g(x) :

(a) is not continuous at x = a.

(b) has a limit when x → a and it is equal to *lm*.

(c) is continuous at x = a.

(d) has a limit when x → a but it is not equal to *lm*.

107. If $f(x) = \begin{cases} \frac{1}{1 + e^{1/x}}, & x \neq 0 \\ 0, & x = 0 \end{cases}$ then f(x) is :

(a) continuous as well as differentiable at x = 0.

(b) continuous but not differentiable at x = 0.

(c) differentiable but not continuous at x = 0.

(d) None of these.

108. If $f(x) = \begin{cases} \frac{e^{1/x} - 1}{e^{1/x} + 1}, & x \neq 0 \\ 0, & x = 0 \end{cases}$, then f(x) is :

(a) continuous as well as differentiable at x = 0.

(b) continuous but not differentiable at x = 0.

(c) differentiable but not continuous at x = 0.

(d) None of these

109. If $g(x) = (x^2 + 2x + 3) f(x)$, f(0) = 5 and $\lim_{x \to 0} \frac{f(x) - 5}{x} = 4$, then g'(0) is equal to :

(a) 22

(b) 20

(c) 18

(d) None of these

110. Let f : R → R be a function defined by f(x) = max {x, x³}. The set of all points where f(x) is not differentiable is :

(a) {-1, 1}

(b) {-1, 0}

(c) {0, 1}

(d) {-1, 0, 1}

111. The function $f(x) = [x] \cos\left(\frac{2x - 1}{2}\right)\pi$, where [.] denotes the greatest integer function, is discontinuous at :

(a) all x

(b) all integer points

(c) no x

(d) x which is not an integer

112. If $f(x) = \lim_{x \to \infty} \left(\sin \dfrac{\pi x}{2} \right)^{2n}$, then the set of points where $f(x)$ is discontinuous, is :

(a) $\{ x \mid x = n, n \in I \}$

(b) $\{ x \mid x = 2n, n \in I \}$

(c) $\{ x \mid x = (2n + 1), n \in I \}$

(d) None of these

113. Let $f(x + y) = f(x) + f(y)$ for all x, y. If $f(x)$ is continuous at $x = 0$, then :

(a) $f(x)$ is continuous for all x.

(b) $f(x)$ is continuous only at finite values of x.

(c) $f(x)$ is discontinuous only at finite values of x.

(d) None of these

114. If $g(x) = \begin{cases} \dfrac{1 - a^x + xa^x \log a}{x^2 \cdot a^x}, & x < 0 \\ \dfrac{(2a)^x - x \log (2a) - 1}{x^2}, & x > 0 \end{cases}$

(where $a > 0$) then the values of a and $g(0)$ so that $g(x)$ is continuous at $x = 0$, are :

(a) $a = \sqrt{2}, g(0) = \dfrac{1}{8} (\log 2)^2$

(b) $a = \dfrac{1}{\sqrt{2}}, g(0) = \dfrac{1}{8} (\log 2)^2$

(c) $a = \dfrac{1}{\sqrt{2}}, g(0) = \dfrac{1}{8} (\log 2)$

(d) None of these

115. The points at which $f(x) = \cos^{-1} \left(\dfrac{x + 1}{2} \right)$ has no finite derivative are :

(a) $x = -3, 2$ (b) $x = -3, 3$

(c) $x = -3, 1$ (d) None of these

116. If $f(x)$ is a continuous function in [2, 3] which takes only irrational values for all $x \in [2, 3]$ and $f(2.5) = \sqrt{5}$ then $f(2.8) =$

(a) 0   (b) $-\sqrt{5}$

(c) $\sqrt{5}$ (d) None of these

117. Let $f(x) = [x]$, $g(x) = \mid x \mid$ and $f[g(x)] = h(x)$, where [.] is the greatest integer function. Then $h'(-1)$ is :

(a) 0   (b) $-\infty$

(c) Non existent   (d) None of these

118. Let $f(x + y) = f(x) - f(y) + 2xy - 1$ for all x, y $\in$ R. If $f(x)$ is differentiable and $f'(0) = \sqrt{3 + a - a^2}$ then :

(a) $f(x) = 0 \ \forall \ x \in R$

(b) $f(x) > 0 \ \forall \ x \in R$

(c) $f(x) < 0 \ \forall \ x \in R$

(d) $f(x) = $ constant $\forall \ x \in R$

119. Let $f(x) = \begin{cases} \dfrac{a + 3 \cos x}{x^2}, & x < 0 \\ b \tan \left(\dfrac{\pi}{[x + 3]} \right), & x \geq 0 \end{cases}$

where [.] represents the greatest integer function. The values of a and b such that $f(x)$ is continuous at $x = 0$, are :

(a) $a = -3, b = \dfrac{\sqrt{3}}{2}$ (b) $a = -3, b = -\dfrac{\sqrt{3}}{2}$

(c) $a = 3, b = \dfrac{-\sqrt{3}}{2}$ (d) None of these

120. The value of $f(0)$ so that the function

$f(x) = \dfrac{2 - (256 - 5x)^{1/8}}{(5x + 32)^{1/5} - 2}$ $(x \neq 0)$

is continuous everywhere, is given by :

(a) -1 (b) 1

(c) 2^6 (d) None of these

121. Let $f(x) = \max \{ x, 2 - x \}$ for all $x \in R$. Then :

(a) $f(x)$ is not continuous everywhere

(b) $f(x)$ is differentiable everywhere

(c) $f(x)$ is continuous at $x = 1$ but not differentiable there

(d) $f(x)$ is neither continuous nor differentiable at $x = 1$

122. If for a continuous function $f(0) = f(1) = 0$, $f'(1) = 2$ and $y(x) = f(e^x) e^{f(x)}$, then $y'(0)$ is equal to :

(a) 1   (b) 2

(c) 0   (d) None of these

123. If $f(x)$ is differentiable, where $f(2) = 3$ and $f(a)\,f(b) = f(a) + f(b) + 3$, then $f\,'(5)$ is :

(a) 17   (b) 26

(c) 3   (d) None of these

124. If $f(x) = x\,(\sqrt{x} - \sqrt{x+1})$ then :

(a) $f(x)$ is continuous but not differentiable at $x = 0$

(b) $f(x)$ is differentiable at $x = 0$

(c) $f(x)$ is not differentiable at $x = 0$

(d) None of these

125. Let $f : R \to R$ be a function such that

$f\left(\dfrac{x+y}{3}\right) = \dfrac{f(x) + f(y)}{3}$, $f(0) = 0$

and $f\,'(0) = 3$, then :

(a) $f(x)$ is a quadratic function

(b) $f(x)$ is continuous but not differentiable

(c) $f(x)$ is differentiable in R

(d) $f(x)$ is bounded in R

126. If f is a differentiable function satisfying $f(0) = 0$, and if $g(x) = \dfrac{f(x)}{x}$, then the value, that should be assigned to $g(0)$, so that g is continuous at '0' is :

(a) 1   (b) 0

(c) $f(0)$ (d) $f\,'(0)$

127. The value of b for which the function

$f(x) = \begin{cases} 5x - 4, & 0 < x \le 1 \\ 4x^2 + 3bx, & 1 < x < 2 \end{cases}$

is continuous at every point of its domain, is :

(a) −1   (b) 0

(c) $\dfrac{13}{3}$ (d) 1

128. If $f(x) = \begin{cases} x \sin\dfrac{1}{x}, & x \ne 0 \\ 0, & x = 0 \end{cases}$ then at $x = 0$, the function $f(x)$ is :

(a) differentiable.

(b) not differentiable.

(c) continuous but not differentiable.

(d) None of these

129. If $f(x) = |x - 3|$, then $f\,'(3)$ is :

(a) −1   (b) 1

(c) 0   (d) Does not exist

130. The function $f(x) = \dfrac{\sin 3x}{x}$, $x \ne 0$

$= \dfrac{k}{2}$, $x = 0$

is continuous at $x = 0$, then $k =$

(a) 3   (b) 6

(c) 9   (d) 12

131. If $f : R \to R$ is a function defined by $f(x) = [x] \cos\left(\dfrac{2x-1}{2}\right)\pi$, where $[x]$ denotes the greatest integer function, then f is :

[AIEEE - 2012]

(a) continuous for every real x

(b) discontinuous only at $x = 0$

(c) discontinuous only at non-zero integral values of x

(d) continuous only at $x = 0$

132. The values of p and q for which the function

[AIEEE - 2011]

$f(x) = \begin{cases} \dfrac{\sin (p+1)\,x + \sin x}{x}, & x < 0 \\ q, & x = 0 \\ \dfrac{\sqrt{x + x^2} - \sqrt{x}}{x^{3/2}}, & x > 0 \end{cases}$

is continuous for all x in R, are

(a) $p = \dfrac{1}{2}, q = \dfrac{3}{2}$ (b) $p = \dfrac{1}{2}, q = -\dfrac{3}{2}$

(c) $p = \dfrac{5}{2}, q = \dfrac{1}{2}$ (d) $p = -\dfrac{3}{2}, q = \dfrac{1}{2}$

133. Let $f(x) = x\,|x|$ and $g(x) = \sin x$. **[AIEEE - 2009]**

Statement 1: gof is differentiable at $x = 0$ and its derivative is continuous at that point.

Statement 2: gof is twice differentiable at $x = 0$.

(a) Statement 1 is true, statement 2 is true; statement 2 is the correct explanation for statement 1.

(b) Statement 1 is true, statement 2 is true; statement 2 is not a correct explanation for statement 1.

(c) Statement 1 is true, statement 2 is false.

(d) Statement 1 is false, statement 2 is true.

134. Let $f(x) = \begin{cases} (x-1)\sin\left(\dfrac{1}{x-1}\right), & \text{if } x \neq 1 \\ 0, & \text{if } x = 1 \end{cases}$.

Then which one of the following is true ?

[AIEEE - 2008]

(a) f is neither differentiable at x = 0 nor at x = 1

(b) f is differentiable at x = 0 and at x = 1

(c) f is differentiable at x = 0 but not at x = 1

(d) f is differentiable at x = 1 but not at x = 0

135. The set of points where $f(x) = \dfrac{x}{1+|x|}$ is differentiable is :   [AIEEE - 2006]

(a) $(-\infty, 0) \cup (0, \infty)$ (b) $(-\infty, -1) \cup (-1, \infty)$

(c) $(-\infty, \infty)$ (d) $(0, \infty)$

136. Suppose f(x) is differentiable at x = 1 and $\lim_{h \to 0} \dfrac{1}{h} f(1+h) = 5$, then f '(1) equals :

[AIEEE - 2005]

(a) 3   (b) 4

(c) 5   (d) 6

137. If f is a real-valued differentiable function satisfying $\left| f(x) - f(y) \right| \leq (x - y)^2$, x, y ∈ R and f(0) = 0, then f(1) equals :   [AIEEE - 2005]

(a) –1   (b) 0

(c) 2   (d) 1

138. If y = sec (tan^{-1} x), then $\dfrac{dy}{dx}$ at x = 1 is equal to

(a) $\sqrt{2}$ (b) $\dfrac{1}{\sqrt{2}}$

(c) $\dfrac{1}{2}$ (d) 1

139. If $y^x - x^y = 1$, then the value of $\dfrac{dy}{dx}$ at x = 1 is

(a) 2 (1 – log 2)   (b) 2 (1 + log 2)

(c) 2 – log 2   (d) 2 + log 2

140. Let y be an implicit function of x defined by $x^{2x} - 2x^x \cot y - 1 = 0$. Then y' (1) is equal to

(a) 1   (b) log 2

(c) – log 2   (d) – 1

141. Let $f(\theta) = \sin\left[\tan^{-1}\left(\dfrac{\sin\theta}{\sqrt{\cos 2\theta}}\right)\right]$, where $-\dfrac{\pi}{4} < \theta < \dfrac{\pi}{4}$. Then the value of $\dfrac{d f(\theta)}{d \tan\theta}$ is

(a) 1   (b) 2

(c) 3   (d) 5

142. The function f(x) = |x log x| where x > 0 is mono- tonically decreasing in the interval

(a) (1, e)   (b) (e, ∞)

(c) $\left(0, \dfrac{1}{e}\right)$ (d) $\left[\dfrac{1}{e}, 1\right]$

ANSWER KEY

1. (c)	2. (a)	3. (b)	4. (b)	5. (c)	6. (c)	7. (b)	8. (b)	9. (b)	10. (b)
11. (a)	12. (b)	13. (c)	14. (a)	15. (d)	16. (b)	17. (b)	18. (c)	19. (a)	20. (b)
21. (b)	22. (c)	23. (b)	24. (c)	25. (a)	26. (b)	27. (d)	28. (b)	29. (d)	30. (b)
31. (a)	32. (c)	33. (d)	34. (a)	35. (b)	36. (c)	37. (b)	38. (a)	39. (b)	40. (c)
41. (d)	42. (c)	43. (d)	44. (b)	45. (b)	46. (c)	47. (a)	48. (d)	49. (d)	50. (a)
51. (a)	52. (b)	53. (d)	54. (b)	55. (a)	56. (c)	57. (a)	58. (b)	59. (d)	60. (b)
61. (b)	62. (c)	63. (a)	64. (b)	65. (d)	66. (b)	67. (a)	68. (d)	69. (b)	70. (b)
71. (a)	72. (d)	73. (c)	74. (b)	75. (c)	76. (a)	77. (a)	78. (b)	79. (c)	80. (b)
81. (b)	82. (b)	83. (a)	84. (b)	85. (c)	86. (a)	87. (c)	88. (c)	89. (d)	90. (d)
91. (c)	92. (a)	93. (a)	94. (b)	95. (d)	96. (c)	97. (b)	98. (d)	99. (a)	100. (c)
101. (d)	102. (a)	103. (d)	104. (a)	105. (b)	106. (b)	107. (d)	108. (d)	109. (a)	110. (d)
111. (c)	112. (c)	113. (a)	114. (b)	115. (c)	116. (c)	117. (c)	118. (b)	119. (b)	120. (d)
121. (c)	122. (b)	123. (d)	124. (b)	125. (c)	126. (d)	127. (a)	128. (c)	129. (d)	130. (b)
131. (a)	132. (d)	133. (c)	134. (a)	135. (c)	136. (c)	137. (b)	138. (b)	139. (a)	140. (d)
141. (a)	142. (d)								

DIFFERENTIATION

MULTIPLE CHOICE QUESTIONS

1. If $f(x) = \left(\dfrac{x^a}{x^b}\right)^{a+b} \cdot \left(\dfrac{x^b}{x^c}\right)^{b+c} \cdot \left(\dfrac{x^c}{x^a}\right)^{c+a}$, then $f'(x) =$

(a) 1

(b) 0

(c) x^{a+b+c}

(d) None of these

2. If $f(x) = \left(\dfrac{\sin^m x}{\sin^n x}\right)^{m+n} \cdot \left(\dfrac{\sin^n x}{\sin^p x}\right)^{n+p} \cdot \left(\dfrac{\sin^p x}{\sin^m x}\right)^{p+m}$, then $f'(x)$ is equal to :

(a) 0

(b) 1

(c) $\cos^{m+n+p} x$

(d) None of these

3. $y = \dfrac{1}{1 + x^{\beta-\alpha} + x^{\gamma+\alpha}} + \dfrac{1}{1 + x^{\alpha-\beta} + x^{\gamma-\beta}} + \dfrac{1}{1 + x^{\alpha-\gamma} + x^{\beta-\gamma}}$, then $\dfrac{dy}{dx} =$

(a) 0

(b) 1

(c) $(\alpha + \beta + \gamma) \cdot x^{\alpha+\beta+\gamma-1}$

(d) None of these

4. If $y = f\left(\dfrac{2x-1}{x^2+1}\right)$ and $f'(x) = \sin x^2$, then $\dfrac{dy}{dx}$ is equal to :

(a) $\sin\left(\dfrac{2x-1}{x^2+1}\right)^2 \cdot \left(\dfrac{2+2x+x^2}{(x^2+1)^2}\right)$

(b) $\sin\left(\dfrac{2x-1}{x^2+1}\right)^2 \left(\dfrac{2+2x-2x^2}{(x^2+1)^2}\right)$

(c) $\sin\left(\dfrac{2x-1}{x^2+1}\right)^2 \left(\dfrac{2+2x-x^2}{(x^2+1)^2}\right)$

(d) None of these

5. If $y = \sec^{-1}\dfrac{\sqrt{x}-1}{x+\sqrt{x}} + \sin^{-1}\dfrac{x+\sqrt{x}}{\sqrt{x}-1}$, then $\dfrac{dy}{dx}$ is equal to :

(a) x

(b) 1

(c) 0

(d) None of these

6. If $f(x) = \dfrac{1-\cos x}{1-\sin x}$, then $f'\left(\dfrac{\pi}{2}\right)$ is equal to :

(a) 1

(b) 0

(c) ∞

(d) Does not exist

7. Differential coefficient w.r.t. x of the function $(\log_{\cos x} \sin x)(\log_{\sin x} \cos x)^{-1} + \sin^{-1}\left(\dfrac{2x}{1+x^2}\right)$ at $x = \dfrac{\pi}{4}$ is :

(a) $\dfrac{8}{\log 2} + \dfrac{32}{\pi^2 + 16}$

(b) $-\dfrac{8}{\log 2} + \dfrac{32}{\pi^2 + 16}$

(c) $-\dfrac{8}{\log 2} - \dfrac{32}{\pi^2 + 16}$

(d) None of these

8. If $y = \tan^{-1}\dfrac{x - \sqrt{1-x^2}}{x + \sqrt{1-x^2}}$, then $\dfrac{dy}{dx}$ is equal to :

(a) $\dfrac{-1}{\sqrt{1-x^2}}$

(b) $\dfrac{1}{\sqrt{1-x^2}}$

(c) $\dfrac{-x}{\sqrt{1-x^2}}$

(d) None of these

9. If g is the inverse of f and $f'(x) = \dfrac{1}{1+x^3}$, then $g'(x)$ is equal to :

(a) $1 + [g(x)]^3$

(b) $\dfrac{1}{1 + [g(x)]^3}$

(c) $[g(x)]^3$

(d) None of these

10. If $y = \log\left(\dfrac{x}{a+bx}\right)^x$, then $x^3 \dfrac{d^2y}{dx^2} =$

(a) $\left(x\dfrac{dy}{dx} - y\right)^2$

(b) $\left(x\dfrac{dx}{dy} - x\right)^2$

(c) $\left(x\dfrac{dy}{dx} + y\right)^2$

(d) None of these

11. If S_n denotes the sum of n terms of a G.P. whose common ratio is r, then $(r-1)\dfrac{dS_n}{dr}$ is equal to :

(a) $(n-1) S_n + n S_{n-1}$

(b) $(n-1)S_n - n S_{n-1}$

(c) $(n-1) S_n$

(d) None of these

12. If $(a - b \cos y)(a + b \cos x) = a^2 - b^2$,

then $\lim\limits_{x \to 0} \dfrac{dy}{dx}$ is equal to :

(a) $\sqrt{\dfrac{a-b}{a+b}}$ (b) $\sqrt{\dfrac{a+b}{a-b}}$

(c) $\dfrac{a-b}{a+b}$ (d) None of these

13. If $y = \tan^{-1} \dfrac{1}{x^2 + x + 1} + \tan^{-1} \dfrac{1}{x^2 + 3x + 3}$

$+ \tan^{-1} \dfrac{1}{x^2 + 5x + 7} + \dots$ to n terms, then $\dfrac{dy}{dx} =$

(a) $\dfrac{1}{1 + (x + n)^2} + \dfrac{1}{1 + x^2}$

(b) $\dfrac{1}{1 + (x + n)^2} - \dfrac{1}{1 + x^2}$

(c) $\dfrac{2}{1 + (x + n)^2} - \dfrac{1}{1 + x^2}$

(d) None of these

14. If $y = e^{\tan x}$, then $\cos^2 x \dfrac{d^2 y}{dx^2} =$

(a) $(1 - \sin 2x) \dfrac{dy}{dx}$ (b) $-(1 + \sin 2x) \dfrac{dy}{dx}$

(c) $(1 + \sin 2x) \dfrac{dy}{dx}$ (d) None of these

15. If $x = x^{(\log x)^{\log \log x}}$, then $\dfrac{dy}{dx}$ is equal to :

(a) $\dfrac{y \log y}{x \log x} (2 \log \log x + 1)$

(b) $\dfrac{x \log x}{y \log y} (2 \log \log x + 1)$

(c) $\dfrac{2y \log y}{x \log x} (\log \log x + 1)$

(d) None of these

16. If $y = a \cos (\log x) + b \sin (\log x)$, then

$x^2 \dfrac{d^2 y}{dx^2} + x \dfrac{dy}{dx} =$

(a) 0 (b) y

(c) $-y$ (d) None of these

17. If $y = e^{x^{e^x}} + x^{e^{e^x}} + e^{x^{x^e}}$, then $\dfrac{dy}{dx}$ is equal to :

(a) $e^{x^{e^x}} \cdot x^{e^x} \cdot e^x \left(\dfrac{1}{x} + \log x \right)$

$+ x^{e^{e^x}} \cdot e^x \cdot \log x \left(e^x + \dfrac{1}{x \log x} \right)$

$+ e^{x^{x^e}} \cdot x^{x^e} \cdot x^{e-1} (e \log x + 1)$

(b) $e^{x^{e^x}} \cdot x^{e^x} \cdot e^x \left(\dfrac{1}{x} + \log x \right)$

$+ x^{e^{e^x}} \cdot e^{e^x} \cdot \log x \left(e^x + \dfrac{1}{x \log x} \right)$

$+ e^{x^{x^e}} \cdot x^{x^e} \cdot x^{e-1} (e \log x + 1)$

(c) $e^{x^{e^x}} \cdot e^x \left(\dfrac{1}{x} + \log x \right)$

$+ x^{e^{e^x}} \cdot e^x \cdot \log x \left(e^x + \dfrac{1}{x \log x} \right)$

$+ e^{x^{x^e}} \cdot x^e \cdot x^{e-1} (e \log x + 1)$

(d) None of these

18. If $y = (\sin^{-1} x)^2$, then $(1 - x^2) \dfrac{d^2 y}{dx^2}$ is equal to :

(a) $x \dfrac{dy}{dx} + 2$ (b) $x \dfrac{dy}{dx} - 2$

(c) $-x \dfrac{dy}{dx} + 2$ (d) None of these

19. If $y = \sum\limits_{r=1}^{x} \tan^{-1} \dfrac{1}{1 + r + r^2}$ then $\dfrac{dy}{dx}$ is equal to :

(a) $\dfrac{1}{1 + x^2}$ (b) $\dfrac{1}{1 + (1 + x)^2}$

(c) 0 (d) None of these

20. The differential coefficient of $\tan^{-1} \dfrac{2x\sqrt{1 - x^2}}{1 - 2x^2}$

w.r.t. $\sec^{-1} \dfrac{1}{2x^2 - 1}$ at $x = \dfrac{1}{2}$ is equal to :

(a) $\dfrac{1}{2}$ (b) $-\dfrac{1}{2}$

(c) -1 (d) None of these

21. If $y^2 = P(x)$, a polynomial of degree $n \geq 3$, then

$2 \dfrac{d}{dx} \left(y^3 \dfrac{d^2 y}{dx^2} \right) =$

(a) $-P(x) \cdot P'''(x)$ (b) $P(x) \cdot P'''(x)$

(c) $P(x) \cdot P''(x)$ (d) None of these

22. If $y = \tan \left(\dfrac{1}{2} \cos^{-1} \dfrac{1 - u^2}{1 + u^2} + \dfrac{1}{2} \sin^{-1} \dfrac{2u}{1 + u^2} \right)$ and

$x = \dfrac{2u}{1 - u^2}$, then $\dfrac{dy}{dx} =$

(a) -1 (b) 0

(c) 1 (d) None of these

23. The derivative of f (tan x) w.r.t. g (sec x) at $x = \dfrac{\pi}{4}$, where $f'(1) = 2$ and $g'(\sqrt{2}) = 4$, is :

(a) $\dfrac{1}{\sqrt{2}}$

(b) $\sqrt{2}$

(c) 1

(d) None of these

24. $x = a(\cos\theta + \theta\sin\theta)$ and $y = a(\sin\theta - \theta\cos\theta)$, where $0 < \theta < \dfrac{\pi}{2}$, then $\dfrac{d^2y}{dx^2}$ at $x = \dfrac{\pi}{4}$ is equal to :

(a) $\dfrac{4\sqrt{2}}{a\pi}$

(b) $\dfrac{8\sqrt{2}}{a\pi}$

(c) $\dfrac{4}{a\pi\sqrt{2}}$

(d) None of these

25. If $x = t^t$ and $y = t^{t^t}$, then $\dfrac{dy}{dx}$ is equal to :

(a) $\dfrac{t^{t^t}\left[(1 + \log t)\log t + \dfrac{1}{t}\right]}{(1 + \log t)}$

(b) $\dfrac{t^{t^t}\left[1 + \log t + \dfrac{1}{t}\right]}{(1 + \log t)}$

(c) $\dfrac{t^{t^t}\left[(1 + \log t)\log t + \dfrac{1}{t}\right]}{(1 + \log t)^2}$

(d) None of these

26. If $ax^2 + 2hxy + by^2 = 1$, then $\dfrac{d^2y}{dx^2}$ is equal to :

(a) $\dfrac{ab - h^2}{(hx + by)^2}$

(b) $\dfrac{h^2 - ab}{(hx + by)^2}$

(c) $\dfrac{h^2 + ab}{(hx + by)^2}$

(d) None of these

27. If $y = 2^{\log_2 (x)^{2x}} + \left(\tan\dfrac{\pi x}{4}\right)^{4/\pi x}$, then $\dfrac{dy}{dx}$ at $x = 1$ is :

(a) 2

(b) -2

(c) 4

(d) None of these

28. If $y = \sin(m\sin^{-1}x)$, then $(1 - x^2)y'' - xy'$ is equal to :

(a) m^2y

(b) my

(c) $-m^2y$

(d) None of these

29. Let f be a twice differentiable function such that :
$f''(x) = -f(x)$ and $f'(x) = g(x)$.
If $h(x) = [f(x)]^2 + [g(x)]^2$ and $h(5) = 11$, then $h(10) =$

(a) 11

(b) 0

(c) -1

(d) None of these

30. If $y^{1/n} + y^{-1/n} = 2x$, then $(x^2 - 1)\dfrac{d^2y}{dx^2} + x\dfrac{dy}{dx} =$

(a) $-n^2y$

(b) n^2y

(c) 0

(d) None of these

31. A function $f(x)$ is so defined that for all x, $[f(x)]^n = f(nx)$. If $f'(x)$ denotes derivative of $f(x)$ w.r.t. x, then $f'(x) \cdot f(nx) =$

(a) $f(x)$

(b) 0

(c) $f(x) \cdot f'(nx)$

(d) None of these

32. If $y = \left[x + \sqrt{1 + x^2}\right]^n$, then $(1 + x^2)\dfrac{d^2y}{dx^2} + x\dfrac{dy}{dx} =$

(a) n^2y

(b) $-n^2y$

(c) $-y$

(d) None of these

33. If $y = \dfrac{ax + b}{x^2 + c}$, where a, b, c are constants, then $(2xy' + y)y'''$ is equal to :

(a) $3(xy'' + y')y''$

(b) $3(xy' + y'')y''$

(c) $3(xy'' + y')y'$

(d) None of these

34. If $f(x) = (ax + b)\sin x + (cx + d)\cos x$, then the values of a, b, c and d such that $f'(x) = x\cos x$ for all x are :

(a) $b = c = 0$, $a = d = 1$

(b) $b = d = 0$, $a = c = 1$

(c) $c = d = 0$, $a = b = 1$

(d) None of these

35. If $y = \dfrac{ax^2}{(x - a)(x - b)(x - c)} + \dfrac{bx}{(x - b)(x - c)} + \dfrac{c}{(x - c)} + 1$, then $\dfrac{y'}{y} =$

(a) $\dfrac{1}{x}\left(\dfrac{a}{a - x} + \dfrac{b}{b - x} + \dfrac{c}{c - x}\right)$

(b) $\left(\dfrac{a}{a - x} + \dfrac{b}{b - x} + \dfrac{c}{c - x}\right)$

(c) $\dfrac{1}{x}\left(\dfrac{a}{x - a} + \dfrac{b}{x - b} + \dfrac{c}{x - c}\right)$

(d) None of these

36. A triangle has two of its vertices P(a, 0), Q(0, b) and the third vertex R(x, y) is moving along the straight line y = x. If A is the area of the triangle, then $\dfrac{dA}{dx}$ =

(a) $\dfrac{a-b}{2}$

(b) $\dfrac{a-b}{4}$

(c) $\dfrac{a+b}{2}$

(d) $\dfrac{a+b}{4}$

37. If $\sqrt{1-y^2}+\sqrt{1-t^2}=\alpha(y-t)$ and $x=\sin^{-1}(t\sqrt{1-t}+\sqrt{t}\sqrt{1-t^2})$, then $\dfrac{dy}{dx}$ =

(a) $\dfrac{2\sqrt{1-y^2}\cdot\sqrt{t}}{2\sqrt{t}+\sqrt{1+t}}$

(b) $\dfrac{\sqrt{1-y^2}\cdot\sqrt{t}}{2\sqrt{t}+\sqrt{1+t}}$

(c) $\dfrac{2\sqrt{1-y^2}\cdot\sqrt{t}}{2\sqrt{t}-\sqrt{1+t}}$

(d) None of these

38. If $x=f(t)$, $y=\phi(t)$, then $\dfrac{d^2y}{dx^2}$ is equal to :

(a) $\dfrac{f_1\phi_2-\phi_1f_2}{f_1^2}$

(b) $\dfrac{f_1\phi_2-\phi_1f_2}{f_1^3}$

(c) $\dfrac{\phi_1f_2-f_1\phi_2}{f_1^3}$

(d) None of these

39. If $y=\sin^{-1}\left(\dfrac{5x+12\sqrt{1-x^2}}{13}\right)$, then $\dfrac{dy}{dx}$ =

(a) $\dfrac{1}{\sqrt{1-x^2}}$

(b) $-\dfrac{1}{\sqrt{1-x^2}}$

(c) $\dfrac{3}{\sqrt{1-x^2}}$

(d) None of these

40. If $x=f(t)\cos t-f'(t)\sin t$, $y=f(t)\sin t+f'(t)\cos t$, then $\left(\dfrac{dx}{dt}\right)^2+\left(\dfrac{dy}{dt}\right)^2$ is equal to :

(a) $f(t)-f''(t)$

(b) $[f(t)-f''(t)]^2$

(c) $[f(t)+f''(t)]^2$

(d) None of these

41. If $x=\sec\theta-\cos\theta$, $y=\sec^n\theta-\cos^n\theta$, then $(x^2+4)\left(\dfrac{dy}{dx}\right)^2$ is equal to :

(a) $n^2(y^2-4)$

(b) $n^2(4-y^2)$

(c) $n^2(y^2+4)$

(d) None of these

42. If $y=\dfrac{2}{\sqrt{a^2-b^2}}\cot^{-1}\left[\sqrt{\dfrac{a-b}{a+b}}\cot\dfrac{x}{2}\right]$, then $\dfrac{dy}{dx}$ =

(a) $\dfrac{1}{a-b\cos x}$

(b) $\dfrac{1}{a+b\cos x}$

(c) $-\dfrac{1}{a+b\cos x}$

(d) None of these

43. If $f_r(x)$, $g_r(x)$, $h_r(x)$, r = 1, 2, 3 are polynomials in x such that $f_r(a)=g_r(a)=h_r(a)$, r = 1, 2, 3 and

$$F(x)=\begin{vmatrix} f_1(x) & f_2(x) & f_3(x) \\ g_1(x) & g_2(x) & g_3(x) \\ h_1(x) & h_2(x) & h_3(x) \end{vmatrix}, \text{ then } F'(a) =$$

(a) a

(b) −a

(c) 0

(d) None of these

44. Let g(x) be a polynomial of degree one and f(x) be defined by $f(x)=\begin{cases} g(x) & ; \ x\le 0 \\ \left(\dfrac{1+x}{2+x}\right)^{1/x} & ; \ x>0 \end{cases}$

If f(x) is continuous at x = 0 and $f'(1)=f(-1)$, then the function g(x) is given by :

(a) $-\dfrac{1}{9}(1+6\log 3)x$

(b) $\dfrac{1}{9}(1+6\log 3)x$

(c) $-\dfrac{1}{9}(1-6\log 3)x$

(d) None of these

45. If y = k sin px, then the value of the determinant

$$\begin{vmatrix} y & y_1 & y_2 \\ y_3 & y_4 & y_5 \\ y_6 & y_7 & y_8 \end{vmatrix} \text{ is equal to :}$$

(where y_n denotes n^{th} derivative of y w.r.t. x)

(a) 1

(b) 0

(c) −1

(d) None of these

46. If f(x), g(x), h(x) are the polynomials in x of degree 2 and $F(x)=\begin{vmatrix} f & g & h \\ f' & g' & h' \\ f'' & g'' & h'' \end{vmatrix}$,

then $F'(x)$ is equal to :

(a) 1

(b) 0

(c) −1

(d) None of these

47. If $y=\log_u |\cos 4x|+|\sin x|$, where u = sec 2x, then $\dfrac{dy}{dx}$ at $x=-\dfrac{\pi}{6}$ is equal to :

(a) $\dfrac{-6\sqrt{3}}{\log 2}-\dfrac{\sqrt{3}}{2}$

(b) $\dfrac{-6\sqrt{3}}{\log 2}+\dfrac{\sqrt{3}}{2}$

(c) $\dfrac{6\sqrt{3}}{\log 2}+\dfrac{\sqrt{3}}{2}$

(d) None of these

48. If f, g, h are differentiable functions of x and

$$\Delta = \begin{vmatrix} f & g & h \\ (xf)' & (xg)' & (xh)' \\ (x^2f)'' & (x^2g)'' & (x^2h)'' \end{vmatrix}$$

then Δ' (the derivative of Δ w.r.t. x) is given by :

(a) $\begin{vmatrix} f' & g' & h' \\ f & g & h \\ (x^3f'')' & (x^3g'')' & (x^3h'')' \end{vmatrix}$

(b) $\begin{vmatrix} f & g & h \\ f' & g' & h' \\ (x^2f'')' & (x^2g'')' & (x^2h'')' \end{vmatrix}$

(c) $\begin{vmatrix} f & g & h \\ f' & g' & h' \\ (x^3f'')' & (x^3g'')' & (x^3h'')' \end{vmatrix}$

(d) None of these

49. If $2x^3 - 3x^2y^2 + 4x - y + 7 = 0$ and $y(1) = 1$, then the value of y''(1) is equal to :

(a) $-\dfrac{343}{474}$ (b) $-\dfrac{474}{343}$

(c) $\dfrac{474}{343}$ (d) $\dfrac{343}{474}$

50. If $\sqrt{1-x^6} + \sqrt{1-y^6} = a^3(x^3 - y^3)$, then $\dfrac{dy}{dx} =$

(a) $\dfrac{x^2}{y^2}\sqrt{\dfrac{1-y^6}{1-x^6}}$ (b) $\dfrac{y^2}{x^2}\sqrt{\dfrac{1-y^6}{1-x^6}}$

(c) $\dfrac{x^2}{y^2}\sqrt{\dfrac{1-x^6}{1-y^6}}$ (d) None of these

51. Let $f\left(\dfrac{x_1 + x_2 + \ldots + x_n}{n}\right) = \dfrac{f(x_1) + f(x_2) + \ldots + f(x_n)}{n}$, where all $x_i \in$ R are independent of each other and $n \in$ N. If f(x) is differentiable and f '(0) = a, f(0) = b, then f '(x) is equal to :

(a) a (b) 0

(c) b (d) None of these

52. If $f(x) = (1-x)^n$, then the value of

$f(0) + f'(0) + \dfrac{f''(0)}{2!} + \ldots + \dfrac{f^n(0)}{n!}$ is equal to :

(a) 2^n (b) 0

(c) 2^{n-1} (d) None of these

53. If $y = f(x^3)$, $z = g(x^5)$, f '(x) = tan x and g'(x) = sec x, then the value of $\dfrac{dy}{dz}$ is :

(a) $\dfrac{3}{5x^2} \cdot \dfrac{\tan x^3}{\sec x^5}$ (b) $\dfrac{5x^2}{3} \cdot \dfrac{\sec x^5}{\tan x^3}$

(c) $\dfrac{3x^2}{5} \cdot \dfrac{\tan x^3}{\sec x^5}$ (d) None of these

54. f '(x) = ϕ(x) and ϕ'(x) = f(x) for all x. Also, f(3) = 5 and f '(3) = 4. Then the value of $[f(10)]^2 - [\phi(10)]^2$ is :

(a) 0 (b) 9

(c) 41 (d) None of these

55. If $8f(x) + 6f\left(\dfrac{1}{x}\right) = x + 5$ & $y = x^2 f(x)$, then $\dfrac{dy}{dx}$ at $x = -1$ is equal to :

(a) 0 (b) $\dfrac{1}{14}$

(c) $-\dfrac{1}{14}$ (d) None of these

56. If $e^x + e^y = e^{x+y}$,

then the value of $\dfrac{dy}{dx}$ at (1, 1) is :

(a) 0 (b) −1

(c) 1 (d) None of these

57. Let f be a function defined for all x $\in$ R. If f is differentiable and $f(x^3) = x^5$ for all x $\in$ R (x $\neq$ 0), then the value of f '(27) is :

(a) 15 (b) 45

(c) 0 (d) None of these

58. If $x^2 + y^2 = t + \dfrac{1}{t}$ and $x^4 + y^4 = t^2 + \dfrac{1}{t^2}$, then $\dfrac{dy}{dx}$ is equal to :

(a) $\dfrac{y}{x}$ (b) $-\dfrac{y}{x}$

(c) $\dfrac{x}{y}$ (d) $-\dfrac{x}{y}$

59. If $f(x) = \sqrt{x^2 - 10x + 25}$, then the derivative of f(x) on the interval [0, 7] is :

(a) 1 (b) −1

(c) 0 (d) Does not exist

60. Let $f(x)$ be a polynomial function satisfying

$f(x) \cdot f\left(\dfrac{1}{x}\right) = f(x) + f\left(\dfrac{1}{x}\right)$. If $f(4) = 65$ and l_1, l_2, l_3

are in G.P., then $f'(l_1)$, $f'(l_2)$, $f'(l_3)$ are in :

(a) A.P.   (b) G.P.

(c) H.P.   (d) None of these

61. If $f(x) = \log\left(\dfrac{m(x)}{n(x)}\right)$, $m(1) = n(1) = 1$ and

$m'(1) = n'(1) = 2$, then $f'(1)$ is equal to :

(a) 0   (b) 1

(c) −1   (d) None of these

62. If $f(x) = \begin{vmatrix} x^n & n! & 2 \\ \cos x & \cos \dfrac{n\pi}{2} & 4 \\ \sin x & \sin \dfrac{n\pi}{2} & 8 \end{vmatrix}$ then the value of

$\dfrac{d^n}{dx^n}[f(x)]_{x=0}$ is :

(a) 0   (b) 1

(c) −1   (d) None of these

63. Let $f(x) = (x^3 + 2)^{30}$. If $f^n(x)$ is a polynomial of degree 20, where $f^n(x)$ denotes the nth derivative of $f(x)$ w.r.t. x, then the value of n is :

(a) 60   (b) 40

(c) 70   (d) None of these

64. If $y = (1 + x)(1 + x^2)(1 + x^4) \dots (1 + x^{2n})$, then

$\dfrac{dy}{dx}$ at $x = 0$ is :

(a) −1   (b) 1

(c) 0   (d) None of these

65. Let $f(x)$ be a polynomial of degree 3 such that $f(3) = 1$, $f'(3) = -1$, $f''(3) = 0$ and $f'''(3) = 12$. Then the value of $f'(1)$ is :

(a) 12   (b) 23

(c) − 13   (d) None of these

66. If $y = \begin{vmatrix} \sin x & \cos x & \sin x \\ \cos x & -\sin x & \cos x \\ x & 1 & 1 \end{vmatrix}$, then $\dfrac{dy}{dx}$ is

equal to :

(a) 1   (b) −1

(c) 0   (d) None of these

67. If $f(x) = (\cos x + i \sin x)(\cos 2x + i \sin 2x)$

$(\cos 3x + i \sin 3x) \dots (\cos nx + i \sin nx)$

and $f(1) = 1$, then $f''(1)$ is equal to :

(a) $\dfrac{n(n+1)}{2}$ (b) $\left(\dfrac{n(n+1)}{2}\right)^2$

(c) $-\left(\dfrac{n(n+1)}{2}\right)^2$ (d) None of these

68. If $f(x) = |x - 3|$ & $\phi(x) = (f \circ f)(x)$, then for $x \geq 10$, $\phi'(x)$ is equal to :

(a) 1   (b) 0

(c) −1   (d) None of these

69. If $y = \sin^{-1}\left(\dfrac{2x}{1 + x^2}\right)$, then $\dfrac{dy}{dx}$ is equal to :

(a) $\dfrac{2}{1 + x^2}$, when $-1 < x < 1$

(b) $\dfrac{2}{1 + x^2}$, when $x < -1$ or $x > 1$

(c) $-\dfrac{2}{1 + x^2}$, when $-1 < x < 1$

(d) None of these

70. If $f(x) = \sqrt{x^2 + 6x + 9}$, then $f'(x)$ is equal to :

(a) 1 for $x < -3$ (b) −1 for $x < -3$

(c) 1 for all $x \in R$ (d) None of these

71. If $f(x) = |(x - 4)(x - 5)|$, then $f'(x)$ is equal to :

(a) $-2x + 9$, for all $x \in R$

(b) $2x - 9$ if $4 < x < 5$

(c) $- 2x + 9$ if $4 < x < 5$

(d) None of these

72. If $xe^{xy} = y + \sin^2 x$, then at $x = 0$, $\dfrac{dy}{dx}$ is equal to :

(a) − 1   (b) 1

(c) 0   (d) None of these

73. If $x^2 + y^2 = 1$, then :

(a) $yy'' - 2(y')^2 + 1 = 0$

(b) $yy'' + (y')^2 + 1 = 0$

(c) $yy'' + (y')^2 - 1 = 0$

(d) $yy'' + 2(y')^2 + 1 = 0$

74. Let $f(x) = \begin{vmatrix} x^3 & \sin x & \cos x \\ 6 & -1 & 0 \\ p & p^2 & p^3 \end{vmatrix}$, where p is a

constant. Then $\dfrac{d^3}{dx^3}[f(x)]$ at x = 0 is

(a) p
(b) $p + p^2$
(c) $p + p^3$
(d) independent of p

75. Let F(x) = f(x) g(x) h(x) for all real x, where f(x), g(x) and h(x) are differentiable functions. At some point x_0, if $F'(x_0) = 21\ F(x_0)$, f '(x_0) = 4f(x_0), g'(x_0) = −7g(x_0) and h'(x_0) = kh(x_0) then k is equal to :

(a) 24
(b) 12
(c) −12
(d) −24

76. If f(x) is a polynomial of degree n (> 2) and f(x) = f(k − x), (where k is a fixed real number), then degree of f '(x) is :

(a) n
(b) n − 1
(c) n − 2
(d) None of these

77. If $\sqrt{x^2 + y^2} = ae^{\tan^{-1}(y/x)}$, a > 0, then, assuming y > 0, y"(0) =

(a) $\dfrac{2}{a}e^{-\pi/2}$
(b) $-\dfrac{2}{a}e^{\pi/2}$
(c) $-\dfrac{2}{a}e^{-\pi/2}$
(d) None of these

78. If α is a repeated root of a quadratic equation f(x) = 0 and A(x), B(x), C(x) are polynomials of degree > 2, then the determinant

$\begin{vmatrix} A(x) & B(x) & C(x) \\ A(\alpha) & B(\alpha) & C(\alpha) \\ A'(\alpha) & B'(\alpha) & C'(\alpha) \end{vmatrix}$ is divisible by :

(a) A(x)
(b) B(x)
(c) C(x)
(d) f(x)

79. The derivative of $\sec^{-1}\dfrac{1}{2x^2 - 1}$ w.r.t. $\sqrt{1 - x^2}$

at $x = \dfrac{1}{2}$ is :

(a) −4
(b) 4
(c) 2
(d) −2

80. If $f(x) = \log_x(\ln x)$ then f '(x) at x = e is :

(a) $\dfrac{1}{e}$
(b) e
(c) $-\dfrac{1}{e}$
(d) 0

81. If $f(x) = \dfrac{x^2 - x}{x^2 + 2x}$, then $\dfrac{df^{-1}(x)}{dx}$ is equal to :

(a) $-\dfrac{3}{(1 - x)^2}$
(b) $\dfrac{3}{(1 - x)^2}$
(c) $\dfrac{1}{(1 - x)^2}$
(d) None of these

82. If y = f(x) is an odd differentiable function defined on (−∞, ∞) such that f '(3) = − 2, then f '(−3) equals :

(a) 4
(b) 2
(c) −2
(d) 0

83. If $y = \tan^{-1}\left(\dfrac{\sin x + \cos x}{\cos x - \sin x}\right)$, then $\dfrac{dy}{dx}$ is equal to :

(a) $\dfrac{1}{2}$
(b) 0
(c) 1
(d) None of these

84. If $y = \sqrt{\sin x + y}$, then $\dfrac{dy}{dx}$ equals :

(a) $\dfrac{\cos x}{2y - 1}$
(b) $\dfrac{\cos x}{1 - 2y}$
(c) $\dfrac{\sin x}{1 - 2y}$
(d) $\dfrac{\sin x}{2y - 1}$

85. Let f and g be differentiable functions satisfying g'(a) = 2, g(a) = b and fog = I (identity function). Then   f '(b) is equal to :

(a) 2
(b) $\dfrac{2}{3}$
(c) $\dfrac{1}{2}$
(d) None of these

86. If $\sqrt{x} + \sqrt{y} = 4$, then $\dfrac{dx}{dy}$ at y = 1, is :

(a) −1
(b) −3
(c) 3
(d) None f these

87. $\dfrac{d}{dx}\left\{\tan^{-1}\left(\dfrac{3x - x^3}{1 - 3x^2}\right)\right\}$ is equal to :

(a) $\dfrac{3}{1 + 9x^2}$
(b) $\dfrac{1}{9 + x^2}$
(c) $\sec^2 3x$
(d) $\dfrac{3}{1 + x^2}$

88. If $y = \left(1 + \dfrac{1}{x}\right)^x$, then $\dfrac{dy}{dx}$ is equal to :

(a) $\left(x + \dfrac{1}{x}\right)^x \left[\log\left(1 + \dfrac{1}{x}\right) + \dfrac{1}{1 + x}\right]$

(b) $\left(x + \dfrac{1}{x}\right)^x \left[\log(x + 1) - \dfrac{x}{x + 1}\right]$

(c) $\left(x + \dfrac{1}{x}\right)^x \left[\log\left(1 + \dfrac{1}{x}\right)\right]$

(d) $\left(1 + \dfrac{1}{x}\right)^x \left[\log\left(1 + \dfrac{1}{x}\right) - \dfrac{1}{1 + x}\right]$

89. If $x^y = e^{x - y}$, then $\dfrac{dy}{dx}$ is equal to :

(a) $\dfrac{\log x}{(1 + \log x)^2}$

(b) $\dfrac{x - y}{(1 + \log x)^2}$

(c) $\dfrac{x - y}{(1 + \log x)^2}$

(d) $\dfrac{1}{1 + \log x}$

90. If $y = \sqrt{\sin x + \sqrt{\sin x + \sqrt{\sin x + \ldots \infty}}}$, then the value of $\dfrac{dy}{dx}$ is :

(a) $\dfrac{\cos x}{2y - 1}$

(b) $\dfrac{\cos x}{2y + 1}$

(c) $\dfrac{\sin x}{y + 1}$

(d) $\dfrac{\sqrt{\sin x}}{y + 1}$

91. If $x = a\left(\cos t + \log \tan \dfrac{t}{2}\right)$ and $y = a \sin t$, then $\dfrac{dy}{dx}$ is equal to :

(a) $-\tan t$

(b) $\tan t$

(c) $\cot t$

(d) None of these

92. If $\sin y = x \cos(a + y)$, then $\dfrac{dy}{dx}$ is equal to :

(a) $\dfrac{\cos^2(a + y)}{\cos a}$

(b) $\dfrac{\cos a}{\cos^2(a + y)}$

(c) $\dfrac{\sin^2 y}{\cos a}$

(d) None of these

93. If $f(x) = \dfrac{\sin^{-1} x}{\sqrt{1 - x^2}}$, then $(1 - x^2)\, f'(x) - x\, f(x) =$

(a) 1

(b) −1

(c) 0

(d) None of these

94. If $y = \tan^{-1}\left[\dfrac{\log(e/x^2)}{\log(ex^2)}\right] + \tan^{-1}\left(\dfrac{3 + 2\log x}{1 - 6\log x}\right)$, then $\dfrac{d^2y}{dx^2} =$

(a) 2

(b) 1

(c) 0

(d) −1

95. Given $F(x) = f(x) \cdot g(x)$ and $f'(x) \cdot g'(x) = c$, then $\dfrac{F''}{F} = \dfrac{f''}{f} + \dfrac{g''}{g} + \dfrac{kc}{fg}$ where $k =$

(a) 1

(b) −1

(c) 2

(d) None of these

96. If $f(x) = \sin(\log x)$ and $y = f\left(\dfrac{2x + 3}{3 - 2x}\right)$ then $\left.\dfrac{dy}{dx}\right]_{x=1} =$

(a) $\dfrac{12}{5} \cos(\log 5)$

(b) $\dfrac{5}{12} \cos(\log 5)$

(c) $\dfrac{12}{5} \sin(\log 5)$

(d) None of these

97. If $f(0) = 1$, $f'(0) = -1$, $f(x) > 0$ for all x, then there exists a function $f(x)$ such that :

(a) $f'(x) < 0$ for all x

(b) $-1 < f''(x) < 0$ for all x

(c) $-2 \le f''(x) \le -1$ for all x

(d) $f''(x) \le -2$ for all x

98. If $\phi(x) = \lambda(x) \cdot f(x)$ and $\psi(x) = \mu(x) \cdot f(x)$, then

$$\begin{vmatrix} f(x) & \phi(x) & \psi(x) \\ f'(x) & \phi'(x) & \psi'(x) \\ f''(x) & \phi''(x) & \psi''(x) \end{vmatrix} = k^3 \cdot \begin{vmatrix} \lambda'(x) & \mu'(x) \\ \lambda''(x) & \mu''(x) \end{vmatrix}$$

where $k =$

(a) $\psi(x)$

(b) $\phi(x)$

(c) $f(x)$

(d) None of these

99. If $\Delta(x) = \begin{vmatrix} x^2 - 1 & x + 1 & x - 2 \\ 2x^2 - 1 & 3x & 3x - 3 \\ x^2 + 4 & 2x - 1 & 3x - 1 \end{vmatrix}$,

then $\Delta(x)$ is :

(a) a constant function

(b) a first degree polynomial

(c) a second degree polynomial

(d) a third degree polynomial

100. If $y = \left(\dfrac{x}{n}\right)^{nx}\left(1 + \log\dfrac{x}{n}\right)$, then $y'(n)$ is :

(a) 0

(b) $\dfrac{1}{n}$

(c) $\left(\dfrac{1}{n}\right)^n$

(d) $\dfrac{n^2 + 1}{n}$

101. If $x = \sqrt{\dfrac{1-t^2}{1+t^2}}$, $y = \dfrac{\sqrt{1+t^2} - \sqrt{1-t^2}}{\sqrt{1+t^2} + \sqrt{1-t^2}}$, then $\dfrac{d^2y}{dx^2}$ at $t = 0$ is :

(a) 0

(b) $\dfrac{1}{2}$

(c) −1

(d) 1

102. If $f(x) = \begin{vmatrix} \sec\theta & \tan^2\theta & 1 \\ \theta\sec x & \tan x & x \\ 1 & \tan x - \tan\theta & 0 \end{vmatrix}$, then $f'(\theta)$ is equal to

(a) 0

(b) 1

(c) −1

(d) None of these

103. If $y = \log_{\phi(x)}\cos^2 x$, $\phi(x) > 0$, $\phi(x) \neq 1$, then $\dfrac{dy}{dx} =$

(a) $-2\dfrac{\phi(x)\tan x \log\phi(x) - \phi'\log\cos x \cdot x}{\phi(x)[\log\phi(x)]^2}$

(b) $2\dfrac{\phi(x)\tan x \log\phi(x) - \phi'\log\cos x \cdot x}{\phi(x)[\log\phi(x)]^2}$

(c) $\dfrac{\phi(x)\tan x \log\phi(x) - \phi'\log\cos x \cdot x}{\phi(x)[\log\phi(x)]^2}$

(d) None of these

104. If $x = \cos\theta$, $y = \sin^3\theta$, then

$$y\dfrac{d^2y}{dx^2} + \left(\dfrac{dy}{dx}\right)^2 = k\sin^2\theta(5\cos^2\theta - 1),$$

where $k =$

(a) 2

(b) 3

(c) −1

(d) None of these

105. If $2^x + 2^y = 2^{x+y}$,

then the value of $\dfrac{dy}{dx}$ at $x = y = 1$ is :

(a) 0

(b) −1

(c) 1

(d) 2

106. The derivative of $\sin^{-1}\left(\dfrac{2x}{1+x^2}\right)$ with respect to $\sin^{-1}\left(\dfrac{1-x^2}{1+x^2}\right)$ is :

(a) −1

(b) 1

(c) 2

(d) $\dfrac{1}{2}$

107. Let f be a polynomial. Then the second derivative of $f(e^x)$ is :

(a) $f''(e^x)e^{2x} + f'(e^x)e^x$

(b) $f''(e^x)e^x + f'(e^x)$

(c) $f''(e^x)e^{2x} + f''(e^x)e^x$

(d) $f''(e^x)$

108. If $y = \log(\sin x)$, then $\dfrac{d^2y}{dx^2}$ equals :

(a) $\sec x \tan x$

(b) $-\operatorname{cosec} x \cot x$

(c) $\sec^2 x$

(d) $-\operatorname{cosec}^2 x$

109. If $y = \cos 2x \sin 3x$, then y_n is equal to :

(a) $6^n \sin\left(2x + \dfrac{n\pi}{2}\right)\cos\left(3x + \dfrac{n\pi}{2}\right)$

(b) $6^n \cos\left(2x + \dfrac{n\pi}{2}\right)\cos\left(3x + \dfrac{n\pi}{2}\right)$

(c) $\dfrac{1}{2}\left[5^n \sin\left(5x + \dfrac{n\pi}{2}\right) + \sin\left(x + \dfrac{n\pi}{2}\right)\right]$

(d) None of these

110. If $y = (\sin x)^{\tan x}$, then $\dfrac{dy}{dx}$ is equal to :

(a) $(\sin x)^{\tan x} \cdot (1 + \sec^2 x \cdot \log\sin x)$

(b) $\tan x \cdot (\sin x)^{\tan x - 1} \cdot \cos x$

(c) $(\sin x)^{\tan x} \cdot \sec^2 x \cdot \log\sin x$

(d) $\tan x \cdot (\sin x)^{\tan x - 1}$

111. If $f(x) = \cot^{-1}\left(\dfrac{x^x - x^{-x}}{2}\right)$, then $f'(1)$ is equal to:

(a) −1

(b) 1

(c) $\log 2$

(d) $-\log 2$

112. If $x = \dfrac{2t}{1+t^2}$, $y = \dfrac{1-t^2}{1+t^2}$, then $\dfrac{dy}{dx} =$

(a) $\dfrac{2t}{t^2 - 1}$

(b) $\dfrac{2t}{t^2 + 1}$

(c) $\dfrac{2t}{1 - t^2}$

(d) None of these

113. Derivative of $\tan^{-1}\left(\dfrac{\sqrt{1+x^2}-1}{x}\right)$ w.r.t. $\tan^{-1}x$ is :

(a) 1   (b) 2

(c) $\dfrac{1}{2}$ (d) None of these

114. If $y = \tan^{-1}\left[\dfrac{3a^2x - x^3}{a(a^2 - 3x^2)}\right]$, then $\dfrac{dy}{dx} =$

(a) $\dfrac{3a^2}{a^2 + x^2}$ (b) $\dfrac{3a}{a^2 + x^2}$

(c) $\dfrac{a}{a^2 + x^2}$ (d) $\dfrac{3}{a^2 + x^2}$

115. Differential coefficient of $e^{\sin^{-1}x}$ w.r.t. $\sin^{-1}x$ is :

(a) $\sin^{-1}x$ (b) $e^{\sin^{-1}x}$

(c) $e^{\cos^{-1}x}$ (d) $\cos^{-1}x$

116. If $y = \tan^{-1}\left(\dfrac{\cos x}{1 + \sin x}\right)$, then $\dfrac{dy}{dx}$ is equal to :

(a) $\dfrac{1}{2}$ (b) $-\dfrac{1}{2}$

(c) 1   (d) None of these

117. Differential coefficient of $\sin^{-1}x$ w.r.t. $\cos^{-1}\sqrt{1-x^2}$ is :

(a) $\dfrac{2}{\sqrt{1-x^2}}$ (b) $\dfrac{1}{\sqrt{1-x^2}}$

(c) $-\dfrac{1}{\sqrt{1+x^2}}$ (d) None of these

118. Differential coefficient of $\tan^{-1}\sqrt{\dfrac{1-x^2}{1+x^2}}$ w.r.t. $\cos^{-1}x^2$ is

(a) $-\dfrac{1}{2}$ (b) 1

(c) $\dfrac{1}{2}$ (d) None of these

119. If $x\sqrt{1+y} + y\sqrt{1+x} = 0$, then $\dfrac{dy}{dx}$ is equal to

(a) $\dfrac{1}{(1+x^2)}$ (b) $-\dfrac{1}{(1+x^2)}$

(c) $\dfrac{1}{1+x^2}$ (d) None of these

120. The differential coefficient of the function $x^{\log_e x}$ w.r.t. x is :

(a) $2x^{(\log_e x - 1)} \cdot \log_e x$ (b) $x^{(\log_e x - 1)}$

(c) $\dfrac{2}{x}\log_e x$ (d) $x^{(\log_e x - 1)} \cdot \log_e x$

121. If $y = \log\log x$, then $e^y \dfrac{dy}{dx} =$

(a) $\dfrac{1}{x \log x}$ (b) $\dfrac{1}{x}$

(c) $\dfrac{1}{\log x}$ (d) e^y

122. Differential coefficient of $\sqrt{\sec\sqrt{x}}$ is :

(a) $\dfrac{1}{4\sqrt{x}}(\sec\sqrt{x})^{3/2}\sin\sqrt{x}$

(b) $\dfrac{1}{4\sqrt{x}}\sec\sqrt{x}\sin\sqrt{x}$

(c) $\dfrac{1}{2}\sqrt{x}(\sec\sqrt{x})^{3/2}\sin\sqrt{x}$

(d) $\dfrac{1}{2}\sqrt{x}\sec\sqrt{x}\sin\sqrt{x}$

123. If $y = \sec x°$, then $\dfrac{dy}{dx} =$

(a) $\sec x \tan x$ (b) $\sec x° \tan x°$

(c) $\dfrac{\pi}{180}\sec x° \tan x°$ (d) $\dfrac{180}{\pi}\sec x° \tan x°$

124. Differential coefficient of $\cos^{-1}\sqrt{x}$ w.r.t. $\sqrt{1-x}$ is :

(a) $\sqrt{x}$ (b) $-\sqrt{x}$

(c) $\dfrac{1}{\sqrt{x}}$ (d) $-\dfrac{1}{\sqrt{x}}$

125. The first derivative of the function $\cos^{-1}\left(\sin\sqrt{\dfrac{1+x}{2}}\right) + x^x$ w.r.t. x at $x = 1$ is :

(a) $\dfrac{3}{4}$ (b) 0

(c) $\dfrac{1}{2}$ (d) $-\dfrac{1}{2}$

126. The values of x, at which the first derivative of the function $\left(\sqrt{x} + \dfrac{1}{\sqrt{x}}\right)^2$ w.r.t. x is $\dfrac{3}{4}$ are :

(a) ± 2 (b) $\pm\dfrac{1}{2}$

(c) $\pm\dfrac{\sqrt{3}}{2}$ (d) $\pm\dfrac{2}{\sqrt{3}}$

127. If $PV = 81$, then $\dfrac{dP}{dV}$ at $V = 9$ equals :

(a) 1 (b) -1

(c) 2 (d) None of these

128. If $f(x) = \log_x (\ln x)$ then $f'(x)$ at $x = e$ is :

(a) 0 (b) e

(c) 2e (d) 1/e

129. $\dfrac{d}{dx} (\cos^{-1} x + \sin^{-1} x)$ is :

(a) $\dfrac{2}{\sqrt{1 - x^2}}$ (b) $\dfrac{\pi}{2}$

(c) 0 (d) None of these

130. $\dfrac{d}{dx} (\sin^{-1} 2x \sqrt{1 - x^2})$ is equal to :

(a) $-\dfrac{2}{\sqrt{1 - x^2}}$ (b) $\dfrac{2}{\sqrt{1 - x^2}}$

(c) $\cos 2x$ (d) None of these

131. If $y = \sqrt{x + \sqrt{x + \sqrt{x + \dots \infty}}}$, then $\dfrac{dy}{dx}$ is equal to :

(a) $-\dfrac{1}{2y - 1}$ (b) $\dfrac{1}{2y - 1}$

(c) $\dfrac{1}{xy}$ (d) 1

132. The differential coefficient of x^6 w.r.t. x^3 is :

(a) $6x^5$ (b) $3x^2$

(c) $2x^3$ (d) x^3

133. Derivative of $\tan^{-1} \left(\dfrac{2x}{1 - x^2}\right)$ with respect to $\sin^{-1} \left(\dfrac{2x}{1 + x^2}\right)$ is :

(a) $\dfrac{1}{1 + x^2}$ (b) $\dfrac{1}{1 - x^2}$

(c) 0 (d) 1

134. $\dfrac{d^2 x}{dy^2}$ equals : **[AIEEE-2011]**

(a) $-\left(\dfrac{d^2 y}{dx^2}\right) \left(\dfrac{dy}{dx}\right)^{-3}$ (b) $\left(\dfrac{d^2 y}{dx^2}\right)^{-1}$

(c) $-\left(\dfrac{d^2 y}{dx^2}\right)^{-1} \left(\dfrac{dy}{dx}\right)^{-3}$ (d) $-\left(\dfrac{d^2 y}{dx^2}\right) \left(\dfrac{dy}{dx}\right)^{-2}$

135. Let $f : (-1, 1) \to R$ be a differentiable function with $f(0) = -1$ and $f'(0) = 1$. **[AIEEE-2010]**

Let $g(x) = [f(2f(x) + 2)]^2$. Then $g'(0) =$

(a) -4 (b) 0

(c) -2 (d) 4

136. Let y be an implicit function of x defined by $x^{2x} - 2x^x \cot y - 1 = 0$. Then $y'(1)$ equals :

[AIEEE-2009]

(a) -1 (b) 1

(c) $\log 2$ (d) $-\log 2$

ANSWER KEY

1. (b)	2. (a)	3. (a)	4. (b)	5. (c)	6. (d)	7. (b)	8. (b)	9. (a)	10. (a)
11. (b)	12. (a)	13. (b)	14. (c)	15. (a)	16. (c)	17. (b)	18. (a)	19. (b)	20. (c)
21. (b)	22. (c)	23. (a)	24. (b)	25. (a)	26. (b)	27. (c)	28. (c)	29. (a)	30. (b)
31. (c)	32. (a)	33. (a)	34. (a)	35. (a)	36. (c)	37. (a)	38. (b)	39. (a)	40. (c)
41. (c)	42. (a)	43. (c)	44. (a)	45. (b)	46. (b)	47. (a)	48. (c)	49. (b)	50. (a)
51. (a)	52. (b)	53. (a)	54. (b)	55. (c)	56. (b)	57. (a)	58. (b)	59. (d)	60. (b)
61. (a)	62. (a)	63. (c)	64. (b)	65. (b)	66. (a)	67. (c)	68. (a)	69. (a)	70. (b)
71. (c)	72. (b)	73. (b)	74. (d)	75. (a)	76. (b)	77. (c)	78. (d)	79. (b)	80. (a)
81. (b)	82. (c)	83. (c)	84. (a)	85. (c)	86. (b)	87. (d)	88. (d)	89. (a)	90. (a)
91. (b)	92. (a)	93. (a)	94. (c)	95. (c)	96. (a)	97. (a)	98. (c)	99. (b)	100. (d)
101. (a)	102. (c)	103. (a)	104. (b)	105. (b)	106. (a)	107. (a)	108. (d)	109. (c)	110. (a)
111. (a)	112. (a)	113. (c)	114. (a)	115. (b)	116. (b)	117. (d)	118. (c)	119. (b)	120. (a)
121. (b)	122. (a)	123. (c)	124. (c)	125. (a)	126. (a)	127. (b)	128. (d)	129. (c)	130. (b)
131. (b)	132. (c)	133. (d)	134. (a)	135. (a)	136. (a)				

Chapter 22

APPLICATIONS OF DERIVATIVES

MULTIPLE CHOICE QUESTIONS

1. The tangent to the curve $\sqrt{x} + \sqrt{y} = 4$ is equally inclined to the axes at the point :
   - (a) $(1, -2)$
   - (b) $(4, 4)$
   - (c) $(4, -4)$
   - (d) $(-4, 4)$

2. The points on the curve $y^2 = 4a \left(x + a \sin \dfrac{x}{a} \right)$ at which the tangent is parallel to x-axis, lie on :
   - (a) a straight line
   - (b) a parabola
   - (c) a circle
   - (d) an ellipse.

3. If m is the slope of a tangent to the curve $e^{2y} = 1 + 4x^2$, then :
   - (a) $m < 1$
   - (b) $|m| \leq 1$
   - (c) $|m| > 1$
   - (d) None of these.

4. If the slope of the curve $y = \dfrac{ax}{b - x}$ at the point $(1, 1)$ is 2, then the values of a and b are :
   - (a) $1, -2$
   - (b) $-1, 2$
   - (c) $1, 2$
   - (d) None of these.

5. If the tangent at each point of the curve
   $$y = \dfrac{2}{3}x^3 - 2ax^2 + 2x + 5$$
   makes an acute angle with the positive direction of x-axis, then :
   - (a) $a \geq 1$
   - (b) $-1 \leq a \leq 1$
   - (c) $a \leq -1$
   - (d) None of these.

6. The angle between the tangents to the curve $y^2 = 2ax$ at the points where $x = \dfrac{a}{2}$ is :
   - (a) $\dfrac{\pi}{6}$
   - (b) $\dfrac{\pi}{4}$
   - (c) $\dfrac{\pi}{3}$
   - (d) $\dfrac{\pi}{2}$

7. The equation of the tangent to the curve $y = \sqrt{9 - 2x^2}$ at the point where the ordinate and the abscissa are equal, is
   - (a) $2x + y - 3\sqrt{3} = 0$
   - (b) $2x + y + 3\sqrt{3} = 0$
   - (c) $2x - y - 3\sqrt{3} = 0$
   - (d) None of these.

8. The angle between the tangents in those points on the curve $y = (x + 1)(x - 3)$ where it meets x-axis is :
   - (a) $\pm \tan^{-1} \left(\dfrac{15}{8} \right)$
   - (b) $\pm \tan^{-1} \left(\dfrac{8}{15} \right)$
   - (c) $\pm \dfrac{\pi}{4}$
   - (d) None of these.

9. The slope of tangent to the curve $x = t^2 + 3t - 8$, $y = 2t^2 - 2t - 5$ at the point $t = 2$ is :
   - (a) $\dfrac{7}{6}$
   - (b) $\dfrac{5}{6}$
   - (c) $\dfrac{6}{7}$
   - (d) 1.

10. The equation of the tangent to the curve $y = 2x^2 + 5x$ at the point where the line $y = 3$ cuts the curve in the first quadrant is :
    - (a) $14x - 2y - 1 = 0$
    - (b) $14x - 2y + 13 = 0$
    - (c) $14x + 2y - 1 = 0$
    - (d) None of these

11. The curves $x^3 - 3xy^2 = a$ and $3x^2y - y^3 = b$, where a and b are constants, cut each other :
    - (a) at an angle $\dfrac{\pi}{3}$
    - (b) at an angle $\dfrac{\pi}{4}$
    - (c) orthogonally
    - (d) None of these.

12. The angle of intersection of the parabolas $y^2 = 4ax$ and $x^2 = 4ay$ at origin is :
    - (a) $\dfrac{\pi}{3}$
    - (b) $\dfrac{\pi}{2}$
    - (c) $\dfrac{\pi}{4}$
    - (d) None of these.

13. The condition that the curves $ax^2 + by^2 = 1$ and $a_1x^2 + b_1y^2 = 1$ may cut each other orthogonally is
    - (a) $\dfrac{1}{a_1} - \dfrac{1}{a} = \dfrac{1}{b_1} - \dfrac{1}{b}$
    - (b) $\dfrac{1}{a} - \dfrac{1}{a_1} = \dfrac{1}{b} - \dfrac{1}{b_1}$
    - (c) $\dfrac{1}{a_1} + \dfrac{1}{b_1} = \dfrac{1}{a} + \dfrac{1}{b}$
    - (d) None of these.

14. The angle at which the curves $y = \sin x$ and $y = \cos x$ intersect in $[0, \pi]$ is :
    (a) $\pm \tan^{-1} 2\sqrt{2}$ (b) $\pm \tan^{-1} \sqrt{2}$
    (c) $\pm \tan^{-1} \left(\dfrac{1}{\sqrt{2}} \right)$ (d) None of these

15. The equation of the normal to the curve $x^2 = 4y$ passing through the point $(1, 2)$ is :
    (a) $x + y + 3 = 0$ (b) $x - y - 3 = 0$
    (c) $x + y - 3 = 0$ (d) None of these.

16. The line $\dfrac{x}{a} + \dfrac{y}{b} = 2$ touches the curve $\left(\dfrac{x}{a} \right)^n + \left(\dfrac{y}{b} \right)^n = 2$ at the point (a, b) for :
    (a) $n = 2$ only
    (b) $n = -3$ only
    (c) n is any real number
    (d) None of these.

17. The length of the perpendicular from the origin to the curve $x = a(\cos \theta + \theta \sin \theta)$, $y = a(\sin \theta - \theta \cos \theta)$ at any point θ is :
    (a) a (b) $\dfrac{a}{2}$
    (c) $\dfrac{a}{3}$ (d) None of these.

18. The tangents to the curve $y = \dfrac{1 + 3x^2}{3 + x^2}$, drawn at the points for which $y = 1$ intersect at the point :
    (a) $(1, -2)$ (b) $(2, 1)$
    (c) $(0, 0)$ (d) None of these

19. The line $x \cos \alpha + y \sin \alpha = p$ is a tangent to the ellipse $b^2 x^2 + a^2 y^2 - a^2 b^2 = 0$ if :
    (a) $p^2 = b^2 \cos^2 \alpha + a^2 \sin^2 \alpha$
    (b) $p^2 = a^2 \cos^2 \alpha + b^2 \sin^2 \alpha$
    (c) $\dfrac{1}{p^2} = \dfrac{a^2}{\cos^2 \alpha} + \dfrac{b^2}{\sin^2 \alpha}$
    (d) None of these.

20. If the normal to the curve $x^{2/3} + y^{2/3} = a^{2/3}$ makes an angle ϕ with the x-axis, then its equation is :
    (a) $y \cos \phi - x \sin \phi = a \cos 2\phi$
    (b) $y \sin \phi - x \cos \phi = a \cos 2\phi$
    (c) $x \cos \phi + y \sin \phi = a \cos 2\phi$
    (d) None of these.

21. The equation of normal at the point θ of the curve $x = a \cos^3 \theta$, $y = a \sin^3 \theta$ is :
    (a) $x \cos \theta + y \sin \theta = a \cos 2\theta$
    (b) $x \cos \theta - y \sin \theta = a \cos 2\theta$
    (c) $x \sin \theta - y \cos \theta = a \cos 2\theta$
    (d) None of these

22. The tangent to the curve $5x^2 + y^2 = 1$ at $\left(\dfrac{1}{3}, -\dfrac{2}{3} \right)$ passes through the point :
    (a) $(0, 0)$ (b) $(1, -1)$
    (c) $(-1, 1)$ (d) None of these

23. If line $y = 2x$ touches the curve $y = ax^2 + bx + c$ at the point where $x = 1$ and the curve passes through the point $(-1, 0)$, then the values of a, b and c are :
    (a) $a = \dfrac{1}{2}$, $b = 1$, $c = \dfrac{1}{2}$
    (b) $a = 1$, $b = \dfrac{1}{2}$, $c = \dfrac{1}{2}$
    (c) $a = \dfrac{1}{2}$, $b = \dfrac{1}{2}$, $c = 1$
    (d) None of these

24. The points where the normal to the curve $\sqrt{xy} = a + x$ makes equal intercepts on the axes are :
    (a) $\pm \left(\dfrac{a}{\sqrt{2}}, \sqrt{2}a - \dfrac{a}{\sqrt{2}} \pm 2a \right)$
    (b) $\pm \left(\dfrac{a}{\sqrt{2}}, -\sqrt{2}a + \dfrac{a}{\sqrt{2}} \pm 2a \right)$
    (c) $\pm \left(\dfrac{a}{\sqrt{2}}, \sqrt{2}a + \dfrac{a}{\sqrt{2}} \pm 2a \right)$
    (d) None of these.

25. The normals to the curve $x = a(\theta + \sin \theta)$, $y = a(1 - \cos \theta)$ at the points $\theta = (2n + 1)\pi$, $n \in I$ are all :
    (a) parallel to x-axis
    (b) parallel to y-axis
    (c) parallel to the line $y = x$
    (d) None of these.

26. The equation of the tangent to the curve $x = \dfrac{3at}{1+t^2}$, $y = \dfrac{3at^2}{1+t^2}$ at the point t = 2 is :

(a) $4x + 3y + a = 120$ (b) $3x + 4y - a = 120$

(c) $4x + 3y - 12a = 0$ (d) None of these.

27. The equation of the tangent to the curve

$$y = \begin{cases} x^2 \sin\dfrac{1}{x}, & x \neq 0 \\ 0, & x = 0 \end{cases}$$

at the origin is :

(a) $x = 0$ (b) $x = y$

(c) $y = 0$ (d) None of these.

28. The condition that the line $lx + my = 1$ may be normal to the curve $y^2 = 4ax$ is :

(a) $al^3 - 2alm^2 = m^2$ (b) $al^2 + 2alm^3 = m^2$

(c) $al^3 + 2alm^2 = m^3$ (d) $al^3 + 2alm^2 = m^2$.

29. The condition that the line $x \cos \alpha + y \sin \alpha = p$ touches the curve $\dfrac{x^n}{a^n} + \dfrac{y^n}{b^n} = 1$ is :

(a) $p^{n/(n-1)} = (a \cos \alpha)^{n/(n-1)} + (b \sin \alpha)^{n/(n-1)}$

(b) $p^{n/(n-1)} = (a \cos \alpha)^{n/(n-1)} - (b \sin \alpha)^{n/(n-1)}$

(c) $p^{(n-1)/n} = (a \cos \alpha)^{(n-1)/n} + (b \sin \alpha)^{(n-1)/n}$

(d) None of these.

30. If the normal at the point t_1 on the curve $xy = c^2$ meets the curve again at t_2, then :

(a) $t_1^3 t_2 = 1$ (b) $t_1^3 t_2 = -1$

(c) $t_1 t_2^3 = -1$ (d) $t_1 t_2^3 = 1$.

31. The tangent to the curve $3xy^2 - 2x^2y = 1$ at (1, 1) meets the curve again at :

(a) $\left(-\dfrac{16}{5}, -\dfrac{1}{20}\right)$ (b) $\left(\dfrac{16}{5}, -\dfrac{1}{20}\right)$

(c) $\left(-\dfrac{16}{5}, \dfrac{1}{20}\right)$ (d) None of these.

32. The sum of intercepts of the tangent to the curve $\sqrt{x} + \sqrt{y} = \sqrt{a}$ upon the coordinate axes is :

(a) $2a$ (b) a

(c) $2\sqrt{2}a$ (d) None of these.

33. The part of the tangent to the curve $xy = c^2$ included between the coordinate axes, is divided by the point of tangency in the ratio :

(a) $1 : 1$ (b) $1 : 2$

(c) $1 : 3$ (d) None of these.

34. The portion of the tangent to the curve

$$x = \sqrt{a^2 - y^2} + \frac{a}{2} \log \frac{a - \sqrt{a^2 - y^2}}{a + \sqrt{a^2 - y^2}}$$

intercepted between the curve and x-axis, is of length :

(a) $\dfrac{a}{2}$ (b) a

(c) $2a$ (d) None of these.

35. The area of the triangle formed by the positive x-axis, the tangent and the normal to the circle $x^2 + y^2 = 9$ at $(2, \sqrt{5})$ is :

(a) $9\sqrt{5}$ (b) $\dfrac{9\sqrt{5}}{2}$

(c) $\dfrac{9\sqrt{5}}{4}$ (d) None of these.

36. If $y = f(x)$ is the equation of an ellipse to which the line $y = 2x + 3$ is a tangent at the point where $x = 2$, then :

(a) $f'(2) = 2$

(b) $f(2) = 2f'(2)$

(c) $f(2) + f'(2) + f''(2) = 2$

(d) None of these.

37. The length of the perpendicular from the origin to the tangent to the curve $y = e^{4x} + 2$ drawn at the point $x = 0$ is :

(a) $\dfrac{4}{\sqrt{17}}$ (b) $\dfrac{3}{\sqrt{17}}$

(c) $\dfrac{2}{\sqrt{17}}$ (d) None of these.

38. Tangents are drawn to the parabola $x^2 = 4y$ at its points of intersection with another parabola $y^2 = 4x$. The point of intersection of the tangents drawn, is given by :

(a) (2, 0) (b) (0, 2)

(c) (-2, 0) (d) None of these.

39. The equation of the normal to the curve $y = \left(\dfrac{1}{x}\right)^x$ at the point of its maxima is :

(a) $x = e$ (b) $x = \dfrac{1}{e}$

(c) $y = \dfrac{1}{e}$ (d) $y = e$.

40. If the tangent at any point on the curve $x = c\sqrt{\cos\theta}$, $y = c\sqrt{\sin\theta}$ cuts off intercepts X and Y on the coordinate axes, then $X^{-4/3} + Y^{-4/3} =$

(a) $c^{-1/2}$ (b) $c^{3/2}$

(c) $c^{-4/3}$ (d) $c^{-3/4}$

41. If T and N are the lengths of perpendiculars from the origin on the tangent and the normal respectively to the curve $x^{2/3} + y^{2/3} = a^{2/3}$, then $4T^2 + N^2 =$

(a) $2a^2$ (b) a^2

(c) $4a^2$ (d) None of these.

42. The normal at any point of the curve

$$x = ae^\theta\left(\sin\frac{\theta}{2} + 2\cos\frac{\theta}{2}\right), \; y = ae^\theta\left(\cos\frac{\theta}{2} - 2\sin\frac{\theta}{2}\right)$$

(a) is at a constant distance from the origin.

(b) passes through the origin.

(c) is twice the distance of the tangent to the curve from the origin.

(d) makes a constant angle with x-axis.

43. The curves $y^2 = 2x$ and $2xy = k$ cut at right angles if :

(a) $k^2 = 8$ (b) $k^2 = 4$

(c) $k^2 = 2$ (d) None of these

44. The sub-normal at any point of the curve $x^2y^2 = a^2(x^2 - a^2)$ varies as :

(a) $(\text{abscissa})^{-3}$ (b) $(\text{abscissa})^3$

(c) $(\text{ordinate})^{-3}$ (d) None of these

45. The sub-tangent at any point of the curve $x^m y^n = a^{m+n}$ varies as :

(a) $(\text{abscissa})^2$ (b) $(\text{ordinate})^2$

(c) abscissa   (d) ordinate

46. The curves $\dfrac{x^2}{a^2 + k_1} + \dfrac{y^2}{b^2 + k_1} = 1$ and

$\dfrac{x^2}{a^2 + k_2} + \dfrac{y^2}{b^2 + k_2} = 1$ intersect at an angle :

(a) $\dfrac{\pi}{4}$ (b) $\dfrac{\pi}{3}$

(c) $\dfrac{\pi}{2}$ (d) None of these.

47. If at any point on a curve the sub-tangent and sub-normal are equal, then the length of the normal is equal to :

(a) $\sqrt{2}$ ordinate   (b) ordinate

(c) $\sqrt{2\text{ ordinate}}$ (d) None of these.

48. For the parabola $y^2 = 4ax$, the ratio of the sub-tangent to the abscissa is :

(a) $1 : 1$ (b) $2 : 1$

(c) $x : y$ (d) $x^2 : y$

49. The sub-tangent, ordinate and sub-normal to the parabola $y^2 = 4ax$ at a point (different from the origin) are in :

(a) G.P.   (b) A.P.

(c) H.P.   (d) None of these.

50. The angle between the tangent at any point P and the line joining P to the origin O, at all points of the curve $\log(x^2 + y^2) = k\tan^{-1}\dfrac{y}{x}$, is :

(a) $\tan^{-1}\left(\dfrac{2}{k}\right)$ (b) $\tan^{-1}\left(\dfrac{k}{2}\right)$

(c) $\tan^{-1}(k)$ (d) $\tan^{-1}\left(\dfrac{1}{k}\right)$.

51. If PG_1 and PG_2 are the normals to the two curves $y^2 = 4ax$ and $ay^2 = 4x^3$ at common point of intersection (which is not origin) meeting the axis of x in G_1 and G_2, then G_1G_2 is equal to :

(a) $2a$ (b) $4a$

(c) a (d) None of these.

52. Any tangent to the curve $y = 3x^7 + 5x + 3$

(a) is parallel to x-axis.

(b) is parallel to y-axis.

(c) makes an acute angle with the x-axis.

(d) makes an obtuse angle with the x-axis.

53. If a tangent at point P_1 other than origin on the curve $y = x^3$ meets the curve again at P_2 and the tangent at P_2 meets the curve again at P_3 and so on, then the abscissae of $P_1, P_2, ..., P_n$ form a :

(a) G.P.   (b) A.P.

(c) H.P.   (d) None of these.

54. The equation of the normal to the curve

$y = (1 + x)^y + \sin^{-1} (\sin^2 x)$ at $x = 0$ is :

(a) $x + y = 2$ (b) $x + y = 1$

(c) $x - y = 1$ (d) None of these.

55. Let P $(a \sec \theta, b \tan \theta)$ and Q $(a \sec \phi, b \tan \phi)$,

where $\phi + \theta = \dfrac{\pi}{2}$ be two points on the hyperbola

$\dfrac{x^2}{a^2} - \dfrac{y^2}{b^2} = 1$. If (h, k) is the point of intersection of

the normals at P and Q, then k is equal to :

(a) $\dfrac{a^2 + b^2}{a}$ (b) $-\left(\dfrac{a^2 + b^2}{a}\right)$

(c) $\dfrac{a^2 + b^2}{b}$ (d) $-\left(\dfrac{a^2 + b^2}{b}\right)$

56. If the normal to the curve $y = f(x)$ at the point

(3, 4) makes an angle $\dfrac{3\pi}{4}$ with the positive x-axis,

then $f'(3) =$

(a) -1 (b) $\dfrac{-3}{4}$

(c) $\dfrac{4}{3}$ (d) 1.

57. A curve $y = f(x)$ passes through the point P(1, 1).
The normal to the curve at P is $a(y - 1) + (x - 1)$
$= 0$. If the slope of the tangent at any point on the
curve is proportional to the ordinate of the point,
then the equation of the curve is :

(a) $y = e^{a(x-1)}$ (b) $y = e^{a(1-x)}$

(c) $y = e^{\frac{a}{2}(x-1)}$ (d) $y = e^{\frac{a}{2}(x+1)}$

58. For the curve $x = t^2 - 1$, $y = t^2 - t$, the tangent is
parallel to x-axis where :

(a) $t = \dfrac{1}{\sqrt{3}}$ (b) $t = -\dfrac{1}{\sqrt{3}}$

(c) $t = 0$ (d) $t = \dfrac{1}{2}$.

59. The curve $y = ax^3 + bx^2 + cx$ is inclined at 45° to
x-axis at (0, 0) but it touches x-axis at (1, 0), then
the values of a, b, c are given by :

(a) $a = 1, b = -2, c = 1$

(b) $a = 1, b = 1, c = -2$

(c) $a = -2, b = 1, c = 1$

(d) $a = -1, b = 2, c = 1$

60. If $f(x) = \begin{cases} x \sin \dfrac{\pi}{x}, & x > 0 \\ 0, & x = 0 \end{cases}$, then in the interval

(0, 1), $f'(x)$ vanishes at :

(a) exactly one point

(b) exactly two points

(c) at no point

(d) infinite number of points.

61. If $f(x)$ and $g(x)$ are differentiable functions for
$0 \le x \le 1$ such that $f(0) = 2$, $g(0) = 0$, $f(1) = 6$,
$g(1) = 2$, then in the interval (0, 1) :

(a) $f'(x) = 0$ for all x.

(b) $f'(x) = 2g'(x)$ for atleast one x.

(c) $f'(x) = 2g'(x)$ for atmost one x.

(d) None of these.

62. If $a + b + c = 0$, then equation $3ax^2 + 2bx + c = 0$
has ...... in the interval (0, 1).

(a) atleast one root   (b) atmost one root

(c) no root   (d) None of these.

63. If α and β $(\alpha < \beta)$ are two different real roots of
the equation $ax^2 + bx + c = 0$, then :

(a) $\alpha > -\dfrac{b}{2a}$ (b) $\beta < -\dfrac{b}{2a}$

(c) $\alpha < -\dfrac{b}{2a} < \beta$ (d) $\beta < -\dfrac{b}{2a} < \alpha$

64. If the equation $a_n x^n + a_{n-1} x^{n-1} + ... + a_1 x = 0$ has
a positive root of $x = \alpha$, then the equation :

$n a_n x^{n-1} + (n - 1) a_{n-1} x^{n-2} + ... + a_1 = 0$ has a
positive root, which is

(a) smaller than α

(b) greater than α

(c) equal to α

(d) greater than or equal to α.

65. If $f(x) = \begin{vmatrix} \sin x & \sin a & \sin b \\ \cos x & \cos a & \cos b \\ \tan x & \tan a & \tan b \end{vmatrix}$,

where $0 < a < b < \dfrac{\pi}{2}$, then the equation $f'(x) = 0$

has ...... in the interval (a, b).

(a) atleast one root   (b) atmost one root

(c) no root   (d) None of these.

66. If $\dfrac{a_0}{n+1} + \dfrac{a_1}{n} + \dfrac{a_2}{n-1} + \dots + \dfrac{a_{n-1}}{2} + a_n = 0$, then the equation $a_0 x^n + a_1 x^{n-1} + \dots + a_{n-1}x + a_n = 0$ has ...... in the interval $(0, 1)$.
   (a) exactly one root
   (b) atleast one root
   (c) atmost one root
   d) no root.

67. The equation $x \log x = 3 - x$ has ...... in the interval $(1, 3)$:
   (a) exactly one root
   (b) atmost one root
   (c) atleast one root
   (d) no root.

68. Between any two real roots of the equation $e^x \sin x = 1$, the equation $e^x \cos x = -1$ has :
   (a) atleast one root
   (b) exactly one root
   (c) atmost one root
   (d) no root.

69. If $f(x)$ is differentiable in the interval $[2, 5]$, where $f(2) = \dfrac{1}{5}$ and $f(5) = \dfrac{1}{2}$, then there exists a number c, such that $2 < c < 5$ for which $f'(c) =$
   (a) $\dfrac{1}{2}$
   (b) $\dfrac{1}{5}$
   (c) $\dfrac{1}{10}$
   (d) None of these.

70. If a, b, c are non-zero real numbers such that
   $$\int_0^1 (1 + \cos^8 x)(ax^2 + bx + c)\, dx$$
   $$= \int_0^1 (1 + \cos^8 x)(ax^2 + bx + c)\, dx = 0,$$
   then the equation $ax^2 + bx + c = 0$ will have :
   (a) one root between 0 and 1 and other root between 1 and 2.
   (b) both the roots between 0 and 1.
   (c) both the roots between 1 and 2.
   (d) None of these.

71. The value of c in Lagrange's theorem for the function $f(x) = \begin{cases} x \cos\left(\dfrac{1}{x}\right), & x \neq 0 \\ 0, & x = 0 \end{cases}$ in the interval $[-1, 1]$ is :
   (a) 0
   (b) $\dfrac{1}{2}$
   (c) $-\dfrac{1}{2}$
   (d) non-existent in the interval.

72. If $27a + 9b + 3c + d = 0$, then the equation $4ax^3 + 3bx^2 + 2cx + d = 0$ has atleast one real root lying between :
   (a) 0 and 1
   (b) 1 and 3
   (c) 0 and 3
   (d) None of these.

73. Let f be a function which is continuous and differentiable for all real x. If $f(2) = -4$ and $f'(x) \geq 6$ for all $x \in [2, 4]$, then :
   (a) $f(4) < 8$
   (b) $f(4) \geq 8$
   (c) $f(4) \geq 12$
   (d) None of these.

74. The function $f(x) = 2x^2 - \log |x|$, $x \neq 0$ is increasing in the interval :
   (a) $\left(-\dfrac{1}{2}, 0\right) \cup \left(\dfrac{1}{2}, \infty\right)$
   (b) $\left(-\infty, -\dfrac{1}{2}\right) \cup \left(0, \dfrac{1}{2}\right)$
   (c) $\left(-\dfrac{1}{2}, \dfrac{1}{2}\right)$
   (d) None of these.

75. The values of x for which $1 + x \ln\left(x + \sqrt{x^2 + 1}\right) \geq \sqrt{1 + x^2}$, are :
   (a) $x \leq 0$
   (b) $0 \leq x \leq 1$
   (c) $x \geq 0$
   (d) None of these.

76. The function $f(x) = x - \log(1 + x)$, $x > -1$ is increasing in the interval :
   (a) $(0, \infty)$
   (b) $(-1, 0)$
   (c) $(-\infty, 0)$
   (d) None of these.

77. The range of values of x for which the function $f(x) = \dfrac{x}{\log x}$, $x > 0$ and $x \neq -1$ may be decreasing is :
   (a) $(0, e)$
   (b) (e, ∞)
   (c) $(0, e) \setminus \{1\}$
   (d) None of these.

78. The function $f(x) = x^{1/x}$ is increasing in the interval :
   (a) (e, ∞)
   (b) $(-\infty, e)$
   (c) $(-e, e)$
   (d) None of these.

79. The function $f(x) = \dfrac{\sin x}{x}$ is decreasing in the interval :
   (a) $\left(-\dfrac{\pi}{2}, 0\right)$
   (b) $\left(0, \dfrac{\pi}{2}\right)$
   (c) $(0, \pi)$
   (d) None of these.

80. If $ax^2 + \dfrac{b}{x} \geq c$ for all positive x, where a, b > 0, then :

(a) $27ab^2 \geq 4c^3$ (b) $27ab^2 < 4c^3$

(c) $4ab^2 \geq 27c^3$ (d) None of these.

81. The function $f(x) = \log x - \dfrac{2x}{2+x}$ is increasing in the interval :

(a) $(-\infty, 0)$ (b) $(0, \infty)$

(c) $(1, \infty)$ (d) $(-\infty, 1)$

82. If $y = x^3 (x-2)^2$, then the values of x for which y increases, are :

(a) $x < \dfrac{6}{5}$ or $x > 3$ (b) $\dfrac{6}{5} < x < 2$

(c) $x < \dfrac{6}{5}$ or $x > 2$ (d) None of these.

83. The function $f(x) = -2x^3 + 21x^2 - 60x + 41$, in the interval $(-\infty, 1)$, is

(a) < 0 (b) ≤ 0

(c) > 0 (d) ≥ 0.

84. If $0 \leq x < \dfrac{\pi}{2}$, then :

(a) $2 \sin x + \tan x > 3x$

(b) $2 \sin x + \tan x < 3x$

(c) $2 \sin x + \tan x \geq 3x$

(d) $2 \sin x + \tan x \leq 3x$.

85. Let $y = x^2 e^{-x}$, then the interval in which y increases w.r.t. x is :

(a) $(-\infty, \infty)$ (b) $(-2, 0)$

(c) $(2, \infty)$ (d) $(0, 2)$.

86. If a < 0, the function $(e^{ax} + e^{-ax})$ is a monotonic decreasing function for all values of x, where :

(a) $x > 0$ (b) $x < 0$

(c) $x > 1$ (d) $x < 1$.

87. The function f defined by $f(x) = (x + 2) e^{-x}$ is :

(a) decreasing for all x

(b) decreasing in $(-\infty, -1)$ and increasing in $(-1, \infty)$

(c) increasing for all x

(d) decreasing in $(-1, \infty)$ and increasing in $(-\infty, -1)$.

88. The function $f(x) = \dfrac{\ln(\pi + x)}{\ln(e + x)}$ is :

(a) increasing on $(0, \infty)$

(b) decreasing on $(0, \infty)$

(c) increasing on $(0, \pi/e)$, decreasing on $(\pi/e, \infty)$

(d) decreasing on $(0, \pi/e)$, increasing on $(\pi/e, \infty)$.

89. The function $f(x) = \tan x - x$:

(a) sometimes increases & sometimes decreases

(b) never increase.

(c) never decrease.

(d) can't say.

90. The range of values of a for which the function

$f(x) = x^3 + (a+2) x^2 + 3ax + 5$

may be monotonic in R, is :

(a) $a < 1$ (b) $1 < a < 4$

(c) $a > 4$ (d) None of these.

91. The values of k for which the function

$f(x) = kx^3 - 9x^2 + 9x + 3$ may be increasing on R are :

(a) $k > 3$ (b) $k < 3$

(c) $k \leq 3$ (d) None of these.

92. The least possible value of k for which the function $f(x) = x^2 + kx + 1$ may be increasing on $[1, 2]$ is :

(a) 2   (b) -2

(c) 0   (d) None of these.

93. If $f(x) = 2x^3 + 9x^2 + \lambda x + 20$ is a decreasing function of x in the largest possible interval $(-2, -1)$ then λ is equal to :

(a) 12   (b) -12

(c) 6   (d) None of these.

94. The function $f(x) = \sin^4 x + \cos^4 x$ increases in the interval :

(a) $\left(0, \dfrac{\pi}{8}\right)$ (b) $\left(\dfrac{\pi}{4}, \dfrac{3\pi}{8}\right)$

(c) $\left(\dfrac{3\pi}{8}, \dfrac{5\pi}{8}\right)$ (d) $\left(\dfrac{5\pi}{8}, \dfrac{3\pi}{4}\right)$.

95. The function $f(x) = 2 \log (x - 1) - x^2 + 2x + 3$ increases in the interval :

(a) $(-\infty, 0) \cup (1, 2)$ (b) $(-\infty, 0) \cup (2, \infty)$

(c) $(0, 1) \cup (2, \infty)$ (d) None of these.

96. The equation $x + e^x = 0$ has :

(a) only one real root   (b) only two real roots

(c) no real root   (d) None of these.

97. If $f(x) = \begin{cases} xe^{ax}, & x \le 0 \\ x + ax^2 - x^3, & x > 0 \end{cases}$ where a is a positive constant, then f '(x) is increasing in the interval :

(a) $\left(-\infty, \dfrac{-2}{a}\right)$ (b) $\left(\dfrac{-2}{a}, \dfrac{a}{3}\right)$

(c) $\left(\dfrac{a}{3}, \infty\right)$ (d) None of these.

98. The interval in which the function $2x^3 + 15$ increases less rapidly than the function $9x^2 - 12x$, is :

(a) $(-\infty, 1)$ (b) $(1, 2)$

(c) $(2, \infty)$ (d) None of these.

99. Consider the following statements S and R :

S : Both sin x and cos x are decreasing functions in the interval $\left(\dfrac{\pi}{2}, \pi\right)$

R : If a differentiable function decreases in an interval (a, b), then its derivative also decreases in (a, b).

Which of the following is true ?

(a) Both S and R are wrong.

(b) Both S and R are correct, but R is not the correct explanation for S.

(c) S is correct and R is the correct explanation for S.

(d) S is correct and R is wrong.

100. Let $f(x) = \int e^x (x - 1) (x - 2) \, dx$. Then f decreases in the interval :

(a) $(-\infty, -2)$ (b) $(-2, -1)$

(c) $(1, 2)$ (d) $(2, +\infty)$

101. If $f(x) = \dfrac{x}{\sin x}$ and $g(x) = \dfrac{x}{\tan x}$, where $0 < x \le 1$, then in this interval :

(a) both f(x) and g(x) are increasing functions.

(b) both f(x) and g(x) are decreasing functions.

(c) f(x) is an increasing function.

(d) g(x) is an increasing function.

102. The value of a in order that

$f(x) = \sin x - \cos x - ax + b$

decreases for all real values is given by :

(a) $a \ge \sqrt{2}$ (b) $a < \sqrt{2}$

(c) $a \ge 1$ (d) $a < 1$

103. If $f(x) = \begin{cases} 3x^2 + 12x - 1, & -1 \le x \le 2 \\ 37 - x, & 2 < x \le 3 \end{cases}$ then :

(a) f(x) is increasing on [−1, 2]

(b) f(x) is continuous on [−1 3]

(c) f '(2) does not exist

(d) All of these.

104. Let f and g be increasing and decreasing functions respectively from [0, ∞) to [0, ∞).. Let $h(x) = f(g(x))$. If $h(0) = 0$, then h(x) is :

(a) always zero   (b) always negative

(c) always positive   (d) strictly increasing

105. The function $y = x^3 + 5x^2 - 1$ is decreasing in the interval :

(a) $-\infty < x < -\dfrac{10}{3}$ (b) $0 < x < \infty$

(c) $-3 < x < 3$ (d) $-\dfrac{10}{3} < x < 0.$

106. If $f''(x) < 0 \; \forall \; x \in (a, b)$, then f '(x) = 0

(a) exactly once in (a, b)

(b) atmost once in (a, b)

(c) atleast once in (a, b)

(d) None of these.

107. The maximum value of $x^{1/x}$, x > 0 is :

(a) $e^{1/e}$ (b) $\left(\dfrac{1}{e}\right)^e$

(c) 1   (d) None of these.

108. The minimum value of $\dfrac{x}{\log x}$ is :

(a) e

(b) $\dfrac{1}{e}$

(c) 1

(d) None of these.

109. The minimum value of $\dfrac{(a + x)(b + x)}{(c + x)}$, $x > -c$, is :

(a) $(\sqrt{c - a} + \sqrt{c - b})^2$

(b) $(\sqrt{a - c} + \sqrt{b - c})^2$

(c) does not exist

(d) None of these.

110. Maximum value of $\sin x + \dfrac{1}{2} \sin 2x + \dfrac{1}{3} \sin 3x$, $0 \le x \le \dfrac{\pi}{2}$ is :

(a) $1 + 2\sqrt{2}$

(b) $2\sqrt{2} - 1$

(c) $1 - 2\sqrt{2}$

(d) None of these.

111. If $P(x) = a_0 + a_1 x^2 + a_2 x^4 + \ldots + a_n x^{2n}$ is a polynomial in $x \in R$ with $0 < a_1 < a_2 \ldots < a_n$, then $P(x)$ has

(a) no point of minimum

(b) only one point of minimum

(c) only two points of minimum

(d) None of these.

112. If $y = a \log_e x + bx^2 + x$ has its extreme values (i.e. maximum or minimum value) at $x = 1$ and $x = 2$, then the values of a and b are :

(a) $a = -\dfrac{1}{6}, b = \dfrac{4}{3}$

(b) $a = -\dfrac{4}{3}, b = \dfrac{1}{6}$

(c) $a = \dfrac{4}{3}, b = -\dfrac{1}{6}$

(d) None of these.

113. If the function $y = \dfrac{ax + b}{(x - 4)(x - 1)}$ has an extremum at $P(2, -1)$ then the values of a and b are :

(a) $a = 0, b = 1$

(b) $a = 0, b = -1$

(c) $a = 1, b = 0$

(d) $a = -1, b = 0$

114. For the function $y = x + \dfrac{1}{x}$,

(a) $x = 1$ is a point of maximum

(b) $x = -1$ is a point of minimum

(c) maximum value > minimum value

(d) maximum value < minimum value.

115. If $xz = 1$, where $x > 0$, then the least value of $x + z$ is :

(a) 1

(b) 2

(c) -2

(d) None of these.

116. The minimum value of $\log_a x + \log_x a$, $0 < x < a$, is :

(a) 1

(b) 2

(c) -2

(d) None of these.

117. The minimum value of $2 \log_{10} x - \log_x 0.01$, $x > 1$, is :

(a) 1

(b) -1

(c) 2

(d) None of these.

118. The coordinates of the point on the curve $y = \dfrac{x}{1 + x^2}$, where the tangent to the curve has the greatest shope, are :

(a) $(0, 0)$

(b) $\left(1, \dfrac{1}{2}\right)$

(c) $\left(-1, -\dfrac{1}{2}\right)$

(d) None of these.

119. The shortest distance of the point $(0, c)$ from the parabola $y = x^2$, where $0 \le c \le 5$, is :

(a) $\sqrt{c - \dfrac{1}{4}}, \dfrac{1}{4} \le c \le 5$

(b) $\sqrt{c - \dfrac{1}{4}}, 0 \le c \le 5$

(c) $\sqrt{c - \dfrac{1}{2}}, \dfrac{1}{2} \le c \le 5$

(d) None of these.

120. The point on the curve $4x^2 + a^2 y^2 = 4a^2$, $4 < a^2 < 8$, that is farthest from the point $(0, -2)$ is :

(a) $(2, 0)$

(b) $(0, 2)$

(c) $(2, -2)$

(d) $(-2, 2)$.

121. The function $f(x) = \int_1^x [2(t - 1)(t - 2)^3 + 3(t - 1)^2 (t - 2)^2]\, dt$ has :

(a) maximum at $x = 1$

(b) minimum at $x = \dfrac{7}{5}$

(c) neither maximum nor minimum at $x = 2$

(d) All the above.

122. The greatest value of the function

$$f(x) = \tan^{-1} x - \frac{1}{2} \log x \text{ in } \left[\frac{1}{\sqrt{3}}, \sqrt{3}\right] \text{ is :}$$

(a) $\frac{\pi}{6} + \frac{1}{4} \log 3$ (b) $\frac{\pi}{3} - \frac{1}{4} \log 3$

(c) $\frac{\pi}{6} - \frac{1}{4} \log 3$ (d) $\frac{\pi}{3} + \frac{1}{4} \log 3$.

123. The maximum value of the function

$$y = x (x - 1)^2, \ 0 \le x \le 2 \text{ is :}$$

(a) 0   (b) $\frac{4}{27}$

(c) −4   (d) None of these.

124. The largest term in the sequence

$$x_n = \frac{n^2}{n^3 + 200}, \ n \in N, \text{ is :}$$

(a) $\frac{49}{543}$ (b) $\frac{8}{89}$

(c) $\frac{1}{52}$ (d) None of these.

125. The greatest height of the graph of the curve
$y = 6 \cos x - 8 \sin x$ above the x-axis is :

(a) 4   (b) 8

(c) 10   (d) None of these.

126. The minimum intercept made by the axes on the
tangent to the ellipse $\frac{x^2}{a^2} + \frac{y^2}{b^2} = 1$ is :

(a) $a + b$ (b) $\frac{a + b}{2}$

(c) $\frac{a + b}{4}$ (d) None of these.

127. The points on the curve $xy^2 = 1$ which are
nearest to the original are :

(a) $\left[\left(\frac{1}{2}\right)^{1/3}, \pm \left(\frac{1}{2}\right)^{-1/6}\right]$ (b) $\left[\left(\frac{1}{2}\right)^{1/3}, 2^{-1/6}\right]$

(c) $\left[2^{1/3}, \pm \left(\frac{1}{2}\right)^{-1/6}\right]$ (d) None of these.

128. If $xy = k$ and $z = lx + my$, where k, l, m are
positive constants, then the minimum value of z
is :

(a) $\sqrt{m/k}$ (b) $2\sqrt{m/k}$

(c) $2m/k$ (d) None of these.

129. The number of values of x where the function
$f(x) = 2 (\cos 3x + \cos \sqrt{3}x)$ attains its maximum
is :

(a) 1   (b) 2

(c) 0   (d) infinite

130. Let $f(x) = 1 + 3x^2 + 3^2x^4 + \ldots + 3^{30} \cdot x^{60}$. Then
$f(x)$ has :

(a) atleast one maximum

(b) exactly one maximum

(c) atleast one minimum

(d) exactly one minimum

131. In a right triangle BAC, $\angle A = \frac{\pi}{2}$ and $a + b = 8$.
The real of the triangle is maximum when $\angle C$
is :

(a) $\frac{\pi}{3}$ (b) $\frac{\pi}{4}$

(c) $\frac{\pi}{6}$ (d) None of these.

132. If the roots of the equation $x^3 - ax^2 + 4x - 8 = 0$
are real and positive, then the minimum value of
a is :

(a) 2   (b) 6

(c) $3\sqrt[3]{4}$ (d) None of these.

133. The difference between the greatest and the
least value of the function

$$f(x) = \int_0^x (6t^2 - 24) \, dt \text{ on } [1, 3] \text{ is :}$$

(a) 14   (b) 10

(c) 4   (d) None of these.

134. The range of values of k for which the function
$f(x) = (k^2 - 7k + 12) \cos x + 2(k - 4) x + \log 2$
does not possess critical points, is :

(a) (1, 5)   (b) (1, 5) − {4}

(c) (1, 4)   (d) None of these.

135. The minimum value of $e^{(x^4 - x^3 + x^2)}$ is :

(a) e (b) e^2

(c) 1   (d) None of these.

136. The maximum value of $x^{2/3} + (x-2)^{2/3}$ is :

   (a) 0   (b) 2

   (c) $2^{2/3}$ (d) None of these.

137. On the interval $[0, 1]$, the function $x^{25} \cdot (1-x)^{75}$ takes its maximum value at the point :

   (a) 0   (b) $\dfrac{1}{4}$

   (c) $\dfrac{1}{2}$ (d) $\dfrac{1}{3}$

138. Rectangle of maximum perimeter which can be inscribed in a circle of radius 'a' is a square of side :

   (a) 2a   (b) $\sqrt{2}a$

   (c) a   (d) None of these.

139. A window of fixed perimeter (including the base of the arch) is in the form of a rectangle surmounted by a semi-circle. The semi-circular portion is fitted with coloured glass while the rectangular part is fitted with clear glass. The clear glass transmits three times as much light per square meter as the coloured glass does. The ratio of the sides of the rectangle, so that the window transmits the maximum light is :

   (a) $\dfrac{6}{(\pi + 6)}$ (b) $\dfrac{4}{(\pi + 4)}$

   (c) $\dfrac{2}{(\pi + 2)}$ (d) None of these.

140. A 12 cm long wire is bent to form a triangle with one of its angles as 60°. If the area of the triangle is largest, then the sides of the triangle are :

   (a) a = 2, b = 4, c = 4

   (d) a = 4, b = 4, c = 4

   (c) a = 4, b = 2, c = 4

   (d) None of these.

141. A private telephone company serving a small community makes a profit of ₹ 12 per subscriber, if it has 725 subscribers. It decides to reduce the rate by a fixed sum for each subscriber over 725, thereby reducing the profit by 1 paise per subscriber. Thus, there will be profit of ₹ 11.99 on each of the 726 subscribers, ₹ 11.98 on each 727 subscribers etc. The number of subscribers which will give the company the maximum profit, is :

   (a) 961   (b) 962

   (c) 963   (d) None of these.

142. Rectangles are inscribed in a circle of radius r. The dimensions of the rectangle which has maximum area, are :

   (a) $\sqrt{2}r, \sqrt{2}r$ (b) $r, \sqrt{2}r$

   (c) $2r, \sqrt{2}r$ (d) None of these.

143. The area of the greatest isosceles triangle that can be inscribed in the ellipse $\dfrac{x^2}{a^2} + \dfrac{y^2}{b^2} = 1$, having its vertex coincident with one extremity of major axis, is :

   (a) $\dfrac{\sqrt{3}ab}{4}$ (b) $\dfrac{\sqrt{3}ab}{2}$

   (c) $\dfrac{3\sqrt{3}ab}{4}$ (d) None of these.

144. A point P is given on the circumference of a circle of radius r. The chord QR is parallel to the tangent line at P. The maximum area of the ΔPQR is :

   (a) $\dfrac{3\sqrt{3}}{4}r^2$ (b) $\dfrac{\sqrt{3}}{4}r^2$

   (c) $\dfrac{\sqrt{3}}{2}r^2$ (d) None of these.

145. The circle $x^2 + y^2 = 1$ cuts the x-axis at P and Q. Another circle with centre at Q and variable radius intercepts the first circle at R above the x-axis and the line segment PQ at S. The maximum area of the ΔQSR is :

   (a) $\dfrac{2\sqrt{3}}{9}$ (b) $\dfrac{4\sqrt{3}}{9}$

   (c) $\dfrac{3\sqrt{3}}{4}$ (d) None of these.

146. A cubic $f(x)$ vanishes at $x = -2$ and has a relative maximum/minimum at $x = \dfrac{1}{3}$ and $x = -1$.

If $\displaystyle\int_{-1}^{1} f(x)\, dx = \dfrac{14}{3}$, then :

   (a) $f(x) = x^3 - x^2 - x + 2$

   (b) $f(x) = x^3 + x^2 + x - 2$

   (c) $f(x) = x^3 + x^2 - x + 2$

   (d) None of these.

147. Let (h, k) be a fixed point, where h > 0, k > 0. A straight line passing through this point cuts the positive direction of the co-ordinate axes at the points P and Q. The minimum area of the ΔOPQ, O being the origin, is :

(a) 2kh   (b) kh

(c) 4kh   (d) None of these.

148. Let f(x) be a polynomial of degree 6. If f(x)

satisfies $\displaystyle\lim_{x \to 0} \left\{ 1 + \frac{f(x)}{x^3} \right\}^{1/x} = e^2$ and has local

maximum at x = 1 and local minimum at x = 0 and x = 2, then :

(a) $f(x) = \frac{2}{3}x^6 - \frac{12}{5}x^5 + 2x^4$

(b) $f(x) = \frac{2}{3}x^6 + \frac{12}{5}x^5 - 2x^4$

(c) $f(x) = \frac{2}{3}x^6 + \frac{12}{5}x^5 + 2x^4$

(d) None of these.

149. If $f(x) = \frac{1}{8}(\ln x - bx + x^2)$, x > 0, where b ≥ 0 is

a constant, then :

(a) f(x) has local minimum at $x = \frac{1}{4}$ for b = 1

(b) f(x) has no extremum for 0 ≤ b < 1

(c) f(x) has local minimum at $x = \frac{b - \sqrt{b^2 - 1}}{4}$,
 b > 1

(d) f(x) has local maximum at $x = \frac{b + \sqrt{b^2 - 1}}{4}$,
 b > 1

150. If $f(x) = \frac{x^2 - 1}{x^2 + 1}$, for every real number x, then

the minimum value of f :

(a) does not exist because f is unbounded.

(b) is not attained even though f is bounded.

(c) is equal to 1.

(d) is equal to –1.

151. The coordinates of the point on the parabola $y^2 = 8x$ which is at a minimum distance from the circle
$x^2 + (y + 6)^2 = 1$ are :

(a) (2, 4)   (b) (2, –4)

(c) (–2, 4)   (d) None of these.

152. If A > 0, B > 0 and A + B = $\frac{\pi}{3}$, then the maximum value of tan A tan B is :

(a) $-\frac{1}{3}$ (b) $\frac{1}{3}$

(c) $\frac{2}{3}$ (d) None of these.

153. The minimum valeu of $27^{\cos 2x} \cdot 81^{\sin 2x}$ is :

(a) $\frac{1}{243}$ (b) –5

(c) $\frac{1}{5}$ (d) None of these.

154. A conical vessel is to be prepared out of a circular sheet of gold of unit radius. The area of the sector, to be removed from the sheet so that vessel has maximum volume, is :

(a) $4\pi^2 \left(1 - \sqrt{\frac{2}{3}}\right)^2$ (b) $2\pi^2 \left(1 - \sqrt{\frac{2}{3}}\right)^2$

(c) $\frac{4\pi^2}{3}$ (d) None of these.

155. If h(x) = f(x) + f(–x), then h(x) has got an extreme value at a point where f '(x) is :

(a) even function   (b) odd function

(c) zero   (d) None of these.

156. The least value of a for which the equation

$\frac{4}{\sin x} + \frac{1}{1 - \sin x} = a$ has atleast one solution on

the interval $\left(0, \frac{\pi}{2}\right)$ is :

(a) 4   (b) 1

(c) 9   (d) 8.

157. If x lies in the interval [0, 1], then the minimum value of $x^2 + x + 1$ is :

(a) 3   (b) $\frac{3}{4}$

(c) 1   (d) None of these.

158. The least value of polynomial $x^3 - 18x^2 + 96x$ in the interval [0, 9] is :

(a) 126   (b) 135

(c) 160   (d) 0

159. The points of extremum of the function

$$F(x) = \int_{1}^{x} e^{-t^2/2} \cdot (1 - t^2)\, dt \text{ are :}$$

(a) $x = 1, -1$
(b) $x = -2$

(c) $x = 0$
(d) $x = \dfrac{1}{2}.$

160. A cone of maximum volume is inscribed in a given sphere. Then the ratio of the height of the cone to the diameter of the sphere is :

(a) $\dfrac{3}{4}$
(b) $\dfrac{1}{3}$

(c) $\dfrac{1}{4}$
(d) $\dfrac{2}{3}.$

161. Let $f(x) = \int_{0}^{x} \dfrac{\cos t}{t} dt$ $(x > 0)$; then for

$x = (2n + 1)\dfrac{\pi}{2}$, $f(x)$ has :

(a) minima when $n = 0, 2, 4, \ldots$
(b) maxima when $n = 0, 2, 4, 6, \ldots$
(c) neither max. nor min. when $n = -1, -3, -5, \ldots$
(d) None of these.

162. The minimum value of $2^{(x^2 - 3)^3} + 27$ is :

(a) 1
(b) 2
(c) 2^{27}
(d) None of these.

163. The maximum value of $12 \sin \theta - 9 \sin^2 \theta$ is :

(a) 4
(b) 5
(c) 3
(d) None.

164. A window is in the form of a rectangle surmounted by a semi-circle. The total area of window is fixed. The ratio of the areas of the semi-circular part and the rectangular part so that the total perimeter may be minimum, is :

(a) $\pi : 4$
(b) $\pi : 6$
(c) $\pi : 2$
(d) None of these.

165. Let $f(x)$ be a polynomial of degree 4 such that $f(x)$ vanishes at $x = -1$ and has local maximum/minimum at $x = 1$, $x = 2$ and $x = 3$. If

$\int_{-2}^{2} f(x)\, dx = -\dfrac{1348}{15}$, then

(a) $f(x) = x^4 - 8x^3 + 22x^2 - 24x - 55$
(b) $f(x) = x^4 + 8x^3 - 22x^2 - 24x - 55$
(c) $f(x) = x^4 - 8x^3 - 22x^2 - 24x - 55$
(d) None of these.

166. Let $f(x) = (1 + b^2) x^2 + 2bx + 1$ and $m(b)$ the minimum values of $f(x)$ for given b. As b varies, the range of $m(b)$ is :

(a) $[0, 1]$
(b) $(0, 1/2]$

(c) $\left[\dfrac{1}{2}, 1\right]$
(d) $(0, 1]$

167. If $f(x) = xe^{x(1-x)}$ then $f(x)$ is :

(a) increasing on $\left[-\dfrac{1}{2}, 1\right]$

(b) decreasing on R

(c) increasing on R

(d) decreasing on $\left[-\dfrac{1}{2}, 1\right].$

168. If $\log_{10}(x^3 + y^3) - \log_{10}(x^2 + y^2 - xy) \le 2$, then the maximum value of xy is :

(a) 2500
(b) 3000
(c) 1200
(d) 3500.

169. The greatest and the least values of the function $f(x)$ defined as

$$f(x) = \begin{cases} \text{Min. of } \{3t^4 - 8t^3 - 6t^2 + 24t;\ 1 \le t \le x\}, \\ \qquad\qquad 1 \le x \le 2 \\ \text{Max. of } \left\{3t + \dfrac{1}{4}\sin^2 \pi t + 2;\ 2 \le t \le x\right\}, \\ \qquad\qquad 2 \le x \le 4 \end{cases}$$

are :

(a) 14, 6
(b) 14, 8
(c) 8, 6
(d) None of these.

170. Let $f(x)$ and $g(x)$ be defined and differentiable for $x \ge x_0$ and $f(x_0) = g(x_0)$, $f'(x) > g'(x)$ for $x > x_0$, then :

(a) $f(x) < g(x), x > x_0$

(b) $f(x) = g(x), x > x_0$

(c) $f(x) > g(x), x > x_0$

(d) None of these.

171. The maximum value of $2 - x^{1/3}$

(a) is 0
(b) is 2
(c) does not exist
(d) None of these.

172. One corner of a rectangular sheet of paper of width 'a' cm is folded over so as to reach the opposite edge of the sheet. The minimum length of crease is :

(a) $\frac{2\sqrt{3}a}{5}$ cm (b) $\frac{3\sqrt{3}a}{4}$ cm

(c) $\frac{\sqrt{3}a}{4}$ cm (d) None of these.

173. $f(x) = x^3 + ax^2 + bx + 5\sin^2 x$ is an increasing function in the set of real numbers if a and b satisfy the condition :

(a) $a^2 - 3b - 15 > 0$ (b) $a^2 - 3b + 15 > 0$

(c) $a^2 - 3b + 15 < 0$ (d) $a > 0,\ b > 0$.

174. The curve $y - e^{xy} + x = 0$ has vertical tangent at the point :

(a) (1, 1) (b) at no point

(c) (0, 1) (d) (1, 0).

175. The shortest distance of the point (0, 0) from the curve $y = \frac{e^x + e^{-x}}{2}$ is :

(a) 2 (b) 3

(c) 1 (d) None of these.

176. The co-ordinates of the points on the ellipse $\frac{x^2}{25} + \frac{9y^2}{400} = 1$, at which the abscissae increases at the same rate as the ordinate decreases, are :

(a) $\left(3, -\frac{16}{3}\right), \left(-3, -\frac{16}{3}\right)$

(b) $\left(3, \frac{16}{3}\right), \left(-3, -\frac{16}{3}\right)$

(c) $\left(3, \frac{16}{3}\right), \left(-3, \frac{16}{3}\right)$

(d) $\left(5, \frac{20}{3}\right), \left(5, -\frac{20}{3}\right)$.

177. The tangent to the graph of the function y = f(x) at the point with abscissa x = 1 form an angle of $\frac{\pi}{6}$, at the point x = 2 an angle of $\frac{\pi}{3}$ and at the point x = 3 an angle of $\frac{\pi}{4}$.

The value of $\int_1^3 f'(x) f''(x) + \int_2^3 f''(x)\, dx$,

(f "(x) being continuous) :

(a) $\frac{4\sqrt{3} - 1}{3\sqrt{3}}$ (b) $\frac{3\sqrt{3} - 1}{2}$

(c) $\frac{4 - \sqrt{3}}{3}$ (d) None of these.

178. Let Q (x) = f (x) + f (1 – x) and f "(x) < 0, $0 \le x \le 1$, then:

(a) Q increases in $\left[\frac{1}{2}, 1\right]$

(b) Q decreases in $\left[\frac{1}{2}, 1\right]$

(c) Q decreases in $\left[0, \frac{1}{2}\right]$

(d) None of these.

179. If the area of ΔABC is maximum where A (1, 4) and B (3, 0) are fixed points on the ellipse $2x^2 + y^2 = 18$ and C is a variable point on the ellipse, then the co-ordinates of C are :

(a) $(\sqrt{6}, -\sqrt{6})$ (b) $(-\sqrt{6}, -\sqrt{6})$

(c) $(-\sqrt{6}, \sqrt{6})$ (d) None of these.

180. Number of possible tangents to the curve $y = \cos(x + y), -3\pi \le x \le 3\pi$, that are parallel to the line x + 2y = 0 are :

(a) 1 (b) 2

(c) 3 (d) 4.

181. The point in the interval [0, 2π] where $f(x) = e^x \sin x$ has maximum slope :

(a) π/4 (b) π/3

(c) π/2 (d) None of these.

182. Let $f(x) = a - (x - 3)^{8/9}$, then greatest value of f (x) is :

(a) 3 (b) a

(c) no maximum value (d) None of these.

183. Let $f(x) = \int_0^x \cos^3 x\, dx$. The function f (x) is :

(a) monotonic increasing in [0, π]

(b) monotonic increasing in $\left[0, \frac{\pi}{2}\right]$

(c) monotonic decreasing in [0, 2π]

(d) monotonic decreasing in $\left[-\frac{\pi}{2}, \frac{3\pi}{2}\right]$.

184. If $f(x) = \dfrac{a \sin x + b \cos x}{c \sin x + d \cos x}$ is decreasing for all x, then :

(a) $ad - ac > 0$
(b) $ad - ac < 0$
(c) $ab - cd > 0$
(d) $ab - cd < 0$.

185. If f(x) is a monotonic increasing function and $a \in R$, then :

(a) $f(a^2 + a + 1) > f(1)$
(b) $f(a^2 + a + 1) < f(a^2 + a)$
(c) $f(a^2 + a + 1) > f\left(\dfrac{3}{4}\right)$
(d) $f(a^2 + a + 1) < f(a + 1)$.

186. The function whose graph passes through the point $\left(0, \dfrac{7}{3}\right)$ and whose derivative is $x\sqrt{1 - x^2}$, is given by :

(a) $f(x) = -\dfrac{1}{3}\{(1 - x^2)^{3/2} - 8\}$
(b) $f(x) = \dfrac{1}{3}\{(1 - x^2)^{3/2} + 8\}$
(c) $f(x) = -\dfrac{1}{3}(\sin^{-1} x + 7)$
(d) None of these.

187. The set of critical points of $\dfrac{|x^2 - 4|}{x}$ is :

(a) $\{0\}$
(b) $\{0, 2, -2\}$
(c) $\{2, -2\}$
(d) $\{2\}$.

188. The value of $(2^{\sin x} + 2^{\cos x})$ for all real values of x is :

(a) greater than $\sqrt{2}$
(b) less than $1 - 1/\sqrt{2}$
(c) greater than or equal to $2^{1 - \frac{1}{\sqrt{2}}}$
(d) lies between 0 and $2^{1 - \frac{1}{\sqrt{2}}}$.

189. The set of all values of a for which the function

$$f(x) = (a^2 - 3a + 2)\left(\cos^2 \dfrac{x}{4} - \sin^2 \dfrac{x}{4}\right)$$
$$+ (a - 1)x + \sin 1$$

does not possess critical points is :

(a) $[1, \infty)$
(b) $(-2, 4)$
(c) $(1, 3) \cup (3, 5)$
(d) $(0, 1) \cup (1, 4)$.

190. Value of a for which the equation $x^2 - 3x + a = 0$ has two distinct roots in $[0, 1]$, is given by :

(a) -1
(b) 1
(c) 3
(d) None of these.

191. If $a < 0$, $f(x) = e^{ax} + e^{-ax}$ and S $\{x : f(x)$ is monotonically decreasing$\}$, then :

(a) $S = \{x : x > 0\}$
(b) $S = \{x : x < 0\}$
(c) $S = \{x : x > 1\}$
(d) $S = \{x : x < 1\}$.

192. The critical points of the function
$f(x) = (x - 2)^{2/3} (2x + 1)$ are

(a) -1 and 2
(b) 1
(c) 1 and $-1/2$
(d) 1 and 2.

193. The co-ordinates of the point P (x, y) on the curve $y = e^{-|x|}$ so that the area formed by the co-ordinate axes and the tangent at P is greatest, are :

(a) $(e, 1)$
(b) $(1, e^{-1})$
(c) $(-1, e^{-1})$
(d) $(0, 1)$.

194. The function $f(x) = \dfrac{\log (\pi + x)}{\log (e + x)}$ is :

(a) increasing on $[0, \infty)$.
(b) decreasing on $[0, \infty)$.
(c) increasing on $[0, \pi/e)$ and decreasing on $[\pi/e, \infty)$.
(d) decreasing on $[0, \pi/e)$ and increasing on $[\pi/e, \infty)$.

195. The function $y = \dfrac{2x^2 - 1}{x^4}$ decreases in the interval :

(a) $(-1, 0) \cup (1, \infty)$
(b) $(0, 1)$
(c) $(-1, 1)$
(d) None of these.

196. An extremum value of the function
$f(x) = (\sin^{-1} x)^3 + (\cos^{-1} x)^3$, $(-1 < x < 1)$ is :

(a) $\dfrac{7\pi^3}{8}$
(b) $\dfrac{\pi^3}{8}$
(c) $\dfrac{\pi^3}{32}$
(d) $\dfrac{\pi^3}{16}$

197. The angle at which the curve $y = ke^{kx}$ intersects the y-axis is :

(a) $\tan^{-1} (k^2)$
(b) $\cot^{-1} (k^2)$
(c) $\sin^{-1} (1/\sqrt{1 + k^4})$
(d) $\sec^{-1} \sqrt{1 + k^4}$.

198. The angle subtended by $x^2 + y^2 = 25$ at the point $(10, 0)$ is :

(a) $\pi/6$ (b) $\pi/4$

(c) $\pi/2$ (d) $\pi/3$.

199. The function $f(x) = x^2(x-2)^2$

(a) decreases on $(0, 1) \cup (2, \infty)$

(b) increases on $(-\infty, 0) \cup (1, 2)$

(c) has a local maximum value 0

(d) has a local maximum value 1.

200. The equation(s) of tangent(s) to $y = x^3$ at $(0, 0)$ is (are) :

(a) $x = 0, y = 0$ (b) $x = 0$

(c) $y = 0$ (d) None of these.

201. For function $f(x) = 2x^2 - \ln |x|$

(a) set of critical points is $\{-1/2, 0, 1/2\}$

(b) $f(x)$ is increasing in $(-\infty, -1/2] \cup (0, 1/2]$

(c) $f(x)$ is decreasing in $[-1/2, 0) \cup [1/2, \infty)$

(d) None of these.

202. Let $f(x) = \cos 2\pi x + x - [x]$ [.] denotes the greatest integer function). Then number of points in $[0, 10]$ at which $f(x)$ assumes its local maximum value is :

(a) 0   (b) 10

(c) 9   (d) infinite.

203. The tangent to a given curve is perpendicular to x-axis if :

(a) $\dfrac{dy}{dx} = 0$ (b) $\dfrac{dx}{dy} = 1$

(c) $\dfrac{dy}{dx} = 1$ (d) $\dfrac{dy}{dx} = 0$.

204. The slope of the normal at the point $(at^2, 2at)$ of parabola $y^2 = 4ax$ is :

(a) $\dfrac{1}{t}$ (b) t

(c) $-t$ (d) $-\dfrac{1}{t}$.

205. Equation of the tangent to the hyperbola $2x^2 - 3y^2 = 6$ which is parallel to the line $y = 3x + 4$ is :

(a) $y = 3x + 5$

(b) $y = 3x - 5$

(c) $y = 3x + 5$ and $y = 3x - 5$

(d) $y = -3x - 5$.

206. The length of the subnormal to the parabola $y^2 = 4ax$ at any point is equal to :

(a) $\sqrt{2}\, a$ (b) $2\sqrt{2}\, a$

(c) $\dfrac{a}{\sqrt{2}}$ (d) $2a$.

207. The normal at the point $(1, 1)$ on the curve $2y = 3 - x^2$ is:

(a) $x + y = 0$ (b) $x + y + 1 = 0$

(c) $x - y + 1 = 0$ (d) $x - y = 0$.

208. Equation of normal to the curve $y = x(2 - x)$ at the point $(2, 0)$ is :

(a) $x - 2y + 2 = 0$ (b) $x - 2y = 2$

(c) $2x + y = 4$ (d) None of these.

209. The normal at the point $(1, 1)$ on the curve $2y = 3 - x^2$ is :

(a) $x - y = 0$ (b) $x - y + 1 = 0$

(c) $x + y + 1 = 0$ (d) $x + y = 0$.

210. The equation of the tangent at $(a, -2a)$ to the parabola $y^2 = 4ax$ is :

(a) $x + y - a = 0$ (b) $x + y + a = 0$

(c) $x - y + a = 0$ (d) $x - y - a = 0$.

211. The equation of the tangent to the parabola $y^2 = 8x$ which is perpendicular to the line $x - 3y + 6 = 0$ is :

(a) $3x + y = 0$ (b) $x + 3y = 8$

(c) $9x + 3y + 2 = 0$ (d) $3x - y = 2$.

212. If f is an increasing function and g is a decreasing function such that gof is defined, then :

(a) gof is increasing

(b) gof is decreasing

(c) gof may not be monotonic

(d) None of these.

213. If $x + y = 8$, then the maximum value of xy is :

(a) 8   (b) 16

(c) 20   (d) 24.

214. The least and greatest values of f when $f(x) = x^3 - 6x^2 + 9x$, where $0 \le x \le 6$, are :

(a) 3, 4   (b) 0, 6

(c) 0, 3   (d) 3, 6.

215. The point on the curve $y^2 = 4x$ which is nearest to the point $(2, 1)$, is :

(a) $(1, 2\sqrt{2})$ (b) $(1, 2)$

(c) $(1, -2)$ (d) $(-2, 1)$.

216. For the curve $y^n = a^{n-1} x$, the subnormal at any point is constant. The value of n must be :

(a) 3   (b) 0

(c) 1   (d) 2.

217. The angle between curve $y = 4x$ and $x^2 + y^2 = 5$ at $(1, 2)$ is :

(a) $\tan^{-1} 2$ (b) $\dfrac{\pi}{2}$

(c) $\dfrac{\pi}{4}$ (d) $\tan^{-1} 3$.

218. The tangent to the curve $y = e^{2x}$ at the point $(0, 1)$ meets the x-axis at :

(a) $(2, 0)$ (b) $(0, 0)$

(c) $\left(-\dfrac{1}{2}, 0\right)$ (d) None of these.

219. The greatest value of

$f(x) = \cos (xe^{|x|} + 7x^2 - 3x)$, $x \in [-1, \infty)$ is :

(a) 0   (b) 1

(c) -1 (d) None of these.

220. For the curve, $y = \dfrac{a}{2} (e^{x/a} + e^{-x/a})$, the length of the portion of the normal intercepted between the curve and x-axis is :

(a) $\dfrac{y^2}{a^2}$ (b) $\dfrac{y}{a}$

(c) $\dfrac{y^2}{a}$ (d) y.

221. The square of the subtangent to the curve $by^2 = (x + a)^3$ is proportional to :

(a) $(\text{Subnormal})^{3/2}$ (b) Subnormal

(c) $(\text{Subnormal})^{1/2}$ (d) None of these.

222. If $x = a (\theta + \sin \theta)$, $y = a (1 - \cos \theta)$, then at $\theta = \dfrac{\pi}{2}$, the length of normal is :

(a) $2a$ (b) $\dfrac{a}{2}$

(c) $a\sqrt{2}$ (d) $\dfrac{a}{\sqrt{2}}$.

223. The function which is neither decreasing nor increasing in $\left(\dfrac{\pi}{2}, \dfrac{3\pi}{2}\right)$ is :

(a) $\csc x$ (b) $\tan x$

(c) x^2 (d) $|x - 1|$.

224. The maximum value of $f(x) = \dfrac{x}{4 - x + x^2}$ on $[-1, 1]$ is :

(a) $-1/4$ (b) $-1/3$

(c) $1/6$ (d) $1/5$.

225. The points on the curve $y = 12x - x^3$ at which the gradient is zero are :

(a) $(0, 2), (2, 16)$ (b) $(0, -2), (2, -16)$

(c) $(2, -16), (-2, 16)$ (d) $(2, 16), (-2, -16)$.

226. If from mean value theorem, $f'(x_1) = \dfrac{f(b) - f(a)}{b - a}$ then

(a) $a < x_1 \le b$ (b) $a \le x_1 < b$

(c) $a < x_1 < b$ (d) $a \le x_1 \le b$.

227. The line $x + y = 2$ is tangent to the curve $x^2 = 3 - 2y$ at the point :

(a) $(1, 1)$ (b) $(-1, 1)$

(c) $(\sqrt{3}, 0)$ (d) $(3, -3)$.

228. The point of the curve $y^2 = 2 (x - 3)$ at which the normal is parallel to the line $y - 2x + 1 = 0$ is :

(a) $(5, 2)$ (b) $\left(-\dfrac{1}{2}, -2\right)$

(c) $(5, -2)$ (d) $\left(\dfrac{3}{2}, 2\right)$.

229. For the function $x + \dfrac{1}{x}$, $x \in [1, 3]$ the value of c for the mean value theorem is :

(a) 1   (b) $\sqrt{3}$

(c) 2   (d) None of these.

230. A spherical balloon is filled with 4500π cubic metres of helium gas. If a leak in the balloon causes the gas to escape at the rate of 72π cubic metres per minute, then the rate (in metres per minute) at which the radius of the balloon decreases 49 minutes after the leakage began is : **[AIEEE - 2012]**

(a) $\dfrac{9}{7}$ (b) $\dfrac{7}{9}$

(c) $\dfrac{2}{9}$ (d) $\dfrac{9}{2}$

231. Let a, b ∈ R be such that the function f given by f (x) = ln | x | + bx² + ax, x ≠ 0 has extreme values at x = −1 and x = 2. **[AIEEE - 2012]**

Statement 1: f has local maximum at x = −1 and at x = 2.

Statement 2: $a = \dfrac{1}{2}$ and $b = \dfrac{-1}{4}$

(a) Statement 1 is false, statement 2 is true.

(b) Statement 1 is true, statement 2 is true; statement 2 is a correct explanation for statement 1.

(c) Statement 1 is true, statement 2 is true; statement 2 is not a correct explanation for statement 1.

(d) Statement 1 is true, statement 2 is false.

232. Consider the function f (x) = | x − 2 | + | x − 5 |, x ∈ R. **[AIEEE - 2012]**

Statement 1 : f '(4) = 0

Statement 2 : f is continuous in [2, 5], differentiable in (2, 5) and f(2) = f(5).

(a) Statement 1 is false, statement 2 is true.

(b) Statement 1 is true, statement 2 is true; statement 2 is a correct explanation for statement 1.

(c) Statement 1 is true, statement 2 is true; statement 2 is not a correct explanation for statement 1.

(d) Statement 1 is true; statement 2 is false.

233. For $x \in \left(0, \dfrac{5\pi}{2}\right)$, define $f(x) = \int_0^x \sqrt{t} \sin t \, dt$.

Then f has **[AIEEE - 2011]**

(a) Local maximum at π and local minimum at 2π

(b) Local maximum at π and 2π

(c) Local minimum at π and 2π

(d) Local minimum at π and local maximum at 2π

234. The equation of the tangent to the curve $y = x + \dfrac{4}{x^2}$, that is parallel to the x-axis, is : **[AIEEE - 2010]**

(a) y = 1   (b) y = 2

(c) y = 3   (d) y = 0

235. Let f : R → R be defined by

$$f(x) = \begin{cases} k - 2x, & \text{if } x \le -1 \\ 2x + 3, & \text{if } x > -1. \end{cases}$$

If f has a local minimum at x = −1, then a possible value of k is : **[AIEEE - 2010]**

(a) 0   (b) $-\dfrac{1}{2}$

(c) −1   (d) 1

236. Given P(x) = x⁴ + ax³ + bx² + cx + d such that x = 0 is the only real root of P'(x) = 0. If P(−1) < P(1), then in the interval [−1, 1] **[AIEEE - 2009]**

(a) P(−1) is the minimum and P(1) is the maximum of P

(b) P(−1) is not minimum but P(1) is the maximum of P

(c) P(−1) is the minimum and P(1) is not the maximum of P

(d) neither P(−1) is the minimum nor P(1) is the maximum of P

237. The normal to a curve at P(x, y) meets the x-axis at G. If the distance of G from the origin is twice the abscissa of P, then the curve is : **[AIEEE - 2007]**

(a) ellipse   (b) parabola

(c) circle   (d) hyperbola

238. A value of C for which the conclusion of Mean Value Theorem holds for the function f(x) = logₑ x on the interval [1, 3] is : **[AIEEE - 2007]**

(a) 2 log₃ e   (b) $\dfrac{1}{2} \log_e x$

(c) log₃ e   (d) logₑ 3

239. The function f (x) = tan⁻¹ (sin x + cos x) is an increasing function in **[AIEEE - 2007]**

(a) $\left(\dfrac{\pi}{4}, \dfrac{\pi}{2}\right)$ (b) $\left(-\dfrac{\pi}{2}, \dfrac{\pi}{4}\right)$

(c) $\left(0, \dfrac{\pi}{2}\right)$ (d) $\left(-\dfrac{\pi}{2}, \dfrac{\pi}{2}\right)$

240. The function $f(x) = \frac{x}{2} + \frac{2}{x}$ has a local minimum at   **[AIEEE - 2006]**

(a) $x = 2$
(b) $x = -2$
(c) $x = 0$
(d) $x = 1$

241. Angle between the tangents to the curve $y = x^2 - 5x + 6$ at the points $(2, 0)$ and $(3, 0)$ is :

[AIEEE - 2006]

(a) $\frac{\pi}{3}$
(b) $\frac{\pi}{2}$
(c) $\frac{\pi}{6}$
(d) $\frac{\pi}{4}$

242. A triangular park is enclosed on two sides by a fence and on the third side by a straight river bank. The two sides having fence are of same length x. The maximum area enclosed by the park is :   **[AIEEE - 2006]**

(a) $\frac{3}{2}x^2$
(b) $\sqrt{\frac{x^3}{8}}$
(c) $\frac{1}{2}x^2$
(d) πx^2

243. Area of the greatest rectangle that can be inscribed in the ellipse $\frac{x^2}{a^2} + \frac{y^2}{b^2} = 1$ is   :

[AIEEE - 2005]

(a) $2ab$
(b) ab
(c) $\sqrt{ab}$
(d) $\frac{a}{b}$

244. The normal to the curve $x = a\,(\cos\theta + \theta \sin\theta)$, $y = a\,(\sin\theta - \theta\cos\theta)$ at any point 'θ' is such that   **[AIEEE - 2005]**

(a) it passes through the origin

(b) it makes angle $\frac{\pi}{2} + \theta$ with the x-axis

(c) it passes through $\left(a\,\frac{\pi}{2},\, -a\right)$

(d) it is at a constant distance from the origin

245. A function is matched below against an interval where it is supposed to be increasing. Which of the following pairs is incorrectly matched ?

[AIEEE - 2005]

Interval	Function
(a) $(-\infty, \infty)$	$x^3 - 3x^2 + 3x + 3$
(b) $[2, \infty)$	$2x^3 - 3x^2 - 12x + 6$
(c) $\left(-\infty, \frac{1}{3}\right)$	$3x^2 - 2x + 1$
(d) $(-\infty, -4]$	$x^3 + 6x^2 + 6$

246. Let f be differentiable for all x. If $f(1) = -2$ and $f'(x) \geq 2$ for $x \in [1, 6]$, then :   **[AIEEE - 2005]**

(a) $f(6) \geq 8$
(b) $f(6) < 8$
(c) $f(6) < 5$
(d) $f(6) = 5$

ANSWER KEY

1. (b)	2. (b)	3. (b)	4. (c)	5. (b)	6. (d)	7. (a)	8. (b)	9. (c)	10. (a)
11. (c)	12. (b)	13. (a)	14. (a)	15. (c)	16. (c)	17. (a)	18. (c)	19. (b)	20. (a)
21. (b)	22. (d)	23. (a)	24. (c)	25. (a)	26. (c)	27. (c)	28. (d)	29. (a)	30. (b)
31. (a)	32. (b)	33. (a)	34. (b)	35. (c)	36. (a)	37. (b)	38. (a)	39. (b)	40. (c)
41. (b)	42. (c)	43. (a)	44. (a)	45. (c)	46. (c)	47. (a)	48. (b)	49. (a)	50. (a)
51. (b)	52. (c)	53. (a)	54. (b)	55. (d)	56. (d)	57. (a)	58. (d)	59. (a)	60. (d)
61. (b)	62. (a)	63. (c)	64. (a)	65. (a)	66. (b)	67. (c)	68. (a)	69. (c)	70. (a)
71. (d)	72. (c)	73. (b)	74. (a)	75. (c)	76. (a)	77. (c)	78. (b)	79. (b)	80. (a)
81. (b)	82. (c)	83. (c)	84. (c)	85. (d)	86. (a)	87. (d)	88. (b)	89. (c)	90. (b)
91. (a)	92. (b)	93. (a)	94. (b)	95. (a)	96. (a)	97. (b)	98. (b)	99. (d)	100. (c)
101. (c)	102. (a)	103. (d)	104. (a)	105. (d)	106. (b)	107. (a)	108. (a)	109. (b)	110. (d)
111. (b)	112. (d)	113. (c)	114. (d)	115. (b)	116. (b)	117. (d)	118. (a)	119. (a)	120. (b)

121. (d)	**122.** (b)	**123.** (b)	**124.** (a)	**125.** (c)	**126.** (a)	**127.** (a)	**128.** (b)	**129.** (a)	**130.** (d)
131. (a)	**132.** (b)	**133.** (a)	**134.** (b)	**135.** (c)	**136.** (b)	**137.** (b)	**138.** (b)	**139.** (a)	**140.** (b)
141. (b)	**142.** (a)	**143.** (c)	**144.** (a)	**145.** (b)	**146.** (c)	**147.** (a)	**148.** (a)	**149.** (b)	**150.** (d)
151. (b)	**152.** (b)	**153.** (a)	**154.** (b)	**155.** (a)	**156.** (c)	**157.** (c)	**158.** (d)	**159.** (a)	**160.** (d)
161. (b)	**162.** (a)	**163.** (a)	**164.** (a)	**165.** (a)	**166.** (d)	**167.** (a)	**168.** (a)	**169.** (b)	**170.** (c)
171. (c)	**172.** (b)	**173.** (c)	**174.** (d)	**175.** (c)	**176.** (b)	**177.** (d)	**178.** (b)	**179.** (b)	**180.** (c)
181. (a)	**182.** (b)	**183.** (b)	**184.** (b)	**185.** (c)	**186.** (a)	**187.** (c)	**188.** (c)	**189.** (d)	**190.** (d)
191. (b)	**192.** (d)	**193.** (c)	**194.** (b)	**195.** (a)	**196.** (c)	**197.** (b)	**198.** (d)	**199.** (d)	**200.** (c)
201. (d)	**202.** (b)	**203.** (a)	**204.** (c)	**205.** (c)	**206.** (d)	**207.** (d)	**208.** (b)	**209.** (a)	**210.** (b)
211. (a)	**212.** (b)	**213.** (b)	**214.** (a)	**215.** (b)	**216.** (d)	**217.** (d)	**218.** (c)	**219.** (b)	**220.** (c)
221. (b)	**222.** (b)	**223.** (a)	**224.** (c)	**225.** (d)	**226.** (c)	**227.** (a)	**228.** (c)	**229.** (b)	**230.** (c)
231. (b)	**232.** (b)	**233.** (a)	**234.** (c)	**235.** (c)	**236.** (b)	**237.** (a,d)	**238.** (a)	**239.** (b)	**240.** (a)
241. (b)	**242.** (c)	**243.** (a)	**244.** (d)	**245.** (c)	**246.** (a)				

INDEFINITE INTEGRATION

MULTIPLE CHOICE QUESTIONS

1. If $\int \sqrt{\dfrac{1-\sqrt{x}}{1+\sqrt{x}}}\,dx$

   $= A \cos^{-1} \sqrt{x} + f(x) (\sqrt{x} - 2) + C$, then :

   (a) $A = 1, f(x) = \sqrt{1-x}$

   (b) $A = -1, f(x) = \sqrt{1-x}$

   (c) $A = 1, f(x) = \sqrt{x-1}$

   (d) $A = -1, f(x) = \sqrt{x-1}$.

2. If $\int (\sin 2x + \cos 2x)\,dx = \dfrac{1}{\sqrt{2}} \sin (2x - c) + a$,

   then :

   (a) $c = \dfrac{\pi}{2}$, a = arbitrary constant

   (b) $c = \dfrac{\pi}{6}$, a = arbitrary constant

   (c) $c = \dfrac{\pi}{4}$, a = arbitrary constant

   (d) None of these.

3. If $\int \sqrt{\dfrac{\cos^3 x}{\sin^{11} x}}\,dx = -2 (A \tan^{-9/2} x + B \tan^{-5/2} x)$
   $+ C$, then :

   (a) $A = \dfrac{1}{9}, B = \dfrac{-1}{5}$ (b) $A = \dfrac{1}{9}, B = \dfrac{1}{5}$

   (c) $A = -\dfrac{1}{9}, B = \dfrac{1}{5}$ (d) None of these.

4. If $\int \sqrt{\dfrac{\sin (x-a)}{\sin (x+a)}}\,dx = A \sin^{-1} \left(\dfrac{\cos x}{\cos a}\right)$

   $+ B \log \left(\sin x + \sqrt{\sin^2 x - \sin^2 a}\right) + C$, then :

   (a) $A = \cos a, B = \sin a$

   (b) $A = \cos a, B = -\sin a$

   (c) $A = -\cos a, B = -\sin a$

   (d) None of these.

5. $\int \dfrac{dx}{\sin x \cdot \sin (x + \alpha)}$ is equal to :

   (a) $\operatorname{cosec} \alpha \log \left|\dfrac{\sin x}{\sin (x + \alpha)}\right| + C$

   (b) $\operatorname{cosec} \alpha \log \left|\dfrac{\sin (x + \alpha)}{\sin x}\right| + C$

   (c) $\operatorname{cosec} \alpha \log \left|\dfrac{\sec (x + \alpha)}{\sec x}\right| + C$

   (d) $\operatorname{cosec} \alpha \log \left|\dfrac{\sec x}{\sec (x + \alpha)}\right| + C$

6. $\int \dfrac{\sqrt{\cos 2x}}{\sin x}\,dx$ is equal to :

   (a) $\log \left|\dfrac{\cot x + \sqrt{\cot^2 x - 1}}{\left(\sqrt{2} \cos x + \sqrt{\cos 2x}\right)^{\sqrt{2}}}\right| + C$

   (b) $\log \left|\dfrac{\left(\sqrt{2} \cos x + \sqrt{\cos 2x}\right)^{\sqrt{2}}}{\left(\cot x + \sqrt{\cot^2 x - 1}\right)^{\sqrt{2}}}\right| + C$

   (c) $\log \left|\dfrac{\tan x + \sqrt{\tan^2 x - 1}}{\left(\sqrt{2} \cos x + \sqrt{\cos 2x}\right)^{\sqrt{2}}}\right| + C$

   (d) $\log \left|\dfrac{\left(\sqrt{2} \cos x + \sqrt{\cos 2x}\right)^{\sqrt{2}}}{\left(\tan x + \sqrt{\tan^2 x - 1}\right)}\right| + C$

7. $\int [1 + \tan x \cdot \tan (x + \alpha)\,dx$ is equal to :

   (a) $\cot \alpha \cdot \log \left|\dfrac{\sin x}{\sin (x + \alpha)}\right| + C$

   (b) $\tan \alpha \cdot \log \left|\dfrac{\sin x}{\sin (x + \alpha)}\right| + C$

   (c) $\cot \alpha \cdot \log \left|\dfrac{\sin (x + \alpha)}{\sin x}\right| + C$

   (d) None of these.

8. $\int \sqrt{\dfrac{e^x - 1}{e^x + 1}}\, dx$ is equal to :

(a) $\log\left(e^x + \sqrt{e^{2x} - 1}\right) - \sec^{-1}(e^x) + C$

(b) $\log\left(e^x + \sqrt{e^{2x} - 1}\right) + \sec^{-1}(e^x) + C$

(c) $\log\left(e^x - \sqrt{e^{2x} - 1}\right) - \sec^{-1}(e^x) + C$

(d) None of these.

9. $\int \tan(x - \alpha)\,\tan(x + \alpha)\,\tan 2x\, dx$ is equal to :

(a) $\log\left|\dfrac{\sqrt{\sec 2x}\ \sec(x + \alpha)}{\sec(x - \alpha)}\right| + C$

(b) $\log\left|\dfrac{\sqrt{\sec 2x}}{\sec(x - \alpha) \cdot \sec(x + \alpha)}\right| + C$

(c) $\log\left|\dfrac{\sqrt{\sec 2x} \cdot \sec(x - \alpha)}{\sec(x + \alpha)}\right| + C$

(d) None of these.

10. If $\int \dfrac{dx}{x^4 + x^3} = \dfrac{A}{x^2} + \dfrac{B}{x} + \log\left|\dfrac{x}{x + 1}\right| + C$, then :

(a) $A = \dfrac{1}{2},\ B = 1$ (b) $A = 1,\ B = -\dfrac{1}{2}$

(c) $A = -\dfrac{1}{2},\ B = 1$ (d) None of these.

11. $\int \dfrac{dx}{x^2 (1 + x^4)^{3/4}}$ is equal to :

(a) $-\dfrac{(1 + x^4)^{1/4}}{x} + C$ (b) $\dfrac{(1 + x^4)^{1/4}}{x} + C$

(c) $-\dfrac{(1 + x^4)^{3/4}}{x} + C$ (d) None of these.

12. $\int \dfrac{dx}{(x + 1)^2 \sqrt{x^2 + 2x + 2}}$ is equal to :

(a) $\dfrac{\sqrt{x^2 + 2x + 2}}{x + 1} + C$ (b) $-\dfrac{\sqrt{x^2 + 2x + 1}}{(x + 1)^2} + C$

(c) $-\dfrac{\sqrt{x^2 + 2x + 2}}{x + 1} + C$ (d) None of these.

13. $\int \dfrac{dx}{\sin^4 x + \cos^4 x}$ is equal to :

(a) $\dfrac{1}{\sqrt{2}} \tan^{-1}\left(\dfrac{1}{\sqrt{2}} \tan 2x\right) + C$

(b) $\sqrt{2} \tan^{-1}\left(\dfrac{1}{\sqrt{2}} \tan 2x\right) + C$

(c) $\dfrac{1}{\sqrt{2}} \tan^{-1}\left(\dfrac{1}{\sqrt{2}} \cot 2x\right) + C$

(d) None of these.

14. If $\int \dfrac{dx}{x^2 (x^2 + a^2)^2}$

$= \dfrac{A}{a^5}\left(\dfrac{2a}{x} + B \tan^{-1}\dfrac{x}{a} + \dfrac{ax}{x^2 + a^2}\right) + C$, then :

(a) $A = -\dfrac{1}{2},\ B = -3$ (b) $A = -\dfrac{1}{2},\ B = 3$

(c) $A = \dfrac{1}{2},\ B = 3$ (d) None of these.

15. If $\int x^{13/2} \cdot (1 + x^{5/2})^{1/2}\, dx$

$= A(1 + x^{5/2})^{7/2} + B(1 + x^{5/2})^{5/2} + C(1 + x^{5/2})^{3/2}$,

then :

(a) $A = -\dfrac{4}{35},\ B = -\dfrac{8}{25},\ C = \dfrac{4}{15}$

(b) $A = \dfrac{4}{35},\ B = -\dfrac{8}{25},\ C = -\dfrac{4}{15}$

(c) $A = \dfrac{4}{35},\ B = -\dfrac{8}{25},\ C = \dfrac{4}{15}$

(d) None of these.

16. If $\int \dfrac{dx}{\sqrt[3]{\sin^{11} x \cos x}} = -\left(\dfrac{3}{8} f(x) + \dfrac{3}{2} g(x)\right) + C$,

then :

(a) $f(x) = \tan^{-8/3} x,\ g(x) = \tan^{-2/3} x$

(b) $f(x) = \tan^{8/3} x,\ g(x) = \tan^{-2/3} x$

(c) $f(x) = \tan^{-8/3} x,\ g(x) = \tan^{2/3} x$

(d) None of these.

17. $\int \dfrac{\sqrt{x}}{\sqrt{x} + \sqrt[3]{x}}\, dx$ is equal to :

(a) $x - \dfrac{6}{5} x^{5/6} - \dfrac{3}{2} x^{2/3} - 2x^{1/2} + 3x^{1/3} + 6x^{1/6}$

$\qquad + 6 \log(1 + x^{1/6}) + C$

(b) $x - \dfrac{6}{5} x^{5/6} + \dfrac{3}{2} x^{2/3} - 2x^{1/2} + 3x^{1/3} - 6x^{1/6}$

$\qquad + 6 \log(1 + x^{1/6}) + C$

(c) $x + \dfrac{6}{5} x^{5/6} + \dfrac{3}{2} x^{2/3} - 2x^{1/2} + 3x^{1/3} - 6x^{1/6}$

$\qquad + 6 \log(1 + x^{1/6}) + C$

(d) None of these.

18. $\int \sqrt{\sec x - 1}\, dx$ is equal to :

(a) $2 \log \left(\cos \frac{x}{2} + \sqrt{\cos^2 \frac{x}{2} - \frac{1}{2}} \right) + C$

(b) $\log \left(\cos \frac{x}{2} + \sqrt{\cos^2 \frac{x}{2} - \frac{1}{2}} \right) + C$

(c) $-2 \log \left(\cos \frac{x}{2} + \sqrt{\cos^2 \frac{x}{2} - \frac{1}{2}} \right) + C$

(d) None of these.

19. $\int \dfrac{dx}{\cos x \sqrt{\cos 2x}}$ is equal to :

(a) $\sqrt{2} \left(\sqrt{\tan x} + \frac{1}{5} \tan^{5/2} x \right) + C$

(b) $\sqrt{2} \left(\sqrt{\cot x} + \frac{1}{5} \tan^{5/2} x \right) + C$

(c) $\sqrt{2} \left(\sqrt{\tan x} - \frac{1}{5} \tan^{5/2} x \right) + C$

(d) None of these.

20. $\int 7^{7^{7^x}} \cdot 7^{7^x}, 7^x \, dx$ is equal to :

(a) $\dfrac{7^{7^x}}{(\log 7)^3} + C$ (b) $\dfrac{7^{7^{7^x}}}{(\log 7)^2} + C$

(c) $7^{7^{7^x}} \cdot (\log 7)^3 + C$ (d) None of these.

21. $\int \dfrac{dx}{\cos^3 x \sqrt{\sin 2x}}$ is equal to :

(a) $\sqrt{2} \left(\sqrt{\cot x} + \frac{1}{5} \tan^{5/2} x \right) + C$

(b) $\sqrt{2} \left(\sqrt{\tan x} + \frac{1}{5} \tan^{5/2} x \right) + C$

(c) $\sqrt{2} \left(\sqrt{\tan x} - \frac{1}{5} \tan^{5/2} x \right) + C$

(d) None of these.

22. If $\int \dfrac{dx}{1 - \sin^4 x} = \frac{1}{2} \tan x + A \tan^{-1} [f(x)] + C$,

then :

(a) $A = \dfrac{\sqrt{2}}{4}$ and $f(x) = \sqrt{2} \tan x$

(b) $A = \sqrt{2}$ and $f(x) = \sqrt{2} \tan x$

(c) $A = -\sqrt{2}$ and $f(x) = \sqrt{2} \tan x$

(d) None of these.

23. If $\int \dfrac{dx}{\sec x + \cosec x} = \frac{1}{2} f(x) - \frac{1}{2\sqrt{2}} g(x)$, then :

(a) $f(x) = \sin x - \cos x$, $g(x) = \log \cot \left(\frac{x}{2} + \frac{\pi}{8} \right)$

(b) $f(x) = \sin x - \cos x$, $g(x) = \log \tan \left(\frac{x}{2} + \frac{\pi}{8} \right)$

(c) $f(x) = \cos x - \sin x$, $g(x) = \log \tan \left(\frac{x}{2} + \frac{\pi}{8} \right)$

(d) $f(x) = \cos x - \sin x$, $g(x) = \log \cot \left(\frac{x}{2} + \frac{\pi}{8} \right)$

24. $\int \dfrac{\log x}{(1 + x)^3}\, dx$ is equal to :

(a) $\dfrac{\log x}{(1 + x)^2} + \frac{1}{2} \log \frac{x}{x + 1} + \frac{1}{2} \cdot \frac{1}{x + 1} + C$

(b) $\dfrac{-\log x}{2(1 + x)^2} + \frac{1}{2} \log \frac{x + 1}{x} + \frac{1}{2} \cdot \frac{1}{x + 1} + C$

(c) $\dfrac{-\log x}{2(1 + x)^2} + \frac{1}{2} \log \frac{x}{x + 1} + \frac{1}{2} \cdot \frac{1}{x + 1} + C$

(d) None of these.

25. $\int \dfrac{\cos x + x \sin x}{x(x + \cos x)}\, dx$ is equal to :

(a) $\log \left| \dfrac{x}{x + \cos x} \right| + C$ (b) $\log \left| \dfrac{x + \cos x}{x} \right| + C$

(c) $\log \left| \dfrac{1}{x + \cos x} \right| + C$ (d) $\log |x + \cos x| + C$.

26. $\int \log \left(x + \sqrt{x^2 + a^2} \right) dx$ is equal to :

(a) $x \log \left(x + \sqrt{x^2 + a^2} \right) + \sqrt{x^2 + a^2} + C$

(b) $x \log \left(x + \sqrt{x^2 + a^2} \right) - 2\sqrt{x^2 + a^2} + C$

(c) $x \log \left(x + \sqrt{x^2 + a^2} \right) - \sqrt{x^2 + a^2} + C$

(d) None of these.

27. $\int \sin^{-1} \sqrt{\dfrac{x}{a + x}}\, dx$ is equal to :

(a) $(x + a) \tan^{-1} \sqrt{\dfrac{x}{a}} - \sqrt{ax} + C$

(b) $(x + a) \tan^{-1} \sqrt{\dfrac{x}{a}} + \sqrt{ax} + C$

(c) $(x + a) \cot^{-1} \sqrt{\dfrac{x}{a}} - \sqrt{ax} + C$

(d) None of these.

28. $\int \dfrac{\tan x}{\sqrt{a + b \tan^2 x}} \, dx$, $a > b > 0$, is equal to :

(a) $\dfrac{1}{\sqrt{a - b}} \log \left(\cos x + \sqrt{\cos^2 x + \dfrac{b}{a - b}} \right) + C$

(b) $\dfrac{1}{\sqrt{a - b}} \log \left(\sin x + \sqrt{\sin^2 x + \dfrac{b}{a - b}} \right) + C$

(c) $-\dfrac{1}{\sqrt{a - b}} \log \left(\cos x + \sqrt{\cos^2 x + \dfrac{b}{a - b}} \right) + C$

(d) None of these.

29. $\int \dfrac{\sin^{-1} \sqrt{x} - \cos^{-1} \sqrt{x}}{\sin^{-1} \sqrt{x} + \cos^{-1} \sqrt{x}} \, dx$ is equal to :

(a) $x - \dfrac{4}{\pi} \left[\left(x - \dfrac{1}{2} \right) \cos^{-1} \sqrt{x} - \dfrac{1}{2} \sqrt{x - x^2} \right] + C$

(b) $x + \dfrac{4}{\pi} \left[\left(x - \dfrac{1}{2} \right) \cos^{-1} \sqrt{x} - \dfrac{1}{2} \sqrt{x - x^2} \right] + C$

(c) $x - \dfrac{4}{\pi} \left[\left(x - \dfrac{1}{2} \right) \cos^{-1} \sqrt{x} + \dfrac{1}{2} \sqrt{x - x^2} \right] + C$

(d) None of these.

30. $\int \dfrac{\tan x}{\sqrt{\sin^4 x + \cos^4 x}} \, dx$ is equal to :

(a) $\log \left(\tan^2 x + \sqrt{1 + \tan^4 x} \right) + C$

(b) $\dfrac{1}{2} \log \left(\tan^2 x + \sqrt{1 + \tan^4 x} \right) + C$

(c) $\dfrac{1}{4} \log \left(\tan^2 x + \sqrt{1 + \tan^4 x} \right) + C$

(d) None of these.

31. $\int \dfrac{dx}{\sqrt{\sin^3 x \sin (x + \alpha)}}$ is equal to

(a) $2 \cosec \alpha \sqrt{\cos \alpha + \sin \alpha \cot x} + C$

(b) $-2 \cosec \alpha \sqrt{\cos \alpha + \sin \alpha \cot x} + C$

(c) $\cosec \alpha \sqrt{\cos \alpha + \sin \alpha \cot x} + C$

(d) None of these.

32. Let $f(x) = \int \dfrac{dx}{(1 + x^2)^{3/2}}$ and $f(0) = 0$, then $f(1) =$

(a) $\dfrac{-1}{\sqrt{2}}$

(b) $\dfrac{1}{\sqrt{2}}$

(c) $\sqrt{2}$

(d) None of these.

33. $\int \dfrac{dx}{(1 + \sqrt{x}) \sqrt{x - x^2}}$ is equal to :

(a) $\dfrac{2 (\sqrt{x} - 1)}{\sqrt{1 - x}} + C$

(b) $\dfrac{2 (1 - \sqrt{x})}{\sqrt{1 - x}} + C$

(c) $\dfrac{(\sqrt{x} - 1)}{\sqrt{1 - x}} + C$

(d) None of these.

34. $\int e^x \left(\dfrac{1 - x}{1 + x} \right)^2 dx$ is equal to :

(a) $e^x \left(\dfrac{1 - x}{1 + x^2} \right) + C$

(b) $e^x \left(\dfrac{x - 1}{1 + x^2} \right) + C$

(c) $e^x \cdot \dfrac{1}{1 + x^2} + C$

(d) None of these.

35. $\int \dfrac{\cos 5x + \cos 4x}{1 - 2 \cos 3x} \, dx$ is equal to :

(a) $\dfrac{\sin 2x}{2} + \sin x + C$

(b) $\dfrac{-\sin 2x}{2} - \sin x + C$

(c) $\dfrac{\sin 2x}{2} - \sin x + C$

(d) $\dfrac{-\sin 2x}{2} + \sin x + C$

36. $\int \dfrac{\sqrt{1 - \sin x}}{1 + \cos x} \cdot e^{-x/2} \, dx$ is equal to :

(a) $\sec \dfrac{x}{2} \cdot e^{-x/2} + C$

(b) $-\sec \dfrac{x}{2} \cdot e^{-x/2} + C$

(c) $\tan \dfrac{x}{2} \cdot e^{-x/2} + C$

(d) None of these.

37. $\int \dfrac{\sin^3 x \, dx}{(1 + \cos^2 x) \sqrt{1 + \cos^2 x + \cos^4 x}}$ is equal to :

(a) $\sec^{-1} (\sec x + \cos x) + C$

(b) $\sec^{-1} (\sec x - \cos x) + C$

(c) $\sec^{-1} (\cos x - \tan x) + C$

(d) None of these.

38. $\int \cos x \cdot \log \tan \dfrac{x}{2} \, dx$ is equal to :

(a) $\sin x \cdot \log \tan \dfrac{x}{2} + x + C$

(b) $\sin x \cdot \log \tan \dfrac{x}{2} - x + C$

(c) $-\sin x \cdot \log \tan \dfrac{x}{2} - x + C$

(d) None of these.

39. If $f(x) = \int \dfrac{(x^2 + \sin^2 x)}{1 + x^2} \sec^2 x\, dx$ and $f(0) = 0$,

the $f(1) =$

(a) $1 - \dfrac{\pi}{4}$

(b) $\dfrac{\pi}{4} - 1$

(c) $\tan 1 - \dfrac{\pi}{4}$

(d) None of these.

40. $\int e^{\sin x} \cdot \dfrac{(x \cos^3 x - \sin x)}{\cos^2 x}\, dx$ is equal to :

(a) $e^{\sin x} (\sec x - x) + C$

(b) $e^{\sin x} (x - \sec x) + C$

(c) $e^{\sin x} (\tan x - x) + C$

(d) None of these.

41. $\int \dfrac{\sqrt{x^2 + 1}\, [\log (x^2 + 1) - 2 \log x]}{x^4}\, dx$ is equal to

(a) $\dfrac{(x^2 + 1)^{3/2}}{x^3} \left[\dfrac{2}{3} - \log \left(\dfrac{x^2 + 1}{x^2}\right)\right] + C$

(b) $\dfrac{(x^2 + 1)^{3/2}}{3x^3} \left[\log \left(\dfrac{x^2 + 1}{x^2}\right) - \dfrac{2}{3}\right] + C$

(c) $\dfrac{(x^2 + 1)^{3/2}}{3x^3} \left[\dfrac{2}{3} - \log \left(\dfrac{x^2 + 1}{x^2}\right)\right] + C$

(d) None of these.

42. If $\int \left(\log (\log x) + \dfrac{1}{(\log x)^2}\right) dx$

$= x\,[f(x) - g(x)] + C$, then :

(a) $f(x) = \log (\log x),\ g(x) = \dfrac{1}{\log x}$

(b) $f(x) = \log x,\ g(x) = \dfrac{1}{\log x}$

(c) $f(x) = \dfrac{1}{\log x},\ g(x) = \log (\log x)$

(d) None of these.

43. $\int \dfrac{3x + 1}{(x - 1)^3 (x + 1)}\, dx$ is equal to :

(a) $\dfrac{1}{(x - 1)^2} + \dfrac{1}{2(x - 1)} - \dfrac{1}{4} \log \left|\dfrac{x + 1}{x - 1}\right| + C$

(b) $\dfrac{-1}{(x - 1)^2} - \dfrac{1}{2(x - 1)} + \dfrac{1}{4} \log \left|\dfrac{x + 1}{x - 1}\right| + C$

(c) $\dfrac{-1}{(x - 1)^2} - \dfrac{1}{2(x - 1)} + \dfrac{1}{4} \log \left|\dfrac{x + 1}{x - 1}\right| + C$

(d) None of these.

44. If $\int \dfrac{x^2}{(x \sin x + \cos x)^2}\, dx$

$= \dfrac{f(x)}{x \sin x + \cos x} + \tan x + C$, then :

(a) $f(x) = \dfrac{x}{\cos x}$

(b) $f(x) = \dfrac{\cos x}{x}$

(c) $f(x) = \dfrac{-x}{\cos x}$

(d) None of these.

45. $\int \dfrac{x^4}{(x - 1)\,(x^2 + 1)}\, dx$ is equal to :

(a) $\dfrac{x^2}{2} + x + \dfrac{1}{2} \log (x - 1) - \dfrac{1}{4} \log (x^2 + 1)$

$\qquad\qquad - \dfrac{1}{2} \tan^{-1} x + C$

(b) $\dfrac{x^2}{2} + x + \dfrac{1}{2} \log (x - 1) + \dfrac{1}{4} \log (x^2 + 1)$

$\qquad\qquad - \dfrac{1}{2} \tan^{-1} x + C$

(c) $\dfrac{x^2}{2} - x + \dfrac{1}{2} \log (x - 1) + \dfrac{1}{4} \log (x^2 + 1)$

$\qquad\qquad + \dfrac{1}{2} \tan^{-1} x + C$

(d) None of these.

46. $\int \log \left(\sqrt{2 - x} + \sqrt{2 + x}\right) dx$ is equal to :

(a) $x \log \left(\sqrt{2 - x} + \sqrt{2 + x}\right) - \sin^{-1} \dfrac{x}{2} + \dfrac{x}{2} + C$

(b) $x \log \left(\sqrt{2 - x} + \sqrt{2 + x}\right) - \sin^{-1} \dfrac{x}{2} - \dfrac{x}{2} + C$

(c) $x \log \left(\sqrt{2 - x} + \sqrt{2 + x}\right) + \sin^{-1} \dfrac{x}{2} - \dfrac{x}{2} + C$

(d) None of these.

47. $\int \dfrac{x^3 - 1}{x^3 + x}\, dx$ is equal to :

(a) $x + \log x + \dfrac{1}{2} \log (x^2 + 1) - \tan^{-1} x + C$

(b) $x - \log x + \dfrac{1}{2} \log (x^2 + 1) - \tan^{-1} x + C$

(c) $x - \log x - \dfrac{1}{2} \log (x^2 + 1) - \tan^{-1} x + C$

(d) None of these.

48. $\int e^x \left(\dfrac{x+2}{x+4}\right)^2 dx$ is equal to :

(a) $\dfrac{xe^x}{x+4} + C$ (b) $e^x \left(\dfrac{x+2}{x+4}\right) + C$

(c) $\dfrac{e^x}{x+4} + C$ (d) None of these.

49. $\int \dfrac{dx}{\sin x + \sin 2x}$ is equal to :

(a) $\dfrac{1}{6} \log (1 - \cos x) - \dfrac{1}{2} \log (1 + \cos x)$

$\qquad\qquad + \dfrac{2}{3} \log (2 \cos x + 1) + C$

(b) $\dfrac{1}{6} \log (1 - \cos x) + \dfrac{1}{2} \log (1 + \cos x)$

$\qquad\qquad - \dfrac{2}{3} \log (2 \cos x + 1) + C$

(c) $\dfrac{1}{6} \log (1 - \cos x) + \dfrac{1}{2} \log (1 + \cos x)$

$\qquad\qquad + \dfrac{2}{3} \log (2 \cos x + 1) + C$

(d) None of these.

50. $\int \dfrac{e^{\tan^{-1} x}}{1 + x^2} (1 + x + x^2) \, dx$ is equal to :

(a) $\dfrac{e^{\tan^{-1} x}}{1 + x^2}$ (b) $e^{\tan^{-1} x} \cdot (1 + x^2)$

(c) $x e^{\tan^{-1} x}$ (d) None of these.

51. $\int \cos 2x \log \left(\dfrac{\cos x + \sin x}{\cos x - \sin x}\right) dx$ is equal to :

(a) $\dfrac{\sin 2x}{2} \log \left(\dfrac{\cos x + \sin x}{\cos x - \sin x}\right) + \dfrac{1}{2} \log \sec 2x + C$

(b) $\dfrac{\sin 2x}{2} \log \left(\dfrac{\cos x + \sin x}{\cos x - \sin x}\right) - \dfrac{1}{2} \log \sec 2x + C$

(c) $\dfrac{\sin 2x}{2} \log \left(\dfrac{\cos x - \sin x}{\cos x + \sin x}\right) - \dfrac{1}{2} \log \sec 2x + C$

(d) None of these.

52. $\int \dfrac{x^2}{(x^2 + a^2)(x^2 + b^2)} \, dx$ is equal to :

(a) $\dfrac{1}{(b^2 - a^2)} \left(b \tan^{-1} \dfrac{x}{b} - a \tan^{-1} \dfrac{x}{a}\right) + C$

(b) $\dfrac{1}{b^2 - a^2} \left(b \tan^{-1} \dfrac{x}{b} + a \tan^{-1} \dfrac{x}{a}\right) + C$

(c) $\dfrac{1}{b^2 - a^2} \left(- b \tan^{-1} \dfrac{x}{b} + a \tan^{-1} \dfrac{x}{a}\right) + C$

(d) None of these.

53. If $\int \dfrac{dx}{1 + \sin \alpha \cdot \cos x} = 2 \sec \alpha \tan^{-1} [f(x)] + C$,

$\left(0 < \alpha < \dfrac{\pi}{2} \text{ and } \alpha \text{ is a constant}\right)$ then :

(a) $f(x) = \cot \dfrac{x}{2} \tan \left(\dfrac{\pi}{4} - \dfrac{\alpha}{2}\right)$

(b) $f(x) = \tan \dfrac{x}{2} \tan \left(\dfrac{\pi}{4} - \dfrac{\alpha}{2}\right)$

(c) $f(x) = \tan \dfrac{x}{2} \tan \left(\dfrac{\alpha}{2} - \dfrac{\pi}{4}\right)$

(d) None of these.

54. $\int \sqrt[3]{\tan x} \, dx$ is equal to :

(a) $\dfrac{1}{6} \log \left|\dfrac{x^2 - x + 1}{(x + 1)^2}\right| + \dfrac{1}{\sqrt{3}} \tan^{-1} \left(\dfrac{2x - 1}{\sqrt{3}}\right) + C$

(b) $\dfrac{1}{6} \log \left|\dfrac{(x + 1)^2}{x^2 - x + 1}\right| + \dfrac{1}{\sqrt{3}} \tan^{-1} \left(\dfrac{2x - 1}{\sqrt{3}}\right) + C$

(c) $\dfrac{1}{6} \log \left|\dfrac{x^2 - x + 1}{(x + 1)^2}\right| - \dfrac{1}{\sqrt{3}} \tan^{-1} \left(\dfrac{2x - 1}{\sqrt{3}}\right) + C$

(d) None of these.

55. $\int \dfrac{1 + x}{1 + \sqrt[3]{x}} \, dx$ is equal to :

(a) $\dfrac{3}{5} x^{5/3} - \dfrac{3}{4} x^{4/3} + x + C$

(b) $\dfrac{3}{5} x^{5/3} + \dfrac{3}{4} x^{4/3} + x + C$

(c) $\dfrac{3}{5} x^{5/3} - \dfrac{3}{4} x^{4/3} - x + C$

(d) None of these.

56. $\int \dfrac{dx}{\sqrt{(x - \alpha)(\beta - x)}}$, where $\beta > \alpha$, is equal to :

(a) $\sin^{-1} \left(\dfrac{2x + \alpha + \beta}{\beta - \alpha}\right) + C$

(b) $\sin^{-1} \left(\dfrac{x - \alpha - \beta}{\beta - \alpha}\right) + C$

(c) $\sin^{-1} \left(\dfrac{2x - \alpha - \beta}{\beta - \alpha}\right) + C$

(d) None of these.

57. $\int \dfrac{dx}{\sqrt[4]{(x-1)^3 (x+2)^5}}$ is equal to :

(a) $\dfrac{3}{4} \sqrt[4]{\dfrac{x-1}{x+2}} + c$

(b) $\dfrac{4}{3} \sqrt[4]{\dfrac{x-1}{x+2}} + C$

(c) $\dfrac{4}{3} \sqrt[4]{\dfrac{x+2}{x-1}} + c$

(d) None of these.

58. If $\int \dfrac{dx}{(1+x^2)\sqrt{1-x^2}} = -\dfrac{1}{\sqrt{2}} \sin^{-1} [f(x)] + C,$

then :

(a) $f(x) = \sqrt{\dfrac{1-x^2}{1+x^2}}$

(b) $f(x) = \sqrt{\dfrac{1+x^2}{1-x^2}}$

(c) $f(x) = \sqrt{\dfrac{x^2-1}{x^2+1}}$

(d) None of these.

59. $\int \dfrac{x}{\sqrt[3]{1+x} + \sqrt[2]{1+x}} \, dx$ is equal to :

(a) $6 \left[\dfrac{(1+x)^{3/2}}{9} + \dfrac{(1+x)^{4/3}}{8} + \dfrac{(1+x)^{7/6}}{7} \right.$

$\left. - \dfrac{(1+x)}{6} + \dfrac{(1+x)^{5/6}}{5} - \dfrac{(1+x)^{2/3}}{4} \right] + C$

(b) $6 \left[\dfrac{(1+x)^{3/2}}{9} - \dfrac{(1+x)^{4/3}}{8} + \dfrac{(1+x)^{7/6}}{7} \right.$

$\left. - \dfrac{(1+x)}{6} + \dfrac{(1+x)^{5/6}}{5} - \dfrac{(1+x)^{2/3}}{4} \right] + C$

(c) $6 \left[\dfrac{(1+x)^{3/2}}{9} + \dfrac{(1+x)^{4/3}}{8} - \dfrac{(1+x)^{7/6}}{7} \right.$

$\left. + \dfrac{(1+x)}{6} + \dfrac{(1+x)^{5/6}}{5} - \dfrac{(1+x)^{2/3}}{4} \right] + C$

(d) None of these.

60. $\int \dfrac{(x^2-1)}{x\sqrt{x^4 + 3x^2 + 1}} \, dx$ is equal to :

(a) $\log \left| x + \dfrac{1}{x} + \sqrt{x^2 + \dfrac{1}{x^2} + 3} \right| + C$

(b) $\log \left| x - \dfrac{1}{x} + \sqrt{x^2 + \dfrac{1}{x^2} - 3} \right| + C$

(c) $\log \left| x + \sqrt{x^2 + 3} \right| + C$

(d) None of these.

61. If $\int \dfrac{dx}{\sin x \sqrt{\cos^3 x}}$

$= \dfrac{2}{\sqrt{\cos x}} + \tan^{-1} [f(x)] - \dfrac{1}{2} \log [g(x)] + C,$ then

(a) $f(x) = \sqrt{\sin x},\ g(x) = \dfrac{1+\sqrt{\cos x}}{1-\sqrt{\cos x}}$

(b) $f(x) = \sqrt{\cos x},\ g(x) = \dfrac{1+\sqrt{\sin x}}{1-\sqrt{\sin x}}$

(c) $f(x) = \sqrt{\cos x},\ g(x) = \dfrac{1-\sqrt{\cos x}}{1+\sqrt{\cos x}}$

(d) $f(x) = \sqrt{\cos x},\ g(x) = \dfrac{1+\sqrt{\cos x}}{1-\sqrt{\cos x}}$

62. $\int \dfrac{x + \sqrt[3]{x^2} + \sqrt[6]{x}}{x \left(1 + \sqrt[3]{x}\right)} \, dx$ is equal to :

(a) $\dfrac{3}{2} x^{2/3} + 6 \tan^{-1} x^{1/6} + C$

(b) $\dfrac{3}{2} x^{2/3} - 6 \tan^{-1} x^{1/6} + C$

(c) $\dfrac{-3}{2} x^{2/3} + 6 \tan^{-1} x^{1/6} + C$

(d) None of these.

63. $\int \left(\sqrt{\tan x} + \sqrt{\cot x} \right) dx$ is equal to :

(a) $\sin^{-1} (\sin x - \cos x) + C$

(b) $\sqrt{2} \sin^{-1} (\sin x - \cos x) + C$

(c) $\sqrt{2} \cos^{-1} (\sin x - \cos x) + C$

(d) None of these.

64. $\int (x-2) \sqrt{\dfrac{1+x}{1-x}} \, dx$ is equal to :

(a) $\dfrac{1}{2} \left[3 \sin^{-1} x + (2-x) \cdot \sqrt{1-x^2} \right] + C$

(b) $\dfrac{1}{2} \left[3 \cos^{-1} x + (x-2) \cdot \sqrt{1-x^2} \right] + C$

(c) $\dfrac{1}{2} \left[3 \cos^{-1} x + (2-x) \cdot \sqrt{1-x^2} \right] + C$

(d) None of these.

65. $\int \dfrac{2}{(2-x)^2} \sqrt[3]{\dfrac{2-x}{2+x}} \, dx$ is equal to :

(a) $\dfrac{4}{3} \left(\dfrac{2+x}{2-x} \right)^{2/3} + C$

(b) $\dfrac{3}{4} \left(\dfrac{2+x}{2-x} \right)^{2/3} + C$

(c) $\dfrac{3}{4} \left(\dfrac{2-x}{2+x} \right)^{2/3} + C$

(d) None of these.

66. If $f(x)$ is a polynomial of second degree such that $f(0) = f(1) = 3f(2) = -3$, then $\int \frac{f(x)}{x^3 - 1} dx$ is equal to :

(a) $\log \frac{1 + x + x^2}{x - 1} + \frac{2}{\sqrt{3}} \tan^{-1}\left(\frac{2x + 1}{\sqrt{3}}\right) + C$

(b) $\log \frac{x - 1}{1 + x + x^2} + \frac{2}{\sqrt{3}} \tan^{-1}\left(\frac{2x + 1}{\sqrt{3}}\right) + C$

(c) $\log \frac{1 + x + x^2}{x - 1} + \frac{1}{\sqrt{3}} \tan^{-1}\left(\frac{2x + 1}{\sqrt{3}}\right) + C$

(d) None of these.

67. If $\int \frac{(\sin\theta - \cos\theta)}{(\sin\theta + \cos\theta)\sqrt{\sin\theta\cos\theta + \sin^2\theta\cos^2\theta}} d\theta = \text{cosec}^{-1}[f(\theta)] + C$, then :

(a) $f(\theta) = \sin 2\theta + 1$ (b) $f(\theta) = 1 - \sin 2\theta$
(c) $f(\theta) = \sin 2\theta - 1$ (d) None of these.

68. $\int \frac{x^4 + 1}{x^6 + 1} dx$ is equal to :

(a) $\tan^{-1} x + \frac{1}{3} \tan^{-1} x^3 + C$

(b) $\tan^{-1} x - \frac{1}{3} \tan^{-1} x^3 + C$

(c) $-\tan x - \frac{1}{3} \tan^{-1} x^3 + C$

(d) None of these.

69. If $\int \sqrt{x + \sqrt{2 + x^2}} \, dx = \frac{[f(x)]^2 - 6}{3\sqrt{f(x)}} + C$ then :

(a) $f(x) = x - \sqrt{2 + x^2}$ (b) $f(x) = x + \sqrt{2 + x^2}$
(c) $f(x) = \sqrt{2 + x^2} - x$ (d) None of these.

70. If $\int \frac{\sin x}{\sin^3 x + \cos^3 x} dx$

$= \frac{1}{6} \log\left|\frac{z^2 - z + 1}{(z + 1)^2}\right| + \frac{1}{\sqrt{3}} \tan^{-1}\left(\frac{2z - 1}{\sqrt{3}}\right) + C$, then

(a) $z = \sin x$ (b) $z = \cos x$
(c) $z = \tan x$ (d) None of these.

71. $\int \frac{(x + 1)}{x(1 + xe^x)^2} dx$ is equal to :

(a) $\log\left(\frac{xe^x}{1 + xe^x}\right) + \frac{1}{1 + xe^x} + C$

(b) $\log\left(\frac{x}{1 + xe^x}\right) + \frac{1}{1 + xe^x} + C$

(c) $\log\left(\frac{1 + xe^x}{xe^x}\right) + \frac{1}{1 + xe^x} + C$

(d) None of these.

72. $\int \frac{x^3}{(1 + x^2)^{1/3}} dx$ is equal to :

(a) $\frac{20}{3} (1 + x^2)^{2/3} (2x^2 - 3) + C$

(b) $\frac{3}{20} (1 + x^2)^{2/3} (2x^2 - 3) + C$

(c) $\frac{3}{20} (1 + x^2)^{2/3} (2x^2 + 3) + C$

(d) None of these.

73. $\int \frac{dx}{\left(\sqrt{1 + x^2} - x\right)^n} \ (n \neq \pm 1)$

$= \frac{1}{2}\left(\frac{z^{n+1}}{n + 1} + \frac{z^{n-1}}{n - 1}\right) + C$, where

(a) $z = x - \sqrt{1 + x^2}$ (b) $z = \sqrt{1 + x^2} - x$
(c) $z = x + \sqrt{1 + x^2}$ (d) None of these.

74. $\int \frac{x - 1}{(x + 1)\sqrt{x^3 + x^2 + x}} dx$ is equal to :

(a) $\tan^{-1}\sqrt{\frac{x^2 + x + 1}{x}} + C$

(b) $2 \tan^{-1}\sqrt{\frac{x^2 + x + 1}{x}} + C$

(c) $3 \tan^{-1}\sqrt{\frac{x^2 + x + 1}{x}} + C$

(d) None of these.

75. $\int \frac{(x^2 - 1)}{(x^4 + 3x^2 + 1) \tan^{-1}\left(\frac{x^2 + 1}{x}\right)} dx$ is equal to :

(a) $\log \tan^{-1}\left(\frac{x^2 + 1}{x}\right) + C$

(b) $\log \tan^{-1}\left(\frac{x}{x^2 + 1}\right) + C$

(c) $2 \log \tan^{-1}\left(\frac{x^2 + 1}{x}\right) + C$

(d) None of these.

76. $\int \dfrac{dx}{\sin^6 x + \cos^6 x}$ is equal to :

(a) $\tan^{-1}(\tan x + \cot x) + C$

(b) $\tan^{-1}(\cot x - \tan x) + C$

(c) $\tan^{-1}(\tan x - \cot x) + C$

(d) None of these.

77. $\int \dfrac{\sec x}{\sqrt{\sin(2x + \alpha) + \sin \alpha}} dx$ is equal to :

(a) $\sqrt{2} \sec \alpha (\tan x + \tan \alpha) + C$

(b) $\sqrt{2} \sec \alpha (\tan x - \tan \alpha) + C$

(c) $\sqrt{2} \sec \alpha (\tan \alpha - \tan x) + C$

(d) None of these.

78. $\int \dfrac{\cos 2x \sin 4x}{\cos^4 x (1 + \cos^2 2x)} dx$ is equal to :

(a) $2\log(1 + \cos 2x) + \sec^2 x - \log(1 + \cos^2 2x) + C$

(b) $\log(1 + \cos 2x) + \sec^2 x - \log(1 + \cos^2 2x) + C$

(c) $2\log(1 + \cos 2x) + \sec^2 x + \log(1 + \cos^2 2x) + C$

(d) None of these.

79. If $\int \dfrac{dx}{x\sqrt{1 - x^3}} = a \log \left| \dfrac{\sqrt{1 - x^3} - 1}{\sqrt{1 - x^3} + 1} \right| + C$,

then $a =$

(a) $1/3$ (b) $2/3$

(c) $-1/3$ (d) $-2/3$.

80. $\int \dfrac{\sqrt{1 + \sqrt{x}}}{x} dx$ is equal to :

(a) $2\sqrt{1 + \sqrt{x}} - 2\log\left(\dfrac{\sqrt{1 + \sqrt{x}} - 1}{\sqrt{1 + \sqrt{x}} + 1}\right) + C$

(b) $4\sqrt{1 + \sqrt{x}} + 2\log\left(\dfrac{\sqrt{1 + \sqrt{x}} + 1}{\sqrt{1 + \sqrt{x}} - 1}\right) + C$

(c) $4\sqrt{1 + \sqrt{x}} + 2\log\left(\dfrac{\sqrt{1 + \sqrt{x}} - 1}{\sqrt{1 + \sqrt{x}} + 1}\right) + C$

(d) None of these.

81. If $\int \dfrac{4e^x + 6e^{-x}}{9e^x - 4e^{-x}} dx = Ax + B \, ln \, (9e^{2x} - 4) + C$,

then :

(a) $A = -\dfrac{3}{2}, B = \dfrac{35}{36}, C = $ constant

(b) $A = \dfrac{3}{2}, B = \dfrac{-35}{36}, C = $ constant

(c) $A = -\dfrac{3}{2}, B = \dfrac{-35}{36}, C = $ constant

(d) None of these.

82. $\int f(x) \sin x \cos x \, dx = \dfrac{1}{2(b^2 - a^2)} \times \log[f(x)] + C$

Then $f(x)$ is equal to :

(a) $\dfrac{1}{a^2 \sin^2 x - b^2 \cos^2 x}$

(b) $\dfrac{1}{a^2 \sin^2 x + b^2 \cos^2 x}$

(c) $\dfrac{1}{a^2 \cos^2 x - b^2 \sin^2 x}$

(d) None of these.

83. $\int \dfrac{(x - x^5)^{1/5}}{x^6} dx$ is equal to :

(a) $\dfrac{5}{24}\left(\dfrac{1}{x^4} - 1\right)^{6/5} + C$

(b) $\dfrac{5}{24}\left(1 - \dfrac{1}{x^4}\right)^{6/5} + C$

(c) $-\dfrac{5}{24}\left(\dfrac{1}{x^4} - 1\right)^{6/5} + C$

(d) None of these.

84. If $\int \dfrac{\cos 8x + 1}{\tan 2x - \cot 2x} dx = a \cos 8x + C$, then :

(a) $a = \dfrac{-1}{16}$ (b) $a = \dfrac{1}{8}$

(c) $a = \dfrac{1}{16}$ (d) $a = \dfrac{-1}{8}$.

85. $\int \dfrac{x^2}{(a + bx^2)^{5/2}} dx$ is equal to :

(a) $-\dfrac{1}{3a}\left(\dfrac{x^2}{a + bx^2}\right)^{3/2} + C$

(b) $\dfrac{1}{3a}\left(\dfrac{x^2}{a + bx^2}\right)^{3/2} + C$

(c) $\dfrac{1}{2a}\left(\dfrac{x^2}{a + bx^2}\right)^{2/3} + C$

(d) None of these.

86. If $\int \frac{\sin^8 x - \cos^8 x}{1 - 2 \sin^2 x \cos^2 x} dx = A \sin 2x + B$, then :

(a) $A = -\frac{1}{2}$

(b) $A = \frac{1}{2}$

(c) $A = -1$

(d) $A = 1$.

87. $\int \frac{dx}{x^{1/2} (1 + x^2)^{5/4}}$ is equal to :

(a) $\frac{-2\sqrt{x}}{\sqrt[4]{1 + x^2}} + C$

(b) $\frac{2\sqrt{x}}{\sqrt[4]{1 + x^2}} + C$

(c) $\frac{-\sqrt{x}}{\sqrt[4]{1 + x^2}} + C$

(d) $\frac{\sqrt{x}}{\sqrt[4]{1 + x^2}} + C$

88. $\int \frac{\sqrt{x^2 + 1}}{x^2} dx$ is equal to :

(a) $\frac{-\sqrt{1 + x^2}}{x} + \log\left(x + \sqrt{1 + x^2}\right) + C$

(b) $\frac{\sqrt{1 + x^2}}{x} + \log\left(x + \sqrt{1 + x^2}\right) + C$

(c) $\frac{x}{\sqrt{1 + x^2}} + \log\left(x + \sqrt{1 + x^2}\right) + C$

(d) None of these.

89. Integral of $\frac{1}{1 + (\log x)^2}$ w.r.t. $\log x$ is :

(a) $\frac{\tan^{-1}(\log x)}{x} + C$

(b) $\tan^{-1}(\log x) + C$

(c) $\frac{\tan^{-1} x}{x} + C$

(d) None of these.

90. Integral of $\frac{1}{\sqrt{x^2 + 4}}$ w.r.t. $(x^2 + 3)$ is equal to :

(a) $\sqrt{x^2 + 4} + C$

(b) $\frac{1}{\sqrt{x^2 + 4}} + C$

(c) $2\sqrt{x^2 + 4} + C$

(d) None of these.

91. $\int x \cdot (x^{x^x}) \cdot (2 \log x + 1) dx$ is equal to :

(a) $x^{(x^x)} + C$

(b) $(x^x)^x + C$

(c) $x^x \cdot \log x + C$

(d) None of these.

92. The equation of a curve passing through origin is given by $y = \int x^3 \cos x^4 dx$. If the equation of the curve is written in the form $x = g(y)$, then :

(a) $g(y) = \sqrt[3]{\sin^{-1}(4y)}$

(b) $g(y) = \sqrt{\sin^{-1}(4y)}$

(c) $g(y) = \sqrt[4]{\sin^{-1}(4y)}$

(d) None of these.

93. Antiderivative of the function $(3x + 4) | \sin x |$, when $0 < x < \pi$, is given by :

(a) $3 \sin x - (3x + 4) \cos x$

(b) $3 \sin x + (3x + 4) \cos x$

(c) $-3 \sin x + (3x + 4) \cos x$

(d) None of these.

94. $\int \frac{[f(x) g'(x) + g(x) f'(x)]}{f(x) \cdot g(x)} [\log f(x) + \log g(x)] dx$ is equal to :

(a) $f(x) g(x) \log [f(x) g(x)] + C$

(b) $\frac{1}{2} [\log \{f(x) g(x)\}]^2 + C$

(c) $[\log \{f(x) \cdot g(x)\}]^2 + C$

(d) $\log \{f(x) \cdot g(x)\} + C$

95. If $f''(x) = \sec^2 x$ and $f(0) = f'(0) = 0$ then :

(a) $f(x) = \log \sec x$

(b) $f(x) = \sec^2 x$

(c) $f(x) = \log \sec x + x$

(d) None of these.

96. The primitive of the function

$$f(x) = \frac{1}{2 + 3 \cos x + 2 \sin x},$$

whose graph passes through origin, is :

(a) $\frac{1}{3} \log \frac{\tan \frac{x}{2} + 1}{5 - \tan \frac{x}{2}}$

(b) $\frac{1}{3} \log \frac{5 + 5 \tan \frac{x}{2}}{5 - \tan \frac{x}{2}}$

(c) $\frac{2}{3} \log \frac{5 + 5 \tan \frac{x}{2}}{5 - \tan \frac{x}{2}}$

(d) None of these.

97. If $\int \dfrac{x^3 - 6x^2 + 11x - 6}{\sqrt{x^2 + 4x + 3}} \, dx$

$= f(x) \cdot \sqrt{x^2 + 4x + 3} - \dfrac{198}{3} g(x) + C$, then :

(a) $f(x) = \dfrac{1}{3}(x^2 - 14x + 111)$,

   $g(x) = \log\left[(x + 2) + \sqrt{x^2 + 4x + 3}\right]$

(b) $f(x) = \dfrac{1}{3}(x^2 + 14x + 111)$,

   $g(x) = \log\left[(x + 2) + \sqrt{x^2 + 4x + 3}\right]$

(c) $f(x) = x^2 - 14x + 111$,

   $g(x) = \log\left[(x + 2) + \sqrt{x^2 + 4x + 3}\right]$

(d) None of these.

98. $\int \sin x \, d(\cos x)$ is equal to :

(a) $\dfrac{\sin 2x}{2} - x + C$ (b) $\dfrac{1}{2}\left(\dfrac{\sin 2x}{2} - x\right) + C$

(c) $\dfrac{1}{2}\left(\dfrac{\sin 2x}{2} + x\right) + C$ (d) None of these.

99. If $\int \dfrac{dx}{\sqrt{2ax - x^2}} = (f \circ g)(x) + C$, then :

(a) $f(x) = \sin^{-1} x,\ g(x) = \dfrac{x + a}{a}$

(b) $f(x) = \sin^{-1} x,\ g(x) = \dfrac{x - a}{a}$

(c) $f(x) = \cos^{-1} x,\ g(x) = \dfrac{x - a}{a}$

(d) $f(x) = \tan^{-1} x,\ g(x) = \dfrac{x - a}{a}$.

100. Let $f(x) = \dfrac{x + 1}{x + 2}$. If $\int \left(\dfrac{f(x)}{x^2}\right)^{1/2} dx$

$= \dfrac{1}{\sqrt{2}} g\left(\dfrac{\sqrt{2f(x)} - 1}{\sqrt{2f(x)} + 1}\right) - h\left(\dfrac{\sqrt{f(x)} - 1}{\sqrt{f(x)} + 1}\right)$, then

(a) $g(x) = \log |x|,\ h(x) = \log |x|$

(b) $g(x) = \log |x|,\ h(x) = \tan^{-1} x$

(c) $g(x) = \tan^{-1} x,\ h(x) = \log |x|$

(d) None of these.

101. Let $f(x)$ be a polynomial of degree three satisfying $f(0) = -1$ and $f(1) = 0$. Also, 0 is a

stationary point of $f(x)$. If $f(x)$ does not have an extremum at $x = 0$, then $\int \dfrac{f(x)}{x^3 - 1} \, dx$ is equal to:

(a) $\dfrac{x^2}{2} + C$ (b) $x + C$

(c) $\dfrac{x^3}{6} + C$ (d) None of these.

102. Let $f(x)$ be a function satisfying $f(0) = 2$, $f'(0) = 3$ and $f''(x) = f(x)$. Then $f(4)$ is equal to

(a) $\dfrac{5e^8 + 1}{2e^4}$ (b) $\dfrac{5e^8 - 1}{2e^4}$

(c) $\dfrac{2e^4}{5e^8 - 1}$ (d) $\dfrac{2e^4}{5e^8 + 1}$.

103. $\int \dfrac{x^3 + 3x + 2}{(x^2 + 1)^2 (x + 1)} \, dx$ is equal to :

(a) $\dfrac{1}{4} \log \left|\dfrac{x^2 + 1}{(x + 1)^2}\right| + \dfrac{3}{2} \tan^{-1} x - \dfrac{x}{x^2 + 1} + C$

(b) $\dfrac{1}{4} \log \left|\dfrac{(x + 1)^2}{x^2 + 1}\right| + \dfrac{3}{2} \tan^{-1} x + \dfrac{x}{x^2 + 1} + C$

(c) $\dfrac{1}{4} \log \left|\dfrac{x^2 + 1}{(x + 1)^2}\right| + \dfrac{3}{2} \tan^{-1} x + \dfrac{x}{x^2 + 1} + C$

(d) None of these.

104. $\int [\sin (\log x) + \cos (\log x)] \, dx$ is equal to :

(a) $\sin (\log x) + \cos (\log x) + C$

(b) $x \sin (\log x) + C$

(c) $x \cos (\log x) + C$

(d) None of these.

105. $\int \dfrac{dx}{x^2 + x + 1}$ is equal to :

(a) $\dfrac{\sqrt{3}}{2} \tan^{-1}\left(\dfrac{2x + 1}{\sqrt{3}}\right) + C$

(b) $\dfrac{2}{\sqrt{3}} \tan^{-1}\left(\dfrac{2x + 1}{\sqrt{3}}\right) + C$

(c) $\dfrac{1}{\sqrt{3}} \tan^{-1}\left(\dfrac{2x + 1}{\sqrt{3}}\right) + C$

(d) None of these.

106. $\int (x - 1) e^{-x} dx$ is equal to :

(a) $- xe^x + C$ (b) $xe^x + C$

(c) $- xe^{-x} + C$ (d) $xe^{-x} + C$.

107. If $\int \dfrac{2^{1/x}}{x^2} dx = K \cdot 2^{1/x}$, then K is equal to :

(a) $\dfrac{-1}{\log 2}$ (b) $- \log 2$

(c) $- 1$ (d) $\dfrac{1}{2}$.

108. $\int \sec^3 x \, dx$ is equal to :

(a) $\dfrac{1}{2} \log |\sec x + \tan x|$

(b) $\dfrac{1}{2} \sec x \tan x + \dfrac{1}{2} \log |\sec x + \tan x|$

(c) $\dfrac{1}{2} \sec x \tan x$

(d) None of these.

109. $\int e^{3 \log x} (x^4 + 1)^{-1} dx$ is equal to :

(a) $\dfrac{1}{4} \log (x^4 + 1) + C$ (b) $- \log (x^4 + 1) + C$

(c) $\log (x^4 + 1) + C$ (d) None of these.

110. $\int \dfrac{\cot x}{\sqrt{\sin x}} dx$ is equal to :

(a) $2 \sqrt{\sin x} + C$ (b) $\dfrac{1}{2 \sqrt{\sin x}} + C$

(c) $\dfrac{-2}{\sqrt{\sin x}} + C$ (d) $\dfrac{2}{\sqrt{\sin x}} + C$.

111. $\int \dfrac{\log (x + 1) - \log x}{x (x + 1)} dx$ is equal to :

(a) $- \dfrac{1}{2} \left[\log \left(\dfrac{x + 1}{x} \right) \right]^2 + C$

(b) $C - [\{\log (x + 1)\}^2 - (\log x)^2]$

(c) $- \log \left[\log \left(\dfrac{x + 1}{x} \right) \right] + C$

(d) $- \log \left(\dfrac{x + 1}{x} \right) + C$.

112. $\int e^{\tan^{-1} x} \left(1 + \dfrac{x}{1 + x^2} \right) dx$ is equal to :

(a) $\dfrac{1}{2} x e^{\tan^{-1} x}$ (b) $\dfrac{1}{2} e^{\tan^{-1} x}$

(c) $x e^{\tan^{-1} x}$ (d) $e^{\tan^{-1} x}$.

113. If $\int f(x) dx = F(x)$, then $\int x^3 f(x^2) dx =$

(a) $\dfrac{1}{2} \left[x^2 (F(x))^2 - \int (F(x))^2 dx \right]$

(b) $\dfrac{1}{2} \left[x^2 \cdot F(x^2) - \int F(x)^2 d(x^2) \right]$

(c) $\dfrac{1}{2} \left[x^2 F(x) - \dfrac{1}{2} \int (F(x))^2 dx \right]$

(d) None of these.

114. $\int \dfrac{1}{1 + x^4} dx$ is equal to :

(a) $\dfrac{1}{2\sqrt{2}} \tan^{-1} \dfrac{x^2 - 1}{\sqrt{2} x} + \dfrac{1}{4\sqrt{2}} \log \left| \dfrac{x^2 - x\sqrt{2} + 1}{x^2 + x\sqrt{2} + 1} \right| + C$

(b) $\dfrac{1}{2\sqrt{2}} \tan^{-1} \dfrac{x^2 - 1}{\sqrt{2} x} - \dfrac{1}{4\sqrt{2}} \log \left| \dfrac{x^2 - x\sqrt{2} + 1}{x^2 + x\sqrt{2} + 1} \right| + C$

(c) $\dfrac{1}{\sqrt{2}} \tan^{-1} \dfrac{x^2 - 1}{\sqrt{2} x} - \dfrac{1}{4\sqrt{2}} \log \left| \dfrac{x^2 - x\sqrt{2} + 1}{x^2 + x\sqrt{2} + 1} \right| + C$

(d) None of these.

115. $\int \dfrac{dx}{x (x^n + 1)}$ is equal to :

(a) $\log x - \dfrac{1}{n} \log (x^n + 1) + C$

(b) $\dfrac{1}{n} \log \left(\dfrac{x^n + 1}{x^n} \right) + C$

(c) $\log x + \dfrac{1}{n} \log (x^n + 1) + C$

(d) None of these.

116. $\int \sqrt{1 + \csc x} \, dx$ is equal to :

(a) $\sin^{-1} (2 \sin x + 1) + C$

(b) $- \sin^{-1} (2 \sin x - 1) + C$

(c) $\sin^{-1} (2 \sin x - 1) + C$

(d) None of these.

117. $\int \dfrac{dx}{1 + \tan x} =$

(a) $\log (x + \sin x) + C$

(b) $\log (\sin x + \cos x) + C$

(c) $2 \sec^2 \dfrac{x}{2} + C$

(d) $\dfrac{1}{2} [x + \log (\sin x + \cos x)] + C$.

118. If $\int \dfrac{(x^2 - 1)}{(x^4 + 3x^2 + 1) \tan^{-1}\left(\dfrac{x^2 + 1}{x}\right)} \, dx$

$= k \log \left| \tan^{-1}\left(\dfrac{x^2 + 1}{x}\right) \right| + C$, then :

(a) $k = 1$ (b) $k = 2$

(c) $k = 3$ (d) None of these.

119. If $f(x) = \int \dfrac{dx}{x - \sqrt{x^2 + 1}}$ and $f(0) = \dfrac{-1}{2} - \dfrac{1}{\sqrt{2}}$,

then $f(1) =$

(a) $\log(1 + \sqrt{2})$ (b) $\log(1 - \sqrt{2})$

(c) $\log(\sqrt{2} - 1)$ (d) None of these.

120. $\int \dfrac{dx}{\sqrt{\sin^3 x \, (\sin x + 2 \cos x)}}$ is equal to :

(a) $\sqrt{1 - \tan \dfrac{x}{2} + \cot \dfrac{x}{2}} + C$

(b) $-\sqrt{1 - \tan \dfrac{x}{2} + \cot \dfrac{x}{2}} + C$

(c) $\sqrt{1 + \tan \dfrac{x}{2} + \cot \dfrac{x}{2}} + C$

(d) None of these.

121. $\int \dfrac{\sin x - \cos x}{\sqrt{2 + \sin 2x}} \, dx$ is equal to :

(a) $\log\left(\sin x + \cos x + \sqrt{2 + \sin 2x}\right) + C$

(b) $-\log\left(\sin x + \cos x + \sqrt{2 + \sin 2x}\right) + C$

(c) $\log\left(\sin x + \cos x - \sqrt{2 + \sin 2x}\right) + C$

(d) None of these.

122. $\int \dfrac{dx}{(1 + x)\sqrt{1 + 2x - x^2}}$ is equal to :

(a) $\sqrt{2} \sin^{-1}\left(\dfrac{x\sqrt{2}}{x + 1}\right) + C$

(b) $\dfrac{1}{\sqrt{2}} \sin^{-1}\left(\dfrac{x\sqrt{2}}{x + 1}\right) + C$

(c) $\sqrt{2} \sin^{-1}\left(\dfrac{x\sqrt{2}}{x + 1}\right) + C$

(d) None of these.

123. $\int \dfrac{x^3}{(1 + x^2)^{1/3}} \, dx$ is equal to :

(a) $\dfrac{20}{3}(1 + x^2)^{2/3}(2x^2 + 3) + C$

(b) $\dfrac{20}{3}(1 + x^2)^{2/3}(2x^2 - 3) + C$

(c) $\dfrac{3}{20}(1 + x^2)^{2/3}(2x^2 - 3) + C$

(d) None of these.

124. $\int \dfrac{1}{e^x + 1 - 2e^{-x}} \, dx$ is equal to :

(a) $\dfrac{1}{3} \log \left| \dfrac{e^x - 1}{e^x + 2} \right| + C$ (b) $\dfrac{1}{3} \log \left| \dfrac{e^x + 2}{e^x - 1} \right| + C$

(c) $3 \log \left| \dfrac{e^x - 1}{e^x + 2} \right| + C$ (d) None of these.

125. The value of $\int \dfrac{\sqrt{1 + x}}{x} \, dx$ is :

(a) $2\sqrt{1 + x} + \ln \left| \dfrac{\sqrt{1 + x} - 1}{\sqrt{1 + x} + 1} \right| + C$

(b) $\ln\left(\dfrac{\sqrt{1 + x} - 1}{\sqrt{1 + x} + 1}\right) + C$

(c) $2\sqrt{1 + x} + C$

(d) $\dfrac{\sqrt{1 + x} - 1}{\sqrt{1 + x} + 1} + C$.

126. $\int \dfrac{1}{\sin x + \cos x} \, dx =$

(a) $\dfrac{1}{\sqrt{2}} \log \tan\left(x + \dfrac{\pi}{4}\right) + C$

(b) $\dfrac{1}{\sqrt{2}} \log \tan\left(\dfrac{x}{2} + \dfrac{\pi}{8}\right) + C$

(c) $\log \tan\left(\dfrac{x}{2} + \dfrac{\pi}{8}\right) + C$

(d) $\dfrac{1}{2} \log \tan\left(\dfrac{x}{2} + \dfrac{\pi}{8}\right) + C$.

127. $\int e^x (1 + \tan x + \tan^2 x) \, dx =$

(a) $e^x \cos x + C$ (b) $e^x \tan x + C$

(c) $e^x \sec x + C$ (d) $e^x \sin x + C$.

128. The value of integral $\int \frac{dx}{x^n (1 + x^n)^{1/n}}$, $n \in N$ is :

(a) $\frac{1}{1 - n} \left\{ 1 + \frac{1}{x^n} \right\}^{1 - \frac{1}{n}} + C$

(b) $\frac{1}{1 + n} \left\{ 1 - \frac{1}{x^n} \right\}^{1 + \frac{1}{n}} + C$

(c) $-\frac{1}{1 - n} \left\{ 1 - \frac{1}{x^n} \right\}^{1 + \frac{1}{n}} + C$

(d) $-\frac{1}{1 + n} \left\{ 1 + \frac{1}{x^n} \right\}^{1 + \frac{1}{n}} + C$

129. If $\int g(x) dx = g(x)$, then $\int g(x) [f(x) + f'(x)] dx$ is equal to :

(a) $g(x) f(x)$

(b) $g(x) f'(x)$

(c) $g(x) f(x) - g(x) f'(x)$

(d) $g(x) f''(x)$.

130. The value of the integral

$\int \frac{\cos^3 x + \cos^5 x}{\sin^2 x + \sin^4 x} dx$ is :

(a) $\sin x - 6 \tan^{-1} (\sin x) + C$

(b) $\sin x - 2 (\sin x)^{-1} + C$

(c) $\sin x - 2 (\sin x)^{-1} - 6 \tan^{-1} (\sin x) + C$

(d) None of these.

131. If $\int \sec^4 x \, \mathrm{cosec}^2 x \, dx = K \tan^3 x + L \tan x + M \cot x + \text{const.}$, then :

(a) $K = -1, L = 0, M = 1$

(b) $K = \frac{1}{3}, L = 1, M = 2$

(c) $K = \frac{1}{3}, L = 2, M = -1$

(d) None of these.

132. If $\int f(x) \sin x \cos x \, dx = \frac{1}{2(b^2 - a^2)} \log f(x) + C$

then $f(x) =$

(a) $\frac{1}{a^2 \sin^2 x + b^2 \cos^2 x}$

(b) $\frac{1}{a^2 \sin^2 x - b^2 \cos^2 x}$

(c) $\frac{1}{a^2 \cos^2 x + b^2 \sin^2 x}$

(d) $\frac{1}{a^2 \cos^2 x - b^2 \sin^2 x}$

133. $\int e^x (1 - \cot x + \cot^2 x) dx =$

(a) $e^x \cot x + c$

(b) $- e^x \cot x + c$

(c) $e^x \, \mathrm{cosec} \, x + c$

(d) $- e^x \, \mathrm{cosec} \, x + c$.

134. $\int x \log \left(1 + \frac{1}{x} \right) dx$

$= f(x) \log (x + 1) + g(x) \log x^2 + Lx - C$ then :

(a) $f(x) = \frac{x^2}{2}$

(b) $g(x) = \log (x)$

(c) $L = 1$

(d) $L = \frac{1}{2}$.

135. $\int \frac{\sin^3 x \, dx}{(\cos^4 x + 3 \cos^2 x + 1) \tan^{-1} (\sec x + \cos x)} =$

(a) $\tan^{-1} (\sec x + \cos x) + C$

(b) $\log \tan^{-1} (\sec x + \cos x) + C$

(c) $\frac{1}{(\sec x + \cos x)^2} + C$

(d) None of these.

136. $\int \frac{\cos 2x - 1}{\cos 2x + 1} dx =$

(a) $\tan x - x + C$

(b) $x + \tan x + C$

(c) $x - \tan x + C$

(d) $- x - \cot x + C$.

137. The integral $\int \frac{(\sin^2 x - \cos^2 x)}{\sin^2 x \cos^2 x} dx =$

(a) $\tan x + \cot x + C$

(b) $\mathrm{cosec} \, x + \sec x + C$

(c) $\tan x + \sec x + C$

(d) $\tan x + \mathrm{cosec} \, x + C$.

138. $\int \frac{x^2 + 1}{x(x^2 - 1)} dx$ is equal to :

(a) $\log \frac{x^2 - 1}{x} + C$

(b) $- \log \frac{x^2 - 1}{x} + C$

(c) $\log \frac{x}{x^2 + 1} + C$

(d) $- \log \frac{x}{x^2 + 1} + C$

139. $\int e^x \sin x \, dx$ is equal to :

(a) $e^x (\sin x - \cos x) + C$

(b) $e^x (\sin x + \cos x) + C$

(c) $\frac{1}{2} e^x (\sin x - \cos x) + C$

(d) $\frac{1}{2} (\tan^{-1} x^2)^3 + C$.

140. The integral $I = \int \dfrac{dx}{x - x^3}$ is equal to :

(a) $\dfrac{1}{2} \log \dfrac{1 - x^2}{x} + C$

(b) $\log \dfrac{1 - x}{x\,(1 + x)} + C$

(c) $\log x\,(1 - x^2) + C$

(d) $\dfrac{1}{2} \log \dfrac{x^2}{1 - x^2} + C.$

141. $\int \dfrac{x^2 \tan^{-1} x^3}{1 + x^6} \, dx$ is equal to :

(a) $\tan^{-1} x^3 + C$

(b) $\dfrac{1}{6} (\tan^{-1} x^3)^2 + C$

(c) $-\dfrac{1}{2} (\tan^{-1} x^3)^2 + C$

(d) $\dfrac{1}{2} (\tan^{-1} x^2)^3 + C.$

142. If $\int \dfrac{dx}{(x^2 + 1)\,(x^2 + 4)} = \dfrac{1}{3} g(x) + \dfrac{2}{3} \tan^{-1} x + C$

then $g(x) =$

(a) $\sin^{-1} x$

(b) $\log\,(1 + x^2)$

(c) $\tan^{-1} x$

(d) None of these.

143. If $\int \dfrac{2x + 3}{(x - 1)\,(x^2 + 1)} \, dx$

$= \log_e [(x - 1)^{5/2} (x^2 + 1)^a] - \dfrac{1}{2} \tan^{-1} x + A,$

where A is any arbitrary constant, then the value of 'a' is :

(a) $\dfrac{5}{4}$

(b) $-\dfrac{5}{3}$

(c) $-\dfrac{5}{6}$

(d) $\dfrac{-5}{4}.$

144. If $\int \dfrac{\sqrt{\cot x}}{\sin x \cos x} \, dx = P \sqrt{\cot x} + Q$, then $P =$

(a) 1

(b) 2

(c) -1

(d) $-2.$

145. $\int e^{\sqrt{x}} \, dx$ is equal to :

(a) $e^{\sqrt{x}} + A$

(b) $\dfrac{1}{2} e^{\sqrt{x}} + A$

(c) $2(\sqrt{x} - 1) e^{\sqrt{x}} + A$

(d) $2(\sqrt{x} + 1) e^{\sqrt{x}} + A$, where A is an arbitrary constant.

146. If $f\left(\dfrac{3x - 4}{3x + 4}\right) = x + 2$, then $\int f(x) \, dx$ is equal to

(a) $e^{x+2} \ln \left|\dfrac{3x - 4}{3x + 4}\right| + C$

(b) $-\dfrac{8}{3} \ln |1 - x| + \dfrac{2}{3} x + C$

(c) $\dfrac{8}{3} \ln |1 - x| + \dfrac{x}{3} + C$

(d) None of these.

147. $\int \dfrac{e^x \,(2 - x^2) \, dx}{(1 - x) \sqrt{1 - x^2}}$ is :

(a) $e^x \sqrt{1 - x^2} + C$

(b) $e^x \sqrt{\dfrac{1 - x^2}{1 - x}} + C$

(c) $\dfrac{e^x \sqrt{1 - x^2}}{(1 - x)} + C$

(d) $\dfrac{e^x}{(1 - x) \sqrt{1 - x^2}} + C.$

148. $\int \dfrac{x e^x}{(x + 1)^2} \, dx =$

(a) $\dfrac{e^x}{1 + x} + C$

(b) $\dfrac{x e^x}{(1 + x)} + C$

(c) $\dfrac{e^x}{(1 + x)^3} + C$

(d) $\dfrac{e^x}{(1 + x)^2} + C$

149. $\int x^x \,(1 + \log x) \, dx =$

(a) $\dfrac{(1 + \log x)^2}{2} + C$

(b) $x^x \log x + C$

(c) $x^{2x} + C$

(d) $x^x + C.$

150. $\int \sin^{-1} x \, dx =$

(a) $x \sin^{-1} x - \sqrt{1 - x^2} + C$

(b) $x \sin^{-1} x + \sqrt{1 - x^2} + C$

(c) $-x \sin^{-1} x + \sqrt{1 - x^2} + C$

(d) None of these.

151. If n is an odd positive integer, then $\int |x^n| \, dx =$

(a) $\left|\dfrac{x^{n+1}}{n + 1}\right| + C$

(b) $\dfrac{x^{n+1}}{n + 1} + C$

(c) $\dfrac{|x^n| x}{n + 1} + C$

(d) None of these.

152. $\int \cos\left(2\cot^{-1}\sqrt{\dfrac{1-x}{1+x}}\right)dx =$

  (a) $\dfrac{1-x^2}{1+x^2}+C$ (b) $-\dfrac{x^2}{2}+C$

  (c) $\dfrac{\sin 2x}{1+x}+C$ (d) None of these

153. If $\int \dfrac{5\tan x}{\tan x - 2}dx = x + a\ln|\sin x - 2\cos x| + k$,

  then a is equal to   [AIEEE - 2012]

  (a) −1   (b) −2

  (c) 1   (d) 2

154. If the integral

  $\int \dfrac{5\tan x}{\tan x - 2}dx = x + a\log|\sin x - 2\cos x| + k$,

  then 'a' is equal to

  (a) 1   (b) 2

  (c) − 1   (d) − 2

155. The integral $\int \dfrac{2x^{12}+5x^9}{(x^5+x^3+1)^3}dx$ is equal to

  (a) $-\dfrac{x^5}{2(x^5+x^3+1)^2}+c$ (b)

  $\dfrac{x^{10}}{2(x^5+x^3+1)^2}+c$

  (c) $\dfrac{x^5}{2(x^5+x^3+1)^2}+c$ (d)

  $\dfrac{-x^{10}}{(x^5+x^3+1)^2}+c$

156. $\int \dfrac{[x+\sqrt{2-x^2}]^{1/3}\,[1-x\sqrt{2-x^2}]^{1/6}}{(1-x^2)^{1/3}}dx$ is

  (a) $\sqrt{1-x^2}+\sqrt[3]{\dfrac{1-x^2}{1+x^2}}+k$

  (b) $2^{1/6}\cdot x + k$

  (c) $\sqrt[3]{\dfrac{1+x^2}{1-x^2}}$

  (d) $2^{1/6}\cdot x^{1/6}+k$

ANSWER KEY

1. (a)	**2.** (c)	**3.** (b)	**4.** (c)	**5.** (a)	**6.** (b)	**7.** (c)	**8.** (a)	**9.** (b)	**10.** (c)
11. (a)	**12.** (c)	**13.** (a)	**14.** (b)	**15.** (c)	**16.** (a)	**17.** (b)	**18.** (c)	**19.** (d)	**20.** (a)
21. (b)	**22.** (a)	**23.** (b)	**24.** (c)	**25.** (a)	**26.** (c)	**27.** (a)	**28.** (c)	**29.** (a)	**30.** (b)
31. (b)	**32.** (b)	**33.** (a)	**34.** (c)	**35.** (b)	**36.** (b)	**37.** (a)	**38.** (b)	**39.** (c)	**40.** (b)
41. (c)	**42.** (a)	**43.** (b)	**44.** (c)	**45.** (a)	**46.** (c)	**47.** (b)	**48.** (a)	**49.** (b)	**50.** (c)
51. (b)	**52.** (a)	**53.** (b)	**54.** (d)	**55.** (a)	**56.** (c)	**57.** (b)	**58.** (a)	**59.** (b)	**60.** (a)
61. (d)	**62.** (a)	**63.** (b)	**64.** (c)	**65.** (b)	**66.** (a)	**67.** (a)	**68.** (a)	**69.** (b)	**70.** (c)
71. (a)	**72.** (b)	**73.** (c)	**74.** (b)	**75.** (a)	**76.** (c)	**77.** (a)	**78.** (a)	**79.** (a)	**80.** (c)
81. (a)	**82.** (b)	**83.** (c)	**84.** (c)	**85.** (b)	**86.** (a)	**87.** (b)	**88.** (a)	**89.** (b)	**90.** (c)
91. (b)	**92.** (c)	**93.** (a)	**94.** (b)	**95.** (a)	**96.** (b)	**97.** (a)	**98.** (b)	**99.** (b)	**100.** (a)
101. (b)	**102.** (b)	**103.** (c)	**104.** (b)	**105.** (b)	**106.** (c)	**107.** (a)	**108.** (b)	**109.** (a)	**110.** (c)
111. (a)	**112.** (c)	**113.** (b)	**114.** (b)	**115.** (a)	**116.** (c)	**117.** (d)	**118.** (b)	**119.** (a)	**120.** (b)
121. (b)	**122.** (b)	**123.** (c)	**124.** (a)	**125.** (a)	**126.** (b)	**127.** (b)	**128.** (a)	**129.** (a)	**130.** (c)
131. (c)	**132.** (c)	**133.** (b)	**134.** (d)	**135.** (b)	**136.** (c)	**137.** (a)	**138.** (a)	**139.** (c)	**140.** (d)
141. (b)	**142.** (d)	**143.** (d)	**144.** (b)	**145.** (c)	**146.** (b)	**147.** (c)	**148.** (a)	**149.** (d)	**150.** (b)
151. (c)	**152.** (b)	**153.** (d)	**154.** (b)	**155.** (b)	**156.** (b)				

Chapter 24

DEFINITE INTEGRAL AND AREA

MULTIPLE CHOICE QUESTIONS

1. The value of the integral

$$\int_0^{\pi} e^{\cos^2 x} \cos^3 (2n+1) x \, dx, \text{ n integer, is :}$$

(a) 0   (b) π

(c) 2π   (d) None of these.

2. $\int_0^{\pi/2} \cos^5 \left(\frac{x}{2}\right) \cdot \sin x \, dx$ is equal to :

(a) $\frac{2}{7}\left(1 - \frac{1}{8\sqrt{2}}\right)$ (b) $\frac{-4}{7}\left(1 - \frac{1}{8\sqrt{2}}\right)$

(c) $\frac{4}{7}\left(1 - \frac{1}{8\sqrt{2}}\right)$ (d) None of these.

3. The value of the integral $\int_0^{\pi} \frac{x \, dx}{1 + \cos \alpha \sin x}$,

$0 < \alpha < \frac{\pi}{2}$, is :

(a) $\frac{\pi\alpha}{\sin \alpha}$ (b) $\frac{\sin \alpha}{\pi\alpha}$

(c) $\frac{2\pi\alpha}{\sin \alpha}$ (d) None of these.

4. $\int_0^{\pi/2} \frac{dx}{(a^2 \cos^2 x + b^2 \sin^2 x)^2}$ is equal to :

(a) $\frac{\pi(a^2 + b^2)}{4a^3 b^3}$ (b) $\frac{\pi(a^2 + b^2)}{2a^3 b^3}$

(c) $\frac{\pi(a^2 + b^2)}{a^3 b^3}$ (d) None of these.

5. The value of the integral $\int_0^{\pi/2} \frac{x \sin x \cos x}{\sin^4 x + \cos^4 x} dx$ is :

(a) $\frac{\pi^2}{8}$ (b) $\frac{\pi^2}{16}$

(c) $\frac{\pi^2}{24}$ (d) None of these.

6. $\int_0^{\pi/4} \frac{\sin^2 x \cdot \cos^2 x}{(\sin^3 x + \cos^3 x)^2} dx$ is equal to :

(a) $\frac{1}{6}$ (b) $\frac{1}{12}$

(c) $\frac{1}{4}$ (d) None of these.

7. The value of the integral $\int_0^{\pi} x(\sin^4 x \cos^4 x) \, dx$ is

(a) $\frac{3\pi^2}{64}$ (b) $\frac{3\pi^2}{128}$

(c) $\frac{3\pi^2}{256}$ (d) None of these.

8. $\int_0^{\pi/4} \frac{\sin x + \cos x}{9 + 16 \sin 2x} dx$ is equal to :

(a) $\frac{1}{20} \log 3$ (b) $\frac{1}{40} \log 3$

(c) $\frac{1}{60} \log 3$ (d) None of these.

9. The value of the integral $\int_{\pi/2}^{\pi} e^x \cdot \frac{1 - \sin x}{1 - \cos x} dx$ is :

(a) $e^{-\pi/2}$ (b) $e^{\pi/4}$

(c) $e^{\pi/2}$ (d) None of these.

10. $\int_0^{\pi} \frac{x \tan x}{\sec x + \tan x} dx$ is equal to :

(a) $\frac{\pi}{2} (\pi - 2)$ (b) $\pi (\pi - 2)$

(c) $\frac{\pi}{4} (\pi - 2)$ (d) None of these.

11. The value of the integral $\int_0^{2\pi} e^x \sin \left(\frac{\pi}{4} + \frac{x}{2}\right) dx$ is :

(a) $\frac{\sqrt{2}}{5} (e^{2\pi} + 1)$ (b) $-\frac{\sqrt{2}}{5} (e^{2\pi} + 1)$

(c) $-\frac{\sqrt{2}}{5} (e^{2\pi} - 1)$ (d) None of these.

12. $\displaystyle\int_{\pi/6}^{\pi/3} \frac{\sqrt{\sin x}}{\sqrt{\sin x} + \sqrt{\cos x}}\, dx$ is equal to :

(a) $\dfrac{\pi}{4}$

(b) $\dfrac{\pi}{6}$

(c) $\dfrac{\pi}{12}$

(d) None of these.

13. $\displaystyle\int_0^1 \log\left(\sqrt{1-x} + \sqrt{1+x}\right) dx =$

(a) $\dfrac{1}{2}\log 2 + \dfrac{\pi-2}{4}$

(b) $\dfrac{1}{2}\log 2 - \dfrac{\pi-2}{4}$

(c) $\dfrac{1}{2}\log 2 + \dfrac{\pi+2}{4}$

(d) None of these.

14. $\displaystyle\int_0^{\pi/2} \log \sin x\, dx$ is equal to :

(a) $\dfrac{\pi}{2}\log 2$

(b) $\dfrac{-\pi}{2}\log 2$

(c) $\pi \log 2$

(d) None of these.

15. The value of the integral $\displaystyle\int_0^{2a} \sqrt{2ax - x^2}\, dx$ is :

(a) πa^2

(b) $\dfrac{\pi a^2}{4}$

(c) $\dfrac{\pi a^2}{2}$

(d) None of these.

16. $\displaystyle\int_0^{\pi} \frac{x}{a^2 \cos^2 x + b^2 \sin^2 x}\, dx$ is equal to :

(a) $\dfrac{\pi^2}{ab}$

(b) $\dfrac{\pi^2}{2ab}$

(c) $\dfrac{\pi^2}{4ab}$

(d) None of these.

17. The value of the integral $\displaystyle\int_0^{\pi} x \log \sin x\, dx$ is :

(a) $-\dfrac{\pi^2}{2}\log 2$

(b) $\dfrac{\pi^2}{2}\log 2$

(c) $\pi^2 \log 2$

(d) None of these.

18. $\displaystyle\int_0^{a} \frac{dx}{a + \sqrt{a^2 - x^2}}$ is equal to :

(a) $\dfrac{\pi}{2} + 1$

(b) $\dfrac{\pi}{2} - 1$

(c) $1 - \dfrac{\pi}{2}$

(d) None of these.

19. $\displaystyle\int_0^{\pi/2} \log(\tan x + \cot x)\, dx$ is equal to :

(a) $\dfrac{\pi}{2}\log 2$

(b) $-\dfrac{\pi}{2}\log 2$

(c) $\pi \log 2$

(d) None of these.

20. $\displaystyle\int_0^{\infty} \frac{x}{(1+x)(1+x^2)}\, dx =$

(a) $\dfrac{\pi}{2}$

(b) $\dfrac{\pi}{4}$

(c) $\dfrac{\pi}{6}$

(d) None of these.

21. The value of the integral $\displaystyle\int_0^{\pi} \log(1 + \cos x)\, dx$ is :

(a) $\dfrac{\pi}{2}\log 2$

(b) $\pi \log 2$

(c) $-\pi \log 2$

(d) None of these.

22. The value of the integral $\displaystyle\int_0^{\pi/2} \sin 2kx \cot x\, dx$, where k is a positive integer, is :

(a) $\dfrac{\pi}{2}$

(b) $-\pi$

(c) π

(d) None of these.

23. $\displaystyle\int_2^3 \frac{2x^5 + x^4 - 2x^3 + 2x^2 + 1}{(x^2+1)(x^4-1)}\, dx$ is equal to :

(a) $\dfrac{1}{2}\left(\log 6 + \dfrac{1}{5}\right)$

(b) $\dfrac{1}{2}\left(\log 6 - \dfrac{1}{5}\right)$

(c) $\dfrac{-1}{2}\left(\log 6 + \dfrac{1}{5}\right)$

(d) None of these.

24. $\displaystyle\int_0^1 \frac{\log(1+x)}{1+x^2}\, dx$ is equal to :

(a) $\dfrac{\pi}{8}\log 2$

(b) $\dfrac{\pi}{8}\log\dfrac{1}{2}$

(c) $\dfrac{\pi}{4}\log 2$

(d) None of these.

25. The value of the integral $\displaystyle\int_0^{\pi} \frac{\sin 2kx}{\sin x}\, dx$, where $k \in I$, is :

(a) $\dfrac{\pi}{2}$

(b) π

(c) 0

(d) None of these.

26. $\displaystyle\int_0^{\pi/2} \frac{\cos^2\theta \, d\theta}{\cos^2\theta + 4\sin^2\theta}$ is equal to :

(a) $\dfrac{\pi}{2}$

(b) 0

(c) $\dfrac{\pi}{6}$

(d) None of these.

27. The value of the integral $\displaystyle\int_0^\infty \log\left(x + \frac{1}{x}\right)\frac{dx}{1+x^2}$ is :

(a) $\dfrac{\pi}{2}\log 2$

(b) $-\dfrac{\pi}{2}\log 2$

(c) $-\pi \log 2$

(d) $\pi \log 2$.

28. $\displaystyle\int_0^\pi \frac{x^2 \sin x}{(2x - \pi)(1 + \cos^2 x)} dx$ is equal to :

(a) $\dfrac{\pi^2}{4}$

(b) $\dfrac{\pi^2}{2}$

(c) $\dfrac{\pi^2}{6}$

(d) None of these.

29. $\displaystyle\int_0^\pi \frac{dx}{1 + \tan^4 x}$ is equal to :

(a) $\dfrac{\pi}{2}$

(b) $\dfrac{\pi}{6}$

(c) 0

(d) $\dfrac{\pi}{4}$

30. The value of the integral $\displaystyle\int_0^{\pi/4} \frac{\sin x \cdot \cos x}{\cos^2 x + \sin^4 x} dx$ is :

(a) $\dfrac{\pi}{\sqrt{3}}$

(b) $\dfrac{\pi}{6\sqrt{3}}$

(c) $\dfrac{\pi}{4\sqrt{3}}$

(d) None of these.

31. $\displaystyle\int_0^\infty \left(\frac{dx}{\left(x + \sqrt{1+x^2}\right)^n}\right)$ where n is an integer > 1, is

(a) $\dfrac{n}{1 - n^2}$

(b) $\dfrac{n}{n^2 - 1}$

(c) $\dfrac{n}{n^2 + 1}$

(d) $\dfrac{-n}{n^2 + 1}$

32. $\displaystyle\int_0^{\pi/2} \frac{\sin^2 x}{\sin^4 x + \cos^4 x} dx$ is equal to :

(a) $\dfrac{\pi}{\sqrt{2}}$

(b) $\dfrac{\pi}{3\sqrt{2}}$

(c) $\dfrac{-\pi}{\sqrt{2}}$

(d) $\dfrac{-\pi}{2\sqrt{2}}$.

33. The value of the integral $\displaystyle\int_0^1 \frac{x}{1 + x^3} dx =$

(a) $-\dfrac{1}{3}\log 2 + \dfrac{\pi}{3\sqrt{3}}$

(b) $\dfrac{1}{3}\log 2 + \dfrac{\pi}{3\sqrt{3}}$

(c) $-\dfrac{1}{3}\log 2 - \dfrac{\pi}{3\sqrt{3}}$

(d) None of these.

34. $\displaystyle\int_1^3 |(x-1)(x-2)(x-3)| \, dx =$

(a) $\dfrac{1}{3}$

(b) $\dfrac{9}{2}$

(c) $\dfrac{9}{4}$

(d) None of these.

35. $\displaystyle\int_{\pi/6}^{\pi/3} \frac{\sin x + \cos x}{\sqrt{\sin 2x}} dx$ is equal to :

(a) $2\sin^{-1}\dfrac{1}{2}(\sqrt{3} - 1)$

(b) $\sin^{-1}\dfrac{1}{2}(\sqrt{3} - 1)$

(c) $2\sin^{-1}\dfrac{1}{2}(\sqrt{3} + 1)$

(d) None of these.

36. $\displaystyle\int_{-1}^{3/2} |x \sin \pi x| \, dx$ is equal to :

(a) $\dfrac{1}{\pi}\left(1 + \dfrac{1}{\pi}\right)$

(b) $\dfrac{1}{\pi}\left(1 - \dfrac{1}{\pi}\right)$

(c) $\dfrac{1}{\pi}\left(\dfrac{1}{\pi} - 1\right)$

(d) None of these.

37. $\displaystyle\int_0^{\pi/2} \frac{x \sin x \cos x}{(a^2 \cos^2 x + b^2 \sin^2 x)^2} dx$ is equal to :

(a) $\dfrac{\pi}{ab^2(a+b)}$

(b) $\dfrac{\pi}{2ab^2(a+b)}$

(c) $\dfrac{\pi}{4ab^2(a+b)}$

(d) None of these.

38. The value of the integral $\int\limits_{0}^{1} |x \cos \pi x| \, dx$ is :

(a) $\dfrac{2}{\pi}$

(b) $\dfrac{1}{\pi}$

(c) $\dfrac{-2}{\pi}$

(d) $\dfrac{-1}{\pi}$.

39. $\int\limits_{0}^{\pi/2} \dfrac{x \sin 2x}{\cos^4 x + \sin^4 x} \, dx$ is equal to :

(a) $\dfrac{\pi^2}{2}$

(b) $\dfrac{\pi^2}{4}$

(c) $\dfrac{\pi^2}{8}$

(d) None of these.

40. The value of the integral $\int\limits_{0}^{2} |x^3 - 3x^2 + 2x| \, dx$ is :

(a) $\dfrac{1}{2}$

(b) $\dfrac{1}{4}$

(c) $\dfrac{1}{16}$

(d) None of these.

41. $\int\limits_{-1}^{1} \log \dfrac{2-x}{2+x} \, dx$ is equal to :

(a) -1

(b) 1

(c) 2

(d) 0.

42. $\int\limits_{0}^{\pi/4} \dfrac{\sec^2 \alpha}{\tan x - \tan \alpha} \, dx$, $\alpha > \dfrac{\pi}{4}$, is equal to :

(a) $\log \dfrac{\sin\left(\alpha - \dfrac{\pi}{4}\right)}{\sin \alpha} + \dfrac{\pi \tan \alpha}{4}$

(b) $\log \dfrac{\sin\left(\alpha - \dfrac{\pi}{4}\right)}{\sin \alpha} - \dfrac{\pi \tan \alpha}{4}$

(c) $\log \dfrac{\sin\left(\dfrac{\pi}{4} - \alpha\right)}{\sin \alpha} - \dfrac{\pi \tan \alpha}{4}$

(d) None of these.

43. The value of the integral $\int\limits_{0}^{2\pi} \dfrac{dx}{(1 + e \cos x)^2}$, $e < 1$, is :

(a) $\dfrac{2\pi}{(1 - e^2)^{3/2}}$

(b) $\dfrac{\pi}{(1 - e^2)^{3/2}}$

(c) $\dfrac{-\pi}{(1 - e^2)^{3/2}}$

(d) None of these.

44. $\int\limits_{0}^{\pi/2} \dfrac{\cos 7\theta - \cos 8\theta}{\cos 2\theta - \cos 3\theta}$ is equal to :

(a) $\dfrac{\pi}{2} + \dfrac{2}{5}$

(b) $\dfrac{\pi}{2} - \dfrac{2}{5}$

(c) $\dfrac{-\pi}{2} + \dfrac{2}{5}$

(d) None of these.

45. $\int\limits_{0}^{\pi} x \sin^6 x \cos^4 x \, dx$ is equal to :

(a) $\dfrac{3\pi^2}{512}$

(b) $\dfrac{3\pi^2}{256}$

(c) $\dfrac{3\pi^2}{1024}$

(d) None of these.

46. $\int\limits_{0}^{\pi/3} \cos^4 3\phi \sin^2 6\phi \, d\phi$ is equal to :

(a) $\dfrac{\pi}{32}$

(b) $\dfrac{7\pi}{96}$

(c) $\dfrac{5\pi}{96}$

(d) None of these.

47. $\int\limits_{0}^{2a} x^{9/2} (2a - x)^{-1/2} \, dx$ is equal to :

(a) $\dfrac{63\pi}{4} a^5$

(b) $\dfrac{63\pi}{2} a^5$

(c) $63\pi \, a^5$

(d) $\dfrac{63\pi}{8} a^5$

48. $\int\limits_{0}^{2} x^3 \sqrt{2x - x^2} \, dx$ is equal to :

(a) $\dfrac{7\pi}{2}$

(b) $\dfrac{7\pi}{4}$

(c) $\dfrac{7\pi}{8}$

(d) $\dfrac{7\pi}{16}$.

49. $\int\limits_{0}^{1} x^5 \sqrt{\dfrac{1 + x^2}{1 - x^2}} \, dx$ is equal to :

(a) $\dfrac{3\pi + 8}{24}$

(b) $\dfrac{\pi + 2}{8}$

(c) $\dfrac{3\pi + 8}{16}$

(d) None of these.

50. $\int\limits_{0}^{\infty} \dfrac{x^2}{\sqrt{(1 + x^6)^7}} \, dx$ is equal to :

(a) $\dfrac{4}{45}$

(b) $\dfrac{8}{45}$

(c) $\dfrac{2}{45}$

(d) None of these.

51. $\int\limits_{-1}^{1}$ [x] dx, where [.] denotes the greatest integer function, is equal to :

(a) 0   (b) 1

(c) – 1   (d) None of these.

52. $\int\limits_{0}^{1.5}$ [x²] dx, where [·] denotes the greatest integer function, is equal to :

(a) $\sqrt{2}-2$ (b) $2-\sqrt{2}$

(c) $2+\sqrt{2}$ (d) None of these.

53. $\int\limits_{0}^{3}$ [√x] dx is equal to :

(a) 1   (b) 2

(c) – 1   (d) – 2.

54. $\int\limits_{-\pi/4}^{\pi/4} \dfrac{x+\pi/4}{2-\cos 2x}$ dx is equal to :

(a) $\dfrac{\pi^2}{6\sqrt{3}}$ (b) $\dfrac{\pi^2}{4\sqrt{3}}$

(c) $\dfrac{\pi^2}{2\sqrt{3}}$ (d) None of these.

55. $\int\limits_{0}^{2} \sin\dfrac{\pi[x]}{2}$ dx is equal to :

(a) 1   (b) – 1

(c) 0   (d) None of these.

56. $\int\limits_{0}^{2\pi} \sqrt{\dfrac{1-\cos 2x}{2}}$ dx is equal to :

(a) 2   (b) – 2

(c) 4   (d) – 4.

57. $\int\limits_{-1}^{2}$ [2x] dx is equal to :

(a) $\dfrac{1}{2}$ (b) $\dfrac{-1}{2}$

(c) $\dfrac{3}{2}$ (d) $\dfrac{-3}{2}$.

58. $\int\limits_{-2}^{1}$ [x + 1] dx is equal to :

(a) 0   (b) 1

(c) – 1   (d) None of these.

59. $\int\limits_{\pi}^{10\pi}$ |sin x| dx is equal to :

(a) 18   (b) 20

(c) 40   (d) None of these.

60. $\int\limits_{0}^{100}$ (x – [x]) dx is equal to :

(a) 50   (b) 100

(c) 200   (d) None of these.

61. If f(x) is an odd function, then $\int\limits_{a}^{x}$ f(t) dt is :

(a) odd

(b) even

(c) neither even nor odd.

62. If f(x) is an even function, then $\int\limits_{0}^{x}$ f(t) dt is :

(a) odd

(b) even

(c) neither even nor odd.

63. If f(x) is a periodic function of period a, then $\int\limits_{0}^{na}$ f(x) dx is equal to :

(a) $\int\limits_{0}^{a}$ f(x) dx   (b) n $\int\limits_{0}^{a}$ f(x) dx

(c) (n – 1) $\int\limits_{0}^{a}$ f(x) dx   (d) None of these.

64. $\lim\limits_{x\to 0}\dfrac{1}{x^3} \int\limits_{0}^{x^2} \sin\sqrt{t}$ dt is equal to :

(a) $\dfrac{1}{3}$ (b) $\dfrac{2}{3}$

(c) $\dfrac{-1}{3}$ (d) $\dfrac{-2}{3}$.

65. $\lim\limits_{h\to 0}\dfrac{1}{h}\displaystyle\int\limits_{x}^{x+h}\dfrac{dz}{z+\sqrt{z^2+1}}$ is equal to :

(a) 0

(b) $\dfrac{1}{x+\sqrt{x^2+1}}$

(c) $\dfrac{1}{\sqrt{x^2+1}}$

(d) None of these.

66. If $f(x)=\displaystyle\int\limits_{1}^{x^3}\dfrac{dt}{1+t^4}$, then $f''(x)$ is equal to :

(a) $\dfrac{6x\,(1-5x^{12})}{(1+x^{12})^2}$

(b) $\dfrac{6x\,(1+5x^{12})}{(1+x^{12})^2}$

(c) $\dfrac{-6x\,(1-5x^{12})}{(1+x^{12})^2}$

(d) None of these.

67. $\lim\limits_{x\to 0}\dfrac{\displaystyle\int\limits_{0}^{x^2}(\tan^{-1}t)^2\,dt}{\displaystyle\int\limits_{0}^{x}\sin\sqrt{t}\,dt}$ is equal to :

(a) 1

(b) – 1

(c) $\dfrac{-1}{2}$

(d) $\dfrac{1}{2}$.

68. The intervals of increase of the function $f(x)$ defined by $f(x)=\displaystyle\int\limits_{-1}^{x}(t^2+2t)\,(t^2-1)\,dt$ are :

(a) $(-\infty,-2)\cup(2,-\infty)$

(b) $(-\infty,-2)\cup(-1,0)\cup(1,-\infty)$

(c) $(-1,0)\cup(1,\infty)$

(d) None of these.

69. If $f(x)$ and $\phi(x)$ are continuous functions on the interval $[0, 4]$ satisfying $f(x)=f(4-x)$, $\phi(x)+\phi(4-x)=3$ and $\displaystyle\int\limits_{0}^{4}f(x)\,dx=2$, then $\displaystyle\int\limits_{0}^{4}f(x)\,\phi(x)\,dx=$

(a) 3

(b) 6

(c) 2

(d) None of these.

70. Let $f(x)$ be a continuous function such that the area bounded by the curve $y=f(x)$, X-axis and the lines $x=0$ & $x=a$ is $\dfrac{a^2}{2}+\dfrac{a}{2}\sin a+\dfrac{\pi}{2}\cos a$, then $f\left(\dfrac{\pi}{2}\right)=$

(a) 1

(b) $\dfrac{1}{2}$

(c) $\dfrac{1}{3}$

(d) None of these.

71. If $2f(x)+3f\left(\dfrac{1}{x}\right)=\dfrac{1}{x}-2x\neq 0$, then $\displaystyle\int\limits_{1}^{2}f(x)\,dx=$

(a) $\dfrac{-2}{5}\log 2+\dfrac{1}{2}$

(b) $\dfrac{-2}{5}\log 2-\dfrac{1}{2}$

(c) $\dfrac{2}{5}\log 2+\dfrac{1}{2}$

(d) None of these.

72. If $a_n=\displaystyle\int\limits_{0}^{\pi/2}\dfrac{\cos^2 nx}{\sin x}\,dx$, then $a_2-a_1,\ a_3-a_2,\ a_4-a_3$ are in :

(a) G.P.

(b) A.P.

(c) H.P.

(d) None of these.

73. If $\phi'(x)=\dfrac{\log(\sin x)}{x}$, $x\neq n\pi,\ n\in I$ and $\displaystyle\int\limits_{1}^{3}\dfrac{3\log(\sin x^3)}{x}\,dx=\phi(k)-\phi(1)$ then, the possible value of k is :

(a) 27

(b) 18

(c) 9

(d) None of these.

74. $\displaystyle\int\limits_{1}^{16}\log x\,dz$, where $z=x^4$, is equal to :

(a) $16\log 2+\dfrac{15}{4}$

(b) $16\log 2-\dfrac{15}{4}$

(c) $-\left(16\log 2+\dfrac{15}{4}\right)$

(d) None of these.

75. If $\phi(x)=\displaystyle\int\limits_{-\pi/3}^{\pi/3}\sin^4 z$, then $\phi(x+2\pi)$ is equal to :

(a) $\phi(x)$

(b) $\phi(x)+\phi(2\pi)$

(c) $\phi(x)-\phi(2\pi)$

(d) $\phi(x)\cdot\phi(2\pi)$.

76. If $\displaystyle\int\limits_{3}^{5}e^{f[\phi(x)]}\cdot f'[\phi(x)]\cdot\phi'(x)\,dx$, where $\phi(3)=\phi(5)$, is equal to :

(a) 1

(b) 0

(c) 3

(d) None of these.

77. If $\displaystyle\int_{-x/3}^{x/3} \left(\frac{a}{3}\, |\tan x| + \frac{b \tan x}{1 + \sec x} + c\right) dx = 0$

where a, b, c are constants, then c =

(a) a log 2

(b) $\dfrac{a}{\pi} \log 2$

(c) $\dfrac{-a}{\pi} \log 2$

(d) $\dfrac{2a}{\pi} \log 2$.

78. The value of the integral $\displaystyle\int_{1}^{e^6} \left[\frac{\log x}{3}\right] dx$, where [.]

denotes the greatest integer function, is :

(a) 0

(b) $e^6 - e^3$

(c) $e^6 + e^3$

(d) $e^3 - e^6$.

79. $\displaystyle\int_{1}^{4} |(1 - x)\, (3 - x)\, \log x|\, dx$ is equal to :

(a) $\dfrac{4}{3} \log 4 + \dfrac{7}{9}$

(b) $\dfrac{4}{3} \log 4 - \dfrac{7}{9}$

(c) $\dfrac{7}{9} - \dfrac{4}{3} \log 4$

(d) None of these.

80. The value of $\displaystyle\int_{-2}^{2} \max\{(1 - x),\, (1 + x),\, 2\}\, dx$ is :

(a) 8

(b) – 8

(c) 9

(d) – 9.

81. $\displaystyle\int_{0}^{2\pi} \frac{dx}{1 + e^{\sin x}}$ is equal to :

(a) π

(b) 2π

(c) $\dfrac{\pi}{2}$

(d) None of these.

82. $\displaystyle\int_{0}^{\pi/6} \sec^2 x\, d(x - [x])$ is equal to :

(a) $\sqrt{3}$

(b) $\dfrac{1}{\sqrt{3}}$

(c) 1

(d) None of these.

83. Let f(x) = minimum $\{x + |x|,\, x - [x]\}$, where [.] denotes the greatest integer function.

Then $\displaystyle\int_{-1}^{1} f(x)\, dx$ is equal to :

(a) $\dfrac{1}{2}$

(b) $\dfrac{-1}{2}$

(c) 1

(d) – 1.

84. If ϕ and f are two continuous functions, then the value of the integral

$\displaystyle\int_{-\pi/4}^{\pi/4} \{f(x) + f(-x)\} \cdot \{g(x) - g(-x)\}\, dx$ is :

(a) $\dfrac{\pi}{4}$

(b) 0

(c) $\dfrac{-\pi}{4}$

(d) None of these.

85. If $f(a - x) = f(x)$ and $\displaystyle\int_{0}^{a/2} f(x)\, dx = p$, then :

$\displaystyle\int_{0}^{a} f(x)\, dx$ is equal to :

(a) 2p

(b) 0

(c) p

(d) None of these.

86. If $f(x) = \displaystyle\int_{2}^{x} (x^3 - 6x^2 + 11x - 6)\, dx$, $2 \le x \le 4$,

then the range of f(x) is :

(a) [0,2]

(b) $\left[\dfrac{-1}{4},\, 2\right]$

(c) $\left[\dfrac{-1}{4},\, 0\right]$

(d) None of these.

87. $\displaystyle\int_{0}^{\infty} e^{-ax} \cos bx\, dx$ equals :

(a) $\dfrac{b}{a^2 + b^2}$

(b) $\dfrac{b}{a^2 - b^2}$

(c) $\dfrac{a}{a^2 + b^2}$

(d) None of these.

88. The value of $\displaystyle\int_{3}^{5} \frac{x^2}{x^2 - 4}\, dx$ is :

(a) $2 - \log_e\left(\dfrac{15}{7}\right)$

(b) $2 + \log_e\left(\dfrac{15}{7}\right)$

(c) $2 + 4 \log_e 3 - 4 \log_e 7 + 4 \log_e 5$

(d) $2 - \tan^{-1}(15/7)$.

89. $\left|\displaystyle\int_{10}^{19} \frac{\sin x\, dx}{1 + x^8}\right|$ is less than $\displaystyle\int_{0}^{1} \frac{dx}{\sqrt{1 + x^4}} \in$ [a, b] is

given by

(a) 10^{-10}

(b) 10^{-11}

(c) 10^{-7}

(d) 10^{-9}.

90. The smallest interval [a, b] such that :

(a) $\left[\dfrac{1}{\sqrt{2}}, 1\right]$

(b) [0, 1]

(c) $\left[\dfrac{1}{2}, 1\right]$

(d) $\left[\dfrac{3}{4}, 1\right]$

91. If f(x + y) = f(x). f(y) for all x, y, where

f '(0) = k ≠ 0, then f(x) can be expressed as :

(a) ae^{kx}

(b) a cos kx + b sin kx

(c) kx

(d) None of these.

92. If $\displaystyle\int_{0}^{1} e^{x^2} (x - \alpha)\, dx = 0$, then :

(a) $1 < \alpha < 2$

(b) $\alpha < 0$

(c) $0 < \alpha < 1$

(d) $\alpha = 0$.

93. $\displaystyle\int_{0}^{1} \dfrac{\tan^{-1} x}{x}\, dx$ equals :

(a) $\displaystyle\int_{0}^{\pi/2} \dfrac{x}{\sin x}\, dx$

(b) $\dfrac{1}{2} \displaystyle\int_{0}^{\pi/2} \dfrac{x}{\sin x}\, dx$

(c) $\displaystyle\int_{0}^{\pi/2} \dfrac{\sin x}{x}\, dx$

(d) None of these.

94. If $\displaystyle\int_{0}^{\pi/3} \dfrac{\cos x}{3 + 4 \sin x}\, dx = k \log\left(\dfrac{3 + 2\sqrt{3}}{3}\right)$, then k is :

(a) $\dfrac{1}{2}$

(b) $\dfrac{1}{3}$

(c) $\dfrac{1}{4}$

(d) $\dfrac{1}{8}$

95. The value of $\displaystyle\int_{0}^{1} (1 + e^{-x^2})\, dx$ is :

(a) – 1

(b) 2

(c) $1 + e^{-1}$

(d) None of these.

96. $\displaystyle\int_{-\pi/2}^{\pi/2} \sin^{10} x\, (6x^9 - 25x^7 + 4x^3 - 2x)\, dx$ equals :

(a) π

(b) 0

(c) 25

(d) None of these.

97. If $f(x) = \begin{bmatrix} x, & x < 1 \\ x - 1, & x \geq 1 \end{bmatrix}$, then $\displaystyle\int_{0}^{2} x^2\, f(x)\, dx =$

(a) 1

(b) $\dfrac{4}{3}$

(c) $\dfrac{5}{3}$

(d) $\dfrac{5}{2}$

98. The value of the integral $\displaystyle\int_{-1}^{1} \sin^{11} x\, dx$ is :

(a) $\dfrac{10}{11} \cdot \dfrac{8}{9} \cdot \dfrac{6}{7} \cdot \dfrac{4}{5} \cdot \dfrac{2}{3}$

(b) $\dfrac{10}{11} \cdot \dfrac{8}{9} \cdot \dfrac{6}{7} \cdot \dfrac{4}{5} \cdot \dfrac{2}{3} \cdot \dfrac{\pi}{2}$

(c) 1

(d) 0.

99. $\displaystyle\int_{0}^{\pi/2} \dfrac{dx}{\sin\left(x - \dfrac{\pi}{3}\right) \cdot \sin\left(x - \dfrac{\pi}{6}\right)}$ equals :

(a) $4 \log \sqrt{3}$

(b) $-4 \log \sqrt{3}$

(c) $2 \log \sqrt{3}$

(d) None of these.

100. $\displaystyle\int_{-\pi}^{\pi} (\cos px - \sin qx)^2\, dx$, where p and q are

integers, is equal to :

(a) – π

(b) 0

(c) π

(d) 2π.

101. $\displaystyle\int_{0}^{1} |\sin 2\pi x|\, dx$ is equal to :

(a) 0

(b) – 1/π

(c) 1/π

(d) 2/π.

102. If $\displaystyle\int_{0}^{\pi} x\, f(\sin^3 x + \cos^2 x)\, dx =$

$k \displaystyle\int_{0}^{\pi/2} x\, f(\sin^3 x + \cos^2 x)\, dx$, then k =

(a) $\dfrac{\pi}{2}$

(b) π

(c) 2π

(d) None of these.

103. $\displaystyle\int_{1}^{4} \log [x]\, dx$ equals :

(a) log 6

(b) log 3

(c) log 2

(d) None of these.

104. If $f(x) = \begin{vmatrix} \sec^2 x & 1 & 1 \\ \cos^2 x & \cos^2 x & \csc^2 x \\ 1 & \cos^2 x & \cot^2 x \end{vmatrix}$,

then $\int\limits_0^{\pi/4} f(x)\, dx =$

(a) $\frac{1}{32}(3\pi - 8)$

(b) $\frac{1}{32}(3\pi + 8)$

(c) $\frac{-1}{32}(3\pi + 8)$

(d) None of these.

105. If

$f(x) = \begin{vmatrix} \sec x & \cos x & \sec^2 x + \csc x \cdot \cot x \\ \cos^2 x & \cos^2 x & \csc^2 x \\ 1 & \cos^2 x & \cos^2 x \end{vmatrix}$

then $\int\limits_0^{\pi/2} f(x)\, dx =$

(a) $-\left(\frac{\pi}{4} + \frac{8}{15}\right)$

(b) $\frac{\pi}{4} - \frac{8}{15}$

(c) $\frac{\pi}{4} + \frac{8}{15}$

(d) $\frac{8}{15} - \frac{\pi}{4}.$

106. $\lim\limits_{n \to \infty}\left[\frac{1}{n+1} + \frac{1}{n+2} \cdots + \frac{1}{n+n}\right]$ is equal to :

(a) $3 \log 2$

(b) $\log 2$

(c) $2 \log 2$

(d) None of these.

107. $\lim\limits_{n \to \infty}\left[\frac{1}{n} + \frac{n^2}{(n+1)^3} + \frac{n^2}{(n+2)^3} + \ldots + \frac{1}{8n}\right] =$

(a) $\frac{3}{8}$

(b) $\frac{1}{4}$

(c) $\frac{1}{8}$

(d) None of these.

108. The value of

$\lim\limits_{n \to \infty}\left[\frac{1}{\sqrt{n^2}} + \frac{1}{\sqrt{n^2 - 1}} + \frac{1}{\sqrt{n^2 - 2^2}} + \ldots + \frac{n^2}{\sqrt{n^2 - (n-1)^2}}\right]$ is

(a) $\frac{\pi}{4}$

(b) $\frac{\pi}{3}$

(c) $\frac{\pi}{2}$

(d) None of these.

109. The value of

$\lim\limits_{n \to \infty}\left[\frac{\sqrt{n}}{(3 + 4\sqrt{n})^2} + \frac{\sqrt{n}}{\sqrt{2}\,(3\sqrt{2} + 4\sqrt{n})^2}\right.$

$\left. + \frac{\sqrt{n}}{\sqrt{3}\,(3\sqrt{3} + 4\sqrt{n})^2} + \ldots + \frac{1}{49n}\right]$ is

(a) 1

(b) $\frac{1}{14}$

(c) $\frac{1}{7}$

(d) None of these.

110. $\lim\limits_{n \to \infty}\left[\frac{n+1}{n^2 + 1^2} + \frac{n+2}{n^2 + 2^2} + \frac{n+3}{n^2 + 3^2} + \ldots + \frac{1}{n}\right] =$

(a) $\frac{\pi}{4} + \frac{1}{2}\log 2$

(b) $\frac{\pi}{4} - \frac{1}{2}\log 2$

(c) $-\left(\frac{\pi}{4} + \frac{1}{2}\log 2\right)$

(d) None of these.

111. $\lim\limits_{x \to \infty}\left[\frac{1}{\sqrt{2n - 1^2}} + \frac{1}{\sqrt{4n - 2^2}} + \frac{1}{\sqrt{6n - 3^2}} + \ldots + \frac{1}{n}\right] =$

(a) $\frac{\pi}{4}$

(b) $\frac{\pi}{2}$

(c) $\frac{\pi}{6}$

(d) $\frac{\pi}{3}.$

112. $\lim\limits_{n \to \infty}\left[\frac{n}{n^2 + 1^2} + \frac{n}{n^2 + 2^2} + \frac{n}{n^2 + 3^2} + \ldots + \frac{1}{2n^2}\right] =$

(a) $\frac{\pi}{4}$

(b) $\frac{\pi}{2}$

(c) π

(d) None of these.

113. $\lim\limits_{n \to \infty} \sum\limits_{r=1}^{n} \frac{r}{n^2} \cdot \sec^2 \frac{r^2}{n^2}$ is equal to :

(a) $\tan 1$

(b) $\frac{1}{3}\tan 1$

(c) $\frac{1}{2}\tan 1$

(d) None of these.

114. $\lim\limits_{n \to \infty} \frac{1}{n} \sum\limits_{r=1}^{n} \sin^{2k}\frac{r\pi}{2n}$ is equal to :

(a) $\frac{2k!}{2^{2k}(k!)^2}$

(b) $\frac{2k!}{2^k (k!)}$

(c) $\frac{2k!}{2^k (k!)^2}$

(d) None of these.

115. $\lim\limits_{n\to\infty} \dfrac{(n!)^{1/n}}{n}$ is equal to :

(a) e (b) $\dfrac{1}{e}$

(c) e^{-1} (d) None of these.

116. $\lim\limits_{n\to\infty}\left[\left(1+\dfrac{1}{n}\right)\left(1+\dfrac{2}{n}\right)\cdots\left(1+\dfrac{n}{n}\right)\right]^{1/n} =$

(a) $\dfrac{2}{e}$ (b) $\dfrac{e}{2}$

(c) $\dfrac{e}{4}$ (d) $\dfrac{4}{e}$.

117. $\lim\limits_{n\to\infty}\left[\left(1+\dfrac{1^2}{n^2}\right)\left(1+\dfrac{2^2}{n^2}\right)\cdots\left(1+\dfrac{n^2}{n^2}\right)\right]^{1/n} =$

(a) $2e^{\frac{\pi+4}{2}}$ (b) $e^{\frac{\pi+4}{2}}$

(c) $2e^{\frac{\pi-4}{2}}$ (d) $e^{\frac{\pi-4}{2}}$

118. $\lim\limits_{n\to\infty} \dfrac{1}{n^{p+1}}[1^p + 2^p + \ldots + n^p)]$, $p > -1$, is equal to :

(a) $\dfrac{1}{p+1}$ (b) $\dfrac{1}{p}$

(c) $\dfrac{1}{p+2}$ (d) None of these.

119. If

$$S_n = \left[\dfrac{1}{2n} + \dfrac{1}{\sqrt{4n^2-1}} + \dfrac{1}{\sqrt{4n^2-4}} + \ldots + \dfrac{1}{\sqrt{3n^2+2n-1}}\right]$$

then $\lim\limits_{n\to\infty} S_n$ is equal to :

(a) $\dfrac{\pi}{4}$ (b) $\dfrac{\pi}{6}$

(c) $\dfrac{\pi}{3}$ (d) $\dfrac{\pi}{2}$

120. If f and g are continuous functions on $[0, \pi]$ satisfying $f(x) + f(\pi - x) = g(x) + g(\pi - x) = 1$, then

$\int\limits_{0}^{\pi} [f(x) + g(x)]\, dx$ is equal to :

(a) π (b) 2π

(c) $\dfrac{\pi}{2}$ (d) $\dfrac{3\pi}{2}$

121. If $f(x) = |2^x - 1| + |x - 1|$, then $\int\limits_{-2}^{2} f(x)\, dx$ is equal to :

(a) $5 - \dfrac{9}{4}\log 2$ (b) $5 + \dfrac{9}{4}\log 2$

(c) $-\left(5 + \dfrac{9}{4}\log 2\right)$ (d) None of these.

122. $\lim\limits_{n\to\infty}\left[\dfrac{1^2}{1^3+n^3} + \dfrac{2^2}{2^3+n^3} + \ldots + \dfrac{1}{2n}\right]$ is equal to :

(a) $\dfrac{1}{3}\log 2$ (b) $\dfrac{1}{2}\log 2$

(c) $\log 2$ (d) None of these.

123. $\lim\limits_{n\to\infty}\left[\tan\dfrac{\pi}{2n}\cdot\tan\dfrac{2\pi}{2n}\cdots\tan\dfrac{n\pi}{2n}\right]^{1/n}$ is equal to :

(a) 0 (b) 1

(c) –1 (d) None of these.

124. $\int\limits_{0}^{1}\tan^{-1}(1 - x + x^2)\, dx =$

(a) $3\log_e 2$ (b) $2\log_e 2$

(c) $\log_e 2$ (d) None of these.

125. The value of the integral $\int\limits_{1/2e}^{e/2}|\log 2x|\, dx$ is :

(a) $1 + e^{-1}$ (b) $1 - e^{-1}$

(c) $e^{-1} - 1$ (d) None of these.

126. The value of α which satisfies

$\int\limits_{0}^{\alpha}\cos x\, dx = \cos 2\alpha$, $\alpha \in [0, 2\pi]$ is :

(a) $\dfrac{\pi}{6}$ (b) $\dfrac{\pi}{3}$

(c) $\dfrac{\pi}{2}$ (d) None of these.

127. The value of the integral $\int\limits_{0}^{100} 2^{x-[x]}\, dx$, where [.] denotes the greatest integer function, is :

(a) $\log 2$ (b) $50\log 2$

(c) $100\log 2$ (d) None of these.

128. Let $I_1 = \int\limits_{\sec^2 z}^{2 - \tan^2 z} x\, f(x(3 - x))\, dx$ and

$I_2 = \int\limits_{\sec^2 z}^{2 - \tan^2 z} f(x(3 - x))\, dx$, where f is a

continuous function and z is any real number, then $I_1/I_2 =$

(a) 3/2   (b) 1/2

(c) 1   (d) None of these.

129. If $I = \int\limits_1^2 \dfrac{dx}{\sqrt{2x^3 - 9x^2 + 12x + 4}}$, then :

(a) $\dfrac{1}{2} < I < \dfrac{1}{3}$ (b) $\dfrac{1}{4} < I < \dfrac{1}{3}$

(c) $\dfrac{1}{4} < I < 1$ (d) None of these.

130. $\int\limits_0^{\pi/2} \cos x \log \cos x\, dx$ is equal to :

(a) $\log \dfrac{4}{e}$ (b) $\log \dfrac{2}{e}$

(c) $\log \dfrac{8}{e}$ (d) None of these.

131. $\int\limits_0^3 \{\sqrt{x}\}\, dx$, where $\{x\}$ denotes the fractional part of x, is equal to :

(a) $\dfrac{5}{2}$ (b) $\dfrac{7}{2}$

(c) $\dfrac{3}{2}$ (d) None of these.

132. The value of the integral

$\int\limits_3^4 \dfrac{[x^2]}{[x^2 - 14x + 49] + [x^2]}\, dx$, where [.] denotes

the greatest integer function, is :

(a) 1   (b) $\dfrac{3}{2}$

(c) $\dfrac{1}{2}$ (d) None of these.

133. If f(x) is function satisfying $f\left(\dfrac{1}{2}\right) + x^2 f(x) = 0$

for all x $(x \neq 0)$, then the value of the

integral $\int\limits_{\tan \theta}^{\cot \theta} f(x)\, dx$ is :

(a) $\tan^2 \theta$ (b) $2 \tan \theta$

(c) 0   (d) None of these.

134. $\int\limits_0^2 \sqrt{\dfrac{2 + x}{2 - x}}\, dx$ is equal to :

(a) $\dfrac{\pi}{2} + 1$ (b) $\pi + \dfrac{3}{2}$

(c) $\pi + 1$ (d) None of these.

135. If $\int\limits_2^e \left[\dfrac{1}{\log x} - \dfrac{1}{(\log x)^2}\right] dx = a + \dfrac{b}{\log 2}$, then :

(a) a = e, b = – 2   (b) a = e, b = 2

(c) a = – e, b = 2   (d) None of these.

136. $\lim\limits_{n \to \infty} \dfrac{1}{n}\left[f\left(\dfrac{1}{n}\right) + f\left(\dfrac{2}{n}\right) + \dots + f\left(\dfrac{n}{n}\right)\right]$ is equal to :

(a) $\int\limits_0^1 f\left(\dfrac{1}{x}\right) dx$ (b) $\int\limits_0^1 x\, f(x)\, dx$

(c) $\int\limits_0^1 \dfrac{1}{x} f\left(\dfrac{1}{x}\right) dx$ (d) $\int\limits_0^1 f(x)\, dx.$

137. If $f(x) = \int\limits_1^x \dfrac{\sin t}{t}\, dt$, then $\lim\limits_{x \to \infty} f'(x) =$

(a) 1   (b) 0

(c) – 1   (d) ∞

138. $\int\limits_0^\infty e^{-ax} \sin bx\, dx$ is equal to :

(a) $\dfrac{b}{a^2 + b^2}$ (b) $\dfrac{a}{a^2 + b^2}$

(c) 1   (d) 0.

139. $\lim\limits_{n \to \infty} \dfrac{1}{n}(e^{1/n} + e^{2/n} + e^{3/n} + \dots + e^{n/n})$ is equal to :

(a) e   (b) e – 1

(c) 1 – e   (d) None of these.

140. $\int_0^{\pi/2} \sin\theta \cos\theta \sqrt{a^2 \sin^2\theta + b^2 \cos^2\theta}\, d\theta =$

(a) $\dfrac{a^2 + ab + b^2}{2(a + b)}$

(b) $\dfrac{a^2 + ab + b^2}{(a + b)}$

(c) $\dfrac{a^2 + ab + b^2}{3(a + b)}$

(d) None of these.

141. $\int_0^{\pi/2} \dfrac{dx}{\sqrt{\tan x} - \sqrt{\cot x}}$ is equal to :

(a) $\dfrac{\pi}{2}$

(b) $\dfrac{\pi}{4}$

(c) 0

(d) None of these.

142. If $\int_{-3}^{2} f(x)\, dx = 2$ and $\int_{2}^{5} [5 + f(x)]\, dx = 9$, then

the value of the integral $\int_{5}^{-3} f(x)\, dx$ is :

(a) 2

(b) 3

(c) 4

(d) 5.

143. The value of the integral

$\int_{2a}^{3a} \sec(x - 2a) \cdot \sec(x - 3a)\, dx$ is

(a) 2 cosec a log sec a

(b) 2 sec a log cosec a

(c) 2 cosec a log cos a

(d) None of these.

144. If $\int_0^{y} e^{-t^2}\, dt + \int_0^{k\pi} \sin^2 t\, dt = 0$, then $\dfrac{dy}{dx} =$

(a) $2x \sin^2 x^2 e^{y^2}$

(b) $-2x \sin^2 x^2 e^{y^2}$

(c) $x \sin^2 x^2 e^{y^2}$

(d) $-x \sin^2 x^2 e^{y^2}$.

145. The integral $\int_0^{kx} \cos^{2n} x\, dx$ is equal to :

(a) $k \int_0^{\pi/2} \cos^{2n} x\, dx$

(b) $2k \int_0^{\pi} \cos^{2n} x\, dx$

(c) $2k \int_0^{\pi/2} \cos^{2n} x\, dx$

(d) None of these.

146. $\lim_{n\to\infty} \left[\dfrac{1^k + 2^k + 3^k + \ldots + n^k}{n^{k+1}} \right]$ is equal to :

(a) $\dfrac{1}{k}$

(b) $\dfrac{1}{k + 1}$

(c) $\dfrac{1}{k + 2}$

(d) None of these.

147. The value of the integral $\int_0^{\pi} \cos^n x\, dx$ is :

(n is even integer)

(a) $\dfrac{\pi(2n)!}{2^{2n} \cdot (n!)^2}$

(b) $\dfrac{\pi \cdot n!}{2^n \cdot \left[\left(\dfrac{n}{2} \right)! \right]^2}$

(c) $\dfrac{\pi \cdot n!}{2^{n+1} \cdot \left[\left(\dfrac{n}{2} \right)! \right]^2}$

(d) None of these.

148. $\int_0^{1} \dfrac{\log(1 - x)}{x}\, dx$ is equal to :

(a) $\dfrac{\pi^2}{8}$

(b) $\dfrac{-\pi^2}{8}$

(c) $\dfrac{\pi^2}{6}$

(d) $\dfrac{-\pi^2}{6}$

149. $\int_0^{1} \dfrac{\log x}{1 + x}\, dx$ is equal to :

(a) $\dfrac{\pi^2}{12}$

(b) $\dfrac{-\pi^2}{12}$

(c) $\dfrac{\pi^2}{6}$

(d) $\dfrac{-\pi^2}{6}$

150. $\int_0^{\pi/2} \tan x \log \sin x\, dx$ is equal to :

(a) $\dfrac{\pi^2}{24}$

(b) $\dfrac{-\pi^2}{24}$

(c) $\dfrac{\pi^2}{12}$

(d) $\dfrac{-\pi^2}{12}$.

151. $\int_0^{\infty} x^n\, e^{-x}\, dx$ (n is a +ve integer) is equal to :

(a) n !

(b) (n – 1)!

(c) (n – 2)!

(d) None of these.

152. $\int\limits_{0}^{\pi/2} \cos^n x \cos nx \, dx$, is equal to :

(a) $\dfrac{\pi}{2^n}$

(b) $\dfrac{\pi}{2^{n+1}}$

(c) $\dfrac{\pi}{2^{n-1}}$

(d) None of these.

153. The area of the smaller part of the circle $x^2 + y^2 = a^2$, cut off by the line $x = \dfrac{a}{\sqrt{2}}$, is given by :

(a) $\dfrac{a^2}{2}\left(\dfrac{\pi}{2} + 1\right)$

(b) $\dfrac{a^2}{2}\left(\dfrac{\pi}{2} - 1\right)$

(c) $a^2\left(\dfrac{\pi}{2} - 1\right)$

(d) None of these.

154. The area bounded by the curve $y = 2\cos x$ and the x-axis from $x = 0$ to $x = 2\pi$ is :

(a) 2

(b) 4

(c) 8

(d) None of these.

155. The area bounded by the semi-circle $y = \sqrt{4 - x^2}$ and its diameter $y = 0$ is :

(a) 2π

(b) π

(c) $\dfrac{\pi}{2}$

(d) None of these.

156. The area bounded by the curve $y = (x - 1)(x - 2)(x - 3)$ lying between the ordinates $x = 0$ and $x = 3$ is :

(a) 11/4

(b) 9/4

(c) 7/4

(d) None of these.

157. The area bounded by $y = \log_e x$, X-axis and the ordinate $x = e$ is given by :

(a) 4

(b) $\dfrac{1}{2}$

(c) 1

(d) None of these.

158. The area bounded by the curve $|x| + y = 1$ and X-axis is given by :

(a) 2

(b) 1

(c) 4

(d) None of these.

159. The area bounded by $y = \cos x$, $y = 0$, $|x| = 1$ is given by :

(a) $\sin 1$

(b) $2 \sin 1$

(c) $4 \sin 1$

(d) None of these.

160. If the ordinate $x = a$ divides the area bounded by X-axis, part of the curve $y = 1 + \dfrac{8}{x^2}$ and the ordinates $x = 2$, $x = 4$, into two equal parts, then a is equal to :

(a) $\sqrt{2}$

(b) $2\sqrt{2}$

(c) $3\sqrt{2}$

(d) None of these.

161. The area of the region bounded by the curves $y = \sqrt{5 - x^2}$ and $y = |x - 1|$ is given by :

(a) $\dfrac{5\pi}{4} - \dfrac{1}{2}$

(b) $\dfrac{3\pi}{4} + \dfrac{1}{2}$

(c) $\dfrac{5\pi}{4} + \dfrac{1}{2}$

(d) $\dfrac{3\pi}{4} - \dfrac{1}{2}$

162. The area bounded by $y = |x - 1|$, $y = 0$ and $|x| = 2$ is :

(a) 4

(b) 5

(c) 3

(d) None of these.

163. The area bounded by $y = |\sin x|$, x-axis and the lines $|x| = \pi$ is :

(a) 2

(b) 1

(c) 4

(d) None of these.

164. The smaller area enclosed by circle $x^2 + y^2 = a^2$ and the line $x + y = a$ is :

(a) $\dfrac{a^2}{4}(\pi - 2)$

(b) $\dfrac{a^2}{4}(\pi + 2)$

(c) $\dfrac{a^2}{4}(2 - \pi)$

(d) None of these.

165. If the area bounded by the curve $y = f(x)$, X-axis and the ordinates $x = 1$ and $x = b$ is $(b - 1)\sin(3b + 4)$, then :

(a) $f(x) = \cos(3x + 4) + 3(x - 1)\sin(3x + 4)$

(b) $f(x) = \sin(3x + 4) + 3(x - 1)\cos(3x + 4)$

(c) $f(x) = \sin(3x + 4) - 3(x - 1)\cos(3x + 4)$

(d) None of these.

166. The area bounded by $y = \cos x$, $y = 1 + x$ and x-axis is:

(a) 1

(b) $\dfrac{1}{2}$

(c) $\dfrac{3}{2}$

(d) None of these.

167. The area bounded by the lines $|x| + |y| = 1$ is

(a) 1   (b) 2

(c) 4   (d) None of these.

168. The area of the portion of circle $x^2 + y^2 = 64$ which is exterior to the parabola $y^2 = 12x$ is :

(a) $\frac{16}{3}(8\pi + \sqrt{3})$ (b) $\frac{8}{3}(8\pi + \sqrt{3})$

(c) $\frac{16}{3}(8\pi - \sqrt{3})$ (d) None of these.

169. The area of one of the curvilinear triangles formed by the curves $y = \sin x$, $y = \cos x$ and X-axis is :

(a) $2 + \sqrt{2}$ (b) $2 - \sqrt{2}$

(c) $2 + 2\sqrt{2}$ (d) None of these

170. The total area enclosed by the lines $y = |x|$, $y = 0$ and $|x| = 1$ is :

(a) 2   (b) 4

(c) 1   (d) None of these.

171. The area bounded by $y = \tan x$, $y = \cot x$, and X-axis in $0 \le x \le \frac{\pi}{2}$ is

(a) 3 log 2   (b) log 2

(c) 2 log 2   (d) None of these.

172. The area bounded by $y = e^x$, $y = e^{-x}$ and $x = 1$ is :

(a) $e + \frac{1}{e} + 2$ (b) $e + \frac{1}{e} - 2$

(c) $e - \frac{1}{e} + 2$ (d) None of these.

173. The area of the region bounded by the curve $y = \sqrt{5 - x^2}$ and $y = |x - 1|$ is :

(a) $\frac{5\pi}{4} + \frac{1}{2}$ (b) $\frac{3\pi}{4} + \frac{1}{2}$

(c) $\frac{5\pi}{4} - \frac{1}{2}$ (d) $\frac{3\pi}{4} - \frac{1}{2}$.

174. The area bounded by the curves $x^2 + y^2 = 25$, $4y = |4 - x^2|$ and $x = 0$, above x-axis is :

(a) $2 + \frac{25}{2}\sin^{-1}\frac{4}{5}$ (b) $2 + \frac{25}{4}\sin^{-1}\frac{4}{5}$

(c) $2 + \frac{25}{2}\sin^{-1}\frac{1}{5}$ (d) None of these.

175. The area bounded by $y = x^3 - 4x$ and X-axis is

(a) 4   (b) 8

(c) 16   (d) None of these.

176. The area bounded by the curve $y = x(3 - x)^2$, the x-axis and the ordinates of the maximum and minimum points of the curve is given by :

(a) 1   (b) 2

(c) 4   (d) None of these.

177. The area bounded by curve $y = \sin x + \cos x$ and the coordinate axes in the first quadrant is

(a) 1   (b) 2

(c) 3   (d) None of these.

178. The area of the region in xy – plane enclosed by curve $a^2y^2 = x^2(a^2 - x^2)$ is :

(a) $\frac{4}{3}a$ (b) $\frac{4}{3}a^2$

(c) $\frac{2}{3}a$ (d) $\frac{2}{3}a^2$.

179. The area bounded by the normal at $(1, 2)$ to the parabola $y^2 = 4x$ $(y \ge 0)$, the curve itself and the axis of the parabola is :

(a) $\frac{2}{3}$ (b) $\frac{4}{3}$

(c) $\frac{8}{3}$ (d) $\frac{10}{3}$.

180. The area of the region bounded by the curve $y = \tan x$, the tangent to it at $x = \frac{\pi}{4}$ and x-axis is :

(a) $\frac{1}{2}\log 2 + \frac{1}{4}$ (b) $\frac{1}{2}\log\frac{1}{2} + \frac{1}{4}$

(c) $\frac{1}{2}\log 2 - \frac{1}{4}$ (d) None of these.

181. The area bounded by the curve $xy^2 = 1$ and the lines $x = 1$, $x = 2$ is :

(a) $4(\sqrt{2} - 1)$ (b) $4(\sqrt{2} + 1)$

(c) $2(\sqrt{2} - 1)$ (d) $2(\sqrt{2} + 1)$.

182. The area bounded by the curve $y = 2x - x$, x-axis and the two ordinates corresponding to the minima of the function, is :

(a) $\frac{3}{120}$ (b) $\frac{5}{120}$

(c) $\frac{1}{20}$ (d) $\frac{7}{120}$.

183. The area contained between the curve $y = \dfrac{a^2}{x^2 + a^2}$ and x-axis is :

(a) πa^2
(b) $2\pi a^2$
(c) $3\pi a^2$
(d) None of these.

184. The area bounded by parabola $y = 6 + 4x - x^2$ and the chord joining the points $(-2, -6)$ and $(4, 6)$ is :

(a) 9
(b) 18
(c) 36
(d) 54.

185. The area bounded by $y = [x]$, X-axis and the two ordinates $x = 1$ and $x = 1.7$ is :

(a) $\dfrac{17}{10}$
(b) 1
(c) $\dfrac{17}{5}$
(d) $\dfrac{7}{10}$.

186. For any real t, $x = \dfrac{e^t + e^{-t}}{2}$ and $y = \dfrac{e^t - e^{-t}}{2}$ is a point on the hyperbola $x^2 - y^2 = 1$. The area bounded by the hyperbola and the lines joining its centre to the points corresponding to t_1 and $-t_2$ is :

(a) $\dfrac{1}{2} t_1$
(b) t_1
(c) $2t_1$
(d) None of these.

187. Area of the region bounded by $x = \dfrac{1}{2}$, $x = 2$, $y = \log_e x$ and $y = 2^x$ is :

(a) $\dfrac{4 - \sqrt{2}}{\log 2} + \dfrac{5}{2} \log 2 + \dfrac{3}{2}$

(b) $\dfrac{4 - \sqrt{2}}{\log 2} - \dfrac{5}{2} \log 2 - \dfrac{3}{2}$

(c) $\dfrac{4 - \sqrt{2}}{\log 2} - \dfrac{5}{2} \log 2 + \dfrac{3}{2}$

(d) None of these.

188. The area of the region bounded by the curves $y = \log_e x$, $y = \sin^4 \pi x$ and $x = 0$ is :

(a) $\dfrac{3}{8}$
(b) 1
(c) $\dfrac{5}{8}$
(d) $\dfrac{11}{8}$.

189. The area included between the parabola $y = \dfrac{x^2}{4a}$ $(a > 0)$ and the witch of Agnessi $y = \dfrac{8a^3}{x^2 + 4a^2}$ is :

(a) $a^2 \left(2\pi - \dfrac{4}{3} \right)$
(b) $a^2 \left(2\pi + \dfrac{4}{3} \right)$
(c) $a^2 \left(\pi + \dfrac{4}{3} \right)$
(d) None of these.

190. If $I_1 = \int\limits_0^{\pi/2} \cos (\sin x)\, dx$; $I_2 = \int\limits_0^{\pi/2} \sin (\cos x)\, dx$ and $I_3 = \int\limits_0^{\pi/2} \cos x\, dx$, then :

(a) $I_1 > I_3 > I_2$
(b) $I_3 > I_1 > I_2$
(c) $I_1 > I_2 > I_3$
(d) $I_3 > I_2 > I_1$.

191. The area bounded by the curves $x^2 + y^2 = 4$; $x^2 = -\sqrt{2}y$ and $x = y$ is :

(a) $2\pi + \dfrac{1}{3}$
(b) $\pi - \dfrac{1}{3}$
(c) $-\pi + \dfrac{1}{3}$
(d) None of these.

192. The area of the region bounded by the curves $y = ex \log_e x$ and $y = \dfrac{\log_e x}{ex}$ is :

(a) $\dfrac{e^2 - 5}{2e}$
(b) $\dfrac{e^2 + 5}{2e}$
(c) $\dfrac{e^2 + 5}{4e}$
(d) $\dfrac{e^2 - 5}{4e}$.

193. The ratio of the areas into which the circle $x^2 + y^2 = 64$ is divided by the parabola $y^2 = 12x$, is :

(a) $\dfrac{4\pi - \sqrt{3}}{8\pi + \sqrt{3}}$
(b) $\dfrac{4\pi + \sqrt{3}}{8\pi - \sqrt{3}}$
(c) $\dfrac{4\pi - \sqrt{3}}{8\pi - \sqrt{3}}$
(d) None of these.

194. The area enclosed between the curves $y = \log_e (x + e)$, $x = \log_e \dfrac{1}{y}$ and the x-axis is :

(a) 2
(b) 1
(c) 4
(d) None of these.

195. The area of the region bounded by the parabola $x = -2y^2$ and $x = 1 - 3y^2$ is :

(a) $\frac{4}{3}$

(b) $\frac{2}{3}$

(c) $\frac{1}{3}$

(d) None of these.

196. The area common to the curves

$y = \sqrt{9 - x^2}$, $x^2 + y^2 = 6x$ in $y \geq 0$ is :

(a) $3\pi + \frac{9\sqrt{3}}{4}$

(b) $3\pi - \frac{9\sqrt{3}}{4}$

(c) $3\pi - \frac{9\sqrt{3}}{2}$

(d) $3\pi + \frac{9\sqrt{3}}{2}$.

197. The area of the region bounded by

$x^2 + y^2 - 2x \leq 0$, $x + y \leq 1$; $y \geq 0$ is :

(a) $\frac{\pi}{8} - \frac{1}{2}$

(b) $\frac{\pi}{8} + \frac{1}{2}$

(c) $\frac{\pi}{4} - \frac{1}{2}$

(d) $\frac{\pi}{4} + \frac{1}{2}$.

198. The curve $y = a\sqrt{x} + bx$ passes through the point $(1, 2)$ and the area enclosed by the curve, the X-axis and the line $x = 4$ is 8 square units. The values of a and b are :

(a) $a = 3, b = 1$

(b) $a = 3, b = -1$

(c) $a = -3, b = 1$

(d) $a = -3, b = -1$.

199. The area of the portion of circle $x^2 + y^2 = 1$, which lies inside the parabola $y^2 = 1 - x$, is :

(a) $\frac{\pi}{2} - \frac{2}{3}$

(b) $\frac{\pi}{2} + \frac{2}{3}$

(c) $\frac{\pi}{2} + \frac{4}{3}$

(d) $\frac{\pi}{2} - \frac{4}{3}$.

200. The area bounded by the parabolas

$y^2 = 4a(x + a)$ and $y^2 = -4a(x - a)$ is :

(a) $\frac{16}{3}a^2$

(b) $\frac{8}{3}a^2$

(c) $\frac{4}{3}a^2$

(d) None of these.

201. The ratio in which the X-axis divides the area of the region bounded by the parabolas $y = 4x - x^2$ and $y = x^2 - x$ is :

(a) $2 : 129$

(b) $8 : 129$

(c) $4 : 129$

(d) None of these.

202. The area lying in the first quadrant inside the circle $x^2 + y^2 = 12$ and bounded by the parabolas $y^2 = 4x$, $x^2 = 4y$ is :

(a) $2\left(\frac{\sqrt{2}}{3} + \frac{3}{2}\sin^{-1}\frac{1}{3}\right)$

(b) $4\left(\frac{\sqrt{2}}{3} + \frac{3}{2}\sin^{-1}\frac{1}{3}\right)$

(c) $\left(\frac{\sqrt{2}}{3} + \frac{3}{2}\sin^{-1}\frac{1}{3}\right)$

(d) None of these.

203. The line $y = mx$ bisects the area enclosed by the lines $x = 0$, $y = 0$, $x = \frac{3}{2}$ and the curve $y = 1 + 4x - x^2$. The value of m is :

(a) $\frac{13}{6}$

(b) $\frac{13}{8}$

(c) $\frac{8}{13}$

(d) $\frac{6}{13}$.

204. The area of the region formed by $x^2 + y^2 - 6x - 4y + 12 \leq 0$, $y \leq x$ and $x \leq 5/2$ is

(a) $\frac{\pi}{6} - \frac{\sqrt{3} + 1}{8}$

(b) $\frac{\pi}{6} + \frac{\sqrt{3} - 1}{8}$

(c) $\frac{\pi}{6} - \frac{\sqrt{3} - 1}{8}$

(d) None of these.

205. Let $f(x) = $ maximum $[x^2, (1 - x)^2, 2x(1 - x)]$, where $0 \leq x \leq 1$. The area of the region bounded by the curves $y = f(x)$, X-axis, $x = 0$ and $x = 1$ is :

(a) $\frac{17}{27}$

(b) $\frac{14}{27}$

(c) $\frac{19}{27}$

(d) None of these.

206. The area of the region enclosed by the curves $y = x \log x$ and $y = 2x - 2x^2$ is :

(a) $\frac{7}{12}$

(b) $\frac{1}{2}$

(c) $\frac{5}{12}$

(d) None of these.

207. The area of the region bounded by $y = |x - 1|$ and $y = 1$ is :

(a) 1

(b) 2

(c) $\frac{1}{2}$

(d) None of these.

208. The area bounded by the curve $y = 2x - x^2$ and the straight line $y = -x$ is given by :

(a) $\frac{9}{2}$

(b) $\frac{43}{6}$

(c) $\frac{35}{6}$

(d) None of these.

209. The slope of the tangent to a curve $y = f(x)$ at $(x, f(x))$ is $2x + 1$. If the curve passes through the point $(1, 2)$, then the area of the region bounded by the curve, the X-axis and the line x = 1 is :

(a) $\frac{5}{6}$

(b) $\frac{6}{5}$

(c) $\frac{1}{6}$

(d) 6.

210. $\int\limits_{-1/2}^{1/2} \left| x \cos \frac{\pi x}{2} \right| dx$ is :

(a) 0

(b) 1

(c) $\frac{\pi\sqrt{2} + 4\sqrt{2} - 8}{\pi^2}$

(d) None of these.

211. The area bounded by the curves $y^2 = 8x$ and $x^2 = 8y$ is :

(a) $\frac{32}{7}$

(b) $\frac{24}{7}$

(c) $\frac{72}{7}$

(d) $\frac{64}{3}$.

212. The points of extremum of the function :

$$F(x) = \int\limits_{1}^{x} e^{-t^2/2} (1 - t^2) \, dt \text{ are :}$$

(a) $x = 1, -1$

(b) $x = -2$

(c) $x = 0$

(d) $x = \frac{1}{2}$

213. The area of the region bounded by the curve $y = x - x^2$, X-axis, x = 0 and x = 1 is :

(a) $\frac{5}{6}$

(b) $\frac{1}{2}$

(c) $\frac{1}{3}$

(d) $\frac{1}{6}$.

214. The area between the curve $y = 1 - |x|$ and X-axis is :

(a) $\frac{1}{3}$

(b) 2

(c) $\frac{1}{2}$

(d) 1.

215. If $\int\limits_{0}^{1} f(x) \, dx = 1$, $\int\limits_{0}^{1} x \, f(x) \, dx = a$,

$$\int\limits_{0}^{1} x^2 \, f(x) \, dx = a^2, \text{ then}$$

$$\int\limits_{0}^{1} (a - x)^2 \, f(x) \, dx \text{ equals :}$$

(a) $4a^2$

(b) 0

(c) $2a^2$

(d) None of the above.

216. Suppose that $f''(x)$ is continuous for all x and $f(0) = f'(1) = 1$. If $\int\limits_{0}^{1} t \, f''(t) \, dt = 0$, then the value of $f(1)$ is :

(a) 3

(b) 2

(c) $4\frac{1}{2}$

(d) None of these.

217. $\int\limits_{-\pi}^{\pi} (1 - x^2) \sin x \cos^2 x \, dx$ is equal to :

(a) $\frac{\pi}{2} - 2\pi^3$

(b) $2\pi - \pi^3$

(c) $\pi - \frac{\pi^3}{3}$

(d) 0.

218. If $\int\limits_{1}^{b} (b - 4x) \, dx \geq 6 - 5b$, b > 1, then b equals

(a) 3

(b) 4

(c) 2

(d) 1.

219. If $I_1 = \int\limits_{0}^{3\pi} f(\cos^2 x) \, dx$ and $I_2 = \int\limits_{0}^{\pi} f(\cos^2 x) \, dx$, then :

(a) $I_1 = 5I_2$

(b) $I_1 = I_2$

(c) $I_1 = 3I_2$

(d) None of these.

220. The area of the curve $x^2 + y^2 = 2ax$ is :

(a) $\frac{\pi a^2}{2}$

(b) $4\pi a^2$

(c) $2\pi a^2$

(d) πa^2.

221. $\lim\limits_{n \to \infty} \left[\frac{n}{1^2 + n^2} + \frac{n}{2^2 + n^2} + \frac{n}{3^2 + n^2} + \ldots + \frac{n}{n^2 + n^2} \right]$ is equal to :

(a) log 2

(b) 0

(c) 1

(d) $\frac{\pi}{4}$.

222. $\lim_{n\to\infty} \dfrac{\sqrt{1}+2\sqrt{2}+3\sqrt{3}+\ldots+m\sqrt{n}}{n^{5/2}}$, is equal to :

(a) $\displaystyle\int_0^1 x\sqrt{x}\,dx$

(b) $\dfrac{5}{2}$

(c) 0

(d) 1.

223. The function $F(x) = \displaystyle\int_0^x \log\left(\dfrac{1-x}{1+x}\right)dx$ is :

(a) an odd function

(b) a periodic function

(c) an even function

(d) None of these.

224. $\displaystyle\int_0^{\log 5} \dfrac{e^x\sqrt{e^x-1}}{e^x+3}\,dx =$

(a) $4+\pi$

(b) $2+\pi$

(c) $4-\pi$

(d) $3+2\pi$.

225. If $u_{10} = \displaystyle\int_0^{\pi/2} x^{10}\sin x\,dx$, then the value of

$u_{10}+90u_8$ is :

(a) $9\left(\dfrac{\pi}{2}\right)^9$

(b) $10\left(\dfrac{\pi}{2}\right)^9$

(c) $\left(\dfrac{\pi}{2}\right)^9$

(d) $9\left(\dfrac{\pi}{2}\right)^8$.

226. Let $f(x) = x - (x)$, for every real number x, where (x) is the integral part of x.

Then $\displaystyle\int_{-1}^1 f(x)\,dx$ is :

(a) 1

(b) 2

(c) 0

(d) $\dfrac{1}{2}$.

227. The value of $\displaystyle\int_0^{\pi/2} \dfrac{\left(\dfrac{\pi}{4}-x\right)}{\sqrt{\sin x+\cos x}}\,dx$ is :

(a) $\dfrac{\pi\sqrt{2}}{4}$

(b) $\dfrac{\pi}{4\sqrt{2}}$

(c) 0

(d) None of these.

228. If $I = \displaystyle\int_0^1 \cos\left(2\cot^{-1}\sqrt{\dfrac{1-x}{1+x}}\right)dx$, then :

(a) $I = -\dfrac{1}{2}$

(b) $0 < I < \dfrac{1}{2}$

(c) $I > \dfrac{1}{2}$

(d) None of these.

229. $\displaystyle\int_0^{\pi/4} \left(\sqrt{\tan x}+\sqrt{\cot x}\right)dx$ is equal to :

(a) $\dfrac{\sqrt{2}\pi}{2}$

(b) $\dfrac{\pi}{2}$

(c) $\dfrac{\sqrt{3}\pi}{2}$

(d) None of these.

230. The area enclosed by the curves $3x^2 + 5y = 32$ and $y = |x-2|$ is :

(a) $\dfrac{17}{2}$

(b) $\dfrac{33}{2}$

(c) $\dfrac{23}{2}$

(d) None of these.

231. $\displaystyle\int_0^{\pi/2} \sin^2 x\cos^2 x\,dx$ is equal to :

(a) $\dfrac{\pi}{16}$

(b) $\dfrac{\pi}{24}$

(c) $\dfrac{\pi}{8}$

(d) None of these.

232. $\displaystyle\int_0^{1/\sqrt{2}} \dfrac{\sin^{-1}x}{(1-x^2)\sqrt{1-x^2}}\,dx$ is equal to :

(a) $\dfrac{\pi}{4}-\dfrac{1}{2}\log 2$

(b) $\dfrac{\pi}{4}+\dfrac{1}{2}\log 2$

(c) $\dfrac{\pi}{4}+\log 2$

(d) $\dfrac{\pi}{4}-\log 2$.

233. $\displaystyle\int_{1/e}^{\tan x} \dfrac{t}{1+t^2}\,dt + \int_{1/e}^{\cot x} \dfrac{dt}{t(1+t^2)}$ is equal to :

(a) 1

(b) -1

(c) 0

(d) None of these.

234. $\displaystyle\int_{-2}^2 |1-x^2|\,dx =$

(a) 4

(b) 2

(c) -2

(d) 0.

235. $\displaystyle\int_0^3 \dfrac{dx}{(x+2)\sqrt{x+1}}$ is equal to :

(a) $\tan^{-1}\dfrac{1}{3}$

(b) $2\tan^{-1}\dfrac{1}{3}$

(c) $3\tan^{-1}\dfrac{1}{3}$

(d) None of these.

236. Let $g(x) = \int_0^x f(t) \ dt$ where $\frac{1}{2} \le f(t) \le 1$,

$t \in [0, 1]$ and $0 \le f(t) \le \frac{1}{2}$ for $t \in (1, 2]$. Then :

(a) $\frac{-3}{2} \le g(2) < \frac{1}{2}$ (b) $0 \le g(2) < 2$

(c) $\frac{3}{2} < g(2) \le \frac{5}{2}$ (d) $2 < g(2) < 4$.

237. The ratio in which the area bounded by the curves $y^2 = 12x$ and $x^2 = 12y$ is divided by the line $x = 3$, is :

(a) $15 : 49$ (b) $13 : 48$

(c) $12 : 37$ (d) None of these.

238. $\int_0^1 \frac{2 - x^2}{(1 + x)\sqrt{1 - x^2}} \ dx$ is equal to :

(a) $\frac{\pi}{4}$ (b) $\frac{\pi}{3}$

(c) $\frac{\pi}{2}$ (d) None of these.

239. $\int_0^1 \frac{1}{(5 + 2x - 2x^2)(1 + e^{(2-4x)})} \ dx$ is equal to :

(a) $\frac{1}{2\sqrt{11}} \log \frac{(\sqrt{11} + 1)^2}{10}$

(b) $\frac{1}{\sqrt{11}} \log \frac{(\sqrt{11} + 1)^2}{10}$

(c) $\frac{1}{2\sqrt{11}} \log \frac{(\sqrt{11} - 1)^2}{10}$

(d) None of these.

240. $\int_0^{\pi/6} \frac{\sqrt{3 \cos 2x - 1}}{\cos x} \ dx$ is equal to :

(a) $2 \tan^{-1} \sqrt{2} + \frac{\pi\sqrt{6}}{3}$ (b) $-2 \tan^{-1} \sqrt{2} + \frac{\pi\sqrt{6}}{3}$

(c) $\tan^{-1} \sqrt{2} + \frac{\pi\sqrt{6}}{3}$ (d) None of these.

241. The area of region lying inside $x^2 + (y - 1)^2 = 1$ and outside $c^2x^2 + y^2 = c^2$ where $c = (\sqrt{2} - 1)$ is :

(a) $(4 - \sqrt{2})\frac{\pi}{4} + \frac{1}{\sqrt{2}}$ (b) $(4 - \sqrt{2})\frac{\pi}{4} - \frac{1}{\sqrt{2}}$

(c) $(4 + \sqrt{2})\frac{\pi}{4} + \frac{1}{\sqrt{2}}$ (d) None of these.

242. If $\int_0^1 \frac{\sin t}{1 + t} \ dt = \alpha$, then the value of the integral

$\int_{4\pi-2}^{4\pi} \frac{\sin t/2}{4\pi + 2 - t} \ dt$ in terms of α is given by :

(a) 2α (b) -2α

(c) α (d) $-\alpha$.

243. The value of $\int_{-\pi/2}^{\pi/2} \left(\left[\frac{x}{\pi}\right] + 0.5\right) dx$ is :

(where [.] denotes the greatest integer function)

(a) π (b) $\pi/2$

(c) 0 (d) $-\pi/2$.

244. $\int_0^{\pi/3} [\sqrt{3} \tan x] \ dx =$

(a) $\frac{5\pi}{6}$ (b) $\frac{5\pi}{6} - \tan^{-1}\left(\frac{2}{\sqrt{3}}\right)$

(c) $\frac{\pi}{2} - \tan^{-1}\left(\frac{2}{\sqrt{3}}\right)$ (d) None of these.

245. $\lim_{n \to \infty} \left[\frac{1}{1 + n^3} + \frac{4}{8 + n^3} + \dots + \frac{r^2}{r^3 + n^3} + \dots + \frac{1}{2n} \right] =$

(a) $\log 2$ (b) $\frac{1}{2} \log 2$

(c) $\frac{1}{3} \log 2$ (d) None of these.

246. The value of $\lim_{n \to \infty} \left\{ \frac{1^k + 2^k + \dots + n^k}{n^{k+1}} \right\}$ is :

(a) $\frac{1}{k + 1}$ (b) $k + 1$

(c) $\frac{1}{k + 2}$ (d) $k + 2$.

247. If $\int_0^1 (3 - 2x) \ dx < a - 3$, then :

(a) $-1 < a < 3$ (b) $a < -1$ or $a > 3$

(c) $a < -1$ (d) $a > 3$.

248. The value of $\int_0^{1000} e^{x - [x]} \ dx =$

(a) 1000 (b) $1000 \ e$

(c) $1000 \ (e - 1)$ (d) None of these.

249. The value of the integral $\int\limits_{0}^{2\pi} [2 \sin x] \, dx$ is :

(a) $-\pi$ (b) -2π

(c) -3π (d) -4π.

250. For any $x \in r$ let f be a continuous function,

Let $I_1 = \int\limits_{\sin^2 t}^{1+\cos^2 t} x \, f \{x \, (2-x)\} \, dx$

and $I_2 = \int\limits_{\sin^2 t}^{1+\cos^2 t} f \{x \, (2-x)\} \, dx$, then I_1/I_2 is :

(a) 0   (b) 1

(c) 2   (d) 3.

251. The value of the integral

$\int\limits_{0}^{n\pi + t} (|\cos x| + |\sin x|) \, dx$ is ... (where $t \in [0, \pi/2]$) :

(a) n   (b) $2n + \sin t + \cos t$

(c) $\cos t$ (d) $4n + \sin t - \cos t + 1$.

252. Suppose for every integer n, $\int\limits_{n}^{n+1} f(x) \, dx = n^2$.

The value of $\int\limits_{-2}^{4} f(x) \, dx$ is :

(a) 16   (b) 14

(c) 19   (d) None of these.

253. The value of $\int\limits_{0}^{2} [x^2 - x + 1] \, dx$, where [.]

denotes the greatest integer function is :

(a) $\dfrac{5 - \sqrt{5}}{2}$ (b) $\dfrac{6 - \sqrt{5}}{2}$

(c) $\dfrac{8 - \sqrt{5}}{2}$ (d) $\dfrac{7 - \sqrt{5}}{2}$

254. If $I = \int\limits_{0}^{1} \cos \left\{ 2 \cot^{-1} \sqrt{\dfrac{1-x}{1+x}} \right\} dx$ then :

(a) $I > 1/2$ (b) $I = -1/2$

(c) $0 < I < 1/2$ (d) None of these.

255. The value of $\int\limits_{0}^{1} [x^2 - 1] \, dx =$

(a) $3 - \sqrt{3} - \sqrt{2}$ (b) 2

(c) 1   (d) None of these.

256. The area bounded by $y = 2 - |2 - x|$ and $y = \dfrac{3}{|x|}$ is :

(a) $\dfrac{4 + 3 \log 3}{2}$ (b) $\dfrac{4 - 3 \log 3}{2}$

(c) $\dfrac{3}{2} \log 3$ (d) $\dfrac{1}{2} \log 3$.

257. If $\int\limits_{-1}^{-4} f(x) \, dx = 4$ and $\int\limits_{2}^{-4} (3 - f) \, (x) \, dx = 7$, then

the value of $\int\limits_{-2}^{1} f(-x) \, dx$ is :

(a) 2   (b) -3

(c) 5   (d) None of these.

258. Let f be a positive function. If

$I_1 = \int\limits_{1-k}^{k} x \, f\{x(1-x)\} \, dx$ and

$I_2 = \int\limits_{1-k}^{k} f\{x(1-x)\} \, dx$ where $2k - 1 > 0$, then

I_1/I_2 is equal to

(a) 2   (b) k

(c) 1/2   (d) None of these.

259. $\lim\limits_{n \to \infty}$ $\left(1 + \dfrac{1}{n^2}\right)^{\frac{2}{n^2}} \left(1 + \dfrac{2^2}{n^2}\right)^{\frac{4}{n^2}} \left(1 + \dfrac{3^2}{n^2}\right)^{\frac{6}{n^2}} \cdots$

$\left(1 + \dfrac{n^2}{n^2}\right)^{\frac{2n}{n^2}}$

is equal to to :

(a) $\dfrac{e}{4}$ (b) $\dfrac{4}{e}$

(c) $\dfrac{e}{2}$ (d) $\dfrac{2}{e}$.

260. If $\int\limits_0^1 e^{x^2} (x - \alpha) \, dx = 0$, then :

(a) $1 < \alpha < 2$ (b) $\alpha < 0$

(c) $0 < \alpha < 1$ (d) $\alpha = 0$.

261. $\int\limits_0^1 \dfrac{1 - 4x + 2x^2}{\sqrt{2x - x^2}} \, dx$ is equal to :

(a) $\dfrac{1}{8} (\beta - \alpha)^2 \, \pi$ (b) $\dfrac{1}{4} (\beta - \alpha)^2 \, \pi$

(c) $\dfrac{1}{2} (\beta - \alpha)^2 \, \pi$ (d) None of these.

262. If $\int\limits_0^{10} f(x) \, dx = 5$, then $\sum\limits_{k=1}^{10} \int\limits_0^1 f(k - 1 + x) \, dx$ is :

(a 50   (b) 10

(c) 5   (d) None of these.

263. $\int\limits_1^\infty \dfrac{dx}{(x - \cos \alpha) \sqrt{x^2 - 1}}$ $(0 < \alpha < \pi)$ is equal to :

(a) $(\pi - \alpha) \sin \alpha$ (b) $(\pi - \alpha) \operatorname{cosec} \alpha$

(c) $(\pi - \alpha) \sec \alpha$ (d) None of these

264. The value of $\int\limits_{-\pi/2}^{\pi/2} \dfrac{dx}{e^{\sin x} + 1} =$

(a) 0   (b) 1

(c) $-\pi/2$ (d) $\pi/2$

265. The value of $\int\limits_0^\pi \max \{\sin x, \cos x\} \, dx$:

(a) does not exist   (b) is 1

(c) is $\sqrt{2}$ (d) is $1 + \sqrt{2}$.

266. $\lim\limits_{n \to \infty} \dfrac{1}{n} \left[\left(\dfrac{1}{n} \right)^m + \left(\dfrac{2}{b} \right)^m + \left(\dfrac{n-1}{n} \right)^m \right]$ is equal to :

(a) $\dfrac{1}{m + 1}$ (b) $\dfrac{1}{m + 2}$

(c) $\dfrac{1}{2}$ (d) None of these.

267. The area of the ellipse $\dfrac{x^2}{a^2} + \dfrac{y^2}{b^2} = 1$ is :

(a) $\dfrac{\pi ab}{4}$ (b) πab

(c) $\pi \left(\dfrac{a^2 + b^2}{4} \right)$ (d) $\pi (a + b)$.

268. The area (in square units) bounded by the curve $y = x^3$, the x-axis and the ordinates at $x = -2$ and $x = 1$ is :

(a) $\dfrac{17}{4}$ (b) $\dfrac{15}{4}$

(c) $\dfrac{15}{2}$ (d) $\dfrac{9}{2}$.

269. $\int\limits_0^{\pi/4} \log (1 + \tan x) \, dx =$

(a) $\dfrac{\pi}{4} \log 2$ (b) $\dfrac{\pi}{8} \log 2$

(c) $\dfrac{\pi}{8} \log 2 \tan x$ (d) $\dfrac{\pi}{8} \log 3$.

270. $\int\limits_0^{\pi/2} \log (\tan x) \, dx =$

(a) $\dfrac{\pi}{4}$ (b) 0

(c) $\dfrac{\pi}{2}$ (d) 2.

271. $\int\limits_0^1 \sin^{-1} \left(\dfrac{2x}{1 + x^2} \right) dx =$

(a) $\dfrac{\pi}{4} + \log 2$ (b) $\dfrac{\pi}{4} - \log 2$

(c) $\dfrac{\pi}{2} + \log 2$ (d) $\dfrac{\pi}{2} - \log 2$.

272. $\int\limits_0^{\pi/2} \dfrac{dx}{a^2 \cos^2 x + b^2 \sin^2 x} =$

(a) $\pi^2 ab$ (b) $\dfrac{\pi}{ab}$

(c) $\dfrac{\pi}{2ab}$ (d) πab

273. $\int\limits_0^{\pi/2} |\sin 2\pi x| \, dx$ is equal to :

(a) $\dfrac{2}{\pi}$ (b) $\dfrac{1}{\pi}$

(c) $\dfrac{-1}{\pi}$ (d) 0

274. The value of $\displaystyle\int_0^{\pi/2} \dfrac{dx}{1 - 2a \cos x + a^2}$ is :

   (a) $\pi (1 - a^2)$
   (b) $\dfrac{\pi}{1 - a^2}$

   (c) $\dfrac{\pi}{2(1 - a^2)}$
   (d) None of these.

275. $\displaystyle\int_{-1}^{0} \dfrac{dx}{x^2 + 2x + 2} =$

   (a) 0
   (b) $\pi/4$

   (c) $\pi/2$
   (d) $-\pi/4$.

276. The value of $\displaystyle\int_0^1 \dfrac{x^4 + 1}{x^2 + 1} dx$ is :

   (a) $\dfrac{1}{6}(3\pi - 4)$
   (b) $\dfrac{1}{6}(3 - 4\pi)$

   (c) $\dfrac{1}{6}(3\pi + 4)$
   (d) $\dfrac{1}{6}(3 + 4\pi)$

277. If $f(x)$ is an odd function of x, then $\displaystyle\int_{-\pi/2}^{\pi/2} f(\cos x) dx$ is equal to :

   (a) 0
   (b) $\displaystyle\int_0^{\pi/2} f(\cos x) dx$

   (c) $2\displaystyle\int_0^{\pi/2} f(\sin x) dx$
   (d) $\displaystyle\int_{-\pi/2}^{\pi/2} f(\cos x) dx$.

278. The ratio of the areas bounded by the curves $y = \cos x$ and $y = \cos 2x$ between $x = 0$, $x = \pi/3$ and x-axis, is :

   (a) $\sqrt{2} : 1$
   (b) $1 : 1$

   (c) $1 : 2$
   (d) $2 : 1$.

279. The area in the first quardrant between $x^2 + y^2 = \pi^2$ and $y = \sin x$ is :

   (a) $\dfrac{(\pi^3 - 8)}{4}$
   (b) $\dfrac{\pi^3}{4}$

   (c) $\dfrac{(\pi^3 - 16)}{4}$
   (d) $\dfrac{(\pi^3 - 8)}{2}$

280. $\displaystyle\lim_{n\to\infty} \left[\dfrac{1}{\sqrt{n^2}} + \dfrac{1}{\sqrt{n^2 + n}} + \dfrac{1}{\sqrt{n^2 + 2n}} + \dots + \dfrac{1}{\sqrt{n^2 + (2n-1)n}} \right]$

   (a) $2\sqrt{2}$
   (b) 2

   (c) $2 - 2\sqrt{2}$
   (d) $2\sqrt{2} - 2$

281. Let $f : (0, \infty) \to R$ and $F(x^2) = \displaystyle\int_0^{x^2} f(t)\, dt$.

   If $F(x^2) = x^2 (1 + x)$, then $f(4)$ equals :

   (a) $\dfrac{5}{4}$
   (b) 7

   (c) 4
   (d) 2.

282. $\displaystyle\lim_{n\to\infty} \left[\dfrac{1}{2n + 1} + \dfrac{1}{2n + 2} + \dots + \dfrac{1}{2n + n} \right] =$

   (a) $\log_e \left(\dfrac{1}{3}\right)$
   (b) $\text{loe}_e \left(\dfrac{2}{3}\right)$

   (c) $\log_e \left(\dfrac{3}{2}\right)$
   (d) $\text{loe}_e \left(\dfrac{4}{3}\right)$.

283. The area of the region bounded by $y = |x - 1|$ and $y = 1$ is :

   (a) 2
   (b) 1

   (c) 1/2
   (d) None of these.

284. The value of $\displaystyle\int_{\pi}^{2\pi} [2 \sin x]\, dx$, where $[.]$ represents the greatest integer function, is :

   (a) $-\dfrac{5\pi}{3}$
   (b) $-\pi$

   (c) $\dfrac{5\pi}{3}$
   (d) -2π.

285. If $f(x) = A \sin\left(\dfrac{\pi x}{2}\right) + B$, $f'\left(\dfrac{1}{2}\right) = \sqrt{2}$ and $\displaystyle\int_0^1 f(x)\, dx = \dfrac{2A}{\pi}$

   then the constants A and B are, respectively :

   (a) $\dfrac{\pi}{2}$ and $-\dfrac{\pi}{2}$
   (b) $\dfrac{\pi}{2}$ and $\dfrac{3}{\pi}$

   (c) 0 and $-\dfrac{4}{\pi}$
   (d) $\dfrac{4}{\pi}$ and 0.

286. $\displaystyle\int_1^2 e^x \left(\dfrac{1}{x} - \dfrac{1}{x^2}\right) dx$ is equal to :

   (a) $e\left(\dfrac{e}{2} - 1\right)$
   (b) $e\,(e - 1)$

   (c) 0
   (d) None of these.

287. $\int\limits_{0}^{1} \dfrac{\tan^{-1} x}{1+ x^2}\, dx$ is equal to :

(a) $\dfrac{\pi}{4}$

(b) $\dfrac{\pi^2}{32}$

(c) 1

(d) None of these.

288. $\int\limits_{0}^{2\pi} \sqrt{1 + \sin \dfrac{x}{2}}\, dx$ is equal to :

(a) zero

(b) 2

(c) 8

(d) 4.

289. The area bounded between the parabolas $x^2 \le \dfrac{y}{4}$ and $x^2 = 9y$ and the straight line $y = 2$ is :

[AIEEE - 2012]

(a) $20\sqrt{2}$

(b) $\dfrac{10\sqrt{2}}{3}$

(c) $\dfrac{20\sqrt{2}}{3}$

(d) $10\sqrt{2}$

290. If $g(x) = \int\limits_{0}^{x} \cos 4t\, dt$, then $g(x + \pi)$ equals :

[AIEEE - 2012]

(a) $\dfrac{g(x)}{g(\pi)}$

(b) $g(x) + g(\pi)$

(c) $g(x) - g(\pi)$

(d) $g(x) \cdot g(\pi)$

291. The value of $\int\limits_{0}^{1} \dfrac{8 \log (1 + x)}{1 + x^2}\, dx$ is :

[AIEEE - 2011]

(a) $\log 2$

(b) $\pi \log 2$

(c) $\dfrac{\pi}{8} \log 2$

(d) $\dfrac{\pi}{2} \log 2$

292. The area of the region enclosed by the curves $y = x$, $x = e$, $y = \dfrac{1}{x}$ and the positive X-axis is :

[AIEEE - 2011]

(a) $\dfrac{5}{2}$ square units

(b) $\dfrac{1}{2}$ square units

(c) 1 square unit

(d) $\dfrac{3}{2}$ square units

293. The area bounded by the curves $y = \cos x$ and $y = \sin x$ between the ordinates $x = 0$ and $x = \dfrac{3\pi}{2}$ is :

[AIEEE - 2010]

(a) $4\sqrt{2} + 2$

(b) $4\sqrt{2} - 1$

(c) $4\sqrt{2} + 1$

(d) $4\sqrt{2} - 2$

294. Let $p(x)$ be a function defined on R such that $p'(x) = p'(1 - x)$, for all $x \in [0, 1]$, $p(0) = 1$ and $p(1) = 41$. Then $\int\limits_{0}^{1} p(x)\, dx$ equals :

[AIEEE - 2010]

(a) 21

(b) 41

(c) 42

(d) $\sqrt{41}$

295. $\int\limits_{0}^{\pi} [\cot x]\, dx$, $[\bullet]$ denotes the greatest integer function, is equal to : **[AIEEE - 2009]**

(a) $\dfrac{\pi}{2}$

(b) 1

(c) -1

(d) $-\dfrac{\pi}{2}$

296. The area of the region bounded by the parabola $(y - 2)^2 = x - 1$, the tangent to the parabola at the point (2, 3) and the x-axis is : **[AIEEE - 2009]**

(a) 3

(b) 6

(c) 9

(d) 12

297. Let $I = \int\limits_{0}^{1} \dfrac{\sin x}{\sqrt{x}}\, dx$ and $J = \int\limits_{0}^{1} \dfrac{\cos x}{\sqrt{x}}\, dx$. Then which one of the following is true?

[AIEEE - 2008]

(a) $I > \dfrac{2}{3}$ and $J > 2$ (b) $I < \dfrac{2}{3}$ and $J < 2$

(c) $I < \dfrac{2}{3}$ and $J > 2$ (d) $I > \dfrac{2}{3}$ and $J < 2$

298. The area of the plane region bounded by the curves $x + 2y^2 = 0$ and $x + 3y^2 = 1$ is equal to :

[AIEEE - 2008]

(a) $\dfrac{5}{3}$

(b) $\dfrac{1}{3}$

(c) $\dfrac{2}{3}$

(d) $\dfrac{4}{3}$

299. The value of the integral, $\int\limits_{3}^{6} \dfrac{\sqrt{x}}{\sqrt{9-x}+\sqrt{x}}\, dx$ is

[AIEEE - 2006]

(a) 1/2 (b) 3/2

(c) 2 (d) 1

300. $\int\limits_{0}^{\pi} x\, f(\sin x)\, dx$ is equal to : **[AIEEE - 2006]**

(a) $\pi \int\limits_{0}^{\pi} f(\cos x)\, dx$ (b) $\pi \int\limits_{0}^{\pi} f(\sin x)\, dx$

(c) $\dfrac{\pi}{2} \int\limits_{0}^{\pi/2} f(\sin x)\, dx$ (d) $\pi \int\limits_{0}^{\pi/2} f(\cos x)\, dx$

301. $\int\limits_{-3\pi/2}^{-\pi/2} [(x+\pi)^3 + \cos^2 (x+3\pi)]\, dx$ is equal to :

[AIEEE – 2006]

(a) $\dfrac{\pi^4}{32}$ (b) $\dfrac{\pi^4}{32}+\dfrac{\pi}{2}$

(c) $\dfrac{\pi}{2}$ (d) $\dfrac{\pi}{4}-1$

302. $\lim\limits_{n\to\infty} \left[\dfrac{1}{n^2} \sec^2 \dfrac{1}{n^2} + \dfrac{2}{n^2} \sec^2 \dfrac{4}{n^2} + \ldots + \dfrac{1}{n^2} \sec^2 1 \right] =$

[AIEEE – 2005]

(a) $\dfrac{1}{2} \sec 1$ (b) $\dfrac{1}{2} \operatorname{cosec} 1$

(c) $\tan 1$ (d) $\dfrac{1}{2} \tan 1$

303. The integral

$\int\limits_{0}^{\pi} \sqrt{1 + 4 \sin^2 \left(\dfrac{x}{2}\right) - 4 \sin \left(\dfrac{x}{2}\right)}\, dx$ equals

(a) $\pi - 4$ (b) $\dfrac{2\pi}{3} - 4 - 4\sqrt{3}$

(c) $4\sqrt{3} - 4$ (d) $4\sqrt{3} - 4 - \dfrac{\pi}{3}$

304. The value of $\int\limits_{0}^{1} \dfrac{8 \log (1+x)}{1+x^2}\, dx$ is

(a) $\log 2$ (b) $\pi \log 2$

(c) $\dfrac{\pi}{8} \log 2$ (d) $\dfrac{\pi}{2} \log 2$

305. If $f(x) = \dfrac{e^x}{1+e^x}$; $I_1 = \int\limits_{f(-a)}^{f(a)} x \cdot g\, (x\, (1-x))\, dx$ and

$I_2 = \int\limits_{f(-a)}^{f(a)} g\, (x\, (1-x))\, dx$ where g is not an identity function, then the value of $\dfrac{I_2}{I_1}$ is

(a) 1 (b) -1

(c) $\dfrac{1}{2}$ (d) 2

306. The value of the integral

$\int\limits_{-\pi/2}^{\pi/2} \left[x^2 + \log \left(\dfrac{\pi+x}{\pi-x}\right) \right] \cos x\, dx$ is

(a) 0 (b) $\dfrac{\pi^2}{2} - 4$

(c) $\dfrac{\pi^2}{2} + 4$ (d) $\dfrac{\pi^2}{2}$

307. The value of the integral $\int\limits_{0}^{2} \dfrac{\log (x^2 + 2)}{(x+2)^2}\, dx$ is

(a) $\dfrac{\sqrt{2}}{3} \tan^{-1} \sqrt{2} + \dfrac{5}{12} \log 2 - \dfrac{1}{4} \log 3$

(b) $\dfrac{\sqrt{2}}{3} \tan^{-1} \sqrt{2} - \dfrac{5}{12} \log 2 - \dfrac{1}{12} \log 3$

(c) $\dfrac{\sqrt{2}}{3} \tan^{-1} \sqrt{2} + \dfrac{5}{12} \log 2 + \dfrac{1}{4} \log 3$

(d) $\dfrac{\sqrt{2}}{3} \tan^{-1} \sqrt{2} - \dfrac{5}{12} \log 2 + \dfrac{1}{12} \log 3$

308. For a real number x, let [x] denote the largest integer less than or equal to x and {x} be the fractional part of x. Then the smallest possible integer value of n for which $\int\limits_{1}^{n} [x]\ \{x\}\ dx > 2013$ is

(a) 63 (b) 64

(c) 90 (d) 91

309. Let $f(x) = \begin{cases} \dfrac{e^{\cos x} \cdot \sin x}{1+x^2} & ; \quad \text{if } |x| < 2 \\ x\, e^{x-2} & ; \quad \text{otherwise} \end{cases}$

Then the value of the integral $\int\limits_{-2}^{4} f(x)\, dx$ is

(a) $1 - 3e^2$ (b) $1 + 3e^2$

(c) $3e^2 - 1$ (d) $3e^2$

310. Let n be a positive integer. For a real number x, let [x] denote the largest integer not exceeding x and $\{x\} = x - [x]$. Then $\int\limits_{1}^{n+1} \dfrac{(\{x\})^{[x]}}{[x]} dx$ is equal to

(a) $\log_e n$

(b) $\dfrac{1}{n+1}$

(c) $\dfrac{n}{n+1}$

(d) $1 + \dfrac{1}{2} + \ldots + \dfrac{1}{n}$

311. The value of $\int\limits_{0}^{1} \dfrac{x^4 (1-x)^4}{1+x^2} dx$ is

(a) $\pi - \dfrac{22}{7}$

(b) $\dfrac{22}{7} - \pi$

(c) 0

(d) $\dfrac{71}{15} - \dfrac{3\pi}{2}$

312. If $f : \left[\dfrac{1}{2}, 1\right] \to \mathbb{R}$ be a positive nonconstant and differentiable function such that

$f'(x) < 2 f(x)$ and $f\left(\dfrac{1}{2}\right) = 1$.

Then the value of $\int\limits_{1/2}^{1} f(x) \, dx$ lies in the interval

(a) $(2e - 1, 2e)$

(b) $(e - 1, 2e - 1)$

(c) $\left(\dfrac{e-1}{2}, e - 1\right)$

(d) $\left(0, \dfrac{e-1}{2}\right)$

313. Let $f : [0, 2] \to \mathbb{R}$ be a function which is continuous on $[0, 2]$ and differentiable on $(0, 2)$. If $F'(x) = f'(x)$ for all $x \in (0, 2)$; where $F(x) = \int\limits_{0}^{x^2} f(\sqrt{t}) \, dt$ then F(2) has value

(a) $e^2 - 1$

(b) $e^4 - 1$

(c) $e - 1$

(d) e^4

314. $\int\limits_{2}^{4} \dfrac{\log (x^2)}{\log (x^2) + \log (36 - 12x + x^2)} dx =$

(a) 1

(b) 6

(c) 2

(d) 4

315. $\int\limits_{\sqrt{\log 2}}^{\sqrt{\log 3}} \dfrac{x \sin (x^2)}{\sin (x^2) + \sin [\log (6 - x^2)]} dx =$

(a) $\dfrac{1}{4} \log \left(\dfrac{3}{2}\right)$

(b) $\dfrac{1}{2} \log \left(\dfrac{3}{2}\right)$

(c) $\log \left(\dfrac{3}{2}\right)$

(d) $\dfrac{1}{6} \log \left(\dfrac{3}{2}\right)$

316. Let $f : \mathbb{R} \to \mathbb{R}$ be a function defined by

$f(x) = \begin{cases} [x] & ; \quad x \le 2 \\ 0 & ; \quad x > 2 \end{cases}$ where [x] denotes the greatest integer not greater than x.

If $I = \int\limits_{-1}^{2} \dfrac{x \, f(x^2)}{2 + f(x+1)} dx$, then the value of $4I - 1$ is

(a) 0

(b) 3

(c) 4

(d) 2

317. The area of the region enclosed by the curves $y = x$, $x = e$, $y = \dfrac{1}{x}$ and the positive x-axis is

(a) $\dfrac{5}{2}$ sq. units

(b) $\dfrac{1}{2}$ sq. units

(c) 1 sq. unit

(d) $\dfrac{3}{2}$ sq. units

318. Let the straight line $x = b$ divides the area enclosed by $y = (1 - x)^2$, $y = 0$ and $x = 0$ into two parts :
$R_1 : 0 \le x \le b$ and $R_2 : b \le x \le 1$ such that $R_1 - R_2 = \dfrac{1}{4}$. Then b is equal to

(a) $\dfrac{3}{4}$

(b) $\dfrac{1}{2}$

(c) $\dfrac{1}{3}$

(d) $\dfrac{1}{4}$

ANSWER KEY

1. (a)	2. (c)	3. (c)	4. (a)	5. (b)	6. (a)	7. (c)	8. (a)	9. (c)	10. (a)
11. (b)	12. (c)	13. (a)	14. (b)	15. (c)	16. (b)	17. (a)	18. (b)	19. (c)	20. (b)

21. (c)	**22.** (a)	**23.** (b)	**24.** (a)	**25.** (c)	**26.** (c)	**27.** (d)	**28.** (a)	**29.** (a)	**30.** (b)
31. (b)	**32.** (d)	**33.** (a)	**34.** (b)	**35.** (a)	**36.** (a)	**37.** (c)	**38.** (b)	**39.** (c)	**40.** (a)
41. (d)	**42.** (b)	**43.** (a)	**44.** (a)	**45.** (a)	**46.** (c)	**47.** (d)	**48.** (c)	**49.** (a)	**50.** (b)
51. (c)	**52.** (b)	**53.** (b)	**54.** (a)	**55.** (a)	**56.** (c)	**57.** (c)	**58.** (a)	**59.** (a)	**60.** (a)
61. (b)	**62.** (a)	**63.** (b)	**64.** (b)	**65.** (b)	**66.** (a)	**67.** (d)	**68.** (b)	**69.** (a)	**70.** (b)
71. (a)	**72.** (c)	**73.** (a)	**74.** (b)	**75.** (b)	**76.** (b)	**77.** (c)	**78.** (b)	**79.** (a)	**80.** (c)
81. (a)	**82.** (b)	**83.** (a)	**84.** (b)	**85.** (a)	**86.** (b)	**87.** (c)	**88.** (b)	**89.** (c)	**90.** (a)
91. (a)	**92.** (c)	**93.** (b)	**94.** (c)	**95.** (d)	**96.** (b)	**97.** (c)	**98.** (d)	**99.** (b)	**100.** (d)
101. (d)	**102.** (b)	**103.** (a)	**104.** (b)	**105.** ((a)	**106.** (b)	**107.** (a)	**108.** (c)	**109.** (b)	**110.** (a)
111. (b)	**112.** (a)	**113.** (c)	**114.** (a)	**115.** (b)	**116.** (d)	**117.** (c)	**118.** (a)	**119.** (b)	**120.** (a)
121. (b)	**122.** (a)	**123.** (b)	**124.** (c)	**125.** (b)	**126.** (a)	**127.** (c)	**128.** (a)	**129.** (c)	**130.** (b)
131. (a)	**132.** (c)	**133.** (c)	**134.** (d)	**135.** (a)	**136.** (d)	**137.** (b)	**138.** (a)	**139.** (b)	**140.** (c)
141. (c)	**142.** (c)	**143.** (a)	**144.** (b)	**145.** (c)	**146.** (b)	**147.** (b)	**148.** (d)	**149.** (b)	**150.** (b)
151. (a)	**152.** (b)	**153.** (b)	**154.** (c)	**155.** (a)	**156.** (b)	**157.** (c)	**158.** (b)	**159.** (b)	**160.** (b)
161. (a)	**162.** (b)	**163.** (c)	**164.** (a)	**165.** (b)	**166.** (c)	**167.** (b)	**168.** (c)	**169.** (b)	**170.** (c)
171. (b)	**172.** (b)	**173.** (c)	**174.** (a)	**175.** (b)	**176.** (c)	**177.** (c)	**178.** (b)	**179.** (d)	**180.** (c)
181. (a)	**182.** (d)	**183.** (a)	**184.** (c)	**185.** (d)	**186.** (b)	**187.** (c)	**188.** (d)	**189.** (a)	**190.** (a)
191. (c)	**192.** (d)	**193.** (b)	**194.** (a)	**195.** (a)	**196.** (b)	**197.** (a)	**198.** (b)	**199.** (c)	**200.** (a)
201. (c)	**202.** (b)	**203.** (a)	**204.** (c)	**205.** (a)	**206.** (a)	**207.** (a)	**208.** (a)	**209.** (a)	**210.** (c)
211. (d)	**212.** (a)	**213.** (d)	**214.** (d)	**215.** (b)	**216.** (b)	**217.** (d)	**218.** (c)	**219.** (c)	**220.** (d)
221. (d)	**222.** (a)	**223.** (c)	**224.** (c)	**225.** (b)	**226.** (a)	**227.** (c)	**228.** (a)	**229.** (a)	**230.** (b)
231. (a)	**232.** (a)	**233.** (a)	**234.** (a)	**235.** (b)	**236.** (b)	**237.** (a)	**238.** (c)	**239.** (a)	**240.** (b)
241. (a)	**242.** (d)	**243.** (c)	**244.** (c)	**245.** (c)	**246.** (a)	**247.** (b)	**248.** (c)	**249.** (a)	**250.** (b)
251. (d)	**252.** (c)	**253.** (d)	**254.** (b)	**255.** (a)	**256.** (b)	**257.** (d)	**258.** (c)	**259.** (b)	**260.** (c)
261. (c)	**262.** (c)	**263.** (b)	**264.** (d)	**265.** (d)	**266.** (a)	**267.** (b)	**268.** (b)	**269.** (b)	**270.** (b)
271. (d)	**272.** (c)	**273.** (a)	**274.** (b)	**275.** (b)	**276.** (a)	**277.** (c)	**278.** (d)	**279.** (a)	**280.** (d)
281. (c)	**282.** (c)	**283.** (b)	**284.** (a)	**285.** (d)	**286.** (a)	**287.** (b)	**288.** (c)	**289.** (c)	**290.** (b,d)
291. (b)	**292.** (d)	**293.** (d)	**294.** (a)	**295.** (d)	**296.** (c)	**297.** (b)	**298.** (d)	**299.** (b)	**300.** (d)
301. (c)	**302.** (d)	**303.** (d)	**304.** (b)	**305.** (c)	**306.** (b)	**307.** (d)	**308.** (b)	**309.** (c)	**310.** (c)
311. (b)	**312.** (d)	**313.** (d)	**314.** (a)	**315.** (a)	**316.** (a)	**317.** (d)	**318.** (b)		

❑❑❑

DIFFERENTIAL EQUATIONS

MULTIPLE CHOICE QUESTIONS

1. The degree of differential equation of which $(x - h)^2 + (y - k)^2 = a^2$, is a solution is :

   (a) 1
   (b) 2
   (c) 3
   (d) None of these

2. The order of the differential equation, of which $xy = ce^x + be^{-x} + x^2$ is a solution, is :

   (a) 1
   (b) 2
   (c) 3
   (d) None of these

3. The differential equation of which $y = Ae^x + Be^{3x} + Ce^{5x}$ is a solution, is :

   (a) $\dfrac{d^3y}{dx^3} - 9\dfrac{d^2y}{dx^2} + 23\dfrac{dy}{dx} - 15y = 0$

   (b) $\dfrac{d^3y}{dx^3} + 9\dfrac{d^2y}{dx^2} + 23\dfrac{dy}{dx} - 15y = 0$

   (c) $\dfrac{d^3y}{dx^3} - 9\dfrac{d^2y}{dx^2} - 23\dfrac{dy}{dx} - 15y = 0$

   (d) None of these

4. The degree of the differential equation, of which $y^2 = 4a(x + a)$ is a solution, is :

   (a) 1
   (b) 2
   (c) 3
   (d) None of these

5. The differential equation of the family of curves $y = e^x (A \cos x + B \sin x)$, where A and B are arbitrary constants, is :

   (a) $\dfrac{d^2y}{dx^2} + 2\dfrac{dy}{dx} + 2y = 0$

   (b) $\dfrac{d^2y}{dx^2} - 2\dfrac{dy}{dx} - 2y = 0$

   (c) $\dfrac{d^2y}{dx^2} - 2\dfrac{dy}{dx} + 2y = 0$

   (d) None of these

6. The differential equation of all the circles passing through the origin and having their centres on the x-axis is :

   (a) $y^2 = x^2 + 2xy \dfrac{dy}{dx}$
   (b) $y^2 = x^2 - 2xy \dfrac{dy}{dx}$

   (c) $x^2 = y^2 + xy \dfrac{dy}{dx}$
   (d) None of these

7. The differential equation of family of parabolas with foci at the origin and axis along the x-axis is :

   (a) $y\left(\dfrac{dy}{dx}\right)^2 + 2x\dfrac{dy}{dx} - y = 0$

   (b) $x\left(\dfrac{dy}{dx}\right)^2 + 2y\dfrac{dy}{dx} - y = 0$

   (c) $y\left(\dfrac{dy}{dx}\right)^2 + 2x\dfrac{dy}{dx} + y = 0$

   (d) None of these

8. The differential equation that represents all the parabolas, each of which has a latus rectum 4a and whose axes are parallel to x-axis is :

   (a) $a\left(\dfrac{d^2y}{dx^2}\right) + \left(\dfrac{dy}{dx}\right)^3 = 0$

   (b) $2a\left(\dfrac{d^2y}{dx^2}\right) + \left(\dfrac{dy}{dx}\right)^3 = 0$

   (c) $2a\left(\dfrac{d^2y}{dx^2}\right) - \left(\dfrac{dy}{dx}\right)^3 = 0$

   (d) None of these

9. The differential equation of all conics whose axes coincide with the axes of coordinates, is :

   (a) $xy\dfrac{d^2y}{dx^2} + x\left(\dfrac{dy}{dx}\right)^2 = y\dfrac{dy}{dx}$

   (b) $x\dfrac{d^2y}{dx^2} + y\left(\dfrac{dy}{dx}\right)^2 = y\dfrac{dy}{dx}$

   (c) $y\dfrac{d^2y}{dx^2} + x\left(\dfrac{dy}{dx}\right)^2 = x\dfrac{dy}{dx}$

   (d) None of these

10. Solution of the equation :

$$y \sqrt{1 + x^2} \, dx + x \sqrt{1 + y^2} \, dy = 0 \text{ is}$$

(a) $\sqrt{1 + x^2} + \sqrt{1 + y^2}$

$$+ \log \left[\frac{(\sqrt{1 + x^2} + 1)(\sqrt{1 + y^2} + 1)}{xy} \right] = C$$

(b) $\sqrt{1 + x^2} + \sqrt{1 + y^2}$

$$- \log \left[\frac{(\sqrt{1 + x^2} + 1)(\sqrt{1 + y^2} + 1)}{xy} \right] = C$$

(c) $\sqrt{1 + x^2} + \sqrt{1 + y^2}$

$$- \log \left[\frac{(\sqrt{1 + x^2} + 1)(\sqrt{1 + y^2} + 1)}{xy} \right] = C$$

(d) None of these

11. The solution of the equation :

$$\sqrt{(1 + x^2)(1 + y^2)} \, dx + xy \, dy = 0 \text{ is}$$

(a) $\sqrt{1 + x^2} + \sqrt{1 + y^2} - \log \dfrac{\sqrt{1 + x^2} + 1}{x} = C$

(b) $\sqrt{1 + x^2} + \sqrt{1 + y^2} + \log \dfrac{\sqrt{1 + x^2} + 1}{x} = C$

(c) $\sqrt{1 + x^2} + \sqrt{1 + y^2} + \log \dfrac{\sqrt{1 + x^2} - 1}{x} = C$

(d) None of these

12. The equation of the curve passing through the point $\left(a, -\dfrac{1}{a} \right)$ and satisfying the differential equation

$$y - x \frac{dy}{dx} = a \left(y^2 + \frac{dy}{dx} \right) \text{ is :}$$

(a) $(x + a)(1 + ay) = -4a^2 y$

(b) $(x + a)(1 - ay) = 4a^2 y$

(c) $(x + a)(1 - ay) = -4a^2 y$

(d) None of these

13. The particular solution of

$$\cos y \, dx + (1 + 2e^{-x}) \sin y \, dy = 0,$$

when $x = 0$, $y = \dfrac{\pi}{4}$ is

(a) $e^x - 2 = 3\sqrt{2} \cos y$

(b) $e^x + 2 = \sqrt{2} \cos y$

(c) $e^x + 2 = 3\sqrt{2} \cos y$

(d) None of these

14. A curve is such that the portion of the x-axis cut off between the origin and the tangent at a point

is twice the abscissa and which passes through the point $(1, 2)$. The equation of the curve is :

(a) $xy = 1$ (b) $xy = 2$

(c) $xy = 3$ (d) None of these

15. The equation of the curve through the point $(1, 1)$ and whose slope is $\dfrac{2ay}{x(y - a)}$, is :

(a) $y^a \cdot x^{2a} = e^{y-1}$ (b) $y^a \cdot x^{2a} = e^y$

(c) $y^{2a} \cdot x^a = e^{y-1}$ (d) None of these

16. Solution of the differential equation $(x + 2y^3) \dfrac{dy}{dx} = y$ is :

(a) $x = y^2 (c + y^2)$ (b) $x = y (c - y^2)$

(c) $x = 2y (c - y^2)$ (d) $x = y (c + y^2)$

17. The equation of a curve passing through $(0, 1)$ and having gradient $\dfrac{-(y + y^3)}{1 + x + xy^2}$ at (x, y) is :

(a) $xy + \tan^{-1} y = \dfrac{\pi}{2}$ (b) $xy + \tan^{-1} y = \dfrac{\pi}{4}$

(c) $xy - \tan^{-1} y = \dfrac{\pi}{2}$ (d) $xy - \tan^{-1} y = \dfrac{\pi}{4}$

18. The equation of the curve satisfying the equation $(1 + y^2) \, dx + (x - e^{\tan^{-1} y}) \, dy = 0$ and passing through origin is :

(a) $x \cdot e^{\tan^{-1} y} = \cot^{-1} y$

(b) $x \cdot e^{\cot^{-1} y} = \tan^{-1} y$

(c) $y \cdot e^{\tan^{-1} x} = \tan^{-1} x$

(d) $x \cdot e^{\tan^{-1} y} = \tan^{-1} y$

19. The solution of the equation $x \dfrac{dy}{dx} + y = y^2 \log x$ satisfying $y(1) = 1$ is :

(a) $1 - \log x = \dfrac{1}{y}$ (b) $1 + \log x = \dfrac{1}{y}$

(c) $1 + \log y = \dfrac{1}{x}$ (d) $1 - \log y = \dfrac{1}{x}$

20. The general solution of the differential equation $\dfrac{dy}{dx} = y \tan x - y^2 \sec x$ is :

(a) $\tan x = (c + \sec x) y$

(b) $\sec y = (c + \tan y) x$

(c) $\sec x = (c + \tan x) y$

(d) None of these

21. The equation of the curve satisfying the equation $(xy - x^2) \dfrac{dy}{dx} = y^2$ and passing through the point $(-1, 1)$ is :

(a) $y = (\log y - 1) x$ (b) $y = (\log y + 1) x$

(c) $x = (\log x - 1) y$ (d) $x = (\log x + 1) y$

22. Solution of the differential equation

$x \sin \dfrac{y}{x} dy = \left(y \sin \dfrac{y}{x} - x \right) dx$ is :

(a) $\log x = \cos \left(\dfrac{y}{x} \right) + C$

(b) $\log y = \cos \left(\dfrac{x}{y} \right) + C$

(c) $\log x = \cos \left(\dfrac{x}{y} \right) + C$

(d) None of these

23. The general solution of the differential equation $\left[2\sqrt{xy} - x \right] dy + y\, dx = 0$ is :

(a) $\log x + \sqrt{\dfrac{y}{x}} = C$ (b) $\log y - \sqrt{\dfrac{x}{y}} = C$

(c) $\log y + \sqrt{\dfrac{x}{y}} = C$ (d) None of these

24. The general solution of the differential equation $(4x + 6y + 5) dx = (2x + 3y + 4) dy$ is :

(a) $\dfrac{1}{8}(2x + 3y) + \dfrac{9}{64} \log (16x + 24y + 23) = x + C$

(b) $\dfrac{1}{64}(2x + 3y) + \dfrac{9}{8} \log (16x + 24y + 23) = x + C$

(c) $\dfrac{1}{8}(2x + 3y) + \dfrac{9}{64} \log (16x + 24y - 23) = x + C$

(d) None of these

25. Solution of the equation

$(x - y)(2dy - dx) = 3dx - 5dy$ is :

(a) $2y - x = \log (x - y + 2) + C$

(b) $2x - y = \log (y - x + 2) + C$

(c) $2y + x = \log (x - y + 2) + C$

(d) None of these

26. Solution of the equation

$x\, dx + y\, dy + \dfrac{x\, dy - y\, dx}{x^2 + y^2} = 0$ is :

(a) $y = x \tan \left(\dfrac{c + x^2 + y^2}{2} \right)$

(b) $x = y \tan \left(\dfrac{c + x^2 + y^2}{2} \right)$

(c) $y = x \tan \left(\dfrac{c - x^2 - y^2}{2} \right)$

(d) None of these

27. The equation of the curve satisfying the differential equation $y (x + y^3)\, dx = x (y^3 - x)\, dy$ and passing through the point $(1, 1)$ is :

(a) $y^3 - 2x + 3x^2 y = 0$ (b) $y^3 + 2x + 3x^2 y = 0$

(c) $y^3 + 2x - 3x^2 y = 0$ (d) None of these

28. The solution of the equation

$\log \dfrac{dy}{dx} = 9x - xy + 6$, given that $y = 1$ when $x = 0$, is :

(a) $3e^{6y} = 2e^{9x-6} + 6e^6$ (b) $3e^{6y} = 2e^{9x+6} - 6e^6$

(c) $3e^{6y} = 2e^{9x+6} + e^6$ (d) None of these

29. The solution of the equation $e^{\frac{dy}{dx}} = x + 3$, given that when $x = -2$, $y = 3$ is :

(a) $y = (x + 3) \log (x + 3) - x + 1$

(b) $y = (x + 3) \log (x + 3) + x + 1$

(c) $y = (x + 3) \log (x + 3) - x - 1$

(d) None of these

30. The solution of the equation

$\left(\dfrac{x + y - 1}{x + y - 2} \right) \dfrac{dy}{dx} = \left(\dfrac{x + y + 1}{x + y + 2} \right)$ given that $y = 1$ when $x = 1$, is :

(a) $\log \left| \dfrac{(x - y)^2 - 2}{2} \right| = 2(x + y)$

(b) $\log \left| \dfrac{(x + y)^2 - 2}{2} \right| = 2(x - y)$

(c) $\log \left| \dfrac{(x + y)^2 + 2}{2} \right| = 2(x - y)$

(d) None of these

31. The solution of the differential equation

$\dfrac{dy}{dx} = \dfrac{y\,(2y - x)}{x\,(2y + x)}$, which satisfies $y = 1$ at $x = 1$, is

(a) $x \log(xy) = 2\,(x - y)$

(b) $y \log(xy) = 2\,(y - x)$

(c) $x \log(xy) = 2\,(x + y)$

(d) None of these

32. The solution of the differential equation

$y \cos \dfrac{y}{x}\,(x\,dy - y\,dx) + x \sin \dfrac{y}{x}\,(x\,dy + y\,dx) = 0$

which satisfies $y\,(1) = \dfrac{\pi}{2}$, is :

(a) $y \sin \dfrac{y}{x} = \dfrac{\pi}{x}$ 　　(b) $y \sin \dfrac{y}{x} = \dfrac{\pi}{3x}$

(c) $y \sin \dfrac{y}{x} = \dfrac{\pi}{2x}$ 　　(d) None of these

33. The general solution of the differential equation $(1 + \tan y)\,(dx - dy) + 2x\,dy = 0$ is :

(a) $x\,(\sin y + \cos y) = \sin y + ce^{y}$

(b) $x\,(\sin y + \cos y) = \sin y + ce^{-y}$

(c) $y\,(\sin x + \cos x) = \sin x + ce^{x}$

(d) None of these

34. Solution of the equation $\dfrac{dy}{dx} = e^{x-y}\,(e^{x} - e^{y})$ is :

(a) $e^{y} = e^{x} - 1 + ce^{-e^{x}}$ 　(b) $e^{y} = e^{x} - 1 + ce^{e^{x}}$

(c) $e^{x} = e^{y} - 1 + ce^{-e^{y}}$ 　(d) None of these

35. Solution of the equation

$x\left(\dfrac{dy}{dx}\right)^{2} + (y - x)\dfrac{dy}{dx} - y = 0$ is :

(a) $(x - y + c)\,(xy - c) = 0$

(b) $(x + y + c)\,(xy - c) = 0$

(c) $(x - y + c)\,(2xy - c) = 0$

(d) $(y - x + c)\,(xy - c) = 0$

36. Solution of equation $(xy^{4} + y)\,dx - x\,dy = 0$ is :

(a) $4x^{4}y^{3} + 3x^{3} = cy^{3}$ 　(b) $3x^{3}y^{4} + 4y^{3} = cx^{3}$

(c) $3x^{4}y^{3} + 4x^{3} = cy^{3}$ 　(d) None of these

37. A curve C has the property that if the tangent drawn at any point P on C meets the coordinate axis at A and B, then P is the mid-point of AB. If the curve passes through the point $(1, 1)$, then the equation of the curve is :

(a) $xy = 2$ 　　　　(b) $xy = 3$

(c) $xy = 1$ 　　　　(d) None of these

38. The equation of the curve passing through origin and satisfying the differential equation

$\dfrac{dy}{dx} = \sin\,(10x + 6y)$ is :

(a) $y = \dfrac{1}{3} \tan^{-1}\left(\dfrac{5 \tan 4x}{4 - 3 \tan 4x}\right) - \dfrac{5x}{3}$

(b) $y = \dfrac{1}{3} \tan^{-1}\left(\dfrac{5 \tan 4x}{4 + 3 \tan 4x}\right) - \dfrac{5x}{3}$

(c) $y = \dfrac{1}{3} \tan^{-1}\left(\dfrac{3 + \tan 4x}{4 - 3 \tan 4x}\right) - \dfrac{5x}{3}$

(d) None of these

39. Solution of the equation

$x^{2}y - x^{3}\dfrac{dy}{dx} = y^{4} \cos x$, when $y(0) = 1$ is :

(a) $y^{3} = 3x^{3} \sin x$ 　　(b) $x^{3} = 3y^{3} \sin x$

(c) $x^{3} = y^{3} \sin x$ 　　(d) None of these

40. Solution of the equation $\cos^{2} x\dfrac{dy}{dx} - (\tan 2x)\,y$

$= \cos^{4} x$, $|x| < \dfrac{\pi}{4}$, when $y\left(\dfrac{\pi}{6}\right) = \dfrac{3\sqrt{3}}{8}$ is :

(a) $y = \tan 2x \cos^{2}x$

(b) $y = \cot 2x \cdot \cos^{2}x$

(c) $y = \dfrac{1}{2} \tan 2x \cdot \cos^{2} x$

(d) $y = \dfrac{1}{2} \cot 2x \cdot \cos^{2} x$

41. The degree of the differential equation of all tangent lines to the parabola $y^{2} = 4ax$ is :

(a) 1 　　　　　(b) 2

(c) 3 　　　　　(d) None of these

42. A solution of the differential equation

$\left(\dfrac{dy}{dx}\right)^{2} - x\dfrac{dy}{dx} + y = 0$ is :

(a) $y = 2$ 　　　　(b) $y = 2x$

(c) $y = 2x - 4$ 　　(d) $y = 2x^{2} - 4$

43. The order of the differential equation whose general solution is given by

$y = c_1 \cos (2x + c_2) - (c_3 + c_4) a^{x + c_5} + c_6 \sin (x - c_7)$

is :

(a) 3   (b) 4

(c) 5   (d) 2

44. The degree of the differential equation

$\left(\dfrac{d^4y}{dx^4}\right)^{3/5} - 5\dfrac{d^3y}{dx^3} + 6\dfrac{d^2y}{dx^2} - 8\dfrac{dy}{dx} + 5 = 0$ is :

(a) 2   (b) 3

(c) 4   (d) 5

45. The degree of the differential equation

$\dfrac{d^3y}{dx^3} + x\left(\dfrac{dy}{dx}\right)^4 = 4 \log \left(\dfrac{d^4y}{dx^4}\right)$ is :

(a) 1   (b) 3

(c) 4   (d) None of these

46. The degree of the differential equation satisfying

$\sqrt{1 + x^2} + \sqrt{1 + y^2} = a (x - y)$ is :

(a) 1   (b) 2

(c) 3   (d) None of these

47. The order of the differential equation whose general solution is given by

$y = (c_1 + c_2) \cos (x + c_3) - c_4 e^{x + c_5}$ where,

c_1, c_2, c_3, c_4, c_5, are arbitrary constants, is :

(a) 5   (b) 4

(c) 3   (d) 2

48. A population grows at the rate of 5% per year. Then the population will be doubled in :

(a) 10 log 2 years   (b) 20 log 2 years

(c) 30 log 2 years   (d) None of these

49. The line normal to a given curve at each point (x, y) on the curve passes through the point (3, 0). If the curve contains the point (3, 4), then its equation is :

(a) $x^2 + y^2 + 6x - 7 = 0$

(b) $x^2 + y^2 - 6x + 7 = 0$

(c) $x^2 + y^2 - 6x - 7 = 0$

(d) None of these

50. The solution of the equation $\dfrac{dy}{dx}(x^2y^3 + xy) = 1$ satisfying $y (1) = \sqrt{2}$ is :

(a) $x\left(2 - y^2 + e^{\frac{-y^2}{2} + 1}\right) = 1$

(b) $x\left(2 + y^2 + e^{\frac{-y^2}{2} + 1}\right) = 1$

(c) $x\left(2 - y^2 + e^{\frac{-y^2}{2} + 1}\right) = 2$

(d) None of these

51. Solution of the equation

$x\, dy - [y + xy^3 (1 + \log x)]\, dx = 0$ is :

(a) $\dfrac{-x^2}{y^2} = \dfrac{2x^3}{3}\left(\dfrac{2}{3} + \log x\right) + C$

(b) $\dfrac{x^2}{y^2} = \dfrac{2x^3}{3}\left(\dfrac{2}{3} + \log x\right) + C$

(c) $\dfrac{-x^2}{y^2} = \dfrac{x^3}{3}\left(\dfrac{2}{3} + \log x\right) + C$

(d) None of these

52. The differential equation satisfied by

$ax^2 + by^2 = 1$ is :

(a) $xy\, y'' + xy'^2 + yy' = 0$

(b) $xy\, y'' + xy'^2 - yy' = 0$

(c) $xy\, y'' - xy'^2 + yy' = 0$

(d) None of these

53. The differential equation of the family of general circles is :

(a) $y''' (1 + y'^2) - 3y' y''^2 = 0$

(b) $y''' (1 + y'^2) + 3y' y''^2 = 0$

(c) $y''' (1 + y'^2) - 3y'' y'^2 = 0$

(d) None of these

54. The equation of the curve passing through the origin if the mid point of the segment of the normal drawn at any point of the curve and x – axis lies on the parabola $2y^2 = x$:

(a) $y^2 = 2x - 1 - e^{2x}$ (b) $y^2 = 2x + 1 + e^{2x}$

(c) $y^2 = 2x + 1 - e^{2x}$ (d) None of these

55. Solution of the equation

$(1 + e^{x/y})\, dx + e^{x/y}\left(1 - \dfrac{x}{y}\right) dy = 0$ is :

(a) $x + ye^{x/y} = C$ (b) $x - ye^{x/y} = C$

(c) $y + xe^{x/y} = C$ (d) None of these

56. The solution of the differential equation $y_1 y_3 = y_2^2$ is :

(a) $x = c_1\, e^{c_2 y} + c_3$ (b) $y = c_1\, e^{c_2 x} + c_3$

(c) $2x = c_1\, e^{c_2 y} + c_3$ (d) None of these

57. If $2f(x) = f'(x)$ and $f(0) = 3$, then $f(2)$ equals :

(a) $4e^3$ (b) $3e^4$

(c) $2e^3$ (d) $3e^2$

58. The equation of the curve satisfying the differential equation $y_2\,(x^2+1) = 4xy_1$, passing through the point $(0, -4)$ and having slope of tangent at $x = 0$ as 4 is :

(a) $y = 4\left(\dfrac{x^5}{5} + x + \dfrac{2x^3}{3} - 1\right)$

(b) $y = 4\left(\dfrac{x^5}{5} - x + \dfrac{2x^3}{3} - 1\right)$

(c) $y = 4\left(\dfrac{x^5}{5} + x + \dfrac{2x^3}{3} + 1\right)$

(d) None of these

59. The differential equation of all ellipses centred at the origin is :

(a) $xyy_2 - xy_1^2 + yy_1 = 0$

(b) $xyy_2 + xy_1^2 - yy_1 = 0$

(c) $xyy_2 + xy_1^2 + yy_1 = 0$

(d) None of these

60. A curve passing through the point $(1, 1)$ has the property that the perpendicular distance of the origin from the normal at any point P of the curve is equal to the distance of P from the x –axis. The equation of the curve is :

(a) $x^2 + y^2 + 2x = 0$ (b) $x^2 + y^2 - 2x = 0$

(c) $x^2 + y^2 - 2y = 0$ (d) None of these

61. A curve $y = f(x)$ passes through the point $P(1, 1)$. The normal to the curve at P is $a(y - 1) + (x - 1) = 0$. If the slope of the tangent at any point on the curve is proportional to the ordinate of the point, then the equation of the curve is :

(a) $y = e^{k\,(x-1)}$ (b) $y = e^{kx}$

(c) $y = e^{k\,(x-2)}$ (d) None of these

62. If the solution of the differential equation

$(x^2 + 4y^2 + 4xy)\, dy = (2x + 4y + 1)\, dx$ is :

$V - 2\log |V^2 + 4V + 2| + \dfrac{3}{\sqrt{2}}\log\left|\dfrac{V + 2 - \sqrt{2}}{V + 2 + \sqrt{2}}\right| = x + C$

then :

(a) $V = x + 2y$ (b) $V = 2x + y$

(c) $V = x + y$ (d) None of these

63. Solution of differential equation $x\, dy - y\, dx = 0$ represents :

(a) parabola whose vertex is at origin

(b) circle whose centre is at origin

(c) a rectangular hyperbola

(d) straight line passing through origin

64. The integrating factor of the differential equation $\dfrac{dy}{dx}\,(x\log x) + y = 2\log x$ is given by :

(a) $\log(\log x)$ (b) e^x

(c) $\log x$ (d) x

65. The general solution of the differential equation $\dfrac{dy}{dx} = \dfrac{y}{x}$ is :

(a) $\log y = kx$ (b) $y = kx$

(c) $y = \dfrac{k}{x}$ (d) $y = k\log x$

66. Integrating factor of differential equation

$\cos x\,\dfrac{dy}{dx} + y\sin x = 1$ is :

(a) $\sin x$ (b) $\sec x$

(c) $\tan x$ (d) $\cos x$

67. D.E. for $y = A \cos \alpha x + B \sin \alpha x$, where A and B are arbitrary constants is :

   (a) $\dfrac{d^2y}{dx^2} + \alpha y = 0$ (b) $\dfrac{d^2y}{dx^2} - \alpha y = 0$

   (c) $\dfrac{d^2y}{dx^2} - \alpha^2 y = 0$ (d) $\dfrac{d^2y}{dx^2} + \alpha^2 y = 0$

68. The solution of $\dfrac{dy}{dx} + \sqrt{\dfrac{1-y^2}{1-x^2}} = 0$ is :

   (a) $\sin^{-1}x \cdot \sin^{-1}y = C$ (b) $\sin^{-1}x = C \sin^{-1}y$
   (c) $\sin^{-1}x - \sin^{-1}y = C$ (d) $\sin^{-1}x + \sin^{-1}y = C$

69. The slope of the tangent at (x, y) to a curve passing through $\left(1, \dfrac{\pi}{4}\right)$ is given by $\dfrac{y}{x} - \cos^2\dfrac{y}{x}$, then the equation of the curve is :

   (a) $y = x \tan^{-1}\left[\log\left(\dfrac{e}{x}\right)\right]$

   (b) $y = x \tan^{-1}\left[\log\left(\dfrac{x}{e}\right)\right]$

   (c) $y = \tan^{-1}\left[\log\left(\dfrac{e}{x}\right)\right]$

   (d) None of these

70. The solution of the differential equation

   $x^2 \dfrac{dy}{dx} - xy = 1 + \cos\dfrac{y}{x}$ is :

   (a) $\cos\dfrac{y}{x} = 1 + \dfrac{c}{x}$

   (b) $x^2 = (c + x^2)\tan\dfrac{y}{x}$

   (c) $\tan\dfrac{y}{2x} = c - \dfrac{1}{2x^2}$

   (d) $\tan\dfrac{y}{x} = c + \dfrac{1}{x}$

71. The solution of the differential equation

   $2x\dfrac{dy}{dx} - y = 3$ represents :

   (a) circle   (b) straight line
   (c) ellipse   (d) parabola

72. Solution of the differential equation

   $\dfrac{dy}{dx} + yf'(x) - f(x) \cdot f'(x) = 0$ is

   (a) $y = f(x) - 1 + ce^{-f(x)}$
   (b) $y = f(x) + 1 + ce^{-f(x)}$
   (c) $y = f(x) - 1 + ce^{f(x)}$
   (d) None of these

73. The equation of family of curves for which the length of the part of the tangent between the point of contact (x, y) and the y-axis is equal to the y-intercept of the tangent, is :

   (a) $x^2 + y^2 + kx = 0$
   (b) $x^2 + y^2 + ky = 0$
   (c) $x^2 + y^2 + k_1 x + k_2 y = 0$
   (d) None of these

74. The orthogonal trajectories of the family of curves $a^{n-1}y = x^n$ is :

   (a) $ny - x^2 = C$ (b) $ny^2 + x^2 = C$
   (c) $nx^2 - y^2 = C$ (d) $nx^2 + y^2 = C$

75. The curve satisfying
   $y\,dx - x\,dy + \log x\,dx = 0 \ (x > 0)$
   passing through $(1, -1)$ is :

   (a) $y + \log x + 1 = 0$
   (b) $-y^2 + \log x + 1 = 0$
   (c) $y^3 + (\log x)^2 + 1 = 0$
   (d) None of these

76. Solution of the equation
   $yy_1 \sin x = \cos x (\sin x - y^2)$ is :

   (a) $y^2 = \sin x + \dfrac{c}{\sin^2 x}$

   (b) $y^2 = \dfrac{1}{3}\sin x + \dfrac{c}{\sin^2 x}$

   (c) $y^2 = \dfrac{2}{3}\sin x + \dfrac{c}{\sin^2 x}$

   (d) None of these

77. Differential equation of all straight lines which are at a fixed distance p from the origin is :

   (a) $(y + xy_1)^2 = p^2(1 + y_1^2)$
   (b) $(y - xy_1)^2 = p^2(1 + y_1^2)$
   (c) $(y + xy_1)^2 = p^2(1 - y_1^2)$
   (d) None of these

78. The equation to the curve $y = f(x)$ such that $\dfrac{d^2y}{dx^2} = \sqrt{1 - \left(\dfrac{dy}{dx}\right)^2}$ and the tangent to the curve at the origin is inclined at $\dfrac{\pi}{4}$ with the positive direction of the x-axis is :

   (a) $y - \sin x = 0$ (b) $y + \sin x = 0$
   (c) $y - \cos x = 0$ (d) $y + \cos x = 0$

79. Solution of the equation

$(1 - xy - x^5y^5) dx = x^2 (x^4y^4 + 1) dy$ is :

(a) $x = ce^{xy + \frac{1}{5}x^5y^5}$ (b) $y = ce^{xy + \frac{1}{5}x^5y^5}$

(c) $y = ce^{xy - \frac{1}{5}x^5y^5}$ (d) None of these

80. If $x\dfrac{dy}{dx} + y = x \cdot \dfrac{f(xy)}{f'(xy)}$ then f(xy) is equal to :

(a) $ke^{x^2/2}$ (b) $ke^{y^2/2}$

(c) $ke^{xy/2}$ (d) None of these

81. If f(x), g(x) are twice differentiable functions on [0, 2] satisfying $f''(x) = g''(x)$, $f'(1) = 2g'(1) = 4$ and f(2) = 3 g(2) = 9, then f(x) – g(x) at x = 4 equals :

(a) 0   (b) 10

(c) 8   (d) 2

82. The differential equation $y + x\dfrac{dx}{dy} = 3$ represents

(a) a family of circles having centre on y-axis

(b) a family of circles having centre on x-axis

(c) a family of ellipses

(d) None of these

83. The function y = f(x) such that,

$\dfrac{dy}{dx} - y \log 2 = 2^{\sin x} (\cos x - 1) \log 2$, y being

bounded when x → ∞, is :

(a) $y = 2^{\cos x}$ (b) $y = 2^{\sin x}$

(c) $y = 2^{\cos 2x}$ (d) $y = 2^{\sin 2x}$

84. Solution of the differential equation

$(2ax + x^2)\dfrac{dy}{dx} = a^2 + 2ax$ is

(a) $x (x + 2a)^3 = ce^{2y/a}$

(b) $x (x - 2a)^3 e^{-2y/a} = c$

(c) $x^3(x + 2a) = ce^{2y/a}$

(d) $x^4(1 + 5a) = ce^{2x/5}$

85. Solution of the equation

$xy\dfrac{dy}{dx} = \dfrac{1 + y^2}{1 + x^2} (1 + x + x^2)$ is :

(a) $\dfrac{1}{2} \log (1 + y^2) = \log x - \tan^{-1} x + C$

(b) $\dfrac{1}{2} \log (1 + y^2) = \log x + \tan^{-1} x + C$

(c) $\dfrac{1}{2} \log (1 + y^2) = - \log x - \tan^{-1} x + C$

(d) None of these

86. Solution of the equation

$\sin y \dfrac{dy}{dx} = \cos y (1 - x \cos y)$ is :

(a) $\cos y = x + 1 + ce^x$ (b) $\sec y = x - 1 + ce^x$

(c) $\sec y = x + 1 + ce^x$ (d) None of these

87. The differential equation of all circles passing through the origin and having their centres on the x-axis is :

(a) $2xyy_1 = y^2 - x^2$ (b) $2xyy_1 = x^2 - y^2$

(c) $xyy_1 = x^2 - y^2$ (d) None of these

88. Solution of the equation

$\dfrac{dy}{dx} - x \tan (y - x) = 1$ is :

(a) $\log \sin (y - x) = \dfrac{1}{2} x^2 + C$

(b) $\log \sin (x - y) = \dfrac{1}{2} x^2 + C$

(c) $\log \cos (y - x) = \dfrac{1}{2} x^2 + C$

(d) $\log \cos (y - x) = -\dfrac{1}{2} x^2 + C$

89. At each point (x, y) of the curve the intercept of the tangent on y–axis is equal to $2xy^2$. The equation of the curve is :

(a) $x + x^2y = cy$ (b) $x - x^2y = cy$

(c) $y + y^2x = cx$ (d) None of these

90. The solution of $\dfrac{dy}{dx} = 2^{y-x}$ is :

(a) $2^x + 2^y = k$ (b) $2^x - 2 \cdot 2^y = k$

(c) $\dfrac{1}{2^x} - \dfrac{1}{2^y} = k$ (d) $\dfrac{1}{2^x} + \dfrac{1}{2^y} = k$

91. If m and n are the order and degree of the differential equation

$\left(\dfrac{d^2y}{dx^2}\right)^5 + 4\dfrac{\left(\dfrac{d^2y}{dx^2}\right)^3}{\left(\dfrac{d^3y}{dx^3}\right)} + \dfrac{d^3y}{dx^3} = x^2 - 1$, then :

(a) m = 3, n = 1   (b) m = 3, n = 3

(c) m = 3, n = 2   (d) m = 3, n = 3

92. The solution of the differential equation

$\frac{dy}{dx} = e^{y+x} e^{y-x}$ is :

(a) $e^x (x + 1) + 1 = y$ (b) $e^x (x - 1) + 1 = y$
(c) $e^x (x + 1) = y$ (d) None of these

93. The curve for which the slope of the tangent at any point equals the ratio of the abscissa to the ordinate of the point is :

(a) a circle
(b) an ellipse
(c) a rectangular hyperbola
(d) None of these

94. Solution of the differential equation

$\frac{dy}{dx} + \frac{y}{x} = \sin x$ is :

(a) $x (y + \cos x) = \cos x + C$
(b) $x (y - \cos x) = \sin x + C$
(c) $x (y + \cos x) = \sin x + C$
(d) None of these

95. The second order differential equation is :

(a) $y'^2 + x = y^2$ (b) $y'y'' + y = \sin x$
(c) $y''' + y'' = y^2$ (d) $y' = y$

96. If $y' = \frac{x - y}{x + y}$, then its solution is :

(a) $y^2 + 2xy - x^2 = C$ (b) $y^2 + 2xy + x^2 = C$
(c) $y^2 - 2xy - x^2 = C$ (d) $y^2 - 2xy + x^2 = C$

97. The solution of $y' = 1 + x + y^2 + xy^2$, $y(0) = 0$ is

(a) $y^2 = \exp \left(x + \frac{x^2}{2} \right) - 1$

(b) $y^2 = 1 + c \exp \left(x + \frac{x^2}{2} \right)$

(c) $y = \tan (c + x + x^2)$

(d) $y = \tan \left(x + \frac{x^2}{2} \right)$

98. Family $y = Ax + A^3$ of curves is represented by the differential equation of degree :

(a) 3   (b) 2
(c) 1   (d) None of these

99. Family of curves $y = e^x (A \cos x + B \sin x)$, represents the differential equation :

(a) $\frac{d^2y}{dx^2} = 2\frac{dy}{dx} - y$ (b) $\frac{d^2y}{dx^2} = 2\frac{dy}{dx} - 2y$

(c) $\frac{d^2y}{dx^2} = \frac{dy}{dx} - 2y$ (d) $\frac{d^2y}{dx^2} = 2\frac{dy}{dx} + y$

100. Solution of $y\, dx - x\, dy = x^2 y\, dx$ is :

(a) $ye^{x^2} = cx^2$ (b) $ye^{-x^2} = cx^2$
(c) $y^2 e^{x^2} = cx^2$ (d) $y^2 e^{-x^2} = cx^2$

101. For solving $\frac{dy}{dx} = (4x + y + 1)$,

suitable substitution is :
(a) $y = Vx$ (b) $y = 4x + V$
(c) $y = 4x$ (d) $y + 4x + 1 = V$

102. If integrating factor of :

$x (1 - x^2)\, dy + (2x^2 y - y - ax^3)\, dx = 0$ is $e^{\int p\, dx}$
then $p =$

(a) $\frac{2x^2 - ax^3}{x (1 - x^2)}$ (b) $2x^2 - 1$

(c) $\frac{2x^2 - 1}{ax^3}$ (d) $\frac{2x^2 - 1}{x (1 - x^2)}$

103. The order and degree of the differential

equation $\frac{d^2y}{dx^2} + \left(\frac{dy}{dx}\right)^{1/3} + x^{1/4} = 0$ are respectively

(a) 2, 3   (b) 3, 3
(c) 2, 6   (d) 2, 4

104. Solution of the differential equation

$\sqrt{a + x}\, \frac{dy}{dx} + xy = 0$ is :

(a) $y = Ae^{2/3} (2a - x) \sqrt{x + a}$
(b) $y = Ae^{-2/3} (a - x) \sqrt{x + a}$
(c) $y = Ae^{2/3} (2a + x) \sqrt{x + a}$
(d) $y = Ae^{-2/3} (2a - x) \sqrt{x + a}$
where A is an arbitrary constant.

105. Degree of the differential equation

$\left(\frac{d^2y}{dx^2}\right)^3 = \left(1 + \frac{dy}{dx}\right)^{1/2}$ is :

(a) 2   (b) 3

(c) $\frac{1}{2}$ (d) 6

106. The solution of $x^2 + y^2 \frac{dy}{dx} = 4$ is :

(a) $x^2 + y^2 = 12x + C$ (b) $x^2 + y^2 = 3x + C$
(c) $x^3 + y^3 = 3x + C$ (d) $x^3 + y^3 = 12x + C$

107. The solution of $x\, dx + y\, dx = x^2 y\, dy - xy^2\, dx$ is

(a) $x^2 - 1 = c (1 + y^2)$ (b) $x^2 + 1 = c (1 - y^2)$
(c) $x^3 - 1 = c (1 + y^3)$ (d) $x^3 + 1 = c (1 - y^3)$

108. The family of curves in which the subtangent at any point of a curve is double the abscissa, is given by :

(a) $x = cy^2$ (b) $y = cx^2$
(c) $x^2 = cy^2$ (d) $y = cx$

109. The population p(t) at time t of a certain mouse species satisfies the differential equation $\frac{dp(t)}{dt} = 0.5\,p(t) - 450$. If p(0) = 850, then the time at which the population becomes zero is :

[AIEEE - 2012]

(a) 2 *ln* 18   (b) *ln* 9

(c) $\frac{1}{2}$ *ln* 18   (d) *ln* 18

110. Let I be the purchase value of an equipment and V(t) be the value after it has been used for t years. The value V(t) depreciates at a rate given by differential equation $\frac{dV(t)}{dt} = -k(T - t)$, where k > 0 is a constant and T is the total life in years of the equipment. Then the scrap value V(T) of the equipment is : **[AIEEE - 2011]**

(a) e^{-kT} (b) $T^2 - \frac{1}{k}$

(c) $I - \frac{kT^2}{2}$ (d) $I - \frac{k(T-t)^2}{2}$

111. If $\frac{dy}{dx} = y + 3 > 0$ and y(0) = 2, then y (*ln* 2) is equal to : **[AIEEE - 2011]**

(a) −2   (b) 7

(c) 5   (d) 13

112. Solution of the differential equation

$\cos x\,dy = y\,(\sin x - y)\,dx$, $0 < x < \frac{\pi}{2}$ is :

[AIEEE - 2010]

(a) y sec x = tan x + c

(b) y tan x = sec x + c

(c) tan x = (sec x + c) y

(d) sec x = (tan x + c) y

113. The differential equation which represents the family of curves $y = c_1 e^{c_2 x}$ where c_1 and c_2 are arbitrary constants is : **[AIEEE - 2009]**

(a) $y' = y^2$ (b) $y'' = y'\,y$

(c) $yy'' = y'$ (d) $yy'' = (y')^2$

114. The solution of the differential equation $\frac{dy}{dx} = \frac{x + y}{x}$ satisfying the condition y(1) = 1 is :

[AIEEE - 2008]

(a) y = *ln* x + x   (b) y = x *ln* x + x^2

(c) y = $xe^{(x-1)}$ (d) y = x *ln* x + x

115. The differential equation of the family of circles with fixed radius 5 units and centre on the line y = 2 is : **[AIEEE - 2008]**

(a) $(x - 2)\,y'^2 = 25 - (y - 2)^2$

(b) $(y - 2)\,y'^2 = 25 - (y - 2)^2$

(c) $(y - 2)^2\,y'^2 = 25 - (y - 2)^2$

(d) $(x - 2)^2\,y'^2 = 25 - (y - 2)^2$

116. The differential equation of all circles passing through the origin and having their centres on the x-axis is : **[AIEEE - 2007]**

(a) $x^2 = y^2 + xy\frac{dy}{dx}$ (b) $x^2 = y^2 + 3xy\frac{dy}{dx}$

(c) $y^2 = x^2 + 2xy\frac{dy}{dx}$ (d) $y^2 = x^2 - 2xy\frac{dy}{dx}$

117. The differential equation representing the family of curves $y^2 = 2c\,(x + \sqrt{c})$, where c > 0, is parameter, is of order and degree as follows :

[AIEEE - 2005]

(a) order 1, degree 2   (b) order 1, degree 1

(c) order 1, degree 3   (d) order 2, degree 2

118. A curve passes through the point $\left(1, \frac{\pi}{6}\right)$. Let the slope of the curve at each point (x, y) be $\frac{y}{x} + \sec\left(\frac{y}{x}\right)$; x > 0. Then the equation of the curve is

(a) $\sin\left(\frac{y}{x}\right) = \log x + \frac{1}{2}$

(b) $\csc\left(\frac{y}{x}\right) = \log x + 2$

(c) $\sec\left(\frac{2y}{x}\right) = \log x + 2$

(d) $\cos\left(\frac{2y}{x}\right) = \log x + \frac{1}{2}$

119. The solution of the differential equation $\dfrac{dy}{dx} = \dfrac{x+y}{x}$ satisfies the condition $y(1) = 1$ is

(a) $y = x \log x + x$

(b) $y = \log x + x$

(c) $y = x \log x + x^2$

(d) $y = x\, e^{(x-1)}$

120. The differential equation of the family of circles with fixed radius 5 units and centre on the line $y = 2$ is

(a) $(x-2)^2\, y'^2 = 25 - (y-2)^2$

(b) $(x-2)\, y'^2 = 25 - (y-2)^2$

(c) $(y-2)\, y'^2 = 25 - (y-2)^2$

(d) $(y-2)^2\, y'^2 = 25 - (y-2)^2$

121. Let y be the solution of the problem $y' - y = 1 + 5e^{-x}$ with $y(0) = y_0$.

If $\lim\limits_{x \to \infty} |y(x)|$ is finite, then y_0 is

(a) $-7/2$

(b) 0

(c) 9

(d) -11

122. Solution of the differential equation

$\cos x\, dy = y\, (\sin x - y)\, dx;\ 0 < x < \pi/2$ is

(a) $y \sec x = \tan x + c$

(b) $y\, (\tan x + c) = \sec x$

(c) $y \tan x = \sec x + c$

(d) $\tan x = (\sec x + c)\, y$

123. The differential equation which represents the family of curves $y = c_1\, e^{c_2 x}$ where c_1 and c_2 are arbitrary constants, is

(a) $y'' = yy'$

(b) $yy'' = y'$

(c) $yy'' = (y')^2$

(d) $y' = y^2$

ANSWER KEY

1. (b)	2. (b)	3. (a)	4. (b)	5. (c)	6. (a)	7. (a)	8. (b)	9. (a)	10. (b)
11. (a)	12. (c)	13. (c)	14. (b)	15. (a)	16. (d)	17. (b)	18. (d)	19. (b)	20. (c)
21. (a)	22. (a)	23. (c)	24. (a)	25. (a)	26. (c)	27. (c)	28. (c)	29. (a)	30. (b)
31. (a)	32. (c)	33. (b)	34. (a)	35. (a)	36. (c)	37. (c)	38. (a)	39. (b)	40. (c)
41. (b)	42. (c)	43. (c)	44. (b)	45. (d)	46. (a)	47. (c)	48. (b)	49. (c)	50. (a)
51. (a)	52. (b)	53. (a)	54. (c)	55. (a)	56. (b)	57. (b)	58. (a)	59. (b)	60. (b)
61. (a)	62. (a)	63. (d)	64. (c)	65. (b)	66. (b)	67. (d)	68. (d)	69. (a)	70. (c)
71. (d)	72. (a)	73. (a)	74. (b)	75. (a)	76. (c)	77. (b)	78. (b)	79. (a)	80. (a)
81. (b)	82. (a)	83. (b)	84. (a)	85. (b)	86. (c)	87. (a)	88. (a)	89. (b)	90. (c)
91. (c)	92. (d)	93. (c)	94. (c)	95. (b)	96. (a)	97. (d)	98. (a)	99. (b)	100. (c)
101. (d)	102. (d)	103. (a)	104. (a)	105. (d)	106. (d)	107. (a)	108. (a)	109. (a)	110. (c)
111. (b)	112. (d)	113. (d)	114. (d)	115. (c)	116. (c)	117. (c)	118. (a)	119. (a)	120. (b)
121. (a)	122. (b)	123. (c)							

Chapter 26

MATRICES

MULTIPLE CHOICE QUESTIONS

1. The matrix $\begin{bmatrix} 0 & 5 & -7 \\ -5 & 0 & 11 \\ 7 & -11 & 0 \end{bmatrix}$ is known as :

   (a) skew-symmetric matrix

   (b) symmetric matrix

   (c) diagonal matrix

   (d) upper triangular matrix

2. If $A = \begin{bmatrix} a & 0 & 0 \\ 0 & a & 0 \\ 0 & 0 & a \end{bmatrix}$ then the value of | adj A | is :

   (a) a^{27} (b) a^9

   (c) a^6 (d) a^2

3. The equations $x + 2y + 3z = 1$, $x - y + 4z = 0$, $2x + y + 7z = 1$ have

   (a) only two solutions

   (b) only one solution

   (c) no solution

   (d) infinitely many solutions

4. If A is a non-zero column matrix of order m × 1 and B is a non-zero row matrix of order 1 × n, then rank of AB is equal to :

   (a) n   (b) m

   (c) 1   (d) None of these

5. The matrix product $\begin{bmatrix} 1 \\ -2 \\ 3 \end{bmatrix} \times [4\ 5\ 2] \times \begin{bmatrix} 2 \\ -3 \\ 5 \end{bmatrix}$ equals

   (a) $\begin{bmatrix} 3 \\ -6 \\ 9 \end{bmatrix}$ (b) $\begin{bmatrix} 3 \\ 6 \\ 9 \end{bmatrix}$

   (c) $\begin{bmatrix} 3 \\ 6 \\ -9 \end{bmatrix}$ (d) None of these

6. If A is a square matrix, then A + A^T is a

   (a) skew-symmetric matrix

   (b) symmetric matrix

   (c) diagonal matrix

   (d) None of these

7. The inverse of a symmetric matrix is :

   (a) diagonal matrix

   (b) symmetric matrix

   (c) skew-symmetric matrix

   (d) None of these

8. If $A = \begin{bmatrix} 1 & 3 \\ 2 & -2 \end{bmatrix}$, then A^{-1} equals

   (a) $-\frac{1}{8}\begin{bmatrix} -2 & -3 \\ -2 & 1 \end{bmatrix}$ (b) $-\frac{1}{8}\begin{bmatrix} 3 & 1 \\ -2 & 2 \end{bmatrix}$

   (c) $\frac{1}{8}\begin{bmatrix} -1 & -3 \\ -2 & 2 \end{bmatrix}$ (d) None of these

9. If $A = \begin{bmatrix} i & 0 \\ 0 & i \end{bmatrix}$, $n \in N$, then A^{4n} equals

   (a) $\begin{bmatrix} 0 & i \\ i & 0 \end{bmatrix}$ (b) $\begin{bmatrix} 0 & 0 \\ 0 & 0 \end{bmatrix}$

   (c) $\begin{bmatrix} 1 & 0 \\ 0 & 1 \end{bmatrix}$ (d) $\begin{bmatrix} 0 & i \\ i & 0 \end{bmatrix}$

10. If $A = \begin{bmatrix} 3 & 4 \\ 2 & 4 \end{bmatrix}$, $B = \begin{bmatrix} -2 & -2 \\ 0 & -1 \end{bmatrix}$, then $(A + B)^{-1} =$

   (a) is a skew symmetric matrix

   (b) A^{-1} + B^{-1}

   (c) does not exist

   (d) None of these

11. Inverse of $\begin{bmatrix} 1 & 2 & 3 \\ 2 & 3 & 4 \\ 3 & 4 & 6 \end{bmatrix}$ is :

(a) $\begin{bmatrix} -2 & 0 & 1 \\ 0 & 3 & -2 \\ 1 & -2 & 1 \end{bmatrix}$ (b) $\begin{bmatrix} 2 & 0 & -1 \\ 0 & -3 & 2 \\ -1 & 2 & -1 \end{bmatrix}$

(c) $\begin{bmatrix} 1 & 2 & 3 \\ 2 & 3 & 4 \\ 3 & 4 & 6 \end{bmatrix}$ (d) None of these

12. If $AB = A$ and $BA = B$, then B^2 is equal to :

(a) B   (b) A   (c) 1   (d) 0

13. If $A = \begin{bmatrix} 1 & 2 \\ 2 & 1 \end{bmatrix}$, then adj A is equal to :

(a) $\begin{bmatrix} -1 & 2 \\ 2 & -1 \end{bmatrix}$ (b) $\begin{bmatrix} 1 & -2 \\ -2 & 1 \end{bmatrix}$

(c) $\begin{bmatrix} 2 & 1 \\ 1 & 1 \end{bmatrix}$ (d) $\begin{bmatrix} 1 & -2 \\ -2 & 1 \end{bmatrix}$

14. If $A = \begin{bmatrix} a & b \\ b & a \end{bmatrix}$, $A^2 = \begin{bmatrix} \alpha & \beta \\ \beta & \alpha \end{bmatrix}$, then :

(a) $\alpha = 2ab,\ \beta = a^2 + b^2$

(b) $\alpha = a^2 + b^2,\ \beta = a^2 - b^2$

(c) $\alpha = a^2 + b^2,\ \beta = 2ab$

(d) $\alpha = a^2 + b^2,\ \beta = ab$

15. If the matrix AB is zero, then :

(a) It is not necessary that either $A = 0$ or $B = 0$

(b) $A = 0$ or $B = 0$

(c) $A = 0$ and $B = 0$

(d) All the above statements are wrong.

16. Let A be an invertible matrix. Which of the following is not ture ?

(a) $(A')^{-1}=(A^{-1})'$ (b) $A^{-1}=|A|^{-1}$

(c) $(A^2)^{-1}= (A^{-1})^2$ (d) None of these

17. If $A = [a_{ij}]$ is a scalar matrix of order n × n such that $a_{ii} = k$ for all i, then trace of A is equal to :

(a) k^n (b) $\dfrac{n}{k}$

(c) nk   (d) None of these

18. If $AB = O$ for the matrices

$A = \begin{bmatrix} \cos^2 \theta & \cos \theta \sin \theta \\ \cos \theta \sin \theta & \sin^2 \theta \end{bmatrix}$

and $B = \begin{bmatrix} \cos^2 \phi & \cos \phi \sin \phi \\ \cos \phi \sin \phi & \sin^2 \phi \end{bmatrix}$, then $\theta - \phi$ is

(a) an odd multiple of $\dfrac{\pi}{2}$

(b) an odd multiple of π

(c) an even multiple of $\dfrac{\pi}{2}$

(d) 0

19. The multiplicative inverse of

$A = \begin{bmatrix} \cos \theta & -\sin \theta \\ \sin \theta & \cos \theta \end{bmatrix}$ is :

(a) $\begin{bmatrix} \cos \theta & \sin \theta \\ \sin \theta & -\cos \theta \end{bmatrix}$ (b) $\begin{bmatrix} -\cos \theta & -\sin \theta \\ \sin \theta & \cos \theta \end{bmatrix}$

(c) $\begin{bmatrix} \cos \theta & \sin \theta \\ -\sin \theta & \cos \theta \end{bmatrix}$ (d) $\begin{bmatrix} -\cos \theta & -\sin \theta \\ -\sin \theta & \cos \theta \end{bmatrix}$

20. Let $A = \begin{bmatrix} 1 & 2 \\ 3 & -5 \end{bmatrix}$ and $B = \begin{bmatrix} 1 & 0 \\ 0 & 2 \end{bmatrix}$ and X be a matrix such that $A = BX$ then X is equal to :

(a) $\dfrac{1}{2}\begin{bmatrix} 2 & 4 \\ 3 & -5 \end{bmatrix}$ (b) $\dfrac{1}{2}\begin{bmatrix} -2 & 4 \\ 3 & 5 \end{bmatrix}$

(c) $\begin{bmatrix} 2 & 4 \\ 3 & -5 \end{bmatrix}$ (d) None of these

21. The value of x for which the matrix product :

$\begin{bmatrix} 2 & 0 & 7 \\ 0 & 1 & 0 \\ 1 & -2 & 1 \end{bmatrix}\begin{bmatrix} -x & 14x & 7x \\ 0 & 1 & 0 \\ x & -4x & -2x \end{bmatrix}$

equals an identity matrix is :

(a) $\dfrac{1}{5}$ (b) $\dfrac{1}{4}$

(c) $\dfrac{1}{3}$ (d) $\dfrac{1}{2}$

22. Let $A = \begin{bmatrix} a & 0 & 0 \\ 0 & a & 0 \\ 0 & 0 & a \end{bmatrix}$, then A^n is equal to :

(a) $\begin{bmatrix} a^n & 0 & 0 \\ 0 & a^n & 0 \\ 0 & 0 & a \end{bmatrix}$ (b) $\begin{bmatrix} a^n & 0 & 0 \\ 0 & a & 0 \\ 0 & 0 & a \end{bmatrix}$

(c) $\begin{bmatrix} a^n & 0 & 0 \\ 0 & a^n & 0 \\ 0 & 0 & a^n \end{bmatrix}$ (d) $\begin{bmatrix} na & 0 & 0 \\ 0 & na & 0 \\ 0 & 0 & na \end{bmatrix}$

23. If A, B are two square matrices such that AB = A and BA = B, then :

(a) only B is idempotent

(b) A, B are idempotent

(c) only A is idempotent

(d) None of these

24. If $[1 \quad x \quad 1] \begin{bmatrix} 1 & 3 & 2 \\ 0 & 5 & 1 \\ 0 & 3 & 2 \end{bmatrix} \begin{bmatrix} x \\ 1 \\ -2 \end{bmatrix} = 0$, then x is :

(a) $-\dfrac{1}{2}$ (b) $\dfrac{1}{2}$

(c) 1 (d) -1

25. If $A = \begin{bmatrix} 0 & c & -b \\ -c & 0 & a \\ b & -a & 0 \end{bmatrix}$ and $B = \begin{bmatrix} a^2 & ab & ac \\ ab & b^2 & bc \\ ac & bc & c^2 \end{bmatrix}$ then

AB is equal to :

(a) B (b) A

(c) 0 (d) I

26. If A is a singular matrix, then adj A is :

(a) non-singular (b) singular

(c) symmetric (d) not defined

27. If A, B are two n × n non-singular matrices, then

(a) AB is non-singular (b) AB is singular

(c) $(AB)^{-1} = A^{-1}B^{-1}$ (d) $(AB)^{-1}$ does not exist

28. If $A = \begin{bmatrix} 1 & 0 & 0 \\ 0 & 1 & 0 \\ 0 & 0 & 1 \end{bmatrix}$, then $A^2 + 2A$ equals :

(a) 4A (b) 3A

(c) 2A (d) A

29. If $A = \begin{bmatrix} 1 & 2 & -1 \\ -1 & 1 & 2 \\ 2 & -1 & 1 \end{bmatrix}$, then det. (adj (adj A)) is:

(a) $(14)^4$ (b) $(14)^3$

(c) $(14)^2$ (d) $(14)^1$

30. If $A = \begin{bmatrix} 1 \\ 2 \\ 3 \end{bmatrix}$ and $B = \begin{bmatrix} -5 & 4 & 0 \\ 0 & 2 & -1 \\ 1 & -3 & 2 \end{bmatrix}$ then :

(a) $AB = \begin{bmatrix} -5 & 8 & 0 \\ 0 & 4 & -2 \\ 3 & -9 & 6 \end{bmatrix}$

(b) $AB = [-2 \quad -1 \quad 4]$

(c) $AB = \begin{bmatrix} -1 \\ 1 \\ 1 \end{bmatrix}$

(d) AB does not exist

31. If $A = \begin{bmatrix} \cos \alpha & \sin \alpha \\ -\sin \alpha & \cos \alpha \end{bmatrix}$, then A^2 is equal to :

(a) $\begin{bmatrix} \sin 2\alpha & \cos 2\alpha \\ \cos 2\alpha & -\sin 2\alpha \end{bmatrix}$ (b) $\begin{bmatrix} \cos 2\alpha & -\sin \alpha \\ -\sin \alpha & \cos 2\alpha \end{bmatrix}$

(c) $\begin{bmatrix} \cos 2\alpha & \sin 2\alpha \\ -\sin 2\alpha & \cos 2\alpha \end{bmatrix}$ (d) $\begin{bmatrix} 1 & 0 \\ 0 & 1 \end{bmatrix}$

32. If B is a non-singular matrix and A is a square matrix, then det $(B^{-1}AB)$ is equal to :

(a) det (A^{-1}) (b) det (B^{-1})

(c) det (A) (d) det (B)

33. If A is a square matrix such that $A^2 = I$, then A^{-1} is equal to :

(a) $A + I$ (b) A

(c) O (d) 2A

34. For any 2 × 2 matrix A, if $A \, (\text{adj } A) = \begin{bmatrix} 10 & 0 \\ 0 & 10 \end{bmatrix}$, then $|A|$ is equal to :

(a) 20 (b) 100

(c) 10 (d) 0

35. If A and B are two matrices such that A + B and AB are both defined, then :

(a) A, B are square matrices of same order

(b) Number of columns of A = Number of rows of B

(c) A and B can be any matrices

(d) None of these

36. If $\begin{bmatrix} 2 & 1 \\ 3 & 2 \end{bmatrix} A \begin{bmatrix} -3 & 2 \\ 5 & -3 \end{bmatrix} = \begin{bmatrix} 1 & 0 \\ 0 & 1 \end{bmatrix}$, then the matrix A is equal to :

(a) $\begin{bmatrix} 1 & 0 \\ 1 & 1 \end{bmatrix}$

(b) $\begin{bmatrix} 0 & 1 \\ 1 & 1 \end{bmatrix}$

(c) $\begin{bmatrix} 1 & 1 \\ 1 & 0 \end{bmatrix}$

(d) $\begin{bmatrix} 1 & 1 \\ 0 & 1 \end{bmatrix}$

37. If $A = (a_{ij})_{2 \times 2}$, where $a_{ij} = i + j$, then A is equal to :

(a) $\begin{bmatrix} 1 & 1 \\ 2 & 2 \end{bmatrix}$

(b) $\begin{bmatrix} 1 & 2 \\ 1 & 2 \end{bmatrix}$

(c) $\begin{bmatrix} 1 & 2 \\ 3 & 4 \end{bmatrix}$

(d) $\begin{bmatrix} 2 & 3 \\ 3 & 4 \end{bmatrix}$

38. If $A = \begin{bmatrix} 3 & 2 \\ 1 & 4 \end{bmatrix}$, then A (adj A) is equal to :

(a) $\begin{bmatrix} 10 & 1 \\ 1 & 10 \end{bmatrix}$

(b) $\begin{bmatrix} 10 & 0 \\ 0 & 10 \end{bmatrix}$

(c) $\begin{bmatrix} 0 & 10 \\ 10 & 0 \end{bmatrix}$

(d) None of the above

39. If A and B are any 2×2 matrices, then det (A + B) = 0 implies :

(a) det A = 0 and det B = 0

(b) det A + det B = 0

(c) det A = 0 or det B = 0

(d) None of these

40. If a 3×3 matrix A has its inverse equal to A, then A^2 is equal to :

(a) $\begin{bmatrix} 0 & 1 & 0 \\ 1 & 1 & 1 \\ 0 & 1 & 0 \end{bmatrix}$

(b) $\begin{bmatrix} 1 & 0 & 1 \\ 0 & 0 & 0 \\ 1 & 0 & 1 \end{bmatrix}$

(c) $\begin{bmatrix} 1 & 0 & 0 \\ 0 & 1 & 0 \\ 0 & 0 & 1 \end{bmatrix}$

(d) $\begin{bmatrix} 1 & 1 & 1 \\ 1 & 1 & 1 \\ 1 & 1 & 1 \end{bmatrix}$

41. The matrix $\begin{bmatrix} \cos \alpha & \sin \alpha \\ -\sin \alpha & \cos \alpha \end{bmatrix}$ is :

(a) Symmetric

(b) Unique

(c) Orthogonal

(d) Scalar

42. The system of equations :

$2x - 3y + 5z = 12$,

$3x + y + \lambda z = \mu$,

$x - 7y + 8z = 17$ has

(a) a unique solution if $\lambda \neq 2$

(b) infinite no. of solutions if $\lambda = 2$ and $\mu = 7$

(c) no solution if $\lambda = 2$, $\mu \neq 7$

(d) All of these

43. The rank of the matrix

$\begin{bmatrix} 1 & 4 & 5 \\ \lambda & 8 & 8\lambda - 6 \\ 1 + \lambda^2 & 8\lambda + 4 & 2\lambda + 21 \end{bmatrix}$ is

(a) 1, if $\lambda = 2$

(b) 2, if $\lambda = -1$

(c) 3, if $\lambda \neq 2$, $\lambda \neq -1$

(d) All of these

44. If A, B are square matrices, such that $A^2 = A$, $B^2 = B$ and A, B commute then :

(a) $(AB)^2 = I$

(b) $(AB)^2 = AB$

(c) $(AB)^2 = BA$

(d) None of these

45. If $A = \begin{bmatrix} 3 & -3 & 4 \\ 2 & -3 & 4 \\ 0 & -1 & 1 \end{bmatrix}$, then $A^3 =$

(a) A

(b) O

(c) A^{-1}

(d) None of these

46. If $[1 \text{ x } 1] \begin{bmatrix} 1 & 3 & 2 \\ 0 & 5 & 1 \\ 0 & 3 & 2 \end{bmatrix} \begin{bmatrix} 1 \\ 1 \\ x \end{bmatrix} = 0$, then x is equal to

(a) 1

(b) −1

(c) $\dfrac{-9 \pm \sqrt{53}}{2}$

(d) None of these

47. If the matrix $\begin{bmatrix} 0 & 2\beta & \gamma \\ \alpha & \beta & -\gamma \\ \alpha & -\beta & \gamma \end{bmatrix}$ is orthogonal, then:

(a) $\alpha = \pm \dfrac{1}{\sqrt{2}}$

(b) $\beta = \pm \dfrac{1}{\sqrt{6}}$

(c) $\gamma = \pm \dfrac{1}{\sqrt{3}}$

(d) All of these

48. The matrix $A = \begin{bmatrix} 1 & 1 & 3 \\ 5 & 2 & 6 \\ -2 & -1 & -3 \end{bmatrix}$ is :

(a) idempotent   (b) involutory

(c) nilpotent   (d) None of these

49. The matrix $A = \begin{bmatrix} -5 & -8 & 0 \\ 3 & 5 & 0 \\ 1 & 2 & -1 \end{bmatrix}$ is :

(a) idempotent   (b) involutory

(c) nilpotent   (d) None of these

50. The rank of the matrix $A = \begin{bmatrix} 4 & 1 & 3 & 8 \\ 6 & 2 & 6 & -1 \\ 10 & 3 & 9 & 7 \\ 16 & 4 & 12 & 15 \end{bmatrix}$ is

(a) 3   (b) 2

(c) 1   (d) 4

51. The rank of the matrix $\begin{bmatrix} 1^2 & 2^2 & 3^2 & 4^2 \\ 2^2 & 3^2 & 4^2 & 5^2 \\ 3^2 & 4^2 & 5^2 & 6^2 \\ 4^2 & 5^2 & 6^2 & 7^2 \end{bmatrix}$ is :

(a) 2   (b) 3

(c) 4   (d) None of these

52. Rank of the matrix $\begin{bmatrix} 1 & 2 & -1 & 4 \\ 2 & 4 & 3 & 4 \\ 1 & 2 & 3 & 4 \\ -1 & -2 & 6 & -7 \end{bmatrix}$ is :

(a) 2   (b) 3

(c) 4   (d) None of these

53. The solution of the system of equations :

$x + y + z = 6$,

$x + 2y - 3z = -4$,

$-x - 4y + 9z = 18$ is

(a) $x = 1, y = 2, z = 3$ (b) $x = 1, y = -2, z = 3$

(c) $x = -1, y = 2, z = 3$ (d) None of these

54. The complete solution of the system of equations

$2x + 3y + 6z = 6$,

$3x - 2y + 4z = 3$,

$2x - y - z = 1$ is

(a) $x = 1, y = \dfrac{2}{3}, z = -\dfrac{1}{3}$

(b) $x = 1, y = \dfrac{2}{3}, z = \dfrac{1}{3}$

(c) $x = -1, y = \dfrac{2}{3}, z = -\dfrac{1}{3}$

(d) None of these

55. The system of equations $5x + 3y + 7z = 4$,

$3x + 26y + 2z = 9$,

$7x + 2y + 10z = 5$ has :

(a) a unique solution

(b) infinite number of solutions

(c) no solution

(d) None of these

56. If the system of equations $\lambda x + 2y - 2z = 1$,

$4x + 2\lambda y - z = 2$,

$6x + 6y + \lambda z = 3$ has a unique solution, then :

(a) $\lambda \neq 1$ (b) $\lambda \neq 2$

(c) $\lambda \neq 3$ (d) None of these

57. The value of λ so that the equations

$2x + y + 2z = 0$,

$x + y + 3z = 0$,

$4x + 3y + \lambda z = 0$ have non-zero solution is :

(a) 2   (b) 4

(c) 8   (d) None of these

58. If A and B are two matrices such that $AB = B$ and $BA = A$, then $A^2 + B^2 =$

(a) $2AB$ (b) $2BA$

(c) $A + B$ (d) AB

59. The system of linear equations

$x + y + z = 2$,

$2x + y - z = 3$,

$3x + 2y + kz = 4$ has a unique solution if

(a) $k \neq 0$ (b) $-1 < k < 1$

(c) $-2 < k < 2$ (d) $k = 0$

60. If $A = \begin{bmatrix} 1 & 0 \\ -1 & 7 \end{bmatrix}$ and $I = \begin{bmatrix} 1 & 0 \\ 0 & 1 \end{bmatrix}$, then the value of k so that $A^2 = 8A + kI$ is :

(a) k = 7 (b) k = –7

(c) k = 0 (d) None of these

61. If $\begin{bmatrix} 2 & -1 \\ 1 & 0 \\ -3 & 4 \end{bmatrix} A = \begin{bmatrix} -1 & -8 & -10 \\ 1 & -2 & -5 \\ 9 & 22 & 15 \end{bmatrix}$, then A =

(a) $\begin{bmatrix} 1 & 2 & -5 \\ 3 & 4 & 0 \end{bmatrix}$ (b) $\begin{bmatrix} 1 & 3 \\ 2 & 4 \\ -5 & 0 \end{bmatrix}$

(c) $\begin{bmatrix} 1 & -2 & -5 \\ 3 & 4 & 0 \end{bmatrix}$ (d) $\begin{bmatrix} 1 & 3 \\ -2 & 4 \\ -5 & 0 \end{bmatrix}$

62. If $A = \begin{bmatrix} 3 & -5 \\ -4 & 2 \end{bmatrix}$, then $A^2 – 5A – 14I$ is equal to

(a) $\begin{bmatrix} 2 & -3 \\ 1 & 0 \end{bmatrix}$ (b) $\begin{bmatrix} 0 & 0 \\ 0 & 0 \end{bmatrix}$

(c) $\begin{bmatrix} 1 & -3 \\ -1 & 0 \end{bmatrix}$ (d) None of these

63. If A and B are non-singular square matrices of the same order, then :

(a) adj AB = (adj A) (adj B)

(b) adj AB = (adj B) (adj A)

(c) adj AB = 1

(d) None of these

64. If A is an invertible matrix, then :

(a) adj A' = (adj A)' (b) adj A' = adj A

(c) adj A' = A' (d) None of these

65. If A is a non-singular square matrix of order n, then adj (adj A) is equal to :

(a) $|A|^n A$ (b) $|A|^{n-1}A$

(c) $|A|^{n-2}A$ (d) None of these

66. The matrix A satisfying the matrix equation

$\begin{bmatrix} 2 & 1 \\ 3 & 2 \end{bmatrix} A \begin{bmatrix} -3 & 2 \\ 5 & -3 \end{bmatrix} = \begin{bmatrix} 1 & 0 \\ 0 & 1 \end{bmatrix}$ is :

(a) $\begin{bmatrix} 1 & 0 \\ 1 & 0 \end{bmatrix}$ (b) $\begin{bmatrix} 1 & -1 \\ 1 & 0 \end{bmatrix}$

(c) $\begin{bmatrix} 1 & 1 \\ 1 & 0 \end{bmatrix}$ (d) $\begin{bmatrix} -1 & 1 \\ 1 & 0 \end{bmatrix}$

67. If A is symmetric as well as skew symmetric matrix, then A is :

(a) Diagonal (b) Null

(c) Triangular (d) None of these

68. If $U = [2 \ -3 \ 4], V = \begin{bmatrix} 3 \\ 2 \\ 1 \end{bmatrix}, X = [0 \ 2 \ 3]$ and

$Y = \begin{bmatrix} 2 \\ 2 \\ 4 \end{bmatrix}$ then UV + XY =

(a) 20 (b) [–20]

(c) –20 (d) [20]

69. If $\begin{bmatrix} 1 & 0 & 1 \\ 0 & 0 & 0 \\ 1 & 0 & 1 \end{bmatrix}$, then $A^2 =$

(a) A (b) –A

(c) 2A (d) –2A

70. If the system of equations
x + 2y – 3z = 1,
(p + 2) z = 3,
(2p + 1) y + z = 2 is inconsistent, then the value of p is :

(a) –2 (b) $-\frac{1}{2}$

(c) 0 (d) 2

71. Let a, b, c be positive real numbers. The following system of equations in x, y and z

$\frac{x^2}{a^2} + \frac{y^2}{b^2} - \frac{z^2}{c^2} = 1$,

$\frac{x^2}{a^2} - \frac{y^2}{b^2} + \frac{z^2}{c^2} = 1$,

$-\frac{x^2}{a^2} + \frac{y^2}{b^2} + \frac{z^2}{c^2} = 1$ has :

(a) no solution

(b) unique solution

(c) infinitely many solutions

(d) finitely many solutions

72. If x, y, z are in A.P. with common difference d

and the rank of the matrix $\begin{vmatrix} 4 & 5 & x \\ 5 & 6 & y \\ 6 & k & z \end{vmatrix}$ is 2, then

the values of d and k are :

(a) $\frac{x}{4}$; arbitrary number

(b) arbitrary number, 7

(c) x, 5

(d) $\frac{x}{2}$, 6

73. If $A = \begin{bmatrix} 2 & 4 & 1 \\ 5 & -6 & 2 \\ 2 & 1 & 5 \end{bmatrix}$, then trace of A is :

(a) -3 (b) 1

(c) 8   (d) 8

74. If A is a skew-symmetric matrix, then trace of A is :

(a) 1   (b) -1

(c) 0   (d) None of these

75. If $D = \text{diag} \ (a_1 \ a_2 \ a_3 \ ... \ a_n)$, where $a_i \neq 0$ for all i = 1, 2, ..., n, then D^{-1} is equal to :

(a) I_n

(b) D

(c) $\text{diag} \ (a_1^{-1} \ a_2^{-1} \ a_3^{-1} \ ... \ a_n^{-1})$

(d) None of these

76. Rank of identity matrix of order 3 is :

(a) 0   (b) 1

(c) 2   (d) 3

77. The system of equations

$6x - 12y + 25z = 4,$

$4x + 15y + 20z = 3,$

$2x + 18y + 15z = 10$ has

(a) unique solution

(b) infinite number of solutions

(c) no solution

(d) None of these

78. The value of λ for which the system of equations

$3x_1 + x_2 - \lambda x_3 = 0,$

$2x_1 + 4x_2 + \lambda x_3 = 0,$

$8x_1 - 4x_2 - 6x_3 = 0$

has a non-trivial solution, is

(a) $\lambda = -1$ (b) $\lambda = 1$

(c) $\lambda = 2$ (d) None of these

79. If the system of equations

$x + y + 4z = 1,$

$x + 2y - 2z = 1,$

$\lambda x + y + z = 1$ has a unique solution, then

(a) $\lambda \neq 2$ (b) $\lambda \neq -1$

(c) $\lambda \neq \frac{7}{10}$ (d) None of these

80. Rank of the matrix $\begin{bmatrix} 1 & 2 & -1 & 3 \\ 4 & 1 & 2 & 1 \\ 3 & -1 & 1 & 2 \\ 1 & 2 & 0 & 1 \end{bmatrix}$ is :

(a) 3   (b) 2

(c) 4   (d) None of these

81. If adj B = A and P, Q are two unimodular matrices such that |P| = 1, |Q| = 1, then $(Q^{-1}BP^{-1}) =$

(a) PAQ   (b) PBQ

(c) QAP   (d) QBP

82. If $A = \begin{bmatrix} 4 & 3 \\ 2 & 5 \end{bmatrix}$ and $A^2 - xA + yI = 0$, then

(a) x = 9, y = −14   (b) x = 9, y = 14

(c) x = −9, y = 14   (d) x = −9, x = −14

83. If $A = \begin{bmatrix} \cos \alpha & -\sin \alpha & 0 \\ \sin \alpha & \cos \alpha & 0 \\ 0 & 0 & 1 \end{bmatrix}$, then A · adj A =

(a) 1   (b) 0

(c) A   (d) adj A

84. If $A = \begin{bmatrix} 5 & 0 & 4 \\ 2 & 3 & 2 \\ 1 & 2 & 1 \end{bmatrix}$ and $B^{-1} = \begin{bmatrix} 1 & 3 & 3 \\ 1 & 4 & 3 \\ 1 & 3 & 4 \end{bmatrix}$

then $(AB)^{-1} =$

(a) $\frac{1}{6} \begin{bmatrix} 2 & -19 & 27 \\ 2 & -18 & 25 \\ 3 & -29 & 42 \end{bmatrix}$

(b) $\frac{1}{6} \begin{bmatrix} -2 & 19 & -27 \\ -2 & 18 & -25 \\ -3 & 29 & -42 \end{bmatrix}$

(c) $\frac{1}{6} \begin{bmatrix} -2 & 19 & 27 \\ 2 & -18 & 25 \\ 3 & -29 & 42 \end{bmatrix}$

(d) None of these

85. If $A = \begin{bmatrix} 0 & 2 \\ 3 & -4 \end{bmatrix}$, $KA = \begin{bmatrix} 0 & 3a \\ 2b & 24 \end{bmatrix}$, then values of

k, a, b are :

(a) $-6, -12, -18$ (b) $-6, -4, 9$

(c) $-6, -4, -9$ (d) $-6, 12, 18$

86. If $A = \begin{bmatrix} 2 & 2 \\ -3 & 2 \end{bmatrix}$, $B = \begin{bmatrix} 0 & -1 \\ 1 & 0 \end{bmatrix}$, then $[B^{-1} A^{-1}]^{-1} =$

(a) $\frac{1}{10} \begin{bmatrix} 2 & -2 \\ 2 & 3 \end{bmatrix}$ (b) $\begin{bmatrix} 3 & -2 \\ 2 & 2 \end{bmatrix}$

(c) $\begin{bmatrix} 2 & -2 \\ 2 & 3 \end{bmatrix}$ (d) $\frac{1}{10} \begin{bmatrix} 3 & 2 \\ -2 & 2 \end{bmatrix}$

87. The element in the first row and third column of

the inverse of the matrix $\begin{bmatrix} 1 & 2 & -3 \\ 0 & 1 & 2 \\ 0 & 0 & 1 \end{bmatrix}$ is :

(a) -2 (b) 0

(c) 1 (d) 7

88. If $A = \begin{bmatrix} 2 & 0 & 0 \\ 0 & 2 & 0 \\ 0 & 0 & 2 \end{bmatrix}$, then $A^5 =$

(a) $5A$ (b) $10A$

(c) $16A$ (d) $32A$

89. If A and B are square matrices of order 3 such
that $|A| = -1$, $|B| = 3$, then $|3AB| =$

(a) -9 (b) -18

(c) -27 (d) 81

90. If $A = \begin{bmatrix} 1 & \tan \frac{\theta}{2} \\ -\tan \frac{\theta}{2} & 1 \end{bmatrix}$ and $AB = 1$, then $B =$

(a) $\cos^2 \frac{\theta}{2} \cdot A$ (b) $\cos^2 \frac{\theta}{2} \cdot A'$

(c) $\cos^2 \frac{\theta}{2} \cdot I$ (d) None of these

91. If for $AX = B$, $B = \begin{bmatrix} 9 \\ 52 \\ 0 \end{bmatrix}$ and

$A^{-1} = \begin{bmatrix} 3 & -1/2 & -1/2 \\ -4 & 3/4 & 5/4 \\ 2 & -1/4 & -3/4 \end{bmatrix}$, then X is equal to

(a) $\begin{bmatrix} 1 \\ 3 \\ 5 \end{bmatrix}$ (b) $\begin{bmatrix} -1/2 \\ -1/2 \\ 2 \end{bmatrix}$

(c) $\begin{bmatrix} -4 \\ 2 \\ 3 \end{bmatrix}$ (d) $\begin{bmatrix} 3 \\ 3/4 \\ -3/4 \end{bmatrix}$

92. If $A = \begin{bmatrix} 0 & i \\ -i & 0 \end{bmatrix}$, then $A^{40} =$

(a) $\begin{bmatrix} 0 & 1 \\ 1 & 0 \end{bmatrix}$ (b) $\begin{bmatrix} 1 & 0 \\ 0 & 1 \end{bmatrix}$

(c) $\begin{bmatrix} -1 & 1 \\ 0 & -1 \end{bmatrix}$ (d) None of these

93. If $A = \begin{bmatrix} 1 & k \\ 0 & 1 \end{bmatrix}$, then $A^n =$

(a) $\begin{bmatrix} n & nk \\ 0 & n \end{bmatrix}$ (b) $\begin{bmatrix} n & k^n \\ 0 & n \end{bmatrix}$

(c) $\begin{bmatrix} 1 & nk \\ 0 & 1 \end{bmatrix}$ (d) $\begin{bmatrix} 1 & k^n \\ 0 & 1 \end{bmatrix}$

94. If $A = \begin{bmatrix} 1 & 0 & 0 \\ 0 & 1 & 0 \\ 0 & 0 & 1 \end{bmatrix}$, then :

(a) adj $A = A^{-1}$

(b) adj $A = A'$

(c) adj $A = A$

(d) All the statements are correct

95. A square matrix A is said to be singular if :

(a) every element of A is equal to zero

(b) the diagonal elements of A are all zero

(c) it is a scalar matrix

(d) $|A| = 0$

96. If $A = \begin{bmatrix} 1 & 2 \\ 3 & -5 \end{bmatrix}$, then adj A is equal to :

(a) $\begin{bmatrix} 5 & 2 \\ 3 & -1 \end{bmatrix}$

(b) $\begin{bmatrix} -5 & -2 \\ 3 & -1 \end{bmatrix}$

(c) $\begin{bmatrix} -5 & -2 \\ -3 & 1 \end{bmatrix}$

(d) $\begin{bmatrix} 5 & -2 \\ -3 & 1 \end{bmatrix}$

97. Consider the system of equations $a_1x + b_1y + c_1z = 0$, $a_2x + b_2y + c_2z = 0$, $a_3x + b_3y + c_3z = 0$

If $\begin{vmatrix} a_1 & b_1 & c_1 \\ a_2 & b_2 & c_2 \\ a_3 & b_3 & c_3 \end{vmatrix} = 0$, then the system has :

(a) more than two solutions

(b) one trivial and one non-trivial solution

(c) no solution

(d) only trivial solution (0, 0, 0)

98. If $A = [a_{ij}]_{m \times n}$ is a matrix of rank ρ, then :

(a) $\rho > \min. (m, n)$

(b) $\rho \leq \min. (m, n)$

(c) $\rho = \min. (m, n)$

(d) None of these

99. Let $A = \begin{bmatrix} 1 & 0 & 0 \\ 2 & 1 & 0 \\ 3 & 2 & 1 \end{bmatrix}$. If u_1 and u_2 are column matrices such that $Au_1 = \begin{bmatrix} 1 \\ 0 \\ 0 \end{bmatrix}$ and $Au_2 = \begin{bmatrix} 0 \\ 1 \\ 0 \end{bmatrix}$, then $u_1 + u_2$ is equal to : **[AIEEE - 2012]**

(a) $\begin{bmatrix} -1 \\ 1 \\ 0 \end{bmatrix}$

(b) $\begin{bmatrix} -1 \\ 1 \\ -1 \end{bmatrix}$

(c) $\begin{bmatrix} -1 \\ -1 \\ 0 \end{bmatrix}$

(d) $\begin{bmatrix} 1 \\ -1 \\ -1 \end{bmatrix}$

100. Let A and B be two symmetric matrices of order 3. **[AIEEE - 2011]**

Statement 1 : A(BA) and (AB)A are symmetric matrices.

Statement 2 : AB is symmetric matrix if matrix multiplication of A with B is commutative.

(a) Statement 1 is false, statement 2 is true.

(b) Statement 1 is true, statement 2 is true; statement 2 is a correct explanation for statement 1.

(c) Statement 1 is true, statement 2 is true; statement 2 is not a correct explanation for statement 1.

(d) Statement 1 is true, statement 2 is false.

101. The number of 3×3 non-singular matrices, with four entries as 1 and all other entries as 0, is :

(a) 5

(b) 6

(c) at least 7

(d) less than 4

102. Let A be a 2×2 matrix with non-zero entries and let $A^2 = I$, where I is 2×2 identity matrix. Define Tr(A) = sum of diagonal elements of A and $|A|$ = determinant of matrix A :

[AIEEE - 2010]

Statement 1 : $Tr(A) = 0$

Statement 2 : $|A| = 1$

(a) Statement 1 is true, statement 2 is true; statement 2 is not a correct explanation for statement 1.

(b) Statement 1 is true, statement 2 is false.

(c) Statement 1 is false, statement 2 is true.

(d) Statement 1 is true, statement 2 is true; statement 2 is the correct explanation for statement 1.

103. Let a, b, c be such that $b(a + c) \neq 0$. If

$\begin{vmatrix} a & a+1 & a-1 \\ -b & b+1 & b-1 \\ c & c-1 & c+1 \end{vmatrix} + \begin{vmatrix} a+1 & b+1 & c-1 \\ a-1 & b-1 & c+1 \\ (-1)^{n+2}a & (-1)^{n+1}b & (-1)^n b \end{vmatrix} = 0$,

then the value of 'n' is : **[AIEEE - 2009]**

(a) zero

(b) any even integer

(c) any odd integer

(d) any integer

104. Let A be a 2×2 matrix with real entries. Let I be the 2×2 identity matrix. Denote by tr (A), the sum of diagonal entries of A. Assume that $A^2 = I$. **[AIEEE - 2008]**

Statement 1: If $A \neq I$ and $A \neq -I$, then det A = −1.

Statement 2: If $A \neq I$ and $A \neq -I$, then tr (A) ≠ 0.

(a) Statement 1 is false, statement 2 is true.

(b) Statement 1 is true, statement 2 is true; statement 2 is a correct explanation for statement 1.

(c) Statement 1 is true, statement 2 is true; Statement 2 is not a correct explanation for statement 1.

(d) Statement 1 is true, statement 2 is false.

105. Let $A = \begin{bmatrix} 5 & 5\alpha & \alpha \\ 0 & \alpha & 5\alpha \\ 0 & 0 & 5 \end{bmatrix}$. If $\left| A^2 \right| = 25$, then $|\alpha|$ equals **[AIEEE - 2007]**

(a) 5^2 (b) 1

(c) 1/5   (d) 5

106. If A and B are square matrices of size n × n such that $A^2 - B^2 = (A - B)(A + B)$, then which of the following will be always true ?

[AIEEE - 2006]

(a) A = B

(b) AB = BA

(c) either of A or B is a zero matrix

(d) either of A or B is an identity matrix

107. Let $A = \begin{bmatrix} 1 & 2 \\ 3 & 4 \end{bmatrix}$ and $B = \begin{bmatrix} a & 0 \\ 0 & b \end{bmatrix}$, a, b ∈ N.

Then : **[AIEEE - 2006]**

(a) there cannot exist any B such that AB = BA

(b) there exist more than one but finite number of B's such that AB = BA

(c) there exists exactly one B such that AB = BA

(d) there exist infinitely many B's such that AB = BA

108. If $A^2 - A + I = 0$, then the inverse of A is :

[AIEEE - 2005]

(a) A + I   (b) A

(c) A − I   (d) I − A

109. If $A = \begin{bmatrix} 1 & 0 \\ 1 & 1 \end{bmatrix}$ and $I = \begin{bmatrix} 1 & 0 \\ 0 & 1 \end{bmatrix}$, then which one of the following holds for all n ≥ 1, by the principle of mathematical induction?

[AIEEE - 2005]

(a) $A^n = nA - (n - 1)I$

(b) $A^n = 2^{n-1}A - (n - 1)I$

(c) $A^n = nA + (n - 1)I$

(d) $A^n = 2^{n-1}A + (n - 1)I$

110. Let $P = [a_{ij}]$ be a 3×3 matrix and let $Q = [b_{ij}]$ where $b_{ij} = 2^{i+j} \cdot a_{ij}$ for $1 \le i, j \le 3$. If the determinant of P is 2, then the determinant of the matrix Q is

(a) 2^{10} (b) 2^{11}

(c) 2^{12} (d) 2^{13}

111. If $S_k = \begin{bmatrix} 1 & k \\ 0 & 1 \end{bmatrix}$; k ∈ ℕ, where ℕ is the set of natural numbers, then $(S_2)^n (S_k)^{-1}$ for n ∈ ℕ, is

(a) $S_{2^n - k}$ (b) $S_{2n - k}$

(c) $S_{2n + k - 1}$ (d) $S_{2^n + k - 1}$

ANSWER KEY

1. (a)	2. (c)	3. (d)	4. (c)	5. (a)	6. (b)	7. (b)	8. (a)	9. (c)	10. (d)
11. (a)	12. (a)	13. (d)	14. (c)	15. (a)	16. (b)	17. (c)	18. (a)	19. (c)	20. (a)
21. (a)	22. (c)	23. (b)	24. (b)	25. (c)	26. (b)	27. (a)	28. (b)	29. (a)	30. (d)
31. (c)	32. (c)	33. (b)	34. (c)	35. (a)	36. (c)	37. (d)	38. (b)	39. (d)	40. (c)

41. (c)	**42.** (d)	**43.** (d)	**44.** (b)	**45.** (c)	**46.** (c)	**47.** (d)	**48.** (c)	**49.** (b)	**50.** (b)
51. (b)	**52.** (b)	**53.** (a)	**54.** (b)	**55.** (b)	**56.** (b)	**57.** (c)	**58.** (c)	**59.** (a)	**60.** (b)
61. (c)	**62.** (b)	**63.** (b)	**64.** (a)	**65.** (c)	**66.** (c)	**67.** (b)	**68.** (d)	**69.** (c)	**70.** (a)
71. (b)	**72.** (b)	**73.** (b)	**74.** (c)	**75.** (c)	**76.** (d)	**77.** (a)	**78.** (b)	**79.** (c)	**80.** (a)
81. (a)	**82.** (b)	**83.** (a)	**84.** (d)	**85.** (c)	**86.** (c)	**87.** (d)	**88.** (c)	**89.** (b)	**90.** (b)
91. (a)	**92.** (b)	**93.** (c)	**94.** (c)	**95.** (d)	**96.** (c)	**97.** (a)	**98.** (b)	**99.** (d)	**100.** (c)
101. (c)	**102.** (b)	**103.** (c)	**104.** (d)	**105.** (c)	**106.** (b)	**107.** (d)	**108.** (d)	**109.** (a)	**110.** (d)
111. (b)									

❑❑❑

Chapter 27

DETERMINANTS

MULTIPLE CHOICE QUESTIONS

1. If the value of the determinant

$$\begin{vmatrix} a-b-c & 2a & 2a \\ 2b & b-c-a & 2b \\ 2c & 2c & c-a-b \end{vmatrix} = (a+b+c)^k,$$

then k is equal to :

(a) 1   (b) 2
(c) 3   (d) None of these

2. The value of the determinant

$$\begin{vmatrix} \sqrt{13}+\sqrt{3} & \sqrt[2]{5} & \sqrt{5} \\ \sqrt{15}+\sqrt{26} & 5 & \sqrt{10} \\ 3+\sqrt{65} & \sqrt{15} & 5 \end{vmatrix} \text{ is :}$$

(a) $-\sqrt[5]{3}\,(5-\sqrt{6})$ (b) $-\sqrt[5]{3}\,(5+\sqrt{6})$

(c) $-\sqrt[5]{3}\,(\sqrt{6}-5)$ (d) None of these

3. The value of the determinant

$$\begin{vmatrix} b^2-ab & b-c & bc-ac \\ ab-a^2 & a-b & b^2-ab \\ bc-ac & c-a & ab-a^2 \end{vmatrix} \text{ is :}$$

(a) 1   (b) 0
(c) −1   (d) None of these

4. If $\begin{vmatrix} b+c & c & b \\ c & c+a & a \\ b & a & a+b \end{vmatrix}$ = k abc, then k is equal

to :

(a) 1   (b) 2
(c) 3   (d) 4

5. The value of the determinant

$$\begin{vmatrix} a^2 & a & 1 \\ \cos nx & \cos(n+1)x & \cos(n+2)x \\ \sin nx & \sin(n+1)x & \sin(n+2)x \end{vmatrix} \text{ is :}$$

(a) independent of n   (b) independent of a
(c) independent of x   (d) None of these

6. The a, b, c are in A.P., then the value of the determinant

$$\begin{vmatrix} x+1 & x+2 & x+a \\ x+2 & x+3 & x+b \\ x+3 & x+4 & x+c \end{vmatrix} \text{ is :}$$

(a) x   (b) 2x
(c) 0   (d) None of these

7. The value of the determinant

$$\begin{vmatrix} a^2+1 & ab & ac \\ ab & b^2+1 & bc \\ ac & bc & c^2+1 \end{vmatrix} \text{ is :}$$

(a) $1+a^2+b^2+c^2$ (b) $a^2+b^2+c^2+abc$
(c) $a^2+b^2+c^2+2abc$ (d) None of these

8. If $\Delta_r = \begin{vmatrix} r-1 & n & 6 \\ (r-1)^2 & 2n^2 & 4n-2 \\ (r-1)^3 & 3n^3 & 3n^2-3n \end{vmatrix}$,

then $\sum\limits_{r=1}^{n} \Delta_r$ is equal to :

(a) 1   (b) 2
(c) 3   (d) 0

9. If $\Delta_r = \begin{vmatrix} r & x & \dfrac{n(n+1)}{2} \\ 2r-1 & y & n^2 \\ 3r-2 & z & \dfrac{n(3n-1)}{2} \end{vmatrix}$,

then $\sum\limits_{r=1}^{n} \Delta_r$ is equal to :

(a) 0   (b) 1
(c) 2   (d) 3

10. If $2s = a + b + c$

and $\begin{vmatrix} a^2 & (s-a)^2 & (s-a)^2 \\ (s-b)^2 & b^2 & (s-b)^2 \\ (s-c)^2 & (s-c)^2 & c^2 \end{vmatrix}$

$= k(s-a)(s-b)(s-c)$, then k is equal to :

(a) 2   (b) 2s

(c) $2s^2$ (d) $2s^3$

11. If a, b, c are p^{th}, q^{th} and r^{th} terms respectively of a

geometric progression, then $\begin{vmatrix} \log a & p & 1 \\ \log b & q & 1 \\ \log c & r & 1 \end{vmatrix}$ is

equal to:

(a) 0   (b) 1

(c) −1   (d) None of these

12. If $U_n = \begin{vmatrix} n & 1 & 5 \\ n^2 & 2N+1 & 2N+1 \\ n^2 & 3N^2 & 3N \end{vmatrix}$,

then $\sum\limits_{n=1}^{N} U_n$ is equal to :

(a) 1   (b) −1

(c) 0   (d) None of these

13. The value of the determinant

$\begin{vmatrix} 1 & 1 & 1 & 1 & 1 \\ 1 & 2 & 3 & 4 & 5 \\ 1 & 3 & 6 & 10 & 15 \\ 1 & 4 & 10 & 20 & 35 \\ 1 & 5 & 15 & 35 & 69 \end{vmatrix}$ is :

(a) 0   (b) 1

(c) 2   (d) 3

14. If A, B and C are the angles of a triangle and

$\begin{vmatrix} 1 & 1 & 1 \\ 1+\sin A & 1+\sin B & 1+\sin C \\ \sin A + \sin^2 A & \sin B + \sin^2 B & \sin C + \sin^2 C \end{vmatrix} = 0$

then the $\triangle ABC$ must be :

(a) right angled   (b) isosceles

(c) equilateral   (d) none of these

15. If $= \begin{vmatrix} b^2+c^2 & ab & ac \\ ab & c^2+a^2 & bc \\ ca & cb & a^2+b^2 \end{vmatrix} = ka^2b^2c^2$, then k is

equal to :

(a) 1   (b) 2

(c) 4   (d) None of these

16. The value of the determinant $\begin{vmatrix} 1^2 & 2^2 & 3^2 & 4^2 \\ 2^2 & 3^2 & 4^2 & 5^2 \\ 3^2 & 4^2 & 5^2 & 6^2 \\ 4^2 & 5^2 & 6^2 & 7^2 \end{vmatrix}$ is :

(a) 1   (b) 0

(c) 2   (d) None of these

17. Let α, β be the roots of the equation $ax^2 + bx + c = 0$. Let $s_n = \alpha^n + \beta^n$ for $n \geq 1$. Then, the value of the determinant

$\begin{vmatrix} 3 & 1+s_1 & 1+s_2 \\ 1+s_1 & 1+s_2 & 1+s_3 \\ 1+s_2 & 1+s_3 & 1+s_4 \end{vmatrix}$ is :

(a) $\dfrac{(a+b+c)(b^2-4ac)}{a^4}$

(b) $\dfrac{(a+b+c)^2(b^2-4ac)}{a^4}$

(c) $\dfrac{(a+b+c)^2(b^2-4ac)}{a^2}$

(d) None of these

18. The value of the determinant $\begin{vmatrix} 1 & bc & bc(b+c) \\ 1 & ca & ca(c+a) \\ 1 & ab & ab(a+b) \end{vmatrix}$

is :

(a) 0   (b) 1

(c) 2   (d) 3

19. The value of the determinant $\begin{vmatrix} 1 & a & a^2-bc \\ 1 & b & b^2-ca \\ 1 & c & c^2-ab \end{vmatrix}$ is :

(a) 0   (b) 1

(c) 2   (d) None of these

20. If $\begin{vmatrix} \cosec \alpha & 1 & 0 \\ 1 & 2\cosec \alpha & 1 \\ 0 & 1 & 2\cosec \alpha \end{vmatrix} = \frac{1}{2}\left(z^3 + \frac{1}{z^3}\right),$

then z is equal to :

(a) $\sin \alpha/2$ (b) $\cos \alpha/2$

(c) $\tan \alpha/2$ (d) None of these

21. The value of the determinant

$\begin{vmatrix} 1 & a & a^2 & a^3 + bcd \\ 1 & b & b^2 & b^3 + cda \\ 1 & c & c^2 & c^3 + abd \\ 1 & d & d^2 & d^3 + abc \end{vmatrix}$ is :

(a) 0   (b) 2

(c) 4   (d) 6

22. If $\begin{vmatrix} a^2 & b^2 & c^2 \\ (a+1)^2 & (b+1)^2 & (c+1)^2 \\ (a-1)^2 & (b-1)^2 & (c-1)^2 \end{vmatrix}$

$= k(a-b)(b-c)(c-a)$, then K is equal to :

(a) 4   (b) –4

(c) 2   (d) –2

23. If $\begin{vmatrix} 2ab & a^2 & b^2 \\ a^2 & b^2 & 2ab \\ b^2 & 2ab & a^2 \end{vmatrix} = -(a^3 + b^3)^n$, then n is equal

to :

(a) 1   (b) 2

(c) 3   (d) 4

24. If A23, 5B1 and 22C are three three-digit numbers, each of which is divisible by k, then

$\Delta = \begin{vmatrix} 2 & 2 & B \\ A & 2 & 5 \\ 3 & C & 1 \end{vmatrix}$ is :

(a) divisible by k   (b) divisible by k^2

(c) divisible by 2k   (d) None of these

25. If $\begin{vmatrix} \dfrac{1}{a+x} & \dfrac{1}{b+x} & \dfrac{1}{c+x} \\ \dfrac{1}{a+y} & \dfrac{1}{b+y} & \dfrac{1}{c+y} \\ \dfrac{1}{a+z} & \dfrac{1}{b+z} & \dfrac{1}{c+z} \end{vmatrix} = \dfrac{P}{Q}$, where Q is the

product of denominators, then P is equal to :

(a) $(a-b)(b-c)(c-a)$

(b) $(x-y)(y-z)(z-x)$

(c) $(a-b)(b-c)(c-a)(x-y)(y-z)(z-x)$

(d) None of these

26. If $\begin{vmatrix} \dfrac{a^2+b^2}{c} & c & c \\ a & \dfrac{b^2+c^2}{a} & a \\ b & b & \dfrac{c^2+a^2}{b} \end{vmatrix} = kabc$, then k is

equal to :

(a) 4   (b) 2

(c) 1   (d) None of these

27. If $a \neq b \neq c$ and $\begin{vmatrix} a & a^3 & a^4 - 1 \\ b & b^3 & b^4 - 1 \\ c & c^3 & c^4 - 1 \end{vmatrix} = 0$, then :

(a) $abc(ab + bc + ca) = a + b + c$

(b) $abc(a + b + c) = (ab + bc + ca)$

(c) $(a + b + c)(ab + bc + ca) = abc$

(d) None of these

28. If A, B and C are the angles of a triangle, then the value of the determinant

$\begin{vmatrix} \sin 2A & \sin C & \sin B \\ \sin C & \sin 2B & \sin A \\ \sin B & \sin A & \sin 2C \end{vmatrix}$ is :

(a) 0   (b) $\sin A \sin B \sin C$

(c) $\cos A \cos B \cos C$ (d) $\sin A + \sin B + \sin C$

29. The determinant $\begin{vmatrix} a^2 + 2a & 2a + 1 & 1 \\ 2a + 1 & a + 2 & 1 \\ 3 & 3 & 1 \end{vmatrix}$ is :

(a) > 0 if $a > 1$ (b) $= 0$ if $a = 1$

(c) < 0 if $a < 1$ (d) All of these

30. The value of the determinant

$$\begin{vmatrix} x^3 & 3x^2 & 3x & 1 \\ x^2 & x^2 + 2x & 2x + 1 & 1 \\ x & 2x + 1 & x + 2 & 1 \\ 1 & 3 & 3 & 1 \end{vmatrix}$$

(a) $(x - 1)^4$ (b) $(x - 1)^5$

(c) $(x - 1)^6$ (d) None of these

31. If $\begin{vmatrix} a & b & c \\ a - b & b - c & c - a \\ b + c & c + a & a + b \end{vmatrix} = a^3 + b^3 + c^3 + k\ abc$,

then k is equal to :

(a) 3 (b) −3

(c) 4 (d) −4

32. The value of the determinant

$$\begin{vmatrix} 1 + x & 2 & 3 & 4 \\ 1 & 2 + x & 3 & 4 \\ 1 & 2 & 3 + x & 4 \\ 1 & 2 & 3 & 4 + x \end{vmatrix} \text{ is :}$$

(a) $x^2 (x + 10)$ (b) $x^3 (x + 10)$

(c) $x^4 (x + 10)$ (d) None of these

33. If $\begin{vmatrix} x & a & a & a \\ a & x & a & a \\ a & a & x & a \\ a & a & a & x \end{vmatrix} = (x + 3a)\ f(x)$, then f(x) is equal

to :

(a) $(x - a)^2$ (b) $(x - a)^3$

(c) $(x + a)^2$ (d) $(x + a)^3$

34. If $\begin{vmatrix} x & 3 & 7 \\ 2 & x & 2 \\ 7 & 6 & x \end{vmatrix} = 0$ then x is equal to :

(a) −9 (b) 2

(c) 7 (d) All of these

35. If $a \neq p$, $b \neq q$, $c \neq r$ and $\begin{vmatrix} p & b & c \\ a & q & c \\ a & b & r \end{vmatrix} = 0$ then the

value of $\dfrac{p}{p - a} + \dfrac{q}{q - b} + \dfrac{r}{r - c}$ is :

(a) 1 (b) 2

(c) 3 (d) None of these

36. If $f(\theta) = \begin{vmatrix} \cos^2 \theta & \cos \theta \sin \theta & -\sin \theta \\ \cos \theta \sin \theta & \sin^2 \theta & \cos \theta \\ \sin \theta & -\cos \theta & 0 \end{vmatrix}$, then

for all θ,

(a) $f(\theta) = 1$ (b) $f(\theta) = 2$

(c) $f(\theta) = 3$ (d) None of these

37. The value of determinant $\begin{vmatrix} {}^xC_1 & {}^xC_2 & {}^xC_3 \\ {}^yC_1 & {}^yC_2 & {}^yC_3 \\ {}^zC_1 & {}^zC_2 & {}^zC_3 \end{vmatrix}$ is :

(a) $xyz\ (x - y)\ (y - z)\ (z - x)$

(b) $\dfrac{xyz}{4}\ (x - y)\ (y - z)\ (z - x)$

(c) $\dfrac{xyz}{12}\ (x - y)\ (y - z)\ (z - x)$

(d) None of these

38. If $f(x) = ax^2 + bx + c$ and $f(0) = 6$, $f(2) = 11$, $f(-3) = 6$, then the value of $f(1)$ is :

(a) 2 (b) 4

(c) 6 (d) 8

39. If $f(x) = \begin{vmatrix} 4 \sin^3 x & 1 & 1 \\ (\sin x - 1)^2 & (\sin x + 2)^2 & (\sin x - 1)^2 \\ (\sin x + 1)^2 & (\sin x + 1)^2 & \sin^2 x \end{vmatrix}$

then $\displaystyle\int_{-\pi/2}^{\pi/2} f(x)\ dx$ is equal to :

(a) 4π (b) -4π

(c) 16π (d) -16π

40. For a fixed positive n, if

$$D = \begin{vmatrix} n! & (n+1)! & (n+2)! \\ (n+1)! & (n+2)! & (n+3)! \\ (n+2)! & (n+3)! & (n+4)! \end{vmatrix},$$

then $\left[\dfrac{D}{(n!)^3} - 4 \right]$ is divisible by :

(a) n
(b) n^2
(c) 2n
(d) None of these

41. If $\begin{vmatrix} a & b+c & a^2 \\ b & c+a & b^2 \\ c & a+b & c^2 \end{vmatrix}$

$= k(a+b+c)(a-b)(b-c)(c-a)$,

then k is equal to :

(a) 1
(b) –1
(c) 4
(d) –4

42. The value of determinant $\begin{vmatrix} x & y & z \\ x^2 & y^2 & z^2 \\ yz & zx & xy \end{vmatrix}$ is :

(a) $(x-y)(y-z)(z-x)(xy+xz+yz)$

(b) $xyz(x-y)(y-z)(z-x)$

(c) $xyz(xy+xz+yz)$

(d) None of these

43. If $f(x) = \begin{vmatrix} \cos x & x & 1 \\ 2\sin x & x^2 & 2x \\ \tan x & x & 1 \end{vmatrix}$, then $\lim\limits_{x \to 0} \left[\dfrac{f'(x)}{x} \right]$ is :

(a) 2
(b) –2
(c) 1
(d) –1

44. If x, y and z are all different and

$$\begin{vmatrix} x & x^2 & 1+x^3 \\ y & y^2 & 1+y^3 \\ z & z^2 & 1+z^3 \end{vmatrix} = 0 , \text{ then :}$$

(a) $xyz = -1$
(b) $xyz = 1$
(c) $xyz = -2$
(d) $xyz = 2$

45. If

$$f(x) = \begin{vmatrix} \sec x & \cos x & \sec^2 x + \cot x \, \csc x \\ \cos^2 x & \cos^2 x & \csc^2 x \\ 1 & \cos^2 x & \cos^2 x \end{vmatrix}$$

then $\int\limits_{0}^{\pi/2} f(x) \, dx$ is equal to :

(a) $(15\pi + 32)/60$
(b) $-(15\pi + 32)/60$
(c) $(15\pi + 32)/4$
(d) None of these

46. The value of the determinant of nth order, being

given by $\begin{vmatrix} x & 1 & 1 & \cdots \\ 1 & x & 1 & \cdots \\ 1 & 1 & x & \cdots \\ \cdots & \cdots & \cdots & \cdots \end{vmatrix}$ is :

(a) $(x-1)^{n-1}(x+n-1)$
(b) $(x-1)^n (x+n-1)$
(c) $(1-x)^{n-1}(x+n-1)$
(d) None of these

47. If f(x), g(x) and h(x) are three polynomials of

degree 2 and $\Delta(x) = \begin{vmatrix} f(x) & g(x) & h(x) \\ f'(x) & g'(x) & h'(x) \\ f''(x) & g''(x) & h''(x) \end{vmatrix}$, then

$\Delta(x)$ is a polynomial of degree :

(a) 2
(b) 3
(c) atmost 2
(d) atmost 3

48. If a, b, c are positive and not all equal, then the

value of the determinant $\begin{vmatrix} a & b & c \\ b & c & a \\ c & a & b \end{vmatrix}$ is :

(a) non-negative
(b) non-positive
(c) negative
(d) positive.

49. If $a = \cos \theta + i \sin \theta$, $b = \cos 2\theta - i \sin 2\theta$,

$c = \cos 3\theta + i \sin 3\theta$ and if $\begin{vmatrix} a & b & c \\ b & c & a \\ c & a & b \end{vmatrix} = 0$ then θ

is equal to :

(a) $n\pi$
(b) $2n\pi$
(c) $(2n+1)\dfrac{\pi}{2}$
(d) None of these

50. The system of equations

$2x + py + 6z = 8$

$x + 2y + qz = 5$

$x + y + 3z = 4$ has :

(a) no solution if $p \neq 2$, $q = 3$

(b) a unique solution if $p \neq 2$, $q \neq 3$

(c) infinitely many solutions

(d) All of these

51. If $a \neq b \neq c$, one value of x which satisfies the equation

$$\begin{vmatrix} 0 & x-a & x-b \\ x+a & 0 & x-c \\ x+b & x+c & 0 \end{vmatrix} = 0 \text{ is given by :}$$

(a) $x = a$ (b) $x = b$

(c) $x = c$ (d) $x = 0$

52. The three roots of the equation $\begin{vmatrix} x & 3 & 7 \\ 2 & x & 2 \\ 7 & 6 & x \end{vmatrix} = 0$

are :

(a) $-9, 2, 7$ (b) $9, -2, 7$

(c) $9, 2, -7$ (d) None of these

53. The solution of the equations $x + 2y + 3z = 6$, $2x + 4y + z = 17$, $3x + 2y + 9z = 2$ is :

(a) $x = 1$, $y = 4$, $z = -1$

(b) $x = 4$, $y = 1$, $z = -1$

(c) $x = -1$, $y = 4$, $z = 1$

(d) None of these

54. The value of the determinant

$$\begin{vmatrix} \dfrac{1}{a} & \dfrac{1}{a(a+d)} & \dfrac{1}{(a+d)(a+2d)} \\ \dfrac{1}{a+d} & \dfrac{1}{(a+d)(a+2d)} & \dfrac{1}{(a+2d)(a+3d)} \\ \dfrac{1}{a+2d} & \dfrac{1}{(a+2d)(a+3d)} & \dfrac{1}{(a+3d)(a+4d)} \end{vmatrix}$$

where a, d > 0, is :

(a) $-\dfrac{4d^4}{a(a+d)^2(a+2d)^3(a+3d)^2(a+4d)}$

(b) $\dfrac{4d^4}{a(a+d)^2(a+2d)^3(a+3d)^2(a+4d)}$

(c) $\dfrac{4d^4}{a(a+d)^2(a+2d)^3(a+3d)^2(a+4d)^2}$

(d) None of these

55. Let λ and α be real. The set of all values of λ for which the system of linear equations

$\lambda x + (\sin \alpha) y + (\cos \alpha) z = 0$

$x + (\cos \alpha) y + (\sin \alpha) z = 0$

$-x + (\sin \alpha) y - (\cos \alpha) z = 0$

has a non-trivial solution, is :

(a) $[0, \sqrt{2}]$ (b) $[-\sqrt{2}, 0]$

(c) $[-\sqrt{2}, \sqrt{2}]$ (d) None of these

56. The value of the determinant

$$\begin{vmatrix} (b+c)^2 & c^2 & b^2 \\ c^2 & (c+a)^2 & a^2 \\ b^2 & a^2 & (a+b)^2 \end{vmatrix} \text{ is}$$

(a) $2(ab + bc + ca)^3$ (b) $(ab + bc + ca)^3$

(c) $4(ab + bc + ca)^3$ (d) None of these

57. The value of k, for which the system of equations

$x + ky + 3z = 0$,

$3x + ky - 2z = 0$,

$2z + 3y - 4z = 0$ possesses a non-trivial solution over the set of rationals, is :

(a) $-\dfrac{33}{2}$ (b) $\dfrac{33}{2}$

(c) 11 (d) None of these

58. If $x = cy + bz$, $y = az + cx$, $z = bx + ay$ where x, y, z are not all zero, then :

(a) $a^2 + b^2 + c^2 + 2abc = 0$

(b) $a^2 + b^2 + c^2 - 2abc = 1$

(c) $a^2 + b^2 + c^2 + 2abc = 1$

(d) None of these

59. Let α_1, α_2 and β_1, β_2 be the roots of equations $ax^2 + bx + c = 0$ and $px^2 + qx + r = 0$ respectively. If the system of equations $\alpha_1 y + \alpha_2 z = 0$ and $\beta_1 y + \beta_2 z = 0$ has a non-trivial solution, then :

(a) $\dfrac{b^2}{q^2} = \dfrac{ac}{pr}$ (b) $\dfrac{c^2}{r^2} = \dfrac{ab}{pq}$

(c) $\dfrac{a^2}{p^2} = \dfrac{bc}{qr}$ (d) None of these

60. The value of the determinant $\begin{vmatrix} -1 & 1 & 1 \\ 1 & -1 & 1 \\ 1 & 1 & -1 \end{vmatrix}$ is :

(a) −4   (b) 0

(c) 1   (d) 4

61. If ω is a cube root of unity, then a root of the equation

$$\begin{vmatrix} x+1 & \omega & \omega^2 \\ \omega & x+\omega^2 & 1 \\ \omega^2 & 1 & x+\omega \end{vmatrix} = 0 \text{ is :}$$

(a) $x = 1$ (b) $x = \omega$

(c) $x = \omega^2$ (d) $x = 0$

62. The value of the determinant

$$\begin{vmatrix} 0 & a-b & a-c \\ b-a & 0 & b-c \\ c-a & c-b & 0 \end{vmatrix} \text{ is :}$$

(a) $a+b+c$ (b) $2abc$

(c) 0   (d) None of these

63. In a third order determinant, each element of the first column consists of sum of two terms, each element of the second column consists of sum of three terms and each element of the third column consists of sum of four terms. Then it can be decomposed into n determinants, where n has the value :

(a) 1   (b) 9

(c) 16   (d) 24

64. If the value of a third order determinant is 11, then the value of the square of the determinant formed by its cofators will be :

(a) 11   (b) 121

(c) 1331   (d) 14641

65. If $\begin{vmatrix} a+b & b+c & c+a \\ b+c & c+a & a+b \\ c+a & a+b & b+c \end{vmatrix} = k \begin{vmatrix} a & b & c \\ b & c & a \\ c & a & b \end{vmatrix}$

then k =

(a) 1   (b) 2

(c) 4   (d) 8

66. If $\omega (\neq 1)$ is a cube root of unity, then

$$\begin{vmatrix} 1 & 1+i+\omega^2 & \omega^2 \\ 1-i & -1 & \omega^2-1 \\ -i & -i+\omega-1 & -1 \end{vmatrix} \text{ equals :}$$

(a) 0   (b) 1

(c) i   (d) ω

67. The system of linear equations $x + y + z = 2$, $2x + y - z = 3$, $3x + 2y + kz = 4$ has a unique solution, if

(a) $k \neq 0$ (b) $-1 < k < 1$

(c) $-2 < k < 2$ (d) $k = 0$

68. If $\begin{vmatrix} a & a+d & a+2d \\ a^2 & (a+d)^2 & (a+2d)^2 \\ 2a+3d & 2(a+d) & 2a+d \end{vmatrix} = 0$, then

(a) $a+d = 0$ (b) $d = 0$

(c) $d = 0$ or $a+d = 0$ (d) None of these

69. If $D_1 = \begin{vmatrix} 1 & 1 & 1 \\ x^2 & y^2 & z^2 \\ x & y & z \end{vmatrix}$ and $D_2 = \begin{vmatrix} 1 & 1 & 1 \\ yz & xz & xy \\ x & y & z \end{vmatrix}$, then

(a) $D_1 = D_2$ (b) $D_1 = -D_2$

(c) $D_1 = -2D_2$ (d) $D_2 = 2D_1$

70. The value of n for which the determinant

$$\begin{vmatrix} {}^8C_3 & {}^9C_5 & {}^{10}C_7 \\ {}^8C_4 & {}^9C_6 & {}^{10}C_8 \\ {}^9C_n & {}^{10}C_{n+2} & {}^{11}C_{n+4} \end{vmatrix} \text{ becomes zero is :}$$

(a) $n = 2$ (b) $n = 3$

(c) $n = 4$ (d) None of these

71. If $f(x) =$

$$\begin{vmatrix} 1 & 2(x-1) & 3(x-1)(x-2) \\ (x-1) & (x-1)(x-2) & (x-1)(x-2)(x-3) \\ x & (x-1)x & (x-1)(x-2)x \end{vmatrix}$$

then $f(41) =$

(a) 41   (b) −41

(c) 0   (d) None of these

72. If $\begin{vmatrix} x^3 + 4x & x + 3 & x - 2 \\ x - 2 & 5x & x - 1 \\ x - 3 & x + 2 & 4x \end{vmatrix}$

$= ax^5 + bx^4 + cx^3 + dx^2 + ex + f,$

be an identity in x, where a, b, c, d, e, f are independent of x, then the value of f is :

(a) 0   (b) 15

(c) 17   (d) None of these

73. Let $\begin{vmatrix} x+3 & x+2 & (x+2)^3 \\ x+2 & x+3 & (x+2)^3 \\ (x+2)^3 & x+2 & x+3 \end{vmatrix}$

$= ax^7 + bx^6 + cx^5 + dx^4 + ex^3 + fx^2 + gx + h$

be an identity in x, where a, b, c, d, e, f, g, h are independent of x, then the value of g is :

(a) −213   (b) 213

(c) 0   (d) None of these

74. $\begin{vmatrix} a^2 & b^2 & c^2 \\ (b-c)^2 & (c-a)^2 & (a-b)^2 \\ bc & ca & ab \end{vmatrix}$ is not divisible by :

(a) $a - b$ (b) $a^2 + b^2 + c^2$

(c) $a + b + c$ (d) None of these

75. If $f(x) = \begin{vmatrix} x+2 & x+3 & x+4 \\ {}^{x+2}P_{x+2} & {}^{x+3}P_{x+3} & {}^{x+4}P_{x+4} \\ {}^{x+2}C_{x+2} & {}^{x+3}C_{x+3} & {}^{x+4}C_{x+4} \end{vmatrix}$, then $f(x)$

is divisible by :

(a) $(x + 2)!$ (b) $(x + 3)!$

(c) $(x + 4)!$ (d) $(x^2 + 5x + 1)$

76. The value of the determinant

$\begin{vmatrix} 1 & \sin(\alpha - \beta)\theta & \cos(\theta - \beta)\theta \\ a & \sin \alpha\theta & \cos \alpha\theta \\ a^2 & \sin(\alpha - \beta)\theta & \cos(\alpha - \beta)\theta \end{vmatrix}$,

is independent of :

(a) α (b) β

(c) θ (d) a

77. If $\alpha + \beta + \gamma = \pi$, then the value of the determinant

$\begin{vmatrix} e^{2i\alpha} & e^{-\gamma} & e^{-i\beta} \\ e^{-i\gamma} & e^{2i\beta} & e^{-i\alpha} \\ e^{-i\beta} & e^{-i\alpha} & e^{2i\gamma} \end{vmatrix}$ is :

(a) 4   (b) −4

(c) 0   (d) None of these

78. If $b^2 - ac < 0$ and $a > 0$ then the value of the determinant

$\begin{vmatrix} a & b & ax + by \\ b & c & bx + cy \\ ax + by & bx + cy & 0 \end{vmatrix}$ is :

(a) positive   (b) negative

(c) zero   (d) $b^2 + ac$

79. If $\sqrt{-1} = i$ and ω is a non-real cube root of unity, then the value of the determinant

$\begin{vmatrix} x + 1 & \omega & \omega^2 \\ \omega & x + \omega^2 & 1 \\ \omega^2 & 1 & x + \omega \end{vmatrix}$ is :

(a) x^3 (b) $x^3 - 1$

(c) $x^3 + 1$ (d) None of these

80. If $U_n = \begin{vmatrix} 1 & k & k \\ 2n & k^2 + k + 1 & k^2 + k \\ 2n - 1 & k^2 & k^2 + k + 1 \end{vmatrix}$

and $\sum\limits_{n=1}^{k} U_n = 72$ then k =

(a) 8   (b) 9

(c) 6   (d) None of these

81. If $f(x) = \begin{vmatrix} x^3 & \cos^2 x & 2^{x^4} \\ \tan^5 x & 1 & \sec 2x \\ \sin^3 x & x^4 & 5 \end{vmatrix}$ then $\int\limits_{-\pi/2}^{\pi/2} f(x)\, dx =$

(a) 2   (b) −2

(c) 0   (d) None of these

82. The sum of the values of the determinants

$$\begin{vmatrix} (-1)^n x & (-1)^{n+1} y & (-1)^{n+3} z \\ x-5 & 3-y & 5+z \\ x-2 & y+6 & 3-z \end{vmatrix}$$

and $\begin{vmatrix} (-1)^{n+3} x & x-5 & x-2 \\ (-1)^{n+2} y & 3-y & y+6 \\ (-1)^{n+4} & 5+z & 3-z \end{vmatrix}$ is

(a) 0   (b) 4

(c) −4   (d) None of these

83. If 4^n is a factor of the determinant

$$\begin{vmatrix} 1 & 1 & 1 \\ {}^nC_1 & {}^{n+4}C_1 & {}^{n+8}C_1 \\ {}^nC_2 & {}^{n+4}C_2 & {}^{n+8}C_2 \end{vmatrix}, \text{ then the maximum value of}$$

n is :

(a) 3   (b) 4

(c) 5   (d) None of these

84. If $\begin{vmatrix} x^n & y^n & z^n \\ x^{n+2} & y^{n+2} & z^{n+2} \\ x^{n+3} & y^{n+3} & z^{n+3} \end{vmatrix}$

$= (x-y)(y-z)(z-x)\left(\dfrac{1}{x}+\dfrac{1}{y}+\dfrac{1}{z}\right)$ then :

(a) n = 1   (b) n = −1

(c) n = 2   (d) n = −2

85. The value of the determinant

$$\begin{vmatrix} \sin\alpha\cos\beta & \cos\alpha\cos\beta & -\sin\alpha\sin\beta \\ \sin\alpha\sin\beta & \cos\alpha\sin\beta & \sin\alpha\cos\beta \\ \cos\alpha & -\sin\alpha & 0 \end{vmatrix} \text{ is :}$$

(a) is independent of α

(b) independent of β

(c) independent of α and β

(d) None of these

86. If $f(x) = \begin{vmatrix} x^{n-1} & \cos x & \dfrac{1}{x+3} \\ 0 & \cos\dfrac{n\pi}{2} & \dfrac{(-1)^n\, n!}{3^{n+1}} \\ \alpha & \alpha^3 & \alpha^5 \end{vmatrix}$

then $\dfrac{d^n}{dx^n}[f(x)]_{x=0} =$

(a) 1   (b) −1

(c) 0   (d) None of these

87. The value of the determinant

$$\begin{vmatrix} 1+\alpha & 1+\alpha z & 1+\alpha z^2 \\ 1+\beta & 1+\beta z & 1+\beta z^2 \\ 1+\gamma & 1+\gamma z & 1+\gamma z^2 \end{vmatrix} \text{ is :}$$

(a) $(\alpha-\beta)(\beta-\gamma)(\gamma-\alpha)$

(b) 0

(c) $\alpha\beta\gamma$

(d) None of these

88. If $a_1, a_2, a_3, \ldots a_n, \ldots$ are in G.P. and $a_i > 0$ for each i, then the determinant

$$\begin{vmatrix} \log a_n & \log a_{n+2} & \log a_{n+4} \\ \log a_{n+6} & \log a_{n+8} & \log a_{n+10} \\ \log a_{n+12} & \log a_{n+14} & \log a_{n+16} \end{vmatrix} \text{ is equal to :}$$

(a) 1   (b) −1

(c) 0   (d) None of these

89. The value of the determinant

$$\begin{vmatrix} \sqrt{x}+\sqrt{y} & \sqrt[2]{z} & \sqrt{z} \\ \sqrt{yz}+\sqrt{2x} & z & \sqrt{2z} \\ y+\sqrt{xz} & \sqrt{yz} & z \end{vmatrix} ; \text{ where x, y, z are}$$

positive real numbers, is :

(a) $z(\sqrt{2}y - z\sqrt{y})$ (b) $y(\sqrt{2}z - y\sqrt{z})$

(c) $x(\sqrt{2}y - z\sqrt{y})$ (d) None of these

90. Let $D_k = \begin{vmatrix} \alpha & \beta & \gamma \\ 2 \cdot 3^k & 16 \cdot 9^k & 26 \cdot 27^k \\ (3^{10}-1) & 2(9^{10}-1) & (27^{10}-1) \end{vmatrix}$

then the value of $\sum\limits_{k=1}^{10} D_k$ is :

(a) $2(\alpha + \beta + \gamma)$ (b) $\alpha\beta + \alpha\gamma + \beta\gamma$

(c) $\alpha\beta\gamma$ (d) 0

91. If $\begin{vmatrix} \alpha & -\beta & 0 \\ 0 & \alpha & \beta \\ \beta & 0 & \alpha \end{vmatrix} = 0$ then :

(a) α/β is one of the cube roots of unity

(b) α is one of the cube roots of unity

(c) β is one of the cube roots of unity

(d) None of these

92. If $f(x) = \begin{vmatrix} x+\lambda & x & x \\ x & x+\lambda & x \\ x & x & x+\lambda \end{vmatrix}$, then $f(3x) - f(x) =$

(a) $3x\lambda^2$ (b) $6x\lambda^2$

(c) $x\lambda^2$ (d) None of these

93. If α, β and γ are roots of equation $x^3 + ax + b = 0$, then the value of the determinant

$\begin{vmatrix} \alpha - \beta - \gamma & 2\alpha & 2\alpha \\ 2\beta & \beta - \gamma - \alpha & 2\beta \\ 2\gamma & 2\gamma & \gamma - \alpha - \beta \end{vmatrix}$ is :

(a) 0   (b) a

(c) $-b$ (d) None of these

94. If α, β, γ are roots of equation $x^3 + px + q = 0$, then the value of the determinant

$\begin{vmatrix} 1+\alpha & 1 & 1 \\ 1 & 1+\beta & 1 \\ 1 & 1 & 1+\gamma \end{vmatrix}$ is :

(a) $p^2 - 2q$ (b) $3pq$

(c) $p - q$ (d) None of these

95. If $1, \omega, \omega^2$ are the cube roots of unity, then

$D = \begin{vmatrix} 1 & \omega^n & \omega^{2n} \\ \omega^{2n} & 1 & \omega^n \\ \omega^n & \omega^{2n} & 1 \end{vmatrix}$ has the value :

(a) 0   (b) ω

(c) ω^2 (d) 1

96. The value of a determinant of third order whose all elements are 1 or -1 is :

(a) an even number   (b) an odd number

(c) a prime number   (d) can't say

97. If $p + q + r = 0$ then $\begin{vmatrix} pa & qb & rc \\ qc & ra & pb \\ rb & pc & qa \end{vmatrix} =$

(a) $pqr (a^3 + b^3 + c^3 - 3abc)$

(b) $abc (p^3 + q^3 + r^3 - 3pqr)$

(c) $pqr (a^3 + b^3 + c^3 + 3abc)$

(d) $abc (p^3 + q^3 + r^3 + 3pqr)$

98. If the determinant

$\begin{vmatrix} b-c & c-a & a-b \\ b'-c' & c'-a' & a'-b' \\ b''-c'' & c''-a'' & a''-b'' \end{vmatrix} = m \begin{vmatrix} a & b & c \\ a' & b' & c' \\ a'' & b'' & c'' \end{vmatrix}$

then the value of m is :

(a) 0   (b) 2

(c) -1 (d) 1

99. If the determinant

$\begin{vmatrix} a & b & 2a\alpha + 3b \\ b & c & 2b\alpha + 3c \\ 2a\alpha + 3b & 2b\alpha + 3c & 0 \end{vmatrix} = 0$, then :

(a) a, b, c are in H.P.

(b) α is root of $4ax^2 + 12bx + 9c = 0$

or a, b, c are in G.P.

(c) a, b, c are in G.P. only

(d) a, b, c are in A.P.

100. If [ ] denotes the greatest integer less than or equal to the real number under consideration, and $-1 \leq x < 0$; $0 \leq y < 1$; $1 \leq z < 2$, then the value of the determinant

$$\begin{vmatrix} [x]+1 & [y] & [z] \\ [x] & [y]+1 & [z] \\ [x] & [y] & [z]+1 \end{vmatrix} \text{ is :}$$

(a) $[z]$ (b) $[y]$

(c) $[x]$ (d) None of these

101. Let m be a + ve integer and

$$\Delta_r = \begin{vmatrix} 2r-1 & {}^mC_r & 1 \\ m^2-1 & 2^m & m+1 \\ \sin^2(m^2) & \sin^2 m & \sin^2(m+1) \end{vmatrix},$$

where $0 \leq r \leq m$, then the value of $\sum\limits_{r=0}^{m} \Delta_r$ is given by :

(a) $2m$ (b) m^2-1

(c) $2^m \sin^2(2^m)$ (d) 0

102. If a, b, c are different, then the value of x satisfying

$$\begin{vmatrix} 0 & x^2-a & x^3-b \\ x^2+a & 0 & x^2+c \\ x^4+b & x-c & 0 \end{vmatrix} = 0 \text{ is}$$

(a) a (b) c

(c) b (d) 0

103. If system of equations $x = a(y+z)$, $y = b(z+x)$, $z = c(x+y)$ $(a, b, c \neq -1)$ has a non-zero solution, then the value of $\dfrac{a}{1+a} + \dfrac{b}{1+b} + \dfrac{c}{1+c}$ is :

(a) -1 (b) 0

(c) 1 (d) 2

104. One root of the equation

$$\begin{vmatrix} 3x-8 & 3 & 3 \\ 3 & 3x-8 & 3 \\ 3 & 3 & 3x-8 \end{vmatrix} = 0$$

is which of the following ?

(a) $\dfrac{2}{3}$ (b) $\dfrac{8}{3}$

(c) $\dfrac{16}{3}$ (d) $\dfrac{1}{3}$

105. If $p\lambda^4 + q\lambda^3 + r\lambda^2 + s\lambda + t =$

$$\begin{vmatrix} \lambda^2+3\lambda & \lambda-1 & \lambda+3 \\ \lambda+1 & 2-\lambda & \lambda-3 \\ \lambda-3 & \lambda+4 & 3\lambda \end{vmatrix}, \text{then t is equal to:}$$

(a) 21 (b) 31

(c) 23 (d) 33

106. If $|A| = \begin{vmatrix} a & b & c \\ x & y & z \\ p & q & r \end{vmatrix}$ and $|B| = \begin{vmatrix} q & -b & y \\ -p & a & -x \\ r & -c & z \end{vmatrix}$, then :

(a) $|A| = 2|B|$ (b) $|A| = |B|$

(c) $|A| = -|B|$ (d) None of these

107. The value of $\begin{vmatrix} b+c & a & a \\ b & c+a & b \\ c & c & a+b \end{vmatrix}$ is :

(a) abc (b) 0

(c) $a+b+c$ (d) $4abc$

108. Solution set of the equations

$$\begin{vmatrix} x & -6 & -1 \\ 2 & -3x & x-3 \\ -3 & 2x & x+2 \end{vmatrix} = 0 \text{ is :}$$

(a) $\{2, 0, 1\}$ (b) $\{2, -3, 1\}$

(c) $\{2, 1, 5\}$ (d) $\{-3, 1, 5\}$

109. If the capital letters denote the cofactors of the corresponding small letters in the determinant

$$\Delta = \begin{vmatrix} a_1 & b_1 & c_1 \\ a_2 & b_2 & c_2 \\ a_3 & b_3 & c_3 \end{vmatrix}, \text{ then the value of}$$

$$\Delta' = \begin{vmatrix} A_1 & B_1 & C_1 \\ A_2 & B_2 & C_2 \\ A_3 & B_3 & C_3 \end{vmatrix} \text{ is :}$$

(a) 0 (b) 2Δ

(c) Δ^2 (d) Δ

110. If $a + b + c = 0$, one root of

$$\begin{vmatrix} a - x & c & b \\ c & b - x & a \\ b & a & c - x \end{vmatrix} = 0 \text{ is :}$$

(a) $x = 0$ (b) $x = 1$

(c) $x = 2$ (d) $x = a^2 + b^2 + c^2$

111. The value of the determinant

$$\begin{vmatrix} 0 & a - b & a - c \\ b - a & 0 & b - c \\ c - a & c - b & 0 \end{vmatrix} \text{ is :}$$

(a) $a + b + c$ (b) $ab + bc + ca$

(c) abc (d) 0

112. The value of the determinant $\begin{vmatrix} 265 & 240 & 219 \\ 240 & 225 & 198 \\ 219 & 198 & 181 \end{vmatrix}$

is :

(a) 679   (b) 0

(c) 729   (d) None of these

113. The repeated factor of the determinant

$$\begin{vmatrix} y + z & x & y \\ z + x & z & x \\ x + y & y & z \end{vmatrix} \text{ is :}$$

(a) $z - x$ (b) $x - y$

(c) $y - z$ (d) None of these

114. The only integral root of the equation

$$\begin{vmatrix} 2 - y & 2 & 3 \\ 2 & 5 - y & 6 \\ 3 & 4 & 10 - y \end{vmatrix} = 0 \text{ is :}$$

(a) $y = 2$ (b) $y = 3$

(c) $y = 1$ (d) None of these

115. The value of $\begin{vmatrix} 1 & 1 & 1 & 1 \\ a & b & c & d \\ a^2 & b^2 & c^2 & d^2 \\ a^3 & b^3 & c^3 & d^3 \end{vmatrix}$ is :

(a) $\dfrac{1}{a} + \dfrac{1}{b} + \dfrac{1}{c} + \dfrac{1}{d}$

(b) $(a - b)(a - c)(a - d)(b - c)(b - d)(c - d)$

(c) $(a - b)(b - c)(c - d)$

(d) $(1 + a + b + c + d)^4$

116. If $a \ne b \ne c$, one value of x which satisfies the equation

$$\begin{vmatrix} 0 & x - a & x - b \\ x + a & 0 & x - c \\ x + b & x + c & 0 \end{vmatrix} = 0 \text{ is given by :}$$

(a) $x = 0$ (b) $x = c$

(c) $x = b$ (d) $x = a$

117. If T_p, T_q, T_r are p^{th}, q^{th}, r^{th} term of an A.P., then

$$\begin{vmatrix} T_p & T_q & T_r \\ p & q & r \\ 1 & 1 & 1 \end{vmatrix} \text{ is equal to :}$$

(a) $p + q + r$ (b) 0

(c) -1 (d) 1

118. The solution set of the equation $\begin{vmatrix} 2 & 3 & x \\ 2 & 1 & x^2 \\ 6 & 7 & 3 \end{vmatrix} = 0$

is :

(a) $\{1, -3\}$ (b) $\{1, -1\}$

(c) $\{1, -3\}$ (d) ϕ

119. If $\Delta = \begin{vmatrix} -1 & 1 & 1 \\ 1 & -1 & 1 \\ 1 & 1 & -1 \end{vmatrix}$, then Δ is equal to :

(a) 2   (b) 0

(c) 1   (d) 4

120. The value of the determinant

$$\begin{vmatrix} \cos\theta & \cos 2\theta & \cos 3\theta \\ \cos 3\theta & \cos\theta & \cos 2\theta \\ \cos 2\theta & \cos 3\theta & \cos\theta \end{vmatrix} \text{ is :}$$

(a) $\sin\dfrac{3\theta}{2}\left(\sin^3\dfrac{5\theta}{2}-\sin^3\dfrac{3\theta}{2}\right)$

(b) $2\sin\dfrac{3\theta}{2}\left(\sin^3\dfrac{5\theta}{2}-\sin^3\dfrac{3\theta}{2}\right)$

(c) $2\sin\dfrac{3\theta}{2}\left(\sin^3\dfrac{3\theta}{2}-\sin^3\dfrac{5\theta}{2}\right)$

(d) None of these

121. The value of the determinant

$$\begin{vmatrix} b^2+c^2 & a^2 & a^2 \\ b^2 & c^2+a^2 & b^2 \\ c^2 & c^2 & a^2+b^2 \end{vmatrix} \text{ is :}$$

(a) $a^2b^2c^2$ (b) $2a^2b^2c^2$

(c) $4a^2b^2c^2$ (d) None of these

122. The set of values of c for which the equations

$2x + 3y = 3$, $(c + 2) x + (c + 4) y = c + 6$,

$(c + 2)^2x + (c + 4)^2y = (c + 6)^2$ are consistent, is

(a) $\{10, 0\}$ (b) $\{-10, 0\}$

(c) $\{-10, 10\}$ (d) None of these

123. The real value of r for which the system of equations $2rx - 2y + 3z = 0$, $x + ry + 2z = 0$, $2x + rz = 0$ have non-trivial solutions is :

(a) $r = 2$ (b) $r = -2$

(c) $r = 0$ (d) None of these

124. Let $f(x) = \begin{vmatrix} x^3 & \sin x & \cos x \\ 6 & -1 & 0 \\ p & p^2 & p^3 \end{vmatrix}$, where p is a

constant. Then $\dfrac{d^3}{dx^3}[f(x)]$ at $x = 0$ is :

(a) p   (b) $p + p^2$

(c) $p + p^3$ (d) independent of p

125. The determinant $\begin{vmatrix} xp+y & x & y \\ yp+z & y & z \\ 0 & xp+y & yp+z \end{vmatrix} = 0$

if :

(a) x, y, z are in A.P. (b) x, y, z are in G.P.

(c) x, y, z are in H.P. (d) xy, yz, zx are in A.P.

126. The value of the determinant $\begin{vmatrix} bc & ca & ab \\ p & q & r \\ 1 & 1 & 1 \end{vmatrix}$

where a, b, c are respectively the pth, q^{th} and r^{th} terms of a harmonic progression, is :

(a) 0   (b) abc

(c) pqr   (d) None of these

127. If $\begin{vmatrix} 6i & -3i & 1 \\ 4 & 3i & -1 \\ 20 & 3 & i \end{vmatrix} = x + iy$, then

(a) $x = 3, y = 1$ (b) $x = 1, y = 3$

(c) $x = 0, y = 3$ (d) $x = 0, y = 0$

128. If

$$f(x) = \begin{vmatrix} 1 & x & x+1 \\ 2x & x(x-1) & (x+1)x \\ 3x(x-1) & x(x-1)(x-2) & (x+1)x(x-1) \end{vmatrix},$$

then f(100) is equal to :

(a) 0   (b) 1

(c) 100   (d) -100

129. If $x = -9$ is a root of the following equation,

then the other roots are $\begin{vmatrix} x & 3 & 7 \\ 2 & x & 2 \\ 7 & 6 & x \end{vmatrix} = 0$

(a) 2, 7   (b) $-2, 7$

(c) $2, -7$ (d) $-2, -7$

130. If $A = \begin{bmatrix} 1 & 3 \\ 2 & 1 \end{bmatrix}$, then the determinant of $A^2 - 2A$

is :

(a) 5   (b) 25

(c) -5 (d) -25

131. If d is the determinant of a square matrix A of order n, then the determinant of its adjoint is :

(a) d^n (b) d^{n-1}

(c) d^{n+1} (d) d

132. If $\Delta = \begin{vmatrix} 1 & 3\cos\theta & 1 \\ \sin\theta & 1 & 3\cos\theta \\ 1 & \sin\theta & 1 \end{vmatrix}$, then maximum

value of Δ is :

(a) 1   (b) 9

(c) 16   (d) None of these

133. If $A = \int_1^{\sin\theta} \frac{t\,dt}{1+t^2}$ and $B = \int_1^{\csc\theta} \frac{dt}{t(1+t^2)}$ then

the value of $\begin{vmatrix} A & A^2 & B \\ e^A e^B & B^2 & -1 \\ 1 & A^2+B^2 & -1 \end{vmatrix}$ is :

(a) $\sin\theta$ (b) $\csc\theta$

(c) 0   (d) 1

134. The value of the determinant $\begin{vmatrix} 1 & a & b+c \\ 1 & b & c+a \\ 1 & c & a+b \end{vmatrix}$ is :

(a) $a+b+c$ (b) $(a+b+c)^2$

(c) 0   (d) $1+a+b+c$

135. $\begin{vmatrix} x+1 & x+2 & x+\lambda \\ x+2 & x+3 & x+\mu \\ x+3 & x+4 & x+\gamma \end{vmatrix} = 0$, where λ, μ, γ are

in A.P., is :

(a) an equation whose all roots are real

(b) an identity in x

(c) an equation with only one real root

(d) None of these

136. The value of determinant $\begin{vmatrix} 2 & 8 & 4 \\ -5 & 6 & -10 \\ 1 & 7 & 2 \end{vmatrix}$ is :

(a) -440 (b) 0

(c) 328   (d) 488

137. If the number of positive integral solutions of $x + y + z = r$ ($r \geq 3$) is denoted by P_r, then the value of

$\begin{vmatrix} P_r & P_{r+1} & P_{r+2} \\ P_{r+1} & P_{r+2} & P_{r+3} \\ P_{r+2} & P_{r+3} & P_{r+4} \end{vmatrix}$ is :

(a) 1   (b) -1

(c) 0   (d) None of these

138. If $\begin{vmatrix} -a^2 & ab & ac \\ ab & -b^2 & bc \\ ac & bc & -c^2 \end{vmatrix} = ka^2b^2c^2$, then k =

(a) 2   (b) 4

(c) -4 (d) 8

139. If $f_1(x) = x + a_1$ and $f_2(x) = x_2 + b_1 x + b_2$ then the

value of the determinant $\begin{vmatrix} 1 & 1 & 1 \\ f_1(x_1) & f_1(x_2) & f_1(x_3) \\ f_2(x_1) & f_2(x_2) & f_2(x_3) \end{vmatrix}$

is :

(a) $x_1 x_2 x_3$

(b) $(x_1 - x_2)(x_2 - x_3)(x_3 - x_1)$

(c) 0

(d) None of these

140. If $\begin{vmatrix} a & b & a\alpha - b \\ b & c & b\alpha - c \\ 2 & 1 & 0 \end{vmatrix} = 0$ and $\alpha \neq \frac{1}{2}$, then :

(a) a, b, c are in A.P. (b) a, b, c are in G.P.

(c) a, b, c are in H.P. (d) None of these

141. If $\Delta_1 = \begin{vmatrix} a & b & 2c \\ d & e & 2f \\ x & y & 2z \end{vmatrix}$ and $\Delta_2 = \begin{vmatrix} f & 2d & e \\ 2z & 4x & 2y \\ c & 2a & b \end{vmatrix}$, then

(a) $\Delta_2 = 2\Delta_1$ (b) $\Delta_2 = \Delta_1$

(c) $\Delta_1 = 2\Delta_2$ (d) None of these

142. $\begin{vmatrix} 1 & \cos(\alpha-\beta) & \cos(\alpha-\gamma) \\ \cos(\alpha-\beta) & 1 & \cos(\beta-\gamma) \\ \cos(\alpha-\gamma) & \cos(\beta-\gamma) & 1 \end{vmatrix} =$

(a) $\begin{vmatrix} \cos\alpha & \sin\alpha & 1 \\ \cos\beta & \sin\beta & 1 \\ \cos\gamma & \sin\gamma & 1 \end{vmatrix}^2$

(b) Zero

(c) $\begin{vmatrix} \cos\alpha & \sin\alpha & 0 \\ \sin\beta & 0 & \cos\beta \\ 0 & \cos\gamma & \sin\gamma \end{vmatrix}$

(d) None of these

143. If $f(\theta) = \begin{vmatrix} \cos^2\theta & \cos\theta\sin\theta & -\sin\theta \\ \cos\theta\sin\theta & \sin^2\theta & \cos\theta \\ \sin\theta & -\cos\theta & 0 \end{vmatrix}$

then $f\left(\dfrac{\pi}{6}\right) =$

(a) 0   (b) 1
(c) 2   (d) None of these

144. If a, b, c are in A.P., then

$\begin{vmatrix} x+3 & x+4 & x+a \\ x+4 & x+5 & x+b \\ x+5 & x+6 & x+c \end{vmatrix}$ is equal to:

(a) 0   (b) $(a+b+c)-9x$
(c) $9x+a+b+c$ (d) None of these

145. If $\begin{vmatrix} e^x & \sin x \\ \cos x & \log_e(1+x^2) \end{vmatrix} = A + Bx + Cx^2 + \dots$

then A and B are :

(a) 0, −1   (b) 0, 1
(c) 1, −1   (d) None of these

146. The number of distinct real roots of

$\begin{vmatrix} \sin x & \cos x & \cos x \\ \cos x & \sin x & \cos x \\ \cos x & \cos x & \sin x \end{vmatrix} = 0$

in the interval $\dfrac{-\pi}{4} \le x \le \dfrac{\pi}{4}$ is :

(a) 0   (b) 2
(c) 1   (d) 3

147. If a, b, c are sides of a triangle and

$\begin{vmatrix} a^2 & b^2 & c^2 \\ (a+1)^2 & (b+1)^2 & (c+1)^2 \\ (a-1)^2 & (b-1)^2 & (c-1)^2 \end{vmatrix} = 0$ then :

(a) $\triangle ABC$ is an equilateral triangle
(b) $\triangle ABC$ is a right angled isosceles triangle
(c) $\triangle ABC$ is an isosceles triangle
(d) None of these

148. The value of the determinant

$\begin{vmatrix} a & a+b & a+2b \\ a+2b & a & a+b \\ a+b & a+2b & a \end{vmatrix}$ is :

(a) $3b^2(a+b)$ (b) $6b^2(a+b)$
(c) $9b^2(a+b)$ (d) None of these

149. The determinant

$\begin{vmatrix} 3 & a+b+c & a^3+b^3+c^3 \\ a+b+c & a^2+b^2+c^2 & a^4+b^4+c^4 \\ a^2+b^2+c^2 & a^3+b^3+c^3 & a^5+b^5+c^5 \end{vmatrix}$

is equal to :

(a) $(a+b+c)(a-b)^2(b-c)^2(c-a)^2$
(b) $(a+b+c)(a-b)(b-c)(c-a)$
(c) $(a+b+c)^2(a-b)(b-c)(c-a)$
(d) None of these

150. The ratio of the determinants

$\begin{vmatrix} 1 & a & a^2 \\ 1 & b & b^2 \\ 1 & c & c^2 \end{vmatrix}$ and $\begin{vmatrix} ab & a+b & 1 \\ bc & b+c & 1 \\ ca & c+a & 1 \end{vmatrix}$ is :

(a) 1 : 2   (b) 2 : 1
(c) 1 : 1   (d) None of these

151. The value of $\begin{vmatrix} \cos\alpha & \sin\alpha & \cos(\alpha+\delta) \\ \cos\beta & \sin\beta & \cos(\beta+\delta) \\ \cos\gamma & \sin\gamma & \cos(\gamma+\delta) \end{vmatrix}$ is :

(a) $\cos(\alpha+\beta+\gamma+\delta)$
(b) $\cos(\alpha+\beta)+\cos(\beta+\gamma)+\cos(\gamma+\delta)$
(c) independent of $\alpha, \beta, \gamma, \delta$
(d) None of these

152. Let $\Delta(x) = \begin{vmatrix} [x] & |x| & 1 \\ [x]^2 & |x|^2 & 1 \\ 1 & 1 & x - [x] \end{vmatrix}$, where [x] is the greatest integer function. If $x > 0$, $x \notin N$, then $\Delta(x) =$

(a) $([x]-x)([x](1-x^2) + x - 1 + x [x]^2)$
(b) $(x-[x])([x](1-x^2) + x - 1 + x [x]^2)$
(c) $([x] - x)([x](1-x^2) - x + 1 + x [x]^2)$
(d) None of these

153. In a $\triangle ABC$, $\begin{vmatrix} 1 & \cos A & c \sin A \\ \cos A & 1 & b \sin A \\ c \sin A & b \sin A & a^2 \end{vmatrix} =$

(a) abc
(b) $\sin A \cos A$
(c) 0
(d) None of these

154. The value of $\begin{vmatrix} a & b & c \\ b & c & a \\ c & a & b \end{vmatrix}$, a, b, c being positive real numbers, is:

(a) positive
(b) negative
(c) non-negative
(d) non-positive

155. The value of the determinant

$\begin{vmatrix} \sqrt{6} & 2i & 3+\sqrt{6} \\ \sqrt{12} & \sqrt{3}+i\sqrt{8} & 3\sqrt{2}+i\sqrt{6} \\ \sqrt{18} & \sqrt{2}+i\sqrt{12} & \sqrt{27}+2i \end{vmatrix}$ is :

(a) complex
(b) imaginary
(c) irrational
(d) none of these

156. The value of the third order determinant is 11. Then the value of the square of the determinant formed by their cofactors is :

(a) 11
(b) 121
(c) 1331
(d) 14641

157. The determinant

$\begin{vmatrix} a^2 & a & 1 \\ \cos nx & \cos(n+1)x & \cos(n+2)x \\ \sin nx & \sin(n+1)x & \sin(n+2)x \end{vmatrix}$

is independent of :

(a) n
(b) a
(c) x
(d) None of these

158. The largest value of a third order determinant whose elements are equal to 1 or 0 is :

(a) 1
(b) 2
(c) 3
(d) None of these

159. For positive numbers x, y and z, the numerical value of the determinant $\begin{vmatrix} 1 & \log_x y & \log_x z \\ \log_y x & 3 & \log_y z \\ \log_z x & \log_z y & 3 \end{vmatrix}$

is :

(a) 2
(b) 4
(c) 10
(d) None of these

160. If $\Delta(x) = \begin{vmatrix} 1 & \cos x & 1- \cos x \\ 1 + \sin x & \cos x & 1 + \sin x - \cos x \\ \sin x & \sin x & 1 \end{vmatrix}$

then $\int_0^{\pi/2} \Delta(x)\, dx$ is equal to :

(a) 1/4
(b) 1/2
(c) 0
(d) −1/2

161. The equation $\begin{vmatrix} 1 + x^4 & 1 + x^8 & -1 \\ x^7 + 1 & 1 + x^{11} & -1 \\ x^2 + x + 1 & x - 1 & x + 1 \end{vmatrix} = 0;$

will have :

(a) no real root
(b) at least one real root
(c) all roots real
(d) none of these

162. The system of equations

$3x + 4y - 2z = -1$
$-3x + 4y - 2z = 8$
$- 3x - 4y + 2z = 5$, will have :

(a) no roots
(b) infinite roots
(c) trivial solution
(d) unique solution

163. If $A + B + C = \pi$, then the value of determinant $\begin{vmatrix} \sin^2 A & \cot A & 2 \\ \sin^2 B & \cot B & 1 \\ \sin^2 C & \cot C & 1 \end{vmatrix}$ is equal to :

(a) 0
(b) 1
(c) −1
(d) None of these

164. If a ($\neq 6$), b, c satisfy $\begin{vmatrix} a & 2b & 2c \\ 3 & b & c \\ 4 & a & b \end{vmatrix} = 0$ then abc =

    (a) $a + b + c$ (b) 0

    (c) b^3 (d) $ab + bc$

165. Let P and Q be 3×3 matrices with $P \neq Q$. If $P^3 = Q^3$ and $P^2Q = Q^2P$, then determinant of $(P^2 + Q^2)$ is equal to :   **[AIEEE - 2012]**

    (a) –2   (b) 1

    (c) 0   (d) –1

166. The number of values of k for which the linear equations :   **[AIEEE - 2011]**

    $4x + ky + 2z = 0$

    $kx + 4y + z = 0$

    $2x + 2y + z = 0$

    possess a non-zero solution is

    (a) 0   (b) 3

    (c) 2   (d) 1

167. Consider the system of linear equations :

    [AIEEE - 2010]

    $x_1 + 2x_2 + x_3 = 3$

    $2x_1 + 3x_2 + x_3 = 3$

    $3x_1 + 5x_2 + 2x_3 = 1$

    The system has

    (a) exactly 3 solutions

    (b) a unique solution

    (c) no solution

    (d) infinite number of solutions

168. Let A be a 2×2 matrix :   **[AIEEE - 2009]**

    Statement 1: adj (adj A) = A

    Statement 2: $|$ adj A $| = |$ A $|$

(a) Statement 1 is true, statement 2 is true; statement 2 is a correct explanation for statement 1.

(b) Statement 1 is true, statement 2 is true; statement 2 is not a correct explanation for statement 1.

(c) Statement 1 is true, statement 2 is false.

(d) Statement 1 is false, statement 2 is true.

169. If $D = \begin{vmatrix} 1 & 1 & 1 \\ 1 & 1+x & 1 \\ 1 & 1 & 1+y \end{vmatrix}$ for $x \neq 0$, $y \neq 0$ then D

    is   **[AIEEE - 2007]**

    (a) divisible by neither x nor y

    (b) divisible by both x and y

    (c) divisible by x but not y

    (d) divisible by y but not x

170. The system of equations :   **[AIEEE - 2005]**

    $\alpha x + y + z = \alpha - 1$,

    $x + \alpha y + z = \alpha - 1$,

    $x + y + \alpha z = \alpha - 1$

    has no solution, if α is

    (a) –2   (b) either –2 or 1

    (c) not –2   (d) 1

171. If $a^2 + b^2 + c^2 = -2$ and

    $f(x) = \begin{vmatrix} 1 + a^2x & (1 + b^2)x & (1 + c^2)x \\ (1 + a^2)x & 1 + b^2x & (1 + c^2)x \\ (1 + a^2)x & (1 + b^2)x & 1 + c^2x \end{vmatrix}$

    then f (x) is a polynomial of degree :

    [AIEEE - 2005]

    (a) 1   (b) 0

    (c) 3   (d) 2

172. If $\begin{vmatrix} 0 & \cos x & -\sin x \\ \sin x & 0 & \cos x \\ \cos x & \sin x & 0 \end{vmatrix}^2 = \begin{vmatrix} 1 & \lambda & -\lambda \\ \lambda & 1 & \lambda \\ -\lambda & \lambda & 1 \end{vmatrix}$

    then λ is

    (a) $- \sin x \cos x$ (b) $\sin x \cos x$

    (c) $\sin x \cos^2 x$ (d) $\cos x \sin^2 x$

ANSWER KEY

1. (c)	**2.** (a)	**3.** (b)	**4.** (d)	**5.** (a)	**6.** (c)	**7.** (a)	**8.** (d)	**9.** (a)	**10.** (d)
11. (a)	**12.** (c)	**13.** (a)	**14.** (b)	**15.** (c)	**16.** (b)	**17.** (b)	**18.** (a)	**19.** (a)	**20.** (c)
21. (a)	**22.** (b)	**23.** (b)	**24.** (a)	**25.** (c)	**26.** (a)	**27.** (a)	**28.** (a)	**29.** (d)	**30.** (c)
31. (b)	**32.** (b)	**33.** (b)	**34.** (d)	**35.** (b)	**36.** (a)	**37.** (c)	**38.** (d)	**39.** (b)	**40.** (a)
41. (b)	**42.** (a)	**43.** (b)	**44.** (a)	**45.** (b)	**46.** (a)	**47.** (c)	**48.** (c)	**49.** (b)	**50.** (d)
51. (d)	**52.** (a)	**53.** (a)	**54.** (b)	**55.** (c)	**56.** (a)	**57.** (b)	**58.** (c)	**59.** (a)	**60.** (d)
61. (d)	**62.** (c)	**63.** (d)	**64.** (b)	**65.** (b)	**66.** (a)	**67.** (a)	**68.** (c)	**69.** (a)	**70.** (c)
71. (c)	**72.** (c)	**73.** (a)	**74.** (d)	**75.** (a)	**76.** (a)	**77.** (b)	**78.** (b)	**79.** (a)	**80.** (a)
81. (c)	**82.** (a)	**83.** (a)	**84.** (b)	**85.** (b)	**86.** (c)	**87.** (b)	**88.** (c)	**89.** (a)	**90.** (d)
91. (a)	**92.** (b)	**93.** (a)	**94.** (c)	**95.** (a)	**96.** (a)	**97.** (a)	**98.** (a)	**99.** (b)	**100.** (a)
101. (d)	**102.** (d)	**103.** (c)	**104.** (a)	**105.** (a)	**106.** (c)	**107.** (d)	**108.** (b)	**109.** (c)	**110.** (a)
111. (d)	**112.** (b)	**113.** (a)	**114.** (b)	**115.** (b)	**116.** (a)	**117.** (b)	**118.** (c)	**119.** (d)	**120.** (b)
121. (c)	**122.** (b)	**123.** (a)	**124.** (d)	**125.** (b)	**126.** (a)	**127.** (d)	**128.** (a)	**129.** (a)	**130.** (b)
131. (b)	**132.** (d)	**133.** (c)	**134.** (c)	**135.** (b)	**136.** (b)	**137.** (b)	**138.** (b)	**139.** (b)	**140.** (b)
141. (a)	**142.** (b)	**143.** (b)	**144.** (a)	**145.** (a)	**146.** (c)	**147.** (c)	**148.** (c)	**149.** (a)	**150.** (c)
151. (c)	**152.** (a)	**153.** (c)	**154.** (d)	**155.** (a)	**156.** (d)	**157.** (a)	**158.** (b)	**159.** (b)	**160.** (d)
161. (b)	**162.** (a)	**163.** (a)	**164.** (c)	**165.** (c)	**166.** (c)	**167.** (c)	**168.** (b)	**169.** (b)	**170.** (a)
171. (d)	**172.** (b)								

❑❑❑

STATISTICS

MULTIPLE CHOICE QUESTIONS

1. Mean of 25 observations was found to be 78.4. But later on it was found that 96 was misread as 69. The correct mean is :

   (a) 79.48   (b) 76.54

   (c) 81.32   (d) 78.4

2. A firm of readymade garments make both men's and women's shirts. Its profit average is 6% of sales. Its profit in men's shirts average 8% of sales and women's shirts comprise 60% of output. The average profit per sales rupee in women's shirts is :

   (a) 0.0466   (b) 0.0166

   (c) 0.0666   (d) None of these

3. The number of runs scored by 11 players of a cricket team of a school are 5, 19, 42, 11, 50, 30, 21, 0, 52, 36, 27. The median is :

   (a) 21   (b) 27

   (c) 30   (d) None of these

4. The median of the items 6, 10, 4, 3, 9, 11, 22, 18 is :

   (a) 9   (b) 10

   (c) 9.5   (d) 11

5. If the value of mode and mean is 60 and 66 respectively, then the value of median is :

   (a) 60   (b) 64

   (c) 68   (d) None of these

6. Geometric mean of 3, 9 and 27 is :

   (a) 18   (b) 6

   (c) 9   (d) None of these

7. Harmonic mean of 2, 4 and 5 is :

   (a) 4.21   (b) 3.16

   (c) 2.98   (d) None of these

8. If the frequencies of first four numbers out of 1, 2, 4, 6, 7, 8 are 2, 3, 3, 2 respectively, then the frequency of 8 if their A.M. is 5, is :

   (a) 4   (b) 5

   (c) 6   (d) None of these

9. The mean weight of 120 students in the second year class of a college is 56 kg. If the mean weights of the boys and that of the girls in the class are 60 kg and 50 kg respectively, then the number of boys and girls separately in the class are :

   (a) 72, 64   (b) 38, 64

   (c) 72, 48   (d) None of these

10. The mean of 10 numbers is 12.5; the mean of the first six is 15 and the last five is 10. The sixth number is :

    (a) 15   (b) 12

    (c) 18   (d) None of these

11. The mean of 100 items is 50 and their S.D. is 4. The sum of all the items and also the sum of the squares of the items is :

    (a) 5000, 251600   (b) 4000, 251600

    (c) 5000, 261600   (d) None of these

12. A student obtained the mean and standard deviation of 100 observations as 40 and 5.1 respectively. It was later found that he had wrongly copied down an observation as 50 instead of 40. The correct mean and standard deviation are :

    (a) 39.9, 6   (b) 36.4, 5

    (c) 39.9, 5   (d) None of these

13. If the A.M. of two numbers is 10 and their G.M. is 8, then their H.M. and the two numbers are :

    (a) 6.4, 16, 4   (b) 4.4, 16, 4

    (c) 6.4, 12, 4   (d) None of these

14. The mean and S.D. of distributions of 100 and 250 items are 50, 5 and 40, 6 respectively. The mean and S.D. of all the 250 items taken together are :

(a) 44, 6.46   (b) 42, 7.46

(c) 44, 7.46   (d) None of these

15. The coefficient of variation of two series are 58% and 69%. If their standard deviations are 21.2 and 15.6, then their A.M.s are :

(a) 36.6, 22.6   (b) 34.8, 22.6

(c) 36.6, 24.4   (d) None of these

16. If $n = 10$, $\bar{x} = 12$, $\sum x^2 = 1530$,

then the coefficient of variation is :

(a) 36%   (b) 41%

(c) 25%   (d) None of these

17. The A.M. and the S.D. of a set of 9 items are 43 and 5 respectively. If an item of value 63 is added to the set, the mean and S.D. of all the 10 items is :

(a) 45, 8.65   (b) 43, 7.65

(c) 45, 7.65   (d) None of these

18. The arithmetic mean of the series $1, 2, 2^2, \ldots 2^{n-1}$ is :

(a) $2^n/n$ (b) $(2^n - 1)/n$

(c) $(2^n + 1)/n$ (d) None of these

19. The arithmetic mean of the series

$^nC_0, ^nC_1, ^nC_2, \ldots, ^nC_n$ is :

(a) $2^n/(n + 1)$ (b) $2^n/n$

(c) $2^{n-1}/(n + 1)$ (d) None of these

20. The A.M. of n observations is M. If the sum of $n - 4$ observations is a, then the mean of remaining 4 observations is :

(a) $\dfrac{nM - a}{4}$ (b) $\dfrac{nM + a}{2}$

(c) $\dfrac{nM - a}{4}$ (d) $n M + a$

21. The weighted mean of first n natural numbers whose weights are equal to the squares of corresponding numbers is :

(a) $\dfrac{n + 1}{2}$ (b) $\dfrac{3n (n + 1)}{2 (2n + 1)}$

(c) $\dfrac{(n + 1) (2n + 1)}{6}$ (d) $\dfrac{n(n + 1)}{2}$

22. Mean deviation of the series, a, a + d, a + 2d ...... a + 2nd from its mean is :

(a) $\dfrac{(n + 1)d}{(2n + 1)}$ (b) $\dfrac{nd}{2n + 1}$

(c) $\dfrac{n (n + 1) d}{(2n + 1)}$ (d) $\dfrac{(2n + 1) d}{n (n + 1)}$

23. In any discrete series (when all values are not same), the relationship between M.D. about mean and S.D. is :

(a) M.D. = S.D.   (b) M.D. $\geq$ S.D.

(c) M.D. < S.D.   (d) M.D. $\leq$ S.D.

24. The mean of n items is $\bar{X}$. If the first item is increased by 1, second by 2 and so on, then the new mean is :

(a) $\bar{X} + n$ (b) $\bar{X} + \dfrac{n}{2}$

(c) $\bar{X} + \dfrac{n + 1}{2}$ (d) None of these

25. If the s.d. of a set of observations is 4 and if each observation is divided by 4, the s.d. of the new set of observations will be :

(a) 4   (b) 3

(c) 2   (d) 1

26. A sample of 35 observations has the mean 80 and s.d. as 4. A second sample of 65 observations from the same population has mean 70 and s.d. 3. The s.d. of the combined sample is :

(a) 5.85   (b) 5.58

(c) 3.42   (d) None of these

27. If μ is the mean of a distribution, then

$\sum f_i (y_i - \mu)$ is equal to :

(a) M.D.   (b) S.D.

(c) 0   (d) None of these

28. The means of five observations is 4 and their variance is 5.2. If three of these observations are 1, 2 and 6, then the other two are :

(a) 2 and 9   (b) 3 and 8

(c) 4 and 7   (d) 5 and 8

29. The quartile deviation for the data :

x	2	3	4	5	6
f	3	4	8	4	1

is :

(a) 0

(b) $\frac{1}{4}$

(c) $\frac{1}{2}$

(d) 1

30. If 25% of the items are less than 20 and 25% are more then 40, the quartile deviation is :

(a) 20

(b) 30

(c) 40

(d) 10

31. If the regression coefficients of X on Y and Y on X are –0.4 and –0.9 respectively, then the correlation coefficient between X and Y is :

(a) – 0.6

(b) 0.6

(c) 0.3

(d) – 0.3

32. If $\Sigma x_i = 60$, $\Sigma y_i = 95$, $\Sigma x_i y_i = 574$, n = 10, then Cov (x, y) is equal to :

(a) –0.2

(b) 0.2

(c) –0.4

(d) 0.4

33. A computer while calculating the correlation coefficient between two variables x and y from 25 pairs of observations obtained the following constants : n = 25, Σx = 125, Σx^2 = 650, Σy = 100, Σy^2 = 460, Σxy = 508. It was, however, later discovered at the time of checking that he had copied down two pairs as (6, 14) and (8, 6), while the correct values were (8, 12) and (6, 8). The correct value of the correlation coefficient is :

(a) $\frac{2}{3}$

(b) $\frac{1}{3}$

(c) $-\frac{2}{3}$

(d) $-\frac{1}{3}$

34. For 5 observations of pairs (x, y) of variables x and y, the following results are obtained :
Σx = 15, Σy = 25, Σx^2 = 55, Σy^2 = 135, Σxy = 83.
The predicted value of x when the value of y is 12, is :

(a) 9

(b) 8

(c) 8.6

(d) None of these

35. If the regression equations of two variables x and y are 4x + 3y + 7 = 0 and 3x + 4y + 8 = 0, then the correlation coefficient between x and y is :

(a) $\frac{4}{3}$

(b) $-\frac{4}{3}$

(c) $\frac{3}{4}$

(d) $-\frac{3}{4}$

36. The lines of regression of y on x and x on y are respectively y = x + 5 and 16x – 9y = 94. If the variance of y is 16, then the variance of x is :

(a) 9

(b) 3

(c) 6

(d) None of these

37. The coefficient of correlation between two variables x and y is 0.8 and their covariance is 20. If variance of x series is 16, then the S.D. of y series is :

(a) 6.25

(b) 4.25

(c) 5.25

(d) None of these

38. If $\bar{x}$ = 15, $\bar{y}$ = 80, σ_x = 12, σ_y = 12 and r = 0.75, then the estimated value of y corresponding to x = 55 is :

(a) 110

(b) 120

(c) 100

(d) None of these

39. If two lines of regression are 3x + 12y – 19 = 0 and 9x + 3y – 46 = 0, then :

(a) $b_{xy} = -\frac{1}{3}$

(b) $b_{xy} = \frac{1}{3}$

(c) $b_{yx} = -\frac{1}{3}$

(d) $b_{yx} = \frac{1}{4}$

40. If the lines of regression of Y on X and X on Y are respectively y = Kx + 4 and x = 4y + 5, then :

(a) $0 \leq K \leq 4$

(b) $0 \leq K \leq \frac{1}{4}$

(c) $K > \frac{1}{4}$

(d) None of these

41. If the correlation coefficient between x and y is 0.6 and if $u = \frac{x-5}{2}$ and $v = \frac{y-3}{3}$ then the coefficient of correlation between u and v is :

(a) 0.8

(b) 0.6

(c) 0.3

(d) 0.2

42. If x and y are two random variables with the same standard deviation and coefficient of correlation r, then the coefficient of correlation between x and x + y is :

(a) $\dfrac{1+r}{2}$

(b) $\sqrt{\dfrac{1+r}{2}}$

(c) $\dfrac{1-r}{2}$

(d) $\sqrt{\dfrac{1-r}{2}}$

43. The two lines of regression are parallel to the axes if r =

(a) 1

(b) – 1

(c) 0

(d) None of these

44. If M.D. is 12, the value of S.D. will be :

(a) 15

(b) 12

(c) 24

(d) None of these

45. If regression coefficient of y on x is 2, then the regression coefficient of x on y is :

(a) 2

(b) $\dfrac{1}{2}$

(c) $\leq \dfrac{1}{2}$

(d) None of these

46. The two regression lines for a bivariate data are $x + y + 50 = 0$ and $2x + 3y + k = 0$. If $\bar{x} = 0$, then $\bar{y} =$:

(a) 50

(b) k – 100

(c) –50

(d) 50 + k

47. If x and y are two variables such that u = – ax and v = by, where a and b are positive constants, then :

(a) r (x, y) = – r (u, v)

(b) r (u, v) = ab.r (x, y)

(c) r (x, y) = ab.r (u, v)

(d) r (x, y) = r (u, v)

48. The S.D. of scores 1, 2, 3, 4, 5 is :

(a) $\sqrt{2}$

(b) $\sqrt{3}$

(c) $\dfrac{2}{5}$

(d) $\dfrac{3}{5}$

49. For a bivariate distribution (x, y) if,

$\Sigma\,x = 50,\ \Sigma\,y = 60,\ \Sigma\,xy = 350,\ \bar{x} = 5,\ \bar{y} = 6,$ variance of x is 4, variance of y is 9, then r_{xy} equals :

(a) $\dfrac{11}{18}$

(b) $\dfrac{11}{3}$

(c) $\dfrac{5}{6}$

(d) $\dfrac{5}{36}$

50. For a symmetrical distribution $Q_1 = 20$ & $Q_3 = 40$. The value of 50th percentile is :

(a) 20

(b) 30

(c) 40

(d) None of these

51. The mean deviation of the numbers 3, 4, 5, 6, 7 is :

(a) 25

(b) 5

(c) 1.2

(d) 0

52. The number of observations in a group is 40. If the average of first 10 is 4.5 and that of the remaining 30 is 3.5, then the average of the whole group is :

(a) $\dfrac{15}{4}$

(b) $\dfrac{1}{5}$

(c) 8

(d) 4

53. The sum of squares of deviations for 10 observations taken from mean 50 is 250. The coefficient of variation is :

(a) 10%

(b) 40%

(c) 50%

(d) None of these

54. The regression coefficient of y on x is $\dfrac{2}{3}$ and x on y is $\dfrac{4}{3}$. If the acute angle between the regression line is θ, then tan θ is equal to :

(a) $\dfrac{1}{9}$

(b) $\dfrac{2}{9}$

(c) $\dfrac{1}{18}$

(d) None of these

55. A person purchases one kg of tomatoes from each of the 4 places at the rate of 1 kg, 2 kg, 3 kg, 4 kg per rupee respectively. On the average he has purchased x kg of tomatoes per rupee, then the value of x is :

(a) 2

(b) 2.5

(c) 1.92

(d) None of these

56. The coefficient of correlation between two variables x and y is 0.8, while the regression coefficient of y on x is 0.2, then the regression coefficient of x on y is :

(a) -3.2 (b) 3.2

(c) 4   (d) 0.16

57. Karl Pearson's coefficient of correlation between the heights (in inches) of teachers and students corresponding to the given data :

Heights of teachers   x :   66   67   68   69   70

Heights of students   y :   68   66   69   72   70

(a) $\dfrac{1}{\sqrt{2}}$ (b) $\sqrt{2}$

(c) $-\dfrac{1}{\sqrt{2}}$ (d) 0

58. Two numbers within the bracket denote the ranks of 10 students of a class in two subjects :

(1, 10), (2, 9), (3, 8), (4, 7), (5, 6), (6, 5), (7, 4), (8, 3), (9, 2), (10, 1), then rank correlation coefficient is :

(a) 0   (b) -1

(c) 1   (d) 0.5

59. If there exists a linear statistical relationship between two variables x and y, then the regression coefficient of y on x is :

(a) $\dfrac{\text{cov}(x, y)}{\sigma_x \, \sigma_y}$ (b) $\dfrac{\text{cov}(x, y)}{\sigma_y^2}$

(c) $\dfrac{\text{cov}(x, y)}{\sigma_x^2}$ (d) $\dfrac{\text{cov}(x, y)}{\sigma_x}$

where σ_x, σ_y are standard deviations of x and y respectively.

60. If $\bar{x} = \bar{y} = 0, \Sigma x_i \, y_i = 12, \sigma_x = 2, \sigma_y = 3$ and $n = 10$, then the coefficient of correlation is :

(a) 0.4   (b) 0.3

(c) 0.2   (d) 0.1

61. If the regression coefficients are 0.8 and 0.2 then the value of coefficient of correlation is :

(a) 0.16   (b) 0.4

(c) 0.04   (d) None of these

62. The A.M. of n numbers of a series is $\bar{X}$. If the sum of the first $(n-1)$ terms is K, then the nth number is :

(a) $\bar{X} - K$ (b) $n\bar{X} - K$

(c) $\bar{X} - nK$ (d) $n\bar{X} - nK$

63. The mean age of a combined group of men and women is 25 years. If the mean age of the group of men is 26 years and that of the group of women is 21 years, then the percentage of men and women in the group is :

(a) 60, 40   (b) 80, 20

(c) 20, 80   (d) 40, 60

64. If the S.D. of a variable X is σ, then the S.D. of $\dfrac{aX + b}{c}$ (a, b, c are constants) is :

(a) $\dfrac{a}{c}\sigma$ (b) $\left|\dfrac{a}{c}\right|\sigma$

(c) $\left|\dfrac{c}{a}\right|\sigma$ (d) $\dfrac{c}{a}\sigma$

65. In a series, the coefficient of variation is 20 and mean 40, the standard deviation shall be :

(a) 6   (b) 8

(c) 4   (d) 2

66. If in a series, the coefficient of variation is 50 and S.D. 20, the A.M. shall be :

(a) 40 .   (b) 30

(c) 20   (d) 10

67. If $y = f(x)$ is a monotonically increasing or decreasing function of x and M is the median of variable x, then the median of y is :

(a) $f(M)$ (b) $\dfrac{M}{2}$

(c) $f^{-1}(M)$ (d) None of these

68. If each observation of a raw data, whose variance is σ^2, is multiplied by h, then the variance of the new set is :

(a) σ^2 (b) $h^2\sigma^2$

(c) $h\sigma^2$ (d) $h + \sigma^2$

69. Let X and Y be two independent variables with means 5 and 10 and variance 4 and 9 respectively. If $U = 3X + 4Y$ and $V = 3X - Y$, then $r(U, V)$ is equal to :

(a) 0   (b) 1

(c) $\dfrac{2}{3}$ (d) None of these

70. The coefficient of correlation between X and Y will have positive sign when :

(a) X is increasing and Y is decreasing

(b) both X and Y are increasing

(c) X is decreasing and Y is increasing

(d) There is no change in X and Y

71. If b_{yx} and b_{xy} are regression coefficients of y on x and x on y respectively, then

(a) $b_{yx} + b_{xy} = 2r(x, y)$

(b) $b_{yx} + b_{xy} < 2r(x, y)$

(c) $b_{yx} + b_{xy} \geq 2r(x, y)$

(d) None of these

72. For two variables x and y with the same mean, the two regression equations are

$y = ax + b$, $x = \alpha y + \beta$, then $\dfrac{b}{\beta}$ is :

(a) $\dfrac{1 - \alpha}{1 - a}$ (b) $\dfrac{1 - a}{1 - \alpha}$

(c) $\dfrac{1 + a}{1 + \alpha}$ (d) $\dfrac{1 + \alpha}{1 + a}$

73. Mean $\pm 3\sigma$ covers :

(a) 93.37 % items   (b) 90% items

(c) 99.9 % items   (d) 99.73 % items

74. Quartile deviation is :

(a) $\dfrac{4}{5}\sigma$ (b) $\dfrac{3}{2}\sigma$

(c) $\dfrac{2}{3}\sigma$ (d) $\dfrac{5}{4}\sigma$

75. In a symmetric distribution :

(a) $(\text{Median} - Q_1) = (Q_3 - \text{Median})$

(b) $(\text{Median} - Q_1) < (Q_3 - \text{Median})$

(c) $(\text{Median} - Q_1) > (Q_3 - \text{Median})$

(d) None of these

76. The reciprocal of the mean of the reciprocals of n observations is their :

(a) A.M.   (b) G.M.

(c) H.M.   (d) None of these

77. The relation between the median M, the second quartile Q_2, the fifth decile D_5 and the fiftieth percentile P_{50}, of a set of observations is :

(a) $M = Q_2 = D_5 = P_{50}$

(b) $M < Q_2 < D_5 < P_{50}$

(c) $M > Q_2 > D_5 > P_{50}$

(d) None of these

78. Which of the following is a unit free number ?

(a) S.D.   (b) Variance

(c) M.D.   (d) C.V.

79. Correlation coefficient is the ...... between the regession coefficients.

(a) A.M.   (b) G.M.

(c) H.M.   (d) None of these

80. When the correlation coefficient is zero, the two regression lines are :

(a) parallel   (b) perpendicular

(c) coincident   (d) None of these

81. Which of the following statements is incorrect ?

(a) Two regression lines are at right angles when r = 0.

(b) If one of the regression coefficients is greater than unity, the other must also be greater than unity.

(c) The product of regression coefficients is always less than one.

(d) b_{yx} and b_{xy} can be obtained if the values of r, σ_y and σ_x are known.

82. If $-1 < r < 0.75$, then the correlation is called a :

(a) perfect negative correlation

(b) low degree of negative correlation

(c) high degree of negative correlation

(d) None of these

83. If the two variables x and y of a bivariate distribution have a perfect correlation, they may be connected by :

(a) $xy = 1$

(b) $\dfrac{a}{x} + \dfrac{b}{y} = 1$

(c) $\dfrac{x}{a} + \dfrac{y}{b} = 1$

(d) None of these

84. The regression coefficients are independent of :

(a) scale, but not origin.

(b) origin, but not of scale.

(c) both origin and scale.

(d) neither origin nor scale.

85. In regression of y on x, x is :

(a) a dependent variable

(b) an independent variable

(c) a constant

(d) None of these

86. The intersecting point of the two regression lines is :

(a) $(0, 0)$

(b) $(\bar{x}, \bar{y})$

(c) (b_{xy}, b_{yx})

(d) None of these

87. For covariance the number of variate values in the two given distributions should be :

(a) unequal.

(b) any number in one and any number in the other.

(c) equal.

(d) None of these

88. The line of regression of x on y estimates :

(a) x for a given value of y

(b) y for a given value of x

(c) x from y and y from x

(d) None of these

89. Let r_{xy} be the coefficient of correlation between two variables x and y. If the variable x is multiplied by 3 and the variable y is increased by 2, then the correlation coefficient of the new set of variables is :

(a) r_{xy}

(b) $3r_{xy}$

(c) $3r_{xy} + 2$

(d) None of these

90. The quartile deviation for the data :

x :	2	3	4	5	6
f :	3	4	8	4	1

(a) 1/2

(b) 1

(c) 1/4

(d) 0

91. Out of the two lines of regression given by $x + 2y = 4$ and $2x + 3y - 5 = 0$, the regression line of x on y is :

(a) $2x + 3y - 5 = 0$

(b) $x + 2y = 4$

(c) $x + 2y = 0$

(d) The given lines cannot be the regression line of x on y.

92. If the two variables x and y or bivariate distribution have a perfect correlation, they may be connected by :

(a) $\dfrac{x}{a} + \dfrac{y}{b} = 1$

(b) $xy = 1$

(c) $\dfrac{a}{x} + \dfrac{b}{y} = 1$

(d) None of these

93. If a, b, c, d are constants such that a and c are both negative and r is the correlation coefficient between x and y, correlation coefficient between $ax + b$ and $cy + d$ is equal to :

(a) $\dfrac{a}{c} r$

(b) $\dfrac{c}{a}$

(c) $- r$

(d) r

94. Quartile deviation for a frequency distribution :

(a) $Q = \dfrac{1}{4}(Q_2 - Q_1)$

(b) $Q = \dfrac{1}{3}(Q_3 - Q_1)$

(c) $Q = \dfrac{1}{2}(Q_3 - Q_1)$

(d) $Q = Q_3 - Q_1$

95. A car completes the first half of its journey with a velocity v_1 and the rest half with a velocity v_2. Then the average velocity of the car for the whole journey is :

(a) $\dfrac{2v_1 v_2}{v_1 + v_2}$

(b) $\dfrac{v_1 + v_2}{2}$

(c) $\sqrt{v_1 v_2}$

(d) None of these

96. If two lines of regression are

8x − 10y + 66 = 0 and 40x − 18y = 214, then

$(\bar{x}, \bar{y})$ is :

(a) (−13, −17)　　　(b) (−17, 13)

(c) (13, 17)　　　(d) (17, 13)

97. Let $x_1, x_2, ..., x_n$ be n observations, and let $\bar{x}$ be their arithmetic mean and σ^2 be their variance.

[AIEEE - 2012]

Statement 1: Variance of $2x_1, 2x_2, ..., 2x_n$ is $4\sigma^2$.

Statement 2: Arithmetic mean of $2x_1, 2x_2, ...,$ $2x_n$ is $4\bar{x}$.

(a) Statement 1 is false, statement 2 is true.

(b) Statement 1 is true, statement 2 is true; statement 2 is a correct explanation for statement 1.

(c) Statement 1 is true, statement 2 is true; statement 2 is not a correct explanation for statement 1.

(d) Statement 1 is true, statement 2 is false.

98. If the mean deviation about the median of the numbers a, 2a, ..., 50a is 50, then | a | equals :

[AIEEE - 2011]

(a) 5　　　(b) 2

(c) 3　　　(d) 4

99. For two data sets, each of size 5, the variances are given to be 4 and 5 and corresponding means are given to be 2 and 4, respectively. The variance of the combined data set is :

[AIEEE - 2010]

(a) $\dfrac{11}{2}$　　　(b) 6

(c) $\dfrac{13}{2}$　　　(d) $\dfrac{5}{2}$

100. If the mean deviation of numbers 1, 1 + d, 1 + 2d, ..., 1 + 100d from their mean is 255, then the value of d is equal to : [AIEEE - 2009]

(a) 10.0　　　(b) 20.0

(c) 10.1　　　(d) 20.2

101. **Statement 1:** The variance of first n even natural numbers is $\dfrac{n^2 - 1}{4}$. [AIEEE - 2009]

Statement 2: The sum of first n natural numbers is $\dfrac{n(n+1)}{2}$ and the sum of squares of first n natural numbers is $\dfrac{n(n+1)(2n+1)}{6}$

(a) Statement 1 is true, statement 2 is true; statement 2 is a correct explanation for statement 1.

(b) Statement 1 is true, statement 2 is true; statement 2 is not a correct explanation for statement 1.

(c) Statement 1 is true, statement 2 is false.

(d) Statement 1 is false, statement 2 is true.

102. The mean of the numbers a, b, 8, 5, 10 is 6 and the variance is 6.80. Then which one of the following gives possible values of a and b?

[AIEEE - 2008]

(a) a = 0, b = 7　　　(b) a = 5, b = 2

(c) a = 1, b = 6　　　(d) a = 3, b = 4

103. The average marks of boys in a class is 52 and that of girls is 42. The average marks of boys and girls combined is 50. The percentage of boys in the class is : [AIEEE - 2007]

(a) 40　　　(b) 20

(c) 80　　　(d) 60

104. Suppose a population A has 100 observations 101, 102, ... , 200, and another population B has 100 observations 151, 152, ... , 250. If V_A and V_B represent the variances of the two populations, respectively, then $\dfrac{V_A}{V_B}$ is :

[AIEEE - 2006]

(a) 1　　　(b) 9/4

(c) 4/9　　　(d) 2/3

105. If in a frequency distribution, the mean and median are 21 and 22 respectively, then its mode is approximately : [AIEEE - 2005]

(a) 22.0　　　(b) 20.5

(c) 25.5　　　(d) 24.0

106. If the mean and standard deviation of 10 observations x_1, x_2, ..., x_{10} are 2 and 3 respectively, then the mean of $(x_1 + 1)^2$, $(x_2 + 1)^2$, ..., $(x_{10} + 1)^2$ is

    (a) 16.0

    (b) 18.0

    (c) 13.5

    (d) 14.4

ANSWER KEY

1. (a)	2. (a)	3. (b)	4. (c)	5. (b)	6. (c)	7. (b)	8. (c)	9. (c)	10. (a)
11. (a)	12. (c)	13. (a)	14. (c)	15. (a)	16. (c)	17. (c)	18. (b)	19. (a)	20. (a)
21. (b)	22. (c)	23. (d)	24. (c)	25. (d)	26. (a)	27. (c)	28. (c)	29. (d)	30. (d)
31. (a)	32. (d)	33. (a)	34. (c)	35. (d)	36. (a)	37. (a)	38. (a)	39. (a,c)	40. (b)
41. (b)	42. (b)	43. (c)	44. (a)	45. (c)	46. (c)	47. (a)	48. (a)	49. (c)	50. (b)
51. (c)	52. (a)	53. (a)	54. (c)	55. (c)	56. (b)	57. (a)	58. (b)	59. (c)	60. (c)
61. (b)	62. (b)	63. (b)	64. (b)	65. (b)	66. (a)	67. (a)	68. (b)	69. (a)	70. (b)
71. (c)	72. (d)	73. (d)	74. (c)	75. (a)	76. (c)	77. (a)	78. (a)	79. (b)	80. (b)
81. (b)	82. (c)	83. (c)	84. (b)	85. (b)	86. (b)	87. (c)	88. (a)	89. (a)	90. (b)
91. (a)	92. (a)	93. (d)	94. (c)	95. (a)	96. (c)	97. (d)	98. (d)	99. (a)	100. (c)
101. (d)	102. (d)	103. (c)	104. (a)	105. (d)	106. (b)				

PROBABILITY

MULTIPLE CHOICE QUESTIONS

1. The probability of throwing more than 15 in one throw with 3 dice is :

   (a) $\dfrac{5}{108}$ (b) $\dfrac{5}{54}$

   (c) $\dfrac{5}{216}$ (d) None of these

2. Two dice are thrown together. The probability that the sum of the numbers on the two faces is neither 9 nor 11 is :

   (a) $\dfrac{1}{2}$ (b) $\dfrac{2}{3}$

   (c) $\dfrac{5}{6}$ (d) None of these

3. In a single throw of three dice, the probability of getting a total of atleast 5 is :

   (a) $\dfrac{1}{3}$ (b) $\dfrac{53}{54}$

   (c) $\dfrac{1}{54}$ (d) None of these

4. The letters of word 'SOCIETY' are placed at random in a row. The probability that three vowels come together, is :

   (a) $\dfrac{6}{7}$ (b) $\dfrac{1}{7}$

   (c) $\dfrac{3}{7}$ (d) None of these

5. The letters of the word 'ARTICLE' are arranged at random. The probability that the vowels may occupy the even places, is :

   (a) $\dfrac{1}{35}$ (b) $\dfrac{4}{35}$

   (c) $\dfrac{7}{35}$ (d) None of these

6. Two unbiased dice are rolled. The probability that the sum of the numbers on the two faces is either divisible by 3 or divisible by 4, is :

   (a) $\dfrac{5}{9}$ (b) $\dfrac{4}{9}$

   (c) $\dfrac{1}{3}$ (d) None of these

7. A drawer contains 50 bolts and 150 nuts. Half of the bolts and half of the nuts are rusted. If one item is chosen at random, the probability that it is rusted or is a bolt, is :

   (a) $\dfrac{3}{8}$ (b) $\dfrac{1}{2}$

   (c) $\dfrac{5}{8}$ (d) None of these

8. The probability that at least one of the events A and B occurs is 0.7 and they occur simultaneously with probability 0.2. Then $P(\bar{A}) + P(\bar{B}) =$

   (a) 1.8 (b) 0.6

   (c) 1.1 (d) 1.4

9. The probability of getting the sum as a prime number when two dice are thrown together, is :

   (a) $\dfrac{1}{2}$ (b) $\dfrac{7}{12}$

   (c) $\dfrac{5}{12}$ (d) None of these

10. The probability of getting the product a perfect square (square of a natural number), when two dice are thrown together, is :

    (a) $\dfrac{2}{9}$ (b) $\dfrac{4}{9}$

    (c) $\dfrac{1}{3}$ (d) None of these

11. There are 100 students in a college class of which 36 are boys studying statistics and 13 are girls not studying statistics. If there are 55 girls in all, the probability that a boy picked up at random is not studying statistics is:

    (a) $\dfrac{3}{5}$ (b) $\dfrac{2}{5}$

    (c) $\dfrac{1}{5}$ (d) None of these

12. A room has 3 lamps. From a collection of 10 light bulbs of which 6 are not good, a person selects 3 at random and puts them in a socket, the probability that he will have light, is :

(a) $\frac{5}{6}$ (b) $\frac{1}{6}$

(c) $\frac{1}{2}$ (d) None of these

13. The probability of getting an even number on the first die or a total of 8 in a single throw of two dice is :

(a) $\frac{5}{9}$ (b) $\frac{4}{9}$

(c) $\frac{2}{9}$ (d) $\frac{1}{9}$

14. One of the two events must happen. Given that the chance of one is two-third of the other, the odds in favour of the other are :

(a) 3 : 5 (b) 2 : 5

(c) 3 : 2 (d) None of these

15. A, B, C are three mutually exclusive and exhaustive events associated with a random experiment. If

P (B) = $\frac{3}{2}$ P(A) and P(C) = $\frac{1}{2}$ P(B), then P(A) =

(a) $\frac{4}{13}$ (b) $\frac{6}{13}$

(c) $\frac{8}{13}$ (d) None of these

16. 100 students appeared for two examinations, 60 passed the first, 50 passed the second and 30 passed both. The probability that a student selected at random has failed in both examinations, is :

(a) 0.4 (b) 0.2

(c) 0.3 (d) None of these

17. The probability that a contractor will get a plumbing contract is $\frac{2}{3}$ and the probability that he will not get an electric contract is $\frac{5}{9}$. If the probability of getting atleast one contract is $\frac{4}{5}$, then the probability that he will get both is :

(a) $\frac{14}{45}$ (b) $\frac{7}{45}$

(c) $\frac{13}{45}$ (d) None of these

18. A police-man fires six bullets on a dacoit. The probability that the dacoit will be killed by one bullet is 0.6. The probability that dacoit is still alive is :

(a) 0.04096 (b) 0.004096

(c) 0.4096 (d) None of these

19. A class consists of 100 students, 25 of them are girls and 75 boys, 20 of them are rich and remaining poor, 40 of them are fair complexioned. The probability of selecting a fair complexioned rich girl is :

(a) 0.02 (b) 0.04

(c) 0.05 (d) 0.08

20. A speaks truth in 60% of the cases and B in 90% of the cases. The percentage of cases they are likely of contradict each other in stating the same fact is :

(a) 36% (b) 48%

(c) 42% (d) None of these

21. Two dice are thrown. The probability that the number appeared have a sum 8 if it is known that the second die always exhibits 4, is :

(a) $\frac{5}{6}$ (b) $\frac{1}{6}$

(c) $\frac{2}{3}$ (d) None of these

22. There are two groups of subjects one of which consists of 5 science subjects and 3 engineering subjects and the other consists of 3 science and 5 engineering subjects. An unbiased die is cast. If number 3 or 5 turns up, a subject is selected at random from the first group, otherwise the subject is selected at random from the second group. The probability that an engineering subject is selected ultimately, is :

(a) $\frac{13}{24}$ (b) $\frac{8}{24}$

(c) $\frac{17}{24}$ (d) None of these

23. Bag A contains 4 red and 5 black balls and bag B contains 3 red and 7 black balls. One ball is drawn from bag A and two from bag B. The probability that out of 3 balls drawn two are black and one is red, is :

(a) $\frac{8}{15}$ (b) $\frac{4}{15}$

(c) $\frac{7}{15}$ (d) None of these

24. A bag contains 6 red and 3 white balls. Four balls are drawn one by one and not replaced. The probability that they are alternatively of different colours is :

(a) $\frac{4}{42}$ (b) $\frac{5}{42}$

(c) $\frac{7}{42}$ (d) None of these

25. Three groups of children contain respectively 3 girls and 1 boy, 2 girls and 2 boys, 1 girl and 3 boys. One child is selected at random from each group. The chance that three selected consist of 1 girl and 2 boys is :

(a) $\frac{13}{32}$ (b) $\frac{15}{32}$

(c) $\frac{17}{32}$ (d) None of these

26. A student takes his examination in four subjects A, B, C and D. He estimates his chance of passing in A as $\frac{4}{5}$, in B as $\frac{3}{4}$, in C as $\frac{5}{6}$ and in D as $\frac{2}{3}$. To qualify he must pass in 3 and at least two other subjects. The probability that he qualifies is :

(a) $\frac{34}{90}$ (b) $\frac{61}{90}$

(c) $\frac{53}{90}$ (d) None of these

27. An urn contains 10 white and 3 black balls, while another urn contains 3 white and 5 black balls. Two are drawn from first urn and put into the second urn and then a ball is drawn from the later. The probability that it is a white ball, is :

(a) $\frac{61}{130}$ (b) $\frac{59}{130}$

(c) $\frac{72}{130}$ (d) None of these

28. A and B throw alternatively with a pair of dice. A wins if he throws 6 before B throws 7 and B wins if he throws 7 before A throws 6. If A begins, his chances of winning are :

(a) $\frac{32}{61}$ (b) $\frac{41}{61}$

(c) $\frac{28}{61}$ (d) $\frac{30}{61}$

29. The odds that A speaks the truth are 3 : 2 and the odds the B speaks that truth are 5 : 3. The percentage of cases they are likely to contradict each other on an identical point is :

(a) 47.5% (b) 32.5%

(c) 42.5% (d) None of these

30. A student appears for tests I, II and III. The student is successful if he passes either in tests I and II or tests I and III. The probabilities of student passing in tests I, II and III are p, q and $\frac{1}{2}$ respectively. If the probability that the student is successful is $\frac{1}{2}$, then :

(a) p = q = 1 (b) p = q = $\frac{1}{2}$

(c) p = 1, q = 0 (d) p = 1, q = $\frac{1}{2}$

31. A bag contains 3 red and 7 black balls. Two balls are selected at random without replacement. If the second selected ball is given to be red, the probability that the first selected ball is also red, is :

(a) $\frac{4}{9}$ (b) $\frac{2}{9}$

(c) $\frac{3}{9}$ (d) None of these

32. The probability that a leap year selected at random contains 53 Sundays is :

(a) $\frac{7}{366}$ (b) $\frac{26}{183}$

(c) $\frac{1}{7}$ (d) $\frac{2}{7}$

33. The probability that an event A happens in a trial is 0.4. Three independent trials are made. The probability that A happens at least once is :

(a) 0.936   (b) 0.216

(c) 0.784   (d) 0.064

34. Seven chits are numbered 1 to 7. Four are drawn one by one with replacements. The probability that the least number on any selected chit is 5, is :

(a) $\left(\dfrac{2}{7}\right)^4$ (b) $4 \cdot \left(\dfrac{2}{7}\right)^4$

(c) $\left(\dfrac{3}{7}\right)^3$ (d) None of these

35. A box contains 5 brown and 4 white socks. A man takes out two socks. The probability that they are of the same colour is :

(a) $\dfrac{5}{108}$ (b) $\dfrac{1}{6}$

(c) $\dfrac{5}{18}$ (d) $\dfrac{4}{9}$

36. For any two independent events E_1 and E_2,

$P\{(E_1 \cup E_2) \cap (\bar{E}_1) \cap (\bar{E}_2)\}$ is :

(a) $< \dfrac{1}{4}$ (b) $> \dfrac{1}{4}$

(c) $\geq \dfrac{1}{2}$ (d) None of these

37. If the probabilities that A and B will die within a year are p and q respectively, then the probability that only one of them will be alive at the end of the year is :

(a) p + q   (b) p + q – 2pq

(c) p + q – pq   (d) p + q + pq

38. In order to get atleast once a head with probability ≥ 0.9, the number of times a coin needs to be tossed is :

(a) 3   (b) 4

(c) 5   (d) None of these

39. A man alternately tosses a coin and throws a dice beginning with the coin. The probability that he gets a 5 or 6 in the dice before getting head is :

(a) $\dfrac{3}{4}$ (b) $\dfrac{1}{2}$

(c) $\dfrac{1}{3}$ (d) None of these

40. You are given a box with 20 cards in it. 10 of these cards have the letter I printed on them. The other ten have the letter T printed on them. If you pick up 3 cards at random and keep them in the same order, the probability of making the word IIT is :

(a) $\dfrac{9}{80}$ (b) $\dfrac{1}{8}$

(c) $\dfrac{4}{27}$ (d) $\dfrac{5}{38}$

41. The probability that Krishna will be alive 10 years hence is $\dfrac{7}{15}$ and Hari will be alive is $\dfrac{7}{10}$. The probability that both Krishna and Hari will be dead 10 years hence is :

(a) $\dfrac{21}{150}$ (b) $\dfrac{24}{150}$

(c) $\dfrac{49}{150}$ (d) $\dfrac{56}{150}$

42. The probabilities of three events A, B and C are P(A) = 0.6, P(B) = 0.4 and P(C) = 0.5.

If $P(A \cup B) = 0.8$, $P(A \cap C) = 0.3$,

$P(A \cap B \cap C) = 0.2$ and $P(A \cup B \cup C) \geq 0.85$, then :

(a) $0.2 \leq P(B \cap C) \leq 0.35$

(b) $0.5 \leq P(B \cap C) \leq 0.85$

(c) $0.1 \leq P(B \cap C) \leq 0.35$

(d) None of these

43. A determinant is chosen at random from the set of all determinants of order 2 with elements 0 or 1 only. The probability that value of the determinant chosen is positive is :

(a) $\dfrac{5}{16}$ (b) $\dfrac{7}{16}$

(c) $\dfrac{3}{16}$ (d) None of these

44. Three faces of a fair die are yellow, two faces red and one blue. The die is tossed three times. The probability that the colours, yellow, red and blue appear in the first, second and third tosses respectively is :

(a) $\dfrac{5}{36}$ (b) $\dfrac{7}{36}$

(c) $\dfrac{1}{36}$ (d) None of these

45. An unbiased die with faces 1, 2, 3, 4, 5 and 6 is rolled 4 times. Out of four face values obtained, the probability that the minimum face value is not less than 2 and the maximum face value is not greater than 5, is :

(a) $\frac{16}{81}$ (b) $\frac{1}{81}$

(c) $\frac{80}{81}$ (d) $\frac{65}{81}$

46. If $(1 - 3p)/2$, $(1 + 4p)/3$ and $(1 + p)/6$ are the probabilities of three mutually exclusive and exhaustive events, then the set of all values of p is :

(a) $(0, 1)$ (b) $[-1/4, 1/3]$

(c) $(0, 1/3)$ (d) $(0, \infty)$

47. A pack of cards contains 4 aces, 4 kings, 4 queens and 4 jacks. Two cards are drawn at random. The probability that atleast one of them is an ace is :

(a) $\frac{1}{5}$ (b) $\frac{3}{16}$

(c) $\frac{9}{20}$ (d) $\frac{1}{9}$

48. A man is known to speak truth 3 out of 4 times. He throws a die and reports that it is six. The probability that it is actually six is :

(a) $\frac{3}{8}$ (b) $\frac{1}{5}$

(c) $\frac{3}{5}$ (d) None of these

49. India plays two matches each with West Indies and Australia. In any match the probabilities of India getting points 0, 1, 2 are 0.45, 0.05 and 0.50 and respectively. Assuming that outcomes are independent, the probability of India getting at least 7 points is :

(a) 0.8750   (b) 0.0875

(c) 0.0624   (d) 0.0250

50. Ram and Shyam throw with one die for a prize of ₹ 88 which is to be won by the player who throws 1 first. If Ram starts, then mathematical expectation for Shyam is :

(a) ₹ 32   (b) ₹ 40

(c) ₹ 48   (d) None of these

51. If\ two events A and B are such that $P(\bar{A}) = 0.3$, $P(B) = 0.4$ and $P(A\bar{B}) = 0.5$, then $P[B|(A \cup \bar{B})] =$

(a) $\frac{1}{2}$ (b) $\frac{1}{3}$

(c) $\frac{1}{4}$ (d) None of these

52. Three of the six vertices of a regular hexagon are chosen at random. The probability that the triangle with three vertices is equilateral equals :

(a) $\frac{1}{2}$ (b) $\frac{1}{5}$

(c) $\frac{1}{10}$ (d) $\frac{1}{20}$

53. Two events A and B have probabilities 0.25 and 0.50 respectively. The probability that both A and B occur simultaneously is 0.14. Then the probability that neither A nor B occurs is :

(a) 0.28   (b) 0.39

(c) 0.61   (d) 0.72

54. In a certain town, 40% of the people have brown hair, 25% have brown eyes and 15% have both brown hair and brown eyes. If a person selected at random from the town, has brown hair, the probability that he also has brown eyes is :

(a) $\frac{1}{5}$ (b) $\frac{3}{8}$

(c) $\frac{1}{3}$ (d) $\frac{2}{3}$

55. An unbiased die is tossed until a number greater than 4 appears. The probability that an even number of tosses is needed is :

(a) $\frac{1}{2}$ (b) $\frac{2}{5}$

(c) $\frac{1}{5}$ (d) $\frac{2}{3}$

56. Three rifle-men take one shot each at the same target. The probability of the first rifle-man hitting the target is 0.4, the probability of the second rifle-man hitting the target is 0.5 and the probability of the third rifle-man hitting the target is 0.8. The probability that exactly two of them hit the target, is :

(a) 0.32   (b) 0.44

(c) 0.54   (d) None of these

57. If p and q are chosen randomly from the set (1, 2, 3, 4, 5, 6, 7, 8, 9, 10) with replacement, then the probability that the roots of the equation $x^2 + px + q = 0$ are real, is :

(a) 0.62

(b) 0.32

(c) 0.44

(d) None of these

58. If $\bar{E}$ and $\bar{F}$ are the complementary events of events E and F respectively and if $0 < P(F) < 1$, then :

(a) $P(E|F) + P(\bar{E}|F) = 1$

(b) $P(E|F) + P(E|\bar{F}) = 1$

(c) $P(\bar{E}|F) + P(E|\bar{F}) = 1$

(d) $P(E|\bar{F}) + P(\bar{E}|\bar{F}) = 1$

59. In a hand at bridge, the chance that 4 kings are held by a specified player, is :

(a) $\dfrac{11}{4165}$

(b) $\dfrac{31}{4165}$

(c) $\dfrac{62}{4165}$

(d) None of these

60. There are 4 envelopes corresponding to 4 letters. If the letters are placed in the envelopes at random, the probability that all the letters are not placed in the right envelopes, is :

(a) $\dfrac{18}{24}$

(b) $\dfrac{23}{24}$

(c) $\dfrac{17}{24}$

(d) None of these

61. The odds in favour of standing first of three students appearing in an examination are 1 : 2, 2 : 5 and 1 : 7 respectively. The probability that either of them will stand first, is :

(a) $\dfrac{125}{168}$

(b) $\dfrac{75}{168}$

(c) $\dfrac{32}{168}$

(d) $\dfrac{4}{168}$

62. Let A, B, C be three events. If the probability of occurring exactly one event out of A and B is $1 - a$, out of B and C is $1 - 2a$, out of C and A is $1 - a$ and that of occurring three events simultaneously is a^2, then the probability that atleast one out of A, B, C will occur, is :

(a) $< \dfrac{1}{2}$

(b) $< \dfrac{1}{3}$

(c) $> \dfrac{1}{2}$

(d) $> \dfrac{1}{3}$

63. The probability that certain electronic component fails when first used is 0.10. If it does not fail immediately, the probability that it lasts for one year is 0.99. The probability that a new component will last for one year is :

(a) 0.891

(b) 0.692

(c) 0.92

(d) None of these

64. Three groups A, B, C are contesting for position on the Board of Directors of a company. The probabilities of their winning are 0.5, 0.3, 0.2 respectively. If the group A wins, the probability of introducing a new product is 0.7 and the corresponding probabilities for groups B and C are 0.6 and 0.5 respectively. The probability that the new product will be introduced, is :

(a) 0.52

(b) 0.63

(c) 0.74

(d) None of these

65. If $E = E_1 \, E_2 \, E_3 \, E_4 \, E_5$ and $P(E_1) = \dfrac{95}{100}$,

$P(E_2|E_1) = \dfrac{94}{99}$, $P(E_3|E_1E_2) = \dfrac{93}{98}$,

$P(E_4 | E_1E_2E_3) = \dfrac{92}{97}$

and $P(E_5 | E_1E_2E_3E_4) = \dfrac{91}{96}$, then $P(E) =$

(a) $\dfrac{91 \cdot 92 \cdot 93 \cdot 94}{97 \cdot 98 \cdot 99 \cdot 100}$

(b) $\dfrac{91 \cdot 92 \cdot 93 \cdot 94 \cdot 95}{96 \cdot 97 \cdot 98 \cdot 99 \cdot 100}$

(c) $\dfrac{94 \cdot 95 \cdot 96}{98 \cdot 99 \cdot 100}$

(d) None of these

66. If a coin is tossed n times, the probability that head will appear an odd number of times, is :

(a) $\dfrac{1}{3}$

(b) $\dfrac{1}{2}$

(c) $\dfrac{2}{3}$

(d) None of these

67. A die is loaded so that the probability of face i is proportional to i, i = 1, 2, ..., 6. The probability of an even number occurring when the die is rolled, is :

(a) $\dfrac{2}{7}$

(b) $\dfrac{4}{7}$

(c) $\dfrac{3}{7}$

(d) None of these

68. Five persons entered the lift cabin on the ground floor of an 8 floor house. Suppose that each of them independently and with equal probability, can leave the cabin at any floor beginning with the first. The probability of all the five persons leaving at different floors, is :

(a) $\dfrac{^8P_5}{7^4}$ (b) $\dfrac{^9P_5}{7^6}$

(c) $\dfrac{^7P_5}{7^5}$ (d) None of these

69. There are three events A, B, C one of which must, and only one can happen. If the odds are 8 to 3 against A, 5 to 2 against B, then the odds against C are :

(a) $32 : 34$ (b) $29 : 34$

(c) $43 : 34$ (d) None of these

70. A student is given a true-false exam with 10 questions. If he gets 8 or more correct answers he passes the exam. Given that he guesses at the answer to each question, the probability that he passes the exam, is :

(a) $\dfrac{6}{128}$ (b) $\dfrac{9}{128}$

(c) $\dfrac{7}{128}$ (d) None of these

71. In a multiple choice question there are four alternative answers, of which one or more are correct. A candidate will get marks in the question only if he ticks all the correct answers. The candidate decides to tick answers at random. If he is allowed upto three chances to answer the question, the probability that he will get marks in the question, is :

(a) $\dfrac{1}{2}$ (b) $\dfrac{1}{5}$

(c) $\dfrac{1}{3}$ (d) None of these

72. An article manufactured by a company consists of two parts X and Y. In the process of manufacture of part X, 9 out of 104 parts may be defective. Similarly, 5 out of 100 are likely to be defective in the manufacture of the part Y. The probability that the assembled product will not be defective, is :

(a) $\dfrac{253}{416}$ (b) $\dfrac{361}{416}$

(c) $\dfrac{322}{416}$ (d) None of these

73. The chance of an event happening is the square of the chance of a second event but the odds against the first are the cubes of the odds against the second. The chances of happening of each event are :

(a) $\dfrac{1}{9}, \dfrac{1}{3}$ (b) $\dfrac{1}{6}, \dfrac{1}{9}$

(c) $\dfrac{1}{3}, \dfrac{1}{6}$ (d) None of these

74. A determinant of the second order is made with the element 0 and 1. The probability that the determinant made is non-negative, is :

(a) $\dfrac{13}{16}$ (b) $\dfrac{5}{16}$

(c) $\dfrac{9}{16}$ (d) None of these

75. Fifteen persons, among whom are A and B, sit down at random at a round table. The probability that there are 4 persons between A and B, is :

(a) $\dfrac{1}{3}$ (b) $\dfrac{1}{7}$

(c) $\dfrac{1}{5}$ (d) None of these

76. In the game odd man out, each of $m \geq 2$ person tosses a coin to determine who will buy refreshments for the entire group. The odd man out is the one with a different outcome from the rest. The probability that there is a loser in any game is :

(a) $\dfrac{m-1}{2^{m-1}}$ (b) $\dfrac{m}{2^{m-1}}$

(c) $\dfrac{m}{2^m}$ (d) None of these

77. A bag contains n white and n red balls. Pairs of balls are drawn without replacement until the bag is empty. The probability that each pair consists of one white and one red ball is :

(a) $\dfrac{2^{n-1}}{^{2n}C_n}$ (b) $\dfrac{2^{n-1}}{^{2n}C_{n-1}}$

(c) $\dfrac{2^n}{^{2n}C_n}$ (d) None of these

78. Three numbers are selected at random without replacement from the set of numbers {1, 2, ...N}. The conditional probability that the third number lies between the first two, if the first number is known to be smaller than the second, is :

(a) $\frac{1}{6}$

(b) $\frac{1}{3}$

(c) $\frac{1}{2}$

(d) None of these

79. Four tickets marked 00, 01, 10 and 11 respectively are placed in a bag. A ticket is drawn at random five times, being replaced each time. The probability that the sum of the numbers on the ticket is 15, is :

(a) $\frac{3}{1024}$

(b) $\frac{5}{1024}$

(c) $\frac{7}{1024}$

(d) None of these

80. A bag contains a white and b black balls. Two players A and B alternately draw a ball from the bag, replacing the ball each time after the draw till one of them draws a white ball and wins the game. If A begins the game and the probability of A winning the game is three times that of B, then a : b =

(a) 2 : 1

(b) 3 : 1

(c) 3 : 2

(d) None of these

81. If X and Y are the independent random variables $B\left(5,\frac{1}{2}\right)$ and $B\left(7,\frac{1}{2}\right)$, then P (X + Y ≥ 1) =

(a) $\frac{4095}{4096}$

(b) $\frac{309}{4096}$

(c) $\frac{4032}{4096}$

(d) None of these

82. Suppose X follows a binomial distribution with parameters n and p, where 0 < p < 1. If P (X = r)/P (X = n − r) is independent of n and r, then p is equal to :

(a) $\frac{1}{3}$

(b) $\frac{1}{2}$

(c) $\frac{1}{4}$

(d) None of these

83. A bag A contains 2 white and 3 red balls, and a bag B contains 4 white and 5 red balls. One ball is drawn at random from one of the bags and it is found to be red. The probability that it was drawn from the bag B, is :

(a) $\frac{25}{52}$

(b) $\frac{13}{52}$

(c) $\frac{27}{52}$

(d) None of these

84. In a test, an examinee either guesses or copies or knows the answer to a multiple choice question with four choices. The probability that he makes a guess is $\frac{1}{3}$ and the probability that he copies the answer is $\frac{1}{6}$. The probability that his answer is correct given that he copied it is $\frac{1}{8}$. The probability that he knows the answer to the question given that he correctly answered it, is :

(a) $\frac{13}{29}$

(b) $\frac{24}{29}$

(c) $\frac{17}{29}$

(d) None of these

85. Numbers are selected at random one at a time, from the numbers 00, 01, 02...., 99 with replacement. An event E occurs if and only if the product of the two digits of a selected number is 18. If four numbers are selected, then the probability that E occurs at least 3 times, is :

(a) $\frac{97}{390625}$

(b) $\frac{68}{390625}$

(c) $\frac{72}{390625}$

(d) None of these

86. A man takes a step forward with probability 0.4 and backward with probability 0.6. The probability that at the end of eleven steps he is one step away from the starting point, is :

(a) 0.37

(b) 0.32

(c) 0.54

(d) None of these

87. The mean and variance of a binomial variable X are 2 and 1 respectively. The probability that X takes values greater than 1, is :
   (a) $\frac{5}{16}$
   (b) $\frac{9}{16}$
   (c) $\frac{11}{16}$
   (d) None of these

88. Three critics review a book. Odds in favour of the book are 5 : 2, 4 : 3 and 3 : 4 respectively for the three critics. The probability that majority are in favour of the book, is :
   (a) $\frac{58}{343}$
   (b) $\frac{209}{343}$
   (c) $\frac{162}{343}$
   (d) None of these

89. If A and B are such events that P (A) > 0 and P (B) ≠1, then $P(\overline{A}|\overline{B})$ is equal to :
   (a) $1 - P(A|B)$
   (b) $1 - P(\overline{A}|B)$
   (c) $\frac{1 - P(A \cup B)}{P(\overline{B})}$
   (d) $\frac{P(\overline{A})}{P(\overline{B})}$

90. An ordinary cube has four blank faces, one face marked 2, another marked 3. Then the probability of obtaining a total of exactly 12 in 5 throws is :
   (a) $\frac{5}{1296}$
   (b) $\frac{5}{1944}$
   (c) $\frac{5}{2592}$
   (d) None of these

91. Three letters are written to different persons, and address on three envelopes are also written. Without looking at the addresses, the probability that the letters go into right envelopes is :
   (a) $\frac{1}{27}$
   (b) $\frac{1}{6}$
   (c) $\frac{1}{9}$
   (d) None of these

92. Probability is 0.45 that a dealer will sell at least 20 television sets during a day, and the probability is 0.74 that he will sell less than 24 televisions. The probability that he will sell 20, 21, 22 or 23 televisions during the day, is :
   (a) 0.19
   (b) 0.32
   (c) 0.21
   (d) None of these

93. An investment consultant predicts that the odds against the price of a certain stock will go up during the next week are 2 : 1 and the odds in favour of the price remaining the same are 1 : 3. The probability that the price of the stock will go down during the next week, is :
   (a) $\frac{4}{12}$
   (b) $\frac{5}{12}$
   (c) $\frac{7}{12}$
   (d) None of these

94. An MBA applies for a job in two firms X and Y. The probability of his being selected in firm X is 0.7 and being rejected at Y is 0.5. The probability of at least one of his applications being rejected is 0.6. The probability that he will be selected in one of the firms, is :
   (a) 0.6
   (b) 0.4
   (c) 0.8
   (d) None of these

95. Out of 1000 persons born only 800 reach the age of 10 and out of every 1000 who reach the age of 10,850 reach the age of 40. Out of every thousand who reach the age of 40, 25 die in one year. The probability that a person would attain the age of 41 years, is :
   (a) 0.563
   (b) 0.663
   (c) 0.78
   (d) None of these

96. A certain player, say X, is known to win with probability 0.3 if the track is fast and 0.4 if the track is slow. For Monday, there is a 0.7 probability of a fast track and 0.3 probability of a slow track. The probability that player X will win a Monday, is :
   (a) 0.22
   (b) 0.11
   (c) 0.33
   (d) None of these

97. Plant I of XYZ manufacturing organization employs 5 production and 3 maintenance foremen, another plant II of same organization employs 4 production and 5 maintenance foremen. From any one of these plants, a single selection of two foremen is made. The probability that one of them would be production and the other maintenance foreman, is :
   (a) $\frac{275}{504}$
   (b) $\frac{263}{504}$
   (c) $\frac{301}{504}$
   (d) $\frac{362}{504}$

98. In a bolt factory machines A, B and C manufacture respectively 25%, 35% and 40% of the total. Of their output 5, 4, 2 percents are defective bolts. A bolt is drawn at random from the product and is found to be defective. The probability that it was manufactured by machine A, is :

(a) $\frac{32}{69}$ (b) $\frac{23}{69}$

(c) $\frac{25}{69}$ (d) None of these

99. Three persons–A, B and C are being considered for the appointments as Vice Chancellor of a University whose chances of being selected for the post are in the proportion 4 : 2 : 3 respectively. The probability that A if selected will introduce democratisation in the university is 0.3, the corresponding probabilities for B and C doing the same are respectively 0.5 and 0.8. The probability that democratisation will be introduced in the university, is :

(a) $\frac{23}{45}$ (b) $\frac{42}{45}$

(c) $\frac{27}{45}$ (d) None of these

100. If a machine is set correctly, it produces 10% of defective items. If it is incorrectly set up, then it produces 10% good items. Chances for a setting to be correct and incorrect are in the ratio 7 : 3. After a setting is made, the first two items produced are found to be good items. The chance that the setting was correct, is :

(a) $\frac{332}{447}$ (b) $\frac{441}{447}$

(c) $\frac{48}{447}$ (d) None of these

101. By examining the chest X-ray probability that T.B. is detected when a person is actually suffering is 0.99. The probability that the doctor diagnose incorrectly that a person has T.B. on the basis of X-ray is 0.001. In a certain city 1 in 1000 persons suffer from T.B. A person selected at random is diagnosed to have T.B. The chance that he actually has T.B., is ;

(a) $\frac{942}{1989}$ (b) $\frac{830}{1989}$

(c) $\frac{990}{1989}$ (d) None of these

102. A is known to tell the truth in 5 cases out of 6 and he states that a white ball was drawn from a bag containing 8 black and 1 white ball. The probability that the white ball was drawn, is :

(a) $\frac{7}{13}$ (b) $\frac{5}{13}$

(c) $\frac{9}{13}$ (d) None of these

103. An article manufactured by a company consists of two parts A and B. In the process of manufacture of part A, 9 out of 100 are likely to be defective. Similarly 5 out of 100 are likely to be defective in the manufacture of part B. The probability that the assembled part will not be defective, is :

(a) 0.8645   (b) 0.6243

(c) 0.9645   (d) None of these

104. A six faced dice is so biased that it is twice as likely to show an even number as an odd number when it is thrown. The probability that the sum of two numbers is even, is :

(a) $\frac{7}{9}$ (b) $\frac{3}{9}$

(c) $\frac{5}{9}$ (d) None of these

105. Suppose that a product is produced in three factories X, Y and Z. It is known that factory X produces twice as many items as factory Y, and that factories Y and Z produce the same number of products. Assume that it is known that 3 percent of items produced by each of the factories X and Z are defective, while 5 percent of those manufactured by factory Y are defective. All the items produced in the three factories are stocked, and an item of product is selected at random. The probability that this item is defective, is :

(a) 0.034   (b) 0.051

(c) 0.042   (d) None of these

106. In a certain recruitment test there are multiple-choice questions. There are 4 possible answers to each question and of which one is correct. An intelligent student knows 90% of the answer while a weak student knows only 20%. If an intelligent student gets the correct answer, then the probability that he was guessing, is :

(a) $\dfrac{1}{37}$

(b) $\dfrac{36}{37}$

(c) $\dfrac{14}{37}$

(d) None of these

107. The sum of two positive quantities is equal to 2n. The probability that their product is not less than $\dfrac{3}{4}$ times their greatest product is :

(a) $\dfrac{3}{4}$

(b) $\dfrac{1}{2}$

(c) $\dfrac{1}{4}$

(d) None of these

108. Four digit numbers are formed using each of the digits 1, 2, ..., 8 only once. One number from these is picked up at random. The probability that the selected number contains unity is :

(a) $\dfrac{1}{2}$

(b) $\dfrac{1}{8}$

(c) $\dfrac{1}{4}$

(d) None of these

109. A book contains 1,000 pages. A page is chosen at random. The probability that the sum of the digits of the marked number on the page is equal to 9, is :

(a) $\dfrac{23}{500}$

(b) $\dfrac{11}{200}$

(c) $\dfrac{7}{100}$

(d) None of these

110. A binary number is made up of 8 digits. Suppose that the probability of an incorrect digit appearing in p and that of errors in different digits are independent of each other. The probability of forming an incorrect number, is :

(a) $\dfrac{p}{8}$

(b) p^8

(c) $(1-p)^8$

(d) $1-(1-p)^8$

111. The following table represents a probability distribution for a random variable X :

X :	1	2	3	4	5	6
p(X = x) :	0.1	2k	k	0.2	3k	0.3

Then, the value of k is :

(a) 0.1

(b) 0.2

(c) 0.3

(d) 0.4

112. If A and B are two independent events such that $P(A \cap B) = 3/25$ and $P(A' \cap B) = 8/25$, then $P(A)$ is :

(a) 11/25

(b) 7/25

(c) 3/11

(d) 9/11

113. If ten objects are distributed at random among ten persons, the probability that at least one of them will not get any thing is :

(a) $\dfrac{10^{10} - 10}{10^{10}}$

(b) $\dfrac{10^{10} - 10!}{10^{10}}$

(c) $\dfrac{10^{10} - 1}{10^{10}}$

(d) None of these

114. For a B.D., the parameters n and p are 16 and $\dfrac{1}{2}$ respectively. Then its S.D. σ is equal to :

(a) 2

(b) $\sqrt{2}$

(c) $2\sqrt{2}$

(d) 4

115. n ($\geq$ 3) persons are sitting in a row. Two of them are selected at random. The probability that they are not together is :

(a) $1 - \dfrac{2}{n}$

(b) $\dfrac{2}{n+1}$

(c) $1 - \dfrac{1}{n}$

(d) None of these

116. 5 girls and 10 boys sit at random in a row having 15 chairs numbered as 1 to 15. The probability that end seats are occupied by the girls and between any two girls odd number of boys sit, is :

(a) $\dfrac{20 \times 10! \times 5!}{15!}$

(b) $\dfrac{20 \times 10!}{15!}$

(c) $\dfrac{20 \times 5!}{15!}$

(d) None of these

117. An artillery target may be either at point I with probability $\frac{8}{9}$ or at point II with probability $\frac{1}{9}$. We have 21 shells each of which can be fired either at point I or II. Each shell may hit the target independently of the other shell with probability $\frac{1}{2}$. The number of shells that must be fired at point 1 to hit the target with maximum probability, is :

(a) 6   (b) 17
(c) 12   (d) 5

118. A fair coin is tossed a fixed number of times. If the probability of getting seven heads is equal to that of getting nine heads, the probability of getting two heads is :

(a) $15/2^8$ (b) 2/15
(c) $15/2^{13}$ (d) None of these

119. The probability that the 13th day of a randomly chosen month is a Friday, is :

(a) $\frac{1}{12}$ (b) $\frac{1}{7}$

(c) $\frac{1}{84}$ (d) None of these

120. Cards are drawn one by one at random from a well shuffled pack of 52 playing cards until 2 aces are obtained for the first time. The probability that 18 draws are required for this is :

(a) $\frac{3}{34}$ (b) $\frac{17}{455}$

(c) $\frac{561}{15925}$ (d) None of these

121. A contest consists of predicting the results win, draw or defeat of 7 football matches. A sent his entry by predicting at random. The probability that his entry will contain exactly 4 correct predictions is :

(a) $8/3^7$ (b) $16/3^7$
(c) $280/3^7$ (d) $560/3^7$

122. A bag contains $(2n + 1)$ coins. It is known that n of these coins have a head on both sides, whereas the remaining $(n +1)$ coins are fair. A coin is picked up at random from the bag and tossed. If the probability that the toss results in a head is 31/42, then n is equal to :

(a) 10   (b) 11
(c) 12   (d) 13

123. Three squares of a chess board are chosen at random, the probability that two are of one colour and one of another is :

(a) $\frac{16}{21}$ (b) $\frac{8}{21}$

(c) $\frac{32}{12}$ (d) None of these

124. A box contains tickets numbers 1 to 20. Three tickets are drawn from the box with replacement. The probability that the largest number on the tickets is 7 is :

(a) $\frac{2}{19}$ (b) $\frac{7}{20}$

(c) $1-\left(\frac{7}{20}\right)^3$ (d) None of these

125. The value of C for which $P(X = k) = Ck^2$ can serve as the probability function of a random variable X that takes value 0, 1, 2, 3, 4 is :

(a) 1/30   (b) 1/10
(c) 1/3   (d) 1/15

126. If the mean of a binomial distribution is 25, then its standard deviation lies in the interval given below :

(a) $[0, 5)$ (b) $(0, 5]$
(c) $[0, 25)$ (d) $(0, 25]$

127. If X follows a binomial distribution with parameters n = 8 & p =1/2, then $P |X - 4| \le 2) =$

(a) $\frac{119}{128}$ (b) $\frac{116}{128}$

(c) $\frac{29}{128}$ (d) None of these

128. There are two purses. The first contains 9 fifty-paise coins and a one rupee coin, while the second purse has 10 fifty-paise coins. Nine coins are transferred from the first purse to the second randomly. Then nine coins are transferred from the second purse to the first randomly. The probability of finding a one rupee coin in the first purse after these transfers is :

(a) $\frac{10}{19}$ (b) $\frac{7}{19}$

(c) $\frac{5}{19}$ (d) None of these

129. A special die is so constructed that the probabilities of throwing 1, 2, 3, 4, 5 and 6 are $(1 - k)/6, (1 + 2k)/6, (1 - k)/6, (1 + k)/6, (1 - 2k)/6$ and $(1 + k)/6$, respectively. If two such dice are thrown and the probability of getting a sum equal to nine lies between 1/9 and 2/9, the set of integral values of k is :

(a) {0} (b) {0, 1}

(c) {1} (d) None of these

130. An urn contains six white and four black balls. A fair die is rolled and a number of balls equal to that appearing on the die is chosen from the urn at random. The probability that all the balls selected are white is :

(a) 1/5 (b) 1/6

(c) 1/7 (d) 1/8

131. One hundred identical coins, each with probability p of showing up heads, are tossed. If $0 < p < 1$ and the probability of heads showing on 50 coins is equal to that of heads showing on 51 coins, the value of p is :

(a) 1/2 (b) 49/101

(c) 50/101 (d) 51/101

132. A point is selected at random from the interior of a circle. The probability that the point is closer to the centre than the boundary of the circle is :

(a) $\dfrac{3}{4}$ (b) $\dfrac{1}{2}$

(c) $\dfrac{1}{4}$ (d) None of these

133. Let A = [2, 3, 4...., 20]. A number is chosen at random from the set A and it is found to be a prime number. The probability that it is more than 10 is :

(a) $\dfrac{9}{10}$ (b) $\dfrac{1}{10}$

(c) $\dfrac{1}{5}$ (d) None of these

134. If the integers m and n are chosen at random between 1 and 100, then the probability that a number of the form $7^m + 7^m$ is divisible by 5 is :

(a) $\dfrac{1}{5}$ (b) $\dfrac{1}{7}$

(c) $\dfrac{1}{4}$ (d) $\dfrac{1}{49}$

135. If A and B are such that $P(A) > 0$ and $P(B) \neq 1$, then $P(\bar{A}|\bar{B})$ is equal to :

(a) $\dfrac{1 - P(A \cup B)}{P(\bar{B})}$ (b) $\dfrac{P(A)}{P(\bar{B})}$

(c) $1 - P(A|B)$ (d) $1 - P(\bar{A}|B)$

136. A and B are any two mutually exclusive events, then :

(a) $P(A) < P(B)$ (b) $P(A) > P(\bar{B})$

(c) $P(A) \leq P(\bar{B})$ (d) None of these

137. In an entrance test there are multiple choice questions. There are four possible answers to each question, of which one is correct. The probability that a student knows the answer to a question is 90%. If he gets the correct answer to a question, then the probability that he was guessing is :

(a) $\dfrac{1}{9}$ (b) $\dfrac{36}{37}$

(c) $\dfrac{1}{37}$ (d) $\dfrac{47}{40}$

138. For a Poisson distribution whose mean is λ, the standard deviation will be :

(a) λ^2 (b) $\dfrac{1}{\lambda}$

(c) $\sqrt{\lambda}$ (d) λ

139. Four positive integers are taken at random and are multiplied together. Then the probability that the product ends in an odd digit other than 5 is :

(a) $\dfrac{3}{5}$ (b) $\dfrac{609}{625}$

(c) $\dfrac{16}{625}$ (d) $\dfrac{2}{5}$

140. If $P(A \cap B) = \dfrac{1}{2}, P(\bar{A} \cap B) = \dfrac{1}{2}$ and $2P(A) = P(B) = p$, then the value of p is equal to :

(a) $\dfrac{1}{2}$ (b) $\dfrac{2}{3}$

(c) $\dfrac{1}{4}$ (d) $\dfrac{1}{3}$

141. The binomial distribution whose mean is 10 and S. D. is $2\sqrt{2}$ is :

(a) $\left(\dfrac{4}{5}+\dfrac{1}{5}\right)^{50}$

(b) $\left(\dfrac{4}{5}+\dfrac{1}{5}\right)^{1/50}$

(c) $\left(\dfrac{4}{5}+\dfrac{5}{1}\right)^{50}$

(d) None of these

142. Given two independent events A and B such that P (A) = 0.30 and P (B) = 0.60. Probability of getting neither A nor B is :

(a) 0.28

(b) 0.13

(c) 0.12

(d) 0.42

143. A and B throw a die. The probability that A's throw is not greater than B's is :

(a) $\dfrac{5}{12}$

(b) $\dfrac{7}{12}$

(c) $\dfrac{1}{6}$

(d) $\dfrac{1}{2}$

144. Let A, B, C be three equally and collectively exhaustive events. If the odds are 3 : 3 against A, 5 : 2 against B, then the odds against C are :

(a) 50 : 31

(b) 77 : 34

(c) 20 : 17

(d) 43 : 34

145. A bag contains 4 tickets numbered 1, 2, 3, 4 and another contains 6 tickets numbered 2, 4, 6, 7, 8, 9. If one bag is chosen at random and two tickets are drawn from the chosen bag, the probability that the tickets drawn bear even numbers is :

(a) $\dfrac{9}{20}$

(b) $\dfrac{17}{60}$

(c) $\dfrac{17}{30}$

(d) None of these

146. n biscuits are distributed among N boys at random. The probability that particular boy gets r (< n) biscuits is :

(a) ${}^{n}C_r \left(\dfrac{1}{N}\right)^{r} \left(\dfrac{N-1}{N}\right)^{n-r}$

(b) ${}^{n}C_r \left(\dfrac{1}{N}\right)^{r}$

(c) ${}^{n}C_r$

(d) $\dfrac{r}{n}$

147. Let 0 < P (A) < 1, 0 < P (B) < 1 and P (A ∪ B) = P (A) + P (B) − P (A) · P (B). Then :

(a) P (A/B) = P (A) + P (B)

(b) P (A ∪ B)ᶜ = P (Aᶜ) − P(Bᶜ)

(c) P (Aᶜ − Bᶜ) = P (Aᶜ) − P (Bᶜ)

(d) P (B/A) = P (B) − P (A)

148. A committee of five is to be chosen from a group of 9 people. The probability that a certain married couple will either serve together or not at all is :

(a) $\dfrac{2}{3}$

(b) $\dfrac{4}{9}$

(c) $\dfrac{1}{2}$

(d) $\dfrac{5}{9}$

149. Cards are drawn from a pack of 52 cards one by one. The probability that exactly 10 cards will be drawn before the first ace is :

(a) $\dfrac{451}{884}$

(b) $\dfrac{241}{1456}$

(c) $\dfrac{164}{4165}$

(d) None of these

150. A sum of money is rounded off to the nearest rupee. The probability that round off error is at least ten paise is :

(a) $\dfrac{81}{100}$

(b) $\dfrac{82}{101}$

(c) $\dfrac{19}{100}$

(d) $\dfrac{19}{101}$

151. n (≥ 3) persons are sitting in a row. Two of them are selected at random. The probability that they are not together is :

(a) $1-\dfrac{1}{n}$

(b) $1-\dfrac{2}{n}$

(c) $\dfrac{2}{n+1}$

(d) None of these

152. A party of 23 persons take their seats at a round table. The odds against two persons sitting together are :

(a) 10 : 1

(b) 1 : 11

(c) 9 : 10

(d) None of these

153. Out of 40 consecutive natural numbers, two are chosen at random. Probability that the sum of the numbers is odd, is :

(a) $\dfrac{14}{29}$

(b) $\dfrac{20}{39}$

(c) $\dfrac{1}{2}$

(d) None of these

154. A five digit number is formed by the digits 1, 2, 3, 4, 5 without repetition. The probability that the number formed is divisible by 4, is :

(a) $\frac{1}{5}$

(b) $\frac{4}{5}$

(c) $\frac{3}{5}$

(d) None of these

155. A pack of playing cards was found to contain only 51 cards. If the first 13 cards, which are examined, are all red, the probability that the missing card is black, is :

(a) $\frac{2}{3}$

(b) $\frac{1}{3}$

(c) $\frac{2}{9}$

(d) None of these

156. Two numbers are selected at random from 1, 2, 3, ... , 100 and multiplied. The probability that the product thus obtained, is divisible by 3, is :

(a) 0.31

(b) 0.44

(c) 0.49

(d) 0.55

157. A ten digit number is formed using the digits from zero to nine, every digit being used exactly once. The probability that the number is divisible by 4, is :

(a) $\frac{16}{81}$

(b) $\frac{20}{81}$

(c) $\frac{32}{81}$

(d) None of these

158. Each coefficient of the equation $ax^2 + bx + c = 0$ is determined by throwing an ordinary die. The probability that the equation has non-real complex roots is :

(a) $\frac{173}{216}$

(b) $\frac{43}{216}$

(c) $\frac{54}{216}$

(d) None of these

159. A committee consists of 9 experts taken from three institutions, A, B and C, of which 2 are from A, 3 from B and 4 from C. If three experts resign, then the probability that they belong to different institutions is :

(a) $\frac{1}{729}$

(b) $\frac{1}{24}$

(c) $\frac{1}{21}$

(d) $\frac{2}{7}$

160. Sixteen players S_1, S_2, ... S_{16} play in a tournament. They are divided into eight pairs at random. From each pair a winner is decided on the basis of a game played between the two players of the pair. Assuming that all the players are of equal strength, the probability that the player S_1 is among the eight winners is :

(a) $\frac{1}{2}$

(b) $\frac{1}{3}$

(c) $\frac{2}{3}$

(d) None of these

161. Three numbers are chosen at random without replacement from {1, 2, ..., 10}. The probability that the minimum of the chosen numbers is 3, or their maximum is 7, is :

(a) $\frac{7}{40}$

(b) $\frac{5}{40}$

(c) $\frac{11}{40}$

(d) None of these

162. Seven white balls and three black balls are randomly placed in a row. The probability that no two black balls are placed adjacently, equals :

(a) $\frac{1}{2}$

(b) $\frac{7}{15}$

(c) $\frac{2}{15}$

(d) $\frac{1}{3}$

163. There are four machines and it is known that exactly two of them are faulty. They are tested one by one, in a random order till both the faulty machines are identified. Then the probability that only two tests are needed is :

(a) $\frac{1}{3}$

(b) $\frac{1}{6}$

(c) $\frac{1}{2}$

(d) $\frac{1}{4}$

164. A fair coin is tossed repeatedly. If tail appears on first four tosses, then the probability of head appearing on the fifth toss equals :

(a) $\frac{1}{2}$

(b) $\frac{1}{32}$

(c) $\frac{31}{32}$

(d) $\frac{1}{5}$

165. Three players A, B and C, toss a coin cyclically in that order (That is A, B, C, A, B, C, A, B,...) till a head is shown. Let p be the probability that the coin shows a head. Let α, β and γ be, respectively, the probabilities that A, B and C get first head, then :

(a) $\alpha = \dfrac{p}{1-q^3}$ (b) $\beta = \dfrac{p(1-p)}{1-q^3}$

(c) $\gamma = \dfrac{p-2p^2+p^3}{1-q^3}$ (d) All of these

166. For the three events A, B and C, (exactly one of the events A or B occurs) = P (exactly one of the events B or C occurs) = P (exactly one of the events C or A occurs) = p and P (all the three events occur simultaneously) = p^2, where $0 < p < 1/2$. Then the probability of at least one of the three events, A, B and C occurring is :

(a) $\dfrac{3p+2p^2}{2}$ (b) $\dfrac{p+3p^2}{4}$

(c) $\dfrac{p+3p^2}{2}$ (d) $\dfrac{3p+2p^2}{4}$

167. An unbiased die is tossed until a number greater than 4 appears. The probability that an even number of tosses is needed is :

(a) 1/2   (b) 2/5

(c) 1/5   (d) 2/3

168. An unbiased coin is tossed. If the result is a head, a pair of unbiased dice is rolled and the number obtained by adding the numbers on the two faces is noted. If the result is a tail, a card from a well shuffled pack of eleven cards numbered 2, 3, 4, ...,12 is picked and the number on the card is noted. The probability that the noted number is either 7 or 8, is :

(a) $\dfrac{193}{792}$ (b) $\dfrac{164}{792}$

(c) $\dfrac{231}{792}$ (d) None of these

169. There are four balls of different colours and four boxes of colours, same as those of the balls. The number of ways in which the balls, one each in a box, could be placed such that a ball does not go to a box of its own colour is :

(a) $\dfrac{5}{8}$ (b) $\dfrac{3}{8}$

(c) $\dfrac{1}{8}$ (d) None of these

170. A sum of money is rounded off to the nearest rupee : the probability that round off error is at least ten paise is :

(a) 19/101   (b) 19/100

(c) 82/101   (d) 81/100

171. A natural number is selected at random from the set X = {x | 1 ≤ x ≤ 100}. The probability that the number satisfies the equation $x^2 - 13x \le 30$, is :

(a) $\dfrac{9}{50}$ (b) $\dfrac{3}{20}$

(c) $\dfrac{2}{11}$ (d) None of these

172. A bag contains four tickets numbered 00, 01,. 10, 11. Four tickets are chosen at random with replacement, the probability that sum of the numbers on the tickets is 23 is :

(a) $\dfrac{3}{32}$ (b) $\dfrac{1}{64}$

(c) $\dfrac{5}{256}$ (d) $\dfrac{7}{256}$

173. Two numbers b and c are chosen at random (with replacement) from the numbers 1, 2, 3, 4, 5, 6, 7, 8 and 9. The probability that $x^2 + bx + c > 0$ for all x ∈ R is :

(a) $\dfrac{17}{123}$ (b) $\dfrac{32}{81}$

(c) $\dfrac{82}{125}$ (d) $\dfrac{45}{143}$

174. A draws two cards at random from a pack of 52 cards. After returning them to the pack and shuffling it, B draws two cards at random. The probability that their draws contain exactly one common card is :

(a) $\dfrac{25}{546}$ (b) $\dfrac{50}{663}$

(c) $\dfrac{25}{663}$ (d) None of these

175. Three numbers are chosen at random without replacement from 1, 2, 3......, 10. The probability that the minimum of the chosen numbers is 4 or their maximum is 8, is :

(a) $\frac{11}{40}$

(b) $\frac{3}{10}$

(c) $\frac{1}{40}$

(d) None of these

176. Let $x = 33^n$. The index n is given a positive integral value at random. The probability that the value of x will have 3 in the units place is :

(a) $\frac{1}{4}$

(b) $\frac{1}{2}$

(c) $\frac{1}{3}$

(d) None of these

177. Six faces of a die are marked with the numbers 1, –1, 0, –2, 2 and 3. The die is thrown thrice. The probability that the sum of the numbers thrown is six, is :

(a) $\frac{1}{72}$

(b) $\frac{1}{12}$

(c) $\frac{5}{108}$

(d) $\frac{1}{36}$

178. Out of 40 consecutive integers, two are chosen at random. The probability that their sum is odd is :

(a) $\frac{14}{29}$

(b) $\frac{20}{39}$

(c) $\frac{1}{2}$

(d) None of these

179. A bag contains m white and n black balls. Two players A and B alternately draw a ball from the bag, replacing the ball each time after draw. A begins the game. If the probability of A winning (i.e. drawing a white ball) is twice the probability of B winning, then the ratio m : n is equal to :

(a) 1 : 2

(b) 2 : 1

(c) 1 : 1

(d) None of these

180. If the mean and variance of a binomial variate X are 2 and 1 respectively, then the probability that X takes a value greater than 1 is :

(a) 2/3

(b) 4/5

(c) 7/8

(d) 15/16

181. Four numbers are multiplied together. Then the probability that the product will be divisible by 5 or 10 is :

(a) $\frac{369}{625}$

(b) $\frac{399}{625}$

(c) $\frac{123}{625}$

(d) $\frac{133}{625}$

182. The numbers 1, 2, 3, ...n, are arranged in a random order. The probability that the digits 1, 2, 3...., k ($n > k$) appear as neighbour is :

(a) $\frac{(n-k)!}{n!}$

(b) $\frac{n-k+1}{{}^nC_k}$

(c) $\frac{n-k}{{}^nC_k}$

(d) $\frac{k!}{n!}$

183. A subset A of set X = {1, 2, 3, ..., 100} is chosen at random. The set X is reconstructed by replacing the elements of A, and another subset B of X is chosen at random. The probability that A ∩ B contains exactly 10 elements is :

(a) ${}^{100}C_{10}\left(\frac{3}{4}\right)^{90}$

(b) ${}^{100}C_{10}\left(\frac{1}{2}\right)^{100}$

(c) ${}^{100}C_{10}\frac{3^{90}}{4^{100}}$

(d) None of these

184. If E_1 and E_2 are independent events such that $0 < P(E_1) < 1$ and $0 < P(E_2) < 1$, then

(a) $P(E_1) + P(E_1^0) = P(E_2)$

(b) $P(E_2) + P(E_2^0) = P(E_1)$

(c) $P(E_1 | E_2) + P(E_1^0 | E_2^0) = 1$

(d) E_1 and E_2 are mutually exclusive

185. For any two independent events E_1 and E_2 in a space S, $P[(E_1 \cup E_2) \cap (\bar{E}_1 \cap \bar{E}_2)]$ is :

(a) $> \frac{1}{2}$

(b) $\geq \frac{1}{2}$

(c) $> \frac{1}{4}$

(d) $\leq \frac{1}{4}$

186. Fifteen coupons are numbered 1 to 15. Seven coupons are selected at random, one at a time with replacement. The probability that the largest number appearing on a selected coupon is 9, is :

(a) $\left(\frac{3}{5}\right)^7$

(b) $\left(\frac{1}{15}\right)^7$

(c) $\left(\frac{8}{15}\right)^7$

(d) None of these

187. A Binomial Probability Distribution is symmetrical if p, the probability of success in a single trial is :

(a) greater than $\frac{1}{2}$

(b) less than $\frac{1}{2}$

(c) less than q where q = 1 – p

(d) equal to $\frac{1}{2}$

188. Two players of equal skill are playing a set of games. They leave off when A requires 3 points to win and B requires 2 points to win. If the stake was Rs. 32, what share would each take ?

(a) 16, 16   (b) 9, 23

(c) 10, 22   (d) None of these

189. A and B are two independent events. The probability that both A and B occur is $\frac{1}{6}$ and the probability that neither of them occurs is $\frac{1}{3}$. Then the probabilities of the two events, respectively, are :

(a) $\frac{2}{3}$ and $\frac{1}{4}$ (b) $\frac{1}{2}$ and $\frac{1}{6}$

(c) $\frac{1}{2}$ and $\frac{1}{3}$ (d) $\frac{1}{5}$ and $\frac{1}{6}$

190. For any two events A and B defined on the same sample space, P (A∪B) – P (A) – P (B) equals :

(a) –P (AB)   (b) 1 – P (AB)

(c) P (AB)   (d) 0

191. Three persons work independently on a problem. If the respective probabilities that they will solve it are $\frac{1}{3}, \frac{1}{4}$ and $\frac{1}{5}$, then the probability that none can solve it is :

(a) $\frac{1}{5}$ (b) $\frac{2}{5}$

(c) $\frac{1}{3}$ (d) None of these

192. If M and N are any two events, the probability that exactly one of them occurs is :

(a) P (M ∩ N°) + P (M° ∩ N)

(b) P (M°) + P (N°) – 2 P (M° ∩ N°)

(c) P (M) + P (N) – P (M ∩ N)

(d) P (M) + P (N) – 2P (M ∩ N)

193. If mean of a Binomial Distribution is 20 and standard deviation is 4, then number of events is :

(a) 80   (b) 100

(c) 25   (d) 50

194. Four persons are chosen at random from a group containing 3 men, 2 women, and 4 children. The chance that exactly 2 of them will be children is :

(a) $\frac{11}{21}$ (b) $\frac{10}{21}$

(c) $\frac{9}{21}$ (d) $\frac{2}{9}$

195. If n integers taken at random are multiplied together, then the probability that the last digit of the product is 2, 4, 6 or 8 is :

(a) $\frac{4^n - 2^n}{5^n}$ (b) $\frac{8^n}{5^n}$

(c) $\frac{8^n - 2^n}{5^n}$ (d) None of these

196. The probability that Krishna will be alive 10 years hence is $\frac{7}{5}$ and Hari will be alive is $\frac{7}{10}$. The probability that both Krishna and Hari will be dead 10 years hence, is :

(a) $\frac{24}{150}$ (b) $\frac{12}{150}$

(c) $\frac{6}{150}$ (d) None of these

197. Two friends Ashok and Baldev have equal number of sons. There are 3 tickets for a cricket match which are to be distributed among the sons. The probability that 2 tickets go to the sons of the one and one ticket go to the sons of the other is 6/7. The number of sons each of the two friends have :

(a) 3   (b) 4

(c) 5   (d) None of these

198. The rifle-men take one shot each at the same target. The probability of the first rifle-man hitting the target is 0.4, the probability of the second rifle-man hitting the target is 0.5 and the probability of the third rifle-man hitting the target is 0.8. The probability of exactly two of them, hitting the target, is :

(a) 0.44   (b) 0.41

(c) 0.49   (d) None of these

199. A purse contains 4 copper coins, 3 silver coins, the second purse contains 6 copper coins, and 2 silver coins. A coin is taken out from any purse. The probability that it is a copper coin is :

(a) $\frac{4}{7}$ (b) $\frac{3}{4}$

(c) $\frac{3}{7}$ (d) $\frac{37}{56}$

200. In a box containing 100 bulbs, 10 are defective. What is the probability that out of a sample of 5 bulbs, none is defective ?

(a) $(10)^{-5}$ (b) $(1/2)^5$

(c) $(9/10)^5$ (d) $9/10$

201. The odds against any event is 5 : 2 and odds in favour of another event is 6 : 5. If both events are independent, then the probability that atleast one happens is :

(a) $\frac{50}{77}$ (b) $\frac{52}{77}$

(c) $\frac{63}{88}$ (d) $\frac{25}{88}$

202. For any two events A and B, $P(A \cap \bar{B})$ is equal to :

(a) $P(A) - P(A \cup B)$

(b) $P(A) - P(\bar{A} \cap B)$

(c) $P(A) + P(\bar{A} \cap \bar{B})$

(d) $P(A) - P(A \cap B)$

203. For two events A and B which of the following statement is true ?

(a) $P(A \cap B) \geq P(A) + P(B) - 1$

(b) $P(A \cap B) \leq P(A) + P(B) - 1$

(c) $P(A \cap B) \geq P(A) + P(B)$

(d) $P(A \cap B) \leq P(A) + P(B)$

204. $P\left(\dfrac{\bar{A}}{A \cup B}\right)$ is equal to :

(a) $\dfrac{P(\bar{B})}{P(A \cup B)}$ (b) $\dfrac{P(\bar{A})}{P(A \cup B)}$

(c) $\dfrac{P(\bar{A} \cap B)}{P(A \cup B)}$ (d) $\dfrac{P(A)}{P(A \cup B)}$

205. One card is drawn from a pack of 52 cards. The probability that it will be an ace or black king or queen of heart is :

(a) $\frac{1}{52}$ (b) $\frac{6}{52}$

(c) $\frac{7}{52}$ (d) $\frac{3}{52}$

206. 15 coins are tossed together, then the probability to come tail on 10 coins and to come head on 5 coins is :

(a) $\dfrac{3005}{32768}$ (b) $\dfrac{3003}{32768}$

(c) $\dfrac{1001}{32768}$ (d) $\dfrac{511}{32768}$

207. Three numbers are selected one by one from whole numbers 1 to 20. The probability that they are consecutive inegers is :

(a) $\frac{1}{3}$ (b) $\frac{5}{190}$

(c) $\frac{3}{190}$ (d) $\frac{7}{190}$

208. The sum of two positive numbers is 100. Probability that their product is greater than 1000 is :

(a) $\frac{7}{9}$ (b) $\frac{7}{10}$

(c) $\frac{2}{5}$ (d) None of these

209. The items produced by a firm are supposed to contain 5% defective items. The probability that a sample of 8 items will contain less than 2 defective items is :

(a) $\frac{27}{20}\left(\frac{19}{20}\right)^7$ (b) $\frac{533}{400}\left(\frac{19}{20}\right)^6$

(c) $\frac{153}{20}\left(\frac{1}{20}\right)^7$ (d) $\frac{35}{16}\left(\frac{1}{20}\right)^6$

210. The probability of happening of an impossible event, i.e. P (ϕ) is :

    (a) 1   (b) 0

    (c) 2   (d) −1

211. A coin is tossed three times in succession. If E is the event that there are at least two heads and F is the event in which first throw is a head, then P (E|F) =

    (a) $\frac{3}{4}$ (b) $\frac{3}{8}$

    (c) $\frac{1}{2}$ (d) $\frac{1}{8}$

212. If E and F are events with $P(E) \leq P(F)$ and $P(E \cap F) > 0$, then :

    (a) occurrence of E $\Rightarrow$ occurrence of F

    (b) occurrence of F $\Rightarrow$ occurrence of E

    (c) non-occurrence of E $\Rightarrow$ non-occurrence of F

    (d) none of the above implications holds

213. Three numbers are chosen at random without replacement from {1, 2, 3, ... 8}. The probability that their minimum is 3, given that their maximum is 6, is : **[AIEEE - 2012]**

    (a) $\frac{3}{8}$ (b) $\frac{1}{5}$

    (c) $\frac{1}{4}$ (d) $\frac{2}{5}$

214. Consider 5 independent Bernoulli's trials each with probability of success p. If the probability of at least one failure is greater than or equal to $\frac{31}{32}$, then p lies in the interval : **[AIEEE - 2011]**

    (a) $\left(\frac{11}{12}, 1\right]$ (b) $\left(\frac{1}{2}, \frac{3}{4}\right)$

    (c) $\left(\frac{3}{4}, \frac{11}{12}\right]$ (d) $\left[0, \frac{1}{2}\right]$

215. If C and D are two events such that $C \subset D$ and $P(D) \neq 0$, then the correct statement among the following is : **[AIEEE - 2011]**

    (a) $P(C|D) = \frac{P(D)}{P(C)}$ (b) $P(C|D) = P(C)$

    (c) $P(C|D) \geq P(C)$ (d) $P(C|D) < P(C)$

216. Four numbers are chosen at random (without replacement) from the set {1, 2, 3, ..., 20}.

    [AIEEE - 2010]

Statement 1: The probability that the chosen numbers when arranged in some order will form an AP is $\frac{1}{85}$.

Statement 2: If the four chosen numbers form an AP, then the set of all possible values of common difference is ($\pm$ 1, $\pm$ 2, $\pm$ 3, $\pm$ 4, $\pm$ 5).

    (a) Statement 1 is true, statement 2 is true; statement 2 is not a correct explanation for statement 1.

    (b) Statement 1 is true, statement 2 is false.

    (c) Statement 1 is false, statement 2 is true.

    (d) Statement 1 is true, statement 2 is true; statement 2 is the correct explanation for statement 1.

217. An urn contains nine balls of which three are red, four are blue and two are green. Three balls are drawn at random without replacement from the urn. The probability that the three balls have different colour is : **[AIEEE - 2010]**

    (a) $\frac{2}{7}$ (b) $\frac{1}{21}$

    (c) $\frac{2}{23}$ (d) $\frac{1}{3}$

218. In a binomial distribution B $\left(n, p = \frac{1}{4}\right)$, if the probability of at least one success is greater than or equal to $\frac{9}{10}$, then n is greater than : **[AIEEE - 2009]**

    (a) $\frac{1}{\log_{10} 4 - \log_{10} 3}$ (b) $\frac{1}{\log_{10} 4 + \log_{10} 3}$

    (c) $\frac{9}{\log_{10} 4 - \log_{10} 3}$ (d) $\frac{4}{\log_{10} 4 - \log_{10} 3}$

219. One ticket is selected at random from 50 tickets numbered 00, 01, 02, ..., 49. Then the probability that the sum of the digits on the selected ticket is 8, given that the product of these digits is zero, equals : **[AIEEE - 2009]**

    (a) $\frac{1}{14}$ (b) $\frac{1}{7}$

    (c) $\frac{5}{14}$ (d) $\frac{1}{50}$

220. It is given that the events A and B are such that $P(A) = \frac{1}{4}$, P(A|B) and $P(B|A) = \frac{2}{3}$. Then P(B) is

[**AIEEE - 2008**]

(a) $\frac{1}{16}$ (b) $\frac{1}{3}$

(c) $\frac{2}{3}$ (d) $\frac{1}{2}$

221. A die is thrown. Let A be the event that the number obtained is greater than 3. Let B be the event that the number obtained is less than 5. Then $P(A \cup B)$ is :   [**AIEEE - 2008**]

(a) $\frac{3}{5}$ (b) 0

(c) 1   (d) $\frac{2}{5}$

222. A pair of fair dice is thrown independently three times. The probability of getting a score of exactly 9 twice is :   [**AIEEE - 2007**]

(a) 1/729   (b) 8/9

(c) 8/729   (d) 8/243

223. At a telephone enquiry system the number of phone cells regarding relevant enquiry follow Poisson distribution with an average of 5 phone calls during 10 minute time intervals. The probability that there is at the most one phone call during a 10 minute time period is :

[**AIEEE - 2006**]

(a) $\frac{6}{5^e}$ (b) $\frac{5}{6}$

(c) $\frac{6}{55}$ (d) $\frac{6}{e^5}$

ANSWER KEY

1. (a)	2. (c)	3. (b)	4. (b)	5. (a)	6. (a)	7. (c)	8. (c)	9. (c)	10. (a)
11. (c)	12. (a)	13. (a)	14. (c)	15. (a)	16. (b)	17. (a)	18. (b)	19. (a)	20. (c)
21. (b)	22. (a)	23. (c)	24. (b)	25. (a)	26. (b)	27. (b)	28. (d)	29. (a)	30. (c)
31. (b)	32. (b)	33. (c)	34. (c)	35. (d)	36. (a)	37. (b)	38. (b)	39. (a)	40. (d)
41. (b)	42. (a)	43. (c)	44. (c)	45. (a)	46. (b)	47. (c)	48. (a)	49. (b)	50. (b)
51. (c)	52. (c)	53. (b)	54. (b)	55. (b)	56. (b)	57. (a)	58. (a)	59. (a)	60. (b)
61. (a)	62. (c)	63. (a)	64. (b)	65. (b)	66. (b)	67. (b)	68. (c)	69. (c)	70. (c)
71. (b)	72. (b)	73. (a)	74. (a)	75. (b)	76. (b)	77. (c)	78. (b)	79. (b)	80. (a)
81. (a)	82. (b)	83. (a)	84. (b)	85. (a)	86. (a)	87. (c)	88. (b)	89. (c)	90. (c)
91. (b)	92. (a)	93. (b)	94. (c)	95. (b)	96. (c)	97. (a)	98. (c)	99. (a)	100. (b)
101. (c)	102. (b)	103. (a)	104. (c)	105. (a)	106. (a)	107. (b)	108. (a)	109. (b)	110. (d)
111. (a)	112. (c)	113. (b)	114. (a)	115. (a)	116. (a)	117. (c)	118. (c)	119. (c)	120. (c)
121. (c)	122. (a)	123. (a)	124. (d)	125. (a)	126. (a)	127. (a)	128. (a)	129. (a)	130. (a)
131. (d)	132. (c)	133. (c)	134. (a)	135. (a)	136. (c)	137. (c)	138. (c)	139. (c)	140. (b)
141. (a)	142. (a)	143. (b)	144. (d)	145. (c)	146. (a)	147. (b)	148. (b)	149. (c)	150. (a)
151. (b)	152. (a)	153. (b)	154. (a)	155. (a)	156. (d)	157. (b)	158. (a)	159. (d)	160. (a)
161. (c)	162. (b)	163. (b)	164. (a)	165. (d)	166. (a)	167. (b)	168. (a)	169. (b)	170. (d)
171. (b)	172. (a)	173. (b)	174. (b)	175. (a)	176. (a)	177. (c)	178. (b)	179. (c)	180. (d)
181. (a)	182. (b)	183. (c)	184. (c)	185. (d)	186. (a)	187. (d)	188. (c)	189. (c)	190. (a)
191. (b)	192. (a)	193. (b)	194. (a)	195. (a)	196. (a)	197. (b)	198. (a)	199. (d)	200. (c)
201. (b)	202. (d)	203. (a)	204. (c)	205. (c)	206. (b)	207. (c)	208. (a)	209. (a)	210. (b)
211. (a)	212. (d)	213. (b)	214. (d)	215. (c)	216. (b)	217. (a)	218. (a)	219. (a)	220. (b)
221. (c)	222. (d)	223. (d)							

VECTORS

MULTIPLE CHOICE QUESTIONS

1. The unit vector parallel to the resultant of the vectors $2\hat{i} + 3\hat{j} - \hat{k}$ and $4\hat{i} - 3\hat{j} + 2\hat{k}$ is :

   (a) $\dfrac{1}{\sqrt{37}}(6\hat{i} + \hat{k})$ (b) $\dfrac{1}{\sqrt{37}}(6\hat{i} + \hat{j})$

   (c) $\dfrac{1}{\sqrt{37}}(6\hat{j} + \hat{k})$ (d) None of these

2. If $\vec{a} = (2, 1, -1)$, $\vec{b} = (1, -1, 0)$ and $\vec{c} = (5, -1, 1)$ then the unit vector parallel to $\vec{a} + \vec{b} - \vec{c}$, but in the opposite direction is :

   (a) $\dfrac{-1}{3}(2\hat{i} - \hat{j} + 2\hat{k})$ (b) $\dfrac{1}{3}(2\hat{i} - \hat{j} + 2\hat{k})$

   (c) $\dfrac{1}{3}(2\hat{i} + \hat{j} - 2\hat{k})$ (d) None of these

3. ABC is any triangle and O any point in the plane of the same. If AO, BO and CO meet the sides BC, CA and AB in D, E, F respectively, then $\dfrac{OD}{AD} + \dfrac{OE}{BE} + \dfrac{OF}{CF} =$

   (a) 1   (b) −1

   (c) 0   (d) None of these

4. Forces P, Q act at O and have a resultant R. If any transversal cuts their lines of action at A, B, C respectively, then :

   (a) $\dfrac{P}{OA} + \dfrac{Q}{OB} + \dfrac{R}{OC} = 0$

   (b) $\dfrac{P}{OA} + \dfrac{Q}{OB} + \dfrac{R}{OC} = 1$

   (c) $\dfrac{P}{OA} + \dfrac{Q}{OB} - \dfrac{R}{OC} = 0$

   (d) $\dfrac{P}{OA} + \dfrac{Q}{OB} - \dfrac{R}{OC} = 1$

5. If G is the centroid of the Δ ABC, then $\vec{GA} + \vec{GB} + \vec{GC} =$

   (a) 0   (b) 1

   (c) −1   (d) None of these

6. In a regular hexagon ABCDEF, $\vec{AB} + \vec{AC} + \vec{AD} + \vec{AE} + \vec{AF} = k\vec{AD}$, where k is equal to :

   (a) 1   (b) 2

   (c) 3   (d) None of these

7. If M and N are the mid points of the diagonals AC and BD respectively of a quadrilateral ABCD, then $\vec{AB} + \vec{AD} + \vec{CB} + \vec{CD} =$

   (a) 4NM   (b) 4MN

   (c) 2MN   (d) None of these

8. Five forces $\vec{AB}, \vec{AC}, \vec{AD}, \vec{AE}, \vec{AF}$ act at the vertex A of a regular hexagon ABCDEF. If O is the centroid of the hexagon, then their resultant is a force given by :

   (a) $4\vec{AO}$ (b) $5\vec{AO}$

   (c) $6\vec{AO}$ (d) None of these

9. ABCD is parallelogram. If L and M are the middle points of BC and CD, then $\vec{AL} + \vec{AM} =$

   (a) $\dfrac{1}{2}\vec{AC}$ (b) $\dfrac{3}{2}\vec{AC}$

   (c) $\vec{AC}$ (d) None of these

10. ABCD is a quadrilateral and E the point of intersection of the lines joining the middle points of opposite sides. If O is any point, then the resultant of $\vec{OA}, \vec{OB}, \vec{OC}$ and $\vec{OD}$ is equal to :

    (a) $2\vec{OE}$ (b) $\vec{OE}$

    (c) $4\vec{OE}$ (d) None of these

11. The vertices of a quadrilateral are A (1, 2, –1), B (–4, 2, –2), C (4, 1, –5) and D (2, –1, 3). At the point A forces of magnitudes 2, 3, 2 kg. act along AB, AC and AD respectively. The magnitude of their resultant is :

(a) $\sqrt{\dfrac{118}{26}}$ (b) $\sqrt{\dfrac{118}{13}}$

(c) $\sqrt{\dfrac{73}{26}}$ (d) None of these

12. Two forces act at the vertex A of a quadrilateral ABCD represented by $\overrightarrow{AB}, \overrightarrow{AD}$ and two at C represented by $\overrightarrow{CB}$ and $\overrightarrow{CD}$. If E and F are the middle points of AC and BD respectively, then their resultant is represented by :

(a) $\overrightarrow{EF}$ (b) $2\overrightarrow{EF}$

(c) $\dfrac{3}{2}\overrightarrow{EF}$ (d) $4\overrightarrow{EF}$

13. If the vectors $\overrightarrow{a}$ and $\overrightarrow{b}$ are non-collinear, then the value of x, for which, the vectors $\overrightarrow{c} = (x - 2)\,\overrightarrow{a} + \overrightarrow{b}$ and $\overrightarrow{d} = (2x + 1)\,\overrightarrow{a} - \overrightarrow{b}$ are collinear is :

(a) $\dfrac{4}{3}$ (b) $\dfrac{2}{3}$

(c) $\dfrac{1}{3}$ (d) None of these

14. Let $\overrightarrow{OA} = \hat{i} + 3\hat{j} - 2\hat{k}$ and $\overrightarrow{OB} = 3\hat{i} + \hat{j} - 2\hat{k}$. The vector $\overrightarrow{OC}$ bisecting the angle AOB where C is a point on the line AB is :

(a) $2(\hat{i} + \hat{j} - \hat{k})$ (b) $4(\hat{i} + \hat{j} - \hat{k})$

(c) $\hat{i} + \hat{j} - \hat{k}$ (d) None of these

15. The vector $\overrightarrow{c}$, directed along the internal bisector of the angle between the vectors $\overrightarrow{a} = 7\hat{i} - 4\hat{j} - 4\hat{k}$ and $\overrightarrow{b} = -2\hat{i} - \hat{j} + 2\hat{k}$ with $|\overrightarrow{c}| = 5\sqrt{6}$ is :

(a) $\dfrac{5}{3}(5\hat{i} + 5\hat{j} + 2\hat{k})$ (b) $\dfrac{5}{3}(\hat{i} + 7\hat{j} + 2\hat{k})$

(c) $\dfrac{5}{3}(-5\hat{i} + 5\hat{j} + 2\hat{k})$ (d) $\dfrac{5}{3}(\hat{i} - 7\hat{j} + 2\hat{k})$

16. A vector $\overrightarrow{A}$ has components A_1, A_2, A_3 in a right handed rectangular cartesian coordinate system Ox, Oy, Oz. The coordinate system is rotated about the z-axis through an angle $\pi/2$. The components of $\overrightarrow{A}$ in the new coordinate system are :

(a) $A_1, -A_2, A_3$ (b) A_2, A_1, A_3

(c) $A_1, A_2, -A_3$ (d) $A_2, -A_1, A_3$

17. The value of 'a' such that the vectors $2\hat{i} - \hat{j} + \hat{k}$, $\hat{i} + 2\hat{j} - 3\hat{k}$ and $3\hat{i} + a\hat{j} + 5\hat{k}$ are coplanar, is :

(a) 4   (b) –4

(c) 2   (d) –2

18. In a △OAB, E is the mid point of OB and D is a point on AB such that AD : DB = 2 : 1. If OD and AE intersect at P, then the ratio OP : PD is :

(a) 1 : 2   (b) 2 : 1

(c) 3 : 2   (d) 2 : 3

19. If the points P, Q, R, S have position vectors $\overrightarrow{p}, \overrightarrow{q}, \overrightarrow{r}, \overrightarrow{s}$, such that $\overrightarrow{p} - \overrightarrow{q} = 2(\overrightarrow{s} - \overrightarrow{r})$, then :

(a) PQ and RS bisect each other

(b) PQ and PR bisect each other

(c) PQ and RS trisect each other

(d) QS and PR trisect each other

20. If $\overrightarrow{a} = \hat{i} + 2\hat{j} - 3\hat{k}$ and $\overrightarrow{b} = 3\hat{i} - \hat{j} + 2\hat{k}$, then the angle between the vector $(\overrightarrow{a} + \overrightarrow{b})$ and $(\overrightarrow{a} - \overrightarrow{b})$ is :

(a) $\dfrac{\pi}{4}$ (b) $\dfrac{\pi}{3}$

(c) $\dfrac{\pi}{2}$ (d) None of these

21. If $|\overrightarrow{a}| = 3, |\overrightarrow{b}| = 1, |\overrightarrow{c}| = 4$ and $\overrightarrow{a} + \overrightarrow{b} + \overrightarrow{c} = 0$, then $\overrightarrow{a} \cdot \overrightarrow{b} + \overrightarrow{b} \cdot \overrightarrow{c} + \overrightarrow{c} \cdot \overrightarrow{a} =$

(a) 12   (b) –12

(c) 13   (d) –13

22. If $a + b + c = 0$ and $|a| = 3$, $|b| = 5$, $|c| = 7$, then the angle between a and b is :

(a) $\dfrac{\pi}{2}$

(b) $\dfrac{\pi}{3}$

(c) $\dfrac{\pi}{4}$

(d) $\dfrac{\pi}{6}$

23. The value of λ for which the vectors $\lambda\hat{i} + 2\hat{j} + \hat{k}$ and $4\hat{i} - 9\hat{j} + 2\hat{k}$ are perpendicular to each other is :

(a) 2

(b) –2

(c) 4

(d) –4

24. Dot products of a vector with vectors $3\hat{i} - 5\hat{k}$, $2\hat{i} + 7\hat{j}$, and $\hat{i} + \hat{j} + \hat{k}$ are respectively –1, 6 and 5. The vector is :

(a) $3\hat{i} + \hat{j} + 2\hat{k}$

(b) $3\hat{i} + 2\hat{k}$

(c) $3\hat{i} - 2\hat{k}$

(d) None of these

25. A unit vector $\hat{a}$ makes an angle $\dfrac{\pi}{4}$ with $\hat{k}$ and is such that $\hat{a} + \hat{i} + \hat{j}$ is also a unit vector, then $\hat{a}$ is equal to :

(a) $\dfrac{1}{2}\hat{i} - \dfrac{1}{2}\hat{j} + \dfrac{1}{\sqrt{2}}\hat{k}$

(b) $\dfrac{-1}{2}\hat{i} - \dfrac{1}{2}\hat{j} + \dfrac{1}{\sqrt{2}}\hat{k}$

(c) $\dfrac{-1}{2}\hat{i} + \dfrac{1}{2}\hat{j} + \dfrac{1}{\sqrt{2}}\hat{k}$

(d) None of these

26. If the scalar projection of $\vec{a} = \lambda\hat{i} + \hat{j} + 4\hat{k}$ on $\vec{b} = 2\hat{i} + 6\hat{j} + 3\hat{k}$ is 4 units then λ is equal to :

(a) 5

(b) 3

(c) 1

(d) –5

27. If $\vec{a} = 4\hat{i} + 6\hat{j}$ and $\vec{b} = 3\hat{j} + 3\hat{k}$, then the vector form of component of $\vec{a}$ along $\vec{b}$ is :

(a) $\dfrac{18}{10\sqrt{3}}(3\hat{i} + 4\hat{k})$

(b) $\dfrac{18}{25}(3\hat{i} + 4\hat{k})$

(c) $\dfrac{18}{\sqrt{3}}(3\hat{i} + 4\hat{k})$

(d) $3\hat{j} + 4\hat{k}$

28. If $\vec{a}$ and $\vec{b}$ are unit vectors and θ is the angle between them, then $|\vec{a} - \vec{b}| =$

(a) $\left|\sin\dfrac{\theta}{2}\right|$

(b) $2\left|\sin\dfrac{\theta}{2}\right|$

(c) $4\left|\sin\dfrac{\theta}{2}\right|$

(d) None of these

29. If the sum of two unit vectors, is a unit vector, then the magnitude of their difference is :

(a) $\sqrt{2}$

(b) $\sqrt{3}$

(c) 1

(d) None of these

30. The angle between any two diagonals of a cube is

(a) $\cos^{-1}\left(\dfrac{1}{3}\right)$

(b) $\cos^{-1}\left(\dfrac{2}{3}\right)$

(c) $\cos^{-1}\left(\dfrac{1}{\sqrt{3}}\right)$

(d) None of these

31. A line makes angles α, β, γ, δ with the diagonals of a cube, then $\cos^2\alpha + \cos^2\beta + \cos^2\gamma + \cos^2\delta =$

(a) $\dfrac{1}{3}$

(b) $\dfrac{2}{3}$

(c) $\dfrac{4}{3}$

(d) None of these

32. The constant forces $\vec{P} = 2\hat{i} - 3\hat{j} + 6\hat{k}$ and $\vec{Q} = -\hat{i} + 2\hat{j} - \hat{k}$ act on a particle. The work done, when the particle is displaced from a point A with position vector $4\hat{i} - 3\hat{j} - 2\hat{k}$ to a point B with position vector $6\hat{i} + \hat{j} - 3\hat{k}$, is given by :

(a) 15 units

(b) 22 units

(c) 18 units

(d) None of these

33. If $\vec{a} = 3\hat{i} - \hat{j} + 2\hat{k}$ and $\vec{b} = -\hat{i} - 2\hat{j} + 4\hat{k}$, then a unit vector along vector $\vec{a} \times \vec{b}$ is :

(a) $\dfrac{-2\hat{j} + \hat{k}}{\sqrt{5}}$

(b) $\dfrac{-\hat{j} - 2\hat{k}}{\sqrt{5}}$

(c) $\dfrac{-2\hat{j} - \hat{k}}{\sqrt{5}}$

(d) None of these

34. A unit vector perpendicular to the plane ABC where A, B, C are the points (3, −1, 2), (1, −1, −3) and (4, −3, 1) respectively is :

(a) $\dfrac{10\hat{i} + 7\hat{j} + 4\hat{k}}{\sqrt{165}}$ (b) $\dfrac{-10\hat{i} + 7\hat{j} + 4\hat{k}}{\sqrt{165}}$

(c) $\dfrac{-10\hat{i} - 7\hat{j} + 4\hat{k}}{\sqrt{165}}$ (d) None of these

35. A vector whose length is 3 and which is perpendicular to each of the vector $\vec{a} = 3\hat{i} + \hat{j} - 4\hat{k}$ and $\vec{b} = 6\hat{i} + 5\hat{j} - 2\hat{k}$ is

(a) $\hat{i} + \hat{j} - 2\hat{k}$ (b) $2\hat{i} + 2\hat{j} + \hat{k}$

(c) $2\hat{i} - 2\hat{j} + \hat{k}$ (d) None of these

36. If $\vec{A} = 2\hat{i} + \hat{k}$, $\vec{B} = \hat{i} + \hat{j} + \hat{k}$ and $\vec{C} = 4\hat{i} - 3\hat{j} + 7\hat{k}$. Then a vector R which satisfies

$\vec{R} \times \vec{B} = \vec{C} \times \vec{B}$ and $\vec{R} \cdot \vec{B} = 0$, is:

(a) $-\hat{i} - 8\hat{j} + 2\hat{k}$ (b) $\hat{i} - 8\hat{j} + 2\hat{k}$

(c) $\hat{i} + 8\hat{j} + 2\hat{k}$ (d) None of these

37. If A, B, C, D are any four points in space, then

$|\vec{AB} \times \vec{CD} + \vec{BC} \times \vec{AD} + \vec{CA} \times \vec{BD}| = k$ (area of $\triangle ABC$), where k is equal to :

(a) 2   (b) $\dfrac{1}{2}$

(c) 4   (d) $\dfrac{1}{4}$

38. If $\vec{A} = (1, 1, 1)$ and $\vec{C} = (0, 1, -1)$ are given vectors, then a vector $\vec{B}$ satisfying the equations $\vec{A} \times \vec{B} = \vec{C}$ and $\vec{A} \cdot \vec{B} = 3$ is :

(a) $\dfrac{1}{3}(5\hat{i} - 2\hat{j} + 2\hat{k})$ (b) $\dfrac{1}{3}(5\hat{i} + 2\hat{j} - 2\hat{k})$

(c) $\dfrac{1}{3}(-5\hat{i} + 2\hat{j} + 2\hat{k})$ (d) $\dfrac{1}{3}(5\hat{i} + 2\hat{j} + 2\hat{k})$

39. Let A (0, 0, 0), B (1, 1, 1), C (3, 2, 1) and D (3, 1, 2) be four points. The angle between the planes through the points A, B, C and through the points A, B, D is :

(a) $\dfrac{\pi}{2}$ (b) $\dfrac{\pi}{6}$

(c) $\dfrac{\pi}{4}$ (d) $\dfrac{\pi}{3}$

40. If $\vec{a}$, $\vec{b}$, $\vec{c}$ are the position vectors of the points A, B, C, then the perpendicular distance from C to the straight line through A and B is :

(a) $\dfrac{|\vec{b} \times \vec{c} + \vec{c} \times \vec{a} + \vec{a} \times \vec{b}|}{|\vec{b} - \vec{a}|}$

(b) $\dfrac{|\vec{b} \times \vec{c} + \vec{c} \times \vec{a} + \vec{a} \times \vec{b}|}{2|\vec{b} - \vec{a}|}$

(c) $\dfrac{|\vec{b} \times \vec{c} + \vec{c} \times \vec{a} + \vec{a} \times \vec{b}|}{4|\vec{b} - \vec{a}|}$

(d) None of these

41. If $\vec{a} = 2\hat{i} - 3\hat{j} + \hat{k}$, $\vec{b} = -\hat{i} + \hat{k}$ and $\vec{c} = 2\hat{j} + \hat{k}$ then the area of the parallelogram having diagonals $\vec{a} + \vec{b}$ and $\vec{b} + \vec{c}$ is :

(a) $\sqrt{21}$ (b) $\dfrac{1}{2}\sqrt{21}$

(c) $\sqrt{23}$ (d) $\dfrac{1}{2}\sqrt{23}$

42. Given $\vec{A} = a\hat{i} + b\hat{j} + c\hat{k}$, $\vec{B} = d\hat{i} + 3\hat{j} + 4\hat{k}$ and $\vec{C} = 3\hat{i} + \hat{j} - 2\hat{k}$. If the vectors A, B and C form a triangle such that A = B + C, then :

(a) a = −8, b = −4, c = 2, d = −11

(b) a = −8, b = 4, c = −2, d = −11

(c) a = −8, b = 4, c = 2, d = −11

(d) None of these

43. The moment of the couple formed by the forces $5\hat{i} + \hat{k}$ and $-5\hat{i} - \hat{k}$ acting at the points (9, −1, 2) and (3, −2, 1) respectively, is :

(a) $\hat{i} + \hat{j} - 5\hat{k}$ (b) $\hat{i} - \hat{j} - 5\hat{k}$

(c) $\hat{i} + \hat{j} + 5\hat{k}$ (d) None of these

44. The torque about the point $3\hat{i} - \hat{j} + 3\hat{k}$ of a force $4\hat{i} + 2\hat{j} + \hat{k}$ through the point $5\hat{i} + 2\hat{j} + 4\hat{k}$, is :

(a) $\hat{i} + 2\hat{j} - 8\hat{k}$ (b) $\hat{i} + 2\hat{j} + 8\hat{k}$

(c) $\hat{i} - 2\hat{j} - 8\hat{k}$ (d) None of these

45. If $\vec{u} = -\hat{i} - 2\hat{j} + \hat{k}$, $\vec{v} = 3\hat{i} + \hat{k}$ and $\vec{w} = \hat{j} - \hat{k}$, then the value of $(\vec{u} + \vec{w}) \cdot [(\vec{u} \times \vec{v}) \times (\vec{v} \times \vec{w})]$ is :

(a) 4   (b) 5

(c) 6   (d) None of these

46. If $\hat{i}, \hat{j}, \hat{k}$ are the unit vectors mutually perpendicular, then $[\hat{i} - \hat{j} \quad \hat{j} - \hat{k} \quad \hat{k} - \hat{i}] =$

(a) 0   (b) 1

(c) -1 (d) None of these

47. The value of λ so that the four points with position vectors $-\hat{i} + 3\hat{j} + 2\hat{k}$, $3\hat{i} + \lambda\hat{j} + 4\hat{k}$, $5\hat{i} + 7\hat{j} + 3\hat{k}$ and $-13\hat{i} + 17\hat{j} - \hat{k}$ are coplanar, is

(a) 2   (b) -2

(c) 4   (d) -4

48. For any three vectors $\vec{a}, \vec{b}, \vec{c}$ $[\vec{a}+\vec{b} \quad \vec{b}+\vec{c} \quad \vec{c}+\vec{a}]$ is equal to :

(a) 0   (b) $[\vec{a}\,\vec{b}\,\vec{c}]$

(c) $2[\vec{a}\,\vec{b}\,\vec{c}]$ (d) None of these

49. If $\hat{i}, \hat{j}, \hat{k}$ are the unit vectors and mutually orthogonal, then for any vector $\vec{a}$, $\hat{i} \times (\vec{a} \times \hat{i}) + \hat{j} \times (\vec{a} \times \hat{j}) + \hat{k} \times (\vec{a} \times \hat{k}) =$

(a) 0   (b) $\vec{a}$

(c) $2\vec{a}$ (d) None of these

50. If $\hat{i}, \hat{j}, \hat{k}$ are the unit vectors and mutually orthogonal, then $\hat{i} \times (\hat{j} \times \hat{k}) + \hat{j} \times (\hat{k} \times \hat{i}) + \hat{k} \times (\hat{i} \times \hat{j}) =$

(a) 0   (b) 1

(c) -1 (d) None of these

51. For any three vectors $\vec{a}, \vec{b}, \vec{c}$ $[\vec{b} \times \vec{c} \quad \vec{c} \times \vec{a} \quad \vec{a} \times \vec{b}]$ is equal to

(a) 0   (b) $[\vec{a}\,\vec{b}\,\vec{c}]$

(c) $[\vec{a}\,\vec{b}\,\vec{c}]^2$ (d) $2[\vec{a}\,\vec{b}\,\vec{c}]$

52. For any four vectors $\vec{a}, \vec{b}\,\vec{c}, \vec{d}$, $(\vec{a} \times \vec{b}) \times (\vec{c} \times \vec{d})$ is equal to :

(a) $[\vec{a}\,\vec{b}\,\vec{d}]\vec{c} - [\vec{a}\,\vec{b}\,\vec{c}]\vec{d}$

(b) $[\vec{a}\,\vec{b}\,\vec{c}]\vec{d} - [\vec{a}\,\vec{b}\,\vec{d}]\vec{c}$

(c) $[\vec{a}\,\vec{c}\,\vec{d}]\vec{b} - [\vec{a}\,\vec{b}\,\vec{d}]\vec{c}$

(d) None of these

53. If $\hat{a}, \hat{b}, \hat{c}$ are three non-parallel unit vectors such that $\hat{a} \times (\hat{b} \times \hat{c}) = \frac{1}{2}\hat{b}$, then the angles which $\hat{a}$ makes with $\hat{b}$ and $\hat{c}$ are :

(a) $90°, 60°$ (b) $45°, 60°$

(c) $30°, 60°$ (d) None of these

54. If $\vec{a} \times (\vec{b} \times \vec{c}) + (\vec{a} \cdot \vec{b})\vec{b} = (4 - 2\beta - \sin\alpha)\vec{b}$ $+ (\beta^2 - 1)\vec{c}$ and $(\vec{c} \cdot \vec{c})\vec{a} = \vec{c}$, while $\vec{b}$ and $\vec{c}$ are non-collinear, then :

(a) $\alpha = \frac{\pi}{2}, \beta = -1$ (b) $\alpha = \frac{\pi}{2}, \beta = 1$

(c) $\alpha = \frac{\pi}{3}, \beta = -1$ (d) None of these

55. A set of vectors reciprocal to the set $-\hat{i} + \hat{j} + \hat{k}$, $\hat{i} - \hat{j} + \hat{k}, \hat{i} + \hat{j} + \hat{k}$, is given by :

(a) $\frac{1}{2}(-\hat{i} + \hat{k}), \frac{1}{2}(\hat{j} - \hat{k}), \frac{1}{2}(\hat{i} + \hat{j})$

(b) $\frac{1}{2}(\hat{i} - \hat{k}), \frac{1}{2}(-\hat{j} + \hat{k}), \frac{1}{2}(\hat{i} + \hat{j})$

(c) $\frac{1}{2}(-\hat{i} + \hat{k}), \frac{1}{2}(-\hat{j} + \hat{k}), \frac{1}{2}(\hat{i} + \hat{j})$

(d) None of these

56. If $\vec{x} = \dfrac{\vec{b} \times \vec{c}}{[\vec{a}\ \vec{b}\ \vec{c}]}$, $\vec{y} = \dfrac{\vec{c} \times \vec{a}}{[\vec{a}\ \vec{b}\ \vec{c}]}$ and

$\vec{z} = \dfrac{\vec{a} \times \vec{b}}{[\vec{a}\ \vec{b}\ \vec{c}]}$ where $\vec{a}, \vec{b}, \vec{c}$ are non-coplanar

vectors, then the value of :

$\vec{x} \cdot (\vec{a} + \vec{b}) + \vec{y} \cdot (\vec{b} + \vec{c}) + \vec{z} \cdot (\vec{c} + \vec{a}) =$

(a) 1   (b) 2

(c) 3   (d) None of these

57. If the angle between the vectors $(x, 3, -7)$ and $(x, -x, 4)$ is acute, the interval in which x lies is :

(a) $(-4, 7)$ (b) $[-4, 7]$

(c) $R - (-4, 7)$ (d) $R - [-4, 7]$

58. The value of c so that for all real x the vectors $cx\hat{i} - 6\hat{j} + 3\hat{k}$ and $x\hat{i} + 2\hat{j} + 2cx\hat{k}$ make an obtuse angle are :

(a) $c < 0$ (b) $0 < c < \dfrac{4}{3}$

(c) $\dfrac{-4}{3} < c < 0$ (d) $c > 0$

59. The point with position vectors $10\hat{i} + 3\hat{j}$, $12\hat{i} - 5\hat{j}$ and $a\hat{i} + 11\hat{j}$ are collinear if the value of a is :

(a) -8 (b) 4

(c) 8   (d) 12

60. If $\hat{a}$ and $\hat{b}$ are two unit vectors inclined at an angle of $60°$ to each other, then :

(a) $|\hat{a} + \hat{b}| > 1$ (b) $|\hat{a} + \hat{b}| < 1$

(c) $|\hat{a} + \hat{b}| = 1$ (d) None of these

61. If $\vec{u} = \vec{a} - \vec{b}$, $\vec{v} = \vec{a} + \vec{b}$ and $|\vec{a}| = |\vec{b}| = 2$ then $|\vec{u} \times \vec{v}| =$

(a) $2\sqrt{[16 - (\vec{a} \cdot \vec{b})^2]}$

(b) $\sqrt{[16 - (\vec{a} \cdot \vec{b})^2]}$

(c) $2\sqrt{[4 - (\vec{a} \cdot \vec{b})^2]}$

(d) $\sqrt{[4 - (\vec{a} \cdot \vec{b})^2]}$

62. If the unit vectors $\vec{a}$ and $\vec{b}$ are inclined at angle 2θ ($0 \le \theta \le \pi$) and $|\vec{a} - \vec{b}| < 1$, then θ lies in the interval:

(a) $\left[0, \dfrac{\pi}{6}\right)$ (b) $\left[\dfrac{\pi}{6}, \dfrac{\pi}{2}\right]$

(c) $\left[\dfrac{\pi}{2}, \dfrac{5\pi}{6}\right]$ (d) None of these

63. The sum of the length of projections of $p\hat{i} + q\hat{j} + 2\hat{k}$ on the coordinate axes, where $p = 2$, $q = 3$ and $r = 1$, is:

(a) 6   (b) 5

(c) 4   (d) 3

64. The value of $\dfrac{[(\vec{a} \times \vec{b})^2 + (\vec{a} \cdot \vec{b})^2]}{2a^2b^2} =$

(a) 1   (b) $\dfrac{1}{2}$

(c) 2   (d) $\dfrac{1}{4}$

65. If $\vec{a}, \vec{b}, \vec{c}$ are three vectors such that $|\vec{a}| = 4$, $|\vec{b}| = 4, |\vec{c}| = 5$ and $\vec{a}, \vec{b}, \vec{c}$ are perpendicular to $\vec{b} + \vec{c}$, $\vec{c} + \vec{a}$, $\vec{a} + \vec{b}$, respectively, then $|\vec{a} + \vec{b} + \vec{c}| =$

(a) $6\sqrt{2}$ (b) $4\sqrt{2}$

(c) $3\sqrt{2}$ (d) $5\sqrt{2}$

66. If $\vec{A} = \hat{i} + \lambda\hat{j} + \hat{k}$, $\vec{B} = \hat{i} + \hat{j} + \hat{k}$ then for $|\vec{A} + \vec{B}| = |\vec{A}| + |\vec{B}|$ to be true, the value of $\lambda =$

(a) -1 (b) 2

(c) -2 (d) 1

67. A parallelogram is constructed on the vectors $\vec{a} = 3\vec{p} - \vec{q}$ & $\vec{b} = \vec{p} + 3\vec{q}$, given that $|\vec{p}| = |\vec{q}| = 2$ and the angle between $\vec{p}$ and $\vec{q}$ is $\dfrac{\pi}{3}$. The length of a diagonal is :

(a) $4\sqrt{5}$ (b) $4\sqrt{3}$

(c) $4\sqrt{7}$ (d) None of these

68. For any vector $\vec{a}$, the value of

$(\vec{a} \times \hat{i})^2 + (\vec{a} \times \hat{j})^2 + (\vec{a} \times \hat{k})^2 =$

(a) a^2

(b) $3a^2$

(c) $4a^2$

(d) $2a^2$

69. If $\vec{a} = (2, 1, 1)$, $\vec{b} = (1, 0, 3)$, $\vec{c} = (2, 1, 3)$ and

$\vec{a} \times (\vec{b} \times \vec{c}) + x\vec{a} + y\vec{b} + z\vec{c}$, then $(x, y, z) =$

(a) $(0, -8, 5)$

(b) $(8, 0, -5)$

(c) $(0, 8, -5)$

(d) $(8, -5, 0)$

70. If $\vec{a}$ is a non-zero vector and k is a scalar such that $|k\,\vec{a}| = 1$, then k is equal to :

(a) $|\vec{a}|$

(b) 1

(c) $\dfrac{1}{|\vec{a}|}$

(d) $\pm \dfrac{1}{|\vec{a}|}$

71. If $\vec{a}$ and $\vec{b}$ are position vectors of A and B respectively, then the position vector of a point C in AB produced such that AC = 3AB is :

(a) $3\vec{a} - \vec{b}$

(b) $3\vec{b} - \vec{a}$

(c) $3\vec{a} - 2\vec{b}$

(d) $3\vec{b} - 2\vec{a}$

72. If $\hat{a}, \hat{b}, \hat{c}$ are unit vectors such that $\hat{a} + \hat{b} + \hat{c} = 0$ then the value of $\hat{a} \cdot \hat{b} + \hat{b} \cdot \hat{c} + \hat{c} \cdot \hat{a} =$

(a) 1

(b) 2

(c) $\dfrac{-3}{2}$

(d) None of these

73. If $|\vec{a}| = 2$, $|\vec{b}| = 5$ and $|\vec{a} \times \vec{b}| = 8$, then $\vec{a} \cdot \vec{b}$ is equal to :

(a) 2

(b) 4

(c) 6

(d) 8

74. Let $\vec{a} = 2\hat{i} - 3\hat{j} - 6\hat{k}$ and $\vec{b} = -2\hat{i} - 2\hat{j} - \hat{k}$ then the value of $\dfrac{\text{The projection of } \vec{a} \text{ on } \vec{b}}{\text{The projection of } \vec{b} \text{ on } \vec{a}}$ is equal to :

(a) $\dfrac{7}{3}$

(b) 2

(c) 4

(d) None of these

75. If $\vec{a} = \hat{i} + \hat{j} - \hat{k}$, $\vec{b} = \hat{i} - \hat{j} + \hat{k}$ and $\hat{c}$ is a unit vector perpendicular to the vector $\vec{a}$ and coplanar with $\vec{a}$ and $\vec{b}$, then a unit vector $\hat{d}$ perpendicular to both $\vec{a}$ and $\hat{c}$ is :

(a) $\dfrac{1}{\sqrt{6}} (2\hat{i} - \hat{j} + \hat{k})$

(b) $\dfrac{1}{\sqrt{2}} (\hat{i} + \hat{j})$

(c) $\dfrac{1}{\sqrt{2}} (\hat{j} + \hat{k})$

(d) $\dfrac{1}{\sqrt{2}} (\hat{i} + \hat{k})$

76. If $\vec{a} = \hat{i} + 2\hat{j} + 3\hat{k}$, $\vec{b} = -\hat{i} + 2\hat{j} + \hat{k}$ and $\vec{c} = 3\hat{i} + \hat{j}$, then t such that $\vec{a} + t\vec{b}$ is at right angles to $\vec{c}$ will be equal to :

(a) 5

(b) 4

(c) 6

(d) 2

77. If $\vec{a} \cdot \vec{b} = \vec{b} \cdot \vec{c} = \vec{c} \cdot \vec{a} = 0$, then $\vec{a} \cdot (\vec{b} \times \vec{c})$ is equal to :

(a) a non-zero vector

(b) 1

(c) -1

(d) $|\vec{a}||\vec{b}||\vec{c}|$

78. A vector $\vec{a}$ has components 2p and 1 w.r.t. a rectangular cartesian system. This system is rotated through a certain angle about the origin in the counter-clockwise sense. If w.r.t. the new system, a has components p + 1 and 1, then :

(a) $p = 0$

(b) $p = 1$ or $p = -\dfrac{1}{3}$

(c) $p = -1$ or $p = \dfrac{1}{3}$

(d) $p = 1$ or $p = -1$

79. If $|\vec{a}| = 3, |\vec{b}| = 4$ and $|\vec{a} + \vec{b}| = 5$, then $|\vec{a} - \vec{b}| =$

(a) 8　　　　　　　　(b) 5

(c) 4　　　　　　　　(d) 3

80. If $\vec{a} \cdot \hat{j} = 4$, then $(\vec{a} \times \hat{j}) \times (2\hat{j} - 3\hat{k}) =$

(a) 12　　　　　　　(b) 2

(c) 0　　　　　　　 (d) –12

81. The sine of the angle between the vectors

$\vec{a} = 3\hat{i} + \hat{j} + \hat{k}, \vec{b} = 2\hat{i} - 2\hat{j} + \hat{k}$ is :

(a) $\sqrt{\dfrac{74}{99}}$　　　　　(b) $\sqrt{\dfrac{25}{99}}$

(c) $\sqrt{\dfrac{37}{99}}$　　　　　(d) $\dfrac{5}{\sqrt{41}}$

82. If the moduli of vectors $\vec{a}, \vec{b}, \vec{c}$ are 3, 4, 5 respectively and $\vec{a}$ and $\vec{b} + \vec{c}, \vec{b}$ and $\vec{c} + \vec{a},$ $\vec{c}$ and $\vec{a} + \vec{b}$ are mutually perpendicular then the modulus of $\vec{a} + \vec{b} + \vec{c} =$

(a) $\sqrt{12}$　　　　　(b) 12

(c) $5\sqrt{2}$　　　　　 (d) 50

83. If $\vec{p} = \hat{i} - 2\hat{j} + 3\hat{k}$ and $\vec{q} = 3\hat{i} + \hat{j} + 2\hat{k}$, then a vector $\vec{r}$ which is linear combination of $\vec{p}$ and $\vec{q}$ also perpendicular to $\vec{q}$ is :

(a) $\hat{i} + 5\hat{j} - 4\hat{k}$　　(b) $\hat{i} - 5\hat{j} + 4\hat{k}$

(c) $\dfrac{-1}{2}(\hat{i} + 5\hat{j} - 4\hat{k})$　(d) None of these

84. A unit vector in XY plane that makes an angle of 45° with the vector $\hat{i} + \hat{j}$ and angle of 60° with the vector $3\hat{i} - 4\hat{j}$ is :

(a) $\hat{i}$　　　　　　　(b) $\dfrac{\hat{i} + \hat{j}}{\sqrt{2}}$

(c) $\dfrac{\hat{i} - \hat{j}}{\sqrt{2}}$　　　　(d) None of these

85. If $\vec{a} \cdot \vec{b} = \beta$ and $\vec{a} \times \vec{b} = \vec{c}$, then $\vec{b}$ is equal to :

(a) $(\beta \vec{a} - \vec{a} \times \vec{c})/a^2$　(b) $(\beta \vec{a} + \vec{a} \times c)/a^2$

(c) $(\beta \vec{c} - \vec{a} \times \vec{c})/a^2$　(d) $(\beta \vec{c} + \vec{a} \times \vec{c})/a^2$

86. If a vector $\vec{\delta}$ is such that it is perpendicular to both $\vec{\alpha} = 4\hat{i} + 5\hat{j} - \hat{k}$ and $\vec{\beta} = \hat{i} - 4\hat{j} + 5\hat{k}$ and $\vec{\delta} \cdot \vec{\gamma} = 21$, where, $\vec{r} = 3\hat{i} + \hat{j} - \hat{k}$, then δ is equal to :

(a) $7(\hat{i} + \hat{j} - \hat{k})$　　(b) $7(\hat{i} + \hat{j} + \hat{k})$

(c) $7(\hat{i} - \hat{j} - \hat{k})$　　(d) None of these

87. If ABCDEF is a regular hexagon, then $\vec{AB} \cdot \vec{AF}$ is equal to :

(a) $\dfrac{1}{2}BC^2$　　　　(b) $-\dfrac{1}{2}BC^2$

(c) $\dfrac{1}{2}AC^2$　　　　(d) $-\dfrac{1}{2}AC^2$

88. The value of the constant S such that the scalar product of the vector $\hat{i} + \hat{j} + \hat{k}$ with the unit vector parallel to the sum of the vectors $5\hat{i} + 4\hat{j} - 5\hat{k}$ and $S\hat{i} + 2\hat{j} + 3\hat{k}$ is equal to one, is

(a) 2　　　　　　　　(b) –2

(c) 1　　　　　　　　(d) None of these

89. A vector $\vec{a}$ is collinear with vector $\vec{b} = \left(6, -8, -7\dfrac{1}{2}\right)$ and makes an acute angle with the positive direction of z-axis. If $|\vec{a}| = 50$, then $\vec{a} =$

(a) (24, 32, 30)　　　(b) (24, –32, 30)

(c) (–24, 32, 30)　　　(d) None of these

90. Let $\vec{a}, \vec{b}, \vec{c}$ be the three vectors such that $\vec{a} \cdot (\vec{b} + \vec{c}) = \vec{b} \cdot (\vec{c} + \vec{a}) = 0$ and $|\vec{a}| = 1, |\vec{b}| = 4, |\vec{c}| = 8$, then $|\vec{a} + \vec{b} + \vec{c}| =$

(a) 13　　　　　　　(b) 81

(c) 9　　　　　　　 (d) 5

91. If r satisfies the equation

$$\vec{r} \times (\hat{i} + 2\hat{j} + \hat{k}) = \hat{i} - \hat{k},$$ then for any scalar t, $\vec{r}$ is equal to :

(a) $\hat{i} + t(\hat{i} + 2\hat{j} + \hat{k})$

(b) $\hat{j} + t(\hat{i} + 2\hat{j} + \hat{k})$

(c) $\hat{k} + t(\hat{i} + 2\hat{j} + \hat{k})$

(d) $\hat{i} + \hat{k} + t(\hat{i} + 2\hat{j} + \hat{k})$

92. $\vec{a}$ and $\vec{b}$ are two unit vectors and θ is the angle between them. Then $\vec{a} + \vec{b}$ is a unit vector if :

(a) $\theta = \pi/3$ (b) $\theta = \pi/4$

(c) $\theta = \pi/2$ (d) $\theta = 2\pi/3$

93. Let A (4, 7, 8), B (2, 3, 4) and C (2, 5, 7) be the p.v's of the vertices of a triangle ABC. The length of the internal bisector of the angle at A is

(a) $\frac{3}{2}\sqrt{34}$ (b) $\frac{2}{3}\sqrt{34}$

(c) $\frac{1}{2}\sqrt{34}$ (d) $\frac{1}{3}\sqrt{34}$

94. The perpendicular distance of a corner of a unit cube form a diagonal not passing through it is :

(a) $\sqrt{6}$ (b) $\frac{\sqrt{6}}{3}$

(c) $\frac{3}{\sqrt{6}}$ (d) None of these

95. The vector $\vec{a}$, $\vec{b}$ and $\vec{c}$ are equal in length and taken pairwise, they make equal angles. If $\vec{a} = \hat{i} + \hat{j}$, $\vec{b} = \hat{j} + \hat{k}$ and $\vec{c}$ makes an obtuse angle with the base vector $\hat{i}$, then $\vec{c}$ is equal to :

(a) $\hat{j} + \hat{k}$ (b) $-\hat{i} + 4\hat{j} - \hat{k}$

(c) $\frac{-1}{3}\hat{i} + \frac{4}{3}\hat{j} - \frac{1}{3}\hat{k}$ (d) $\frac{1}{3}\hat{i} + \frac{-4}{3}\hat{j} + \frac{1}{3}\hat{k}$

96. A vector $\vec{a}$ is collinear with vector $6\hat{i} - 8\hat{j} - \frac{15}{2}\hat{k}$ of magnitude 50 making an obtuse angle with z-axis is :

(a) $24\hat{i} - 32\hat{j} - 30\hat{k}$ (b) $-24\hat{i} + 32\hat{j} + 30\hat{k}$

(c) $24\hat{i} + 32\hat{j} - 30\hat{k}$ (d) None of these

97. If p^{th}, q^{th}, r^{th} terms of a G.P. are the positive numbers a, b, c then the angle between the vectors : $\log a^2 \hat{i} + \log b^2 \hat{j} + \log c^2 \hat{k}$ and $(q - r) \hat{i} + (r - p) \hat{j} + (p - q) \hat{k}$ is :

(a) $\frac{\pi}{3}$ (b) $\frac{\pi}{2}$

(c) $\sin^{-1} 1/\sqrt{a^2 + b^2 + c^2}$ (d)   None of these

98. If $\vec{a}, \vec{b}, \vec{c}$ be three non-zero vectors, then the equation $\vec{a} \cdot \vec{b} = \vec{a} \times \vec{c}$ implies :

(a) $\vec{b} = \vec{c}$

(b) $\vec{a}$ is orthogonal to $\vec{b} - \vec{c}$

(c) either $\vec{a}$ is orthogonal to both $\vec{b}$ and $\vec{c}$ is or $\vec{a}$ orthogonal to $\vec{b} - \vec{c}$

(d) either $\vec{b} = \vec{c}$ or $\vec{a}$ is orthogonal to $\vec{b} - \vec{c}$

99. Let a, b, c be distinct non-negative numbers. If the vectors $a\hat{i} + a\hat{j} + c\hat{k}$; $\hat{i} + \hat{k}$ and $c\hat{i} + c\hat{j} + b\hat{k}$ lie in a plane, then c is :

(a) the Arithmetic mean of a and b

(b) the Geometric mean of a and b

(c) the Harmonic mean of a and b

(d) equal to zero

100. Vector $\vec{a} + 3\vec{b}$ is perpendicular to $7\vec{a} - 5\vec{b}$ and $\vec{a} - 5\vec{b}$ is perpendicular to $7\vec{a} + 3\vec{b}$. The angle between $\vec{a}$ and $\vec{b}$ is :

(a) $\frac{\pi}{6}$ (b) $\frac{\pi}{2}$

(c) $\frac{\pi}{4}$ (d) None of these

101. If $|\vec{a} + \vec{b}| = |\vec{a} - \vec{b}|$, then

(a) $\vec{a}$ and $\vec{b}$ are $\perp$ to each other

(b) $\vec{a}$ is parallel to $\vec{b}$

(c) $\vec{a} = 0$

(d) $\vec{b} = 0$

102. Let $\overrightarrow{OA} = \vec{a}$, $\overrightarrow{OB} = 10\vec{a} + 2\vec{b}$ and $\overrightarrow{OC} = \vec{b}$ where O, A, C are non-collinear. Let p denote the area of the quadrilateral OABC and q denote the area of the parallelogram with OA and OC as adjacent sides. Then $\dfrac{p}{q}$ is equal to :

(a) 4

(b) 6

(c) $\dfrac{1}{2} \dfrac{|\vec{a} - \vec{b}|}{|\vec{a}|}$

(d) None of these

103. If A, B, C, D are any four points in space, then

$|\overrightarrow{AB} \times \overrightarrow{CD} + \overrightarrow{BC} \times \overrightarrow{AD} + \overrightarrow{CA} \times \overrightarrow{BD}|$

= k (area of $\triangle$ABC), where k =

(a) 4

(b) 2

(c) 1

(d) None of these

104. The triangle ABC is defined by the vertices A(1, –2, 2), B(1, 4, 0) and C(–4, 1, 1). Let M be the foot of the altitude drawn from the vertex B to side AC. Then $\overrightarrow{BM} =$

(a) $\left(-\dfrac{20}{7}, -\dfrac{30}{7}, \dfrac{10}{7}\right)$ (b) (–20, –30, 10)

(c) (2, 3, –1)

(d) None of these

105. If $\hat{e}_1$, $\hat{e}_2$ are two unit vectors and θ is the angle between them, then $\cos\dfrac{\theta}{2}$ is :

(a) $\dfrac{1}{2}|\hat{e}_1 + \hat{e}_2|$

(b) $\dfrac{1}{2}|\hat{e}_1 - \hat{e}_2|$

(c) $\dfrac{|\hat{e}_1 \hat{e}_2|}{2}$

(d) $\dfrac{|\hat{e}_1 + \hat{e}_2|}{2|\hat{e}_1| \cdot |\hat{e}_2|}$

106. Let $\vec{a} = \hat{i} - \hat{j}$, $\vec{b} = \hat{j} - \hat{k}$, $\vec{c} = \hat{k} = \hat{i}$. If $\hat{d}$ is a unit vector such that $\vec{a} \cdot \hat{d} = 0 = [\vec{b} \; \vec{c} \; \hat{d}] = 0$ then $\hat{d}$ is equal to :

(a) $\pm\dfrac{\hat{i} + \hat{j} - \hat{k}}{\sqrt{3}}$

(b) $\pm\dfrac{\hat{i} + \hat{j} + \hat{k}}{\sqrt{3}}$

(c) $\pm\dfrac{\hat{i} + \hat{j} - 2\hat{k}}{\sqrt{6}}$

(d) $\pm\hat{k}$

107. Two planes are perpendicular to one another. One of them contains vectors $\vec{a}$ and $\vec{b}$ and the other contains vectors eq $\vec{c}$ and $\vec{d}$, then $(\vec{a} \times \vec{b}) \cdot (\vec{c} \times \vec{d})$ is equal to :

(a) 1

(b) 0

(c) $[\vec{a} \; \vec{b} \; \vec{c}]\vec{d}$

(d) $[\vec{b} \; \vec{c} \; \vec{d}]\vec{a}$

108. If $\vec{e_1}'$, $\vec{e_2}'$, $\vec{e_3}'$ are vectors reciprocal to the non-coplanar vectors $\vec{e}_1$, $\vec{e}_2$, $\vec{e}_3$ then $[\vec{e_1}', \vec{e_2}', \vec{e_3}'][\vec{e}_1, \vec{e}_2, \vec{e}_3] =$

(a) $\dfrac{-1}{2}$

(b) 1

(c) 0

(d) 4

109. If the vector $\vec{c}$, $\vec{a} = x\hat{i} + y\hat{j} + z\hat{k}$ and $\vec{b} = \hat{j}$ are such that $\vec{a}$, $\vec{c}$ and $\vec{b}$ form a right handed system then $\vec{c}$ is :

(a) $z\hat{i} - x\hat{k}$

(b) 0

(c) $y\hat{j}$

(d) $-z\hat{i} - x\hat{k}$

110. The three vectors $7\hat{i} - 11\hat{j} + 5\hat{k}, 5\hat{i} + 3\hat{j} - 2\hat{k}$ and $12\hat{i} - 8\hat{j} - \hat{k}$ form :

(a) an equilateral triangle

(b) a right angled triangle

(c) an isosceles triangle

(d) collinear vectors

111. ABCD is a quadrilateral with $\overrightarrow{AB} = \overrightarrow{a}$, $\overrightarrow{AD} = \overrightarrow{b}$ and $\overrightarrow{AC} = 2\overrightarrow{a} + 3\overrightarrow{b}$. If its area is α times the area of the parallelogram with AB, AD as adjacent sides, then α is equal to :

(a) 5   (b) $\dfrac{5}{2}$

(c) 1   (d) $\dfrac{1}{2}$

112. If the position vectors of $\overrightarrow{A}$ and $\overrightarrow{B}$ are $6\hat{i} + \hat{j} - 3\hat{k}$ and $4\hat{i} - 3\hat{j} - 2\hat{k}$, then the work done by the force $\overrightarrow{F} = \hat{i} - 3\hat{j} + 5\hat{k}$ in displacing a particle from A to B is :

(a) 15 units   (b) 17 units
(c) −15 units   (d) None of these

113. If $\overrightarrow{r} \cdot \overrightarrow{a} = 0$, $\overrightarrow{r} \cdot \overrightarrow{b} = 0$ and $\overrightarrow{r} \cdot \overrightarrow{c} = 0$ for some non-zero vector r, then the value of $[\overrightarrow{a}\ \overrightarrow{b}\ \overrightarrow{c}]$ is :

(a) 0   (b) 1/2
(c) 1   (d) 2

114. Given three unit vectors $\overrightarrow{a}, \overrightarrow{b}, \overrightarrow{c}$, no two of which are collinear satisfying in equation

$$\overrightarrow{a} \times (\overrightarrow{b} \times \overrightarrow{c}) = \dfrac{1}{2}\overrightarrow{b}.$$

The angle between $\overrightarrow{a}$ and $\overrightarrow{b}$ is :

(a) $\dfrac{\pi}{3}$ (b) $\dfrac{\pi}{4}$

(c) $\dfrac{\pi}{2}$ (d) None of these

115. A, B, C and D are four points such that

$\overrightarrow{AB} = m(2\hat{i} - 6\hat{j} + 2\hat{k})$, $\overrightarrow{BC} = \hat{i} - 2\hat{j}$ and $\overrightarrow{CD} = n(-6\hat{i} + 15\hat{j} - 3\hat{k})$.
If AB and CD intersect at some point E, then :

(a) $m \geq \dfrac{1}{2}$

(b) $n \geq \dfrac{1}{3}$

(c) area of $\Delta BCE = \dfrac{1}{2}\sqrt{6}$

(d) All of these

116. If the four vectors $\overrightarrow{a}, \overrightarrow{b}, \overrightarrow{c}, \overrightarrow{d}$ are coplanar, then

$[\overrightarrow{b}\ \overrightarrow{c}\ \overrightarrow{d}] + [\overrightarrow{c}\ \overrightarrow{a}\ \overrightarrow{d}] + [\overrightarrow{a}\ \overrightarrow{b}\ \overrightarrow{d}] =$

(a) 0   (b) 1
(c) −1   (d) $[a\ b\ c]$

117. The points O, A, B, C, D are such that $\overrightarrow{OA} = \overrightarrow{a}$, $\overrightarrow{OB} = \overrightarrow{b}$, $\overrightarrow{OC} = 2\overrightarrow{a} + 3\overrightarrow{b}$ and $\overrightarrow{OD} = \overrightarrow{a} - 2\overrightarrow{b}$. If $|\overrightarrow{a}| = 3|\overrightarrow{b}|$, then the angle between BD and AC is :

(a) π (b) $\dfrac{\pi}{2}$

(c) $\dfrac{\pi}{3}$ (d) None of these

118. In a trapezoid the vector $\overrightarrow{BC} = \lambda\overrightarrow{AD}$ and $\overrightarrow{p} = \mu\overrightarrow{AD}$ and $\overrightarrow{p} = \overrightarrow{AC} + \overrightarrow{BD}$ is collinear with $\overrightarrow{AD}$. Then :

(a) $\mu = \lambda + 1$ (b) $\lambda = \mu + 1$
(c) $\lambda + \mu = 1$ (d) $\mu = 2 + \lambda$

119. If $\overrightarrow{AC} = 3\hat{i} + \hat{j} - \hat{k}$ and $\overrightarrow{AC} = \hat{i} - \hat{j} + 3\hat{k}$. If the point P on the line segment BC is equidistant from AB and AC, then $\overrightarrow{AP}$ is :

(a) $2\hat{i} - \hat{k}$ (b) $\hat{i} - 2\hat{k}$
(c) $2\hat{i} + \hat{k}$ (d) None of these

120. A, B, C, D are four points on a plane with position vectors $\overrightarrow{a}, \overrightarrow{b}, \overrightarrow{c}, \overrightarrow{d}$ respectively such that $(\overrightarrow{a} - \overrightarrow{d}) \cdot (\overrightarrow{b} - \overrightarrow{c}) = (\overrightarrow{b} - \overrightarrow{d}) \cdot (\overrightarrow{c} - \overrightarrow{a}) = 0$. For ΔABC, D is the :

(a) Incentre   (b) Orthocentre
(c) Centroid   (d) None of these

121. If $\hat{a}$ and $\hat{b}$ are two unit vectors, then the vector $(\hat{a} + \hat{b}) \times (\hat{a} \times \hat{b})$ is parallel to the vector

(a) $\hat{a} - \hat{b}$ (b) $\hat{a} + \hat{b}$
(c) $2\hat{a} - \hat{b}$ (d) $2\hat{a} + \hat{b}$

122. If $\hat{a}$ and $\hat{b}$ are two unit vectors inclined to X-axis at angles 30° and 120°, then $|\hat{a} + \hat{b}| =$

(a) $\sqrt{\dfrac{2}{3}}$ (b) $\sqrt{2}$

(c) $\sqrt{3}$ (d) 2

123. The vectors $\vec{a}$ and $\vec{b}$ are non-collinear. The value of x for which the vectors

$\vec{c} = (x - 2)\,\vec{a} + \vec{b}$ and $\vec{d} = (2x + 1)\,\vec{a} - \vec{b}$

are collinear is :

(a) $\dfrac{-1}{3}$ (b) $\dfrac{1}{3}$

(c) $\dfrac{2}{3}$ (d) None of these

124. If $\vec{r} = \lambda\,(\vec{a} \times \vec{b}) + \mu\,(\vec{b} \times \vec{c}) + \upsilon\,(\vec{c} \times \vec{a})$

and $[\vec{a}\ \vec{b}\ \vec{c}] = \dfrac{1}{8}$, then $\lambda + \mu + \upsilon$ is equal to :

(a) $\vec{r}\,\cdot(\vec{a} + \vec{b} + \vec{c})$

(b) $8\vec{r}\cdot(\vec{a} + \vec{b} + \vec{c})$

(c) $4\vec{r}\,\cdot(\vec{a} + \vec{b} + \vec{c})$

(d) None of these

125. If $\vec{a}$, $\vec{b}$ and $\vec{c}$ are any three vectors, then

$\vec{a} \times (\vec{b} \times \vec{c}) = (\vec{a} \times \vec{b}) \times \vec{c}$ only if :

(a) $\vec{b}$ and $\vec{c}$ are collinear

(b) $\vec{a}$ and $\vec{c}$ are collinear

(c) $\vec{a}$ and $\vec{b}$ are collinear

(d) None of these

126. The position vectors $\vec{a}, \vec{b}, \vec{c}$ and $\vec{d}$ of four distinct points A, B, C and D lie on a plane are such that $|\vec{a} - \vec{d}| = |\vec{b} - \vec{d}| = |\vec{c} - \vec{d}|$ then the point D is the:

(a) centroid of ΔABC

(b) orthocentre of ΔABC

(c) circumcentre of ΔABC

(d) None of these

127. The values of x for which the angle between the vectors $\vec{a} = x\hat{i} - 3\hat{j} - \hat{k}$ and $\vec{b} = 2x\hat{i} + x\hat{j} - \hat{k}$ is acute and the angle between the vector $\vec{b}$ and the y-axis lies between $\dfrac{\pi}{2}$ and π are :

(a) $1, \dfrac{1}{2}$ (b) $0 < x < \dfrac{1}{2}$

(c) all $x < 0$ (d) $x < 0$ or $x > 1$

128. A unit vector in xy plane that makes an angle of 45° with the vector $\hat{i} + \hat{j}$ and an angle of 60° with the vector $3\hat{i} - 4\hat{j}$ is :

(a) $\hat{i}$ (b) $(\hat{i} + \hat{j})/\sqrt{2}$

(c) $(\hat{i} - \hat{j})/\sqrt{2}$ (d) None of these

129. Consider a tetrahedron with faces F_1, F_2, F_3, F_4. Let $\vec{V}_1, \vec{V}_2, \vec{V}_3, \vec{V}_4$ be the vectors whose magnitudes are respectively equal to areas of F_1, F_2, F_3, F_4 and whose directions are perpendicular to their faces in outward direction. Then $|\vec{V}_1 + \vec{V}_2 + \vec{V}_3 + \vec{V}_4|$ equals :

(a) 1   (b) 4

(c) 0   (d) None of these

130. Let $\vec{a}, \vec{b}$ and $\vec{c}$ be three non-zero and non-coplanar vectors and $\vec{p}, \vec{q}$ and $\vec{r}$ be three vectors given by

$\vec{p} = \vec{a} + \vec{b} - 2\vec{c}, \quad \vec{q} = 3\vec{a} - 2\vec{b} + \vec{c}$

and $\vec{r} = \vec{a} - 4\vec{b} + 2\vec{c}$

If the volume of the parallelopiped determined by $\vec{a}, \vec{b}$ and $\vec{c}$ is V_1 and the volume of the parallelopiped determined by $\vec{p}, \vec{q}$ and $\vec{r}$ is V_2 then $V_2 : V_1 =$

(a) 3 : 1   (b) 7 : 1

(c) 11 : 1   (d) 15 : 1

131. If $\vec{a} = 2\hat{i} - \hat{j} + \hat{k}$, $\vec{b} = \hat{i} + 2\hat{j} - 3\hat{k}$ and $\vec{c} = 3\hat{i} + \mu\hat{j} + 5\hat{k}$ are coplanar, then μ is a root of the equation :

(a) $x^2 + 3x = 4$
(b) $x^2 + 2x = 6$
(c) $x^2 + 3x = 6$
(d) None of these

132. $p\hat{i} + 3\hat{j} + 4\hat{k}$ and $\sqrt{q\hat{i} + 5\hat{j}}$ are two vectors, where p, q $\geq$ 0 are two scalars, then the length of the vectors is equal for :

(a) all values of (p, q)

(b) only finite number of values of (p, q)

(c) infinite number of values of (p, q)

(d) no value of (p, q)

133. If $\vec{a}, \vec{b}, \vec{c}$ are three unit vectors such that $|\vec{a} + \vec{b} + \vec{c}| = 1$ and $\vec{a} \perp \vec{b}$. If $\vec{c}$ makes angles α and β with $\vec{a}$ and $\vec{b}$ respectively, then $\cos \alpha + \cos \beta$ is equal to :

(a) $\dfrac{3}{2}$
(b) 1

(c) -1
(d) None of these

134. The three vectors $\hat{i} + \hat{j}$, $\hat{j} + \hat{k}$, $\hat{k} + \hat{i}$ taken two at a time form three planes. The three unit vectors drawn perpendicular to these three planes form a parallelopiped of volume :

(a) $\dfrac{1}{3}$
(b) 4

(c) $\dfrac{3\sqrt{3}}{4}$
(d) $\dfrac{4}{3\sqrt{3}}$

135. If ABCDEF is a regular hexagon inscribed in a circle with centre O, then $(\overrightarrow{AB} + \overrightarrow{AC} + \overrightarrow{AD} + \overrightarrow{AE} + \overrightarrow{AF})$ equals :

(a) $4\overrightarrow{AO}$
(b) $5\overrightarrow{AO}$

(c) $6\overrightarrow{AO}$
(d) $8\overrightarrow{AO}$

136. For a non-zero vector $\vec{a}$, set of real numbers satisfying the inequality $|(5 - x)\vec{a}| < |2\vec{a}|$ consists of all x such that :

(a) $0 < x < 3$
(b) $3 < x < 7$
(c) $-7 < x < -3$
(d) $-7 < x < 3$

137. A tetrahedron has vertices at O(0, 0, 0), A(1, 2, 1), B(2, 1, 3) and C(–1, 1, 2). Then the angle between the faces OAB and ABC will be :

(a) $\cos^{-1}\left(\dfrac{19}{35}\right)$
(b) $\cos^{-1}\left(\dfrac{71}{31}\right)$

(c) $30°$
(d) $90°$

138. If force represented by $5\hat{i} + \hat{k}$ is acting through the point $9\hat{i} - \hat{j} + 2\hat{k}$, the moment about the point $3\hat{i} + 2\hat{j} + \hat{k}$ is :

(a) $3\hat{i} + \hat{j} + 15\hat{k}$
(b) $3\hat{i} - \hat{j} + 15\hat{k}$
(c) $-3\hat{i} - \hat{j} + 15\hat{k}$
(d) $3\hat{i} + \hat{j} - 15\hat{k}$

139. For non-zero vectors $\vec{a}, \vec{b}, \vec{c}$, $|(\vec{a} \times \vec{b}) \cdot \vec{c}| = |\vec{a}||\vec{b}||\vec{c}|$ holds if and only if :

(a) $\vec{a} \cdot \vec{b} = 0$, $\vec{b} \cdot \vec{c} = 0$

(b) $\vec{b} \cdot \vec{c} = 0$, $\vec{c} \cdot \vec{a} = 0$

(c) $\vec{c} \cdot \vec{a} = 0$, $\vec{a} \cdot \vec{b} = 0$

(d) $\vec{a} \cdot \vec{b} = \vec{b} \cdot \vec{c} = \vec{c} \cdot \vec{a} = 0$

140. Let $\vec{a} = \hat{i} + \hat{j}$ and $\vec{b} = 2\hat{i} - \hat{j}$, the point of intersection of the lines $\vec{r} \times \vec{a} = \vec{b} \times \vec{a}$ and $\vec{r} \times \vec{b} = \vec{a} \times \vec{b}$ is :

(a) $-\hat{i} + \hat{j} + \hat{k}$
(b) $3\hat{i} - \hat{j} + \hat{k}$
(c) $3\hat{i} + \hat{j} - \hat{k}$
(d) $\hat{i} - \hat{j} - \hat{k}$

141. If the vectors $a\hat{i} + \hat{j} + \hat{k}$, $\hat{i} + b\hat{j} + \hat{k}$ and $\hat{i} + \hat{j} + c\hat{k}$ ($a \neq b \neq c \neq 1$) are coplanar then the value of $\dfrac{1}{1-a} + \dfrac{1}{1-b} + \dfrac{1}{1-c}$ is :

(a) 0
(b) 1

(c) -1
(d) None of these

142. If C is the mid point of AB and P is any point outside AB, then : **[AIEEE – 2005]**

(a) $\overrightarrow{PA} + \overrightarrow{PB} = 2\overrightarrow{PC}$

(b) $\overrightarrow{PA} + \overrightarrow{PB} = \overrightarrow{PC}$

(c) $\overrightarrow{PA} + p\overrightarrow{B} + 2\overrightarrow{PC} = 0$

(d) $\overrightarrow{PA} + \overrightarrow{PB} + \overrightarrow{PC} = 0$

143. Vectors $2\hat{i} - m\hat{j} + 3m\hat{k}$ and $(1 + m)\,\hat{i} - 2m\hat{j} + \hat{k}$ include an acute angle for :

(a) all values of m   (b) $m < -2$ or $m > \dfrac{-1}{2}$

(c) $m = \dfrac{-1}{2}$ (d) $m \in \left[-2, \dfrac{-1}{2}\right]$

144. Let $\overrightarrow{p}$ and $\overrightarrow{q}$ be the position vectors of P and Q respectively w.r.t. O and $|\overrightarrow{p}| = p, |\overrightarrow{q}| = q$. The points R and S divide PQ internally and externally in the ratio 2 : 3 respectively. If $\overrightarrow{OR}$ and $\overrightarrow{OS}$ are perpendicular, then :

(a) $9p^2 = 4q^2$ (b) $4p^2 = 9q^2$

(c) $9p = 4q$ (d) $4p = 9q$

145. Vectors $\overrightarrow{AB} = 3\hat{i} + 4\hat{k}$ and $\overrightarrow{AC} = 5\hat{i} - 2\hat{j} + 4\hat{k}$ are the sides of a triangle ABC. The length of the median through A is :

(a) $3\sqrt{2}$ (b) $\dfrac{6}{\sqrt{2}}$

(c) $\dfrac{3}{\sqrt{2}}$ (d) None of these

146. If $\overrightarrow{A}, \overrightarrow{B}, \overrightarrow{C}$ are three non-coplanar vectors, then $\dfrac{\overrightarrow{A} \cdot \overrightarrow{B} \times \overrightarrow{C}}{\overrightarrow{C} \times \overrightarrow{A} \cdot \overrightarrow{B}} + \dfrac{\overrightarrow{B} \cdot \overrightarrow{A} \times \overrightarrow{C}}{\overrightarrow{C} \cdot \overrightarrow{A} \times \overrightarrow{B}} =$

(a) 0   (b) 1

(c) –1   (d) None of these

147. If $\overrightarrow{p} = \dfrac{\overrightarrow{b} \times \overrightarrow{c}}{[\overrightarrow{a}\ \overrightarrow{b}\ \overrightarrow{c}]}$, $\overrightarrow{q} = \dfrac{\overrightarrow{c} \times \overrightarrow{a}}{[\overrightarrow{a}\ \overrightarrow{b}\ \overrightarrow{c}]}$, $\overrightarrow{r} = \dfrac{\overrightarrow{a} \times \overrightarrow{b}}{[\overrightarrow{a}\ \overrightarrow{b}\ \overrightarrow{c}]}$

where $\overrightarrow{a}, \overrightarrow{b}, \overrightarrow{c}$ are three non-coplanar vectors then the value of $(\overrightarrow{a} + \overrightarrow{b} + \overrightarrow{c}) \cdot (\overrightarrow{p} + \overrightarrow{q} + \overrightarrow{r})$ is :

(a) 3   (b) 2

(c) 1   (d) 0

148. Given the vectors $\overrightarrow{a}$ (2, 1, –1), $\overrightarrow{b}$ (1, 2, 1), $\overrightarrow{c}$ (2, –1, 3), $\overrightarrow{d}$ (3, –1, 2), the projection of the vector $\overrightarrow{a} + \overrightarrow{c}$ on the vector $(\overrightarrow{b} - \overrightarrow{d}) \times \overrightarrow{c}$ is :

(a) $\sqrt{2}$ (b) $\sqrt{3}$

(c) $\sqrt{6}$ (d) None of these

149. The position vectors of three points A, B and C are $\hat{i} + \hat{j}$, $\hat{i} - \hat{j}$ and $l\hat{i} + m\hat{j} + n\hat{k}$ respectively. The vectors OA, OB, OC are coplanar if :

(a) $l = m = n = 1$

(b) $l = 1$, m and n are any scalars

(c) $n = 0$, l, m are scalars

(d) $m = 0, n = 1, l$ is any scalar

150. $[\overrightarrow{a}\ \overrightarrow{b}\ \overrightarrow{a} \times \overrightarrow{b}]$ is equal to :

(a) $|\overrightarrow{a} \times \overrightarrow{b}|$ (b) $|\overrightarrow{a} \times \overrightarrow{b}|^2$

(c) $|\overrightarrow{a} \cdot \overrightarrow{b}|$ (d) $|\overrightarrow{a}||\overrightarrow{b}|$

151. If $\overrightarrow{d} = x(\overrightarrow{a} \times \overrightarrow{b}) + y(\overrightarrow{b} \times \overrightarrow{c}) + z(\overrightarrow{c} \times \overrightarrow{a})$ and $[a\ b\ c] = \dfrac{1}{8}$, then $x + y + z = k(\overrightarrow{a} + \overrightarrow{b} + \overrightarrow{c}) \cdot \overrightarrow{d}$, where k =

(a) 2   (b) 4

(c) 8   (d) None of these

152. If $\overrightarrow{a}, \overrightarrow{b}, \overrightarrow{c}, \overrightarrow{d}$ are non-coplanar vectors and $\overrightarrow{d} \cdot \{\overrightarrow{a} \times [\overrightarrow{b} \times (\overrightarrow{c} \times \overrightarrow{d})]\}$ is equal to :

(a) $(\overrightarrow{b} \cdot \overrightarrow{d})[\overrightarrow{a}\ \overrightarrow{c}\ \overrightarrow{d}]$

(b) $(\overrightarrow{a} \cdot \overrightarrow{d})[\overrightarrow{a}\ \overrightarrow{c}\ \overrightarrow{d}]$

(c) $(\overrightarrow{c} \cdot \overrightarrow{d})[\overrightarrow{a}\ \overrightarrow{c}\ \overrightarrow{d}]$

(d) None of these

153. $(\vec{r} \cdot \hat{i})(\vec{r} \times \hat{i}) + (\vec{r} \cdot \hat{j})(\vec{r} \times \hat{j}) + (\vec{r} \cdot \hat{k})(\vec{r} \times \hat{k})$

is equal to :

(a) $3\vec{r}$ (b) $\vec{r}$

(c) 0   (d) None of these

154. Let $\vec{a} = 2\hat{i} + \hat{j} - 2\hat{k}$ and $\vec{b} = \hat{i} + \hat{j}$. If $\vec{c}$ is a vector such that $\vec{a} \cdot \vec{c} = |\vec{c}|, |\vec{c} - \vec{a}| = 2\sqrt{2}$ and the angle between $\vec{a} \times \vec{b}$ and $\vec{c}$ is $30°$ then $|(\vec{a} \times \vec{b}) \times \vec{c}|$ is equal to :

(a) 2/3   (b) 3/2

(c) 2   (d) 3

155. Let $\vec{a}, \vec{b}, \vec{c}$ be three vectors such that $a \neq 0$ and $\vec{a} \times \vec{b} = 2\vec{a} \times \vec{c}, |\vec{a}| = |\vec{c}| = 1, |\vec{b}| = 4$ $|\vec{b} \times \vec{c}| = \sqrt{15}$, if $\vec{b} - 2\vec{c} = \lambda\vec{a}$. Then λ equals

(a) 1   (b) –1

(c) 2   (d) –4

156. If the non-zero vectors $\vec{a}$ and $\vec{b}$ are perpendicular to each other then the solution of the equation $\vec{r} \times \vec{a} = \vec{b}$ is :

(a) $\vec{r} = x\vec{a} + \dfrac{1}{\vec{a} \cdot \vec{a}}(\vec{a} \times \vec{b})$

(b) $\vec{r} = x\vec{b} - \dfrac{1}{\vec{b} \cdot \vec{b}}(\vec{a} \times \vec{b})$

(c) $\vec{r} = x(\vec{a} \times \vec{b})$

(d) None of these

157. If $\vec{a}, \vec{b}, \vec{c}$ are three non-coplanar non-zero vectors and $\vec{r}$ is any vector in space then $(\vec{a} \times \vec{b}) \times (\vec{r} \times \vec{c}) + (\vec{b} \times \vec{c}) \times (\vec{r} \times \vec{a}) + (\vec{c} \times \vec{a}) \times (\vec{r} \times \vec{b})$

is equal to :

(a) $2[\vec{a} \ \vec{b} \ \vec{c}]\vec{r}$ (b) $3[\vec{a} \ \vec{b} \ \vec{c}]\vec{r}$

(c) $[\vec{a} \ \vec{b} \ \vec{c}]\vec{r}$ (d) None of these

158. If $\vec{a}, \vec{b}, \vec{c}$ are three non-coplanar, non-zero vectors then $(\vec{a} \cdot \vec{a})\vec{b} \times \vec{c} + (\vec{a} \cdot \vec{b})\vec{c} \times \vec{a} + (\vec{a} \cdot \vec{c})\vec{a} \times \vec{b}$

is equal to :

(a) $[\vec{b} \ \vec{c} \ \vec{a}]\vec{a}$ (b) $[\vec{c} \ \vec{a} \ \vec{b}]\vec{b}$

(c) $[\vec{a} \ \vec{b} \ \vec{c}]\vec{c}$ (d) None of these

159. Let the unit vectors $\hat{a}$ and $\hat{b}$ be perpendicular to each other and the unit vector $\hat{c}$ be inclined at an angle θ to both $\hat{a}$ and $\hat{b}$.

If $\hat{c} = x\hat{a} + y\hat{b} + z(\hat{a} \times \hat{b})$, then :

(a) $x = \cos \theta, y = \sin \theta, z = \cos 2\theta$

(b) $x = \sin \theta, y = \cos \theta, z = -\cos 2\theta$

(c) $x = y = \cos \theta, z^2 = \cos 2\theta$

(d) $x = y = \cos \theta, z^2 = -\cos 2\theta$

160. If $\hat{n}_1, \hat{n}_2$ are two unit vectors and θ is the angle between them, then $\cos \dfrac{\theta}{2} =$

(a) $\dfrac{1}{2}|\hat{n}_1 + \hat{n}_2|$ (b) $\dfrac{1}{2}|\hat{n}_1 - \hat{n}_2|$

(c) $\dfrac{1}{2}(\hat{n}_1 + \hat{n}_2)$ (d) $\dfrac{|\hat{n}_1 \times \hat{n}_2|}{2|\hat{n}_1||\hat{n}_2|}$

161. $\begin{vmatrix} \vec{a} \cdot \vec{a} & \vec{a} \cdot \vec{b} & \vec{a} \cdot \vec{c} \\ \vec{b} \cdot \vec{a} & \vec{b} \cdot \vec{b} & \vec{b} \cdot \vec{c} \\ \vec{c} \cdot \vec{a} & \vec{c} \cdot \vec{b} & \vec{c} \cdot \vec{c} \end{vmatrix}$ is equal to :

(a) $[\vec{a} \ \vec{b} \ \vec{c}]^2$ (b) $[\vec{a} \ \vec{b} \ \vec{c}]$

(c) $[\vec{a} \ \vec{b} \ \vec{c}]^3$ (d) None of these

162. If $\vec{a}, \vec{b}, \vec{c}$ and $\vec{p}, \vec{q}, \vec{r}$ are reciprocal system of vectors, then $\vec{a} \times \vec{p} + \vec{b} \times \vec{q} + \vec{c} \times \vec{r}$ equals:

(a) $[\vec{a} \ \vec{b} \ \vec{c}]$ (b) $[\vec{p} + \vec{q} + \vec{r}]$

(c) 0   (d) $\vec{a} + \vec{b} + \vec{c}$

163. If S is the circumcentre, O is the orthocentre of $\triangle ABC$, then $\overrightarrow{SA} + \overrightarrow{SB} + \overrightarrow{SC} =$

(a) $\overrightarrow{SO}$

(b) $2\overrightarrow{SO}$

(c) $\overrightarrow{OS}$

(d) $2\overrightarrow{OS}$

164. If $(\vec{a} \times \vec{b})^2 + (\vec{a} \cdot \vec{b})^2 = 144$ then $|\vec{a}|$ and $|\vec{b}| =$

(a) 16

(b) 8

(c) 3

(d) 12

165. The median AD of the triangle ABC is bisected at E, BE meets AC in F, then AF : AC =

(a) 3/4

(b) 1/3

(c) 1/2

(d) 1/4

166. If $\hat{i}, \hat{j}, \hat{k}$ are unit orthonormal vectors and $\vec{b}$ is a vector, if $\vec{a} \times \vec{r} = \hat{j}$, then $\vec{a} \cdot \vec{r}$ is :

(a) 0

(b) 1

(c) –1

(d) Arbitrary scalar

167. Let $\vec{a} = x\hat{i} + y\hat{j} + z\hat{k}$, $\vec{b} = \hat{j}$. The value of $\vec{c}$, for which $\vec{a}, \vec{b}, \vec{c}$ form a right handed system is :

(a) $y\hat{j}$

(b) $-z\hat{i} + x\hat{k}$

(c) 0

(d) $z\hat{i} - x\hat{k}$

168. Vectors $\vec{a} = \hat{i} + \hat{j} + (m+l)\hat{k}$, $\vec{b} = \hat{i} + \hat{j} + lm\hat{k}$, and $\vec{c} = \hat{i} - \hat{j} + m\hat{k}$ are coplanar for :

(a) $m = 2$

(b) $m = \dfrac{1}{2}$

(c) $m = -\dfrac{1}{2}$

(d) no value of m

169. The area of the parallelogram whose diagonals are given by the vectors $3\hat{i} + \hat{j} - 2\hat{k}$ and $\hat{i} - 3\hat{j} + 4\hat{k}$ is :

(a) $5\sqrt{3}$

(b) 4

(c) $0\sqrt{3}$

(d) 8

170. The value of $(\vec{a} - \vec{b}) \cdot [(\vec{b} - \vec{c}) \times (\vec{a} - \vec{a})]$ is :

(a) $2[\vec{a}\ \vec{b}\ \vec{c}]$

(b) $3[\vec{a}\ \vec{b}\ \vec{c}]$

(c) 0

(d) None of these

171. Let $\hat{A}, \hat{B}, \hat{C}$ be unit vectors.

Suppose $\hat{A} \cdot \hat{B} = \hat{A} \cdot \hat{C} = 0$ and the angle between $\hat{B}$ and $\hat{C}$ is $\dfrac{\pi}{6}$.

Then $\hat{A}$ equals:

(a) $\pm 2(\hat{B} \times \hat{C})$

(b) $-2(\hat{B} \times \hat{C})$

(c) $2(\hat{B} \times \hat{C})$

(d) $\hat{B} \times \hat{C}$

172. A constant force $\vec{F} = 2\hat{i} - 3\hat{j} + 2\hat{k}$ is acting on a particle such that the particle is displaced from the point A (1, 2, 3) to the point B (3, 4, 5). The work done by the force is :

(a) $2\sqrt{51}$

(b) $\sqrt{17}$

(c) 3

(d) 2

173. If a parallelogram is constructed on the vectors $\vec{a} = 3\vec{p} - \vec{q}$, $\vec{b} = 3\vec{q}$ and $|\vec{p}| = |\vec{q}| = 2$ and angle between $\vec{p}$ and $\vec{q}$ is $\dfrac{\pi}{3}$, then the ratio of the lengths of the sides is :

(a) $\sqrt{7} : \sqrt{13}$

(b) $\sqrt{6} : \sqrt{2}$

(c) $\sqrt{3} : \sqrt{5}$

(d) None of these

174. If the vectors $\vec{a}$ and $\vec{b}$ are perpendicular to each other, then a vector $\vec{v}$ in terms of $\vec{a}$ and $\vec{b}$ satisfying the equations $\vec{v} \cdot \vec{a} = 0$, $\vec{v} \cdot \vec{b} = 1$ and $[\vec{v}\ \vec{a}\ \vec{b}] = 1$ is :

(a) $\dfrac{1}{|\vec{b}|^2}\vec{b} + \dfrac{1}{|\vec{a} \times \vec{b}|^2}\vec{a} \times \vec{b}$

(b) $\dfrac{\vec{b}}{|\vec{b}|} + \dfrac{\vec{a} \times \vec{b}}{|\vec{a} \times \vec{b}|^2}$

(c) $\dfrac{\vec{b}}{|\vec{b}|^2} + \dfrac{\vec{a} \times \vec{b}}{|\vec{a} \times \vec{b}|}$

(d) None of these

175. $\hat{a}, \hat{b}, \hat{c}$ are three unit vectors such that $\hat{a} \times (\hat{b} \times \hat{c}) = \frac{1}{2}(\hat{b} + \hat{c})$. If the vectors $\hat{b}$ and $\hat{c}$ are non-parallel, then the angle between $\hat{a}$ and $\hat{b}$ is :

(a) $\frac{\pi}{3}$

(b) $\frac{2\pi}{3}$

(c) $\frac{5\pi}{6}$

(d) None of these

176. If $\vec{a}, \vec{b}, \vec{c}$ are non-coplanar vectors and $\hat{d}$ is a unit vector, then the value of

$|(\vec{a} \cdot \hat{d})(\vec{b} \times \vec{c}) + (\vec{b} \cdot \hat{d})(\vec{c} \times \vec{a}) + (\vec{c} \cdot \hat{d})(\vec{a} \times \vec{b})| =$

(a) 1

(b) −1

(c) $1[\vec{a} \ \vec{b} \ \vec{c}]$

(d) None of these

177. The distance of the point $B(\hat{i} + 2\hat{j} + 3\hat{k})$ from the line which is passing through $A(4\hat{i} + 2\hat{j} + 2\hat{k})$ and which is parallel to the vector $C = 2\hat{i} + 3\hat{j} + 6\hat{k}$, is :

(a) 10

(b) $\sqrt{10}$

(c) $2\sqrt{10}$

(d) None of these

178. Let $\hat{a}$ be a unit vector and $\vec{b}$ be a non-zero vector not parallel to $\hat{a}$. If two sides of the triangle are represented by the vectors $\sqrt{3}(\hat{a} \times \vec{b})$ and $\vec{b} \cdot (\hat{a} \cdot \vec{b})\hat{a}$, then the angles of the triangle are :

(a) 30°, 90°, 60°

(b) 45°, 45°, 90°

(c) 60°, 60°, 60°

(d) None of these

179. Let the vectors $\vec{a}, \vec{b}, \vec{c}$ and $\vec{d}$ be such that $(\vec{a} \times \vec{b}) \times (\vec{c} \times \vec{d}) = 0$. Let P_1 and P_2 be planes determined by the pairs of vectors $\vec{a}, \vec{b}$ and $\vec{c}, \vec{d}$ respectively, then the angle between P_1 and P_2 is :

(a) 0

(b) $\frac{\pi}{4}$

(c) $\frac{\pi}{3}$

(d) $\frac{\pi}{2}$

180. If $\hat{a}, \hat{b}$ and $\hat{c}$ are unit coplanar vectors, then the scalar triple product $[2\hat{a} - \hat{b}, 2\hat{b} - \hat{c}, 2\hat{c} - \hat{a}] =$

(a) 0

(b) 1

(c) $-\sqrt{3}$

(d) $\sqrt{3}$

181. If $\vec{a} = \hat{i} + \hat{j} + \hat{k}$, $\vec{b} = 4\hat{i} + 3\hat{j} + 4\hat{k}$ and $\vec{c} = \hat{i} + \alpha\hat{j} + \beta\hat{k}$ are linearly dependent vectors and $|\vec{c}| = \sqrt{3}$, then :

(a) $\alpha = 1, \beta = -1$

(b) $\alpha = 1, \beta = \pm 1$

(c) $\alpha = -1, \beta = \pm 1$

(d) $\alpha = \pm 1, \beta = 1$

182. For three vectors, $\vec{u}, \vec{v}, \vec{w}$ which of the following expressions is not equal to any of the remaining three ?

(a) $\vec{u} \cdot (\vec{v} \times \vec{w})$

(b) $(\vec{v} \times \vec{w}) \cdot \vec{u}$

(c) $\vec{v} \cdot (\vec{u} \times \vec{w})$

(d) $(\vec{u} \times \vec{v}) \cdot \vec{w}$

183. For any two vectors $\vec{u}$ and $\vec{v}$,

$(\vec{u} \cdot \vec{v})^2 + |\vec{u} \times \vec{v}|^2 =$

(a) $|\vec{u}|^2 |\vec{v}|^2$

(b) $2|\vec{u}|^2 \cdot |\vec{v}|^2$

(c) $4|\vec{u}|^2 |\vec{v}|^2$

(d) None of these

184. For any two vectors $\vec{u}$ and $\vec{v}$,

$(1 - \vec{u} \cdot \vec{v})^2 + |\vec{u} + \vec{v} + (\vec{u} \times \vec{v})|^2$ is equal to :

(a) $(1 - |\vec{u}|^2)(1 - |\vec{v}|^2)$

(b) $(1 + |\vec{u}|^2)(1 + |\vec{v}|^2)$

(c) $(1 - |\vec{u}|)(1 - |\vec{v}|)$

(d) None of these

185. Let $\vec{OA} = \vec{a}$, $\vec{OB} = 10\vec{a} + 2\vec{b}$ and $\vec{OC} = \vec{b}$ where O, A and C are non-collinear points. Let p denote the area of the quadrilateral OABC, and let q denote the area of the parallelogram with OA and OC as adjacent sides. If $p = kq$, then $k =$

(a) 3

(b) 4

(c) 5

(d) 6

186. If $\vec{A}, \vec{B}$ and $\vec{C}$ are vectors such that $|\vec{B}| = |\vec{C}|$, then $[(\vec{A}+\vec{B}) \times (\vec{A}+\vec{C})] \times (\vec{B}\times\vec{C}) \cdot (\vec{B}+\vec{C}) =$

(a) 1

(b) –1

(c) 0

(d) None of these

187. Let $\vec{a} = 2\hat{i} + \hat{j} - 2\hat{k}$ and $\vec{b} = \hat{i} + \hat{j}$. If $\vec{c}$ is a vector such that $|\vec{a} \cdot \vec{c}| = |\vec{c}|, |\vec{c} - \vec{a}| = 2\sqrt{2}$ and the angle between $(\vec{a}\times\vec{b})$ and $\vec{c}$ is 30°, then $|(\vec{a}\times\vec{b}) \times \vec{c}| =$

(a) 2/3

(b) 3/2

(c) 2

(d) 3

188. Let $\vec{a} = 2\hat{i} + \hat{j} + \hat{k}$, $\vec{b} = \hat{i} + 2\hat{j} - \hat{k}$ and a unit vector $\vec{c}$ be coplanar. If $\vec{c}$ is perpendicular to $\vec{a}$, then $\vec{c} =$

(a) $\frac{1}{\sqrt{2}}(-\hat{i} + \hat{k})$

(b) $\frac{1}{\sqrt{3}}(-\hat{i} - \hat{j} - \hat{k})$

(c) $\frac{1}{\sqrt{5}}(\hat{i} - 2\hat{j})$

(d) $\frac{1}{\sqrt{3}}(\hat{i} - \hat{j} - \hat{k})$

189. Let $\hat{u}$ and $\hat{v}$ be unit vectors. If $\vec{w}$ is a vector such that $\vec{w} + (\vec{w}\times\hat{u}) = \hat{v}$ then $|(\hat{u}\times\hat{v}) \cdot \vec{w}|$

(a) $\le \frac{1}{3}$

(b) $\le \frac{1}{2}$

(c) $> \frac{1}{3}$

(d) $\ge \frac{1}{2}$

190. If $\hat{b}$ and $\hat{c}$ are any two non-collinear unit vectors and $\vec{a}$ is any vector, then

$(\vec{a} \cdot \hat{b})\hat{b} + (\vec{a} \cdot \hat{c})\hat{c} + \frac{\vec{a} \cdot (\hat{b} + \hat{c})}{|\hat{b} + \hat{c}|^2}(\hat{b} \times \hat{c}) =$

(a) $\overline{\vec{a}}$

(b) $\hat{b}$

(c) $\hat{c}$

(d) None of these

191. Let $\vec{p}, \vec{q}, \vec{r}$ be three mutually perpendicular vectors of the same magnitude. If a vector $\vec{x}$ satisfies the equation

$\vec{p} \times [(\vec{x} - \vec{q}) \times \vec{p}] + \vec{q} \times [(\vec{x} - \vec{r}) \times \vec{q}]$
$+ \vec{r}[(\vec{x} - \vec{p}) \times \vec{r}] = 0$, then $\vec{x}$ is given by :

(a) $\frac{1}{2}(\vec{p} + \vec{q} - 2\vec{r})$

(b) $\frac{1}{2}(\vec{p} + \vec{q} + \vec{r})$

(c) $\frac{1}{3}(\vec{p} + \vec{q} + \vec{r})$

(d) $\frac{1}{3}(2\vec{p} + \vec{q} - \vec{r})$

192. Let $\vec{a}, \vec{b}$ and $\vec{c}$ be three vectors having magnitudes 1, 1 and 2 respectively.

If $\vec{a} \times (\vec{a}\times\vec{c}) + \vec{b} = 0$, then the acute angle between $\vec{a}$ and $\vec{c}$ is :

(a) $\frac{\pi}{4}$

(b) $\frac{\pi}{6}$

(c) $\frac{\pi}{3}$

(d) None of these

193. A unit vector perpendicular to the plane determined by the points P(1, –1, 2), Q(2, 0, –1) and R (0, 2, 1) is :

(a) $\frac{2\hat{i} + \hat{j} + \hat{k}}{\sqrt{6}}$

(b) $\frac{\hat{i} + 2\hat{j} + \hat{k}}{\sqrt{6}}$

(c) $\frac{\hat{i} + \hat{j} + 2\hat{k}}{\sqrt{6}}$

(d) None of these

194. Given that $\vec{a} = (1, 1, 1)$, $\vec{c} = (0, 1, -1)$ and $\vec{a} \cdot \vec{b} = 3$, $\vec{a} \times \vec{b} = \vec{c}$ then $\vec{b} =$

(a) $\left(\frac{5}{3}, \frac{2}{3}, \frac{-2}{3}\right)$

(b) $\left(\frac{5}{3}, \frac{-2}{3}, \frac{2}{3}\right)$

(c) $\left(\frac{5}{3}, \frac{2}{3}, \frac{2}{3}\right)$

(d) None of these

195. If $\vec{A} = 2\hat{i} + \hat{k}$, $\vec{B} = \hat{i} + \hat{j} + \hat{k}$ and $\vec{C} = 4\hat{i} + 3\hat{j} + 7\hat{k}$ then a vector $\vec{R}$ satisfying $\vec{R} \times \vec{B} = \vec{C} \times \vec{B}$ and $\vec{R} \cdot \vec{A} = 0$ is :

(a) $-\hat{i} - 8\hat{j} + 2\hat{k}$

(b) $-\hat{i} + 8\hat{j} + 2\hat{k}$

(c) $\hat{i} - 8\hat{j} + 2\hat{k}$

(d) None of these

196. If the vectors $\vec{a}$, $\vec{b}$, $\vec{c}$ are coplanar, then

$$\begin{vmatrix} \vec{a} & \vec{b} & \vec{c} \\ \vec{a}\cdot\vec{a} & \vec{a}\cdot\vec{b} & \vec{a}\cdot\vec{c} \\ \vec{b}\cdot\vec{a} & \vec{b}\cdot\vec{b} & \vec{b}\cdot\vec{c} \end{vmatrix} =$$

(a) 1   (b) 0

(c) −1   (d) None of these

197. In a $\triangle$ OAB, E is the mid point of OB and D is a point on AB such that AD : DB = 2 : 1. If OD and AE intersect at P, then the ratio OP : PD is :

(a) 2 : 3   (b) 3 : 2

(c) 1 : 3   (d) 3 : 1

198. The number of vectors of unit length perpendicular to vectors $\vec{a}$ = (1, 1, 0) and $\vec{b}$ = (0, 1, 1) is :

(a) one   (b) two

(c) three   (d) infinite

199. Let $\vec{a} = a_1\hat{i} + a_2\hat{j} + a_3\hat{k}$, $\vec{b} = b_1\hat{i} + b_2\hat{j} + b_3\hat{k}$ and $\vec{c} = c_1\hat{i} + c_2\hat{j} + c_3\hat{k}$ be three non-zero vectors such that $\hat{c}$ is a unit vector perpendicular to both vectors $\vec{a}$ and $\vec{b}$. If the angle between vectors $\vec{a}$ and $\vec{b}$ is π/6, then $\begin{vmatrix} a_1 & a_2 & a_3 \\ b_1 & b_2 & b_3 \\ c_1 & c_2 & c_3 \end{vmatrix}^2$

is equal to

(a) 0   (b) 1

(c) $\frac{1}{4}(a_1^2 + a_2^2 + a_3^2)(b_1^2 + b_2^2 + b_3^2)$

(d) $\frac{3}{4}(a_1^2 + a_2^2 + a_3^2)(b_1^2 + b_2^2 + b_3^2)(c_1^2 + c_2^2 + c_3^2)$

200. Position vectors of the points A, B, C and D are $-3\hat{i} - 2\hat{j} - \hat{k}, 2\hat{i} + 3\hat{j} - 4\hat{k}, -\hat{i} + \hat{j} + 2\hat{k}$ and $4\hat{i} + 5\hat{j} + \lambda\hat{k}$ respectively. If the points A, B, C and D are on a plane, then the value of λ is :

(a) $\frac{146}{17}$ (b) $\frac{-146}{17}$

(c) $\frac{17}{146}$ (d) None of these

201. If $\hat{a}, \hat{b}$ and $\hat{c}$ are unit vectors then $|\hat{a} - \hat{b}|^2 + |\hat{b} - \hat{c}|^2 + |\hat{c} - \hat{a}|^2$ does not exceed :

(a) 4   (b) 9

(c) 8   (d) 6

202. Let $\vec{a} = \hat{i} - \hat{k}$, $\vec{b} = x\hat{i} + \hat{j} + (1 - x)\hat{k}$ and $\vec{c} = y\hat{i} + x\hat{j} + (1 + x - y)\hat{k}$. Then $[\vec{a}\ \vec{b}\ \vec{c}]$ depends on :

(a) only x   (b) only y

(c) neither x nor y   (d) both x and y

203. Let $\vec{a} = \hat{i} - \hat{j}$, $\vec{b} = \hat{j} - \hat{k}$, $\vec{c} = \hat{k} - \hat{i}$. If $\hat{d}$ is unit vector such that $\vec{a}\cdot\vec{d} = 0 = [\vec{b}\ \vec{c}\ \vec{d}]$, then $\hat{d}$ equals :

(a) $\pm\dfrac{\hat{i} + \hat{j} - 2\hat{k}}{\sqrt{6}}$ (b) $\pm\dfrac{\hat{i} + \hat{j} - \hat{k}}{\sqrt{3}}$

(c) $\pm\dfrac{\hat{i} + \hat{j} + \hat{k}}{\sqrt{3}}$ (d) $\pm\hat{k}$

204. If $\vec{A}, \vec{B}$ and $\vec{C}$ are three non-coplanar vectors, then $(\vec{A} + \vec{B} + \vec{C})\cdot[(\vec{A} + \vec{B})\times(\vec{A} + \vec{C})]$ equals :

(a) 0   (b) $[\vec{A},\ \vec{B},\ \vec{C}]$

(c) $2[\vec{A},\ \vec{B},\ \vec{C}]$ (d) $-[\vec{A},\ \vec{B},\ \vec{C}]$

205. If $\hat{a}, \hat{b}, \hat{c}$ are non-coplanar unit vectors such that $\hat{a}\times(\hat{b}\times\hat{c}) = \dfrac{\hat{b} + \hat{c}}{\sqrt{2}}$, then the angle between $\hat{a}$ and $\hat{b}$ is :

(a) $\frac{3\pi}{4}$ (b) $\frac{\pi}{4}$

(c) $\frac{\pi}{2}$ (d) π

206. If the sum of two unit vectors is a unit vector, then the angle between them is equal to :

(a) $\pi/6$ (b) $\pi/3$

(c) $\pi/2$ (d) $2\pi/3$

207. If three points A, B, C whose position vectors are respectively

$\hat{i} - 2\hat{j} - 8\hat{k}, 5\hat{i} - 2\hat{k}$ and $11\hat{i} + 3\hat{j} + 7\hat{k}$ are collinear, then the ratio in which B divides AC is ?

(a) $1 : 2$ (b) $2 : 3$

(c) $2 : 1$ (d) None of these

208. If $\vec{a}, \vec{b}, \vec{c}$ are p.v. of vertices of a Δ ABC, then unit vector perpendicular to its plane is :

(a) $\vec{a} \times \vec{b} + \vec{b} \times \vec{c} + \vec{c} \times \vec{a}$

(b) $\dfrac{\vec{a} \times \vec{b} + \vec{b} \times \vec{c} + \vec{c} \times \vec{a}}{|\vec{a} \times \vec{b} + \vec{b} \times \vec{c} + \vec{c} \times \vec{a}|}$

(c) $\dfrac{\vec{a} \times \vec{b}}{|\vec{a} \times \vec{b}|}$

(d) None of these

209. If $|\vec{a} + \vec{b}| = |\vec{a} - \vec{b}|$, then angle between $\vec{a}$ and $\vec{b}$ is :

(a) $0°$ (b) $45°$

(c) $60°$ (d) $90°$

210. A and B are two points. The position vector $\vec{A}$ is $6\vec{b} - 2\vec{a}$. A point P divides the line AB in the ratio $1 : 2$. If $\vec{a} - \vec{b}$ is the position vector of P, then the position vector of B is given by :

(a) $7\vec{a} - 15\vec{b}$ (b) $7\vec{a} + 15\vec{b}$

(c) $15\vec{a} - 7\vec{b}$ (d) $15\vec{a} + 7\vec{b}$

211. The perimeter of the triangle whose vertices have the position vectors

$(\hat{i} + \hat{j} + \hat{k}), (5\hat{i} + 3\hat{j} - 3\hat{k})$ and $(2\hat{i} + 5\hat{j} + 9\hat{k})$, is given by :

(a) $15 + \sqrt{157}$ (b) $15 - \sqrt{157}$

(c) $\sqrt{15} - \sqrt{157}$ (d) $\sqrt{15} - \sqrt{157}$

212. The moment about the point M $(-2, 4, -6)$ of the force represented in magnitude and position by $\overrightarrow{AB}$ where the points A and B have the coordinates $(1, 2, -3)$ and $(3, -4, 2)$ respectively, is :

(a) $8\hat{i} - 9\hat{j} - 14\hat{k}$ (b) $2\hat{i} - 6\hat{j} + 5\hat{k}$

(c) $-3\hat{i} + 2\hat{j} - 3\hat{k}$ (d) $-5\hat{i} + 8\hat{j} - 8\hat{k}$

213. If $\vec{a}, \vec{b}, \vec{c}$ and $\vec{d}$ are the position vectors of points A, B, C, D such that no three of them are collinear and $\vec{a} + \vec{c} = \vec{b} + \vec{d}$, then ABCD is :

(a) a rhombus   (b) a rectangle

(c) a square   (d) a parallelogram

214. If $4\hat{i} + 7\hat{j} + 8\hat{k}, 2\hat{i} + 7\hat{j} + 7\hat{k}$ and $3\hat{i} + 5\hat{j} + 7\hat{k}$ are the position vectors of the vertices A, B and C respectively of triangle ABC. The position vector of the point where the bisector of angle A meets is :

(a) $\dfrac{1}{3}(5\hat{j} + 12\hat{k})$ (b) $\dfrac{1}{3}(6\hat{i} + 13\hat{j} + 18\hat{k})$

(c) $\dfrac{2}{3}(6\hat{i} + 8\hat{j} + 6\hat{k})$ (d) $\dfrac{2}{3}(-6\hat{i} - 8\hat{j} - 6\hat{k})$

215. If A = $(1, 1, 1)$, C = $(0, 1, -1)$ are two given vectors, then a vector $\vec{B}$ satisfying the equation $\vec{A} \times \vec{B} = \vec{C}$ and $\vec{A} \cdot \vec{B} = 3$ is :

(a) $\left(\dfrac{5}{3}, \dfrac{2}{3}, \dfrac{-2}{3}\right)$ (b) $\left(\dfrac{5}{3}, \dfrac{-2}{3}, \dfrac{2}{3}\right)$

(c) $\left(-\dfrac{5}{3}, \dfrac{2}{3}, \dfrac{2}{3}\right)$ (d) $\left(\dfrac{5}{3}, \dfrac{2}{3}, \dfrac{2}{3}\right)$

216. The vector $\vec{b} = 3\hat{i} + 4\hat{k}$ is to be written as the sum of a vector $\vec{b_1}$ parallel to $\vec{a} = \hat{i} + \hat{j}$ and a vector $\vec{b_2}$ perpendicular to $\vec{a}$, then $\vec{b_1}$ equals :

(a) $\dfrac{1}{3}(\hat{i} + \hat{j})$ (b) $\dfrac{1}{2}(\hat{i} + \hat{j})$

(c) $\dfrac{2}{3}(\hat{i} + \hat{j})$ (d) $\dfrac{3}{2}(\hat{i} + \hat{j})$

217. If a vector $\vec{r}$ of magnitude $3\sqrt{6}$ is directed along the bisector of the angle between the vectors $\vec{a} = 7\hat{i} - 4\hat{j} - 4\hat{k}$ and $\vec{b} = -2\hat{i} - \hat{j} + 2\hat{k}$, then $\vec{r}$ is equal to :

(a) $-\hat{i} - 7\hat{j} - 2\hat{k}$ (b) $\hat{i} - 7\hat{j} - 2\hat{k}$

(c) $\hat{i} + 7\hat{j} - 2\hat{k}$ (d) $\pm(\hat{i} - 7\hat{j} + 2\hat{k})$

218. If $\vec{a}$, $\vec{b}$, $\vec{c}$ are three non-zero vectors, no two of which are collinear and the vector $\vec{a} + \vec{b}$ is collinear with $\vec{c}$ and $\vec{b} + \vec{c}$ is collinear with $\vec{a}$, then $\vec{a} + \vec{b} + \vec{c}$ is equal to:

(a) $2a$ (b) 0

(c) b (d) None of these

219. Given the two vectors $\hat{i} - \hat{j}$ and $\hat{i} + 2\hat{j}$, the unit vector coplanar with the two vectors and perpendicular to the first is :

(a) $\dfrac{2\hat{i} + \hat{j}}{\sqrt{5}}$ (b) $\dfrac{2\hat{i} + 2\hat{j}}{2\sqrt{2}}$

(c) $\dfrac{\hat{i} + \hat{j}}{2\sqrt{2}}$ (d) None of these

220. If $\hat{v}$ and $\hat{w}$ are two mutually perpendicular unit vectors and $\vec{u} = a\hat{v} + b\hat{w}$, where a and b are non-zero real numbers, then the angle between $\vec{u}$ and $\hat{w}$ is :

(a) $\cos^{-1}\left(\dfrac{b}{\sqrt{a^2 + b^2}}\right)$ (b) $\cos^{-1}\left(\dfrac{a}{\sqrt{a^2 + b^2}}\right)$

(c) $\cos^{-1}(b)$ (d) $\cos^{-1}(a)$

221. If $\hat{a}$ is a unit vector, $\hat{a} \times \vec{r} = \vec{b}$, $\hat{a} \cdot \vec{r} = \vec{c}$, $\hat{a} \cdot \vec{b} = 0$, then $\vec{r}$ is :

(a) $c\vec{b} + (\vec{a} \times \vec{b})$ (b) $c\vec{a} + (\vec{a} \times \vec{b})$

(c) $c\vec{b} - (\vec{a} \times \vec{b})$ (d) $c\vec{a} - (\vec{a} \times \vec{b})$

222. If $\vec{a}$, $\vec{b}$, $\vec{c}$ are three non-zero vectors, no two of which are collinear, $\vec{a} + 2\vec{b}$ is collinear with $\vec{c}$ and $\vec{b} + 3\vec{c}$ is collinear with $\vec{a}$ then $\vec{a} + 2\vec{b} + 6\vec{c}$ will be equal to :

(a) zero   (b) 1

(c) 9   (d) None of these

223. If $\vec{a}$ is perpendicular to $\vec{b} + \vec{c}$, $\vec{b}$ is perpendicular to $\vec{c} + \vec{a}$ and $\vec{c}$ is perpendicular to $\vec{a} + \vec{b}$ and $|\vec{a}| = 1$, $|\vec{b}| = 2$, $|\vec{c}| = 3$, then $|\vec{a} + \vec{b} + \vec{c}| = 1$

(a) $2\sqrt{3}$ (b) $\sqrt{7}$

(c) $\sqrt{14}$ (d) $3\sqrt{2}$

224. Let $\vec{a} = 2\hat{i} + 3\hat{j} + 4\hat{k}$, $\vec{b} = \hat{i} - 2\hat{j} + \hat{k}$, then $\vec{r}$, satisfying $\vec{a} \times \vec{r} = 3\vec{b}$, $\vec{a} \cdot \vec{r} = 2$ is :

(a) $\hat{i} + \hat{j} + \hat{k}$ (b) $\hat{i} - \hat{j}$

(c) $\hat{i} - \hat{k}$ (d) $-\hat{i} + \hat{k}$

225. Angle between the line

$$r = (2\hat{i} - \hat{j} + \hat{k}) + \lambda(-\hat{i} + \hat{j} + \hat{k})$$

and the plane $r \cdot (3\hat{i} + 2\hat{j} - \hat{k}) = 4$ is :

(a) $\cos^{-1}\left(\dfrac{2}{\sqrt{45}}\right)$ (b) $\cos^{-1}\left(-\dfrac{2}{\sqrt{42}}\right)$

(c) $\sin^{-1}\left(\dfrac{2}{\sqrt{42}}\right)$ (d) $\sin^{-1}\left(-\dfrac{2}{\sqrt{42}}\right)$

226. The projection of the vector $\hat{i} + \hat{j} + \hat{k}$ on the line whose vector equation is

$$\vec{r} = (3 + t)\,\hat{i} + (2t - 1)\,\hat{j} + 3t\hat{k},$$

t being the scalar parameter, is :

(a) $\dfrac{1}{\sqrt{14}}$ (b) 6

(c) $\dfrac{6}{\sqrt{14}}$ (d) None of these

227. If $\vec{a}$, $\vec{b}$ and $\vec{c}$ are three non-collinear vectors, then the length of projection of vector $\vec{a}$ along the plane of the vector $\vec{b}$ and $\vec{c}$ may be given as :

(a) $\dfrac{|\vec{a} \cdot (\vec{b} \times \vec{c})|}{|(\vec{b} \times \vec{c})|}$

(b) $\dfrac{|\vec{a} \times (\vec{b} \times \vec{c})|}{|\vec{b} \times \vec{c}|}$

(c) $\dfrac{|\vec{a} \cdot \vec{b} \cdot \vec{c}|}{\vec{b} \cdot \vec{c}}$

(d) None of these

228. P is a point on the line through the point A whose position vector is $\vec{a}$ and the line is parallel to the vector $\vec{b}$. If PA = 6, the position vector of P is :

(a) $\vec{a} + 6\vec{b}$

(b) $\vec{a} + \dfrac{6}{|\vec{b}|}\vec{b}$

(c) $\vec{a} - 6\vec{b}$

(d) $\vec{b} + \dfrac{6}{|\vec{a}|}\vec{a}$

229. The three concurrent edges of a parallelopied represent the vectors $\vec{a}$, $\vec{b}$, $\vec{c}$ such that $[\vec{a}\ \vec{b}\ \vec{c}] = \lambda$. Then the volume of parallelopiped whose three concurrent edges are the three concurrent diagonals of the three faces of the given parallelopiped is :

(a) 2λ

(b) 3λ

(c) λ

(d) None of these

230. If $\vec{a} = (a_1, a_2, a_3)$, $\vec{b} = (b_1, b_2, b_3)$ and $\vec{c} = (c_1, c_2, c_3)$ are non-zero vectors such that $|\vec{c}|$ and $\vec{c}$ makes an angle $\pi/3$ with plane consisting of vectors $\vec{a}$ and $\vec{b}$ and angle between $\vec{a}$ and $\vec{b}$ is $\pi/6$, then the value of $\begin{vmatrix} a_1 & a_2 & a_3 \\ b_1 & b_2 & b_3 \\ c_1 & c_2 & c_3 \end{vmatrix}^2$ is :

(a) $\dfrac{1}{16}|\vec{a}|^2|\vec{b}|^2$

(b) $\dfrac{3}{16}|\vec{a}|^2|\vec{b}|^2$

(c) $\dfrac{1}{4}|\vec{a}|^2|\vec{b}|^2$

(d) $\dfrac{3}{4}|\vec{a}|^2|\vec{b}|^2$

231. Let $\vec{a} = 2\hat{i} - \hat{j} + \hat{k}$, $\vec{b} = \hat{i} + 2\hat{j} - \hat{k}$, $\vec{c} = \hat{i} + \hat{j} - \hat{k}$. A vector in the plane of $\vec{b}$ and $\vec{c}$ whose projection on $\vec{a}$ has the magnitude $\sqrt{2/3}$ is :

(a) $2\hat{i} + 3\hat{j} - 3\hat{k}$

(b) $2\hat{i} + 3\hat{j} + 3\hat{k}$

(c) $-2\hat{i} - \hat{j} + 5\hat{k}$

(b) $2\hat{i} + 3\hat{j} + 5\hat{k}$

232. If the vectors $\sec^2 A\hat{i} + \hat{j} + \hat{k}$, $\hat{i} + \sec^2 B\hat{j} + \hat{k}$, $\hat{i} + \hat{j} + \sec^2 C\hat{k}$ are coplanar, then $\csc^2 A + \csc^2 B + \csc^2 C$ is :

(a) -1

(b) 3

(c) greater than 3

(d) less than 3

233. The unit vector perpendicular to both the vectors $\vec{a} = \hat{i} + \hat{j} + \hat{k}$ and $\vec{b} = \hat{i} - \hat{j} + 3\hat{k}$ and making an acute angle with the vector $\hat{k}$ is :

(a) $\dfrac{-1}{\sqrt{26}}(4\hat{i} - \hat{j} - 3\hat{k})$

(b) $\dfrac{1}{\sqrt{26}}(4\hat{i} - \hat{j} - 3\hat{k})$

(c) $\dfrac{1}{\sqrt{26}}(4\hat{i} - \hat{j} + 3\hat{k})$

(d) None of these

234. The image of a point $2\hat{i} + 2\hat{j} - \hat{k}$ in the line passing through the points $\hat{i} - \hat{j} + 2\hat{k}$ and $3\hat{i} + \hat{j} - 2\hat{k}$ is :

(a) $3\hat{i} + 11\hat{j} + 7\hat{k}$

(b) $\dfrac{-\hat{i} - 11\hat{j} + 7\hat{k}}{3}$

(c) $-\hat{i} - 2\hat{j} + \hat{k}$

(d) None of these

235. The position vectors of the points A, B and C are $\hat{i} + \hat{j} + \hat{k}$, $\hat{i} + 5\hat{j} - \hat{k}$ and $2\hat{i} + 3\hat{j} + 5\hat{k}$ respectively. The greatest angle of the Δ ABC is

(a) $120°$

(b) $90°$

(c) $\cos^{-1}(2/3)$

(d) $\cos^{-1}(5/7)$

236. Find the value of λ so that the points P, Q, R, S on the sides OA, OB, OC and AB of a regular tetrahedron are coplanar. You are given that

(a) $\dfrac{\overrightarrow{OP}}{\overrightarrow{OA}} = \dfrac{1}{3}$; $\dfrac{\overrightarrow{OQ}}{\overrightarrow{OB}} = \dfrac{1}{2}$, $\dfrac{\overrightarrow{OR}}{\overrightarrow{OC}} = \dfrac{1}{3}$ and $\dfrac{\overrightarrow{OS}}{\overrightarrow{AB}} = \lambda$

(a) λ = 1/2   (b) λ = −1

(c) λ = 0   (d) For no value of λ

237. Points X and Y lie on the sides QR and RS of a parallelogram PQRS such that $\overrightarrow{OX} = 2\overrightarrow{XR}$ and $\overrightarrow{RY} = 2\overrightarrow{YS}$. The diagonal PR meets the line XY at Z. If PZ = λPR, then the value of 'λ' is :

(a) $\dfrac{21}{25}$ (b) $\dfrac{10}{13}$

(c) $\dfrac{7}{9}$ (d) None of these

238. x and y are two mutually perpendicular unit vectors. If the vectors

$a\,\hat{x} + a\hat{y} + c(\hat{x} + \hat{y}),\quad \hat{x} + (\hat{x} \times \hat{y})$ and

$c\hat{x} + c\hat{y} + b(\hat{x} \times \hat{y})$, lie in a plane then c is :

(a) A.M. of a and b   (b) G.M. of a and b

(c) H.M. of a and b   (d) equal to zero

239. A vector $\overrightarrow{a}$ has components 2p and 1 with respect a rectangular certain system. This system is rotated through a certain angle about the origin in the counter- clockwise sense. If, with respect to the new system, $\overrightarrow{a}$ has components p + 1 and 1, then :

(a) p = 0   (b) p = 1 or p = $\dfrac{1}{3}$

(c) p = −1 or p = $\dfrac{1}{3}$ (d) p = 1 or p = −1

240. If $\overrightarrow{a} + \overrightarrow{b} + \overrightarrow{c} = \alpha \cdot \overrightarrow{d}$ and $\overrightarrow{b} + \overrightarrow{c} + \overrightarrow{d} = -\beta\, \overrightarrow{a}$ where $\overrightarrow{a},\overrightarrow{b},\overrightarrow{c}$ are non-coplanar vectors and α, β are non-zero real numbers then :

(a) $\overrightarrow{a} + \overrightarrow{b} + \overrightarrow{c} = \overrightarrow{d}$

(b) $\overrightarrow{a} + \overrightarrow{b} + \overrightarrow{c} + \overrightarrow{d} = 0$

(c) $\overrightarrow{a} + \overrightarrow{b} + \overrightarrow{c} + 2\overrightarrow{d} = 0$

(d) None of these

241. Given vectors $\overrightarrow{a} = (3, -1, 5)$ and $\overrightarrow{b} = (1, 2, -3)$. A vector $\overrightarrow{c}$ which is perpendicular to z-axis and satisfying $\overrightarrow{c} \cdot \overrightarrow{a} = 9$ and $\overrightarrow{c} \cdot \overrightarrow{b} = -4$ is :

(a) (2, −2, 0)   (b) (4, −2, 0)

(c) (2, −3, 0)   (d) (1, 2, 4)

242. If $\overrightarrow{p} \times \overrightarrow{q} = \overrightarrow{r}$ and $\overrightarrow{p} \cdot \overrightarrow{q} = c$ then $\overrightarrow{q} =$

(a) $\dfrac{(c\overrightarrow{p} - \overrightarrow{p} \times \overrightarrow{r})}{|\overrightarrow{p}|^2}$ (b) $\dfrac{(c\overrightarrow{p} + \overrightarrow{p} \times \overrightarrow{r})}{|\overrightarrow{p}|^2}$

(c) $\dfrac{(c\overrightarrow{r} - \overrightarrow{p} \times \overrightarrow{r})}{|\overrightarrow{p}|^2}$ (d) $\dfrac{(c\overrightarrow{r} + \overrightarrow{p} \times \overrightarrow{r})}{|\overrightarrow{p}|^2}$

243. The locus of a point equidistant from two points whose position vectors are $\overrightarrow{a}$ and $\overrightarrow{b}$ is :

(a) $[\overrightarrow{r}(\overrightarrow{a} + \overrightarrow{b})] \cdot \overrightarrow{b} = 0$

(b) $\left(\overrightarrow{r} - \dfrac{1}{2}(\overrightarrow{a} + \overrightarrow{b})\right) \cdot \overrightarrow{a} = 0$

(c) $\left(\overrightarrow{r} - \dfrac{1}{2}(\overrightarrow{a} + \overrightarrow{b})\right) \cdot (\overrightarrow{a} - \overrightarrow{b}) = 0$

(d) $\left(\overrightarrow{r} - \dfrac{1}{2}(\overrightarrow{a} + \overrightarrow{b})\right) \cdot (\overrightarrow{a} + \overrightarrow{b}) = 0$

244. If $\overrightarrow{x}$ and $\overrightarrow{y}$ are two non-collinear vectors and Δ ABC is a triangle with side lengths a, b, c satisfying

$(20a - 15b)\,\overrightarrow{x} + (15b - 12c)\,\overrightarrow{y} + (12c - 20a)(\overrightarrow{x} \times \overrightarrow{y}) = 0$

then Δ ABC is :

(a) an acute angled triangle

(b) an obtuse angled triangle

(c) a right angled triangle

(d) an isosceles triangle

245. A vector $\vec{a} = (x, y, z)$ of length $2\sqrt{3}$ which makes equal angles with the vectors $\vec{b} = (y, -2z, 3x)$ and $\vec{c} = (2z, 3x, -y)$ and is perpendicular to $\vec{d} = (1, -1, 2)$ and makes an obtuse angle with y-axis is :

(a) $(-2, 2, 2)$ (b) $(1, 1, \sqrt{10})$

(c) $(2, -2, -2)$ (d) None of these

246. Let $\vec{a} = \hat{i} + \hat{j} + 2\hat{k}$ and $\vec{b} = 2\hat{i} - \hat{j} - \hat{k}$. Then the point of intersection of the lines $\vec{r} \times \vec{a} = \vec{b} \times \vec{a}$ and $\vec{r} \times \vec{b} = \vec{a} \times \vec{b}$ is :

(a) $-\hat{i} + 2\hat{j} + 2\hat{k}$ (b) $\hat{i} - 2\hat{j} - 3\hat{k}$

(c) $3\hat{i} + \hat{k}$ (d) $-3\hat{i} - \hat{k}$

247. A unit vector $\hat{n}$ perpendicular to the plane determined by points $A(0, -2, 1)$, $B(1, -1, -2)$ and $C(-1, 1, 0)$ is :

(a) $\frac{1}{3}(2\hat{i} + \hat{j} + 2\hat{k})$ (b) $\frac{1}{4\sqrt{6}}(8\hat{i} + 4\hat{j} + 4\hat{k})$

(c) $\frac{1}{\sqrt{3}}(\hat{i} - \hat{j} + \hat{k})$ (d) $\frac{1}{\sqrt{14}}(3\hat{i} + \hat{j} + 2\hat{k})$

248. If $\vec{a}, \vec{b}, \vec{c}$ are such that $|\vec{a} + \vec{b} + \vec{c}| = 1$, $\vec{c} = \lambda\, \vec{a} \times \vec{b}$ & $|\vec{a}| = \frac{1}{\sqrt{2}}, |\vec{b}| = \frac{1}{\sqrt{3}}, |\vec{c}| = \frac{1}{\sqrt{6}}$, then the angle between $\vec{a}$ and $\vec{b}$ is :

(a) $\frac{\pi}{6}$ (b) $\frac{\pi}{4}$

(c) $\frac{\pi}{3}$ (d) $\frac{\pi}{2}$

249. Consider a parallelopiped with sides $\vec{a} = 3\hat{i} + 2\hat{j} + \hat{k}$, $\vec{b} = \hat{i} + \hat{j} + 2\hat{k}$ and $\vec{c} = \hat{i} + 3\hat{j} + 3\hat{k}$. Then the angle between $\vec{a}$ and the plane containing the face determined by $\vec{b}$ and $\vec{c}$ is :

(a) $\sin^{-1} \frac{1}{3}$ (b) $\cos^{-1} \frac{9}{14}$

(c) $\sin^{-1} \frac{9}{14}$ (d) $\sin^{-1} \frac{2}{3}$

250. The volume of the tetrahedron whose vertices are the points $\hat{i}, \hat{i} + \hat{j}, \hat{i} + \hat{j} + \hat{k}$ & $2\hat{i} + 3\hat{j} + \lambda\hat{k}$ is $\frac{1}{6}$ units. Then the value of λ

(a) does not exist   (b) is 7

(c) is -1 (d) is any real value

251. A unit tangent vector at $t = 2$ on the curve $x = t^2 + 2$, $y = 4t - 5$, $z = 2t^2 - 6t$ is :

(a) $\frac{1}{\sqrt{3}}(\hat{i} + \hat{j} + \hat{k})$ (b) $\frac{1}{3}(2\hat{i} + 2\hat{j} + \hat{k})$

(c) $\frac{1}{\sqrt{6}}(2\hat{i} + \hat{j} + \hat{k})$ (d) None of these

252. The value of $|\hat{i} \times \vec{a}|^2 + |\hat{j} \times \vec{a}|^2 + |\hat{k} \times \vec{a}|^2 =$

(a) a^2 (b) $2a^2$

(c) $3a^2$ (d) None of these

253. If $\vec{a} = 4\hat{i} + 2\hat{j} - 5\hat{k}$, $\vec{b} = -12\hat{i} - 6\hat{j} + 15\hat{k}$, then the vectors $\vec{a}, \vec{b}$ are :

(a) orthogonal   (b) parallel

(c) non-coplanar   (d) none of these

254. $\vec{r} \times \vec{a} = \vec{b} \times \vec{a}$; $\vec{r} \times \vec{b} = \vec{a} \times \vec{b}$; $\vec{a} \neq 0, \vec{b} \neq 0$, $\vec{a} \neq \lambda \vec{b}$; a is not perpendicular to $\vec{b} \Rightarrow \vec{r} =$

(a) $\vec{a} - \vec{b}$ (b) $\vec{a} + \vec{b}$

(c) $\vec{a} \times \vec{b} + \vec{a}$ (d) $\vec{a} \times \vec{b} + \vec{b}$

255. A unit vector in the xy plane that makes an angle of 45° with the vector $\hat{i} + \hat{j}$ and an angle of 60° with the vector $3\hat{i} - 4\hat{j}$ is :

(a) $\frac{1}{2}(\hat{i} + \hat{j})$ (b) $\frac{1}{\sqrt{2}}(\hat{i} + \hat{j})$

(c) $\hat{i}$ (d) None of these

256. Let $p\hat{i} + 3\hat{j} + 4\hat{k}$ and $\sqrt{q}\hat{i} + 5\hat{k}$ be two vectors where $p, q \neq 0$, then their lengths are equal if :

(a) $p = q^2$ (b) $p^2 = q$

(c) $p = q = 1$ (d) $p = 2, q = 4$

257. If the vectors $a\hat{i} + 2\hat{j} + 3\hat{k}$ and $-\hat{i} + 5\hat{j} + a\hat{k}$ are perpendicular to each other, then a =

(a) −6   (b) −5

(c) 6   (d) 5

258. If $\vec{a}, \vec{b}, \vec{c}$ are three vectors such that $\vec{a} + \vec{b} = \vec{c}$, then $\vec{b}$ is called :

(a) a projection of $\vec{c}$ (b) a complement of $\vec{c}$

(c) a component of $\vec{c}$ (d) None of these

259. The vector $\vec{a}$ is equal to :

(a) $(\vec{a} \cdot \vec{a})(\hat{i} + \hat{j} + \hat{k})$

(b) $(\vec{a} \cdot \hat{i})\hat{i} + (\vec{a} \cdot \hat{j})\hat{j} + (\vec{a} \cdot \hat{k})\hat{k}$

(c) $(\vec{a} \cdot \hat{i})\hat{i} + (\vec{a} \cdot \hat{k})\hat{i} + (\vec{a} \cdot \hat{i})\hat{k}$

(d) $(\vec{a} \cdot \hat{k})\hat{i} + (\vec{a} \cdot \hat{i})\hat{j} + (\vec{a} \cdot \hat{j})\hat{k}$

260. The angle between the vectors $\vec{a} \times \vec{b}$ and $\vec{b} \times \vec{a}$ is :

(a) 180°   (b) 90°

(c) 0°   (d) 45°

261. If $\vec{a} = (1, -1)$ and $\vec{b} = (-2, m)$ are two collinear vectors, then m =

(a) 4   (b) 3

(c) 2   (d) 0

262. The position vectors of three vertices A, B, C of a tetrahedron OABC with respect to its vertex O are $6\hat{i}, 6\hat{j}, \hat{k}$. Its volume is :

(a) 1/3   (b) 1/6

(c) 3   (d) 6

263. $\hat{i} \times (\hat{j} \times \hat{k}) =$

(a) 1   (b) 0

(c) −1   (d) None of these

264. The work done in moving an object along the vector $3\hat{i} + 2\hat{j} - 5\hat{k}$, if the applied force is $\vec{F} = 2\hat{i} - \hat{j} - \hat{k}$ is :

(a) 11   (b) 8

(c) 9   (d) None of these

265. $(\vec{b} \times \vec{c}) \times (\vec{c} \times \vec{a}) =$

(a) $[\vec{b}, \vec{c}, \vec{a}]\vec{a}$ (b) $[\vec{c}, \vec{a}, \vec{b}]\vec{b}$

(c) $[\vec{a}, \vec{b}, \vec{c}]\vec{c}$ (d) $[\vec{a}, \vec{c}, \vec{b}]\vec{b}$

266. If $\vec{a} \times \vec{b} = \vec{b} \times \vec{b} \neq 0$, where $\vec{a}, \vec{b}, \vec{c}$ are coplanar vectors, then true statement is :

(a) $\vec{a} + \vec{c} = 0$ (b) $\vec{a} + \vec{c} = k\vec{b}$

(c) $\vec{a} + \vec{c} = k\vec{c}$ (d) $\vec{a} + \vec{c} = k\vec{a}$

267. If position vectors of vertices A, B and C of any triangle are $4\hat{i} - 2\hat{j}, \hat{i} + 4\hat{j} - 3\hat{k}$ and $-\hat{i} + 5\hat{j} + \hat{k}$ respectively, then $\angle$ ABC is equal to :

(a) $\frac{\pi}{6}$ (b) $\frac{\pi}{4}$

(c) $\frac{\pi}{3}$ (d) $\frac{\pi}{2}$

268. If $\vec{a} \cdot (\vec{b} \times \vec{c}) = 0$, then true statement is :

(a) $\vec{a}, \vec{b}, \vec{c}$ are caplaner.

(b) Any two are parallel from $\vec{a}, \vec{b}, \vec{c}$.

(c) Any two are same from $\vec{a}, \vec{b}, \vec{c}$.

(d) Atleast one is correct from above three choices.

269. For a non-zero vector $\vec{a}$, which of the following statement is true ?

(a) $\vec{a} \cdot \vec{a} \geq 0$ (b) $\vec{a} \cdot \vec{a} > 0$

(c) $\vec{a} \cdot \vec{a} = 0$ (d) $\vec{a} \cdot \vec{a} \leq 0$

270. If $\hat{i} + 2\hat{j} + 3\hat{k}$ is parallel to the sum of vectors $3\hat{i} + \lambda\hat{j} + 2\hat{k}$ and $-2\hat{i} + 3\hat{j} + \hat{k}$, then λ is equal to :

(a) 1   (b) -1

(c) 2   (d) -2

271. The unit vector perpendicular to both $\hat{i} + \hat{j}$ and $\hat{j} + \hat{k}$ is :

(a) $(\hat{i} - \hat{j} + \hat{k})$ (b) $(\hat{i} - \hat{j} + \hat{k})/\sqrt{3}$

(c) $(\hat{i} + \hat{j} + \hat{k})/\sqrt{3}$ (d) $(\hat{i} + \hat{j} - \hat{k})/\sqrt{3}$

272. If the points A, B, C and D have positive vectors $\vec{a}$, $2\vec{a} + \vec{b}$, $4\vec{a} + 4\vec{b}$ and $5\vec{a} + 4\vec{b}$ respectively. Then the three collinear points are :

(a) A, B and D   (b) B, C and D

(c) A, B and C   (d) A, B and D

273. If $\vec{a}$ and $\vec{b}$ are adjacent sides of a parallelogram, then $|\vec{a} + \vec{b}| = |\vec{a} - \vec{b}|$ is a necessary and sufficient condition for the parallelogram to be a :

(a) trapezium   (b) rectangle

(c) rhombus   (d) square

274. Which of the following is a true statement ?

(a) $(\vec{a} \times \vec{b}) \times \vec{c}$ is perpendicular to $\vec{c}$.

(b) $(\vec{a} \times \vec{b}) \times \vec{c}$ is perpendicular to $\vec{b}$.

(c) $(\vec{a} \times \vec{b}) \times \vec{c}$ is perpendicular to $\vec{a}$.

(d) $(\vec{a} \times \vec{b}) \times \vec{c}$ is coplanar with $\vec{c}$.

275. Let $\hat{a}$ and $\hat{b}$ be two unit vectors. If the vectors $\vec{c} = \hat{a} + 2\hat{b}$ and $\vec{d} = 5\hat{a} - 4\hat{b}$ are perpendicular to each other, then the angle between $\hat{a}$ and $\hat{b}$ is : **[AIEEE – 2012]**

(a) $\dfrac{\pi}{6}$ (b) $\dfrac{\pi}{2}$

(c) $\dfrac{\pi}{3}$ (d) $\dfrac{\pi}{4}$

276. Let ABCD be a parallelogram such that $\overrightarrow{AB} = \vec{q}$, $\overrightarrow{AD} = \vec{p}$ and $\angle$ BAD be an acute angle. If $\vec{r}$ is the vector that coincides with the altitude directed from the vertex B to the side AB, then $\vec{r}$ is given by : **[AIEEE – 2012]**

(a) $\vec{r} = 3\vec{q} - \dfrac{3(\vec{p} \cdot \vec{q})}{(\vec{p} \cdot \vec{p})}\vec{p}$

(b) $\vec{r} = -\vec{q} + \left(\dfrac{\vec{p} \cdot \vec{q}}{\vec{p} \cdot \vec{p}}\right)\vec{p}$

(c) $\vec{r} = \vec{q} - \left(\dfrac{\vec{p} \cdot \vec{q}}{\vec{p} \cdot \vec{p}}\right)\vec{p}$

(d) $\vec{r} = -3\vec{q} + \left[\dfrac{3(\vec{p} \cdot \vec{q})}{\vec{p} \cdot \vec{p}}\right]\vec{p}$

277. If $\vec{a} = \dfrac{1}{\sqrt{10}}(3\hat{i} + \hat{k})$ and $\vec{b} = \dfrac{1}{7}(2\hat{i} + 3\hat{j} - 6\hat{k})$, then the value of $(2\vec{a} - \vec{b}) \cdot [(\vec{a} \times \vec{b}) \times (\vec{a} \times 2\vec{b})]$ is : **[AIEEE – 2011]**

(a) 3   (b) -5

(c) -3 (d) 5

278. The vectors $\vec{a}$ and $\vec{b}$ are not perpendicular and $\vec{c}$ and $\vec{d}$ are two vectors satisfying $\vec{b} \times \vec{c} = \vec{b} \times \vec{d}$ and $\vec{a} \cdot \vec{d} = 0$. Then the vector $\vec{d}$ is equal to : **[AIEEE – 2011]**

(a) $\vec{c} - \left(\dfrac{\vec{a} \cdot \vec{c}}{\vec{a} \cdot \vec{b}}\right)\vec{b}$ (b) $\vec{b} - \left(\dfrac{\vec{b} \cdot \vec{c}}{\vec{a} \cdot \vec{b}}\right)\vec{c}$

(c) $\vec{c} + \left(\dfrac{\vec{a} \cdot \vec{c}}{\vec{a} \cdot \vec{b}}\right)\vec{b}$ (d) $\vec{b} + \left(\dfrac{\vec{b} \cdot \vec{c}}{\vec{a} \cdot \vec{b}}\right)\vec{c}$

279. Let $\vec{a} = \hat{j} - \hat{k}$ & $\vec{c} = \hat{i} - \hat{j} - \hat{k}$. Then vector $\vec{b}$ satisfying $\vec{a} \times \vec{b} + \vec{c} = 0$ and $\vec{a} \cdot \vec{b} = 3$ is :

[AIEEE – 2010]

(a) $2\hat{i} - \hat{j} + 2\hat{k}$ (b) $\hat{i} - \hat{j} - 2\hat{k}$

(c) $\hat{i} + \hat{j} - 2\hat{k}$ (d) $-\hat{i} + \hat{j} - 2\hat{k}$

280. If the vectors $\vec{a} = \hat{i} - \hat{j} + 2\hat{k}$, $\vec{b} = 2\hat{i} + 4\hat{j} + \hat{k}$ and $\vec{c} = \lambda\hat{i} + \hat{j} + \mu\hat{k}$ are mutually orthogonal, then $(\lambda, \mu) =$ [AIEEE – 2010]

(a) $(2, -3)$ (b) $(-2, 3)$

(c) $(3, -2)$ (d) $(-3, 2)$

281. If $\vec{u}, \vec{v}, \vec{w}$ are non-coplanar vectors and p, q are real numbers, then the equality

[AIEEE-2009]

$[3\vec{u}\ \vec{p}\vec{v}\ \vec{p}\vec{w}] - [\vec{p}\vec{v}\ \vec{w}\ q\vec{u}] - [2\vec{w}\ q\vec{v}\ q\vec{u}] = 0$

holds for

(a) exactly one value of (p, q)

(b) exactly two values of (p, q)

(c) more than two but not all values of (p, q)

(d) all values of (p, q)

282. The projections of a vector on the three coordinate axes are 6, –3, 2 respectively. The direction cosines of the vectors are :

[AIEEE – 2009]

(a) $6, -3, 2$ (b) $\dfrac{6}{5}, -\dfrac{3}{5}, \dfrac{2}{5}$

(c) $\dfrac{6}{7}, -\dfrac{3}{7}, \dfrac{2}{7}$ (d) $-\dfrac{6}{7}, -\dfrac{3}{7}, \dfrac{2}{7}$

283. The vector $\vec{a} = \alpha\hat{i} + 2\hat{j} + \beta\hat{k}$ lies in the plane of the vectors $\vec{b} = \hat{i} + \hat{j}$ and $\vec{c} = \hat{j} + \hat{k}$ and bisects the angle between $\vec{b}$ and $\vec{c}$. Then which one of the following gives possible values of α and β ?   [AIEEE – 2008]

(a) $\alpha = 2, \beta = 2$ (b) $\alpha = 1, \beta = 2$

(c) $\alpha = 2, \beta = 1$ (d) $\alpha = 1, \beta = 1$

284. The non-zero vectors $\vec{a}, \vec{b}$ and $\vec{c}$ are related by $\vec{a} = 8\vec{b}$ and $\vec{c} = -7\vec{b}$. Then the angle between $\vec{a}$ and $\vec{c}$ is :   [AIEEE – 2008]

(a) 0   (b) $\pi/4$

(c) $\pi/2$ (d) π

285. If $\hat{u}$ and $\hat{v}$ are unit vectors and θ is the acute angle between them, then $2\hat{u} \times 3\hat{v}$ is a unit vector for :

(a) exactly two values of θ [AIEEE – 2007]

(b) more than two values of θ

(c) no value of θ

(d) exactly one value of θ

286. Let $\vec{a} = \hat{i} + \hat{j} + \hat{k}$, $\vec{b} = \hat{i} - \hat{j} + 2\hat{k}$ and $\vec{c} = x\hat{i} + (x - 2)\hat{j} - \hat{k}$. If the vector $\vec{c}$ lies in the plane of $\vec{a}$ and $\vec{b}$, then x equals :

[AIEEE – 2007]

(a) 0   (b) 1

(c) –4   (d) –2

287. If $(\vec{a} \times \vec{b}) \times \vec{c} = \vec{a} \times (\vec{b} \times \vec{c})$, where $\vec{a}, \vec{b}$ and $\vec{c}$ are any three vectors such that $\vec{a} \cdot \vec{b} \neq 0$, $\vec{b} \cdot \vec{c} \neq 0$, then $\vec{a}$ and $\vec{c}$ are :

[AIEEE – 2006]

(a) inclined at an angle of $\pi/3$ between them

(b) inclined at an angle of $\pi/6$ between them

(c) perpendicular

(d) parallel

288. The values of a, for which the points A, B, C with position vectors $2\hat{i} - \hat{j} + \hat{k}$, $\hat{i} - 3\hat{j} - 5\hat{k}$ and $a\hat{i} - 3\hat{j} + \hat{k}$ respectively are the vertices of a right-angled triangle with $C = \dfrac{\pi}{2}$ are :

[AIEEE – 2006]

(a) 2 and 1   (b) –2 and –1

(c) –2 and 1   (d) 2 and –1

289. If $\vec{a} = \dfrac{1}{\sqrt{10}} (3\vec{i} + \vec{k})$ and

$\vec{b} = \dfrac{1}{7}(2\vec{i} + 3\vec{j} - 6\vec{k})$ then the value of

$(2\vec{a} - \vec{b}) \cdot [(\vec{a} \times \vec{b}) \times (\vec{a} + 2\vec{b})]$ is

(a) 3   (b) -5

(c) -3 (d) 5

290. Let $\vec{a}, \vec{b}, \vec{c}$ be three unit vectors such that

$\vec{a} \times (\vec{b} \times \vec{c}) = \dfrac{\sqrt{3}}{2}(\vec{b} + \vec{c})$.

If $\vec{b}$ is not parallel to $\vec{c}$, then the angle between $\vec{a}$ and $\vec{b}$ is

(a) $\dfrac{3\pi}{4}$ (b) $\dfrac{\pi}{2}$

(c) $\dfrac{2\pi}{3}$ (d) $\dfrac{5\pi}{6}$

291. Let $\vec{a}, \vec{b}, \vec{c}$ be three vectors, each non-zero; such that no two of them are collinear and $(\vec{a} \times \vec{b}) \times \vec{c} = \dfrac{1}{3}|\vec{b}||\vec{c}|\vec{a}$. If θ is the angle between vectors $\vec{b}$ and $\vec{c}$, then the value of $\sin \theta$ is

(a) $\dfrac{2}{3}$ (b) $\dfrac{2\sqrt{2}}{3}$

(c) $-\dfrac{2\sqrt{3}}{3}$ (d) $-\dfrac{\sqrt{2}}{3}$

292. Let $\vec{a} = \vec{j} - \vec{k}$ and $\vec{c} = \vec{i} - \vec{j} - \vec{k}$. Then the vector $\vec{b}$ satisfying $\vec{a} \times \vec{b} + \vec{c} = \vec{0}$ and $\vec{a} \cdot \vec{b} = 3$ is

(a) $-\vec{i} + \vec{j} - 2\vec{k}$ (b) $2\vec{i} - \vec{j} + 2\vec{k}$

(c) $\vec{i} - \vec{j} - 2\vec{k}$ (d) $\vec{i} + \vec{j} - 2\vec{k}$

293. If $\vec{a}, \vec{b}, \vec{c}$ are unit vectors satisfying

$|\vec{a} - \vec{b}|^2 + |\vec{b} - \vec{c}|^2 + |\vec{c} - \vec{a}|^2 = 9$

then $|2\vec{a} + 5\vec{b} + 5\vec{c}|$ is

(a) 4   (b) 7

(c) 3   (d) 2

294. If $[\vec{a} \times \vec{b} \quad \vec{b} \times \vec{c} \quad \vec{c} \times \vec{a}] = \lambda [\vec{a} \ \vec{b} \ \vec{c}]^2$ then λ is equal to

(a) 2   (b) 3

(c) 0   (d) 1

295. The three vectors $\vec{a}, \vec{b}, \vec{c}$ are represented in magnitude and direction by the sides BC, CA, AB respectively, of a triangle ABC. Then the vector equation $\vec{a} \cdot (\vec{a} + \vec{b} + \vec{c}) = 0$ represents

(a) sine rule   (b) cosine rule

(c) projection rule   (d) Pappu's theorem

ANSWER KEY

1. (a)	2. (b)	3. (a)	4. (c)	5. (a)	6. (c)	7. (b)	8. (c)	9. (b)	10. (c)
11. (a)	12. (d)	13. (c)	14. (a)	15. (d)	16. (d)	17. (b)	18. (c)	19. (d)	20. (c)
21. (d)	22. (b)	23. (c)	24. (b)	25. (b)	26. (a)	27. (b)	28. (b)	29. (b)	30. (a)
31. (c)	32. (a)	33. (c)	34. (c)	35. (c)	36. (a)	37. (c)	38. (c)	39. (d)	40. (a)
41. (b)	42. (c)	43. (b)	44. (a)	45. (c)	46. (a)	47. (b)	48. (c)	49. (c)	50. (a)
51. (c)	52. (a)	53. (a)	54. (b)	55. (c)	56. (c)	57. (c)	58. (d)	59. (c)	60. (a)
61. (a)	62. (a)	63. (a)	64. (b)	65. (d)	66. (d)	67. (b)	68. (d)	69. (c)	70. (d)
71. (d)	72. (c)	73. (c)	74. (a)	75. (c)	76. (a)	77. (d)	78. (b)	79. (b)	80. (d)
81. (a)	82. (c)	83. (c)	84. (d)	85. (a)	86. (c)	87. (b)	88. (c)	89. (c)	90. (c)

91. (b)	**92.** (d)	**93.** (b)	**94.** (b)	**95.** (c)	**96.** (a)	**97.** (b)	**98.** (d)	**99.** (b)	**100.** (c)
101. (a)	**102.** (b)	**103.** (a)	**104.** (a)	**105.** (a)	**106.** (c)	**107.** (b)	**108.** (b)	**109.** (a)	**110.** (b)
111. (b)	**112.** (a)	**113.** (a)	**114.** (c)	**115.** (d)	**116.** (d)	**117.** (b)	**118.** (a)	**119.** (c)	**120.** (b)
121. (a)	**122.** (b)	**123.** (b)	**124.** (b)	**125.** (b)	**126.** (c)	**127.** (c)	**128.** (d)	**129.** (c)	**130.** (d)
131. (a)	**132.** (c)	**133.** (c)	**134.** (d)	**135.** (c)	**136.** (b)	**137.** (a)	**138.** (c)	**139.** (d)	**140.** (c)
141. (b)	**142.** (a)	**143.** (b)	**144.** (a)	**145.** (d)	**146.** (a)	**147.** (a)	**148.** (c)	**149.** (c)	**150.** (b)
151. (c)	**152.** (a)	**153.** (c)	**154.** (b)	**155.** (d)	**156.** (a)	**157.** (a)	**158.** (a)	**159.** (d)	**160.** (a)
161. (a)	**162.** (c)	**163.** (a)	**164.** (c)	**165.** (b)	**166.** (d)	**167.** (b)	**168.** (d)	**169.** (a)	**170.** (c)
171. (a)	**172.** (d)	**173.** (a)	**174.** (a)	**175.** (b)	**176.** (c)	**177.** (b)	**178.** (a)	**179.** (a)	**180.** (a)
181. (d)	**182.** (c)	**183.** (a)	**184.** (b)	**185.** (d)	**186.** (c)	**187.** (b)	**188.** (a)	**189.** (b)	**190.** (a)
191. (b)	**192.** (b)	**193.** (a)	**194.** (c)	**195.** (a)	**196.** (b)	**197.** (b)	**198.** (b)	**199.** (c)	**200.** (b)
201. (b)	**202.** (c)	**203.** (a)	**204.** (d)	**205.** (a)	**206.** (d)	**207.** (b)	**208.** (b)	**209.** (d)	**210.** (a)
211. (a)	**212.** (a)	**213.** (d)	**214.** (b)	**215.** (d)	**216.** (d)	**217.** (d)	**218.** (b)	**219.** (c)	**220.** (a)
221. (d)	**222.** (a)	**223.** (c)	**224.** (d)	**225.** (d)	**226.** (c)	**227.** (b)	**228.** (b)	**229.** (a)	**230.** (b)
231. (c)	**232.** (c)	**233.** (a)	**234.** (d)	**235.** (b)	**236.** (b)	**237.** (b)	**238.** (b)	**239.** (c)	**240.** (b)
241. (c)	**242.** (a)	**243.** (c)	**244.** (c)	**245.** (c)	**246.** (c)	**247.** (b)	**248.** (d)	**249.** (c)	**250.** (d)
251. (b)	**252.** (b)	**253.** (b)	**254.** (b)	**255.** (d)	**256.** (b)	**257.** (d)	**258.** (c)	**259.** (b)	**260.** (a)
261. (c)	**262.** (d)	**263.** (b)	**264.** (c)	**265.** (c)	**266.** (b)	**267.** (d)	**268.** (d)	**269.** (b)	**270.** (b)
271. (b)	**272.** (d)	**273.** (b)	**274.** (a)	**275.** (c)	**276.** (b)	**277.** (b)	**278.** (a)	**279.** (d)	**280.** (d)
281. (a)	**282.** (c)	**283.** (d)	**284.** (d)	**285.** (d)	**286.** (d)	**287.** (d)	**288.** (a)	**289.** (b)	**290.** (d)
291. (b)	**292.** (a)	**293.** (c)	**294.** (d)	**295.** (c)					

❑❑❑

THREE DIMENSIONAL GEOMETRY

MULTIPLE CHOICE QUESTIONS

1. The angle between the straight lines whose direction cosines are given by $2l + 2m - n = 0$, $mn + nl - lm = 0$, is :

   (a) $\dfrac{\pi}{2}$

   (b) $\dfrac{\pi}{3}$

   (c) $\dfrac{\pi}{4}$

   (d) None of these

2. The acute angle between the lines whose direction cosines are proportional to $(2, 3, -6)$ and $(3, -4, 5)$ is :

   (a) $\dfrac{36}{7\sqrt{48}}$

   (b) $\dfrac{36}{7\sqrt{50}}$

   (c) $\dfrac{18}{7\sqrt{50}}$

   (d) None of these

3. If a variable line in two adjacent positions has direction cosines l, m, n and $l + \delta l$, $m + \delta m$, $n + \delta n$, then the small angle $\delta\theta$ between the two positions is given by :

   (a) $\delta\theta^2 = 4\,(\delta l^2 + \delta m^2 + \delta n^2)$

   (b) $\delta\theta^2 = 2\,(\delta l^2 + \delta m^2 + \delta n^2)$

   (c) $\delta\theta^2 = (\delta l^2 + \delta m^2 + \delta n^2)$

   (d) None of these

4. The lines whose direction cosines are given by $al + bm + cn$ and $ul^2 + vm^2 + wn^2 = 0$ are parallel if $\dfrac{a^2}{u} + \dfrac{b^2}{v} + \dfrac{c^2}{w} =$

   (a) 0

   (b) 1

   (c) –1

   (d) None of these

5. The angle between the straight lines whose direction cosines are given by $l + m + n = 0$ and $fmn + gln + hlm = 0$ is $\dfrac{\pi}{3}$ if $\dfrac{1}{f} + \dfrac{1}{g} + \dfrac{1}{h} =$

   (a) 1

   (b) 0

   (c) –1

   (d) None of these

6. The coordinates of the point where the line joining A(3, 4, 1) and B(5, 1, 6) crosses the xy-plane, are :

   (a) $\left(\dfrac{13}{5}, \dfrac{23}{5}, 0\right)$

   (b) $\left(\dfrac{13}{5}, -\dfrac{23}{5}, 0\right)$

   (c) $\left(-\dfrac{13}{5}, \dfrac{23}{5}, 0\right)$

   (d) None of these

7. The ratio in which the line joining $(1, 2, 3)$ and $(-3, 4, -5)$ is divided by xy-plane is :

   (a) 5 : 3

   (b) 3 : 5

   (c) 2 : 3

   (d) None of these

8. A(3, 2, 0), B(5, 3, 2), C(–9, 6, –3) are three points forming a triangle. If AD, the bisector of $\angle$BAC meets BC in D, then coordinates of D are :

   (a) $\left(-\dfrac{19}{8}, \dfrac{57}{16}, \dfrac{17}{16}\right)$

   (b) $\left(\dfrac{19}{8}, -\dfrac{57}{16}, \dfrac{17}{16}\right)$

   (c) $\left(\dfrac{19}{8}, \dfrac{57}{16}, -\dfrac{17}{16}\right)$

   (d) $\left(\dfrac{19}{8}, \dfrac{57}{16}, \dfrac{17}{16}\right)$

9. The ratio in which the plane $x - 2y + 3z = 17$ divides the line joining the points $(2, -4, 7)$ and $(3, -5, 8)$ is :

   (a) 1 : 5

   (b) 5 : 1

   (c) 3 : 10

   (d) 10 : 3

10. If the projection of a line segment on x, y and z axes are respectively, 3, 4 and 5, then the length of the line segment is :

    (a) $3\sqrt{2}$

    (b) $5\sqrt{2}$

    (c) $7\sqrt{2}$

    (d) None of these

11. The direction cosines of the line which is perpendicular to the lines whose direction cosines are proportional to $(1, -1, 2)$ and $(2, 1, -1)$, are :

    (a) $\dfrac{1}{\sqrt{35}}, -\dfrac{5}{\sqrt{35}}, \dfrac{3}{\sqrt{35}}$

    (b) $-\dfrac{1}{\sqrt{35}}, \dfrac{5}{\sqrt{35}}, \dfrac{3}{\sqrt{35}}$

    (c) $\dfrac{1}{\sqrt{35}}, \dfrac{5}{\sqrt{35}}, \dfrac{3}{\sqrt{35}}$

    (d) None of these

12. The projection of the line segment joining the points (–1, 0, 3) and (2, 5, 1) on the line whose direction ratios are 6, 2, 3, is :

(a) $\frac{22}{7}$

(b) $\frac{15}{7}$

(c) $\frac{9}{7}$

(d) None of these

13. The coordinates of the foot of the perpendicular drawn from the point A (1, 0, 3) to the join of the points B (4, 7, 1) and C (3, 5, 3) is :

(a) $\left(\frac{5}{3}, -\frac{7}{3}, \frac{17}{3}\right)$

(b) $\left(\frac{5}{3}, \frac{7}{3}, -\frac{17}{3}\right)$

(c) $\left(\frac{5}{3}, -\frac{7}{3}, -\frac{17}{3}\right)$

(d) $\left(\frac{5}{3}, \frac{7}{3}, \frac{17}{3}\right)$

14. The angle between two diagonals of a cube is :

(a) $\cos^{-1}\left(\frac{1}{\sqrt{3}}\right)$

(b) $\cos^{-1}\left(\frac{2}{\sqrt{3}}\right)$

(c) $\cos^{-1}\left(\frac{1}{3}\right)$

(d) None of these

15. If a line makes α, β, γ angles with the positive directions of the axes, then $\sin^2\alpha + \sin^2\beta + \sin^2\gamma$ is equal to :

(a) 1

(b) 2

(c) 0

(d) None of these

16. The direction cosines of any normal to the xy-plane are :

(a) 1, 0, 0

(b) 0, 1, 0

(c) 1, 1, 0

(d) 0, 0, 1

17. If r is a vector of magnitude 21 and has DRs 2, –3, 6, then r is equal to :

(a) $6\hat{i} - 9\hat{j} + 18\hat{k}$

(b) $6\hat{i} + 9\hat{j} + 18\hat{k}$

(c) $6\hat{i} - 9\hat{j} - 18\hat{k}$

(d) $6\hat{i} + 9\hat{j} - 18\hat{k}$

18. A plane meets the coordinate axes at A, B, C such that the centroid of the Δ ABC is the point (a, b, c). The equation of the plane is $\frac{x}{a} + \frac{y}{b} + \frac{z}{c} = k$, where k =

(a) 1

(b) 2

(c) 3

(d) None of these

19. If the axes are rectangular and P is the point (2, 3, –1), then the equation of the plane through P at right angles to OP is :

(a) 2x + 3y + z = 14

(b) 2x + 3y – z = 14

(c) 2x – 3y + z = 14

(d) None of these

20. The equation of the plane that passes through (2, –3, 1) and is perpendicular to the line joining the points (3, 4, –1) and (2, –1, 5) is :

(a) x + 5y – 6z + 19 = 0

(b) x + 5y + 6z + 19 = 0

(c) x – 5y + 6z + 19 = 0

(d) None of these

21. The equation of the plane through the points (2, 3, 1) and (4, –5, 3) and parallel to x-axis is :

(a) x – z – 1 = 0

(b) 4x + y – 11 = 0

(c) y + 4z – 7 = 0

(d) None of these

22. The plane $lx + my = 0$ is rotated about its line of intersection with the plane z = 0 through an angle α. The equation of the plane in its new position is

(a) $lx + my \pm z\sqrt{l^2 + m^2}\ \sin\alpha = 0$

(b) $lx + my \pm z\sqrt{l^2 + m^2}\ \tan\alpha = 0$

(c) $lx + my \pm z\sqrt{l^2 + m^2}\ \cot\alpha = 0$

(d) None of these

23. The equation of the plane perpendicular to the yz-plane and passing through the points (1, –2, 4) and (3, –4, 5) is :

(a) y + 2z = 5

(b) 2y + z = 5

(c) y + 2z = 6

(d) 2y + z = 6

24. The equation of the plane through (1, 1, 1) and passing through the line of intersection of the planes :

x + 2y – z + 1 = 0 and 3x – y – 4z + 3 = 0 is :

(a) 8x + 5y – 11z + 8 = 0

(b) 8x + 5y + 11z + 8 = 0

(c) 8x – 5y – 11z + 8 = 0

(d) None of these

25. The equation of the plane passing through the line of intersection of the planes $2x - y = 0$ and $3z - y = 0$ and perpendicular to the plane $4x + 5y - 3z = 8$, is :

(a) $2x + 17y + 9z = 0$

(b) $2x - 17y + 9z = 0$

(c) $2x + 17y - 9z = 0$

(d) None of these

26. The equation of the plane through the point $(-1, 3, 2)$ and perpendicular to the planes $x + 2y + 2z = 5$ and $3x + 3y + 2z = 8$, is :

(a) $2x - 4y + 3z + 8 = 0$

(b) $2x + 4y + 3z + 8 = 0$

(c) $2x + 4y - 3z + 8 = 0$

(d) None of these

27. The equation of the plane through the points $(1, 1, 0)$, $(-2, 2, -1)$ and $(1, 2, 1)$ is :

(a) $2x + 3y + 3z = 5$ (b) $2x - 3y + 3z = 5$

(c) $2x + 3y - 3z = 3$ (d) $2x + 3y - 3z = 5$

28. A variable plane is at a constant distance p from the origin and meets the axes, which are rectangular, in A, B, C. Through A, B, C planes are drawn parallel to the coordinate planes. The locus of their point of intersection is given by $x^{-2} + y^{-2} + z^{-2} = kp^{-2}$, where k is equal to :

(a) 1 (b) 2

(c) 4 (d) None of these

29. The coordinates of the point of intersection of the line $\dfrac{x+1}{1} = \dfrac{y+3}{3} = \dfrac{z-2}{-2}$ with the plane $3x + 4y + 5z = 25$ are :

(a) $(5, 15, 10)$ (b) $(5, 15, -10)$

(c) $(5, -15, 10)$ (d) None of these

30. If the axes are rectangular, the distance from the point $(3, 4, 5)$ to the point where the line $\dfrac{x-3}{1} = \dfrac{y-4}{2} = \dfrac{z-5}{2}$ meets the plane $x + y + z = 17$ is :

(a) 1 (b) 2

(c) 3 (d) None of these

31. The distance of the point $(1, -2, 3)$ from the plane $x - y + z = 5$ measured parallel to the line $\dfrac{x}{2} = \dfrac{y}{3} = \dfrac{z-1}{-6}$ is :

(a) 1 (b) 2

(c) 4 (d) None of these

32. The planes $3x - y + z + 1 = 0$, $5x + y + 3z = 0$ intersect in the line PQ. The equation of the plane through the point $(2, 1, 4)$ and perpendicular to PQ is :

(a) $x + y - 2z = 5$ (b) $x + y - 2z = -5$

(c) $x + y + 2z = 5$ (d) $x + y + 2z = -5$

33. The equation of the plane through the line $x + y + z + 3 = 0 = 2x - y + 3z + 1$ and parallel to the line $\dfrac{x}{1} = \dfrac{y}{2} = \dfrac{z}{3}$ is :

(a) $x - 5y + 3z = 7$ (b) $x - 5y + 3z = -7$

(c) $x + 5y + 3z = 7$ (d) $x + 5y + 3z = -7$

34. The equation of the plane containing the line $\dfrac{x+1}{-3} = \dfrac{y-3}{2} = \dfrac{z+2}{1}$ and the point $(0, 7, -7)$ is :

(a) $x + y + z = 2$ (b) $x + y + z = 3$

(c) $x + y + z = 0$ (d) None of these

35. The equation of the plane passing through the straight line $\dfrac{x-1}{2} = \dfrac{y+1}{-1} = \dfrac{z-3}{4}$

and perpendicular to the plane $x + 2y + z = 12$ is

(a) $9x + 2y - 5z + 4 = 0$

(b) $9x - 2y - 5z + 4 = 0$

(c) $9x + 2y + 5z + 4 = 0$

(d) None of these

36. The equation of the plane through the points $(2, -1, 0)$, $(3, -4, 5)$ and parallel to the line $2x = 3y = 4z$ is :

(a) $29 (x - 2) + 27 (y + 1) - 22z = 0$

(b) $29 (x - 2) - 27 (y + 1) - 22z = 0$

(c) $29 (x - 2) + 27 (y + 1) + 22z = 0$

(d) None of these

37. A plane parallel to the lines $x - 1 = 2y - 5 = 2z$ and $3x = 4y - 11 = 3z - 4$ passes through the point (2, 3, 3). The equation of the plane is :

    (a) $x - 4y + 2z + 4 = 0$

    (b) $x + 4y + 2z + 4 = 0$

    (c) $x - 4y + 2z - 4 = 0$

    (d) None of these

38. The position vectors of points A and B are $\hat{i} - \hat{j} + 3\hat{k}$ and $3\hat{i} + 3\hat{j} + 3\hat{k}$ respectively. The equation of a plane is $\vec{r} \cdot (5\hat{i} + 2\hat{j} - 7\hat{k}) + 9 = 0$. The points A and B :

    (a) lie on the plane

    (b) are on the same side of the plane

    (c) are on the opposite sides of the plane

    (d) None of these

39. The distance from the point $-\hat{i} + 2\hat{j} + 6\hat{k}$ to the straight line through the point (2, 3, –4) and parallel to the vector $6\hat{i} + 3\hat{j} - 4\hat{k}$ is :

    (a) 7   (b) 10

    (c) 9   (d) None of these

40. The line of intersection of the planes $\vec{r} \cdot (3\hat{i} - \hat{j} + \hat{k}) = 1$ and $r \cdot (\hat{i} + 4\hat{j} - 2\hat{k}) = 2$ is parallel to the vector :

    (a) $-2\hat{i} + 7\hat{j} + 13\hat{k}$ (b) $2\hat{i} + 7\hat{j} - 13\hat{k}$

    (c) $-2\hat{i} - 7\hat{j} + 13\hat{k}$ (d) $2\hat{i} + 7\hat{j} + 13\hat{k}$

41. The angle between the planes $\vec{r} \cdot (3\hat{i} + \hat{j} - \hat{k}) = 1$ and $\vec{r} \cdot (\hat{i} + 4\hat{j} - 2\hat{k}) = 2$ is

    (a) $\cos^{-1}\left(\dfrac{9}{\sqrt{231}}\right)$ (b) $\cos^{-1}\left(\dfrac{4}{\sqrt{231}}\right)$

    (c) $\cos^{-1}\left(\dfrac{11}{\sqrt{231}}\right)$ (d) None of these

42. If the planes $\vec{r} \cdot (2\hat{i} + \lambda\hat{j} - 3\hat{k})$ and $\vec{r} \cdot (\lambda\hat{i} + 3\hat{j} + \hat{k}) = 5$ are perpendicular, then λ is equal to :

    (a) 2   (b) –2

    (c) 3   (d) –3

43. The equation of the plane through the point (4, 2, 4) and perpendicular to the planes $\vec{r} \cdot (2\hat{i} + 5\hat{j} + 4\hat{k}) = -1$ and $\vec{r} \cdot (4\hat{i} + 7\hat{j} + 6\hat{k}) = -2$ is :

    (a) $\vec{r} \cdot (\hat{i} + 2\hat{j} - 6\hat{k}) = 4$

    (b) $\vec{r} \cdot (\hat{i} + 2\hat{j} - 3\hat{k}) = -4$

    (c) $\vec{r} \cdot (\hat{i} + 2\hat{j} + 3\hat{k}) = -4$

    (d) None of these

44. The distance between the planes $\vec{r} \cdot (2\hat{i} - \hat{j} + 3\hat{k}) = 4$ and $\vec{r} \cdot (6\hat{i} - 3\hat{j} + 9\hat{k}) + 13 = 0$ is :

    (a) $\dfrac{5}{3\sqrt{14}}$ (b) $\dfrac{10}{3\sqrt{14}}$

    (c) $\dfrac{25}{3\sqrt{14}}$ (d) None of these

45. The distance of the line L whose vector equation is $\vec{r} = 2\hat{i} - 2\hat{j} + 3\hat{k} + \lambda(\hat{i} - \hat{j} + 4\hat{k})$ from the plane π whose vector equation is $\vec{r} \cdot (\hat{i} + 5\hat{j} + \hat{k}) = 5$, is :

    (a) $\dfrac{5}{3\sqrt{3}}$ (b) $\dfrac{10}{3\sqrt{3}}$

    (c) $\dfrac{25}{3\sqrt{3}}$ (d) None of these

46. The equation of the plane bisecting the obtuse angle between the planes $x + 2y + 2z - 3 = 0$ and $3x + 4y + 12z + 1 = 0$ is :

    (a) $2x + 7y - 5z - 21 = 0$

    (b) $11x + 19y + 31z - 18 = 0$

    (c) $2x + 7y - 5z + 21 = 0$

    (d) $11x + 19y + 31z + 18 = 0$

47. Chord AB is a diameter of the sphere $|\vec{r} - 2\hat{i} - \hat{j} + 6\hat{k}| = \sqrt{18}$. If the coordinates of A are (3, 2, –2), then the coordinates of B are :

    (a) (1, 0, 10)   (b) (1, 0, –10)

    (c) (–1, 0, 10)   (d) None of these

48. The equation of the sphere inscribed in a tetrahedron, whose faces are x = 0, y = 0, z = 0 and x + 2y + 2z = 1 is :

(a) $32(x^2 + y^2 + z^2) + 8(x + y + z) + 1 = 0$

(b) $32(x^2 + y^2 + z^2) - 8(x + y + z) - 1 = 0$

(c) $32(x^2 + y^2 + z^2) - 8(x + y + z) + 1 = 0$

(d) None of these

49. A plane passes through a fixed point (a, b, c). The locus of the foot of the perpendicular to it from the origin is the sphere :

(a) $x^2 + y^2 + z^2 - ax - by - cz = 0$

(b) $x^2 + y^2 + z^2 - 2ax - 2by - 2cz = 0$

(c) $x^2 + y^2 + z^2 - 4ax - 4by - 4cz = 0$

(d) None of these

50. A plane passes through a fixed point (a, b, c) and cuts the axes in A, B, C. The locus of the centre of the sphere OABC is $\dfrac{a}{x} + \dfrac{b}{y} + \dfrac{c}{z} = k$, where k is equal to :

(a) 1   (b) 2

(c) 4   (d) None of these

51. The radius of the circular section of the sphere $|\vec{r}| = 5$ by the plane $\vec{r} \cdot (\hat{i} + \hat{j} + \hat{k}) = 3\sqrt{3}$ is :

(a) 16   (b) 8

(c) 4   (d) None of these

52. The equation of the sphere whose centre has the position vector $(3\hat{i} + 6\hat{j} - 4\hat{k})$ and which touches the plane $\vec{r} \cdot (2\hat{i} - 2\hat{j} - \hat{k}) = 10$ is :

(a) $|\vec{r} - (3\hat{i} + 6\hat{j} - 4\hat{k})| = 4$

(b) $|\vec{r} - (3\hat{i} + 6\hat{j} + 4\hat{k})| = 4$

(c) $|\vec{r} - (3\hat{i} + 6\hat{j} - 4\hat{k})| = 2$

(d) None of these

53. The point of contact of plane 2x–2y + z +12 = 0 and the sphere $x^2 + y^2 + z^2 - 2x - 4y + 2z - 3 = 0$ is :

(a) (1, 4, –2)   (b) (–1, –4, –2)

(c) (–1, 4, 2)   (d) (–1, 4, –2)

54. The vector equation of the plane $\vec{r} = \hat{i} - \hat{j} + \lambda(\hat{i} + \hat{j} + \hat{k}) + \mu(\hat{i} - 2\hat{j} + 3\hat{k})$ is :

(a) $\vec{r} \cdot (5\hat{i} - 2\hat{j} - 3\hat{k}) = 7$

(b) $\vec{r} \cdot (5\hat{i} + 2\hat{j} - 3\hat{k}) = 7$

(c) $\vec{r} \cdot (5\hat{i} - 2\hat{j} + 3\hat{k}) = 7$

(d) None of these

55. The image of the point (1, 3, 4) in the plane 2x – y + z + 3 = 0 is :

(a) (3, 5, 2)   (b) (–3, 5, 2)

(c) (3, 5, –2)   (d) (3, –5, 2)

56. The equation of the line passing through the point with position vector $2\hat{i} - 3\hat{j} - 5\hat{k}$ and perpendicular to the plane $\vec{r} \cdot (6\hat{i} - 3\hat{j} - 5\hat{k}) + 2 = 0$ is :

(a) $\vec{r} = 2\hat{i} - 3\hat{j} - 5\hat{k} + \lambda(-6\hat{i} + 3\hat{j} + 5\hat{k})$

(b) $\vec{r} = 2\hat{i} + 3\hat{j} - 5\hat{k} + \lambda(-6\hat{i} + 3\hat{j} + 5\hat{k})$

(c) $\vec{r} = 2\hat{i} - 3\hat{j} - 5\hat{k} + \lambda(6\hat{i} + 3\hat{j} + 5\hat{k})$

(d) None of these

57. The shortest distance between the lines whose vector equations are

$\vec{r} = \hat{i} + 2\hat{j} + 3\hat{k} + \lambda(2\hat{i} + 3\hat{j} + 4\hat{k})$

and $\vec{r} = 2\hat{i} + 4\hat{j} + 5\hat{k} + \mu(3\hat{i} + 4\hat{j} + 5\hat{k})$ is :

(a) $\dfrac{5}{\sqrt{6}}$ (b) $\dfrac{4}{\sqrt{6}}$

(c) $\dfrac{1}{\sqrt{6}}$ (d) None of these

58. The equation $|\vec{r}|^2 - \vec{r} \cdot (2\hat{i} + 4\hat{j} - 2\hat{k}) - 10 = 0$ represents a :

(a) circle

(b) plane

(c) sphere of radius 4

(d) sphere of radius 3

(e) None of these

59. The equation of a sphere which passes through the points $(1, 0, 0)$, $(0, 1, 0)$, $(0, 0, 1)$ and having radius as small as possible,

(a) $3(x^2 + y^2 + z^2) - 2(x + y + z) - 1 = 0$

(b) $x^2 + y^2 + z^2 - x - y - z - 1 = 0$

(c) $3(x^2 + y^2 + z^2) - 2(x + y + z) + 1 = 0$

(d) None of these

60. A sphere of constant radius k passes through origin and meets axes in A, B, C. The centroid of the triangle ABC lies on the sphere :

(a) $9(x^2 + y^2 + z^2) = 4k^2$

(b) $3(x^2 + y^2 + z^2) = 4k^2$

(c) $x^2 + y^2 + z^2 = 4k^2$

(d) None of these

61. The radius of the circle $x^2 + y^2 + z^2 = 49$,

$2x + 3y - z - 5\sqrt{14} = 0$ is :

(a) $\sqrt{6}$

(b) $2\sqrt{6}$

(c) $4\sqrt{6}$

(d) None of these

62. The perpendicular distance of $P(1, 2, 3)$ from the line $\dfrac{x - 6}{3} = \dfrac{y - 7}{2} = \dfrac{z - 7}{-2}$ is :

(a) 7

(b) 5

(c) 0

(d) None of these

63. The ratio in which the plane

$\vec{r} \cdot (\hat{i} - 2\hat{j} + 2\hat{k}) = 17$ divides the line joining the points $-2\hat{i} + 4\hat{j} + 7\hat{k}$ and $3\hat{i} - 5\hat{j} + 8\hat{k}$ is :

(a) $3 : 5$

(b) $1 : 10$

(c) $3 : 10$

(d) $1 : 5$

64. The equation of the plane containing the line

$\vec{r} = \hat{i} + \hat{j} + \lambda(2\hat{i} + \hat{j} + 4\hat{k})$ is :

(a) $\vec{r} \cdot (-\hat{i} - 2\hat{j} + \hat{k}) = 3$

(b) $\vec{r} \cdot (\hat{i} + 2\hat{j} - \hat{k}) = 0$

(c) $\vec{r} \cdot (\hat{i} + 2\hat{j} - \hat{k}) = 3$

(d) None of these

65. Given the line $L : \dfrac{x - 1}{3} = \dfrac{y + 1}{2} = \dfrac{z - 3}{-1}$ and the plane $\pi : x - 2y = 0$. Of the following assertions, the only one that is always true is :

(a) L is $\perp$ to π

(b) L lies in π

(c) L is parallel to π

(d) None of these

66. Radius of the circle

$\vec{r}^2 + \vec{r} \cdot (2\hat{i} - 2\hat{j} - 4\hat{k}) - 19 = 0$

$\vec{r} \cdot (\hat{i} - 2\hat{j} + 4\hat{k}) + 8 = 0$:

(a) 5

(b) 4

(c) 3

(d) 2

67. The line of intersection of the planes

$\vec{r} \cdot (3\hat{i} - \hat{j} + \hat{k}) = 1$ and $\vec{r} \cdot (\hat{i} + 4\hat{j} - 2\hat{k}) = 2$ is parallel to the vector :

(a) $2\hat{i} + 7\hat{j} + 13\hat{k}$

(b) $-2\hat{i} - 7\hat{j} + 13\hat{k}$

(c) $2\hat{i} + 7\hat{j} - 13\hat{k}$

(d) $-2\hat{i} + 7\hat{j} + 13\hat{k}$

68. A straight line which makes an angle of 60° with each of y and z-axis, inclines with x-axis at an angle :

(a) 30°

(b) 60°

(c) 75°

(d) 45°

69. Equation of the sphere with centre $(1, -1, 1)$ and radius equal to that of sphere $2x^2 + 2y^2 + 2z^2 - 2x + 4y - 6z = 1$ is :

(a) $x^2 + y^2 + z^2 - 2x + 2y - 2z + 1 = 0$

(b) $x^2 + y^2 + z^2 + 2x - 2y + 2z + 1 = 0$

(c) $x^2 + y^2 + z^2 - 2x + 2y - 2z - 1 = 0$

(d) None of the above

70. The shortest distance between the lines

$\dfrac{x - 1}{2} = \dfrac{y - 2}{3} = \dfrac{z - 3}{4}$ and $\dfrac{x - 2}{3} = \dfrac{y - 4}{4} = \dfrac{z - 5}{5}$

is :

(a) $\dfrac{1}{\sqrt{6}}$

(b) $\dfrac{1}{6}$

(c) $\dfrac{1}{3}$

(d) $\dfrac{1}{\sqrt{3}}$

71. The distance between the line

$$\vec{r} = 2\hat{i} - 2\hat{j} + 3\hat{k} + \lambda(\hat{i} - \hat{j} + 4\hat{k}) \text{ and the plane}$$

$$\vec{r} \cdot (\hat{i} + 5\hat{j} + \hat{k}) = 5 \text{ is :}$$

(a) $\dfrac{10}{9}$ (b) $\dfrac{10}{3\sqrt{3}}$

(c) $\dfrac{10}{3}$ (d) None of these

72. The points (5, 2, 4), (6, –1, 2) and (8, –7, k) are collinear if k is equal to :

(a) –1   (b) 3

(c) 2   (d) –2

73. The equation of the plane through (2, 3, 4) and parallel to the plane x + 2y + 4z = 5 is :

(a) x + 2y + 4z = 24   (b) x + y + 2z = 2

(c) x + 2y + 4z = 3   (d) x + 2y + 4z = 10

74. The intercepts of the plane 2x – 3y + 4z = 12 on the coordinate axes are given by :

(a) 3, –2, 1.5   (b) 6, –4, 3

(c) 6, –4, –3   (d) 2, –3, 4

75. The locus of $x^2 + y^2 + z^2 = 0$ is :

(a) a circle   (b) a sphere

(c) (0, 0, 0)   (d) None of these

76. Perpendicular distance of the point (3, 4, 5) from the y-axis is :

(a) $\sqrt{34}$ (b) $\sqrt{41}$

(c) 4   (d) 5

77. If r is position vector of any point on a sphere and a and b are respectively position vectors of the extremities of a diameter, then :

(a) $\vec{r} \cdot (a - b) = 0$

(b) $\vec{r} \cdot (\vec{r} - a) = 0$

(c) $(\vec{r} + a) \cdot (\vec{r} + b) = 0$

(d) $(\vec{r} - a) \cdot (\vec{r} - b) = 0$

78. The angle between the lines 2x = 3y = – z and 6x = – y = –4z is :

(a) 0°   (b) 30°

(c) 45°   (d) 90°

79. The number of straight lines that are equally inclined to three dimensional coordinate axes, is :

(a) 2   (b) 4

(c) 6   (d) 8

80. The ratio in which the line joining the points (a, b, c) and (–a, –c, –b) is divided by the xy-plane is

(a) a : b   (b) b : c

(c) c : a   (d) c : b

81. The equation of straight line passing through the point (a, b, c) and parallel to z-axis is :

(a) $\dfrac{x - a}{1} = \dfrac{y - b}{1} = \dfrac{z - c}{0}$

(b) $\dfrac{x - a}{0} = \dfrac{y - b}{1} = \dfrac{z - c}{1}$

(c) $\dfrac{x - a}{1} = \dfrac{y - b}{0} = \dfrac{z - c}{0}$

(d) $\dfrac{x - a}{0} = \dfrac{y - b}{0} = \dfrac{z - c}{1}$

82. The direction ratios of the diagonals of a cube which join the origin to the opposite corner are (when the three concurrent edges of the cube are coordinate axes) :

(a) $\dfrac{2}{\sqrt{3}}, \dfrac{2}{\sqrt{3}}, \dfrac{2}{\sqrt{3}}$ (b) 1, 1, 1

(c) 2, –2, 1   (d) 1, 2, 3

83. The equation of the plane through (2, 3, 4) and parallel to the plane x + 2y + 4z = 5 is :

(a) x + 2y + 4z = 10   (b) x + 2y + 4z = 3

(c) x + y + 2z = 2   (d) x + 2y + 4z = 24

84. The angle between the straight lines

$$\dfrac{x + 1}{2} = \dfrac{y - 2}{5} = \dfrac{z + 3}{4} \text{ and } \dfrac{x - 1}{1} = \dfrac{y + 2}{2} = \dfrac{z - 3}{-3} \text{ is}$$

(a) 45°   (b) 30°

(c) 60°   (d) 90°

85. The equation of the plane containing the two lines and $\dfrac{x - 1}{2} = \dfrac{y + 1}{-1} = \dfrac{z}{3}$ and $\dfrac{x}{2} = \dfrac{y - 2}{-1} = \dfrac{z + 1}{3}$ is :

(a) 8x + y – 5z – 7 = 0   (b) 8x + y + 5z – 7 = 0

(c) 8x – y – 5z – 7 = 0   (d) None of these

86. If a plane passes through the point $(1, 1, 1)$ and is perpendicular to the line $\frac{x-1}{3} = \frac{y-1}{0} = \frac{z-1}{4}$, then its perpendicular distance from the origin is

(a) 3/4   (b) 4/3

(c) 7/5   (d) 1

87. The direction ratios of the line

$x - y + z - 5 = 0 = x - 3y - 6$ are :

(a) 3, 1, –2   (b) 2, –4, 1

(c) $\frac{3}{\sqrt{14}}, \frac{1}{\sqrt{14}}, \frac{-2}{\sqrt{14}}$ (d) $\frac{2}{\sqrt{41}}, \frac{-4}{\sqrt{41}}, \frac{1}{\sqrt{41}}$

88. The angle between the line $\frac{x-1}{2} = \frac{y-2}{1} = \frac{z+3}{-2}$ and the plane $x + y + 4 = 0$ is :

(a) 0°   (b) 30°

(c) 45°   (d) 90°

89. The centre of the sphere which touches the lines $y = x$, $z = c$ and $y = -x$, $z = -c$ lies on :

(a) $xy + 2cz = 0$ (b) $yz + 2cx = 0$

(c) $zx + 2cy = 0$ (d) None of these

90. The plane passing through the point $(-2, -2, 2)$ and containing the line joining the points $(1, 1, 1)$ and $(1, -1, 2)$ makes intercepts on the coordinate axes, the sum of whose lengths is :

(a) 3   (b) 4

(c) 6   (d) 12

91. A line segment has length 63 and direction ratios are $(3, -2, 6)$. If the line makes an obtuse angle with x-axis, the components of the line vector are

(a) 27, –18, 54   (b) –27, 18, –54

(c) 27, 18, –54   (d) 27, –18, –54

92. A line passes through the points $(6, -7, -1)$ and $(2, -3, 1)$. If the angle α, which the line makes with the positive direction of x-axis, is acute; the direction cosines of the line are :

(a) 2/3, –2/3, –1/3   (b) 2/3, 2/3, –1/3

(c) 2/3, –2/3, 1/3   (d) 2/3, 2/3, 1/3

93. The equation of the plane containing the lines

$\vec{r} = \vec{a}_1 + \lambda \vec{a}_2, \ \vec{r} = \vec{a}_2 + \lambda \vec{a}_1$ is

(a) $[\vec{r} \ \vec{a}_1 \ \vec{a}_2] = 0$

(b) $[\vec{r} \ \vec{a}_1 \ \vec{a}_2] = \vec{a}_1 \cdot \vec{a}_2$

(c) $[\vec{r} \ \vec{a}_2 \ \vec{a}_1] = \vec{a}_1 \cdot \vec{a}_2$

(d) None of these

94. The line of intersection of the planes $\vec{r} \cdot (3\hat{i} - \hat{j} + \hat{k}) = 1$ and $\vec{r} \cdot (\hat{i} + 4\hat{j} - 2\hat{k}) = 2$ is parallel to the vector :

(a) $-2\hat{i} + 7\hat{j} - 13\hat{k}$ (b) $2\hat{i} + 7\hat{j} - 13\hat{k}$

(c) $-2\hat{i} - 7\hat{j} + 13\hat{k}$ (d) $2\hat{i} + 7\hat{j} + 13\hat{k}$

95. The vector equation of the plane containing the lines $\vec{r} = (\hat{i} + \hat{j}) + \lambda (\hat{i} + 2\hat{j} - \hat{k})$ and $\vec{r} = (\hat{i} + \hat{j}) + \mu (-\hat{i} + \hat{j} - 2\hat{k})$ is :

(a) $\vec{r} \cdot (\hat{i} + \hat{j} + \hat{k}) = 0$

(b) $\vec{r} \cdot (\hat{i} - \hat{j} - \hat{k}) = 0$

(c) $\vec{r} \cdot (\hat{i} + \hat{j} + \hat{k}) = 3$

(d) None of these

96. The length of the perpendicular from the origin to the plane passing through the point a and containing the line $\vec{r} = \vec{b} + \lambda \vec{c}$ is :

(a) $\dfrac{[\vec{a} \ \vec{b} \ \vec{c}]}{|\vec{a} \times \vec{b} + \vec{b} \times \vec{c} + \vec{c} \times \vec{a}|}$ (b) $\dfrac{[\vec{a} \ \vec{b} \ \vec{c}]}{|\vec{a} \times \vec{b} + \vec{b} \times \vec{c}|}$

(c) $\dfrac{[\vec{a} \ \vec{b} \ \vec{c}]}{|\vec{b} \times \vec{c} + \vec{c} \times \vec{a}|}$ (d) $\dfrac{[\vec{a} \ \vec{b} \ \vec{c}]}{|\vec{c} \times \vec{a} + \vec{a} \times \vec{b}|}$

97. The direction cosines of a line equally inclined to three mutually perpendicular lines having direction cosines as $l_1, m_1, n_1; l_2, m_2, n_2 ; l_3, m_3, n_3$ are :

(a) $l_1 + l_2 + l_3, m_1 + m_2 + m_3, n_1 + n_2 + n_3$

(b) $\dfrac{l_1 + l_2 + l_3}{\sqrt{3}}, \dfrac{m_1 + m_2 + m_3}{\sqrt{3}}, \dfrac{n_1 + n_2 + n_3}{\sqrt{3}}$

(c) $\dfrac{l_1 + l_2 + l_3}{3}, \dfrac{m_1 + m_2 + m_3}{3}, \dfrac{n_1 + n_2 + n_3}{3}$

(d) None of these

98. The vector equation of the plane through the point $2\hat{i} - \hat{j} - 4\hat{k}$ and parallel to the plane $\vec{r} \cdot (4\hat{i} - 12\hat{j} - 3\hat{k}) - 7 = 0$ is :

(a) $\vec{r} \cdot (4\hat{i} - 12\hat{j} - 3\hat{k}) = 0$

(b) $\vec{r} \cdot (4\hat{i} - 12\hat{j} - 3\hat{k}) = 32$

(c) $\vec{r} \cdot (4\hat{i} - 12\hat{j} - 3\hat{k}) = 12$

(d) None of these

99. The vector equation of the plane through the point $(2, 1, -1)$ and passing through the line of intersection of the planes $\vec{r} \cdot (\hat{i} + 3\hat{j} - \hat{k}) = 0$ and $\vec{r} \cdot (\hat{i} + 2\hat{k}) = 0$, is :

(a) $\vec{r} \cdot (\hat{i} + 9\hat{j} + 11\hat{k}) = 0$

(b) $\vec{r} \cdot (\hat{i} + 9\hat{j} + 11\hat{k}) = 6$

(c) $\vec{r} \cdot (\hat{i} - 3\hat{j} - 13\hat{k}) = 0$

(d) None of these

100. The perpendicular distance from the origin to the plane through the point $(2, 3, -1)$ and $\perp$ to the vector $3\hat{i} - 4\hat{j} + 7\hat{k}$ is :

(a) $\dfrac{13}{\sqrt{74}}$

(b) $\dfrac{-13}{\sqrt{74}}$

(c) 13

(d) None of these

101. The equation of the plane perpendicular to the line $\dfrac{x-1}{1} = \dfrac{y-2}{-1} = \dfrac{z+1}{2}$ and passing through the point $(2, 3, 1)$ is :

(a) $\vec{r} \cdot (\hat{i} + \hat{j} + 2\hat{k}) = 1$

(b) $\vec{r} \cdot (\hat{i} - \hat{j} + 2\hat{k}) = 1$

(c) $\vec{r} \cdot (\hat{i} - \hat{j} + 2\hat{k}) = 7$

(d) None of these

102. The vector equation of the line of intersection of the planes $\vec{r} \cdot (\hat{i} + 2\hat{j} + 3\hat{k}) = 0$ and $\vec{r} \cdot (3\hat{i} + 2\hat{j} + 3\hat{k}) = 0$ is :

(a) $\vec{r} = \lambda(\hat{i} + 2\hat{j} + \hat{k})$

(b) $\vec{r} = \lambda(\hat{i} - 2\hat{j} + 3\hat{k})$

(c) $\vec{r} = \lambda(\hat{i} + 2\hat{j} - 3\hat{k})$

(d) None of these

103. Two lines with direction cosines $< l_1, m_1, n_1 >$ and $< l_2, m_2, n_2 >$ are at right angles if :

(a) $l_1 l_2 + m_1 m_2 + n_1 n_2 = 1$

(b) $l_1 l_2 + m_1 m_2 + n_1 n_2 = 0$

(c) $\dfrac{l_1}{l_2} = \dfrac{m_1}{m_2} = \dfrac{n_1}{n_2}$

(d) $l_1 = l_2, m_1 = m_2, n_1 = n_2$

104. The equation of the line joining the points $(-2, 4, 2)$ and $(7, -2, 5)$ are :

(a) $\dfrac{x+2}{3} = \dfrac{y-4}{-2} = \dfrac{z-2}{1}$

(b) $\dfrac{x}{-2} = \dfrac{y}{4} = \dfrac{z}{2}$

(c) $\dfrac{x}{7} = \dfrac{y}{-2} = \dfrac{z}{5}$

(d) None of these

105. The direction cosines of the normal to the plane $x + 2y - 3z + 4 = 0$ are :

(a) $\dfrac{1}{\sqrt{14}}, \dfrac{2}{\sqrt{14}}, -\dfrac{3}{\sqrt{14}}$

(b) $-\dfrac{1}{\sqrt{14}}, \dfrac{2}{\sqrt{14}}, \dfrac{3}{\sqrt{14}}$

(c) $\dfrac{1}{\sqrt{14}}, \dfrac{2}{\sqrt{14}}, \dfrac{3}{\sqrt{14}}$

(d) $\dfrac{1}{\sqrt{14}}, -\dfrac{2}{\sqrt{14}}, \dfrac{3}{\sqrt{14}}$

106. Equation of the plane parallel to x-axis is :

(a) $ax + cz + d = 0$ (b) $by + cz + d = 0$

(c) $ax + by + d = 0$ (d) $ax + by + cz + d = 0$

107. The angle between two lines $\dfrac{x+1}{2} = \dfrac{y+3}{2} = \dfrac{z-4}{-1}$ and $\dfrac{x-4}{1} = \dfrac{y+4}{2} = \dfrac{z+1}{2}$ is :

(a) $\cos^{-1}\left(\dfrac{2}{9}\right)$

(b) $\cos^{-1}\left(\dfrac{4}{9}\right)$

(c) $\cos^{-1}\left(\dfrac{1}{9}\right)$

(d) $\cos^{-1}\left(\dfrac{3}{9}\right)$

108. The straight line through (a, b, c) and parallel to x-axis is :

(a) $\dfrac{x-a}{1}=\dfrac{y-b}{1}=\dfrac{z-c}{1}$

(b) $\dfrac{x-a}{0}=\dfrac{y-b}{0}=\dfrac{z-c}{1}$

(c) $\dfrac{x-a}{1}=\dfrac{y-b}{0}=\dfrac{z-c}{0}$

(d) $\dfrac{x-a}{0}=\dfrac{y-b}{1}=\dfrac{z-c}{0}$

109. The lines $\dfrac{x}{1}=\dfrac{y}{2}=\dfrac{z}{3}$ and $\dfrac{x-1}{-2}=\dfrac{y-2}{-4}=\dfrac{z-3}{-6}$ are

(a) coincident (b) skew

(c) intersecting (d) parallel

110. Angle between the two planes 3x–4y +5z = 0 and 2x – y – 2z = 5 is :

(a) $\dfrac{\pi}{4}$ (b) $\dfrac{\pi}{6}$

(c) $\dfrac{\pi}{2}$ (d) $\dfrac{\pi}{3}$

111. The direction cosines of the line joining the points (4, 3, –5) and (–2, 1, –8) are :

(a) < 6, 2, 3 > (b) $\left<\dfrac{6}{7},\dfrac{2}{7},\dfrac{3}{7}\right>$

(c) < 2, 4, –13 > (d) None of these

112. The equation $|\vec{r}|^2 -2(\vec{r}\cdot\vec{a})+\lambda=0$ represents

(a) a sphere (b) a straight line

(c) a plane (d) None of these

113. In three dimensional space, equation 3y + 4z = 0 represents :

(a) a plane containing z-axis

(b) a line with direction numbers 0, 3, 4

(c) a plane containing x-axis

(d) a plane containing y-axis

114. The radius of the sphere

$x^2 + y^2 + z^2 – 6x + 8y – 10z + 1 = 0$ is :

(a) 5 (b) 15

(c) 7 (d) 2

115. The angle between the lines whose direction cosines satisfy the equations

$l + m + n = 0, l^2 + m^2 + n^2 = 0$, is given by :

(a) $\dfrac{2\pi}{3}$ (b) $\dfrac{\pi}{6}$

(c) $\dfrac{5\pi}{6}$ (d) $\dfrac{\pi}{3}$

116. The equation of a plane which passes through (2, –3, 1) and is normal to the line joining the points (3, 4, –1) and (2, –1, 5) is given by :

(a) x + 5y – 6z + 19 = 0

(b) x – 5y + 6z – 19 = 0

(c) x + 5y + 6z + 19 = 0

(d) x – 5y – 6z – 19 = 0

117. The equation of straight line passing through the points (a, b, c) and (a – b, b – c, c – a) is :

(a) $\dfrac{x-a}{a-b}=\dfrac{y-b}{b-c}=\dfrac{z-c}{c-a}$

(b) $\dfrac{x-a}{b}=\dfrac{y-b}{c}=\dfrac{z-c}{a}$

(c) $\dfrac{x-a}{a}=\dfrac{y-b}{b}=\dfrac{z-c}{c}$

(d) $\dfrac{x-a}{2a-b}=\dfrac{y-b}{2b-c}=\dfrac{z-c}{2c-a}$

118. Distance between the two parallel planes 2x–2y + z + 3 = 0 and 4x – 4y + 2z + 5 = 0 is :

(a) $\dfrac{2}{3}$ (b) $\dfrac{1}{3}$

(c) $\dfrac{1}{6}$ (d) 2

119. If the planes $3x – 2y + 2z + 17 = 0$ and $4x + 3y – kz = 25$ are mutually perpendicular, then k =

(a) 3 (b) –3

(c) 9 (d) –6

120. The equation of a plane which cuts equal intercepts of unit length on the axes, is :

(a) x + y + z = 0 (b) x + y + z = 1

(c) x + y – z = 1 (d) $\dfrac{x}{a}+\dfrac{y}{a}+\dfrac{z}{a}=1$

121. The co-ordinates of the point which divides the join of the points $(2, -1, 3)$ and $(4, 3, 1)$ in the ratio $3 : 4$ internally are given by :

(a) $\frac{2}{7}, \frac{20}{7}, \frac{10}{7}$ (b) $\frac{15}{7}, \frac{20}{7}, \frac{3}{7}$

(c) $\frac{10}{7}, \frac{15}{7}, \frac{2}{7}$ (d) $\frac{20}{7}, \frac{5}{7}, \frac{15}{7}$

122. The angle between the pair of lines with direction ratios $(1, 1, 2)$ & $(\sqrt{3} - 1, -\sqrt{3} - 1, 4)$ is :

(a) $30°$ (b) $45°$

(c) $60°$ (d) $90°$

123. The coordinates of the points where the line $\frac{x-6}{-1} = \frac{y+1}{0} = \frac{z+3}{4}$ meets the plane

$x + y - z = 3$, are :

(a) $(2, 1, 0)$ (b) $(7, -1, -7)$

(c) $(1, 2, -6)$ (d) $(5, -1, 1)$

124. The acute angle between the line joining the points $(2, 1, -3)$, $(-3, 4, 7)$ and a line parallel to $\frac{x-1}{3} = \frac{y}{4} = \frac{z+3}{4}$ through the point $(-1, 0, 4)$ is

(a) $\cos^{-1}\left(\frac{7}{5\sqrt{10}}\right)$ (b) $\cos^{-1}\left(\frac{7}{\sqrt{10}}\right)$

(c) $\cos^{-1}\left(\frac{3}{5\sqrt{10}}\right)$ (d) $\cos^{-1}\left(\frac{1}{5\sqrt{10}}\right)$

125. If the plane $x - 3y + 5z = d$ passes through the point $(1, 2, 4)$, then the lengths of intercepts cut by it on the axes of x, y, z are respectively :

(a) $15, -5, 3$ (b) $1, -5, 3$

(c) $-15, 5, 3$ (d) $1, -6, 20$

126. If the length of perpendicular drawn from origin on a plane is 7 units and its direction ratios are $-3, 2$ and 6, then that plane is :

(a) $-3x + 2y + 6z - 7 = 0$

(b) $-3x + 2y + 6z - 49 = 0$

(c) $3x - 2y + 6z + 7 = 0$

(d) $-3x + 2y - 6z - 49 = 0$

127. A line makes angles α, β and γ with the axes respectively, then $\cos 2\alpha + \cos 2\beta + \cos 2\gamma =$

(a) -2 (b) -1

(c) 1 (d) 2

128. The angle between the lines $2x = 3y = -z$ is :

(a) $0°$ (b) $30°$

(c) $45°$ (d) $90°$

129. An equation of a plane parallel to the plane $x - 2y + 2z - 5 = 0$ and at a unit distance from the origin is : **[AIEEE - 2012]**

(a) $x - 2y + 2z - 3 = 0$

(b) $x - 2y + 2z + 1 = 0$

(c) $x - 2y + 2z - 1 = 0$

(d) $x - 2y + 2z + 5 = 0$

130. If the lines $\frac{x-1}{2} = \frac{y+1}{3} = \frac{z-1}{4}$ and

$\frac{x-3}{1} = \frac{y-k}{2} = \frac{z}{1}$ intersect, then k is equal to :

(a) -1 (b) $\frac{2}{9}$

(c) $\frac{9}{2}$ (d) 0

131. **Statement 1:** The point A $(1, 0, 7)$ is the mirror image of the point B $(1, 6, 3)$ in the line :

$\frac{x}{1} = \frac{y-1}{2} = \frac{z-2}{3}$ **[AIEEE - 2011]**

Statement 2: The line : $\frac{x}{1} = \frac{y-1}{2} = \frac{z-2}{3}$

bisects the line segment joining A $(1, 0, 7)$ and B $(1, 6, 3)$.

(a) Statement 1 is false, statement 2 is true.

(b) Statement 1 is true, statement 2 is true and statement 2 is a correct explanation for statement 1.

(c) Statement 1 is true, statement 2 is true and statement 2 is not a correct explanation for statement 1.

(d) Statement 1 is true, statement 2 is false.

132. If the angle between the line $x = \frac{y-1}{2} = \frac{z-3}{\lambda}$

and the plane $x + 2y + 3z = 4$ is $\cos^{-1}\left(\sqrt{\frac{5}{14}}\right)$,

then λ equals : **[AIEEE – 2011]**

(a) $\frac{5}{3}$ (b) $\frac{2}{3}$

(c) $\frac{3}{2}$ (d) $\frac{2}{5}$

133. **Statement 1:** The point A (3, 1, 6) is the mirror image of the point B (1, 3, 4) in the plane $x - y + z = 5$.

    Statement 2: The plane $x - y + z = 5$ bisects the line segment joining A (3, 1, 6) and B (1, 3, 4). **[AIEEE - 2010]**

    (a) Statement 1 is true, statement 2 is true; statement 2 is not a correct explanation for statement 1.

    (b) Statement 1 is true, statement 2 is false.

    (c) Statement 1 is false, statement 2 is true.

    (d) Statement 1 is true, statement 2 is true; statement 2 is the correct explanation for statement 1.

134. A line AB in three-dimensional space makes angles 45° and 120° with the positive X-axis and the positive Y-axis respectively. If AB makes an acute angle θ with the positive z-axis, then θ equals : **[AIEEE - 2010]**

    (a) 45° (b) 60°
    (c) 75° (d) 30°

135. Let the line $\dfrac{x-2}{3} = \dfrac{y-1}{-5} = \dfrac{z+2}{2}$ lies in the plane $x + 3y - \alpha z + \beta = 0$. Then (α, β) equals:
    [AIEEE - 2009]

    (a) (6, -17) (b) (-6, 7)
    (c) (5, -15) (d) (-5, 15)

136. The line passing through the points (5, 1, a) and (3, b, 1) crosses the yz-plane at the point $\left(0, \dfrac{17}{2}, \dfrac{-13}{2}\right)$. Then : **[AIEEE - 2008]**

    (a) $a = 2, b = 8$ (b) $a = 4, b = 6$
    (c) $a = 6, b = 4$ (d) $a = 8, b = 2$

137. If the straight lines $\dfrac{x-1}{k} = \dfrac{y-2}{2} = \dfrac{z-3}{3}$ and $\dfrac{x-2}{3} = \dfrac{y-3}{k} = \dfrac{z-1}{2}$ intersect at a point, then the integer k is equal to : **[AIEEE - 2008]**

    (a) -5 (b) 5
    (c) 2 (d) -2

138. Let L be the line of intersection of the planes $2x + 3y + z = 1$ and $x + 3y + 2z = 2$. If L makes an angle α with the positive x-axis, then $\cos \alpha$ equals : **[AIEEE - 2007]**

    (a) $\dfrac{1}{\sqrt{3}}$ (b) $\dfrac{1}{2}$

    (c) 1 (d) $\dfrac{1}{\sqrt{2}}$

139. If a line makes an angle of $\dfrac{\pi}{4}$ with the positive directions of each of X-axis and Y-axis, then the angle that the line makes with the positive direction of the Z-axis is: **[AIEEE - 2007]**

    (a) $\dfrac{\pi}{6}$ (b) $\dfrac{\pi}{3}$

    (c) $\dfrac{\pi}{4}$ (d) $\dfrac{\pi}{2}$

140. If (2, 3, 5) is one end of a diameter of the sphere $x^2 + y^2 + z^2 - 6x - 12y - 2z + 20 = 0$, then the coordinates of the other end of the diameter are : **[AIEEE - 2007]**

    (a) (4, 9, -3) (b) (4, -3, 3)
    (c) (4, 3, 5) (d) (4, 3, -3)

141. The two lines $x = ay + b, z = cy + d$; and $x = a'y + b', z = c'y + d'$ are perpendicular to each other if **[AIEEE - 2006]**

    (a) $aa' + cc' = -1$ (b) $aa' + cc' = 1$
    (c) $\dfrac{a}{a'} + \dfrac{c}{c'} = -1$ (d) $\dfrac{a}{a'} + \dfrac{c}{c'} = 1$

142. Equation of the plane containing the straight line $\dfrac{x}{2} = \dfrac{y}{3} = \dfrac{z}{4}$ and perpendicular to the plane containing the straight lines $\dfrac{x}{3} = \dfrac{y}{4} = \dfrac{z}{2}$ and $\dfrac{x}{4} = \dfrac{y}{2} = \dfrac{z}{3}$ is

    (a) $x + 2y - 2z = 0$ (b) $3x + 2y - 2z = 0$
    (c) $x - 2y + z = 0$ (d) $5x + 2y - 4z = 0$

143. Consider the line $L_1 : \dfrac{x+1}{-3} = \dfrac{y-2}{1} = \dfrac{z+3}{-1}$ and the plane $\alpha : 2x + 3y + z + 3 = 0$. The line L_2 is the image of L_1 in the plane α. Then L_2 is given by

(a) $\dfrac{x+4}{13} = \dfrac{y-3}{-19} = \dfrac{z+4}{3}$

(b) $\dfrac{x-4}{13} = \dfrac{y+3}{-19} = \dfrac{z-4}{3}$

(c) $\dfrac{x+4}{11} = \dfrac{y-3}{-21} = \dfrac{z+4}{5}$

(d) $\dfrac{x+4}{14} = \dfrac{y-3}{7} = \dfrac{z+4}{-1}$

ANSWER KEY

1. (a)	**2.** (b)	**3.** (c)	**4.** (a)	**5.** (b)	**6.** (a)	**7.** (b)	**8.** (d)	**9.** (c)	**10.** (b)
11. (b)	**12.** (a)	**13.** (d)	**14.** (c)	**15.** (b)	**16.** (d)	**17.** (a)	**18.** (c)	**19.** (b)	**20.** (a)
21. (c)	**22.** (b)	**23.** (c)	**24.** (c)	**25.** (b)	**26.** (a)	**27.** (d)	**28.** (a)	**29.** (b)	**30.** (c)
31. (a)	**32.** (b)	**33.** (a)	**34.** (c)	**35.** (b)	**36.** (b)	**37.** (a)	**38.** (c)	**39.** (a)	**40.** (a)
41. (a)	**42.** (d)	**43.** (b)	**44.** (c)	**45.** (b)	**46.** (a)	**47.** (b)	**48.** (c)	**49.** (a)	**50.** (b)
51. (c)	**52.** (a)	**53.** (d)	**54.** (a)	**55.** (b)	**56.** (a)	**57.** (c)	**58.** (c)	**59.** (a)	**60.** (a)
61. (b)	**62.** (a)	**63.** (c)	**64.** (c)	**65.** (b)	**66.** (b)	**67.** (d)	**68.** (d)	**69.** (c)	**70.** (a)
71. (b)	**72.** (d)	**73.** (a)	**74.** (b)	**75.** (c)	**76.** (a)	**77.** (d)	**78.** (d)	**79.** (b)	**80.** (d)
81. (d)	**82.** (b)	**83.** (d)	**84.** (d)	**85.** (a)	**86.** (c)	**87.** (a)	**88.** (c)	**89.** (a)	**90.** (d)
91. (b)	**92.** (a)	**93.** (a)	**94.** (a)	**95.** (b)	**96.** (c)	**97.** (b)	**98.** (b)	**99.** (a)	**100.** (a)
101. (b)	**102.** (b)	**103.** (b)	**104.** (a)	**105.** (a)	**106.** (b)	**107.** (b)	**108.** (c)	**109.** (d)	**110.** (c)
111. (b)	**112.** (a)	**113.** (c)	**114.** (c)	**115.** (a)	**116.** (a)	**117.** (b)	**118.** (c)	**119.** (a)	**120.** (b)
121. (d)	**122.** (c)	**123.** (d)	**124.** (a)	**125.** (a)	**126.** (b)	**127.** (b)	**128.** (d)	**129.** (a)	**130.** (c)
131. (c)	**132.** (b)	**133.** (a)	**134.** (b)	**135.** (b)	**136.** (c)	**137.** (a)	**138.** (a)	**139.** (d)	**140.** (a)
141. (a)	**142.** (c)	**143.** (a)							

MATHEMATICAL LOGIC

MULTIPLE CHOICE QUESTIONS

1. Which of the following is equivalent to $p \rightarrow q$?

   (a) $\sim q \rightarrow \sim p$ (b) $\sim p \wedge q$

   (c) $p \wedge \sim q$ (d) None of these

2. Which of the following is equivalent to $\sim p \vee q$?

   (a) $p \leftrightarrow q$ (b) $q \rightarrow p$

   (c) $\sim p \rightarrow q$ (d) $p \rightarrow q$

3. Which of these is not equivalent to $\sim (p \leftrightarrow q)$?

   (a) $\sim p \leftrightarrow q$ (b) $q \rightarrow p$

   (c) $p \leftrightarrow \sim q$ (d) None of these

4. Which of the following is a logical statement ?

   (a) Open the door.

   (b) What a beautiful girl !

   (c) Are you in Delhi ?

   (d) All prime numbers are odd numbers.

5. Which of the following is not a logical statement?

   (a) 3 multiplied by 4 is 10.

   (b) All men have short hair.

   (c) Today is Friday.

   (d) Every equilateral triangle is isosceles.

6. Which of the following is a logical statement ?

   (a) She is a maths post graduate.

   (b) All months have 30 days.

   (c) How many days are there is a week ?

   (d) Maths is fun.

7. Which of the following is not a logical statement ?

   (a) 9 is greater than 12.

   (b) All sets are not infinite.

   (c) Delhi is capital of India.

   (d) The airport is far-off from here.

8. Which of the following is not a logical statement ?

   (a) Today is not Thursday.

   (b) It rains only when its cloudy.

   (c) If the diagonals of a quadrilateral bisect each other then it is a parallelogram.

   (d) Perfect squares are always positive.

9. p : 'New Delhi is a capital'. Which of the following is not $\sim p$.

   (a) New Delhi is not a capital.

   (b) 'New Delhi is a capital' is false.

   (c) Jaipur is a capital.

   (d) None of these

10. p : "Every one in India speaks Hindi". Which of the following is not negation of p ?

    (a) Not everyone in India speaks Hindi.

    (b) No one in India speaks Hindi.

    (c) There are people in India who do not speak Hindi.

    (d) None of these.

11. Negation of a statement is "Every natural number is greater than 0". The statement is

    (a) Every natural number is less than 0.

    (b) Every natural number is less than or equal to zero.

    (c) There exists a natural number which is not greater than 0.

    (d) None of these.

12. Negation of which of the following statements is "sum of 3 and 4 is equal to 9".

    (a) Sum of 3 and 4 is not equal to 9.

    (b) Sum of 3 and 4 is greater than 9.

    (c) Sum of 3 and 4 is equal to 7.

    (d) None of these

13. p → q is not equivalent to

  (a) p is sufficient for q

  (b) q is necessary for p

  (c) p only if q

  (d) None of these

14. Which of the following is not a fallacy ? (f is a false statement).

  (a) p ∧ ~p   (b) p ∧ f

  (c) p ∨ f   (d) None of these

15. Which of the following is a tautology ?

  (a) p ∧ f   (b) p ∨ f

  (c) p ∨ (~p)   (d) p ∧ t

16. If each of the statements p → ~q, ~r → q and p is true, then

  (a) r is false   (b) r is true

  (c) q is true   (d) None of these

17. If each of the statements p → q, q → r, ~r is true, then

  (a) p is false   (b) p is true

  (c) q is true   (d) None of these

18. Which of the following is true ?

  (a) p ∧ ~p ≡ t

  (b) p ∨ ~p ≡ f

  (c) p ⇒ q ≡ q → p

  (d) p ⇒ q ≡ ~q → (~p)

19. In which of the following compound statements; the connective 'or' is exclusive ?

  (a) If x is a real number; then x is either rational or irrational

  (b) If x is an integer, then either x ≥ 0 or x ≤ 0.

  (c) If x is any real number, then either x ≥ 0 or x ≤ 0.

  (d) If A and B are comparable sets, then either A ⊂ B or B ⊂ A.

20. If both p and q are false then

  (a) p ∧ q is true   (b) p ∨ q is true

  (c) p → q is true   (d) p ↔ q is false

21. If both p and q are true then

  (a) p ∧ q is false   (b) p ∨ q is false

  (c) p → q is true   (d) None of these

22. If p is true and q is false, then which of the following statements is not true ?

  (a) p ∨ q   (b) p → q

  (c) p ∧ (~q)   (d) q → p

23. If p is false and q is true, then

  (a) p ∧ q is true   (b) p ∨ (~q) is true

  (c) q → p is true   (d) p → q is true

24. The converse of p → q is

  (a) ~q → ~p   (b) p ↔ q

  (c) q → p   (d) None of these

25. Contrapositive of the statement p → q is

  (a) ~q → ~q   (b) p ↔ q

  (c) q → p   (d) None of these

26. The negation of the statement, "If I become a teacher, then I will open a school" is

                              [AIEEE - 2012]

  (a) I will become a teacher and I will not open a school.

  (b) Either I will not become a teacher or I will not open a school.

  (c) Neither I will become a teacher nor I will open a school.

  (d) I will not become a teacher or I will open a school.

27. Consider the following statements :

  P : Suman is brilliant.

  Q : Suman is rich.

  R : Suman is honest.

  The negation of the statement "Suman is brilliant and dishonest if and only if Suman is rich", can be expressed as   **[AIEEE - 2011]**

  (a) ~ (P ∧ ~ R) ↔ Q

  (b) ~ P ∧ (Q ↔ ~ R)

  (c) ~ (Q ↔ (P ∧ ~R))

  (d) ~ Q ↔ ~ P ∧ R

28. Let S be a non-empty subset of R. Consider the following statements :

P : There is a rational number $x \in S$ such that $x > 0$. Which of the following statements is the negation of the statement P ?   **[AIEEE - 2010]**

(a) There is no rational number $x \in S$, such that $x \le 0$.

(b) Every rational number $x \in S$ satisfies $x \le 0$.

(c) $x \in S$ and $x \le 0 \Rightarrow x$ is not rational.

(d) There is a rational number $x \in S$, such that $x \le 0$.

29. Statement 1 : $\sim (p \leftrightarrow \sim q) \equiv p \leftrightarrow q$

[AIEEE - 2009]

Statement 2 : $\sim (p \leftrightarrow \sim q)$ is a tautology

(a) Statement 1 is true, statement 2 is true and statement 2 is correct explanation of statement 1.

(b) Statement 1 and 2 are both true but statement 2 is not the correct explanation for 1.

(c) Statement 1 is true, statement 2 is false.

(d) Statement 1 is false and statement 2 is true.

30. p : x is an irrational number.

q : y is a trancsendental number.

r : x is a rational number iff y is a transcendental number.

Statement 1 : r is equivalent to either q or p.

Statement 2 : r is equivalent to $\sim (p \leftrightarrow \sim q)$.

(a) Statement 1 is true, statement 2 is true and statement 2 is the correct explanation of statement 1.

(b) Statement 1 and 2 are both true but statement 2 is not the correct explanation for statement 1.

(c) Statement 1 is true, statement 2 is false.

(d) Statement 1 is false and statement 2 is true.

ANSWER KEY

1. (a)	**2.** (d)	**3.** (b)	**4.** d)	**5.** (c)	**6.** (b)	**7.** (d)	**8.** (a)	**9.** (c)	**10.** (b)
11. (c)	**12.** (a)	**13.** (d)	**14.** (c)	**15.** (c)	**16.** (b)	**17.** (a)	**18.** (d)	**19.** (a)	**20.** (c)
21. (c)	**22.** (b)	**23.** (d)	**24.** (c)	**25.** (a)	**26.** (a)	**27.** (c)	**28.** (b)	**29.** (c)	**30.** (d)

1. Distance between the two parallel planes $2x + y + 2z = 8$ and $4x + 2y + 4z + 5 = 0$ is :

   (a) $\dfrac{3}{2}$ (b) $\dfrac{5}{2}$

   (c) $\dfrac{7}{2}$ (d) $\dfrac{9}{2}$

2. At present, a firm is manufacturing 2000 items. It is estimated that the rate of change of production P.w.r.t. additional number of workers x is given by $\dfrac{dP}{dx} = 100 - 12\sqrt{x}$. If the firm employs 25 more workers, then the new level of production of items is :

   (a) 2500   (b) 3000

   (c) 3500   (d) 4500

3. Let A and B be two sets containing 2 elements and 4 elements respectively. The number of subsets of $A \times B$ having 3 or more elements is :

   (a) 256   (b) 220

   (c) 219   (d) 211

4. If the lines $\dfrac{x-2}{1} = \dfrac{y-3}{1} = \dfrac{z-4}{-k}$ and $\dfrac{x-1}{k} = \dfrac{y-4}{2} = \dfrac{z-5}{1}$ are coplanar, then k can have :

   (a) any value
   (b) exactly one value
   (c) exactly two value
   (d) exactly three values

5. If the vectors $\overline{AB} = 3\hat{i} + 4\hat{k}$ and $\overline{AC} = 5\hat{i} - 2\hat{j} + 4\hat{k}$ are the sides of a triangle ABC, then the length of the median through A is :

   (a) $\sqrt{18}$ (b) $\sqrt{22}$
   (c) $\sqrt{33}$ (d) $\sqrt{45}$

6. The real number k for which the equation, $2x^3 + 3x + k = 0$ has two distinct real roots in $[0, 1]$:

   (a) lies between 1 and 2
   (b) lies between 2 and 3

   (c) lies between -1 and 0
   (d) does not exist

7. The sum of first 20 terms of the sequence 0.7, 0.77, 0.777, ……, is :

   (a) $\dfrac{7}{81}(179 - 10^{-20})$ (b) $\dfrac{7}{9}(99 - 10^{-20})$

   (c) $\dfrac{7}{81}(179 + 10^{-20})$ (d) $\dfrac{7}{9}(99 + 10^{-20})$

8. A ray of light along $x + \sqrt{3}y = \sqrt{3}$ gets reflected upon reaching x-axis, the equation of the reflected ray is :

   (a) $y = x + \sqrt{3}$ (b) $\sqrt{3}y = x - \sqrt{3}$
   (c) $y = \sqrt{3}x - \sqrt{3}$ (d) $\sqrt{3}y = x - 1$

9. The number of values of k, for which the system of equations,

   $(k + 1)x + 8y = 4k$

   $kx + (k + 3)y = 3k - 1$

   has no solution, is :

   (a) infinite   (b) 1

   (c) 2   (d) 3

10. If equations $x^2 + 2x + 3 = 0$ and $ax^2 + bx + c = 0$, a, b, c $\in$ R, have a common root, then a : b : c : is :

    (a) $1 : 2 : 3$ (b) $3 : 2 : 1$

    (c) $1 : 3 : 2$ (d) $3 : 1 : 2$

11. The circle passing through $(1, -2)$ and touching the axis of x at $(3, 0)$ also passes through the point :

    (a) $(-5, 2)$ (b) $(2, -5)$

    (c) $(5, -2)$ (d) $(-2, 5)$

12. If x, y, z are in A.P. and $\tan^{-1} x$, $\tan^{-1} y$ and $\tan^{-1} z$ are also in A.P. then :

    (a) $x = y = z$ (b) $2x = 3y = 6z$

    (c) $3x = 3y = 2z$ (d) $6x = 4y = 3z$

13. Consider,

Statement - I : $(p \wedge \sim q) \wedge (\sim p \wedge q)$ is a fallacy.

Statement - II : $(p \to q) \leftrightarrow (\sim q \to \sim p)$ is a tautology.

(a) Statement - I is true, Statement - II is true; Statement - II is a correct explanation for Statement – I.

(b) Statement - I is true; Statement - II is true; Statement - II is not a correct explanation for Statement - I.

(c) Statement - I is true; Statement - II is false.

(d) Statement - I is false; Statement - II is true.

14. If $\int f(x)\,dx = \psi(x)$, then $\int x^5 f(x^3)\,dx$ is equal to :

(a) $\frac{1}{3}[x^3\psi(x^3) - \int x^2\psi(x^3)\,dx] + C$

(b) $\frac{1}{3}x^3\psi(x^3) - 3\int x^3\psi(x^3)\,dx + C$

(c) $\frac{1}{3}x^3\psi(x^3) - \int x^2\psi(x^3)\,dx + C$

(d) $\frac{1}{3}[x^3\psi(x^3) - \int x^3\psi(x^3)\,dx] + C$

15. $\lim\limits_{x\to0} \dfrac{(1 - \cos 2x)(3 + \cos x)}{x \tan 4x}$ is equal to :

(a) $-\dfrac{1}{4}$

(b) $\dfrac{1}{2}$

(c) 1

(d) 2

16. Statement - I :

The value of integral $\displaystyle\int_{\pi/6}^{\pi/3} \dfrac{dx}{1 + \sqrt{\tan x}}$ is equal to $\dfrac{\pi}{6}$.

Statement - II :

$\displaystyle\int_a^b f(x)\,dx = \int_a^b f(a + b - x)\,dx$

(a) Statement - I is true; Statement - II is true; Statement - II is a correct explanation for Statement - I.

(b) Statement - I is true; Statement - II is true; Statement - II is not a correct explanation for Statement - I.

(c) Statement - I is true; Statement - II is false.

(d) Statement - I is false; Statement - II is true.

17. The equation of the circle passing through the foci of the ellipse $\dfrac{x^2}{16} + \dfrac{y^2}{9} = 1$, and having centre at $(0, 3)$ is :

(a) $x^2 + y^2 - 6y - 7 = 0$

(b) $x^2 + y^2 - 6y + 7 = 0$

(c) $x^2 + y^2 - 6y - 5 = 0$

(d) $x^2 + y^2 - 6y + 5 = 0$

18. A multiple choice examination has 5 questions. Each question has three alternative answers of which exactly one is correct. The probability that a student will get 4 or more correct answers just by guessing is:

(a) $\dfrac{17}{3^5}$

(b) $\dfrac{13}{3^5}$

(c) $\dfrac{11}{3^5}$

(d) $\dfrac{10}{3^5}$

19. The x-coordinate of the incentre of the triangle that has the coordinates of mid points of its sides as $(0, 1)$ $(1, 1)$ and $(1, 0)$ is :

(a) $2 + \sqrt{2}$

(b) $2 - \sqrt{2}$

(c) $1 + \sqrt{2}$

(d) $1 - \sqrt{2}$

20. The term independent of x in expansion of

$\left(\dfrac{x+1}{x^{2/3} - x^{1/3} + 1} - \dfrac{x-1}{x - x^{1/2}}\right)^{10}$ is :

(a) 4

(b) 120

(c) 210

(d) 310

21. The area (in square units) bounded by the curves $y = \sqrt{x}$, $2y - x + 3 = 0$, x-axis, and lying in the first quadrant is :

(a) 9

(b) 36

(c) 18

(d) $\dfrac{27}{4}$

22. Let T_n be the number of all possible triangles formed by joining vertices of a n-sided regular polygon. If $T_{n+1} - T_n = 10$ then the value of n is :

(a) 1

(b) 5

(c) 10

(d) 8

23. If z is a complex number of unit modulus and argument θ, then $\arg\left(\dfrac{1+z}{1+\bar{z}}\right)$ equals :

    (a) − θ
    (b) $\dfrac{\pi}{2} - \theta$
    (c) θ
    (d) π − θ

24. ABCD is a trapezium such that AB and CD are parallel and BC ⊥ CD. If ∠ ADB = θ, BC = p and CD = q, then AB is equal to :

    (a) $\dfrac{(p^2 + q^2)\sin\theta}{p\cos\theta + q\sin\theta}$

    (b) $\dfrac{p^2 + q^2\cos\theta}{p\cos\theta + q\sin\theta}$

    (c) $\dfrac{p^2 + q^2}{p^2\cos\theta + q^2\sin\theta}$

    (d) $\dfrac{(p^2 + q^2)\sin\theta}{(p\cos\theta + q\sin\theta)^2}$

25. If $P = \begin{bmatrix} 1 & \alpha & 3 \\ 1 & 3 & 3 \\ 2 & 4 & 4 \end{bmatrix}$ is the adjoint of 3 × 3 matrix A and $|A| = 4$, then α is equal to :

    (a) 4
    (b) 11
    (c) 5
    (d) 0

26. The intercepts on x-axis made by tangents to the curve, $y = \int\limits_0^x |t|\, dt$, x ∈ R, which are parallel to the line y = 2x, are equal to :

    (a) ± 1
    (b) ± 2
    (c) ± 3
    (d) ± 4

27. Given : A circle, $2x^2 + 2y^2 = 5$ and a parabola, $y^2 = 4\sqrt{5}x$.

    Statement - I : An equation of a common tangent to these curves is $y = x + \sqrt{5}$.

    Statement - II : If the line, $y = mx + \dfrac{\sqrt{5}}{m}$ (m ≠ 0) is their common tangent, then 'm' satisfies, $m^4 - 3m^2 + 2 = 0$.

    (a) Statement - I is true; Statement - II is true; Statement - II is a correct explanation for Statement - I.

    (b) Statement - I is true; Statement - II is true; Statement - II is not a correct explanation for Statement - I.

    (c) Statement - I is true; Statement - II is false.

    (d) Statement - I is false; Statement - II is true.

28. If $y = \sec(\tan^{-1} x)$, then $\dfrac{dy}{dx}$ at x = 1 is equal to :

    (a) $\dfrac{1}{\sqrt{2}}$
    (b) $\dfrac{1}{2}$
    (c) 1
    (d) $\sqrt{2}$

29. The expression $\dfrac{\tan A}{1 - \cot A} + \dfrac{\cot A}{1 - \tan A}$ can be written as :

    (a) sin A ·cos A + 1
    (b) sec A ·cosec A + 1
    (c) tan A + cot A
    (d) sec A + cosec A

30. All the students of a class performed poorly in Mathematics. The teacher decided to give grace marks of 10 to each of the students. Which of the following statistical measures will not change even after the grace marks were given ?

    (a) Mean
    (b) Median
    (c) Mode
    (d) Variance

ANSWER KEY

1. (c)	2. (c)	3. (c)	4. (c)	5. (c)	6. (d)	7. (c)	8. (b)	9. (b)	10. (a)
11. (c)	12. (a)	13. (b)	14. (c)	15. (d)	16. (d)	17. (a)	18. (c)	19. (b)	20. (c)
21. (a)	22. (b)	23. (c)	24. (a)	25. (b)	26. (a)	27. (b)	28. (a)	29. (b)	30. (d)

❑❑❑

1. The image of the line $\frac{x-1}{3} = \frac{y-3}{1} = \frac{z-4}{-5}$ in the plane $2x - y + z + 3 = 0$ is the line

   (a) $\frac{x+3}{3} = \frac{y-5}{1} = \frac{z-2}{-5}$

   (b) $\frac{x+3}{-3} = \frac{y-5}{-1} = \frac{z+2}{5}$

   (c) $\frac{x-3}{3} = \frac{y+5}{1} = \frac{z-2}{-5}$

   (d) $\frac{x-3}{-3} = \frac{y+5}{-1} = \frac{z-2}{5}$

2. If the coefficients of x^3 and x^4 in the expansion of $(1 + ax + bx^2)(1 - 2x)^{18}$ in powers of x are both zero, then (a, b) is equal to

   (a) $\left(16, \frac{251}{3}\right)$

   (b) $\left(14, \frac{251}{3}\right)$

   (c) $\left(14, \frac{272}{3}\right)$

   (d) $\left(16, \frac{272}{3}\right)$

3. If $a \in R$ and equation
   $-3(x - [x])^2 + 2(x - [x]) + a^2 = 0$
   (where [x] denotes the greatest integer $\leq x$) has no integral solution, then all possible values of a lie in the interval

   (a) $(-1, 0) \cup (0, 1)$

   (b) $(1, 2)$

   (c) $(-2, -1)$

   (d) $(-\infty, -2) \cup (2, \infty)$

4. If $[\vec{a} \times \vec{b} \quad \vec{b} \times \vec{c} \quad \vec{c} \times \vec{a}] = \lambda [\vec{a} \quad \vec{b} \quad \vec{c}]^2$, then λ is equal to

   (a) 2

   (b) 3

   (c) 0

   (d) 1

5. The variance of first 50 even natural numbers is

   (a) $\frac{833}{4}$

   (b) 833

   (c) 437

   (d) $\frac{437}{4}$

6. A bird is sitting on the top of a vertical pole 20 m high and its elevation from a point O on the ground is 45°. It flies off horizontally straight away from the point O. After one second, the elevation of the bird from O is reduced to 30°. Then the speed (in m/s) of the bird is

   (a) $40(\sqrt{2} - 1)$

   (b) $40\sqrt{3} - \sqrt{2})$

   (c) $20\sqrt{2}$

   (d) $20(\sqrt{3} - 1)$

7. The integral $\int_0^{\pi} \sqrt{1 + 4\sin^2\frac{x}{2} - 4\sin\frac{x}{2}} \, dx$ equals

   (a) $\pi - 4$

   (b) $\frac{2\pi}{3} - 4 - 4\sqrt{3}$

   (c) $4\sqrt{3} - 4$

   (d) $4\sqrt{3} - 4 - \frac{\pi}{3}$

8. The statement $\sim (p \leftrightarrow \sim q)$ is

   (a) equivalent to $p \leftrightarrow q$

   (b) equivalent to $\sim p \leftrightarrow q$

   (c) a tautology

   (d) a fallacy

9. If A is an 3×3 non-singular matrix such that $AA' = A'A$ and $B = A^{-1}A'$, then BB' equals

   (a) $I + B$

   (B) I

   (c) B^{-1}

   (d) $(B^{-1})'$

10. The integral $\int \left(1 + x - \frac{1}{x}\right) e^{x + \frac{1}{x}} \, dx$ is equal to

    (a) $(x - 1) e^{x + \frac{1}{x}} + c$

    (b) $x\, e^{x + \frac{1}{x}} + c$

    (c) $(x + 1) e^{x + \frac{1}{x}} + c$

    (d) $-x\, e^{x + \frac{1}{x}} + c$

11. If z is a complex number such that $|z| \geq 2$, then the minimum value of $\left| z + \frac{1}{2} \right|$

    (a) is equal to $\frac{5}{2}$

    (b) lies in the interval $(1, 2)$

    (c) is strictly greater than $\frac{5}{2}$

    (d) is strictly greater than $\frac{3}{2}$ but less than $\frac{5}{2}$

12. If g is the inverse of a function f and $f'(x) = \frac{1}{1 + x^5}$, then $g'(x)$ is equal to

    (a) $1 + x^5$

    (b) $5x^4$

    (c) $\frac{1}{1 + \{g(x)\}^5}$

    (d) $1 + \{g(x)\}^5$

13. If α, $\beta = 0$ and $f(n) = \alpha^n + \beta^n$ and

$$\begin{vmatrix} 3 & 1 + f(1) & 1 + f(2) \\ 1 + f(1) & 1 + f(2) & 1 + f(3) \\ 1 + f(2) & 1 + f(3) & 1 + f(4) \end{vmatrix}$$

$= K (1 - \alpha)^2 (1 - \beta)^2 (\alpha - \beta)^2$, then K is equal to

(a) $\alpha\beta$

(b) $\dfrac{1}{\alpha\beta}$

(c) 1

(d) -1

14. Let $f_K(x) = \dfrac{1}{k} (\sin^k x + \cos^k x)$ where $x \in R$ and $k \geq 1$. Then $f_4(x) - f_6(x)$ equals

(a) $\dfrac{1}{6}$

(b) $\dfrac{1}{3}$

(c) $\dfrac{1}{4}$

(d) $\dfrac{1}{12}$

15. Let α and β be roots of equation $px^2 + qx + r = 0$, $p \neq 0$. If p, q, r are in A.P. and $\dfrac{1}{\alpha} + \dfrac{1}{\beta} = 4$, then the value of $|\alpha - \beta|$ is

(a) $\dfrac{\sqrt{61}}{9}$

(b) $\dfrac{2\sqrt{17}}{9}$

(c) $\dfrac{\sqrt{34}}{9}$

(d) $\dfrac{2\sqrt{13}}{9}$

16. Let A and B be two events such that

$$P\,(\overline{A \cup B}) = \frac{1}{6}, \; P\,(A \cap B) = \frac{1}{4} \text{ and } P\,(\overline{A}) = \frac{1}{4},$$

where $\overline{A}$ stands for the complement of the event A. Then the events A and B are

(a) mutually exclusive and independent

(b) equally likely but not independent

(c) independent but not equally likely

(d) independent and equally likely

17. If f and g are differentiable functions in [0, 1] satisfying $f(0) = 2 = g(1)$, $g(0) = 0$ and $f(1) = 6$, then for some $c \in \,]0, 1[$.

(a) $2f\,'(c) = g'(c)$

(b) $2f\,'(c) = 3g'(c)$

(c) $f\,'(c) = g'(c)$

(d) $f\,'(c) = 2g'(c)$

18. Let the population of rabbit surviving at a time t be governed by the differential equation $\dfrac{dp(t)}{dt} = \dfrac{1}{2} p(t) - 200$. If $p(0) = 100$, then $p(t)$ equals

(a) $400 - 300\, e^{t/2}$

(b) $300 - 200\, e^{-t/2}$

(c) $600 - 500\, e^{t/2}$

(d) $400 - 300\, e^{-t/2}$

19. Let C be the circle with centre at (1, 1) and radius $= 1$. If T is the circle centred at (0, y), passing through origin and touching the circle C externally, then the radius of T is equal to

(a) $\dfrac{\sqrt{3}}{\sqrt{2}}$

(b) $\dfrac{\sqrt{3}}{2}$

(c) $\dfrac{1}{2}$

(d) $\dfrac{1}{4}$

20. The area of the region described by $A = \{(x, y) : x^2 + y^2 \leq 1 \text{ and } y^2 \leq 1 - x\}$ is

(a) $\dfrac{\pi}{2} + \dfrac{4}{3}$

(b) $\dfrac{\pi}{2} - \dfrac{4}{3}$

(c) $\dfrac{\pi}{2} - \dfrac{2}{3}$

(D) $\dfrac{\pi}{2} + \dfrac{2}{3}$

21. Let a, b, c and d be non-zero numbers. If the point of intersection of the lines $4ax + 2ay + c = 0$ and $5bx + 2by + d = 0$ lies in the fourth quadrant and is equidistant from the two axes then

(a) $2bc - 3ad = 0$

(b) $2bc + 3ad = 0$

(c) $3bc - 2ad = 0$

(d) $3bc + 2ad = 0$

22. Let PS be the median of the triangle with vertices P (2, 2), Q (6, $-$ 1) and R (7, 3). The equation of the line passing through (1, $-$ 1) and parallel to PS is

(a) $4x - 7y - 11 = 0$

(b) $2x + 9y + 7 = 0$

(c) $4x + 7y + 3 = 0$

(d) $2x - 9y - 11 = 0$

23. $\lim\limits_{x \to 0} \dfrac{\sin\,(\pi \cos^2 x)}{x^2}$ is equal to

(a) $\dfrac{\pi}{2}$

(b) 1

(c) $-\pi$

(d) π

24. If $X = \{4^n - 3n - 1 : n \in N\}$ and $Y = \{9(n-1) : n \in N\}$, where N is the set of natural numbers, then $X \cup Y$ is equal to

(a) N

(b) $Y - X$

(c) X

(d) Y

25. The locus of the foot of perpendicular drawn from the centre of the ellipse $x^2 + 3y^2 = 6$ on any tangent to it is

(a) $(x^2 - y^2)^2 = 6x^2 + 2y^2$

(b) $(x^2 - y^2)^2 = 6x^2 - 2y^2$

(c) $(x^2 + y^2)^2 = 6x^2 + 2y^2$

(d) $(x^2 + y^2)^2 = 6x^2 - 2y^2$

26. Three positive numbers from an increasing G.P. If the middle term in this G.P. is doubled, the new numbers are in A.P. Then the common ratio of the G.P. is

(a) $\sqrt{2} + \sqrt{3}$

(b) $3 + \sqrt{2}$

(c) $2 - \sqrt{3}$

(d) $2 + \sqrt{3}$

27. If $(10)^9 + 2(11)^1(10)^8 + 3(11)^2(10)^7 + \ldots + 10(11)^9 = k(10)^9$, then k is equal to

(a) $\dfrac{121}{10}$

(b) $\dfrac{441}{100}$

(c) 100

(d) 110

28. The angle between the lines whose direction cosines satisfy the equations $l + m + n = 0$ and $l^2 = m^2 + n^2$ is

(a) $\dfrac{\pi}{3}$

(b) $\dfrac{\pi}{4}$

(c) $\dfrac{\pi}{6}$

(d) $\dfrac{\pi}{2}$

29. The slope of the line touching both the parabolas $y^2 = 4x$ and $x^2 = -32y$ is

(a) $\dfrac{1}{2}$

(b) $\dfrac{3}{2}$

(c) $\dfrac{1}{8}$

(d) $\dfrac{2}{3}$

30. If $x = -1$ and $x = 2$ are extreme points of $f(x) = \alpha \log |x| + \beta x^2 + x$, then

(a) $\alpha = -6, \beta = \dfrac{1}{2}$

(b) $\alpha = -6, \beta = -\dfrac{1}{2}$

(c) $\alpha = 2, \beta = -\dfrac{1}{2}$

(d) $\alpha = 2, \beta = \dfrac{1}{2}$

ANSWER KEY

1. (a)	2. (d)	3. (a)	4. (d)	5. (b)	6. (d)	7. (d)	8. (a)	9. (b)	10. (b)
11. (b)	12. (d)	13. (c)	14. (d)	15. (d)	16. (c)	17. (d)	18. (a)	19. (d)	20. (a)
21. (c)	22. (b)	23. (d)	24. (d)	25. (c)	26. (d)	27. (c)	28. (a)	29. (a)	30. (c)

1. Let A and B be two sets containing four and two elements respectively. Then the number of subsets of the set A × B, each having at least three elements is

   (a) 219
   (b) 256
   (c) 275
   (d) 510

2. A complex number z is said to be unimodular, if $|z| = 1$. Suppose z_1 and z_2 are complex numbers such that $\dfrac{z_1 - 2z_2}{2 - z_1 z_2}$ is unimodular and z_2 is not unimodular. Then the point z_1 lies on a

   (a) straight line parallel to x-axis
   (b) straight line parallel to y-axis
   (c) circle of radius 2
   (d) circle of radius $\sqrt{2}$

3. Let α and β be the roots of equation $x^2 - 6x - 2 = 0$. If $a_n = \alpha^n - \beta^n$, for $n \geq 1$, then the value of $\dfrac{a_{10} - 2a_8}{2a_9}$ is equal to

   (a) 6
   (b) −6
   (c) 3
   (d) −3

4. If $A = \begin{bmatrix} 1 & 2 & 2 \\ 2 & 1 & -2 \\ a & 2 & b \end{bmatrix}$ is a matrix satisfying the equation $AA^T = 9I$, where I is 3 × 3 identity matrix, then the ordered pair (a, b) is equal to

   (a) (2, −1)
   (b) (−2, 1)
   (c) (2, 1)
   (d) (−2, −1)

5. The set of all of values of λ for which the system of linear equations :

   $2x_1 - 2x_2 + x_3 = \lambda x_1$
   $2x_1 - 3x_2 + 2x_3 = \lambda x_2$
   $-x_1 + 2x_2 = \lambda x_3$

   has a non-trivial solution,

   (a) is an empty set
   (b) is a singleton set
   (c) contains two elements
   (d) contains more than two elements

6. The number of integers greater than 6,000 that can be formed, using the digits 3, 5, 6, 7 and 8, without repetition, is

   (a) 216
   (b) 192
   (c) 120
   (d) 72

7. The sum of coefficients of integral powers of x in the binomial expansion of $\left(1 - 2\sqrt{x}\right)^{50}$ is

   (a) $\dfrac{1}{2}(3^{50} + 1)$
   (b) $\dfrac{1}{2}(3^{50})$
   (c) $\dfrac{1}{2}(3^{50} - 1)$
   (d) $\dfrac{1}{2}(2^{50} + 1)$

8. If m is the A.M. of two distinct real numbers l and n (l, n > 1) and G_1, G_2 and G_3 are three geometric means between l and n, $G_1^4 + 2G_2^4 + G_3^4$ equals,

   (a) $4 l^2 mn$
   (b) $4 lm^2 n$
   (c) $4 lmn^2$
   (d) $4 l^2 m^2 n^2$

9. The sum of first 9 terms of the series
   $\dfrac{1^3}{1} + \dfrac{1^3 + 2^3}{1 + 3} + \dfrac{1^3 + 2^3 + 3^3}{1 + 3 + 5} + \dots$ is

   (a) 71
   (b) 96
   (c) 142
   (d) 192

10. $\displaystyle\lim_{x \to 0} \dfrac{(1 - \cos 2x)(3 + \cos x)}{x \tan 4x}$ is equal to

    (a) 4
    (b) 3
    (c) 2
    (d) $\dfrac{1}{2}$

11. If the function, $g(x) = \begin{cases} k\sqrt{x + 1} , & 0 \leq x \leq 3 \\ mx + 2 , & 3 < x \leq 5 \end{cases}$ is differentiable, then the value of k + m is

    (a) 2
    (b) $\dfrac{16}{5}$
    (c) $\dfrac{10}{3}$
    (d) 4

12. The normal to the curve, $x^2 + 2xy - 3y^2 = 0$, at (1, 1)

    (a) does not meet the curve again
    (b) meets the curve again in the second quadrant
    (c) meets the curve again in the third quadrant
    (d) meets the curve again in the fourth quadrant

13. Let $f(x)$ be a polynomial of degree four having extreme values at $x = 1$, and $x = 2$.

    If $\lim\limits_{x \to 0}\left[1 + \dfrac{f(x)}{x^2}\right] = 3$, then $f(2)$ is equal to

    (a) -8
    (b) -4
    (c) 0
    (d) 4

14. The integral $\displaystyle\int \dfrac{dx}{x^2\,(x^4 + 1)^{3/4}}$ equals

    (a) $\left(\dfrac{x^4 + 1}{x^4}\right)^{1/4} + c$
    (b) $(x^4 + 1)^{1/4} + c$

    (c) $-(x^4 + 1)^{1/4} + c$
    (d) $-\left(\dfrac{x^4 + 1}{x^4}\right)^{1/4} + c$

15. The integral $\displaystyle\int_{2}^{4} \dfrac{\log x^2}{\log x^2 + \log (36 - 12x + x^2)}\, dx$ is

    equal to

    (a) 2
    (b) 4
    (c) 1
    (d) 6

16. The area (in sq. units) of the region described by

    $\{(x, y) : y^2 \le 2x \text{ and } y \ge 4x - 1)\}$ is

    (a) $\dfrac{7}{32}$
    (b) $\dfrac{5}{64}$

    (c) $\dfrac{15}{64}$
    (d) $\dfrac{9}{32}$

17. Let $y(x)$ be the solution of the differential equation

    $(x \log x)\dfrac{dy}{dx} + y = 2x \log x$, $(x \ge 1)$.

    Then $y(e)$ is equal to

    (a) e
    (b) 0
    (c) 2
    (4) $2e$

18. The number of points, having both co-ordinates as integers, that lie in the interior of the triangle with vertices $(0, 0)$, $(0, 41)$ and $(41, 0)$, is ......

    (a) 901
    (b) 861
    (c) 820
    (d) 780

19. Locus of the image of the point $(2, 3)$ in the line $(2x - 3y + 4) + k(x - 2y + 3) = 0$, $k \in R$, is a

    (a) straight line parallel to x-axis
    (b) straight line parallel to y-axis
    (c) circle of radius $\sqrt{2}$
    (d) circle of radius $\sqrt{3}$

20. The number of common tangents to the circles $x^2 + y^2 - 4x - 6y - 12 = 0$ and

    $x^2 + y^2 + 6x + 18y + 26 = 0$, is

    (a) 1
    (b) 2
    (c) 3
    (d) 4

21. The area (in sq. units) of the quadrilateral formed by the tangents at the end points of the lateral

    recta to the ellipse $\dfrac{x^2}{9} + \dfrac{y^2}{5} = 1$, is ......

    (a) $\dfrac{27}{4}$ sq. units
    (b) 18 sq. units

    (c) $\dfrac{27}{2}$ sq. units
    (d) 27 sq. units

22. Let O be the vertex and Q be any points on the parabola, $x^2 = 8y$. If the point P divides the line segment OQ internally in the ratio $1 : 3$, then the locus of P is

    (a) $x^2 = y$
    (b) $y^2 = x$
    (c) $y^2 = 2x$
    (d) $x^2 = 2y$

23. The distance of the point $(1, 0, 2)$ from the point

    of intersection of the line $\dfrac{x - 2}{3} = \dfrac{y + 1}{4} = \dfrac{z - 2}{12}$

    and the plane $x - y + z = 16$, is ......

    (a) $2\sqrt{14}$
    (b) 8
    (c) $3\sqrt{21}$
    (d) 13

24. The equation of the plane containing the line $2x - 5y + z = 3$; $x + y + 4z = 5$, and parallel to the plane, $x + 3y + 6z = 1$, is

    (a) $2x + 6y + 12z = 13$
    (b) $x + 3y + 6z = -7$
    (c) $x + 3y + 6z = 7$
    (d) $2x + 6y + 12z = -13$

25. Let $\vec{a}$, $\vec{b}$ and $\vec{c}$ be three non-zero vectors such that no two of them are collinear and $(\vec{a} \times \vec{b}) \times \vec{c} = \frac{1}{3}\ |\vec{b}|,\ |\vec{c}|,\ \vec{a}$. If θ is the angle between vectors $\vec{b}$ and $\vec{c}$, then a value of $\sin \theta$ is

(a) $\frac{2\sqrt{2}}{3}$

(b) $\frac{-\sqrt{2}}{3}$

(c) $\frac{2}{3}$

(d) $\frac{-2\sqrt{3}}{3}$

26. If 12 identical balls are to be placed in 3 identical boxes, then the probability that one of the boxes contains exactly 3 balls is

(a) $\frac{55}{3}\left(\frac{2}{3}\right)^{11}$

(b) $55\left(\frac{2}{3}\right)^{10}$

(c) $220\left(\frac{1}{3}\right)^{12}$

(d) $22\left(\frac{1}{3}\right)^{11}$

27. The mean of the data set comprising of 16 observations is 16. If one of the observation valued 16 is deleted and three new observations valued 3, 4 and 5 are added to the data, then the mean of the resultant data, is

(a) 16.8

(b) 16.0

(c) 15.8

(d) 14.0

28. If the angles of elevation of the top of a tower from three collinear points A, B and C, on a line leading to the foot of the tower, are 30°, 45° and 60° respectively, then the ratio, AB : BC, is ......

(a) $\sqrt{3} : 1$

(b) $\sqrt{3} : \sqrt{2}$

(c) $1 : \sqrt{3}$

(d) $2 : 3$

29. Let $\tan^{-1} y = \tan^{-1} x + \tan^{-1}\left(\frac{2x}{1 - x^2}\right)$, where $|x| < \frac{1}{\sqrt{3}}$. Then a value of y is

(a) $\frac{3x - x^3}{1 - 3x^2}$

(b) $\frac{3x + x^3}{1 - 3x^2}$

(c) $\frac{3x - x^3}{1 + 3x^2}$

(d) $\frac{3x + x^3}{1 + 3x^2}$

30. The negation of $\sim s \vee (\sim r \wedge s)$ is equivalent to

(a) $s \wedge \sim r$

(b) $s \wedge (r \wedge \sim s)$

(c) $s \vee (r \vee \sim s)$

(d) $s \wedge r$

ANSWER KEY

1. (a)	2. (c)	3. (c)	4. (d)	5. (c)	6. (b)	7. (a)	8. (b)	9. (b)	10. (c)
11. (a)	12. (d)	13. (c)	14. (d)	15. (c)	16. (d)	17. (c)	18. (d)	19. (c)	20. (c)
21. (d)	22. (d)	23. (d)	24. (c)	25. (a)	26. (a)	27. (d)	28. (a)	29. (a)	30. (d)

1. If $f(x) + 2f\left(\dfrac{1}{x}\right) = 3x$,

   $x \neq 0$ and $S = \{x \neq R : f(x) = f(-x)\}$; then S

   (a) is an empty set

   (b) contains exactly one element

   (c) contains exactly two elements

   (d) contains more than two elements

2. A value of θ for which $\dfrac{2 + 3i \sin \theta}{1 - 2i \sin \theta}$ is purely imaginary, is

   (a) $\dfrac{\pi}{3}$

   (b) $\dfrac{\pi}{6}$

   (c) $\sin^{-1}\left(\dfrac{\sqrt{3}}{4}\right)$

   (d) $\sin^{-1}\left(\dfrac{1}{\sqrt{3}}\right)$

3. The sum of all real values of x satisfying the equation $(x^2 - 5x + 5)^{x^2 + 4x - 60} = 1$ is

   (a) 3

   (b) -4

   (c) 6

   (d) 5

4. If $A = \begin{bmatrix} 5a & -b \\ 3 & 2 \end{bmatrix}$ and A adj $A = AA^T$, then $5a + b$ is equal to

   (a) -1

   (b) 5

   (c) 4

   (d) 13

5. The system of linear equations

   $x + \lambda y - z = 0$; $\lambda x - y - z = 0$; $x + y - \lambda z = 0$

   has a non-trivial solution for

   (a) infinitely many values of λ

   (b) exactly one value of λ

   (c) exactly two values of λ

   (d) exactly three values of λ

6. If all the words (with or without meaning having five letters, formed using the letters of the word SMALL and arranged as in a dictionary, then the position of the word SMALL is

   (a) 46th

   (b) 59th

   (c) 52nd

   (d) 58th

7. If the number of terms in the expansion of $\left(1 - \dfrac{2}{x} + \dfrac{4}{x^2}\right)^n$, $x \neq = 0$, is 28, then the sum of the coefficients of all the terms in this expansion, is

   (a) 64

   (b) 2187

   (c) 243

   (d) 729

8. If the 2nd, 5th and 9th terms of a non-constant AP are in GP, then the common ratio of this GP is

   (a) $\dfrac{8}{5}$

   (b) $\dfrac{4}{3}$

   (c) 1

   (d) $\dfrac{7}{4}$

9. If the sum of the first ten terms of the series

   $\left(1\dfrac{3}{5}\right)^2 + \left(2\dfrac{2}{5}\right)^2 + \left(3\dfrac{1}{5}\right)^2 + 4^2 + \left(4\dfrac{4}{5}\right)^2 + ...$, is $\dfrac{16}{5}$ m, then m is equal to

   (a) 102

   (b) 101

   (c) 100

   (d) 99

10. Let $p = \lim\limits_{x \to 0^+} (1 + \tan^2 \sqrt{x})^{1/2x}$, then log p is equal to

    (a) 2

    (b) 1

    (c) $\dfrac{1}{2}$

    (d) $\dfrac{1}{4}$

11. For $x \in R$, $f(x) = |\log 2 - \sin x|$ and $g(x) = f(f(x))$, then

    (a) g is not differentiable at $x = 0$

    (b) $g'(0) = \cos (\log 2)$

    (c) $g'(0) = -\cos (\log 2)$

    (d) g is differentiable at $x = 0$ and $g'(0) = -\sin (\log 2)$

12. Consider $f(x) = \tan^{-1}\left(\sqrt{\dfrac{1 + \sin x}{1 - \sin x}}\right)$, $x \in \left(0, \dfrac{\pi}{2}\right)$.

    A normal to $y = f(x)$ at $x = \dfrac{\pi}{6}$ also passes through the point

    (a) $(0, 0)$

    (b) $\left(0, \dfrac{2\pi}{3}\right)$

    (c) $\left(\dfrac{\pi}{6}, 0\right)$

    (d) $\left(\dfrac{\pi}{4}, 0\right)$

13. A wire of length 2 units is cut into two parts which are bent respectively to form a square of side = x units and a circle of radius = r units. If the sum of the areas of the square and the circle of formed is minimum, then

(a) $2x = (\pi + 4)\, r$ (b) $(4 - \pi)\, x = \pi r$

(c) $x = 2r$ (d) $2x = r$

14. The integral $\displaystyle\int \frac{2x^{12} + 5x^9}{(x^5 + x^3 + 1)^3}\, dx$ is equal to

(a) $\dfrac{-x^5}{(x^5 + x^3 + 1)^2} + C$

(b) $\dfrac{x^{10}}{2\,(x^5 + x^3 + 1)^2} + C$

(c) $\dfrac{x^5}{2\,(x^5 + x^3 + 1)^2} + C$

(d) $\dfrac{-x^{10}}{2\,(x^5 + x^3 + 1)^2} + C$

15. $\displaystyle\lim_{n\to\infty} \left(\frac{(n+1)\,(n+2)\,\dots\,3n}{n^{2n}}\right)^{1/n}$ is equal to

(a) $\dfrac{18}{e^4}$ (b) $\dfrac{27}{e^2}$

(c) $\dfrac{9}{e^2}$ (d) $3 \log 3 - 2$

16. The area (in sq. units) of the region $\{(x, y) : y^2 > 2x \text{ and } x^2 + y^2 < 4x, x \geq 0, y \geq 0\}$ is

(a) $\pi - \dfrac{4}{3}$ (b) $\pi - \dfrac{8}{3}$

(c) $\pi - \dfrac{4\sqrt{2}}{3}$ (d) $\dfrac{\pi}{2} - \dfrac{2\sqrt{2}}{3}$

17. If a curve $y = f(x)$ passes through the point $(1, -1)$ and satisfies the differential equation, $y(1 + xy)\, dx = x\, dy$, then $f\left(-\dfrac{1}{2}\right)$ is equal to

(a) $-\dfrac{2}{5}$ (b) $-\dfrac{4}{5}$

(c) $\dfrac{2}{5}$ (d) $\dfrac{4}{5}$

18. Two sides of a rhombus are along the lines, $x - y + 1 = 0$ and $7x - y - 5 = 0$. If its diagonals intersect at $(-1, -2)$, then which one of the following is a vertex of this rhombus ?

(a) $(-3, -9)$ (b) $(-3, -8)$

(c) $\left(\dfrac{1}{3}, \dfrac{8}{3}\right)$ (d) $\left(-\dfrac{10}{3}, -\dfrac{7}{3}\right)$

19. The centres of those circles which touch the cirlce, $x^2 + y^2 - 8x - 8y - 4 = 0$, externally and also touch the X-axis, lie on

(a) a circle

(b) an ellipse which is not a circle

(c) a hyperbola

(d) a parabola

20. If one of the diameters of the circle, given by the equation, $x^2 + y^2 - 4x + 6y - 12 = 0$, is a chord of a circle S, whose centre is at $(-3, 2)$, then the radius of S is

(a) $5\sqrt{2}$ (b) $5\sqrt{3}$

(c) 5 (d) 10

21. Let P be the point on the parabola, $y^2 = 8x$, which is at a minimum distance from the centre C of the circle, $x^2 + (y + 6)^2 = 1$. Then, the equation of the circle, passing through C and having its centre at P is

(a) $x^2 + y^2 - 4x + 8y + 12 = 0$

(b) $x^2 + y^2 - x + 4y - 12 = 0$

(c) $x^2 + y^2 - \dfrac{x}{4} + 2y - 24 = 0$

(d) $x^2 + y^2 - 4x + 9y + 18 = 0$

22. The eccentricity of the hyperbola whose length of the latus rectum is equal to 8 and the length of its conjugate axis is equal to half of the distance between its foci, is

(a) $\dfrac{4}{3}$ (b) $\dfrac{4}{\sqrt{3}}$

(c) $\dfrac{2}{\sqrt{3}}$ (d) $\sqrt{3}$

23. The distance of the point $(1, -5, 9)$ from the plane $x - y + z = 5$ measured along the line $x = y = z$ is

(a) $3\sqrt{10}$ (b) $10\sqrt{3}$

(c) $\dfrac{10}{\sqrt{3}}$ (d) $\dfrac{20}{3}$

24. If the line, $\dfrac{x-3}{2} = \dfrac{y+2}{-1} = \dfrac{z+4}{3}$ lies in the plane, $lx + my - z = 9$, then $l^2 + m^2$ is equal to

(a) 26 (b) 18

(c) 5 (d) 2

25. Let a, b and c be three units vectors such that $a \times (b \times c) = \dfrac{\sqrt{3}}{2}(b + c)$. If b is not parallel to c, then the angle between a and b is

(a) $\dfrac{3\pi}{4}$ (b) $\dfrac{\pi}{2}$

(c) $\dfrac{2\pi}{3}$ (d) $\dfrac{5\pi}{6}$

26. If the standard deviation of the numbers 2, 3, a and 11 is 3.5, then which of the following is true ?

(a) $3a^2 - 26a + 55 = 0$

(b) $3a^2 - 32a + 84 = 0$

(c) $3a^2 - 34a + 91 = 0$

(d) $3a^2 - 23a + 44 = 0$

27. Let two fair six-faced dice A and B be thrown simultaneously. If E_1 is the event that die A shows up four, E_2 is the event that die B shows up two and E_3 is the event that the sum of numbers on both dice is odd, then which of the following statements is not true ?

(a) E_1 and E_2 are independent.

(b) E_2 and E_3 are independent.

(c) E_1 and E_3 are independent.

(d) E_1, E_2 and E_3 are independent.

28. $0 \le x \le 2\pi$, then the number of real values of x, which satisfy the equation $\cos x + \cos 2x + \cos 3x + \cos 4x = 0$, is

(a) 3 (b) 5

(c) 7 (d) 9

29. A man is walking towards a vertical pillar in a straight path, at a uniform speed. At a certain point A on the path, he observes that the angle of elevation of the top of the pillar is 30°. After walking for 10 min from A in the same direction, at a point B, he observes that the angle of elevation of the top of the pillar is 60°. Then the time taken (in minutes) by him, from B to reach the pillar, is

(a) 6 (b) 10

(c) 20 (d) 5

30. The Boolean experssion

$(p \wedge \sim q) \vee q \vee (\sim p \wedge q)$ is equivalent to

(a) $\sim p \wedge q$ (b) $p \wedge q$

(c) $p \vee q$ (d) $p \vee \sim q$

ANSWER KEY

1. (c)	2. (d)	3. (a)	4. (b)	5. (d)	6. (d)	7. (d)	8. (b)	9. (b)	10. (c)
11. (b)	12. (b)	13. (c)	14. (b)	15. (b)	16. (b)	17. (d)	18. (c)	19. (d)	20. (b)
21. (a)	22. (c)	23. (b)	24. (d)	25. (d)	26. (b)	27. (d)	28. (c)	29. (d)	30. (c)

NOTES